The Ultimate Wodehouse Collection
P.G. Wodehouse

GRAPEVINE INDIA

Published by

GRAPEVINE INDIA PUBLISHERS PVT LTD

www.grapevineindia.com
Delhi | Mumbai
email: grapevineindiapublishers@gmail.com

Ordering Information:
Quantity sales: Special discounts are available on quantity purchases by corporations, associations, and others. For details, reach out to the publisher.

First published by Grapevine India 2023
Copyright © Grapevine 2023
All rights reserved

THE GOLD BAT

I
THE FIFTEENTH PLACE

"Outside!"

"Don't be an idiot, man. I bagged it first."

"My dear chap, I've been waiting here a month."

"When you fellows have quite finished rotting about in front of that bath don't let me detain you."

"Anybody seen that sponge?"

"Well, look here"——this in a tone of compromise——"let's toss for it."

"All right. Odd man out."

All of which, being interpreted, meant that the first match of the Easter term had just come to an end, and that those of the team who, being day boys, changed over at the pavilion, instead of performing the operation at leisure and in comfort, as did the members of houses, were discussing the vital question——who was to have first bath?

The Field Sports Committee at Wrykyn——that is, at the school which stood some half-mile outside that town and took its name from it——were not lavish in their expenditure as regarded the changing accommodation in the pavilion. Letters appeared in every second number of the Wrykinian, some short, others long, some from members of the school, others from Old Boys, all protesting against the condition of the first, second, and third fifteen dressing-rooms. "Indignant" would inquire acidly, in half a page of small type, if the editor happened to be aware that there was no hair-brush in the second room, and only half a comb. "Disgusted O. W." would remark that when he came down with the Wandering Zephyrs to play against the third fifteen, the water supply had suddenly and mysteriously failed, and the W.Z.'s had been obliged to go home as they were, in a state of primeval grime, and he thought that this was "a very bad thing in a school of over six hundred boys", though what the number of boys had to do with the fact that there was no water he omitted to explain. The editor would express his regret in brackets, and things would go on as before.

There was only one bath in the first fifteen room, and there were on the present occasion six claimants to it. And each claimant was of the fixed opinion that, whatever happened subsequently, he was going to have it first. Finally, on the suggestion of Otway, who had reduced tossing to a fine art, a mystic game of Tommy Dodd was played. Otway having triumphantly obtained first innings, the conversation reverted to the subject of the match.

The Easter term always opened with a scratch game against a mixed team of masters and old boys, and the school usually won without any great exertion. On this occasion the match had been rather more even than the average, and the team had only just pulled the thing off by a couple of tries to a goal. Otway expressed an opinion that the school had played badly.

"Why on earth don't you forwards let the ball out occasionally?" he asked. Otway was one of the first fifteen halves.

"They were so jolly heavy in the scrum," said Maurice, one of the forwards. "And when we did let it out, the outsides nearly always mucked it."

"Well, it wasn't the halves' fault. We always got it out to the centres."

"It wasn't the centres," put in Robinson. "They played awfully well. Trevor was ripping."

"Trevor always is," said Otway; "I should think he's about the best captain we've had here for a long time. He's certainly one of the best centres."

"Best there's been since Rivers-Jones," said Clephane.

Rivers-Jones was one of those players who mark an epoch. He had been in the team fifteen years ago, and had left Wrykyn to captain Cambridge and play three years in succession for Wales. The school regarded the standard set by him as one that did not admit of comparison. However good a Wrykyn centre three-quarter might be, the most he could hope to be considered was "the best since Rivers-Jones". "Since" Rivers-Jones, however, covered fifteen years, and to be looked on as the best centre the school could boast of during that time, meant something. For Wrykyn knew how to play football.

Since it had been decided thus that the faults in the school attack did not lie with the halves, forwards, or centres, it was more or less evident that they must be attributable to the wings. And the search for the weak spot was even further narrowed down by the general verdict that Clowes, on the left wing, had played well. With a beautiful unanimity the six occupants of the first fifteen room came to the conclusion that the man who had let the team down that day had been the man on the right——Rand-Brown, to wit, of Seymour's.

"I'll bet he doesn't stay in the first long," said Clephane, who was now in the bath, vice Otway, retired. "I suppose they had to try him, as he was the senior wing three-quarter of the second, but he's no earthly good."

"He only got into the second because he's big," was Robinson's opinion. "A man who's big and strong can always get his second colours."

"Even if he's a funk, like Rand-Brown," said Clephane. "Did any of you chaps notice the way he let Paget through that time he scored for them? He simply didn't attempt to tackle him. He could have brought him down like a shot if he'd only gone for him. Paget was running straight along the touch-line, and hadn't any room to dodge. I know Trevor was jolly sick about it. And then he let him through once before in just the same way in the first half, only Trevor got round and stopped him. He was rank."

"Missed every other pass, too," said Otway.

Clephane summed up.

"He was rank," he said again. "Trevor won't keep him in the team long."

"I wish Paget hadn't left," said Otway, referring to the wing three-quarter who, by leaving unexpectedly at the end of the Christmas term, had let Rand-Brown into the team. His loss was likely to be felt. Up till Christmas Wrykyn had done well, and Paget had been their scoring man. Rand-Brown had occupied a similar position in the second fifteen. He was big and speedy, and in second fifteen matches these qualities make up for a great deal. If a man scores one or two tries in nearly every match, people are inclined to overlook in him such failings as timidity and clumsiness. It is only when he comes to be tried in football of a higher class that he is seen through. In the second fifteen the fact that Rand-Brown was afraid to tackle his man had almost escaped notice. But the habit would not do in first fifteen circles.

"All the same," said Clephane, pursuing his subject, "if they don't play him, I don't see who they're going to get. He's the best of the second three-quarters, as far as I can see."

It was this very problem that was puzzling Trevor, as he walked off the field with Paget and Clowes, when they had got into their blazers after the match. Clowes was in the same house as Trevor—¬Donaldson's—¬and Paget was staying there, too. He had been head of Donaldson's up to Christmas.

"It strikes me," said Paget, "the school haven't got over the holidays yet. I never saw such a lot of slackers. You ought to have taken thirty points off the sort of team you had against you today."

"Have you ever known the school play well on the second day of term?" asked Clowes. "The forwards always play as if the whole thing bored them to death."

"It wasn't the forwards that mattered so much," said Trevor. "They'll shake down all right after a few matches. A little running and passing will put them right."

"Let's hope so," Paget observed, "or we might as well scratch to Ripton at once. There's a jolly sight too much of the mince-pie and Christmas pudding about their play at present." There was a pause. Then Paget brought out the question towards which he had been moving all the time.

"What do you think of Rand-Brown?" he asked.

It was pretty clear by the way he spoke what he thought of that player himself, but in discussing with a football captain the capabilities of the various members of his team, it is best to avoid a too positive statement one way or the other before one has heard his views on the subject. And Paget was one of those people who like to know the opinions of others before committing themselves.

Clowes, on the other hand, was in the habit of forming his views on his own account, and expressing them. If people agreed with them, well and good: it afforded strong presumptive evidence of their sanity. If they disagreed, it was unfortunate, but he was not going to alter his opinions for that, unless convinced at great length that they were unsound. He summed things up, and gave you the result. You could take it or leave it, as you preferred.

"I thought he was bad," said Clowes.

"Bad!" exclaimed Trevor, "he was a disgrace. One can understand a chap having his off-days at any game, but one doesn't expect a man in the Wrykyn first to funk. He mucked five out of every six passes I gave him, too, and the ball wasn't a bit slippery. Still, I shouldn't mind that so much if he had only gone for his man properly. It isn't being out of practice that makes you funk. And even when he did have a try at you, Paget, he always went high."

"That," said Clowes thoughtfully, "would seem to show that he was game."

Nobody so much as smiled. Nobody ever did smile at Clowes' essays in wit, perhaps because of the solemn, almost sad, tone of voice in which he delivered them. He was tall and dark and thin, and had a pensive eye, which encouraged the more soulful of his female relatives to entertain hopes that he would some day take orders.

"Well," said Paget, relieved at finding that he did not stand alone in his views on Rand-Brown's performance, "I must say I thought he was awfully bad myself."

"I shall try somebody else next match," said Trevor. "It'll be rather hard, though. The man one would naturally put in, Bryce, left at Christmas, worse luck."

Bryce was the other wing three-quarter of the second fifteen.

"Isn't there anybody in the third?" asked Paget.

"Barry," said Clowes briefly.

"Clowes thinks Barry's good," explained Trevor.

"He is good," said Clowes. "I admit he's small, but he can tackle."

"The question is, would he be any good in the first? A chap might do jolly well for the third, and still not be worth trying for the first."

"I don't remember much about Barry," said Paget, "except being collared by him when we played Seymour's last year in the final. I certainly came away with a sort of impression that he could tackle. I thought he marked me jolly well."

"There you are, then," said Clowes. "A year ago Barry could tackle Paget. There's no reason for supposing that he's fallen off since then. We've seen that Rand-Brown can't tackle Paget. Ergo, Barry is better worth playing for the team than Rand-Brown. Q.E.D."

"All right, then," replied Trevor. "There can't be any harm in trying him. We'll have another scratch game on Thursday. Will you be here then, Paget?"

"Oh, yes. I'm stopping till Saturday."

"Good man. Then we shall be able to see how he does against you. I wish you hadn't left, though, by Jove. We should have had Ripton on toast, the same as last term."

Wrykyn played five schools, but six school matches. The school that they played twice in the season was Ripton. To win one Ripton match meant that, however many losses it might have sustained in the other matches, the school had had, at any rate, a passable season. To win two Ripton matches in the same year was almost unheard of. This year there had seemed every likelihood of it. The match before Christmas on the Ripton ground had resulted in a win for Wrykyn by two goals and a try to a try. But the calculations of the school had been upset by the sudden departure of Paget at the end of term, and also of Bryce, who had hitherto been regarded as his understudy. And in the first Ripton match the two goals had both been scored by Paget, and both had been brilliant bits of individual play, which a lesser man could not have carried through.

The conclusion, therefore, at which the school reluctantly arrived, was that their chances of winning the second match could not be judged by their previous success. They would have to approach the Easter term fixture from another——¬a non-Paget——¬standpoint. In these circumstances it became a serious problem: who was to get the fifteenth place? Whoever played in Paget's stead against Ripton would be certain, if the match were won, to receive his colours. Who, then, would fill the vacancy?

"Rand-Brown, of course," said the crowd.

But the experts, as we have shown, were of a different opinion.

II
THE GOLD BAT

Trevor did not take long to resume a garb of civilisation. He never wasted much time over anything. He was gifted with a boundless energy, which might possibly have made him unpopular had he not justified it by results. The football of the school had never been in such a flourishing condition as it had attained to on his succeeding to the captaincy. It was not only that the first fifteen was good. The excellence of a first fifteen does not always depend on the captain. But the games, even down to the very humblest junior game, had woken up one morning—at the beginning of the previous term—to find themselves, much to their surprise, organised going concerns. Like the immortal Captain Pott, Trevor was "a terror to the shirker and the lubber". And the resemblance was further increased by the fact that he was "a toughish lot", who was "little, but steel and India-rubber". At first sight his appearance was not imposing. Paterfamilias, who had heard his son's eulogies on Trevor's performances during the holidays, and came down to watch the school play a match, was generally rather disappointed on seeing five feet six where he had looked for at least six foot one, and ten stone where he had expected thirteen. But then, what there was of Trevor was, as previously remarked, steel and india-rubber, and he certainly played football like a miniature Stoddart. It was characteristic of him that, though this was the first match of the term, his condition seemed to be as good as possible. He had done all his own work on the field and most of Rand-Brown's, and apparently had not turned a hair. He was one of those conscientious people who train in the holidays.

When he had changed, he went down the passage to Clowes' study. Clowes was in the position he frequently took up when the weather was good—wedged into his window in a sitting position, one leg in the study, the other hanging outside over space. The indoor leg lacked a boot, so that it was evident that its owner had at least had the energy to begin to change. That he had given the thing up after that, exhausted with the effort, was what one naturally expected from Clowes. He would have made a splendid actor: he was so good at resting.

"Hurry up and dress," said Trevor; "I want you to come over to the baths."

"What on earth do you want over at the baths?"

"I want to see O'Hara."

"Oh, yes, I remember. Dexter's are camping out there, aren't they? I heard they were. Why is it?"

"One of the Dexter kids got measles in the last week of the holidays, so they shunted all the beds and things across, and the chaps went back there instead of to the house."

In the winter term the baths were always boarded over and converted into a sort of extra gymnasium where you could go and box or fence when there was no room to do it in the real gymnasium. Socker and stump-cricket were also largely played there, the floor being admirably suited to such games, though the light was always rather tricky, and prevented heavy scoring.

"I should think," said Clowes, "from what I've seen of Dexter's beauties, that Dexter would like them to camp out at the bottom of the baths all the year round. It would be a happy release for him if they were all drowned. And I suppose if he had to choose any one of them for a violent death, he'd pick O'Hara. O'Hara must be a boon to a house-master. I've known chaps break rules when the spirit moved them, but he's the only one I've met who breaks them all day long and well into the night simply for amusement. I've often thought of writing to the S.P.C.A. about it. I suppose you could call Dexter an animal all right?"

"O'Hara's right enough, really. A man like Dexter would make any fellow run amuck. And then O'Hara's an Irishman to start with, which makes a difference."

There is usually one house in every school of the black sheep sort, and, if you go to the root of the matter, you will generally find that the fault is with the master of that house. A house-master who enters into the life of his house, coaches them in games—¬if an athlete—¬or, if not an athlete, watches the games, umpiring at cricket and refereeing at football, never finds much difficulty in keeping order. It may be accepted as fact that the juniors of a house will never be orderly of their own free will, but disturbances in the junior day-room do not make the house undisciplined. The prefects are the criterion. If you find them joining in the general "rags", and even starting private ones on their own account, then you may safely say that it is time the master of that house retired from the business, and took to chicken-farming. And that was the state of things in Dexter's. It was the most lawless of the houses. Mr Dexter belonged to a type of master almost unknown at a public school—¬the usher type. In a private school he might have passed. At Wrykyn he was out of place. To him the whole duty of a house-master appeared to be to wage war against his house.

When Dexter's won the final for the cricket cup in the summer term of two years back, the match lasted four afternoons—¬four solid afternoons of glorious, up-and-down cricket. Mr Dexter did not see a single ball of that match bowled. He was prowling in sequestered lanes and broken-down barns out of bounds on the off-chance that he might catch some member of his house smoking there. As if the whole of the house, from the head to the smallest fag, were not on the field watching Day's best bats collapse before Henderson's bowling, and Moriarty hit up that marvellous and unexpected fifty-three at the end of the second innings!

That sort of thing definitely stamps a master.

"What do you want to see O'Hara about?" asked Clowes.

"He's got my little gold bat. I lent it him in the holidays."

A remark which needs a footnote. The bat referred to was made of gold, and was about an inch long by an eighth broad. It had come into existence some ten years previously, in the following manner. The inter-house cricket cup at Wrykyn had originally been a rather tarnished and unimpressive vessel, whose only merit consisted in the fact that it was of silver. Ten years ago an Old Wrykinian, suddenly reflecting that it would not be a bad idea to do something for the school in a small way, hied him to the nearest jeweller's and purchased another silver cup, vast withal and cunningly decorated with filigree work, and standing on a massive ebony plinth, round which were little silver lozenges just big enough to hold the name of the winning house and the year of grace. This he presented with his blessing to be competed for by the dozen houses that made up the school of Wrykyn, and it was formally established as the house cricket cup. The question now arose: what was to be done with the other cup? The School House, who happened to be the holders at the time, suggested disinterestedly that it should become the property of the house which had won it last. "Not so," replied the Field Sports Committee, "but far otherwise. We will have it melted down in a fiery furnace, and thereafter fashioned into eleven little silver bats. And these little silver bats shall be the guerdon of the eleven members of the winning team, to have and to hold for the space of one year, unless, by winning the cup twice in succession, they gain the right of keeping the bat for yet another year. How is that, umpire?" And the authorities replied, "O men of infinite resource and sagacity, verily is it a cold day when you get left behind. Forge ahead." But, when they had forged ahead, behold! it would not run to eleven little silver bats, but only to ten little silver bats. Thereupon the headmaster, a man liberal with his cash, caused an eleventh little bat to be fashioned——for the captain of the winning team to have and to hold in the manner aforesaid. And, to single it out from the others, it was wrought, not of silver, but of gold. And so it came to pass that at the time of our story Trevor was in possession of the little gold bat, because Donaldson's had won the cup in the previous summer, and he had captained them——and, incidentally, had scored seventy-five without a mistake.

"Well, I'm hanged if I would trust O'Hara with my bat," said Clowes, referring to the silver ornament on his own watch-chain; "he's probably pawned yours in the holidays. Why did you lend it to him?"

"His people wanted to see it. I know him at home, you know. They asked me to lunch the last day but one of the holidays, and we got talking about the bat, because, of course, if we hadn't beaten Dexter's in the final, O'Hara would have had it himself. So I sent it over next day with a note asking O'Hara to bring it back with him here."

"Oh, well, there's a chance, then, seeing he's only had it so little time, that he hasn't pawned it yet. You'd better rush off and get it back as soon as possible. It's no good waiting for me. I shan't be ready for weeks."

"Where's Paget?"

"Teaing with Donaldson. At least, he said he was going to."

"Then I suppose I shall have to go alone. I hate walking alone."

"If you hurry," said Clowes, scanning the road from his post of vantage, "you'll be able to go with your fascinating pal Ruthven. He's just gone out."

Trevor dashed downstairs in his energetic way, and overtook the youth referred to.

Clowes brooded over them from above like a sorrowful and rather disgusted Providence. Trevor's liking for Ruthven, who was a Donaldsonite like himself, was one of the few points on which the two had any real disagreement. Clowes could not understand how any person in his senses could of his own free will make an intimate friend of Ruthven.

"Hullo, Trevor," said Ruthven.

"Come over to the baths," said Trevor, "I want to see O'Hara about something. Or were you going somewhere else."

"I wasn't going anywhere in particular. I never know what to do in term-time. It's deadly dull."

Trevor could never understand how any one could find term-time dull. For his own part, there always seemed too much to do in the time.

"You aren't allowed to play games?" he said, remembering something about a doctor's certificate in the past.

"No," said Ruthven. "Thank goodness," he added.

Which remark silenced Trevor. To a person who thanked goodness that he was not allowed to play games he could find nothing to say. But he ceased to wonder how it was that Ruthven was dull.

They proceeded to the baths together in silence. O'Hara, they were informed by a Dexter's fag who met them outside the door, was not about.

"When he comes back," said Trevor, "tell him I want him to come to tea tomorrow directly after school, and bring my bat. Don't forget."

The fag promised to make a point of it.

III
THE MAYOR'S STATUE

One of the rules that governed the life of Donough O'Hara, the light-hearted descendant of the O'Haras of Castle Taterfields, Co. Clare, Ireland, was "Never refuse the offer of a free tea". So, on receipt—per the Dexter's fag referred to—of Trevor's invitation, he scratched one engagement (with his mathematical master—not wholly unconnected with the working-out of Examples 200 to 206 in Hall and Knight's Algebra), postponed another (with his friend and ally Moriarty, of Dexter's, who wished to box with him in the gymnasium), and made his way at a leisurely pace towards Donaldson's. He was feeling particularly pleased with himself today, for several reasons. He had begun the day well by scoring brilliantly off Mr Dexter across the matutinal rasher and coffee. In morning school he had been put on to translate the one passage which he happened to have prepared—the first ten lines, in fact, of the hundred which formed the morning's lesson. And in the final hour of afternoon school, which was devoted to French, he had discovered and exploited with great success an entirely new and original form of ragging. This, he felt, was the strenuous life; this was living one's life as one's life should be lived.

He met Trevor at the gate. As they were going in, a carriage and pair dashed past. Its cargo consisted of two people, the headmaster, looking bored, and a small, dapper man, with a very red face, who looked excited, and was talking volubly. Trevor and O'Hara raised their caps as the chariot swept by, but the salute passed unnoticed. The Head appeared to be wrapped in thought.

"What's the Old Man doing in a carriage, I wonder," said Trevor, looking after them. "Who's that with him?"

"That," said O'Hara, "is Sir Eustace Briggs."

"Who's Sir Eustace Briggs?"

O'Hara explained, in a rich brogue, that Sir Eustace was Mayor of Wrykyn, a keen politician, and a hater of the Irish nation, judging by his letters and speeches.

They went into Trevor's study. Clowes was occupying the window in his usual manner.

"Hullo, O'Hara," he said, "there is an air of quiet satisfaction about you that seems to show that you've been ragging Dexter. Have you?"

"Oh, that was only this morning at breakfast. The best rag was in French," replied O'Hara, who then proceeded to explain in detail the methods he had employed to embitter the existence of the hapless Gallic exile with whom he had come in contact. It was that gentleman's custom to sit on a certain desk while conducting the lesson. This desk chanced to be O'Hara's. On the principle that a man may do what he likes with his own, he had entered the room privily in the dinner-hour, and removed the screws from his desk, with the result that for the first half-hour of the lesson the class had been occupied in excavating M. Gandinois from the ruins. That gentleman's first act on regaining his equilibrium had been to send O'Hara out of the room, and O'Hara, who had foreseen this emergency, had spent a very pleasant half-hour in the passage with some mixed chocolates and a copy of Mr Hornung's Amateur Cracksman. It was his notion of a cheerful and instructive French lesson.

"What were you talking about when you came in?" asked Clowes. "Who's been slanging

Ireland, O'Hara?"

"The man Briggs."

"What are you going to do about it? Aren't you going to take any steps?"

"Is it steps?" said O'Hara, warmly, "and haven't we———"

He stopped.

"Well?"

"Ye know," he said, seriously, "ye mustn't let it go any further. I shall get sacked if it's found out. An' so will Moriarty, too."

"Why?" asked Trevor, looking up from the tea-pot he was filling, "what on earth have you been doing?"

"Wouldn't it be rather a cheery idea," suggested Clowes, "if you began at the beginning."

"Well, ye see," O'Hara began, "it was this way. The first I heard of it was from Dexter. He was trying to score off me as usual, an' he said, 'Have ye seen the paper this morning, O'Hara?' I said, no, I had not. Then he said, 'Ah,' he said, 'ye should look at it. There's something there that ye'll find interesting.' I said, 'Yes, sir?' in me respectful way. 'Yes,' said he, 'the Irish members have been making their customary disturbances in the House. Why is it, O'Hara,' he said, 'that Irishmen are always thrusting themselves forward and making disturbances for purposes of self-advertisement?' 'Why, indeed, sir?' said I, not knowing what else to say, and after that the conversation ceased."

"Go on," said Clowes.

"After breakfast Moriarty came to me with a paper, and showed me what they had been saying about the Irish. There was a letter from the man Briggs on the subject. 'A very sensible and temperate letter from Sir Eustace Briggs', they called it, but bedad! if that was a temperate letter, I should like to know what an intemperate one is. Well, we read it through, and Moriarty said to me, 'Can we let this stay as it is?' And I said, 'No. We can't.' 'Well,' said Moriarty to me, 'what are we to do about it? I should like to tar and feather the man,' he said. 'We can't do that,' I said, 'but why not tar and feather his statue?' I said. So we thought we would. Ye know where the statue is, I suppose? It's in the recreation ground just across the river."

"I know the place," said Clowes. "Go on. This is ripping. I always knew you were pretty mad, but this sounds as if it were going to beat all previous records."

"Have ye seen the baths this term," continued O'Hara, "since they shifted Dexter's house into them? The beds are in two long rows along each wall. Moriarty's and mine are the last two at the end farthest from the door."

"Just under the gallery," said Trevor. "I see."

"That's it. Well, at half-past ten sharp every night Dexter sees that we're all in, locks the door, and goes off to sleep at the Old Man's, and we don't see him again till breakfast. He turns the gas off from outside. At half-past seven the next morning, Smith"———"Smith was one of the school porters———"unlocks the door and calls us, and we go over to the Hall to breakfast."

"Well?"

"Well, directly everybody was asleep last night———it wasn't till after one, as there was a rag on———Moriarty and I got up, dressed, and climbed up into the gallery. Ye know the gallery windows? They open at the top, an' it's rather hard to get out of them. But we managed it, and dropped on to the gravel outside."

"Long drop," said Clowes.

"Yes. I hurt myself rather. But it was in a good cause. I dropped first, and while I was on the ground, Moriarty came on top of me. That's how I got hurt. But it wasn't much, and we cut across the grounds, and over the fence, and down to the river. It was a fine night, and not very dark, and everything smelt ripping down by the river."

"Don't get poetical," said Clowes. "Stick to the point."

"We got into the boat-house——"

"How?" asked the practical Trevor, for the boat-house was wont to be locked at one in the morning. "Moriarty had a key that fitted," explained O'Hara, briefly. "We got in, and launched a boat——a big tub——put in the tar and a couple of brushes——there's always tar in the boat-house——and rowed across."

"Wait a bit," interrupted Trevor, "you said tar and feathers. Where did you get the feathers?"

"We used leaves. They do just as well, and there were heaps on the bank. Well, when we landed, we tied up the boat, and bucked across to the Recreation Ground. We got over the railings——beastly, spiky railings——and went over to the statue. Ye know where the statue stands? It's right in the middle of the place, where everybody can see it. Moriarty got up first, and I handed him the tar and a brush. Then I went up with the other brush, and we began. We did his face first. It was too dark to see really well, but I think we made a good job of it. When we had put about as much tar on as we thought would do, we took out the leaves——which we were carrying in our pockets——and spread them on. Then we did the rest of him, and after about half an hour, when we thought we'd done about enough, we got into our boat again, and came back."

"And what did you do till half-past seven?"

"We couldn't get back the way we'd come, so we slept in the boat-house."

"Well——I'm——hanged," was Trevor's comment on the story.

Clowes roared with laughter. O'Hara was a perpetual joy to him.

As O'Hara was going, Trevor asked him for his gold bat.

"You haven't lost it, I hope?" he said.

O'Hara felt in his pocket, but brought his hand out at once and transferred it to another pocket. A look of anxiety came over his face, and was reflected in Trevor's.

"I could have sworn it was in that pocket," he said.

"You haven't lost it?" queried Trevor again.

"He has," said Clowes, confidently. "If you want to know where that bat is, I should say you'd find it somewhere between the baths and the statue. At the foot of the statue, for choice. It seems to me——correct me if I am wrong——that you have been and gone and done it, me broth av a bhoy."

O'Hara gave up the search.

"It's gone," he said. "Man, I'm most awfully sorry. I'd sooner have lost a ten-pound note."

"I don't see why you should lose either," snapped Trevor. "Why the blazes can't you be more careful."

O'Hara was too penitent for words. Clowes took it on himself to point out the bright side.

"There's nothing to get sick about, really," he said. "If the thing doesn't turn up, though it probably will, you'll simply have to tell the Old Man that it's lost. He'll have another made. You won't be asked for it till just before Sports Day either, so you will have plenty of time to find it."

The challenge cups, and also the bats, had to be given to the authorities before the sports, to be formally presented on Sports Day.

"Oh, I suppose it'll be all right," said Trevor, "but I hope it won't be found anywhere near the statue."

O'Hara said he hoped so too.

IV
THE LEAGUE'S WARNING

The team to play in any match was always put upon the notice-board at the foot of the stairs in the senior block a day before the date of the fixture. Both first and second fifteens had matches on the Thursday of this week. The second were playing a team brought down by an old Wrykinian. The first had a scratch game.

When Barry, accompanied by M'Todd, who shared his study at Seymour's and rarely left him for two minutes on end, passed by the notice-board at the quarter to eleven interval, it was to the second fifteen list that he turned his attention. Now that Bryce had left, he thought he might have a chance of getting into the second. His only real rival, he considered, was Crawford, of the School House, who was the other wing three-quarter of the third fifteen. The first name he saw on the list was Crawford's. It seemed to be written twice as large as any of the others, and his own was nowhere to be seen. The fact that he had half expected the calamity made things no better. He had set his heart on playing for the second this term.

Then suddenly he noticed a remarkable phenomenon. The other wing three-quarter was Rand-Brown. If Rand-Brown was playing for the second, who was playing for the first?

He looked at the list.

"Come on," he said hastily to M'Todd. He wanted to get away somewhere where his agitated condition would not be noticed. He felt quite faint at the shock of seeing his name on the list of the first fifteen. There it was, however, as large as life. "M. Barry." Separated from the rest by a thin red line, but still there. In his most optimistic moments he had never dreamed of this. M'Todd was reading slowly through the list of the second. He did everything slowly, except eating.

"Come on," said Barry again.

M'Todd had, after much deliberation, arrived at a profound truth. He turned to Barry, and imparted his discovery to him in the weighty manner of one who realises the importance of his words.

"Look here," he said, "your name's not down here."

"I know. Come on."

"But that means you're not playing for the second."

"Of course it does. Well, if you aren't coming, I'm off."

"But, look here——¬"

Barry disappeared through the door. After a moment's pause, M'Todd followed him. He came up with him on the senior gravel.

"What's up?" he inquired.

"Nothing," said Barry.

"Are you sick about not playing for the second?"

"No."

"You are, really. Come and have a bun."

In the philosophy of M'Todd it was indeed a deep-rooted sorrow that could not be cured by the internal application of a new, hot bun. It had never failed in his own case.

"Bun!" Barry was quite shocked at the suggestion. "I can't afford to get myself out of condition with beastly buns."

"But if you aren't playing———"

"You ass. I'm playing for the first. Now, do you see?"

M'Todd gaped. His mind never worked very rapidly. "What about Rand-Brown, then?" he said.

"Rand-Brown's been chucked out. Can't you understand? You are an idiot. Rand-Brown's playing for the second, and I'm playing for the first."

"But you're———"

He stopped. He had been going to point out that Barry's tender years—he was only sixteen—and smallness would make it impossible for him to play with success for the first fifteen. He refrained owing to a conviction that the remark would not be wholly judicious. Barry was touchy on the subject of his size, and M'Todd had suffered before now for commenting on it in a disparaging spirit.

"I tell you what we'll do after school," said Barry, "we'll have some running and passing. It'll do you a lot of good, and I want to practise taking passes at full speed. You can trot along at your ordinary pace, and I'll sprint up from behind."

M'Todd saw no objection to that. Trotting along at his ordinary pace—five miles an hour—would just suit him.

"Then after that," continued Barry, with a look of enthusiasm, "I want to practise passing back to my centre. Paget used to do it awfully well last term, and I know Trevor expects his wing to. So I'll buck along, and you race up to take my pass. See?"

This was not in M'Todd's line at all. He proposed a slight alteration in the scheme.

"Hadn't you better get somebody else—?" he began.

"Don't be a slack beast," said Barry. "You want exercise awfully badly."

And, as M'Todd always did exactly as Barry wished, he gave in, and spent from four-thirty to five that afternoon in the prescribed manner. A suggestion on his part at five sharp that it wouldn't be a bad idea to go and have some tea was not favourably received by the enthusiastic three-quarter, who proposed to devote what time remained before lock-up to practising drop-kicking. It was a painful alternative that faced M'Todd. His allegiance to Barry demanded that he should consent to the scheme. On the other hand, his allegiance to afternoon tea—equally strong—called him back to the house, where there was cake, and also muffins. In the end the question was solved by the appearance of Drummond, of Seymour's, garbed in football things, and also anxious to practise drop-kicking. So M'Todd was dismissed to his tea with opprobrious epithets, and Barry and Drummond settled down to a little serious and scientific work.

Making allowances for the inevitable attack of nerves that attends a first appearance in higher football circles than one is accustomed to, Barry did well against the scratch team—certainly far better than Rand-Brown had done. His smallness was, of course, against him, and, on the only occasion on which he really got away, Paget overtook him and brought him down. But then Paget was exceptionally fast. In the two most important branches of the game, the taking of passes and tackling, Barry did well. As far as pluck went he had enough for two, and when the whistle blew for no-side he had not let Paget through once, and Trevor felt that his inclusion in the team had been justified. There was another scratch game on the Saturday. Barry played in it, and did much better. Paget had gone away by an early train, and the man he had to mark now was one of the masters, who had been good in his time, but was getting a trifle old for football. Barry scored twice, and on one occasion, by passing back to Trevor after the manner of Paget, enabled the captain to run in. And Trevor, like the captain in Billy Taylor, "werry much approved of what he'd done." Barry began to be regarded in the school as a regular member of the fifteen. The first of the fixture-card matches, versus the Town, was due on the following Saturday, and it was generally expected that he would play. M'Todd's devotion increased every day. He even went to the length of taking long runs with him. And if there was one thing in the world that M'Todd loathed, it was a long run.

On the Thursday before the match against the Town, Clowes came chuckling to Trevor's study after preparation, and asked him if he had heard the latest.

"Have you ever heard of the League?" he said.

Trevor pondered.

"I don't think so," he replied.

"How long have you been at the school?"

"Let's see. It'll be five years at the end of the summer term."

"Ah, then you wouldn't remember. I've been here a couple of terms longer than you, and the row about the League was in my first term."

"What was the row?"

"Oh, only some chaps formed a sort of secret society in the place. Kind of Vehmgericht, you know. If they got their knife into any one, he usually got beans, and could never find out where they came from. At first, as a matter of fact, the thing was quite a philanthropical concern. There used to be a good deal of bullying in the place then—¬at least, in some of the houses—¬and, as the prefects couldn't or wouldn't stop it, some fellows started this League."

"Did it work?"

"Work! By Jove, I should think it did. Chaps who previously couldn't get through the day without making some wretched kid's life not worth living used to go about as nervous as cats, looking over their shoulders every other second. There was one man in particular, a chap called Leigh. He was hauled out of bed one night, blindfolded, and ducked in a cold bath. He was in the School House."

"Why did the League bust up?"

"Well, partly because the fellows left, but chiefly because they didn't stick to the philanthropist idea. If anybody did anything they didn't like, they used to go for him. At last they put their foot into it badly. A chap called Robinson—¬in this house by the way—¬offended them in some way, and one morning he was found tied up in the bath, up to his neck in cold water. Apparently he'd been there about an hour. He got pneumonia, and almost died, and then the authorities began to get going. Robinson thought he had recognised the voice of one of the chaps—¬I forget his name. The chap was had up by the Old Man, and gave the show away entirely. About a dozen fellows were sacked, clean off the reel. Since then the thing has been dropped."

"But what about it? What were you going to say when you came in?"

"Why, it's been revived!"

"Rot!"

"It's a fact. Do you know Mill, a prefect, in Seymour's?"

"Only by sight."

"I met him just now. He's in a raving condition. His study's been wrecked. You never saw such a sight. Everything upside down or smashed. He has been showing me the ruins."

"I believe Mill is awfully barred in Seymour's," said Trevor. "Anybody might have ragged his study."

"That's just what I thought. He's just the sort of man the League used to go for."

"That doesn't prove that it's been revived, all the same," objected Trevor.

"No, friend; but this does. Mill found it tied to a chair."

It was a small card. It looked like an ordinary visiting card. On it, in neat print, were the words, "With the compliments of the League".

"That's exactly the same sort of card as they used to use," said Clowes. "I've seen some of them. What do you think of that?"

"I think whoever has started the thing is a pretty average-sized idiot. He's bound to get caught some time or other, and then out he goes. The Old Man wouldn't think twice about sacking a chap of that sort."

"A chap of that sort," said Clowes, "will take jolly good care he isn't caught. But it's rather sport, isn't it?"

And he went off to his study.

Next day there was further evidence that the League was an actual going concern. When Trevor came down to breakfast, he found a letter by his plate. It was printed, as the card had been. It was signed "The President of the League." And the purport of it was that the League did not wish Barry to continue to play for the first fifteen.

V
MILL RECEIVES VISITORS

Trevor's first idea was that somebody had sent the letter for a joke,—¬Clowes for choice. He sounded him on the subject after breakfast.

"Did you send me that letter?" he inquired, when Clowes came into his study to borrow a Sportsman.

"What letter? Did you send the team for tomorrow up to the sporter? I wonder what sort of a lot the Town are bringing."

"About not giving Barry his footer colours?"

Clowes was reading the paper.

"Giving whom?" he asked.

"Barry. Can't you listen?"

"Giving him what?"

"Footer colours."

"What about them?"

Trevor sprang at the paper, and tore it away from him. After which he sat on the fragments.

"Did you send me a letter about not giving Barry his footer colours?"

Clowes surveyed him with the air of a nurse to whom the family baby has just said some more than usually good thing.

"Don't stop," he said, "I could listen all day."

Trevor felt in his pocket for the note, and flung it at him. Clowes picked it up, and read it gravely.

"What are footer colours?" he asked.

"Well," said Trevor, "it's a pretty rotten sort of joke, whoever sent it. You haven't said yet whether you did or not."

"What earthly reason should I have for sending it? And I think you're making a mistake if you think this is meant as a joke."

"You don't really believe this League rot?"

"You didn't see Mill's study 'after treatment'. I did. Anyhow, how do you account for the card I showed you?"

"But that sort of thing doesn't happen at school."

"Well, it has happened, you see."

"Who do you think did send the letter, then?"

"The President of the League."

"And who the dickens is the President of the League when he's at home?"

"If I knew that, I should tell Mill, and earn his blessing. Not that I want it."

"Then, I suppose," snorted Trevor, "you'd suggest that on the strength of this letter I'd better leave Barry out of the team?"

"Satirically in brackets," commented Clowes.

"It's no good your jumping on me," he added. "I've done nothing. All I suggest is that you'd better keep more or less of a look-out. If this League's anything like the old one, you'll find they've all sorts of ways of getting at people they don't love. I shouldn't like to come down for a bath some morning, and find you already in possession, tied up like Robinson. When they found Robinson, he was quite blue both as to the face and speech. He didn't speak very clearly, but what one could catch was well worth hearing. I should advise you to sleep with a loaded revolver under your pillow."

"The first thing I shall do is find out who wrote this letter."

"I should," said Clowes, encouragingly. "Keep moving."

In Seymour's house the Mill's study incident formed the only theme of conversation that morning. Previously the sudden elevation to the first fifteen of Barry, who was popular in the house, at the expense of Rand-Brown, who was unpopular, had given Seymour's something to talk about. But the ragging of the study put this topic entirely in the shade. The study was still on view in almost its original condition of disorder, and all day comparative strangers flocked to see Mill in his den, in order to inspect things. Mill was a youth with few friends, and it is probable that more of his fellow-Seymourites crossed the threshold of his study on the day after the occurrence than had visited him in the entire course of his school career. Brown would come in to borrow a knife, would sweep the room with one comprehensive glance, and depart, to be followed at brief intervals by Smith, Robinson, and Jones, who came respectively to learn the right time, to borrow a book, and to ask him if he had seen a pencil anywhere. Towards the end of the day, Mill would seem to have wearied somewhat of the proceedings, as was proved when Master Thomas Renford, aged fourteen (who fagged for Milton, the head of the house), burst in on the thin pretence that he had mistaken the study for that of his rightful master, and gave vent to a prolonged whistle of surprise and satisfaction at the sight of the ruins. On that occasion, the incensed owner of the dismantled study, taking a mean advantage of the fact that he was a prefect, and so entitled to wield the rod, produced a handy swagger-stick from an adjacent corner, and, inviting Master Renford to bend over, gave him six of the best to remember him by. Which ceremony being concluded, he kicked him out into the passage, and Renford went down to the junior day-room to tell his friend Harvey about it.

"Gave me six, the cad," said he, "just because I had a look at his beastly study. Why shouldn't I look at his study if I like? I've a jolly good mind to go up and have another squint."

Harvey warmly approved the scheme.

"No, I don't think I will," said Renford with a yawn. "It's such a fag going upstairs."

"Yes, isn't it?" said Harvey.

"And he's such a beast, too."

"Yes, isn't he?" said Harvey.

"I'm jolly glad his study has been ragged," continued the vindictive Renford.

"It's jolly exciting, isn't it?" added Harvey. "And I thought this term was going to be slow. The Easter term generally is."

This remark seemed to suggest a train of thought to Renford, who made the following cryptic observation. "Have you seen them today?"

To the ordinary person the words would have conveyed little meaning. To Harvey they appeared to teem with import.

"Yes," he said, "I saw them early this morning."

"Were they all right?"

"Yes. Splendid."

"Good," said Renford.

Barry's friend Drummond was one of those who had visited the scene of the disaster early, before Mill's energetic hand had repaired the damage done, and his narrative was consequently in some demand.

"The place was in a frightful muck," he said. "Everything smashed except the table; and ink all over the place. Whoever did it must have been fairly sick with him, or he'd never have taken the trouble to do it so thoroughly. Made a fair old hash of things, didn't he, Bertie?"

"Bertie" was the form in which the school elected to serve up the name of De Bertini. Raoul de Bertini was a French boy who had come to Wrykyn in the previous term. Drummond's father had met his father in Paris, and Drummond was supposed to be looking after Bertie. They shared a study together. Bertie could not speak much English, and what he did speak was, like Mill's furniture, badly broken.

"Pardon?" he said.

"Doesn't matter," said Drummond, "it wasn't anything important. I was only appealing to you for corroborative detail to give artistic verisimilitude to a bald and unconvincing narrative."

Bertie grinned politely. He always grinned when he was not quite equal to the intellectual pressure of the conversation. As a consequence of which, he was generally, like Mrs Fezziwig, one vast, substantial smile.

"I never liked Mill much," said Barry, "but I think it's rather bad luck on the man."

"Once," announced M'Todd, solemnly, "he kicked me——¬for making a row in the passage." It was plain that the recollection rankled.

Barry would probably have pointed out what an excellent and praiseworthy act on Mill's part that had been, when Rand-Brown came in.

"Prefects' meeting?" he inquired. "Or haven't they made you a prefect yet, M'Todd?"

M'Todd said they had not.

Nobody present liked Rand-Brown, and they looked at him rather inquiringly, as if to ask what he had come for. A friend may drop in for a chat. An acquaintance must justify his intrusion.

Rand-Brown ignored the silent inquiry. He seated himself on the table, and dragged up a chair to rest his legs on.

"Talking about Mill, of course?" he said.

"Yes," said Drummond. "Have you seen his study since it happened?"

"Yes."

Rand-Brown smiled, as if the recollection amused him. He was one of those people who do not look their best when they smile.

"Playing for the first tomorrow, Barry?"

"I don't know," said Barry, shortly. "I haven't seen the list."

He objected to the introduction of the topic. It is never pleasant to have to discuss games with the very man one has ousted from the team.

Drummond, too, seemed to feel that the situation was an embarrassing one, for a few minutes later he got up to go over to the gymnasium.

"Any of you chaps coming?" he asked.

Barry and M'Todd thought they would, and the three left the room.

"Nothing like showing a man you don't want him, eh, Bertie? What do you think?" said Rand-Brown.

Bertie grinned politely.

VI
TREVOR REMAINS FIRM

The most immediate effect of telling anybody not to do a thing is to make him do it, in order to assert his independence. Trevor's first act on receipt of the letter was to include Barry in the team against the Town. It was what he would have done in any case, but, under the circumstances, he felt a peculiar pleasure in doing it. The incident also had the effect of recalling to his mind the fact that he had tried Barry in the first instance on his own responsibility, without consulting the committee. The committee of the first fifteen consisted of the two old colours who came immediately after the captain on the list. The powers of a committee varied according to the determination and truculence of the members of it. On any definite and important step, affecting the welfare of the fifteen, the captain theoretically could not move without their approval. But if the captain happened to be strong-minded and the committee weak, they were apt to be slightly out of it, and the captain would develop a habit of consulting them a day or so after he had done a thing. He would give a man his colours, and inform the committee of it on the following afternoon, when the thing was done and could not be repealed.

Trevor was accustomed to ask the advice of his lieutenants fairly frequently. He never gave colours, for instance, off his own bat. It seemed to him that it might be as well to learn what views Milton and Allardyce had on the subject of Barry, and, after the Town team had gone back across the river, defeated by a goal and a try to nil, he changed and went over to Seymour's to interview Milton.

Milton was in an arm-chair, watching Renford brew tea. His was one of the few studies in the school in which there was an arm-chair. With the majority of his contemporaries, it would only run to the portable kind that fold up.

"Come and have some tea, Trevor," said Milton.

"Thanks. If there's any going."

"Heaps. Is there anything to eat, Renford?"

The fag, appealed to on this important point, pondered darkly for a moment.

"There was some cake," he said.

"That's all right," interrupted Milton, cheerfully. "Scratch the cake. I ate it before the match. Isn't there anything else?"

Milton had a healthy appetite.

"Then there used to be some biscuits."

"Biscuits are off. I finished 'em yesterday. Look here, young Renford, what you'd better do is cut across to the shop and get some more cake and some more biscuits, and tell 'em to put it down to me. And don't be long."

"A miles better idea would be to send him over to Donaldson's to fetch something from my study," suggested Trevor. "It isn't nearly so far, and I've got heaps of stuff."

"Ripping. Cut over to Donaldson's, young Renford. As a matter of fact," he added, confidentially, when the emissary had vanished, "I'm not half sure that the other dodge would have worked. They seem to think at the shop that I've had about enough things on tick lately. I haven't settled up for last term yet. I've spent all I've got on this study. What do you think of those photographs?"

Trevor got up and inspected them. They filled the mantelpiece and most of the wall above it. They were exclusively theatrical photographs, and of a variety to suit all tastes. For the earnest student of the drama there was Sir Henry Irving in The Bells, and Mr Martin Harvey in The Only Way. For the admirers of the merely beautiful there were Messrs Dan Leno and Herbert Campbell.

"Not bad," said Trevor. "Beastly waste of money."

"Waste of money!" Milton was surprised and pained at the criticism. "Why, you must spend your money on something."

"Rot, I call it," said Trevor. "If you want to collect something, why don't you collect something worth having?"

Just then Renford came back with the supplies.

"Thanks," said Milton, "put 'em down. Does the billy boil, young Renford?"

Renford asked for explanatory notes.

"You're a bit of an ass at times, aren't you?" said Milton, kindly. "What I meant was, is the tea ready? If it is, you can scoot. If it isn't, buck up with it."

A sound of bubbling and a rush of steam from the spout of the kettle proclaimed that the billy did boil. Renford extinguished the Etna, and left the room, while Milton, murmuring vague formulae about "one spoonful for each person and one for the pot", got out of his chair with a groan——for the Town match had been an energetic one——and began to prepare tea.

"What I really came round about——" began Trevor.

"Half a second. I can't find the milk."

He went to the door, and shouted for Renford. On that overworked youth's appearance, the following dialogue took place.

"Where's the milk?"

"What milk?"

"My milk."

"There isn't any." This in a tone not untinged with triumph, as if the speaker realised that here was a distinct score to him.

"No milk?"

"No."

"Why not?"

"You never had any."

"Well, just cut across——no, half a second. What are you doing downstairs?"

"Having tea."

"Then you've got milk."

"Only a little." This apprehensively.

"Bring it up. You can have what we leave."

Disgusted retirement of Master Renford.

"What I really came about," said Trevor again, "was business."

"Colours?" inquired Milton, rummaging in the tin for biscuits with sugar on them. "Good brand of biscuit you keep, Trevor."

"Yes. I think we might give Alexander and Parker their third."

"All right. Any others?"

"Barry his second, do you think?"

"Rather. He played a good game today. He's an improvement on Rand-Brown."

"Glad you think so. I was wondering whether it was the right thing to do, chucking Rand-Brown out after one trial like that. But still, if you think Barry's better——"

"Streets better. I've had heaps of chances of watching them and comparing them, when they've been playing for the house. It isn't only that Rand-Brown can't tackle, and Barry can. Barry takes his passes much better, and doesn't lose his head when he's pressed."

"Just what I thought," said Trevor. "Then you'd go on playing him for the first?"

"Rather. He'll get better every game, you'll see, as he gets more used to playing in the first three-quarter line. And he's as keen as anything on getting into the team. Practises taking passes and that sort of thing every day."

"Well, he'll get his colours if we lick Ripton."

"We ought to lick them. They've lost one of their forwards, Clifford, a red-haired chap, who was good out of touch. I don't know if you remember him."

"I suppose I ought to go and see Allardyce about these colours, now. Good-bye."

There was running and passing on the Monday for every one in the three teams. Trevor and Clowes met Mr Seymour as they were returning. Mr Seymour was the football master at Wrykyn.

"I see you've given Barry his second, Trevor."

"Yes, sir."

"I think you're wise to play him for the first. He knows the game, which is the great thing, and he will improve with practice," said Mr Seymour, thus corroborating Milton's words of the previous Saturday.

"I'm glad Seymour thinks Barry good," said Trevor, as they walked on. "I shall go on playing him now."

"Found out who wrote that letter yet?"

Trevor laughed.

"Not yet," he said.

"Probably Rand-Brown," suggested Clowes. "He's the man who would gain most by Barry's not playing. I hear he had a row with Mill just before his study was ragged."

"Everybody in Seymour's has had rows with Mill some time or other," said Trevor.

Clowes stopped at the door of the junior day-room to find his fag. Trevor went on upstairs. In the passage he met Ruthven.

Ruthven seemed excited.

"I say. Trevor," he exclaimed, "have you seen your study?"

"Why, what's the matter with it?"

"You'd better go and look."

VII
"WITH THE COMPLIMENTS OF THE LEAGUE"

Trevor went and looked.

It was rather an interesting sight. An earthquake or a cyclone might have made it a little more picturesque, but not much more. The general effect was not unlike that of an American saloon, after a visit from Mrs Carrie Nation (with hatchet). As in the case of Mill's study, the only thing that did not seem to have suffered any great damage was the table. Everything else looked rather off colour. The mantelpiece had been swept as bare as a bone, and its contents littered the floor. Trevor dived among the debris and retrieved the latest addition to his art gallery, the photograph of this year's first fifteen. It was a wreck. The glass was broken and the photograph itself slashed with a knife till most of the faces were unrecognisable. He picked up another treasure, last year's first eleven. Smashed glass again. Faces cut about with knife as before. His collection of snapshots was torn into a thousand fragments, though, as Mr Jerome said of the papier-mâché trout, there may only have been nine hundred. He did not count them. His bookshelf was empty. The books had gone to swell the contents of the floor. There was a Shakespeare with its cover off. Pages twenty-two to thirty-one of Vice Versa had parted from the parent establishment, and were lying by themselves near the door. The Rogues' March lay just beyond them, and the look of the cover suggested that somebody had either been biting it or jumping on it with heavy boots.

There was other damage. Over the mantelpiece in happier days had hung a dozen sea gulls' eggs, threaded on a string. The string was still there, as good as new, but of the eggs nothing was to be seen, save a fine parti-coloured powder—¬on the floor, like everything else in the study. And a good deal of ink had been upset in one place and another.

Trevor had been staring at the ruins for some time, when he looked up to see Clowes standing in the doorway.

"Hullo," said Clowes, "been tidying up?"

Trevor made a few hasty comments on the situation. Clowes listened approvingly.

"Don't you think," he went on, eyeing the study with a critical air, "that you've got too many things on the floor, and too few anywhere else? And I should move some of those books on to the shelf, if I were you."

Trevor breathed very hard.

"I should like to find the chap who did this," he said softly.

Clowes advanced into the room and proceeded to pick up various misplaced articles of furniture in a helpful way.

"I thought so," he said presently, "come and look here."

Tied to a chair, exactly as it had been in the case of Mill, was a neat white card, and on it were the words, "With the Compliments of the League".

"What are you going to do about this?" asked Clowes. "Come into my room and talk it over."

"I'll tidy this place up first," said Trevor. He felt that the work would be a relief. "I don't want people to see this. It mustn't get about. I'm not going to have my study turned into a sort of side-show, like Mill's. You go and change. I shan't be long."

"I will never desert Mr Micawber," said Clowes. "Friend, my place is by your side. Shut the door and let's get to work."

Ten minutes later the room had resumed a more or less——though principally less——normal appearance. The books and chairs were back in their places. The ink was sopped up. The broken photographs were stacked in a neat pile in one corner, with a rug over them. The mantelpiece was still empty, but, as Clowes pointed out, it now merely looked as if Trevor had been pawning some of his household gods. There was no sign that a devastating secret society had raged through the study.

Then they adjourned to Clowes' study, where Trevor sank into Clowes' second-best chair——Clowes, by an adroit movement, having appropriated the best one——with a sigh of enjoyment. Running and passing, followed by the toil of furniture-shifting, had made him feel quite tired.

"It doesn't look so bad now," he said, thinking of the room they had left. "By the way, what did you do with that card?"

"Here it is. Want it?"

"You can keep it. I don't want it."

"Thanks. If this sort of things goes on, I shall get quite a nice collection of these cards. Start an album some day."

"You know," said Trevor, "this is getting serious."

"It always does get serious when anything bad happens to one's self. It always strikes one as rather funny when things happen to other people. When Mill's study was wrecked, I bet you regarded it as an amusing and original 'turn'. What do you think of the present effort?"

"Who on earth can have done it?"

"The Pres——"

"Oh, dry up. Of course it was. But who the blazes is he?"

"Nay, children, you have me there," quoted Clowes. "I'll tell you one thing, though. You remember what I said about it's probably being Rand-Brown. He can't have done this, that's certain, because he was out in the fields the whole time. Though I don't see who else could have anything to gain by Barry not getting his colours."

"There's no reason to suspect him at all, as far as I can see. I don't know much about him, bar the fact that he can't play footer for nuts, but I've never heard anything against him. Have you?"

"I scarcely know him myself. He isn't liked in Seymour's, I believe."

"Well, anyhow, this can't be his work."

"That's what I said."

"For all we know, the League may have got their knife into Barry for some reason. You said they used to get their knife into fellows in that way. Anyhow, I mean to find out who ragged my room."

"It wouldn't be a bad idea," said Clowes.

* * * * *

O'Hara came round to Donaldson's before morning school next day to tell Trevor that he had not yet succeeded in finding the lost bat. He found Trevor and Clowes in the former's den, trying to put a few finishing touches to the same.

"Hullo, an' what's up with your study?" he inquired. He was quick at noticing things. Trevor looked annoyed. Clowes asked the visitor if he did not think the study presented a neat and gentlemanly appearance.

"Where are all your photographs, Trevor?" persisted the descendant of Irish kings.

"It's no good trying to conceal anything from the bhoy," said Clowes. "Sit down, O'Hara—¬mind that chair; it's rather wobbly—¬and I will tell ye the story."

"Can you keep a thing dark?" inquired Trevor.

O'Hara protested that tombs were not in it.

"Well, then, do you remember what happened to Mill's study? That's what's been going on here."

O'Hara nearly fell off his chair with surprise. That some philanthropist should rag Mill's study was only to be expected. Mill was one of the worst. A worm without a saving grace. But Trevor! Captain of football! In the first eleven! The thing was unthinkable.

"But who—?" he began.

"That's just what I want to know," said Trevor, shortly. He did not enjoy discussing the affair.

"How long have you been at Wrykyn, O'Hara?" said Clowes.

O'Hara made a rapid calculation. His fingers twiddled in the air as he worked out the problem.

"Six years," he said at last, leaning back exhausted with brain work.

"Then you must remember the League?"

"Remember the League? Rather."

"Well, it's been revived."

O'Hara whistled.

"This'll liven the old place up," he said. "I've often thought of reviving it meself. An' so has Moriarty. If it's anything like the Old League, there's going to be a sort of Donnybrook before it's done with. I wonder who's running it this time."

"We should like to know that. If you find out, you might tell us."

"I will."

"And don't tell anybody else," said Trevor. "This business has got to be kept quiet. Keep it dark about my study having been ragged."

"I won't tell a soul."

"Not even Moriarty."

"Oh, hang it, man," put in Clowes, "you don't want to kill the poor bhoy, surely? You must let him tell one person."

"All right," said Trevor, "you can tell Moriarty. But nobody else, mind."

O'Hara promised that Moriarty should receive the news exclusively.

"But why did the League go for ye?"

"They happen to be down on me. It doesn't matter why. They are."

"I see," said O'Hara. "Oh," he added, "about that bat. The search is being 'vigorously prosecuted'——that's a newspaper quotation——"

"Times?" inquired Clowes.

"Wrykyn Patriot," said O'Hara, pulling out a bundle of letters. He inspected each envelope in turn, and from the fifth extracted a newspaper cutting.

"Read that," he said.

It was from the local paper, and ran as follows:——

"Hooligan Outrage——A painful sensation has been caused in the town by a deplorable ebullition of local Hooliganism, which has resulted in the wanton disfigurement of the splendid statue of Sir Eustace Briggs which stands in the New Recreation Grounds. Our readers will recollect that the statue was erected to commemorate the return of Sir Eustace as member for the borough of Wrykyn, by an overwhelming majority, at the last election. Last Tuesday some youths of the town, passing through the Recreation Grounds early in the morning, noticed that the face and body of the statue were completely covered with leaves and some black substance, which on examination proved to be tar. They speedily lodged information at the police station. Everything seems to point to party spite as the motive for the outrage. In view of the forth-coming election, such an act is highly significant, and will serve sufficiently to indicate the tactics employed by our opponents. The search for the perpetrator (or perpetrators) of the dastardly act is being vigorously prosecuted, and we learn with satisfaction that the police have already several clues."

"Clues!" said Clowes, handing back the paper, "that means the bat. That gas about 'our opponents' is all a blind to put you off your guard. You wait. There'll be more painful sensations before you've finished with this business."

"They can't have found the bat, or why did they not say so?" observed O'Hara.

"Guile," said Clowes, "pure guile. If I were you, I should escape while I could. Try Callao. There's no extradition there.

'On no petition

Is extradition

Allowed in Callao.'

Either of you chaps coming over to school?"

VIII
O'HARA ON THE TRACK

Tuesday mornings at Wrykyn were devoted—¬up to the quarter to eleven interval—¬to the study of mathematics. That is to say, instead of going to their form-rooms, the various forms visited the out-of-the-way nooks and dens at the top of the buildings where the mathematical masters were wont to lurk, and spent a pleasant two hours there playing round games or reading fiction under the desk. Mathematics being one of the few branches of school learning which are of any use in after life, nobody ever dreamed of doing any work in that direction, least of all O'Hara. It was a theory of O'Hara's that he came to school to enjoy himself. To have done any work during a mathematics lesson would have struck him as a positive waste of time, especially as he was in Mr Banks' class. Mr Banks was a master who simply cried out to be ragged. Everything he did and said seemed to invite the members of his class to amuse themselves, and they amused themselves accordingly. One of the advantages of being under him was that it was possible to predict to a nicety the moment when one would be sent out of the room. This was found very convenient.

O'Hara's ally, Moriarty, was accustomed to take his mathematics with Mr Morgan, whose room was directly opposite Mr Banks'. With Mr Morgan it was not quite so easy to date one's expulsion from the room under ordinary circumstances, and in the normal wear and tear of the morning's work, but there was one particular action which could always be relied upon to produce the desired result.

In one corner of the room stood a gigantic globe. The problem—¬how did it get into the room?—¬was one that had exercised the minds of many generations of Wrykinians. It was much too big to have come through the door. Some thought that the block had been built round it, others that it had been placed in the room in infancy, and had since grown. To refer the question to Mr Morgan would, in six cases out of ten, mean instant departure from the room. But to make the event certain, it was necessary to grasp the globe firmly and spin it round on its axis. That always proved successful. Mr Morgan would dash down from his dais, address the offender in spirited terms, and give him his marching orders at once and without further trouble.

Moriarty had arranged with O'Hara to set the globe rolling at ten sharp on this particular morning. O'Hara would then so arrange matters with Mr Banks that they could meet in the passage at that hour, when O'Hara wished to impart to his friend his information concerning the League.

O'Hara promised to be at the trysting-place at the hour mentioned.

He did not think there would be any difficulty about it. The news that the League had been revived meant that there would be trouble in the very near future, and the prospect of trouble was meat and drink to the Irishman in O'Hara. Consequently he felt in particularly good form for mathematics (as he interpreted the word). He thought that he would have no difficulty whatever in keeping Mr Banks bright and amused. The first step had to be to arouse in him an interest in life, to bring him into a frame of mind which would induce him to look severely rather than leniently on the next offender. This was effected as follows:—¬

It was Mr Banks' practice to set his class sums to work out, and, after some three-quarters of an hour had elapsed, to pass round the form what he called "solutions". These were large sheets of paper, on which he had worked out each sum in his neat handwriting to a happy ending. When the head of the form, to whom they were passed first, had finished with them, he would make a slight tear in one corner, and, having done so, hand them on to his neighbour. The neighbour, before giving them to his neighbour, would also tear them slightly. In time they would return to their patentee and proprietor, and it was then that things became exciting.

"Who tore these solutions like this?" asked Mr Banks, in the repressed voice of one who is determined that he will be calm.

No answer. The tattered solutions waved in the air.

He turned to Harringay, the head of the form.

"Harringay, did you tear these solutions like this?"

Indignant negative from Harringay. What he had done had been to make the small tear in the top left-hand corner. If Mr Banks had asked, "Did you make this small tear in the top left-hand corner of these solutions?" Harringay would have scorned to deny the impeachment. But to claim the credit for the whole work would, he felt, be an act of flat dishonesty, and an injustice to his gifted collaborateurs.

"No, sir," said Harringay.

"Browne!"

"Yes, sir?"

"Did you tear these solutions in this manner?"

"No, sir."

And so on through the form.

Then Harringay rose after the manner of the debater who is conscious that he is going to say the popular thing.

"Sir——" he began.

"Sit down, Harringay."

Harringay gracefully waved aside the absurd command.

"Sir," he said, "I think I am expressing the general consensus of opinion among my—¬ahem——¬fellow-students, when I say that this class sincerely regrets the unfortunate state the solutions have managed to get themselves into."

"Hear, hear!" from a back bench.

"It is with——¬"

"Sit down, Harringay."

"It is with heartfelt——¬"

"Harringay, if you do not sit down——¬"

"As your ludship pleases." This sotto voce.

And Harringay resumed his seat amidst applause. O'Hara got up.

"As me frind who has just sat down was about to observe——¬"

"Sit down, O'Hara. The whole form will remain after the class."

"——¬the unfortunate state the solutions have managed to get thimsilves into is sincerely regretted by this class. Sir, I think I am ixprissing the general consensus of opinion among my fellow-students whin I say that it is with heart-felt sorrow——¬"

"O'Hara!"

"Yes, sir?"

"Leave the room instantly."

"Yes, sir."

From the tower across the gravel came the melodious sound of chimes. The college clock was beginning to strike ten. He had scarcely got into the passage, and closed the door after him, when a roar as of a bereaved spirit rang through the room opposite, followed by a string of words, the only intelligible one being the noun-substantive "globe", and the next moment the door opened and Moriarty came out. The last stroke of ten was just booming from the clock.

There was a large cupboard in the passage, the top of which made a very comfortable seat. They climbed on to this, and began to talk business.

"An' what was it ye wanted to tell me?" inquired Moriarty.

O'Hara related what he had learned from Trevor that morning.

"An' do ye know," said Moriarty, when he had finished, "I half suspected, when I heard that Mill's study had been ragged, that it might be the League that had done it. If ye remember, it was what they enjoyed doing, breaking up a man's happy home. They did it frequently."

"But I can't understand them doing it to Trevor at all."

"They'll do it to anybody they choose till they're caught at it."

"If they are caught, there'll be a row."

"We must catch 'em," said Moriarty. Like O'Hara, he revelled in the prospect of a disturbance. O'Hara and he were going up to Aldershot at the end of the term, to try and bring back the light and middle-weight medals respectively. Moriarty had won the light-weight in the previous year, but, by reason of putting on a stone since the competition, was now no longer eligible for that class. O'Hara had not been up before, but the Wrykyn instructor, a good judge of pugilistic form, was of opinion that he ought to stand an excellent chance. As the prize-fighter in Rodney Stone says, "When you get a good Irishman, you can't better 'em, but they're dreadful 'asty." O'Hara was attending the gymnasium every night, in order to learn to curb his "dreadful 'astiness", and acquire skill in its place.

"I wonder if Trevor would be any good in a row," said Moriarty.

"He can't box," said O'Hara, "but he'd go on till he was killed entirely. I say, I'm getting rather tired of sitting here, aren't you? Let's go to the other end of the passage and have some cricket."

So, having unearthed a piece of wood from the debris at the top of the cupboard, and rolled a handkerchief into a ball, they adjourned.

Recalling the stirring events of six years back, when the League had first been started, O'Hara remembered that the members of that enterprising society had been wont to hold meetings in a secluded spot, where it was unlikely that they would be disturbed. It seemed to him that the first thing he ought to do, if he wanted to make their nearer acquaintance now, was to find their present rendezvous. They must have one. They would never run the risk involved in holding mass-meetings in one another's studies. On the last occasion, it had been an old quarry away out on the downs. This had been proved by the not-to-be-shaken testimony of three school-house fags, who had wandered out one half-holiday with the unconcealed intention of finding the League's place of meeting. Unfortunately for them, they had found it. They were going down the path that led to the quarry before-mentioned, when they were unexpectedly seized, blindfolded, and carried off. An impromptu court-martial was held——¬in whispers——¬and the three explorers forthwith received the most spirited "touching-up" they had ever experienced. Afterwards they were released, and returned to their house with their zeal for detection quite quenched. The episode had created a good deal of excitement in the school at the time.

On three successive afternoons, O'Hara and Moriarty scoured the downs, and on each occasion they drew blank. On the fourth day, just before lock-up, O'Hara, who had been to tea with Gregson, of Day's, was going over to the gymnasium to keep a pugilistic appointment with Moriarty, when somebody ran swiftly past him in the direction of the boarding-houses. It was almost dark, for the days were still short, and he did not recognise the runner. But it puzzled him a little to think where he had sprung from. O'Hara was walking quite close to the wall of the College buildings, and the runner had passed between it and him. And he had not heard his footsteps. Then he understood, and his pulse quickened as he felt that he was on the track. Beneath the block was a large sort of cellar-basement. It was used as a store-room for chairs, and was never opened except when prize-day or some similar event occurred, when the chairs were needed. It was supposed to be locked at other times, but never was. The door was just by the spot where he was standing. As he stood there, half-a-dozen other vague forms dashed past him in a knot. One of them almost brushed against him. For a moment he thought of stopping him, but decided not to. He could wait.

On the following afternoon he slipped down into the basement soon after school. It was as black as pitch in the cellar. He took up a position near the door.

It seemed hours before anything happened. He was, indeed, almost giving up the thing as a bad job, when a ray of light cut through the blackness in front of him, and somebody slipped through the door. The next moment, a second form appeared dimly, and then the light was shut off again.

O'Hara could hear them groping their way past him. He waited no longer. It is difficult to tell where sound comes from in the dark. He plunged forward at a venture. His hand, swinging round in a semicircle, met something which felt like a shoulder. He slipped his grasp down to the arm, and clutched it with all the force at his disposal.

IX
MAINLY ABOUT FERRETS

"Ow!" exclaimed the captive, with no uncertain voice. "Let go, you ass, you're hurting."

The voice was a treble voice. This surprised O'Hara. It looked very much as if he had put up the wrong bird. From the dimensions of the arm which he was holding, his prisoner seemed to be of tender years.

"Let go, Harvey, you idiot. I shall kick."

Before the threat could be put into execution, O'Hara, who had been fumbling all this while in his pocket for a match, found one loose, and struck a light. The features of the owner of the arm——he was still holding it——were lit up for a moment.

"Why, it's young Renford!" he exclaimed. "What are you doing down here?"

Renford, however, continued to pursue the topic of his arm, and the effect that the vice-like grip of the Irishman had had upon it.

"You've nearly broken it," he said, complainingly.

"I'm sorry. I mistook you for somebody else. Who's that with you?"

"It's me," said an ungrammatical voice.

"Who's me?"

"Harvey."

At this point a soft yellow light lit up the more immediate neighbourhood. Harvey had brought a bicycle lamp into action.

"That's more like it," said Renford. "Look here, O'Hara, you won't split, will you?"

"I'm not an informer by profession, thanks," said O'Hara.

"Oh, I know it's all right, really, but you can't be too careful, because one isn't allowed down here, and there'd be a beastly row if it got out about our being down here."

"And they would be cobbed," put in Harvey.

"Who are they?" asked O'Hara.

"Ferrets. Like to have a look at them?"

"Ferrets!"

"Yes. Harvey brought back a couple at the beginning of term. Ripping little beasts. We couldn't keep them in the house, as they'd have got dropped on in a second, so we had to think of somewhere else, and thought why not keep them down here?"

"Why, indeed?" said O'Hara. "Do ye find they like it?"

"Oh, they don't mind," said Harvey. "We feed 'em twice a day. Once before breakfast——we take it in turns to get up early——and once directly after school. And on half-holidays and Sundays we take them out on to the downs."

"What for?"

"Why, rabbits, of course. Renford brought back a saloon-pistol with him. We keep it locked up in a box—¬don't tell any one."

"And what do ye do with the rabbits?"

"We pot at them as they come out of the holes."

"Yes, but when ye hit 'em?"

"Oh," said Renford, with some reluctance, "we haven't exactly hit any yet."

"We've got jolly near, though, lots of times," said Harvey. "Last Saturday I swear I wasn't more than a quarter of an inch off one of them. If it had been a decent-sized rabbit, I should have plugged it middle stump; only it was a small one, so I missed. But come and see them. We keep 'em right at the other end of the place, in case anybody comes in."

"Have you ever seen anybody down here?" asked O'Hara.

"Once," said Renford. "Half-a-dozen chaps came down here once while we were feeding the ferrets. We waited till they'd got well in, then we nipped out quietly. They didn't see us."

"Did you see who they were?"

"No. It was too dark. Here they are. Rummy old crib this, isn't it? Look out for your shins on the chairs. Switch on the light, Harvey. There, aren't they rippers? Quite tame, too. They know us quite well. They know they're going to be fed, too. Hullo, Sir Nigel! This is Sir Nigel. Out of the 'White Company', you know. Don't let him nip your fingers. This other one's Sherlock Holmes."

"Cats-s-s—¬s!!" said O'Hara. He had a sort of idea that that was the right thing to say to any animal that could chase and bite.

Renford was delighted to be able to show his ferrets off to so distinguished a visitor.

"What were you down here about?" inquired Harvey, when the little animals had had their meal, and had retired once more into private life.

O'Hara had expected this question, but he did not quite know what answer to give. Perhaps, on the whole, he thought, it would be best to tell them the real reason. If he refused to explain, their curiosity would be roused, which would be fatal. And to give any reason except the true one called for a display of impromptu invention of which he was not capable. Besides, they would not be likely to give away his secret while he held this one of theirs connected with the ferrets. He explained the situation briefly, and swore them to silence on the subject.

Renford's comment was brief.

"By Jove!" he observed.

Harvey went more deeply into the question.

"What makes you think they meet down here?" he asked.

"I saw some fellows cutting out of here last night. And you say ye've seen them here, too. I don't see what object they could have down here if they weren't the League holding a meeting. I don't see what else a chap would be after."

"He might be keeping ferrets," hazarded Renford.

"The whole school doesn't keep ferrets," said O'Hara. "You're unique in that way. No, it must be the League, an' I mean to wait here till they come."

"Not all night?" asked Harvey. He had a great respect for O'Hara, whose reputation in the school for out-of-the-way doings was considerable. In the bright lexicon of O'Hara he believed there to be no such word as "impossible."

"No," said O'Hara, "but till lock-up. You two had better cut now."

"Yes, I think we'd better," said Harvey.

"And don't ye breathe a word about this to a soul"——a warning which extracted fervent promises of silence from both youths.

"This," said Harvey, as they emerged on to the gravel, "is something like. I'm jolly glad we're in it."

"Rather. Do you think O'Hara will catch them?"

"He must if he waits down there long enough. They're certain to come again. Don't you wish you'd been here when the League was on before?"

"I should think I did. Race you over to the shop. I want to get something before it shuts."

"Right ho!" And they disappeared.

O'Hara waited where he was till six struck from the clock-tower, followed by the sound of the bell as it rang for lock-up. Then he picked his way carefully through the groves of chairs, barking his shins now and then on their out-turned legs, and, pushing open the door, went out into the open air. It felt very fresh and pleasant after the brand of atmosphere supplied in the vault. He then ran over to the gymnasium to meet Moriarty, feeling a little disgusted at the lack of success that had attended his detective efforts up to the present. So far he had nothing to show for his trouble except a good deal of dust on his clothes, and a dirty collar, but he was full of determination. He could play a waiting game.

It was a pity, as it happened, that O'Hara left the vault when he did. Five minutes after he had gone, six shadowy forms made their way silently and in single file through the doorway of the vault, which they closed carefully behind them. The fact that it was after lock-up was of small consequence. A good deal of latitude in that way was allowed at Wrykyn. It was the custom to go out, after the bell had sounded, to visit the gymnasium. In the winter and Easter terms, the gymnasium became a sort of social club. People went there with a very small intention of doing gymnastics. They went to lounge about, talking to cronies, in front of the two huge stoves which warmed the place. Occasionally, as a concession to the look of the thing, they would do an easy exercise or two on the horse or parallels, but, for the most part, they preferred the rôle of spectator. There was plenty to see. In one corner O'Hara and Moriarty would be sparring their nightly six rounds (in two batches of three rounds each). In another, Drummond, who was going up to Aldershot as a feather-weight, would be putting in a little practice with the instructor. On the apparatus, the members of the gymnastic six, including the two experts who were to carry the school colours to Aldershot in the spring, would be performing their usual marvels. It was worth dropping into the gymnasium of an evening. In no other place in the school were so many sights to be seen.

When you were surfeited with sightseeing, you went off to your house. And this was where the peculiar beauty of the gymnasium system came in. You went up to any master who happened to be there——there was always one at least——and observed in suave accents, "Please, sir, can I have a paper?" Whereupon, he, taking a scrap of paper, would write upon it, "J. O. Jones (or A. B. Smith or C. D. Robinson) left gymnasium at such-and-such a time". And, by presenting this to the menial who opened the door to you at your house, you went in rejoicing, and all was peace.

Now, there was no mention on the paper of the hour at which you came to the gymnasium—¬only of the hour at which you left. Consequently, certain lawless spirits would range the neighbourhood after lock-up, and, by putting in a quarter of an hour at the gymnasium before returning to their houses, escape comment. To this class belonged the shadowy forms previously mentioned.

O'Hara had forgotten this custom, with the result that he was not at the vault when they arrived. Moriarty, to whom he confided between the rounds the substance of his evening's discoveries, reminded him of it. "It's no good watching before lock-up," he said. "After six is the time they'll come, if they come at all."

"Bedad, ye're right," said O'Hara. "One of these nights we'll take a night off from boxing, and go and watch."

"Right," said Moriarty. "Are ye ready to go on?"

"Yes. I'm going to practise that left swing at the body this round. The one Fitzsimmons does." And they "put 'em up" once more.

X
BEING A CHAPTER OF ACCIDENTS

On the evening following O'Hara's adventure in the vaults, Barry and M'Todd were in their study, getting out the tea-things. Most Wrykinians brewed in the winter and Easter terms, when the days were short and lock-up early. In the summer term there were other things to do—¬nets, which lasted till a quarter to seven (when lock-up was), and the baths—¬and brewing practically ceased. But just now it was at its height, and every evening, at a quarter past five, there might be heard in the houses the sizzling of the succulent sausage and other rare delicacies. As a rule, one or two studies would club together to brew, instead of preparing solitary banquets. This was found both more convivial and more economical. At Seymour's, studies numbers five, six, and seven had always combined from time immemorial, and Barry, on obtaining study six, had carried on the tradition. In study five were Drummond and his friend De Bertini. In study seven, which was a smaller room and only capable of holding one person with any comfort, one James Rupert Leather-Twigg (that was his singular name, as Mr Gilbert has it) had taken up his abode. The name of Leather-Twigg having proved, at an early date in his career, too great a mouthful for Wrykyn, he was known to his friends and acquaintances by the euphonious title of Shoeblossom. The charm about the genial Shoeblossom was that you could never tell what he was going to do next. All that you could rely on with any certainty was that it would be something which would have been better left undone.

It was just five o'clock when Barry and M'Todd started to get things ready. They were not high enough up in the school to have fags, so that they had to do this for themselves.

Barry was still in football clothes. He had been out running and passing with the first fifteen. M'Todd, whose idea of exercise was winding up a watch, had been spending his time since school ceased in the study with a book. He was in his ordinary clothes. It was therefore fortunate that, when he upset the kettle (he nearly always did at some period of the evening's business), the contents spread themselves over Barry, and not over himself. Football clothes will stand any amount of water, whereas M'Todd's "Youth's winter suiting at forty-two shillings and sixpence" might have been injured. Barry, however, did not look upon the episode in this philosophical light. He spoke to him eloquently for a while, and then sent him downstairs to fetch more water. While he was away, Drummond and De Bertini came in.

"Hullo," said Drummond, "tea ready?"

"Not much," replied Barry, bitterly, "not likely to be, either, at this rate. We'd just got the kettle going when that ass M'Todd plunged against the table and upset the lot over my bags. Lucky the beastly stuff wasn't boiling. I'm soaked."

"While we wait—¬the sausages—¬Yes?—¬a good idea—¬M'Todd, he is downstairs—¬but to wait? No, no. Let us. Shall we? Is it not so? Yes?" observed Bertie, lucidly.

"Now construe," said Barry, looking at the linguist with a bewildered expression. It was a source of no little inconvenience to his friends that De Bertini was so very fixed in his determination to speak English. He was a trier all the way, was De Bertini. You rarely caught him helping out his remarks with the language of his native land. It was English or nothing with him. To most of his circle it might as well have been Zulu.

Drummond, either through natural genius or because he spent more time with him, was generally able to act as interpreter. Occasionally there would come a linguistic effort by which even he freely confessed himself baffled, and then they would pass on unsatisfied. But, as a rule, he was equal to the emergency. He was so now.

"What Bertie means," he explained, "is that it's no good us waiting for M'Todd to come back. He never could fill a kettle in less than ten minutes, and even then he's certain to spill it coming upstairs and have to go back again. Let's get on with the sausages."

The pan had just been placed on the fire when M'Todd returned with the water. He tripped over the mat as he entered, and spilt about half a pint into one of his football boots, which stood inside the door, but the accident was comparatively trivial, and excited no remark.

"I wonder where that slacker Shoeblossom has got to," said Barry. "He never turns up in time to do any work. He seems to regard himself as a beastly guest. I wish we could finish the sausages before he comes. It would be a sell for him."

"Not much chance of that," said Drummond, who was kneeling before the fire and keeping an excited eye on the spluttering pan, "you see. He'll come just as we've finished cooking them. I believe the man waits outside with his ear to the keyhole. Hullo! Stand by with the plate. They'll be done in half a jiffy."

Just as the last sausage was deposited in safety on the plate, the door opened, and Shoeblossom, looking as if he had not brushed his hair since early childhood, sidled in with an attempt at an easy nonchalance which was rendered quite impossible by the hopeless state of his conscience.

"Ah," he said, "brewing, I see. Can I be of any use?"

"We've finished years ago," said Barry.

"Ages ago," said M'Todd.

A look of intense alarm appeared on Shoeblossom's classical features.

"You've not finished, really?"

"We've finished cooking everything," said Drummond. "We haven't begun tea yet. Now, are you happy?"

Shoeblossom was. So happy that he felt he must do something to celebrate the occasion. He felt like a successful general. There must be something he could do to show that he regarded the situation with approval. He looked round the study. Ha! Happy thought—¬the frying-pan. That useful culinary instrument was lying in the fender, still bearing its cargo of fat, and beside it—¬a sight to stir the blood and make the heart beat faster—¬were the sausages, piled up on their plate.

Shoeblossom stooped. He seized the frying-pan. He gave it one twirl in the air. Then, before any one could stop him, he had turned it upside down over the fire. As has been already remarked, you could never predict exactly what James Rupert Leather-Twigg would be up to next.

When anything goes out of the frying-pan into the fire, it is usually productive of interesting by-products. The maxim applies to fat. The fat was in the fire with a vengeance. A great sheet of flame rushed out and up. Shoeblossom leaped back with a readiness highly creditable in one who was not a professional acrobat. The covering of the mantelpiece caught fire. The flames went roaring up the chimney.

Drummond, cool while everything else was so hot, without a word moved to the mantelpiece to beat out the fire with a football shirt. Bertie was talking rapidly to himself in French.

Nobody could understand what he was saying, which was possibly fortunate.

By the time Drummond had extinguished the mantelpiece, Barry had also done good work by knocking the fire into the grate with the poker. M'Todd, who had been standing up till now in the far corner of the room, gaping vaguely at things in general, now came into action. Probably it was force of habit that suggested to him that the time had come to upset the kettle. At any rate, upset it he did——most of it over the glowing, blazing mass in the grate, the rest over Barry. One of the largest and most detestable smells the study had ever had to endure instantly assailed their nostrils. The fire in the study was out now, but in the chimney it still blazed merrily.

"Go up on to the roof and heave water down," said Drummond, the strategist. "You can get out from Milton's dormitory window. And take care not to chuck it down the wrong chimney."

Barry was starting for the door to carry out these excellent instructions, when it flew open.

"Pah! What have you boys been doing? What an abominable smell. Pah!" said a muffled voice. It was Mr Seymour. Most of his face was concealed in a large handkerchief, but by the look of his eyes, which appeared above, he did not seem pleased. He took in the situation at a glance. Fires in the house were not rarities. One facetious sportsman had once made a rule of setting the senior day-room chimney on fire every term. He had since left (by request), but fires still occurred.

"Is the chimney on fire?"

"Yes, sir," said Drummond.

"Go and find Herbert, and tell him to take some water on to the roof and throw it down." Herbert was the boot and knife cleaner at Seymour's.

Barry went. Soon afterwards a splash of water in the grate announced that the intrepid Herbert was hard at it. Another followed, and another. Then there was a pause. Mr Seymour thought he would look up to see if the fire was out. He stooped and peered into the darkness, and, even as he gazed, splash came the contents of the fourth pail, together with some soot with which they had formed a travelling acquaintance on the way down. Mr Seymour staggered back, grimy and dripping. There was dead silence in the study. Shoeblossom's face might have been seen working convulsively.

The silence was broken by a hollow, sepulchral voice with a strong Cockney accent.

"Did yer see any water come down then, sir?" said the voice.

Shoeblossom collapsed into a chair, and began to sob feebly.

* * * * *

"——¬disgraceful … scandalous … get up, Leather-Twigg … not to be trusted … babies … three hundred lines, Leather-Twigg … abominable … surprised … ought to be ashamed of yourselves … double, Leather-Twigg … not fit to have studies … atrocious …——¬"

Such were the main heads of Mr Seymour's speech on the situation as he dabbed desperately at the soot on his face with his handkerchief. Shoeblossom stood and gurgled throughout. Not even the thought of six hundred lines could quench that dauntless spirit.

"Finally," perorated Mr Seymour, as he was leaving the room, "as you are evidently not to be trusted with rooms of your own, I forbid you to enter them till further notice. It is disgraceful that such a thing should happen. Do you hear, Barry? And you, Drummond? You are not to enter your studies again till I give you leave. Move your books down to the senior day-room tonight."

And Mr Seymour stalked off to clean himself.

"Anyhow," said Shoeblossom, as his footsteps died away, "we saved the sausages."

It is this indomitable gift of looking on the bright side that makes us Englishmen what we are.

XI
THE HOUSE-MATCHES

It was something of a consolation to Barry and his friends—at any rate, to Barry and Drummond—that directly after they had been evicted from their study, the house-matches began. Except for the Ripton match, the house-matches were the most important event of the Easter term. Even the sports at the beginning of April were productive of less excitement. There were twelve houses at Wrykyn, and they played on the "knocking-out" system. To be beaten once meant that a house was no longer eligible for the competition. It could play "friendlies" as much as it liked, but, play it never so wisely, it could not lift the cup. Thus it often happened that a weak house, by fluking a victory over a strong rival, found itself, much to its surprise, in the semi-final, or sometimes even in the final. This was rarer at football than at cricket, for at football the better team generally wins.

The favourites this year were Donaldson's, though some fancied Seymour's. Donaldson's had Trevor, whose leadership was worth almost more than his play. In no other house was training so rigid. You could tell a Donaldson's man, if he was in his house-team, at a glance. If you saw a man eating oatmeal biscuits in the shop, and eyeing wistfully the while the stacks of buns and pastry, you could put him down as a Donaldsonite without further evidence. The captains of the other houses used to prescribe a certain amount of self-abnegation in the matter of food, but Trevor left his men barely enough to support life—enough, that is, of the things that are really worth eating. The consequence was that Donaldson's would turn out for an important match all muscle and bone, and on such occasions it was bad for those of their opponents who had been taking life more easily. Besides Trevor they had Clowes, and had had bad luck in not having Paget. Had Paget stopped, no other house could have looked at them. But by his departure, the strength of the team had become more nearly on a level with that of Seymour's.

Some even thought that Seymour's were the stronger. Milton was as good a forward as the school possessed. Besides him there were Barry and Rand-Brown on the wings. Drummond was a useful half, and five of the pack had either first or second fifteen colours. It was a team that would take some beating.

Trevor came to that conclusion early. "If we can beat Seymour's, we'll lift the cup," he said to Clowes.

"We'll have to do all we know," was Clowes' reply.

They were watching Seymour's pile up an immense score against a scratch team got up by one of the masters. The first round of the competition was over. Donaldson's had beaten Templar's, Seymour's the School House. Templar's were rather stronger than the School House, and Donaldson's had beaten them by a rather larger score than that which Seymour's had run up in their match. But neither Trevor nor Clowes was inclined to draw any augury from this. Seymour's had taken things easily after half-time; Donaldson's had kept going hard all through.

"That makes Rand-Brown's fourth try," said Clowes, as the wing three-quarter of the second fifteen raced round and scored in the corner.

"Yes. This is the sort of game he's all right in. The man who's marking him is no good. Barry's scored twice, and both good tries, too."

"Oh, there's no doubt which is the best man," said Clowes. "I only mentioned that it was Rand-Brown's fourth as an item of interest."

The game continued. Barry scored a third try.

"We're drawn against Appleby's next round," said Trevor. "We can manage them all right."

"When is it?"

"Next Thursday. Nomads' match on Saturday. Then Ripton, Saturday week."

"Who've Seymour's drawn?"

"Day's. It'll be a good game, too. Seymour's ought to win, but they'll have to play their best. Day's have got some good men."

"Fine scrum," said Clowes. "Yes. Quick in the open, too, which is always good business. I wish they'd beat Seymour's."

"Oh, we ought to be all right, whichever wins."

Appleby's did not offer any very serious resistance to the Donaldson attack. They were outplayed at every point of the game, and, before half-time, Donaldson's had scored their thirty points. It was a rule in all in-school matches—and a good rule, too—that, when one side led by thirty points, the match stopped. This prevented those massacres which do so much towards crushing all the football out of the members of the beaten team; and it kept the winning team from getting slack, by urging them on to score their thirty points before half-time. There were some houses—notoriously slack—which would go for a couple of seasons without ever playing the second half of a match.

Having polished off the men of Appleby, the Donaldson team trooped off to the other game to see how Seymour's were getting on with Day's. It was evidently an exciting match. The first half had been played to the accompaniment of much shouting from the ropes. Though coming so early in the competition, it was really the semi-final, for whichever team won would be almost certain to get into the final. The school had turned up in large numbers to watch.

"Seymour's looking tired of life," said Clowes. "That would seem as if his fellows weren't doing well."

"What's been happening here?" asked Trevor of an enthusiast in a Seymour's house cap whose face was crimson with yelling.

"One goal all," replied the enthusiast huskily. "Did you beat Appleby's?"

"Yes. Thirty points before half-time. Who's been doing the scoring here?"

"Milton got in for us. He barged through out of touch. We've been pressing the whole time. Barry got over once, but he was held up. Hullo, they're beginning again. Buck up, Sey-mour's."

His voice cracking on the high note, he took an immense slab of vanilla chocolate as a remedy for hoarseness.

"Who scored for Day's?" asked Clowes.

"Strachan. Rand-Brown let him through from their twenty-five. You never saw anything so rotten as Rand-Brown. He doesn't take his passes, and Strachan gets past him every time."

"Is Strachan playing on the wing?"

Strachan was the first fifteen full-back.

"Yes. They've put young Bassett back instead of him. Sey-mour's. Buck up, Seymour's. We-ell played! There, did you ever see anything like it?" he broke off disgustedly.

The Seymourite playing centre next to Rand-Brown had run through to the back and passed out to his wing, as a good centre should. It was a perfect pass, except that it came at his head instead of his chest. Nobody with any pretensions to decent play should have missed it. Rand-Brown, however, achieved that feat. The ball struck his hands and bounded forward. The referee blew his whistle for a scrum, and a certain try was lost.

From the scrum the Seymour's forwards broke away to the goal-line, where they were pulled up by Bassett. The next minute the defence had been pierced, and Drummond was lying on the ball a yard across the line. The enthusiast standing by Clowes expended the last relics of his voice in commemorating the fact that his side had the lead.

"Drummond'll be good next year," said Trevor. And he made a mental note to tell Allardyce, who would succeed him in the command of the school football, to keep an eye on the player in question.

The triumph of the Seymourites was not long lived. Milton failed to convert Drummond's try. From the drop-out from the twenty-five line Barry got the ball, and punted into touch. The throw-out was not straight, and a scrum was formed. The ball came out to the Day's halves, and went across to Strachan. Rand-Brown hesitated, and then made a futile spring at the first fifteen man's neck. Strachan handed him off easily, and ran. The Seymour's full-back, who was a poor player, failed to get across in time. Strachan ran round behind the posts, the kick succeeded, and Day's now led by two points.

After this the game continued in Day's half. Five minutes before time was up, Drummond got the ball from a scrum nearly on the line, passed it to Barry on the wing instead of opening up the game by passing to his centres, and Barry slipped through in the corner. This put Seymour's just one point ahead, and there they stayed till the whistle blew for no-side.

Milton walked over to the boarding-houses with Clowes and Trevor. He was full of the match, particularly of the iniquity of Rand-Brown. "I slanged him on the field," he said. "It's a thing I don't often do, but what else can you do when a man plays like that? He lost us three certain tries."

"When did you administer your rebuke?" inquired Clowes.

"When he had let Strachan through that second time, in the second half. I asked him why on earth he tried to play footer at all. I told him a good kiss-in-the-ring club was about his form. It was rather cheap, but I felt so frightfully sick about it. It's sickening to be let down like that when you've been pressing the whole time, and ought to be scoring every other minute."

"What had he to say on the subject?" asked Clowes.

"Oh, he gassed a bit until I told him I'd kick him if he said another word. That shut him up."

"You ought to have kicked him. You want all the kicking practice you can get. I never saw anything feebler than that shot of yours after Drummond's try."

"I'd like to see you take a kick like that. It was nearly on the touch-line. Still, when we play you, we shan't need to convert any of our tries. We'll get our thirty points without that. Perhaps you'd like to scratch?"

"As a matter of fact," said Clowes confidentially, "I am going to score seven tries against you off my own bat. You'll be sorry you ever turned out when we've finished with you."

XII
NEWS OF THE GOLD BAT

Shoeblossom sat disconsolately on the table in the senior day-room. He was not happy in exile. Brewing in the senior day-room was a mere vulgar brawl, lacking all the refining influences of the study. You had to fight for a place at the fire, and when you had got it 'twas not always easy to keep it, and there was no privacy, and the fellows were always bear-fighting, so that it was impossible to read a book quietly for ten consecutive minutes without some ass heaving a cushion at you or turning out the gas. Altogether Shoeblossom yearned for the peace of his study, and wished earnestly that Mr Seymour would withdraw the order of banishment. It was the not being able to read that he objected to chiefly. In place of brewing, the ex-proprietors of studies five, six, and seven now made a practice of going to the school shop. It was more expensive and not nearly so comfortable—there is a romance about a study brew which you can never get anywhere else—but it served, and it was not on this score that he grumbled most. What he hated was having to live in a bear-garden. For Shoeblossom was a man of moods. Give him two or three congenial spirits to back him up, and he would lead the revels with the abandon of a Mr Bultitude (after his return to his original form). But he liked to choose his accomplices, and the gay sparks of the senior day-room did not appeal to him. They were not intellectual enough. In his lucid intervals, he was accustomed to be almost abnormally solemn and respectable. When not promoting some unholy rag, Shoeblossom resembled an elderly gentleman of studious habits. He liked to sit in a comfortable chair and read a book. It was the impossibility of doing this in the senior day-room that led him to try and think of some other haven where he might rest. Had it been summer, he would have taken some literature out on to the cricket-field or the downs, and put in a little steady reading there, with the aid of a bag of cherries. But with the thermometer low, that was impossible.

He felt very lonely and dismal. He was not a man with many friends. In fact, Barry and the other three were almost the only members of the house with whom he was on speaking-terms. And of these four he saw very little. Drummond and Barry were always out of doors or over at the gymnasium, and as for M'Todd and De Bertini, it was not worth while talking to the one, and impossible to talk to the other. No wonder Shoeblossom felt dull. Once Barry and Drummond had taken him over to the gymnasium with them, but this had bored him worse than ever. They had been hard at it all the time—for, unlike a good many of the school, they went to the gymnasium for business, not to lounge—and he had had to sit about watching them. And watching gymnastics was one of the things he most loathed. Since then he had refused to go.

That night matters came to a head. Just as he had settled down to read, somebody, in flinging a cushion across the room, brought down the gas apparatus with a run, and before light was once more restored it was tea-time. After that there was preparation, which lasted for two hours, and by the time he had to go to bed he had not been able to read a single page of the enthralling work with which he was at present occupied.

He had just got into bed when he was struck with a brilliant idea. Why waste the precious hours in sleep? What was that saying of somebody's, "Five hours for a wise man, six for somebody else—he forgot whom—eight for a fool, nine for an idiot," or words to that effect? Five hours sleep would mean that he need not go to bed till half past two. In the meanwhile he could be finding out exactly what the hero did do when he found out (to his horror) that it was his cousin Jasper who had really killed the old gentleman in the wood. The only question was——how was he to do his reading? Prefects were allowed to work on after lights out in their dormitories by the aid of a candle, but to the ordinary mortal this was forbidden.

Then he was struck with another brilliant idea. It is a curious thing about ideas. You do not get one for over a month, and then there comes a rush of them, all brilliant. Why, he thought, should he not go and read in his study with a dark lantern? He had a dark lantern. It was one of the things he had found lying about at home on the last day of the holidays, and had brought with him to school. It was his custom to go about the house just before the holidays ended, snapping up unconsidered trifles, which might or might not come in useful. This term he had brought back a curious metal vase (which looked Indian, but which had probably been made in Birmingham the year before last), two old coins (of no mortal use to anybody in the world, including himself), and the dark lantern. It was reposing now in the cupboard in his study nearest the window.

He had brought his book up with him on coming to bed, on the chance that he might have time to read a page or two if he woke up early. (He had always been doubtful about that man Jasper. For one thing, he had been seen pawning the old gentleman's watch on the afternoon of the murder, which was a suspicious circumstance, and then he was not a nice character at all, and just the sort of man who would be likely to murder old gentlemen in woods.) He waited till Mr Seymour had paid his nightly visit——he went the round of the dormitories at about eleven——and then he chuckled gently. If Mill, the dormitory prefect, was awake, the chuckle would make him speak, for Mill was of a suspicious nature, and believed that it was only his unintermitted vigilance which prevented the dormitory ragging all night.

Mill was awake.

"Be quiet, there," he growled. "Shut up that noise."

Shoeblossom felt that the time was not yet ripe for his departure. Half an hour later he tried again. There was no rebuke. To make certain he emitted a second chuckle, replete with sinister meaning. A slight snore came from the direction of Mill's bed. Shoeblossom crept out of the room, and hurried to his study. The door was not locked, for Mr Seymour had relied on his commands being sufficient to keep the owner out of it. He slipped in, found and lit the dark lantern, and settled down to read. He read with feverish excitement. The thing was, you see, that though Claud Trevelyan (that was the hero) knew jolly well that it was Jasper who had done the murder, the police didn't, and, as he (Claud) was too noble to tell them, he had himself been arrested on suspicion. Shoeblossom was skimming through the pages with starting eyes, when suddenly his attention was taken from his book by a sound. It was a footstep. Somebody was coming down the passage, and under the door filtered a thin stream of light. To snap the dark slide over the lantern and dart to the door, so that if it opened he would be behind it, was with him, as Mr Claud Trevelyan might have remarked, the work of a moment. He heard the door of study number five flung open, and then the footsteps passed on, and stopped opposite his own den. The handle turned, and the light of a candle flashed into the room, to be extinguished instantly as the draught of the moving door caught it.

Shoeblossom heard his visitor utter an exclamation of annoyance, and fumble in his pocket for matches. He recognised the voice. It was Mr Seymour's. The fact was that Mr Seymour had had the same experience as General Stanley in The Pirates of Penzance:

The man who finds his conscience ache,

No peace at all enjoys;

And, as I lay in bed awake,

I thought I heard a noise.

Whether Mr Seymour's conscience ached or not, cannot, of course, be discovered. But he had certainly thought he heard a noise, and he had come to investigate.

The search for matches had so far proved fruitless. Shoeblossom stood and quaked behind the door. The reek of hot tin from the dark lantern grew worse momentarily. Mr Seymour sniffed several times, until Shoeblossom thought that he must be discovered. Then, to his immense relief, the master walked away. Shoeblossom's chance had come. Mr Seymour had probably gone to get some matches to relight his candle. It was far from likely that the episode was closed. He would be back again presently. If Shoeblossom was going to escape, he must do it now, so he waited till the footsteps had passed away, and then darted out in the direction of his dormitory.

As he was passing Milton's study, a white figure glided out of it. All that he had ever read or heard of spectres rushed into Shoeblossom's petrified brain. He wished he was safely in bed. He wished he had never come out of it. He wished he had led a better and nobler life. He wished he had never been born.

The figure passed quite close to him as he stood glued against the wall, and he saw it disappear into the dormitory opposite his own, of which Rigby was prefect. He blushed hotly at the thought of the fright he had been in. It was only somebody playing the same game as himself.

He jumped into bed and lay down, having first plunged the lantern bodily into his jug to extinguish it. Its indignant hiss had scarcely died away when Mr Seymour appeared at the door. It had occurred to Mr Seymour that he had smelt something very much out of the ordinary in Shoeblossom's study, a smell uncommonly like that of hot tin. And a suspicion dawned on him that Shoeblossom had been in there with a dark lantern. He had come to the dormitory to confirm his suspicions. But a glance showed him how unjust they had been. There was Shoeblossom fast asleep. Mr Seymour therefore followed the excellent example of my Lord Tomnoddy on a celebrated occasion, and went off to bed.

* * * * *

It was the custom for the captain of football at Wrykyn to select and publish the team for the Ripton match a week before the day on which it was to be played. On the evening after the Nomads' match, Trevor was sitting in his study writing out the names, when there came a knock at the door, and his fag entered with a letter.

"This has just come, Trevor," he said.

"All right. Put it down."

The fag left the room. Trevor picked up the letter. The handwriting was strange to him. The words had been printed. Then it flashed upon him that he had received a letter once before addressed in the same way——the letter from the League about Barry. Was this, too, from that address? He opened it.

It was.

He read it, and gasped. The worst had happened. The gold bat was in the hands of the enemy.

XIII
VICTIM NUMBER THREE

"With reference to our last communication," ran the letter——the writer evidently believed in the commercial style——"it may interest you to know that the bat you lost by the statue on the night of the 26th of January has come into our possession. We observe that Barry is still playing for the first fifteen."

"And will jolly well continue to," muttered Trevor, crumpling the paper viciously into a ball.

He went on writing the names for the Ripton match. The last name on the list was Barry's.

Then he sat back in his chair, and began to wrestle with this new development. Barry must play. That was certain. All the bluff in the world was not going to keep him from playing the best man at his disposal in the Ripton match. He himself did not count. It was the school he had to think of. This being so, what was likely to happen? Though nothing was said on the point, he felt certain that if he persisted in ignoring the League, that bat would find its way somehow——by devious routes, possibly——to the headmaster or someone else in authority. And then there would be questions——awkward questions——and things would begin to come out. Then a fresh point struck him, which was, that whatever might happen would affect, not himself, but O'Hara. This made it rather more of a problem how to act. Personally, he was one of those dogged characters who can put up with almost anything themselves. If this had been his affair, he would have gone on his way without hesitating. Evidently the writer of the letter was under the impression that he had been the hero (or villain) of the statue escapade.

If everything came out it did not require any great effort of prophecy to predict what the result would be. O'Hara would go. Promptly. He would receive his marching orders within ten minutes of the discovery of what he had done. He would be expelled twice over, so to speak, once for breaking out at night——one of the most heinous offences in the school code——and once for tarring the statue. Anything that gave the school a bad name in the town was a crime in the eyes of the powers, and this was such a particularly flagrant case. Yes, there was no doubt of that. O'Hara would take the first train home without waiting to pack up. Trevor knew his people well, and he could imagine their feelings when the prodigal strolled into their midst——an old Wrykinian malgré lui. As the philosopher said of falling off a ladder, it is not the falling that matters: it is the sudden stopping at the other end. It is not the being expelled that is so peculiarly objectionable: it is the sudden homecoming. With this gloomy vision before him, Trevor almost wavered. But the thought that the selection of the team had nothing whatever to do with his personal feelings strengthened him. He was simply a machine, devised to select the fifteen best men in the school to meet Ripton. In his official capacity of football captain he was not supposed to have any feelings. However, he yielded in so far that he went to Clowes to ask his opinion.

Clowes, having heard everything and seen the letter, unhesitatingly voted for the right course. If fifty mad Irishmen were to be expelled, Barry must play against Ripton. He was the best man, and in he must go.

"That's what I thought," said Trevor. "It's bad for O'Hara, though."

Clowes remarked somewhat tritely that business was business.

"Besides," he went on, "you're assuming that the thing this letter hints at will really come off. I don't think it will. A man would have to be such an awful blackguard to go as low as that. The least grain of decency in him would stop him. I can imagine a man threatening to do it as a piece of bluff——by the way, the letter doesn't actually say anything of the sort, though I suppose it hints at it——but I can't imagine anybody out of a melodrama doing it."

"You can never tell," said Trevor. He felt that this was but an outside chance. The forbearance of one's antagonist is but a poor thing to trust to at the best of times.

"Are you going to tell O'Hara?" asked Clowes.

"I don't see the good. Would you?"

"No. He can't do anything, and it would only give him a bad time. There are pleasanter things, I should think, than going on from day to day not knowing whether you're going to be sacked or not within the next twelve hours. Don't tell him."

"I won't. And Barry plays against Ripton."

"Certainly. He's the best man."

"I'm going over to Seymour's now," said Trevor, after a pause, "to see Milton. We've drawn Seymour's in the next round of the house-matches. I suppose you knew. I want to get it over before the Ripton match, for several reasons. About half the fifteen are playing on one side or the other, and it'll give them a good chance of getting fit. Running and passing is all right, but a good, hard game's the thing for putting you into form. And then I was thinking that, as the side that loses, whichever it is——"

"Seymour's, of course."

"Hope so. Well, they're bound to be a bit sick at losing, so they'll play up all the harder on Saturday to console themselves for losing the cup."

"My word, what strategy!" said Clowes. "You think of everything. When do you think of playing it, then?"

"Wednesday struck me as a good day. Don't you think so?"

"It would do splendidly. It'll be a good match. For all practical purposes, of course, it's the final. If we beat Seymour's, I don't think the others will trouble us much."

There was just time to see Milton before lock-up. Trevor ran across to Seymour's, and went up to his study.

"Come in," said Milton, in answer to his knock.

Trevor went in, and stood surprised at the difference in the look of the place since the last time he had visited it. The walls, once covered with photographs, were bare. Milton, seated before the fire, was ruefully contemplating what looked like a heap of waste cardboard.

Trevor recognised the symptoms. He had had experience.

"You don't mean to say they've been at you, too!" he cried.

Milton's normally cheerful face was thunderous and gloomy.

"Yes. I was thinking what I'd like to do to the man who ragged it."

"It's the League again, I suppose?"

Milton looked surprised.

"Again?" he said, "where did you hear of the League? This is the first time I've heard of its existence, whatever it is. What is the confounded thing, and why on earth have they played the fool here? What's the meaning of this bally rot?"

He exhibited one of the variety of cards of which Trevor had already seen two specimens. Trevor explained briefly the style and nature of the League, and mentioned that his study also had been wrecked.

"Your study? Why, what have they got against you?"

"I don't know," said Trevor. Nothing was to be gained by speaking of the letters he had received.

"Did they cut up your photographs?"

"Every one."

"I tell you what it is, Trevor, old chap," said Milton, with great solemnity, "there's a lunatic in the school. That's what I make of it. A lunatic whose form of madness is wrecking studies."

"But the same chap couldn't have done yours and mine. It must have been a Donaldson's fellow who did mine, and one of your chaps who did yours and Mill's."

"Mill's? By Jove, of course. I never thought of that. That was the League, too, I suppose?"

"Yes. One of those cards was tied to a chair, but Clowes took it away before anybody saw it."

Milton returned to the details of the disaster.

"Was there any ink spilt in your room?"

"Pints," said Trevor, shortly. The subject was painful.

"So there was here," said Milton, mournfully. "Gallons."

There was silence for a while, each pondering over his wrongs.

"Gallons," said Milton again. "I was ass enough to keep a large pot full of it here, and they used it all, every drop. You never saw such a sight."

Trevor said he had seen one similar spectacle.

"And my photographs! You remember those photographs I showed you? All ruined. Slit across with a knife. Some torn in half. I wish I knew who did that."

Trevor said he wished so, too.

"There was one of Mrs Patrick Campbell," Milton continued in heartrending tones, "which was torn into sixteen pieces. I counted them. There they are on the mantelpiece. And there was one of Little Tich" (here he almost broke down), "which was so covered with ink that for half an hour I couldn't recognise it. Fact."

Trevor nodded sympathetically.

"Yes," said Milton. "Soaked."

There was another silence. Trevor felt it would be almost an outrage to discuss so prosaic a topic as the date of a house-match with one so broken up. Yet time was flying, and lock-up was drawing near.

"Are you willing to play——" he began.

"I feel as if I could never play again," interrupted Milton. "You'd hardly believe the amount of blotting-paper I've used today. It must have been a lunatic, Dick, old man."

When Milton called Trevor "Dick", it was a sign that he was moved. When he called him "Dick, old man", it gave evidence of an internal upheaval without parallel.

"Why, who else but a lunatic would get up in the night to wreck another chap's study? All this was done between eleven last night and seven this morning. I turned in at eleven, and when I came down here again at seven the place was a wreck. It must have been a lunatic."

"How do you account for the printed card from the League?"

Milton murmured something about madmen's cunning and diverting suspicion, and relapsed into silence. Trevor seized the opportunity to make the proposal he had come to make, that Donaldson's v. Seymour's should be played on the following Wednesday.

Milton agreed listlessly.

"Just where you're standing," he said, "I found a photograph of Sir Henry Irving so slashed about that I thought at first it was Huntley Wright in San Toy."

"Start at two-thirty sharp," said Trevor.

"I had seventeen of Edna May," continued the stricken Seymourite, monotonously. "In various attitudes. All destroyed."

"On the first fifteen ground, of course," said Trevor. "I'll get Aldridge to referee. That'll suit you, I suppose?"

"All right. Anything you like. Just by the fireplace I found the remains of Arthur Roberts in H.M.S. Irresponsible. And part of Seymour Hicks. Under the table——"

Trevor departed.

XIV
THE WHITE FIGURE

"Suppose," said Shoe blossom to Barry, as they were walking over to school on the morning following the day on which Milton's study had passed through the hands of the League, "suppose you thought somebody had done something, but you weren't quite certain who, but you knew it was someone, what would you do?"

"What on earth do you mean?" inquired Barry.

"I was trying to make an A.B. case of it," explained Shoeblossom.

"What's an A.B. case?"

"I don't know," admitted Shoeblossom, frankly. "But it comes in a book of Stevenson's. I think it must mean a sort of case where you call everyone A. and B. and don't tell their names."

"Well, go ahead."

"It's about Milton's study."

"What! what about it?"

"Well, you see, the night it was ragged I was sitting in my study with a dark lantern——"

"What!"

Shoeblossom proceeded to relate the moving narrative of his night-walking adventure. He dwelt movingly on his state of mind when standing behind the door, waiting for Mr Seymour to come in and find him. He related with appropriate force the hair-raising episode of the weird white figure. And then he came to the conclusions he had since drawn (in calmer moments) from that apparition's movements.

"You see," he said, "I saw it coming out of Milton's study, and that must have been about the time the study was ragged. And it went into Rigby's dorm. So it must have been a chap in that dorm, who did it."

Shoeblossom was quite clever at rare intervals. Even Barry, whose belief in his sanity was of the smallest, was compelled to admit that here, at any rate, he was talking sense.

"What would you do?" asked Shoeblossom.

"Tell Milton, of course," said Barry.

"But he'd give me beans for being out of the dorm, after lights-out."

This was a distinct point to be considered. The attitude of Barry towards Milton was different from that of Shoeblossom. Barry regarded him——through having played with him in important matches——as a good sort of fellow who had always behaved decently to him. Leather-Twigg, on the other hand, looked on him with undisguised apprehension, as one in authority who would give him lines the first time he came into contact with him, and cane him if he ever did it again. He had a decided disinclination to see Milton on any pretext whatever.

"Suppose I tell him?" suggested Barry.

"You'll keep my name dark?" said Shoeblossom, alarmed.

Barry said he would make an A.B. case of it.

After school he went to Milton's study, and found him still brooding over its departed glories.

"I say, Milton, can I speak to you for a second?"

"Hullo, Barry. Come in."

Barry came in.

"I had forty-three photographs," began Milton, without preamble. "All destroyed. And I've no money to buy any more. I had seventeen of Edna May."

Barry, feeling that he was expected to say something, said, "By Jove! Really?"

"In various positions," continued Milton. "All ruined."

"Not really?" said Barry.

"There was one of Little Tich——"

But Barry felt unequal to playing the part of chorus any longer. It was all very thrilling, but, if Milton was going to run through the entire list of his destroyed photographs, life would be too short for conversation on any other topic.

"I say, Milton," he said, "it was about that that I came. I'm sorry——"

Milton sat up.

"It wasn't you who did this, was it?"

"No, no," said Barry, hastily.

"Oh, I thought from your saying you were sorry——"

"I was going to say I thought I could put you on the track of the chap who did do it——"

For the second time since the interview began Milton sat up.

"Go on," he said.

"——But I'm sorry I can't give you the name of the fellow who told me about it."

"That doesn't matter," said Milton. "Tell me the name of the fellow who did it. That'll satisfy me."

"I'm afraid I can't do that, either."

"Have you any idea what you can do?" asked Milton, satirically.

"I can tell you something which may put you on the right track."

"That'll do for a start. Well?"

"Well, the chap who told me——I'll call him A.; I'm going to make an A.B. case of it——was coming out of his study at about one o'clock in the morning——"

"What the deuce was he doing that for?"

"Because he wanted to go back to bed," said Barry.

"About time, too. Well?"

"As he was going past your study, a white figure emerged——"

"I should strongly advise you, young Barry," said Milton, gravely, "not to try and rot me in any way. You're a jolly good wing three-quarters, but you shouldn't presume on it. I'd slay the Old Man himself if he rotted me about this business."

Barry was quite pained at this sceptical attitude in one whom he was going out of his way to assist.

"I'm not rotting," he protested. "This is all quite true."

"Well, go on. You were saying something about white figures emerging."

"Not white figures. A white figure," corrected Barry. "It came out of your study——"

"——And vanished through the wall?"

"It went into Rigby's dorm.," said Barry, sulkily. It was maddening to have an exclusive bit of news treated in this way.

"Did it, by Jove!" said Milton, interested at last. "Are you sure the chap who told you wasn't pulling your leg? Who was it told you?"

"I promised him not to say."

"Out with it, young Barry."

"I won't," said Barry.

"You aren't going to tell me?"

"No."

Milton gave up the point with much cheerfulness. He liked Barry, and he realised that he had no right to try and make him break his promise.

"That's all right," he said. "Thanks very much, Barry. This may be useful."

"I'd tell you his name if I hadn't promised, you know, Milton."

"It doesn't matter," said Milton. "It's not important."

"Oh, there was one thing I forgot. It was a biggish chap the fellow saw."

"How big! My size?"

"Not quite so tall, I should think. He said he was about Seymour's size."

"Thanks. That's worth knowing. Thanks very much, Barry."

When his visitor had gone, Milton proceeded to unearth one of the printed lists of the house which were used for purposes of roll-call. He meant to find out who were in Rigby's dormitory. He put a tick against the names. There were eighteen of them. The next thing was to find out which of them was about the same height as Mr Seymour. It was a somewhat vague description, for the house-master stood about five feet nine or eight, and a good many of the dormitory were that height, or near it. At last, after much brain-work, he reduced the number of "possibles" to seven. These seven were Rigby himself, Linton, Rand-Brown, Griffith, Hunt, Kershaw, and Chapple. Rigby might be scratched off the list at once. He was one of Milton's greatest friends. Exeunt also Griffith, Hunt, and Kershaw. They were mild youths, quite incapable of any deed of devilry. There remained, therefore, Chapple, Linton, and Rand-Brown. Chapple was a boy who was invariably late for breakfast. The inference was that he was not likely to forego his sleep for the purpose of wrecking studies. Chapple might disappear from the list. Now there were only Linton and Rand-Brown to be considered. His suspicions fell on Rand-Brown. Linton was the last person, he thought, to do such a low thing. He was a cheerful, rollicking individual, who was popular with everyone and seemed to like everyone. He was not an orderly member of the house, certainly, and on several occasions Milton had found it necessary to

[61] P.G. WODEHOUSE

drop on him heavily for creating disturbances. But he was not the sort that bears malice. He took it all in the way of business, and came up smiling after it was over. No, everything pointed to Rand-Brown. He and Milton had never got on well together, and quite recently they had quarrelled openly over the former's play in the Day's match. Rand-Brown must be the man. But Milton was sensible enough to feel that so far he had no real evidence whatever. He must wait.

On the following afternoon Seymour's turned out to play Donaldson's.

The game, like most house-matches, was played with the utmost keenness. Both teams had good three-quarters, and they attacked in turn. Seymour's had the best of it forward, where Milton was playing a great game, but Trevor in the centre was the best outside on the field, and pulled up rush after rush. By half-time neither side had scored.

After half-time Seymour's, playing downhill, came away with a rush to the Donaldsonites' half, and Rand-Brown, with one of the few decent runs he had made in good class football that term, ran in on the left. Milton took the kick, but failed, and Seymour's led by three points. For the next twenty minutes nothing more was scored. Then, when five minutes more of play remained, Trevor gave Clowes an easy opening, and Clowes sprinted between the posts. The kick was an easy one, and what sporting reporters term "the major points" were easily added.

When there are five more minutes to play in an important house-match, and one side has scored a goal and the other a try, play is apt to become spirited. Both teams were doing all they knew. The ball came out to Barry on the right. Barry's abilities as a three-quarter rested chiefly on the fact that he could dodge well. This eel-like attribute compensated for a certain lack of pace. He was past the Donaldson's three-quarters in an instant, and running for the line, with only the back to pass, and with Clowes in hot pursuit. Another wriggle took him past the back, but it also gave Clowes time to catch him up. Clowes was a far faster runner, and he got to him just as he reached the twenty-five line. They came down together with a crash, Clowes on top, and as they fell the whistle blew.

"No-side," said Mr. Aldridge, the master who was refereeing.

Clowes got up.

"All over," he said. "Jolly good game. Hullo, what's up?"

For Barry seemed to be in trouble.

"You might give us a hand up," said the latter. "I believe I've twisted my beastly ankle or something."

XV
A SPRAIN AND A VACANT PLACE

"I say," said Clowes, helping him up, "I'm awfully sorry. Did I do it? How did it happen?"

Barry was engaged in making various attempts at standing on the injured leg. The process seemed to be painful.

"Shall I get a stretcher or anything? Can you walk?"

"If you'd help me over to the house, I could manage all right. What a beastly nuisance! It wasn't your fault a bit. Only you tackled me when I was just trying to swerve, and my ankle was all twisted."

Drummond came up, carrying Barry's blazer and sweater.

"Hullo, Barry," he said, "what's up? You aren't crocked?"

"Something gone wrong with my ankle. That my blazer? Thanks. Coming over to the house? Clowes was just going to help me over."

Clowes asked a Donaldson's junior, who was lurking near at hand, to fetch his blazer and carry it over to the house, and then made his way with Drummond and the disabled Barry to Seymour's. Having arrived at the senior day-room, they deposited the injured three-quarter in a chair, and sent M'Todd, who came in at the moment, to fetch the doctor.

Dr Oakes was a big man with a breezy manner, the sort of doctor who hits you with the force of a sledge-hammer in the small ribs, and asks you if you felt anything then. It was on this principle that he acted with regard to Barry's ankle. He seized it in both hands and gave it a wrench.

"Did that hurt?" he inquired anxiously.

Barry turned white, and replied that it did.

Dr Oakes nodded wisely.

"Ah! H'm! Just so. 'Myes. Ah."

"Is it bad?" asked Drummond, awed by these mystic utterances.

"My dear boy," replied the doctor, breezily, "it is always bad when one twists one's ankle."

"How long will it do me out of footer?" asked Barry.

"How long? How long? How long? Why, fortnight. Fortnight," said the doctor.

"Then I shan't be able to play next Saturday?"

"Next Saturday? Next Saturday? My dear boy, if you can put your foot to the ground by next Saturday, you may take it as evidence that the age of miracles is not past. Next Saturday, indeed! Ha, ha."

It was not altogether his fault that he treated the matter with such brutal levity. It was a long time since he had been at school, and he could not quite realise what it meant to Barry not to be able to play against Ripton. As for Barry, he felt that he had never loathed and detested any one so thoroughly as he loathed and detested Dr Oakes at that moment.

"I don't see where the joke comes in," said Clowes, when he had gone. "I bar that man."

"He's a beast," said Drummond. "I can't understand why they let a tout like that be the school doctor."

Barry said nothing. He was too sore for words.

What Dr Oakes said to his wife that evening was: "Over at the school, my dear, this afternoon. This afternoon. Boy with a twisted ankle. Nice young fellow. Very much put out when I told him he could not play football for a fortnight. But I chaffed him, and cheered him up in no time. I cheered him up in no time, my dear."

"I'm sure you did, dear," said Mrs Oakes. Which shows how differently the same thing may strike different people. Barry certainly did not look as if he had been cheered up when Clowes left the study and went over to tell Trevor that he would have to find a substitute for his right wing three-quarter against Ripton.

Trevor had left the field without noticing Barry's accident, and he was tremendously pleased at the result of the game.

"Good man," he said, when Clowes came in, "you saved the match."

"And lost the Ripton match probably," said Clowes, gloomily.

"What do you mean?"

"That last time I brought down Barry I crocked him. He's in his study now with a sprained ankle. I've just come from there. Oakes has seen him, and says he mustn't play for a fortnight."

"Great Scott!" said Trevor, blankly. "What on earth shall we do?"

"Why not move Strachan up to the wing, and put somebody else back instead of him? Strachan is a good wing."

Trevor shook his head.

"No. There's nobody good enough to play back for the first. We mustn't risk it."

"Then I suppose it must be Rand-Brown?"

"I suppose so."

"He may do better than we think. He played quite a decent game today. That try he got wasn't half a bad one."

"He'd be all right if he didn't funk. But perhaps he wouldn't funk against Ripton. In a match like that anybody would play up. I'll ask Milton and Allardyce about it."

"I shouldn't go to Milton today," said Clowes. "I fancy he'll want a night's rest before he's fit to talk to. He must be a bit sick about this match. I know he expected Seymour's to win."

He went out, but came back almost immediately.

"I say," he said, "there's one thing that's just occurred to me. This'll please the League. I mean, this ankle business of Barry's."

The same idea had struck Trevor. It was certainly a respite. But he regretted it for all that. What he wanted was to beat Ripton, and Barry's absence would weaken the team. However, it was good in its way, and cleared the atmosphere for the time. The League would hardly do anything with regard to the carrying out of their threat while Barry was on the sick-list.

Next day, having given him time to get over the bitterness of defeat in accordance with

Clowes' thoughtful suggestion, Trevor called on Milton, and asked him what his opinion was on the subject of the inclusion of Rand-Brown in the first fifteen in place of Barry.

"He's the next best man," he added, in defence of the proposal.

"I suppose so," said Milton. "He'd better play, I suppose. There's no one else."

"Clowes thought it wouldn't be a bad idea to shove Strachan on the wing, and put somebody else back."

"Who is there to put?"

"Jervis?"

"Not good enough. No, it's better to be weakish on the wing than at back. Besides, Rand-Brown may do all right. He played well against you."

"Yes," said Trevor. "Study looks a bit better now," he added, as he was going, having looked round the room. "Still a bit bare, though."

Milton sighed. "It will never be what it was."

"Forty-three theatrical photographs want some replacing, of course," said Trevor. "But it isn't bad, considering."

"How's yours?"

"Oh, mine's all right, except for the absence of photographs."

"I say, Trevor."

"Yes?" said Trevor, stopping at the door. Milton's voice had taken on the tone of one who is about to disclose dreadful secrets.

"Would you like to know what I think?"

"What?"

"Why, I'm pretty nearly sure who it was that ragged my study?"

"By Jove! What have you done to him?"

"Nothing as yet. I'm not quite sure of my man."

"Who is the man?"

"Rand-Brown."

"By Jove! Clowes once said he thought Rand-Brown must be the President of the League. But then, I don't see how you can account for my study being wrecked. He was out on the field when it was done."

"Why, the League, of course. You don't suppose he's the only man in it? There must be a lot of them."

"But what makes you think it was Rand-Brown?"

Milton told him the story of Shoeblossom, as Barry had told it to him. The only difference was that Trevor listened without any of the scepticism which Milton had displayed on hearing it. He was getting excited. It all fitted in so neatly. If ever there was circumstantial evidence against a man, here it was against Rand-Brown. Take the two cases. Milton had quarrelled with him. Milton's study was wrecked "with the compliments of the League". Trevor had turned him out of the first fifteen. Trevor's study was wrecked "with the compliments of the League". As Clowes had pointed out, the man with the most obvious motive for not wishing Barry to play for the school was Rand-Brown. It seemed a true bill.

"I shouldn't wonder if you're right," he said, "but of course one can't do anything yet. You want a lot more evidence. Anyhow, we must play him against Ripton, I suppose. Which is his study? I'll go and tell him now."

"Ten."

Trevor knocked at the door of study Ten. Rand-Brown was sitting over the fire, reading. He jumped up when he saw that it was Trevor who had come in, and to his visitor it seemed that his face wore a guilty look.

"What do you want?" said Rand-Brown.

It was not the politest way of welcoming a visitor. It increased Trevor's suspicions. The man was afraid. A great idea darted into his mind. Why not go straight to the point and have it out with him here and now? He had the League's letter about the bat in his pocket. He would confront him with it and insist on searching the study there and then. If Rand-Brown were really, as he suspected, the writer of the letter, the bat must be in this room somewhere. Search it now, and he would have no time to hide it. He pulled out the letter.

"I believe you wrote that," he said.

Trevor was always direct.

Rand-Brown seemed to turn a little pale, but his voice when he replied was quite steady.

"That's a lie," he said.

"Then, perhaps," said Trevor, "you wouldn't object to proving it."

"How?"

"By letting me search your study?"

"You don't believe my word?"

"Why should I? You don't believe mine."

Rand-Brown made no comment on this remark.

"Was that what you came here for?" he asked.

"No," said Trevor; "as a matter of fact, I came to tell you to turn out for running and passing with the first tomorrow afternoon. You're playing against Ripton on Saturday."

Rand-Brown's attitude underwent a complete transformation at the news. He became friendliness itself.

"All right," he said. "I say, I'm sorry I said what I did about lying. I was rather sick that you should think I wrote that rot you showed me. I hope you don't mind."

"Not a bit. Do you mind my searching your study?"

For a moment Rand-Brown looked vicious. Then he sat down with a laugh.

"Go on," he said; "I see you don't believe me. Here are the keys if you want them."

Trevor thanked him, and took the keys. He opened every drawer and examined the writing-desk. The bat was in none of these places. He looked in the cupboards. No bat there.

"Like to take up the carpet?" inquired Rand-Brown.

"No, thanks."

"Search me if you like. Shall I turn out my pockets?"

"Yes, please," said Trevor, to his surprise. He had not expected to be taken literally.

Rand-Brown emptied them, but the bat was not there. Trevor turned to go.

"You've not looked inside the legs of the chairs yet," said Rand-Brown. "They may be hollow. There's no knowing."

"It doesn't matter, thanks," said Trevor. "Sorry for troubling you. Don't forget tomorrow afternoon."

And he went, with the very unpleasant feeling that he had been badly scored off.

XVI
THE RIPTON MATCH

It was a curious thing in connection with the matches between Ripton and Wrykyn, that Ripton always seemed to be the bigger team. They always had a gigantic pack of forwards, who looked capable of shoving a hole through one of the pyramids. Possibly they looked bigger to the Wrykinians than they really were. Strangers always look big on the football field. When you have grown accustomed to a person's appearance, he does not look nearly so large. Milton, for instance, never struck anybody at Wrykyn as being particularly big for a school forward, and yet today he was the heaviest man on the field by a quarter of a stone. But, taken in the mass, the Ripton pack were far heavier than their rivals. There was a legend current among the lower forms at Wrykyn that fellows were allowed to stop on at Ripton till they were twenty-five, simply to play football. This is scarcely likely to have been based on fact. Few lower form legends are.

Jevons, the Ripton captain, through having played opposite Trevor for three seasons—he was the Ripton left centre-three-quarter—had come to be quite an intimate of his. Trevor had gone down with Milton and Allardyce to meet the team at the station, and conduct them up to the school.

"How have you been getting on since Christmas?" asked Jevons.

"Pretty well. We've lost Paget, I suppose you know?"

"That was the fast man on the wing, wasn't it?"

"Yes."

"Well, we've lost a man, too."

"Oh, yes, that red-haired forward. I remember him."

"It ought to make us pretty even. What's the ground like?"

"Bit greasy, I should think. We had some rain late last night."

The ground was a bit greasy. So was the ball. When Milton kicked off up the hill with what wind there was in his favour, the outsides of both teams found it difficult to hold the ball. Jevons caught it on his twenty-five line, and promptly handed it forward. The first scrum was formed in the heart of the enemy's country.

A deep, swelling roar from either touch-line greeted the school's advantage. A feature of a big match was always the shouting. It rarely ceased throughout the whole course of the game, the monotonous but impressive sound of five hundred voices all shouting the same word. It was worth hearing. Sometimes the evenness of the noise would change to an excited crescendo as a school three-quarter got off, or the school back pulled up the attack with a fine piece of defence. Sometimes the shouting would give place to clapping when the school was being pressed and somebody had found touch with a long kick. But mostly the man on the ropes roared steadily and without cessation, and with the full force of his lungs, the word "Wrykyn!"

The scrum was a long one. For two minutes the forwards heaved and strained, now one side, now the other, gaining a few inches. The Wrykyn pack were doing all they knew to heel, but their opponents' superior weight was telling. Ripton had got the ball, and were keeping it. Their game was to break through with it and rush. Then suddenly one of their forwards kicked it on, and just at that moment the opposition of the Wrykyn pack gave way, and the scrum broke up. The ball came out on the Wrykyn side, and Allardyce whipped it out to Deacon, who was playing half with him.

"Ball's out," cried the Ripton half who was taking the scrum. "Break up. It's out."

And his colleague on the left darted across to stop Trevor, who had taken Deacon's pass, and was running through on the right.

Trevor ran splendidly. He was a three-quarter who took a lot of stopping when he once got away. Jevons and the Ripton half met him almost simultaneously, and each slackened his pace for the fraction of a second, to allow the other to tackle. As they hesitated, Trevor passed them. He had long ago learned that to go hard when you have once started is the thing that pays.

He could see that Rand-Brown was racing up for the pass, and, as he reached the back, he sent the ball to him, waist-high. Then the back got to him, and he came down with a thud, with a vision, seen from the corner of his eye, of the ball bounding forward out of the wing three-quarter's hands into touch. Rand-Brown had bungled the pass in the old familiar way, and lost a certain try.

The touch-judge ran up with his flag waving in the air, but the referee had other views.

"Knocked on inside," he said; "scrum here."

"Here" was, Trevor saw with unspeakable disgust, some three yards from the goal-line. Rand-Brown had only had to take the pass, and he must have scored.

The Ripton forwards were beginning to find their feet better now, and they carried the scrum. A truculent-looking warrior in one of those ear-guards which are tied on by strings underneath the chin, and which add fifty per cent to the ferocity of a forward's appearance, broke away with the ball at his feet, and swept down the field with the rest of the pack at his heels. Trevor arrived too late to pull up the rush, which had gone straight down the right touch-line, and it was not till Strachan fell on the ball on the Wrykyn twenty-five line that the danger ceased to threaten.

Even now the school were in a bad way. The enemy were pressing keenly, and a real piece of combination among their three-quarters would only too probably end in a try. Fortunately for them, Allardyce and Deacon were a better pair of halves than the couple they were marking. Also, the Ripton forwards heeled slowly, and Allardyce had generally got his man safely buried in the mud before he could pass.

He was just getting round for the tenth time to bottle his opponent as before, when he slipped. When the ball came out he was on all fours, and the Ripton exponent, finding to his great satisfaction that he had not been tackled, whipped the ball out on the left, where a wing three-quarter hovered.

This was the man Rand-Brown was supposed to be marking, and once again did Barry's substitute prove of what stuff his tackling powers were made. After his customary moment of hesitation, he had at the Riptonian's neck. The Riptonian handed him off in a manner that recalled the palmy days of the old Prize Ring——handing off was always slightly vigorous in the Ripton v. Wrykyn match——and dashed over the line in the extreme corner.

There was anguish on the two touch-lines. Trevor looked savage, but made no comment. The team lined up in silence.

It takes a very good kick to convert a try from the touch-line. Jevons' kick was a long one, but it fell short. Ripton led by a try to nothing.

A few more scrums near the halfway line, and a fine attempt at a dropped goal by the Ripton back, and it was half-time, with the score unaltered.

During the interval there were lemons. An excellent thing is your lemon at half-time. It cools the mouth, quenches the thirst, stimulates the desire to be at them again, and improves the play.

Possibly the Wrykyn team had been happier in their choice of lemons on this occasion, for no sooner had the game been restarted than Clowes ran the whole length of the field, dodged through the three-quarters, punted over the back's head, and scored a really brilliant try, of the sort that Paget had been fond of scoring in the previous term. The man on the touch-line brightened up wonderfully, and began to try and calculate the probable score by the end of the game, on the assumption that, as a try had been scored in the first two minutes, ten would be scored in the first twenty, and so on.

But the calculations were based on false premises. After Strachan had failed to convert, and the game had been resumed with the score at one try all, play settled down in the centre, and neither side could pierce the other's defence. Once Jevons got off for Ripton, but Trevor brought him down safely, and once Rand-Brown let his man through, as before, but Strachan was there to meet him, and the effort came to nothing. For Wrykyn, no one did much except tackle. The forwards were beaten by the heavier pack, and seldom let the ball out. Allardyce intercepted a pass when about ten minutes of play remained, and ran through to the back. But the back, who was a capable man and in his third season in the team, laid him low scientifically before he could reach the line.

Altogether it looked as if the match were going to end in a draw. The Wrykyn defence, with the exception of Rand-Brown, was too good to be penetrated, while the Ripton forwards, by always getting the ball in the scrums, kept them from attacking. It was about five minutes from the end of the game when the Ripton right centre-three-quarter, in trying to punt across to the wing, miskicked and sent the ball straight into the hands of Trevor's colleague in the centre. Before his man could get round to him he had slipped through, with Trevor backing him up. The back, as a good back should, seeing two men coming at him, went for the man with the ball. But by the time he had brought him down, the ball was no longer where it had originally been. Trevor had got it, and was running in between the posts.

This time Strachan put on the extra two points without difficulty.

Ripton played their hardest for the remaining minutes, but without result. The game ended with Wrykyn a goal ahead——a goal and a try to a try. For the second time in one season the Ripton match had ended in a victory——a thing it was very rarely in the habit of doing.

* * * * *

The senior day-room at Seymour's rejoiced considerably that night. The air was dark with flying cushions, and darker still, occasionally, when the usual humorist turned the gas out. Milton was out, for he had gone to the dinner which followed the Ripton match, and the man in command of the house in his absence was Mill. And the senior day-room had no respect whatever for Mill.

Barry joined in the revels as well as his ankle would let him, but he was not feeling happy. The disappointment of being out of the first still weighed on him.

At about eight, when things were beginning to grow really lively, and the noise seemed likely to crack the window at any moment, the door was flung open and Milton stalked in.

"What's all this row?" he inquired. "Stop it at once."

As a matter of fact, the row had stopped——¬directly he came in.

"Is Barry here?" he asked.

"Yes," said that youth.

"Congratulate you on your first, Barry. We've just had a meeting and given you your colours. Trevor told me to tell you."

XVII
THE WATCHERS IN THE VAULT

For the next three seconds you could have heard a cannonball drop. And that was equivalent, in the senior day-room at Seymour's, to a dead silence. Barry stood in the middle of the room leaning on the stick on which he supported life, now that his ankle had been injured, and turned red and white in regular rotation, as the magnificence of the news came home to him.

Then the small voice of Linton was heard.

"That'll be six d. I'll trouble you for, young Sammy," said Linton. For he had betted an even sixpence with Master Samuel Menzies that Barry would get his first fifteen cap this term, and Barry had got it.

A great shout went up from every corner of the room. Barry was one of the most popular members of the house, and every one had been sorry for him when his sprained ankle had apparently put him out of the running for the last cap.

"Good old Barry," said Drummond, delightedly. Barry thanked him in a dazed way.

Every one crowded in to shake his hand. Barry thanked then all in a dazed way.

And then the senior day-room, in spite of the fact that Milton had returned, gave itself up to celebrating the occasion with one of the most deafening uproars that had ever been heard even in that factory of noise. A babel of voices discussed the match of the afternoon, each trying to outshout the other. In one corner Linton was beating wildly on a biscuit-tin with part of a broken chair. Shoeblossom was busy in the opposite corner executing an intricate step-dance on somebody else's box. M'Todd had got hold of the red-hot poker, and was burning his initials in huge letters on the seat of a chair. Every one, in short, was enjoying himself, and it was not until an advanced hour that comparative quiet was restored. It was a great evening for Barry, the best he had ever experienced.

Clowes did not learn the news till he saw it on the notice-board, on the following Monday. When he saw it he whistled softly.

"I see you've given Barry his first," he said to Trevor, when they met. "Rather sensational."

"Milton and Allardyce both thought he deserved it. If he'd been playing instead of Rand-Brown, they wouldn't have scored at all probably, and we should have got one more try."

"That's all right," said Clowes. "He deserves it right enough, and I'm jolly glad you've given it him. But things will begin to move now, don't you think? The League ought to have a word to say about the business. It'll be a facer for them."

"Do you remember," asked Trevor, "saying that you thought it must be Rand-Brown who wrote those letters?"

"Yes. Well?"

"Well, Milton had an idea that it was Rand-Brown who ragged his study."

"What made him think that?"

Trevor related the Shoeblossom incident.

Clowes became quite excited.

"Then Rand-Brown must be the man," he said. "Why don't you go and tackle him? Probably he's got the bat in his study."

"It's not in his study," said Trevor, "because I looked everywhere for it, and got him to turn out his pockets, too. And yet I'll swear he knows something about it. One thing struck me as a bit suspicious. I went straight into his study and showed him that last letter——about the bat, you know, and accused him of writing it. Now, if he hadn't been in the business somehow, he wouldn't have understood what was meant by their saying 'the bat you lost'. It might have been an ordinary cricket-bat for all he knew. But he offered to let me search the study. It didn't strike me as rum till afterwards. Then it seemed fishy. What do you think?"

Clowes thought so too, but admitted that he did not see of what use the suspicion was going to be. Whether Rand-Brown knew anything about the affair or not, it was quite certain that the bat was not with him.

O'Hara, meanwhile, had decided that the time had come for him to resume his detective duties. Moriarty agreed with him, and they resolved that that night they would patronise the vault instead of the gymnasium, and take a holiday as far as their boxing was concerned. There was plenty of time before the Aldershot competition.

Lock-up was still at six, so at a quarter to that hour they slipped down into the vault, and took up their position.

A quarter of an hour passed. The lock-up bell sounded faintly. Moriarty began to grow tired.

"Is it worth it?" he said, "an' wouldn't they have come before, if they meant to come?"

"We'll give them another quarter of an hour," said O'Hara. "After that——"

"Sh!" whispered Moriarty.

The door had opened. They could see a figure dimly outlined in the semi-darkness. Footsteps passed down into the vault, and there came a sound as if the unknown had cannoned into a chair, followed by a sharp intake of breath, expressive of pain. A scraping sound, and a flash of light, and part of the vault was lit by a candle. O'Hara caught a glimpse of the unknown's face as he rose from lighting the candle, but it was not enough to enable him to recognise him. The candle was standing on a chair, and the light it gave was too feeble to reach the face of any one not on a level with it.

The unknown began to drag chairs out into the neighbourhood of the light. O'Hara counted six.

The sixth chair had scarcely been placed in position when the door opened again. Six other figures appeared in the opening one after the other, and bolted into the vault like rabbits into a burrow. The last of them closed the door after them.

O'Hara nudged Moriarty, and Moriarty nudged O'Hara; but neither made a sound. They were not likely to be seen——the blackness of the vault was too Egyptian for that——but they were so near to the chairs that the least whisper must have been heard. Not a word had proceeded from the occupants of the chairs so far. If O'Hara's suspicion was correct, and this was really the League holding a meeting, their methods were more secret than those of any other secret society in existence. Even the Nihilists probably exchanged a few remarks from time to time, when they met together to plot. But these men of mystery never opened their lips. It puzzled O'Hara.

The light of the candle was obscured for a moment, and a sound of puffing came from the darkness.

O'Hara nudged Moriarty again.

"Smoking!" said the nudge.

Moriarty nudged O'Hara.

"Smoking it is!" was the meaning of the movement.

A strong smell of tobacco showed that the diagnosis had been a true one. Each of the figures in turn lit his pipe at the candle, and sat back, still in silence. It could not have been very pleasant, smoking in almost pitch darkness, but it was breaking rules, which was probably the main consideration that swayed the smokers. They puffed away steadily, till the two Irishmen were wrapped about in invisible clouds.

Then a strange thing happened. I know that I am infringing copyright in making that statement, but it so exactly suits the occurrence, that perhaps Mr Rider Haggard will not object. It was a strange thing that happened.

A rasping voice shattered the silence.

"You boys down there," said the voice, "come here immediately. Come here, I say."

It was the well-known voice of Mr Robert Dexter, O'Hara and Moriarty's beloved house-master.

The two Irishmen simultaneously clutched one another, each afraid that the other would think—¬from force of long habit—¬that the house-master was speaking to him. Both stood where they were. It was the men of mystery and tobacco that Dexter was after, they thought.

But they were wrong. What had brought Dexter to the vault was the fact that he had seen two boys, who looked uncommonly like O'Hara and Moriarty, go down the steps of the vault at a quarter to six. He had been doing his usual after-lock-up prowl on the junior gravel, to intercept stragglers, and he had been a witness—¬from a distance of fifty yards, in a very bad light—¬of the descent into the vault. He had remained on the gravel ever since, in the hope of catching them as they came up; but as they had not come up, he had determined to make the first move himself. He had not seen the six unknowns go down, for, the evening being chilly, he had paced up and down, and they had by a lucky accident chosen a moment when his back was turned.

"Come up immediately," he repeated.

Here a blast of tobacco-smoke rushed at him from the darkness. The candle had been extinguished at the first alarm, and he had not realised—¬though he had suspected it—¬that smoking had been going on.

A hurried whispering was in progress among the unknowns. Apparently they saw that the game was up, for they picked their way towards the door.

As each came up the steps and passed him, Mr Dexter observed "Ha!" and appeared to make a note of his name. The last of the six was just leaving him after this process had been completed, when Mr Dexter called him back.

"That is not all," he said, suspiciously.

"Yes, sir," said the last of the unknowns.

Neither of the Irishmen recognised the voice. Its owner was a stranger to them.

"I tell you it is not," snapped Mr Dexter. "You are concealing the truth from me. O'Hara and Moriarty are down there—two boys in my own house. I saw them go down there."

"They had nothing to do with us, sir. We saw nothing of them."

"I have no doubt," said the house-master, "that you imagine that you are doing a very chivalrous thing by trying to hide them, but you will gain nothing by it. You may go."

He came to the top of the steps, and it seemed as if he intended to plunge into the darkness in search of the suspects. But, probably realising the futility of such a course, he changed his mind, and delivered an ultimatum from the top step.

"O'Hara and Moriarty."

No reply.

"O'Hara and Moriarty, I know perfectly well that you are down there. Come up immediately."

Dignified silence from the vault.

"Well, I shall wait here till you do choose to come up. You would be well advised to do so immediately. I warn you you will not tire me out."

He turned, and the door slammed behind him.

"What'll we do?" whispered Moriarty. It was at last safe to whisper.

"Wait," said O'Hara, "I'm thinking."

O'Hara thought. For many minutes he thought in vain. At last there came flooding back into his mind a memory of the days of his faghood. It was after that that he had been groping all the time. He remembered now. Once in those days there had been an unexpected function in the middle of term. There were needed for that function certain chairs. He could recall even now his furious disgust when he and a select body of fellow fags had been pounced upon by their form-master, and coerced into forming a line from the junior block to the cloisters, for the purpose of handing chairs. True, his form-master had stood ginger-beer after the event, with princely liberality, but the labour was of the sort that gallons of ginger-beer will not make pleasant. But he ceased to regret the episode now. He had been at the extreme end of the chair-handling chain. He had stood in a passage in the junior block, just by the door that led to the masters' garden, and which—he remembered—was never locked till late at night. And while he stood there, a pair of hands—apparently without a body—had heaved up chair after chair through a black opening in the floor. In other words, a trap-door connected with the vault in which he now was.

He imparted these reminiscences of childhood to Moriarty. They set off to search for the missing door, and, after wanderings and barkings of shins too painful to relate, they found it. Moriarty lit a match. The light fell on the trap-door, and their last doubts were at an end. The thing opened inwards. The bolt was on their side, not in the passage above them. To shoot the bolt took them one second, to climb into the passage one minute. They stood at the side of the opening, and dusted their clothes.

"Bedad!" said Moriarty, suddenly.

"What?"

"Why, how are we to shut it?"

This was a problem that wanted some solving. Eventually they managed it, O'Hara leaning over and fishing for it, while Moriarty held his legs.

As luck would have it—and luck had stood by them well all through—there was a bolt on top of the trap-door, as well as beneath it.

"Supposing that had been shot!" said O'Hara, as they fastened the door in its place.

Moriarty did not care to suppose anything so unpleasant.

Mr Dexter was still prowling about on the junior gravel, when the two Irishmen ran round and across the senior gravel to the gymnasium. Here they put in a few minutes' gentle sparring, and then marched boldly up to Mr Day (who happened to have looked in five minutes after their arrival) and got their paper.

"What time did O'Hara and Moriarty arrive at the gymnasium?" asked Mr Dexter of Mr Day next morning.

"O'Hara and Moriarty? Really, I can't remember. I know they left at about a quarter to seven."

That profound thinker, Mr Tony Weller, was never so correct as in his views respecting the value of an alibi. There are few better things in an emergency.

XVIII
O'HARA EXCELS HIMSELF

It was Renford's turn next morning to get up and feed the ferrets. Harvey had done it the day before.

Renford was not a youth who enjoyed early rising, but in the cause of the ferrets he would have endured anything, so at six punctually he slid out of bed, dressed quietly, so as not to disturb the rest of the dormitory, and ran over to the vault. To his utter amazement he found it locked. Such a thing had never been done before in the whole course of his experience. He tugged at the handle, but not an inch or a fraction of an inch would the door yield. The policy of the Open Door had ceased to find favour in the eyes of the authorities.

A feeling of blank despair seized upon him. He thought of the dismay of the ferrets when they woke up and realised that there was no chance of breakfast for them. And then they would gradually waste away, and some day somebody would go down to the vault to fetch chairs, and would come upon two mouldering skeletons, and wonder what they had once been. He almost wept at the vision so conjured up.

There was nobody about. Perhaps he might break in somehow. But then there was nothing to get to work with. He could not kick the door down. No, he must give it up, and the ferrets' breakfast-hour must be postponed. Possibly Harvey might be able to think of something.

"Fed 'em?" inquired Harvey, when they met at breakfast.

"No, I couldn't."

"Why on earth not? You didn't oversleep yourself?"

Renford poured his tale into his friend's shocked ears.

"My hat!" said Harvey, when he had finished, "what on earth are we to do? They'll starve."

Renford nodded mournfully.

"Whatever made them go and lock the door?" he said.

He seemed to think the authorities should have given him due notice of such an action.

"You're sure they have locked it? It isn't only stuck or something?"

"I lugged at the handle for hours. But you can go and see for yourself if you like."

Harvey went, and, waiting till the coast was clear, attached himself to the handle with a prehensile grasp, and put his back into one strenuous tug. It was even as Renford had said. The door was locked beyond possibility of doubt.

Renford and he went over to school that morning with long faces and a general air of acute depression. It was perhaps fortunate for their purpose that they did, for had their appearance been normal it might not have attracted O'Hara's attention. As it was, the Irishman, meeting them on the junior gravel, stopped and asked them what was wrong. Since the adventure in the vault, he had felt an interest in Renford and Harvey.

The two told their story in alternate sentences like the Strophe and Antistrophe of a Greek chorus. ("Steichomuthics," your Greek scholar calls it, I fancy. Ha, yes! Just so.)

"So ye can't get in because they've locked the door, an' ye don't know what to do about it?" said O'Hara, at the conclusion of the narrative.

Renford and Harvey informed him in chorus that that was the state of the game up to present date.

"An' ye want me to get them out for you?"

Neither had dared to hope that he would go so far as this. What they had looked for had been at the most a few thoughtful words of advice. That such a master-strategist as O'Hara should take up their cause was an unexampled piece of good luck.

"If you only would," said Harvey.

"We should be most awfully obliged," said Renford.

"Very well," said O'Hara.

They thanked him profusely.

O'Hara replied that it would be a privilege.

He should be sorry, he said, to have anything happen to the ferrets.

Renford and Harvey went on into school feeling more cheerful. If the ferrets could be extracted from their present tight corner, O'Hara was the man to do it.

O'Hara had not made his offer of assistance in any spirit of doubt. He was certain that he could do what he had promised. For it had not escaped his memory that this was a Tuesday——in other words, a mathematics morning up to the quarter to eleven interval. That meant, as has been explained previously, that, while the rest of the school were in the form-rooms, he would be out in the passage, if he cared to be. There would be no witnesses to what he was going to do.

But, by that curious perversity of fate which is so often noticeable, Mr Banks was in a peculiarly lamb-like and long-suffering mood this morning. Actions for which O'Hara would on other days have been expelled from the room without hope of return, today were greeted with a mild "Don't do that, please, O'Hara," or even the ridiculously inadequate "O'Hara!" It was perfectly disheartening. O'Hara began to ask himself bitterly what was the use of ragging at all if this was how it was received. And the moments were flying, and his promise to Renford and Harvey still remained unfulfilled.

He prepared for fresh efforts.

So desperate was he, that he even resorted to crude methods like the throwing of paper balls and the dropping of books. And when your really scientific ragger sinks to this, he is nearing the end of his tether. O'Hara hated to be rude, but there seemed no help for it.

The striking of a quarter past ten improved his chances. It had been privily agreed upon beforehand amongst the members of the class that at a quarter past ten every one was to sneeze simultaneously. The noise startled Mr Banks considerably. The angelic mood began to wear off. A man may be long-suffering, but he likes to draw the line somewhere.

"Another exhibition like that," he said, sharply, "and the class stays in after school, O'Hara!"

"Sir?"

"Silence."

"I said nothing, sir, really."

"Boy, you made a cat-like noise with your mouth."

"What sort of noise, sir?"

The form waited breathlessly. This peculiarly insidious question had been invented for mathematical use by one Sandys, who had left at the end of the previous summer. It was but rarely that the master increased the gaiety of nations by answering the question in the manner desired.

Mr Banks, off his guard, fell into the trap.

"A noise like this," he said curtly, and to the delighted audience came the melodious sound of a "Mi-aou", which put O'Hara's effort completely in the shade, and would have challenged comparison with the war-cry of the stoutest mouser that ever trod a tile.

A storm of imitations arose from all parts of the room. Mr Banks turned pink, and, going straight to the root of the disturbance, forthwith evicted O'Hara.

O'Hara left with the satisfying feeling that his duty had been done.

Mr Banks' room was at the top of the middle block. He ran softly down the stairs at his best pace. It was not likely that the master would come out into the passage to see if he was still there, but it might happen, and it would be best to run as few risks as possible.

He sprinted over to the junior block, raised the trap-door, and jumped down. He knew where the ferrets had been placed, and had no difficulty in finding them. In another minute he was in the passage again, with the trap-door bolted behind him.

He now asked himself—what should he do with them? He must find a safe place, or his labours would have been in vain.

Behind the fives-court, he thought, would be the spot. Nobody ever went there. It meant a run of three hundred yards there and the same distance back, and there was more than a chance that he might be seen by one of the Powers. In which case he might find it rather hard to explain what he was doing in the middle of the grounds with a couple of ferrets in his possession when the hands of the clock pointed to twenty minutes to eleven.

But the odds were against his being seen. He risked it.

When the bell rang for the quarter to eleven interval the ferrets were in their new home, happily discussing a piece of meat—Renford's contribution, held over from the morning's meal,—and O'Hara, looking as if he had never left the passage for an instant, was making his way through the departing mathematical class to apologise handsomely to Mr Banks—as was his invariable custom—for his disgraceful behaviour during the morning's lesson.

XIX
THE MAYOR'S VISIT

School prefects at Wrykyn did weekly essays for the headmaster. Those who had got their scholarships at the 'Varsity, or who were going up in the following year, used to take their essays to him after school and read them to him——an unpopular and nerve-destroying practice, akin to suicide. Trevor had got his scholarship in the previous November. He was due at the headmaster's private house at six o'clock on the present Tuesday. He was looking forward to the ordeal not without apprehension. The essay subject this week had been "One man's meat is another man's poison", and Clowes, whose idea of English Essay was that it should be a medium for intempestive frivolity, had insisted on his beginning with, "While I cannot conscientiously go so far as to say that one man's meat is another man's poison, yet I am certainly of opinion that what is highly beneficial to one man may, on the other hand, to another man, differently constituted, be extremely deleterious, and, indeed, absolutely fatal."

Trevor was not at all sure how the headmaster would take it. But Clowes had seemed so cut up at his suggestion that it had better be omitted, that he had allowed it to stand.

He was putting the final polish on this gem of English literature at half-past five, when Milton came in.

"Busy?" said Milton.

Trevor said he would be through in a minute.

Milton took a chair, and waited.

Trevor scratched out two words and substituted two others, made a couple of picturesque blots, and, laying down his pen, announced that he had finished.

"What's up?" he said.

"It's about the League," said Milton.

"Found out anything?"

"Not anything much. But I've been making inquiries. You remember I asked you to let me look at those letters of yours?"

Trevor nodded. This had happened on the Sunday of that week.

"Well, I wanted to look at the post-marks."

"By Jove, I never thought of that."

Milton continued with the business-like air of the detective who explains in the last chapter of the book how he did it.

"I found, as I thought, that both letters came from the same place."

Trevor pulled out the letters in question. "So they do," he said, "Chesterton."

"Do you know Chesterton?" asked Milton.

"Only by name."

"It's a small hamlet about two miles from here across the downs. There's only one shop in the place, which acts as post-office and tobacconist and everything else. I thought that if I went there and asked about those letters, they might remember who it was that sent them, if I showed them a photograph."

"By Jove," said Trevor, "of course! Did you? What happened?"

"I went there yesterday afternoon. I took about half-a-dozen photographs of various chaps, including Rand-Brown."

"But wait a bit. If Chesterton's two miles off, Rand-Brown couldn't have sent the letters. He wouldn't have the time after school. He was on the grounds both the afternoons before I got the letters."

"I know," said Milton; "I didn't think of that at the time."

"Well?"

"One of the points about the Chesterton post-office is that there's no letter-box outside. You have to go into the shop and hand anything you want to post across the counter. I thought this was a tremendous score for me. I thought they would be bound to remember who handed in the letters. There can't be many at a place like that."

"Did they remember?"

"They remembered the letters being given in distinctly, but as for knowing anything beyond that, they were simply futile. There was an old woman in the shop, aged about three hundred and ten, I should think. I shouldn't say she had ever been very intelligent, but now she simply gibbered. I started off by laying out a shilling on some poisonous-looking sweets. I gave the lot to a village kid when I got out. I hope they didn't kill him. Then, having scattered ground-bait in that way, I lugged out the photographs, mentioned the letters and the date they had been sent, and asked her to weigh in and identify the sender."

"Did she?"

"My dear chap, she identified them all, one after the other. The first was one of Clowes. She was prepared to swear on oath that that was the chap who had sent the letters. Then I shot a photograph of you across the counter, and doubts began to creep in. She said she was certain it was one of those two 'la-ads', but couldn't quite say which. To keep her amused I fired in photograph number three——Allardyce's. She identified that, too. At the end of ten minutes she was pretty sure that it was one of the six——¬the other three were Paget, Clephane, and Rand-Brown——¬but she was not going to bind herself down to any particular one. As I had come to the end of my stock of photographs, and was getting a bit sick of the game, I got up to go, when in came another ornament of Chesterton from a room at the back of the shop. He was quite a kid, not more than a hundred and fifty at the outside, so, as a last chance, I tackled him on the subject. He looked at the photographs for about half an hour, mumbling something about it not being 'thiccy 'un' or 'that 'un', or 'that 'ere tother 'un', until I began to feel I'd had enough of it. Then it came out that the real chap who had sent the letters was a 'la-ad' with light hair, not so big as me——¬"

"That doesn't help us much," said Trevor.

"——¬And a 'prarper little gennlemun'. So all we've got to do is to look for some young duke of polished manners and exterior, with a thatch of light hair."

"There are three hundred and sixty-seven fellows with light hair in the school," said Trevor, calmly.

"Thought it was three hundred and sixty-eight myself," said Milton, "but I may be wrong. Anyhow, there you have the results of my investigations. If you can make anything out of them, you're welcome to it. Good-bye."

"Half a second," said Trevor, as he got up; "had the fellow a cap of any sort?"

"No. Bareheaded. You wouldn't expect him to give himself away by wearing a house-cap?"

Trevor went over to the headmaster's revolving this discovery in his mind. It was not much of a clue, but the smallest clue is better than nothing. To find out that the sender of the League letters had fair hair narrowed the search down a little. It cleared the more raven-locked members of the school, at any rate. Besides, by combining his information with Milton's, the search might be still further narrowed down. He knew that the polite letter-writer must be either in Seymour's or in Donaldson's. The number of fair-haired youths in the two houses was not excessive. Indeed, at the moment he could not recall any; which rather complicated matters.

He arrived at the headmaster's door, and knocked. He was shown into a room at the side of the hall, near the door. The butler informed him that the headmaster was engaged at present. Trevor, who knew the butler slightly through having constantly been to see the headmaster on business via the front door, asked who was there.

"Sir Eustace Briggs," said the butler, and disappeared in the direction of his lair beyond the green baize partition at the end of the hall.

Trevor went into the room, which was a sort of spare study, and sat down, wondering what had brought the mayor of Wrykyn to see the headmaster at this advanced hour.

A quarter of an hour later the sound of voices broke in upon his peace. The headmaster was coming down the hall with the intention of showing his visitor out. The door of Trevor's room was ajar, and he could hear distinctly what was being said. He had no particular desire to play the eavesdropper, but the part was forced upon him.

Sir Eustace seemed excited.

"It is far from being my habit," he was saying, "to make unnecessary complaints respecting the conduct of the lads under your care." (Sir Eustace Briggs had a distaste for the shorter and more colloquial forms of speech. He would have perished sooner than have substituted "complain of your boys" for the majestic formula he had used. He spoke as if he enjoyed choosing his words. He seemed to pause and think before each word. Unkind people—who were jealous of his distinguished career—used to say that he did this because he was afraid of dropping an aitch if he relaxed his vigilance.)

"But," continued he, "I am reluctantly forced to the unpleasant conclusion that the dastardly outrage to which both I and the Press of the town have called your attention is to be attributed to one of the lads to whom I 'ave—have (this with a jerk) referred."

"I will make a thorough inquiry, Sir Eustace," said the bass voice of the headmaster.

"I thank you," said the mayor. "It would, under the circumstances, be nothing more, I think, than what is distinctly advisable. The man Samuel Wapshott, of whose narrative I have recently afforded you a brief synopsis, stated in no uncertain terms that he found at the foot of the statue on which the dastardly outrage was perpetrated a diminutive ornament, in shape like the bats that are used in the game of cricket. This ornament, he avers (with what truth I know not), was handed by him to a youth of an age coeval with that of the lads in the upper division of this school. The youth claimed it as his property, I was given to understand."

"A thorough inquiry shall be made, Sir Eustace."

"I thank you."

And then the door shut, and the conversation ceased.

XX
THE FINDING OF THE BAT

Trevor waited till the headmaster had gone back to his library, gave him five minutes to settle down, and then went in.

The headmaster looked up inquiringly.

"My essay, sir," said Trevor.

"Ah, yes. I had forgotten."

Trevor opened the notebook and began to read what he had written. He finished the paragraph which owed its insertion to Clowes, and raced hurriedly on to the next. To his surprise the flippancy passed unnoticed, at any rate, verbally. As a rule the headmaster preferred that quotations from back numbers of Punch should be kept out of the prefects' English Essays. And he generally said as much. But today he seemed strangely preoccupied. A split infinitive in paragraph five, which at other times would have made him sit up in his chair stiff with horror, elicited no remark. The same immunity was accorded to the insertion (inspired by Clowes, as usual) of a popular catch phrase in the last few lines. Trevor finished with the feeling that luck had favoured him nobly.

"Yes," said the headmaster, seemingly roused by the silence following on the conclusion of the essay. "Yes." Then, after a long pause, "Yes," again.

Trevor said nothing, but waited for further comment.

"Yes," said the headmaster once more, "I think that is a very fair essay. Very fair. It wants a little more——er——not quite so much——um——yes."

Trevor made a note in his mind to effect these improvements in future essays, and was getting up, when the headmaster stopped him.

"Don't go, Trevor. I wish to speak to you."

Trevor's first thought was, perhaps naturally, that the bat was going to be brought into discussion. He was wondering helplessly how he was going to keep O'Hara and his midnight exploit out of the conversation, when the headmaster resumed. "An unpleasant thing has happened, Trevor——"

"Now we're coming to it," thought Trevor.

"It appears, Trevor, that a considerable amount of smoking has been going on in the school."

Trevor breathed freely once more. It was only going to be a mere conventional smoking row after all. He listened with more enjoyment as the headmaster, having stopped to turn down the wick of the reading-lamp which stood on the table at his side, and which had begun, appropriately enough, to smoke, resumed his discourse.

"Mr Dexter——"

Of course, thought Trevor. If there ever was a row in the school, Dexter was bound to be at the bottom of it.

"Mr Dexter has just been in to see me. He reported six boys. He discovered them in the vault beneath the junior block. Two of them were boys in your house."

Trevor murmured something wordless, to show that the story interested him.

"You knew nothing of this, of course——"

"No, sir."

"No. Of course not. It is difficult for the head of a house to know all that goes on in that house."

Was this his beastly sarcasm? Trevor asked himself. But he came to the conclusion that it was not. After all, the head of a house is only human. He cannot be expected to keep an eye on the private life of every member of his house.

"This must be stopped, Trevor. There is no saying how widespread the practice has become or may become. What I want you to do is to go straight back to your house and begin a complete search of the studies."

"Tonight, sir?" It seemed too late for such amusement.

"Tonight. But before you go to your house, call at Mr Seymour's, and tell Milton I should like to see him. And, Trevor."

"Yes, sir?"

"You will understand that I am leaving this matter to you to be dealt with by you. I shall not require you to make any report to me. But if you should find tobacco in any boy's room, you must punish him well, Trevor. Punish him well."

This meant that the culprit must be "touched up" before the house assembled in the dining-room. Such an event did not often occur. The last occasion had been in Paget's first term as head of Donaldson's, when two of the senior day-room had been discovered attempting to revive the ancient and dishonourable custom of bullying. This time, Trevor foresaw, would set up a record in all probability. There might be any number of devotees of the weed, and he meant to carry out his instructions to the full, and make the criminals more unhappy than they had been since the day of their first cigar. Trevor hated the habit of smoking at school. He was so intensely keen on the success of the house and the school at games, that anything which tended to damage the wind and eye filled him with loathing. That anybody should dare to smoke in a house which was going to play in the final for the House Football Cup made him rage internally, and he proposed to make things bad and unrestful for such.

To smoke at school is to insult the divine weed. When you are obliged to smoke in odd corners, fearing every moment that you will be discovered, the whole meaning, poetry, romance of a pipe vanishes, and you become like those lost beings who smoke when they are running to catch trains. The boy who smokes at school is bound to come to a bad end. He will degenerate gradually into a person that plays dominoes in the smoking-rooms of A.B.C. shops with friends who wear bowler hats and frock coats.

Much of this philosophy Trevor expounded to Clowes in energetic language when he returned to Donaldson's after calling at Seymour's to deliver the message for Milton.

Clowes became quite animated at the prospect of a real row.

"We shall be able to see the skeletons in their cupboards," he observed. "Every man has a skeleton in his cupboard, which follows him about wherever he goes. Which study shall we go to first?"

"We?" said Trevor.

"We," repeated Clowes firmly. "I am not going to be left out of this jaunt. I need bracing up—¬I'm not strong, you know—¬and this is just the thing to do it. Besides, you'll want a bodyguard of some sort, in case the infuriated occupant turns and rends you."

"I don't see what there is to enjoy in the business," said Trevor, gloomily. "Personally, I bar this kind of thing. By the time we've finished, there won't be a chap in the house I'm on speaking terms with."

"Except me, dearest," said Clowes. "I will never desert you. It's of no use asking me, for I will never do it. Mr Micawber has his faults, but I will never desert Mr Micawber."

"You can come if you like," said Trevor; "we'll take the studies in order. I suppose we needn't look up the prefects?"

"A prefect is above suspicion. Scratch the prefects."

"That brings us to Dixon."

Dixon was a stout youth with spectacles, who was popularly supposed to do twenty-two hours' work a day. It was believed that he put in two hours sleep from eleven to one, and then got up and worked in his study till breakfast.

He was working when Clowes and Trevor came in. He dived head foremost into a huge Liddell and Scott as the door opened. On hearing Trevor's voice he slowly emerged, and a pair of round and spectacled eyes gazed blankly at the visitors. Trevor briefly explained his errand, but the interview lost in solemnity owing to the fact that the bare notion of Dixon storing tobacco in his room made Clowes roar with laughter. Also, Dixon stolidly refused to understand what Trevor was talking about, and at the end of ten minutes, finding it hopeless to try and explain, the two went. Dixon, with a hazy impression that he had been asked to join in some sort of round game, and had refused the offer, returned again to his Liddell and Scott, and continued to wrestle with the somewhat obscure utterances of the chorus in AEschylus' Agamemnon. The results of this fiasco on Trevor and Clowes were widely different. Trevor it depressed horribly. It made him feel savage. Clowes, on the other hand, regarded the whole affair in a spirit of rollicking farce, and refused to see that this was a serious matter, in which the honour of the house was involved.

The next study was Ruthven's. This fact somewhat toned down the exuberances of Clowes's demeanour. When one particularly dislikes a person, one has a curious objection to seeming in good spirits in his presence. One feels that he may take it as a sort of compliment to himself, or, at any rate, contribute grins of his own, which would be hateful. Clowes was as grave as Trevor when they entered the study.

Ruthven's study was like himself, overdressed and rather futile. It ran to little china ornaments in a good deal of profusion. It was more like a drawing-room than a school study.

"Sorry to disturb you, Ruthven," said Trevor.

"Oh, come in," said Ruthven, in a tired voice. "Please shut the door; there is a draught. Do you want anything?"

"We've got to have a look round," said Clowes.

"Can't you see everything there is?"

Ruthven hated Clowes as much as Clowes hated him.

Trevor cut into the conversation again.

"It's like this, Ruthven," he said. "I'm awfully sorry, but the Old Man's just told me to search the studies in case any of the fellows have got baccy."

Ruthven jumped up, pale with consternation.

"You can't. I won't have you disturbing my study."

"This is rot," said Trevor, shortly, "I've got to. It's no good making it more unpleasant for me than it is."

"But I've no tobacco. I swear I haven't."

"Then why mind us searching?" said Clowes affably.

"Come on, Ruthven," said Trevor, "chuck us over the keys. You might as well."

"I won't."

"Don't be an ass, man."

"We have here," observed Clowes, in his sad, solemn way, "a stout and serviceable poker." He stooped, as he spoke, to pick it up.

"Leave that poker alone," cried Ruthven.

Clowes straightened himself.

"I'll swop it for your keys," he said.

"Don't be a fool."

"Very well, then. We will now crack our first crib."

Ruthven sprang forward, but Clowes, handing him off in football fashion with his left hand, with his right dashed the poker against the lock of the drawer of the table by which he stood.

The lock broke with a sharp crack. It was not built with an eye to such onslaught.

"Neat for a first shot," said Clowes, complacently. "Now for the Umustaphas and shag."

But as he looked into the drawer he uttered a sudden cry of excitement. He drew something out, and tossed it over to Trevor.

"Catch, Trevor," he said quietly. "Something that'll interest you."

Trevor caught it neatly in one hand, and stood staring at it as if he had never seen anything like it before. And yet he had——¬often. For what he had caught was a little golden bat, about an inch long by an eighth of an inch wide.

XXI
THE LEAGUE REVEALED

"What do you think of that?" said Clowes.

Trevor said nothing. He could not quite grasp the situation. It was not only that he had got the idea so firmly into his head that it was Rand-Brown who had sent the letters and appropriated the bat. Even supposing he had not suspected Rand-Brown, he would never have dreamed of suspecting Ruthven. They had been friends. Not very close friends—¬Trevor's keenness for games and Ruthven's dislike of them prevented that—¬but a good deal more than acquaintances. He was so constituted that he could not grasp the frame of mind required for such an action as Ruthven's. It was something absolutely abnormal.

Clowes was equally surprised, but for a different reason. It was not so much the enormity of Ruthven's proceedings that took him aback. He believed him, with that cheerful intolerance which a certain type of mind affects, capable of anything. What surprised him was the fact that Ruthven had had the ingenuity and even the daring to conduct a campaign of this description. Cribbing in examinations he would have thought the limit of his crimes. Something backboneless and underhand of that kind would not have surprised him in the least. He would have said that it was just about what he had expected all along. But that Ruthven should blossom out suddenly as quite an ingenious and capable criminal in this way, was a complete surprise.

"Well, perhaps you'll make a remark?" he said, turning to Ruthven.

Ruthven, looking very much like a passenger on a Channel steamer who has just discovered that the motion of the vessel is affecting him unpleasantly, had fallen into a chair when Clowes handed him off. He sat there with a look on his pasty face which was not good to see, as silent as Trevor. It seemed that whatever conversation there was going to be would have to take the form of a soliloquy from Clowes.

Clowes took a seat on the corner of the table.

"It seems to me, Ruthven," he said, "that you'd better say something. At present there's a lot that wants explaining. As this bat has been found lying in your drawer, I suppose we may take it that you're the impolite letter-writer?"

Ruthven found his voice at last.

"I'm not," he cried; "I never wrote a line."

"Now we're getting at it," said Clowes. "I thought you couldn't have had it in you to carry this business through on your own. Apparently you've only been the sleeping partner in this show, though I suppose it was you who ragged Trevor's study? Not much sleeping about that. You took over the acting branch of the concern for that day only, I expect. Was it you who ragged the study?"

Ruthven stared into the fire, but said nothing.

"Must be polite, you know, Ruthven, and answer when you're spoken to. Was it you who ragged Trevor's study?"

"Yes," said Ruthven.

"Thought so."

"Why, of course, I met you just outside," said Trevor, speaking for the first time. "You were the chap who told me what had happened."

Ruthven said nothing.

"The ragging of the study seems to have been all the active work he did," remarked Clowes.

"No," said Trevor, "he posted the letters, whether he wrote them or not. Milton was telling me——you remember? I told you. No, I didn't. Milton found out that the letters were posted by a small, light-haired fellow."

"That's him," said Clowes, as regardless of grammar as the monks of Rheims, pointing with the poker at Ruthven's immaculate locks. "Well, you ragged the study and posted the letters. That was all your share. Am I right in thinking Rand-Brown was the other partner?"

Silence from Ruthven.

"Am I?" persisted Clowes.

"You may think what you like. I don't care."

"Now we're getting rude again," complained Clowes. "Was Rand-Brown in this?"

"Yes," said Ruthven.

"Thought so. And who else?"

"No one."

"Try again."

"I tell you there was no one else. Can't you believe a word a chap says?"

"A word here and there, perhaps," said Clowes, as one making a concession, "but not many, and this isn't one of them. Have another shot."

Ruthven relapsed into silence.

"All right, then," said Clowes, "we'll accept that statement. There's just a chance that it may be true. And that's about all, I think. This isn't my affair at all, really. It's yours, Trevor. I'm only a spectator and camp-follower. It's your business. You'll find me in my study." And putting the poker carefully in its place, Clowes left the room. He went into his study, and tried to begin some work. But the beauties of the second book of Thucydides failed to appeal to him. His mind was elsewhere. He felt too excited with what had just happened to translate Greek. He pulled up a chair in front of the fire, and gave himself up to speculating how Trevor was getting on in the neighbouring study. He was glad he had left him to finish the business. If he had been in Trevor's place, there was nothing he would so greatly have disliked as to have some one——however familiar a friend——interfering in his wars and settling them for him. Left to himself, Clowes would probably have ended the interview by kicking Ruthven into the nearest approach to pulp compatible with the laws relating to manslaughter. He had an uneasy suspicion that Trevor would let him down far too easily.

The handle turned. Trevor came in, and pulled up another chair in silence. His face wore a look of disgust. But there were no signs of combat upon him. The toe of his boot was not worn and battered, as Clowes would have liked to have seen it. Evidently he had not chosen to adopt active and physical measures for the improvement of Ruthven's moral well-being.

"Well?" said Clowes.

"My word, what a hound!" breathed Trevor, half to himself.

"My sentiments to a hair," said Clowes, approvingly. "But what have you done?"

"I didn't do anything."

"I was afraid you wouldn't. Did he give any explanation? What made him go in for the thing at all? What earthly motive could he have for not wanting Barry to get his colours, bar the fact that Rand-Brown didn't want him to? And why should he do what Rand-Brown told him? I never even knew they were pals, before today."

"He told me a good deal," said Trevor. "It's one of the beastliest things I ever heard. They neither of them come particularly well out of the business, but Rand-Brown comes worse out of it even than Ruthven. My word, that man wants killing."

"That'll keep," said Clowes, nodding. "What's the yarn?"

"Do you remember about a year ago a chap named Patterson getting sacked?"

Clowes nodded again. He remembered the case well. Patterson had had gambling transactions with a Wrykyn tradesman, had been found out, and had gone.

"You remember what a surprise it was to everybody. It wasn't one of those cases where half the school suspects what's going on. Those cases always come out sooner or later. But Patterson nobody knew about."

"Yes. Well?"

"Nobody," said Trevor, "except Ruthven, that is. Ruthven got to know somehow. I believe he was a bit of a pal of Patterson's at the time. Anyhow,—they had a row, and Ruthven went to Dexter—¬Patterson was in Dexter's—¬and sneaked. Dexter promised to keep his name out of the business, and went straight to the Old Man, and Patterson got turfed out on the spot. Then somehow or other Rand-Brown got to know about it—¬I believe Ruthven must have told him by accident some time or other. After that he simply had to do everything Rand-Brown wanted him to. Otherwise he said that he would tell the chaps about the Patterson affair. That put Ruthven in a dead funk."

"Of course," said Clowes; "I should imagine friend Ruthven would have got rather a bad time of it. But what made them think of starting the League? It was a jolly smart idea. Rand-Brown's, of course?"

"Yes. I suppose he'd heard about it, and thought something might be made out of it if it were revived."

"And were Ruthven and he the only two in it?"

"Ruthven swears they were, and I shouldn't wonder if he wasn't telling the truth, for once in his life. You see, everything the League's done so far could have been done by him and Rand-Brown, without anybody else's help. The only other studies that were ragged were Mill's and Milton's—¬both in Seymour's.

"Yes," said Clowes.

There was a pause. Clowes put another shovelful of coal on the fire.

"What are you going to do to Ruthven?"

"Nothing."

"Nothing? Hang it, he doesn't deserve to get off like that. He isn't as bad as Rand-Brown—¬quite—¬but he's pretty nearly as finished a little beast as you could find."

"Finished is just the word," said Trevor. "He's going at the end of the week."

"Going? What! sacked?"

"Yes. The Old Man's been finding out things about him, apparently, and this smoking row has just added the finishing-touch to his discoveries. He's particularly keen against smoking just now for some reason."

"But was Ruthven in it?"

"Yes. Didn't I tell you? He was one of the fellows Dexter caught in the vault. There were two in this house, you remember?"

"Who was the other?"

"That man Dashwood. Has the study next to Paget's old one. He's going, too."

"Scarcely knew him. What sort of a chap was he?"

"Outsider. No good to the house in any way. He won't be missed."

"And what are you going to do about Rand-Brown?"

"Fight him, of course. What else could I do?"

"But you're no match for him."

"We'll see."

"But you aren't," persisted Clowes. "He can give you a stone easily, and he's not a bad boxer either. Moriarty didn't beat him so very cheaply in the middle-weight this year. You wouldn't have a chance."

Trevor flared up.

"Heavens, man," he cried, "do you think I don't know all that myself? But what on earth would you have me do? Besides, he may be a good boxer, but he's got no pluck at all. I might outstay him."

"Hope so," said Clowes.

But his tone was not hopeful.

XXII
A DRESS REHEARSAL

Some people in Trevor's place might have taken the earliest opportunity of confronting Rand-Brown, so as to settle the matter in hand without delay. Trevor thought of doing this, but finally decided to let the matter rest for a day, until he should have found out with some accuracy what chance he stood.

After four o'clock, therefore, on the next day, having had tea in his study, he went across to the baths, in search of O'Hara. He intended that before the evening was over the Irishman should have imparted to him some of his skill with the hands. He did not know that for a man absolutely unscientific with his fists there is nothing so fatal as to take a boxing lesson on the eve of battle. A little knowledge is a dangerous thing. He is apt to lose his recklessness—which might have stood by him well—in exchange for a little quite useless science. He is neither one thing nor the other, neither a natural fighter nor a skilful boxer.

This point O'Hara endeavoured to press upon him as soon as he had explained why it was that he wanted coaching on this particular afternoon.

The Irishman was in the gymnasium, punching the ball, when Trevor found him. He generally put in a quarter of an hour with the punching-ball every evening, before Moriarty turned up for the customary six rounds.

"Want me to teach ye a few tricks?" he said. "What's that for?"

"I've got a mill coming on soon," explained Trevor, trying to make the statement as if it were the most ordinary thing in the world for a school prefect, who was also captain of football, head of a house, and in the cricket eleven, to be engaged for a fight in the near future.

"Mill!" exclaimed O'Hara. "You! An' why?"

"Never mind why," said Trevor. "I'll tell you afterwards, perhaps. Shall I put on the gloves now?"

"Wait," said O'Hara, "I must do my quarter of an hour with the ball before I begin teaching other people how to box. Have ye a watch?"

"Yes."

"Then time me. I'll do four rounds of three minutes each, with a minute's rest in between. That's more than I'll do at Aldershot, but it'll get me fit. Ready?"

"Time," said Trevor.

He watched O'Hara assailing the swinging ball with considerable envy. Why, he wondered, had he not gone in for boxing? Everybody ought to learn to box. It was bound to come in useful some time or other. Take his own case. He was very much afraid—no, afraid was not the right word, for he was not that. He was very much of opinion that Rand-Brown was going to have a most enjoyable time when they met. And the final house-match was to be played next Monday. If events turned out as he could not help feeling they were likely to turn out, he would be too battered to play in that match. Donaldson's would probably win whether he played or not, but it would be bitter to be laid up on such an occasion. On the other hand, he must go through with it. He did not believe in letting other people take a hand in settling his private quarrels.

But he wished he had learned to box. If only he could hit that dancing, jumping ball with a fifth of the skill that O'Hara was displaying, his wiriness and pluck might see him through. O'Hara finished his fourth round with his leathern opponent, and sat down, panting.

"Pretty useful, that," commented Trevor, admiringly.

"Ye should see Moriarty," gasped O'Hara.

"Now, will ye tell me why it is you're going to fight, and with whom you're going to fight?"

"Very well. It's with Rand-Brown."

"Rand-Brown!" exclaimed O'Hara. "But, me dearr man, he'll ate you."

Trevor gave a rather annoyed laugh. "I must say I've got a nice, cheery, comforting lot of friends," he said. "That's just what Clowes has been trying to explain to me."

"Clowes is quite right," said O'Hara, seriously. "Has the thing gone too far for ye to back out? Without climbing down, of course," he added.

"Yes," said Trevor, "there's no question of my getting out of it. I daresay I could. In fact, I know I could. But I'm not going to."

"But, me dearr man, ye haven't an earthly chance. I assure ye ye haven't. I've seen Rand-Brown with the gloves on. That was last term. He's not put them on since Moriarty bate him in the middles, so he may be out of practice. But even then he'd be a bad man to tackle. He's big an' he's strong, an' if he'd only had the heart in him he'd have been going up to Aldershot instead of Moriarty. That's what he'd be doing. An' you can't box at all. Never even had the gloves on."

"Never. I used to scrap when I was a kid, though."

"That's no use," said O'Hara, decidedly. "But you haven't said what it is that ye've got against Rand-Brown. What is it?"

"I don't see why I shouldn't tell you. You're in it as well. In fact, if it hadn't been for the bat turning up, you'd have been considerably more in it than I am."

"What!" cried O'Hara. "Where did you find it? Was it in the grounds? When was it you found it?"

Whereupon Trevor gave him a very full and exact account of what had happened. He showed him the two letters from the League, touched on Milton's connection with the affair, traced the gradual development of his suspicions, and described with some approach to excitement the scene in Ruthven's study, and the explanations that had followed it.

"Now do you wonder," he concluded, "that I feel as if a few rounds with Rand-Brown would do me good."

O'Hara breathed hard.

"My word!" he said, "I'd like to see ye kill him."

"But," said Trevor, "as you and Clowes have been pointing out to me, if there's going to be a corpse, it'll be me. However, I mean to try. Now perhaps you wouldn't mind showing me a few tricks."

"Take my advice," said O'Hara, "and don't try any of that foolery."

"Why, I thought you were such a believer in science," said Trevor in surprise.

"So I am, if you've enough of it. But it's the worst thing ye can do to learn a trick or two just before a fight, if you don't know anything about the game already. A tough, rushing fighter is ten times as good as a man who's just begun to learn what he oughtn't to do."

"Well, what do you advise me to do, then?" asked Trevor, impressed by the unwonted earnestness with which the Irishman delivered this pugilistic homily, which was a paraphrase of the views dinned into the ears of every novice by the school instructor.

"I must do something."

"The best thing ye can do," said O'Hara, thinking for a moment, "is to put on the gloves and have a round or two with me. Here's Moriarty at last. We'll get him to time us."

As much explanation as was thought good for him having been given to the newcomer, to account for Trevor's newly-acquired taste for things pugilistic, Moriarty took the watch, with instructions to give them two minutes for the first round.

"Go as hard as you can," said O'Hara to Trevor, as they faced one another, "and hit as hard as you like. It won't be any practice if you don't. I sha'n't mind being hit. It'll do me good for Aldershot. See?"

Trevor said he saw.

"Time," said Moriarty.

Trevor went in with a will. He was a little shy at first of putting all his weight into his blows. It was hard to forget that he felt friendly towards O'Hara. But he speedily awoke to the fact that the Irishman took his boxing very seriously, and was quite a different person when he had the gloves on. When he was so equipped, the man opposite him ceased to be either friend or foe in a private way. He was simply an opponent, and every time he hit him was one point. And, when he entered the ring, his only object in life for the next three minutes was to score points. Consequently Trevor, sparring lightly and in rather a futile manner at first, was woken up by a stinging flush hit between the eyes. After that he, too, forgot that he liked the man before him, and rushed him in all directions. There was no doubt as to who would have won if it had been a competition. Trevor's guard was of the most rudimentary order, and O'Hara got through when and how he liked. But though he took a good deal, he also gave a good deal, and O'Hara confessed himself not altogether sorry when Moriarty called "Time".

"Man," he said regretfully, "why ever did ye not take up boxing before? Ye'd have made a splendid middle-weight."

"Well, have I a chance, do you think?" inquired Trevor.

"Ye might do it with luck," said O'Hara, very doubtfully. "But," he added, "I'm afraid ye've not much chance."

And with this poor encouragement from his trainer and sparring-partner, Trevor was forced to be content.

XXIII
WHAT RENFORD SAW

The health of Master Harvey of Seymour's was so delicately constituted that it was an absolute necessity that he should consume one or more hot buns during the quarter of an hour's interval which split up morning school. He was tearing across the junior gravel towards the shop on the morning following Trevor's sparring practice with O'Hara, when a melodious treble voice called his name. It was Renford. He stopped, to allow his friend to come up with him, and then made as if to resume his way to the shop. But Renford proposed an amendment. "Don't go to the shop," he said, "I want to talk."

"Well, can't you talk in the shop?"

"Not what I want to tell you. It's private. Come for a stroll."

Harvey hesitated. There were few things he enjoyed so much as exclusive items of school gossip (scandal preferably), but hot new buns were among those few things. However, he decided on this occasion to feed the mind at the expense of the body. He accepted Renford's invitation.

"What is it?" he asked, as they made for the football field. "What's been happening?"

"It's frightfully exciting," said Renford.

"What's up?"

"You mustn't tell any one."

"All right. Of course not."

"Well, then, there's been a big fight, and I'm one of the only chaps who know about it so far."

"A fight?" Harvey became excited. "Who between?"

Renford paused before delivering his news, to emphasise the importance of it.

"It was between O'Hara and Rand-Brown," he said at length.

"By Jove!" said Harvey. Then a suspicion crept into his mind.

"Look here, Renford," he said, "if you're trying to green me——¬"

"I'm not, you ass," replied Renford indignantly. "It's perfectly true. I saw it myself."

"By Jove, did you really? Where was it? When did it come off? Was it a good one? Who won?"

"It was the best one I've ever seen."

"Did O'Hara beat him? I hope he did. O'Hara's a jolly good sort."

"Yes. They had six rounds. Rand-Brown got knocked out in the middle of the sixth."

"What, do you mean really knocked out, or did he just chuck it?"

"No. He was really knocked out. He was on the floor for quite a time. By Jove, you should have seen it. O'Hara was ripping in the sixth round. He was all over him."

"Tell us about it," said Harvey, and Renford told.

"I'd got up early," he said, "to feed the ferrets, and I was just cutting over to the fives-courts with their grub, when, just as I got across the senior gravel, I saw O'Hara and Moriarty standing waiting near the second court. O'Hara knows all about the ferrets, so I didn't try and cut or anything. I went up and began talking to him. I noticed he didn't look particularly keen on seeing me at first. I asked him if he was going to play fives. Then he said no, and told me what he'd really come for. He said he and Rand-Brown had had a row, and they'd agreed to have it out that morning in one of the fives-courts. Of course, when I heard that, I was all on to see it, so I said I'd wait, if he didn't mind. He said he didn't care, so long as I didn't tell everybody, so I said I wouldn't tell anybody except you, so he said all right, then, I could stop if I wanted to. So that was how I saw it. Well, after we'd been waiting a few minutes, Rand-Brown came in sight, with that beast Merrett in our house, who'd come to second him. It was just like one of those duels you read about, you know. Then O'Hara said that as I was the only one there with a watch——¬he and Rand-Brown were in footer clothes, and Merrett and Moriarty hadn't got their tickers on them——¬I'd better act as timekeeper. So I said all right, I would, and we went to the second fives-court. It's the biggest of them, you know. I stood outside on the bench, looking through the wire netting over the door, so as not to be in the way when they started scrapping. O'Hara and Rand-Brown took off their blazers and sweaters, and chucked them to Moriarty and Merrett, and then Moriarty and Merrett went and stood in two corners, and O'Hara and Rand-Brown walked into the middle and stood up to one another. Rand-Brown was miles the heaviest——¬by a stone, I should think——¬and he was taller and had a longer reach. But O'Hara looked much fitter. Rand-Brown looked rather flabby.

"I sang out 'Time' through the wire netting, and they started off at once. O'Hara offered to shake hands, but Rand-Brown wouldn't. So they began without it.

"The first round was awfully fast. They kept having long rallies all over the place. O'Hara was a jolly sight quicker, and Rand-Brown didn't seem able to guard his hits at all. But he hit frightfully hard himself, great, heavy slogs, and O'Hara kept getting them in the face. At last he got one bang in the mouth which knocked him down flat. He was up again in a second, and was starting to rush, when I looked at the watch, and found that I'd given them nearly half a minute too much already. So I shouted 'Time', and made up my mind I'd keep more of an eye on the watch next round. I'd got so jolly excited, watching them, that I'd forgot I was supposed to be keeping time for them. They had only asked for a minute between the rounds, but as I'd given them half a minute too long in the first round, I chucked in a bit extra in the rest, so that they were both pretty fit by the time I started them again.

"The second round was just like the first, and so was the third. O'Hara kept getting the worst of it. He was knocked down three or four times more, and once, when he'd rushed Rand-Brown against one of the walls, he hit out and missed, and barked his knuckles jolly badly against the wall. That was in the middle of the third round, and Rand-Brown had it all his own way for the rest of the round——¬for about two minutes, that is to say. He hit O'Hara about all over the shop. I was so jolly keen on O'Hara's winning, that I had half a mind to call time early, so as to give him time to recover. But I thought it would be a low thing to do, so I gave them their full three minutes.

"Directly they began the fourth round, I noticed that things were going to change a bit. O'Hara had given up his rushing game, and was waiting for his man, and when he came at him he'd put in a hot counter, nearly always at the body. After a bit Rand-Brown began to get cautious, and wouldn't rush, so the fourth round was the quietest there had been. In the last minute they didn't hit each other at all. They simply sparred for openings. It was in the fifth round that O'Hara began to forge ahead. About half way through he got in a ripper, right in the wind, which almost doubled Rand-Brown up, and then he started rushing again. Rand-Brown looked awfully bad at the end of the round. Round six was ripping. I never saw two chaps go for each other so. It was one long rally. Then——how it happened I couldn't see, they were so quick——just as they had been at it a minute and a half, there was a crack, and the next thing I saw was Rand-Brown on the ground, looking beastly. He went down absolutely flat; his heels and head touched the ground at the same time.

"I counted ten out loud in the professional way like they do at the National Sporting Club, you know, and then said 'O'Hara wins'. I felt an awful swell. After about another half-minute, Rand-Brown was all right again, and he got up and went back to the house with Merrett, and O'Hara and Moriarty went off to Dexter's, and I gave the ferrets their grub, and cut back to breakfast."

"Rand-Brown wasn't at breakfast," said Harvey.

"No. He went to bed. I wonder what'll happen. Think there'll be a row about it?"

"Shouldn't think so," said Harvey. "They never do make rows about fights, and neither of them is a prefect, so I don't see what it matters if they do fight. But, I say——"

"What's up?"

"I wish," said Harvey, his voice full of acute regret, "that it had been my turn to feed those ferrets."

"I don't," said Renford cheerfully. "I wouldn't have missed that mill for something. Hullo, there's the bell. We'd better run."

When Trevor called at Seymour's that afternoon to see Rand-Brown, with a view to challenging him to deadly combat, and found that O'Hara had been before him, he ought to have felt relieved. His actual feeling was one of acute annoyance. It seemed to him that O'Hara had exceeded the limits of friendship. It was all very well for him to take over the Rand-Brown contract, and settle it himself, in order to save Trevor from a very bad quarter of an hour, but Trevor was one of those people who object strongly to the interference of other people in their private business. He sought out O'Hara and complained. Within two minutes O'Hara's golden eloquence had soothed him and made him view the matter in quite a different light. What O'Hara pointed out was that it was not Trevor's affair at all, but his own. Who, he asked, had been likely to be damaged most by Rand-Brown's manoeuvres in connection with the lost bat? Trevor was bound to admit that O'Hara was that person. Very well, then, said O'Hara, then who had a better right to fight Rand-Brown? And Trevor confessed that no one else had a better.

"Then I suppose," he said, "that I shall have to do nothing about it?"

"That's it," said O'Hara.

"It'll be rather beastly meeting the man after this," said Trevor, presently. "Do you think he might possibly leave at the end of term?"

"He's leaving at the end of the week," said O'Hara. "He was one of the fellows Dexter caught in the vault that evening. You won't see much more of Rand-Brown."

"I'll try and put up with that," said Trevor.

"And so will I," replied O'Hara. "And I shouldn't think Milton would be so very grieved."

"No," said Trevor. "I tell you what will make him sick, though, and that is your having milled with Rand-Brown. It's a job he'd have liked to have taken on himself."

[97] P.G. WODEHOUSE

XXIV
CONCLUSION

Into the story at this point comes the narrative of Charles Mereweather Cook, aged fourteen, a day-boy.

Cook arrived at the school on the tenth of March, at precisely nine o'clock, in a state of excitement.

He said there was a row on in the town.

Cross-examined, he said there was no end of a row on in the town.

During morning school, he explained further, whispering his tale into the attentive ear of Knight of the School House, who sat next to him.

What sort of a row, Knight wanted to know.

Cook deposed that he had been riding on his bicycle past the entrance to the Recreation Grounds on his way to school, when his eye was attracted by the movements of a mass of men just inside the gate. They appeared to be fighting. Witness did not stop to watch, much as he would have liked to do so. Why not? Why, because he was late already, and would have had to scorch anyhow, in order to get to school in time. And he had been late the day before, and was afraid that old Appleby (the master of the form) would give him beans if he were late again. Wherefore he had no notion of what the men were fighting about, but he betted that more would be heard about it. Why? Because, from what he saw of it, it seemed a jolly big thing. There must have been quite three hundred men fighting. (Knight, satirically, "Pile it on!") Well, quite a hundred, anyhow. Fifty a side. And fighting like anything. He betted there would be something about it in the Wrykyn Patriot tomorrow. He shouldn't wonder if somebody had been killed. What were they scrapping about? How should he know!

Here Mr Appleby, who had been trying for the last five minutes to find out where the whispering noise came from, at length traced it to its source, and forthwith requested Messrs Cook and Knight to do him two hundred lines, adding that, if he heard them talking again, he would put them into the extra lesson. Silence reigned from that moment.

Next day, while the form was wrestling with the moderately exciting account of Caesar's doings in Gaul, Master Cook produced from his pocket a newspaper cutting. This, having previously planted a forcible blow in his friend's ribs with an elbow to attract the latter's attention, he handed to Knight, and in dumb show requested him to peruse the same. Which Knight, feeling no interest whatever in Caesar's doings in Gaul, and having, in consequence, a good deal of time on his hands, proceeded to do. The cutting was headed "Disgraceful Fracas", and was written in the elegant style that was always so marked a feature of the Wrykyn Patriot.

"We are sorry to have to report," it ran, "another of those deplorable ebullitions of local Hooliganism, to which it has before now been our painful duty to refer. Yesterday the Recreation Grounds were made the scene of as brutal an exhibition of savagery as has ever marred the fair fame of this town. Our readers will remember how on a previous occasion, when the fine statue of Sir Eustace Briggs was found covered with tar, we attributed the act to the malevolence of the Radical section of the community. Events have proved that we were right. Yesterday a body of youths, belonging to the rival party, was discovered in the very act of repeating the offence. A thick coating of tar had already been administered, when several members of the rival faction appeared. A free fight of a peculiarly violent nature immediately ensued, with the result that, before the police could interfere, several of the combatants had received severe bruises. Fortunately the police then arrived on the scene, and with great difficulty succeeded in putting a stop to the fracas. Several arrests were made.

"We have no desire to discourage legitimate party rivalry, but we feel justified in strongly protesting against such dastardly tricks as those to which we have referred. We can assure our opponents that they can gain nothing by such conduct."

There was a good deal more to the effect that now was the time for all good men to come to the aid of the party, and that the constituents of Sir Eustace Briggs must look to it that they failed not in the hour of need, and so on. That was what the Wrykyn Patriot had to say on the subject.

O'Hara managed to get hold of a copy of the paper, and showed it to Clowes and Trevor.

"So now," he said, "it's all right, ye see. They'll never suspect it wasn't the same people that tarred the statue both times. An' ye've got the bat back, so it's all right, ye see."

"The only thing that'll trouble you now," said Clowes, "will be your conscience."

O'Hara intimated that he would try and put up with that.

"But isn't it a stroke of luck," he said, "that they should have gone and tarred Sir Eustace again so soon after Moriarty and I did it?"

Clowes said gravely that it only showed the force of good example.

"Yes. They wouldn't have thought of it, if it hadn't been for us," chortled O'Hara. "I wonder, now, if there's anything else we could do to that statue!" he added, meditatively.

"My good lunatic," said Clowes, "don't you think you've done almost enough for one term?"

"Well, 'myes," replied O'Hara thoughtfully, "perhaps we have, I suppose."

The term wore on. Donaldson's won the final house-match by a matter of twenty-six points. It was, as they had expected, one of the easiest games they had had to play in the competition. Bryant's, who were their opponents, were not strong, and had only managed to get into the final owing to their luck in drawing weak opponents for the trial heats. The real final, that had decided the ownership of the cup, had been Donaldson's v. Seymour's.

Aldershot arrived, and the sports. Drummond and O'Hara covered themselves with glory, and brought home silver medals. But Moriarty, to the disappointment of the school, which had counted on his pulling off the middles, met a strenuous gentleman from St Paul's in the final, and was prematurely outed in the first minute of the third round. To him, therefore, there fell but a medal of bronze.

It was on the Sunday after the sports that Trevor's connection with the bat ceased——as far, that is to say, as concerned its unpleasant character (as a piece of evidence that might be used to his disadvantage). He had gone to supper with the headmaster, accompanied by Clowes and Milton. The headmaster nearly always invited a few of the house prefects to Sunday supper during the term. Sir Eustace Briggs happened to be there. He had withdrawn his insinuations concerning the part supposedly played by a member of the school in the matter of the tarred statue, and the headmaster had sealed the entente cordiale by asking him to supper.

An ordinary man might have considered it best to keep off the delicate subject. Not so Sir Eustace Briggs. He was on to it like glue. He talked of little else throughout the whole course of the meal.

"My suspicions," he boomed, towards the conclusion of the feast, "which have, I am rejoiced to say, proved so entirely void of foundation and significance, were aroused in the first instance, as I mentioned before, by the narrative of the man Samuel Wapshott."

Nobody present showed the slightest desire to learn what the man Samuel Wapshott had had to say for himself, but Sir Eustace, undismayed, continued as if the whole table were hanging on his words.

"The man Samuel Wapshott," he said, "distinctly asserted that a small gold ornament, shaped like a bat, was handed by him to a lad of age coeval with these lads here."

The headmaster interposed. He had evidently heard more than enough of the man Samuel Wapshott.

"He must have been mistaken," he said briefly. "The bat which Trevor is wearing on his watch-chain at this moment is the only one of its kind that I know of. You have never lost it, Trevor?"

Trevor thought for a moment. He had never lost it. He replied diplomatically, "It has been in a drawer nearly all the term, sir," he said.

"A drawer, hey?" remarked Sir Eustace Briggs. "Ah! A very sensible place to keep it in, my boy. You could have no better place, in my opinion."

And Trevor agreed with him, with the mental reservation that it rather depended on whom the drawer belonged to.

PSMITH IN THE CITY

1. Mr Bickersdyke Walks behind the Bowler's Arm

Considering what a prominent figure Mr John Bickersdyke was to be in Mike Jackson's life, it was only appropriate that he should make a dramatic entry into it. This he did by walking behind the bowler's arm +when Mike had scored ninety-eight, causing him thereby to be clean bowled by a long-hop.

It was the last day of the Ilsworth cricket week, and the house team were struggling hard on a damaged wicket. During the first two matches of the week all had been well. Warm sunshine, true wickets, tea in the shade of the trees. But on the Thursday night, as the team champed their dinner contentedly after defeating the Incogniti by two wickets, a pattering of rain made itself heard upon the windows. By bedtime it had settled to a steady downpour. On Friday morning, when the team of the local regiment arrived in their brake, the sun was shining once more in a watery, melancholy way, but play was not possible before lunch. After lunch the bowlers were in their element. The regiment, winning the toss, put together a hundred and thirty, due principally to a last wicket stand between two enormous corporals, who swiped at everything and had luck enough for two whole teams. The house team followed with seventy-eight, of which Psmith, by his usual golf methods, claimed thirty. Mike, who had gone in first as the star bat of the side, had been run out with great promptitude off the first ball of the innings, which his partner had hit in the immediate neighbourhood of point. At close of play the regiment had made five without loss. This, on the Saturday morning, helped by another shower of rain which made the wicket easier for the moment, they had increased to a hundred and forty-eight, leaving the house just two hundred to make on a pitch which looked as if it were made of linseed.

It was during this week that Mike had first made the acquaintance of Psmith's family. Mr Smith had moved from Shropshire, and taken Ilsworth Hall in a neighbouring county. This he had done, as far as could be ascertained, simply because he had a poor opinion of Shropshire cricket. And just at the moment cricket happened to be the pivot of his life.

'My father,' Psmith had confided to Mike, meeting him at the station in the family motor on the Monday, 'is a man of vast but volatile brain. He has not that calm, dispassionate outlook on life which marks your true philosopher, such as myself. I—'

'I say,' interrupted Mike, eyeing Psmith's movements with apprehension, 'you aren't going to drive, are you?'

'Who else? As I was saying, I am like some contented spectator of a Pageant. My pater wants to jump in and stage-manage. He is a man of hobbies. He never has more than one at a time, and he never has that long. But while he has it, it's all there. When I left the house this morning he was all for cricket. But by the time we get to the ground he may have chucked cricket and taken up the Territorial Army. Don't be surprised if you find the wicket being dug up into trenches, when we arrive, and the pro. moving in echelon towards the pavilion. No,' he added, as the car turned into the drive, and they caught a glimpse of white flannels and blazers in the distance, and heard the sound of bat meeting ball, 'cricket seems still to be topping the bill. Come along, and I'll show you your room. It's next to mine, so that, if brooding on Life in the still hours of the night, I hit on any great truth, I shall pop in and discuss it with you.'

While Mike was changing, Psmith sat on his bed, and continued to discourse.

'I suppose you're going to the 'Varsity?' he said.

'Rather,' said Mike, lacing his boots. 'You are, of course? Cambridge, I hope. I'm going to King's.'

'Between ourselves,' confided Psmith, 'I'm dashed if I know what's going to happen to me. I am the thingummy of what's-its-name.'

'You look it,' said Mike, brushing his hair.

'Don't stand there cracking the glass,' said Psmith. 'I tell you I am practically a human three-shies-a-penny ball. My father is poising me lightly in his hand, preparatory to flinging me at one of the milky cocos of Life. Which one he'll aim at I don't know. The least thing fills him with a whirl of new views as to my future. Last week we were out shooting together, and he said that the life of the gentleman-farmer was the most manly and independent on earth, and that he had a good mind to start me on that. I pointed out that lack of early training had rendered me unable to distinguish between a threshing-machine and a mangel-wurzel, so he chucked that. He has now worked round to Commerce. It seems that a blighter of the name of Bickersdyke is coming here for the week-end next Saturday. As far as I can say without searching the Newgate Calendar, the man Bickersdyke's career seems to have been as follows. He was at school with my pater, went into the City, raked in a certain amount of doubloons—probably dishonestly—and is now a sort of Captain of Industry, manager of some bank or other, and about to stand for Parliament. The result of these excesses is that my pater's imagination has been fired, and at time of going to press he wants me to imitate Comrade Bickersdyke. However, there's plenty of time. That's one comfort. He's certain to change his mind again. Ready? Then suppose we filter forth into the arena?'

Out on the field Mike was introduced to the man of hobbies. Mr Smith, senior, was a long, earnest-looking man who might have been Psmith in a grey wig but for his obvious energy. He was as wholly on the move as Psmith was wholly statuesque. Where Psmith stood like some dignified piece of sculpture, musing on deep questions with a glassy eye, his father would be trying to be in four places at once. When Psmith presented Mike to him, he shook hands warmly with him and started a sentence, but broke off in the middle of both performances to dash wildly in the direction of the pavilion in an endeavour to catch an impossible catch some thirty yards away. The impetus so gained carried him on towards Bagley, the Ilsworth Hall ground-man, with whom a moment later he was carrying on an animated discussion as to whether he had or had not seen a dandelion on the field that morning. Two minutes afterwards he had skimmed away again. Mike, as he watched him, began to appreciate Psmith's reasons for feeling some doubt as to what would be his future walk in life.

At lunch that day Mike sat next to Mr Smith, and improved his acquaintance with him; and by the end of the week they were on excellent terms. Psmith's father had Psmith's gift of getting on well with people.

On this Saturday, as Mike buckled on his pads, Mr Smith bounded up, full of advice and encouragement.

'My boy,' he said, 'we rely on you. These others'—he indicated with a disparaging wave of the hand the rest of the team, who were visible through the window of the changing-room—'are all very well. Decent club bats. Good for a few on a billiard-table. But you're our hope on a wicket like this. I have studied cricket all my life'—till that summer it is improbable that Mr Smith had ever handled a bat—'and I know a first-class batsman when I see one. I've seen your brothers play. Pooh, you're better than any of them. That century of yours against the Green Jackets was a wonderful innings, wonderful. Now look here, my boy. I want you to be careful. We've a lot of runs to make, so we mustn't take any risks. Hit plenty of boundaries, of course, but be careful. Careful. Dash it, there's a youngster trying to climb up the elm. He'll break his neck. It's young Giles, my keeper's boy. Hi! Hi, there!'

He scudded out to avert the tragedy, leaving Mike to digest his expert advice on the art of batting on bad wickets.

Possibly it was the excellence of this advice which induced Mike to play what was, to date, the best innings of his life. There are moments when the batsman feels an almost super-human fitness. This came to Mike now. The sun had begun to shine strongly. It made the wicket more difficult, but it added a cheerful touch to the scene. Mike felt calm and masterful. The bowling had no terrors for him. He scored nine off his first over and seven off his second, half-way through which he lost his partner. He was to undergo a similar bereavement several times that afternoon, and at frequent intervals. However simple the bowling might seem to him, it had enough sting in it to worry the rest of the team considerably. Batsmen came and went at the other end with such rapidity that it seemed hardly worth while their troubling to come in at all. Every now and then one would give promise of better things by lifting the slow bowler into the pavilion or over the boundary, but it always happened that a similar stroke, a few balls later, ended in an easy catch. At five o'clock the Ilsworth score was eighty-one for seven wickets, last man nought, Mike not out fifty-nine. As most of the house team, including Mike, were dispersing to their homes or were due for visits at other houses that night, stumps were to be drawn at six. It was obvious that they could not hope to win. Number nine on the list, who was Bagley, the ground-man, went in with instructions to play for a draw, and minute advice from Mr Smith as to how he was to do it. Mike had now begun to score rapidly, and it was not to be expected that he could change his game; but Bagley, a dried-up little man of the type which bowls for five hours on a hot August day without exhibiting any symptoms of fatigue, put a much-bound bat stolidly in front of every ball he received; and the Hall's prospects of saving the game grew brighter.

At a quarter to six the professional left, caught at very silly point for eight. The score was a hundred and fifteen, of which Mike had made eighty-five.

A lengthy young man with yellow hair, who had done some good fast bowling for the Hall during the week, was the next man in. In previous matches he had hit furiously at everything, and against the Green Jackets had knocked up forty in twenty minutes while Mike was putting the finishing touches to his century. Now, however, with his host's warning ringing in his ears, he adopted the unspectacular, or Bagley, style of play. His manner of dealing with the ball was that of one playing croquet. He patted it gingerly back to the bowler when it was straight, and left it icily alone when it was off the wicket. Mike, still in the brilliant vein, clumped a half-volley past point to the boundary, and with highly scientific late cuts and glides brought his score to ninety-eight. With Mike's score at this, the total at a hundred and thirty, and the hands of the clock at five minutes to six, the yellow-haired croquet exponent fell, as Bagley had fallen, a victim to silly point, the ball being the last of the over.

Mr Smith, who always went in last for his side, and who so far had not received a single ball during the week, was down the pavilion steps and half-way to the wicket before the retiring batsman had taken half a dozen steps.

'Last over,' said the wicket-keeper to Mike. 'Any idea how many you've got? You must be near your century, I should think.'

'Ninety-eight,' said Mike. He always counted his runs.

'By Jove, as near as that? This is something like a finish.'

Mike left the first ball alone, and the second. They were too wide of the off-stump to be hit at safely. Then he felt a thrill as the third ball left the bowler's hand. It was a long-hop. He faced square to pull it.

And at that moment Mr John Bickersdyke walked into his life across the bowling-screen.

He crossed the bowler's arm just before the ball pitched. Mike lost sight of it for a fraction of a second, and hit wildly. The next moment his leg stump was askew; and the Hall had lost the match.

'I'm sorry,' he said to Mr Smith. 'Some silly idiot walked across the screen just as the ball was bowled.'

'What!' shouted Mr Smith. 'Who was the fool who walked behind the bowler's arm?' he yelled appealingly to Space.

'Here he comes, whoever he is,' said Mike.

A short, stout man in a straw hat and a flannel suit was walking towards them. As he came nearer Mike saw that he had a hard, thin-lipped mouth, half-hidden by a rather ragged moustache, and that behind a pair of gold spectacles were two pale and slightly protruding eyes, which, like his mouth, looked hard.

'How are you, Smith,' he said.

'Hullo, Bickersdyke.' There was a slight internal struggle, and then Mr Smith ceased to be the cricketer and became the host. He chatted amiably to the new-comer.

'You lost the game, I suppose,' said Mr Bickersdyke.

The cricketer in Mr Smith came to the top again, blended now, however, with the host. He was annoyed, but restrained in his annoyance.

'I say, Bickersdyke, you know, my dear fellow,' he said complainingly, 'you shouldn't have walked across the screen. You put Jackson off, and made him get bowled.'

'The screen?'

'That curious white object,' said Mike. 'It is not put up merely as an ornament. There's a sort of rough idea of giving the batsman a chance of seeing the ball, as well. It's a great help to him when people come charging across it just as the bowler bowls.'

Mr Bickersdyke turned a slightly deeper shade of purple, and was about to reply, when what sporting reporters call 'the veritable ovation' began.

Quite a large crowd had been watching the game, and they expressed their approval of Mike's performance.

There is only one thing for a batsman to do on these occasions. Mike ran into the pavilion, leaving Mr Bickersdyke standing.

2. Mike Hears Bad News

It seemed to Mike, when he got home, that there was a touch of gloom in the air. His sisters were as glad to see him as ever. There was a good deal of rejoicing going on among the female Jacksons because Joe had scored his first double century in first-class cricket. Double centuries are too common, nowadays, for the papers to take much notice of them; but, still, it is not everybody who can make them, and the occasion was one to be marked. Mike had read the news in the evening paper in the train, and had sent his brother a wire from the station, congratulating him. He had wondered whether he himself would ever achieve the feat in first-class cricket. He did not see why he should not. He looked forward through a long vista of years of county cricket. He had a birth qualification for the county in which Mr Smith had settled, and he had played for it once already at the beginning of the holidays. His debut had not been sensational, but it had been promising. The fact that two members of the team had made centuries, and a third seventy odd, had rather eclipsed his own twenty-nine not out; but it had been a faultless innings, and nearly all the papers had said that here was yet another Jackson, evidently well up to the family standard, who was bound to do big things in the future.

The touch of gloom was contributed by his brother Bob to a certain extent, and by his father more noticeably. Bob looked slightly thoughtful. Mr Jackson seemed thoroughly worried.

Mike approached Bob on the subject in the billiard-room after dinner. Bob was practising cannons in rather a listless way.

'What's up, Bob?' asked Mike.

Bob laid down his cue.

'I'm hanged if I know,' said Bob. 'Something seems to be. Father's worried about something.'

'He looked as if he'd got the hump rather at dinner.'

'I only got here this afternoon, about three hours before you did. I had a bit of a talk with him before dinner. I can't make out what's up. He seemed awfully keen on my finding something to do now I've come down from Oxford. Wanted to know whether I couldn't get a tutoring job or a mastership at some school next term. I said I'd have a shot. I don't see what all the hurry's about, though. I was hoping he'd give me a bit of travelling on the Continent somewhere before I started in.'

'Rough luck,' said Mike. 'I wonder why it is. Jolly good about Joe, wasn't it? Let's have fifty up, shall we?'

Bob's remarks had given Mike no hint of impending disaster. It seemed strange, of course, that his father, who had always been so easy-going, should have developed a hustling Get On or Get Out spirit, and be urging Bob to Do It Now; but it never occurred to him that there could be any serious reason for it. After all, fellows had to start working some time or other. Probably his father had merely pointed this out to Bob, and Bob had made too much of it.

Half-way through the game Mr Jackson entered the room, and stood watching in silence.

'Want a game, father?' asked Mike.

'No, thanks, Mike. What is it? A hundred up?'

'Fifty.'

[105] P.G. WODEHOUSE

'Oh, then you'll be finished in a moment. When you are, I wish you'd just look into the study for a moment, Mike. I want to have a talk with you.'

'Rum,' said Mike, as the door closed. 'I wonder what's up?'

For a wonder his conscience was free. It was not as if a bad school-report might have arrived in his absence. His Sedleigh report had come at the beginning of the holidays, and had been, on the whole, fairly decent—nothing startling either way. Mr Downing, perhaps through remorse at having harried Mike to such an extent during the Sammy episode, had exercised a studied moderation in his remarks. He had let Mike down far more easily than he really deserved. So it could not be a report that was worrying Mr Jackson. And there was nothing else on his conscience.

Bob made a break of sixteen, and ran out. Mike replaced his cue, and walked to the study.

His father was sitting at the table. Except for the very important fact that this time he felt that he could plead Not Guilty on every possible charge, Mike was struck by the resemblance in the general arrangement of the scene to that painful ten minutes at the end of the previous holidays, when his father had announced his intention of taking him away from Wrykyn and sending him to Sedleigh. The resemblance was increased by the fact that, as Mike entered, Mr Jackson was kicking at the waste-paper basket—a thing which with him was an infallible sign of mental unrest.

'Sit down, Mike,' said Mr Jackson. 'How did you get on during the week?'

'Topping. Only once out under double figures. And then I was run out. Got a century against the Green Jackets, seventy-one against the Incogs, and today I made ninety-eight on a beast of a wicket, and only got out because some silly goat of a chap—'

He broke off. Mr Jackson did not seem to be attending. There was a silence. Then Mr Jackson spoke with an obvious effort.

'Look here, Mike, we've always understood one another, haven't we?'

'Of course we have.'

'You know I wouldn't do anything to prevent you having a good time, if I could help it. I took you away from Wrykyn, I know, but that was a special case. It was necessary. But I understand perfectly how keen you are to go to Cambridge, and I wouldn't stand in the way for a minute, if I could help it.'

Mike looked at him blankly. This could only mean one thing. He was not to go to the 'Varsity. But why? What had happened? When he had left for the Smith's cricket week, his name had been down for King's, and the whole thing settled. What could have happened since then?

'But I can't help it,' continued Mr Jackson.

'Aren't I going up to Cambridge, father?' stammered Mike.

'I'm afraid not, Mike. I'd manage it if I possibly could. I'm just as anxious to see you get your Blue as you are to get it. But it's kinder to be quite frank. I can't afford to send you to Cambridge. I won't go into details which you would not understand; but I've lost a very large sum of money since I saw you last. So large that we shall have to economize in every way. I shall let this house and take a much smaller one. And you and Bob, I'm afraid, will have to start earning your living. I know it's a terrible disappointment to you, old chap.'

'Oh, that's all right,' said Mike thickly. There seemed to be something sticking in his throat, preventing him from speaking.

'If there was any possible way—'

'No, it's all right, father, really. I don't mind a bit. It's awfully rough luck on you losing all that.'

There was another silence. The clock ticked away energetically on the mantelpiece, as if glad to make itself heard at last. Outside, a plaintive snuffle made itself heard. John, the bull-dog, Mike's inseparable companion, who had followed him to the study, was getting tired of waiting on the mat. Mike got up and opened the door. John lumbered in.

The movement broke the tension.

'Thanks, Mike,' said Mr Jackson, as Mike started to leave the room, 'you're a sportsman.'

3. The New Era Begins

Details of what were in store for him were given to Mike next morning. During his absence at Ilsworth a vacancy had been got for him in that flourishing institution, the New Asiatic Bank; and he was to enter upon his duties, whatever they might be, on the Tuesday of the following week. It was short notice, but banks have a habit of swallowing their victims rather abruptly. Mike remembered the case of Wyatt, who had had just about the same amount of time in which to get used to the prospect of Commerce.

On the Monday morning a letter arrived from Psmith. Psmith was still perturbed. 'Commerce,' he wrote, 'continues to boom. My pater referred to Comrade Bickersdyke last night as a Merchant Prince. Comrade B. and I do not get on well together. Purely for his own good, I drew him aside yesterday and explained to him at great length the frightfulness of walking across the bowling-screen. He seemed restive, but I was firm. We parted rather with the Distant Stare than the Friendly Smile. But I shall persevere. In many ways the casual observer would say that he was hopeless. He is a poor performer at Bridge, as I was compelled to hint to him on Saturday night. His eyes have no animated sparkle of intelligence. And the cut of his clothes jars my sensitive soul to its foundations. I don't wish to speak ill of a man behind his back, but I must confide in you, as my Boyhood's Friend, that he wore a made-up tie at dinner. But no more of a painful subject. I am working away at him with a brave smile. Sometimes I think that I am succeeding. Then he seems to slip back again. However,' concluded the letter, ending on an optimistic note, 'I think that I shall make a man of him yet—some day.'

Mike re-read this letter in the train that took him to London. By this time Psmith would know that his was not the only case in which Commerce was booming. Mike had written to him by return, telling him of the disaster which had befallen the house of Jackson. Mike wished he could have told him in person, for Psmith had a way of treating unpleasant situations as if he were merely playing at them for his own amusement. Psmith's attitude towards the slings and arrows of outrageous Fortune was to regard them with a bland smile, as if they were part of an entertainment got up for his express benefit.

Arriving at Paddington, Mike stood on the platform, waiting for his box to emerge from the luggage-van, with mixed feelings of gloom and excitement. The gloom was in the larger quantities, perhaps, but the excitement was there, too. It was the first time in his life that he had been entirely dependent on himself. He had crossed the Rubicon. The occasion was too serious for him to feel the same helplessly furious feeling with which he had embarked on life at Sedleigh. It was possible to look on Sedleigh with quite a personal enmity. London was too big to be angry with. It took no notice of him. It did not care whether he was glad to be there or sorry, and there was no means of making it care. That is the peculiarity of London. There is a sort of cold unfriendliness about it. A city like New York makes the new arrival feel at home in half an hour; but London is a specialist in what Psmith in his letter had called the Distant Stare. You have to buy London's good-will.

Mike drove across the Park to Victoria, feeling very empty and small. He had settled on Dulwich as the spot to get lodgings, partly because, knowing nothing about London, he was under the impression that rooms anywhere inside the four-mile radius were very expensive, but principally because there was a school at Dulwich, and it would be a comfort being near a school. He might get a game of fives there sometimes, he thought, on a Saturday afternoon, and, in the summer, occasional cricket.

Wandering at a venture up the asphalt passage which leads from Dulwich station in the direction of the College, he came out into Acacia Road. There is something about Acacia Road which inevitably suggests furnished apartments. A child could tell at a glance that it was bristling with bed-sitting rooms.

Mike knocked at the first door over which a card hung.

There is probably no more depressing experience in the world than the process of engaging furnished apartments. Those who let furnished apartments seem to take no joy in the act. Like Pooh-Bah, they do it, but it revolts them.

In answer to Mike's knock, a female person opened the door. In appearance she resembled a pantomime 'dame', inclining towards the restrained melancholy of Mr Wilkie Bard rather than the joyous abandon of Mr George Robey. Her voice she had modelled on the gramophone. Her most recent occupation seemed to have been something with a good deal of yellow soap in it. As a matter of fact—there are no secrets between our readers and ourselves—she had been washing a shirt. A useful occupation, and an honourable, but one that tends to produce a certain homeliness in the appearance.

She wiped a pair of steaming hands on her apron, and regarded Mike with an eye which would have been markedly expressionless in a boiled fish.

'Was there anything?' she asked.

Mike felt that he was in for it now. He had not sufficient ease of manner to back gracefully away and disappear, so he said that there was something. In point of fact, he wanted a bed-sitting room.

'Orkup stays,' said the pantomime dame. Which Mike interpreted to mean, would he walk upstairs?

The procession moved up a dark flight of stairs until it came to a door. The pantomime dame opened this, and shuffled through. Mike stood in the doorway, and looked in.

It was a repulsive room. One of those characterless rooms which are only found in furnished apartments. To Mike, used to the comforts of his bedroom at home and the cheerful simplicity of a school dormitory, it seemed about the most dismal spot he had ever struck. A sort of Sargasso Sea among bedrooms.

He looked round in silence. Then he said: 'Yes.' There did not seem much else to say.

'It's a nice room,' said the pantomime dame. Which was a black lie. It was not a nice room. It never had been a nice room. And it did not seem at all probable that it ever would be a nice room. But it looked cheap. That was the great thing. Nobody could have the assurance to charge much for a room like that. A landlady with a conscience might even have gone to the length of paying people some small sum by way of compensation to them for sleeping in it.

'About what?' queried Mike. Cheapness was the great consideration. He understood that his salary at the bank would be about four pounds ten a month, to begin with, and his father was allowing him five pounds a month. One does not do things en prince on a hundred and fourteen pounds a year.

The pantomime dame became slightly more animated. Prefacing her remarks by a repetition of her statement that it was a nice room, she went on to say that she could 'do' it at seven and sixpence per week 'for him'—giving him to understand, presumably, that, if the Shah of Persia or Mr Carnegie ever applied for a night's rest, they would sigh in vain for such easy terms. And that included lights. Coals were to be looked on as an extra. 'Sixpence a scuttle.' Attendance was thrown in.

Having stated these terms, she dribbled a piece of fluff under the bed, after the manner of a professional Association footballer, and relapsed into her former moody silence.

Mike said he thought that would be all right. The pantomime dame exhibited no pleasure.

"Bout meals?' she said. 'You'll be wanting breakfast. Bacon, aigs, an' that, I suppose?'

Mike said he supposed so.

'That'll be extra,' she said. 'And dinner? A chop, or a nice steak?'

Mike bowed before this original flight of fancy. A chop or a nice steak seemed to be about what he might want.

'That'll be extra,' said the pantomime dame in her best Wilkie Bard manner.

Mike said yes, he supposed so. After which, having put down seven and sixpence, one week's rent in advance, he was presented with a grubby receipt and an enormous latchkey, and the seance was at an end. Mike wandered out of the house. A few steps took him to the railings that bounded the College grounds. It was late August, and the evenings had begun to close in. The cricket-field looked very cool and spacious in the dim light, with the school buildings looming vague and shadowy through the slight mist. The little gate by the railway bridge was not locked. He went in, and walked slowly across the turf towards the big clump of trees which marked the division between the cricket and football fields. It was all very pleasant and soothing after the pantomime dame and her stuffy bed-sitting room. He sat down on a bench beside the second eleven telegraph-board, and looked across the ground at the pavilion. For the first time that day he began to feel really home-sick. Up till now the excitement of a strange venture had borne him up; but the cricket-field and the pavilion reminded him so sharply of Wrykyn. They brought home to him with a cutting distinctness, the absolute finality of his break with the old order of things. Summers would come and go, matches would be played on this ground with all the glory of big scores and keen finishes; but he was done. 'He was a jolly good bat at school. Top of the Wrykyn averages two years. But didn't do anything after he left. Went into the city or something.' That was what they would say of him, if they didn't quite forget him.

The clock on the tower over the senior block chimed quarter after quarter, but Mike sat on, thinking. It was quite late when he got up, and began to walk back to Acacia Road. He felt cold and stiff and very miserable.

4. First Steps in a Business Career

The city received Mike with the same aloofness with which the more western portion of London had welcomed him on the previous day. Nobody seemed to look at him. He was permitted to alight at St Paul's and make his way up Queen Victoria Street without any demonstration. He followed the human stream till he reached the Mansion House, and eventually found himself at the massive building of the New Asiatic Bank, Limited.

The difficulty now was to know how to make an effective entrance. There was the bank, and here was he. How had he better set about breaking it to the authorities that he had positively arrived and was ready to start earning his four pound ten per mensem? Inside, the bank seemed to be in a state of some confusion. Men were moving about in an apparently irresolute manner. Nobody seemed actually to be working. As a matter of fact, the business of a bank does not start very early in the morning. Mike had arrived before things had really begun to move. As he stood near the doorway, one or two panting figures rushed up the steps, and flung themselves at a large book which stood on the counter near the door. Mike was to come to know this book well. In it, if you were an employe of the New Asiatic Bank, you had to inscribe your name every morning. It was removed at ten sharp to the accountant's room, and if you reached the bank a certain number of times in the year too late to sign, bang went your bonus.

After a while things began to settle down. The stir and confusion gradually ceased. All down the length of the bank, figures could be seen, seated on stools and writing hieroglyphics in large letters. A benevolent-looking man, with spectacles and a straggling grey beard, crossed the gangway close to where Mike was standing. Mike put the thing to him, as man to man.

'Could you tell me,' he said, 'what I'm supposed to do? I've just joined the bank.' The benevolent man stopped, and looked at him with a pair of mild blue eyes. 'I think, perhaps, that your best plan would be to see the manager,' he said. 'Yes, I should certainly do that. He will tell you what work you have to do. If you will permit me, I will show you the way.'

'It's awfully good of you,' said Mike. He felt very grateful. After his experience of London, it was a pleasant change to find someone who really seemed to care what happened to him. His heart warmed to the benevolent man.

'It feels strange to you, perhaps, at first, Mr—'

'Jackson.'

'Mr Jackson. My name is Waller. I have been in the City some time, but I can still recall my first day. But one shakes down. One shakes down quite quickly. Here is the manager's room. If you go in, he will tell you what to do.'

'Thanks awfully,' said Mike.

'Not at all.' He ambled off on the quest which Mike had interrupted, turning, as he went, to bestow a mild smile of encouragement on the new arrival. There was something about Mr Waller which reminded Mike pleasantly of the White Knight in 'Alice through the Looking-glass.'

Mike knocked at the managerial door, and went in.

Two men were sitting at the table. The one facing the door was writing when Mike went in. He continued to write all the time he was in the room. Conversation between other people in his presence had apparently no interest for him, nor was it able to disturb him in any way.

The other man was talking into a telephone. Mike waited till he had finished. Then he coughed. The man turned round. Mike had thought, as he looked at his back and heard his voice, that something about his appearance or his way of speaking was familiar. He was right. The man in the chair was Mr Bickersdyke, the cross-screen pedestrian.

These reunions are very awkward. Mike was frankly unequal to the situation. Psmith, in his place, would have opened the conversation, and relaxed the tension with some remark on the weather or the state of the crops. Mike merely stood wrapped in silence, as in a garment.

That the recognition was mutual was evident from Mr Bickersdyke's look. But apart from this, he gave no sign of having already had the pleasure of making Mike's acquaintance. He merely stared at him as if he were a blot on the arrangement of the furniture, and said, 'Well?'

The most difficult parts to play in real life as well as on the stage are those in which no 'business' is arranged for the performer. It was all very well for Mr Bickersdyke. He had been 'discovered sitting'. But Mike had had to enter, and he wished now that there was something he could do instead of merely standing and speaking.

'I've come,' was the best speech he could think of. It was not a good speech. It was too sinister. He felt that even as he said it. It was the sort of thing Mephistopheles would have said to Faust by way of opening conversation. And he was not sure, either, whether he ought not to have added, 'Sir.'

Apparently such subtleties of address were not necessary, for Mr Bickersdyke did not start up and shout, 'This language to me!' or anything of that kind. He merely said, 'Oh! And who are you?'

'Jackson,' said Mike. It was irritating, this assumption on Mr Bickersdyke's part that they had never met before.

'Jackson? Ah, yes. You have joined the staff?'

Mike rather liked this way of putting it. It lent a certain dignity to the proceedings, making him feel like some important person for whose services there had been strenuous competition. He seemed to see the bank's directors being reassured by the chairman. ('I am happy to say, gentlemen, that our profits for the past year are 3,000,006-2-2 1/2 pounds—(cheers)—and'—impressively—'that we have finally succeeded in inducing Mr Mike Jackson—(sensation)—to—er—in fact, to join the staff!' (Frantic cheers, in which the chairman joined.)

'Yes,' he said.

Mr Bickersdyke pressed a bell on the table beside him, and picking up a pen, began to write. Of Mike he took no further notice, leaving that toy of Fate standing stranded in the middle of the room.

After a few moments one of the men in fancy dress, whom Mike had seen hanging about the gangway, and whom he afterwards found to be messengers, appeared. Mr Bickersdyke looked up.

'Ask Mr Bannister to step this way,' he said.

The messenger disappeared, and presently the door opened again to admit a shock-headed youth with paper cuff-protectors round his wrists.

'This is Mr Jackson, a new member of the staff. He will take your place in the postage department. You will go into the cash department, under Mr Waller. Kindly show him what he has to do.'

Mike followed Mr Bannister out. On the other side of the door the shock-headed one became communicative.

'Whew!' he said, mopping his brow. 'That's the sort of thing which gives me the pip. When William came and said old Bick wanted to see me, I said to him, "William, my boy, my number is up. This is the sack." I made certain that Rossiter had run me in for something. He's been waiting for a chance to do it for weeks, only I've been as good as gold and haven't given it him. I pity you going into the postage. There's one thing, though. If you can stick it for about a month, you'll get through all right. Men are always leaving for the East, and then you get shunted on into another department, and the next new man goes into the postage. That's the best of this place. It's not like one of those banks where you stay in London all your life. You only have three years here, and then you get your orders, and go to one of the branches in the East, where you're the dickens of a big pot straight away, with a big screw and a dozen native Johnnies under you. Bit of all right, that. I shan't get my orders for another two and a half years and more, worse luck. Still, it's something to look forward to.'

'Who's Rossiter?' asked Mike.

'The head of the postage department. Fussy little brute. Won't leave you alone. Always trying to catch you on the hop. There's one thing, though. The work in the postage is pretty simple. You can't make many mistakes, if you're careful. It's mostly entering letters and stamping them.'

They turned in at the door in the counter, and arrived at a desk which ran parallel to the gangway. There was a high rack running along it, on which were several ledgers. Tall, green-shaded electric lamps gave it rather a cosy look.

As they reached the desk, a little man with short, black whiskers buzzed out from behind a glass screen, where there was another desk.

'Where have you been, Bannister, where have you been? You must not leave your work in this way. There are several letters waiting to be entered. Where have you been?'

'Mr Bickersdyke sent for me,' said Bannister, with the calm triumph of one who trumps an ace.

'Oh! Ah! Oh! Yes, very well. I see. But get to work, get to work. Who is this?'

'This is a new man. He's taking my place. I've been moved on to the cash.'

'Oh! Ah! Is your name Smith?' asked Mr Rossiter, turning to Mike.

Mike corrected the rash guess, and gave his name. It struck him as a curious coincidence that he should be asked if his name were Smith, of all others. Not that it is an uncommon name.

'Mr Bickersdyke told me to expect a Mr Smith. Well, well, perhaps there are two new men. Mr Bickersdyke knows we are short-handed in this department. But, come along, Bannister, come along. Show Jackson what he has to do. We must get on. There is no time to waste.'

He buzzed back to his lair. Bannister grinned at Mike. He was a cheerful youth. His normal expression was a grin.

'That's a sample of Rossiter,' he said. 'You'd think from the fuss he's made that the business of the place was at a standstill till we got to work. Perfect rot! There's never anything to do here till after lunch, except checking the stamps and petty cash, and I've done that ages ago. There are three letters. You may as well enter them. It all looks like work. But you'll find the best way is to wait till you get a couple of dozen or so, and then work them off in a batch. But if you see Rossiter about, then start stamping something or writing something, or he'll run you in for neglecting your job. He's a nut. I'm jolly glad I'm under old Waller now. He's the pick of the bunch. The other heads of departments are all nuts, and Bickersdyke's the nuttiest of the lot. Now, look here. This is all you've got to do. I will just show you, and then you can manage for yourself. I shall have to be shunting off to my own work in a minute.'

5. The Other Man

As Bannister had said, the work in the postage department was not intricate. There was nothing much to do except enter and stamp letters, and, at intervals, take them down to the post office at the end of the street. The nature of the work gave Mike plenty of time for reflection.

His thoughts became gloomy again. All this was very far removed from the life to which he had looked forward. There are some people who take naturally to a life of commerce. Mike was not of these. To him the restraint of the business was irksome. He had been used to an open-air life, and a life, in its way, of excitement. He gathered that he would not be free till five o'clock, and that on the following day he would come at ten and go at five, and the same every day, except Saturdays and Sundays, all the year round, with a ten days' holiday. The monotony of the prospect appalled him. He was not old enough to know what a narcotic is Habit, and that one can become attached to and interested in the most unpromising jobs. He worked away dismally at his letters till he had finished them. Then there was nothing to do except sit and wait for more.

He looked through the letters he had stamped, and re-read the addresses. Some of them were directed to people living in the country, one to a house which he knew quite well, near to his own home in Shropshire. It made him home-sick, conjuring up visions of shady gardens and country sounds and smells, and the silver Severn gleaming in the distance through the trees. About now, if he were not in this dismal place, he would be lying in the shade in the garden with a book, or wandering down to the river to boat or bathe. That envelope addressed to the man in Shropshire gave him the worst moment he had experienced that day.

The time crept slowly on to one o'clock. At two minutes past Mike awoke from a day-dream to find Mr Waller standing by his side. The cashier had his hat on.

'I wonder,' said Mr Waller, 'if you would care to come out to lunch. I generally go about this time, and Mr Rossiter, I know, does not go out till two. I thought perhaps that, being unused to the City, you might have some difficulty in finding your way about.'

'It's awfully good of you,' said Mike. 'I should like to.'

The other led the way through the streets and down obscure alleys till they came to a chop-house. Here one could have the doubtful pleasure of seeing one's chop in its various stages of evolution. Mr Waller ordered lunch with the care of one to whom lunch is no slight matter. Few workers in the City do regard lunch as a trivial affair. It is the keynote of their day. It is an oasis in a desert of ink and ledgers. Conversation in city office deals, in the morning, with what one is going to have for lunch, and in the afternoon with what one has had for lunch.

At intervals during the meal Mr Waller talked. Mike was content to listen. There was something soothing about the grey-bearded one.

'What sort of a man is Bickersdyke?' asked Mike.

'A very able man. A very able man indeed. I'm afraid he's not popular in the office. A little inclined, perhaps, to be hard on mistakes. I can remember the time when he was quite different. He and I were fellow clerks in Morton and Blatherwick's. He got on better than I did. A great fellow for getting on. They say he is to be the Unionist candidate for Kenningford when the time comes. A great worker, but perhaps not quite the sort of man to be generally popular in an office.'

'He's a blighter,' was Mike's verdict. Mr Waller made no comment. Mike was to learn later that the manager and the cashier, despite the fact that they had been together in less prosperous days—or possibly because of it—were not on very good terms. Mr Bickersdyke was a man of strong prejudices, and he disliked the cashier, whom he looked down upon as one who had climbed to a lower rung of the ladder than he himself had reached.

As the hands of the chop-house clock reached a quarter to two, Mr Waller rose, and led the way back to the office, where they parted for their respective desks. Gratitude for any good turn done to him was a leading characteristic of Mike's nature, and he felt genuinely grateful to the cashier for troubling to seek him out and be friendly to him.

His three-quarters-of-an-hour absence had led to the accumulation of a small pile of letters on his desk. He sat down and began to work them off. The addresses continued to exercise a fascination for him. He was miles away from the office, speculating on what sort of a man J. B. Garside, Esq, was, and whether he had a good time at his house in Worcestershire, when somebody tapped him on the shoulder.

He looked up.

Standing by his side, immaculately dressed as ever, with his eye-glass fixed and a gentle smile on his face, was Psmith.

Mike stared.

'Commerce,' said Psmith, as he drew off his lavender gloves, 'has claimed me for her own. Comrade of old, I, too, have joined this blighted institution.'

As he spoke, there was a whirring noise in the immediate neighbourhood, and Mr Rossiter buzzed out from his den with the esprit and animation of a clock-work toy.

'Who's here?' said Psmith with interest, removing his eye-glass, polishing it, and replacing it in his eye.

'Mr Jackson,' exclaimed Mr Rossiter. 'I really must ask you to be good enough to come in from your lunch at the proper time. It was fully seven minutes to two when you returned, and—'

'That little more,' sighed Psmith, 'and how much is it!'

'Who are you?' snapped Mr Rossiter, turning on him.

'I shall be delighted, Comrade—'

'Rossiter,' said Mike, aside.

'Comrade Rossiter. I shall be delighted to furnish you with particulars of my family history. As follows. Soon after the Norman Conquest, a certain Sieur de Psmith grew tired of work—a family failing, alas!—and settled down in this country to live peacefully for the remainder of his life on what he could extract from the local peasantry. He may be described as the founder of the family which ultimately culminated in Me. Passing on—'

Mr Rossiter refused to pass on.

'What are you doing here? What have you come for?'

'Work,' said Psmith, with simple dignity. 'I am now a member of the staff of this bank. Its interests are my interests. Psmith, the individual, ceases to exist, and there springs into being Psmith, the cog in the wheel of the New Asiatic Bank; Psmith, the link in the bank's chain; Psmith, the Worker. I shall not spare myself,' he proceeded earnestly. 'I shall toil with all the accumulated energy of one who, up till now, has only known what work is like from hearsay. Whose is that form sitting on the steps of the bank in the morning, waiting eagerly for the place to open? It is the form of Psmith, the Worker. Whose is that haggard, drawn face which bends over a ledger long after the other toilers have sped blithely westwards to dine at Lyons' Popular Cafe? It is the face of Psmith, the Worker.'

'I—' began Mr Rossiter.

'I tell you,' continued Psmith, waving aside the interruption and tapping the head of the department rhythmically in the region of the second waistcoat-button with a long finger, 'I tell you, Comrade Rossiter, that you have got hold of a good man. You and I together, not forgetting Comrade Jackson, the pet of the Smart Set, will toil early and late till we boost up this Postage Department into a shining model of what a Postage Department should be. What that is, at present, I do not exactly know. However. Excursion trains will be run from distant shires to see this Postage Department. American visitors to London will do it before going on to the Tower. And now,' he broke off, with a crisp, businesslike intonation, 'I must ask you to excuse me. Much as I have enjoyed this little chat, I fear it must now cease. The time has come to work. Our trade rivals are getting ahead of us. The whisper goes round, "Rossiter and Psmith are talking, not working," and other firms prepare to pinch our business. Let me Work.'

Two minutes later, Mr Rossiter was sitting at his desk with a dazed expression, while Psmith, perched gracefully on a stool, entered figures in a ledger.

6. Psmith Explains

For the space of about twenty-five minutes Psmith sat in silence, concentrated on his ledger, the picture of the model bank-clerk. Then he flung down his pen, slid from his stool with a satisfied sigh, and dusted his waistcoat. 'A commercial crisis,' he said, 'has passed. The job of work which Comrade Rossiter indicated for me has been completed with masterly skill. The period of anxiety is over. The bank ceases to totter. Are you busy, Comrade Jackson, or shall we chat awhile?'

Mike was not busy. He had worked off the last batch of letters, and there was nothing to do but to wait for the next, or—happy thought—to take the present batch down to the post, and so get out into the sunshine and fresh air for a short time. 'I rather think I'll nip down to the post-office,' said he, 'You couldn't come too, I suppose?'

'On the contrary,' said Psmith, 'I could, and will. A stroll will just restore those tissues which the gruelling work of the last half-hour has wasted away. It is a fearful strain, this commercial toil. Let us trickle towards the post office. I will leave my hat and gloves as a guarantee of good faith. The cry will go round, "Psmith has gone! Some rival institution has kidnapped him!" Then they will see my hat,'—he built up a foundation of ledgers, planted a long ruler in the middle, and hung his hat on it—'my gloves,'—he stuck two pens into the desk and hung a lavender glove on each—'and they will sink back swooning with relief. The awful suspense will be over. They will say, "No, he has not gone permanently. Psmith will return. When the fields are white with daisies he'll return." And now, Comrade Jackson, lead me to this picturesque little post-office of yours of which I have heard so much.'

Mike picked up the long basket into which he had thrown the letters after entering the addresses in his ledger, and they moved off down the aisle. No movement came from Mr Rossiter's lair. Its energetic occupant was hard at work. They could just see part of his hunched-up back.

'I wish Comrade Downing could see us now,' said Psmith. 'He always set us down as mere idlers. Triflers. Butterflies. It would be a wholesome corrective for him to watch us perspiring like this in the cause of Commerce.'

'You haven't told me yet what on earth you're doing here,' said Mike. 'I thought you were going to the 'Varsity. Why the dickens are you in a bank? Your pater hasn't lost his money, has he?'

'No. There is still a tolerable supply of doubloons in the old oak chest. Mine is a painful story.'

'It always is,' said Mike.

'You are very right, Comrade Jackson. I am the victim of Fate. Ah, so you put the little chaps in there, do you?' he said, as Mike, reaching the post-office, began to bundle the letters into the box. 'You seem to have grasped your duties with admirable promptitude. It is the same with me. I fancy we are both born men of Commerce. In a few years we shall be pinching Comrade Bickersdyke's job. And talking of Comrade B. brings me back to my painful story. But I shall never have time to tell it to you during our walk back. Let us drift aside into this tea-shop. We can order a buckwheat cake or a butter-nut, or something equally succulent, and carefully refraining from consuming these dainties, I will tell you all.'

'Right O!' said Mike.

'When last I saw you,' resumed Psmith, hanging Mike's basket on the hat-stand and ordering two portions of porridge, 'you may remember that a serious crisis in my affairs had arrived. My father inflamed with the idea of Commerce had invited Comrade Bickersdyke—'

'When did you know he was a manager here?' asked Mike.

'At an early date. I have my spies everywhere. However, my pater invited Comrade Bickersdyke to our house for the weekend. Things turned out rather unfortunately. Comrade B. resented my purely altruistic efforts to improve him mentally and morally. Indeed, on one occasion he went so far as to call me an impudent young cub, and to add that he wished he had me under him in his bank, where, he asserted, he would knock some of the nonsense out of me. All very painful. I tell you, Comrade Jackson, for the moment it reduced my delicately vibrating ganglions to a mere frazzle. Recovering myself, I made a few blithe remarks, and we then parted. I cannot say that we parted friends, but at any rate I bore him no ill-will. I was still determined to make him a credit to me. My feelings towards him were those of some kindly father to his prodigal son. But he, if I may say so, was fairly on the hop. And when my pater, after dinner the same night, played into his hands by mentioning that he thought I ought to plunge into a career of commerce, Comrade B. was, I gather, all over him. Offered to make a vacancy for me in the bank, and to take me on at once. My pater, feeling that this was the real hustle which he admired so much, had me in, stated his case, and said, in effect, "How do we go?" I intimated that Comrade Bickersdyke was my greatest chum on earth. So the thing was fixed up and here I am. But you are not getting on with your porridge, Comrade Jackson. Perhaps you don't care for porridge? Would you like a finnan haddock, instead? Or a piece of shortbread? You have only to say the word.'

'It seems to me,' said Mike gloomily, 'that we are in for a pretty rotten time of it in this bally bank. If Bickersdyke's got his knife into us, he can make it jolly warm for us. He's got his knife into me all right about that walking-across-the-screen business.'

'True,' said Psmith, 'to a certain extent. It is an undoubted fact that Comrade Bickersdyke will have a jolly good try at making life a nuisance to us; but, on the other hand, I propose, so far as in me lies, to make things moderately unrestful for him, here and there.'

'But you can't,' objected Mike. 'What I mean to say is, it isn't like a school. If you wanted to score off a master at school, you could always rag and so on. But here you can't. How can you rag a man who's sitting all day in a room of his own while you're sweating away at a desk at the other end of the building?'

'You put the case with admirable clearness, Comrade Jackson,' said Psmith approvingly. 'At the hard-headed, common-sense business you sneak the biscuit every time with ridiculous ease. But you do not know all. I do not propose to do a thing in the bank except work. I shall be a model as far as work goes. I shall be flawless. I shall bound to do Comrade Rossiter's bidding like a highly trained performing dog. It is outside the bank, when I have staggered away dazed with toil, that I shall resume my attention to the education of Comrade Bickersdyke.'

'But, dash it all, how can you? You won't see him. He'll go off home, or to his club, or—'

Psmith tapped him earnestly on the chest.

'There, Comrade Jackson,' he said, 'you have hit the bull's-eye, rung the bell, and gathered in the cigar or cocoanut according to choice. He will go off to his club. And I shall do precisely the same.'

'How do you mean?'

'It is this way. My father, as you may have noticed during your stay at our stately home of England, is a man of a warm, impulsive character. He does not always do things as other people would do them. He has his own methods. Thus, he has sent me into the City to do the hard-working, bank-clerk act, but at the same time he is allowing me just as large an allowance as he would have given me if I had gone to the 'Varsity. Moreover, while I was still at Eton he put my name up for his clubs, the Senior Conservative among others. My pater belongs to four clubs altogether, and in course of time, when my name comes up for election, I shall do the same. Meanwhile, I belong to one, the Senior Conservative. It is a bigger club than the others, and your name comes up for election sooner. About the middle of last month a great yell of joy made the West End of London shake like a jelly. The three thousand members of the Senior Conservative had just learned that I had been elected.'

Psmith paused, and ate some porridge.

'I wonder why they call this porridge,' he observed with mild interest. 'It would be far more manly and straightforward of them to give it its real name. To resume. I have gleaned, from casual chit-chat with my father, that Comrade Bickersdyke also infests the Senior Conservative. You might think that that would make me, seeing how particular I am about whom I mix with, avoid the club. Error. I shall go there every day. If Comrade Bickersdyke wishes to emend any little traits in my character of which he may disapprove, he shall never say that I did not give him the opportunity. I shall mix freely with Comrade Bickersdyke at the Senior Conservative Club. I shall be his constant companion. I shall, in short, haunt the man. By these strenuous means I shall, as it were, get a bit of my own back. And now,' said Psmith, rising, 'it might be as well, perhaps, to return to the bank and resume our commercial duties. I don't know how long you are supposed to be allowed for your little trips to and from the post-office, but, seeing that the distance is about thirty yards, I should say at a venture not more than half an hour. Which is exactly the space of time which has flitted by since we started out on this important expedition. Your devotion to porridge, Comrade Jackson, has led to our spending about twenty-five minutes in this hostelry.'

'Great Scott,' said Mike, 'there'll be a row.'

'Some slight temporary breeze, perhaps,' said Psmith. 'Annoying to men of culture and refinement, but not lasting. My only fear is lest we may have worried Comrade Rossiter at all. I regard Comrade Rossiter as an elder brother, and would not cause him a moment's heart-burning for worlds. However, we shall soon know,' he added, as they passed into the bank and walked up the aisle, 'for there is Comrade Rossiter waiting to receive us in person.'

The little head of the Postage Department was moving restlessly about in the neighbourhood of Psmith's and Mike's desk.

'Am I mistaken,' said Psmith to Mike, 'or is there the merest suspicion of a worried look on our chief's face? It seems to me that there is the slightest soupcon of shadow about that broad, calm brow.'

7. Going into Winter Quarters

There was.

Mr Rossiter had discovered Psmith's and Mike's absence about five minutes after they had left the building. Ever since then, he had been popping out of his lair at intervals of three minutes, to see whether they had returned. Constant disappointment in this respect had rendered him decidedly jumpy. When Psmith and Mike reached the desk, he was a kind of human soda-water bottle. He fizzed over with questions, reproofs, and warnings.

'What does it mean? What does it mean?' he cried. 'Where have you been? Where have you been?'

'Poetry,' said Psmith approvingly.

'You have been absent from your places for over half an hour. Why? Why? Why? Where have you been? Where have you been? I cannot have this. It is preposterous. Where have you been? Suppose Mr Bickersdyke had happened to come round here. I should not have known what to say to him.'

'Never an easy man to chat with, Comrade Bickersdyke,' agreed Psmith.

'You must thoroughly understand that you are expected to remain in your places during business hours.'

'Of course,' said Psmith, 'that makes it a little hard for Comrade Jackson to post letters, does it not?'

'Have you been posting letters?'

'We have,' said Psmith. 'You have wronged us. Seeing our absent places you jumped rashly to the conclusion that we were merely gadding about in pursuit of pleasure. Error. All the while we were furthering the bank's best interests by posting letters.'

'You had no business to leave your place. Jackson is on the posting desk.'

'You are very right,' said Psmith, 'and it shall not occur again. It was only because it was the first day, Comrade Jackson is not used to the stir and bustle of the City. His nerve failed him. He shrank from going to the post-office alone. So I volunteered to accompany him. And,' concluded Psmith, impressively, 'we won safely through. Every letter has been posted.'

'That need not have taken you half an hour.'

'True. And the actual work did not. It was carried through swiftly and surely. But the nerve-strain had left us shaken. Before resuming our more ordinary duties we had to refresh. A brief breathing-space, a little coffee and porridge, and here we are, fit for work once more.'

'If it occurs again, I shall report the matter to Mr Bickersdyke.'

'And rightly so,' said Psmith, earnestly. 'Quite rightly so. Discipline, discipline. That is the cry. There must be no shirking of painful duties. Sentiment must play no part in business. Rossiter, the man, may sympathise, but Rossiter, the Departmental head, must be adamant.'

Mr Rossiter pondered over this for a moment, then went off on a side-issue.

'What is the meaning of this foolery?' he asked, pointing to Psmith's gloves and hat. 'Suppose Mr Bickersdyke had come round and seen them, what should I have said?'

'You would have given him a message of cheer. You would have said, "All is well. Psmith has not left us. He will come back. And Comrade Bickersdyke, relieved, would have—"'

'You do not seem very busy, Mr Smith.'

Both Psmith and Mr Rossiter were startled.

Mr Rossiter jumped as if somebody had run a gimlet into him, and even Psmith started slightly. They had not heard Mr Bickersdyke approaching. Mike, who had been stolidly entering addresses in his ledger during the latter part of the conversation, was also taken by surprise.

Psmith was the first to recover. Mr Rossiter was still too confused for speech, but Psmith took the situation in hand.

'Apparently no,' he said, swiftly removing his hat from the ruler. 'In reality, yes. Mr Rossiter and I were just scheming out a line of work for me as you came up. If you had arrived a moment later, you would have found me toiling.'

'H'm. I hope I should. We do not encourage idling in this bank.'

'Assuredly not,' said Psmith warmly. 'Most assuredly not. I would not have it otherwise. I am a worker. A bee, not a drone. A Lusitania, not a limpet. Perhaps I have not yet that grip on my duties which I shall soon acquire; but it is coming. It is coming. I see daylight.'

'H'm. I have only your word for it.' He turned to Mr Rossiter, who had now recovered himself, and was as nearly calm as it was in his nature to be. 'Do you find Mr Smith's work satisfactory, Mr Rossiter?'

Psmith waited resignedly for an outburst of complaint respecting the small matter that had been under discussion between the head of the department and himself; but to his surprise it did not come.

'Oh—ah—quite, quite, Mr Bickersdyke. I think he will very soon pick things up.'

Mr Bickersdyke turned away. He was a conscientious bank manager, and one can only suppose that Mr Rossiter's tribute to the earnestness of one of his employes was gratifying to him. But for that, one would have said that he was disappointed.

'Oh, Mr Bickersdyke,' said Psmith.

The manager stopped.

'Father sent his kind regards to you,' said Psmith benevolently.

Mr Bickersdyke walked off without comment.

'An uncommonly cheery, companionable feller,' murmured Psmith, as he turned to his work.

The first day anywhere, if one spends it in a sedentary fashion, always seemed unending; and Mike felt as if he had been sitting at his desk for weeks when the hour for departure came. A bank's day ends gradually, reluctantly, as it were. At about five there is a sort of stir, not unlike the stir in a theatre when the curtain is on the point of falling. Ledgers are closed with a bang. Men stand about and talk for a moment or two before going to the basement for their hats and coats. Then, at irregular intervals, forms pass down the central aisle and out through the swing doors. There is an air of relaxation over the place, though some departments are still working as hard as ever under a blaze of electric light. Somebody begins to sing, and an instant chorus of protests and maledictions rises from all sides. Gradually, however, the electric lights go out. The procession down the centre aisle becomes more regular; and eventually the place is left to darkness and the night watchman.

The postage department was one of the last to be freed from duty. This was due to the inconsiderateness of the other departments, which omitted to disgorge their letters till the last moment. Mike as he grew familiar with the work, and began to understand it, used to prowl round the other departments during the afternoon and wrest letters from them, usually receiving with them much abuse for being a nuisance and not leaving honest workers alone. Today, however, he had to sit on till nearly six, waiting for the final batch of correspondence.

Psmith, who had waited patiently with him, though his own work was finished, accompanied him down to the post office and back again to the bank to return the letter basket; and they left the office together.

'By the way,' said Psmith, 'what with the strenuous labours of the bank and the disturbing interviews with the powers that be, I have omitted to ask you where you are digging. Wherever it is, of course you must clear out. It is imperative, in this crisis, that we should be together. I have acquired a quite snug little flat in Clement's Inn. There is a spare bedroom. It shall be yours.'

'My dear chap,' said Mike, 'it's all rot. I can't sponge on you.'

'You pain me, Comrade Jackson. I was not suggesting such a thing. We are business men, hard-headed young bankers. I make you a business proposition. I offer you the post of confidential secretary and adviser to me in exchange for a comfortable home. The duties will be light. You will be required to refuse invitations to dinner from crowned heads, and to listen attentively to my views on Life. Apart from this, there is little to do. So that's settled.'

'It isn't,' said Mike. 'I—'

'You will enter upon your duties tonight. Where are you suspended at present?'

'Dulwich. But, look here—'

'A little more, and you'll get the sack. I tell you the thing is settled. Now, let us hail yon taximeter cab, and desire the stern-faced aristocrat on the box to drive us to Dulwich. We will then collect a few of your things in a bag, have the rest off by train, come back in the taxi, and go and bite a chop at the Carlton. This is a momentous day in our careers, Comrade Jackson. We must buoy ourselves up.'

Mike made no further objections. The thought of that bed-sitting room in Acacia Road and the pantomime dame rose up and killed them. After all, Psmith was not like any ordinary person. There would be no question of charity. Psmith had invited him to the flat in exactly the same spirit as he had invited him to his house for the cricket week.

'You know,' said Psmith, after a silence, as they flitted through the streets in the taximeter, 'one lives and learns. Were you so wrapped up in your work this afternoon that you did not hear my very entertaining little chat with Comrade Bickersdyke, or did it happen to come under your notice? It did? Then I wonder if you were struck by the singular conduct of Comrade Rossiter?'

'I thought it rather decent of him not to give you away to that blighter Bickersdyke.'

'Admirably put. It was precisely that that struck me. He had his opening, all ready made for him, but he refrained from depositing me in the soup. I tell you, Comrade Jackson, my rugged old heart was touched. I said to myself, "There must be good in Comrade Rossiter, after all. I must cultivate him." I shall make it my business to be kind to our Departmental head. He deserves the utmost consideration. His action shone like a good deed in a wicked world. Which it was, of course. From today onwards I take Comrade Rossiter under my wing. We seem to be getting into a tolerably benighted quarter. Are we anywhere near? "Through Darkest Dulwich in a Taximeter.'"

The cab arrived at Dulwich station, and Mike stood up to direct the driver. They whirred down Acacia Road. Mike stopped the cab and got out. A brief and somewhat embarrassing interview with the pantomime dame, during which Mike was separated from a week's rent in lieu of notice, and he was in the cab again, bound for Clement's Inn.

His feelings that night differed considerably from the frame of mind in which he had gone to bed the night before. It was partly a very excellent dinner and partly the fact that Psmith's flat, though at present in some disorder, was obviously going to be extremely comfortable, that worked the change. But principally it was due to his having found an ally. The gnawing loneliness had gone. He did not look forward to a career of Commerce with any greater pleasure than before; but there was no doubt that with Psmith, it would be easier to get through the time after office hours. If all went well in the bank he might find that he had not drawn such a bad ticket after all.

8. The Friendly Native

'The first principle of warfare,' said Psmith at breakfast next morning, doling out bacon and eggs with the air of a medieval monarch distributing largesse, 'is to collect a gang, to rope in allies, to secure the cooperation of some friendly native. You may remember that at Sedleigh it was partly the sympathetic cooperation of that record blitherer, Comrade Jellicoe, which enabled us to nip the pro-Spiller movement in the bud. It is the same in the present crisis. What Comrade Jellicoe was to us at Sedleigh, Comrade Rossiter must be in the city. We must make an ally of that man. Once I know that he and I are as brothers, and that he will look with a lenient and benevolent eye on any little shortcomings in my work, I shall be able to devote my attention whole-heartedly to the moral reformation of Comrade Bickersdyke, that man of blood. I look on Comrade Bickersdyke as a bargee of the most pronounced type; and anything I can do towards making him a decent member of Society shall be done freely and ungrudgingly. A trifle more tea, Comrade Jackson?'

'No, thanks,' said Mike. 'I've done. By Jove, Smith, this flat of yours is all right.'

'Not bad,' assented Psmith, 'not bad. Free from squalor to a great extent. I have a number of little objects of vertu coming down shortly from the old homestead. Pictures, and so on. It will be by no means un-snug when they are up. Meanwhile, I can rough it. We are old campaigners, we Psmiths. Give us a roof, a few comfortable chairs, a sofa or two, half a dozen cushions, and decent meals, and we do not repine. Reverting once more to Comrade Rossiter—'

'Yes, what about him?' said Mike. 'You'll have a pretty tough job turning him into a friendly native, I should think. How do you mean to start?'

Psmith regarded him with a benevolent eye.

'There is but one way,' he said. 'Do you remember the case of Comrade Outwood, at Sedleigh? How did we corral him, and become to him practically as long-lost sons?'

'We got round him by joining the Archaeological Society.'

'Precisely,' said Psmith. 'Every man has his hobby. The thing is to find it out. In the case of comrade Rossiter, I should say that it would be either postage stamps, dried seaweed, or Hall Caine. I shall endeavour to find out today. A few casual questions, and the thing is done. Shall we be putting in an appearance at the busy hive now? If we are to continue in the running for the bonus stakes, it would be well to start soon.'

Mike's first duty at the bank that morning was to check the stamps and petty cash. While he was engaged on this task, he heard Psmith conversing affably with Mr Rossiter.

'Good morning,' said Psmith.

'Morning,' replied his chief, doing sleight-of-hand tricks with a bundle of letters which lay on his desk. 'Get on with your work, Psmith. We have a lot before us.'

'Undoubtedly. I am all impatience. I should say that in an institution like this, dealing as it does with distant portions of the globe, a philatelist would have excellent opportunities of increasing his collection. With me, stamp-collecting has always been a positive craze. I—'

'I have no time for nonsense of that sort myself,' said Mr Rossiter. 'I should advise you, if you mean to get on, to devote more time to your work and less to stamps.'

'I will start at once. Dried seaweed, again—'

'Get on with your work, Smith.'

Psmith retired to his desk.

'This,' he said to Mike, 'is undoubtedly something in the nature of a set-back. I have drawn blank. The papers bring out posters, "Psmith Baffled." I must try again. Meanwhile, to work. Work, the hobby of the philosopher and the poor man's friend.'

The morning dragged slowly on without incident. At twelve o'clock Mike had to go out and buy stamps, which he subsequently punched in the punching-machine in the basement, a not very exhilarating job in which he was assisted by one of the bank messengers, who discoursed learnedly on roses during the seance. Roses were his hobby. Mike began to see that Psmith had reason in his assumption that the way to every man's heart was through his hobby. Mike made a firm friend of William, the messenger, by displaying an interest and a certain knowledge of roses. At the same time the conversation had the bad effect of leading to an acute relapse in the matter of homesickness. The rose-garden at home had been one of Mike's favourite haunts on a summer afternoon. The contrast between it and the basement of the new Asiatic Bank, the atmosphere of which was far from being roselike, was too much for his feelings. He emerged from the depths, with his punched stamps, filled with bitterness against Fate.

He found Psmith still baffled.

'Hall Caine,' said Psmith regretfully, 'has also proved a frost. I wandered round to Comrade Rossiter's desk just now with a rather brainy excursus on "The Eternal City", and was received with the Impatient Frown rather than the Glad Eye. He was in the middle of adding up a rather tricky column of figures, and my remarks caused him to drop a stitch. So far from winning the man over, I have gone back. There now exists between Comrade Rossiter and myself a certain coldness. Further investigations will be postponed till after lunch.'

The postage department received visitors during the morning. Members of other departments came with letters, among them Bannister. Mr Rossiter was away in the manager's room at the time.

'How are you getting on?' said Bannister to Mike.

'Oh, all right,' said Mike.

'Had any trouble with Rossiter yet?'

'No, not much.'

'He hasn't run you in to Bickersdyke?'

'No.'

'Pardon my interrupting a conversation between old college chums,' said Psmith courteously, 'but I happened to overhear, as I toiled at my desk, the name of Comrade Rossiter.'

Bannister looked somewhat startled. Mike introduced them.

'This is Smith,' he said. 'Chap I was at school with. This is Bannister, Smith, who used to be on here till I came.'

'In this department?' asked Psmith.

'Yes.'

'Then, Comrade Bannister, you are the very man I have been looking for. Your knowledge will be invaluable to us. I have no doubt that, during your stay in this excellently managed department, you had many opportunities of observing Comrade Rossiter?'

'I should jolly well think I had,' said Bannister with a laugh. 'He saw to that. He was always popping out and cursing me about something.'

'Comrade Rossiter's manners are a little restive,' agreed Psmith. 'What used you to talk to him about?'

'What used I to talk to him about?'

'Exactly. In those interviews to which you have alluded, how did you amuse, entertain Comrade Rossiter?'

'I didn't. He used to do all the talking there was.'

Psmith straightened his tie, and clicked his tongue, disappointed.

'This is unfortunate,' he said, smoothing his hair. 'You see, Comrade Bannister, it is this way. In the course of my professional duties, I find myself continually coming into contact with Comrade Rossiter.'

'I bet you do,' said Bannister.

'On these occasions I am frequently at a loss for entertaining conversation. He has no difficulty, as apparently happened in your case, in keeping up his end of the dialogue. The subject of my shortcomings provides him with ample material for speech. I, on the other hand, am dumb. I have nothing to say.'

'I should think that was a bit of a change for you, wasn't it?'

'Perhaps, so,' said Psmith, 'perhaps so. On the other hand, however restful it may be to myself, it does not enable me to secure Comrade Rossiter's interest and win his esteem.'

'What Smith wants to know,' said Mike, 'is whether Rossiter has any hobby of any kind. He thinks, if he has, he might work it to keep in with him.'

Psmith, who had been listening with an air of pleased interest, much as a father would listen to his child prattling for the benefit of a visitor, confirmed this statement.

'Comrade Jackson,' he said, 'has put the matter with his usual admirable clearness. That is the thing in a nutshell. Has Comrade Rossiter any hobby that you know of? Spillikins, brass-rubbing, the Near Eastern Question, or anything like that? I have tried him with postage-stamps (which you'd think, as head of a postage department, he ought to be interested in), and dried seaweed, Hall Caine, but I have the honour to report total failure. The man seems to have no pleasures. What does he do with himself when the day's toil is ended? That giant brain must occupy itself somehow.'

'I don't know,' said Bannister, 'unless it's football. I saw him once watching Chelsea. I was rather surprised.'

'Football,' said Psmith thoughtfully, 'football. By no means a scaly idea. I rather fancy, Comrade Bannister, that you have whanged the nail on the head. Is he strong on any particular team? I mean, have you ever heard him, in the intervals of business worries, stamping on his desk and yelling, "Buck up Cottagers!" or "Lay 'em out, Pensioners!" or anything like that? One moment.' Psmith held up his hand. 'I will get my Sherlock Holmes system to work. What was the other team in the modern gladiatorial contest at which you saw Comrade Rossiter?'

'Manchester United.'

'And Comrade Rossiter, I should say, was a Manchester man.'

'I believe he is.'

'Then I am prepared to bet a small sum that he is nuts on Manchester United. My dear Holmes, how—! Elementary, my dear fellow, quite elementary. But here comes the lad in person.'

Mr Rossiter turned in from the central aisle through the counter-door, and, observing the conversational group at the postage-desk, came bounding up. Bannister moved off.

'Really, Smith,' said Mr Rossiter, 'you always seem to be talking. I have overlooked the matter once, as I did not wish to get you into trouble so soon after joining; but, really, it cannot go on. I must take notice of it.'

Psmith held up his hand.

'The fault was mine,' he said, with manly frankness. 'Entirely mine. Bannister came in a purely professional spirit to deposit a letter with Comrade Jackson. I engaged him in conversation on the subject of the Football League, and I was just trying to correct his view that Newcastle United were the best team playing, when you arrived.'

'It is perfectly absurd,' said Mr Rossiter, 'that you should waste the bank's time in this way. The bank pays you to work, not to talk about professional football.'

'Just so, just so,' murmured Psmith.

'There is too much talking in this department.'

'I fear you are right.'

'It is nonsense.'

'My own view,' said Psmith, 'was that Manchester United were by far the finest team before the public.'

'Get on with your work, Smith.'

Mr Rossiter stumped off to his desk, where he sat as one in thought.

'Smith,' he said at the end of five minutes.

Psmith slid from his stool, and made his way deferentially towards him.

'Bannister's a fool,' snapped Mr Rossiter.

'So I thought,' said Psmith.

'A perfect fool. He always was.'

Psmith shook his head sorrowfully, as who should say, 'Exit Bannister.'

'There is no team playing today to touch Manchester United.'

'Precisely what I said to Comrade Bannister.'

'Of course. You know something about it.'

'The study of League football,' said Psmith, 'has been my relaxation for years.'

'But we have no time to discuss it now.'

'Assuredly not, sir. Work before everything.'

'Some other time, when—'

'—We are less busy. Precisely.'

Psmith moved back to his seat.

'I fear,' he said to Mike, as he resumed work, 'that as far as Comrade Rossiter's friendship and esteem are concerned, I have to a certain extent landed Comrade Bannister in the bouillon; but it was in a good cause. I fancy we have won through. Half an hour's thoughtful perusal of the "Footballers' Who's Who", just to find out some elementary facts about Manchester United, and I rather think the friendly Native is corralled. And now once more to work. Work, the hobby of the hustler and the deadbeat's dread.'

9. The Haunting of Mr Bickersdyke

Anything in the nature of a rash and hasty move was wholly foreign to Psmith's tactics. He had the patience which is the chief quality of the successful general. He was content to secure his base before making any offensive movement. It was a fortnight before he turned his attention to the education of Mr Bickersdyke. During that fortnight he conversed attractively, in the intervals of work, on the subject of League football in general and Manchester United in particular. The subject is not hard to master if one sets oneself earnestly to it; and Psmith spared no pains. The football editions of the evening papers are not reticent about those who play the game: and Psmith drank in every detail with the thoroughness of the conscientious student. By the end of the fortnight, he knew what was the favourite breakfast-food of J. Turnbull; what Sandy Turnbull wore next his skin; and who, in the opinion of Meredith, was England's leading politician. These facts, imparted to and discussed with Mr Rossiter, made the progress of the entente cordiale rapid. It was on the eighth day that Mr Rossiter consented to lunch with the Old Etonian. On the tenth he played the host. By the end of the fortnight the flapping of the white wings of Peace over the Postage Department was setting up a positive draught. Mike, who had been introduced by Psmith as a distant relative of Moger, the goalkeeper, was included in the great peace.

'So that now,' said Psmith, reflectively polishing his eye-glass, 'I think that we may consider ourselves free to attend to Comrade Bickersdyke. Our bright little Mancunian friend would no more run us in now than if we were the brothers Turnbull. We are as inside forwards to him.'

The club to which Psmith and Mr Bickersdyke belonged was celebrated for the steadfastness of its political views, the excellence of its cuisine, and the curiously Gorgonzolaesque marble of its main staircase. It takes all sorts to make a world. It took about four thousand of all sorts to make the Senior Conservative Club. To be absolutely accurate, there were three thousand seven hundred and eighteen members.

To Mr Bickersdyke for the next week it seemed as if there was only one.

There was nothing crude or overdone about Psmith's methods. The ordinary man, having conceived the idea of haunting a fellow clubman, might have seized the first opportunity of engaging him in conversation. Not so Psmith. The first time he met Mr Bickersdyke in the club was on the stairs after dinner one night. The great man, having received practical proof of the excellence of cuisine referred to above, was coming down the main staircase at peace with all men, when he was aware of a tall young man in the 'faultless evening dress' of which the female novelist is so fond, who was regarding him with a fixed stare through an eye-glass. The tall young man, having caught his eye, smiled faintly, nodded in a friendly but patronizing manner, and passed on up the staircase to the library. Mr Bickersdyke sped on in search of a waiter.

As Psmith sat in the library with a novel, the waiter entered, and approached him.

'Beg pardon, sir,' he said. 'Are you a member of this club?'

Psmith fumbled in his pocket and produced his eye-glass, through which he examined the waiter, button by button.

'I am Psmith,' he said simply.

'A member, sir?'

'The member,' said Psmith. 'Surely you participated in the general rejoicings which ensued when it was announced that I had been elected? But perhaps you were too busy working to pay any attention. If so, I respect you. I also am a worker. A toiler, not a flatfish. A sizzler, not a squab. Yes, I am a member. Will you tell Mr Bickersdyke that I am sorry, but I have been elected, and have paid my entrance fee and subscription.'

'Thank you, sir.'

The waiter went downstairs and found Mr Bickersdyke in the lower smoking-room.

'The gentleman says he is, sir.'

'H'm,' said the bank-manager. 'Coffee and Benedictine, and a cigar.'

'Yes, sir.'

On the following day Mr Bickersdyke met Psmith in the club three times, and on the day after that seven. Each time the latter's smile was friendly, but patronizing. Mr Bickersdyke began to grow restless.

On the fourth day Psmith made his first remark. The manager was reading the evening paper in a corner, when Psmith sinking gracefully into a chair beside him, caused him to look up.

'The rain keeps off,' said Psmith.

Mr Bickersdyke looked as if he wished his employee would imitate the rain, but he made no reply.

Psmith called a waiter.

'Would you mind bringing me a small cup of coffee?' he said. 'And for you,' he added to Mr Bickersdyke.

'Nothing,' growled the manager.

'And nothing for Mr Bickersdyke.'

The waiter retired. Mr Bickersdyke became absorbed in his paper.

'I see from my morning paper,' said Psmith, affably, 'that you are to address a meeting at the Kenningford Town Hall next week. I shall come and hear you. Our politics differ in some respects, I fear—I incline to the Socialist view—but nevertheless I shall listen to your remarks with great interest, great interest.'

The paper rustled, but no reply came from behind it.

'I heard from father this morning,' resumed Psmith.

Mr Bickersdyke lowered his paper and glared at him.

'I don't wish to hear about your father,' he snapped.

An expression of surprise and pain came over Psmith's face.

'What!' he cried. 'You don't mean to say that there is any coolness between my father and you? I am more grieved than I can say. Knowing, as I do, what a genuine respect my father has for your great talents, I can only think that there must have been some misunderstanding. Perhaps if you would allow me to act as a mediator—'

Mr Bickersdyke put down his paper and walked out of the room.

Psmith found him a quarter of an hour later in the card-room. He sat down beside his table, and began to observe the play with silent interest. Mr Bickersdyke, never a great performer at the best of times, was so unsettled by the scrutiny that in the deciding game of the rubber he revoked, thereby presenting his opponents with the rubber by a very handsome majority of points. Psmith clicked his tongue sympathetically.

Dignified reticence is not a leading characteristic of the bridge-player's manner at the Senior Conservative Club on occasions like this. Mr Bickersdyke's partner did not bear his calamity with manly resignation. He gave tongue on the instant. 'What on earth's', and 'Why on earth's' flowed from his mouth like molten lava. Mr Bickersdyke sat and fermented in silence. Psmith clicked his tongue sympathetically throughout.

Mr Bickersdyke lost that control over himself which every member of a club should possess. He turned on Psmith with a snort of frenzy.

'How can I keep my attention fixed on the game when you sit staring at me like a—like a—'

'I am sorry,' said Psmith gravely, 'if my stare falls short in any way of your ideal of what a stare should be; but I appeal to these gentlemen. Could I have watched the game more quietly?'

'Of course not,' said the bereaved partner warmly. 'Nobody could have any earthly objection to your behaviour. It was absolute carelessness. I should have thought that one might have expected one's partner at a club like this to exercise elementary—'

But Mr Bickersdyke had gone. He had melted silently away like the driven snow.

Psmith took his place at the table.

'A somewhat nervous excitable man, Mr Bickersdyke, I should say,' he observed.

'A somewhat dashed, blanked idiot,' emended the bank-manager's late partner. 'Thank goodness he lost as much as I did. That's some light consolation.'

Psmith arrived at the flat to find Mike still out. Mike had repaired to the Gaiety earlier in the evening to refresh his mind after the labours of the day. When he returned, Psmith was sitting in an armchair with his feet on the mantelpiece, musing placidly on Life.

'Well?' said Mike.

'Well? And how was the Gaiety? Good show?'

'Jolly good. What about Bickersdyke?'

Psmith looked sad.

'I cannot make Comrade Bickersdyke out,' he said. 'You would think that a man would be glad to see the son of a personal friend. On the contrary, I may be wronging Comrade B., but I should almost be inclined to say that my presence in the Senior Conservative Club tonight irritated him. There was no bonhomie in his manner. He seemed to me to be giving a spirited imitation of a man about to foam at the mouth. I did my best to entertain him. I chatted. His only reply was to leave the room. I followed him to the card-room, and watched his very remarkable and brainy tactics at bridge, and he accused me of causing him to revoke. A very curious personality, that of Comrade Bickersdyke. But let us dismiss him from our minds. Rumours have reached me,' said Psmith, 'that a very decent little supper may be obtained at a quaint, old-world eating-house called the Savoy. Will you accompany me thither on a tissue-restoring expedition? It would be rash not to probe these rumours to their foundation, and ascertain their exact truth.'

10. Mr Bickersdyke Addresses His Constituents

It was noted by the observant at the bank next morning that Mr Bickersdyke had something on his mind. William, the messenger, knew it, when he found his respectful salute ignored. Little Briggs, the accountant, knew it when his obsequious but cheerful 'Good morning' was acknowledged only by a 'Morn" which was almost an oath. Mr Bickersdyke passed up the aisle and into his room like an east wind. He sat down at his table and pressed the bell. Harold, William's brother and co-messenger, entered with the air of one ready to duck if any missile should be thrown at him. The reports of the manager's frame of mind had been circulated in the office, and Harold felt somewhat apprehensive. It was on an occasion very similar to this that George Barstead, formerly in the employ of the New Asiatic Bank in the capacity of messenger, had been rash enough to laugh at what he had taken for a joke of Mr Bickersdyke's, and had been instantly presented with the sack for gross impertinence.

'Ask Mr Smith—' began the manager. Then he paused. 'No, never mind,' he added.

Harold remained in the doorway, puzzled.

'Don't stand there gaping at me, man,' cried Mr Bickersdyke, 'Go away.'

Harold retired and informed his brother, William, that in his, Harold's, opinion, Mr Bickersdyke was off his chump.

'Off his onion,' said William, soaring a trifle higher in poetic imagery.

'Barmy,' was the terse verdict of Samuel Jakes, the third messenger. 'Always said so.' And with that the New Asiatic Bank staff of messengers dismissed Mr Bickersdyke and proceeded to concentrate themselves on their duties, which consisted principally of hanging about and discussing the prophecies of that modern seer, Captain Coe.

What had made Mr Bickersdyke change his mind so abruptly was the sudden realization of the fact that he had no case against Psmith. In his capacity of manager of the bank he could not take official notice of Psmith's behaviour outside office hours, especially as Psmith had done nothing but stare at him. It would be impossible to make anybody understand the true inwardness of Psmith's stare. Theoretically, Mr Bickersdyke had the power to dismiss any subordinate of his whom he did not consider satisfactory, but it was a power that had to be exercised with discretion. The manager was accountable for his actions to the Board of Directors. If he dismissed Psmith, Psmith would certainly bring an action against the bank for wrongful dismissal, and on the evidence he would infallibly win it. Mr Bickersdyke did not welcome the prospect of having to explain to the Directors that he had let the shareholders of the bank in for a fine of whatever a discriminating jury cared to decide upon, simply because he had been stared at while playing bridge. His only hope was to catch Psmith doing his work badly.

He touched the bell again, and sent for Mr Rossiter.

The messenger found the head of the Postage Department in conversation with Psmith. Manchester United had been beaten by one goal to nil on the previous afternoon, and Psmith was informing Mr Rossiter that the referee was a robber, who had evidently been financially interested in the result of the game. The way he himself looked at it, said Psmith, was that the thing had been a moral victory for the United. Mr Rossiter said yes, he thought so too. And it was at this moment that Mr Bickersdyke sent for him to ask whether Psmith's work was satisfactory.

The head of the Postage Department gave his opinion without hesitation. Psmith's work was about the hottest proposition he had ever struck. Psmith's work—well, it stood alone. You couldn't compare it with anything. There are no degrees in perfection. Psmith's work was perfect, and there was an end to it.

He put it differently, but that was the gist of what he said.

Mr Bickersdyke observed he was glad to hear it, and smashed a nib by stabbing the desk with it.

It was on the evening following this that the bank-manager was due to address a meeting at the Kenningford Town Hall.

He was looking forward to the event with mixed feelings. He had stood for Parliament once before, several years back, in the North. He had been defeated by a couple of thousand votes, and he hoped that the episode had been forgotten. Not merely because his defeat had been heavy. There was another reason. On that occasion he had stood as a Liberal. He was standing for Kenningford as a Unionist. Of course, a man is at perfect liberty to change his views, if he wishes to do so, but the process is apt to give his opponents a chance of catching him (to use the inspired language of the music-halls) on the bend. Mr Bickersdyke was rather afraid that the light-hearted electors of Kenningford might avail themselves of this chance.

Kenningford, S.E., is undoubtedly by way of being a tough sort of place. Its inhabitants incline to a robust type of humour, which finds a verbal vent in catch phrases and expends itself physically in smashing shop-windows and kicking policemen. He feared that the meeting at the Town Hall might possibly be a trifle rowdy.

All political meetings are very much alike. Somebody gets up and introduces the speaker of the evening, and then the speaker of the evening says at great length what he thinks of the scandalous manner in which the Government is behaving or the iniquitous goings-on of the Opposition. From time to time confederates in the audience rise and ask carefully rehearsed questions, and are answered fully and satisfactorily by the orator. When a genuine heckler interrupts, the orator either ignores him, or says haughtily that he can find him arguments but cannot find him brains. Or, occasionally, when the question is an easy one, he answers it. A quietly conducted political meeting is one of England's most delightful indoor games. When the meeting is rowdy, the audience has more fun, but the speaker a good deal less.

Mr Bickersdyke's introducer was an elderly Scotch peer, an excellent man for the purpose in every respect, except that he possessed a very strong accent.

The audience welcomed that accent uproariously. The electors of Kenningford who really had any definite opinions on politics were fairly equally divided. There were about as many earnest Liberals as there were earnest Unionists. But besides these there was a strong contingent who did not care which side won. These looked on elections as Heaven-sent opportunities for making a great deal of noise. They attended meetings in order to extract amusement from them; and they voted, if they voted at all, quite irresponsibly. A funny story at the expense of one candidate told on the morning of the polling, was quite likely to send these brave fellows off in dozens filling in their papers for the victim's opponent.

There was a solid block of these gay spirits at the back of the hall. They received the Scotch peer with huge delight. He reminded them of Harry Lauder and they said so. They addressed him affectionately as 'Arry', throughout his speech, which was rather long. They implored him to be a pal and sing 'The Saftest of the Family'. Or, failing that, 'I love a lassie'. Finding they could not induce him to do this, they did it themselves. They sang it several times.

When the peer, having finished his remarks on the subject of Mr Bickersdyke, at length sat down, they cheered for seven minutes, and demanded an encore.

The meeting was in excellent spirits when Mr Bickersdyke rose to address it.

The effort of doing justice to the last speaker had left the free and independent electors at the back of the hall slightly limp. The bank-manager's opening remarks were received without any demonstration.

Mr Bickersdyke spoke well. He had a penetrating, if harsh, voice, and he said what he had to say forcibly. Little by little the audience came under his spell. When, at the end of a well-turned sentence, he paused and took a sip of water, there was a round of applause, in which many of the admirers of Mr Harry Lauder joined.

He resumed his speech. The audience listened intently. Mr Bickersdyke, having said some nasty things about Free Trade and the Alien Immigrant, turned to the Needs of the Navy and the necessity of increasing the fleet at all costs.

'This is no time for half-measures,' he said. 'We must do our utmost. We must burn our boats—'

'Excuse me,' said a gentle voice.

Mr Bickersdyke broke off. In the centre of the hall a tall figure had risen. Mr Bickersdyke found himself looking at a gleaming eye-glass which the speaker had just polished and inserted in his eye.

The ordinary heckler Mr Bickersdyke would have taken in his stride. He had got his audience, and simply by continuing and ignoring the interruption, he could have won through in safety. But the sudden appearance of Psmith unnerved him. He remained silent.

'How,' asked Psmith, 'do you propose to strengthen the Navy by burning boats?'

The inanity of the question enraged even the pleasure-seekers at the back.

'Order! Order!' cried the earnest contingent.

'Sit down, face!' roared the pleasure-seekers.

Psmith sat down with a patient smile.

Mr Bickersdyke resumed his speech. But the fire had gone out of it. He had lost his audience. A moment before, he had grasped them and played on their minds (or what passed for minds down Kenningford way) as on a stringed instrument. Now he had lost his hold.

He spoke on rapidly, but he could not get into his stride. The trivial interruption had broken the spell. His words lacked grip. The dead silence in which the first part of his speech had been received, that silence which is a greater tribute to the speaker than any applause, had given place to a restless medley of little noises; here a cough; there a scraping of a boot along the floor, as its wearer moved uneasily in his seat; in another place a whispered conversation. The audience was bored.

Mr Bickersdyke left the Navy, and went on to more general topics. But he was not interesting. He quoted figures, saw a moment later that he had not quoted them accurately, and instead of carrying on boldly, went back and corrected himself.

'Gow up top!' said a voice at the back of the hall, and there was a general laugh.

Mr Bickersdyke galloped unsteadily on. He condemned the Government. He said they had betrayed their trust.

And then he told an anecdote.

'The Government, gentlemen,' he said, 'achieves nothing worth achieving, and every individual member of the Government takes all the credit for what is done to himself. Their methods remind me, gentlemen, of an amusing experience I had while fishing one summer in the Lake District.'

In a volume entitled 'Three Men in a Boat' there is a story of how the author and a friend go into a riverside inn and see a very large trout in a glass case. They make inquiries about it, have men assure them, one by one, that the trout was caught by themselves. In the end the trout turns out to be made of plaster of Paris.

Mr Bickersdyke told that story as an experience of his own while fishing one summer in the Lake District.

It went well. The meeting was amused. Mr Bickersdyke went on to draw a trenchant comparison between the lack of genuine merit in the trout and the lack of genuine merit in the achievements of His Majesty's Government.

There was applause.

When it had ceased, Psmith rose to his feet again.

'Excuse me,' he said.

11. Misunderstood

Mike had refused to accompany Psmith to the meeting that evening, saying that he got too many chances in the ordinary way of business of hearing Mr Bickersdyke speak, without going out of his way to make more. So Psmith had gone off to Kenningford alone, and Mike, feeling too lazy to sally out to any place of entertainment, had remained at the flat with a novel.

He was deep in this, when there was the sound of a key in the latch, and shortly afterwards Psmith entered the room. On Psmith's brow there was a look of pensive care, and also a slight discoloration. When he removed his overcoat, Mike saw that his collar was burst and hanging loose and that he had no tie. On his erstwhile speckless and gleaming shirt front were number of finger-impressions, of a boldness and clearness of outline which would have made a Bertillon expert leap with joy.

'Hullo!' said Mike dropping his book.

Psmith nodded in silence, went to his bedroom, and returned with a looking-glass. Propping this up on a table, he proceeded to examine himself with the utmost care. He shuddered slightly as his eye fell on the finger-marks; and without a word he went into his bathroom again. He emerged after an interval of ten minutes in sky-blue pyjamas, slippers, and an Old Etonian blazer. He lit a cigarette; and, sitting down, stared pensively into the fire.

'What the dickens have you been playing at?' demanded Mike.

Psmith heaved a sigh.

'That,' he replied, 'I could not say precisely. At one moment it seemed to be Rugby football, at another a jiu-jitsu seance. Later, it bore a resemblance to a pantomime rally. However, whatever it was, it was all very bright and interesting. A distinct experience.'

'Have you been scrapping?' asked Mike. 'What happened? Was there a row?'

'There was,' said Psmith, 'in a measure what might be described as a row. At least, when you find a perfect stranger attaching himself to your collar and pulling, you begin to suspect that something of that kind is on the bill.'

'Did they do that?'

Psmith nodded.

'A merchant in a moth-eaten bowler started warbling to a certain extent with me. It was all very trying for a man of culture. He was a man who had, I should say, discovered that alcohol was a food long before the doctors found it out. A good chap, possibly, but a little boisterous in his manner. Well, well.'

Psmith shook his head sadly.

'He got you one on the forehead,' said Mike, 'or somebody did. Tell us what happened. I wish the dickens I'd come with you. I'd no notion there would be a rag of any sort. What did happen?'

'Comrade Jackson,' said Psmith sorrowfully, 'how sad it is in this life of ours to be consistently misunderstood. You know, of course, how wrapped up I am in Comrade Bickersdyke's welfare. You know that all my efforts are directed towards making a decent man of him; that, in short, I am his truest friend. Does he show by so much as a word that he appreciates my labours? Not he. I believe that man is beginning to dislike me, Comrade

Jackson.'

'What happened, anyhow? Never mind about Bickersdyke.'

'Perhaps it was mistaken zeal on my part.... Well, I will tell you all. Make a long arm for the shovel, Comrade Jackson, and pile on a few more coals. I thank you. Well, all went quite smoothly for a while. Comrade B. in quite good form. Got his second wind, and was going strong for the tape, when a regrettable incident occurred. He informed the meeting, that while up in the Lake country, fishing, he went to an inn and saw a remarkably large stuffed trout in a glass case. He made inquiries, and found that five separate and distinct people had caught—'

'Why, dash it all,' said Mike, 'that's a frightful chestnut.'

Psmith nodded.

'It certainly has appeared in print,' he said. 'In fact I should have said it was rather a well-known story. I was so interested in Comrade Bickersdyke's statement that the thing had happened to himself that, purely out of good-will towards him, I got up and told him that I thought it was my duty, as a friend, to let him know that a man named Jerome had pinched his story, put it in a book, and got money by it. Money, mark you, that should by rights have been Comrade Bickersdyke's. He didn't appear to care much about sifting the matter thoroughly. In fact, he seemed anxious to get on with his speech, and slur the matter over. But, tactlessly perhaps, I continued rather to harp on the thing. I said that the book in which the story had appeared was published in 1889. I asked him how long ago it was that he had been on his fishing tour, because it was important to know in order to bring the charge home against Jerome. Well, after a bit, I was amazed, and pained, too, to hear Comrade Bickersdyke urging certain bravoes in the audience to turn me out. If ever there was a case of biting the hand that fed him.... Well, well.... By this time the meeting had begun to take sides to some extent. What I might call my party, the Earnest Investigators, were whistling between their fingers, stamping on the floor, and shouting, "Chestnuts!" while the opposing party, the bravoes, seemed to be trying, as I say, to do jiu-jitsu tricks with me. It was a painful situation. I know the cultivated man of affairs should have passed the thing off with a short, careless laugh; but, owing to the above-mentioned alcohol-expert having got both hands under my collar, short, careless laughs were off. I was compelled, very reluctantly, to conclude the interview by tapping the bright boy on the jaw. He took the hint, and sat down on the floor. I thought no more of the matter, and was making my way thoughtfully to the exit, when a second man of wrath put the above on my forehead. You can't ignore a thing like that. I collected some of his waistcoat and one of his legs, and hove him with some vim into the middle distance. By this time a good many of the Earnest Investigators were beginning to join in; and it was just there that the affair began to have certain points of resemblance to a pantomime rally. Everybody seemed to be shouting a good deal and hitting everybody else. It was no place for a man of delicate culture, so I edged towards the door, and drifted out. There was a cab in the offing. I boarded it. And, having kicked a vigorous politician in the stomach, as he was endeavouring to climb in too, I drove off home.'

Psmith got up, looked at his forehead once more in the glass, sighed, and sat down again.

'All very disturbing,' he said.

'Great Scott,' said Mike, 'I wish I'd come. Why on earth didn't you tell me you were going to rag? I think you might as well have done. I wouldn't have missed it for worlds.'

Psmith regarded him with raised eyebrows.

'Rag!' he said. 'Comrade Jackson, I do not understand you. You surely do not think that I had any other object in doing what I did than to serve Comrade Bickersdyke? It's terrible how one's motives get distorted in this world of ours.'

'Well,' said Mike, with a grin, 'I know one person who'll jolly well distort your motives, as you call it, and that's Bickersdyke.'

Psmith looked thoughtful.

'True,' he said, 'true. There is that possibility. I tell you, Comrade Jackson, once more that my bright young life is being slowly blighted by the frightful way in which that man misunderstands me. It seems almost impossible to try to do him a good turn without having the action misconstrued.'

'What'll you say to him tomorrow?'

'I shall make no allusion to the painful affair. If I happen to meet him in the ordinary course of business routine, I shall pass some light, pleasant remark—on the weather, let us say, or the Bank rate—and continue my duties.'

'How about if he sends for you, and wants to do the light, pleasant remark business on his own?'

'In that case I shall not thwart him. If he invites me into his private room, I shall be his guest, and shall discuss, to the best of my ability, any topic which he may care to introduce. There shall be no constraint between Comrade Bickersdyke and myself.'

'No, I shouldn't think there would be. I wish I could come and hear you.'

'I wish you could,' said Psmith courteously.

'Still, it doesn't matter much to you. You don't care if you do get sacked.'

Psmith rose.

'In that way possibly, as you say, I am agreeably situated. If the New Asiatic Bank does not require Psmith's services, there are other spheres where a young man of spirit may carve a place for himself. No, what is worrying me, Comrade Jackson, is not the thought of the push. It is the growing fear that Comrade Bickersdyke and I will never thoroughly understand and appreciate one another. A deep gulf lies between us. I do what I can do to bridge it over, but he makes no response. On his side of the gulf building operations appear to be at an entire standstill. That is what is carving these lines of care on my forehead, Comrade Jackson. That is what is painting these purple circles beneath my eyes. Quite inadvertently to be disturbing Comrade Bickersdyke, annoying him, preventing him from enjoying life. How sad this is. Life bulges with these tragedies.'

Mike picked up the evening paper.

'Don't let it keep you awake at night,' he said. 'By the way, did you see that Manchester United were playing this afternoon? They won. You'd better sit down and sweat up some of the details. You'll want them tomorrow.'

'You are very right, Comrade Jackson,' said Psmith, reseating himself. 'So the Mancunians pushed the bulb into the meshes beyond the uprights no fewer than four times, did they? Bless the dear boys, what spirits they do enjoy, to be sure. Comrade Jackson, do not disturb me. I must concentrate myself. These are deep waters.'

12. In a Nutshell

Mr Bickersdyke sat in his private room at the New Asiatic Bank with a pile of newspapers before him. At least, the casual observer would have said that it was Mr Bickersdyke. However, it was an active volcano in the shape and clothes of the bank-manager. It was freely admitted in the office that morning that the manager had lowered all records with ease. The staff had known him to be in a bad temper before—frequently; but his frame of mind on all previous occasions had been, compared with his present frame of mind, that of a rather exceptionally good-natured lamb. Within ten minutes of his arrival the entire office was on the jump. The messengers were collected in a pallid group in the basement, discussing the affair in whispers and endeavouring to restore their nerve with about sixpenn'orth of the beverage known as 'unsweetened'. The heads of departments, to a man, had bowed before the storm. Within the space of seven minutes and a quarter Mr Bickersdyke had contrived to find some fault with each of them. Inward Bills was out at an A.B.C. shop snatching a hasty cup of coffee, to pull him together again. Outward Bills was sitting at his desk with the glazed stare of one who has been struck in the thorax by a thunderbolt. Mr Rossiter had been torn from Psmith in the middle of a highly technical discussion of the Manchester United match, just as he was showing—with the aid of a ball of paper—how he had once seen Meredith centre to Sandy Turnbull in a Cup match, and was now leaping about like a distracted grasshopper. Mr Waller, head of the Cash Department, had been summoned to the Presence, and after listening meekly to a rush of criticism, had retired to his desk with the air of a beaten spaniel.

Only one man of the many in the building seemed calm and happy—Psmith.

Psmith had resumed the chat about Manchester United, on Mr Rossiter's return from the lion's den, at the spot where it had been broken off; but, finding that the head of the Postage Department was in no mood for discussing football (or anything else), he had postponed his remarks and placidly resumed his work.

Mr Bickersdyke picked up a paper, opened it, and began searching the columns. He had not far to look. It was a slack season for the newspapers, and his little trouble, which might have received a paragraph in a busy week, was set forth fully in three-quarters of a column.

The column was headed, 'Amusing Heckling'.

Mr Bickersdyke read a few lines, and crumpled the paper up with a snort.

The next he examined was an organ of his own shade of political opinion. It too, gave him nearly a column, headed 'Disgraceful Scene at Kenningford'. There was also a leaderette on the subject.

The leaderette said so exactly what Mr Bickersdyke thought himself that for a moment he was soothed. Then the thought of his grievance returned, and he pressed the bell.

'Send Mr Smith to me,' he said.

William, the messenger, proceeded to inform Psmith of the summons.

Psmith's face lit up.

'I am always glad to sweeten the monotony of toil with a chat with Little Clarence,' he said. 'I shall be with him in a moment.'

He cleaned his pen very carefully, placed it beside his ledger, flicked a little dust off his coatsleeve, and made his way to the manager's room.

Mr Bickersdyke received him with the ominous restraint of a tiger crouching for its spring. Psmith stood beside the table with languid grace, suggestive of some favoured confidential secretary waiting for instructions.

A ponderous silence brooded over the room for some moments. Psmith broke it by remarking that the Bank Rate was unchanged. He mentioned this fact as if it afforded him a personal gratification.

Mr Bickersdyke spoke.

'Well, Mr Smith?' he said.

'You wished to see me about something, sir?' inquired Psmith, ingratiatingly.

'You know perfectly well what I wished to see you about. I want to hear your explanation of what occurred last night.'

'May I sit, sir?'

He dropped gracefully into a chair, without waiting for permission, and, having hitched up the knees of his trousers, beamed winningly at the manager.

'A deplorable affair,' he said, with a shake of his head. 'Extremely deplorable. We must not judge these rough, uneducated men too harshly, however. In a time of excitement the emotions of the lower classes are easily stirred. Where you or I would—'

Mr Bickersdyke interrupted.

'I do not wish for any more buffoonery, Mr Smith—'

Psmith raised a pained pair of eyebrows.

'Buffoonery, sir!'

'I cannot understand what made you act as you did last night, unless you are perfectly mad, as I am beginning to think.'

'But, surely, sir, there was nothing remarkable in my behaviour? When a merchant has attached himself to your collar, can you do less than smite him on the other cheek? I merely acted in self-defence. You saw for yourself—'

'You know what I am alluding to. Your behaviour during my speech.'

'An excellent speech,' murmured Psmith courteously.

'Well?' said Mr Bickersdyke.

'It was, perhaps, mistaken zeal on my part, sir, but you must remember that I acted purely from the best motives. It seemed to me—'

'That is enough, Mr Smith. I confess that I am absolutely at a loss to understand you—'

'It is too true, sir,' sighed Psmith.

'You seem,' continued Mr Bickersdyke, warming to his subject, and turning gradually a richer shade of purple, 'you seem to be determined to endeavour to annoy me.' ('No no,' from Psmith.) 'I can only assume that you are not in your right senses. You follow me about in my club—'

'Our club, sir,' murmured Psmith.

'Be good enough not to interrupt me, Mr Smith. You dog my footsteps in my club—'

'Purely accidental, sir. We happen to meet—that is all.'

'You attend meetings at which I am speaking, and behave in a perfectly imbecile manner.'

Psmith moaned slightly.

'It may seem humorous to you, but I can assure you it is extremely bad policy on your part. The New Asiatic Bank is no place for humour, and I think—'

'Excuse me, sir,' said Psmith.

The manager started at the familiar phrase. The plum-colour of his complexion deepened.

'I entirely agree with you, sir,' said Psmith, 'that this bank is no place for humour.'

'Very well, then. You—'

'And I am never humorous in it. I arrive punctually in the morning, and I work steadily and earnestly till my labours are completed. I think you will find, on inquiry, that Mr Rossiter is satisfied with my work.'

'That is neither here nor—'

'Surely, sir,' said Psmith, 'you are wrong? Surely your jurisdiction ceases after office hours? Any little misunderstanding we may have at the close of the day's work cannot affect you officially. You could not, for instance, dismiss me from the service of the bank if we were partners at bridge at the club and I happened to revoke.'

'I can dismiss you, let me tell you, Mr Smith, for studied insolence, whether in the office or not.'

'I bow to superior knowledge,' said Psmith politely, 'but I confess I doubt it. And,' he added, 'there is another point. May I continue to some extent?'

'If you have anything to say, say it.'

Psmith flung one leg over the other, and settled his collar.

'It is perhaps a delicate matter,' he said, 'but it is best to be frank. We should have no secrets. To put my point quite clearly, I must go back a little, to the time when you paid us that very welcome week-end visit at our house in August.'

'If you hope to make capital out of the fact that I have been a guest of your father—'

'Not at all,' said Psmith deprecatingly. 'Not at all. You do not take me. My point is this. I do not wish to revive painful memories, but it cannot be denied that there was, here and there, some slight bickering between us on that occasion. The fault,' said Psmith magnanimously, 'was possibly mine. I may have been too exacting, too capricious. Perhaps so. However, the fact remains that you conceived the happy notion of getting me into this bank, under the impression that, once I was in, you would be able to—if I may use the expression—give me beans. You said as much to me, if I remember. I hate to say it, but don't you think that if you give me the sack, although my work is satisfactory to the head of my department, you will be by way of admitting that you bit off rather more than you could chew? I merely make the suggestion.'

Mr Bickersdyke half rose from his chair.

'You—'

'Just so, just so, but—to return to the main point—don't you? The whole painful affair reminds me of the story of Agesilaus and the Petulant Pterodactyl, which as you have never heard, I will now proceed to relate. Agesilaus—'

Mr Bickersdyke made a curious clucking noise in his throat.

'I am boring you,' said Psmith, with ready tact. 'Suffice it to say that Comrade Agesilaus interfered with the pterodactyl, which was doing him no harm; and the intelligent creature, whose motto was "Nemo me impune lacessit", turned and bit him. Bit him good and hard, so that Agesilaus ever afterwards had a distaste for pterodactyls. His reluctance to disturb them became quite a byword. The Society papers of the period frequently commented upon it. Let us draw the parallel.'

Here Mr Bickersdyke, who had been clucking throughout this speech, essayed to speak; but Psmith hurried on.

'You are Agesilaus,' he said. 'I am the Petulant Pterodactyl. You, if I may say so, butted in of your own free will, and took me from a happy home, simply in order that you might get me into this place under you, and give me beans. But, curiously enough, the major portion of that vegetable seems to be coming to you. Of course, you can administer the push if you like; but, as I say, it will be by way of a confession that your scheme has sprung a leak. Personally,' said Psmith, as one friend to another, 'I should advise you to stick it out. You never know what may happen. At any moment I may fall from my present high standard of industry and excellence; and then you have me, so to speak, where the hair is crisp.'

He paused. Mr Bickersdyke's eyes, which even in their normal state protruded slightly, now looked as if they might fall out at any moment. His face had passed from the plum-coloured stage to something beyond. Every now and then he made the clucking noise, but except for that he was silent. Psmith, having waited for some time for something in the shape of comment or criticism on his remarks, now rose.

'It has been a great treat to me, this little chat,' he said affably, 'but I fear that I must no longer allow purely social enjoyments to interfere with my commercial pursuits. With your permission, I will rejoin my department, where my absence is doubtless already causing comment and possibly dismay. But we shall be meeting at the club shortly, I hope. Good-bye, sir, good-bye.'

He left the room, and walked dreamily back to the Postage Department, leaving the manager still staring glassily at nothing.

13. Mike is Moved On

This episode may be said to have concluded the first act of the commercial drama in which Mike and Psmith had been cast for leading parts. And, as usually happens after the end of an act, there was a lull for a while until things began to work up towards another climax. Mike, as day succeeded day, began to grow accustomed to the life of the bank, and to find that it had its pleasant side after all. Whenever a number of people are working at the same thing, even though that thing is not perhaps what they would have chosen as an object in life, if left to themselves, there is bound to exist an atmosphere of good-fellowship; something akin to, though a hundred times weaker than, the public-school spirit. Such a community lacks the main motive of the public-school spirit, which is pride in the school and its achievements. Nobody can be proud of the achievements of a bank. When the business of arranging a new Japanese loan was given to the New Asiatic Bank, its employees did not stand on stools, and cheer. On the contrary, they thought of the extra work it would involve; and they cursed a good deal, though there was no denying that it was a big thing for the bank—not unlike winning the Ashburton would be to a school. There is a cold impersonality about a bank. A school is a living thing.

Setting aside this important difference, there was a good deal of the public school about the New Asiatic Bank. The heads of departments were not quite so autocratic as masters, and one was treated more on a grown-up scale, as man to man; but, nevertheless, there remained a distinct flavour of a school republic. Most of the men in the bank, with the exception of certain hard-headed Scotch youths drafted in from other establishments in the City, were old public school men. Mike found two Old Wrykinians in the first week. Neither was well known to him. They had left in his second year in the team. But it was pleasant to have them about, and to feel that they had been educated at the right place.

As far as Mike's personal comfort went, the presence of these two Wrykinians was very much for the good. Both of them knew all about his cricket, and they spread the news. The New Asiatic Bank, like most London banks, was keen on sport, and happened to possess a cricket team which could make a good game with most of the second-rank clubs. The disappearance to the East of two of the best bats of the previous season caused Mike's advent to be hailed with a good deal of enthusiasm. Mike was a county man. He had only played once for his county, it was true, but that did not matter. He had passed the barrier which separates the second-class bat from the first-class, and the bank welcomed him with awe. County men did not come their way every day.

Mike did not like being in the bank, considered in the light of a career. But he bore no grudge against the inmates of the bank, such as he had borne against the inmates of Sedleigh. He had looked on the latter as bound up with the school, and, consequently, enemies. His fellow workers in the bank he regarded as companions in misfortune. They were all in the same boat together. There were men from Tonbridge, Dulwich, Bedford, St Paul's, and a dozen other schools. One or two of them he knew by repute from the pages of Wisden. Bannister, his cheerful predecessor in the Postage Department, was the Bannister, he recollected now, who had played for Geddington against Wrykyn in his second year in the Wrykyn team. Munroe, the big man in the Fixed Deposits, he remembered as leader of the Ripton pack. Every day brought fresh discoveries of this sort, and each made Mike more reconciled to his lot. They were a pleasant set of fellows in the New Asiatic Bank, and but for the dreary outlook which the future held—for Mike, unlike most of his follow workers, was not attracted by the idea of a life in the East—he would have been very fairly content.

The hostility of Mr Bickersdyke was a slight drawback. Psmith had developed a habit of taking Mike with him to the club of an evening; and this did not do anything towards wiping out of the manager's mind the recollection of his former passage of arms with the Old Wrykinian. The glass remaining Set Fair as far as Mr Rossiter's approval was concerned, Mike was enabled to keep off the managerial carpet to a great extent; but twice, when he posted letters without going through the preliminary formality of stamping them, Mr Bickersdyke had opportunities of which he availed himself. But for these incidents life was fairly enjoyable. Owing to Psmith's benevolent efforts, the Postage Department became quite a happy family, and ex-occupants of the postage desk, Bannister especially, were amazed at the change that had come over Mr Rossiter. He no longer darted from his lair like a pouncing panther. To report his subordinates to the manager seemed now to be a lost art with him. The sight of Psmith and Mr Rossiter proceeding high and disposedly to a mutual lunch became quite common, and ceased to excite remark.

'By kindness,' said Psmith to Mike, after one of these expeditions. 'By tact and kindness. That is how it is done. I do not despair of training Comrade Rossiter one of these days to jump through paper hoops.'

So that, altogether, Mike's life in the bank had become very fairly pleasant.

Out of office-hours he enjoyed himself hugely. London was strange to him, and with Psmith as a companion, he extracted a vast deal of entertainment from it. Psmith was not unacquainted with the West End, and he proved an excellent guide. At first Mike expostulated with unfailing regularity at the other's habit of paying for everything, but Psmith waved aside all objections with languid firmness.

'I need you, Comrade Jackson,' he said, when Mike lodged a protest on finding himself bound for the stalls for the second night in succession. 'We must stick together. As my confidential secretary and adviser, your place is by my side. Who knows but that between the acts tonight I may not be seized with some luminous thought? Could I utter this to my next-door neighbour or the programme-girl? Stand by me, Comrade Jackson, or we are undone.'

So Mike stood by him.

By this time Mike had grown so used to his work that he could tell to within five minutes when a rush would come; and he was able to spend a good deal of his time reading a surreptitious novel behind a pile of ledgers, or down in the tea-room. The New Asiatic Bank supplied tea to its employees. In quality it was bad, and the bread-and-butter associated with it was worse. But it had the merit of giving one an excuse for being away from one's desk. There were large printed notices all over the tea-room, which was in the basement, informing gentlemen that they were only allowed ten minutes for tea, but one took just as long as one thought the head of one's department would stand, from twenty-five minutes to an hour and a quarter.

This state of things was too good to last. Towards the beginning of the New Year a new man arrived, and Mike was moved on to another department.

14. Mr Waller Appears in a New Light

The department into which Mike was sent was the Cash, or, to be more exact, that section of it which was known as Paying Cashier. The important task of shooting doubloons across the counter did not belong to Mike himself, but to Mr Waller. Mike's work was less ostentatious, and was performed with pen, ink, and ledgers in the background. Occasionally, when Mr Waller was out at lunch, Mike had to act as substitute for him, and cash cheques; but Mr Waller always went out at a slack time, when few customers came in, and Mike seldom had any very startling sum to hand over.

He enjoyed being in the Cash Department. He liked Mr Waller. The work was easy; and when he did happen to make mistakes, they were corrected patiently by the grey-bearded one, and not used as levers for boosting him into the presence of Mr Bickersdyke, as they might have been in some departments. The cashier seemed to have taken a fancy to Mike; and Mike, as was usually the way with him when people went out of their way to be friendly, was at his best. Mike at his ease and unsuspicious of hostile intentions was a different person from Mike with his prickles out.

Psmith, meanwhile, was not enjoying himself. It was an unheard-of thing, he said, depriving a man of his confidential secretary without so much as asking his leave.

'It has caused me the greatest inconvenience,' he told Mike, drifting round in a melancholy way to the Cash Department during a slack spell one afternoon. 'I miss you at every turn. Your keen intelligence and ready sympathy were invaluable to me. Now where am I? In the cart. I evolved a slightly bright thought on life just now. There was nobody to tell it to except the new man. I told it him, and the fool gaped. I tell you, Comrade Jackson, I feel like some lion that has been robbed of its cub. I feel as Marshall would feel if they took Snelgrove away from him, or as Peace might if he awoke one morning to find Plenty gone. Comrade Rossiter does his best. We still talk brokenly about Manchester United—they got routed in the first round of the Cup yesterday and Comrade Rossiter is wearing black—but it is not the same. I try work, but that is no good either. From ledger to ledger they hurry me, to stifle my regret. And when they win a smile from me, they think that I forget. But I don't. I am a broken man. That new exhibit they've got in your place is about as near to the Extreme Edge as anything I've ever seen. One of Nature's blighters. Well, well, I must away. Comrade Rossiter awaits me.'

Mike's successor, a youth of the name of Bristow, was causing Psmith a great deal of pensive melancholy. His worst defect—which he could not help—was that he was not Mike. His others—which he could—were numerous. His clothes were cut in a way that harrowed Psmith's sensitive soul every time he looked at them. The fact that he wore detachable cuffs, which he took off on beginning work and stacked in a glistening pile on the desk in front of him, was no proof of innate viciousness of disposition, but it prejudiced the Old Etonian against him. It was part of Psmith's philosophy that a man who wore detachable cuffs had passed beyond the limit of human toleration. In addition, Bristow wore a small black moustache and a ring and that, as Psmith informed Mike, put the lid on it.

Mike would sometimes stroll round to the Postage Department to listen to the conversations between the two. Bristow was always friendliness itself. He habitually addressed Psmith as Smithy, a fact which entertained Mike greatly but did not seem to amuse Psmith to any overwhelming extent. On the other hand, when, as he generally did, he called Mike 'Mister

Cricketer', the humour of the thing appeared to elude Mike, though the mode of address always drew from Psmith a pale, wan smile, as of a broken heart made cheerful against its own inclination.

The net result of the coming of Bristow was that Psmith spent most of his time, when not actually oppressed by a rush of work, in the precincts of the Cash Department, talking to Mike and Mr Waller. The latter did not seem to share the dislike common among the other heads of departments of seeing his subordinates receiving visitors. Unless the work was really heavy, in which case a mild remonstrance escaped him, he offered no objection to Mike being at home to Psmith. It was this tolerance which sometimes got him into trouble with Mr Bickersdyke. The manager did not often perambulate the office, but he did occasionally, and the interview which ensued upon his finding Hutchinson, the underling in the Cash Department at that time, with his stool tilted comfortably against the wall, reading the sporting news from a pink paper to a friend from the Outward Bills Department who lay luxuriously on the floor beside him, did not rank among Mr Waller's pleasantest memories. But Mr Waller was too soft-hearted to interfere with his assistants unless it was absolutely necessary. The truth of the matter was that the New Asiatic Bank was over-staffed. There were too many men for the work. The London branch of the bank was really only a nursery. New men were constantly wanted in the Eastern branches, so they had to be put into the London branch to learn the business, whether there was any work for them to do or not.

It was after one of these visits of Psmith's that Mr Waller displayed a new and unsuspected side to his character. Psmith had come round in a state of some depression to discuss Bristow, as usual. Bristow, it seemed, had come to the bank that morning in a fancy waistcoat of so emphatic a colour-scheme that Psmith stoutly refused to sit in the same department with it.

'What with Comrades Bristow and Bickersdyke combined,' said Psmith plaintively, 'the work is becoming too hard for me. The whisper is beginning to circulate, "Psmith's number is up—As a reformer he is merely among those present. He is losing his dash." But what can I do? I cannot keep an eye on both of them at the same time. The moment I concentrate myself on Comrade Bickersdyke for a brief spell, and seem to be doing him a bit of good, what happens? Why, Comrade Bristow sneaks off and buys a sort of woollen sunset. I saw the thing unexpectedly. I tell you I was shaken. It is the suddenness of that waistcoat which hits you. It's discouraging, this sort of thing. I try always to think well of my fellow man. As an energetic Socialist, I do my best to see the good that is in him, but it's hard. Comrade Bristow's the most striking argument against the equality of man I've ever come across.'

Mr Waller intervened at this point.

'I think you must really let Jackson go on with his work, Smith,' he said. 'There seems to be too much talking.'

'My besetting sin,' said Psmith sadly. 'Well, well, I will go back and do my best to face it, but it's a tough job.'

He tottered wearily away in the direction of the Postage Department.

'Oh, Jackson,' said Mr Waller, 'will you kindly take my place for a few minutes? I must go round and see the Inward Bills about something. I shall be back very soon.'

Mike was becoming accustomed to deputizing for the cashier for short spaces of time. It generally happened that he had to do so once or twice a day. Strictly speaking, perhaps, Mr Waller was wrong to leave such an important task as the actual cashing of cheques to an inexperienced person of Mike's standing; but the New Asiatic Bank differed from most banks in that there was not a great deal of cross-counter work. People came in fairly frequently to cash cheques of two or three pounds, but it was rare that any very large dealings took place.

Having completed his business with the Inward Bills, Mr Waller made his way back by a circuitous route, taking in the Postage desk.

He found Psmith with a pale, set face, inscribing figures in a ledger. The Old Etonian greeted him with the faint smile of a persecuted saint who is determined to be cheerful even at the stake.

'Comrade Bristow,' he said.

'Hullo, Smithy?' said the other, turning.

Psmith sadly directed Mr Waller's attention to the waistcoat, which was certainly definite in its colouring.

'Nothing,' said Psmith. 'I only wanted to look at you.'

'Funny ass,' said Bristow, resuming his work. Psmith glanced at Mr Waller, as who should say, 'See what I have to put up with. And yet I do not give way.'

'Oh—er—Smith,' said Mr Waller, 'when you were talking to Jackson just now—'

'Say no more,' said Psmith. 'It shall not occur again. Why should I dislocate the work of your department in my efforts to win a sympathetic word? I will bear Comrade Bristow like a man here. After all, there are worse things at the Zoo.'

'No, no,' said Mr Waller hastily, 'I did not mean that. By all means pay us a visit now and then, if it does not interfere with your own work. But I noticed just now that you spoke to Bristow as Comrade Bristow.'

'It is too true,' said Psmith. 'I must correct myself of the habit. He will be getting above himself.'

'And when you were speaking to Jackson, you spoke of yourself as a Socialist.'

'Socialism is the passion of my life,' said Psmith.

Mr Waller's face grew animated. He stammered in his eagerness.

'I am delighted,' he said. 'Really, I am delighted. I also—'

'A fellow worker in the Cause?' said Psmith.

'Er—exactly.'

Psmith extended his hand gravely. Mr Waller shook it with enthusiasm.

'I have never liked to speak of it to anybody in the office,' said Mr Waller, 'but I, too, am heart and soul in the movement.'

'Yours for the Revolution?' said Psmith.

'Just so. Just so. Exactly. I was wondering—the fact is, I am in the habit of speaking on Sundays in the open air, and—'

'Hyde Park?'

'No. No. Clapham Common. It is—er—handier for me where I live. Now, as you are interested in the movement, I was thinking that perhaps you might care to come and hear me speak next Sunday. Of course, if you have nothing better to do.'

'I should like to excessively,' said Psmith.

'Excellent. Bring Jackson with you, and both of you come to supper afterwards, if you will.'

'Thanks very much.'

'Perhaps you would speak yourself?'

'No,' said Psmith. 'No. I think not. My Socialism is rather of the practical sort. I seldom speak. But it would be a treat to listen to you. What—er—what type of oratory is yours?'

'Oh, well,' said Mr Waller, pulling nervously at his beard, 'of course I—. Well, I am perhaps a little bitter—'

'Yes, yes.'

'A little mordant and ironical.'

'You would be,' agreed Psmith. 'I shall look forward to Sunday with every fibre quivering. And Comrade Jackson shall be at my side.'

'Excellent,' said Mr Waller. 'I will go and tell him now.'

15. Stirring Times on the Common

'The first thing to do,' said Psmith, 'is to ascertain that such a place as Clapham Common really exists. One has heard of it, of course, but has its existence ever been proved? I think not. Having accomplished that, we must then try to find out how to get to it. I should say at a venture that it would necessitate a sea-voyage. On the other hand, Comrade Waller, who is a native of the spot, seems to find no difficulty in rolling to the office every morning. Therefore—you follow me, Jackson? —it must be in England. In that case, we will take a taximeter cab, and go out into the unknown, hand in hand, trusting to luck.'

'I expect you could get there by tram,' said Mike.

Psmith suppressed a slight shudder.

'I fear, Comrade Jackson,' he said, 'that the old noblesse oblige traditions of the Psmiths would not allow me to do that. No. We will stroll gently, after a light lunch, to Trafalgar Square, and hail a taxi.'

'Beastly expensive.'

'But with what an object! Can any expenditure be called excessive which enables us to hear Comrade Waller being mordant and ironical at the other end?'

'It's a rum business,' said Mike. 'I hope the dickens he won't mix us up in it. We should look frightful fools.'

'I may possibly say a few words,' said Psmith carelessly, 'if the spirit moves me. Who am I that I should deny people a simple pleasure?'

Mike looked alarmed.

'Look here,' he said, 'I say, if you are going to play the goat, for goodness' sake don't go lugging me into it. I've got heaps of troubles without that.'

Psmith waved the objection aside.

'You,' he said, 'will be one of the large, and, I hope, interested audience. Nothing more. But it is quite possible that the spirit may not move me. I may not feel inspired to speak. I am not one of those who love speaking for speaking's sake. If I have no message for the many-headed, I shall remain silent.'

'Then I hope the dickens you won't have,' said Mike. Of all things he hated most being conspicuous before a crowd—except at cricket, which was a different thing—and he had an uneasy feeling that Psmith would rather like it than otherwise.

'We shall see,' said Psmith absently. 'Of course, if in the vein, I might do something big in the way of oratory. I am a plain, blunt man, but I feel convinced that, given the opportunity, I should haul up my slacks to some effect. But—well, we shall see. We shall see.'

And with this ghastly state of doubt Mike had to be content.

It was with feelings of apprehension that he accompanied Psmith from the flat to Trafalgar Square in search of a cab which should convey them to Clapham Common.

They were to meet Mr Waller at the edge of the Common nearest the old town of Clapham. On the journey down Psmith was inclined to be debonnaire. Mike, on the other hand, was silent and apprehensive. He knew enough of Psmith to know that, if half an opportunity were offered him, he would extract entertainment from this affair after his own fashion; and then the odds were that he himself would be dragged into it. Perhaps—his scalp bristled at the mere idea—he would even be let in for a speech.

This grisly thought had hardly come into his head, when Psmith spoke.

'I'm not half sure,' he said thoughtfully, 'I sha'n't call on you for a speech, Comrade Jackson.'

'Look here, Psmith—' began Mike agitatedly.

'I don't know. I think your solid, incisive style would rather go down with the masses. However, we shall see, we shall see.'

Mike reached the Common in a state of nervous collapse.

Mr Waller was waiting for them by the railings near the pond. The apostle of the Revolution was clad soberly in black, except for a tie of vivid crimson. His eyes shone with the light of enthusiasm, vastly different from the mild glow of amiability which they exhibited for six days in every week. The man was transformed.

'Here you are,' he said. 'Here you are. Excellent. You are in good time. Comrades Wotherspoon and Prebble have already begun to speak. I shall commence now that you have come. This is the way. Over by these trees.'

They made their way towards a small clump of trees, near which a fair-sized crowd had already begun to collect. Evidently listening to the speakers was one of Clapham's fashionable Sunday amusements. Mr Waller talked and gesticulated incessantly as he walked. Psmith's demeanour was perhaps a shade patronizing, but he displayed interest. Mike proceeded to the meeting with the air of an about-to-be-washed dog. He was loathing the whole business with a heartiness worthy of a better cause. Somehow, he felt he was going to be made to look a fool before the afternoon was over. But he registered a vow that nothing should drag him on to the small platform which had been erected for the benefit of the speaker.

As they drew nearer, the voices of Comrades Wotherspoon and Prebble became more audible. They had been audible all the time, very much so, but now they grew in volume. Comrade Wotherspoon was a tall, thin man with side-whiskers and a high voice. He scattered his aitches as a fountain its sprays in a strong wind. He was very earnest. Comrade Prebble was earnest, too. Perhaps even more so than Comrade Wotherspoon. He was handicapped to some extent, however, by not having a palate. This gave to his profoundest thoughts a certain weirdness, as if they had been uttered in an unknown tongue. The crowd was thickest round his platform. The grown-up section plainly regarded him as a comedian, pure and simple, and roared with happy laughter when he urged them to march upon Park Lane and loot the same without mercy or scruple. The children were more doubtful. Several had broken down, and been led away in tears.

When Mr Waller got up to speak on platform number three, his audience consisted at first only of Psmith, Mike, and a fox-terrier. Gradually however, he attracted others. After wavering for a while, the crowd finally decided that he was worth hearing. He had a method of his own. Lacking the natural gifts which marked Comrade Prebble out as an entertainer, he made up for this by his activity. Where his colleagues stood comparatively still, Mr Waller behaved with the vivacity generally supposed to belong only to peas on shovels and cats on hot bricks. He crouched to denounce the House of Lords. He bounded from side to side while dissecting the methods of the plutocrats. During an impassioned onslaught on the monarchical system he stood on one leg and hopped. This was more the sort of thing the crowd had come to see. Comrade Wotherspoon found himself deserted, and even Comrade Prebble's shortcomings in the way of palate were insufficient to keep his flock together.

The entire strength of the audience gathered in front of the third platform.

Mike, separated from Psmith by the movement of the crowd, listened with a growing depression. That feeling which attacks a sensitive person sometimes at the theatre when somebody is making himself ridiculous on the stage—the illogical feeling that it is he and not the actor who is floundering—had come over him in a wave. He liked Mr Waller, and it made his gorge rise to see him exposing himself to the jeers of a crowd. The fact that Mr Waller himself did not know that they were jeers, but mistook them for applause, made it no better. Mike felt vaguely furious.

His indignation began to take a more personal shape when the speaker, branching off from the main subject of Socialism, began to touch on temperance. There was no particular reason why Mr Waller should have introduced the subject of temperance, except that he happened to be an enthusiast. He linked it on to his remarks on Socialism by attributing the lethargy of the masses to their fondness for alcohol; and the crowd, which had been inclined rather to pat itself on the back during the assaults on Rank and Property, finding itself assailed in its turn, resented it. They were there to listen to speakers telling them that they were the finest fellows on earth, not pointing out their little failings to them. The feeling of the meeting became hostile. The jeers grew more frequent and less good-tempered.

'Comrade Waller means well,' said a voice in Mike's ear, 'but if he shoots it at them like this much more there'll be a bit of an imbroglio.'

'Look here, Smith,' said Mike quickly, 'can't we stop him? These chaps are getting fed up, and they look bargees enough to do anything. They'll be going for him or something soon.'

'How can we switch off the flow? I don't see. The man is wound up. He means to get it off his chest if it snows. I feel we are by way of being in the soup once more, Comrade Jackson. We can only sit tight and look on.'

The crowd was becoming more threatening every minute. A group of young men of the loafer class who stood near Mike were especially fertile in comment. Psmith's eyes were on the speaker; but Mike was watching this group closely. Suddenly he saw one of them, a thick-set youth wearing a cloth cap and no collar, stoop.

When he rose again there was a stone in his hand.

The sight acted on Mike like a spur. Vague rage against nobody in particular had been simmering in him for half an hour. Now it concentrated itself on the cloth-capped one.

Mr Waller paused momentarily before renewing his harangue. The man in the cloth cap raised his hand. There was a swirl in the crowd, and the first thing that Psmith saw as he turned was Mike seizing the would-be marksman round the neck and hurling him to the ground, after the manner of a forward at football tackling an opponent during a line-out from touch.

There is one thing which will always distract the attention of a crowd from any speaker, and that is a dispute between two of its units. Mr Waller's views on temperance were forgotten in an instant. The audience surged round Mike and his opponent.

The latter had scrambled to his feet now, and was looking round for his assailant.

'That's 'im, Bill!' cried eager voices, indicating Mike.

"E's the bloke wot 'it yer, Bill,' said others, more precise in detail.

Bill advanced on Mike in a sidelong, crab-like manner.

"Oo're you, I should like to know?' said Bill.

Mike, rightly holding that this was merely a rhetorical question and that Bill had no real thirst for information as to his family history, made no reply. Or, rather, the reply he made was not verbal. He waited till his questioner was within range, and then hit him in the eye. A reply far more satisfactory, if not to Bill himself, at any rate to the interested onlookers, than any flow of words.

A contented sigh went up from the crowd. Their Sunday afternoon was going to be spent just as they considered Sunday afternoons should be spent.

'Give us your coat,' said Psmith briskly, 'and try and get it over quick. Don't go in for any fancy sparring. Switch it on, all you know, from the start. I'll keep a thoughtful eye open to see that none of his friends and relations join in.'

Outwardly Psmith was unruffled, but inwardly he was not feeling so composed. An ordinary turn-up before an impartial crowd which could be relied upon to preserve the etiquette of these matters was one thing. As regards the actual little dispute with the cloth-capped Bill, he felt that he could rely on Mike to handle it satisfactorily. But there was no knowing how long the crowd would be content to remain mere spectators. There was no doubt which way its sympathies lay. Bill, now stripped of his coat and sketching out in a hoarse voice a scenario of what he intended to do—knocking Mike down and stamping him into the mud was one of the milder feats he promised to perform for the entertainment of an indulgent audience—was plainly the popular favourite.

Psmith, though he did not show it, was more than a little apprehensive.

Mike, having more to occupy his mind in the immediate present, was not anxious concerning the future. He had the great advantage over Psmith of having lost his temper. Psmith could look on the situation as a whole, and count the risks and possibilities. Mike could only see Bill shuffling towards him with his head down and shoulders bunched.

'Gow it, Bill!' said someone.

'Pliy up, the Arsenal!' urged a voice on the outskirts of the crowd.

A chorus of encouragement from kind friends in front: 'Step up, Bill!'

And Bill stepped.

16. Further Developments

Bill (surname unknown) was not one of your ultra-scientific fighters. He did not favour the American crouch and the artistic feint. He had a style wholly his own. It seemed to have been modelled partly on a tortoise and partly on a windmill. His head he appeared to be trying to conceal between his shoulders, and he whirled his arms alternately in circular sweeps.

Mike, on the other hand, stood upright and hit straight, with the result that he hurt his knuckles very much on his opponent's skull, without seeming to disturb the latter to any great extent. In the process he received one of the windmill swings on the left ear. The crowd, strong pro-Billites, raised a cheer.

This maddened Mike. He assumed the offensive. Bill, satisfied for the moment with his success, had stepped back, and was indulging in some fancy sparring, when Mike sprang upon him like a panther. They clinched, and Mike, who had got the under grip, hurled Bill forcibly against a stout man who looked like a publican. The two fell in a heap, Bill underneath.

At the same time Bill's friends joined in.

The first intimation Mike had of this was a violent blow across the shoulders with a walking-stick. Even if he had been wearing his overcoat, the blow would have hurt. As he was in his jacket it hurt more than anything he had ever experienced in his life. He leapt up with a yell, but Psmith was there before him. Mike saw his assailant lift the stick again, and then collapse as the old Etonian's right took him under the chin.

He darted to Psmith's side.

'This is no place for us,' observed the latter sadly. 'Shift ho, I think. Come on.'

They dashed simultaneously for the spot where the crowd was thinnest. The ring which had formed round Mike and Bill had broken up as the result of the intervention of Bill's allies, and at the spot for which they ran only two men were standing. And these had apparently made up their minds that neutrality was the best policy, for they made no movement to stop them. Psmith and Mike charged through the gap, and raced for the road.

The suddenness of the move gave them just the start they needed. Mike looked over his shoulder. The crowd, to a man, seemed to be following. Bill, excavated from beneath the publican, led the field. Lying a good second came a band of three, and after them the rest in a bunch.

They reached the road in this order.

Some fifty yards down the road was a stationary tram. In the ordinary course of things it would probably have moved on long before Psmith and Mike could have got to it; but the conductor, a man with sporting blood in him, seeing what appeared to be the finish of some Marathon Race, refrained from giving the signal, and moved out into the road to observe events more clearly, at the same time calling to the driver, who joined him. Passengers on the roof stood up to get a good view. There was some cheering.

Psmith and Mike reached the tram ten yards to the good; and, if it had been ready to start then, all would have been well. But Bill and his friends had arrived while the driver and conductor were both out in the road.

The affair now began to resemble the doings of Horatius on the bridge. Psmith and Mike turned to bay on the platform at the foot of the tram steps. Bill, leading by three yards, sprang on to it, grabbed Mike, and fell with him on to the road. Psmith, descending with a dignity somewhat lessened by the fact that his hat was on the side of his head, was in time to engage the runners-up.

Psmith, as pugilist, lacked something of the calm majesty which characterized him in the more peaceful moments of life, but he was undoubtedly effective. Nature had given him an enormous reach and a lightness on his feet remarkable in one of his size; and at some time in his career he appeared to have learned how to use his hands. The first of the three runners, the walking-stick manipulator, had the misfortune to charge straight into the old Etonian's left. It was a well-timed blow, and the force of it, added to the speed at which the victim was running, sent him on to the pavement, where he spun round and sat down. In the subsequent proceedings he took no part.

The other two attacked Psmith simultaneously, one on each side. In doing so, the one on the left tripped over Mike and Bill, who were still in the process of sorting themselves out, and fell, leaving Psmith free to attend to the other. He was a tall, weedy youth. His conspicuous features were a long nose and a light yellow waistcoat. Psmith hit him on the former with his left and on the latter with his right. The long youth emitted a gurgle, and collided with Bill, who had wrenched himself free from Mike and staggered to his feet. Bill, having received a second blow in the eye during the course of his interview on the road with Mike, was not feeling himself. Mistaking the other for an enemy, he proceeded to smite him in the parts about the jaw. He had just upset him, when a stern official voice observed, "Ere, now, what's all this?'

There is no more unfailing corrective to a scene of strife than the 'What's all this?' of the London policeman. Bill abandoned his intention of stamping on the prostrate one, and the latter, sitting up, blinked and was silent.

'What's all this?' asked the policeman again. Psmith, adjusting his hat at the correct angle again, undertook the explanations.

'A distressing scene, officer,' he said. 'A case of that unbridled brawling which is, alas, but too common in our London streets. These two, possibly till now the closest friends, fall out over some point, probably of the most trivial nature, and what happens? They brawl. They—'

'He 'it me,' said the long youth, dabbing at his face with a handkerchief and pointing an accusing finger at Psmith, who regarded him through his eyeglass with a look in which pity and censure were nicely blended.

Bill, meanwhile, circling round restlessly, in the apparent hope of getting past the Law and having another encounter with Mike, expressed himself in a stream of language which drew stern reproof from the shocked constable.

'You 'op it,' concluded the man in blue. 'That's what you do. You 'op it.'

'I should,' said Psmith kindly. 'The officer is speaking in your best interests. A man of taste and discernment, he knows what is best. His advice is good, and should be followed.'

The constable seemed to notice Psmith for the first time. He turned and stared at him. Psmith's praise had not had the effect of softening him. His look was one of suspicion.

'And what might you have been up to?' he inquired coldly. 'This man says you hit him.'

Psmith waved the matter aside.

'Purely in self-defence,' he said, 'purely in self-defence. What else could the man of spirit do? A mere tap to discourage an aggressive movement.'

The policeman stood silent, weighing matters in the balance. He produced a notebook and sucked his pencil. Then he called the conductor of the tram as a witness.

'A brainy and admirable step,' said Psmith, approvingly. 'This rugged, honest man, all unused to verbal subtleties, shall give us his plain account of what happened. After which, as I presume this tram—little as I know of the habits of trams—has got to go somewhere today, I would suggest that we all separated and moved on.'

He took two half-crowns from his pocket, and began to clink them meditatively together. A slight softening of the frigidity of the constable's manner became noticeable. There was a milder beam in the eyes which gazed into Psmith's.

Nor did the conductor seem altogether uninfluenced by the sight.

The conductor deposed that he had bin on the point of pushing on, seeing as how he'd hung abart long enough, when he see'd them two gents, the long 'un with the heye-glass (Psmith bowed) and t'other 'un, a-legging of it dahn the road towards him, with the other blokes pelting after 'em. He added that, when they reached the trem, the two gents had got aboard, and was then set upon by the blokes. And after that, he concluded, well, there was a bit of a scrap, and that's how it was.

'Lucidly and excellently put,' said Psmith. 'That is just how it was. Comrade Jackson, I fancy we leave the court without a stain on our characters. We win through. Er—constable, we have given you a great deal of trouble. Possibly—?'

'Thank you, sir.' There was a musical clinking. 'Now then, all of you, you 'op it. You're all bin poking your noses in 'ere long enough. Pop off. Get on with that tram, conductor.'

Psmith and Mike settled themselves in a seat on the roof. When the conductor came along, Psmith gave him half a crown, and asked after his wife and the little ones at home. The conductor thanked goodness that he was a bachelor, punched the tickets, and retired.

'Subject for a historical picture,' said Psmith. 'Wounded leaving the field after the Battle of Clapham Common. How are your injuries, Comrade Jackson?'

'My back's hurting like blazes,' said Mike. 'And my ear's all sore where that chap got me. Anything the matter with you?'

'Physically,' said Psmith, 'no. Spiritually much. Do you realize, Comrade Jackson, the thing that has happened? I am riding in a tram. I, Psmith, have paid a penny for a ticket on a tram. If this should get about the clubs! I tell you, Comrade Jackson, no such crisis has ever occurred before in the course of my career.'

'You can always get off, you know,' said Mike.

'He thinks of everything,' said Psmith, admiringly. 'You have touched the spot with an unerring finger. Let us descend. I observe in the distance a cab. That looks to me more the sort of thing we want. Let us go and parley with the driver.'

17. Sunday Supper

The cab took them back to the flat, at considerable expense, and Psmith requested Mike to make tea, a performance in which he himself was interested purely as a spectator. He had views on the subject of tea-making which he liked to expound from an armchair or sofa, but he never got further than this. Mike, his back throbbing dully from the blow he had received, and feeling more than a little sore all over, prepared the Etna, fetched the milk, and finally produced the finished article.

Psmith sipped meditatively.

'How pleasant,' he said, 'after strife is rest. We shouldn't have appreciated this simple cup of tea had our sensibilities remained unstirred this afternoon. We can now sit at our ease, like warriors after the fray, till the time comes for setting out to Comrade Waller's once more.'

Mike looked up.

'What! You don't mean to say you're going to sweat out to Clapham again?'

'Undoubtedly. Comrade Waller is expecting us to supper.'

'What absolute rot! We can't fag back there.'

'Noblesse oblige. The cry has gone round the Waller household, "Jackson and Psmith are coming to supper," and we cannot disappoint them now. Already the fatted blanc-mange has been killed, and the table creaks beneath what's left of the midday beef. We must be there; besides, don't you want to see how the poor man is? Probably we shall find him in the act of emitting his last breath. I expect he was lynched by the enthusiastic mob.'

'Not much,' grinned Mike. 'They were too busy with us. All right, I'll come if you really want me to, but it's awful rot.'

One of the many things Mike could never understand in Psmith was his fondness for getting into atmospheres that were not his own. He would go out of his way to do this. Mike, like most boys of his age, was never really happy and at his ease except in the presence of those of his own years and class. Psmith, on the contrary, seemed to be bored by them, and infinitely preferred talking to somebody who lived in quite another world. Mike was not a snob. He simply had not the ability to be at his ease with people in another class from his own. He did not know what to talk to them about, unless they were cricket professionals. With them he was never at a loss.

But Psmith was different. He could get on with anyone. He seemed to have the gift of entering into their minds and seeing things from their point of view.

As regarded Mr Waller, Mike liked him personally, and was prepared, as we have seen, to undertake considerable risks in his defence; but he loathed with all his heart and soul the idea of supper at his house. He knew that he would have nothing to say. Whereas Psmith gave him the impression of looking forward to the thing as a treat.

The house where Mr Waller lived was one of a row of semi-detached villas on the north side of the Common. The door was opened to them by their host himself. So far from looking battered and emitting last breaths, he appeared particularly spruce. He had just returned from Church, and was still wearing his gloves and tall hat. He squeaked with surprise when he saw who were standing on the mat.

'Why, dear me, dear me,' he said. 'Here you are! I have been wondering what had happened to you. I was afraid that you might have been seriously hurt. I was afraid those ruffians might have injured you. When last I saw you, you were being—'

'Chivvied,' interposed Psmith, with dignified melancholy. 'Do not let us try to wrap the fact up in pleasant words. We were being chivvied. We were legging it with the infuriated mob at our heels. An ignominious position for a Shropshire Psmith, but, after all, Napoleon did the same.'

'But what happened? I could not see. I only know that quite suddenly the people seemed to stop listening to me, and all gathered round you and Jackson. And then I saw that Jackson was engaged in a fight with a young man.'

'Comrade Jackson, I imagine, having heard a great deal about all men being equal, was anxious to test the theory, and see whether Comrade Bill was as good a man as he was. The experiment was broken off prematurely, but I personally should be inclined to say that Comrade Jackson had a shade the better of the exchanges.'

Mr Waller looked with interest at Mike, who shuffled and felt awkward. He was hoping that Psmith would say nothing about the reason of his engaging Bill in combat. He had an uneasy feeling that Mr Waller's gratitude would be effusive and overpowering, and he did not wish to pose as the brave young hero. There are moments when one does not feel equal to the role.

Fortunately, before Mr Waller had time to ask any further questions, the supper-bell sounded, and they went into the dining-room.

Sunday supper, unless done on a large and informal scale, is probably the most depressing meal in existence. There is a chill discomfort in the round of beef, an icy severity about the open jam tart. The blancmange shivers miserably.

Spirituous liquor helps to counteract the influence of these things, and so does exhilarating conversation. Unfortunately, at Mr Waller's table there was neither. The cashier's views on temperance were not merely for the platform; they extended to the home. And the company was not of the exhilarating sort. Besides Psmith and Mike and their host, there were four people present—Comrade Prebble, the orator; a young man of the name of Richards; Mr Waller's niece, answering to the name of Ada, who was engaged to Mr Richards; and Edward.

Edward was Mr Waller's son. He was ten years old, wore a very tight Eton suit, and had the peculiarly loathsome expression which a snub nose sometimes gives to the young.

It would have been plain to the most casual observer that Mr Waller was fond and proud of his son. The cashier was a widower, and after five minutes' acquaintance with Edward, Mike felt strongly that Mrs Waller was the lucky one. Edward sat next to Mike, and showed a tendency to concentrate his conversation on him. Psmith, at the opposite end of the table, beamed in a fatherly manner upon the pair through his eyeglass.

Mike got on with small girls reasonably well. He preferred them at a distance, but, if cornered by them, could put up a fairly good show. Small boys, however, filled him with a sort of frozen horror. It was his view that a boy should not be exhibited publicly until he reached an age when he might be in the running for some sort of colours at a public school.

Edward was one of those well-informed small boys. He opened on Mike with the first mouthful.

'Do you know the principal exports of Marseilles?' he inquired.

'What?' said Mike coldly.

'Do you know the principal exports of Marseilles? I do.'

'Oh?' said Mike.

'Yes. Do you know the capital of Madagascar?'

Mike, as crimson as the beef he was attacking, said he did not.

'I do.'

'Oh?' said Mike.

'Who was the first king—'

'You mustn't worry Mr Jackson, Teddy,' said Mr Waller, with a touch of pride in his voice, as who should say 'There are not many boys of his age, I can tell you, who could worry you with questions like that.'

'No, no, he likes it,' said Psmith, unnecessarily. 'He likes it. I always hold that much may be learned by casual chit-chat across the dinner-table. I owe much of my own grasp of—'

'I bet you don't know what's the capital of Madagascar,' interrupted Mike rudely.

'I do,' said Edward. 'I can tell you the kings of Israel?' he added, turning to Mike. He seemed to have no curiosity as to the extent of Psmith's knowledge. Mike's appeared to fascinate him.

Mike helped himself to beetroot in moody silence.

His mouth was full when Comrade Prebble asked him a question. Comrade Prebble, as has been pointed out in an earlier part of the narrative, was a good chap, but had no roof to his mouth.

'I beg your pardon?' said Mike.

Comrade Prebble repeated his observation. Mike looked helplessly at Psmith, but Psmith's eyes were on his plate.

Mike felt he must venture on some answer.

'No,' he said decidedly.

Comrade Prebble seemed slightly taken aback. There was an awkward pause. Then Mr Waller, for whom his fellow Socialist's methods of conversation held no mysteries, interpreted.

'The mustard, Prebble? Yes, yes. Would you mind passing Prebble the mustard, Mr Jackson?'

'Oh, sorry,' gasped Mike, and, reaching out, upset the water-jug into the open jam-tart.

Through the black mist which rose before his eyes as he leaped to his feet and stammered apologies came the dispassionate voice of Master Edward Waller reminding him that mustard was first introduced into Peru by Cortez.

His host was all courtesy and consideration. He passed the matter off genially. But life can never be quite the same after you have upset a water-jug into an open jam-tart at the table of a comparative stranger. Mike's nerve had gone. He ate on, but he was a broken man.

At the other end of the table it became gradually apparent that things were not going on altogether as they should have done. There was a sort of bleakness in the atmosphere. Young Mr Richards was looking like a stuffed fish, and the face of Mr Waller's niece was cold and set.

'Why, come, come, Ada,' said Mr Waller, breezily, 'what's the matter? You're eating nothing. What's George been saying to you?' he added jocularly.

'Thank you, uncle Robert,' replied Ada precisely, 'there's nothing the matter. Nothing that Mr Richards can say to me can upset me.'

'Mr Richards!' echoed Mr Waller in astonishment. How was he to know that, during the walk back from church, the world had been transformed, George had become Mr Richards, and all was over?

'I assure you, Ada—' began that unfortunate young man. Ada turned a frigid shoulder towards him.

'Come, come,' said Mr Waller disturbed. 'What's all this? What's all this?'

His niece burst into tears and left the room.

If there is anything more embarrassing to a guest than a family row, we have yet to hear of it. Mike, scarlet to the extreme edges of his ears, concentrated himself on his plate. Comrade Prebble made a great many remarks, which were probably illuminating, if they could have been understood. Mr Waller looked, astonished, at Mr Richards. Mr Richards, pink but dogged, loosened his collar, but said nothing. Psmith, leaning forward, asked Master Edward Waller his opinion on the Licensing Bill.

'We happened to have a word or two,' said Mr Richards at length, 'on the way home from church on the subject of Women's Suffrage.'

'That fatal topic!' murmured Psmith.

'In Australia—' began Master Edward Waller.

'I was rayther—well, rayther facetious about it,' continued Mr Richards.

Psmith clicked his tongue sympathetically.

'In Australia—' said Edward.

'I went talking on, laughing and joking, when all of a sudden she flew out at me. How was I to know she was 'eart and soul in the movement? You never told me,' he added accusingly to his host.

'In Australia—' said Edward.

'I'll go and try and get her round. How was I to know?'

Mr Richards thrust back his chair and bounded from the room.

'Now, iawinyaw, iear oiler—' said Comrade Prebble judicially, but was interrupted.

'How very disturbing!' said Mr Waller. 'I am so sorry that this should have happened. Ada is such a touchy, sensitive girl. She—'

'In Australia,' said Edward in even tones, 'they've got Women's Suffrage already. Did you know that?' he said to Mike.

Mike made no answer. His eyes were fixed on his plate. A bead of perspiration began to roll down his forehead. If his feelings could have been ascertained at that moment, they would have been summed up in the words, 'Death, where is thy sting?'

18. Psmith Makes a Discovery

'Women,' said Psmith, helping himself to trifle, and speaking with the air of one launched upon his special subject, 'are, one must recollect, like—like—er, well, in fact, just so. Passing on lightly from that conclusion, let us turn for a moment to the Rights of Property, in connection with which Comrade Prebble and yourself had so much that was interesting to say this afternoon. Perhaps you'—he bowed in Comrade Prebble's direction—'would resume, for the benefit of Comrade Jackson—a novice in the Cause, but earnest—your very lucid—'

Comrade Prebble beamed, and took the floor. Mike began to realize that, till now, he had never known what boredom meant. There had been moments in his life which had been less interesting than other moments, but nothing to touch this for agony. Comrade Prebble's address streamed on like water rushing over a weir. Every now and then there was a word or two which was recognizable, but this happened so rarely that it amounted to little. Sometimes Mr Waller would interject a remark, but not often. He seemed to be of the opinion that Comrade Prebble's was the master mind and that to add anything to his views would be in the nature of painting the lily and gilding the refined gold. Mike himself said nothing. Psmith and Edward were equally silent. The former sat like one in a trance, thinking his own thoughts, while Edward, who, prospecting on the sideboard, had located a rich biscuit-mine, was too occupied for speech.

After about twenty minutes, during which Mike's discomfort changed to a dull resignation, Mr Waller suggested a move to the drawing-room, where Ada, he said, would play some hymns.

The prospect did not dazzle Mike, but any change, he thought, must be for the better. He had sat staring at the ruin of the blancmange so long that it had begun to hypnotize him. Also, the move had the excellent result of eliminating the snub-nosed Edward, who was sent to bed. His last words were in the form of a question, addressed to Mike, on the subject of the hypotenuse and the square upon the same.

'A remarkably intelligent boy,' said Psmith. 'You must let him come to tea at our flat one day. I may not be in myself—I have many duties which keep me away—but Comrade Jackson is sure to be there, and will be delighted to chat with him.'

On the way upstairs Mike tried to get Psmith to himself for a moment to suggest the advisability of an early departure; but Psmith was in close conversation with his host. Mike was left to Comrade Prebble, who, apparently, had only touched the fringe of his subject in his lecture in the dining-room.

When Mr Waller had predicted hymns in the drawing-room, he had been too sanguine (or too pessimistic). Of Ada, when they arrived, there were no signs. It seemed that she had gone straight to bed. Young Mr Richards was sitting on the sofa, moodily turning the leaves of a photograph album, which contained portraits of Master Edward Waller in geometrically progressing degrees of repulsiveness—here, in frocks, looking like a gargoyle; there, in sailor suit, looking like nothing on earth. The inspection of these was obviously deepening Mr Richards' gloom, but he proceeded doggedly with it.

Comrade Prebble backed the reluctant Mike into a corner, and, like the Ancient Mariner, held him with a glittering eye. Psmith and Mr Waller, in the opposite corner, were looking at something with their heads close together. Mike definitely abandoned all hope of a rescue from Psmith, and tried to buoy himself up with the reflection that this could not last for ever.

Hours seemed to pass, and then at last he heard Psmith's voice saying good-bye to his host.

He sprang to his feet. Comrade Prebble was in the middle of a sentence, but this was no time for polished courtesy. He felt that he must get away, and at once. 'I fear,' Psmith was saying, 'that we must tear ourselves away. We have greatly enjoyed our evening. You must look us up at our flat one day, and bring Comrade Prebble. If I am not in, Comrade Jackson is certain to be, and he will be more than delighted to hear Comrade Prebble speak further on the subject of which he is such a master.' Comrade Prebble was understood to say that he would certainly come. Mr Waller beamed. Mr Richards, still steeped in gloom, shook hands in silence.

Out in the road, with the front door shut behind them, Mike spoke his mind.

'Look here, Smith,' he said definitely, 'if being your confidential secretary and adviser is going to let me in for any more of that sort of thing, you can jolly well accept my resignation.'

'The orgy was not to your taste?' said Psmith sympathetically.

Mike laughed. One of those short, hollow, bitter laughs.

'I am at a loss, Comrade Jackson,' said Psmith, 'to understand your attitude. You fed sumptuously. You had fun with the crockery—that knockabout act of yours with the water-jug was alone worth the money—and you had the advantage of listening to the views of a master of his subject. What more do you want?'

'What on earth did you land me with that man Prebble for?'

'Land you! Why, you courted his society. I had practically to drag you away from him. When I got up to say good-bye, you were listening to him with bulging eyes. I never saw such a picture of rapt attention. Do you mean to tell me, Comrade Jackson, that your appearance belied you, that you were not interested? Well, well. How we misread our fellow creatures.'

'I think you might have come and lent a hand with Prebble. It was a bit thick.'

'I was too absorbed with Comrade Waller. We were talking of things of vital moment. However, the night is yet young. We will take this cab, wend our way to the West, seek a cafe, and cheer ourselves with light refreshments.'

Arrived at a cafe whose window appeared to be a sort of museum of every kind of German sausage, they took possession of a vacant table and ordered coffee. Mike soon found himself soothed by his bright surroundings, and gradually his impressions of blancmange, Edward, and Comrade Prebble faded from his mind. Psmith, meanwhile, was preserving an unusual silence, being deep in a large square book of the sort in which Press cuttings are pasted. As Psmith scanned its contents a curious smile lit up his face. His reflections seemed to be of an agreeable nature.

'Hullo,' said Mike, 'what have you got hold of there? Where did you get that?'

'Comrade Waller very kindly lent it to me. He showed it to me after supper, knowing how enthusiastically I was attached to the Cause. Had you been less tensely wrapped up in Comrade Prebble's conversation, I would have desired you to step across and join us. However, you now have your opportunity.'

'But what is it?' asked Mike.

'It is the record of the meetings of the Tulse Hill Parliament,' said Psmith impressively. 'A faithful record of all they said, all the votes of confidence they passed in the Government, and also all the nasty knocks they gave it from time to time.'

'What on earth's the Tulse Hill Parliament?'

'It is, alas,' said Psmith in a grave, sad voice, 'no more. In life it was beautiful, but now it has done the Tom Bowling act. It has gone aloft. We are dealing, Comrade Jackson, not with the live, vivid present, but with the far-off, rusty past. And yet, in a way, there is a touch of the live, vivid present mixed up in it.'

'I don't know what the dickens you're talking about,' said Mike. 'Let's have a look, anyway.'

Psmith handed him the volume, and, leaning back, sipped his coffee, and watched him. At first Mike's face was bored and blank, but suddenly an interested look came into it.

'Aha!' said Psmith.

'Who's Bickersdyke? Anything to do with our Bickersdyke?'

'No other than our genial friend himself.'

Mike turned the pages, reading a line or two on each.

'Hullo!' he said, chuckling. 'He lets himself go a bit, doesn't he!'

'He does,' acknowledged Psmith. 'A fiery, passionate nature, that of Comrade Bickersdyke.'

'He's simply cursing the Government here. Giving them frightful beans.'

Psmith nodded.

'I noticed the fact myself.'

'But what's it all about?'

'As far as I can glean from Comrade Waller,' said Psmith, 'about twenty years ago, when he and Comrade Bickersdyke worked hand-in-hand as fellow clerks at the New Asiatic, they were both members of the Tulse Hill Parliament, that powerful institution. At that time Comrade Bickersdyke was as fruity a Socialist as Comrade Waller is now. Only, apparently, as he began to get on a bit in the world, he altered his views to some extent as regards the iniquity of freezing on to a decent share of the doubloons. And that, you see, is where the dim and rusty past begins to get mixed up with the live, vivid present. If any tactless person were to publish those very able speeches made by Comrade Bickersdyke when a bulwark of the Tulse Hill Parliament, our revered chief would be more or less caught bending, if I may employ the expression, as regards his chances of getting in as Unionist candidate at Kenningford. You follow me, Watson? I rather fancy the light-hearted electors of Kenningford, from what I have seen of their rather acute sense of humour, would be, as it were, all over it. It would be very, very trying for Comrade Bickersdyke if these speeches of his were to get about.'

'You aren't going to—!'

'I shall do nothing rashly. I shall merely place this handsome volume among my treasured books. I shall add it to my "Books that have helped me" series. Because I fancy that, in an emergency, it may not be at all a bad thing to have about me. And now,' he concluded, 'as the hour is getting late, perhaps we had better be shoving off for home.'

19. The Illness of Edward

Life in a bank is at its pleasantest in the winter. When all the world outside is dark and damp and cold, the light and warmth of the place are comforting. There is a pleasant air of solidity about the interior of a bank. The green shaded lamps look cosy. And, the outside world offering so few attractions, the worker, perched on his stool, feels that he is not so badly off after all. It is when the days are long and the sun beats hot on the pavement, and everything shouts to him how splendid it is out in the country, that he begins to grow restless.

Mike, except for a fortnight at the beginning of his career in the New Asiatic Bank, had not had to stand the test of sunshine. At present, the weather being cold and dismal, he was almost entirely contented. Now that he had got into the swing of his work, the days passed very quickly; and with his life after office-hours he had no fault to find at all.

His life was very regular. He would arrive in the morning just in time to sign his name in the attendance-book before it was removed to the accountant's room. That was at ten o'clock. From ten to eleven he would potter. There was nothing going on at that time in his department, and Mr Waller seemed to take it for granted that he should stroll off to the Postage Department and talk to Psmith, who had generally some fresh grievance against the ring-wearing Bristow to air. From eleven to half past twelve he would put in a little gentle work. Lunch, unless there was a rush of business or Mr Waller happened to suffer from a spasm of conscientiousness, could be spun out from half past twelve to two. More work from two till half past three. From half past three till half past four tea in the tearoom, with a novel. And from half past four till five either a little more work or more pottering, according to whether there was any work to do or not. It was by no means an unpleasant mode of spending a late January day.

Then there was no doubt that it was an interesting little community, that of the New Asiatic Bank. The curiously amateurish nature of the institution lent a certain air of light-heartedness to the place. It was not like one of those banks whose London office is their main office, where stern business is everything and a man becomes a mere machine for getting through a certain amount of routine work. The employees of the New Asiatic Bank, having plenty of time on their hands, were able to retain their individuality. They had leisure to think of other things besides their work. Indeed, they had so much leisure that it is a wonder they thought of their work at all.

The place was full of quaint characters. There was West, who had been requested to leave Haileybury owing to his habit of borrowing horses and attending meets in the neighbourhood, the same being always out of bounds and necessitating a complete disregard of the rules respecting evening chapel and lock-up. He was a small, dried-up youth, with black hair plastered down on his head. He went about his duties in a costume which suggested the sportsman of the comic papers.

There was also Hignett, who added to the meagre salary allowed him by the bank by singing comic songs at the minor music halls. He confided to Mike his intention of leaving the bank as soon as he had made a name, and taking seriously to the business. He told him that he had knocked them at the Bedford the week before, and in support of the statement showed him a cutting from the Era, in which the writer said that 'Other acceptable turns were the Bounding Zouaves, Steingruber's Dogs, and Arthur Hignett.' Mike wished him luck.

And there was Raymond who dabbled in journalism and was the author of 'Straight Talks to Housewives' in Trifles, under the pseudonym of 'Lady Gussie'; Wragge, who believed that the earth was flat, and addressed meetings on the subject in Hyde Park on Sundays; and many others, all interesting to talk to of a morning when work was slack and time had to be filled in.

Mike found himself, by degrees, growing quite attached to the New Asiatic Bank.

One morning, early in February, he noticed a curious change in Mr Waller. The head of the Cash Department was, as a rule, mildly cheerful on arrival, and apt (excessively, Mike thought, though he always listened with polite interest) to relate the most recent sayings and doings of his snub-nosed son, Edward. No action of this young prodigy was withheld from Mike. He had heard, on different occasions, how he had won a prize at his school for General Information (which Mike could well believe); how he had trapped young Mr Richards, now happily reconciled to Ada, with an ingenious verbal catch; and how he had made a sequence of diverting puns on the name of the new curate, during the course of that cleric's first Sunday afternoon visit.

On this particular day, however, the cashier was silent and absent-minded. He answered Mike's good-morning mechanically, and sitting down at his desk, stared blankly across the building. There was a curiously grey, tired look on his face.

Mike could not make it out. He did not like to ask if there was anything the matter. Mr Waller's face had the unreasonable effect on him of making him feel shy and awkward. Anything in the nature of sorrow always dried Mike up and robbed him of the power of speech. Being naturally sympathetic, he had raged inwardly in many a crisis at this devil of dumb awkwardness which possessed him and prevented him from putting his sympathy into words. He had always envied the cooing readiness of the hero on the stage when anyone was in trouble. He wondered whether he would ever acquire that knack of pouring out a limpid stream of soothing words on such occasions. At present he could get no farther than a scowl and an almost offensive gruffness.

The happy thought struck him of consulting Psmith. It was his hour for pottering, so he pottered round to the Postage Department, where he found the old Etonian eyeing with disfavour a new satin tie which Bristow was wearing that morning for the first time.

'I say, Smith,' he said, 'I want to speak to you for a second.'

Psmith rose. Mike led the way to a quiet corner of the Telegrams Department.

'I tell you, Comrade Jackson,' said Psmith, 'I am hard pressed. The fight is beginning to be too much for me. After a grim struggle, after days of unremitting toil, I succeeded yesterday in inducing the man Bristow to abandon that rainbow waistcoat of his. Today I enter the building, blythe and buoyant, worn, of course, from the long struggle, but seeing with aching eyes the dawn of another, better era, and there is Comrade Bristow in a satin tie. It's hard, Comrade Jackson, it's hard, I tell you.'

'Look here, Smith,' said Mike, 'I wish you'd go round to the Cash and find out what's up with old Waller. He's got the hump about something. He's sitting there looking absolutely fed up with things. I hope there's nothing up. He's not a bad sort. It would be rot if anything rotten's happened.'

Psmith began to display a gentle interest.

'So other people have troubles as well as myself,' he murmured musingly. 'I had almost forgotten that. Comrade Waller's misfortunes cannot but be trivial compared with mine, but possibly it will be as well to ascertain their nature. I will reel round and make inquiries.'

'Good man,' said Mike. 'I'll wait here.'

Psmith departed, and returned, ten minutes later, looking more serious than when he had left.

'His kid's ill, poor chap,' he said briefly. 'Pretty badly too, from what I can gather. Pneumonia. Waller was up all night. He oughtn't to be here at all today. He doesn't know what he's doing half the time. He's absolutely fagged out. Look here, you'd better nip back and do as much of the work as you can. I shouldn't talk to him much if I were you. Buck along.'

Mike went. Mr Waller was still sitting staring out across the aisle. There was something more than a little gruesome in the sight of him. He wore a crushed, beaten look, as if all the life and fight had gone out of him. A customer came to the desk to cash a cheque. The cashier shovelled the money to him under the bars with the air of one whose mind is elsewhere. Mike could guess what he was feeling, and what he was thinking about. The fact that the snub-nosed Edward was, without exception, the most repulsive small boy he had ever met in this world, where repulsive small boys crowd and jostle one another, did not interfere with his appreciation of the cashier's state of mind. Mike's was essentially a sympathetic character. He had the gift of intuitive understanding, where people of whom he was fond were concerned. It was this which drew to him those who had intelligence enough to see beyond his sometimes rather forbidding manner, and to realize that his blunt speech was largely due to shyness. In spite of his prejudice against Edward, he could put himself into Mr Waller's place, and see the thing from his point of view.

Psmith's injunction to him not to talk much was unnecessary. Mike, as always, was rendered utterly dumb by the sight of suffering. He sat at his desk, occupying himself as best he could with the driblets of work which came to him.

Mr Waller's silence and absentness continued unchanged. The habit of years had made his work mechanical. Probably few of the customers who came to cash cheques suspected that there was anything the matter with the man who paid them their money. After all, most people look on the cashier of a bank as a sort of human slot-machine. You put in your cheque, and out comes money. It is no affair of yours whether life is treating the machine well or ill that day.

The hours dragged slowly by till five o'clock struck, and the cashier, putting on his coat and hat, passed silently out through the swing doors. He walked listlessly. He was evidently tired out.

Mike shut his ledger with a vicious bang, and went across to find Psmith. He was glad the day was over.

20. Concerning a Cheque

Things never happen quite as one expects them to. Mike came to the office next morning prepared for a repetition of the previous day. He was amazed to find the cashier not merely cheerful, but even exuberantly cheerful. Edward, it appeared, had rallied in the afternoon, and, when his father had got home, had been out of danger. He was now going along excellently, and had stumped Ada, who was nursing him, with a question about the Thirty Years' War, only a few minutes before his father had left to catch his train. The cashier was overflowing with happiness and goodwill towards his species. He greeted customers with bright remarks on the weather, and snappy views on the leading events of the day: the former tinged with optimism, the latter full of a gentle spirit of toleration. His attitude towards the latest actions of His Majesty's Government was that of one who felt that, after all, there was probably some good even in the vilest of his fellow creatures, if one could only find it.

Altogether, the cloud had lifted from the Cash Department. All was joy, jollity, and song.

'The attitude of Comrade Waller,' said Psmith, on being informed of the change, 'is reassuring. I may now think of my own troubles. Comrade Bristow has blown into the office today in patent leather boots with white kid uppers, as I believe the technical term is. Add to that the fact that he is still wearing the satin tie, the waistcoat, and the ring, and you will understand why I have definitely decided this morning to abandon all hope of his reform. Henceforth my services, for what they are worth, are at the disposal of Comrade Bickersdyke. My time from now onward is his. He shall have the full educative value of my exclusive attention. I give Comrade Bristow up. Made straight for the corner flag, you understand,' he added, as Mr Rossiter emerged from his lair, 'and centred, and Sandy Turnbull headed a beautiful goal. I was just telling Jackson about the match against Blackburn Rovers,' he said to Mr Rossiter.

'Just so, just so. But get on with your work, Smith. We are a little behind-hand. I think perhaps it would be as well not to leave it just yet.'

'I will leap at it at once,' said Psmith cordially.

Mike went back to his department.

The day passed quickly. Mr Waller, in the intervals of work, talked a good deal, mostly of Edward, his doings, his sayings, and his prospects. The only thing that seemed to worry Mr Waller was the problem of how to employ his son's almost superhuman talents to the best advantage. Most of the goals towards which the average man strives struck him as too unambitious for the prodigy.

By the end of the day Mike had had enough of Edward. He never wished to hear the name again.

We do not claim originality for the statement that things never happen quite as one expects them to. We repeat it now because of its profound truth. The Edward's pneumonia episode having ended satisfactorily (or, rather, being apparently certain to end satisfactorily, for the invalid, though out of danger, was still in bed), Mike looked forward to a series of days unbroken by any but the minor troubles of life. For these he was prepared. What he did not expect was any big calamity.

At the beginning of the day there were no signs of it. The sky was blue and free from all suggestions of approaching thunderbolts. Mr Waller, still chirpy, had nothing but good news of Edward. Mike went for his morning stroll round the office feeling that things had settled down and had made up their mind to run smoothly.

When he got back, barely half an hour later, the storm had burst.

There was no one in the department at the moment of his arrival; but a few minutes later he saw Mr Waller come out of the manager's room, and make his way down the aisle.

It was his walk which first gave any hint that something was wrong. It was the same limp, crushed walk which Mike had seen when Edward's safety still hung in the balance.

As Mr Waller came nearer, Mike saw that the cashier's face was deadly pale.

Mr Waller caught sight of him and quickened his pace.

'Jackson,' he said.

Mike came forward.

'Do you—remember—' he spoke slowly, and with an effort, 'do you remember a cheque coming through the day before yesterday for a hundred pounds, with Sir John Morrison's signature?'

'Yes. It came in the morning, rather late.'

Mike remembered the cheque perfectly well, owing to the amount. It was the only three-figure cheque which had come across the counter during the day. It had been presented just before the cashier had gone out to lunch. He recollected the man who had presented it, a tallish man with a beard. He had noticed him particularly because of the contrast between his manner and that of the cashier. The former had been so very cheery and breezy, the latter so dazed and silent.

'Why,' he said.

'It was a forgery,' muttered Mr Waller, sitting down heavily.

Mike could not take it in all at once. He was stunned. All he could understand was that a far worse thing had happened than anything he could have imagined.

'A forgery?' he said.

'A forgery. And a clumsy one. Oh it's hard. I should have seen it on any other day but that. I could not have missed it. They showed me the cheque in there just now. I could not believe that I had passed it. I don't remember doing it. My mind was far away. I don't remember the cheque or anything about it. Yet there it is.'

Once more Mike was tongue-tied. For the life of him he could not think of anything to say. Surely, he thought, he could find something in the shape of words to show his sympathy. But he could find nothing that would not sound horribly stilted and cold. He sat silent.

'Sir John is in there,' went on the cashier. 'He is furious. Mr Bickersdyke, too. They are both furious. I shall be dismissed. I shall lose my place. I shall be dismissed.' He was talking more to himself than to Mike. It was dreadful to see him sitting there, all limp and broken.

'I shall lose my place. Mr Bickersdyke has wanted to get rid of me for a long time. He never liked me. I shall be dismissed. What can I do? I'm an old man. I can't make another start. I am good for nothing. Nobody will take an old man like me.'

His voice died away. There was a silence. Mike sat staring miserably in front of him.

Then, quite suddenly, an idea came to him. The whole pressure of the atmosphere seemed to lift. He saw a way out. It was a curious crooked way, but at that moment it stretched clear and broad before him. He felt lighthearted and excited, as if he were watching the development of some interesting play at the theatre.

He got up, smiling.

The cashier did not notice the movement. Somebody had come in to cash a cheque, and he was working mechanically.

Mike walked up the aisle to Mr Bickersdyke's room, and went in.

The manager was in his chair at the big table. Opposite him, facing slightly sideways, was a small, round, very red-faced man. Mr Bickersdyke was speaking as Mike entered.

'I can assure you, Sir John—' he was saying.

He looked up as the door opened.

'Well, Mr Jackson?'

Mike almost laughed. The situation was tickling him.

'Mr Waller has told me—' he began.

'I have already seen Mr Waller.'

'I know. He told me about the cheque. I came to explain.'

'Explain?'

'Yes. He didn't cash it at all.'

'I don't understand you, Mr Jackson.'

'I was at the counter when it was brought in,' said Mike. 'I cashed it.'

21. Psmith Makes Inquiries

Psmith, as was his habit of a morning when the fierce rush of his commercial duties had abated somewhat, was leaning gracefully against his desk, musing on many things, when he was aware that Bristow was standing before him.

Focusing his attention with some reluctance upon this blot on the horizon, he discovered that the exploiter of rainbow waistcoats and satin ties was addressing him.

'I say, Smithy,' said Bristow. He spoke in rather an awed voice.

'Say on, Comrade Bristow,' said Psmith graciously. 'You have our ear. You would seem to have something on your chest in addition to that Neapolitan ice garment which, I regret to see, you still flaunt. If it is one tithe as painful as that, you have my sympathy. Jerk it out, Comrade Bristow.'

'Jackson isn't half copping it from old Bick.'

'Isn't—? What exactly did you say?'

'He's getting it hot on the carpet.'

'You wish to indicate,' said Psmith, 'that there is some slight disturbance, some passing breeze between Comrades Jackson and Bickersdyke?'

Bristow chuckled.

'Breeze! Blooming hurricane, more like it. I was in Bick's room just now with a letter to sign, and I tell you, the fur was flying all over the bally shop. There was old Bick cursing for all he was worth, and a little red-faced buffer puffing out his cheeks in an armchair.'

'We all have our hobbies,' said Psmith.

'Jackson wasn't saying much. He jolly well hadn't a chance. Old Bick was shooting it out fourteen to the dozen.'

'I have been privileged,' said Psmith, 'to hear Comrade Bickersdyke speak both in his sanctum and in public. He has, as you suggest, a ready flow of speech. What, exactly was the cause of the turmoil?'

'I couldn't wait to hear. I was too jolly glad to get away. Old Bick looked at me as if he could eat me, snatched the letter out of my hand, signed it, and waved his hand at the door as a hint to hop it. Which I jolly well did. He had started jawing Jackson again before I was out of the room.'

'While applauding his hustle,' said Psmith, 'I fear that I must take official notice of this. Comrade Jackson is essentially a Sensitive Plant, highly strung, neurotic. I cannot have his nervous system jolted and disorganized in this manner, and his value as a confidential secretary and adviser impaired, even though it be only temporarily. I must look into this. I will go and see if the orgy is concluded. I will hear what Comrade Jackson has to say on the matter. I shall not act rashly, Comrade Bristow. If the man Bickersdyke is proved to have had good grounds for his outbreak, he shall escape uncensured. I may even look in on him and throw him a word of praise. But if I find, as I suspect, that he has wronged Comrade Jackson, I shall be forced to speak sharply to him.'

Mike had left the scene of battle by the time Psmith reached the Cash Department, and was sitting at his desk in a somewhat dazed condition, trying to clear his mind sufficiently to enable him to see exactly how matters stood as concerned himself. He felt confused and rattled. He had known, when he went to the manager's room to make his statement, that there would be trouble. But, then, trouble is such an elastic word. It embraces a hundred degrees of meaning. Mike had expected sentence of dismissal, and he had got it. So far he had nothing to complain of. But he had not expected it to come to him riding high on the crest of a great, frothing wave of verbal denunciation. Mr Bickersdyke, through constantly speaking in public, had developed the habit of fluent denunciation to a remarkable extent. He had thundered at Mike as if Mike had been his Majesty's Government or the Encroaching Alien, or something of that sort. And that kind of thing is a little overwhelming at short range. Mike's head was still spinning.

It continued to spin; but he never lost sight of the fact round which it revolved, namely, that he had been dismissed from the service of the bank. And for the first time he began to wonder what they would say about this at home.

Up till now the matter had seemed entirely a personal one. He had charged in to rescue the harassed cashier in precisely the same way as that in which he had dashed in to save him from Bill, the Stone-Flinging Scourge of Clapham Common. Mike's was one of those direct, honest minds which are apt to concentrate themselves on the crisis of the moment, and to leave the consequences out of the question entirely.

What would they say at home? That was the point.

Again, what could he do by way of earning a living? He did not know much about the City and its ways, but he knew enough to understand that summary dismissal from a bank is not the best recommendation one can put forward in applying for another job. And if he did not get another job in the City, what could he do? If it were only summer, he might get taken on somewhere as a cricket professional. Cricket was his line. He could earn his pay at that. But it was very far from being summer.

He had turned the problem over in his mind till his head ached, and had eaten in the process one-third of a wooden penholder, when Psmith arrived.

'It has reached me,' said Psmith, 'that you and Comrade Bickersdyke have been seen doing the Hackenschmidt-Gotch act on the floor. When my informant left, he tells me, Comrade B. had got a half-Nelson on you, and was biting pieces out of your ear. Is this so?'

Mike got up. Psmith was the man, he felt, to advise him in this crisis. Psmith's was the mind to grapple with his Hard Case.

'Look here, Smith,' he said, 'I want to speak to you. I'm in a bit of a hole, and perhaps you can tell me what to do. Let's go out and have a cup of coffee, shall we? I can't tell you about it here.'

'An admirable suggestion,' said Psmith. 'Things in the Postage Department are tolerably quiescent at present. Naturally I shall be missed, if I go out. But my absence will not spell irretrievable ruin, as it would at a period of greater commercial activity. Comrades Rossiter and Bristow have studied my methods. They know how I like things to be done. They are fully competent to conduct the business of the department in my absence. Let us, as you say, scud forth. We will go to a Mecca. Why so-called I do not know, nor, indeed, do I ever hope to know. There we may obtain, at a price, a passable cup of coffee, and you shall tell me your painful story.'

The Mecca, except for the curious aroma which pervades all Meccas, was deserted. Psmith, moving a box of dominoes on to the next table, sat down.

'Dominoes,' he said, 'is one of the few manly sports which have never had great attractions for me. A cousin of mine, who secured his chess blue at Oxford, would, they tell me, have represented his University in the dominoes match also, had he not unfortunately dislocated the radius bone of his bazooka while training for it. Except for him, there has been little dominoes talent in the Psmith family. Let us merely talk. What of this slight brass-rag-parting to which I alluded just now? Tell me all.'

He listened gravely while Mike related the incidents which had led up to his confession and the results of the same. At the conclusion of the narrative he sipped his coffee in silence for a moment.

'This habit of taking on to your shoulders the harvest of other people's bloomers,' he said meditatively, 'is growing upon you, Comrade Jackson. You must check it. It is like dram-drinking. You begin in a small way by breaking school rules to extract Comrade Jellicoe (perhaps the supremest of all the blitherers I have ever met) from a hole. If you had stopped there, all might have been well. But the thing, once started, fascinated you. Now you have landed yourself with a splash in the very centre of the Oxo in order to do a good turn to Comrade Waller. You must drop it, Comrade Jackson. When you were free and without ties, it did not so much matter. But now that you are confidential secretary and adviser to a Shropshire Psmith, the thing must stop. Your secretarial duties must be paramount. Nothing must be allowed to interfere with them. Yes. The thing must stop before it goes too far.'

'It seems to me,' said Mike, 'that it has gone too far. I've got the sack. I don't know how much farther you want it to go.'

Psmith stirred his coffee before replying.

'True,' he said, 'things look perhaps a shade rocky just now, but all is not yet lost. You must recollect that Comrade Bickersdyke spoke in the heat of the moment. That generous temperament was stirred to its depths. He did not pick his words. But calm will succeed storm, and we may be able to do something yet. I have some little influence with Comrade Bickersdyke. Wrongly, perhaps,' added Psmith modestly, 'he thinks somewhat highly of my judgement. If he sees that I am opposed to this step, he may possibly reconsider it. What Psmith thinks today, is his motto, I shall think tomorrow. However, we shall see.'

'I bet we shall!' said Mike ruefully.

'There is, moreover,' continued Psmith, 'another aspect to the affair. When you were being put through it, in Comrade Bickersdyke's inimitably breezy manner, Sir John What's-his-name was, I am given to understand, present. Naturally, to pacify the aggrieved bart., Comrade B. had to lay it on regardless of expense. In America, as possibly you are aware, there is a regular post of mistake-clerk, whose duty it is to receive in the neck anything that happens to be coming along when customers make complaints. He is hauled into the presence of the foaming customer, cursed, and sacked. The customer goes away appeased. The mistake-clerk, if the harangue has been unusually energetic, applies for a rise of salary. Now, possibly, in your case—'

'In my case,' interrupted Mike, 'there was none of that rot. Bickersdyke wasn't putting it on. He meant every word. Why, dash it all, you know yourself he'd be only too glad to sack me, just to get some of his own back with me.'

Psmith's eyes opened in pained surprise.

'Get some of his own back!' he repeated.

'Are you insinuating, Comrade Jackson, that my relations with Comrade Bickersdyke are not of the most pleasant and agreeable nature possible? How do these ideas get about? I yield to nobody in my respect for our manager. I may have had occasion from time to time to correct him in some trifling matter, but surely he is not the man to let such a thing rankle? No! I prefer to think that Comrade Bickersdyke regards me as his friend and well-wisher, and will lend a courteous ear to any proposal I see fit to make. I hope shortly to be able to prove this to you. I will discuss this little affair of the cheque with him at our ease at the club, and I shall be surprised if we do not come to some arrangement.'

'Look here, Smith,' said Mike earnestly, 'for goodness' sake don't go playing the goat. There's no earthly need for you to get lugged into this business. Don't you worry about me. I shall be all right.'

'I think,' said Psmith, 'that you will—when I have chatted with Comrade Bickersdyke.'

22. And Take Steps

On returning to the bank, Mike found Mr Waller in the grip of a peculiarly varied set of mixed feelings. Shortly after Mike's departure for the Mecca, the cashier had been summoned once more into the Presence, and had there been informed that, as apparently he had not been directly responsible for the gross piece of carelessness by which the bank had suffered so considerable a loss (here Sir John puffed out his cheeks like a meditative toad), the matter, as far as he was concerned, was at an end. On the other hand—! Here Mr Waller was hauled over the coals for Incredible Rashness in allowing a mere junior subordinate to handle important tasks like the paying out of money, and so on, till he felt raw all over. However, it was not dismissal. That was the great thing. And his principal sensation was one of relief.

Mingled with the relief were sympathy for Mike, gratitude to him for having given himself up so promptly, and a curiously dazed sensation, as if somebody had been hitting him on the head with a bolster.

All of which emotions, taken simultaneously, had the effect of rendering him completely dumb when he saw Mike. He felt that he did not know what to say to him. And as Mike, for his part, simply wanted to be let alone, and not compelled to talk, conversation was at something of a standstill in the Cash Department.

After five minutes, it occurred to Mr Waller that perhaps the best plan would be to interview Psmith. Psmith would know exactly how matters stood. He could not ask Mike point-blank whether he had been dismissed. But there was the probability that Psmith had been informed and would pass on the information.

Psmith received the cashier with a dignified kindliness.

'Oh, er, Smith,' said Mr Waller, 'I wanted just to ask you about Jackson.'

Psmith bowed his head gravely.

'Exactly,' he said. 'Comrade Jackson. I think I may say that you have come to the right man. Comrade Jackson has placed himself in my hands, and I am dealing with his case. A somewhat tricky business, but I shall see him through.'

'Has he—?' Mr Waller hesitated.

'You were saying?' said Psmith.

'Does Mr Bickersdyke intend to dismiss him?'

'At present,' admitted Psmith, 'there is some idea of that description floating—nebulously, as it were—in Comrade Bickersdyke's mind. Indeed, from what I gather from my client, the push was actually administered, in so many words. But tush! And possibly bah! we know what happens on these occasions, do we not? You and I are students of human nature, and we know that a man of Comrade Bickersdyke's warm-hearted type is apt to say in the heat of the moment a great deal more than he really means. Men of his impulsive character cannot help expressing themselves in times of stress with a certain generous strength which those who do not understand them are inclined to take a little too seriously. I shall have a chat with Comrade Bickersdyke at the conclusion of the day's work, and I have no doubt that we shall both laugh heartily over this little episode.'

Mr Waller pulled at his beard, with an expression on his face that seemed to suggest that he was not quite so confident on this point. He was about to put his doubts into words when

Mr Rossiter appeared, and Psmith, murmuring something about duty, turned again to his ledger. The cashier drifted back to his own department.

It was one of Psmith's theories of Life, which he was accustomed to propound to Mike in the small hours of the morning with his feet on the mantelpiece, that the secret of success lay in taking advantage of one's occasional slices of luck, in seizing, as it were, the happy moment. When Mike, who had had the passage to write out ten times at Wrykyn on one occasion as an imposition, reminded him that Shakespeare had once said something about there being a tide in the affairs of men, which, taken at the flood, &c., Psmith had acknowledged with an easy grace that possibly Shakespeare had got on to it first, and that it was but one more proof of how often great minds thought alike.

Though waiving his claim to the copyright of the maxim, he nevertheless had a high opinion of it, and frequently acted upon it in the conduct of his own life.

Thus, when approaching the Senior Conservative Club at five o'clock with the idea of finding Mr Bickersdyke there, he observed his quarry entering the Turkish Baths which stand some twenty yards from the club's front door, he acted on his maxim, and decided, instead of waiting for the manager to finish his bath before approaching him on the subject of Mike, to corner him in the Baths themselves.

He gave Mr Bickersdyke five minutes' start. Then, reckoning that by that time he would probably have settled down, he pushed open the door and went in himself. And, having paid his money, and left his boots with the boy at the threshold, he was rewarded by the sight of the manager emerging from a box at the far end of the room, clad in the mottled towels which the bather, irrespective of his personal taste in dress, is obliged to wear in a Turkish bath.

Psmith made for the same box. Mr Bickersdyke's clothes lay at the head of one of the sofas, but nobody else had staked out a claim. Psmith took possession of the sofa next to the manager's. Then, humming lightly, he undressed, and made his way downstairs to the Hot Rooms. He rather fancied himself in towels. There was something about them which seemed to suit his figure. They gave him, he though, rather a debonnaire look. He paused for a moment before the looking-glass to examine himself, with approval, then pushed open the door of the Hot Rooms and went in.

23. Mr Bickersdyke Makes a Concession

Mr Bickersdyke was reclining in an easy-chair in the first room, staring before him in the boiled-fish manner customary in a Turkish Bath. Psmith dropped into the next seat with a cheery 'Good evening.' The manager started as if some firm hand had driven a bradawl into him. He looked at Psmith with what was intended to be a dignified stare. But dignity is hard to achieve in a couple of parti-coloured towels. The stare did not differ to any great extent from the conventional boiled-fish look, alluded to above.

Psmith settled himself comfortably in his chair. 'Fancy finding you here,' he said pleasantly. 'We seem always to be meeting. To me,' he added, with a reassuring smile, 'it is a great pleasure. A very great pleasure indeed. We see too little of each other during office hours. Not that one must grumble at that. Work before everything. You have your duties, I mine. It is merely unfortunate that those duties are not such as to enable us to toil side by side, encouraging each other with word and gesture. However, it is idle to repine. We must make the most of these chance meetings when the work of the day is over.'

Mr Bickersdyke heaved himself up from his chair and took another at the opposite end of the room. Psmith joined him.

'There's something pleasantly mysterious, to my mind,' said he chattily, 'in a Turkish Bath. It seems to take one out of the hurry and bustle of the everyday world. It is a quiet backwater in the rushing river of Life. I like to sit and think in a Turkish Bath. Except, of course, when I have a congenial companion to talk to. As now. To me—'

Mr Bickersdyke rose, and went into the next room.

'To me,' continued Psmith, again following, and seating himself beside the manager, 'there is, too, something eerie in these places. There is a certain sinister air about the attendants. They glide rather than walk. They say little. Who knows what they may be planning and plotting? That drip-drip again. It may be merely water, but how are we to know that it is not blood? It would be so easy to do away with a man in a Turkish Bath. Nobody has seen him come in. Nobody can trace him if he disappears. These are uncomfortable thoughts, Mr Bickersdyke.'

Mr Bickersdyke seemed to think them so. He rose again, and returned to the first room.

'I have made you restless,' said Psmith, in a voice of self-reproach, when he had settled himself once more by the manager's side. 'I am sorry. I will not pursue the subject. Indeed, I believe that my fears are unnecessary. Statistics show, I understand, that large numbers of men emerge in safety every year from Turkish Baths. There was another matter of which I wished to speak to you. It is a somewhat delicate matter, and I am only encouraged to mention it to you by the fact that you are so close a friend of my father's.'

Mr Bickersdyke had picked up an early edition of an evening paper, left on the table at his side by a previous bather, and was to all appearances engrossed in it. Psmith, however, not discouraged, proceeded to touch upon the matter of Mike.

'There was,' he said, 'some little friction, I hear, in the office today in connection with a cheque.' The evening paper hid the manager's expressive face, but from the fact that the hands holding it tightened their grip Psmith deduced that Mr Bickersdyke's attention was not wholly concentrated on the City news. Moreover, his toes wriggled. And when a man's toes wriggle, he is interested in what you are saying.

'All these petty breezes,' continued Psmith sympathetically, 'must be very trying to a man in your position, a man who wishes to be left alone in order to devote his entire thought to the niceties of the higher Finance. It is as if Napoleon, while planning out some intricate scheme of campaign, were to be called upon in the midst of his meditations to bully a private for not cleaning his buttons. Naturally, you were annoyed. Your giant brain, wrenched temporarily from its proper groove, expended its force in one tremendous reprimand of Comrade Jackson. It was as if one had diverted some terrific electric current which should have been controlling a vast system of machinery, and turned it on to annihilate a black-beetle. In the present case, of course, the result is as might have been expected. Comrade Jackson, not realizing the position of affairs, went away with the absurd idea that all was over, that you meant all you said—briefly, that his number was up. I assured him that he was mistaken, but no! He persisted in declaring that all was over, that you had dismissed him from the bank.'

Mr Bickersdyke lowered the paper and glared bulbously at the old Etonian.

'Mr Jackson is perfectly right,' he snapped. 'Of course I dismissed him.'

'Yes, yes,' said Psmith, 'I have no doubt that at the moment you did work the rapid push. What I am endeavouring to point out is that Comrade Jackson is under the impression that the edict is permanent, that he can hope for no reprieve.'

'Nor can he.'

'You don't mean—'

'I mean what I say.'

'Ah, I quite understand,' said Psmith, as one who sees that he must make allowances. 'The incident is too recent. The storm has not yet had time to expend itself. You have not had leisure to think the matter over coolly. It is hard, of course, to be cool in a Turkish Bath. Your ganglions are still vibrating. Later, perhaps—'

'Once and for all,' growled Mr Bickersdyke, 'the thing is ended. Mr Jackson will leave the bank at the end of the month. We have no room for fools in the office.'

'You surprise me,' said Psmith. 'I should not have thought that the standard of intelligence in the bank was extremely high. With the exception of our two selves, I think that there are hardly any men of real intelligence on the staff. And comrade Jackson is improving every day. Being, as he is, under my constant supervision he is rapidly developing a stranglehold on his duties, which—'

'I have no wish to discuss the matter any further.'

'No, no. Quite so, quite so. Not another word. I am dumb.'

'There are limits you see, to the uses of impertinence, Mr Smith.'

Psmith started.

'You are not suggesting—! You do not mean that I—!'

'I have no more to say. I shall be glad if you will allow me to read my paper.'

Psmith waved a damp hand.

'I should be the last man,' he said stiffly, 'to force my conversation on another. I was under the impression that you enjoyed these little chats as keenly as I did. If I was wrong—'

He relapsed into a wounded silence. Mr Bickersdyke resumed his perusal of the evening paper, and presently, laying it down, rose and made his way to the room where muscular attendants were in waiting to perform that blend of Jiu-Jitsu and Catch-as-catch-can which is the most valuable and at the same time most painful part of a Turkish Bath.

It was not till he was resting on his sofa, swathed from head to foot in a sheet and smoking a cigarette, that he realized that Psmith was sharing his compartment.

He made the unpleasant discovery just as he had finished his first cigarette and lighted his second. He was blowing out the match when Psmith, accompanied by an attendant, appeared in the doorway, and proceeded to occupy the next sofa to himself. All that feeling of dreamy peace, which is the reward one receives for allowing oneself to be melted like wax and kneaded like bread, left him instantly. He felt hot and annoyed. To escape was out of the question. Once one has been scientifically wrapped up by the attendant and placed on one's sofa, one is a fixture. He lay scowling at the ceiling, resolved to combat all attempt at conversation with a stony silence.

Psmith, however, did not seem to desire conversation. He lay on his sofa motionless for a quarter of an hour, then reached out for a large book which lay on the table, and began to read.

When he did speak, he seemed to be speaking to himself. Every now and then he would murmur a few words, sometimes a single name. In spite of himself, Mr Bickersdyke found himself listening.

At first the murmurs conveyed nothing to him. Then suddenly a name caught his ear. Strowther was the name, and somehow it suggested something to him. He could not say precisely what. It seemed to touch some chord of memory. He knew no one of the name of Strowther. He was sure of that. And yet it was curiously familiar. An unusual name, too. He could not help feeling that at one time he must have known it quite well.

'Mr Strowther,' murmured Psmith, 'said that the hon. gentleman's remarks would have been nothing short of treason, if they had not been so obviously the mere babblings of an irresponsible lunatic. Cries of "Order, order," and a voice, "Sit down, fat-head!"'

For just one moment Mr Bickersdyke's memory poised motionless, like a hawk about to swoop. Then it darted at the mark. Everything came to him in a flash. The hands of the clock whizzed back. He was no longer Mr John Bickersdyke, manager of the London branch of the New Asiatic Bank, lying on a sofa in the Cumberland Street Turkish Baths. He was Jack Bickersdyke, clerk in the employ of Messrs Norton and Biggleswade, standing on a chair and shouting 'Order! order!' in the Masonic Room of the 'Red Lion' at Tulse Hill, while the members of the Tulse Hill Parliament, divided into two camps, yelled at one another, and young Tom Barlow, in his official capacity as Mister Speaker, waved his arms dumbly, and banged the table with his mallet in his efforts to restore calm.

He remembered the whole affair as if it had happened yesterday. It had been a speech of his own which had called forth the above expression of opinion from Strowther. He remembered Strowther now, a pale, spectacled clerk in Baxter and Abrahams, an inveterate upholder of the throne, the House of Lords and all constituted authority. Strowther had objected to the socialistic sentiments of his speech in connection with the Budget, and there had been a disturbance unparalleled even in the Tulse Hill Parliament, where disturbances were frequent and loud....

Psmith looked across at him with a bright smile. 'They report you verbatim,' he said. 'And rightly. A more able speech I have seldom read. I like the bit where you call the Royal Family "blood-suckers". Even then, it seems you knew how to express yourself fluently and well.'

Mr Bickersdyke sat up. The hands of the clock had moved again, and he was back in what Psmith had called the live, vivid present.

'What have you got there?' he demanded.

'It is a record,' said Psmith, 'of the meeting of an institution called the Tulse Hill Parliament. A bright, chatty little institution, too, if one may judge by these reports. You in particular, if I may say so, appear to have let yourself go with refreshing vim. Your political views have changed a great deal since those days, have they not? It is extremely interesting. A most fascinating study for political students. When I send these speeches of yours to the Clarion—'

Mr Bickersdyke bounded on his sofa.

'What!' he cried.

'I was saying,' said Psmith, 'that the Clarion will probably make a most interesting comparison between these speeches and those you have been making at Kenningford.'

'I—I—I forbid you to make any mention of these speeches.'

Psmith hesitated.

'It would be great fun seeing what the papers said,' he protested.

'Great fun!'

'It is true,' mused Psmith, 'that in a measure, it would dish you at the election. From what I saw of those light-hearted lads at Kenningford the other night, I should say they would be so amused that they would only just have enough strength left to stagger to the poll and vote for your opponent.'

Mr Bickersdyke broke out into a cold perspiration.

'I forbid you to send those speeches to the papers,' he cried.

Psmith reflected.

'You see,' he said at last, 'it is like this. The departure of Comrade Jackson, my confidential secretary and adviser, is certain to plunge me into a state of the deepest gloom. The only way I can see at present by which I can ensure even a momentary lightening of the inky cloud is the sending of these speeches to some bright paper like the Clarion. I feel certain that their comments would wring, at any rate, a sad, sweet smile from me. Possibly even a hearty laugh. I must, therefore, look on these very able speeches of yours in something of the light of an antidote. They will stand between me and black depression. Without them I am in the cart. With them I may possibly buoy myself up.'

Mr Bickersdyke shifted uneasily on his sofa. He glared at the floor. Then he eyed the ceiling as if it were a personal enemy of his. Finally he looked at Psmith. Psmith's eyes were closed in peaceful meditation.

'Very well,' said he at last. 'Jackson shall stop.'

Psmith came out of his thoughts with a start. 'You were observing—?' he said.

'I shall not dismiss Jackson,' said Mr Bickersdyke.

Psmith smiled winningly.

'Just as I had hoped,' he said. 'Your very justifiable anger melts before reflection. The storm subsides, and you are at leisure to examine the matter dispassionately. Doubts begin to creep in. Possibly, you say to yourself, I have been too hasty, too harsh. Justice must be tempered with mercy. I have caught Comrade Jackson bending, you add (still to yourself), but shall I press home my advantage too ruthlessly? No, you cry, I will abstain. And I applaud your action. I like to see this spirit of gentle toleration. It is bracing and comforting. As for these excellent speeches,' he added, 'I shall, of course, no longer have any need of their consolation. I can lay them aside. The sunlight can now enter and illumine my life through more ordinary channels. The cry goes round, "Psmith is himself again."'

Mr Bickersdyke said nothing. Unless a snort of fury may be counted as anything.

24. The Spirit of Unrest

During the following fortnight, two things happened which materially altered Mike's position in the bank.

The first was that Mr Bickersdyke was elected a member of Parliament. He got in by a small majority amidst scenes of disorder of a nature unusual even in Kenningford. Psmith, who went down on the polling-day to inspect the revels and came back with his hat smashed in, reported that, as far as he could see, the electors of Kenningford seemed to be in just that state of happy intoxication which might make them vote for Mr Bickersdyke by mistake. Also it had been discovered, on the eve of the poll, that the bank manager's opponent, in his youth, had been educated at a school in Germany, and had subsequently spent two years at Heidelberg University. These damaging revelations were having a marked effect on the warm-hearted patriots of Kenningford, who were now referring to the candidate in thick but earnest tones as 'the German Spy'.

'So that taking everything into consideration,' said Psmith, summing up, 'I fancy that Comrade Bickersdyke is home.'

And the papers next day proved that he was right.

'A hundred and fifty-seven,' said Psmith, as he read his paper at breakfast. 'Not what one would call a slashing victory. It is fortunate for Comrade Bickersdyke, I think, that I did not send those very able speeches of his to the *Clarion*'.

Till now Mike had been completely at a loss to understand why the manager had sent for him on the morning following the scene about the cheque, and informed him that he had reconsidered his decision to dismiss him. Mike could not help feeling that there was more in the matter than met the eye. Mr Bickersdyke had not spoken as if it gave him any pleasure to reprieve him. On the contrary, his manner was distinctly brusque. Mike was thoroughly puzzled. To Psmith's statement, that he had talked the matter over quietly with the manager and brought things to a satisfactory conclusion, he had paid little attention. But now he began to see light.

'Great Scott, Smith,' he said, 'did you tell him you'd send those speeches to the papers if he sacked me?'

Psmith looked at him through his eye-glass, and helped himself to another piece of toast.

'I am unable,' he said, 'to recall at this moment the exact terms of the very pleasant conversation I had with Comrade Bickersdyke on the occasion of our chance meeting in the Turkish Bath that afternoon; but, thinking things over quietly now that I have more leisure, I cannot help feeling that he may possibly have read some such intention into my words. You know how it is in these little chats, Comrade Jackson. One leaps to conclusions. Some casual word I happened to drop may have given him the idea you mention. At this distance of time it is impossible to say with any certainty. Suffice it that all has ended well. He did reconsider his resolve. I shall be only too happy if it turns out that the seed of the alteration in his views was sown by some careless word of mine. Perhaps we shall never know.'

Mike was beginning to mumble some awkward words of thanks, when Psmith resumed his discourse.

'Be that as it may, however,' he said, 'we cannot but perceive that Comrade Bickersdyke's election has altered our position to some extent. As you have pointed out, he may have been influenced in this recent affair by some chance remark of mine about those speeches. Now, however, they will cease to be of any value. Now that he is elected he has nothing to lose by their publication. I mention this by way of indicating that it is possible that, if another painful episode occurs, he may be more ruthless.'

'I see what you mean,' said Mike. 'If he catches me on the hop again, he'll simply go ahead and sack me.'

'That,' said Psmith, 'is more or less the position of affairs.'

The other event which altered Mike's life in the bank was his removal from Mr Waller's department to the Fixed Deposits. The work in the Fixed Deposits was less pleasant, and Mr Gregory, the head of the department was not of Mr Waller's type. Mr Gregory, before joining the home-staff of the New Asiatic Bank, had spent a number of years with a firm in the Far East, where he had acquired a liver and a habit of addressing those under him in a way that suggested the mate of a tramp steamer. Even on the days when his liver was not troubling him, he was truculent. And when, as usually happened, it did trouble him, he was a perfect fountain of abuse. Mike and he hated each other from the first. The work in the Fixed Deposits was not really difficult, when you got the hang of it, but there was a certain amount of confusion in it to a beginner; and Mike, in commercial matters, was as raw a beginner as ever began. In the two other departments through which he had passed, he had done tolerably well. As regarded his work in the Postage Department, stamping letters and taking them down to the post office was just about his form. It was the sort of work on which he could really get a grip. And in the Cash Department, Mr Waller's mild patience had helped him through. But with Mr Gregory it was different. Mike hated being shouted at. It confused him. And Mr Gregory invariably shouted. He always spoke as if he were competing against a high wind. With Mike he shouted more than usual. On his side, it must be admitted that Mike was something out of the common run of bank clerks. The whole system of banking was a horrid mystery to him. He did not understand why things were done, or how the various departments depended on and dove-tailed into one another. Each department seemed to him something separate and distinct. Why they were all in the same building at all he never really gathered. He knew that it could not be purely from motives of sociability, in order that the clerks might have each other's company during slack spells. That much he suspected, but beyond that he was vague.

It naturally followed that, after having grown, little by little, under Mr Waller's easy-going rule, to enjoy life in the bank, he now suffered a reaction. Within a day of his arrival in the Fixed Deposits he was loathing the place as earnestly as he had loathed it on the first morning.

Psmith, who had taken his place in the Cash Department, reported that Mr Waller was inconsolable at his loss.

'I do my best to cheer him up,' he said, 'and he smiles bravely every now and then. But when he thinks I am not looking, his head droops and that wistful expression comes into his face. The sunshine has gone out of his life.'

It had just come into Mike's, and, more than anything else, was making him restless and discontented. That is to say, it was now late spring: the sun shone cheerfully on the City; and cricket was in the air. And that was the trouble.

In the dark days, when everything was fog and slush, Mike had been contented enough to spend his mornings and afternoons in the bank, and go about with Psmith at night. Under such conditions, London is the best place in which to be, and the warmth and light of the bank were pleasant.

But now things had changed. The place had become a prison. With all the energy of one who had been born and bred in the country, Mike hated having to stay indoors on days when all the air was full of approaching summer. There were mornings when it was almost more than he could do to push open the swing doors, and go out of the fresh air into the stuffy atmosphere of the bank.

The days passed slowly, and the cricket season began. Instead of being a relief, this made matters worse. The little cricket he could get only made him want more. It was as if a starving man had been given a handful of wafer biscuits.

If the summer had been wet, he might have been less restless. But, as it happened, it was unusually fine. After a week of cold weather at the beginning of May, a hot spell set in. May passed in a blaze of sunshine. Large scores were made all over the country.

Mike's name had been down for the M.C.C. for some years, and he had become a member during his last season at Wrykyn. Once or twice a week he managed to get up to Lord's for half an hour's practice at the nets; and on Saturdays the bank had matches, in which he generally managed to knock the cover off rather ordinary club bowling. But it was not enough for him.

June came, and with it more sunshine. The atmosphere of the bank seemed more oppressive than ever.

25. At the Telephone

If one looks closely into those actions which are apparently due to sudden impulse, one generally finds that the sudden impulse was merely the last of a long series of events which led up to the action. Alone, it would not have been powerful enough to effect anything. But, coming after the way has been paved for it, it is irresistible. The hooligan who bonnets a policeman is apparently the victim of a sudden impulse. In reality, however, the bonneting is due to weeks of daily encounters with the constable, at each of which meetings the dislike for his helmet and the idea of smashing it in grow a little larger, till finally they blossom into the deed itself.

This was what happened in Mike's case. Day by day, through the summer, as the City grew hotter and stuffier, his hatred of the bank became more and more the thought that occupied his mind. It only needed a moderately strong temptation to make him break out and take the consequences.

Psmith noticed his restlessness and endeavoured to soothe it.

'All is not well,' he said, 'with Comrade Jackson, the Sunshine of the Home. I note a certain wanness of the cheek. The peach-bloom of your complexion is no longer up to sample. Your eye is wild; your merry laugh no longer rings through the bank, causing nervous customers to leap into the air with startled exclamations. You have the manner of one whose only friend on earth is a yellow dog, and who has lost the dog. Why is this, Comrade Jackson?'

They were talking in the flat at Clement's Inn. The night was hot. Through the open windows the roar of the Strand sounded faintly. Mike walked to the window and looked out.

'I'm sick of all this rot,' he said shortly.

Psmith shot an inquiring glance at him, but said nothing. This restlessness of Mike's was causing him a good deal of inconvenience, which he bore in patient silence, hoping for better times. With Mike obviously discontented and out of tune with all the world, there was but little amusement to be extracted from the evenings now. Mike did his best to be cheerful, but he could not shake off the caged feeling which made him restless.

'What rot it all is!' went on Mike, sitting down again. 'What's the good of it all? You go and sweat all day at a desk, day after day, for about twopence a year. And when you're about eighty-five, you retire. It isn't living at all. It's simply being a bally vegetable.'

'You aren't hankering, by any chance, to be a pirate of the Spanish main, or anything like that, are you?' inquired Psmith.

'And all this rot about going out East,' continued Mike. 'What's the good of going out East?'

'I gather from casual chit-chat in the office that one becomes something of a blood when one goes out East,' said Psmith. 'Have a dozen native clerks under you, all looking up to you as the Last Word in magnificence, and end by marrying the Governor's daughter.'

'End by getting some foul sort of fever, more likely, and being booted out as no further use to the bank.'

'You look on the gloomy side, Comrade Jackson. I seem to see you sitting in an armchair, fanned by devoted coolies, telling some Eastern potentate that you can give him five minutes. I understand that being in a bank in the Far East is one of the world's softest jobs. Millions of natives hang on your lightest word. Enthusiastic rajahs draw you aside and press jewels into your hand as a token of respect and esteem. When on an elephant's back you pass, somebody beats on a booming brass gong! The Banker of Bhong! Isn't your generous young heart stirred to any extent by the prospect? I am given to understand—'

'I've a jolly good mind to chuck up the whole thing and become a pro. I've got a birth qualification for Surrey. It's about the only thing I could do any good at.'

Psmith's manner became fatherly.

'You're all right,' he said. 'The hot weather has given you that tired feeling. What you want is a change of air. We will pop down together hand in hand this week-end to some seaside resort. You shall build sand castles, while I lie on the beach and read the paper. In the evening we will listen to the band, or stroll on the esplanade, not so much because we want to, as to give the natives a treat. Possibly, if the weather continues warm, we may even paddle. A vastly exhilarating pastime, I am led to believe, and so strengthening for the ankles. And on Monday morning we will return, bronzed and bursting with health, to our toil once more.'

'I'm going to bed,' said Mike, rising.

Psmith watched him lounge from the room, and shook his head sadly. All was not well with his confidential secretary and adviser.

The next day, which was a Thursday, found Mike no more reconciled to the prospect of spending from ten till five in the company of Mr Gregory and the ledgers. He was silent at breakfast, and Psmith, seeing that things were still wrong, abstained from conversation. Mike propped the Sportsman up against the hot-water jug, and read the cricket news. His county, captained by brother Joe, had, as he had learned already from yesterday's evening paper, beaten Sussex by five wickets at Brighton. Today they were due to play Middlesex at Lord's. Mike thought that he would try to get off early, and go and see some of the first day's play.

As events turned out, he got off a good deal earlier, and saw a good deal more of the first day's play than he had anticipated.

He had just finished the preliminary stages of the morning's work, which consisted mostly of washing his hands, changing his coat, and eating a section of a pen-holder, when William, the messenger, approached.

'You're wanted on the 'phone, Mr Jackson.'

The New Asiatic Bank, unlike the majority of London banks, was on the telephone, a fact which Psmith found a great convenience when securing seats at the theatre. Mike went to the box and took up the receiver.

'Hullo!' he said.

'Who's that?' said an agitated voice. 'Is that you, Mike? I'm Joe.'

'Hullo, Joe,' said Mike. 'What's up? I'm coming to see you this evening. I'm going to try and get off early.'

'Look here, Mike, are you busy at the bank just now?'

'Not at the moment. There's never anything much going on before eleven.'

'I mean, are you busy today? Could you possibly manage to get off and play for us against Middlesex?'

Mike nearly dropped the receiver.

'What?' he cried.

'There's been the dickens of a mix-up. We're one short, and you're our only hope. We can't possibly get another man in the time. We start in half an hour. Can you play?'

For the space of, perhaps, one minute, Mike thought.

'Well?' said Joe's voice.

The sudden vision of Lord's ground, all green and cool in the morning sunlight, was too much for Mike's resolution, sapped as it was by days of restlessness. The feeling surged over him that whatever happened afterwards, the joy of the match in perfect weather on a perfect wicket would make it worth while. What did it matter what happened afterwards?

'All right, Joe,' he said. 'I'll hop into a cab now, and go and get my things.'

'Good man,' said Joe, hugely relieved.

26. Breaking the News

Dashing away from the call-box, Mike nearly cannoned into Psmith, who was making his way pensively to the telephone with the object of ringing up the box office of the Haymarket Theatre.

'Sorry,' said Mike. 'Hullo, Smith.'

'Hullo indeed,' said Psmith, courteously. 'I rejoice, Comrade Jackson, to find you going about your commercial duties like a young bomb. How is it, people repeatedly ask me, that Comrade Jackson contrives to catch his employer's eye and win the friendly smile from the head of his department? My reply is that where others walk, Comrade Jackson runs. Where others stroll, Comrade Jackson legs it like a highly-trained mustang of the prairie. He does not loiter. He gets back to his department bathed in perspiration, in level time. He—'

'I say, Smith,' said Mike, 'you might do me a favour.'

'A thousand. Say on.'

'Just look in at the Fixed Deposits and tell old Gregory that I shan't be with him today, will you? I haven't time myself. I must rush!'

Psmith screwed his eyeglass into his eye, and examined Mike carefully.

'What exactly—?' be began.

'Tell the old ass I've popped off.'

'Just so, just so,' murmured Psmith, as one who assents to a thoroughly reasonable proposition. 'Tell him you have popped off. It shall be done. But it is within the bounds of possibility that Comrade Gregory may inquire further. Could you give me some inkling as to why you are popping?'

'My brother Joe has just rung me up from Lords. The county are playing Middlesex and they're one short. He wants me to roll up.'

Psmith shook his head sadly.

'I don't wish to interfere in any way,' he said, 'but I suppose you realize that, by acting thus, you are to some extent knocking the stuffing out of your chances of becoming manager of this bank? If you dash off now, I shouldn't count too much on that marrying the Governor's daughter scheme I sketched out for you last night. I doubt whether this is going to help you to hold the gorgeous East in fee, and all that sort of thing.'

'Oh, dash the gorgeous East.'

'By all means,' said Psmith obligingly. 'I just thought I'd mention it. I'll look in at Lord's this afternoon. I shall send my card up to you, and trust to your sympathetic cooperation to enable me to effect an entry into the pavilion on my face. My father is coming up to London today. I'll bring him along, too.'

'Right ho. Dash it, it's twenty to. So long. See you at Lord's.'

Psmith looked after his retreating form till it had vanished through the swing-door, and shrugged his shoulders resignedly, as if disclaiming all responsibility.

'He has gone without his hat,' he murmured. 'It seems to me that this is practically a case of running amok. And now to break the news to bereaved Comrade Gregory.'

He abandoned his intention of ringing up the Haymarket Theatre, and turning away from the call-box, walked meditatively down the aisle till he came to the Fixed Deposits Department, where the top of Mr Gregory's head was to be seen over the glass barrier, as he applied himself to his work.

Psmith, resting his elbows on the top of the barrier and holding his head between his hands, eyed the absorbed toiler for a moment in silence, then emitted a hollow groan.

Mr Gregory, who was ruling a line in a ledger—most of the work in the Fixed Deposits Department consisted of ruling lines in ledgers, sometimes in black ink, sometimes in red—started as if he had been stung, and made a complete mess of the ruled line. He lifted a fiery, bearded face, and met Psmith's eye, which shone with kindly sympathy.

He found words.

'What the dickens are you standing there for, mooing like a blanked cow?' he inquired.

'I was groaning,' explained Psmith with quiet dignity. 'And why was I groaning?' he continued. 'Because a shadow has fallen on the Fixed Deposits Department. Comrade Jackson, the Pride of the Office, has gone.'

Mr Gregory rose from his seat.

'I don't know who the dickens you are—' he began.

'I am Psmith,' said the old Etonian,

'Oh, you're Smith, are you?'

'With a preliminary P. Which, however, is not sounded.'

'And what's all this dashed nonsense about Jackson?'

'He is gone. Gone like the dew from the petal of a rose.'

'Gone! Where's he gone to?'

'Lord's.'

'What lord's?'

Psmith waved his hand gently.

'You misunderstand me. Comrade Jackson has not gone to mix with any member of our gay and thoughtless aristocracy. He has gone to Lord's cricket ground.'

Mr Gregory's beard bristled even more than was its wont.

'What!' he roared. 'Gone to watch a cricket match! Gone—!'

'Not to watch. To play. An urgent summons I need not say. Nothing but an urgent summons could have wrenched him from your very delightful society, I am sure.'

Mr Gregory glared.

'I don't want any of your impudence,' he said.

Psmith nodded gravely.

'We all have these curious likes and dislikes,' he said tolerantly. 'You do not like my impudence. Well, well, some people don't. And now, having broken the sad news, I will return to my own department.'

'Half a minute. You come with me and tell this yarn of yours to Mr Bickersdyke.'

'You think it would interest, amuse him? Perhaps you are right. Let us buttonhole Comrade

Bickersdyke.'

Mr Bickersdyke was disengaged. The head of the Fixed Deposits Department stumped into the room. Psmith followed at a more leisurely pace.

'Allow me,' he said with a winning smile, as Mr Gregory opened his mouth to speak, 'to take this opportunity of congratulating you on your success at the election. A narrow but well-deserved victory.'

There was nothing cordial in the manager's manner.

'What do you want?' he said.

'Myself, nothing,' said Psmith. 'But I understand that Mr Gregory has some communication to make.'

'Tell Mr Bickersdyke that story of yours,' said Mr Gregory.

'Surely,' said Psmith reprovingly, 'this is no time for anecdotes. Mr Bickersdyke is busy. He—'

'Tell him what you told me about Jackson.'

Mr Bickersdyke looked up inquiringly.

'Jackson,' said Psmith, 'has been obliged to absent himself from work today owing to an urgent summons from his brother, who, I understand, has suffered a bereavement.'

'It's a lie,' roared Mr Gregory. 'You told me yourself he'd gone to play in a cricket match.'

'True. As I said, he received an urgent summons from his brother.'

'What about the bereavement, then?'

'The team was one short. His brother was very distressed about it. What could Comrade Jackson do? Could he refuse to help his brother when it was in his power? His generous nature is a byword. He did the only possible thing. He consented to play.'

Mr Bickersdyke spoke.

'Am I to understand,' he asked, with sinister calm, 'that Mr Jackson has left his work and gone off to play in a cricket match?'

'Something of that sort has, I believe, happened,' said Psmith. 'He knew, of course,' he added, bowing gracefully in Mr Gregory's direction, 'that he was leaving his work in thoroughly competent hands.'

'Thank you,' said Mr Bickersdyke. 'That will do. You will help Mr Gregory in his department for the time being, Mr Smith. I will arrange for somebody to take your place in your own department.'

'It will be a pleasure,' murmured Psmith.

'Show Mr Smith what he has to do, Mr Gregory,' said the manager.

They left the room.

'How curious, Comrade Gregory,' mused Psmith, as they went, 'are the workings of Fate! A moment back, and your life was a blank. Comrade Jackson, that prince of Fixed Depositors, had gone. How, you said to yourself despairingly, can his place be filled? Then the cloud broke, and the sun shone out again. I came to help you. What you lose on the swings, you make up on the roundabouts. Now show me what I have to do, and then let us make this department sizzle. You have drawn a good ticket, Comrade Gregory.'

27. At Lord's

Mike got to Lord's just as the umpires moved out into the field. He raced round to the pavilion. Joe met him on the stairs.

'It's all right,' he said. 'No hurry. We've won the toss. I've put you in fourth wicket.'

'Right ho,' said Mike. 'Glad we haven't to field just yet.'

'We oughtn't to have to field today if we don't chuck our wickets away.'

'Good wicket?'

'Like a billiard-table. I'm glad you were able to come. Have any difficulty in getting away?'

Joe Jackson's knowledge of the workings of a bank was of the slightest. He himself had never, since he left Oxford, been in a position where there were obstacles to getting off to play in first-class cricket. By profession he was agent to a sporting baronet whose hobby was the cricket of the county, and so, far from finding any difficulty in playing for the county, he was given to understand by his employer that that was his chief duty. It never occurred to him that Mike might find his bank less amenable in the matter of giving leave. His only fear, when he rang Mike up that morning, had been that this might be a particularly busy day at the New Asiatic Bank. If there was no special rush of work, he took it for granted that Mike would simply go to the manager, ask for leave to play in the match, and be given it with a beaming smile.

Mike did not answer the question, but asked one on his own account.

'How did you happen to be short?' he said.

'It was rotten luck. It was like this. We were altering our team after the Sussex match, to bring in Ballard, Keene, and Willis. They couldn't get down to Brighton, as the 'Varsity had a match, but there was nothing on for them in the last half of the week, so they'd promised to roll up.'

Ballard, Keene, and Willis were members of the Cambridge team, all very capable performers and much in demand by the county, when they could get away to play for it.

'Well?' said Mike.

'Well, we all came up by train from Brighton last night. But these three asses had arranged to motor down from Cambridge early today, and get here in time for the start. What happens? Why, Willis, who fancies himself as a chauffeur, undertakes to do the driving; and naturally, being an absolute rotter, goes and smashes up the whole concern just outside St Albans. The first thing I knew of it was when I got to Lord's at half past ten, and found a wire waiting for me to say that they were all three of them crocked, and couldn't possibly play. I tell you, it was a bit of a jar to get half an hour before the match started. Willis has sprained his ankle, apparently; Keene's damaged his wrist; and Ballard has smashed his collar-bone. I don't suppose they'll be able to play in the 'Varsity match. Rotten luck for Cambridge. Well, fortunately we'd had two reserve pros, with us at Brighton, who had come up to London with the team in case they might be wanted, so, with them, we were only one short. Then I thought of you. That's how it was.'

'I see,' said Mike. 'Who are the pros?'

'Davis and Brockley. Both bowlers. It weakens our batting a lot. Ballard or Willis might have got a stack of runs on this wicket. Still, we've got a certain amount of batting as it is.

We oughtn't to do badly, if we're careful. You've been getting some practice, I suppose, this season?'

'In a sort of a way. Nets and so on. No matches of any importance.'

'Dash it, I wish you'd had a game or two in decent class cricket. Still, nets are better than nothing, I hope you'll be in form. We may want a pretty long knock from you, if things go wrong. These men seem to be settling down all right, thank goodness,' he added, looking out of the window at the county's first pair, Warrington and Mills, two professionals, who, as the result of ten minutes' play, had put up twenty.

'I'd better go and change,' said Mike, picking up his bag. 'You're in first wicket, I suppose?'

'Yes. And Reggie, second wicket.'

Reggie was another of Mike's brothers, not nearly so fine a player as Joe, but a sound bat, who generally made runs if allowed to stay in.

Mike changed, and went out into the little balcony at the top of the pavilion. He had it to himself. There were not many spectators in the pavilion at this early stage of the game.

There are few more restful places, if one wishes to think, than the upper balconies of Lord's pavilion. Mike, watching the game making its leisurely progress on the turf below, set himself seriously to review the situation in all its aspects. The exhilaration of bursting the bonds had begun to fade, and he found himself able to look into the matter of his desertion and weigh up the consequences. There was no doubt that he had cut the painter once and for all. Even a friendly-disposed management could hardly overlook what he had done. And the management of the New Asiatic Bank was the very reverse of friendly. Mr Bickersdyke, he knew, would jump at this chance of getting rid of him. He realized that he must look on his career in the bank as a closed book. It was definitely over, and he must now think about the future.

It was not a time for half-measures. He could not go home. He must carry the thing through, now that he had begun, and find something definite to do, to support himself.

There seemed only one opening for him. What could he do, he asked himself. Just one thing. He could play cricket. It was by his cricket that he must live. He would have to become a professional. Could he get taken on? That was the question. It was impossible that he should play for his own county on his residential qualification. He could not appear as a professional in the same team in which his brothers were playing as amateurs. He must stake all on his birth qualification for Surrey.

On the other hand, had he the credentials which Surrey would want? He had a school reputation. But was that enough? He could not help feeling that it might not be.

Thinking it over more tensely than he had ever thought over anything in his whole life, he saw clearly that everything depended on what sort of show he made in this match which was now in progress. It was his big chance. If he succeeded, all would be well. He did not care to think what his position would be if he did not succeed.

A distant appeal and a sound of clapping from the crowd broke in on his thoughts. Mills was out, caught at the wicket. The telegraph-board gave the total as forty-eight. Not sensational. The success of the team depended largely on what sort of a start the two professionals made.

The clapping broke out again as Joe made his way down the steps. Joe, as an All England player, was a favourite with the crowd.

Mike watched him play an over in his strong, graceful style: then it suddenly occurred to him that he would like to know how matters had gone at the bank in his absence.

He went down to the telephone, rang up the bank, and asked for Psmith.

Presently the familiar voice made itself heard.

'Hullo, Smith.'

'Hullo. Is that Comrade Jackson? How are things progressing?'

'Fairly well. We're in first. We've lost one wicket, and the fifty's just up. I say, what's happened at the bank?'

'I broke the news to Comrade Gregory. A charming personality. I feel that we shall be friends.'

'Was he sick?'

'In a measure, yes. Indeed, I may say he practically foamed at the mouth. I explained the situation, but he was not to be appeased. He jerked me into the presence of Comrade Bickersdyke, with whom I had a brief but entertaining chat. He had not a great deal to say, but he listened attentively to my narrative, and eventually told me off to take your place in the Fixed Deposits. That melancholy task I am now performing to the best of my ability. I find the work a little trying. There is too much ledger-lugging to be done for my simple tastes. I have been hauling ledgers from the safe all the morning. The cry is beginning to go round, "Psmith is willing, but can his physique stand the strain?" In the excitement of the moment just now I dropped a somewhat massive tome on to Comrade Gregory's foot, unfortunately, I understand, the foot in which he has of late been suffering twinges of gout. I passed the thing off with ready tact, but I cannot deny that there was a certain temporary coolness, which, indeed, is not yet past. These things, Comrade Jackson, are the whirlpools in the quiet stream of commercial life.'

'Have I got the sack?'

'No official pronouncement has been made to me as yet on the subject, but I think I should advise you, if you are offered another job in the course of the day, to accept it. I cannot say that you are precisely the pet of the management just at present. However, I have ideas for your future, which I will divulge when we meet. I propose to slide coyly from the office at about four o'clock. I am meeting my father at that hour. We shall come straight on to Lord's.'

'Right ho,' said Mike. 'I'll be looking out for you.'

'Is there any little message I can give Comrade Gregory from you?'

'You can give him my love, if you like.'

'It shall be done. Good-bye.'

'Good-bye.'

Mike replaced the receiver, and went up to his balcony again.

As soon as his eye fell on the telegraph-board he saw with a start that things had been moving rapidly in his brief absence. The numbers of the batsmen on the board were three and five.

'Great Scott!' he cried. 'Why, I'm in next. What on earth's been happening?'

He put on his pads hurriedly, expecting every moment that a wicket would fall and find him unprepared. But the batsmen were still together when he rose, ready for the fray, and went downstairs to get news.

He found his brother Reggie in the dressing-room.

'What's happened?' he said. 'How were you out?'

'L.b.w.,' said Reggie. 'Goodness knows how it happened. My eyesight must be going. I mistimed the thing altogether.'

'How was Warrington out?'

'Caught in the slips.'

'By Jove!' said Mike. 'This is pretty rocky. Three for sixty-one. We shall get mopped.'

'Unless you and Joe do something. There's no earthly need to get out. The wicket's as good as you want, and the bowling's nothing special. Well played, Joe!'

A beautiful glide to leg by the greatest of the Jacksons had rolled up against the pavilion rails. The fieldsmen changed across for the next over.

'If only Peters stops a bit—' began Mike, and broke off. Peters' off stump was lying at an angle of forty-five degrees.

'Well, he hasn't,' said Reggie grimly. 'Silly ass, why did he hit at that one? All he'd got to do was to stay in with Joe. Now it's up to you. Do try and do something, or we'll be out under the hundred.'

Mike waited till the outcoming batsman had turned in at the professionals' gate. Then he walked down the steps and out into the open, feeling more nervous than he had felt since that far-off day when he had first gone in to bat for Wrykyn against the M.C.C. He found his thoughts flying back to that occasion. Today, as then, everything seemed very distant and unreal. The spectators were miles away. He had often been to Lord's as a spectator, but the place seemed entirely unfamiliar now. He felt as if he were in a strange land.

He was conscious of Joe leaving the crease to meet him on his way. He smiled feebly. 'Buck up,' said Joe in that robust way of his which was so heartening. 'Nothing in the bowling, and the wicket like a shirt-front. Play just as if you were at the nets. And for goodness' sake don't try to score all your runs in the first over. Stick in, and we've got them.'

Mike smiled again more feebly than before, and made a weird gurgling noise in his throat.

It had been the Middlesex fast bowler who had destroyed Peters. Mike was not sorry. He did not object to fast bowling. He took guard, and looked round him, taking careful note of the positions of the slips.

As usual, once he was at the wicket the paralysed feeling left him. He became conscious again of his power. Dash it all, what was there to be afraid of? He was a jolly good bat, and he would jolly well show them that he was, too.

The fast bowler, with a preliminary bound, began his run. Mike settled himself into position, his whole soul concentrated on the ball. Everything else was wiped from his mind.

28. Psmith Arranges his Future

It was exactly four o'clock when Psmith, sliding unostentatiously from his stool, flicked divers pieces of dust from the leg of his trousers, and sidled towards the basement, where he was wont to keep his hat during business hours. He was aware that it would be a matter of some delicacy to leave the bank at that hour. There was a certain quantity of work still to be done in the Fixed Deposits Department—work in which, by rights, as Mike's understudy, he should have lent a sympathetic and helping hand. 'But what of that?' he mused, thoughtfully smoothing his hat with his knuckles. 'Comrade Gregory is a man who takes such an enthusiastic pleasure in his duties that he will go singing about the office when he discovers that he has got a double lot of work to do.'

With this comforting thought, he started on his perilous journey to the open air. As he walked delicately, not courting observation, he reminded himself of the hero of 'Pilgrim's Progress'. On all sides of him lay fearsome beasts, lying in wait to pounce upon him. At any moment Mr Gregory's hoarse roar might shatter the comparative stillness, or the sinister note of Mr Bickersdyke make itself heard.

'However,' said Psmith philosophically, 'these are Life's Trials, and must be borne patiently.'

A roundabout route, via the Postage and Inwards Bills Departments, took him to the swing-doors. It was here that the danger became acute. The doors were well within view of the Fixed Deposits Department, and Mr Gregory had an eye compared with which that of an eagle was more or less bleared.

Psmith sauntered to the door and pushed it open in a gingerly manner.

As he did so a bellow rang through the office, causing a timid customer, who had come in to arrange about an overdraft, to lose his nerve completely and postpone his business till the following afternoon.

Psmith looked up. Mr Gregory was leaning over the barrier which divided his lair from the outer world, and gesticulating violently.

'Where are you going,' roared the head of the Fixed Deposits.

Psmith did not reply. With a benevolent smile and a gesture intended to signify all would come right in the future, he slid through the swing-doors, and began to move down the street at a somewhat swifter pace than was his habit.

Once round the corner he slackened his speed.

'This can't go on,' he said to himself. 'This life of commerce is too great a strain. One is practically a hunted hare. Either the heads of my department must refrain from View Halloos when they observe me going for a stroll, or I abandon Commerce for some less exacting walk in life.'

He removed his hat, and allowed the cool breeze to play upon his forehead. The episode had been disturbing.

He was to meet his father at the Mansion House. As he reached that land-mark he saw with approval that punctuality was a virtue of which he had not the sole monopoly in the Smith family. His father was waiting for him at the tryst.

'Certainly, my boy,' said Mr Smith senior, all activity in a moment, when Psmith had suggested going to Lord's. 'Excellent. We must be getting on. We must not miss a moment of the match. Bless my soul: I haven't seen a first-class match this season. Where's a cab? Hi, cabby! No, that one's got some one in it. There's another. Hi! Here, lunatic! Are you blind? Good, he's seen us. That's right. Here he comes. Lord's Cricket Ground, cabby, as quick as you can. Jump in, Rupert, my boy, jump in.'

Psmith rarely jumped. He entered the cab with something of the stateliness of an old Roman Emperor boarding his chariot, and settled himself comfortably in his seat. Mr Smith dived in like a rabbit.

A vendor of newspapers came to the cab thrusting an evening paper into the interior. Psmith bought it.

'Let's see how they're getting on,' he said, opening the paper. 'Where are we? Lunch scores. Lord's. Aha! Comrade Jackson is in form.'

'Jackson?' said Mr Smith, 'is that the same youngster you brought home last summer? The batsman? Is he playing today?'

'He was not out thirty at lunch-time. He would appear to be making something of a stand with his brother Joe, who has made sixty-one up to the moment of going to press. It's possible he may still be in when we get there. In which case we shall not be able to slide into the pavilion.'

'A grand bat, that boy. I said so last summer. Better than any of his brothers. He's in the bank with you, isn't he?'

'He was this morning. I doubt, however, whether he can be said to be still in that position.'

'Eh? what? How's that?'

'There was some slight friction between him and the management. They wished him to be glued to his stool; he preferred to play for the county. I think we may say that Comrade Jackson has secured the Order of the Boot.'

'What? Do you mean to say—?'

Psmith related briefly the history of Mike's departure.

Mr Smith listened with interest.

'Well,' he said at last, 'hang me if I blame the boy. It's a sin cooping up a fellow who can bat like that in a bank. I should have done the same myself in his place.'

Psmith smoothed his waistcoat.

'Do you know, father,' he said, 'this bank business is far from being much of a catch. Indeed, I should describe it definitely as a bit off. I have given it a fair trial, and I now denounce it unhesitatingly as a shade too thick.'

'What? Are you getting tired of it?'

'Not precisely tired. But, after considerable reflection, I have come to the conclusion that my talents lie elsewhere. At lugging ledgers I am among the also-rans—a mere cipher. I have been wanting to speak to you about this for some time. If you have no objection, I should like to go to the Bar.'

'The Bar? Well—'

'I fancy I should make a pretty considerable hit as a barrister.'

Mr Smith reflected. The idea had not occurred to him before. Now that it was suggested, his always easily-fired imagination took hold of it readily. There was a good deal to be said for the Bar as a career. Psmith knew his father, and he knew that the thing was practically as good as settled. It was a new idea, and as such was bound to be favourably received.

'What I should do, if I were you,' he went on, as if he were advising a friend on some course of action certain to bring him profit and pleasure, 'is to take me away from the bank at once. Don't wait. There is no time like the present. Let me hand in my resignation tomorrow. The blow to the management, especially to Comrade Bickersdyke, will be a painful one, but it is the truest kindness to administer it swiftly. Let me resign tomorrow, and devote my time to quiet study. Then I can pop up to Cambridge next term, and all will be well.'

'I'll think it over—' began Mr Smith.

'Let us hustle,' urged Psmith. 'Let us Do It Now. It is the only way. Have I your leave to shoot in my resignation to Comrade Bickersdyke tomorrow morning?'

Mr Smith hesitated for a moment, then made up his mind.

'Very well,' he said. 'I really think it is a good idea. There are great opportunities open to a barrister. I wish we had thought of it before.'

'I am not altogether sorry that we did not,' said Psmith. 'I have enjoyed the chances my commercial life has given me of associating with such a man as Comrade Bickersdyke. In many ways a master-mind. But perhaps it is as well to close the chapter. How it happened it is hard to say, but somehow I fancy I did not precisely hit it off with Comrade Bickersdyke. With Psmith, the worker, he had no fault to find; but it seemed to me sometimes, during our festive evenings together at the club, that all was not well. From little, almost imperceptible signs I have suspected now and then that he would just as soon have been without my company. One cannot explain these things. It must have been some incompatibility of temperament. Perhaps he will manage to bear up at my departure. But here we are,' he added, as the cab drew up. 'I wonder if Comrade Jackson is still going strong.'

They passed through the turnstile, and caught sight of the telegraph-board.

'By Jove!' said Psmith, 'he is. I don't know if he's number three or number six. I expect he's number six. In which case he has got ninety-eight. We're just in time to see his century.'

29. And Mike's

For nearly two hours Mike had been experiencing the keenest pleasure that it had ever fallen to his lot to feel. From the moment he took his first ball till the luncheon interval he had suffered the acutest discomfort. His nervousness had left him to a great extent, but he had never really settled down. Sometimes by luck, and sometimes by skill, he had kept the ball out of his wicket; but he was scratching, and he knew it. Not for a single over had he been comfortable. On several occasions he had edged balls to leg and through the slips in quite an inferior manner, and it was seldom that he managed to hit with the centre of the bat.

Nobody is more alive to the fact that he is not playing up to his true form than the batsman. Even though his score mounted little by little into the twenties, Mike was miserable. If this was the best he could do on a perfect wicket, he felt there was not much hope for him as a professional.

The poorness of his play was accentuated by the brilliance of Joe's. Joe combined science and vigour to a remarkable degree. He laid on the wood with a graceful robustness which drew much cheering from the crowd. Beside him Mike was oppressed by that leaden sense of moral inferiority which weighs on a man who has turned up to dinner in ordinary clothes when everybody else has dressed. He felt awkward and conspicuously out of place.

Then came lunch—and after lunch a glorious change.

Volumes might be written on the cricket lunch and the influence it has on the run of the game; how it undoes one man, and sends another back to the fray like a giant refreshed; how it turns the brilliant fast bowler into the sluggish medium, and the nervous bat into the masterful smiter.

On Mike its effect was magical. He lunched wisely and well, chewing his food with the concentration of a thirty-three-bites a mouthful crank, and drinking dry ginger-ale. As he walked out with Joe after the interval he knew that a change had taken place in him. His nerve had come back, and with it his form.

It sometimes happens at cricket that when one feels particularly fit one gets snapped in the slips in the first over, or clean bowled by a full toss; but neither of these things happened to Mike. He stayed in, and began to score. Now there were no edgings through the slips and snicks to leg. He was meeting the ball in the centre of the bat, and meeting it vigorously. Two boundaries in successive balls off the fast bowler, hard, clean drives past extra-cover, put him at peace with all the world. He was on top. He had found himself.

Joe, at the other end, resumed his brilliant career. His century and Mike's fifty arrived in the same over. The bowling began to grow loose.

Joe, having reached his century, slowed down somewhat, and Mike took up the running. The score rose rapidly.

A leg-theory bowler kept down the pace of the run-getting for a time, but the bowlers at the other end continued to give away runs. Mike's score passed from sixty to seventy, from seventy to eighty, from eighty to ninety. When the Smiths, father and son, came on to the ground the total was ninety-eight. Joe had made a hundred and thirty-three.

Mike reached his century just as Psmith and his father took their seats. A square cut off the slow bowler was just too wide for point to get to. By the time third man had sprinted across and returned the ball the batsmen had run two.

Mr Smith was enthusiastic.

'I tell you,' he said to Psmith, who was clapping in a gently encouraging manner, 'the boy's a wonderful bat. I said so when he was down with us. I remember telling him so myself. "I've seen your brothers play," I said, "and you're better than any of them." I remember it distinctly. He'll be playing for England in another year or two. Fancy putting a cricketer like that into the City! It's a crime.'

'I gather,' said Psmith, 'that the family coffers had got a bit low. It was necessary for Comrade Jackson to do something by way of saving the Old Home.'

'He ought to be at the University. Look, he's got that man away to the boundary again. They'll never get him out.'

At six o'clock the partnership was broken, Joe running himself out in trying to snatch a single where no single was. He had made a hundred and eighty-nine.

Mike flung himself down on the turf with mixed feelings. He was sorry Joe was out, but he was very glad indeed of the chance of a rest. He was utterly fagged. A half-day match once a week is no training for first-class cricket. Joe, who had been playing all the season, was as tough as india-rubber, and trotted into the pavilion as fresh as if he had been having a brief spell at the nets. Mike, on the other hand, felt that he simply wanted to be dropped into a cold bath and left there indefinitely. There was only another half-hour's play, but he doubted if he could get through it.

He dragged himself up wearily as Joe's successor arrived at the wickets. He had crossed Joe before the latter's downfall, and it was his turn to take the bowling.

Something seemed to have gone out of him. He could not time the ball properly. The last ball of the over looked like a half-volley, and he hit out at it. But it was just short of a half-volley, and his stroke arrived too soon. The bowler, running in the direction of mid-on, brought off an easy c.-and-b.

Mike turned away towards the pavilion. He heard the gradually swelling applause in a sort of dream. It seemed to him hours before he reached the dressing-room.

He was sitting on a chair, wishing that somebody would come along and take off his pads, when Psmith's card was brought to him. A few moments later the old Etonian appeared in person.

'Hullo, Smith,' said Mike, 'By Jove! I'm done.'

'"How Little Willie Saved the Match,"' said Psmith. 'What you want is one of those gin and ginger-beers we hear so much about. Remove those pads, and let us flit downstairs in search of a couple. Well, Comrade Jackson, you have fought the good fight this day. My father sends his compliments. He is dining out, or he would have come up. He is going to look in at the flat latish.'

'How many did I get?' asked Mike. 'I was so jolly done I didn't think of looking.'

'A hundred and forty-eight of the best,' said Psmith. 'What will they say at the old homestead about this? Are you ready? Then let us test this fruity old ginger-beer of theirs.'

The two batsmen who had followed the big stand were apparently having a little stand all of their own. No more wickets fell before the drawing of stumps. Psmith waited for Mike while he changed, and carried him off in a cab to Simpson's, a restaurant which, as he justly observed, offered two great advantages, namely, that you need not dress, and, secondly, that you paid your half-crown, and were then at liberty to eat till you were helpless, if you felt so disposed, without extra charge.

Mike stopped short of this giddy height of mastication, but consumed enough to make him feel a great deal better. Psmith eyed his inroads on the menu with approval.

'There is nothing,' he said, 'like victualling up before an ordeal.'

'What's the ordeal?' said Mike.

'I propose to take you round to the club anon, where I trust we shall find Comrade Bickersdyke. We have much to say to one another.'

'Look here, I'm hanged—' began Mike.

'Yes, you must be there,' said Psmith. 'Your presence will serve to cheer Comrade B. up. Fate compels me to deal him a nasty blow, and he will want sympathy. I have got to break it to him that I am leaving the bank.'

'What, are you going to chuck it?'

Psmith inclined his head.

'The time,' he said, 'has come to part. It has served its turn. The startled whisper runs round the City. "Psmith has had sufficient."'

'What are you going to do?'

'I propose to enter the University of Cambridge, and there to study the intricacies of the Law, with a view to having a subsequent dash at becoming Lord Chancellor.'

'By Jove!' said Mike, 'you're lucky. I wish I were coming too.'

Psmith knocked the ash off his cigarette.

'Are you absolutely set on becoming a pro?' he asked.

'It depends on what you call set. It seems to me it's about all I can do.'

'I can offer you a not entirely scaly job,' said Smith, 'if you feel like taking it. In the course of conversation with my father during the match this afternoon, I gleaned the fact that he is anxious to secure your services as a species of agent. The vast Psmith estates, it seems, need a bright boy to keep an eye upon them. Are you prepared to accept the post?'

Mike stared.

'Me! Dash it all, how old do you think I am? I'm only nineteen.'

'I had suspected as much from the alabaster clearness of your unwrinkled brow. But my father does not wish you to enter upon your duties immediately. There would be a preliminary interval of three, possibly four, years at Cambridge, during which I presume, you would be learning divers facts concerning spuds, turmuts, and the like. At least,' said Psmith airily, 'I suppose so. Far be it from me to dictate the line of your researches.'

'Then I'm afraid it's off,' said Mike gloomily. 'My pater couldn't afford to send me to Cambridge.'

'That obstacle,' said Psmith, 'can be surmounted. You would, of course, accompany me to Cambridge, in the capacity, which you enjoy at the present moment, of my confidential secretary and adviser. Any expenses that might crop up would be defrayed from the Psmith family chest.'

Mike's eyes opened wide again.

'Do you mean,' he asked bluntly, 'that your pater would pay for me at the 'Varsity? No I say—dash it—I mean, I couldn't—'

'Do you suggest,' said Psmith, raising his eyebrows, 'that I should go to the University without a confidential secretary and adviser?'

'No, but I mean—' protested Mike.

'Then that's settled,' said Psmith. 'I knew you would not desert me in my hour of need, Comrade Jackson. "What will you do," asked my father, alarmed for my safety, "among these wild undergraduates? I fear for my Rupert." "Have no fear, father," I replied. "Comrade Jackson will be beside me." His face brightened immediately. "Comrade Jackson," he said, "is a man in whom I have the supremest confidence. If he is with you I shall sleep easy of nights." It was after that that the conversation drifted to the subject of agents.'

Psmith called for the bill and paid it in the affable manner of a monarch signing a charter. Mike sat silent, his mind in a whirl. He saw exactly what had happened. He could almost hear Psmith talking his father into agreeing with his scheme. He could think of nothing to say. As usually happened in any emotional crisis in his life, words absolutely deserted him. The thing was too big. Anything he could say would sound too feeble. When a friend has solved all your difficulties and smoothed out all the rough places which were looming in your path, you cannot thank him as if he had asked you to lunch. The occasion demanded some neat, polished speech; and neat, polished speeches were beyond Mike.

'I say, Psmith—' he began.

Psmith rose.

'Let us now,' he said, 'collect our hats and meander to the club, where, I have no doubt, we shall find Comrade Bickersdyke, all unconscious of impending misfortune, dreaming pleasantly over coffee and a cigar in the lower smoking-room.'

30. The Last Sad Farewells

As it happened, that was precisely what Mr Bickersdyke was doing. He was feeling thoroughly pleased with life. For nearly nine months Psmith had been to him a sort of spectre at the feast inspiring him with an ever-present feeling of discomfort which he had found impossible to shake off. And tonight, he saw his way of getting rid of him.

At five minutes past four Mr Gregory, crimson and wrathful, had plunged into his room with a long statement of how Psmith, deputed to help in the life and thought of the Fixed Deposits Department, had left the building at four o'clock, when there was still another hour and a half's work to be done.

Moreover, Mr Gregory deposed, the errant one, seen sliding out of the swinging door, and summoned in a loud, clear voice to come back, had flatly disobeyed and had gone upon his ways 'Grinning at me,' said the aggrieved Mr Gregory, 'like a dashed ape.' A most unjust description of the sad, sweet smile which Psmith had bestowed upon him from the doorway.

Ever since that moment Mr Bickersdyke had felt that there was a silver lining to the cloud. Hitherto Psmith had left nothing to be desired in the manner in which he performed his work. His righteousness in the office had clothed him as in a suit of mail. But now he had slipped. To go off an hour and a half before the proper time, and to refuse to return when summoned by the head of his department—these were offences for which he could be dismissed without fuss. Mr Bickersdyke looked forward to tomorrow's interview with his employee.

Meanwhile, having enjoyed an excellent dinner, he was now, as Psmith had predicted, engaged with a cigar and a cup of coffee in the lower smoking-room of the Senior Conservative Club.

Psmith and Mike entered the room when he was about half through these luxuries.

Psmith's first action was to summon a waiter, and order a glass of neat brandy. 'Not for myself,' he explained to Mike. 'For Comrade Bickersdyke. He is about to sustain a nasty shock, and may need a restorative at a moment's notice. For all we know, his heart may not be strong. In any case, it is safest to have a pick-me-up handy.'

He paid the waiter, and advanced across the room, followed by Mike. In his hand, extended at arm's length, he bore the glass of brandy.

Mr Bickersdyke caught sight of the procession, and started. Psmith set the brandy down very carefully on the table, beside the manager's coffee cup, and, dropping into a chair, regarded him pityingly through his eyeglass. Mike, who felt embarrassed, took a seat some little way behind his companion. This was Psmith's affair, and he proposed to allow him to do the talking.

Mr Bickersdyke, except for a slight deepening of the colour of his complexion, gave no sign of having seen them. He puffed away at his cigar, his eyes fixed on the ceiling.

'An unpleasant task lies before us,' began Psmith in a low, sorrowful voice, 'and it must not be shirked. Have I your ear, Mr Bickersdyke?'

Addressed thus directly, the manager allowed his gaze to wander from the ceiling. He eyed Psmith for a moment like an elderly basilisk, then looked back at the ceiling again.

'I shall speak to you tomorrow,' he said.

Psmith heaved a heavy sigh.

'You will not see us tomorrow,' he said, pushing the brandy a little nearer.

Mr Bickersdyke's eyes left the ceiling once more.

'What do you mean?' he said.

'Drink this,' urged Psmith sympathetically, holding out the glass. 'Be brave,' he went on rapidly. 'Time softens the harshest blows. Shocks stun us for the moment, but we recover. Little by little we come to ourselves again. Life, which we had thought could hold no more pleasure for us, gradually shows itself not wholly grey.'

Mr Bickersdyke seemed about to make an observation at this point, but Psmith, with a wave of the hand, hurried on.

'We find that the sun still shines, the birds still sing. Things which used to entertain us resume their attraction. Gradually we emerge from the soup, and begin—'

'If you have anything to say to me,' said the manager, 'I should be glad if you would say it, and go.'

'You prefer me not to break the bad news gently?' said Psmith. 'Perhaps you are wise. In a word, then,'—he picked up the brandy and held it out to him—'Comrade Jackson and myself are leaving the bank.'

'I am aware of that,' said Mr Bickersdyke drily.

Psmith put down the glass.

'You have been told already?' he said. 'That accounts for your calm. The shock has expended its force on you, and can do no more. You are stunned. I am sorry, but it had to be. You will say that it is madness for us to offer our resignations, that our grip on the work of the bank made a prosperous career in Commerce certain for us. It may be so. But somehow we feel that our talents lie elsewhere. To Comrade Jackson the management of the Psmith estates seems the job on which he can get the rapid half-Nelson. For my own part, I feel that my long suit is the Bar. I am a poor, unready speaker, but I intend to acquire a knowledge of the Law which shall outweigh this defect. Before leaving you, I should like to say—I may speak for you as well as myself, Comrade Jackson—?'

Mike uttered his first contribution to the conversation—a gurgle—and relapsed into silence again.

'I should like to say,' continued Psmith, 'how much Comrade Jackson and I have enjoyed our stay in the bank. The insight it has given us into your masterly handling of the intricate mechanism of the office has been a treat we would not have missed. But our place is elsewhere.'

He rose. Mike followed his example with alacrity. It occurred to Mr Bickersdyke, as they turned to go, that he had not yet been able to get in a word about their dismissal. They were drifting away with all the honours of war.

'Come back,' he cried.

Psmith paused and shook his head sadly.

'This is unmanly, Comrade Bickersdyke,' he said. 'I had not expected this. That you should be dazed by the shock was natural. But that you should beg us to reconsider our resolve and return to the bank is unworthy of you. Be a man. Bite the bullet. The first keen pang will pass. Time will soften the feeling of bereavement. You must be brave. Come, Comrade

Jackson.'

Mike responded to the call without hesitation.

'We will now,' said Psmith, leading the way to the door, 'push back to the flat. My father will be round there soon.' He looked over his shoulder. Mr Bickersdyke appeared to be wrapped in thought.

'A painful business,' sighed Psmith. 'The man seems quite broken up. It had to be, however. The bank was no place for us. An excellent career in many respects, but unsuitable for you and me. It is hard on Comrade Bickersdyke, especially as he took such trouble to get me into it, but I think we may say that we are well out of the place.'

Mike's mind roamed into the future. Cambridge first, and then an open-air life of the sort he had always dreamed of. The Problem of Life seemed to him to be solved. He looked on down the years, and he could see no troubles there of any kind whatsoever. Reason suggested that there were probably one or two knocking about somewhere, but this was no time to think of them. He examined the future, and found it good.

'I should jolly well think,' he said simply, 'that we might.'

PSMITH, JOURNALIST

PREFACE

THE conditions of life in New York are so different from those of London that a story of this kind calls for a little explanation. There are several million inhabitants of New York. Not all of them eke out a precarious livelihood by murdering one another, but there is a definite section of the population which murders—not casually, on the spur of the moment, but on definitely commercial lines at so many dollars per murder. The "gangs" of New York exist in fact. I have not invented them. Most of the incidents in this story are based on actual happenings. The Rosenthal case, where four men, headed by a genial individual calling himself "Gyp the Blood" shot a fellow-citizen in cold blood in a spot as public and fashionable as Piccadilly Circus and escaped in a motor-car, made such a stir a few years ago that the noise of it was heard all over the world and not, as is generally the case with the doings of the gangs, in New York only. Rosenthal cases on a smaller and less sensational scale are frequent occurrences on Manhattan Island. It was the prominence of the victim rather than the unusual nature of the occurrence that excited the New York press. Most gang victims get a quarter of a column in small type.

P. G. WODEHOUSE New York, 1915

CHAPTER I — "COSY MOMENTS"

The man in the street would not have known it, but a great crisis was imminent in New York journalism.

Everything seemed much as usual in the city. The cars ran blithely on Broadway. Newsboys shouted "Wux-try!" into the ears of nervous pedestrians with their usual Caruso-like vim. Society passed up and down Fifth Avenue in its automobiles, and was there a furrow of anxiety upon Society's brow? None. At a thousand street corners a thousand policemen preserved their air of massive superiority to the things of this world. Not one of them showed the least sign of perturbation. Nevertheless, the crisis was at hand. Mr. J. Fillken Wilberfloss, editor-in-chief of Cosy Moments, was about to leave his post and start on a ten weeks' holiday.

In New York one may find every class of paper which the imagination can conceive. Every grade of society is catered for. If an Esquimau came to New York, the first thing he would find on the bookstalls in all probability would be the Blubber Magazine, or some similar production written by Esquimaux for Esquimaux. Everybody reads in New York, and reads all the time. The New Yorker peruses his favourite paper while he is being jammed into a crowded compartment on the subway or leaping like an antelope into a moving Street car.

There was thus a public for Cosy Moments. Cosy Moments, as its name (an inspiration of Mr. Wilberfloss's own) is designed to imply, is a journal for the home. It is the sort of paper which the father of the family is expected to take home with him from his office and read aloud to the chicks before bed-time. It was founded by its proprietor, Mr. Benjamin White, as an antidote to yellow journalism. One is forced to admit that up to the present yellow journalism seems to be competing against it with a certain measure of success. Headlines are still of as generous a size as heretofore, and there is no tendency on the part of editors to scamp the details of the last murder-case.

Nevertheless, Cosy Moments thrives. It has its public.

Its contents are mildly interesting, if you like that sort of thing. There is a "Moments in the Nursery" page, conducted by Luella Granville Waterman, to which parents are invited to contribute the bright speeches of their offspring, and which bristles with little stories about the nursery canary, by Jane (aged six), and other works of rising young authors. There is a "Moments of Meditation" page, conducted by the Reverend Edwin T. Philpotts; a "Moments Among the Masters" page, consisting of assorted chunks looted from the literature of the past, when foreheads were bulgy and thoughts profound, by Mr. Wilberfloss himself; one or two other pages; a short story; answers to correspondents on domestic matters; and a "Moments of Mirth" page, conducted by an alleged humorist of the name of B. Henderson Asher, which is about the most painful production ever served up to a confiding public.

The guiding spirit of Cosy Moments was Mr. Wilberfloss. Circumstances had left the development of the paper mainly to him. For the past twelve months the proprietor had been away in Europe, taking the waters at Carlsbad, and the sole control of Cosy Moments had passed into the hands of Mr. Wilberfloss. Nor had he proved unworthy of the trust or unequal to the duties. In that year Cosy Moments had reached the highest possible level of domesticity. Anything not calculated to appeal to the home had been rigidly excluded. And as a result the circulation had increased steadily. Two extra pages had been added, "Moments Among the Shoppers" and "Moments with Society." And the advertisements had grown in volume. But the work had told upon the Editor. Work of that sort carries its penalties with it. Success means absorption, and absorption spells softening of the brain.

Whether it was the strain of digging into the literature of the past every week, or the effort of reading B. Henderson Asher's "Moments of Mirth" is uncertain. At any rate, his duties, combined with the heat of a New York summer, had sapped Mr. Wilberfloss's health to such an extent that the doctor had ordered him ten weeks' complete rest in the mountains. This Mr. Wilberfloss could, perhaps, have endured, if this had been all. There are worse places than the mountains of America in which to spend ten weeks of the tail-end of summer, when the sun has ceased to grill and the mosquitoes have relaxed their exertions. But it was not all. The doctor, a far-seeing man who went down to first causes, had absolutely declined to consent to Mr. Wilberfloss's suggestion that he should keep in touch with the paper during his vacation. He was adamant. He had seen copies of Cosy Moments once or twice, and he refused to permit a man in the editor's state of health to come in contact with Luella Granville Waterman's "Moments in the Nursery" and B. Henderson Asher's "Moments of Mirth." The medicine-man put his foot down firmly.

"You must not see so much as the cover of the paper for ten weeks," he said. "And I'm not so sure that it shouldn't be longer. You must forget that such a paper exists. You must dismiss the whole thing from your mind, live in the open, and develop a little flesh and muscle."

To Mr. Wilberfloss the sentence was almost equivalent to penal servitude. It was with tears in his voice that he was giving his final instructions to his sub-editor, in whose charge the paper would be left during his absence. He had taken a long time doing this. For two days he had been fussing in and out of the office, to the discontent of its inmates, more especially Billy Windsor, the sub-editor, who was now listening moodily to the last harangue of the series, with the air of one whose heart is not in the subject. Billy Windsor was a tall, wiry, loose-jointed young man, with unkempt hair and the general demeanour of a caged eagle. Looking at him, one could picture him astride of a bronco, rounding up cattle, or cooking his dinner at a camp-fire. Somehow he did not seem to fit into the Cosy Moments atmosphere.

"Well, I think that that is all, Mr. Windsor," chirruped the editor. He was a little man with a long neck and large pince-nez, and he always chirruped. "You understand the general lines on which I think the paper should be conducted?" The sub-editor nodded. Mr. Wilberfloss made him tired. Sometimes he made him more tired than at other times. At the present moment he filled him with an aching weariness. The editor meant well, and was full of zeal, but he had a habit of covering and recovering the ground. He possessed the art of saying the same obvious thing in a number of different ways to a degree which is found usually only in politicians. If Mr. Wilberfloss had been a politician, he would have been one of those dealers in glittering generalities who used to be fashionable in American politics.

"There is just one thing," he continued "Mrs. Julia Burdett Parslow is a little inclined—I may have mentioned this before—"

"You did," said the sub-editor.

Mr. Wilberfloss chirruped on, unchecked.

"A little inclined to be late with her 'Moments with Budding Girlhood'. If this should happen while I am away, just write her a letter, quite a pleasant letter, you understand, pointing out the necessity of being in good time. The machinery of a weekly paper, of course, cannot run smoothly unless contributors are in good time with their copy. She is a very sensible woman, and she will understand, I am sure, if you point it out to her."

The sub-editor nodded.

"And there is just one other thing. I wish you would correct a slight tendency I have noticed lately in Mr. Asher to be just a trifle—well, not precisely risky, but perhaps a shade broad in his humour."

"His what?" said Billy Windsor.

"Mr. Asher is a very sensible man, and he will be the first to acknowledge that his sense of humour has led him just a little beyond the bounds. You understand? Well, that is all, I think. Now I must really be going, or I shall miss my train. Good-bye, Mr. Windsor."

"Good-bye," said the sub-editor thankfully.

At the door Mr. Wilberfloss paused with the air of an exile bidding farewell to his native land, sighed, and trotted out.

Billy Windsor put his feet upon the table, and with a deep scowl resumed his task of reading the proofs of Luella Granville Waterman's "Moments in the Nursery."

CHAPTER II — BILLY WINDSOR

Billy Windsor had started life twenty-five years before this story opens on his father's ranch in Wyoming. From there he had gone to a local paper of the type whose Society column consists of such items as "Pawnee Jim Williams was to town yesterday with a bunch of other cheap skates. We take this opportunity of once more informing Jim that he is a liar and a skunk," and whose editor works with a revolver on his desk and another in his hip-pocket. Graduating from this, he had proceeded to a reporter's post on a daily paper in a Kentucky town, where there were blood feuds and other Southern devices for preventing life from becoming dull. All this time New York, the magnet, had been tugging at him. All reporters dream of reaching New York. At last, after four years on the Kentucky paper, he had come East, minus the lobe of one ear and plus a long scar that ran diagonally across his left shoulder, and had worked without much success as a free-lance. He was tough and ready for anything that might come his way, but these things are a great deal a matter of luck. The cub-reporter cannot make a name for himself unless he is favoured by fortune. Things had not come Billy Windsor's way. His work had been confined to turning in reports of fires and small street accidents, which the various papers to which he supplied them cut down to a couple of inches.

Billy had been in a bad way when he had happened upon the sub-editorship of Cosy Moments. He despised the work with all his heart, and the salary was infinitesimal. But it was regular, and for a while Billy felt that a regular salary was the greatest thing on earth. But he still dreamed of winning through to a post on one of the big New York dailies, where there was something doing and a man would have a chance of showing what was in him.

The unfortunate thing, however, was that Cosy Moments took up his time so completely. He had no chance of attracting the notice of big editors by his present work, and he had no leisure for doing any other.

All of which may go to explain why his normal aspect was that of a caged eagle.

To him, brooding over the outpourings of Luella Granville Waterman, there entered Pugsy Maloney, the office-boy, bearing a struggling cat.

"Say!" said Pugsy.

He was a nonchalant youth, with a freckled, mask-like face, the expression of which never varied. He appeared unconscious of the cat. Its existence did not seem to occur to him.

"Well?" said Billy, looking up. "Hello, what have you got there?"

Master Maloney eyed the cat, as if he were seeing it for the first time.

"It's a kitty what I got in de street," he said.

"Don't hurt the poor brute. Put her down."

Master Maloney obediently dropped the cat, which sprang nimbly on to an upper shelf of the book-case.

"I wasn't hoitin' her," he said, without emotion. "Dere was two fellers in de street sickin' a dawg on to her. An' I comes up an' says, 'G'wan! What do youse t'ink you're doin', fussin' de poor dumb animal?' An' one of de guys, he says, 'G'wan! Who do youse t'ink youse is?' An' I says, 'I'm de guy what's goin' to swat youse one on de coco if youse don't quit fussin' de poor dumb animal.' So wit dat he makes a break at swattin' me one, but I swats him one, an' I swats de odder feller one, an' den I swats dem bote some more, an' I gets de kitty, an' I brings her in here, cos I t'inks maybe youse'll look after her."

And having finished this Homeric narrative, Master Maloney fixed an expressionless eye on the ceiling, and was silent.

Billy Windsor, like most men of the plains, combined the toughest of muscle with the softest of hearts. He was always ready at any moment to become the champion of the oppressed on the slightest provocation. His alliance with Pugsy Maloney had begun on the occasion when he had rescued that youth from the clutches of a large negro, who, probably from the soundest of motives, was endeavouring to slay him. Billy had not inquired into the rights and wrongs of the matter: he had merely sailed in and rescued the office-boy. And Pugsy, though he had made no verbal comment on the affair, had shown in many ways that he was not ungrateful.

"Bully for you, Pugsy!" he cried. "You're a little sport. Here"—he produced a dollar-bill—"go out and get some milk for the poor brute. She's probably starving. Keep the change."

"Sure thing," assented Master Maloney. He strolled slowly out, while Billy Windsor, mounting a chair, proceeded to chirrup and snap his fingers in the effort to establish the foundations of an entente cordiale with the rescued cat.

By the time that Pugsy returned, carrying a five-cent bottle of milk, the animal had vacated the book-shelf, and was sitting on the table, washing her face. The milk having been poured into the lid of a tobacco-tin, in lieu of a saucer, she suspended her operations and adjourned for refreshments. Billy, business being business, turned again to Luella Granville Waterman, but Pugsy, having no immediate duties on hand, concentrated himself on the cat.

"Say!" he said.

"Well?"

"Dat kitty."

"What about her?"

"Pipe de leather collar she's wearing."

Billy had noticed earlier in the proceedings that a narrow leather collar encircled the cat's neck. He had not paid any particular attention to it. "What about it?" he said.

"Guess I know where dat kitty belongs. Dey all have dose collars. I guess she's one of Bat Jarvis's kitties. He's got a lot of dem for fair, and every one wit one of dem collars round deir neck."

"Who's Bat Jarvis? Do you mean the gang-leader?"

"Sure. He's a cousin of mine," said Master Maloney with pride.

"Is he?" said Billy. "Nice sort of fellow to have in the family. So you think that's his cat?"

"Sure. He's got twenty-t'ree of dem, and dey all has dose collars."

"Are you on speaking terms with the gentleman?"

"Huh?"

"Do you know Bat Jarvis to speak to?"

"Sure. He's me cousin."

"Well, tell him I've got the cat, and that if he wants it he'd better come round to my place. You know where I live?"

"Sure."

"Fancy you being a cousin of Bat's, Pugsy. Why did you never tell us? Are you going to join the gang some day?"

"Nope. Nothin' doin'. I'm goin' to be a cow-boy."

"Good for you. Well, you tell him when you see him. And now, my lad, out you get, because if I'm interrupted any more I shan't get through to-night."

"Sure," said Master Maloney, retiring.

"Oh, and Pugsy . . ."

"Huh?"

"Go out and get a good big basket. I shall want one to carry this animal home in."

"Sure," said Master Maloney.

CHAPTER III — AT "THE GARDENIA"

"It would ill beseem me, Comrade Jackson," said Psmith, thoughtfully sipping his coffee, "to run down the metropolis of a great and friendly nation, but candour compels me to state that New York is in some respects a singularly blighted town."

"What's the matter with it?" asked Mike.

"Too decorous, Comrade Jackson. I came over here principally, it is true, to be at your side, should you be in any way persecuted by scoundrels. But at the same time I confess that at the back of my mind there lurked a hope that stirring adventures might come my way. I had heard so much of the place. Report had it that an earnest seeker after amusement might have a tolerably spacious rag in this modern Byzantium. I thought that a few weeks here might restore that keen edge to my nervous system which the languor of the past term had in a measure blunted. I wished my visit to be a tonic rather than a sedative. I anticipated that on my return the cry would go round Cambridge, 'Psmith has been to New York. He is full of oats. For he on honey-dew hath fed, and drunk the milk of Paradise. He is hot stuff. Rah!' But what do we find?"

He paused, and lit a cigarette.

"What do we find?" he asked again.

"I don't know," said Mike. "What?"

"A very judicious query, Comrade Jackson. What, indeed? We find a town very like London. A quiet, self-respecting town, admirable to the apostle of social reform, but disappointing to one who, like myself, arrives with a brush and a little bucket of red paint, all eager for a treat. I have been here a week, and I have not seen a single citizen clubbed by a policeman. No negroes dance cake-walks in the street. No cow-boy has let off his revolver at random in Broadway. The cables flash the message across the ocean, 'Psmith is losing his illusions.'"

Mike had come to America with a team of the M.C.C. which was touring the cricket-playing section of the United States. Psmith had accompanied him in a private capacity. It was the end of their first year at Cambridge, and Mike, with a century against Oxford to his credit, had been one of the first to be invited to join the tour. Psmith, who had played cricket in a rather desultory way at the University, had not risen to these heights. He had merely taken the opportunity of Mike's visit to the other side to accompany him. Cambridge had proved pleasant to Psmith, but a trifle quiet. He had welcomed the chance of getting a change of scene.

So far the visit had failed to satisfy him. Mike, whose tastes in pleasure were simple, was delighted with everything. The cricket so far had been rather of the picnic order, but it was very pleasant; and there was no limit to the hospitality with which the visitors were treated. It was this more than anything which had caused Psmith's grave disapproval of things American. He was not a member of the team, so that the advantages of the hospitality did not reach him. He had all the disadvantages. He saw far too little of Mike. When he wished to consult his confidential secretary and adviser on some aspect of Life, that invaluable official was generally absent at dinner with the rest of the team. To-night was one of the rare occasions when Mike could get away. Psmith was becoming bored. New York is a better city than London to be alone in, but it is never pleasant to be alone in any big city.

As they sat discussing New York's shortcomings over their coffee, a young man passed them, carrying a basket, and seated himself at the next table. He was a tall, loose-jointed young man, with unkempt hair.

A waiter made an ingratiating gesture towards the basket, but the young man stopped him. "Not on your life, sonny," he said. "This stays right here." He placed it carefully on the floor beside his chair, and proceeded to order dinner.

Psmith watched him thoughtfully.

"I have a suspicion, Comrade Jackson," he said, "that this will prove to be a somewhat stout fellow. If possible, we will engage him in conversation. I wonder what he's got in the basket. I must get my Sherlock Holmes system to work. What is the most likely thing for a man to have in a basket? You would reply, in your unthinking way, 'sandwiches.' Error. A man with a basketful of sandwiches does not need to dine at restaurants. We must try again."

The young man at the next table had ordered a jug of milk to be accompanied by a saucer. These having arrived, he proceeded to lift the basket on to his lap, pour the milk into the saucer, and remove the lid from the basket. Instantly, with a yell which made the young man's table the centre of interest to all the diners, a large grey cat shot up like a rocket, and darted across the room. Psmith watched with silent interest.

It is hard to astonish the waiters at a New York restaurant, but when the cat performed this feat there was a squeal of surprise all round the room. Waiters rushed to and fro, futile but energetic. The cat, having secured a strong strategic position on the top of a large oil-painting which hung on the far wall, was expressing loud disapproval of the efforts of one of the waiters to drive it from its post with a walking-stick. The young man, seeing these manoeuvres, uttered a wrathful shout, and rushed to the rescue.

"Comrade Jackson," said Psmith, rising, "we must be in this."

When they arrived on the scene of hostilities, the young man had just possessed himself of the walking-stick, and was deep in a complex argument with the head-waiter on the ethics of the matter. The head-waiter, a stout impassive German, had taken his stand on a point of etiquette. "Id is," he said, "to bring gats into der grill-room vorbidden. No gendleman would gats into der grill-room bring. Der gendleman—"

The young man meanwhile was making enticing sounds, to which the cat was maintaining an attitude of reserved hostility. He turned furiously on the head-waiter.

"For goodness' sake," he cried, "can't you see the poor brute's scared stiff? Why don't you clear your gang of German comedians away, and give her a chance to come down?"

"Der gendleman—" argued the head-waiter.

Psmith stepped forward and touched him on the arm.

"May I have a word with you in private?"

"Zo?"

Psmith drew him away.

"You don't know who that is?" he whispered, nodding towards the young man.

"No gendleman he is," asserted the head-waiter. "Der gendleman would not der gat into—"

Psmith shook his head pityingly.

"These petty matters of etiquette are not for his Grace—but, hush, he wishes to preserve his incognito."

"Ingognito?"

"You understand. You are a man of the world, Comrade—may I call you Freddie? You understand, Comrade Freddie, that in a man in his Grace's position a few little eccentricities may be pardoned. You follow me, Frederick?"

The head-waiter's eye rested upon the young man with a new interest and respect.

"He is noble?" he inquired with awe.

"He is here strictly incognito, you understand," said Psmith warningly. The head-waiter nodded.

The young man meanwhile had broken down the cat's reserve, and was now standing with her in his arms, apparently anxious to fight all-comers in her defence. The head-waiter approached deferentially.

"Der gendleman," he said, indicating Psmith, who beamed in a friendly manner through his eye-glass, "haf everything exblained. All will now quite satisfactory be."

The young man looked inquiringly at Psmith, who winked encouragingly. The head-waiter bowed.

"Let me present Comrade Jackson," said Psmith, "the pet of our English Smart Set. I am Psmith, one of the Shropshire Psmiths. This is a great moment. Shall we be moving back? We were about to order a second instalment of coffee, to correct the effects of a fatiguing day. Perhaps you would care to join us?"

"Sure," said the alleged duke.

"This," said Psmith, when they were seated, and the head-waiter had ceased to hover, "is a great meeting. I was complaining with some acerbity to Comrade Jackson, before you introduced your very interesting performing-animal speciality, that things in New York were too quiet, too decorous. I have an inkling, Comrade—"

"Windsor's my name."

"I have an inkling, Comrade Windsor, that we see eye to eye on the subject."

"I guess that's right. I was raised in the plains, and I lived in Kentucky a while. There's more doing there in a day than there is here in a month. Say, how did you fix it with the old man?"

"With Comrade Freddie? I have a certain amount of influence with him. He is content to order his movements in the main by my judgment. I assured him that all would be well, and he yielded." Psmith gazed with interest at the cat, which was lapping milk from the saucer. "Are you training that animal for a show of some kind, Comrade Windsor, or is it a domestic pet?"

"I've adopted her. The office-boy on our paper got her away from a dog this morning, and gave her to me."

"Your paper?"

"Cosy Moments," said Billy Windsor, with a touch of shame.

"Cosy Moments?" said Psmith reflectively. "I regret that the bright little sheet has not come my way up to the present. I must seize an early opportunity of perusing it."

"Don't you do it."

"You've no paternal pride in the little journal?"

"It's bad enough to hurt," said Billy Windsor disgustedly. "If you really want to see it, come along with me to my place, and I'll show you a copy."

"It will be a pleasure," said Psmith. "Comrade Jackson, have you any previous engagement for to-night?"

"I'm not doing anything," said Mike.

"Then let us stagger forth with Comrade Windsor. While he is loading up that basket, we will be collecting our hats. . . . I am not half sure, Comrade Jackson," he added, as they walked out, "that Comrade Windsor may not prove to be the genial spirit for whom I have been searching. If you could give me your undivided company, I should ask no more. But with you constantly away, mingling with the gay throng, it is imperative that I have some solid man to accompany me in my ramblings hither and thither. It is possible that Comrade Windsor may possess the qualifications necessary for the post. But here he comes. Let us foregather with him and observe him in private life before arriving at any premature decision."

CHAPTER IV — BAT JARVIS

Billy Windsor lived in a single room on East Fourteenth Street. Space in New York is valuable, and the average bachelor's apartments consist of one room with a bathroom opening off it. During the daytime this one room loses all traces of being used for sleeping purposes at night. Billy Windsor's room was very much like a public-school study. Along one wall ran a settee. At night this became a bed; but in the daytime it was a settee and nothing but a settee. There was no space for a great deal of furniture. There was one rocking-chair, two ordinary chairs, a table, a book-stand, a typewriter—nobody uses pens in New York—and on the walls a mixed collection of photographs, drawings, knives, and skins, relics of their owner's prairie days. Over the door was the head of a young bear.

Billy's first act on arriving in this sanctum was to release the cat, which, having moved restlessly about for some moments, finally came to the conclusion that there was no means of getting out, and settled itself on a corner of the settee. Psmith, sinking gracefully down beside it, stretched out his legs and lit a cigarette. Mike took one of the ordinary chairs; and Billy Windsor, planting himself in the rocker, began to rock rhythmically to and fro, a performance which he kept up untiringly all the time.

"A peaceful scene," observed Psmith. "Three great minds, keen, alert, restless during business hours, relax. All is calm and pleasant chit-chat. You have snug quarters up here, Comrade Windsor. I hold that there is nothing like one's own roof-tree. It is a great treat to one who, like myself, is located in one of these vast caravanserai—to be exact, the Astor—to pass a few moments in the quiet privacy of an apartment such as this."

"It's beastly expensive at the Astor," said Mike.

"The place has that drawback also. Anon, Comrade Jackson, I think we will hunt around for some such cubby-hole as this, built for two. Our nervous systems must be conserved."

"On Fourth Avenue," said Billy Windsor, "you can get quite good flats very cheap. Furnished, too. You should move there. It's not much of a neighbourhood. I don't know if you mind that?"

"Far from it, Comrade Windsor. It is my aim to see New York in all its phases. If a certain amount of harmless revelry can be whacked out of Fourth Avenue, we must dash there with the vim of highly-trained smell-dogs. Are you with me, Comrade Jackson?"

"All right," said Mike.

"And now, Comrade Windsor, it would be a pleasure to me to peruse that little journal of which you spoke. I have had so few opportunities of getting into touch with the literature of this great country."

Billy Windsor stretched out an arm and pulled a bundle of papers from the book-stand. He tossed them on to the settee by Psmith's side.

"There you are," he said, "if you really feel like it. Don't say I didn't warn you. If you've got the nerve, read on."

Psmith had picked up one of the papers when there came a shuffling of feet in the passage outside, followed by a knock upon the door. The next moment there appeared in the doorway a short, stout young man. There was an indescribable air of toughness about him, partly due to the fact that he wore his hair in a well-oiled fringe almost down to his eyebrows, which gave him the appearance of having no forehead at all. His eyes were small and set close together. His mouth was wide, his jaw prominent. Not, in short, the sort of man you would have picked out on sight as a model citizen.

His entrance was marked by a curious sibilant sound, which, on acquaintance, proved to be a whistled tune. During the interview which followed, except when he was speaking, the visitor whistled softly and unceasingly.

"Mr. Windsor?" he said to the company at large.

Psmith waved a hand towards the rocking-chair. "That," he said, "is Comrade Windsor. To your right is Comrade Jackson, England's favourite son. I am Psmith."

The visitor blinked furtively, and whistled another tune. As he looked round the room, his eye fell on the cat. His face lit up.

"Say!" he said, stepping forward, and touching the cat's collar, "mine, mister."

"Are you Bat Jarvis?" asked Windsor with interest.

"Sure," said the visitor, not without a touch of complacency, as of a monarch abandoning his incognito.

For Mr. Jarvis was a celebrity.

By profession he was a dealer in animals, birds, and snakes. He had a fancier's shop in Groome street, in the heart of the Bowery. This was on the ground-floor. His living abode was in the upper story of that house, and it was there that he kept the twenty-three cats whose necks were adorned with leather collars, and whose numbers had so recently been reduced to twenty-two. But it was not the fact that he possessed twenty-three cats with leather collars that made Mr. Jarvis a celebrity.

A man may win a purely local reputation, if only for eccentricity, by such means. But Mr. Jarvis's reputation was far from being purely local. Broadway knew him, and the Tenderloin. Tammany Hall knew him. Long Island City knew him. In the underworld of New York his name was a by-word. For Bat Jarvis was the leader of the famous Groome Street Gang, the most noted of all New York's collections of Apaches. More, he was the founder and originator of it. And, curiously enough, it had come into being from motives of sheer benevolence. In Groome Street in those days there had been a dance-hall, named the Shamrock and presided over by one Maginnis, an Irishman and a friend of Bat's. At the Shamrock nightly dances were given and well attended by the youth of the neighbourhood at ten cents a head. All might have been well, had it not been for certain other youths of the neighbourhood who did not dance and so had to seek other means of getting rid of their surplus energy. It was the practice of these light-hearted sportsmen to pay their ten cents for admittance, and once in, to make hay. And this habit, Mr. Maginnis found, was having a marked effect on his earnings. For genuine lovers of the dance fought shy of a place where at any moment Philistines might burst in and break heads and furniture. In this crisis the proprietor thought of his friend Bat Jarvis. Bat at that time had a solid reputation as a man of his hands. It is true that, as his detractors pointed out, he had killed no one—a defect which he had subsequently corrected; but his admirers based his claim to respect on his many meritorious performances with fists and with the black-jack. And Mr. Maginnis for one held him in the very highest esteem. To Bat accordingly he went, and laid his painful case before him. He offered him a handsome salary to be on hand at the nightly dances and check undue revelry by his own robust methods. Bat had accepted the offer. He had gone to Shamrock Hall; and with him, faithful adherents, had gone such stalwarts as Long Otto, Red Logan, Tommy Jefferson, and Pete Brodie. Shamrock Hall became a place of joy and order; and—more important still—the nucleus of the Groome Street Gang had been formed. The work progressed. Off-shoots of the main gang sprang up here and there about the East Side. Small thieves, pickpockets and the like, flocked to Mr. Jarvis as their tribal leader and protector and he protected them. For he, with his followers, were of use to the politicians. The New York gangs, and especially the Groome Street Gang, have brought to a fine art the gentle practice of "repeating"; which, broadly speaking, is the art of voting a number of different times at different polling-stations on election days. A man who can vote, say, ten times in a single day for you, and who controls a great number of followers who are also prepared, if they like you, to vote ten times in a single day for you, is worth cultivating. So the politicians passed the word to the police, and the police left the Groome Street Gang unmolested and they waxed fat and flourished.

Such was Bat Jarvis.

* * *

"Pipe de collar," said Mr. Jarvis, touching the cat's neck. "Mine, mister."

"Pugsy said it must be," said Billy Windsor. "We found two fellows setting a dog on to it, so we took it in for safety."

Mr. Jarvis nodded approval.

"There's a basket here, if you want it," said Billy.

"Nope. Here, kit."

Mr. Jarvis stooped, and, still whistling softly, lifted the cat. He looked round the company, met Psmith's eye-glass, was transfixed by it for a moment, and finally turned again to Billy Windsor.

"Say!" he said, and paused. "Obliged," he added.

He shifted the cat on to his left arm, and extended his right hand to Billy.

"Shake!" he said.

Billy did so.

Mr. Jarvis continued to stand and whistle for a few moments more.

"Say!" he said at length, fixing his roving gaze once more upon Billy. "Obliged. Fond of de kit, I am."

Psmith nodded approvingly.

"And rightly," he said. "Rightly, Comrade Jarvis. She is not unworthy of your affection. A most companionable animal, full of the highest spirits. Her knockabout act in the restaurant would have satisfied the most jaded critic. No diner-out can afford to be without such a cat. Such a cat spells death to boredom."

Mr. Jarvis eyed him fixedly, as if pondering over his remarks. Then he turned to Billy again.

"Say!" he said. "Any time you're in bad. Glad to be of service. You know the address. Groome Street. Bat Jarvis. Good night. Obliged."

He paused and whistled a few more bars, then nodded to Psmith and Mike, and left the room. They heard him shuffling downstairs.

"A blithe spirit," said Psmith. "Not garrulous, perhaps, but what of that? I am a man of few words myself. Comrade Jarvis's massive silences appeal to me. He seems to have taken a fancy to you, Comrade Windsor."

Billy Windsor laughed.

"I don't know that he's just the sort of side-partner I'd go out of my way to choose, from what I've heard about him. Still, if one got mixed up with any of that East-Side crowd, he would be a mighty useful friend to have. I guess there's no harm done by getting him grateful."

"Assuredly not," said Psmith. "We should not despise the humblest. And now, Comrade Windsor," he said, taking up the paper again, "let me concentrate myself tensely on this very entertaining little journal of yours. Comrade Jackson, here is one for you. For sound, clear-headed criticism," he added to Billy, "Comrade Jackson's name is a by-word in our English literary salons. His opinion will be both of interest and of profit to you, Comrade Windsor."

CHAPTER V — PLANNING IMPROVEMENTS

"By the way," said Psmith, "what is your exact position on this paper? Practically, we know well, you are its back-bone, its life-blood; but what is your technical position? When your proprietor is congratulating himself on having secured the ideal man for your job, what precise job does he congratulate himself on having secured the ideal man for?"

"I'm sub-editor."

"Merely sub? You deserve a more responsible post than that, Comrade Windsor. Where is your proprietor? I must buttonhole him and point out to him what a wealth of talent he is allowing to waste itself. You must have scope."

"He's in Europe. At Carlsbad, or somewhere. He never comes near the paper. He just sits tight and draws the profits. He lets the editor look after things. Just at present I'm acting as editor."

"Ah! then at last you have your big chance. You are free, untrammelled."

"You bet I'm not," said Billy Windsor. "Guess again. There's no room for developing free untrammelled ideas on this paper. When you've looked at it, you'll see that each page is run by some one. I'm simply the fellow who minds the shop."

Psmith clicked his tongue sympathetically. "It is like setting a gifted French chef to wash up dishes," he said. "A man of your undoubted powers, Comrade Windsor, should have more scope. That is the cry, 'more scope!' I must look into this matter. When I gaze at your broad, bulging forehead, when I see the clear light of intelligence in your eyes, and hear the grey matter splashing restlessly about in your cerebellum, I say to myself without hesitation, 'Comrade Windsor must have more scope.'" He looked at Mike, who was turning over the leaves of his copy of Cosy Moments in a sort of dull despair. "Well, Comrade Jackson, and what is your verdict?"

Mike looked at Billy Windsor. He wished to be polite, yet he could find nothing polite to say. Billy interpreted the look.

"Go on," he said. "Say it. It can't be worse than what I think."

"I expect some people would like it awfully," said Mike.

"They must, or they wouldn't buy it. I've never met any of them yet, though."

Psmith was deep in Luella Granville Waterman's "Moments in the Nursery." He turned to Billy Windsor.

"Luella Granville Waterman," he said, "is not by any chance your nom-de-plume, Comrade Windsor?"

"Not on your life. Don't think it."

"I am glad," said Psmith courteously. "For, speaking as man to man, I must confess that for sheer, concentrated bilge she gets away with the biscuit with almost insolent ease. Luella Granville Waterman must go."

"How do you mean?"

"She must go," repeated Psmith firmly. "Your first act, now that you have swiped the editorial chair, must be to sack her."

"But, say, I can't. The editor thinks a heap of her stuff."

"We cannot help his troubles. We must act for the good of the paper. Moreover, you said, I think, that he was away?"

"So he is. But he'll come back."

"Sufficient unto the day, Comrade Windsor. I have a suspicion that he will be the first to approve your action. His holiday will have cleared his brain. Make a note of improvement number one—the sacking of Luella Granville Waterman."

"I guess it'll be followed pretty quick by improvement number two—the sacking of William Windsor. I can't go monkeying about with the paper that way."

Psmith reflected for a moment.

"Has this job of yours any special attractions for you, Comrade Windsor?"

"I guess not."

"As I suspected. You yearn for scope. What exactly are your ambitions?"

"I want to get a job on one of the big dailies. I don't see how I'm going to fix it, though, at the present rate."

Psmith rose, and tapped him earnestly on the chest.

"Comrade Windsor, you have touched the spot. You are wasting the golden hours of your youth. You must move. You must hustle. You must make Windsor of Cosy Moments a name to conjure with. You must boost this sheet up till New York rings with your exploits. On the present lines that is impossible. You must strike out a line for yourself. You must show the world that even Cosy Moments cannot keep a good man down."

He resumed his seat.

"How do you mean?" said Billy Windsor.

Psmith turned to Mike.

"Comrade Jackson, if you were editing this paper, is there a single feature you would willingly retain?"

"I don't think there is," said Mike. "It's all pretty bad rot."

"My opinion in a nutshell," said Psmith, approvingly. "Comrade Jackson," he explained, turning to Billy, "has a secure reputation on the other side for the keenness and lucidity of his views upon literature. You may safely build upon him. In England when Comrade Jackson says 'Turn' we all turn. Now, my views on the matter are as follows. Cosy Moments, in my opinion (worthless, were it not backed by such a virtuoso as Comrade Jackson), needs more snap, more go. All these putrid pages must disappear. Letters must be despatched tomorrow morning, informing Luella Granville Waterman and the others (and in particular B. Henderson Asher, who from a cursory glance strikes me as an ideal candidate for a lethal chamber) that, unless they cease their contributions instantly, you will be compelled to place yourself under police protection. After that we can begin to move."

Billy Windsor sat and rocked himself in his chair without replying. He was trying to assimilate this idea. So far the grandeur of it had dazed him. It was too spacious, too revolutionary. Could it be done? It would undoubtedly mean the sack when Mr. J. Fillken Wilberfloss returned and found the apple of his eye torn asunder and, so to speak, deprived of its choicest pips. On the other hand . . . His brow suddenly cleared. After all, what was the sack? One crowded hour of glorious life is worth an age without a name, and he would have no name as long as he clung to his present position. The editor would be away ten weeks. He would have ten weeks in which to try himself out. Hope leaped within him. In ten weeks he could change Cosy Moments into a real live paper. He wondered that the idea had not occurred to him before. The trifling fact that the despised journal was the property of Mr. Benjamin White, and that he had no right whatever to tinker with it without that gentleman's approval, may have occurred to him, but, if it did, it occurred so momentarily that he did not notice it. In these crises one cannot think of everything.

"I'm on," he said, briefly.

Psmith smiled approvingly.

"That," he said, "is the right spirit. You will, I fancy, have little cause to regret your decision. Fortunately, if I may say so, I happen to have a certain amount of leisure just now. It is at your disposal. I have had little experience of journalistic work, but I foresee that I shall be a quick learner. I will become your sub-editor, without salary."

"Bully for you," said Billy Windsor.

"Comrade Jackson," continued Psmith, "is unhappily more fettered. The exigencies of his cricket tour will compel him constantly to be gadding about, now to Philadelphia, now to Saskatchewan, anon to Onehorseville, Ga. His services, therefore, cannot be relied upon continuously. From him, accordingly, we shall expect little but moral support. An occasional congratulatory telegram. Now and then a bright smile of approval. The bulk of the work will devolve upon our two selves."

"Let it devolve," said Billy Windsor, enthusiastically.

"Assuredly," said Psmith. "And now to decide upon our main scheme. You, of course, are the editor, and my suggestions are merely suggestions, subject to your approval. But, briefly, my idea is that Cosy Moments should become red-hot stuff. I could wish its tone to be such that the public will wonder why we do not print it on asbestos. We must chronicle all the live events of the day, murders, fires, and the like in a manner which will make our readers' spines thrill. Above all, we must be the guardians of the People's rights. We must be a search-light, showing up the dark spot in the souls of those who would endeavour in any way to do the PEOPLE in the eye. We must detect the wrong-doer, and deliver him such a series of resentful buffs that he will abandon his little games and become a model citizen. The details of the campaign we must think out after, but I fancy that, if we follow those main lines, we shall produce a bright, readable little sheet which will in a measure make this city sit up and take notice. Are you with me, Comrade Windsor?"

"Surest thing you know," said Billy with fervour.

CHAPTER VI — THE TENEMENTS

To alter the scheme of a weekly from cover to cover is not a task that is completed without work. The dismissal of Cosy Moments' entire staff of contributors left a gap in the paper which had to be filled, and owing to the nearness of press day there was no time to fill it before the issue of the next number. The editorial staff had to be satisfied with heading every page with the words "Look out! Look out!! Look out!!! See foot of page!!!!" printing in the space at the bottom the legend, "Next Week! See Editorial!" and compiling in conjunction a snappy editorial, setting forth the proposed changes. This was largely the work of Psmith.

"Comrade Jackson," he said to Mike, as they set forth one evening in search of their new flat, "I fancy I have found my metier. Commerce, many considered, was the line I should take; and doubtless, had I stuck to that walk in life, I should soon have become a financial magnate. But something seemed to whisper to me, even in the midst of my triumphs in the New Asiatic Bank, that there were other fields. For the moment it seems to me that I have found the job for which nature specially designed me. At last I have Scope. And without Scope, where are we? Wedged tightly in among the ribstons. There are some very fine passages in that editorial. The last paragraph, beginning 'Cosy Moments cannot be muzzled,' in particular. I like it. It strikes the right note. It should stir the blood of a free and independent people till they sit in platoons on the doorstep of our office, waiting for the next number to appear."

"How about that next number?" asked Mike. "Are you and Windsor going to fill the whole paper yourselves?"

"By no means. It seems that Comrade Windsor knows certain stout fellows, reporters on other papers, who will be delighted to weigh in with stuff for a moderate fee."

"How about Luella What's-her-name and the others? How have they taken it?"

"Up to the present we have no means of ascertaining. The letters giving them the miss-in-baulk in no uncertain voice were only despatched yesterday. But it cannot affect us how they writhe beneath the blow. There is no reprieve."

Mike roared with laughter.

"It's the rummiest business I ever struck," he said. "I'm jolly glad it's not my paper. It's pretty lucky for you two lunatics that the proprietor's in Europe."

Psmith regarded him with pained surprise.

"I do not understand you, Comrade Jackson. Do you insinuate that we are not acting in the proprietor's best interests? When he sees the receipts, after we have handled the paper for a while, he will go singing about his hotel. His beaming smile will be a by-word in Carlsbad. Visitors will be shown it as one of the sights. His only doubt will be whether to send his money to the bank or keep it in tubs and roll in it. We are on to a big thing, Comrade Jackson. Wait till you see our first number."

"And how about the editor? I should think that first number would bring him back foaming at the mouth."

"I have ascertained from Comrade Windsor that there is nothing to fear from that quarter. By a singular stroke of good fortune Comrade Wilberfloss—his name is Wilberfloss—has been ordered complete rest during his holiday. The kindly medico, realising the fearful strain inflicted by reading Cosy Moments in its old form, specifically mentioned that the paper was to be withheld from him until he returned."

"And when he does return, what are you going to do?"

"By that time, doubtless, the paper will be in so flourishing a state that he will confess how wrong his own methods were and adopt ours without a murmur. In the meantime, Comrade Jackson, I would call your attention to the fact that we seem to have lost our way. In the exhilaration of this little chat, our footsteps have wandered. Where we are, goodness only knows. I can only say that I shouldn't care to have to live here."

"There's a name up on the other side of that lamp-post."

"Let us wend in that direction. Ah, Pleasant Street? I fancy that the master-mind who chose that name must have had the rudiments of a sense of humour."

It was indeed a repellent neighbourhood in which they had arrived. The New York slum stands in a class of its own. It is unique. The height of the houses and the narrowness of the streets seem to condense its unpleasantness. All the smells and noises, which are many and varied, are penned up in a sort of canyon, and gain in vehemence from the fact. The masses of dirty clothes hanging from the fire-escapes increase the depression. Nowhere in the city does one realise so fully the disadvantages of a lack of space. New York, being an island, has had no room to spread. It is a town of human sardines. In the poorer quarters the congestion is unbelievable.

Psmith and Mike picked their way through the groups of ragged children who covered the roadway. There seemed to be thousands of them.

"Poor kids!" said Mike. "It must be awful living in a hole like this."

Psmith said nothing. He was looking thoughtful. He glanced up at the grimy buildings on each side. On the lower floors one could see into dark, bare rooms. These were the star apartments of the tenement-houses, for they opened on to the street, and so got a little light and air. The imagination jibbed at the thought of the back rooms.

"I wonder who owns these places," said Psmith. "It seems to me that there's what you might call room for improvement. It wouldn't be a scaly idea to turn that Cosy Moments search-light we were talking about on to them."

They walked on a few steps.

"Look here," said Psmith, stopping. "This place makes me sick. I'm going in to have a look round. I expect some muscular householder will resent the intrusion and boot us out, but we'll risk it."

Followed by Mike, he turned in at one of the doors. A group of men leaning against the opposite wall looked at them without curiosity. Probably they took them for reporters hunting for a story. Reporters were the only tolerably well-dressed visitors Pleasant Street ever entertained.

It was almost pitch dark on the stairs. They had to feel their way up. Most of the doors were shut but one on the second floor was ajar. Through the opening they had a glimpse of a number of women sitting round on boxes. The floor was covered with little heaps of linen. All the women were sewing. Mike, stumbling in the darkness, almost fell against the door. None of the women looked up at the noise. Time was evidently money in Pleasant Street.

On the fourth floor there was an open door. The room was empty. It was a good representative Pleasant Street back room. The architect in this case had given rein to a passion for originality. He had constructed the room without a window of any sort whatsoever. There was a square opening in the door. Through this, it was to be presumed, the entire stock of air used by the occupants was supposed to come.

They stumbled downstairs again and out into the street. By contrast with the conditions indoors the street seemed spacious and breezy.

"This," said Psmith, as they walked on, "is where Cosy Moments gets busy at a singularly early date."

"What are you going to do?" asked Mike.

"I propose, Comrade Jackson," said Psmith, "if Comrade Windsor is agreeable, to make things as warm for the owner of this place as I jolly well know how. What he wants, of course," he proceeded in the tone of a family doctor prescribing for a patient, "is disembowelling. I fancy, however, that a mawkishly sentimental legislature will prevent our performing that national service. We must endeavour to do what we can by means of kindly criticism in the paper. And now, having settled that important point, let us try and get out of this place of wrath, and find Fourth Avenue."

CHAPTER VII — VISITORS AT THE OFFICE

On the following morning Mike had to leave with the team for Philadelphia. Psmith came down to the ferry to see him off, and hung about moodily until the time of departure.

"It is saddening me to a great extent, Comrade Jackson," he said, "this perpetual parting of the ways. When I think of the happy moments we have spent hand-in-hand across the seas, it fills me with a certain melancholy to have you flitting off in this manner without me. Yet there is another side to the picture. To me there is something singularly impressive in our unhesitating reply to the calls of Duty. Your Duty summons you to Philadelphia, to knock the cover off the local bowling. Mine retains me here, to play my part in the great work of making New York sit up. By the time you return, with a century or two, I trust, in your bag, the good work should, I fancy, be getting something of a move on. I will complete the arrangements with regard to the flat."

After leaving Pleasant Street they had found Fourth Avenue by a devious route, and had opened negotiations for a large flat near Thirtieth Street. It was immediately above a saloon, which was something of a drawback, but the landlord had assured them that the voices of the revellers did not penetrate to it.

* * *

When the ferry-boat had borne Mike off across the river, Psmith turned to stroll to the office of Cosy Moments. The day was fine, and on the whole, despite Mike's desertion, he felt pleased with life. Psmith's was a nature which required a certain amount of stimulus in the way of gentle excitement; and it seemed to him that the conduct of the remodelled Cosy Moments might supply this. He liked Billy Windsor, and looked forward to a not unenjoyable time till Mike should return.

The offices of Cosy Moments were in a large building in the street off Madison Avenue. They consisted of a sort of outer lair, where Pugsy Maloney spent his time reading tales of life in the prairies and heading off undesirable visitors; a small room, which would have belonged to the stenographer if Cosy Moments had possessed one; and a larger room beyond, which was the editorial sanctum.

As Psmith passed through the front door, Pugsy Maloney rose.

"Say!" said Master Maloney.

"Say on, Comrade Maloney," said Psmith.

"Dey're in dere."

"Who, precisely?"

"A whole bunch of dem."

Psmith inspected Master Maloney through his eye-glass. "Can you give me any particulars?" he asked patiently. "You are well-meaning, but vague, Comrade Maloney. Who are in there?"

"De whole bunch of dem. Dere's Mr. Asher and the Rev. Philpotts and a gazebo what calls himself Waterman and about 'steen more of dem."

A faint smile appeared upon Psmith's face.

"And is Comrade Windsor in there, too, in the middle of them?"

"Nope. Mr. Windsor's out to lunch."

"Comrade Windsor knows his business. Why did you let them in?"

"Sure, dey just butted in," said Master Maloney complainingly. "I was sittin' here, readin' me book, when de foist of de guys blew in. 'Boy,' says he, 'is de editor in?' 'Nope,' I says. 'I'll go in an' wait,' says he. 'Nuttin' doin',' says I. 'Nix on de goin' in act.' I might as well have saved me breat'. In he butts, and he's in der now. Well, in about t'ree minutes along comes another gazebo. 'Boy,' says he, 'is de editor in?' 'Nope,' I says. 'I'll wait,' says he lightin' out for de door. Wit dat I sees de proposition's too fierce for muh. I can't keep dese big husky guys out if dey's for buttin' in. So when de rest of de bunch comes along, I don't try to give dem de t'run down. I says, 'Well, gents,' I says, 'it's up to youse. De editor ain't in, but if youse wants to join de giddy t'rong, push t'roo inter de inner room. I can't be boddered.'"

"And what more could you have said?" agreed Psmith approvingly. "Tell me, Comrade Maloney, what was the general average aspect of these determined spirits?"

"Huh?"

"Did they seem to you to be gay, lighthearted? Did they carol snatches of song as they went? Or did they appear to be looking for some one with a hatchet?"

"Dey was hoppin'-mad, de whole bunch of dem."

"As I suspected. But we must not repine, Comrade Maloney. These trifling contretemps are the penalties we pay for our high journalistic aims. I will interview these merchants. I fancy that with the aid of the Diplomatic Smile and the Honeyed Word I may manage to pull through. It is as well, perhaps, that Comrade Windsor is out. The situation calls for the handling of a man of delicate culture and nice tact. Comrade Windsor would probably have endeavoured to clear the room with a chair. If he should arrive during the seance, Comrade Maloney, be so good as to inform him of the state of affairs, and tell him not to come in. Give him my compliments, and tell him to go out and watch the snowdrops growing in Madison Square Garden."

"Sure," said Master Maloney.

Then Psmith, having smoothed the nap of his hat and flicked a speck of dust from his coat-sleeve, walked to the door of the inner room and went in.

CHAPTER VIII — THE HONEYED WORD

Master Maloney's statement that "about 'steen visitors" had arrived in addition to Messrs. Asher, Waterman, and the Rev. Philpotts proved to have been due to a great extent to a somewhat feverish imagination. There were only five men in the room.

As Psmith entered, every eye was turned upon him. To an outside spectator he would have seemed rather like a very well-dressed Daniel introduced into a den of singularly irritable lions. Five pairs of eyes were smouldering with a long-nursed resentment. Five brows were corrugated with wrathful lines. Such, however, was the simple majesty of Psmith's demeanour that for a moment there was dead silence. Not a word was spoken as he paced, wrapped in thought, to the editorial chair. Stillness brooded over the room as he carefully dusted that piece of furniture, and, having done so to his satisfaction, hitched up the knees of his trousers and sank gracefully into a sitting position.

This accomplished, he looked up and started. He gazed round the room.

"Ha! I am observed!" he murmured.

The words broke the spell. Instantly, the five visitors burst simultaneously into speech.

"Are you the acting editor of this paper?"

"I wish to have a word with you, sir."

"Mr. Windsor, I presume?"

"Pardon me!"

"I should like a few moments' conversation."

The start was good and even; but the gentleman who said "Pardon me!" necessarily finished first with the rest nowhere.

Psmith turned to him, bowed, and fixed him with a benevolent gaze through his eye-glass.

"Are you Mr. Windsor, sir, may I ask?" inquired the favoured one.

The others paused for the reply.

"Alas! no," said Psmith with manly regret.

"Then who are you?"

"I am Psmith."

There was a pause.

"Where is Mr. Windsor?"

"He is, I fancy, champing about forty cents' worth of lunch at some neighbouring hostelry."

"When will he return?"

"Anon. But how much anon I fear I cannot say."

The visitors looked at each other.

"This is exceedingly annoying," said the man who had said "Pardon me!" "I came for the express purpose of seeing Mr. Windsor."

"So did I," chimed in the rest. "Same here. So did I."

Psmith bowed courteously.

"Comrade Windsor's loss is my gain. Is there anything I can do for you?"

"Are you on the editorial staff of this paper?"

"I am acting sub-editor. The work is not light," added Psmith gratuitously. "Sometimes the cry goes round, 'Can Psmith get through it all? Will his strength support his unquenchable spirit?' But I stagger on. I do not repine."

"Then maybe you can tell me what all this means?" said a small round gentleman who so far had done only chorus work.

"If it is in my power to do so, it shall be done, Comrade—I have not the pleasure of your name."

"My name is Waterman, sir. I am here on behalf of my wife, whose name you doubtless know."

"Correct me if I am wrong," said Psmith, "but I should say it, also, was Waterman."

"Luella Granville Waterman, sir," said the little man proudly. Psmith removed his eye-glass, polished it, and replaced it in his eye. He felt that he must run no risk of not seeing clearly the husband of one who, in his opinion, stood alone in literary circles as a purveyor of sheer bilge.

"My wife," continued the little man, producing an envelope and handing it to Psmith, "has received this extraordinary communication from a man signing himself W. Windsor. We are both at a loss to make head or tail of it."

Psmith was reading the letter.

"It seems reasonably clear to me," he said.

"It is an outrage. My wife has been a contributor to this journal from its foundation. Her work has given every satisfaction to Mr. Wilberfloss. And now, without the slightest warning, comes this peremptory dismissal from W. Windsor. Who is W. Windsor? Where is Mr. Wilberfloss?"

The chorus burst forth. It seemed that that was what they all wanted to know: Who was W. Windsor? Where was Mr. Wilberfloss?

"I am the Reverend Edwin T. Philpotts, sir," said a cadaverous-looking man with pale blue eyes and a melancholy face. "I have contributed 'Moments of Meditation' to this journal for a very considerable period of time."

"I have read your page with the keenest interest," said Psmith. "I may be wrong, but yours seems to me work which the world will not willingly let die."

The Reverend Edwin's frosty face thawed into a bleak smile.

"And yet," continued Psmith, "I gather that Comrade Windsor, on the other hand, actually wishes to hurry on its decease. It is these strange contradictions, these clashings of personal taste, which make up what we call life. Here we have, on the one hand—"

A man with a face like a walnut, who had hitherto lurked almost unseen behind a stout person in a serge suit, bobbed into the open, and spoke his piece.

"Where's this fellow Windsor? W. Windsor. That's the man we want to see. I've been working for this paper without a break, except when I had the mumps, for four years, and I've reason to know that my page was as widely read and appreciated as any in New York. And now up comes this Windsor fellow, if you please, and tells me in so many words the paper's got no use for me."

"These are life's tragedies," murmured Psmith.

"What's he mean by it? That's what I want to know. And that's what these gentlemen want to know—See here—"

"I am addressing—?" said Psmith.

"Asher's my name. B. Henderson Asher. I write 'Moments of Mirth.'"

A look almost of excitement came into Psmith's face, such a look as a visitor to a foreign land might wear when confronted with some great national monument. That he should be privileged to look upon the author of "Moments of Mirth" in the flesh, face to face, was almost too much.

"Comrade Asher," he said reverently, "may I shake your hand?"

The other extended his hand with some suspicion.

"Your 'Moments of Mirth,'" said Psmith, shaking it, "have frequently reconciled me to the toothache."

He reseated himself.

"Gentlemen," he said, "this is a painful case. The circumstances, as you will readily admit when you have heard all, are peculiar. You have asked me where Mr. Wilberfloss is. I do not know."

"You don't know!" exclaimed Mr. Waterman.

"I don't know. You don't know. They," said Psmith, indicating the rest with a wave of the hand, "don't know. Nobody knows. His locality is as hard to ascertain as that of a black cat in a coal-cellar on a moonless night. Shortly before I joined this journal, Mr. Wilberfloss, by his doctor's orders, started out on a holiday, leaving no address. No letters were to be forwarded. He was to enjoy complete rest. Where is he now? Who shall say? Possibly legging it down some rugged slope in the Rockies, with two bears and a wild cat in earnest pursuit. Possibly in the midst of some Florida everglade, making a noise like a piece of meat in order to snare crocodiles. Possibly in Canada, baiting moose-traps. We have no data."

Silent consternation prevailed among the audience. Finally the Rev. Edwin T. Philpotts was struck with an idea.

"Where is Mr. White?" he asked.

The point was well received.

"Yes, where's Mr. Benjamin White?" chorused the rest.

Psmith shook his head.

"In Europe. I cannot say more."

The audience's consternation deepened.

"Then, do you mean to say," demanded Mr. Asher, "that this fellow Windsor's the boss here, that what he says goes?"

Psmith bowed.

"With your customary clear-headedness, Comrade Asher, you have got home on the bull's-eye first pop. Comrade Windsor is indeed the boss. A man of intensely masterful character, he will brook no opposition. I am powerless to sway him. Suggestions from myself as to the conduct of the paper would infuriate him. He believes that radical changes are necessary in the programme of Cosy Moments, and he means to put them through if it snows. Doubtless he would gladly consider your work if it fitted in with his ideas. A snappy account of a glove-fight, a spine-shaking word-picture of a railway smash, or something on those lines, would be welcomed. But—"

"I have never heard of such a thing," said Mr. Waterman indignantly.

Psmith sighed.

"Some time ago," he said, "—how long it seems!—I remember saying to a young friend of mine of the name of Spiller, 'Comrade Spiller, never confuse the unusual with the impossible.' It is my guiding rule in life. It is unusual for the substitute-editor of a weekly paper to do a Captain Kidd act and take entire command of the journal on his own account; but is it impossible? Alas no. Comrade Windsor has done it. That is where you, Comrade Asher, and you, gentlemen, have landed yourselves squarely in the broth. You have confused the unusual with the impossible."

"But what is to be done?" cried Mr. Asher.

"I fear that there is nothing to be done, except wait. The present rigime is but an experiment. It may be that when Comrade Wilberfloss, having dodged the bears and eluded the wild cat, returns to his post at the helm of this journal, he may decide not to continue on the lines at present mapped out. He should be back in about ten weeks."

"Ten weeks!"

"I fancy that was to be the duration of his holiday. Till then my advice to you gentlemen is to wait. You may rely on me to keep a watchful eye upon your interests. When your thoughts tend to take a gloomy turn, say to yourselves, 'All is well. Psmith is keeping a watchful eye upon our interests.'"

"All the same, I should like to see this W. Windsor," said Mr. Asher.

Psmith shook his head.

"I shouldn't," he said. "I speak in your best interests. Comrade Windsor is a man of the fiercest passions. He cannot brook interference. Were you to question the wisdom of his plans, there is no knowing what might not happen. He would be the first to regret any violent action, when once he had cooled off, but would that be any consolation to his victim? I think not. Of course, if you wish it, I could arrange a meeting—"

Mr. Asher said no, he thought it didn't matter.

"I guess I can wait," he said.

"That," said Psmith approvingly, "is the right spirit. Wait. That is the watch-word. And now," he added, rising, "I wonder if a bit of lunch somewhere might not be a good thing? We have had an interesting but fatiguing little chat. Our tissues require restoring. If you gentlemen would care to join me—"

Ten minutes later the company was seated in complete harmony round a table at the Knickerbocker. Psmith, with the dignified bonhomie of a seigneur of the old school, was ordering the wine; while B. Henderson Asher, brimming over with good-humour, was relating to an attentive circle an anecdote which should have appeared in his next instalment of "Moments of Mirth."

CHAPTER IX — FULL STEAM AHEAD

When Psmith returned to the office, he found Billy Windsor in the doorway, just parting from a thick-set young man, who seemed to be expressing his gratitude to the editor for some good turn. He was shaking him warmly by the hand.

Psmith stood aside to let him pass.

"An old college chum, Comrade Windsor?" he asked.

"That was Kid Brady."

"The name is unfamiliar to me. Another contributor?"

"He's from my part of the country—Wyoming. He wants to fight any one in the world at a hundred and thirty-three pounds."

"We all have our hobbies. Comrade Brady appears to have selected a somewhat exciting one. He would find stamp-collecting less exacting."

"It hasn't given him much excitement so far, poor chap," said Billy Windsor. "He's in the championship class, and here he has been pottering about New York for a month without being able to get a fight. It's always the way in this rotten East," continued Billy, warming up as was his custom when discussing a case of oppression and injustice. "It's all graft here. You've got to let half a dozen brutes dip into every dollar you earn, or you don't get a chance. If the kid had a manager, he'd get all the fights he wanted. And the manager would get nearly all the money. I've told him that we will back him up."

"You have hit it, Comrade Windsor," said Psmith with enthusiasm. "Cosy Moments shall be Comrade Brady's manager. We will give him a much-needed boost up in our columns. A sporting section is what the paper requires more than anything."

"If things go on as they've started, what it will require still more will be a fighting-editor. Pugsy tells me you had visitors while I was out."

"A few," said Psmith. "One or two very entertaining fellows. Comrades Asher, Philpotts, and others. I have just been giving them a bite of lunch at the Knickerbocker."

"Lunch!"

"A most pleasant little lunch. We are now as brothers. I fear I have made you perhaps a shade unpopular with our late contributors; but these things must be. We must clench our teeth and face them manfully. If I were you, I think I should not drop in at the house of Comrade Asher and the rest to take pot-luck for some little time to come. In order to soothe the squad I was compelled to curse you to some extent."

"Don't mind me."

"I think I may say I didn't."

"Say, look here, you must charge up the price of that lunch to the office. Necessary expenses, you know."

"I could not dream of doing such a thing, Comrade Windsor. The whole affair was a great treat to me. I have few pleasures. Comrade Asher alone was worth the money. I found his society intensely interesting. I have always believed in the Darwinian theory. Comrade Asher confirmed my views."

They went into the inner office. Psmith removed his hat and coat.

"And now once more to work," he said. "Psmith the flaneur of Fifth Avenue ceases to exist. In his place we find Psmith the hard-headed sub-editor. Be so good as to indicate a job of work for me, Comrade Windsor. I am champing at my bit."

Billy Windsor sat down, and lit his pipe.

"What we want most," he said thoughtfully, "is some big topic. That's the only way to get a paper going. Look at Everybody's Magazine. They didn't amount to a row of beans till Lawson started his 'Frenzied Finance' articles. Directly they began, the whole country was squealing for copies. Everybody's put up their price from ten to fifteen cents, and now they lead the field."

"The country must squeal for Cosy Moments," said Psmith firmly. "I fancy I have a scheme which may not prove wholly scaly. Wandering yesterday with Comrade Jackson in a search for Fourth Avenue, I happened upon a spot called Pleasant Street. Do you know it?"

Billy Windsor nodded.

"I went down there once or twice when I was a reporter. It's a beastly place."

"It is a singularly beastly place. We went into one of the houses."

"They're pretty bad."

"Who owns them?"

"I don't know. Probably some millionaire. Those tenement houses are about as paying an investment as you can have."

"Hasn't anybody ever tried to do anything about them?"

"Not so far as I know. It's pretty difficult to get at these fellows, you see. But they're fierce, aren't they, those houses!"

"What," asked Psmith, "is the precise difficulty of getting at these merchants?"

"Well, it's this way. There are all sorts of laws about the places, but any one who wants can get round them as easy as falling off a log. The law says a tenement house is a building occupied by more than two families. Well, when there's a fuss, all the man has to do is to clear out all the families but two. Then, when the inspector fellow comes along, and says, let's say, 'Where's your running water on each floor? That's what the law says you've got to have, and here are these people having to go downstairs and out of doors to fetch their water supplies,' the landlord simply replies, 'Nothing doing. This isn't a tenement house at all. There are only two families here.' And when the fuss has blown over, back come the rest of the crowd, and things go on the same as before."

"I see," said Psmith. "A very cheery scheme."

"Then there's another thing. You can't get hold of the man who's really responsible, unless you're prepared to spend thousands ferreting out evidence. The land belongs in the first place to some corporation or other. They lease it to a lessee. When there's a fuss, they say they aren't responsible, it's up to the lessee. And he lies so low that you can't find out who he is. It's all just like the East. Everything in the East is as crooked as Pearl Street. If you want a square deal, you've got to come out Wyoming way."

"The main problem, then," said Psmith, "appears to be the discovery of the lessee, lad? Surely a powerful organ like Cosy Moments, with its vast ramifications, could bring off a thing like that?"

"I doubt it. We'll try, anyway. There's no knowing but what we may have luck."

"Precisely," said Psmith. "Full steam ahead, and trust to luck. The chances are that, if we go on long enough, we shall eventually arrive somewhere. After all, Columbus didn't know that America existed when he set out. All he knew was some highly interesting fact about an egg. What that was, I do not at the moment recall, but it bucked Columbus up like a tonic. It made him fizz ahead like a two-year-old. The facts which will nerve us to effort are two. In the first place, we know that there must be some one at the bottom of the business. Secondly, as there appears to be no law of libel whatsoever in this great and free country, we shall be enabled to haul up our slacks with a considerable absence of restraint."

"Sure," said Billy Windsor. "Which of us is going to write the first article?"

"You may leave it to me, Comrade Windsor. I am no hardened old journalist, I fear, but I have certain qualifications for the post. A young man once called at the office of a certain newspaper, and asked for a job. 'Have you any special line?' asked the editor. 'Yes,' said the bright lad, 'I am rather good at invective.' 'Any special kind of invective?' queried the man up top. 'No,' replied our hero, 'just general invective.' Such is my own case, Comrade Windsor. I am a very fair purveyor of good, general invective. And as my visit to Pleasant Street is of such recent date, I am tolerably full of my subject. Taking full advantage of the benevolent laws of this country governing libel, I fancy I will produce a screed which will make this anonymous lessee feel as if he had inadvertently seated himself upon a tin-tack. Give me pen and paper, Comrade Windsor, instruct Comrade Maloney to suspend his whistling till such time as I am better able to listen to it; and I think we have got a success."

CHAPTER X — GOING SOME

There was once an editor of a paper in the Far West who was sitting at his desk, musing pleasantly of life, when a bullet crashed through the window and embedded itself in the wall at the back of his head. A happy smile lit up the editor's face. "Ah," he said complacently, "I knew that Personal column of ours was going to be a success!"

What the bullet was to the Far West editor, the visit of Mr. Francis Parker to the offices of Cosy Moments was to Billy Windsor.

It occurred in the third week of the new rigime of the paper. Cosy Moments, under its new management, had bounded ahead like a motor-car when the throttle is opened. Incessant work had been the order of the day. Billy Windsor's hair had become more dishevelled than ever, and even Psmith had at moments lost a certain amount of his dignified calm. Sandwiched in between the painful case of Kid Brady and the matter of the tenements, which formed the star items of the paper's contents, was a mass of bright reading dealing with the events of the day. Billy Windsor's newspaper friends had turned in some fine, snappy stuff in their best Yellow Journal manner, relating to the more stirring happenings in the city. Psmith, who had constituted himself guardian of the literary and dramatic interests of the paper, had employed his gift of general invective to considerable effect, as was shown by a conversation between Master Maloney and a visitor one morning, heard through the open door.

"I wish to see the editor of this paper," said the visitor.

"Editor not in," said Master Maloney, untruthfully.

"Ha! Then when he returns I wish you to give him a message."

"Sure."

"I am Aubrey Bodkin, of the National Theatre. Give him my compliments, and tell him that Mr. Bodkin does not lightly forget."

An unsolicited testimonial which caused Psmith the keenest satisfaction.

The section of the paper devoted to Kid Brady was attractive to all those with sporting blood in them. Each week there appeared in the same place on the same page a portrait of the Kid, looking moody and important, in an attitude of self-defence, and under the portrait the legend, "Jimmy Garvin must meet this boy." Jimmy was the present holder of the light-weight title. He had won it a year before, and since then had confined himself to smoking cigars as long as walking-sticks and appearing nightly as the star in a music-hall sketch entitled "A Fight for Honour." His reminiscences were appearing weekly in a Sunday paper. It was this that gave Psmith the idea of publishing Kid Brady's autobiography in Cosy Moments, an idea which made the Kid his devoted adherent from then on. Like most pugilists, the Kid had a passion for bursting into print, and his life had been saddened up to the present by the refusal of the press to publish his reminiscences. To appear in print is the fighter's accolade. It signifies that he has arrived. Psmith extended the hospitality of page four of Cosy Moments to Kid Brady, and the latter leaped at the chance. He was grateful to Psmith for not editing his contributions. Other pugilists, contributing to other papers, groaned under the supervision of a member of the staff who cut out their best passages and altered the rest into Addisonian English. The readers of Cosy Moments got Kid Brady raw.

"Comrade Brady," said Psmith to Billy, "has a singularly pure and pleasing style. It is bound to appeal powerfully to the many-headed. Listen to this bit. Our hero is fighting Battling Jack Benson in that eminent artist's native town of Louisville, and the citizens have given their native son the Approving Hand, while receiving Comrade Brady with chilly silence. Here is the Kid on the subject: 'I looked around that house, and I seen I hadn't a friend in it. And then the gong goes, and I says to myself how I has one friend, my poor old mother way out in Wyoming, and I goes in and mixes it, and then I seen Benson losing his goat, so I ups with an awful half-scissor hook to the plexus, and in the next round I seen Benson has a chunk of yellow, and I gets in with a hay-maker and I picks up another sleep-producer from the floor and hands it him, and he takes the count all right.' . . Crisp, lucid, and to the point. That is what the public wants. If this does not bring Comrade Garvin up to the scratch, nothing will."

But the feature of the paper was the "Tenement" series. It was late summer now, and there was nothing much going on in New York. The public was consequently free to take notice. The sale of Cosy Moments proceeded briskly. As Psmith had predicted, the change of policy had the effect of improving the sales to a marked extent. Letters of complaint from old subscribers poured into the office daily. But, as Billy Windsor complacently remarked, they had paid their subscriptions, so that the money was safe whether they read the paper or not. And, meanwhile, a large new public had sprung up and was growing every week. Advertisements came trooping in. Cosy Moments, in short, was passing through an era of prosperity undreamed of in its history.

"Young blood," said Psmith nonchalantly, "young blood. That is the secret. A paper must keep up to date, or it falls behind its competitors in the race. Comrade Wilberfloss's methods were possibly sound, but too limited and archaic. They lacked ginger. We of the younger generation have our fingers more firmly on the public pulse. We read off the public's unspoken wishes as if by intuition. We know the game from A to Z."

At this moment Master Maloney entered, bearing in his hand a card.

"'Francis Parker'?" said Billy, taking it. "Don't know him."

"Nor I," said Psmith. "We make new friends daily."

"He's a guy with a tall-shaped hat," volunteered Master Maloney, "an' he's wearin' a dude suit an' shiny shoes."

"Comrade Parker," said Psmith approvingly, "has evidently not been blind to the importance of a visit to Cosy Moments. He has dressed himself in his best. He has felt, rightly, that this is no occasion for the old straw hat and the baggy flannels. I would not have it otherwise. It is the right spirit. Shall we give him audience, Comrade Windsor?"

"I wonder what he wants."

"That," said Psmith, "we shall ascertain more clearly after a personal interview. Comrade Maloney, show the gentleman in. We can give him three and a quarter minutes."

Pugsy withdrew.

Mr. Francis Parker proved to be a man who might have been any age between twenty-five and thirty-five. He had a smooth, clean-shaven face, and a cat-like way of moving. As Pugsy had stated in effect, he wore a tail-coat, trousers with a crease which brought a smile of kindly approval to Psmith's face, and patent-leather boots of pronounced shininess. Gloves and a tall hat, which he carried, completed an impressive picture.

He moved softly into the room.

"I wished to see the editor."

Psmith waved a hand towards Billy.

"The treat has not been denied you," he said. "Before you is Comrade Windsor, the Wyoming cracker-jack. He is our editor. I myself—I am Psmith—though but a subordinate, may also claim the title in a measure. Technically, I am but a sub-editor; but such is the mutual esteem in which Comrade Windsor and I hold each other that we may practically be said to be inseparable. We have no secrets from each other. You may address us both impartially. Will you sit for a space?"

He pushed a chair towards the visitor, who seated himself with the care inspired by a perfect trouser-crease. There was a momentary silence while he selected a spot on the table on which to place his hat.

"The style of the paper has changed greatly, has it not, during the past few weeks?" he said. "I have never been, shall I say, a constant reader of Cosy Moments, and I may be wrong. But is not its interest in current affairs a recent development?"

"You are very right," responded Psmith. "Comrade Windsor, a man of alert and restless temperament, felt that a change was essential if Cosy Moments was to lead public thought. Comrade Wilberfloss's methods were good in their way. I have no quarrel with Comrade Wilberfloss. But he did not lead public thought. He catered exclusively for children with water on the brain, and men and women with solid ivory skulls. Comrade Windsor, with a broader view, feels that there are other and larger publics. He refuses to content himself with ladling out a weekly dole of mental predigested breakfast food. He provides meat. He—"

"Then—excuse me—" said Mr. Parker, turning to Billy, "You, I take it, are responsible for this very vigorous attack on the tenement-house owners?"

"You can take it I am," said Billy.

Psmith interposed.

"We are both responsible, Comrade Parker. If any husky guy, as I fancy Master Maloney would phrase it, is anxious to aim a swift kick at the man behind those articles, he must distribute it evenly between Comrade Windsor and myself."

"I see." Mr. Parker paused. "They are—er—very outspoken articles," he added.

"Warm stuff," agreed Psmith. "Distinctly warm stuff."

"May I speak frankly?" said Mr. Parker.

"Assuredly, Comrade Parker. There must be no secrets, no restraint between us. We would not have you go away and say to yourself, 'Did I make my meaning clear? Was I too elusive?' Say on."

"I am speaking in your best interests."

"Who would doubt it, Comrade Parker. Nothing has buoyed us up more strongly during the hours of doubt through which we have passed than the knowledge that you wish us well."

Billy Windsor suddenly became militant. There was a feline smoothness about the visitor which had been jarring upon him ever since he first spoke. Billy was of the plains, the home of blunt speech, where you looked your man in the eye and said it quick. Mr. Parker was too bland for human consumption. He offended Billy's honest soul.

"See here," cried he, leaning forward, "what's it all about? Let's have it. If you've anything to say about those articles, say it right out. Never mind our best interests. We can look after them. Let's have what's worrying you."

Psmith waved a deprecating hand.

"Do not let us be abrupt on this happy occasion. To me it is enough simply to sit and chat with Comrade Parker, irrespective of the trend of his conversation. Still, as time is money, and this is our busy day, possibly it might be as well, sir, if you unburdened yourself as soon as convenient. Have you come to point out some flaw in those articles? Do they fall short in any way of your standard for such work?"

Mr. Parker's smooth face did not change its expression, but he came to the point.

"I should not go on with them if I were you," he said.

"Why?" demanded Billy.

"There are reasons why you should not," said Mr. Parker.

"And there are reasons why we should."

"Less powerful ones."

There proceeded from Billy a noise not describable in words. It was partly a snort, partly a growl. It resembled more than anything else the preliminary sniffing snarl a bull-dog emits before he joins battle. Billy's cow-boy blood was up. He was rapidly approaching the state of mind in which the men of the plains, finding speech unequal to the expression of their thoughts, reach for their guns.

Psmith intervened.

"We do not completely gather your meaning, Comrade Parker. I fear we must ask you to hand it to us with still more breezy frankness. Do you speak from purely friendly motives? Are you advising us to discontinue the articles merely because you fear that they will damage our literary reputation? Or are there other reasons why you feel that they should cease? Do you speak solely as a literary connoisseur? Is it the style or the subject-matter of which you disapprove?"

Mr. Parker leaned forward.

"The gentleman whom I represent—"

"Then this is no matter of your own personal taste? You are an emissary?"

"These articles are causing a certain inconvenience to the gentleman whom I represent. Or, rather, he feels that, if continued, they may do so."

"You mean," broke in Billy explosively, "that if we kick up enough fuss to make somebody start a commission to inquire into this rotten business, your friend who owns the private Hades we're trying to get improved, will have to get busy and lose some of his money by making the houses fit to live in? Is that it?"

"It is not so much the money, Mr. Windsor, though, of course, the expense would be considerable. My employer is a wealthy man."

"I bet he is," said Billy disgustedly. "I've no doubt he makes a mighty good pile out of Pleasant Street."

"It is not so much the money," repeated Mr. Parker, "as the publicity involved. I speak quite frankly. There are reasons why my employer would prefer not to come before the public just now as the owner of the Pleasant Street property. I need not go into those reasons. It is sufficient to say that they are strong ones."

"Well, he knows what to do, I guess. The moment he starts in to make those houses decent, the articles stop. It's up to him."

Psmith nodded.

"Comrade Windsor is correct. He has hit the mark and rung the bell. No conscientious judge would withhold from Comrade Windsor a cigar or a cocoanut, according as his private preference might dictate. That is the matter in a nutshell. Remove the reason for those very scholarly articles, and they cease."

Mr. Parker shook his head.

"I fear that is not feasible. The expense of reconstructing the houses makes that impossible."

"Then there's no use in talking," said Billy. "The articles will go on."

Mr. Parker coughed. A tentative cough, suggesting that the situation was now about to enter upon a more delicate phase. Billy and Psmith waited for him to begin. From their point of view the discussion was over. If it was to be reopened on fresh lines, it was for their visitor to effect that reopening.

"Now, I'm going to be frank, gentlemen," said he, as who should say, "We are all friends here. Let us be hearty." "I'm going to put my cards on the table, and see if we can't fix something up. Now, see here: We don't want unpleasantness. You aren't in this business for your healths, eh? You've got your living to make, just like everybody else, I guess. Well, see here. This is how it stands. To a certain extant, I don't mind admitting, seeing that we're being frank with one another, you two gentlemen have got us—that's to say, my employer—in a cleft stick. Frankly, those articles are beginning to attract attention, and if they go on there's going to be a lot of inconvenience for my employer. That's clear, I reckon. Well, now, here's a square proposition. How much do you want to stop those articles? That's straight. I've been frank with you, and I want you to be frank with me. What's your figure? Name it, and, if it's not too high, I guess we needn't quarrel."

He looked expectantly at Billy. Billy's eyes were bulging. He struggled for speech. He had got as far as "Say!" when Psmith interrupted him. Psmith, gazing sadly at Mr. Parker through his monocle, spoke quietly, with the restrained dignity of some old Roman senator dealing with the enemies of the Republic.

"Comrade Parker," he said, "I fear that you have allowed constant communication with the conscienceless commercialism of this worldly city to undermine your moral sense. It is useless to dangle rich bribes before our eyes. Cosy Moments cannot be muzzled. You doubtless mean well, according to your—if I may say so—somewhat murky lights, but we are not for sale, except at ten cents weekly. From the hills of Maine to the Everglades of Florida, from Sandy Hook to San Francisco, from Portland, Oregon, to Melonsquashville, Tennessee, one sentence is in every man's mouth. And what is that sentence? I give you three guesses. You give it up? It is this: 'Cosy Moments cannot be muzzled!'"

Mr. Parker rose.

"There's nothing more to be done then," he said.

"Nothing," agreed Psmith, "except to make a noise like a hoop and roll away."

"And do it quick," yelled Billy, exploding like a fire-cracker.

Psmith bowed.

"Speed," he admitted, "would be no bad thing. Frankly—if I may borrow the expression—your square proposition has wounded us. I am a man of powerful self-restraint, one of those strong, silent men, and I can curb my emotions. But I fear that Comrade Windsor's generous temperament may at any moment prompt him to start throwing ink-pots. And in Wyoming his deadly aim with the ink-pot won him among the admiring cowboys the sobriquet of Crack-Shot Cuthbert. As man to man, Comrade Parker, I should advise you to bound swiftly away."

"I'm going," said Mr. Parker, picking up his hat. "And I'll give you a piece of advice, too. Those articles are going to be stopped, and if you've any sense between you, you'll stop them yourselves before you get hurt. That's all I've got to say, and that goes."

He went out, closing the door behind him with a bang that added emphasis to his words.

"To men of nicely poised nervous organisation such as ourselves, Comrade Windsor," said Psmith, smoothing his waistcoat thoughtfully, "these scenes are acutely painful. We wince before them. Our ganglions quiver like cinematographs. Gradually recovering command of ourselves, we review the situation. Did our visitor's final remarks convey anything definite to you? Were they the mere casual badinage of a parting guest, or was there something solid behind them?"

Billy Windsor was looking serious.

"I guess he meant it all right. He's evidently working for somebody pretty big, and that sort of man would have a pull with all kinds of Thugs. We shall have to watch out. Now that they find we can't be bought, they'll try the other way. They mean business sure enough. But, by George, let 'em! We're up against a big thing, and I'm going to see it through if they put every gang in New York on to us."

"Precisely, Comrade Windsor. Cosy Moments, as I have had occasion to observe before, cannot be muzzled."

"That's right," said Billy Windsor. "And," he added, with the contented look the Far West editor must have worn as the bullet came through the window, "we must have got them scared, or they wouldn't have shown their hand that way. I guess we're making a hit. Cosy Moments is going some now."

CHAPTER XI — THE MAN AT THE ASTOR

The duties of Master Pugsy Maloney at the offices of Cosy Moments were not heavy; and he was accustomed to occupy his large store of leisure by reading narratives dealing with life in the prairies, which he acquired at a neighbouring shop at cut rates in consideration of their being shop-soiled. It was while he was engrossed in one of these, on the morning following the visit of Mr. Parker, that the seedy-looking man made his appearance. He walked in from the street, and stood before Master Maloney.

"Hey, kid," he said.

Pugsy looked up with some hauteur. He resented being addressed as "kid" by perfect strangers.

"Editor in, Tommy?" inquired the man.

Pugsy by this time had taken a thorough dislike to him. To be called "kid" was bad. The subtle insult of "Tommy" was still worse.

"Nope," he said curtly, fixing his eyes again on his book. A movement on the part of the visitor attracted his attention. The seedy man was making for the door of the inner room. Pugsy instantly ceased to be the student and became the man of action. He sprang from his seat and wriggled in between the man and the door.

"Youse can't butt in dere," he said authoritatively. "Chase yerself."

The man eyed him with displeasure.

"Fresh kid!" he observed disapprovingly.

"Fade away," urged Master Maloney.

The visitor's reply was to extend a hand and grasp Pugsy's left ear between a long finger and thumb. Since time began, small boys in every country have had but one answer for this action. Pugsy made it. He emitted a piercing squeal in which pain, fear, and resentment strove for supremacy.

The noise penetrated into the editorial sanctum, losing only a small part of its strength on the way. Psmith, who was at work on a review of a book of poetry, looked up with patient sadness.

"If Comrade Maloney," he said, "is going to take to singing as well as whistling, I fear this journal must put up its shutters. Concentrated thought will be out of the question."

A second squeal rent the air. Billy Windsor jumped up.

"Somebody must be hurting the kid," he exclaimed.

He hurried to the door and flung it open. Psmith followed at a more leisurely pace. The seedy man, caught in the act, released Master Maloney, who stood rubbing his ear with resentment written on every feature.

On such occasions as this Billy was a man of few words. He made a dive for the seedy man; but the latter, who during the preceding moment had been eyeing the two editors as if he were committing their appearance to memory, sprang back, and was off down the stairs with the agility of a Marathon runner.

"He blows in," said Master Maloney, aggrieved, "and asks is de editor dere. I tells him no, 'cos youse said youse wasn't, and he nips me by the ear when I gets busy to stop him gettin' t'roo."

"Comrade Maloney," said Psmith, "you are a martyr. What would Horatius have done if somebody had nipped him by the ear when he was holding the bridge? The story does not consider the possibility. Yet it might have made all the difference. Did the gentleman state his business?"

"Nope. Just tried to butt t'roo."

"Another of these strong silent men. The world is full of us. These are the perils of the journalistic life. You will be safer and happier when you are rounding up cows on your mustang."

"I wonder what he wanted," said Billy, when they were back again in the inner room.

"Who can say, Comrade Windsor? Possibly our autographs. Possibly five minutes' chat on general subjects."

"I don't like the look of him," said Billy.

"Whereas what Comrade Maloney objected to was the feel of him. In what respect did his look jar upon you? His clothes were poorly cut, but such things, I know, leave you unmoved."

"It seems to me," said Billy thoughtfully, "as if he came just to get a sight of us."

"And he got it. Ah, Providence is good to the poor."

"Whoever's behind those tenements isn't going to stick at any odd trifle. We must watch out. That man was probably sent to mark us down for one of the gangs. Now they'll know what we look like, and they can get after us."

"These are the drawbacks to being public men, Comrade Windsor. We must bear them manfully, without wincing."

Billy turned again to his work.

"I'm not going to wince," he said, "so's you could notice it with a microscope. What I'm going to do is to buy a good big stick. And I'd advise you to do the same."

* * *

It was by Psmith's suggestion that the editorial staff of Cosy Moments dined that night in the roof-garden at the top of the Astor Hotel.

"The tired brain," he said, "needs to recuperate. To feed on such a night as this in some low-down hostelry on the level of the street, with German waiters breathing heavily down the back of one's neck and two fiddles and a piano whacking out 'Beautiful Eyes' about three feet from one's tympanum, would be false economy. Here, fanned by cool breezes and surrounded by fair women and brave men, one may do a bit of tissue-restoring. Moreover, there is little danger up here of being slugged by our moth-eaten acquaintance of this morning. A man with trousers like his would not be allowed in. We shall probably find him waiting for us at the main entrance with a sand-bag, when we leave, but, till then—"

He turned with gentle grace to his soup.

It was a warm night, and the roof-garden was full. From where they sat they could see the million twinkling lights of the city. Towards the end of the meal, Psmith's gaze concentrated itself on the advertisement of a certain brand of ginger-ale in Times Square. It is a mass of electric light arranged in the shape of a great bottle, and at regular intervals there proceed from the bottle's mouth flashes of flame representing ginger-ale. The thing began to exercise a hypnotic effect on Psmith. He came to himself with a start, to find Billy Windsor in conversation with a waiter.

"Yes, my name's Windsor," Billy was saying.

The waiter bowed and retired to one of the tables where a young man in evening clothes was seated. Psmith recollected having seen this solitary diner looking in their direction once or twice during dinner, but the fact had not impressed him.

"What is happening, Comrade Windsor?" he inquired. "I was musing with a certain tenseness at the moment, and the rush of events has left me behind."

"Man at that table wanted to know if my name was Windsor," said Billy.

"Ah?" said Psmith, interested; "and was it?"

"Here he comes. I wonder what he wants. I don't know the man from Adam."

The stranger was threading his way between the tables.

"Can I have a word with you, Mr. Windsor?" he said.

Billy looked at him curiously. Recent events had made him wary of strangers.

"Won't you sit down?" he said.

A waiter was bringing a chair. The young man seated himself.

"By the way," added Billy; "my friend, Mr. Smith."

"Pleased to meet you," said the other.

"I don't know your name," Billy hesitated.

"Never mind about my name," said the stranger. "It won't be needed. Is Mr. Smith on your paper? Excuse my asking."

Psmith bowed. "That's all right, then. I can go ahead." He bent forward.

"Neither of you gentlemen are hard of hearing, eh?"

"In the old prairie days," said Psmith, "Comrade Windsor was known to the Indians as Boola-Ba-Na-Gosh, which, as you doubtless know, signifies Big-Chief-Who-Can-Hear-A-Fly-Clear-Its-Throat. I too can hear as well as the next man. Why?"

"That's all right, then. I don't want to have to shout it. There's some things it's better not to yell."

He turned to Billy, who had been looking at him all the while with a combination of interest and suspicion. The man might or might not be friendly. In the meantime, there was no harm in being on one's guard. Billy's experience as a cub-reporter had given him the knowledge that is only given in its entirety to police and newspaper men: that there are two New Yorks. One is a modern, well-policed city, through which one may walk from end to end without encountering adventure. The other is a city as full of sinister intrigue, of whisperings and conspiracies, of battle, murder, and sudden death in dark by-ways, as any town of mediaeval Italy. Given certain conditions, anything may happen to any one in New York. And Billy realised that these conditions now prevailed in his own case. He had come into conflict with New York's underworld. Circumstances had placed him below the surface, where only his wits could help him.

"It's about that tenement business," said the stranger.

Billy bristled. "Well, what about it?" he demanded truculently.

The stranger raised a long and curiously delicately shaped hand. "Don't bite at me," he said. "This isn't my funeral. I've no kick coming. I'm a friend."

"Yet you don't tell us your name."

"Never mind my name. If you were in my line of business, you wouldn't be so durned stuck on this name thing. Call me Smith, if you like."

"You could select no nobler pseudonym," said Psmith cordially.

"Eh? Oh, I see. Well, make it Brown, then. Anything you please. It don't signify. See here, let's get back. About this tenement thing. You understand certain parties have got it in against you?"

"A charming conversationalist, one Comrade Parker, hinted at something of the sort," said Psmith, "in a recent interview. Cosy Moments, however, cannot be muzzled."

"Well?" said Billy.

"You're up against a big proposition."

"We can look after ourselves."

"Gum! you'll need to. The man behind is a big bug."

Billy leaned forward eagerly.

"Who is he?"

The other shrugged his shoulders.

"I don't know. You wouldn't expect a man like that to give himself away."

"Then how do you know he's a big bug?"

"Precisely," said Psmith. "On what system have you estimated the size of the gentleman's bughood?"

The stranger lit a cigar.

"By the number of dollars he was ready to put up to have you done in."

Billy's eyes snapped.

"Oh?" he said. "And which gang has he given the job to?"

"I wish I could tell you. He—his agent, that is—came to Bat Jarvis."

"The cat-expert?" said Psmith. "A man of singularly winsome personality."

"Bat turned the job down."

"Why was that?" inquired Billy.

"He said he needed the money as much as the next man, but when he found out who he was supposed to lay for, he gave his job the frozen face. Said you were a friend of his and none of his fellows were going to put a finger on you. I don't know what you've been doing to Bat, but he's certainly Willie the Long-Lost Brother with you."

"A powerful argument in favour of kindness to animals!" said Psmith. "Comrade Windsor came into possession of one of Comrade Jarvis's celebrated stud of cats. What did he do? Instead of having the animal made into a nourishing soup, he restored it to its bereaved owner. Observe the sequel. He is now as a prize tortoiseshell to Comrade Jarvis."

"So Bat wouldn't stand for it?" said Billy.

"Not on his life. Turned it down without a blink. And he sent me along to find you and tell you so."

"We are much obliged to Comrade Jarvis," said Psmith.

"He told me to tell you to watch out, because another gang is dead sure to take on the job. But he said you were to know he wasn't mixed up in it. He also said that any time you were in bad, he'd do his best for you. You've certainly made the biggest kind of hit with Bat. I haven't seen him so worked up over a thing in years. Well, that's all, I reckon. Guess I'll be pushing along. I've a date to keep. Glad to have met you. Glad to have met you, Mr. Smith. Pardon me, you have an insect on your coat."

He flicked at Psmith's coat with a quick movement. Psmith thanked him gravely.

"Good night," concluded the stranger, moving off. For a few moments after he had gone, Psmith and Billy sat smoking in silence. They had plenty to think about.

"How's the time going?" asked Billy at length. Psmith felt for his watch, and looked at Billy with some sadness.

"I am sorry to say, Comrade Windsor—"

"Hullo," said Billy, "here's that man coming back again."

The stranger came up to their table, wearing a light overcoat over his dress clothes. From the pocket of this he produced a gold watch.

"Force of habit," he said apologetically, handing it to Psmith. "You'll pardon me. Good night, gentlemen, again."

CHAPTER XII — A RED TAXIMETER

The Astor Hotel faces on to Times Square. A few paces to the right of the main entrance the Times Building towers to the sky; and at the foot of this the stream of traffic breaks, forming two channels. To the right of the building is Seventh Avenue, quiet, dark, and dull. To the left is Broadway, the Great White Way, the longest, straightest, brightest, wickedest street in the world.

Psmith and Billy, having left the Astor, started to walk down Broadway to Billy's lodgings in Fourteenth Street. The usual crowd was drifting slowly up and down in the glare of the white lights.

They had reached Herald Square, when a voice behind them exclaimed, "Why, it's Mr. Windsor!"

They wheeled round. A flashily dressed man was standing with outstetched hand.

"I saw you come out of the Astor," he said cheerily. "I said to myself, 'I know that man.' Darned if I could put a name to you, though. So I just followed you along, and right here it came to me."

"It did, did it?" said Billy politely.

"It did, sir. I've never set eyes on you before, but I've seen so many photographs of you that I reckon we're old friends. I know your father very well, Mr. Windsor. He showed me the photographs. You may have heard him speak of me—Jack Lake? How is the old man? Seen him lately?"

"Not for some time. He was well when he last wrote."

"Good for him. He would be. Tough as a plank, old Joe Windsor. We always called him Joe."

"You'd have known him down in Missouri, of course?" said Billy.

"That's right. In Missouri. We were side-partners for years. Now, see here, Mr. Windsor, it's early yet. Won't you and your friend come along with me and have a smoke and a chat? I live right here in Thirty-Third Street. I'd be right glad for you to come."

"I don't doubt it," said Billy, "but I'm afraid you'll have to excuse us."

"In a hurry, are you?"

"Not in the least."

"Then come right along."

"No, thanks."

"Say, why not? It's only a step."

"Because we don't want to. Good night."

He turned, and started to walk away. The other stood for a moment, staring; then crossed the road.

Psmith broke the silence.

"Correct me if I am wrong, Comrade Windsor," he said tentatively, "but were you not a trifle—shall we say abrupt?—with the old family friend?"

Billy Windsor laughed.

"If my father's name was Joseph," he said, "instead of being William, the same as mine, and if he'd ever been in Missouri in his life, which he hasn't, and if I'd been photographed since I was a kid, which I haven't been, I might have gone along. As it was, I thought it better not to."

"These are deep waters, Comrade Windsor. Do you mean to intimate—?"

"If they can't do any better than that, we shan't have much to worry us. What do they take us for, I wonder? Farmers? Playing off a comic-supplement bluff like that on us!"

There was honest indignation in Billy's voice.

"You think, then, that if we had accepted Comrade Lake's invitation, and gone along for a smoke and a chat, the chat would not have been of the pleasantest nature?"

"We should have been put out of business."

"I have heard so much," said Psmith, thoughtfully, "of the lavish hospitality of the American."

"Taxi, sir?"

A red taximeter cab was crawling down the road at their side. Billy shook his head.

"Not that a taxi would be an unsound scheme," said Psmith.

"Not that particular one, if you don't mind."

"Something about it that offends your aesthetic taste?" queried Psmith sympathetically.

"Something about it makes my aesthetic taste kick like a mule," said Billy.

"Ah, we highly strung literary men do have these curious prejudices. We cannot help it. We are the slaves of our temperaments. Let us walk, then. After all, the night is fine, and we are young and strong."

They had reached Twenty-Third Street when Billy stopped. "I don't know about walking," he said. "Suppose we take the Elevated?"

"Anything you wish, Comrade Windsor. I am in your hands."

They cut across into Sixth Avenue, and walked up the stairs to the station of the Elevated Railway. A train was just coming in.

"Has it escaped your notice, Comrade Windsor," said Psmith after a pause, "that, so far from speeding to your lodgings, we are going in precisely the opposite direction? We are in an up-town train."

"I noticed it," said Billy briefly.

"Are we going anywhere in particular?"

"This train goes as far as Hundred and Tenth Street. We'll go up to there."

"And then?"

"And then we'll come back."

"And after that, I suppose, we'll make a trip to Philadelphia, or Chicago, or somewhere? Well, well, I am in your hands, Comrade Windsor. The night is yet young. Take me where you will. It is only five cents a go, and we have money in our purses. We are two young men out for reckless dissipation. By all means let us have it."

At Hundred and Tenth Street they left the train, went down the stairs, and crossed the street. Half-way across Billy stopped.

"What now, Comrade Windsor?" inquired Psmith patiently. "Have you thought of some new form of entertainment?"

Billy was making for a spot some few yards down the road. Looking in that direction, Psmith saw his objective. In the shadow of the Elevated there was standing a taximeter cab.

"Taxi, sir?" said the driver, as they approached.

"We are giving you a great deal of trouble," said Billy. "You must be losing money over this job. All this while you might be getting fares down-town."

"These meetings, however," urged Psmith, "are very pleasant."

"I can save you worrying," said Billy. "My address is 84 East Fourteenth Street. We are going back there now."

"Search me," said the driver, "I don't know what you're talking about."

"I thought perhaps you did," replied Billy. "Good night."

"These things are very disturbing," said Psmith, when they were in the train. "Dignity is impossible when one is compelled to be the Hunted Fawn. When did you begin to suspect that yonder merchant was doing the sleuth-hound act?"

"When I saw him in Broadway having a heart-to-heart talk with our friend from Missouri."

"He must be something of an expert at the game to have kept on our track."

"Not on your life. It's as easy as falling off a log. There are only certain places where you can get off an Elevated train. All he'd got to do was to get there before the train, and wait. I didn't expect to dodge him by taking the Elevated. I just wanted to make certain of his game."

The train pulled up at the Fourteenth Street station. In the roadway at the foot of the opposite staircase was a red taximeter cab.

CHAPTER XIII — REVIEWING THE SITUATION

Arriving at the bed-sitting-room, Billy proceeded to occupy the rocking-chair, and, as was his wont, began to rock himself rhythmically to and fro. Psmith seated himself gracefully on the couch-bed. There was a silence.

The events of the evening had been a revelation to Psmith. He had not realised before the extent of the ramifications of New York's underworld. That members of the gangs should crop up in the Astor roof-garden and in gorgeous raiment in the middle of Broadway was a surprise. When Billy Windsor had mentioned the gangs, he had formed a mental picture of low-browed hooligans, keeping carefully to their own quarter of the town. This picture had been correct, as far as it went, but it had not gone far enough. The bulk of the gangs of New York are of the hooligan class, and are rarely met with outside their natural boundaries. But each gang has its more prosperous members; gentlemen, who, like the man of the Astor roof-garden, support life by more delicate and genteel methods than the rest. The main body rely for their incomes, except at election-time, on such primitive feats as robbing intoxicated pedestrians. The aristocracy of the gangs soar higher.

It was a considerable time before Billy spoke.

"Say," he said, "this thing wants talking over."

"By all means, Comrade Windsor."

"It's this way. There's no doubt now that we're up against a mighty big proposition."

"Something of the sort would seem to be the case."

"It's like this. I'm going to see this through. It isn't only that I want to do a bit of good to the poor cusses in those tenements, though I'd do it for that alone. But, as far as I'm concerned, there's something to it besides that. If we win out, I'm going to get a job out of one of the big dailies. It'll give me just the chance I need. See what I mean? Well, it's different with you. I don't see that it's up to you to run the risk of getting yourself put out of business with a black-jack, and maybe shot. Once you get mixed up with the gangs there's no saying what's going to be doing. Well, I don't see why you shouldn't quit. All this has got nothing to do with you. You're over here on a vacation. You haven't got to make a living this side. You want to go about and have a good time, instead of getting mixed up with—"

He broke off.

"Well, that's what I wanted to say, anyway," he concluded.

Psmith looked at him reproachfully.

"Are you trying to sack me, Comrade Windsor?"

"How's that?"

"In various treatises on 'How to Succeed in Literature,'" said Psmith sadly, "which I have read from time to time, I have always found it stated that what the novice chiefly needed was an editor who believed in him. In you, Comrade Windsor, I fancied that I had found such an editor."

"What's all this about?" demanded Billy. "I'm making no kick about your work."

"I gathered from your remarks that you were anxious to receive my resignation."

"Well, I told you why. I didn't want you be black-jacked."

"Was that the only reason?"

"Sure."

"Then all is well," said Psmith, relieved. "For the moment I fancied that my literary talents had been weighed in the balance and adjudged below par. If that is all—why, these are the mere everyday risks of the young journalist's life. Without them we should be dull and dissatisfied. Our work would lose its fire. Men such as ourselves, Comrade Windsor, need a certain stimulus, a certain fillip, if they are to keep up their high standards. The knowledge that a low-browed gentleman is waiting round the corner with a sand-bag poised in air will just supply that stimulus. Also that fillip. It will give our output precisely the edge it requires."

"Then you'll stay in this thing? You'll stick to the work?"

"Like a conscientious leech, Comrade Windsor."

"Bully for you," said Billy.

It was not Psmith's habit, when he felt deeply on any subject, to exhibit his feelings; and this matter of the tenements had hit him harder than any one who did not know him intimately would have imagined. Mike would have understood him, but Billy Windsor was too recent an acquaintance. Psmith was one of those people who are content to accept most of the happenings of life in an airy spirit of tolerance. Life had been more or less of a game with him up till now. In his previous encounters with those with whom fate had brought him in contact there had been little at stake. The prize of victory had been merely a comfortable feeling of having had the best of a battle of wits; the penalty of defeat nothing worse than the discomfort of having failed to score. But this tenement business was different. Here he had touched the realities. There was something worth fighting for. His lot had been cast in pleasant places, and the sight of actual raw misery had come home to him with an added force from that circumstance. He was fully aware of the risks that he must run. The words of the man at the Astor, and still more the episodes of the family friend from Missouri and the taximeter cab, had shown him that this thing was on a different plane from anything that had happened to him before. It was a fight without the gloves, and to a finish at that. But he meant to see it through. Somehow or other those tenement houses had got to be cleaned up. If it meant trouble, as it undoubtedly did, that trouble would have to be faced.

"Now that Comrade Jarvis," he said, "showing a spirit of forbearance which, I am bound to say, does him credit, has declined the congenial task of fracturing our occiputs, who should you say, Comrade Windsor, would be the chosen substitute?"

Billy shook his head. "Now that Bat has turned up the job, it might be any one of three gangs. There are four main gangs, you know. Bat's is the biggest. But the smallest of them's large enough to put us away, if we give them the chance."

"I don't quite grasp the nice points of this matter. Do you mean that we have an entire gang on our trail in one solid mass, or will it be merely a section?"

"Well, a section, I guess, if it comes to that. Parker, or whoever fixed this thing up, would go to the main boss of the gang. If it was the Three Points, he'd go to Spider Reilly. If it was the Table Hill lot, he'd look up Dude Dawson. And so on."

"And what then?"

"And then the boss would talk it over with his own special partners. Every gang-leader has about a dozen of them. A sort of Inner Circle. They'd fix it up among themselves. The rest of the gang wouldn't know anything about it. The fewer in the game, you see, the fewer to split up the dollars."

"I see. Then things are not so black. All we have to do is to look out for about a dozen hooligans with a natural dignity in their bearing, the result of intimacy with the main boss. Carefully eluding these aristocrats, we shall win through. I fancy, Comrade Windsor, that all may yet be well. What steps do you propose to take by way of self-defence?"

"Keep out in the middle of the street, and not go off the Broadway after dark. You're pretty safe on Broadway. There's too much light for them there."

"Now that our sleuth-hound friend in the taximeter has ascertained your address, shall you change it?"

"It wouldn't do any good. They'd soon find where I'd gone to. How about yours?"

"I fancy I shall be tolerably all right. A particularly massive policeman is on duty at my very doors. So much for our private lives. But what of the day-time? Suppose these sandbag-specialists drop in at the office during business hours. Will Comrade Maloney's frank and manly statement that we are not in be sufficient to keep them out? I doubt it. All unused to the nice conventions of polite society, these rugged persons will charge through. In such circumstances good work will be hard to achieve. Your literary man must have complete quiet if he is to give the public of his best. But stay. An idea!"

"Well?"

"Comrade Brady. The Peerless Kid. The man Cosy Moments is running for the light-weight championship. We are his pugilistic sponsors. You may say that it is entirely owing to our efforts that he has obtained this match with—who exactly is the gentleman Comrade Brady fights at the Highfield Club on Friday night?"

"Cyclone Al. Wolmann, isn't it?"

"You are right. As I was saying, but for us the privilege of smiting Comrade Cyclone Al. Wolmann under the fifth rib on Friday night would almost certainly have been denied to him."

It almost seemed as if he were right. From the moment the paper had taken up his cause, Kid Brady's star had undoubtedly been in the ascendant. People began to talk about him as a likely man. Edgren, in the Evening World, had a paragraph about his chances for the light-weight title. Tad, in the Journal, drew a picture of him. Finally, the management of the Highfield Club had signed him for a ten-round bout with Mr. Wolmann. There were, therefore, reasons why Cosy Moments should feel a claim on the Kid's services.

"He should," continued Psmith, "if equipped in any degree with finer feelings, be bubbling over with gratitude towards us. 'But for Cosy Moments,' he should be saying to himself, 'where should I be? Among the also-rans.' I imagine that he will do any little thing we care to ask of him. I suggest that we approach Comrade Brady, explain the facts of the case, and offer him at a comfortable salary the post of fighting-editor of Cosy Moments. His duties will be to sit in the room opening out of ours, girded as to the loins and full of martial spirit, and apply some of those half-scissor hooks of his to the persons of any who overcome the opposition of Comrade Maloney. We, meanwhile, will enjoy that leisure and freedom from interruption which is so essential to the artist."

"It's not a bad idea," said Billy.

"It is about the soundest idea," said Psmith, "that has ever been struck. One of your newspaper friends shall supply us with tickets, and Friday night shall see us at the Highfield."

CHAPTER XIV — THE HIGHFIELD

Far up at the other end of the island, on the banks of the Harlem River, there stands the old warehouse which modern progress has converted into the Highfield Athletic and Gymnastic Club. The imagination, stimulated by the title, conjures up a sort of National Sporting Club, with pictures on the walls, padding on the chairs, and a sea of white shirt-fronts from roof to floor. But the Highfield differs in some respects from this fancy picture. Indeed, it would be hard to find a respect in which it does not differ. But these names are so misleading. The title under which the Highfield used to be known till a few years back was "Swifty Bob's." It was a good, honest title. You knew what to expect; and if you attended siances at Swifty Bob's you left your gold watch and your little savings at home. But a wave of anti-pugilistic feeling swept over the New York authorities. Promoters of boxing contests found themselves, to their acute disgust, raided by the police. The industry began to languish. People avoided places where at any moment the festivities might be marred by an inrush of large men in blue uniforms armed with locust-sticks.

And then some big-brained person suggested the club idea, which stands alone as an example of American dry humour. There are now no boxing contests in New York. Swifty Bob and his fellows would be shocked at the idea of such a thing. All that happens now is exhibition sparring bouts between members of the club. It is true that next day the papers very tactlessly report the friendly exhibition spar as if it had been quite a serious affair, but that is not the fault of Swifty Bob.

Kid Brady, the chosen of Cosy Moments, was billed for a "ten-round exhibition contest," to be the main event of the evening's entertainment. No decisions are permitted at these clubs. Unless a regrettable accident occurs, and one of the sparrers is knocked out, the verdict is left to the newspapers next day. It is not uncommon to find a man win easily in the World, draw in the American, and be badly beaten in the Evening Mail. The system leads to a certain amount of confusion, but it has the merit of offering consolation to a much-smitten warrior.

The best method of getting to the Highfield is by the Subway. To see the Subway in its most characteristic mood one must travel on it during the rush-hour, when its patrons are packed into the carriages in one solid jam by muscular guards and policemen, shoving in a manner reminiscent of a Rugby football scrum. When Psmith and Billy entered it on the Friday evening, it was comparatively empty. All the seats were occupied, but only a few of the straps and hardly any of the space reserved by law for the conductor alone.

Conversation on the Subway is impossible. The ingenious gentlemen who constructed it started with the object of making it noisy. Not ordinarily noisy, like a ton of coal falling on to a sheet of tin, but really noisy. So they fashioned the pillars of thin steel, and the sleepers of thin wood, and loosened all the nuts, and now a Subway train in motion suggests a prolonged dynamite explosion blended with the voice of some great cataract.

Psmith, forced into temporary silence by this combination of noises, started to make up for lost time on arriving in the street once more.

"A thoroughly unpleasant neighbourhood," he said, critically surveying the dark streets. "I fear me, Comrade Windsor, that we have been somewhat rash in venturing as far into the middle west as this. If ever there was a blighted locality where low-browed desperadoes might be expected to spring with whoops of joy from every corner, this blighted locality is that blighted locality. But we must carry on. In which direction, should you say, does this arena lie?"

It had begun to rain as they left Billy's lodgings. Psmith turned up the collar of his Burberry.

"We suffer much in the cause of Literature," he said. "Let us inquire of this genial soul if he knows where the Highfield is."

The pedestrian referred to proved to be going there himself. They went on together, Psmith courteously offering views on the weather and forecasts of the success of Kid Brady in the approaching contest.

Rattling on, he was alluding to the prominent part Cosy Moments had played in the affair, when a rough thrust from Windsor's elbow brought home to him his indiscretion.

He stopped suddenly, wishing he had not said as much. Their connection with that militant journal was not a thing even to be suggested to casual acquaintances, especially in such a particularly ill-lighted neighbourhood as that through which they were now passing.

Their companion, however, who seemed to be a man of small speech, made no comment. Psmith deftly turned the conversation back to the subject of the weather, and was deep in a comparison of the respective climates of England and the United States, when they turned a corner and found themselves opposite a gloomy, barn-like building, over the door of which it was just possible to decipher in the darkness the words "Highfield Athletic and Gymnastic Club."

The tickets which Billy Windsor had obtained from his newspaper friend were for one of the boxes. These proved to be sort of sheep-pens of unpolished wood, each with four hard chairs in it. The interior of the Highfield Athletic and Gymnastic Club was severely free from anything in the shape of luxury and ornament. Along the four walls were raised benches in tiers. On these were seated as tough-looking a collection of citizens as one might wish to see. On chairs at the ring-side were the reporters, with tickers at their sides, by means of which they tapped details of each round through to their down-town offices, where write-up reporters were waiting to read off and elaborate the messages. In the centre of the room, brilliantly lighted by half a dozen electric chandeliers, was the ring.

There were preliminary bouts before the main event. A burly gentleman in shirt-sleeves entered the ring, followed by two slim youths in fighting costume and a massive person in a red jersey, blue serge trousers, and yellow braces, who chewed gum with an abstracted air throughout the proceedings.

The burly gentleman gave tongue in a voice that cleft the air like a cannon-ball.

"Ex-hib-it-i-on four-round bout between Patsy Milligan and Tommy Goodley, members of this club. Patsy on my right, Tommy on my left. Gentlemen will kindly stop smokin'."

The audience did nothing of the sort. Possibly they did not apply the description to themselves. Possibly they considered the appeal a mere formula. Somewhere in the background a gong sounded, and Patsy, from the right, stepped briskly forward to meet Tommy, approaching from the left.

The contest was short but energetic. At intervals the combatants would cling affectionately to one another, and on these occasions the red-jerseyed man, still chewing gum and still wearing the same air of being lost in abstract thought, would split up the mass by the simple method of ploughing his way between the pair. Towards the end of the first round Thomas, eluding a left swing, put Patrick neatly to the floor, where the latter remained for the necessary ten seconds.

The remaining preliminaries proved disappointing. So much so that in the last of the series a soured sportsman on one of the benches near the roof began in satirical mood to whistle the "Merry Widow Waltz." It was here that the red-jerseyed thinker for the first and last time came out of his meditative trance. He leaned over the ropes, and spoke—without heat, but firmly.

"If that guy whistling back up yonder thinks he can do better than these boys, he can come right down into the ring."

The whistling ceased.

There was a distinct air of relief when the last preliminary was finished and preparations for the main bout began. It did not commence at once. There were formalities to be gone through, introductions and the like. The burly gentleman reappeared from nowhere, ushering into the ring a sheepishly-grinning youth in a flannel suit.

"In-ter-doo-cin' Young Leary," he bellowed impressively, "a noo member of this chub, who will box some good boy here in September."

He walked to the other side of the ring and repeated the remark. A raucous welcome was accorded to the new member.

Two other notable performers were introduced in a similar manner, and then the building became suddenly full of noise, for a tall youth in a bath-robe, attended by a little army of assistants, had entered the ring. One of the army carried a bright green bucket, on which were painted in white letters the words "Cyclone Al. Wolmann." A moment later there was another, though a far lesser, uproar, as Kid Brady, his pleasant face wearing a self-conscious smirk, ducked under the ropes and sat down in the opposite corner.

"Ex-hib-it-i-on ten-round bout," thundered the burly gentleman, "between Cyclone. Al. Wolmann—"

Loud applause. Mr. Wolmann was one of the famous, a fighter with a reputation from New York to San Francisco. He was generally considered the most likely man to give the hitherto invincible Jimmy Garvin a hard battle for the light-weight championship.

"Oh, you Al.!" roared the crowd.

Mr. Wolmann bowed benevolently.

"—and Kid Brady, members of this—"

There was noticeably less applause for the Kid. He was an unknown. A few of those present had heard of his victories in the West, but these were but a small section of the crowd. When the faint applause had ceased, Psmith rose to his feet.

"Oh, you Kid!" he observed encouragingly.

"I should not like Comrade Brady," he said, reseating himself, "to think that he has no friend but his poor old mother, as, you will recollect, occurred on a previous occasion."

The burly gentleman, followed by the two armies of assistants, dropped down from the ring, and the gong sounded.

Mr. Wolmann sprang from his corner as if somebody had touched a spring. He seemed to be of the opinion that if you are a cyclone, it is never too soon to begin behaving like one. He danced round the Kid with an india-rubber agility. The Cosy Moments representative exhibited more stolidity. Except for the fact that he was in fighting attitude, with one gloved hand moving slowly in the neighbourhood of his stocky chest, and the other pawing the air on a line with his square jaw, one would have said that he did not realise the position of affairs. He wore the friendly smile of the good-natured guest who is led forward by his hostess to join in some round game.

Suddenly his opponent's long left shot out. The Kid, who had been strolling forward, received it under the chin, and continued to stroll forward as if nothing of note had happened. He gave the impression of being aware that Mr. Wolmann had committed a breach of good taste and of being resolved to pass it off with ready tact.

The Cyclone, having executed a backward leap, a forward leap, and a feint, landed heavily with both hands. The Kid's genial smile did not even quiver, but he continued to move forward. His opponent's left flashed out again, but this time, instead of ignoring the matter, the Kid replied with a heavy right swing; and Mr. Wolmann, leaping back, found himself against the ropes. By the time he had got out of that uncongenial position, two more of the Kid's swings had found their mark. Mr. Wolmann, somewhat perturbed, scuttered out into the middle of the ring, the Kid following in his self-contained, solid way.

The Cyclone now became still more cyclonic. He had a left arm which seemed to open out in joints like a telescope. Several times when the Kid appeared well out of distance there was a thud as a brown glove ripped in over his guard and jerked his head back. But always he kept boring in, delivering an occasional right to the body with the pleased smile of an infant destroying a Noah's Ark with a tack-hammer. Despite these efforts, however, he was plainly getting all the worst of it. Energetic Mr. Wolmann, relying on his long left, was putting in three blows to his one. When the gong sounded, ending the first round, the house was practically solid for the Cyclone. Whoops and yells rose from everywhere. The building rang with shouts of, "Oh, you Al.!"

Psmith turned sadly to Billy.

"It seems to me, Comrade Windsor," he said, "that this merry meeting looks like doing Comrade Brady no good. I should not be surprised at any moment to see his head bounce off on to the floor."

"Wait," said Billy. "He'll win yet."

"You think so?"

"Sure. He comes from Wyoming," said Billy with simple confidence.

Rounds two and three were a repetition of round one. The Cyclone raged almost unchecked about the ring. In one lightning rally in the third he brought his right across squarely on to the Kid's jaw. It was a blow which should have knocked any boxer out. The Kid merely staggered slightly and returned to business, still smiling.

"See!" roared Billy enthusiastically in Psmith's ear, above the uproar. "He doesn't mind it! He likes it! He comes from Wyoming!"

With the opening of round four there came a subtle change. The Cyclone's fury was expending itself. That long left shot out less sharply. Instead of being knocked back by it, the Cosy Moments champion now took the hits in his stride, and came shuffling in with his damaging body-blows. There were cheers and "Oh, you Al.'s!" at the sound of the gong, but there was an appealing note in them this time. The gallant sportsmen whose connection with boxing was confined to watching other men fight, and betting on what they considered a certainty, and who would have expired promptly if any one had tapped them sharply on their well-filled waistcoats, were beginning to fear that they might lose their money after all.

In the fifth round the thing became a certainty. Like the month of March, the Cyclone, who had come in like a lion, was going out like a lamb. A slight decrease in the pleasantness of the Kid's smile was noticeable. His expression began to resemble more nearly the gloomy importance of the Cosy Moments photographs. Yells of agony from panic-stricken speculators around the ring began to smite the rafters. The Cyclone, now but a gentle breeze, clutched repeatedly, hanging on like a leech till removed by the red-jerseyed referee.

Suddenly a grisly silence fell upon the house. It was broken by a cow-boy yell from Billy Windsor. For the Kid, battered, but obviously content, was standing in the middle of the ring, while on the ropes the Cyclone, drooping like a wet sock, was sliding slowly to the floor.

"Cosy Moments wins," said Psmith. "An omen, I fancy, Comrade Windsor."

CHAPTER XV — AN ADDITION TO THE STAFF

Penetrating into the Kid's dressing-room some moments later, the editorial staff found the winner of the ten-round exhibition bout between members of the club seated on a chair, having his right leg rubbed by a shock-headed man in a sweater, who had been one of his seconds during the conflict. The Kid beamed as they entered.

"Gents," he said, "come right in. Mighty glad to see you."

"It is a relief to me, Comrade Brady," said Psmith, "to find that you can see us. I had expected to find that Comrade Wolmann's purposeful buffs had completely closed your star-likes."

"Sure, I never felt them. He's a good quick boy, is Al., but," continued the Kid with powerful imagery, "he couldn't hit a hole in a block of ice-cream, not if he was to use a hammer."

"And yet at one period in the proceedings, Comrade Brady," said Psmith, "I fancied that your head would come unglued at the neck. But the fear was merely transient. When you began to administer those—am I correct in saying?—half-scissor hooks to the body, why, then I felt like some watcher of the skies when a new planet swims into his ken; or like stout Cortez when with eagle eyes he stared at the Pacific."

The Kid blinked.

"How's that?" he inquired.

"And why did I feel like that, Comrade Brady? I will tell you. Because my faith in you was justified. Because there before me stood the ideal fighting-editor of Cosy Moments. It is not a post that any weakling can fill. There charm of manner cannot qualify a man for the position. No one can hold down the job simply by having a kind heart or being good at farmyard imitations. No. We want a man of thews and sinews, a man who would rather be hit on the head with a half-brick than not. And you, Comrade Brady, are such a man."

The Kid turned appealingly to Billy.

"Say, this gets past me, Mr. Windsor. Put me wise."

"Can we have a couple of words with you alone, Kid?" said Billy. "We want to talk over something with you."

"Sure. Sit down, gents. Jack'll be through in a minute."

Jack, who during this conversation had been concentrating himself on his subject's left leg, now announced that he guessed that would about do, and having advised the Kid not to stop and pick daisies, but to get into his clothes at once before he caught a chill, bade the company good night and retired.

Billy shut the door.

"Kid," he said, "you know those articles about the tenements we've been having in the paper?"

"Sure. I read 'em. They're to the good."

Psmith bowed.

"You stimulate us, Comrade Brady. This is praise from Sir Hubert Stanley."

"It was about time some strong josher came and put it across to 'em," added the Kid.

"So we thought. Comrade Parker, however, totally disagreed with us."

"Parker?"

"That's what I'm coming to," said Billy. "The day before yesterday a man named Parker called at the office and tried to buy us off."

Billy's voice grew indignant at the recollection.

"You gave him the hook, I guess?" queried the interested Kid.

"To such an extent, Comrade Brady," said Psmith, "that he left breathing threatenings and slaughter. And it is for that reason that we have ventured to call upon you."

"It's this way," said Billy. "We're pretty sure by this time that whoever the man is this fellow Parker's working for has put one of the gangs on to us."

"You don't say!" exclaimed the Kid. "Gum! Mr. Windsor, they're tough propositions, those gangs."

"We've been followed in the streets, and once they put up a bluff to get us where they could do us in. So we've come along to you. We can look after ourselves out of the office, you see, but what we want is some one to help in case they try to rush us there."

"In brief, a fighting-editor," said Psmith. "At all costs we must have privacy. No writer can prune and polish his sentences to his satisfaction if he is compelled constantly to break off in order to eject boisterous hooligans. We therefore offer you the job of sitting in the outer room and intercepting these bravoes before they can reach us. The salary we leave to you. There are doubloons and to spare in the old oak chest. Take what you need and put the rest—if any—back. How does the offer strike you, Comrade Brady?"

"We don't want to get you in under false pretences, Kid," said Billy. "Of course, they may not come anywhere near the office. But still, if they did, there would be something doing. What do you feel about it?"

"Gents," said the Kid, "it's this way."

He stepped into his coat, and resumed.

"Now that I've made good by getting the decision over Al., they'll be giving me a chance of a big fight. Maybe with Jimmy Garvin. Well, if that happens, see what I mean? I'll have to be going away somewhere and getting into training. I shouldn't be able to come and sit with you. But, if you gents feel like it, I'd be mighty glad to come in till I'm wanted to go into training-camp."

"Great," said Billy; "that would suit us all the way up. If you'd do that, Kid, we'd be tickled to death."

"And touching salary—" put in Psmith.

"Shucks!" said the Kid with emphasis. "Nix on the salary thing. I wouldn't take a dime. If it hadn't a-been for you gents, I'd have been waiting still for a chance of lining up in the championship class. That's good enough for me. Any old thing you gents want me to do, I'll do it. And glad, too."

"Comrade Brady," said Psmith warmly, "you are, if I may say so, the goods. You are, beyond a doubt, supremely the stuff. We three, then, hand-in-hand, will face the foe; and if the foe has good, sound sense, he will keep right away. You appear to be ready. Shall we meander forth?"

The building was empty and the lights were out when they emerged from the dressing-room. They had to grope their way in darkness. It was still raining when they reached the street, and the only signs of life were a moist policeman and the distant glare of public-house lights down the road.

They turned off to the left, and, after walking some hundred yards, found themselves in a blind alley.

"Hullo!" said Billy. "Where have we come to?"

Psmith sighed.

"In my trusting way," he said, "I had imagined that either you or Comrade Brady was in charge of this expedition and taking me by a known route to the nearest Subway station. I did not think to ask. I placed myself, without hesitation, wholly in your hands."

"I thought the Kid knew the way," said Billy.

"I was just taggin' along with you gents," protested the light-weight, "I thought you was taking me right. This is the first time I been up here."

"Next time we three go on a little jaunt anywhere," said Psmith resignedly, "it would be as well to take a map and a corps of guides with us. Otherwise we shall start for Broadway and finish up at Minneapolis."

They emerged from the blind alley and stood in the dark street, looking doubtfully up and down it.

"Aha!" said Psmith suddenly, "I perceive a native. Several natives, in fact. Quite a little covey of them. We will put our case before them, concealing nothing, and rely on their advice to take us to our goal."

A little knot of men was approaching from the left. In the darkness it was impossible to say how many of them there were. Psmith stepped forward, the Kid at his side.

"Excuse me, sir," he said to the leader, "but if you can spare me a moment of your valuable time—"

There was a sudden shuffle of feet on the pavement, a quick movement on the part of the Kid, a chunky sound as of wood striking wood, and the man Psmith had been addressing fell to the ground in a heap.

As he fell, something dropped from his hand on to the pavement with a bump and a rattle. Stooping swiftly, the Kid picked it up, and handed it to Psmith. His fingers closed upon it. It was a short, wicked-looking little bludgeon, the black-jack of the New York tough.

"Get busy," advised the Kid briefly.

CHAPTER XVI — THE FIRST BATTLE

The promptitude and despatch with which the Kid had attended to the gentleman with the black-jack had not been without its effect on the followers of the stricken one. Physical courage is not an outstanding quality of the New York hooligan. His personal preference is for retreat when it is a question of unpleasantness with a stranger. And, in any case, even when warring among themselves, the gangs exhibit a lively distaste for the hard knocks of hand-to-hand fighting. Their chosen method of battling is to lie down on the ground and shoot. This is more suited to their physique, which is rarely great. The gangsman, as a rule, is stunted and slight of build.

The Kid's rapid work on the present occasion created a good deal of confusion. There was no doubt that much had been hoped for from speedy attack. Also, the generalship of the expedition had been in the hands of the fallen warrior. His removal from the sphere of active influence had left the party without a head. And, to add to their discomfiture, they could not account for the Kid. Psmith they knew, and Billy Windsor they knew, but who was this stranger with the square shoulders and the upper-cut that landed like a cannon-ball? Something approaching a panic prevailed among the gang.

It was not lessened by the behaviour of the intended victims. Billy Windsor, armed with the big stick which he had bought after the visit of Mr. Parker, was the first to join issue. He had been a few paces behind the others during the black-jack incident; but, dark as it was, he had seen enough to show him that the occasion was, as Psmith would have said, one for the Shrewd Blow rather than the Prolonged Parley. With a whoop of the purest Wyoming brand, he sprang forward into the confused mass of the enemy. A moment later Psmith and the Kid followed, and there raged over the body of the fallen leader a battle of Homeric type.

It was not a long affair. The rules and conditions governing the encounter offended the delicate sensibilities of the gang. Like artists who feel themselves trammelled by distasteful conventions, they were damped and could not do themselves justice. Their forte was long-range fighting with pistols. With that they felt en rapport. But this vulgar brawling in the darkness with muscular opponents who hit hard and often with sticks and hands was distasteful to them. They could not develop any enthusiasm for it. They carried pistols, but it was too dark and the combatants were too entangled to allow them to use these. Besides, this was not the dear, homely old Bowery, where a gentleman may fire a pistol without exciting vulgar comment. It was up-town, where curious crowds might collect at the first shot.

There was but one thing to be done. Reluctant as they might be to abandon their fallen leader, they must tear themselves away. Already they were suffering grievously from the stick, the black-jack, and the lightning blows of the Kid. For a moment they hung, wavering; then stampeded in half a dozen different directions, melting into the night whence they had come.

Billy, full of zeal, pursued one fugitive some fifty yards down the street, but his quarry, exhibiting a rare turn of speed, easily outstripped him.

He came back, panting, to find Psmith and the Kid examining the fallen leader of the departed ones with the aid of a match, which went out just as Billy arrived.

"It is our friend of the earlier part of the evening, Comrade Windsor," said Psmith. "The merchant with whom we hob-nobbed on our way to the Highfield. In a moment of imprudence I mentioned Cosy Moments. I fancy that this was his first intimation that we were in the offing. His visit to the Highfield was paid, I think, purely from sport-loving motives. He was not on our trail. He came merely to see if Comrade Brady was proficient with his hands. Subsequent events must have justified our fighting editor in his eyes. It seems to be a moot point whether he will ever recover consciousness."

"Mighty good thing if he doesn't," said Billy uncharitably.

"From one point of view, Comrade Windsor, yes. Such an event would undoubtedly be an excellent thing for the public good. But from our point of view, it would be as well if he were to sit up and take notice. We could ascertain from him who he is and which particular collection of horny-handeds he represents. Light another match, Comrade Brady."

The Kid did so. The head of it fell off and dropped upon the up-turned face. The hooligan stirred, shook himself, sat up, and began to mutter something in a foggy voice.

"He's still woozy," said the Kid.

"Still—what exactly, Comrade Brady?"

"In the air," explained the Kid. "Bats in the belfry. Dizzy. See what I mean? It's often like that when a feller puts one in with a bit of weight behind it just where that one landed. Gum! I remember when I fought Martin Kelly; I was only starting to learn the game then. Martin and me was mixing it good and hard all over the ring, when suddenly he puts over a stiff one right on the point. What do you think I done? Fall down and take the count? Not on your life. I just turns round and walks straight out of the ring to my dressing-room. Willie Harvey, who was seconding me, comes tearing in after me, and finds me getting into my clothes. 'What's doing, Kid?' he asks. 'I'm going fishin', Willie,' I says. 'It's a lovely day.' 'You've lost the fight,' he says. 'Fight?' says I. 'What fight?' See what I mean? I hadn't a notion of what had happened. It was a half an hour and more before I could remember a thing."

During this reminiscence, the man on the ground had contrived to clear his mind of the mistiness induced by the Kid's upper-cut. The first sign he showed of returning intelligence was a sudden dash for safety up the road. But he had not gone five yards when he sat down limply.

The Kid was inspired to further reminiscence. "Guess he's feeling pretty poor," he said. "It's no good him trying to run for a while after he's put his chin in the way of a real live one. I remember when Joe Peterson put me out, way back when I was new to the game—it was the same year I fought Martin Kelly. He had an awful punch, had old Joe, and he put me down and out in the eighth round. After the fight they found me on the fire-escape outside my dressing-room. 'Come in, Kid,' says they. 'It's all right, chaps,' I says, 'I'm dying.' Like that. 'It's all right, chaps, I'm dying.' Same with this guy. See what I mean?"

They formed a group about the fallen black-jack expert.

"Pardon us," said Psmith courteously, "for breaking in upon your reverie; but, if you could spare us a moment of your valuable time, there are one or two things which we should like to know."

"Sure thing," agreed the Kid.

"In the first place," continued Psmith, "would it be betraying professional secrets if you told us which particular bevy of energetic sandbaggers it is to which you are attached?"

"Gent," explained the Kid, "wants to know what's your gang."

The man on the ground muttered something that to Psmith and Billy was unintelligible.

"It would be a charity," said the former, "if some philanthropist would give this blighter elocution lessons. Can you interpret, Comrade Brady?"

"Says it's the Three Points," said the Kid.

"The Three Points? Let me see, is that Dude Dawson, Comrade Windsor, or the other gentleman?"

"It's Spider Reilly. Dude Dawson runs the Table Hill crowd."

"Perhaps this is Spider Reilly?"

"Nope," said the Kid. "I know the Spider. This ain't him. This is some other mutt."

"Which other mutt in particular?" asked Psmith. "Try and find out, Comrade Brady. You seem to be able to understand what he says. To me, personally, his remarks sound like the output of a gramophone with a hot potato in its mouth."

"Says he's Jack Repetto," announced the interpreter.

There was another interruption at this moment. The bashful Mr. Repetto, plainly a man who was not happy in the society of strangers, made another attempt to withdraw. Reaching out a pair of lean hands, he pulled the Kid's legs from under him with a swift jerk, and, wriggling to his feet, started off again down the road. Once more, however, desire outran performance. He got as far as the nearest street-lamp, but no farther. The giddiness seemed to overcome him again, for he grasped the lamp-post, and, sliding slowly to the ground, sat there motionless.

The Kid, whose fall had jolted and bruised him, was inclined to be wrathful and vindictive. He was the first of the three to reach the elusive Mr. Repetto, and if that worthy had happened to be standing instead of sitting it might have gone hard with him. But the Kid was not the man to attack a fallen foe. He contented himself with brushing the dust off his person and addressing a richly abusive flow of remarks to Mr. Repetto.

Under the rays of the lamp it was possible to discern more closely the features of the black-jack exponent. There was a subtle but noticeable resemblance to those of Mr. Bat Jarvis. Apparently the latter's oiled forelock, worn low over the forehead, was more a concession to the general fashion prevailing in gang circles than an expression of personal taste. Mr. Repetto had it, too. In his case it was almost white, for the fallen warrior was an albino. His eyes, which were closed, had white lashes and were set as near together as Nature had been able to manage without actually running them into one another. His under-lip protruded and drooped. Looking at him, one felt instinctively that no judging committee of a beauty contest would hesitate a moment before him.

It soon became apparent that the light of the lamp, though bestowing the doubtful privilege of a clearer view of Mr. Repetto's face, held certain disadvantages. Scarcely had the staff of Cosy Moments reached the faint yellow pool of light, in the centre of which Mr. Repetto reclined, than, with a suddenness which caused them to leap into the air, there sounded from the darkness down the road the crack-crack-crack of a revolver. Instantly from the opposite direction came other shots. Three bullets flicked grooves in the roadway almost at Billy's feet. The Kid gave a sudden howl. Psmith's hat, suddenly imbued with life, sprang into the air and vanished, whirling into the night.

The thought did not come to them consciously at the moment, there being little time to think, but it was evident as soon as, diving out of the circle of light into the sheltering darkness, they crouched down and waited for the next move, that a somewhat skilful ambush had been effected. The other members of the gang, who had fled with such remarkable speed, had by no means been eliminated altogether from the game. While the questioning of Mr. Repetto had been in progress, they had crept back, unperceived except by Mr. Repetto himself. It being too dark for successful shooting, it had become Mr. Repetto's task to lure his captors into the light, which he had accomplished with considerable skill.

For some minutes the battle halted. There was dead silence. The circle of light was empty now. Mr. Repetto had vanished. A tentative shot from nowhere ripped through the air close to where Psmith lay flattened on the pavement. And then the pavement began to vibrate and give out a curious resonant sound. To Psmith it conveyed nothing, but to the opposing army it meant much. They knew it for what it was. Somewhere—it might be near or far—a policeman had heard the shots, and was signalling for help to other policemen along the line by beating on the flag-stones with his night-stick, the New York constable's substitute for the London police-whistle.

The noise grew, filling the still air. From somewhere down the road sounded the ring of running feet.

"De cops!" cried a voice. "Beat it!"

Next moment the night was full of clatter. The gang was "beating it."

Psmith rose to his feet and dusted his clothes ruefully. For the first time he realised the horrors of war. His hat had gone for ever. His trousers could never be the same again after their close acquaintance with the pavement.

The rescue party was coming up at the gallop.

The New York policeman may lack the quiet dignity of his London rival, but he is a hustler.

"What's doing?"

"Nothing now," said the disgusted voice of Billy Windsor from the shadows. "They've beaten it."

The circle of lamplight became as if by mutual consent a general rendezvous. Three grey-clad policemen, tough, clean-shaven men with keen eyes and square jaws, stood there, revolver in one hand, night-stick in the other. Psmith, hatless and dusty, joined them. Billy Windsor and the Kid, the latter bleeding freely from his left ear, the lobe of which had been chipped by a bullet, were the last to arrive.

"What's bin the rough house?" inquired one of the policemen, mildly interested.

"Do you know a sportsman of the name of Repetto?" inquired Psmith.

"Jack Repetto! Sure."

"He belongs to the Three Points," said another intelligent officer, as one naming some fashionable club.

"When next you see him," said Psmith, "I should be obliged if you would use your authority to make him buy me a new hat. I could do with another pair of trousers, too; but I will not press the trousers. A new hat, is, however, essential. Mine has a six-inch hole in it."

"Shot at you, did they?" said one of the policemen, as who should say, "Dash the lads, they're always up to some of their larks."

"Shot at us!" burst out the ruffled Kid. "What do you think's bin happening? Think an aeroplane ran into my ear and took half of it off? Think the noise was somebody opening bottles of pop? Think those guys that sneaked off down the road was just training for a Marathon?"

"Comrade Brady," said Psmith, "touches the spot. He—"

"Say, are you Kid Brady?" inquired one of the officers. For the first time the constabulary had begun to display any real animation.

"Reckoned I'd seen you somewhere!" said another. "You licked Cyclone Al. all right, Kid, I hear."

"And who but a bone-head thought he wouldn't?" demanded the third warmly. "He could whip a dozen Cyclone Al.'s in the same evening with his eyes shut."

"He's the next champeen," admitted the first speaker.

"If he puts it over Jimmy Garvin," argued the second.

"Jimmy Garvin!" cried the third. "He can whip twenty Jimmy Garvins with his feet tied. I tell you—"

"I am loath," observed Psmith, "to interrupt this very impressive brain-barbecue, but, trivial as it may seem to you, to me there is a certain interest in this other little matter of my ruined hat. I know that it may strike you as hypersensitive of us to protest against being riddled with bullets, but—"

"Well, what's bin doin'?" inquired the Force. It was a nuisance, this perpetual harping on trifles when the deep question of the light-weight Championship of the World was under discussion, but the sooner it was attended to, the sooner it would be over.

Billy Windsor undertook to explain.

"The Three Points laid for us," he said. "Jack Repetto was bossing the crowd. I don't know who the rest were. The Kid put one over on to Jack Repetto's chin, and we were asking him a few questions when the rest came back, and started into shooting. Then we got to cover quick, and you came up and they beat it."

"That," said Psmith, nodding, "is a very fair pricis of the evening's events. We should like you, if you will be so good, to corral this Comrade Repetto, and see that he buys me a new hat."

"We'll round Jack up," said one of the policemen indulgently.

"Do it nicely," urged Psmith. "Don't go hurting his feelings."

The second policeman gave it as his opinion that Jack was getting too gay. The third policeman conceded this. Jack, he said, had shown signs for some time past of asking for it in the neck. It was an error on Jack's part, he gave his hearers to understand, to assume that the lid was completely off the great city of New York.

"Too blamed fresh he's gettin'," the trio agreed. They could not have been more disapproving if they had been prefects at Haileybury and Mr. Repetto a first-termer who had been detected in the act of wearing his cap on the back of his head.

They seemed to think it was too bad of Jack.

"The wrath of the Law," said Psmith, "is very terrible. We will leave the matter, then, in your hands. In the meantime, we should be glad if you would direct us to the nearest Subway station. Just at the moment, the cheerful lights of the Great White Way are what I seem to chiefly need."

CHAPTER XVII — GUERILLA WARFARE

Thus ended the opening engagement of the campaign, seemingly in a victory for the Cosy Moments army. Billy Windsor, however, shook his head.

"We've got mighty little out of it," he said.

"The victory," said Psmith, "was not bloodless. Comrade Brady's ear, my hat—these are not slight casualties. On the other hand, surely we are one up? Surely we have gained ground? The elimination of Comrade Repetto from the scheme of things in itself is something. I know few men I would not rather meet in a lonely road than Comrade Repetto. He is one of Nature's sand-baggers. Probably the thing crept upon him slowly. He started, possibly, in a merely tentative way by slugging one of the family circle. His nurse, let us say, or his young brother. But, once started, he is unable to resist the craving. The thing grips him like dram-drinking. He sandbags now not because he really wants to, but because he cannot help himself. To me there is something consoling in the thought that Comrade Repetto will no longer be among those present."

"What makes you think that?"

"I should imagine that a benevolent Law will put him away in his little cell for at least a brief spell."

"Not on your life," said Billy. "He'll prove an alibi."

Psmith's eyeglass dropped out of his eye. He replaced it, and gazed, astonished, at Billy.

"An alibi? When three keen-eyed men actually caught him at it?"

"He can find thirty toughs to swear he was five miles away."

"And get the court to believe it?" said Psmith.

"Sure," said Billy disgustedly. "You don't catch them hurting a gangsman unless they're pushed against the wall. The politicians don't want the gangs in gaol, especially as the Aldermanic elections will be on in a few weeks. Did you ever hear of Monk Eastman?"

"I fancy not, Comrade Windsor. If I did, the name has escaped me. Who was this cleric?"

"He was the first boss of the East Side gang, before Kid Twist took it on."

"Yes?"

"He was arrested dozens of times, but he always got off. Do you know what he said once, when they pulled him for thugging a fellow out in New Jersey?"

"I fear not, Comrade Windsor. Tell me all."

"He said, 'You're arresting me, huh? Say, you want to look where you're goin'; I cut some ice in this town. I made half the big politicians in New York!' That was what he said."

"His small-talk," said Psmith, "seems to have been bright and well-expressed. What happened then? Was he restored to his friends and his relations?"

"Sure, he was. What do you think? Well, Jack Repetto isn't Monk Eastman, but he's in with Spider Reilly, and the Spider's in with the men behind. Jack'll get off."

"It looks to me, Comrade Windsor," said Psmith thoughtfully, "as if my stay in this great city were going to cost me a small fortune in hats."

Billy's prophecy proved absolutely correct. The police were as good as their word. In due season they rounded up the impulsive Mr. Repetto, and he was haled before a magistrate. And then, what a beautiful exhibition of brotherly love and auld-lang-syne camaraderie was witnessed! One by one, smirking sheepishly, but giving out their evidence with unshaken earnestness, eleven greasy, wandering-eyed youths mounted the witness-stand and affirmed on oath that at the time mentioned dear old Jack had been making merry in their company in a genial and law-abiding fashion, many, many blocks below the scene of the regrettable assault. The magistrate discharged the prisoner, and the prisoner, meeting Billy and Psmith in the street outside, leered triumphantly at them.

Billy stepped up to him. "You may have wriggled out of this," he said furiously, "but if you don't get a move on and quit looking at me like that, I'll knock you over the Singer Building. Hump yourself."

Mr. Repetto humped himself.

So was victory turned into defeat, and Billy's jaw became squarer and his eye more full of the light of battle than ever. And there was need of a square jaw and a battle-lit eye, for now began a period of guerilla warfare such as no New York paper had ever had to fight against.

It was Wheeler, the gaunt manager of the business side of the journal, who first brought it to the notice of the editorial staff. Wheeler was a man for whom in business hours nothing existed but his job; and his job was to look after the distribution of the paper. As to the contents of the paper he was absolutely ignorant. He had been with Cosy Moments from its start, but he had never read a line of it. He handled it as if it were so much soap. The scholarly writings of Mr. Wilberfloss, the mirth-provoking sallies of Mr. B. Henderson Asher, the tender outpourings of Louella Granville Waterman—all these were things outside his ken. He was a distributor, and he distributed.

A few days after the restoration of Mr. Repetto to East Side Society, Mr. Wheeler came into the editorial room with information and desire for information.

He endeavoured to satisfy the latter first.

"What's doing, anyway?" he asked. He then proceeded to his information. "Some one's got it in against the paper, sure," he said. "I don't know what it's all about. I ha'n't never read the thing. Don't see what any one could have against a paper with a name like Cosy Moments, anyway. The way things have been going last few days, seems it might be the organ of a blamed mining-camp what the boys have took a dislike to."

"What's been happening?" asked Billy with gleaming eyes.

"Why, nothing in the world to fuss about, only our carriers can't go out without being beaten up by gangs of toughs. Pat Harrigan's in the hospital now. Just been looking in on him. Pat's a feller who likes to fight. Rather fight he would than see a ball-game. But this was too much for him. Know what happened? Why, see here, just like this it was. Pat goes out with his cart. Passing through a low-down street on his way up-town he's held up by a bunch of toughs. He shows fight. Half a dozen of them attend to him, while the rest gets clean away with every copy of the paper there was in the cart. When the cop comes along, there's Pat in pieces on the ground and nobody in sight but a Dago chewing gum. Cop asks the Dago what's been doing, and the Dago says he's only just come round the corner and ha'n't seen nothing of anybody. What I want to know is, what's it all about? Who's got it in for us and why?"

Mr. Wheeler leaned back in his chair, while Billy, his hair rumpled more than ever and his eyes glowing, explained the situation. Mr. Wheeler listened absolutely unmoved, and, when the narrative had come to an end, gave it as his opinion that the editorial staff had sand. That was his sole comment. "It's up to you," he said, rising. "You know your business. Say, though, some one had better get busy right quick and do something to stop these guys rough-housing like this. If we get a few more carriers beat up the way Pat was, there'll be a strike. It's not as if they were all Irishmen. The most of them are Dagoes and such, and they don't want any more fight than they can get by beating their wives and kicking kids off the sidewalk. I'll do my best to get this paper distributed right and it's a shame if it ain't, because it's going big just now—but it's up to you. Good day, gents."

He went out. Psmith looked at Billy.

"As Comrade Wheeler remarks," he said, "it is up to us. What do you propose to do about it? This is a move of the enemy which I have not anticipated. I had fancied that their operations would be confined exclusively to our two selves. If they are going to strew the street with our carriers, we are somewhat in the soup."

Billy said nothing. He was chewing the stem of an unlighted pipe. Psmith went on.

"It means, of course, that we must buck up to a certain extent. If the campaign is to be a long one, they have us where the hair is crisp. We cannot stand the strain. Cosy Moments cannot be muzzled, but it can undoubtedly be choked. What we want to do is to find out the name of the man behind the tenements as soon as ever we can and publish it; and, then, if we perish, fall yelling the name."

Billy admitted the soundness of this scheme, but wished to know how it was to be done.

"Comrade Windsor," said Psmith. "I have been thinking this thing over, and it seems to me that we are on the wrong track, or rather we aren't on any track at all; we are simply marking time. What we want to do is to go out and hustle round till we stir up something. Our line up to the present has been to sit at home and scream vigorously in the hope of some stout fellow hearing and rushing to help. In other words, we've been saying in the paper what an out-size in scugs the merchant must be who owns those tenements, in the hope that somebody else will agree with us and be sufficiently interested to get to work and find out who the blighter is. That's all wrong. What we must do now, Comrade Windsor, is put on our hats, such hats as Comrade Repetto has left us, and sally forth as sleuth-hounds on our own account."

"Yes, but how?" demanded Billy. "That's all right in theory, but how's it going to work in practice? The only thing that can corner the man is a commission."

"Far from it, Comrade Windsor. The job may be worked more simply. I don't know how often the rents are collected in these places, but I should say at a venture once a week. My idea is to hang negligently round till the rent-collector arrives, and when he has loomed up on the horizon, buttonhole him and ask him quite politely, as man to man, whether he is collecting those rents for himself or for somebody else, and if somebody else, who that somebody else is. Simple, I fancy? Yet brainy. Do you take me, Comrade Windsor?"

Billy sat up, excited. "I believe you've hit it."

Psmith shot his cuffs modestly.

CHAPTER XVIII — AN EPISODE BY THE WAY

It was Pugsy Maloney who, on the following morning, brought to the office the gist of what is related in this chapter. Pugsy's version was, however, brief and unadorned, as was the way with his narratives. Such things as first causes and piquant details he avoided, as tending to prolong the telling excessively, thus keeping him from perusal of his cowboy stories. The way Pugsy put it was as follows. He gave the thing out merely as an item of general interest, a bubble on the surface of the life of a great city. He did not know how nearly interested were his employers in any matter touching that gang which is known as the Three Points. Pugsy said: "Dere's trouble down where I live. Dude Dawson's mad at Spider Reilly, an' now de Table Hills are layin' for de T'ree Points. Sure." He had then retired to his outer fastness, yielding further details jerkily and with the distrait air of one whose mind is elsewhere.

Skilfully extracted and pieced together, these details formed themselves into the following typical narrative of East Side life in New York.

The really important gangs of New York are four. There are other less important institutions, but these are little more than mere friendly gatherings of old boyhood chums for purposes of mutual companionship. In time they may grow, as did Bat Jarvis's coterie, into formidable organisations, for the soil is undoubtedly propitious to such growth. But at present the amount of ice which good judges declare them to cut is but small. They "stick up" an occasional wayfarer for his "cush," and they carry "canisters" and sometimes fire them off, but these things do not signify the cutting of ice. In matters political there are only four gangs which count, the East Side, the Groome Street, the Three Points, and the Table Hill. Greatest of these by virtue of their numbers are the East Side and the Groome Street, the latter presided over at the time of this story by Mr. Bat Jarvis. These two are colossal, and, though they may fight each other, are immune from attack at the hands of lesser gangs. But between the other gangs, and especially between the Table Hill and the Three Points, which are much of a size, warfare rages as briskly as among the republics of South America. There has always been bad blood between the Table Hill and the Three Points, and until they wipe each other out after the manner of the Kilkenny cats, it is probable that there always will be. Little events, trifling in themselves, have always occurred to shatter friendly relations just when there has seemed a chance of their being formed. Thus, just as the Table Hillites were beginning to forgive the Three Points for shooting the redoubtable Paul Horgan down at Coney Island, a Three Pointer injudiciously wiped out another of the rival gang near Canal Street. He pleaded self-defence, and in any case it was probably mere thoughtlessness, but nevertheless the Table Hillites were ruffled.

That had been a month or so back. During that month things had been simmering down, and peace was just preparing to brood when there occurred the incident to which Pugsy had alluded, the regrettable falling out of Dude Dawson and Spider Reilly at Mr. Maginnis's dancing saloon, Shamrock Hall, the same which Bat Jarvis had been called in to protect in the days before the Groome Street gang began to be.

Shamrock Hall, being under the eyes of the great Bat, was, of course, forbidden ground; and it was with no intention of spoiling the harmony of the evening that Mr. Dawson had looked in. He was there in a purely private and peaceful character.

As he sat smoking, sipping, and observing the revels, there settled at the next table Mr. Robert ("Nigger") Coston, an eminent member of the Three Points.

There being temporary peace between the two gangs, the great men exchanged a not unfriendly nod and, after a short pause, a word or two. Mr. Coston, alluding to an Italian who had just pirouetted past, remarked that there sure was some class to the way that wop hit it up. Mr. Dawson said Yup, there sure was. You would have said that all Nature smiled.

Alas! The next moment the sky was covered with black clouds and the storm broke. For Mr. Dawson, continuing in this vein of criticism, rather injudiciously gave it as his opinion that one of the lady dancers had two left feet.

For a moment Mr. Coston did not see which lady was alluded to.

"De goil in de pink skoit," said Mr. Dawson, facilitating the other's search by pointing with a much-chewed cigarette. It was at this moment that Nature's smile was shut off as if by a tap. For the lady in the pink skirt had been in receipt of Mr. Coston's respectful devotion for the past eight days.

From this point onwards the march of events was rapid.

Mr. Coston, rising, asked Mr. Dawson who he thought he, Mr. Dawson, was.

Mr. Dawson, extinguishing his cigarette and placing it behind his ear, replied that he was the fellow who could bite his, Mr. Coston's, head off.

Mr. Coston said: "Huh?"

Mr. Dawson said: "Sure."

Mr. Coston called Mr. Dawson a pie-faced rubber-necked four-flusher.

Mr. Dawson called Mr. Coston a coon.

And that was where the trouble really started.

It was secretly a great grief to Mr. Coston that his skin was of so swarthy a hue. To be permitted to address Mr. Coston face to face by his nickname was a sign of the closest friendship, to which only Spider Reilly, Jack Repetto, and one or two more of the gang could aspire. Others spoke of him as Nigger, or, more briefly, Nig—strictly behind his back. For Mr. Coston had a wide reputation as a fighter, and his particular mode of battling was to descend on his antagonist and bite him. Into this action he flung himself with the passionate abandonment of the artist. When he bit he bit. He did not nibble.

If a friend had called Mr. Coston "Nig" he would have been running grave risks. A stranger, and a leader of a rival gang, who addressed him as "coon" was more than asking for trouble. He was pleading for it.

Great men seldom waste time. Mr. Coston, leaning towards Mr. Dawson, promptly bit him on the cheek. Mr. Dawson bounded from his seat. Such was the excitement of the moment that, instead of drawing his "canister," he forgot that he had one on his person, and, seizing a mug which had held beer, bounced it vigorously on Mr. Coston's skull, which, being of solid wood, merely gave out a resonant note and remained unbroken.

So far the honours were comparatively even, with perhaps a slight balance in favour of Mr. Coston. But now occurred an incident which turned the scale, and made war between the gangs inevitable. In the far corner of the room, surrounded by a crowd of admiring friends, sat Spider Reilly, monarch of the Three Points. He had noticed that there was a slight disturbance at the other side of the hall, but had given it little attention till, the dancing ceasing suddenly and the floor emptying itself of its crowd, he had a plain view of Mr. Dawson and Mr. Coston squaring up at each other for the second round. We must assume that Mr. Reilly was not thinking what he did, for his action was contrary to all rules of gang-etiquette. In the street it would have been perfectly legitimate, even praiseworthy, but in a dance-hall belonging to a neutral power it was unpardonable.

What he did was to produce his "canister" and pick off the unsuspecting Mr. Dawson just as that exquisite was preparing to get in some more good work with the beer-mug. The leader of the Table Hillites fell with a crash, shot through the leg; and Spider Reilly, together with Mr. Coston and others of the Three Points, sped through the doorway for safety, fearing the wrath of Bat Jarvis, who, it was known, would countenance no such episodes at the dance-hall which he had undertaken to protect.

Mr. Dawson, meanwhile, was attended to and helped home. Willing informants gave him the name of his aggressor, and before morning the Table Hill camp was in ferment. Shooting broke out in three places, though there were no casualties. When the day dawned there existed between the two gangs a state of war more bitter than any in their record; for this time it was no question of obscure nonentities. Chieftain had assaulted chieftain; royal blood had been spilt.

* * *

"Comrade Windsor," said Psmith, when Master Maloney had spoken his last word, "we must take careful note of this little matter. I rather fancy that sooner or later we may be able to turn it to our profit. I am sorry for Dude Dawson, anyhow. Though I have never met him, I have a sort of instinctive respect for him. A man such as he would feel a bullet through his trouser-leg more than one of common clay who cared little how his clothes looked."

CHAPTER XIX — IN PLEASANT STREET

Careful inquiries, conducted incognito by Master Maloney among the denizens of Pleasant Street, brought the information that rents in the tenements were collected not weekly but monthly, a fact which must undoubtedly cause a troublesome hitch in the campaign. Rent-day, announced Pugsy, fell on the last day of the month.

"I rubbered around," he said, "and did de sleut' act, and I finds t'ings out. Dere's a feller comes round 'bout supper time dat day, an' den it's up to de fam'lies what lives in de tenements to dig down into deir jeans fer de stuff, or out dey goes dat same night."

"Evidently a hustler, our nameless friend," said Psmith.

"I got dat from a kid what knows anuder kid what lives dere," explained Master Maloney. "Say," he proceeded confidentially, "dat kid's in bad, sure he is. Dat second kid, de one what lives dere. He's a wop kid, an—"

"A what, Comrade Maloney?"

"A wop. A Dago. Why, don't you get next? Why, an Italian. Sure, dat's right. Well, dis kid, he is sure to de bad, 'cos his father come over from Italy to work on de Subway."

"I don't see why that puts him in bad," said Billy Windsor wonderingly.

"Nor I," agreed Psmith. "Your narratives, Comrade Maloney, always seem to me to suffer from a certain lack of construction. You start at the end, and then you go back to any portion of the story which happens to appeal to you at the moment, eventually winding up at the beginning. Why should the fact that this stripling's father has come over from Italy to work on the Subway be a misfortune?"

"Why, sure, because he got fired an' went an' swatted de foreman one on de coco, an' de magistrate gives him t'oity days."

"And then, Comrade Maloney? This thing is beginning to get clearer. You are like Sherlock Holmes. After you've explained a thing from start to finish—or, as you prefer to do, from finish to start—it becomes quite simple."

"Why, den dis kid's in bad for fair, 'cos der ain't nobody to pungle de bones."

"Pungle de what, Comrade Maloney?"

"De bones. De stuff. Dat's right. De dollars. He's all alone, dis kid, so when de rent-guy blows in, who's to slip him over de simoleons? It'll be outside for his, quick."

Billy warmed up at this tale of distress in his usual way. "Somebody ought to do something. It's a vile shame the kid being turned out like that."

"We will see to it, Comrade Windsor. Cosy Moments shall step in. We will combine business with pleasure, paying the stripling's rent and corralling the rent-collector at the same time. What is today? How long before the end of the month? Another week! A murrain on it, Comrade Windsor. Two murrains. This delay may undo us."

But the days went by without any further movement on the part of the enemy. A strange quiet seemed to be brooding over the other camp. As a matter of fact, the sudden outbreak of active hostilities with the Table Hill contingent had had the effect of taking the minds of Spider Reilly and his warriors off Cosy Moments and its affairs, much as the unexpected appearance of a mad bull would make a man forget that he had come out butterfly-hunting.

Psmith and Billy could wait; they were not likely to take the offensive; but the Table Hillites demanded instant attention.

War had broken out, as was usual between the gangs, in a somewhat tentative fashion at first sight. There had been sniping and skirmishes by the wayside, but as yet no pitched battle. The two armies were sparring for an opening.

The end of the week arrived, and Psmith and Billy, conducted by Master Maloney, made their way to Pleasant Street. To get there it was necessary to pass through a section of the enemy's country; but the perilous passage was safely negotiated. The expedition reached its unsavoury goal intact.

The wop kid, whose name, it appeared, was Giuseppe Orloni, inhabited a small room at the very top of the building next to the one Psmith and Mike had visited on their first appearance in Pleasant Street. He was out when the party, led by Pugsy up dark stairs, arrived; and, on returning, seemed both surprised and alarmed to see visitors. Pugsy undertook to do the honours. Pugsy as interpreter was energetic but not wholly successful. He appeared to have a fixed idea that the Italian language was one easily mastered by the simple method of saying "da" instead of "the," and tacking on a final "a" to any word that seemed to him to need one.

"Say, kid," he began, "has da rent-a-man come yet-a?"

The black eyes of the wop kid clouded. He gesticulated, and said something in his native language.

"He hasn't got next," reported Master Maloney. "He can't git on to me curves. Dese wop kids is all boneheads. Say, kid, look-a here." He walked out of the room and closed the door; then, rapping on it smartly from the outside, re-entered and, assuming a look of extreme ferocity, stretched out his hand and thundered: "Unbelt-a! Slip-a me da stuff!"

The wop kid's puzzlement became pathetic.

"This," said Psmith, deeply interested, "is getting about as tense as anything I ever struck. Don't give in, Comrade Maloney. Who knows but that you may yet win through? I fancy the trouble is that your too perfect Italian accent is making the youth home-sick. Once more to the breach, Comrade Maloney."

Master Maloney made a gesture of disgust. "I'm t'roo. Dese Dagoes makes me tired. Dey don't know enough to go upstairs to take de Elevated. Beat it, you mutt," he observed with moody displeasure to the wop kid, accompanying the words with a gesture which conveyed its own meaning. The wop kid, plainly glad to get away, slipped out of the door like a shadow.

Pugsy shrugged his shoulders.

"Gents," he said resignedly, "it's up to youse."

"I fancy," said Psmith, "that this is one of those moments when it is necessary for me to unlimber my Sherlock Holmes system. As thus. If the rent collector had been here, it is certain, I think, that Comrade Spaghetti, or whatever you said his name was, wouldn't have been. That is to say, if the rent collector had called and found no money waiting for him, surely Comrade Spaghetti would have been out in the cold night instead of under his own roof-tree. Do you follow me, Comrade Maloney?"

"That's right," said Billy Windsor. "Of course."

"Elementary, my dear Watson, elementary," murmured Psmith.

"So all we have to do is to sit here and wait."

"All?" said Psmith sadly. "Surely it is enough. For of all the scaly localities I have struck this seems to me the scaliest. The architect of this Stately Home of America seems to have had a positive hatred for windows. His idea of ventilation was to leave a hole in the wall about the size of a lima bean and let the thing go at that. If our friend does not arrive shortly, I shall pull down the roof. Why, gadzooks! Not to mention stap my vitals! Isn't that a trap-door up there? Make a long-arm, Comrade Windsor."

Billy got on a chair and pulled the bolt. The trap-door opened downwards. It fell, disclosing a square of deep blue sky.

"Gum!" he said. "Fancy living in this atmosphere when you don't have to. Fancy these fellows keeping that shut all the time."

"I expect it is an acquired taste," said Psmith, "like Limburger cheese. They don't begin to appreciate air till it is thick enough to scoop chunks out of with a spoon. Then they get up on their hind legs and inflate their chests and say, 'This is fine! This beats ozone hollow!' Leave it open, Comrade Windsor. And now, as to the problem of dispensing with Comrade Maloney's services?"

"Sure," said Billy. "Beat it, Pugsy, my lad."

Pugsy looked up, indignant.

"Beat it?" he queried.

"While your shoe leather's good," said Billy. "This is no place for a minister's son. There may be a rough house in here any minute, and you would be in the way."

"I want to stop and pipe de fun," objected Master Maloney.

"Never mind. Cut off. We'll tell you all about it to-morrow."

Master Maloney prepared reluctantly to depart. As he did so there was a sound of a well-shod foot on the stairs, and a man in a snuff-coloured suit, wearing a brown Homburg hat and carrying a small notebook in one hand, walked briskly into the room. It was not necessary for Psmith to get his Sherlock Holmes system to work. His whole appearance proclaimed the new-comer to be the long-expected collector of rents.

CHAPTER XX — CORNERED

He stood in the doorway looking with some surprise at the group inside. He was a smallish, pale-faced man with protruding eyes and teeth which gave him a certain resemblance to a rabbit.

"Hello," he said.

"Welcome to New York," said Psmith.

Master Maloney, who had taken advantage of the interruption to edge farther into the room, now appeared to consider the question of his departure permanently shelved. He sidled to a corner and sat down on an empty soap-box with the air of a dramatic critic at the opening night of a new play. The scene looked good to him. It promised interesting developments. Master Maloney was an earnest student of the drama, as exhibited in the theatres of the East Side, and few had ever applauded the hero of "Escaped from Sing-Sing," or hissed the villain of "Nellie, the Beautiful Cloak-Model" with more fervour than he. He liked his drama to have plenty of action, and to his practised eye this one promised well. Psmith he looked upon as a quite amiable lunatic, from whom little was to be expected; but there was a set expression on Billy Windsor's face which suggested great things.

His pleasure was abruptly quenched. Billy Windsor, placing a firm hand on his collar, led him to the door and pushed him out, closing the door behind him.

The rent collector watched these things with a puzzled eye. He now turned to Psmith.

"Say, seen anything of the wops that live here?" he inquired.

"I am addressing—?" said Psmith courteously.

"My name's Gooch."

Psmith bowed.

"Touching these wops, Comrade Gooch," he said, "I fear there is little chance of your seeing them to-night, unless you wait some considerable time. With one of them—the son and heir of the family, I should say—we have just been having a highly interesting and informative chat. Comrade Maloney, who has just left us, acted as interpreter. The father, I am told, is in the dungeon below the castle moat for a brief spell for punching his foreman in the eye. The result? The rent is not forthcoming."

"Then it's outside for theirs," said Mr. Gooch definitely.

"It's a big shame," broke in Billy, "turning the kid out. Where's he to go?"

"That's up to him. Nothing to do with me. I'm only acting under orders from up top."

"Whose orders, Comrade Gooch?" inquired Psmith.

"The gent who owns this joint."

"Who is he?" said Billy.

Suspicion crept into the protruding eyes of the rent collector. He waxed wroth. "Say!" he demanded. "Who are you two guys, anyway, and what do you think you're doing here? That's what I'd like to know. What do you want with the name of the owner of this place? What business is it of yours?"

"The fact is, Comrade Gooch, we are newspaper men."

"I guessed you were," said Mr. Gooch with triumph. "You can't bluff me. Well, it's no good, boys. I've nothing for you. You'd better chase off and try something else."

He became more friendly.

"Say, though," he said, "I just guessed you were from some paper. I wish I could give you a story, but I can't. I guess it's this Cosy Moments business that's been and put your editor on to this joint, ain't it? Say, though, that's a queer thing, that paper. Why, only a few weeks ago it used to be a sort of take-home-and-read-to-the-kids affair. A friend of mine used to buy it regular. And then suddenly it comes out with a regular whoop, and started knocking these tenements and boosting Kid Brady, and all that. I can't understand it. All I know is that it's begun to get this place talked about. Why, you see for yourselves how it is. Here is your editor sending you down to get a story about it. But, say, those Cosy Moments guys are taking big risks. I tell you straight they are, and that goes. I happen to know a thing or two about what's going on on the other side, and I tell you there's going to be something doing if they don't cut it out quick. Mr.—" he stopped and chuckled, "Mr. Jones isn't the man to sit still and smile. He's going to get busy. Say, what paper do you boys come from?"

"Cosy Moments, Comrade Gooch," Psmith replied. "Immediately behind you, between you and the door, is Comrade Windsor, our editor. I am Psmith. I sub-edit."

For a moment the inwardness of the information did not seem to come home to Mr. Gooch. Then it hit him. He spun round. Billy Windsor was standing with his back against the door and a more than nasty look on his face.

"What's all this?" demanded Mr. Gooch.

"I will explain all," said Psmith soothingly. "In the first place, however, this matter of Comrade Spaghetti's rent. Sooner than see that friend of my boyhood slung out to do the wandering-child-in-the-snow act, I will brass up for him."

"Confound his rent. Let me out."

"Business before pleasure. How much is it? Twelve dollars? For the privilege of suffocating in this compact little Black Hole? By my halidom, Comrade Gooch, that gentleman whose name you are so shortly to tell us has a very fair idea of how to charge! But who am I that I should criticise? Here are the simoleons, as our young friend, Comrade Maloney, would call them. Push me over a receipt."

"Let me out."

"Anon, gossip, anon.—Shakespeare. First, the receipt."

Mr. Gooch scribbled a few words in his notebook and tore out the page. Psmith thanked him.

"I will see that it reaches Comrade Spaghetti," he said. "And now to a more important matter. Don't put away that notebook. Turn to a clean page, moisten your pencil, and write as follows. Are you ready? By the way, what is your Christian name? . . . Gooch, Gooch, this is no way to speak! Well, if you are sensitive on the point, we will waive the Christian name. It is my duty to tell you, however, that I suspect it to be Percy. Let us push on. Are you ready, once more? Pencil moistened? Very well, then. 'I'—comma—'being of sound mind and body'—comma—'and a bright little chap altogether'—comma—Why, you're not writing."

"Let me out," bellowed Mr. Gooch. "I'll summon you for assault and battery. Playing a fool game like this! Get away from that door."

"There has been no assault and battery yet, Comrade Gooch, but who shall predict how long so happy a state of things will last? Do not be deceived by our gay and smiling faces, Comrade Gooch. We mean business. Let me put the whole position of affairs before you; and I am sure a man of your perception will see that there is only one thing to be done."

He dusted the only chair in the room with infinite care and sat down. Billy Windsor, who had not spoken a word or moved an inch since the beginning of the interview, continued to stand and be silent. Mr. Gooch shuffled restlessly in the middle of the room.

"As you justly observed a moment ago," said Psmith, "the staff of Cosy Moments is taking big risks. We do not rely on your unsupported word for that. We have had practical demonstration of the fact from one J. Repetto, who tried some few nights ago to put us out of business. Well, it struck us both that we had better get hold of the name of the blighter who runs these tenements as quickly as possible, before Comrade Repetto's next night out. That is what we should like you to give us, Comrade Gooch. And we should like it in writing. And, on second thoughts, in ink. I have one of those patent non-leakable fountain pens in my pocket. The Old Journalist's Best Friend. Most of the ink has come out and is permeating the lining of my coat, but I think there is still sufficient for our needs. Remind me later, Comrade Gooch, to continue on the subject of fountain pens. I have much to say on the theme. Meanwhile, however, business, business. That is the cry."

He produced a pen and an old letter, the last page of which was blank, and began to write.

"How does this strike you?" he said. "'I'—(I have left a blank for the Christian name: you can write it in yourself later)—'I, blank Gooch, being a collector of rents in Pleasant Street, New York, do hereby swear'—hush, Comrade Gooch, there is no need to do it yet—'that the name of the owner of the Pleasant Street tenements, who is responsible for the perfectly foul conditions there, is—' And that is where you come in, Comrade Gooch. That is where we need your specialised knowledge. Who is he?"

Billy Windsor reached out and grabbed the rent collector by the collar. Having done this, he proceeded to shake him.

Billy was muscular, and his heart was so much in the business that Mr. Gooch behaved as if he had been caught in a high wind. It is probable that in another moment the desired information might have been shaken out of him, but before this could happen there was a banging at the door, followed by the entrance of Master Maloney. For the first time since Psmith had known him, Pugsy was openly excited.

"Say," he began, "youse had better beat it quick, you had. Dey's coming!"

"And now go back to the beginning, Comrade Maloney," said Psmith patiently, "which in the exuberance of the moment you have skipped. Who are coming?"

"Why, dem. De guys."

Psmith shook his head.

"Your habit of omitting essentials, Comrade Maloney, is going to undo you one of these days. When you get to that ranch of yours, you will probably start out to gallop after the cattle without remembering to mount your mustang. There are four million guys in New York. Which section is it that is coming?"

"Gum! I don't know how many dere is ob dem. I seen Spider Reilly an' Jack Repetto an'—"

"Say no more," said Psmith. "If Comrade Repetto is there, that is enough for me. I am going to get on the roof and pull it up after me."

Billy released Mr. Gooch, who fell, puffing, on to the low bed, which stood in one corner of the room.

"They must have spotted us as we were coming here," he said, "and followed us. Where did you see them, Pugsy?"

"On de Street just outside. Dere was a bunch of dem talkin' togedder, and I hears dem say you was in here. One of dem seen you come in, an dere ain't no ways out but de front, so dey ain't hurryin'! Dey just reckon to pike along upstairs, lookin' into each room till dey finds you. An dere's a bunch of dem goin' to wait on de Street in case youse beat it past down de stairs while de udder guys is rubberin' for youse. Say, gents, it's pretty fierce, dis proposition. What are youse goin' to do?"

Mr. Gooch, from the bed, laughed unpleasantly.

"I guess you ain't the only assault-and-battery artists in the business," he said. "Looks to me as if some one else was going to get shaken up some."

Billy looked at Psmith.

"Well?" he said. "What shall we do? Go down and try and rush through?"

Psmith shook his head.

"Not so, Comrade Windsor, but about as much otherwise as you can jolly well imagine."

"Well, what then?"

"We will stay here. Or rather we will hop nimbly up on to the roof through that skylight. Once there, we may engage these varlets on fairly equal terms. They can only get through one at a time. And while they are doing it I will give my celebrated imitation of Horatius. We had better be moving. Our luggage, fortunately, is small. Merely Comrade Gooch. If you will get through the skylight, I will pass him up to you."

Mr. Gooch, with much verbal embroidery, stated that he would not go. Psmith acted promptly. Gripping the struggling rent collector round the waist, and ignoring his frantic kicks as mere errors in taste, he lifted him to the trap-door, whence the head, shoulders and arms of Billy Windsor protruded into the room. Billy collected the collector, and then Psmith turned to Pugsy.

"Comrade Maloney."

"Huh?"

"Have I your ear?"

"Huh?"

"Are you listening till you feel that your ears are the size of footballs? Then drink this in. For weeks you have been praying for a chance to show your devotion to the great cause; or if you haven't, you ought to have been. That chance has come. You alone can save us. In a sense, of course, we do not need to be saved. They will find it hard to get at us, I fancy, on the roof. But it ill befits the dignity of the editorial staff of a great New York weekly to roost like pigeons for any length of time; and consequently it is up to you."

"Shall I go for de cops, Mr. Smith?"

"No, Comrade Maloney, I thank you. I have seen the cops in action, and they did not impress me. We do not want allies who will merely shake their heads at Comrade Repetto and the others, however sternly. We want some one who will swoop down upon these merry roisterers, and, as it were, soak to them good. Do you know where Dude Dawson lives?"

The light of intelligence began to shine in Master Maloney's face. His eye glistened with respectful approval. This was strategy of the right sort.

"Dude Dawson? Nope. But I can ask around."

"Do so, Comrade Maloney. And when found, tell him that his old college chum, Spider Reilly, is here. He will not be able to come himself, I fear, but he can send representatives."

"Sure."

"That's all, then. Go downstairs with a gay and jaunty air, as if you had no connection with the old firm at all. Whistle a few lively bars. Make careless gestures. Thus shall you win through. And now it would be no bad idea, I fancy, for me to join the rest of the brains of the paper up aloft. Off you go, Comrade Maloney. And, in passing, don't take a week about it. Leg it with all the speed you possess."

Pugsy vanished, and Psmith closed the door behind him. Inspection revealed the fact that it possessed no lock. As a barrier it was useless. He left it ajar, and, jumping up, gripped the edge of the opening in the roof and pulled himself through.

Billy Windsor was seated comfortably on Mr. Gooch's chest a few feet away. By his side was his big stick. Psmith possessed himself of this, and looked about him. The examination was satisfactory. The trap-door appeared to be the only means of access to the roof, and between their roof and that of the next house there was a broad gulf.

"Practically impregnable," he murmured. "Only one thing can dish us, Comrade Windsor; and that is if they have the sense to get on to the roof next door and start shooting. Even in that case, however, we have cover in the shape of the chimneys. I think we may fairly say that all is well. How are you getting along? Has the patient responded at all?"

"Not yet," said Billy. "But he's going to."

"He will be in your charge. I must devote myself exclusively to guarding the bridge. It is a pity that the trap has not got a bolt this side. If it had, the thing would be a perfect picnic. As it is, we must leave it open. But we mustn't expect everything."

Billy was about to speak, but Psmith suddenly held up his hand warningly. From the room below came a sound of feet.

For a moment the silence was tense. Then from Mr. Gooch's lips there escaped a screech.

"This way! They're up—"

The words were cut short as Billy banged his hand over the speaker's mouth. But the thing was done.

"On top de roof," cried a voice. "Dey've beaten it for de roof."

The chair rasped over the floor. Feet shuffled. And then, like a jack-in-the-box, there popped through the opening a head and shoulders.

CHAPTER XXI — THE BATTLE OF PLEASANT STREET

The new arrival was a young man with a shock of red hair, an ingrowing Roman nose, and a mouth from which force or the passage of time had removed three front teeth. He held on to the edges of the trap with his hands, and stared in a glassy manner into Psmith's face, which was within a foot of his own.

There was a momentary pause, broken by an oath from Mr. Gooch, who was still undergoing treatment in the background.

"Aha!" said Psmith genially. "Historic picture. 'Doctor Cook discovers the North Pole.'"

The red-headed young man blinked. The strong light of the open air was trying to his eyes.

"Youse had better come down," he observed coldly. "We've got youse."

"And," continued Psmith, unmoved, "is instantly handed a gum-drop by his faithful Esquimaux."

As he spoke, he brought the stick down on the knuckles which disfigured the edges of the trap. The intruder uttered a howl and dropped out of sight. In the room below there were whisperings and mutterings, growing gradually louder till something resembling coherent conversation came to Psmith's ears, as he knelt by the trap making meditative billiard-shots with the stick at a small pebble.

"Aw g'wan! Don't be a quitter!"

"Who's a quitter?"

"Youse is a quitter. Get on top de roof. He can't hoit youse."

"De guy's gotten a big stick." Psmith nodded appreciatively. "I and Roosevelt," he murmured.

A somewhat baffled silence on the part of the attacking force was followed by further conversation.

"Gum! some guy's got to go up." Murmur of assent from the audience. A voice, in inspired tones: "Let Sam do it!"

This suggestion made a hit. There was no doubt about that. It was a success from the start. Quite a little chorus of voices expressed sincere approval of the very happy solution to what had seemed an insoluble problem. Psmith, listening from above, failed to detect in the choir of glad voices one that might belong to Sam himself. Probably gratification had rendered the chosen one dumb.

"Yes, let Sam do it!" cried the unseen chorus. The first speaker, unnecessarily, perhaps—for the motion had been carried almost unanimously—but possibly with the idea of convincing the one member of the party in whose bosom doubts might conceivably be harboured, went on to adduce reasons.

"Sam bein' a coon," he argued, "ain't goin' to git hoit by no stick. Youse can't hoit a coon by soakin' him on de coco, can you, Sam?"

Psmith waited with some interest for the reply, but it did not come. Possibly Sam did not wish to generalise on insufficient experience.

"Solvitur ambulando," said Psmith softly, turning the stick round in his fingers. "Comrade Windsor!"

"Hullo?"

"Is it possible to hurt a coloured gentleman by hitting him on the head with a stick?"

"If you hit him hard enough."

"I knew there was some way out of the difficulty," said Psmith with satisfaction. "How are you getting on up at your end of the table, Comrade Windsor?"

"Fine."

"Any result yet?"

"Not at present."

"Don't give up."

"Not me."

"The right spirit, Comrade Win—"

A report like a cannon in the room below interrupted him. It was merely a revolver shot, but in the confined space it was deafening. The bullet sang up into the sky.

"Never hit me!" said Psmith with dignified triumph.

The noise was succeeded by a shuffling of feet. Psmith grasped his stick more firmly. This was evidently the real attack. The revolver shot had been a mere demonstration of artillery to cover the infantry's advance.

Sure enough, the next moment a woolly head popped through the opening, and a pair of rolling eyes gleamed up at the old Etonian.

"Why, Sam!" said Psmith cordially, "this is well met! I remember you. Yes, indeed, I do. Wasn't you the feller with the open umbereller that I met one rainy morning on the Av-en-ue? What, are you coming up? Sam, I hate to do it, but—"

A yell rang out.

"What was that?" asked Billy Windsor over his shoulder.

"Your statement, Comrade Windsor, has been tested and proved correct."

By this time the affair had begun to draw a "gate." The noise of the revolver had proved a fine advertisement. The roof of the house next door began to fill up. Only a few of the occupants could get a clear view of the proceedings, for a large chimney-stack intervened. There was considerable speculation as to what was passing between Billy Windsor and Mr. Gooch. Psmith's share in the entertainment was more obvious. The early comers had seen his interview with Sam, and were relating it with gusto to their friends. Their attitude towards Psmith was that of a group of men watching a terrier at a rat-hole. They looked to him to provide entertainment for them, but they realised that the first move must be with the attackers. They were fair-minded men, and they did not expect Psmith to make any aggressive move.

Their indignation, when the proceedings began to grow slow, was directed entirely at the dilatory Three Pointers. With an aggrieved air, akin to that of a crowd at a cricket match when batsmen are playing for a draw, they began to "barrack." They hooted the Three Pointers. They begged them to go home and tuck themselves up in bed. The men on the roof were mostly Irishmen, and it offended them to see what should have been a spirited fight so grossly bungled.

"G'wan away home, ye quitters!" roared one.

"Call yersilves the Three Points, do ye? An' would ye know what I call ye? The Young Ladies' Seminary!" bellowed another with withering scorn.

A third member of the audience alluded to them as "stiffs."

"I fear, Comrade Windsor," said Psmith, "that our blithe friends below are beginning to grow a little unpopular with the many-headed. They must be up and doing if they wish to retain the esteem of Pleasant Street. Aha!"

Another and a longer explosion from below, and more bullets wasted themselves on air. Psmith sighed.

"They make me tired," he said. "This is no time for a feu de joie. Action! That is the cry. Action! Get busy, you blighters!"

The Irish neighbours expressed the same sentiment in different and more forcible words. There was no doubt about it—as warriors, the Three Pointers had failed to give satisfaction.

A voice from the room called up to Psmith.

"Say!"

"You have our ear," said Psmith.

"What's that?"

"I said you had our ear."

"Are youse stiffs comin' down off out of dat roof?"

"Would you mind repeating that remark?"

"Are youse guys goin' to quit off out of dat roof?"

"Your grammar is perfectly beastly," said Psmith severely.

"Hey!"

"Well?"

"Are youse guys—?"

"No, my lad," said Psmith, "since you ask, we are not. And why? Because the air up here is refreshing, the view pleasant, and we are expecting at any moment an important communication from Comrade Gooch."

"We're goin' to wait here till youse come down."

"If you wish it," said Psmith courteously, "by all means do. Who am I that I should dictate your movements? The most I aspire to is to check them when they take an upward direction."

There was silence below. The time began to pass slowly. The Irishmen on the other roof, now definitely abandoning hope of further entertainment, proceeded with hoots of scorn to climb down one by one into the recesses of their own house.

Suddenly from the street far below there came a fusillade of shots and a babel of shouts and counter-shouts. The roof of the house next door, which had been emptying itself slowly and reluctantly, filled again with a magical swiftness, and the low wall facing into the street became black with the backs of those craning over.

"What's that?" inquired Billy.

"I rather fancy," said Psmith, "that our allies of the Table Hill contingent must have arrived. I sent Comrade Maloney to explain matters to Dude Dawson, and it seems as if that golden-hearted sportsman had responded. There appear to be great doings in the street."

In the room below confusion had arisen. A scout, clattering upstairs, had brought the news of the Table Hillites' advent, and there was doubt as to the proper course to pursue. Certain voices urged going down to help the main body. Others pointed out that that would mean abandoning the siege of the roof. The scout who had brought the news was eloquent in favour of the first course.

"Gum!" he cried, "don't I keep tellin' youse dat de Table Hills is here? Sure, dere's a whole bunch of dem, and unless youse come on down dey'll bite de hull head off of us lot. Leave those stiffs on de roof. Let Sam wait here with his canister, and den dey can't get down, 'cos Sam'll pump dem full of lead while dey're beatin' it t'roo de trap-door. Sure."

Psmith nodded reflectively.

"There is certainly something in what the bright boy says," he murmured. "It seems to me the grand rescue scene in the third act has sprung a leak. This will want thinking over."

In the street the disturbance had now become terrific. Both sides were hard at it, and the Irishmen on the roof, rewarded at last for their long vigil, were yelling encouragement promiscuously and whooping with the unfettered ecstasy of men who are getting the treat of their lives without having paid a penny for it.

The behaviour of the New York policeman in affairs of this kind is based on principles of the soundest practical wisdom. The unthinking man would rush in and attempt to crush the combat in its earliest and fiercest stages. The New York policeman, knowing the importance of his own safety, and the insignificance of the gangsman's, permits the opposing forces to hammer each other into a certain distaste for battle, and then, when both sides have begun to have enough of it, rushes in himself and clubs everything in sight. It is an admirable process in its results, but it is sure rather than swift.

Proceedings in the affair below had not yet reached the police interference stage. The noise, what with the shots and yells from the street and the ear-piercing approval of the roof-audience, was just working up to a climax.

Psmith rose. He was tired of kneeling by the trap, and there was no likelihood of Sam making another attempt to climb through. He walked towards Billy.

As he did so, Billy got up and turned to him. His eyes were gleaming with excitement. His whole attitude was triumphant. In his hand he waved a strip of paper.

"I've got it," he cried.

"Excellent, Comrade Windsor," said Psmith. "Surely we must win through now. All we have to do is to get off this roof, and fate cannot touch us. Are two mammoth minds such as ours unequal to such a feat? It can hardly be. Let us ponder."

"Why not go down through the trap? They've all gone to the street."

Psmith shook his head.

"All," he replied, "save Sam. Sam was the subject of my late successful experiment, when I proved that coloured gentlemen's heads could be hurt with a stick. He is now waiting below, armed with a pistol, ready—even anxious—to pick us off as we climb through the trap. How would it be to drop Comrade Gooch through first, and so draw his fire? Comrade Gooch, I am sure, would be delighted to do a little thing like that for old friends of our standing or—but what's that!"

"What's the matter?"

"Is that a ladder that I see before me, its handle to my hand? It is! Comrade Windsor, we win through. Cosy Moments' editorial staff may be tree'd, but it cannot be put out of business. Comrade Windsor, take the other end of that ladder and follow me."

The ladder was lying against the farther wall. It was long, more than long enough for the purpose for which it was needed. Psmith and Billy rested it on the coping, and pushed it till the other end reached across the gulf to the roof of the house next door, Mr. Gooch eyeing them in silence the while.

Psmith turned to him.

"Comrade Gooch," he said, "do nothing to apprise our friend Sam of these proceedings. I speak in your best interests. Sam is in no mood to make nice distinctions between friend and foe. If you bring him up here, he will probably mistake you for a member of the staff of Cosy Moments, and loose off in your direction without waiting for explanations. I think you had better come with us. I will go first, Comrade Windsor, so that if the ladder breaks, the paper will lose merely a sub-editor, not an editor."

He went down on all-fours, and in this attitude wormed his way across to the opposite roof, whose occupants, engrossed in the fight in the street, in which the police had now joined, had their backs turned and did not observe him. Mr. Gooch, pallid and obviously ill-attuned to such feats, followed him; and finally Billy Windsor reached the other side.

"Neat," said Psmith complacently. "Uncommonly neat. Comrade Gooch reminded me of the untamed chamois of the Alps, leaping from crag to crag."

In the street there was now comparative silence. The police, with their clubs, had knocked the last remnant of fight out of the combatants. Shooting had definitely ceased.

"I think," said Psmith, "that we might now descend. If you have no other engagements, Comrade Windsor, I will take you to the Knickerbocker, and buy you a square meal. I would ask for the pleasure of your company also, Comrade Gooch, were it not that matters of private moment, relating to the policy of the paper, must be discussed at the table. Some other day, perhaps. We are infinitely obliged to you for your sympathetic co-operation in this little matter. And now good-bye. Comrade Windsor, let us debouch."

CHAPTER XXII — CONCERNING MR. WARING

Psmith pushed back his chair slightly, stretched out his legs, and lit a cigarette. The resources of the Knickerbocker Hotel had proved equal to supplying the fatigued staff of Cosy Moments with an excellent dinner, and Psmith had stoutly declined to talk business until the coffee arrived. This had been hard on Billy, who was bursting with his news. Beyond a hint that it was sensational he had not been permitted to go.

"More bright young careers than I care to think of," said Psmith, "have been ruined by the fatal practice of talking shop at dinner. But now that we are through, Comrade Windsor, by all means let us have it. What's the name which Comrade Gooch so eagerly divulged?"

Billy leaned forward excitedly.

"Stewart Waring," he whispered.

"Stewart who?" asked Psmith.

Billy stared.

"Great Scott, man!" he said, "haven't you heard of Stewart Waring?"

"The name seems vaguely familiar, like Isinglass or Post-toasties. I seem to know it, but it conveys nothing to me."

"Don't you ever read the papers?"

"I toy with my American of a morning, but my interest is confined mainly to the sporting page which reminds me that Comrade Brady has been matched against one Eddie Wood a month from to-day. Gratifying as it is to find one of the staff getting on in life, I fear this will cause us a certain amount of inconvenience. Comrade Brady will have to leave the office temporarily in order to go into training, and what shall we do then for a fighting editor? However, possibly we may not need one now. Cosy Moments should be able shortly to give its message to the world and ease up for a while. Which brings us back to the point. Who is Stewart Waring?"

"Stewart Waring is running for City Alderman. He's one of the biggest men in New York!"

"Do you mean in girth? If so, he seems to have selected the right career for himself."

"He's one of the bosses. He used to be Commissioner of Buildings for the city."

"Commissioner of Buildings? What exactly did that let him in for?"

"It let him in for a lot of graft."

"How was that?"

"Oh, he took it off the contractors. Shut his eyes and held out his hands when they ran up rotten buildings that a strong breeze would have knocked down, and places like that Pleasant Street hole without any ventilation."

"Why did he throw up the job?" inquired Psmith. "It seems to me that it was among the World's Softest. Certain drawbacks to it, perhaps, to the man with the Hair-Trigger Conscience; but I gather that Comrade Waring did not line up in that class. What was his trouble?"

"His trouble," said Billy, "was that he stood in with a contractor who was putting up a music-hall, and the contractor put it up with material about as strong as a heap of meringues, and it collapsed on the third night and killed half the audience."

"And then?"

"The papers raised a howl, and they got after the contractor, and the contractor gave Waring away. It killed him for the time being."

"I should have thought it would have had that excellent result permanently," said Psmith thoughtfully. "Do you mean to say he got back again after that?"

"He had to quit being Commissioner, of course, and leave the town for a time; but affairs move so fast here that a thing like that blows over. He made a bit of a pile out of the job, and could afford to lie low for a year or two."

"How long ago was that?"

"Five years. People don't remember a thing here that happened five years back unless they're reminded of it."

Psmith lit another cigarette.

"We will remind them," he said.

Billy nodded.

"Of course," he said, "one or two of the papers against him in this Aldermanic Election business tried to bring the thing up, but they didn't cut any ice. The other papers said it was a shame, hounding a man who was sorry for the past and who was trying to make good now; so they dropped it. Everybody thought that Waring was on the level now. He's been shooting off a lot of hot air lately about philanthropy and so on. Not that he has actually done a thing—not so much as given a supper to a dozen news-boys; but he's talked, and talk gets over if you keep it up long enough."

Psmith nodded adhesion to this dictum.

"So that naturally he wants to keep it dark about these tenements. It'll smash him at the election when it gets known."

"Why is he so set on becoming an Alderman," inquired Psmith.

"There's a lot of graft to being an Alderman," explained Billy.

"I see. No wonder the poor gentleman was so energetic in his methods. What is our move now, Comrade Windsor?"

Billy stared.

"Why, publish the name, of course."

"But before then? How are we going to ensure the safety of our evidence? We stand or fall entirely by that slip of paper, because we've got the beggar's name in the writing of his own collector, and that's proof positive."

"That's all right," said Billy, patting his breast-pocket. "Nobody's going to get it from me."

Psmith dipped his hand into his trouser-pocket.

"Comrade Windsor," he said, producing a piece of paper, "how do we go?"

He leaned back in his chair, surveying Billy blandly through his eye-glass. Billy's eyes were goggling. He looked from Psmith to the paper and from the paper to Psmith.

"What—what the—?" he stammered. "Why, it's it!"

Psmith nodded.

"How on earth did you get it?"

Psmith knocked the ash off his cigarette.

"Comrade Windsor," he said, "I do not wish to cavil or carp or rub it in in any way. I will merely remark that you pretty nearly landed us in the soup, and pass on to more congenial topics. Didn't you know we were followed to this place?"

"Followed!"

"By a merchant in what Comrade Maloney would call a tall-shaped hat. I spotted him at an early date, somewhere down by Twenty-ninth Street. When we dived into Sixth Avenue for a space at Thirty-third Street, did he dive, too? He did. And when we turned into Forty-second Street, there he was. I tell you, Comrade Windsor, leeches were aloof, and burrs non-adhesive compared with that tall-shaped-hatted blighter."

"Yes?"

"Do you remember, as you came to the entrance of this place, somebody knocking against you?"

"Yes, there was a pretty big crush in the entrance."

"There was; but not so big as all that. There was plenty of room for this merchant to pass if he had wished. Instead of which he butted into you. I happened to be waiting for just that, so I managed to attach myself to his wrist with some vim and give it a fairly hefty wrench. The paper was inside his hand."

Billy was leaning forward with a pale face.

"Jove!" he muttered.

"That about sums it up," said Psmith.

Billy snatched the paper from the table and extended it towards him.

"Here," he said feverishly, "you take it. Gum, I never thought I was such a mutt! I'm not fit to take charge of a toothpick. Fancy me not being on the watch for something of that sort. I guess I was so tickled with myself at the thought of having got the thing, that it never struck me they might try for it. But I'm through. No more for me. You're the man in charge now."

Psmith shook his head.

"These stately compliments," he said, "do my old heart good, but I fancy I know a better plan. It happened that I chanced to have my eye on the blighter in the tall-shaped hat, and so was enabled to land him among the ribstones; but who knows but that in the crowd on Broadway there may not lurk other, unidentified blighters in equally tall-shaped hats, one of whom may work the same sleight-of-hand speciality on me? It was not that you were not capable of taking care of that paper: it was simply that you didn't happen to spot the man. Now observe me closely, for what follows is an exhibition of Brain."

He paid the bill, and they went out into the entrance-hall of the hotel. Psmith, sitting down at a table, placed the paper in an envelope and addressed it to himself at the address of Cosy Moments. After which, he stamped the envelope and dropped it into the letter-box at the back of the hall.

"And now, Comrade Windsor," he said, "let us stroll gently homewards down the Great White Way. What matter though it be fairly stiff with low-browed bravoes in tall-shaped hats? They cannot harm us. From me, if they search me thoroughly, they may scoop a matter of eleven dollars, a watch, two stamps, and a packet of chewing-gum. Whether they would do any better with you I do not know. At any rate, they wouldn't get that paper; and that's the main thing."

"You're a genius," said Billy Windsor.

"You think so?" said Psmith diffidently. "Well, well, perhaps you are right, perhaps you are right. Did you notice the hired ruffian in the flannel suit who just passed? He wore a baffled look, I fancy. And hark! Wasn't that a muttered 'Failed!' I heard? Or was it the breeze moaning in the tree-tops? To-night is a cold, disappointing night for Hired Ruffians, Comrade Windsor."

CHAPTER XXIII — REDUCTIONS IN THE STAFF

The first member of the staff of Cosy Moments to arrive at the office on the following morning was Master Maloney. This sounds like the beginning of a "Plod and Punctuality," or "How Great Fortunes have been Made" story; but, as a matter of fact, Master Maloney was no early bird. Larks who rose in his neighbourhood, rose alone. He did not get up with them. He was supposed to be at the office at nine o'clock. It was a point of honour with him, a sort of daily declaration of independence, never to put in an appearance before nine-thirty. On this particular morning he was punctual to the minute, or half an hour late, whichever way you choose to look at it.

He had only whistled a few bars of "My Little Irish Rose," and had barely got into the first page of his story of life on the prairie when Kid Brady appeared. The Kid, as was his habit when not in training, was smoking a big black cigar. Master Maloney eyed him admiringly. The Kid, unknown to that gentleman himself, was Pugsy's ideal. He came from the Plains; and had, indeed, once actually been a cowboy; he was a coming champion; and he could smoke black cigars. It was, therefore, without his usual well-what-is-it-now? air that Pugsy laid down his book, and prepared to converse.

"Say, Mr. Smith or Mr. Windsor about, Pugsy?" asked the Kid.

"Naw, Mr. Brady, they ain't came yet," replied Master Maloney respectfully.

"Late, ain't they?"

"Sure. Mr. Windsor generally blows in before I do."

"Wonder what's keepin' them."

"P'raps, dey've bin put out of business," suggested Pugsy nonchalantly.

"How's that?"

Pugsy related the events of the previous day, relaxing something of his austere calm as he did so. When he came to the part where the Table Hill allies swooped down on the unsuspecting Three Pointers, he was almost animated.

"Say," said the Kid approvingly, "that Smith guy's got more grey matter under his thatch than you'd think to look at him. I—"

"Comrade Brady," said a voice in the doorway, "you do me proud."

"Why, say," said the Kid, turning, "I guess the laugh's on me. I didn't see you, Mr. Smith. Pugsy's been tellin' me how you sent him for the Table Hills yesterday. That was cute. It was mighty smart. But say, those guys are goin' some, ain't they now! Seems as if they was dead set on puttin' you out of business."

"Their manner yesterday, Comrade Brady, certainly suggested the presence of some sketchy outline of such an ideal in their minds. One Sam, in particular, an ebony-hued sportsman, threw himself into the task with great vim. I rather fancy he is waiting for us with his revolver to this moment. But why worry? Here we are, safe and sound, and Comrade Windsor may be expected to arrive at any moment. I see, Comrade Brady, that you have been matched against one Eddie Wood."

"It's about that I wanted to see you, Mr. Smith. Say, now that things have been and brushed up so, what with these gang guys layin' for you the way they're doin', I guess you'll be needin' me around here. Isn't that right? Say the word and I'll call off this Eddie Wood fight."

"Comrade Brady," said Psmith with some enthusiasm, "I call that a sporting offer. I'm very much obliged. But we mustn't stand in your way. If you eliminate this Comrade Wood, they will have to give you a chance against Jimmy Garvin, won't they?"

"I guess that's right, sir," said the Kid. "Eddie stayed nineteen rounds against Jimmy, and if I can put him away, it gets me into line with Jimmy, and he can't side-step me."

"Then go in and win, Comrade Brady. We shall miss you. It will be as if a ray of sunshine had been removed from the office. But you mustn't throw a chance away. We shall be all right, I think."

"I'll train at White Plains," said the Kid. "That ain't far from here, so I'll be pretty near in case I'm wanted. Hullo, who's here?"

He pointed to the door. A small boy was standing there, holding a note.

"Mr. Smith?"

"Sir to you," said Psmith courteously.

"P. Smith?"

"The same. This is your lucky day."

"Cop at Jefferson Market give me dis to take to youse."

"A cop in Jefferson Market?" repeated Psmith. "I did not know I had friends among the constabulary there. Why, it's from Comrade Windsor." He opened the envelope and read the letter. "Thanks," he said, giving the boy a quarter-dollar.

It was apparent the Kid was politely endeavouring to veil his curiosity. Master Maloney had no such scruples.

"What's in de letter, boss?" he inquired.

"The letter, Comrade Maloney, is from our Mr. Windsor, and relates in terse language the following facts, that our editor last night hit a policeman in the eye, and that he was sentenced this morning to thirty days on Blackwell's Island."

"He's de guy!" admitted Master Maloney approvingly.

"What's that?" said the Kid. "Mr. Windsor bin punchin' cops! What's he bin doin' that for?"

"He gives no clue. I must go and find out. Could you help Comrade Maloney mind the shop for a few moments while I push round to Jefferson Market and make inquiries?"

"Sure. But say, fancy Mr. Windsor cuttin' loose that way!" said the Kid admiringly.

The Jefferson Market Police Court is a little way down town, near Washington Square. It did not take Psmith long to reach it, and by the judicious expenditure of a few dollars he was enabled to obtain an interview with Billy in a back room.

The chief editor of Cosy Moments was seated on a bench, looking upon the world through a pair of much blackened eyes. His general appearance was dishevelled. He had the air of a man who has been caught in the machinery.

"Hullo, Smith," he said. "You got my note all right then?"

Psmith looked at him, concerned.

"Comrade Windsor," he said, "what on earth has been happening to you?"

"Oh, that's all right," said Billy. "That's nothing."

"Nothing! You look as if you had been run over by a motor-car."

"The cops did that," said Billy, without any apparent resentment. "They always turn nasty if you put up a fight. I was a fool to do it, I suppose, but I got so mad. They knew perfectly well that I had nothing to do with any pool-room downstairs."

Psmith's eye-glass dropped from his eye.

"Pool-room, Comrade Windsor?"

"Yes. The house where I live was raided late last night. It seems that some gamblers have been running a pool-room on the ground floor. Why the cops should have thought I had anything to do with it, when I was sleeping peacefully upstairs, is more than I can understand. Anyway, at about three in the morning there was the dickens of a banging at my door. I got up to see what was doing, and found a couple of Policemen there. They told me to come along with them to the station. I asked what on earth for. I might have known it was no use arguing with a New York cop. They said they had been tipped off that there was a pool-room being run in the house, and that they were cleaning up the house, and if I wanted to say anything I'd better say it to the magistrate. I said, all right, I'd put on some clothes and come with them. They said they couldn't wait about while I put on clothes. I said I wasn't going to travel about New York in pyjamas, and started to get into my shirt. One of them gave me a shove in the ribs with his night-stick, and told me to come along quick. And that made me so mad I hit out." A chuckle escaped Billy. "He wasn't expecting it, and I got him fair. He went down over the bookcase. The other cop took a swipe at me with his club, but by that time I was so mad I'd have taken on Jim Jeffries, if he had shown up and got in my way. I just sailed in, and was beginning to make the man think that he had stumbled on Stanley Ketchel or Kid Brady or a dynamite explosion by mistake, when the other fellow loosed himself from the bookcase, and they started in on me together, and there was a general rough house, in the middle of which somebody seemed to let off about fifty thousand dollars' worth of fireworks all in a bunch; and I didn't remember anything more till I found myself in a cell, pretty nearly knocked to pieces. That's my little life-history. I guess I was a fool to cut loose that way, but I was so mad I didn't stop to think."

Psmith sighed.

"You have told me your painful story," he said. "Now hear mine. After parting with you last night, I went meditatively back to my Fourth Avenue address, and, with a courtly good night to the large policeman who, as I have mentioned in previous conversations, is stationed almost at my very door, I passed on into my room, and had soon sunk into a dreamless slumber. At about three o'clock in the morning I was aroused by a somewhat hefty banging on the door."

"What!"

"A banging at the door," repeated Psmith. "There, standing on the mat, were three policemen. From their remarks I gathered that certain bright spirits had been running a gambling establishment in the lower regions of the building—where, I think I told you, there is a saloon—and the Law was now about to clean up the place. Very cordially the honest fellows invited me to go with them. A conveyance, it seemed, waited in the street without. I pointed out, even as you appear to have done, that sea-green pyjamas with old rose frogs were not the costume in which a Shropshire Psmith should be seen abroad in one of the world's greatest cities; but they assured me—more by their manner than their words—that my misgivings were out of place, so I yielded. These men, I told myself, have lived longer in New York than I. They know what is done and what is not done. I will bow to their views. So I went with them, and after a very pleasant and cosy little ride in the patrol waggon, arrived at the police station. This morning I chatted a while with the courteous magistrate, convinced him by means of arguments and by silent evidence of my open, honest face and unwavering eye that I was not a professional gambler, and came away without a stain on my character."

Billy Windsor listened to this narrative with growing interest.

"Gum! it's them!" he cried.

"As Comrade Maloney would say," said Psmith, "meaning what, Comrade Windsor?"

"Why, the fellows who are after that paper. They tipped the police off about the pool-rooms, knowing that we should be hauled off without having time to take anything with us. I'll bet anything you like they have been in and searched our rooms by now."

"As regards yours, Comrade Windsor, I cannot say. But it is an undoubted fact that mine, which I revisited before going to the office, in order to correct what seemed to me even on reflection certain drawbacks to my costume, looks as if two cyclones and a threshing machine had passed through it."

"They've searched it?"

"With a fine-toothed comb. Not one of my objects of vertu but has been displaced."

Billy Windsor slapped his knee.

"It was lucky you thought of sending that paper by post," he said. "We should have been done if you hadn't. But, say," he went on miserably, "this is awful. Things are just warming up for the final burst, and I'm out of it all."

"For thirty days," sighed Psmith. "What Cosy Moments really needs is a sitz-redacteur."

"A what?"

"A sitz-redacteur, Comrade Windsor, is a gentleman employed by German newspapers with a taste for lhse majesti to go to prison whenever required in place of the real editor. The real editor hints in his bright and snappy editorial, for instance, that the Kaiser's moustache reminds him of a bad dream. The police force swoops down en masse on the office of the journal, and are met by the sitz-redacteur, who goes with them peaceably, allowing the editor to remain and sketch out plans for his next week's article on the Crown Prince. We need a sitz-redacteur on Cosy Moments almost as much as a fighting editor; and we have neither."

"The Kid has had to leave then?"

"He wants to go into training at once. He very sportingly offered to cancel his match, but of course that would never do. Unless you consider Comrade Maloney equal to the job, I must look around me for some one else. I shall be too fully occupied with purely literary matters to be able to deal with chance callers. But I have a scheme."

"What's that?"

"It seems to me that we are allowing much excellent material to lie unused in the shape of Comrade Jarvis."

"Bat Jarvis."

"The same. The cat-specialist to whom you endeared yourself somewhat earlier in the proceedings by befriending one of his wandering animals. Little deeds of kindness, little acts of love, as you have doubtless heard, help, etc. Should we not give Comrade Jarvis an opportunity of proving the correctness of this statement? I think so. Shortly after you—if you will forgive me for touching on a painful subject—have been haled to your dungeon, I will push round to Comrade Jarvis's address, and sound him on the subject. Unfortunately, his affection is confined, I fancy, to you. Whether he will consent to put himself out on my behalf remains to be seen. However, there is no harm in trying. If nothing else comes of the visit, I shall at least have had the opportunity of chatting with one of our most prominent citizens."

A policeman appeared at the door.

"Say, pal," he remarked to Psmith, "you'll have to be fading away soon, I guess. Give you three minutes more. Say it quick."

He retired. Billy leaned forward to Psmith.

"I guess they won't give me much chance," he whispered, "but if you see me around in the next day or two, don't be surprised."

"I fail to follow you, Comrade Windsor."

"Men have escaped from Blackwell's Island before now. Not many, it's true; but it has been done."

Psmith shook his head.

"I shouldn't," he said. "They're bound to catch you, and then you will be immersed in the soup beyond hope of recovery. I shouldn't wonder if they put you in your little cell for a year or so."

"I don't care," said Billy stoutly. "I'd give a year later on to be round and about now."

"I shouldn't," urged Psmith. "All will be well with the paper. You have left a good man at the helm."

"I guess I shan't get a chance, but I'll try it if I do."

The door opened and the policeman reappeared.

"Time's up, I reckon."

"Well, good-bye, Comrade Windsor," said Psmith regretfully. "Abstain from undue worrying. It's a walk-over from now on, and there's no earthly need for you to be around the office. Once, I admit, this could not have been said. But now things have simplified themselves. Have no fear. This act is going to be a scream from start to finish."

CHAPTER XXIV — A GATHERING OF CAT-SPECIALISTS

Master Maloney raised his eyes for a moment from his book as Psmith re-entered the office.

"Dere's a guy in dere waitin' ter see youse," he said briefly, jerking his head in the direction of the inner room.

"A guy waiting to see me, Comrade Maloney? With or without a sand-bag?"

"Says his name's Jackson," said Master Maloney, turning a page.

Psmith moved quickly to the door of the inner room.

"Why, Comrade Jackson," he said, with the air of a father welcoming home the prodigal son, "this is the maddest, merriest day of all the glad New Year. Where did you come from?"

Mike, looking very brown and in excellent condition, put down the paper he was reading.

"Hullo, Psmith," he said. "I got back this morning. We're playing a game over in Brooklyn to-morrow."

"No engagements of any importance to-day?"

"Not a thing. Why?"

"Because I propose to take you to visit Comrade Jarvis, whom you will doubtless remember."

"Jarvis?" said Mike, puzzled. "I don't remember any Jarvis."

"Let your mind wander back a little through the jungle of the past. Do you recollect paying a visit to Comrade Windsor's room—"

"By the way, where is Windsor?"

"In prison. Well, on that evening—"

"In prison?"

"For thirty days. For slugging a policeman. More of this, however, anon. Let us return to that evening. Don't you remember a certain gentleman with just about enough forehead to keep his front hair from getting all tangled up with his eye-brows?"

"Oh, the cat chap? I know."

"As you very justly observe, Comrade Jackson, the cat chap. For going straight to the mark and seizing on the salient point of a situation, I know of no one who can last two minutes against you. Comrade Jarvis may have other sides to his character—possibly many—but it is as a cat chap that I wish to approach him to-day."

"What's the idea? What are you going to see him for?"

"We," corrected Psmith. "I will explain all at a little luncheon at which I trust that you will be my guest. Already, such is the stress of this journalistic life, I hear my tissues crying out imperatively to be restored. An oyster and a glass of milk somewhere round the corner, Comrade Jackson? I think so, I think so."

* * *

"I was reading Cosy Moments in there," said Mike, as they lunched. "You certainly seem to have bucked it up rather. Kid Brady's reminiscences are hot stuff."

"Somewhat sizzling, Comrade Jackson," admitted Psmith. "They have, however, unfortunately cost us a fighting editor."

"How's that?"

"Such is the boost we have given Comrade Brady, that he is now never without a match. He has had to leave us to-day to go to White Plains to train for an encounter with a certain Mr. Wood, a four-ounce-glove juggler of established fame."

"I expect you need a fighting editor, don't you?"

"He is indispensable, Comrade Jackson, indispensable."

"No rotting. Has anybody cut up rough about the stuff you've printed?"

"Cut up rough? Gadzooks! I need merely say that one critical reader put a bullet through my hat—"

"Rot! Not really?"

"While others kept me tree'd on top of a roof for the space of nearly an hour. Assuredly they have cut up rough, Comrade Jackson."

"Great Scott! Tell us."

Psmith briefly recounted the adventures of the past few weeks.

"But, man," said Mike, when he had finished "why on earth don't you call in the police?"

"We have mentioned the matter to certain of the force. They appeared tolerably interested, but showed no tendency to leap excitedly to our assistance. The New York policeman, Comrade Jackson, like all great men, is somewhat peculiar. If you go to a New York policeman and exhibit a black eye, he will examine it and express some admiration for the abilities of the citizen responsible for the same. If you press the matter, he becomes bored, and says, 'Ain't youse satisfied with what youse got? G'wan!' His advice in such cases is good, and should be followed. No; since coming to this city I have developed a habit of taking care of myself, or employing private help. That is why I should like you, if you will, to come with me to call upon Comrade Jarvis. He is a person of considerable influence among that section of the populace which is endeavouring to smash in our occiputs. Indeed, I know of nobody who cuts a greater quantity of ice. If I can only enlist Comrade Jarvis's assistance, all will be well. If you are through with your refreshment, shall we be moving in his direction? By the way, it will probably be necessary in the course of our interview to allude to you as one of our most eminent living cat-fanciers. You do not object? Remember that you have in your English home seventy-four fine cats, mostly Angoras. Are you on to that? Then let us be going. Comrade Maloney has given me the address. It is a goodish step down on the East side. I should like to take a taxi, but it might seem ostentatious. Let us walk."

* * *

They found Mr. Jarvis in his Groome Street fancier's shop, engaged in the intellectual occupation of greasing a cat's paws with butter. He looked up as they entered, and began to breathe a melody with a certain coyness.

"Comrade Jarvis," said Psmith, "we meet again. You remember me?"

"Nope," said Mr. Jarvis, pausing for a moment in the middle of a bar, and then taking up the air where he had left off. Psmith was not discouraged.

"Ah," he said tolerantly, "the fierce rush of New York life. How it wipes from the retina of to-day the image impressed on it but yesterday. Are you with me, Comrade Jarvis?"

The cat-expert concentrated himself on the cat's paws without replying.

"A fine animal," said Psmith, adjusting his eyeglass. "To which particular family of the Felis Domestica does that belong? In colour it resembles a Neapolitan ice more than anything."

Mr. Jarvis's manner became unfriendly.

"Say, what do youse want? That's straight ain't it? If youse want to buy a boid or a snake why don't youse say so?"

"I stand corrected," said Psmith. "I should have remembered that time is money. I called in here partly on the strength of being a colleague and side-partner of Comrade Windsor—"

"Mr. Windsor! De gent what caught my cat?"

"The same—and partly in order that I might make two very eminent cat-fanciers acquainted. This," he said, with a wave of his hand in the direction of the silently protesting Mike, "is Comrade Jackson, possibly the best known of our English cat-fanciers. Comrade Jackson's stud of Angoras is celebrated wherever the King's English is spoken, and in Hoxton."

Mr. Jarvis rose, and, having inspected Mike with silent admiration for a while, extended a well-buttered hand towards him. Psmith looked on benevolently.

"What Comrade Jackson does not know about cats," he said, "is not knowledge. His information on Angoras alone would fill a volume."

"Say,"—Mr. Jarvis was evidently touching on a point which had weighed deeply upon him—"why's catnip called catnip?"

Mike looked at Psmith helplessly. It sounded like a riddle, but it was obvious that Mr. Jarvis's motive in putting the question was not frivolous. He really wished to know.

"The word, as Comrade Jackson was just about to observe," said Psmith, "is a corruption of cat-mint. Why it should be so corrupted I do not know. But what of that? The subject is too deep to be gone fully into at the moment. I should recommend you to read Comrade Jackson's little brochure on the matter. Passing lightly on from that—"

"Did youse ever have a cat dat ate beetles?" inquired Mr. Jarvis.

"There was a time when many of Comrade Jackson's felidae supported life almost entirely on beetles."

"Did they git thin?"

Mike felt that it was time, if he was to preserve his reputation, to assert himself.

"No," he replied firmly.

Mr. Jarvis looked astonished.

"English beetles," said Psmith, "don't make cats thin. Passing lightly—"

"I had a cat oncest," said Mr. Jarvis, ignoring the remark and sticking to his point, "dat ate beetles and got thin and used to tie itself into knots."

"A versatile animal," agreed Psmith.

"Say," Mr. Jarvis went on, now plainly on a subject near to his heart, "dem beetles is fierce. Sure. Can't keep de cats off of eatin' dem, I can't. First t'ing you know dey've swallowed dem, and den dey gits thin and ties theirselves into knots."

"You should put them into strait-waistcoats," said Psmith. "Passing, however, lightly—"

"Say, ever have a cross-eyed cat?"

"Comrade Jackson's cats," said Psmith, "have happily been almost free from strabismus."

"Dey's lucky, cross-eyed cats is. You has a cross-eyed cat, and not'in' don't never go wrong. But, say, was dere ever a cat wit one blue eye and one yaller one in your bunch? Gum, it's fierce when it's like dat. It's a real skiddoo, is a cat wit one blue eye and one yaller one. Puts you in bad, surest t'ing you know. Oncest a guy give me a cat like dat, and first t'ing you know I'm in bad all round. It wasn't till I give him away to de cop on de corner and gets me one dat's cross-eyed dat I lifts de skiddoo off of me."

"And what happened to the cop?" inquired Psmith, interested.

"Oh, he got in bad, sure enough," said Mr. Jarvis without emotion. "One of de boys what he'd pinched and had sent to de Island once lays for him and puts one over him wit a black-jack. Sure. Dat's what comes of havin' a cat wit one blue eye and one yaller one."

Mr. Jarvis relapsed into silence. He seemed to be meditating on the inscrutable workings of Fate. Psmith took advantage of the pause to leave the cat topic and touch on matter of more vital import.

"Tense and exhilarating as is this discussion of the optical peculiarities of cats," he said, "there is another matter on which, if you will permit me, I should like to touch. I would hesitate to bore you with my own private troubles, but this is a matter which concerns Comrade Windsor as well as myself, and I know that your regard for Comrade Windsor is almost an obsession."

"How's that?"

"I should say," said Psmith, "that Comrade Windsor is a man to whom you give the glad hand."

"Sure. He's to the good, Mr. Windsor is. He caught me cat."

"He did. By the way, was that the one that used to tie itself into knots?"

"Nope. Dat was anudder."

"Ah! However, to resume. The fact is, Comrade Jarvis, we are much persecuted by scoundrels. How sad it is in this world! We look to every side. We look north, east, south, and west, and what do we see? Mainly scoundrels. I fancy you have heard a little about our troubles before this. In fact, I gather that the same scoundrels actually approached you with a view to engaging your services to do us in, but that you very handsomely refused the contract."

"Sure," said Mr. Jarvis, dimly comprehending.

"A guy comes to me and says he wants you and Mr. Windsor put through it, but I gives him de t'run down. 'Nuttin' done,' I says. 'Mr. Windsor caught me cat.'"

"So I was informed," said Psmith. "Well, failing you, they went to a gentleman of the name of Reilly."

"Spider Reilly?"

"You have hit it, Comrade Jarvis. Spider Reilly, the lessee and manager of the Three Points gang."

"Dose T'ree Points, dey're to de bad. Dey're fresh."

"It is too true, Comrade Jarvis."

"Say," went on Mr. Jarvis, waxing wrathful at the recollection, "what do youse t'ink dem fresh stiffs done de udder night. Started some rough woik in me own dance-joint."

"Shamrock Hall?" said Psmith.

"Dat's right. Shamrock Hall. Got gay, dey did, wit some of de Table Hillers. Say, I got it in for dem gazebos, sure I have. Surest t'ing you know."

Psmith beamed approval.

"That," he said, "is the right spirit. Nothing could be more admirable. We are bound together by our common desire to check the ever-growing spirit of freshness among the members of the Three Points. Add to that the fact that we are united by a sympathetic knowledge of the manners and customs of cats, and especially that Comrade Jackson, England's greatest fancier, is our mutual friend, and what more do we want? Nothing."

"Mr. Jackson's to de good," assented Mr. Jarvis, eyeing Mike in friendly fashion.

"We are all to de good," said Psmith. "Now the thing I wished to ask you is this. The office of the paper on which I work was until this morning securely guarded by Comrade Brady, whose name will be familiar to you."

"De Kid?"

"On the bull's-eye, as usual, Comrade Jarvis. Kid Brady, the coming light-weight champion of the world. Well, he has unfortunately been compelled to leave us, and the way into the office is consequently clear to any sand-bag specialist who cares to wander in. Matters connected with the paper have become so poignant during the last few days that an inrush of these same specialists is almost a certainty, unless—and this is where you come in."

"Me?"

"Will you take Comrade Brady's place for a few days?"

"How's that?"

"Will you come in and sit in the office for the next day or so and help hold the fort? I may mention that there is money attached to the job. We will pay for your services. How do we go, Comrade Jarvis?"

Mr. Jarvis reflected but a brief moment.

"Why, sure," he said. "Me fer dat. When do I start?"

"Excellent, Comrade Jarvis. Nothing could be better. I am obliged. I rather fancy that the gay band of Three Pointers who will undoubtedly visit the offices of Cosy Moments in the next few days, probably to-morrow, are due to run up against the surprise of their lives. Could you be there at ten to-morrow morning?"

"Sure t'ing. I'll bring me canister."

"I should," said Psmith. "In certain circumstances one canister is worth a flood of rhetoric. Till to-morrow, then, Comrade Jarvis. I am very much obliged to you."

* * *

"Not at all a bad hour's work," said Psmith complacently, as they turned out of Groome Street. "A vote of thanks to you, Comrade Jackson, for your invaluable assistance."

"It strikes me I didn't do much," said Mike with a grin.

"Apparently, no. In reality, yes. Your manner was exactly right. Reserved, yet not haughty. Just what an eminent cat-fancier's manner should be. I could see that you made a pronounced hit with Comrade Jarvis. By the way, if you are going to show up at the office to-morrow, perhaps it would be as well if you were to look up a few facts bearing on the feline world. There is no knowing what thirst for information a night's rest may not give Comrade Jarvis. I do not presume to dictate, but if you were to make yourself a thorough master of the subject of catnip, for instance, it might quite possibly come in useful."

CHAPTER XXV — TRAPPED

Mr. Jarvis was as good as his word. On the following morning, at ten o'clock to the minute, he made his appearance at the office of Cosy Moments, his fore-lock more than usually well-oiled in honour of the occasion, and his right coat-pocket bulging in a manner that betrayed to the initiated eye the presence of the faithful "canister." With him, in addition to his revolver, he brought a long, thin young man who wore under his brown tweed coat a blue-and-red striped jersey. Whether he brought him as an ally in case of need or merely as a kindred soul with whom he might commune during his vigil, was not ascertained.

Pugsy, startled out of his wonted calm by the arrival of this distinguished company, observed the pair, as they passed through into the inner office, with protruding eyes, and sat speechless for a full five minutes. Psmith received the new-corners in the editorial sanctum with courteous warmth. Mr. Jarvis introduced his colleague.

"Thought I'd bring him along. Long Otto's his monaker."

"You did very rightly, Comrade Jarvis," Psmith assured him. "Your unerring instinct did not play you false when it told you that Comrade Otto would be as welcome as the flowers in May. With Comrade Otto I fancy we shall make a combination which will require a certain amount of tackling."

Mr. Jarvis confirmed this view. Long Otto, he affirmed, was no rube, but a scrapper from Biffville-on-the-Slosh. The hardiest hooligan would shrink from introducing rough-house proceedings into a room graced by the combined presence of Long Otto and himself.

"Then," said Psmith, "I can go about my professional duties with a light heart. I may possibly sing a bar or two. You will find cigars in that box. If you and Comrade Otto will select one apiece and group yourselves tastefully about the room in chairs, I will start in to hit up a slightly spicy editorial on the coming election."

Mr. Jarvis regarded the paraphernalia of literature on the table with interest. So did Long Otto, who, however, being a man of silent habit, made no comment. Throughout the seance and the events which followed it he confined himself to an occasional grunt. He seemed to lack other modes of expression. A charming chap, however.

"Is dis where youse writes up pieces fer de paper?" inquired Mr. Jarvis, eyeing the table.

"It is," said Psmith. "In Comrade Windsor's pre-dungeon days he was wont to sit where I am sitting now, while I bivouacked over there at the smaller table. On busy mornings you could hear our brains buzzing in Madison Square Garden. But wait! A thought strikes me." He called for Pugsy.

"Comrade Maloney," he said, "if the Editorial Staff of this paper were to give you a day off, could you employ it to profit?"

"Surest t'ing you know," replied Pugsy with some fervour. "I'd take me goil to de Bronx Zoo."

"Your girl?" said Psmith inquiringly. "I had heard no inkling of this, Comrade Maloney. I had always imagined you one of those strong, rugged, blood-and-iron men who were above the softer emotions. Who is she?"

"Aw, she's a kid," said Pugsy. "Her pa runs a delicatessen shop down our street. She ain't a bad mutt," added the ardent swain. "I'm her steady."

"See that I have a card for the wedding, Comrade Maloney," said Psmith, "and in the meantime take her to the Bronx, as you suggest."

"Won't youse be wantin' me to-day."

"Not to-day. You need a holiday. Unflagging toil is sapping your physique. Go up and watch the animals, and remember me very kindly to the Peruvian Llama, whom friends have sometimes told me I resemble in appearance. And if two dollars would in any way add to the gaiety of the jaunt . . ."

"Sure t'ing. T'anks, boss."

"It occurred to me," said Psmith, when he had gone, "that the probable first move of any enterprising Three Pointer who invaded this office would be to knock Comrade Maloney on the head to prevent his announcing him. Comrade Maloney's services are too valuable to allow him to be exposed to unnecessary perils. Any visitors who call must find their way in for themselves. And now to work. Work, the what's-its-name of the thingummy and the thing-um-a-bob of the what d'you-call-it."

For about a quarter of an hour the only sound that broke the silence of the room was the scratching of Psmith's pen and the musical expectoration of Messrs. Otto and Jarvis. Finally Psmith leaned back in his chair with a satisfied expression, and spoke.

"While, as of course you know, Comrade Jarvis," he said, "there is no agony like the agony of literary composition, such toil has its compensations. The editorial I have just completed contains its measure of balm. Comrade Otto will bear me out in my statement that there is a subtle joy in the manufacture of the well-formed phrase. Am I not right, Comrade Otto?"

The long one gazed appealingly at Mr. Jarvis, who spoke for him.

"He's a bit shy on handin' out woids, is Otto," he said.

Psmith nodded.

"I understand. I am a man of few words myself. All great men are like that. Von Moltke, Comrade Otto, and myself. But what are words? Action is the thing. That is the cry. Action. If that is Comrade Otto's forte, so much the better, for I fancy that action rather than words is what we may be needing in the space of about a quarter of a minute. At least, if the footsteps I hear without are, as I suspect, those of our friends of the Three Points."

Jarvis and Long Otto turned towards the door. Psmith was right. Some one was moving stealthily in the outer office. Judging from the sound, more than one person.

"It is just as well," said Psmith softly, "that Comrade Maloney is not at his customary post. Now, in about a quarter of a minute, as I said—Aha!"

The handle of the door began to revolve slowly and quietly. The next moment three figures tumbled into the room. It was evident that they had not expected to find the door unlocked, and the absence of resistance when they applied their weight had had surprising effects. Two of the three did not pause in their career till they cannoned against the table. The third, who was holding the handle, was more fortunate.

Psmith rose with a kindly smile to welcome his guests.

"Why, surely!" he said in a pleased voice. "I thought I knew the face. Comrade Repetto, this is a treat. Have you come bringing me a new hat?"

The white-haired leader's face, as he spoke, was within a few inches of his own. Psmith's observant eye noted that the bruise still lingered on the chin where Kid Brady's upper-cut had landed at their previous meeting.

"I cannot offer you all seats," he went on, "unless you care to dispose yourselves upon the tables. I wonder if you know my friend, Mr. Bat Jarvis? And my friend, Mr. L. Otto? Let us all get acquainted on this merry occasion."

The three invaders had been aware of the presence of the great Bat and his colleague for some moments, and the meeting seemed to be causing them embarrassment. This may have been due to the fact that both Mr. Jarvis and Mr. Otto had produced and were toying meditatively with distinctly ugly-looking pistols.

Mr. Jarvis spoke.

"Well," he said, "what's doin'?"

Mr. Repetto, to whom the remark was directly addressed, appeared to have some difficulty in finding a reply. He shuffled his feet, and looked at the floor. His two companions seemed equally at a loss.

"Goin' to start any rough stuff?" inquired Mr. Jarvis casually.

"The cigars are on the table," said Psmith hospitably. "Draw up your chairs, and let's all be jolly. I will open the proceedings with a song."

In a rich baritone, with his eyeglass fixed the while on Mr. Repetto, he proceeded to relieve himself of the first verse of "I only know I love thee."

"Chorus, please," he added, as he finished. "Come along, Comrade Repetto. Why this shrinking coyness? Fling out your chest, and cut loose."

But Mr. Repetto's eye was fastened on Mr. Jarvis's revolver. The sight apparently had the effect of quenching his desire for song.

"'Lov' muh, ahnd ther world is—ah—mine!'" concluded Psmith.

He looked round the assembled company.

"Comrade Otto," he observed, "will now recite that pathetic little poem 'Baby's Sock is now a Blue-bag.' Pray, gentlemen, silence for Comrade Otto."

He looked inquiringly at the long youth, who remained mute. Psmith clicked his tongue regretfully.

"Comrade Jarvis," he said, "I fear that as a smoking-concert this is not going to be a success. I understand, however. Comrade Repetto and his colleagues have come here on business, and nothing will make them forget it. Typical New York men of affairs, they close their minds to all influences that might lure them from their business. Let us get on, then. What did you wish to see me about, Comrade Repetto?"

Mr. Repetto's reply was unintelligible.

Mr. Jarvis made a suggestion.

"Youse had better beat it," he said.

Long Otto grunted sympathy with this advice.

"And youse had better go back to Spider Reilly," continued Mr. Jarvis, "and tell him that there's nothin' doin' in the way of rough house wit dis gent here." He indicated Psmith, who bowed. "And you can tell de Spider," went on Bat with growing ferocity, "dat next time he gits gay and starts in to shoot guys in me dance-joint I'll bite de head off'n him. See? Does dat go? If he t'inks his little two-by-four gang can put it across de Groome Street, he can try. Dat's right. An' don't fergit dis gent here and me is pals, and any one dat starts anyt'ing wit dis gent is going to have to git busy wit me. Does dat go?"

Psmith coughed, and shot his cuffs.

"I do not know," he said, in the manner of a chairman addressing a meeting, "that I have anything to add to the very well-expressed remarks of my friend, Comrade Jarvis. He has, in my opinion, covered the ground very thoroughly and satisfactorily. It now only remains for me to pass a vote of thanks to Comrade Jarvis and to declare this meeting at an end."

"Beat it," said Mr. Jarvis, pointing to the door.

The delegation then withdrew.

"I am very much obliged," said Psmith, "for your courtly assistance, Comrade Jarvis. But for you I do not care to think with what a splash I might not have been immersed in the gumbo. Thank you, Comrade Jarvis. And you, Comrade Otto."

"Aw chee!" said Mr. Jarvis, handsomely dismissing the matter. Mr. Otto kicked the leg of the table, and grunted.

* * *

For half an hour after the departure of the Three Pointers Psmith chatted amiably to his two assistants on matters of general interest. The exchange of ideas was somewhat one-sided, though Mr. Jarvis had one or two striking items of information to impart, notably some hints on the treatment of fits in kittens.

At the end of this period the conversation was once more interrupted by the sound of movements in the outer office.

"If dat's dose stiffs come back—" began Mr. Jarvis, reaching for his revolver.

"Stay your hand, Comrade Jarvis," said as a sharp knock sounded on the door. "I do not think it can be our late friends. Comrade Repetto's knowledge of the usages of polite society is too limited, I fancy, to prompt him to knock on doors. Come in."

The door opened. It was not Mr. Repetto or his colleagues, but another old friend. No other, in fact, than Mr. Francis Parker, he who had come as an embassy from the man up top in the very beginning of affairs, and had departed, wrathful, mouthing declarations of war. As on his previous visit, he wore the dude suit, the shiny shoes, and the tall-shaped hat.

"Welcome, Comrade Parker," said Psmith. "It is too long since we met. Comrade Jarvis I think you know. If I am right, that is to say, in supposing that it was you who approached him at an earlier stage in the proceedings with a view to engaging his sympathetic aid in the great work of putting Comrade Windsor and myself out of business. The gentleman on your left is Comrade Otto."

Mr. Parker was looking at Bat in bewilderment. It was plain that he had not expected to find Psmith entertaining such company.

"Did you come purely for friendly chit-chat, Comrade Parker," inquired Psmith, "or was there, woven into the social motives of your call, a desire to talk business of any kind?"

"My business is private. I didn't expect a crowd."

"Especially of ancient friends such as Comrade Jarvis. Well, well, you are breaking up a most interesting little symposium. Comrade Jarvis, I think I shall be forced to postpone our very entertaining discussion of fits in kittens till a more opportune moment. Meanwhile, as Comrade Parker wishes to talk over some private business—"

Bat Jarvis rose.

"I'll beat it," he said.

"Reluctantly, I hope, Comrade Jarvis. As reluctantly as I hint that I would be alone. If I might drop in some time at your private residence?"

"Sure," said Mr. Jarvis warmly.

"Excellent. Well, for the present, good-bye. And many thanks for your invaluable co-operation."

"Aw chee!" said Mr. Jarvis.

"And now, Comrade Parker," said Psmith, when the door had closed, "let her rip. What can I do for you?"

"You seem to be all to the merry with Bat Jarvis," observed Mr. Parker.

"The phrase exactly expresses it, Comrade Parker. I am as a tortoiseshell kitten to him. But, touching your business?"

Mr. Parker was silent for a moment.

"See here," he said at last, "aren't you going to be good? Say, what's the use of keeping on at this fool game? Why not quit it before you get hurt?"

Psmith smoothed his waistcoat reflectively.

"I may be wrong, Comrade Parker," he said, "but it seems to me that the chances of my getting hurt are not so great as you appear to imagine. The person who is in danger of getting hurt seems to me to be the gentleman whose name is on that paper which is now in my possession."

"Where is it?" demanded Mr. Parker quickly.

Psmith eyed him benevolently.

"If you will pardon the expression, Comrade Parker," he said, "'Aha!' Meaning that I propose to keep that information to myself."

Mr. Parker shrugged his shoulders.

"You know your own business, I guess."

Psmith nodded.

"You are absolutely correct, Comrade Parker. I do. Now that Cosy Moments has our excellent friend Comrade Jarvis on its side, are you not to a certain extent among the Blenheim Oranges? I think so. I think so."

As he spoke there was a rap at the door. A small boy entered. In his hand was a scrap of paper.

"Guy asks me give dis to gazebo named Smiff," he said.

"There are many gazebos of that name, my lad. One of whom I am which, as Artemus Ward was wont to observe. Possibly the missive is for me."

He took the paper. It was dated from an address on the East Side.

"Dear Smith," it ran. "Come here as quick as you can, and bring some money. Explain when I see you."

It was signed "W. W."

So Billy Windsor had fulfilled his promise. He had escaped.

A feeling of regret for the futility of the thing was Psmith's first emotion. Billy could be of no possible help in the campaign at its present point. All the work that remained to be done could easily be carried through without his assistance. And by breaking out from the Island he had committed an offence which was bound to carry with it serious penalties. For the first time since his connection with Cosy Moments began Psmith was really disturbed.

He turned to Mr. Parker.

"Comrade Parker," he said, "I regret to state that this office is now closing for the day. But for this, I should be delighted to sit chatting with you. As it is—"

"Very well," said Mr. Parker. "Then you mean to go on with this business?"

"Though it snows, Comrade Parker."

They went out into the street, Psmith thoughtful and hardly realising the other's presence. By the side of the pavement a few yards down the road a taximeter-cab was standing. Psmith hailed it.

Mr. Parker was still beside him. It occurred to Psmith that it would not do to let him hear the address Billy Windsor had given in his note.

"Turn and go on down the street," he said to the driver.

He had taken his seat and was closing the door, when it was snatched from his grasp and Mr. Parker darted on to the seat opposite. The next moment the cab had started up the street instead of down and the hard muzzle of a revolver was pressing against Psmith's waistcoat.

"Now what?" said Mr. Parker smoothly, leaning back with the pistol resting easily on his knee.

CHAPTER XXVI — A FRIEND IN NEED

"The point is well taken," said Psmith thoughtfully.

"You think so?" said Mr. Parker.

"I am convinced of it."

"Good. But don't move. Put that hand back where it was."

"You think of everything, Comrade Parker."

He dropped his hand on to the seat, and remained silent for a few moments. The taxi-cab was buzzing along up Fifth Avenue now. Looking towards the window, Psmith saw that they were nearing the park. The great white mass of the Plaza Hotel showed up on the left.

"Did you ever stop at the Plaza, Comrade Parker?"

"No," said Mr. Parker shortly.

"Don't bite at me, Comrade Parker. Why be brusque on so joyous an occasion? Better men than us have stopped at the Plaza. Ah, the Park! How fresh the leaves, Comrade Parker, how green the herbage! Fling your eye at yonder grassy knoll."

He raised his hand to point. Instantly the revolver was against his waistcoat, making an unwelcome crease in that immaculate garment.

"I told you to keep that hand where it was."

"You did, Comrade Parker, you did. The fault," said Psmith handsomely, "was entirely mine. Carried away by my love of nature, I forgot. It shall not occur again."

"It had better not," said Mr. Parker unpleasantly. "If it does, I'll blow a hole through you."

Psmith raised his eyebrows.

"That, Comrade Parker," he said, "is where you make your error. You would no more shoot me in the heart of the metropolis than, I trust, you would wear a made-up tie with evening dress. Your skin, however unhealthy to the eye of the casual observer, is doubtless precious to yourself, and you are not the man I take you for if you would risk it purely for the momentary pleasure of plugging me with a revolver. The cry goes round criminal circles in New York, 'Comrade Parker is not such a fool as he looks.' Think for a moment what would happen. The shot would ring out, and instantly bicycle-policemen would be pursuing this taxi-cab with the purposeful speed of greyhounds trying to win the Waterloo Cup. You would be headed off and stopped. Ha! What is this? Psmith, the People's Pet, weltering in his gore? Death to the assassin! I fear nothing could save you from the fury of the mob, Comrade Parker. I seem to see them meditatively plucking you limb from limb. 'She loves me!' Off comes an arm. 'She loves me not.' A leg joins the little heap of limbs on the ground. That is how it would be. And what would you have left out of it? Merely, as I say, the momentary pleasure of potting me. And it isn't as if such a feat could give you the thrill of successful marksmanship. Anybody could hit a man with a pistol at an inch and a quarter. I fear you have not thought this matter out with sufficient care, Comrade Parker. You said to yourself, 'Happy thought, I will kidnap Psmith!' and all your friends said, 'Parker is the man with the big brain!' But now, while it is true that I can't get out, you are moaning, 'What on earth shall I do with him, now that I have got him?'"

"You think so, do you?"

"I am convinced of it. Your face is contorted with the anguish of mental stress. Let this be a lesson to you, Comrade Parker, never to embark on any enterprise of which you do not see the end."

"I guess I see the end of this all right."

"You have the advantage of me then, Comrade Parker. It seems to me that we have nothing before us but to go on riding about New York till you feel that my society begins to pall."

"You figure you're clever, I guess."

"There are few brighter brains in this city, Comrade Parker. But why this sudden tribute?"

"You reckon you've thought it all out, eh?"

"There may be a flaw in my reasoning, but I confess I do not at the moment see where it lies. Have you detected one?"

"I guess so."

"Ah! And what is it?"

"You seem to think New York's the only place on the map."

"Meaning what, Comrade Parker?"

"It might be a fool trick to shoot you in the city as you say, but, you see, we aren't due to stay in the city. This cab is moving on."

"Like John Brown's soul," said Psmith, nodding. "I see. Then you propose to make quite a little tour in this cab?"

"You've got it."

"And when we are out in the open country, where there are no witnesses, things may begin to move."

"That's it."

"Then," said Psmith heartily, "till that moment arrives what we must do is to entertain each other with conversation. You can take no step of any sort for a full half-hour, possibly more, so let us give ourselves up to the merriment of the passing instant. Are you good at riddles, Comrade Parker? How much wood would a wood-chuck chuck, assuming for purposes of argument that it was in the power of a wood-chuck to chuck wood?"

Mr. Parker did not attempt to solve this problem. He was sitting in the same attitude of watchfulness, the revolver resting on his knee. He seemed mistrustful of Psmith's right hand, which was hanging limply at his side. It was from this quarter that he seemed to expect attack. The cab was bowling easily up the broad street, past rows on rows of high houses, all looking exactly the same. Occasionally, to the right, through a break in the line of buildings, a glimpse of the river could be seen.

Psmith resumed the conversation.

"You are not interested in wood-chucks, Comrade Parker? Well, well, many people are not. A passion for the flora and fauna of our forests is innate rather than acquired. Let us talk of something else. Tell me about your home-life, Comrade Parker. Are you married? Are there any little Parkers running about the house? When you return from this very pleasant excursion will baby voices crow gleefully, 'Fahzer's come home'?"

Mr. Parker said nothing.

"I see," said Psmith with ready sympathy. "I understand. Say no more. You are unmarried.

She wouldn't have you. Alas, Comrade Parker! However, thus it is! We look around us, and what do we see? A solid phalanx of the girls we have loved and lost. Tell me about her, Comrade Parker. Was it your face or your manners at which she drew the line?"

Mr. Parker leaned forward with a scowl. Psmith did not move, but his right hand, as it hung, closed. Another moment and Mr. Parker's chin would be in just the right position for a swift upper-cut. . .

This fact appeared suddenly to dawn on Mr. Parker himself. He drew back quickly, and half raised the revolver. Psmith's hand resumed its normal attitude.

"Leaving more painful topics," said Psmith, "let us turn to another point. That note which the grubby stripling brought to me at the office purported to come from Comrade Windsor, and stated that he had escaped from Blackwell's Island, and was awaiting my arrival at some address in the Bowery. Would you mind telling me, purely to satisfy my curiosity, if that note was genuine? I have never made a close study of Comrade Windsor's handwriting, and in an unguarded moment I may have assumed too much."

Mr. Parker permitted himself a smile.

"I guess you aren't so clever after all," he said. "The note was a fake all right."

"And you had this cab waiting for me on the chance?"

Mr. Parker nodded.

"Sherlock Holmes was right," said Psmith regretfully. "You may remember that he advised Doctor Watson never to take the first cab, or the second. He should have gone further, and urged him not to take cabs at all. Walking is far healthier."

"You'll find it so," said Mr. Parker.

Psmith eyed him curiously.

"What are you going to do with me, Comrade Parker?" he asked.

Mr. Parker did not reply. Psmith's eye turned again to the window. They had covered much ground since last he had looked at the view. They were off Manhattan Island now, and the houses were beginning to thin out. Soon, travelling at their present rate, they must come into the open country. Psmith relapsed into silence. It was necessary for him to think. He had been talking in the hope of getting the other off his guard; but Mr. Parker was evidently too keenly on the look-out. The hand that held the revolver never wavered. The muzzle, pointing in an upward direction, was aimed at Psmith's waist. There was no doubt that a move on his part would be fatal. If the pistol went off, it must hit him. If it had been pointed at his head in the orthodox way he might have risked a sudden blow to knock it aside, but in the present circumstances that would be useless. There was nothing to do but wait.

The cab moved swiftly on. Now they had reached the open country. An occasional wooden shack was passed, but that was all. At any moment the climax of the drama might be reached. Psmith's muscles stiffened for a spring. There was little chance of its being effective, but at least it would be better to put up some kind of a fight. And he had a faint hope that the suddenness of his movement might upset the other's aim. He was bound to be hit somewhere. That was certain. But quickness might save him to some extent.

He braced his leg against the back of the cab. In another moment he would have sprung; but just then the smooth speed of the cab changed to a series of jarring bumps, each more emphatic than the last. It slowed down, then came to a halt. One of the tyres had burst.

There was a thud, as the chauffeur jumped down. They heard him fumbling in the tool-box.

Presently the body of the machine was raised slightly as he got to work with the jack.

It was about a minute later that somebody in the road outside spoke.

"Had a breakdown?" inquired the voice. Psmith recognised it. It was the voice of Kid Brady.

CHAPTER XXVII — PSMITH CONCLUDES HIS RIDE

The Kid, as he had stated to Psmith at their last interview that he intended to do, had begun his training for his match with Eddie Wood, at White Plains, a village distant but a few miles from New York. It was his practice to open a course of training with a little gentle road-work; and it was while jogging along the highway a couple of miles from his training-camp, in company with the two thick-necked gentlemen who acted as his sparring-partners, that he had come upon the broken-down taxi-cab.

If this had happened after his training had begun in real earnest, he would have averted his eyes from the spectacle, however alluring, and continued on his way without a pause. But now, as he had not yet settled down to genuine hard work, he felt justified in turning aside and looking into the matter. The fact that the chauffeur, who seemed to be a taciturn man, lacking the conversational graces, manifestly objected to an audience, deterred him not at all. One cannot have everything in this world, and the Kid and his attendant thick-necks were content to watch the process of mending the tyre, without demanding the additional joy of sparkling small-talk from the man in charge of the operations.

"Guy's had a breakdown, sure," said the first of the thick-necks.

"Surest thing you know," agreed his colleague.

"Seems to me the tyre's punctured," said the Kid.

All three concentrated their gaze on the machine

"Kid's right," said thick-neck number one. "Guy's been an' bust a tyre."

"Surest thing you know," said thick-neck number two.

They observed the perspiring chauffeur in silence for a while.

"Wonder how he did that, now?" speculated the Kid.

"Guy ran over a nail, I guess," said thick-neck number one.

"Surest thing you know," said the other, who, while perhaps somewhat lacking in the matter of original thought, was a most useful fellow to have by one. A sort of Boswell.

"Did you run over a nail?" the Kid inquired of the chauffeur.

The chauffeur ignored the question.

"This is his busy day," said the first thick-neck with satire. "Guy's too full of work to talk to us."

"Deaf, shouldn't wonder," surmised the Kid.

"Say, wonder what he's doin' with a taxi so far out of the city."

"Some guy tells him to drive him out here, I guess. Say, it'll cost him something, too. He'll have to strip off a few from his roll to pay for this."

Psmith, in the interior of the cab, glanced at Mr. Parker.

"You heard, Comrade Parker? He is right, I fancy. The bill—"

Mr. Parker dug viciously at him with the revolver.

"Keep quiet," he whispered, "or you'll get hurt."

Psmith suspended his remarks.

Outside, the conversation had begun again.

"Pretty rich guy inside," said the Kid, following up his companion's train of thought. "I'm goin' to rubber in at the window."

Psmith, meeting Mr. Parker's eye, smiled pleasantly. There was no answering smile on the other's face.

There came the sound of the Kid's feet grating on the road as he turned; and as he heard it Mr. Parker, that eminent tactician, for the first time lost his head. With a vague idea of screening Psmith from the eyes of the man in the road he half rose. For an instant the muzzle of the pistol ceased to point at Psmith's waistcoat. It was the very chance Psmith had been waiting for. His left hand shot out, grasped the other's wrist, and gave it a sharp wrench. The revolver went off with a deafening report, the bullet passing through the back of the cab; then fell to the floor, as the fingers lost their hold. The next moment Psmith's right fist, darting upwards, took Mr. Parker neatly under the angle of the jaw.

The effect was instantaneous. Psmith had risen from his seat as he delivered the blow, and it consequently got the full benefit of his weight, which was not small. Mr. Parker literally crumpled up. His head jerked back, then fell limply on his chest. He would have slipped to the floor had not Psmith pushed him on to the seat.

The interested face of the Kid appeared at the window. Behind him could be seen portions of the faces of the two thick-necks.

"Ah, Comrade Brady!" said Psmith genially. "I heard your voice, and was hoping you might look in for a chat."

"What's doin', Mr. Smith?" queried the excited Kid.

"Much, Comrade Brady, much. I will tell you all anon. Meanwhile, however, kindly knock that chauffeur down and sit on his head. He's a bad person."

"De guy's beat it," volunteered the first thick-neck.

"Surest thing you know," said the other.

"What's been doin', Mr. Smith?" asked the Kid.

"I'll tell you about it as we go, Comrade Brady," said Psmith, stepping into the road. "Riding in a taxi is pleasant provided it is not overdone. For the moment I have had sufficient. A bit of walking will do me good."

"What are you going to do with this guy, Mr. Smith?" asked the Kid, pointing to Parker, who had begun to stir slightly.

Psmith inspected the stricken one gravely.

"I have no use for him, Comrade Brady," he said. "Our ride together gave me as much of his society as I desire for to-day. Unless you or either of your friends are collecting Parkers, I propose that we leave him where he is. We may as well take the gun, however. In my opinion, Comrade Parker is not the proper man to have such a weapon. He is too prone to go firing it off in any direction at a moment's notice, causing inconvenience to all." He groped on the floor of the cab for the revolver. "Now, Comrade Brady," he said, straightening himself up, "I am at your disposal. Shall we be pushing on?"

* * *

It was late in the evening when Psmith returned to the metropolis, after a pleasant afternoon at the Brady training-camp. The Kid, having heard the details of the ride, offered once more to abandon his match with Eddie Wood, but Psmith would not hear of it. He was fairly satisfied that the opposition had fired their last shot, and that their next move would be to endeavour to come to terms. They could not hope to catch him off his guard a second time, and, as far as hired assault and battery were concerned, he was as safe in New York, now that Bat Jarvis had declared himself on his side, as he would have been in the middle of a desert. What Bat said was law on the East Side. No hooligan, however eager to make money, would dare to act against a protigi of the Groome Street leader.

The only flaw in Psmith's contentment was the absence of Billy Windsor. On this night of all nights the editorial staff of Cosy Moments should have been together to celebrate the successful outcome of their campaign. Psmith dined alone, his enjoyment of the rather special dinner which he felt justified in ordering in honour of the occasion somewhat diminished by the thought of Billy's hard case. He had seen Mr William Collier in The Man from Mexico, and that had given him an understanding of what a term of imprisonment on Blackwell's Island meant. Billy, during these lean days, must be supporting life on bread, bean soup, and water. Psmith, toying with the hors d'oeuvre, was somewhat saddened by the thought.

* * *

All was quiet at the office on the following day. Bat Jarvis, again accompanied by the faithful Otto, took up his position in the inner room, prepared to repel all invaders; but none arrived. No sounds broke the peace of the outer office except the whistling of Master Maloney.

Things were almost dull when the telephone bell rang. Psmith took down the receiver.

"Hullo?" he said.

"I'm Parker," said a moody voice.

Psmith uttered a cry of welcome.

"Why, Comrade Parker, this is splendid! How goes it? Did you get back all right yesterday? I was sorry to have to tear myself away, but I had other engagements. But why use the telephone? Why not come here in person? You know how welcome you are. Hire a taxi-cab and come right round."

Mr. Parker made no reply to the invitation.

"Mr. Waring would like to see you."

"Who, Comrade Parker?"

"Mr. Stewart Waring."

"The celebrated tenement house-owner?"

Silence from the other end of the wire. "Well," said Psmith, "what step does he propose to take towards it?"

"He tells me to say that he will be in his office at twelve o'clock to-morrow morning. His office is in the Morton Building, Nassau Street."

Psmith clicked his tongue regretfully.

"Then I do not see how we can meet," he said. "I shall be here."

"He wishes to see you at his office."

"I am sorry, Comrade Parker. It is impossible. I am very busy just now, as you may know, preparing the next number, the one in which we publish the name of the owner of the Pleasant Street Tenements. Otherwise, I should be delighted. Perhaps later, when the rush of work has diminished somewhat."

"Am I to tell Mr. Waring that you refuse?"

"If you are seeing him at any time and feel at a loss for something to say, perhaps you might mention it. Is there anything else I can do for you, Comrade Parker?"

"See here—"

"Nothing? Then good-bye. Look in when you're this way."

He hung up the receiver.

As he did so, he was aware of Master Maloney standing beside the table.

"Yes, Comrade Maloney?"

"Telegram," said Pugsy. "For Mr. Windsor."

Psmith ripped open the envelope.

The message ran:

"Returning to-day. Will be at office to-morrow morning," and it was signed "Wilberfloss."

"See who's here!" said Psmith softly.

CHAPTER XXVIII — STANDING ROOM ONLY

In the light of subsequent events it was perhaps the least bit unfortunate that Mr. Jarvis should have seen fit to bring with him to the office of Cosy Moments on the following morning two of his celebrated squad of cats, and that Long Otto, who, as usual, accompanied him, should have been fired by his example to the extent of introducing a large and rather boisterous yellow dog. They were not to be blamed, of course. They could not know that before the morning was over space in the office would be at a premium. Still, it was unfortunate.

Mr. Jarvis was slightly apologetic.

"T'ought I'd bring de kits along," he said. "Dey started in scrappin' yesterday when I was here, so to-day I says I'll keep my eye on dem."

Psmith inspected the menagerie without resentment.

"Assuredly, Comrade Jarvis," he said. "They add a pleasantly cosy and domestic touch to the scene. The only possible criticism I can find to make has to do with their probable brawling with the dog."

"Oh, dey won't scrap wit de dawg. Dey knows him."

"But is he aware of that? He looks to me a somewhat impulsive animal. Well, well, the matter's in your hands. If you will undertake to look after the refereeing of any pogrom that may arise, I say no more."

Mr. Jarvis's statement as to the friendly relations between the animals proved to be correct. The dog made no attempt to annihilate the cats. After an inquisitive journey round the room he lay down and went to sleep, and an era of peace set in. The cats had settled themselves comfortably, one on each of Mr. Jarvis's knees, and Long Otto, surveying the ceiling with his customary glassy stare, smoked a long cigar in silence. Bat breathed a tune, and scratched one of the cats under the ear. It was a soothing scene.

But it did not last. Ten minutes had barely elapsed when the yellow dog, sitting up with a start, uttered a whine. In the outer office could be heard a stir and movement. The next moment the door burst open and a little man dashed in. He had a peeled nose and showed other evidences of having been living in the open air. Behind him was a crowd of uncertain numbers. Psmith recognised the leaders of this crowd. They were the Reverend Edwin T. Philpotts and Mr. B. Henderson Asher.

"Why, Comrade Asher," he said, "this is indeed a Moment of Mirth. I have been wondering for weeks where you could have got to. And Comrade Philpotts! Am I wrong in saying that this is the maddest, merriest day of all the glad New Year?"

The rest of the crowd had entered the room.

"Comrade Waterman, too!" cried Psmith. "Why we have all met before. Except—"

He glanced inquiringly at the little man with the peeled nose.

"My name is Wilberfloss," said the other with austerity. "Will you be so good as to tell me where Mr. Windsor is?"

A murmur of approval from his followers.

"In one moment," said Psmith. "First, however, let me introduce two important members of our staff. On your right, Mr. Bat Jarvis. On your left, Mr. Long Otto. Both of Groome Street."

The two Bowery boys rose awkwardly. The cats fell in an avalanche to the floor. Long Otto, in his haste, trod on the dog, which began barking, a process which it kept up almost without a pause during the rest of the interview.

"Mr. Wilberfloss," said Psmith in an aside to Bat, "is widely known as a cat fancier in Brooklyn circles."

"Honest?" said Mr. Jarvis. He tapped Mr. Wilberfloss in friendly fashion on the chest. "Say," he asked, "did youse ever have a cat wit one blue and one yellow eye?"

Mr. Wilberfloss side-stepped and turned once more to Psmith, who was offering B. Henderson Asher a cigarette.

"Who are you?" he demanded.

"Who am I?" repeated Psmith in an astonished tone.

"Who are you?"

"I am Psmith," said the old Etonian reverently. "There is a preliminary P before the name. This, however, is silent. Like the tomb. Compare such words as ptarmigan, psalm, and phthisis."

"These gentlemen tell me you're acting editor. Who appointed you?"

Psmith reflected.

"It is rather a nice point," he said. "It might be claimed that I appointed myself. You may say, however, that Comrade Windsor appointed me."

"Ah! And where is Mr. Windsor?"

"In prison," said Psmith sorrowfully.

"In prison!"

Psmith nodded.

"It is too true. Such is the generous impulsiveness of Comrade Windsor's nature that he hit a policeman, was promptly gathered in, and is now serving a sentence of thirty days on Blackwell's Island."

Mr. Wilberfloss looked at Mr. Philpotts. Mr. Asher looked at Mr. Wilberfloss. Mr. Waterman started, and stumbled over a cat.

"I never heard of such a thing," said Mr. Wilberfloss.

A faint, sad smile played across Psmith's face.

"Do you remember, Comrade Waterman—I fancy it was to you that I made the remark—my commenting at our previous interview on the rashness of confusing the unusual with the improbable? Here we see Comrade Wilberfloss, big-brained though he is, falling into error."

"I shall dismiss Mr. Windsor immediately," said the big-brained one.

"From Blackwell's Island?" said Psmith. "I am sure you will earn his gratitude if you do. They live on bean soup there. Bean soup and bread, and not much of either."

He broke off, to turn his attention to Mr. Jarvis and Mr. Waterman, between whom bad blood seemed to have arisen. Mr. Jarvis, holding a cat in his arms, was glowering at Mr.

Waterman, who had backed away and seemed nervous.

"What is the trouble, Comrade Jarvis?"

"Dat guy dere wit two left feet," said Bat querulously, "goes and treads on de kit. I—"

"I assure you it was a pure accident. The animal—"

Mr. Wilberfloss, eyeing Bat and the silent Otto with disgust, intervened.

"Who are these persons, Mr. Smith?" he inquired.

"Poisson yourself," rejoined Bat, justly incensed. "Who's de little guy wit de peeled breezer, Mr. Smith?"

Psmith waved his hands.

"Gentlemen, gentlemen," he said, "let us not descend to mere personalities. I thought I had introduced you. This, Comrade Jarvis, is Mr. Wilberfloss, the editor of this journal. These, Comrade Wilberfloss—Zam-buk would put your nose right in a day—are, respectively, Bat Jarvis and Long Otto, our acting fighting-editors, vice Kid Brady, absent on unavoidable business."

"Kid Brady!" shrilled Mr. Wilberfloss. "I insist that you give me a full explanation of this matter. I go away by my doctor's orders for ten weeks, leaving Mr. Windsor to conduct the paper on certain well-defined lines. I return yesterday, and, getting into communication with Mr. Philpotts, what do I find? Why, that in my absence the paper has been ruined."

"Ruined?" said Psmith. "On the contrary. Examine the returns, and you will see that the circulation has gone up every week. Cosy Moments was never so prosperous and flourishing. Comrade Otto, do you think you could use your personal influence with that dog to induce it to suspend its barking for a while? It is musical, but renders conversation difficult."

Long Otto raised a massive boot and aimed it at the animal, which, dodging with a yelp, cannoned against the second cat and had its nose scratched. Piercing shrieks cleft the air.

"I demand an explanation," roared Mr. Wilberfloss above the din.

"I think, Comrade Otto," said Psmith, "it would make things a little easier if you removed that dog."

He opened the door. The dog shot out. They could hear it being ejected from the outer office by Master Maloney. When there was silence, Psmith turned courteously to the editor.

"You were saying, Comrade Wilberfloss?"

"Who is this person Brady? With Mr. Philpotts I have been going carefully over the numbers which have been issued since my departure—"

"An intellectual treat," murmured Psmith.

"—and in each there is a picture of this young man in a costume which I will not particularise—"

"There is hardly enough of it to particularise."

"—together with a page of disgusting autobiographical matter."

Psmith held up his hand.

"I protest," he said. "We court criticism, but this is mere abuse. I appeal to these gentlemen to say whether this, for instance, is not bright and interesting."

He picked up the current number of Cosy Moments, and turned to the Kid's page.

"This," he said. "Describing a certain ten-round unpleasantness with one Mexican Joe. 'Joe comes up for the second round and he gives me a nasty look, but I thinks of my mother and swats him one in the lower ribs. He hollers foul, but nix on that. Referee says, "Fight on." Joe gives me another nasty look. "All right, Kid," he says; "now I'll knock you up into the gallery." And with that he cuts loose with a right swing, but I falls into the clinch, and then—-!'"

"Bah!" exclaimed Mr. Wilberfloss.

"Go on, boss," urged Mr. Jarvis approvingly. "It's to de good, dat stuff."

"There!" said Psmith triumphantly. "You heard? Comrade Jarvis, one of the most firmly established critics east of Fifth Avenue, stamps Kid Brady's reminiscences with the hall-mark of his approval."

"I falls fer de Kid every time," assented Mr. Jarvis.

"Assuredly, Comrade Jarvis. You know a good thing when you see one. Why," he went on warmly, "there is stuff in these reminiscences which would stir the blood of a jelly-fish. Let me quote you another passage to show that they are not only enthralling, but helpful as well. Let me see, where is it? Ah, I have it. 'A bully good way of putting a guy out of business is this. You don't want to use it in the ring, because by Queensberry Rules it's a foul; but you will find it mighty useful if any thick-neck comes up to you in the street and tries to start anything. It's this way. While he's setting himself for a punch, just place the tips of the fingers of your left hand on the right side of his chest. Then bring down the heel of your left hand. There isn't a guy living that could stand up against that. The fingers give you a leverage to beat the band. The guy doubles up, and you upper-cut him with your right, and out he goes.' Now, I bet you never knew that before, Comrade Philpotts. Try it on your parishioners."

"Cosy Moments," said Mr. Wilberfloss irately, "is no medium for exploiting low prize-fighters."

"Low prize-fighters! Comrade Wilberfloss, you have been misinformed. The Kid is as decent a little chap as you'd meet anywhere. You do not seem to appreciate the philanthropic motives of the paper in adopting Comrade Brady's cause. Think of it, Comrade Wilberfloss. There was that unfortunate stripling with only two pleasures in life, to love his mother and to knock the heads off other youths whose weight coincided with his own; and misfortune, until we took him up, had barred him almost completely from the second pastime. Our editorial heart was melted. We adopted Comrade Brady. And look at him now! Matched against Eddie Wood! And Comrade Waterman will support me in my statement that a victory over Eddie Wood means that he gets a legitimate claim to meet Jimmy Garvin for the championship."

"It is abominable," burst forth Mr. Wilberfloss. "It is disgraceful. I never heard of such a thing. The paper is ruined."

"You keep reverting to that statement, Comrade Wilberfloss. Can nothing reassure you? The returns are excellent. Prosperity beams on us like a sun. The proprietor is more than satisfied."

"The proprietor?" gasped Mr. Wilberfloss. "Does he know how you have treated the paper?"

"He is cognisant of our every move."

"And he approves?"

"He more than approves."

Mr. Wilberfloss snorted.

"I don't believe it," he said.

The assembled ex-contributors backed up this statement with a united murmur. B. Henderson Asher snorted satirically.

"They don't believe it," sighed Psmith. "Nevertheless, it is true."

"It is not true," thundered Mr. Wilberfloss, hopping to avoid a perambulating cat. "Nothing will convince me of it. Mr. Benjamin White is not a maniac."

"I trust not," said Psmith. "I sincerely trust not. I have every reason to believe in his complete sanity. What makes you fancy that there is even a possibility of his being—er—?"

"Nobody but a lunatic would approve of seeing his paper ruined."

"Again!" said Psmith. "I fear that the notion that this journal is ruined has become an obsession with you, Comrade Wilberfloss. Once again I assure you that it is more than prosperous."

"If," said Mr. Wilberfloss, "you imagine that I intend to take your word in this matter, you are mistaken. I shall cable Mr. White to-day, and inquire whether these alterations in the paper meet with his approval."

"I shouldn't, Comrade Wilberfloss. Cables are expensive, and in these hard times a penny saved is a penny earned. Why worry Comrade White? He is so far away, so out of touch with our New York literary life. I think it is practically a certainty that he has not the slightest inkling of any changes in the paper."

Mr. Wilberfloss uttered a cry of triumph.

"I knew it," he said, "I knew it. I knew you would give up when it came to the point, and you were driven into a corner. Now, perhaps, you will admit that Mr. White has given no sanction for the alterations in the paper?"

A puzzled look crept into Psmith's face.

"I think, Comrade Wilberfloss," he said, "we are talking at cross-purposes. You keep harping on Comrade White and his views and tastes. One would almost imagine that you fancied that Comrade White was the proprietor of this paper."

Mr. Wilberfloss stared. B. Henderson Asher stared. Every one stared, except Mr. Jarvis, who, since the readings from the Kid's reminiscences had ceased, had lost interest in the discussion, and was now entertaining the cats with a ball of paper tied to a string.

"Fancied that Mr. White . . .?" repeated Mr. Wilberfloss. "I don't follow you. Who is, if he isn't?"

Psmith removed his monocle, polished it thoughtfully, and put it back in its place.

"I am," he said.

CHAPTER XXIX — THE KNOCK-OUT FOR MR. WARING

"You!" cried Mr. Wilberfloss.

"The same," said Psmith.

"You!" exclaimed Messrs. Waterman, Asher, and the Reverend Edwin Philpotts.

"On the spot!" said Psmith.

Mr. Wilberfloss groped for a chair and sat down.

"Am I going mad?" he demanded feebly.

"Not so, Comrade Wilberfloss," said Psmith encouragingly. "All is well. The cry goes round New York, 'Comrade Wilberfloss is to the good. He does not gibber.'"

"Do I understand you to say that you own this paper?"

"I do."

"Since when?"

"Roughly speaking, about a month."

Among his audience (still excepting Mr. Jarvis, who was tickling one of the cats and whistling a plaintive melody) there was a tendency toward awkward silence. To start bally-ragging a seeming nonentity and then to discover he is the proprietor of the paper to which you wish to contribute is like kicking an apparently empty hat and finding your rich uncle inside it. Mr. Wilberfloss in particular was disturbed. Editorships of the kind which he aspired to are not easy to get. If he were to be removed from Cosy Moments, he would find it hard to place himself anywhere else. Editors, like manuscripts, are rejected from want of space.

"Very early in my connection with this journal," said Psmith, "I saw that I was on to a good thing. I had long been convinced that about the nearest approach to the perfect job in this world, where good jobs are so hard to acquire, was to own a paper. All you had to do, once you had secured your paper, was to sit back and watch the other fellows work, and from time to time forward big cheques to the bank. Nothing could be more nicely attuned to the tastes of a Shropshire Psmith. The glimpses I was enabled to get of the workings of this little journal gave me the impression that Comrade White was not attached with any paternal fervour to Cosy Moments. He regarded it, I deduced, not so much as a life-work as in the light of an investment. I assumed that Comrade White had his price, and wrote to my father, who was visiting Carlsbad at the moment, to ascertain what that price might be. He cabled it to me. It was reasonable. Now it so happens that an uncle of mine some years ago left me a considerable number of simoleons, and though I shall not be legally entitled actually to close in on the opulence for a matter of nine months or so, I anticipated that my father would have no objection to staking me to the necessary amount on the security of my little bit of money. My father has spent some time of late hurling me at various professions, and we had agreed some time ago that the Law was to be my long suit. Paper-owning, however, may be combined with being Lord Chancellor, and I knew he would have no objection to my being a Napoleon of the Press on this side. So we closed with Comrade White, and—"

There was a knock at the door, and Master Maloney entered with a card.

"Guy's waiting outside," he said.

"Mr. Stewart Waring," read Psmith. "Comrade Maloney, do you know what Mahomet did when the mountain would not come to him?"

"Search me," said the office-boy indifferently.

"He went to the mountain. It was a wise thing to do. As a general rule in life you can't beat it. Remember that, Comrade Maloney."

"Sure," said Pugsy. "Shall I send the guy in?"

"Surest thing you know, Comrade Maloney."

He turned to the assembled company.

"Gentlemen," he said, "you know how I hate to have to send you away, but would you mind withdrawing in good order? A somewhat delicate and private interview is in the offing. Comrade Jarvis, we will meet anon. Your services to the paper have been greatly appreciated. If I might drop in some afternoon and inspect the remainder of your zoo—?"

"Any time you're down Groome Street way. Glad."

"I will make a point of it. Comrade Wilberfloss, would you mind remaining? As editor of this journal, you should be present. If the rest of you would look in about this time tomorrow—Show Mr. Waring in, Comrade Maloney."

He took a seat.

"We are now, Comrade Wilberfloss," he said, "at a crisis in the affairs of this journal, but I fancy we shall win through."

The door opened, and Pugsy announced Mr. Waring.

The owner of the Pleasant Street Tenements was of what is usually called commanding presence. He was tall and broad, and more than a little stout. His face was clean-shaven and curiously expressionless. Bushy eyebrows topped a pair of cold grey eyes. He walked into the room with the air of one who is not wont to apologise for existing. There are some men who seem to fill any room in which they may be. Mr. Waring was one of these.

He set his hat down on the table without speaking. After which he looked at Mr. Wilberfloss, who shrank a little beneath his gaze.

Psmith had risen to greet him.

"Won't you sit down?" he said.

"I prefer to stand."

"Just as you wish. This is Liberty Hall."

Mr. Waring again glanced at Mr. Wilberfloss.

"What I have to say is private," he said.

"All is well," said Psmith reassuringly. "It is no stranger that you see before you, no mere irresponsible lounger who has butted in by chance. That is Comrade J. Fillken Wilberfloss, the editor of this journal."

"The editor? I understood—"

"I know what you would say. You have Comrade Windsor in your mind. He was merely acting as editor while the chief was away hunting sand-eels in the jungles of Texas. In his absence Comrade Windsor and I did our best to keep the old journal booming along, but it lacked the master-hand. But now all is well: Comrade Wilberfloss is once more doing stunts at the old stand. You may speak as freely before him as you would before well, let us say Comrade Parker."

"Who are you, then, if this gentleman is the editor?"

"I am the proprietor."

"I understood that a Mr. White was the proprietor."

"Not so," said Psmith. "There was a time when that was the case, but not now. Things move so swiftly in New York journalistic matters that a man may well be excused for not keeping abreast of the times, especially one who, like yourself, is interested in politics and house-ownership rather than in literature. Are you sure you won't sit down?"

Mr. Waring brought his hand down with a bang on the table, causing Mr. Wilberfloss to leap a clear two inches from his chair.

"What are you doing it for?" he demanded explosively. "I tell you, you had better quit it. It isn't healthy."

Psmith shook his head.

"You are merely stating in other—and, if I may say so, inferior—words what Comrade Parker said to us. I did not object to giving up valuable time to listen to Comrade Parker. He is a fascinating conversationalist, and it was a privilege to hob-nob with him. But if you are merely intending to cover the ground covered by him, I fear I must remind you that this is one of our busy days. Have you no new light to fling upon the subject?"

Mr. Waring wiped his forehead. He was playing a lost game, and he was not the sort of man who plays lost games well. The Waring type is dangerous when it is winning, but it is apt to crumple up against strong defence.

His next words proved his demoralisation.

"I'll sue you for libel," said he.

Psmith looked at him admiringly.

"Say no more," he said, "for you will never beat that. For pure richness and whimsical humour it stands alone. During the past seven weeks you have been endeavouring in your cheery fashion to blot the editorial staff of this paper off the face of the earth in a variety of ingenious and entertaining ways; and now you propose to sue us for libel! I wish Comrade Windsor could have heard you say that. It would have hit him right."

Mr. Waring accepted the invitation he had refused before. He sat down.

"What are you going to do?" he said.

It was the white flag. The fight had gone out of him.

Psmith leaned back in his chair.

"I'll tell you," he said. "I've thought the whole thing out. The right plan would be to put the complete kybosh (if I may use the expression) on your chances of becoming an alderman. On the other hand, I have been studying the papers of late, and it seems to me that it doesn't much matter who gets elected. Of course the opposition papers may have allowed their zeal to run away with them, but even assuming that to be the case, the other candidates appear to be a pretty fair contingent of blighters. If I were a native of New York, perhaps I might take a more fervid interest in the matter, but as I am merely passing through your beautiful little city, it doesn't seem to me to make any very substantial difference who gets in. To be absolutely candid, my view of the thing is this. If the People are chumps enough to elect you, then they deserve you. I hope I don't hurt your feelings in any way. I am merely stating my own individual opinion."

Mr. Waring made no remark.

"The only thing that really interests me," resumed Psmith, "is the matter of these tenements. I shall shortly be leaving this country to resume the strangle-hold on Learning which I relinquished at the beginning of the Long Vacation. If I were to depart without bringing off improvements down Pleasant Street way, I shouldn't be able to enjoy my meals. The startled cry would go round Cambridge: 'Something is the matter with Psmith. He is off his feed. He should try Blenkinsop's Balm for the Bilious.' But no balm would do me any good. I should simply droop and fade slowly away like a neglected lily. And you wouldn't like that, Comrade Wilberfloss, would you?"

Mr. Wilberfloss, thus suddenly pulled into the conversation, again leaped in his seat.

"What I propose to do," continued Psmith, without waiting for an answer, "is to touch you for the good round sum of five thousand and three dollars."

Mr. Waring half rose.

"Five thousand dollars!"

"Five thousand and three dollars," said Psmith. "It may possibly have escaped your memory, but a certain minion of yours, one J. Repetto, utterly ruined a practically new hat of mine. If you think that I can afford to come to New York and scatter hats about as if they were mere dross, you are making the culminating error of a misspent life. Three dollars are what I need for a new one. The balance of your cheque, the five thousand, I propose to apply to making those tenements fit for a tolerably fastidious pig to live in."

"Five thousand!" cried Mr. Waring. "It's monstrous."

"It isn't," said Psmith. "It's more or less of a minimum. I have made inquiries. So out with the good old cheque-book, and let's all be jolly."

"I have no cheque-book with me."

"I have," said Psmith, producing one from a drawer. "Cross out the name of my bank, substitute yours, and fate cannot touch us."

Mr. Waring hesitated for a moment, then capitulated. Psmith watched, as he wrote, with an indulgent and fatherly eye.

"Finished?" he said. "Comrade Maloney."

"Youse hollering fer me?" asked that youth, appearing at the door.

"Bet your life I am, Comrade Maloney. Have you ever seen an untamed mustang of the prairie?"

"Nope. But I've read about dem."

"Well, run like one down to Wall Street with this cheque, and pay it in to my account at the International Bank."

Pugsy disappeared.

"Cheques," said Psmith, "have been known to be stopped. Who knows but what, on reflection, you might not have changed your mind?"

"What guarantee have I," asked Mr. Waring, "that these attacks on me in your paper will stop?"

"If you like," said Psmith, "I will write you a note to that effect. But it will not be necessary. I propose, with Comrade Wilberfloss's assistance, to restore Cosy Moments to its old style. Some days ago the editor of Comrade Windsor's late daily paper called up on the telephone and asked to speak to him. I explained the painful circumstances, and, later, went round and hob-nobbed with the great man. A very pleasant fellow. He asks to re-engage Comrade Windsor's services at a pretty sizeable salary, so, as far as our prison expert is concerned, all may be said to be well. He has got where he wanted. Cosy Moments may therefore ease up a bit. If, at about the beginning of next month, you should hear a deafening squeal of joy ring through this city, it will be the infants of New York and their parents receiving the news that Cosy Moments stands where it did. May I count on your services, Comrade Wilberfloss? Excellent. I see I may. Then perhaps you would not mind passing the word round among Comrades Asher, Waterman, and the rest of the squad, and telling them to burnish their brains and be ready to wade in at a moment's notice. I fear you will have a pretty tough job roping in the old subscribers again, but it can be done. I look to you, Comrade Wilberfloss. Are you on?"

Mr. Wilberfloss, wriggling in his chair, intimated that he was.

CONCLUSION

IT was a drizzly November evening. The streets of Cambridge were a compound of mud, mist, and melancholy. But in Psmith's rooms the fire burned brightly, the kettle droned, and all, as the proprietor had just observed, was joy, jollity, and song. Psmith, in pyjamas and a college blazer, was lying on the sofa. Mike, who had been playing football, was reclining in a comatose state in an arm-chair by the fire.

"How pleasant it would be," said Psmith dreamily, "if all our friends on the other side of the Atlantic could share this very peaceful moment with us! Or perhaps not quite all. Let us say, Comrade Windsor in the chair over there, Comrades Brady and Maloney on the table, and our old pal Wilberfloss sharing the floor with B. Henderson Asher, Bat Jarvis, and the cats. By the way, I think it would be a graceful act if you were to write to Comrade Jarvis from time to time telling him how your Angoras are getting on. He regards you as the World's Most Prominent Citizen. A line from you every now and then would sweeten the lad's existence."

Mike stirred sleepily in his chair.

"What?" he said drowsily.

"Never mind, Comrade Jackson. Let us pass lightly on. I am filled with a strange content to-night. I may be wrong, but it seems to me that all is singularly to de good, as Comrade Maloney would put it. Advices from Comrade Windsor inform me that that prince of blighters, Waring, was rejected by an intelligent electorate. Those keen, clear-sighted citizens refused to vote for him to an extent that you could notice without a microscope. Still, he has one consolation. He owns what, when the improvements are completed, will be the finest and most commodious tenement houses in New York. Millionaires will stop at them instead of going to the Plaza. Are you asleep, Comrade Jackson?"

"Um-m," said Mike.

"That is excellent. You could not be better employed. Keep listening. Comrade Windsor also stated—as indeed did the sporting papers—that Comrade Brady put it all over friend Eddie Wood, administering the sleep-producer in the eighth round. My authorities are silent as to whether or not the lethal blow was a half-scissor hook, but I presume such to have been the case. The Kid is now definitely matched against Comrade Garvin for the championship, and the experts seem to think that he should win. He is a stout fellow, is Comrade Brady, and I hope he wins through. He will probably come to England later on. When he does, we must show him round. I don't think you ever met him, did you, Comrade Jackson?"

"Ur-r," said Mike.

"Say no more," said Psmith. "I take you."

He reached out for a cigarette.

"These," he said, comfortably, "are the moments in life to which we look back with that wistful pleasure. What of my boyhood at Eton? Do I remember with the keenest joy the brain-tourneys in the old form-room, and the bally rot which used to take place on the Fourth of June? No. Burned deeply into my memory is a certain hot bath I took after one of the foulest cross-country runs that ever occurred outside Dante's Inferno. So with the present moment. This peaceful scene, Comrade Jackson, will remain with me when I have forgotten that such a person as Comrade Repetto ever existed. These are the real Cosy Moments. And while on that subject you will be glad to hear that the little sheet is going strong. The man Wilberfloss is a marvel in his way. He appears to have gathered in the majority of the old subscribers again. Hopping mad but a brief while ago, they now eat out of his hand. You've really no notion what a feeling of quiet pride it gives you owning a paper. I try not to show it, but I seem to myself to be looking down on the world from some lofty peak. Yesterday night, when I was looking down from the peak without a cap and gown, a proctor slid up. To-day I had to dig down into my jeans for a matter of two plunks. But what of it? Life must inevitably be dotted with these minor tragedies. I do not repine. The whisper goes round, 'Psmith bites the bullet, and wears a brave smile.' Comrade Jackson—"

A snore came from the chair.

Psmith sighed. But he did not repine. He bit the bullet. His eyes closed.

Five minutes later a slight snore came from the sofa, too. The man behind Cosy Moments slept.

A DAMSEL IN DISTRESS

CHAPTER 1.

Inasmuch as the scene of this story is that historic pile, Belpher Castle, in the county of Hampshire, it would be an agreeable task to open it with a leisurely description of the place, followed by some notes on the history of the Earls of Marshmoreton, who have owned it since the fifteenth century. Unfortunately, in these days of rush and hurry, a novelist works at a disadvantage. He must leap into the middle of his tale with as little delay as he would employ in boarding a moving tramcar. He must get off the mark with the smooth swiftness of a jack-rabbit surprised while lunching. Otherwise, people throw him aside and go out to picture palaces.

I may briefly remark that the present Lord Marshmoreton is a widower of some forty-eight years: that he has two children—a son, Percy Wilbraham Marsh, Lord Belpher, who is on the brink of his twenty-first birthday, and a daughter, Lady Patricia Maud Marsh, who is just twenty: that the chatelaine of the castle is Lady Caroline Byng, Lord Marshmoreton's sister, who married the very wealthy colliery owner, Clifford Byng, a few years before his death (which unkind people say she hastened): and that she has a step-son, Reginald. Give me time to mention these few facts and I am done. On the glorious past of the Marshmoretons I will not even touch.

Luckily, the loss to literature is not irreparable. Lord Marshmoreton himself is engaged upon a history of the family, which will doubtless be on every bookshelf as soon as his lordship gets it finished. And, as for the castle and its surroundings, including the model dairy and the amber drawing-room, you may see them for yourself any Thursday, when Belpher is thrown open to the public on payment of a fee of one shilling a head. The money is collected by Keggs the butler, and goes to a worthy local charity. At least, that is the idea. But the voice of calumny is never silent, and there exists a school of thought, headed by Albert, the page-boy, which holds that Keggs sticks to these shillings like glue, and adds them to his already considerable savings in the Farmers' and Merchants' Bank, on the left side of the High Street in Belpher village, next door to the Oddfellows' Hall.

With regard to this, one can only say that Keggs looks far too much like a particularly saintly bishop to indulge in any such practices. On the other hand, Albert knows Keggs. We must leave the matter open.

Of course, appearances are deceptive. Anyone, for instance, who had been standing outside the front entrance of the castle at eleven o'clock on a certain June morning might easily have made a mistake. Such a person would probably have jumped to the conclusion that the middle-aged lady of a determined cast of countenance who was standing near the rose-garden, talking to the gardener and watching the young couple strolling on the terrace below, was the mother of the pretty girl, and that she was smiling because the latter had recently become engaged to the tall, pleasant-faced youth at her side.

Sherlock Holmes himself might have been misled. One can hear him explaining the thing to Watson in one of those lightning flashes of inductive reasoning of his. "It is the only explanation, my dear Watson. If the lady were merely complimenting the gardener on his rose-garden, and if her smile were merely caused by the excellent appearance of that rose-garden, there would be an answering smile on the face of the gardener. But, as you see, he looks morose and gloomy."

As a matter of fact, the gardener—that is to say, the stocky, brown-faced man in shirt sleeves and corduroy trousers who was frowning into a can of whale-oil solution—was the

Earl of Marshmoreton, and there were two reasons for his gloom. He hated to be interrupted while working, and, furthermore, Lady Caroline Byng always got on his nerves, and never more so than when, as now, she speculated on the possibility of a romance between her step-son Reggie and his lordship's daughter Maud.

Only his intimates would have recognized in this curious corduroy-trousered figure the seventh Earl of Marshmoreton. The Lord Marshmoreton who made intermittent appearances in London, who lunched among bishops at the Athenaeum Club without exciting remark, was a correctly dressed gentleman whom no one would have suspected of covering his sturdy legs in anything but the finest cloth. But if you will glance at your copy of Who's Who, and turn up the "M's", you will find in the space allotted to the Earl the words "Hobby—Gardening". To which, in a burst of modest pride, his lordship has added "Awarded first prize for Hybrid Teas, Temple Flower Show, 1911". The words tell their own story.

Lord Marshmoreton was the most enthusiastic amateur gardener in a land of enthusiastic amateur gardeners. He lived for his garden. The love which other men expend on their nearest and dearest Lord Marshmoreton lavished on seeds, roses and loamy soil. The hatred which some of his order feel for Socialists and Demagogues Lord Marshmoreton kept for rose slugs, rose-beetles and the small, yellowish-white insect which is so depraved and sinister a character that it goes through life with an alias—being sometimes called a rose-hopper and sometimes a thrip. A simple soul, Lord Marshmoreton—mild and pleasant. Yet put him among the thrips, and he became a dealer-out of death and slaughter, a destroyer in the class of Attila the Hun and Genghis Khan. Thrips feed on the underside of rose leaves, sucking their juice and causing them to turn yellow; and Lord Marshmoreton's views on these things were so rigid that he would have poured whale-oil solution on his grandmother if he had found her on the underside of one of his rose leaves sucking its juice.

The only time in the day when he ceased to be the horny-handed toiler and became the aristocrat was in the evening after dinner, when, egged on by Lady Caroline, who gave him no rest in the matter—he would retire to his private study and work on his History of the Family, assisted by his able secretary, Alice Faraday. His progress on that massive work was, however, slow. Ten hours in the open air make a man drowsy, and too often Lord Marshmoreton would fall asleep in mid-sentence to the annoyance of Miss Faraday, who was a conscientious girl and liked to earn her salary.

The couple on the terrace had turned. Reggie Byng's face, as he bent over Maud, was earnest and animated, and even from a distance it was possible to see how the girl's eyes lit up at what he was saying. She was hanging on his words. Lady Caroline's smile became more and more benevolent.

"They make a charming pair," she murmured. "I wonder what dear

Reggie is saying. Perhaps at this very moment—"

She broke off with a sigh of content. She had had her troubles over this affair. Dear Reggie, usually so plastic in her hands, had displayed an unaccountable reluctance to offer his agreeable self to Maud—in spite of the fact that never, not even on the public platform which she adorned so well, had his step-mother reasoned more clearly than she did when pointing out to him the advantages of the match. It was not that Reggie disliked Maud. He admitted that she was a "topper", on several occasions going so far as to describe her as "absolutely priceless". But he seemed reluctant to ask her to marry him. How could Lady Caroline know that Reggie's entire world—or such of it as was not occupied by racing cars and golf—was filled by Alice Faraday? Reggie had never told her. He had not even told

Miss Faraday.

"Perhaps at this very moment," went on Lady Caroline, "the dear boy is proposing to her."

Lord Marshmoreton grunted, and continued to peer with a questioning eye in the awesome brew which he had prepared for the thrips.

"One thing is very satisfactory," said Lady Caroline. "I mean that Maud seems entirely to have got over that ridiculous infatuation of hers for that man she met in Wales last summer. She could not be so cheerful if she were still brooding on that. I hope you will admit now, John, that I was right in keeping her practically a prisoner here and never allowing her a chance of meeting the man again either by accident or design. They say absence makes the heart grow fonder. Stuff! A girl of Maud's age falls in and out of love half a dozen times a year. I feel sure she has almost forgotten the man by now."

"Eh?" said Lord Marshmoreton. His mind had been far away, dealing with green flies.

"I was speaking about that man Maud met when she was staying with

Brenda in Wales."

"Oh, yes!"

"Oh, yes!" echoed Lady Caroline, annoyed. "Is that the only comment you can find to make? Your only daughter becomes infatuated with a perfect stranger—a man we have never seen—of whom we know nothing, not even his name—nothing except that he is an American and hasn't a penny—Maud admitted that. And all you say is 'Oh, yes'!"

"But it's all over now, isn't it? I understood the dashed affair was all over."

"We hope so. But I should feel safer if Maud were engaged to

Reggie. I do think you might take the trouble to speak to Maud."

"Speak to her? I do speak to her." Lord Marshmoreton's brain moved slowly when he was pre-occupied with his roses. "We're on excellent terms."

Lady Caroline frowned impatiently. Hers was an alert, vigorous mind, bright and strong like a steel trap, and her brother's vagueness and growing habit of inattention irritated her.

"I mean to speak to her about becoming engaged to Reggie. You are her father. Surely you can at least try to persuade her."

"Can't coerce a girl."

"I never suggested that you should coerce her, as you put it. I merely meant that you could point out to her, as a father, where her duty and happiness lie."

"Drink this!" cried his lordship with sudden fury, spraying his can over the nearest bush, and addressing his remark to the invisible thrips. He had forgotten Lady Caroline completely. "Don't stint yourselves! There's lots more!"

A girl came down the steps of the castle and made her way towards them. She was a good-looking girl, with an air of quiet efficiency about her. Her eyes were grey and whimsical. Her head was uncovered, and the breeze stirred her dark hair. She made a graceful picture in the morning sunshine, and Reggie Byng, sighting her from the terrace, wobbled in his tracks, turned pink, and lost the thread of his remarks.

The sudden appearance of Alice Faraday always affected him like that.

"I have copied out the notes you made last night, Lord

Marshmoreton. I typed two copies."

Alice Faraday spoke in a quiet, respectful, yet subtly authoritative voice. She was a girl of great character. Previous employers of her services as secretary had found her a jewel. To Lord Marshmoreton she was rapidly becoming a perfect incubus. Their views on the relative importance of gardening and family histories did not coincide. To him the history of the Marshmoreton family was the occupation of the idle hour: she seemed to think that he ought to regard it as a life-work. She was always coming and digging him out of the garden and dragging him back to what should have been a purely after-dinner task. It was Lord Marshmoreton's habit, when he awoke after one of his naps too late to resume work, to throw out some vague promise of "attending to it tomorrow"; but, he reflected bitterly, the girl ought to have tact and sense to understand that this was only polite persiflage, and not to be taken literally.

"They are very rough," continued Alice, addressing her conversation to the seat of his lordship's corduroy trousers. Lord Marshmoreton always assumed a stooping attitude when he saw Miss Faraday approaching with papers in her hand; for he laboured under a pathetic delusion, of which no amount of failures could rid him, that if she did not see his face she would withdraw. "You remember last night you promised you would attend to them this morning." She paused long enough to receive a non-committal grunt by way of answer. "Of course, if you're busy—" she said placidly, with a half-glance at Lady Caroline. That masterful woman could always be counted on as an ally in these little encounters.

"Nothing of the kind!" said Lady Caroline crisply. She was still ruffled by the lack of attention which her recent utterances had received, and welcomed the chance of administering discipline. "Get up at once, John, and go in and work."

"I am working," pleaded Lord Marshmoreton.

Despite his forty-eight years his sister Caroline still had the power at times to make him feel like a small boy. She had been a great martinet in the days of their mutual nursery.

"The Family History is more important than grubbing about in the dirt. I cannot understand why you do not leave this sort of thing to MacPherson. Why you should pay him liberal wages and then do his work for him, I cannot see. You know the publishers are waiting for the History. Go and attend to these notes at once."

"You promised you would attend to them this morning, Lord

Marshmoreton," said Alice invitingly.

Lord Marshmoreton clung to his can of whale-oil solution with the clutch of a drowning man. None knew better than he that these interviews, especially when Caroline was present to lend the weight of her dominating personality, always ended in the same way.

"Yes, yes, yes!" he said. "Tonight, perhaps. After dinner, eh? Yes, after dinner. That will be capital."

"I think you ought to attend to them this morning," said Alice, gently persistent. It really perturbed this girl to feel that she was not doing work enough to merit her generous salary. And on the subject of the history of the Marshmoreton family she was an enthusiast. It had a glamour for her.

Lord Marshmoreton's fingers relaxed their hold. Throughout the rose-garden hundreds of spared thrips went on with their morning meal, unwitting of doom averted.

"Oh, all right, all right, all right! Come into the library."

"Very well, Lord Marshmoreton." Miss Faraday turned to Lady

Caroline. "I have been looking up the trains, Lady Caroline. The best is the twelve-fifteen. It has a dining-car, and stops at Belpher if signalled."

"Are you going away, Caroline?" inquired Lord Marshmoreton hopefully.

"I am giving a short talk to the Social Progress League at Lewisham. I shall return tomorrow."

"Oh!" said Marshmoreton, hope fading from his voice.

"Thank you, Miss Faraday," said Lady Caroline. "The twelve-fifteen."

"The motor will be round at a quarter to twelve."

"Thank you. Oh, by the way, Miss Faraday, will you call to Reggie as you pass, and tell him I wish to speak to him."

Maud had left Reggie by the time Alice Faraday reached him, and that ardent youth was sitting on a stone seat, smoking a cigarette and entertaining himself with meditations in which thoughts of Alice competed for precedence with graver reflections connected with the subject of the correct stance for his approach-shots. Reggie's was a troubled spirit these days. He was in love, and he had developed a bad slice with his mid-iron. He was practically a soul in torment.

"Lady Caroline asked me to tell you that she wishes to speak to you, Mr. Byng."

Reggie leaped from his seat.

"Hullo-ullo-ullo! There you are! I mean to say, what?"

He was conscious, as was his custom in her presence, of a warm, prickly sensation in the small of the back. Some kind of elephantiasis seemed to have attacked his hands and feet, swelling them to enormous proportions. He wished profoundly that he could get rid of his habit of yelping with nervous laughter whenever he encountered the girl of his dreams. It was calculated to give her a wrong impression of a chap—make her think him a fearful chump and what not!

"Lady Caroline is leaving by the twelve-fifteen."

"That's good! What I mean to say is—oh, she is, is she? I see what you mean." The absolute necessity of saying something at least moderately coherent gripped him. He rallied his forces. "You wouldn't care to come for a stroll, after I've seen the mater, or a row on the lake, or any rot like that, would you?"

"Thank you very much, but I must go in and help Lord Marshmoreton with his book."

"What a rotten—I mean, what a dam' shame!"

The pity of it tore at Reggie's heart strings. He burned with generous wrath against Lord Marshmoreton, that modern Simon Legree, who used his capitalistic power to make a slave of this girl and keep her toiling indoors when all the world was sunshine.

"Shall I go and ask him if you can't put it off till after dinner?"

"Oh, no, thanks very much. I'm sure Lord Marshmoreton wouldn't dream of it."

She passed on with a pleasant smile. When he had recovered from the effect of this Reggie proceeded slowly to the upper level to meet his step-mother.

"Hullo, mater. Pretty fit and so forth? What did you want to see me about?"

"Well, Reggie, what is the news?"

"Eh? What? News? Didn't you get hold of a paper at breakfast? Nothing much in it. Tam Duggan beat Alec Fraser three up and two to play at Prestwick. I didn't notice anything else much. There's a new musical comedy at the Regal. Opened last night, and seems to be just like mother makes. The Morning Post gave it a topping notice. I must trickle up to town and see it some time this week."

Lady Caroline frowned. This slowness in the uptake, coming so soon after her brother's inattention, displeased her.

"No, no, no. I mean you and Maud have been talking to each other for quite a long time, and she seemed very interested in what you were saying. I hoped you might have some good news for me."

Reggie's face brightened. He caught her drift.

"Oh, ah, yes, I see what you mean. No, there wasn't anything of that sort or shape or order."

"What were you saying to her, then, that interested her so much?"

"I was explaining how I landed dead on the pin with my spoon out of a sand-trap at the eleventh hole yesterday. It certainly was a pretty ripe shot, considering. I'd sliced into this baby bunker, don't you know; I simply can't keep 'em straight with the iron nowadays—and there the pill was, grinning up at me from the sand. Of course, strictly speaking, I ought to have used a niblick, but—"

"Do you mean to say, Reggie, that, with such an excellent opportunity, you did not ask Maud to marry you?"

"I see what you mean. Well, as a matter of absolute fact, I, as it were, didn't."

Lady Caroline uttered a wordless sound.

"By the way, mater," said Reggie, "I forgot to tell you about that.

It's all off."

"What!"

"Absolutely. You see, it appears there's a chappie unknown for whom Maud has an absolute pash. It seems she met this sportsman up in Wales last summer. She was caught in the rain, and he happened to be passing and rallied round with his rain-coat, and one thing led to another. Always raining in Wales, what! Good fishing, though, here and there. Well, what I mean is, this cove was so deucedly civil, and all that, that now she won't look at anybody else. He's the blue-eyed boy, and everybody else is an also-ran, with about as much chance as a blind man with one arm trying to get out of a bunker with a tooth-pick."

"What perfect nonsense! I know all about that affair. It was just a passing fancy that never meant anything. Maud has got over that long ago."

"She didn't seem to think so."

"Now, Reggie," said Lady Caroline tensely, "please listen to me. You know that the castle will be full of people in a day or two for Percy's coming-of-age, and this next few days may be your last chance of having a real, long, private talk with Maud. I shall be seriously annoyed if you neglect this opportunity. There is no excuse for the way you are behaving. Maud is a charming girl—"

"Oh, absolutely! One of the best."

"Very well, then!"

"But, mater, what I mean to say is—"

"I don't want any more temporizing, Reggie!"

"No, no! Absolutely not!" said Reggie dutifully, wishing he knew what the word meant, and wishing also that life had not become so frightfully complex.

"Now, this afternoon, why should you not take Maud for a long ride in your car?"

Reggie grew more cheerful. At least he had an answer for that.

"Can't be done, I'm afraid. I've got to motor into town to meet Percy. He's arriving from Oxford this morning. I promised to meet him in town and tool him back in the car."

"I see. Well, then, why couldn't you—?"

"I say, mater, dear old soul," said Reggie hastily, "I think you'd better tear yourself away and what not. If you're catching the twelve-fifteen, you ought to be staggering round to see you haven't forgotten anything. There's the car coming round now."

"I wish now I had decided to go by a later train."

"No, no, mustn't miss the twelve-fifteen. Good, fruity train. Everybody speaks well of it. Well, see you anon, mater. I think you'd better run like a hare."

"You will remember what I said?"

"Oh, absolutely!"

"Good-bye, then. I shall be back tomorrow."

Reggie returned slowly to his stone seat. He breathed a little heavily as he felt for his cigarette case. He felt like a hunted fawn.

Maud came out of the house as the car disappeared down the long avenue of elms. She crossed the terrace to where Reggie sat brooding on life and its problem.

"Reggie!"

Reggie turned.

"Hullo, Maud, dear old thing. Take a seat."

Maud sat down beside him. There was a flush on her pretty face, and when she spoke her voice quivered with suppressed excitement.

"Reggie," she said, laying a small hand on his arm. "We're friends, aren't we?"

Reggie patted her back paternally. There were few people he liked better than Maud.

"Always have been since the dear old days of childhood, what!"

"I can trust you, can't I?"

"Absolutely!"

"There's something I want you to do for me, Reggie. You'll have to keep it a dead secret of course."

"The strong, silent man. That's me. What is it?"

"You're driving into town in your car this afternoon, aren't you, to meet Percy?"

"That was the idea."

"Could you go this morning instead—and take me?"

"Of course."

Maud shook her head.

"You don't know what you are letting yourself in for, Reggie, or I'm sure you wouldn't agree so lightly. I'm not allowed to leave the castle, you know, because of what I was telling you about."

"The chappie?"

"Yes. So there would be terrible scenes if anybody found out."

"Never mind, dear old soul. I'll risk it. None shall learn your secret from these lips."

"You're a darling, Reggie."

"But what's the idea? Why do you want to go today particularly?"

Maud looked over her shoulder.

"Because—" She lowered her voice, though there was no one near. "Because he is back in London! He's a sort of secretary, you know, Reggie, to his uncle, and I saw in the paper this morning that the uncle returned yesterday after a long voyage in his yacht. So—he must have come back, too. He has to go everywhere his uncle goes."

"And everywhere the uncle went, the chappie was sure to go!" murmured Reggie. "Sorry. Didn't mean to interrupt."

"I must see him. I haven't seen him since last summer—nearly a whole year! And he hasn't written to me, and I haven't dared to write to him, for fear of the letter going wrong. So, you see, I must go. Today's my only chance. Aunt Caroline has gone away. Father will be busy in the garden, and won't notice whether I'm here or not. And, besides, tomorrow it will be too late, because Percy will be here. He was more furious about the thing than anyone."

"Rather the proud aristocrat, Percy," agreed Reggie. "I understand absolutely. Tell me just what you want me to do."

"I want you to pick me up in the car about half a mile down the road. You can drop me somewhere in Piccadilly. That will be near enough to where I want to go. But the most important thing is about Percy. You must persuade him to stay and dine in town and come back here after dinner. Then I shall be able to get back by an afternoon train, and no one will know I've been gone."

"That's simple enough, what? Consider it done. When do you want to start?"

"At once."

"I'll toddle round to the garage and fetch the car." Reggie chuckled amusedly. "Rum thing! The mater's just been telling me I ought to take you for a drive."

"You are a darling, Reggie, really!"

Reggie gave her back another paternal pat.

"I know what it means to be in love, dear old soul. I say, Maud, old thing, do you find love puts you off your stroke? What I mean is, does it make you slice your approach-shots?"

Maud laughed.

"No. It hasn't had any effect on my game so far. I went round in eighty-six the other day."

Reggie sighed enviously.

"Women are wonderful!" he said. "Well, I'll be legging it and fetching the car. When you're ready, stroll along down the road and wait for me."

* * *

When he had gone Maud pulled a small newspaper clipping from her pocket. She had extracted it from yesterday's copy of the Morning Post's society column. It contained only a few words:

"Mr. Wilbur Raymond has returned to his residence at

No. 11a Belgrave Square from a prolonged voyage in his

yacht, the Siren."

Maud did not know Mr. Wilbur Raymond, and yet that paragraph had sent the blood tingling through every vein in her body. For as she had indicated to Reggie, when the Wilbur Raymonds of this world return to their town residences, they bring with them their nephew and secretary, Geoffrey Raymond. And Geoffrey Raymond was the man Maud had loved ever since the day when she had met him in Wales.

CHAPTER 2.

The sun that had shone so brightly on Belpher Castle at noon, when Maud and Reggie Byng set out on their journey, shone on the West-End of London with equal pleasantness at two o'clock. In Little Gooch Street all the children of all the small shopkeepers who support life in that backwater by selling each other vegetables and singing canaries were out and about playing curious games of their own invention. Cats washed themselves on doorsteps, preparatory to looking in for lunch at one of the numerous garbage cans which dotted the sidewalk. Waiters peered austerely from the windows of the two Italian restaurants which carry on the Lucretia Borgia tradition by means of one shilling and sixpenny table d'hôte luncheons. The proprietor of the grocery store on the corner was bidding a silent farewell to a tomato which even he, though a dauntless optimist, had been compelled to recognize as having outlived its utility. On all these things the sun shone with a genial smile. Round the corner, in Shaftesbury Avenue, an east wind was doing its best to pierce the hardened hides of the citizenry; but it did not penetrate into Little Gooch Street, which, facing south and being narrow and sheltered, was enabled practically to bask.

Mac, the stout guardian of the stage door of the Regal Theatre, whose gilded front entrance is on the Avenue, emerged from the little glass case in which the management kept him, and came out to observe life and its phenomena with an indulgent eye. Mac was feeling happy this morning. His job was a permanent one, not influenced by the success or failure of the productions which followed one another at the theatre throughout the year; but he felt, nevertheless, a sort of proprietary interest in these ventures, and was pleased when they secured the approval of the public. Last night's opening, a musical piece by an American author and composer, had undoubtedly made a big hit, and Mac was glad, because he liked what he had seen of the company, and, in the brief time in which he had known him, had come to entertain a warm regard for George Bevan, the composer, who had travelled over from New York to help with the London production.

George Bevan turned the corner now, walking slowly, and, it seemed to Mac, gloomily towards the stage door. He was a young man of about twenty-seven, tall and well knit, with an agreeable, clean-cut face, of which a pair of good and honest eyes were the most noticeable feature. His sensitive mouth was drawn down a little at the corners, and he looked tired.

"Morning, Mac."

"Good morning, sir."

"Anything for me?"

"Yes, sir. Some telegrams. I'll get 'em. Oh, I'll get 'em," said Mac, as if reassuring some doubting friend and supporter as to his ability to carry through a labour of Hercules.

He disappeared into his glass case. George Bevan remained outside in the street surveying the frisking children with a sombre glance. They seemed to him very noisy, very dirty and very young. Disgustingly young. Theirs was joyous, exuberant youth which made a fellow feel at least sixty. Something was wrong with George today, for normally he was fond of children. Indeed, normally he was fond of most things. He was a good-natured and cheerful young man, who liked life and the great majority of those who lived it contemporaneously with himself. He had no enemies and many friends.

But today he had noticed from the moment he had got out of bed that something was amiss with the world. Either he was in the grip of some divine discontent due to the highly developed condition of his soul, or else he had a grouch. One of the two. Or it might have been the reaction from the emotions of the previous night. On the morning after an opening your sensitive artist is always apt to feel as if he had been dried over a barrel.

Besides, last night there had been a supper party after the performance at the flat which the comedian of the troupe had rented in Jermyn Street, a forced, rowdy supper party where a number of tired people with over-strained nerves had seemed to feel it a duty to be artificially vivacious. It had lasted till four o'clock when the morning papers with the notices arrived, and George had not got to bed till four-thirty. These things colour the mental outlook.

Mac reappeared.

"Here you are, sir."

"Thanks."

George put the telegrams in his pocket. A cat, on its way back from lunch, paused beside him in order to use his leg as a serviette. George tickled it under the ear abstractedly. He was always courteous to cats, but today he went through the movements perfunctorily and without enthusiasm.

The cat moved on. Mac became conversational.

"They tell me the piece was a hit last night, sir."

"It seemed to go very well."

"My Missus saw it from the gallery, and all the first-nighters was speaking very 'ighly of it. There's a regular click, you know, sir, over here in London, that goes to all the first nights in the gallery. 'Ighly critical they are always. Specially if it's an American piece like this one. If they don't like it, they precious soon let you know. My missus ses they was all speakin' very 'ighly of it. My missus says she ain't seen a livelier show for a long time, and she's a great theatregoer. My missus says they was all specially pleased with the music."

"That's good."

"The Morning Leader give it a fine write-up. How was the rest of the papers?"

"Splendid, all of them. I haven't seen the evening papers yet. I came out to get them."

Mac looked down the street.

"There'll be a rehearsal this afternoon, I suppose, sir? Here's

Miss Dore coming along."

George followed his glance. A tall girl in a tailor-made suit of blue was coming towards them. Even at a distance one caught the genial personality of the new arrival. It seemed to go before her like a heartening breeze. She picked her way carefully through the children crawling on the side walk. She stopped for a moment and said something to one of them. The child grinned. Even the proprietor of the grocery store appeared to brighten up at the sight of her, as at the sight of some old friend.

"How's business, Bill?" she called to him as she passed the spot where he stood brooding on the mortality of tomatoes. And, though he replied "Rotten", a faint, grim smile did nevertheless flicker across his tragic mask.

Billie Dore, who was one of the chorus of George Bevan's musical comedy, had an attractive face, a mouth that laughed readily, rather bright golden hair (which, she was

[335] P.G. WODEHOUSE

fond of insisting with perfect truth, was genuine though appearances were against it), and steady blue eyes. The latter were frequently employed by her in quelling admirers who were encouraged by the former to become too ardent. Billie's views on the opposite sex who forgot themselves were as rigid as those of Lord Marshmoreton concerning thrips. She liked men, and she would signify this liking in a practical manner by lunching and dining with them, but she was entirely self-supporting, and when men overlooked that fact she reminded them of it in no uncertain voice; for she was a girl of ready speech and direct.

"'Morning, George. 'Morning, Mac. Any mail?"

"I'll see, miss."

"How did your better four-fifths like the show, Mac?"

"I was just telling Mr. Bevan, miss, that the missus said she 'adn't seen a livelier show for a long time."

"Fine. I knew I'd be a hit. Well, George, how's the boy this bright afternoon?"

"Limp and pessimistic."

"That comes of sitting up till four in the morning with festive hams."

"You were up as late as I was, and you look like Little Eva after a night of sweet, childish slumber."

"Yes, but I drank ginger ale, and didn't smoke eighteen cigars. And yet, I don't know. I think I must be getting old, George. All-night parties seem to have lost their charm. I was ready to quit at one o'clock, but it didn't seem matey. I think I'll marry a farmer and settle down."

George was amazed. He had not expected to find his present view of life shared in this quarter.

"I was just thinking myself," he said, feeling not for the first time how different Billie was from the majority of those with whom his profession brought him in contact, "how flat it all was. The show business I mean, and these darned first nights, and the party after the show which you can't sidestep. Something tells me I'm about through."

Billie Dore nodded.

"Anybody with any sense is always about through with the show business. I know I am. If you think I'm wedded to my art, let me tell you I'm going to get a divorce the first chance that comes along. It's funny about the show business. The way one drifts into it and sticks, I mean. Take me, for example. Nature had it all doped out for me to be the Belle of Hicks Corners. What I ought to have done was to buy a gingham bonnet and milk cows. But I would come to the great city and help brighten up the tired business man."

"I didn't know you were fond of the country, Billie."

"Me? I wrote the words and music. Didn't you know I was a country kid? My dad ran a Bide a Wee Home for flowers, and I used to know them all by their middle names. He was a nursery gardener out in Indiana. I tell you, when I see a rose nowadays, I shake its hand and say: 'Well, well, Cyril, how's everything with you? And how are Joe and Jack and Jimmy and all the rest of the boys at home?' Do you know how I used to put in my time the first few nights I was over here in London? I used to hang around Covent Garden with my head back, sniffing. The boys that mess about with the flowers there used to stub their toes on me so often that they got to look on me as part of the scenery."

"That's where we ought to have been last night."

"We'd have had a better time. Say, George, did you see the awful mistake on Nature's part that Babe Sinclair showed up with towards the middle of the proceedings? You must have noticed him, because he took up more room than any one man was entitled to. His name was Spenser Gray."

George recalled having been introduced to a fat man of his own age who answered to that name.

"It's a darned shame," said Billie indignantly. "Babe is only a kid. This is the first show she's been in. And I happen to know there's an awfully nice boy over in New York crazy to marry her. And I'm certain this gink is giving her a raw deal. He tried to get hold of me about a week ago, but I turned him down hard; and I suppose he thinks Babe is easier. And it's no good talking to her; she thinks he's wonderful. That's another kick I have against the show business. It seems to make girls such darned chumps. Well, I wonder how much longer Mr. Arbuckle is going to be retrieving my mail. What ho, within there, Fatty!"

Mac came out, apologetic, carrying letters.

"Sorry, miss. By an oversight I put you among the G's."

"All's well that ends well. 'Put me among the G's.' There's a good title for a song for you, George. Excuse me while I grapple with the correspondence. I'll bet half of these are mash notes. I got three between the first and second acts last night. Why the nobility and gentry of this burg should think that I'm their affinity just because I've got golden hair—which is perfectly genuine, Mac; I can show you the pedigree—and because I earn an honest living singing off the key, is more than I can understand."

Mac leaned his massive shoulders comfortably against the building, and resumed his chat.

"I expect you're feeling very 'appy today, sir?"

George pondered. He was certainly feeling better since he had seen

Billie Dore, but he was far from being himself.

"I ought to be, I suppose. But I'm not."

"Ah, you're getting blarzy, sir, that's what it is. You've 'ad too much of the fat, you 'ave. This piece was a big 'it in America, wasn't it?"

"Yes. It ran over a year in New York, and there are three companies of it out now."

"That's 'ow it is, you see. You've gone and got blarzy. Too big a 'elping of success, you've 'ad." Mac wagged a head like a harvest moon. "You aren't a married man, are you, sir?"

Billie Dore finished skimming through her mail, and crumpled the letters up into a large ball, which she handed to Mac.

"Here's something for you to read in your spare moments, Mac. Glance through them any time you have a suspicion you may be a chump, and you'll have the comfort of knowing that there are others. What were you saying about being married?"

"Mr. Bevan and I was 'aving a talk about 'im being blarzy, miss."

"Are you blarzy, George?"

"So Mac says."

"And why is he blarzy, miss?" demanded Mac rhetorically.

"Don't ask me," said Billie. "It's not my fault."

"It's because, as I was saying, 'e's 'ad too big a 'elping of success, and because 'e ain't a married man. You did say you wasn't a married man, didn't you, sir?"

"I didn't. But I'm not."

"That's 'ow it is, you see. You pretty soon gets sick of pulling off good things, if you ain't got nobody to pat you on the back for doing of it. Why, when I was single, if I got 'old of a sure thing for the three o'clock race and picked up a couple of quid, the thrill of it didn't seem to linger somehow. But now, if some of the gentlemen that come 'ere put me on to something safe and I make a bit, 'arf the fascination of it is taking the stuff 'ome and rolling it on to the kitchen table and 'aving 'er pat me on the back."

"How about when you lose?"

"I don't tell 'er," said Mac simply.

"You seem to understand the art of being happy, Mac."

"It ain't an art, sir. It's just gettin' 'old of the right little woman, and 'aving a nice little 'ome of your own to go back to at night."

"Mac," said Billie admiringly, "you talk like a Tin Pan Alley song hit, except that you've left out the scent of honeysuckle and Old Mister Moon climbing up over the trees. Well, you're quite right. I'm all for the simple and domestic myself. If I could find the right man, and he didn't see me coming and duck, I'd become one of the Mendelssohn's March Daughters right away. Are you going, George? There's a rehearsal at two-thirty for cuts."

"I want to get the evening papers and send off a cable or two. See you later."

"We shall meet at Philippi."

Mac eyed George's retreating back till he had turned the corner.

"A nice pleasant gentleman, Mr. Bevan," he said. "Too bad 'e's got the pip the way 'e 'as, just after 'avin' a big success like this 'ere. Comes of bein' a artist, I suppose."

Miss Dore dived into her vanity case and produced a puff with which she proceeded to powder her nose.

"All composers are nuts, Mac. I was in a show once where the manager was panning the composer because there wasn't a number in the score that had a tune to it. The poor geek admitted they weren't very tuney, but said the thing about his music was that it had such a wonderful aroma. They all get that way. The jazz seems to go to their heads. George is all right, though, and don't let anyone tell you different."

"Have you know him long, miss?"

"About five years. I was a stenographer in the house that published his songs when I first met him. And there's another thing you've got to hand it to George for. He hasn't let success give him a swelled head. The money that boy makes is sinful, Mac. He wears thousand dollar bills next to his skin winter and summer. But he's just the same as he was when I first knew him, when he was just hanging around Broadway, looking out for a chance to be allowed to slip a couple of interpolated numbers into any old show that came along. Yes. Put it in your diary, Mac, and write it on your cuff, George Bevan's all right. He's an ace."

Unconscious of these eulogies, which, coming from one whose judgment he respected, might have cheered him up, George wandered down Shaftesbury Avenue feeling more depressed than ever. The sun had gone in for the time being, and the east wind was frolicking round him like a playful puppy, patting him with a cold paw, nuzzling his ankles, bounding away and bounding back again, and behaving generally as east winds do when they discover a victim who has come out without his spring overcoat. It was plain to George now that the sun and the wind were a couple of confidence tricksters working together as a team. The sun had disarmed him with specious promises and an air of cheery goodfellowship, and had delivered him into the hands of the wind, which was now going through him with the swift thoroughness of the professional hold-up artist. He quickened his steps, and began to wonder if he was so sunk in senile decay as to have acquired a liver.

He discarded the theory as repellent. And yet there must be a reason for his depression. Today of all days, as Mac had pointed out, he had everything to make him happy. Popular as he was in America, this was the first piece of his to be produced in London, and there was no doubt that it was a success of unusual dimensions. And yet he felt no elation.

He reached Piccadilly and turned westwards. And then, as he passed the gates of the In and Out Club, he had a moment of clear vision and understood everything. He was depressed because he was bored, and he was bored because he was lonely. Mac, that solid thinker, had been right. The solution of the problem of life was to get hold of the right girl and have a home to go back to at night. He was mildly surprised that he had tried in any other direction for an explanation of his gloom. It was all the more inexplicable in that fully 80 per cent of the lyrics which he had set in the course of his musical comedy career had had that thought at the back of them.

George gave himself up to an orgy of sentimentality. He seemed to be alone in the world which had paired itself off into a sort of seething welter of happy couples. Taxicabs full of happy couples rolled by every minute. Passing omnibuses creaked beneath the weight of happy couples. The very policeman across the Street had just grinned at a flitting shop girl, and she had smiled back at him. The only female in London who did not appear to be attached was a girl in brown who was coming along the sidewalk at a leisurely pace, looking about her in a manner that suggested that she found Piccadilly a new and stimulating spectacle.

As far as George could see she was an extremely pretty girl, small and dainty, with a proud little tilt to her head and the jaunty walk that spoke of perfect health. She was, in fact, precisely the sort of girl that George felt he could love with all the stored-up devotion of an old buffer of twenty-seven who had squandered none of his rich nature in foolish flirtations. He had just begun to weave a rose-tinted romance about their two selves, when a cold reaction set in. Even as he paused to watch the girl threading her way through the crowd, the east wind jabbed an icy finger down the back of his neck, and the chill of it sobered him. After all, he reflected bitterly, this girl was only alone because she was on her way somewhere to meet some confounded man. Besides there was no earthly chance of getting to know her. You can't rush up to pretty girls in the street and tell them you are lonely. At least, you can, but it doesn't get you anywhere except the police station. George's gloom deepened—a thing he would not have believed possible a moment before. He felt that he had been born too late. The restraints of modern civilization irked him. It was not, he told himself, like this in the good old days.

In the Middle Ages, for example, this girl would have been a Damsel; and in that happy time practically everybody whose technical rating was that of Damsel was in distress and only too willing to waive the formalities in return for services rendered by the casual passer-by. But the twentieth century is a prosaic age, when girls are merely girls and have no troubles at all. Were he to stop this girl in brown and assure her that his aid and comfort were at her disposal, she would undoubtedly call that large policeman from across the way, and the romance would begin and end within the space of thirty seconds, or, if the policeman were a quick mover, rather less.

Better to dismiss dreams and return to the practical side of life by buying the evening papers from the shabby individual beside him, who had just thrust an early edition in his face. After all notices are notices, even when the heart is aching. George felt in his pocket for the necessary money, found emptiness, and remembered that he had left all his ready funds at his hotel. It was just one of the things he might have expected on a day like this.

The man with the papers had the air of one whose business is conducted on purely cash principles. There was only one thing to be done, return to the hotel, retrieve his money, and try to forget the weight of the world and its cares in lunch. And from the hotel he could despatch the two or three cables which he wanted to send to New York.

The girl in brown was quite close now, and George was enabled to get a clearer glimpse of her. She more than fulfilled the promise she had given at a distance. Had she been constructed to his own specifications, she would not have been more acceptable in George's sight. And now she was going out of his life for ever. With an overwhelming sense of pathos, for there is no pathos more bitter than that of parting from someone we have never met, George hailed a taxicab which crawled at the side of the road; and, with all the refrains of all the sentimental song hits he had ever composed ringing in his ears, he got in and passed away.

"A rotten world," he mused, as the cab, after proceeding a couple of yards, came to a standstill in a block of the traffic. "A dull, flat bore of a world, in which nothing happens or ever will happen. Even when you take a cab it just sticks and doesn't move."

At this point the door of the cab opened, and the girl in brown jumped in.

"I'm so sorry," she said breathlessly, "but would you mind hiding me, please."

CHAPTER 3.

George hid her. He did it, too, without wasting precious time by asking questions. In a situation which might well have thrown the quickest-witted of men off his balance, he acted with promptitude, intelligence and despatch. The fact is, George had for years been an assiduous golfer; and there is no finer school for teaching concentration and a strict attention to the matter in hand. Few crises, however unexpected, have the power to disturb a man who has so conquered the weakness of the flesh as to have trained himself to bend his left knee, raise his left heel, swing his arms well out from the body, twist himself into the shape of a corkscrew and use the muscle of the wrist, at the same time keeping his head still and his eye on the ball. It is estimated that there are twenty-three important points to be borne in mind simultaneously while making a drive at golf; and to the man who has mastered the art of remembering them all the task of hiding girls in taxicabs is mere child's play. To pull down the blinds on the side of the vehicle nearest the kerb was with George the work of a moment. Then he leaned out of the centre window in such a manner as completely to screen the interior of the cab from public view.

"Thank you so much," murmured a voice behind him. It seemed to come from the floor.

"Not at all," said George, trying a sort of vocal chip-shot out of the corner of his mouth, designed to lift his voice backwards and lay it dead inside the cab.

He gazed upon Piccadilly with eyes from which the scales had fallen. Reason told him that he was still in Piccadilly. Otherwise it would have seemed incredible to him that this could be the same street which a moment before he had passed judgment upon and found flat and uninteresting. True, in its salient features it had altered little. The same number of stodgy-looking people moved up and down. The buildings retained their air of not having had a bath since the days of the Tudors. The east wind still blew. But, though superficially the same, in reality Piccadilly had altered completely. Before it had been just Piccadilly. Now it was a golden street in the City of Romance, a main thoroughfare of Bagdad, one of the principal arteries of the capital of Fairyland. A rose-coloured mist swam before George's eyes. His spirits, so low but a few moments back, soared like a good niblick shot out of the bunker of Gloom. The years fell away from him till, in an instant, from being a rather poorly preserved, liverish greybeard of sixty-five or so, he became a sprightly lad of twenty-one in a world of springtime and flowers and laughing brooks. In other words, taking it by and large, George felt pretty good. The impossible had happened; Heaven had sent him an adventure, and he didn't care if it snowed.

It was possibly the rose-coloured mist before his eyes that prevented him from observing the hurried approach of a faultlessly attired young man, aged about twenty-one, who during George's preparations for ensuring privacy in his cab had been galloping in pursuit in a resolute manner that suggested a well-dressed bloodhound somewhat overfed and out of condition. Only when this person stopped and began to pant within a few inches of his face did he become aware of his existence.

"You, sir!" said the bloodhound, removing a gleaming silk hat, mopping a pink forehead, and replacing the luminous superstructure once more in position. "You, sir!"

Whatever may be said of the possibility of love at first sight, in which theory George was now a confirmed believer, there can be no doubt that an exactly opposite phenomenon is of frequent occurrence. After one look at some people even friendship is impossible. Such a one, in George's opinion, was this gurgling excrescence underneath the silk hat. He comprised in his single person practically all the qualities which George disliked most. He was, for a young man, extraordinarily obese. Already a second edition of his chin had been published, and the perfectly-cut morning coat which encased his upper section bulged out in an opulent semi-circle. He wore a little moustache, which to George's prejudiced eye seemed more a complaint than a moustache. His face was red, his manner dictatorial, and he was touched in the wind. Take him for all in all he looked like a bit of bad news.

George had been educated at Lawrenceville and Harvard, and had subsequently had the privilege of mixing socially with many of New York's most prominent theatrical managers; so he knew how to behave himself. No Vere de Vere could have exhibited greater repose of manner.

"And what," he inquired suavely, leaning a little further out of the cab, "is eating you, Bill?"

A messenger boy, two shabby men engaged in non-essential industries, and a shop girl paused to observe the scene. Time was not of the essence to these confirmed sightseers. The shop girl was late already, so it didn't matter if she was any later; the messenger boy had nothing on hand except a message marked "Important: Rush"; and as for the two shabby men, their only immediate plans consisted of a vague intention of getting to some public house and leaning against the wall; so George's time was their time. One of the pair put his head on one side and said: "What ho!"; the other picked up a cigar stub from the gutter and began to smoke.

"A young lady just got into your cab," said the stout young man.

"Surely not?" said George.

"What the devil do you mean—surely not?"

"I've been in the cab all the time, and I should have noticed it."

At this juncture the block in the traffic was relieved, and the cab bowled smartly on for some fifty yards when it was again halted. George, protruding from the window like a snail, was entertained by the spectacle of the pursuit. The hunt was up. Short of throwing his head up and baying, the stout young man behaved exactly as a bloodhound in similar circumstances would have conducted itself. He broke into a jerky gallop, attended by his self-appointed associates; and, considering that the young man was so stout, that the messenger boy considered it unprofessional to hurry, that the shop girl had doubts as to whether sprinting was quite ladylike, and that the two Bohemians were moving at a quicker gait than a shuffle for the first occasion in eleven years, the cavalcade made good time. The cab was still stationary when they arrived in a body.

"Here he is, guv'nor," said the messenger boy, removing a bead of perspiration with the rush message.

"Here he is, guv'nor," said the non-smoking Bohemian. "What oh!"

"Here I am!" agreed George affably. "And what can I do for you?"

The smoker spat appreciatively at a passing dog. The point seemed to him well taken. Not for many a day had he so enjoyed himself. In an arid world containing too few goes of gin and too many policemen, a world in which the poor were oppressed and could seldom even enjoy a quiet cigar without having their fingers trodden upon, he found himself for the moment contented, happy, and expectant. This looked like a row between toffs, and of all things which most intrigued him a row between toffs ranked highest.

"R!" he said approvingly. "Now you're torkin'!"

The shop girl had espied an acquaintance in the crowd. She gave tongue.

"Mordee! Cummere! Cummere quick! Sumfin' hap'nin'!" Maudie, accompanied by perhaps a dozen more of London's millions, added herself to the audience. These all belonged to the class which will gather round and watch silently while a motorist mends a tyre. They are not impatient. They do not call for rapid and continuous action. A mere hole in the ground, which of all sights is perhaps the least vivid and dramatic, is enough to grip their attention for hours at a time. They stared at George and George's cab with unblinking gaze. They did not know what would happen or when it would happen, but they intended to wait till something did happen. It might be for years or it might be for ever, but they meant to be there when things began to occur.

Speculations became audible.

"Wot is it? 'Naccident?"

"Nah! Gent 'ad 'is pocket picked!"

"Two toffs 'ad a scrap!"

"Feller bilked the cabman!"

A sceptic made a cynical suggestion.

"They're doin' of it for the pictures."

The idea gained instant popularity.

"Jear that? It's a fillum!"

"Wot o', Charlie!"

"The kemerer's 'idden in the keb."

"Wot'll they be up to next!"

A red-nosed spectator with a tray of collar-studs harnessed to his stomach started another school of thought. He spoke with decision as one having authority.

"Nothin' of the blinkin' kind! The fat 'un's bin 'avin' one or two around the corner, and it's gorn and got into 'is 'ead!"

The driver of the cab, who till now had been ostentatiously unaware that there was any sort of disturbance among the lower orders, suddenly became humanly inquisitive.

"What's it all about?" he asked, swinging around and addressing

George's head.

"Exactly what I want to know," said George. He indicated the collar-stud merchant. "The gentleman over there with the portable Woolworth-bargain-counter seems to me to have the best theory."

The stout young man, whose peculiar behaviour had drawn all this flattering attention from the many-headed and who appeared considerably ruffled by the publicity, had been puffing noisily during the foregoing conversation. Now, having recovered sufficient breath to resume the attack, he addressed himself to George once more.

"Damn you, sir, will you let me look inside that cab?"

"Leave me," said George, "I would be alone."

"There is a young lady in that cab. I saw her get in, and I have been watching ever since, and she has not got out, so she is there now."

George nodded approval of this close reasoning.

"Your argument seems to be without a flaw. But what then? We applaud the Man of Logic, but what of the Man of Action? What are you going to do about it?"

"Get out of my way!"

"I won't."

"Then I'll force my way in!"

"If you try it, I shall infallibly bust you one on the jaw."

The stout young man drew back a pace.

"You can't do that sort of thing, you know."

"I know I can't," said George, "but I shall. In this life, my dear sir, we must be prepared for every emergency. We must distinguish between the unusual and the impossible. It would be unusual for a comparative stranger to lean out of a cab window and sock you one, but you appear to have laid your plans on the assumption that it would be impossible. Let this be a lesson to you!"

"I tell you what it is—"

"The advice I give to every young man starting life is 'Never confuse the unusual with the impossible!' Take the present case, for instance. If you had only realized the possibility of somebody some day busting you on the jaw when you tried to get into a cab, you might have thought out dozens of crafty schemes for dealing with the matter. As it is, you are unprepared. The thing comes on you as a surprise. The whisper flies around the clubs: 'Poor old What's-his-name has been taken unawares. He cannot cope with the situation!'"

The man with the collar-studs made another diagnosis. He was seeing clearer and clearer into the thing every minute.

"Looney!" he decided. "This 'ere one's bin moppin' of it up, and the one in the keb's orf 'is bloomin' onion. That's why 'e 's standin' up instead of settin'. 'E won't set down 'cept you bring 'im a bit o' toast, 'cos he thinks 'e 's a poached egg."

George beamed upon the intelligent fellow.

"Your reasoning is admirable, but—"

He broke off here, not because he had not more to say, but for the reason that the stout young man, now in quite a Berserk frame of mind, made a sudden spring at the cab door and clutched the handle, which he was about to wrench when George acted with all the promptitude and decision which had marked his behaviour from the start.

It was a situation which called for the nicest judgment. To allow the assailant free play with the handle or even to wrestle with him for its possession entailed the risk that the door might open and reveal the girl. To bust the young man on the jaw, as promised, on the other hand, was not in George's eyes a practical policy. Excellent a deterrent as the threat of such a proceeding might be, its actual accomplishment was not to be thought of. Gaols yawn and actions for assault lie in wait for those who go about the place busting their fellows on the jaw. No. Something swift, something decided and immediate was indicated, but something that stopped short of technical battery.

George brought his hand round with a sweep and knocked the stout young man's silk hat off.

The effect was magical. We all of us have our Achilles heel, and—paradoxically enough—in the case of the stout young man that heel was his hat. Superbly built by the only hatter in London who can construct a silk hat that is a silk hat, and freshly ironed by loving hands but a brief hour before at the only shaving-parlour in London where ironing is ironing and not a brutal attack, it was his pride and joy. To lose it was like losing his trousers. It made him feel insufficiently clad. With a passionate cry like that of some wild creature deprived of its young, the erstwhile Berserk released the handle and sprang in pursuit. At the same moment the traffic moved on again.

The last George saw was a group scene with the stout young man in the middle of it. The hat had been popped up into the infield, where it had been caught by the messenger boy. The stout young man was bending over it and stroking it with soothing fingers. It was too far off for anything to be audible, but he seemed to George to be murmuring words of endearment to it. Then, placing it on his head, he darted out into the road and George saw him no more. The audience remained motionless, staring at the spot where the incident had happened. They would continue to do this till the next policeman came along and moved them on.

With a pleasant wave of farewell, in case any of them might be glancing in his direction, George drew in his body and sat down.

The girl in brown had risen from the floor, if she had ever been there, and was now seated composedly at the further end of the cab.

CHAPTER 4.

"Well, that's that!" said George.

"I'm so much obliged," said the girl.

"It was a pleasure," said George.

He was enabled now to get a closer, more leisurely and much more satisfactory view of this distressed damsel than had been his good fortune up to the present. Small details which, when he had first caught sight of her, distance had hidden from his view, now presented themselves. Her eyes, he discovered, which he had supposed brown, were only brown in their general colour-scheme. They were shot with attractive little flecks of gold, matching perfectly the little streaks of gold which the sun, coming out again on one of his flying visits and now shining benignantly once more on the world, revealed in her hair. Her chin was square and determined, but its resoluteness was contradicted by a dimple and by the pleasant good-humour of the mouth; and a further softening of the face was effected by the nose, which seemed to have started out with the intention of being dignified and aristocratic but had defeated its purpose by tilting very slightly at the tip. This was a girl who would take chances, but would take them with a smile and laugh when she lost.

George was but an amateur physiognomist, but he could read what was obvious in the faces he encountered; and the more he looked at this girl, the less he was able to understand the scene which had just occurred. The thing mystified him completely. For all her good-humour, there was an air, a manner, a something capable and defensive, about this girl with which he could not imagine any man venturing to take liberties. The gold-brown eyes, as they met his now, were friendly and smiling, but he could imagine them freezing into a stare baleful enough and haughty enough to quell such a person as the silk-hatted young man with a single glance. Why, then, had that super-fatted individual been able to demoralize her to the extent of flying to the shelter of strange cabs? She was composed enough now, it was true, but it had been quite plain that at the moment when she entered the taxi her nerve had momentarily forsaken her. There were mysteries here, beyond George.

The girl looked steadily at George and George looked steadily at her for the space of perhaps ten seconds. She seemed to George to be summing him up, weighing him. That the inspection proved satisfactory was shown by the fact that at the end of this period she smiled. Then she laughed, a clear pealing laugh which to George was far more musical than the most popular song-hit he had ever written.

"I suppose you are wondering what it's all about?" she said.

This was precisely what George was wondering most consumedly.

"No, no," he said. "Not at all. It's not my business."

"And of course you're much too well bred to be inquisitive about other people's business?"

"Of course I am. What was it all about?"

"I'm afraid I can't tell you."

"But what am I to say to the cabman?"

"I don't know. What do men usually say to cabmen?"

"I mean he will feel very hurt if I don't give him a full explanation of all this. He stooped from his pedestal to make enquiries just now. Condescension like that deserves some recognition."

"Give him a nice big tip."

George was reminded of his reason for being in the cab.

"I ought to have asked before," he said. "Where can I drive you?"

"Oh, I mustn't steal your cab. Where were you going?"

"I was going back to my hotel. I came out without any money, so I shall have to go there first to get some."

The girl started.

"What's the matter?" asked George.

"I've lost my purse!"

"Good Lord! Had it much in it?"

"Not very much. But enough to buy a ticket home."

"Any use asking where that is?"

"None, I'm afraid."

"I wasn't going to, of course."

"Of course not. That's what I admire so much in you. You aren't inquisitive."

George reflected.

"There's only one thing to be done. You will have to wait in the cab at the hotel, while I go and get some money. Then, if you'll let me, I can lend you what you require."

"It's much too kind of you. Could you manage eleven shillings?"

"Easily. I've just had a legacy."

"Of course, if you think I ought to be economical, I'll go third-class. That would only be five shillings. Ten-and-six is the first-class fare. So you see the place I want to get to is two hours from London."

"Well, that's something to know."

"But not much, is it?"

"I think I had better lend you a sovereign. Then you'll be able to buy a lunch-basket."

"You think of everything. And you're perfectly right. I shall be starving. But how do you know you will get the money back?"

"I'll risk it."

"Well, then, I shall have to be inquisitive and ask your name. Otherwise I shan't know where to send the money."

"Oh, there's no mystery about me. I'm an open book."

"You needn't be horrid about it. I can't help being mysterious."

"I didn't mean that."

"It sounded as if you did. Well, who is my benefactor?"

"My name is George Bevan. I am staying at the Carlton at present."

"I'll remember."

The taxi moved slowly down the Haymarket. The girl laughed.

"Yes?" said George.

"I was only thinking of back there. You know, I haven't thanked you nearly enough for all you did. You were wonderful."

"I'm very glad I was able to be of any help."

"What did happen? You must remember I couldn't see a thing except your back, and I could only hear indistinctly."

"Well, it started by a man galloping up and insisting that you had got into the cab. He was a fellow with the appearance of a before-using advertisement of an anti-fat medicine and the manners of a ring-tailed chimpanzee."

The girl nodded.

"Then it was Percy! I knew I wasn't mistaken."

"Percy?"

"That is his name."

"It would be! I could have betted on it."

"What happened then?"

"I reasoned with the man, but didn't seem to soothe him, and finally he made a grab for the door-handle, so I knocked off his hat, and while he was retrieving it we moved on and escaped."

The girl gave another silver peal of laughter.

"Oh, what a shame I couldn't see it. But how resourceful of you! How did you happen to think of it?"

"It just came to me," said George modestly.

A serious look came into the girl's face. The smile died out of her eyes. She shivered.

"When I think how some men might have behaved in your place!"

"Oh, no. Any man would have done just what I did. Surely, knocking off Percy's hat was an act of simple courtesy which anyone would have performed automatically!"

"You might have been some awful bounder. Or, what would have been almost worse, a slow-witted idiot who would have stopped to ask questions before doing anything. To think I should have had the luck to pick you out of all London!"

"I've been looking on it as a piece of luck—but entirely from my viewpoint."

She put a small hand on his arm, and spoke earnestly.

"Mr. Bevan, you mustn't think that, because I've been laughing a good deal and have seemed to treat all this as a joke, you haven't saved me from real trouble. If you hadn't been there and hadn't acted with such presence of mind, it would have been terrible!"

"But surely, if that fellow was annoying you, you could have called a policeman?"

"Oh, it wasn't anything like that. It was much, much worse. But I mustn't go on like this. It isn't fair on you." Her eyes lit up again with the old shining smile. "I know you have no curiosity about me, but still there's no knowing whether I might not arouse some if I went on piling up the mystery. And the silly part is that really there's no mystery at all. It's just that I can't tell anyone about it."

"That very fact seems to me to constitute the makings of a pretty fair mystery."

"Well, what I mean is, I'm not a princess in disguise trying to escape from anarchists, or anything like those things you read about in books. I'm just in a perfectly simple piece of trouble. You would be bored to death if I told you about it."

"Try me."

She shook her head.

"No. Besides, here we are." The cab had stopped at the hotel, and a commissionaire was already opening the door. "Now, if you haven't repented of your rash offer and really are going to be so awfully kind as to let me have that money, would you mind rushing off and getting it, because I must hurry. I can just catch a good train, and it's hours to the next."

"Will you wait here? I'll be back in a moment."

"Very well."

The last George saw of her was another of those exhilarating smiles of hers. It was literally the last he saw of her, for, when he returned not more than two minutes later, the cab had gone, the girl had gone, and the world was empty.

To him, gaping at this wholly unforeseen calamity the commissionaire vouchsafed information.

"The young lady took the cab on, sir."

"Took the cab on?"

"Almost immediately after you had gone, sir, she got in again and told the man to drive to Waterloo."

George could make nothing of it. He stood there in silent perplexity, and might have continued to stand indefinitely, had not his mind been distracted by a dictatorial voice at his elbow.

"You, sir! Dammit!"

A second taxi-cab had pulled up, and from it a stout, scarlet-faced young man had sprung. One glance told George all. The hunt was up once more. The bloodhound had picked up the trail. Percy was in again!

For the first time since he had become aware of her flight, George was thankful that the girl had disappeared. He perceived that he had too quickly eliminated Percy from the list of the Things That Matter. Engrossed with his own affairs, and having regarded their late skirmish as a decisive battle from which there would be no rallying, he had overlooked the possibility of this annoying and unnecessary person following them in another cab—a task which, in the congested, slow-moving traffic, must have been a perfectly simple one. Well, here he was, his soul manifestly all stirred up and his blood-pressure at a far higher figure than his doctor would have approved of, and the matter would have to be opened all over again.

"Now then!" said the stout young man.

George regarded him with a critical and unfriendly eye. He disliked this fatty degeneration excessively. Looking him up and down, he could find no point about him that gave him the least pleasure, with the single exception of the state of his hat, in the side of which he was rejoiced to perceive there was a large and unshapely dent.

"You thought you had shaken me off! You thought you'd given me the slip! Well, you're wrong!"

George eyed him coldly.

"I know what's the matter with you," he said. "Someone's been feeding you meat."

The young man bubbled with fury. His face turned a deeper scarlet.

He gesticulated.

"You blackguard! Where's my sister?"

At this extraordinary remark the world rocked about George dizzily. The words upset his entire diagnosis of the situation. Until that moment he had looked upon this man as a Lothario, a pursuer of damsels. That the other could possibly have any right on his side had never occurred to him. He felt unmanned by the shock. It seemed to cut the ground from under his feet.

"Your sister!"

"You heard what I said. Where is she?"

George was still endeavouring to adjust his scattered faculties. He felt foolish and apologetic. He had imagined himself unassailably in the right, and it now appeared that he was in the wrong.

For a moment he was about to become conciliatory. Then the recollection of the girl's panic and her hints at some trouble which threatened her—presumably through the medium of this man, brother or no brother—checked him. He did not know what it was all about, but the one thing that did stand out clearly in the welter of confused happenings was the girl's need for his assistance. Whatever might be the rights of the case, he was her accomplice, and must behave as such.

"I don't know what you're talking about," he said.

The young man shook a large, gloved fist in his face.

"You blackguard!"

A rich, deep, soft, soothing voice slid into the heated scene like the Holy Grail sliding athwart a sunbeam.

"What's all this?"

A vast policeman had materialized from nowhere. He stood beside them, a living statue of Vigilant Authority. One thumb rested easily on his broad belt. The fingers of the other hand caressed lightly a moustache that had caused more heart-burnings among the gentler sex than any other two moustaches in the C-division. The eyes above the moustache were stern and questioning.

"What's all this?"

George liked policemen. He knew the way to treat them. His voice, when he replied, had precisely the correct note of respectful deference which the Force likes to hear.

"I really couldn't say, officer," he said, with just that air of having in a time of trouble found a kind elder brother to help him out of his difficulties which made the constable his ally on the spot. "I was standing here, when this man suddenly made his extraordinary attack on me. I wish you would ask him to go away."

The policeman tapped the stout young man on the shoulder.

"This won't do, you know!" he said austerely. "This sort o' thing won't do, 'ere, you know!"

"Take your hands off me!" snorted Percy.

A frown appeared on the Olympian brow. Jove reached for his thunderbolts.

"'Ullo! 'Ullo! 'Ullo!" he said in a shocked voice, as of a god defied by a mortal. "'Ullo! 'Ullo! 'Ul-lo!"

His fingers fell on Percy's shoulder again, but this time not in a mere warning tap. They rested where they fell—in an iron clutch.

"It won't do, you know," he said. "This sort o' thing won't do!" Madness came upon the stout young man. Common prudence and the lessons of a carefully-taught youth fell from him like a garment. With an incoherent howl he wriggled round and punched the policeman smartly in the stomach.

"Ho!" quoth the outraged officer, suddenly becoming human. His left hand removed itself from the belt, and he got a businesslike grip on his adversary's collar. "Will you come along with me!"

It was amazing. The thing had happened in such an incredibly brief space of time. One moment, it seemed to George, he was the centre of a nasty row in one of the most public spots in London; the next, the focus had shifted; he had ceased to matter; and the entire attention of the metropolis was focused on his late assailant, as, urged by the arm of the Law, he made that journey to Vine Street Police Station which so many a better man than he had trod.

George watched the pair as they moved up the Haymarket, followed by a growing and increasingly absorbed crowd; then he turned into the hotel.

"This," he said to himself; "is the middle of a perfect day! And I thought London dull!"

CHAPTER 5.

George awoke next morning with a misty sense that somehow the world had changed. As the last remnants of sleep left him, he was aware of a vague excitement. Then he sat up in bed with a jerk. He had remembered that he was in love.

There was no doubt about it. A curious happiness pervaded his entire being. He felt young and active. Everything was emphatically for the best in this best of all possible worlds. The sun was shining. Even the sound of someone in the street below whistling one of his old compositions, of which he had heartily sickened twelve months before, was pleasant to his ears, and this in spite of the fact that the unseen whistler only touched the key in odd spots and had a poor memory for tunes. George sprang lightly out of bed, and turned on the cold tap in the bath-room. While he lathered his face for its morning shave he beamed at himself in the mirror.

It had come at last. The Real Thing.

George had never been in love before. Not really in love. True, from the age of fifteen, he had been in varying degrees of intensity attracted sentimentally by the opposite sex. Indeed, at that period of life of which Mr. Booth Tarkington has written so searchingly—the age of seventeen—he had been in love with practically every female he met and with dozens whom he had only seen in the distance; but ripening years had mellowed his taste and robbed him of that fine romantic catholicity. During the last five years women had found him more or less cold. It was the nature of his profession that had largely brought about this cooling of the emotions. To a man who, like George, has worked year in and year out at the composition of musical comedies, woman comes to lose many of those attractive qualities which ensnare the ordinary male. To George, of late years, it had begun to seem that the salient feature of woman as a sex was her disposition to kick. For five years he had been wandering in a world of women, many of them beautiful, all of them superficially attractive, who had left no other impress on his memory except the vigour and frequency with which they had kicked. Some had kicked about their musical numbers, some about their love-scenes; some had grumbled about their exit lines, others about the lines of their second-act frocks. They had kicked in a myriad differing ways—wrathfully, sweetly, noisily, softly, smilingly, tearfully, pathetically and patronizingly; but they had all kicked; with the result that woman had now become to George not so much a flaming inspiration or a tender goddess as something to be dodged—tactfully, if possible; but, if not possible, by open flight. For years he had dreaded to be left alone with a woman, and had developed a habit of gliding swiftly away when he saw one bearing down on him.

The psychological effect of such a state of things is not difficult to realize. Take a man of naturally quixotic temperament, a man of chivalrous instincts and a feeling for romance, and cut him off for five years from the exercise of those qualities, and you get an accumulated store of foolishness only comparable to an escape of gas in a sealed room or a cellarful of dynamite. A flicker of a match, and there is an explosion.

This girl's tempestuous irruption into his life had supplied flame for George. Her bright eyes, looking into his, had touched off the spiritual trinitrotoluol which he had been storing up for so long. Up in the air in a million pieces had gone the prudence and self-restraint of a lifetime. And here he was, as desperately in love as any troubadour of the Middle Ages.

It was not till he had finished shaving and was testing the temperature of his bath with a shrinking toe that the realization came over him in a wave that, though he might be in love, the fairway of love was dotted with more bunkers than any golf course he had ever played on in his life. In the first place, he did not know the girl's name. In the second place, it seemed practically impossible that he would ever see her again. Even in the midst of his optimism George could not deny that these facts might reasonably be considered in the nature of obstacles. He went back into his bedroom, and sat on the bed. This thing wanted thinking over.

He was not depressed—only a little thoughtful. His faith in his luck sustained him. He was, he realized, in the position of a man who has made a supreme drive from the tee, and finds his ball near the green but in a cuppy lie. He had gained much; it now remained for him to push his success to the happy conclusion. The driver of Luck must be replaced by the spoon—or, possibly, the niblick—of Ingenuity. To fail now, to allow this girl to pass out of his life merely because he did not know who she was or where she was, would stamp him a feeble adventurer. A fellow could not expect Luck to do everything for him. He must supplement its assistance with his own efforts.

What had he to go on? Well, nothing much, if it came to that, except the knowledge that she lived some two hours by train out of London, and that her journey started from Waterloo Station. What would Sherlock Holmes have done? Concentrated thought supplied no answer to the question; and it was at this point that the cheery optimism with which he had begun the day left George and gave place to a grey gloom. A dreadful phrase, haunting in its pathos, crept into his mind. "Ships that pass in the night!" It might easily turn out that way. Indeed, thinking over the affair in all its aspects as he dried himself after his tub, George could not see how it could possibly turn out any other way.

He dressed moodily, and left the room to go down to breakfast. Breakfast would at least alleviate this sinking feeling which was unmanning him. And he could think more briskly after a cup or two of coffee.

He opened the door. On a mat outside lay a letter.

The handwriting was feminine. It was also in pencil, and strange to him. He opened the envelope.

"Dear Mr. Bevan" (it began).

With a sudden leap of the heart he looked at the signature.

The letter was signed "The Girl in the Cab."

"DEAR MR. BEVAN,

"I hope you won't think me very rude, running off without waiting to say good-bye. I had to. I saw Percy driving up in a cab, and knew that he must have followed us. He did not see me, so I got away all right. I managed splendidly about the money, for I remembered that I was wearing a nice brooch, and stopped on the way to the station to pawn it.

"Thank you ever so much again for all your wonderful

kindness.

Yours,

THE GIRL IN THE CAB."

George read the note twice on the way down to the breakfast room, and three times more during the meal; then, having committed its contents to memory down to the last comma, he gave himself up to glowing thoughts.

What a girl! He had never in his life before met a woman who could write a letter without a postscript, and this was but the smallest of her unusual gifts. The resource of her, to think of pawning that brooch! The sweetness of her to bother to send him a note! More than ever before was he convinced that he had met his ideal, and more than ever before was he determined that a triviality like being unaware of her name and address should not keep him from her. It was not as if he had no clue to go upon. He knew that she lived two hours from London and started home from Waterloo. It narrowed the thing down absurdly. There were only about three counties in which she could possibly live; and a man must be a poor fellow who is incapable of searching through a few small counties for the girl he loves. Especially a man with luck like his.

Luck is a goddess not to be coerced and forcibly wooed by those who seek her favours. From such masterful spirits she turns away. But it happens sometimes that, if we put our hand in hers with the humble trust of a little child, she will have pity on us, and not fail us in our hour of need. On George, hopefully watching for something to turn up, she smiled almost immediately.

It was George's practice, when he lunched alone, to relieve the tedium of the meal with the assistance of reading matter in the shape of one or more of the evening papers. Today, sitting down to a solitary repast at the Piccadilly grill-room, he had brought with him an early edition of the Evening News. And one of the first items which met his eye was the following, embodied in a column on one of the inner pages devoted to humorous comments in prose and verse on the happenings of the day. This particular happening the writer had apparently considered worthy of being dignified by rhyme. It was headed:

"THE PEER AND THE POLICEMAN."

"Outside the 'Carlton,' 'tis averred, these stirring happenings occurred. The hour, 'tis said (and no one doubts) was half-past two, or thereabouts. The day was fair, the sky was blue, and everything was peaceful too, when suddenly a well-dressed gent engaged in heated argument and roundly to abuse began another well-dressed gentleman. His suede-gloved fist he raised on high to dot the other in the eye. Who knows what horrors might have been, had there not come upon the scene old London city's favourite son, Policeman C. 231. 'What means this conduct? Prithee stop!' exclaimed that admirable slop. With which he placed a warning hand upon the brawler's collarband. We simply hate to tell the rest. No subject here for flippant jest. The mere remembrance of the tale has made our ink turn deadly pale. Let us be brief. Some demon sent stark madness on the well-dressed gent. He gave the constable a punch just where the latter kept his lunch. The constable said 'Well! Well! Well!' and marched him to a dungeon cell. At Vine Street Station out it came—Lord Belpher was the culprit's name. But British Justice is severe alike on pauper and on peer; with even hand she holds the scale; a thumping fine, in lieu of gaol, induced Lord B. to feel remorse and learn he mustn't punch the Force."

George's mutton chop congealed on the plate, untouched. The French fried potatoes cooled off, unnoticed. This was no time for food. Rightly indeed had he relied upon his luck. It had stood by him nobly. With this clue, all was over except getting to the nearest Free Library and consulting Burke's Peerage. He paid his bill and left the restaurant.

Ten minutes later he was drinking in the pregnant information that Belpher was the family name of the Earl of Marshmoreton, and that the present earl had one son, Percy Wilbraham Marsh, educ. Eton and Christ Church, Oxford, and what the book with its customary curtness called "one d."—Patricia Maud. The family seat, said Burke, was Belpher Castle, Belpher, Hants.

Some hours later, seated in a first-class compartment of a train that moved slowly out of

Waterloo Station, George watched London vanish behind him. In the pocket closest to his throbbing heart was a single ticket to Belpher.

CHAPTER 6.

At about the time that George Bevan's train was leaving Waterloo, a grey racing car drew up with a grinding of brakes and a sputter of gravel in front of the main entrance of Belpher Castle. The slim and elegant young man at the wheel removed his goggles, pulled out a watch, and addressed the stout young man at his side.

"Two hours and eighteen minutes from Hyde Park Corner, Boots. Not so dusty, what?"

His companion made no reply. He appeared to be plunged in thought. He, too, removed his goggles, revealing a florid and gloomy face, equipped, in addition to the usual features, with a small moustache and an extra chin. He scowled forbiddingly at the charming scene which the goggles had hidden from him.

Before him, a symmetrical mass of grey stone and green ivy, Belpher Castle towered against a light blue sky. On either side rolling park land spread as far as the eye could see, carpeted here and there with violets, dotted with great oaks and ashes and Spanish chestnuts, orderly, peaceful and English. Nearer, on his left, were rose-gardens, in the centre of which, tilted at a sharp angle, appeared the seat of a pair of corduroy trousers, whose wearer seemed to be engaged in hunting for snails. Thrushes sang in the green shrubberies; rooks cawed in the elms. Somewhere in the distance sounded the tinkle of sheep bells and the lowing of cows. It was, in fact, a scene which, lit by the evening sun of a perfect spring day and fanned by a gentle westerly wind, should have brought balm and soothing meditations to one who was the sole heir to all this Paradise.

But Percy, Lord Belpher, remained uncomforted by the notable co-operation of Man and Nature, and drew no solace from the reflection that all these pleasant things would one day be his own. His mind was occupied at the moment, to the exclusion of all other thoughts, by the recollection of that painful scene in Bow Street Police Court. The magistrate's remarks, which had been tactless and unsympathetic, still echoed in his ears. And that infernal night in Vine Street police station . . . The darkness . . . The hard bed. . . The discordant vocalising of the drunk and disorderly in the next cell. . . . Time might soften these memories, might lessen the sharp agony of them; but nothing could remove them altogether.

Percy had been shaken to the core of his being. Physically, he was still stiff and sore from the plank bed. Mentally, he was a volcano. He had been marched up the Haymarket in the full sight of all London by a bounder of a policeman. He had been talked to like an erring child by a magistrate whom nothing could convince that he had not been under the influence of alcohol at the moment of his arrest. (The man had said things about his liver, kindly be-warned-in-time-and-pull-up-before-it-is-too-late things, which would have seemed to Percy indecently frank if spoken by his medical adviser in the privacy of the sick chamber.) It is perhaps not to be wondered at that Belpher Castle, for all its beauty of scenery and architecture, should have left Lord Belpher a little cold. He was seething with a fury which the conversation of Reggie Byng had done nothing to allay in the course of the journey from London. Reggie was the last person he would willingly have chosen as a companion in his hour of darkness. Reggie was not soothing. He would insist on addressing him by his old Eton nickname of Boots which Percy detested. And all the way down he had been breaking out at intervals into ribald comments on the recent unfortunate occurrence which were very hard to bear.

He resumed this vein as they alighted and rang the bell.

"This," said Reggie, "is rather like a bit out of a melodrama. Convict son totters up the steps of the old home and punches the bell. What awaits him beyond? Forgiveness? Or the raspberry? True, the white-haired butler who knew him as a child will sob on his neck, but what of the old dad? How will dad take the blot of the family escutcheon?"

Lord Belpher's scowl deepened.

"It's not a joking matter," he said coldly.

"Great Heavens, I'm not joking. How could I have the heart to joke at a moment like this, when the friend of my youth has suddenly become a social leper?"

"I wish to goodness you would stop."

"Do you think it is any pleasure to me to be seen about with a man who is now known in criminal circles as Percy, the Piccadilly Policeman-Puncher? I keep a brave face before the world, but inwardly I burn with shame and agony and what not."

The great door of the castle swung open, revealing Keggs, the butler. He was a man of reverend years, portly and dignified, with a respectfully benevolent face that beamed gravely on the young master and Mr. Byng, as if their coming had filled his cup of pleasure. His light, slightly protruding eyes expressed reverential good will. He gave just that touch of cosy humanity to the scene which the hall with its half lights and massive furniture needed to make it perfect to the returned wanderer. He seemed to be intimating that this was a moment to which he had looked forward long, and that from now on quiet happiness would reign supreme. It is distressing to have to reveal the jarring fact that, in his hours of privacy when off duty, this apparently ideal servitor was so far from being a respecter of persons that he was accustomed to speak of Lord Belpher as "Percy", and even as "His Nibs". It was, indeed, an open secret among the upper servants at the castle, and a fact hinted at with awe among the lower, that Keggs was at heart a Socialist.

"Good evening, your lordship. Good evening, sir."

Lord Belpher acknowledged the salutation with a grunt, but Reggie was more affable.

"How are you, Keggs? Now's your time, if you're going to do it." He stepped a little to one side and indicated Lord Belpher's crimson neck with an inviting gesture.

"I beg your pardon, sir?"

"Ah. You'd rather wait till you can do it a little more privately.

Perhaps you're right."

The butler smiled indulgently. He did not understand what Reggie was talking about, but that did not worry him. He had long since come to the conclusion that Reggie was slightly mad, a theory supported by the latter's valet, who was of the same opinion. Keggs did not dislike Reggie, but intellectually he considered him negligible.

"Send something to drink into the library, Keggs," said Lord

Belpher.

"Very good, your lordship."

"A topping idea," said Reggie. "I'll just take the old car round to the garage, and then I'll be with you."

He climbed to the steering wheel, and started the engine. Lord Belpher proceeded to the library, while Keggs melted away through the green baize door at the end of the hall which divided the servants' quarters from the rest of the house.

Reggie had hardly driven a dozen yards when he perceived his stepmother and Lord

Marshmoreton coming towards him from the direction of the rose-garden. He drew up to greet them.

"Hullo, mater. What ho, uncle! Back again at the old homestead, what?"

Beneath Lady Caroline's aristocratic front agitation seemed to lurk.

"Reggie, where is Percy?"

"Old Boots? I think he's gone to the library. I just decanted him out of the car."

Lady Caroline turned to her brother.

"Let us go to the library, John."

"All right. All right. All right," said Lord Marshmoreton irritably. Something appeared to have ruffled his calm.

Reggie drove on. As he was strolling back after putting the car away he met Maud.

"Hullo, Maud, dear old thing."

"Why, hullo, Reggie. I was expecting you back last night."

"Couldn't get back last night. Had to stick in town and rally round

old Boots. Couldn't desert the old boy in his hour of trial."

Reggie chuckled amusedly. "'Hour of trial,' is rather good, what?

What I mean to say is, that's just what it was, don't you know."

"Why, what happened to Percy?"

"Do you mean to say you haven't heard? Of course not. It wouldn't have been in the morning papers. Why, Percy punched a policeman."

"Percy did what?"

"Slugged a slop. Most dramatic thing. Sloshed him in the midriff.

Absolutely. The cross marks the spot where the tragedy occurred."

Maud caught her breath. Somehow, though she could not trace the connection, she felt that this extraordinary happening must be linked up with her escapade. Then her sense of humour got the better of apprehension. Her eyes twinkled delightedly.

"You don't mean to say Percy did that?"

"Absolutely. The human tiger, and what not. Menace to Society and all that sort of thing. No holding him. For some unexplained reason the generous blood of the Belphers boiled over, and then—zing. They jerked him off to Vine Street. Like the poem, don't you know. 'And poor old Percy walked between with gyves upon his wrists.' And this morning, bright and early, the beak parted him from ten quid. You know, Maud, old thing, our duty stares us plainly in the eyeball. We've got to train old Boots down to a reasonable weight and spring him on the National Sporting Club. We've been letting a champion middleweight blush unseen under our very roof tree."

Maud hesitated a moment.

"I suppose you don't know," she asked carelessly, "why he did it? I mean, did he tell you anything?"

"Couldn't get a word out of him. Oysters garrulous and tombs chatty in comparison. Absolutely. All I know is that he popped one into the officer's waistband. What led up to it is more than I can tell you. How would it be to stagger to the library and join the post-mortem?"

"The post-mortem?"

"Well, I met the mater and his lordship on their way to the library, and it looked to me very much as if the mater must have got hold of an evening paper on her journey from town. When did she arrive?"

"Only a short while ago."

"Then that's what's happened. She would have bought an evening paper to read in the train. By Jove, I wonder if she got hold of the one that had the poem about it. One chappie was so carried away by the beauty of the episode that he treated it in verse. I think we ought to look in and see what's happening."

Maud hesitated again. But she was a girl of spirit. And she had an intuition that her best defence would be attack. Bluff was what was needed. Wide-eyed, innocent wonder . . . After all, Percy couldn't be certain he had seen her in Piccadilly.

"All right."

"By the way, dear old girl," inquired Reggie, "did your little business come out satisfactorily? I forgot to ask."

"Not very. But it was awfully sweet of you to take me into town."

"How would it be," said Reggie nervously, "not to dwell too much on that part of it? What I mean to say is, for heaven's sake don't let the mater know I rallied round."

"Don't worry," said Maud with a laugh. "I'm not going to talk about the thing at all."

Lord Belpher, meanwhile, in the library, had begun with the aid of a whisky and soda to feel a little better. There was something about the library with its sombre half tones that soothed his bruised spirit. The room held something of the peace of a deserted city. The world, with its violent adventures and tall policemen, did not enter here. There was balm in those rows and rows of books which nobody ever read, those vast writing tables at which nobody ever wrote. From the broad mantel-piece the bust of some unnamed ancient looked down almost sympathetically. Something remotely resembling peace had begun to steal into Percy's soul, when it was expelled by the abrupt opening of the door and the entry of Lady Caroline Byng and his father. One glance at the face of the former was enough to tell Lord Belpher that she knew all.

He rose defensively.

"Let me explain."

Lady Caroline quivered with repressed emotion. This masterly woman had not lost control of herself, but her aristocratic calm had seldom been so severely tested. As Reggie had surmised, she had read the report of the proceedings in the evening paper in the train, and her world had been reeling ever since. Caesar, stabbed by Brutus, could scarcely have experienced a greater shock. The other members of her family had disappointed her often. She had become inured to the spectacle of her brother working in the garden in corduroy trousers and in other ways behaving in a manner beneath the dignity of an Earl of Marshmoreton. She had resigned herself to the innate flaw in the character of Maud which had allowed her to fall in love with a nobody whom she had met without an introduction. Even Reggie had exhibited at times democratic traits of which she thoroughly disapproved. But of her nephew Percy she had always been sure. He was solid rock. He, at least, she had always felt, would never do anything to injure the family prestige. And now, so to speak, "Lo, Ben Adhem's name led all the rest." In other words, Percy was the worst of the lot. Whatever indiscretions the rest had committed, at least they had never got the family into the comic columns of the evening papers. Lord Marshmoreton might wear corduroy trousers and refuse to entertain the County at garden parties and go to bed with a book when it was his duty to act as host at a formal ball; Maud might give her heart to an impossible person whom nobody had ever heard of; and Reggie might be seen at fashionable restaurants with pugilists; but at any rate evening paper poets had never written facetious verses about their exploits. This crowning degradation had been reserved for the hitherto blameless Percy, who, of all the young men of Lady Caroline's acquaintance, had till now appeared to have the most scrupulous sense of his position, the most rigid regard for the dignity of his great name. Yet, here he was, if the carefully considered reports in the daily press were to be believed, spending his time in the very spring-tide of his life running about London like a frenzied Hottentot, brutally assaulting the police. Lady Caroline felt as a bishop might feel if he suddenly discovered that some favourite curate had gone over to the worship of Mumbo Jumbo.

"Explain?" she cried. "How can you explain? You—my nephew, the heir to the title, behaving like a common rowdy in the streets of London . . . your name in the papers . . . "

"If you knew the circumstances."

"The circumstances? They are in the evening paper. They are in print."

"In verse," added Lord Marshmoreton. He chuckled amiably at the recollection. He was an easily amused man. "You ought to read it, my boy. Some of it was capital . . ."

"John!"

"But deplorable, of course," added Lord Marshmoreton hastily. "Very deplorable." He endeavoured to regain his sister's esteem by a show of righteous indignation. "What do you mean by it, damn it? You're my only son. I have watched you grow from child to boy, from boy to man, with tender solicitude. I have wanted to be proud of you. And all the time, dash it, you are prowling about London like a lion, seeking whom you may devour, terrorising the metropolis, putting harmless policemen in fear of their lives. . ."

"Will you listen to me for a moment?" shouted Percy. He began to speak rapidly, as one conscious of the necessity of saying his say while the saying was good. "The facts are these. I was walking along Piccadilly on my way to lunch at the club, when, near Burlington Arcade, I was amazed to see Maud."

Lady Caroline uttered an exclamation.

"Maud? But Maud was here."

"I can't understand it," went on Lord Marshmoreton, pursuing his remarks. Righteous indignation had, he felt, gone well. It might be judicious to continue in that vein, though privately he held the opinion that nothing in Percy's life so became him as this assault on the Force. Lord Marshmoreton, who in his time had committed all the follies of youth, had come to look on his blameless son as scarcely human. "It's not as if you were wild. You've never got into any scrapes at Oxford. You've spent your time collecting old china and prayer rugs. You wear flannel next your skin . . ."

"Will you please be quiet," said Lady Caroline impatiently. "Go on, Percy."

"Oh, very well," said Lord Marshmoreton. "I only spoke. I merely made a remark."

"You say you saw Maud in Piccadilly, Percy?"

"Precisely. I was on the point of putting it down to an extraordinary resemblance, when suddenly she got into a cab. Then I knew."

Lord Marshmoreton could not permit this to pass in silence. He was a fair-minded man.

"Why shouldn't the girl have got into a cab? Why must a girl walking along Piccadilly be my daughter Maud just because she got into a cab. London," he proceeded, warming to the argument and thrilled by the clearness and coherence of his reasoning, "is full of girls who take cabs."

"She didn't take a cab."

"You just said she did," said Lord Marshmoreton cleverly.

"I said she got into a cab. There was somebody else already in the cab. A man. Aunt Caroline, it was the man."

"Good gracious," ejaculated Lady Caroline, falling into a chair as if she had been hamstrung.

"I am absolutely convinced of it," proceeded Lord Belpher solemnly. "His behaviour was enough to confirm my suspicions. The cab had stopped in a block of the traffic, and I went up and requested him in a perfectly civil manner to allow me to look at the lady who had just got in. He denied that there was a lady in the cab. And I had seen her jump in with my own eyes. Throughout the conversation he was leaning out of the window with the obvious intention of screening whoever was inside from my view. I followed him along Piccadilly in another cab, and tracked him to the Carlton. When I arrived there he was standing on the pavement outside. There were no signs of Maud. I demanded that he tell me her whereabouts. . ."

"That reminds me," said Lord Marshmoreton cheerfully, "of a story I read in one of the papers. I daresay it's old. Stop me if you've heard it. A woman says to the maid: 'Do you know anything of my husband's whereabouts?' And the maid replies—"

"Do be quiet," snapped Lady Caroline. "I should have thought that you would be interested in a matter affecting the vital welfare of your only daughter."

"I am. I am," said Lord Marshmoreton hastily. "The maid replied: 'They're at the wash.' Of course I am. Go on, Percy. Good God, boy, don't take all day telling us your story."

"At that moment the fool of a policeman came up and wanted to know what the matter was. I lost my head. I admit it freely. The policeman grasped my shoulder, and I struck him."

"Where?" asked Lord Marshmoreton, a stickler for detail.

"What does that matter?" demanded Lady Caroline. "You did quite right, Percy. These insolent jacks in office ought not to be allowed to manhandle people. Tell me, what this man was like?"

"Extremely ordinary-looking. In fact, all I can remember about him was that he was clean-shaven. I cannot understand how Maud could have come to lose her head over such a man. He seemed to me to have no attraction whatever," said Lord Belpher, a little unreasonably, for Apollo himself would hardly appear attractive when knocking one's best hat off.

"It must have been the same man."

"Precisely. If we wanted further proof, he was an American. You recollect that we heard that the man in Wales was American."

There was a portentous silence. Percy stared at the floor. Lady Caroline breathed deeply. Lord Marshmoreton, feeling that something was expected of him, said "Good Gad!" and gazed seriously at a stuffed owl on a bracket. Maud and Reggie Byng came in.

"What ho, what ho, what ho!" said Reggie breezily. He always believed in starting a conversation well, and putting people at their ease. "What ho! What ho!"

Maud braced herself for the encounter.

"Hullo, Percy, dear," she said, meeting her brother's accusing eye with the perfect composure that comes only from a thoroughly guilty conscience. "What's all this I hear about your being the Scourge of London? Reggie says that policemen dive down manholes when they see you coming."

The chill in the air would have daunted a less courageous girl. Lady Caroline had risen, and was staring sternly. Percy was puffing the puffs of an overwrought soul. Lord Marshmoreton, whose thoughts had wandered off to the rose garden, pulled himself together and tried to look menacing. Maud went on without waiting for a reply. She was all bubbling gaiety and insouciance, a charming picture of young English girlhood that nearly made her brother foam at the mouth.

"Father dear," she said, attaching herself affectionately to his buttonhole, "I went round the links in eighty-three this morning. I did the long hole in four. One under par, a thing I've never done before in my life." ("Bless my soul," said Lord Marshmoreton weakly, as, with an apprehensive eye on his sister, he patted his daughter's shoulder.) "First, I sent a screecher of a drive right down the middle of the fairway. Then I took my brassey and put the ball just on the edge of the green. A hundred and eighty yards if it was an inch. My approach putt—"

Lady Caroline, who was no devotee of the royal and ancient game, interrupted the recital.

"Never mind what you did this morning. What did you do yesterday afternoon?"

"Yes," said Lord Belpher. "Where were you yesterday afternoon?"

Maud's gaze was the gaze of a young child who has never even attempted to put anything over in all its little life.

"Whatever do you mean?"

"What were you doing in Piccadilly yesterday afternoon?" said Lady

Caroline.

"Piccadilly? The place where Percy fights policemen? I don't understand."

Lady Caroline was no sportsman. She put one of those direct questions, capable of being answered only by "Yes" or "No", which ought not to be allowed in controversy. They are the verbal equivalent of shooting a sitting bird.

"Did you or did you not go to London yesterday, Maud?"

The monstrous unfairness of this method of attack pained Maud. From childhood up she had held the customary feminine views upon the Lie Direct. As long as it was a question of suppression of the true or suggestion of the false she had no scruples. But she had a distaste for deliberate falsehood. Faced now with a choice between two evils, she chose the one which would at least leave her self-respect.

"Yes, I did."

Lady Caroline looked at Lord Belpher. Lord Belpher looked at

Lady Caroline.

"You went to meet that American of yours?"

Reggie Byng slid softly from the room. He felt that he would be happier elsewhere. He had been an acutely embarrassed spectator of this distressing scene, and had been passing the time by shuffling his feet, playing with his coat buttons and perspiring.

"Don't go, Reggie," said Lord Belpher.

"Well, what I mean to say is—family row and what not—if you see what I mean—I've one or two things I ought to do—"

He vanished. Lord Belpher frowned a sombre frown. "Then it was that man who knocked my hat off?"

"What do you mean?" said Lady Caroline. "Knocked your hat off? You never told me he knocked your hat off."

"It was when I was asking him to let me look inside the cab. I had grasped the handle of the door, when he suddenly struck my hat, causing it to fly off. And, while I was picking it up, he drove away."

"C'k," exploded Lord Marshmoreton. "C'k, c'k, c'k." He twisted his face by a supreme exertion of will power into a mask of indignation. "You ought to have had the scoundrel arrested," he said vehemently. "It was a technical assault."

"The man who knocked your hat off, Percy," said Maud, "was not . . . He was a different man altogether. A stranger."

"As if you would be in a cab with a stranger," said Lady Caroline caustically. "There are limits, I hope, to even your indiscretions."

Lord Marshmoreton cleared his throat. He was sorry for Maud, whom he loved.

"Now, looking at the matter broadly—"

"Be quiet," said Lady Caroline.

Lord Marshmoreton subsided.

"I wanted to avoid you," said Maud, "so I jumped into the first cab I saw."

"I don't believe it," said Percy.

"It's the truth."

"You are simply trying to put us off the scent."

Lady Caroline turned to Maud. Her manner was plaintive. She looked like a martyr at the stake who deprecatingly lodges a timid complaint, fearful the while lest she may be hurting the feelings of her persecutors by appearing even for a moment out of sympathy with their activities.

"My dear child, why will you not be reasonable in this matter? Why will you not let yourself be guided by those who are older and wiser than you?"

"Exactly," said Lord Belpher.

"The whole thing is too absurd."

"Precisely," said Lord Belpher.

Lady Caroline turned on him irritably.

"Please do not interrupt, Percy. Now, you've made me forget what I was going to say."

"To my mind," said Lord Marshmoreton, coming to the surface once more, "the proper attitude to adopt on occasions like the present—"

"Please," said Lady Caroline.

Lord Marshmoreton stopped, and resumed his silent communion with the stuffed bird.

"You can't stop yourself being in love, Aunt Caroline," said Maud.

"You can be stopped if you've somebody with a level head looking after you."

Lord Marshmoreton tore himself away from the bird.

"Why, when I was at Oxford in the year '87," he said chattily, "I fancied myself in love with the female assistant at a tobacconist shop. Desperately in love, dammit. Wanted to marry her. I recollect my poor father took me away from Oxford and kept me here at Belpher under lock and key. Lock and key, dammit. I was deucedly upset at the time, I remember." His mind wandered off into the glorious past. "I wonder what that girl's name was. Odd one can't remember names. She had chestnut hair and a mole on the side of her chin. I used to kiss it, I recollect—"

Lady Caroline, usually such an advocate of her brother's researches into the family history, cut the reminiscences short.

"Never mind that now."

"I don't. I got over it. That's the moral."

"Well," said Lady Caroline, "at any rate poor father acted with great good sense on that occasion. There seems nothing to do but to treat Maud in just the same way. You shall not stir a step from the castle till you have got over this dreadful infatuation. You will be watched."

"I shall watch you," said Lord Belpher solemnly, "I shall watch your every movement."

A dreamy look came into Maud's brown eyes.

"Stone walls do not a prison make nor iron bars a cage," she said softly.

"That wasn't your experience, Percy, my boy," said Lord

Marshmoreton.

"They make a very good imitation," said Lady Caroline coldly, ignoring the interruption.

Maud faced her defiantly. She looked like a princess in captivity facing her gaolers.

"I don't care. I love him, and I always shall love him, and nothing is ever going to stop me loving him—because I love him," she concluded a little lamely.

"Nonsense," said Lady Caroline. "In a year from now you will have forgotten his name. Don't you agree with me, Percy?"

"Quite," said Lord Belpher.

"I shan't."

"Deuced hard things to remember, names," said Lord Marshmoreton. "If I've tried once to remember that tobacconist girl's name, I've tried a hundred times. I have an idea it began with an 'L.' Muriel or Hilda or something."

"Within a year," said Lady Caroline, "you will be wondering how you ever came to be so foolish. Don't you think so, Percy?"

"Quite," said Lord Belpher.

Lord Marshmoreton turned on him irritably.

"Good God, boy, can't you answer a simple question with a plain affirmative? What do you mean—quite? If somebody came to me and pointed you out and said, 'Is that your son?' do you suppose I should say 'Quite?' I wish the devil you didn't collect prayer rugs. It's sapped your brain."

"They say prison life often weakens the intellect, father," said Maud. She moved towards the door and turned the handle. Albert, the page boy, who had been courting earache by listening at the keyhole, straightened his small body and scuttled away. "Well, is that all, Aunt Caroline? May I go now?"

"Certainly. I have said all I wished to say."

"Very well. I'm sorry to disobey you, but I can't help it."

"You'll find you can help it after you've been cooped up here for a few more months," said Percy.

A gentle smile played over Maud's face.

"Love laughs at locksmiths," she murmured softly, and passed from the room.

"What did she say?" asked Lord Marshmoreton, interested. "Something about somebody laughing at a locksmith? I don't understand. Why should anyone laugh at locksmiths? Most respectable men. Had one up here only the day before yesterday, forcing open the drawer of my desk. Watched him do it. Most interesting. He smelt rather strongly of a damned bad brand of tobacco. Fellow must have a throat of leather to be able to smoke the stuff. But he didn't strike me as an object of derision. From first to last, I was never tempted to laugh once."

Lord Belpher wandered moodily to the window and looked out into the gathering darkness.

"And this has to happen," he said bitterly, "on the eve of my twenty-first birthday."

CHAPTER 7.

The first requisite of an invading army is a base. George, having entered Belpher village and thus accomplished the first stage in his foreward movement on the castle, selected as his base the Marshmoreton Arms. Selected is perhaps hardly the right word, as it implies choice, and in George's case there was no choice. There are two inns at Belpher, but the Marshmoreton Arms is the only one that offers accommodation for man and beast, assuming—that is to say—that the man and beast desire to spend the night. The other house, the Blue Boar, is a mere beerhouse, where the lower strata of Belpher society gather of a night to quench their thirst and to tell one another interminable stories without any point whatsoever. But the Marshmoreton Arms is a comfortable, respectable hostelry, catering for the village plutocrats. There of an evening you will find the local veterinary surgeon smoking a pipe with the grocer, the baker, and the butcher, with perhaps a sprinkling of neighbouring farmers to help the conversation along. On Saturdays there is a "shilling ordinary"—which is rural English for a cut off the joint and a boiled potato, followed by hunks of the sort of cheese which believes that it pays to advertise, and this is usually well attended. On the other days of the week, until late in the evening, however, the visitor to the Marshmoreton Arms has the place almost entirely to himself.

It is to be questioned whether in the whole length and breadth of the world there is a more admirable spot for a man in love to pass a day or two than the typical English village. The Rocky Mountains, that traditional stamping-ground for the heartbroken, may be well enough in their way; but a lover has to be cast in a pretty stern mould to be able to be introspective when at any moment he may meet an annoyed cinnamon bear. In the English village there are no such obstacles to meditation. It combines the comforts of civilization with the restfulness of solitude in a manner equalled by no other spot except the New York Public Library. Here your lover may wander to and fro unmolested, speaking to nobody, by nobody addressed, and have the satisfaction at the end of the day of sitting down to a capitally cooked chop and chips, lubricated by golden English ale.

Belpher, in addition to all the advantages of the usual village, has a quiet charm all its own, due to the fact that it has seen better days. In a sense, it is a ruin, and ruins are always soothing to the bruised soul. Ten years before, Belpher had been a flourishing centre of the South of England oyster trade. It is situated by the shore, where Hayling Island, lying athwart the mouth of the bay, forms the waters into a sort of brackish lagoon, in much the same way as Fire Island shuts off the Great South Bay of Long Island from the waves of the Atlantic. The water of Belpher Creek is shallow even at high tide, and when the tide runs out it leaves glistening mud flats, which it is the peculiar taste of the oyster to prefer to any other habitation. For years Belpher oysters had been the mainstay of gay supper parties at the Savoy, the Carlton and Romano's. Dukes doted on them; chorus girls wept if they were not on the bill of fare. And then, in an evil hour, somebody discovered that what made the Belpher Oyster so particularly plump and succulent was the fact that it breakfasted, lunched and dined almost entirely on the local sewage. There is but a thin line ever between popular homage and execration. We see it in the case of politicians, generals and prize-fighters; and oysters are no exception to the rule. There was a typhoid scare—quite a passing and unjustified scare, but strong enough to do its deadly work; and almost overnight Belpher passed from a place of flourishing industry to the sleepy, by-the-world-forgotten spot which it was when George Bevan discovered it. The shallow water is still there; the mud is still there; even the oyster-beds are still there; but not the oysters nor the little world of activity which had sprung up around them. The glory of Belpher is dead; and over its gates Ichabod is written. But, if it has lost in importance, it has gained in charm; and George, for one, had no regrets. To him, in his present state of mental upheaval, Belpher was the ideal spot.

It was not at first that George roused himself to the point of asking why he was here and what—now that he was here—he proposed to do. For two languorous days he loafed, sufficiently occupied with his thoughts. He smoked long, peaceful pipes in the stable-yard, watching the ostlers as they groomed the horses; he played with the Inn puppy, bestowed respectful caresses on the Inn cat. He walked down the quaint cobbled street to the harbour, sauntered along the shore, and lay on his back on the little beach at the other side of the lagoon, from where he could see the red roofs of the village, while the imitation waves splashed busily on the stones, trying to conceal with bustle and energy the fact that the water even two hundred yards from the shore was only eighteen inches deep. For it is the abiding hope of Belpher Creek that it may be able to deceive the occasional visitor into mistaking it for the open sea.

And presently the tide would ebb. The waste of waters became a sea of mud, cheerfully covered as to much of its surface with green grasses. The evening sun struck rainbow colours from the moist softness. Birds sang in the thickets. And George, heaving himself up, walked back to the friendly cosiness of the Marshmoreton Arms. And the remarkable part of it was that everything seemed perfectly natural and sensible to him, nor had he any particular feeling that in falling in love with Lady Maud Marsh and pursuing her to Belpher he had set himself anything in the nature of a hopeless task. Like one kissed by a goddess in a dream, he walked on air; and, while one is walking on air, it is easy to overlook the boulders in the path.

Consider his position, you faint-hearted and self-pitying young men who think you have a tough row to hoe just because, when you pay your evening visit with the pound box of candy under your arm, you see the handsome sophomore from Yale sitting beside her on the porch, playing the ukulele. If ever the world has turned black to you in such a situation and the moon gone in behind a cloud, think of George Bevan and what he was up against. You are at least on the spot. You can at least put up a fight. If there are ukuleles in the world, there are also guitars, and tomorrow it may be you and not he who sits on the moonlit porch; it may be he and not you who arrives late. Who knows? Tomorrow he may not show up till you have finished the Bedouin's Love Song and are annoying the local birds, roosting in the trees, with Poor Butterfly.

What I mean to say is, you are on the map. You have a sporting chance. Whereas George... Well, just go over to England and try wooing an earl's daughter whom you have only met once—and then without an introduction; whose brother's hat you have smashed beyond repair; whose family wishes her to marry some other man: who wants to marry some other man herself—and not the same other man, but another other man; who is closely immured in a mediaeval castle . . . Well, all I say is—try it. And then go back to your porch with a chastened spirit and admit that you might be a whole lot worse off.

George, as I say, had not envisaged the peculiar difficulties of his position. Nor did he until the evening of his second day at the Marshmoreton Arms. Until then, as I have indicated, he roamed in a golden mist of dreamy meditation among the soothing by-ways of the village of Belpher. But after lunch on the second day it came upon him that all this sort of thing was pleasant but not practical. Action was what was needed. Action.

The first, the obvious move was to locate the castle. Inquiries at the Marshmoreton Arms elicited the fact that it was "a step" up the road that ran past the front door of the inn. But this wasn't the day of the week when the general public was admitted. The sightseer could invade Belpher Castle on Thursdays only, between the hours of two and four. On other days of the week all he could do was to stand like Moses on Pisgah and take in the general effect from a distance. As this was all that George had hoped to be able to do, he set forth.

It speedily became evident to George that "a step" was a euphemism. Five miles did he tramp before, trudging wearily up a winding lane, he came out on a breeze-swept hill-top, and saw below him, nestling in its trees, what was now for him the centre of the world. He sat on a stone wall and lit a pipe. Belpher Castle. Maud's home. There it was. And now what?

The first thought that came to him was practical, even prosaic— the thought that he couldn't possibly do this five-miles-there and-five-miles-back walk, every time he wanted to see the place. He must shift his base nearer the scene of operations. One of those trim, thatched cottages down there in the valley would be just the thing, if he could arrange to take possession of it. They sat there all round the castle, singly and in groups, like small dogs round their master. They looked as if they had been there for centuries. Probably they had, as they were made of stone as solid as that of the castle. There must have been a time, thought George, when the castle was the central rallying-point for all those scattered homes; when rumour of danger from marauders had sent all that little community scuttling for safety to the sheltering walls.

For the first time since he had set out on his expedition, a certain chill, a discomforting sinking of the heart, afflicted George as he gazed down at the grim grey fortress which he had undertaken to storm. So must have felt those marauders of old when they climbed to the top of this very hill to spy out the land. And George's case was even worse than theirs. They could at least hope that a strong arm and a stout heart would carry them past those solid walls; they had not to think of social etiquette. Whereas George was so situated that an unsympathetic butler could put him to rout by refusing him admittance.

The evening was drawing in. Already, in the brief time he had spent on the hill-top, the sky had turned from blue to saffron and from saffron to grey. The plaintive voices of homing cows floated up to him from the valley below. A bat had left its shelter and was wheeling around him, a sinister blot against the sky. A sickle moon gleamed over the trees. George felt cold. He turned. The shadows of night wrapped him round, and little things in the hedgerows chirped and chittered mockery at him as he stumbled down the lane.

George's request for a lonely furnished cottage somewhere in the neighbourhood of the castle did not, as he had feared, strike the Belpher house-agent as the demand of a lunatic. Every well-dressed stranger who comes to Belpher is automatically set down by the natives as an artist, for the picturesqueness of the place has caused it to be much infested by the brothers and sisters of the brush. In asking for a cottage, indeed, George did precisely as Belpher society expected him to do; and the agent was reaching for his list almost before the words were out of his mouth. In less than half an hour George was out in the street again, the owner for the season of what the agent described as a "gem" and the employer of a farmer's wife who lived near-by and would, as was her custom with artists, come in the morning and evening to "do" for him. The interview would have taken but a few minutes, had it not been prolonged by the chattiness of the agent on the subject of the occupants of the castle, to which George listened attentively. He was not greatly encouraged by what he heard of Lord Marshmoreton. The earl had made himself notably unpopular in the village recently by his firm—the house-agent said "pig-headed"—attitude in respect to a certain dispute about a right-of-way. It was Lady Caroline, and not the easy-going peer, who was really to blame in the matter; but the impression that George got from the house-agent's description of Lord Marshmoreton was that the latter was a sort of Nero, possessing, in addition to the qualities of a Roman tyrant, many of the least lovable traits of the ghila monster of Arizona. Hearing this about her father, and having already had the privilege of meeting her brother and studying him at first hand, his heart bled for Maud. It seemed to him that existence at the castle in such society must be little short of torture.

"I must do something," he muttered. "I must do something quick."

"Beg pardon," said the house-agent.

"Nothing," said George. "Well, I'll take that cottage. I'd better write you a cheque for the first month's rent now."

So George took up his abode, full of strenuous—if vague—purpose, in the plainly-furnished but not uncomfortable cottage known locally as "the one down by Platt's." He might have found a worse billet. It was a two-storied building of stained red brick, not one of the thatched nests on which he had looked down from the hill. Those were not for rent, being occupied by families whose ancestors had occupied them for generations back. The one down by Platt's was a more modern structure—a speculation, in fact, of the farmer whose wife came to "do" for George, and designed especially to accommodate the stranger who had the desire and the money to rent it. It so departed from type that it possessed a small but undeniable bath-room. Besides this miracle, there was a cosy sitting-room, a larger bedroom on the floor above and next to this an empty room facing north, which had evidently served artist occupants as a studio. The remainder of the ground floor was taken up by kitchen and scullery. The furniture had been constructed by somebody who would probably have done very well if he had taken up some other line of industry; but it was mitigated by a very fine and comfortable wicker easy chair, left there by one of last year's artists; and other artists had helped along the good work by relieving the plainness of the walls with a landscape or two. In fact, when George had removed from the room two antimacassars, three group photographs of the farmer's relations, an illuminated text, and a china statuette of the Infant Samuel, and stacked them in a corner of the empty studio, the place became almost a home from home.

Solitude can be very unsolitary if a man is in love. George never even began to be bored. The only thing that in any way troubled his peace was the thought that he was not accomplishing a great deal in the matter of helping Maud out of whatever trouble it was that had befallen her. The most he could do was to prowl about roads near the castle in the hope of an accidental meeting. And such was his good fortune that, on the fourth day of his vigil, the accidental meeting occurred.

Taking his morning prowl along the lanes, he was rewarded by the sight of a grey racing-car at the side of the road. It was empty, but from underneath it protruded a pair of long legs, while beside it stood a girl, at the sight of whom George's heart began to thump so violently that the long-legged one might have been pardoned had he supposed that his engine had started again of its own volition.

Until he spoke the soft grass had kept her from hearing his approach. He stopped close behind her, and cleared his throat. She started and turned, and their eyes met.

For a moment hers were empty of any recognition. Then they lit up. She caught her breath quickly, and a faint flush came into her face.

"Can I help you?" asked George.

The long legs wriggled out into the road followed by a long body. The young man under the car sat up, turning a grease-streaked and pleasant face to George.

"Eh, what?"

"Can I help you? I know how to fix a car."

The young man beamed in friendly fashion.

"It's awfully good of you, old chap, but so do I. It's the only thing I can do well. Thanks very much and so forth all the same."

George fastened his eyes on the girl's. She had not spoken.

"If there is anything in the world I can possibly do for you," he said slowly, "I hope you will let me know. I should like above all things to help you."

The girl spoke.

"Thank you," she said in a low voice almost inaudible.

George walked away. The grease-streaked young man followed him with his gaze.

"Civil cove, that," he said. "Rather gushing though, what? American, wasn't he?"

"Yes. I think he was."

"Americans are the civillest coves I ever struck. I remember asking the way of a chappie at Baltimore a couple of years ago when I was there in my yacht, and he followed me for miles, shrieking advice and encouragement. I thought it deuced civil of him."

"I wish you would hurry up and get the car right, Reggie. We shall be awfully late for lunch."

Reggie Byng began to slide backwards under the car.

"All right, dear heart. Rely on me. It's something quite simple."

"Well, do be quick."

"Imitation of greased lightning—very difficult," said Reggie encouragingly. "Be patient. Try and amuse yourself somehow. Ask yourself a riddle. Tell yourself a few anecdotes. I'll be with you in a moment. I say, I wonder what the cove is doing at Belpher? Deuced civil cove," said Reggie approvingly. "I liked him. And now, business of repairing breakdown."

His smiling face vanished under the car like the Cheshire cat. Maud stood looking thoughtfully down the road in the direction in which George had disappeared.

CHAPTER 8.

The following day was a Thursday and on Thursdays, as has been stated, Belpher Castle was thrown open to the general public between the hours of two and four. It was a tradition of long standing, this periodical lowering of the barriers, and had always been faithfully observed by Lord Marshmoreton ever since his accession to the title. By the permanent occupants of the castle the day was regarded with mixed feelings. Lord Belpher, while approving of it in theory, as he did of all the family traditions—for he was a great supporter of all things feudal, and took his position as one of the hereditary aristocracy of Great Britain extremely seriously—heartily disliked it in practice. More than once he had been obliged to exit hastily by a further door in order to keep from being discovered by a drove of tourists intent on inspecting the library or the great drawing-room; and now it was his custom to retire to his bedroom immediately after lunch and not to emerge until the tide of invasion had ebbed away.

Keggs, the butler, always looked forward to Thursdays with pleasurable anticipation. He enjoyed the sense of authority which it gave him to herd these poor outcasts to and fro among the surroundings which were an everyday commonplace to himself. Also he liked hearing the sound of his own voice as it lectured in rolling periods on the objects of interest by the way-side. But even to Keggs there was a bitter mixed with the sweet. No one was better aware than himself that the nobility of his manner, excellent as a means of impressing the mob, worked against him when it came to a question of tips. Again and again had he been harrowed by the spectacle of tourists, huddled together like sheep, debating among themselves in nervous whispers as to whether they could offer this personage anything so contemptible as half a crown for himself and deciding that such an insult was out of the question. It was his endeavour, especially towards the end of the proceedings, to cultivate a manner blending a dignity fitting his position with a sunny geniality which would allay the timid doubts of the tourist and indicate to him that, bizarre as the idea might seem, there was nothing to prevent him placing his poor silver in more worthy hands.

Possibly the only member of the castle community who was absolutely indifferent to these public visits was Lord Marshmoreton. He made no difference between Thursday and any other day. Precisely as usual he donned his stained corduroys and pottered about his beloved garden; and when, as happened on an average once a quarter, some visitor, strayed from the main herd, came upon him as he worked and mistook him for one of the gardeners, he accepted the error without any attempt at explanation, sometimes going so far as to encourage it by adopting a rustic accent in keeping with his appearance. This sort of thing tickled the simple-minded peer.

George joined the procession punctually at two o'clock, just as Keggs was clearing his throat preparatory to saying, "We are now in the main 'all, and before going any further I would like to call your attention to Sir Peter Lely's portrait of—" It was his custom to begin his Thursday lectures with this remark, but today it was postponed; for, no sooner had George appeared, than a breezy voice on the outskirts of the throng spoke in a tone that made competition impossible.

"For goodness' sake, George."

And Billie Dore detached herself from the group, a trim vision in blue. She wore a dust-coat and a motor veil, and her eyes and cheeks were glowing from the fresh air.

"For goodness' sake, George, what are you doing here?"

"I was just going to ask you the same thing."

"Oh, I motored down with a boy I know. We had a breakdown just outside the gates. We were on our way to Brighton for lunch. He suggested I should pass the time seeing the sights while he fixed up the sprockets or the differential gear or whatever it was. He's coming to pick me up when he's through. But, on the level, George, how do you get this way? You sneak out of town and leave the show flat, and nobody has a notion where you are. Why, we were thinking of advertising for you, or going to the police or something. For all anybody knew, you might have been sandbagged or dropped in the river."

This aspect of the matter had not occurred to George till now. His sudden descent on Belpher had seemed to him the only natural course to pursue. He had not realized that he would be missed, and that his absence might have caused grave inconvenience to a large number of people.

"I never thought of that. I—well, I just happened to come here."

"You aren't living in this old castle?"

"Not quite. I've a cottage down the road. I wanted a few days in the country so I rented it."

"But what made you choose this place?"

Keggs, who had been regarding these disturbers of the peace with dignified disapproval, coughed.

"If you would not mind, madam. We are waiting."

"Eh? How's that?" Miss Dore looked up with a bright smile. "I'm sorry. Come along, George. Get in the game." She nodded cheerfully to the butler. "All right. All set now. You may fire when ready, Gridley."

Keggs bowed austerely, and cleared his throat again.

"We are now in the main 'all, and before going any further I would like to call your attention to Sir Peter Lely's portrait of the fifth countess. Said by experts to be in his best manner."

There was an almost soundless murmur from the mob, expressive of wonder and awe, like a gentle breeze rustling leaves. Billie Dore resumed her conversation in a whisper.

"Yes, there was an awful lot of excitement when they found that you had disappeared. They were phoning the Carlton every ten minutes trying to get you. You see, the summertime number flopped on the second night, and they hadn't anything to put in its place. But it's all right. They took it out and sewed up the wound, and now you'd never know there had been anything wrong. The show was ten minutes too long, anyway."

"How's the show going?"

"It's a riot. They think it will run two years in London. As far as I can make it out you don't call it a success in London unless you can take your grandchildren to see the thousandth night."

"That's splendid. And how is everybody? All right?"

"Fine. That fellow Gray is still hanging round Babe. It beats me what she sees in him. Anybody but an infant could see the man wasn't on the level. Well, I don't blame you for quitting London, George. This sort of thing is worth fifty Londons."

The procession had reached one of the upper rooms, and they were looking down from a window that commanded a sweep of miles of the countryside, rolling and green and wooded. Far away beyond the last covert Belpher Bay gleamed like a streak of silver. Billie

Dore gave a little sigh.

"There's nothing like this in the world. I'd like to stand here for the rest of my life, just lapping it up."

"I will call your attention," boomed Keggs at their elbow, "to this window, known in the fem'ly tredition as Leonard's Leap. It was in the year seventeen 'undred and eighty-seven that Lord Leonard Forth, eldest son of 'Is Grace the Dook of Lochlane, 'urled 'imself out of this window in order to avoid compromising the beautiful Countess of Marshmoreton, with oom 'e is related to 'ave 'ad a ninnocent romance. Surprised at an advanced hour by 'is lordship the earl in 'er ladyship's boudoir, as this room then was, 'e leaped through the open window into the boughs of the cedar tree which stands below, and was fortunate enough to escape with a few 'armless contusions."

A murmur of admiration greeted the recital of the ready tact of this eighteenth-century Steve Brodie.

"There," said Billie enthusiastically, "that's exactly what I mean about this country. It's just a mass of Leonard's Leaps and things. I'd like to settle down in this sort of place and spend the rest of my life milking cows and taking forkfuls of soup to the deserving villagers."

"We will now," said Keggs, herding the mob with a gesture, "proceed to the Amber Drawing-Room, containing some Gobelin Tapestries 'ighly spoken of by connoozers."

The obedient mob began to drift out in his wake.

"What do you say, George," asked Billie in an undertone, "if we side-step the Amber Drawing-Room? I'm wild to get into that garden. There's a man working among those roses. Maybe he would show us round."

George followed her pointing finger. Just below them a sturdy, brown-faced man in corduroys was pausing to light a stubby pipe.

"Just as you like."

They made their way down the great staircase. The voice of Keggs, saying complimentary things about the Gobelin Tapestry, came to their ears like the roll of distant drums. They wandered out towards the rose-garden. The man in corduroys had lit his pipe and was bending once more to his task.

"Well, dadda," said Billie amiably, "how are the crops?"

The man straightened himself. He was a nice-looking man of middle age, with the kind eyes of a friendly dog. He smiled genially, and started to put his pipe away.

Billie stopped him.

"Don't stop smoking on my account," she said. "I like it. Well, you've got the right sort of a job, haven't you! If I was a man, there's nothing I'd like better than to put in my eight hours in a rose-garden." She looked about her. "And this," she said with approval, "is just what a rose-garden ought to be."

"Are you fond of roses—missy?"

"You bet I am! You must have every kind here that was ever invented. All the fifty-seven varieties."

"There are nearly three thousand varieties," said the man in corduroys tolerantly.

"I was speaking colloquially, dadda. You can't teach me anything about roses. I'm the guy that invented them. Got any Ayrshires?"

The man in corduroys seemed to have come to the conclusion that Billie was the only thing on earth that mattered. This revelation of a kindred spirit had captured him completely. George was merely among those present.

"Those—them—over there are Ayrshires, missy."

"We don't get Ayrshires in America. At least, I never ran across them. I suppose they do have them."

"You want the right soil."

"Clay and lots of rain."

"You're right."

There was an earnest expression on Billie Dore's face that George had never seen there before.

"Say, listen, dadda, in this matter of rose-beetles, what would you do if—"

George moved away. The conversation was becoming too technical for him, and he had an idea that he would not be missed. There had come to him, moreover, in a flash one of those sudden inspirations which great generals get. He had visited the castle this afternoon without any settled plan other than a vague hope that he might somehow see Maud. He now perceived that there was no chance of doing this. Evidently, on Thursdays, the family went to earth and remained hidden until the sightseers had gone. But there was another avenue of communication open to him. This gardener seemed an exceptionally intelligent man. He could be trusted to deliver a note to Maud.

In his late rambles about Belpher Castle in the company of Keggs and his followers, George had been privileged to inspect the library. It was an easily accessible room, opening off the main hall. He left Billie and her new friend deep in a discussion of slugs and plant-lice, and walked quickly back to the house. The library was unoccupied.

George was a thorough young man. He believed in leaving nothing to chance. The gardener had seemed a trustworthy soul, but you never knew. It was possible that he drank. He might forget or lose the precious note. So, with a wary eye on the door, George hastily scribbled it in duplicate. This took him but a few minutes. He went out into the garden again to find Billie Dore on the point of stepping into a blue automobile.

"Oh, there you are, George. I wondered where you had got to. Say, I made quite a hit with dadda. I've given him my address, and he's promised to send me a whole lot of roses. By the way, shake hands with Mr. Forsyth. This is George Bevan, Freddie, who wrote the music of our show."

The solemn youth at the wheel extended a hand.

"Topping show. Topping music. Topping all round."

"Well, good-bye, George. See you soon, I suppose?"

"Oh, yes. Give my love to everybody."

"All right. Let her rip, Freddie. Good-bye."

"Good-bye."

The blue car gathered speed and vanished down the drive. George returned to the man in corduroys, who had bent himself double in pursuit of a slug.

"Just a minute," said George hurriedly. He pulled out the first of the notes. "Give this to Lady Maud the first chance you get. It's important. Here's a sovereign for your trouble."

He hastened away. He noticed that gratification had turned the other nearly purple in the face, and was anxious to leave him. He was a modest young man, and effusive thanks always embarrassed him.

There now remained the disposal of the duplicate note. It was hardly worth while, perhaps, taking such a precaution, but George knew that victories are won by those who take no chances. He had wandered perhaps a hundred yards from the rose-garden when he encountered a small boy in the many-buttoned uniform of a page. The boy had appeared from behind a big cedar, where, as a matter of fact, he had been smoking a stolen cigarette.

"Do you want to earn half a crown?" asked George.

The market value of messengers had slumped.

The stripling held his hand out.

"Give this note to Lady Maud."

"Right ho!"

"See that it reaches her at once."

George walked off with the consciousness of a good day's work done. Albert the page, having bitten his half-crown, placed it in his pocket. Then he hurried away, a look of excitement and gratification in his deep blue eyes.

CHAPTER 9.

While George and Billie Dore wandered to the rose garden to interview the man in corduroys, Maud had been seated not a hundred yards away—in a very special haunt of her own, a cracked stucco temple set up in the days of the Regency on the shores of a little lily-covered pond. She was reading poetry to Albert the page.

Albert the page was a recent addition to Maud's inner circle. She had interested herself in him some two months back in much the same spirit as the prisoner in his dungeon cell tames and pets the conventional mouse. To educate Albert, to raise him above his groove in life and develop his soul, appealed to her romantic nature as a worthy task, and as a good way of filling in the time. It is an exceedingly moot point—and one which his associates of the servants' hall would have combated hotly—whether Albert possessed a soul. The most one could say for certain is that he looked as if he possessed one. To one who saw his deep blue eyes and their sweet, pensive expression as they searched the middle distance he seemed like a young angel. How was the watcher to know that the thought behind that far-off gaze was simply a speculation as to whether the bird on the cedar tree was or was not within range of his catapult? Certainly, Maud had no such suspicion. She worked hopefully day by day to rouse Albert to an appreciation of the nobler things of life.

Not but what it was tough going. Even she admitted that. Albert's soul did not soar readily. It refused to leap from the earth. His reception of the poem she was reading could scarcely have been called encouraging. Maud finished it in a hushed voice, and looked pensively across the dappled water of the pool. A gentle breeze stirred the water-lilies, so that they seemed to sigh.

"Isn't that beautiful, Albert?" she said.

Albert's blue eyes lit up. His lips parted eagerly,

"That's the first hornet I seen this year," he said pointing.

Maud felt a little damped.

"Haven't you been listening, Albert?"

"Oh, yes, m'lady! Ain't he a wopper, too?"

"Never mind the hornet, Albert."

"Very good, m'lady."

"I wish you wouldn't say 'Very good, m'lady'. It's like—like—" She paused. She had been about to say that it was like a butler, but, she reflected regretfully, it was probably Albert's dearest ambition to be like a butler. "It doesn't sound right. Just say 'Yes'."

"Yes, m'lady."

Maud was not enthusiastic about the 'M'lady', but she let it go. After all, she had not quite settled in her own mind what exactly she wished Albert's attitude towards herself to be. Broadly speaking, she wanted him to be as like as he could to a medieval page, one of those silk-and-satined little treasures she had read about in the Ingoldsby Legends. And, of course, they presumably said 'my lady'. And yet—she felt—not for the first time—that it is not easy, to revive the Middle Ages in these curious days. Pages like other things, seem to have changed since then.

"That poem was written by a very clever man who married one of my ancestresses. He ran away with her from this very castle in the seventeenth century."

"Lor'", said Albert as a concession, but he was still interested in the hornet.

"He was far below her in the eyes of the world, but she knew what a wonderful man he was, so she didn't mind what people said about her marrying beneath her."

"Like Susan when she married the pleeceman."

"Who was Susan?"

"Red-'eaded gel that used to be cook 'ere. Mr. Keggs says to 'er, 'e says, 'You're marrying beneath you, Susan', 'e says. I 'eard 'im. I was listenin' at the door. And she says to 'im, she says, 'Oh, go and boil your fat 'ead', she says."

This translation of a favourite romance into terms of the servants' hall chilled Maud like a cold shower. She recoiled from it.

"Wouldn't you like to get a good education, Albert," she said perseveringly, "and become a great poet and write wonderful poems?"

Albert considered the point, and shook his head.

"No, m'lady."

It was discouraging. But Maud was a girl of pluck. You cannot leap into strange cabs in Piccadilly unless you have pluck. She picked up another book from the stone seat.

"Read me some of this," she said, "and then tell me if it doesn't make you feel you want to do big things."

Albert took the book cautiously. He was getting a little fed up with all this sort of thing. True, 'er ladyship gave him chocolates to eat during these sessions, but for all that it was too much like school for his taste. He regarded the open page with disfavour.

"Go on," said Maud, closing her eyes. "It's very beautiful."

Albert began. He had a husky voice, due, it is to be feared, to precocious cigarette smoking, and his enunciation was not as good as it might have been.

> "Wiv' blekest morss the flower-ports
> Was-I mean were-crusted one and orl;
> Ther rusted niles fell from the knorts
> That 'eld the pear to the garden-worll.
> Ther broken sheds looked sed and stringe;
> Unlifted was the clinking latch;
> Weeded and worn their ancient thatch
> Er-pon ther lownely moated gringe,
> She only said 'Me life is dreary,
> 'E cometh not,' she said."

Albert rather liked this part. He was never happy in narrative unless it could be sprinkled with a plentiful supply of "he said's" and "she said's." He finished with some gusto.

> "She said - I am aweary, aweary,
> I would that I was dead."

Maud had listened to this rendition of one of her most adored poems with much the same feeling which a composer with an over-sensitive ear would suffer on hearing his pet opus assassinated by a schoolgirl. Albert, who was a willing lad and prepared, if such should be her desire, to plough his way through the entire seven stanzas, began the second verse, but Maud gently took the book away from him. Enough was sufficient.

"Now, wouldn't you like to be able to write a wonderful thing like that, Albert?"

"Not me, m'lady."

"You wouldn't like to be a poet when you grow up?"

Albert shook his golden head.

"I want to be a butcher when I grow up, m'lady."

Maud uttered a little cry.

"A butcher?"

"Yus, m'lady. Butchers earn good money," he said, a light of enthusiasm in his blue eyes, for he was now on his favourite subject. "You've got to 'ave meat, yer see, m'lady. It ain't like poetry, m'lady, which no one wants."

"But, Albert," cried Maud faintly. "Killing poor animals. Surely you wouldn't like that?"

Albert's eyes glowed softly, as might an acolyte's at the sight of the censer.

"Mr. Widgeon down at the 'ome farm," he murmured reverently, "he says, if I'm a good boy, 'e'll let me watch 'im kill a pig Toosday."

He gazed out over the water-lilies, his thoughts far away. Maud shuddered. She wondered if medieval pages were ever quite as earthy as this.

"Perhaps you had better go now, Albert. They may be needing you in the house."

"Very good, m'lady."

Albert rose, not unwilling to call it a day. He was conscious of the need for a quiet cigarette. He was fond of Maud, but a man can't spend all his time with the women.

"Pigs squeal like billy-o, m'lady!" he observed by way of adding a parting treasure to Maud's stock of general knowledge. "Oo! 'Ear 'em a mile orf, you can!"

Maud remained where she was, thinking, a wistful figure. Tennyson's "Mariana" always made her wistful even when rendered by Albert. In the occasional moods of sentimental depression which came to vary her normal cheerfulness, it seemed to her that the poem might have been written with a prophetic eye to her special case, so nearly did it crystallize in magic words her own story.

> *"With blackest moss the flower-pots*
>
> *Were thickly crusted, one and all."*

Well, no, not that particular part, perhaps. If he had found so much as one flower-pot of his even thinly crusted with any foreign substance, Lord Marshmoreton would have gone through the place like an east wind, dismissing gardeners and under-gardeners with every breath. But—

> *"She only said 'My life is dreary,*
>
> *He cometh not,' she said.*
>
> *She said 'I am aweary, aweary.*

I would that I were dead!"

How exactly—at these moments when she was not out on the links picking them off the turf with a midiron or engaged in one of those other healthful sports which tend to take the mind off its troubles—those words summed up her case.

Why didn't Geoffrey come? Or at least write? She could not write to him. Letters from the castle left only by way of the castle post-bag, which Rogers, the chauffeur, took down to the village every evening. Impossible to entrust the kind of letter she wished to write to any mode of delivery so public—especially now, when her movements were watched. To open and read another's letters is a low and dastardly act, but she believed that Lady Caroline would do it like a shot. She longed to pour out her heart to Geoffrey in a long, intimate letter, but she did not dare to take the risk of writing for a wider public. Things were bad enough as it was, after that disastrous sortie to London.

At this point a soothing vision came to her—the vision of George Bevan knocking off her brother Percy's hat. It was the only pleasant thing that had happened almost as far back as she could remember. And then, for the first time, her mind condescended to dwell for a moment on the author of that act, George Bevan, the friend in need, whom she had met only the day before in the lane. What was George doing at Belpher? His presence there was significant, and his words even more so. He had stated explicitly that he wished to help her.

She found herself oppressed by the irony of things. A knight had come to the rescue—but the wrong knight. Why could it not have been Geoffrey who waited in ambush outside the castle, and not a pleasant but negligible stranger? Whether, deep down in her consciousness, she was aware of a fleeting sense of disappointment in Geoffrey, a swiftly passing thought that he had failed her, she could hardly have said, so quickly did she crush it down.

She pondered on the arrival of George. What was the use of his being somewhere in the neighbourhood if she had no means of knowing where she could find him? Situated as she was, she could not wander at will about the countryside, looking for him. And, even if she found him, what then? There was not much that any stranger, however pleasant, could do.

She flushed at a sudden thought. Of course there was something George could do for her if he were willing. He could receive, despatch and deliver letters. If only she could get in touch with him, she could—through him—get in touch with Geoffrey.

The whole world changed for her. The sun was setting and chill little winds had begun to stir the lily-pads, giving a depressing air to the scene, but to Maud it seemed as if all Nature smiled. With the egotism of love, she did not perceive that what she proposed to ask George to do was practically to fulfil the humble role of the hollow tree in which lovers dump letters, to be extracted later; she did not consider George's feelings at all. He had offered to help her, and this was his job. The world is full of Georges whose task it is to hang about in the background and make themselves unobtrusively useful.

She had reached this conclusion when Albert, who had taken a short cut the more rapidly to accomplish his errand, burst upon her dramatically from the heart of a rhododendron thicket.

"M'lady! Gentleman give me this to give yer!"

Maud read the note. It was brief, and to the point.

"I am staying near the castle at a cottage they call 'the one down by Platt's'. It is a rather new, red-brick place. You can easily find it. I shall be waiting there if you want me."

It was signed "The Man in the Cab".

"Do you know a cottage called 'the one down by Platt's', Albert?" asked Maud.

"Yes, m'lady. It's down by Platt's farm. I see a chicken killed there Wednesday week. Do you know, m'lady, after a chicken's 'ead is cut orf, it goes running licketty-split?"

Maud shivered slightly. Albert's fresh young enthusiasms frequently jarred upon her.

"I find a friend of mine is staying there. I want you to take a note to him from me."

"Very good, m'lady."

"And, Albert—"

"Yes, m'lady?"

"Perhaps it would be as well if you said nothing about this to any of your friends."

In Lord Marshmoreton's study a council of three was sitting in debate. The subject under discussion was that other note which George had written and so ill-advisedly entrusted to one whom he had taken for a guileless gardener. The council consisted of Lord Marshmoreton, looking rather shamefaced, his son Percy looking swollen and serious, and Lady Caroline Byng, looking like a tragedy queen.

"This," Lord Belpher was saying in a determined voice, "settles it.

From now on Maud must not be allowed out of our sight."

Lord Marshmoreton spoke.

"I rather wish," he said regretfully, "I hadn't spoken about the note. I only mentioned it because I thought you might think it amusing."

"Amusing!" Lady Caroline's voice shook the furniture.

"Amusing that the fellow should have handed me of all people a letter for Maud," explained her brother. "I don't want to get Maud into trouble."

"You are criminally weak," said Lady Caroline severely. "I really honestly believe that you were capable of giving the note to that poor, misguided girl, and saying nothing about it." She flushed. "The insolence of the man, coming here and settling down at the very gates of the castle! If it was anybody but this man Platt who was giving him shelter I should insist on his being turned out. But that man Platt would be only too glad to know that he is causing us annoyance."

"Quite!" said Lord Belpher.

"You must go to this man as soon as possible," continued Lady Caroline, fixing her brother with a commanding stare, "and do your best to make him see how abominable his behaviour is."

"Oh, I couldn't!" pleaded the earl. "I don't know the fellow. He'd throw me out."

"Nonsense. Go at the very earliest opportunity."

"Oh, all right, all right, all right. Well, I think I'll be slipping out to the rose garden again now. There's a clear hour before dinner."

There was a tap at the door. Alice Faraday entered bearing papers, a smile of sweet helpfulness on her pretty face.

"I hoped I should find you here, Lord Marshmoreton. You promised to go over these notes with me, the ones about the Essex branch—"

The hunted peer looked as if he were about to dive through the window.

"Some other time, some other time. I—I have important matters—"

"Oh, if you're busy—"

"Of course, Lord Marshmoreton will be delighted to work on your notes, Miss Faraday," said Lady Caroline crisply. "Take this chair. We are just going."

Lord Marshmoreton gave one wistful glance through the open window.

Then he sat down with a sigh, and felt for his reading-glasses.

CHAPTER 10.

Your true golfer is a man who, knowing that life is short and perfection hard to attain, neglects no opportunity of practising his chosen sport, allowing neither wind nor weather nor any external influence to keep him from it. There is a story, with an excellent moral lesson, of a golfer whose wife had determined to leave him for ever. "Will nothing alter your decision?" he says. "Will nothing induce you to stay? Well, then, while you're packing, I think I'll go out on the lawn and rub up my putting a bit." George Bevan was of this turn of mind. He might be in love; romance might have sealed him for her own; but that was no reason for blinding himself to the fact that his long game was bound to suffer if he neglected to keep himself up to the mark. His first act on arriving at Belpher village had been to ascertain whether there was a links in the neighbourhood; and thither, on the morning after his visit to the castle and the delivery of the two notes, he repaired.

At the hour of the day which he had selected the club-house was empty, and he had just resigned himself to a solitary game, when, with a whirr and a rattle, a grey racing-car drove up, and from it emerged the same long young man whom, a couple of days earlier, he had seen wriggle out from underneath the same machine. It was Reggie Byng's habit also not to allow anything, even love, to interfere with golf; and not even the prospect of hanging about the castle grounds in the hope of catching a glimpse of Alice Faraday and exchanging timorous words with her had been enough to keep him from the links.

Reggie surveyed George with a friendly eye. He had a dim recollection of having seen him before somewhere at some time or other, and Reggie had the pleasing disposition which caused him to rank anybody whom he had seen somewhere at some time or other as a bosom friend.

"Hullo! Hullo! Hullo!" he observed.

"Good morning," said George.

"Waiting for somebody?"

"No."

"How about it, then? Shall we stagger forth?"

"Delighted."

George found himself speculating upon Reggie. He was unable to place him. That he was a friend of Maud he knew, and guessed that he was also a resident of the castle. He would have liked to question Reggie, to probe him, to collect from him inside information as to the progress of events within the castle walls; but it is a peculiarity of golf, as of love, that it temporarily changes the natures of its victims; and Reggie, a confirmed babbler off the links, became while in action a stern, silent, intent person, his whole being centred on the game. With the exception of a casual remark of a technical nature when he met George on the various tees, and an occasional expletive when things went wrong with his ball, he eschewed conversation. It was not till the end of the round that he became himself again.

"If I'd known you were such hot stuff," he declared generously, as George holed his eighteenth putt from a distance of ten feet, "I'd have got you to give me a stroke or two."

"I was on my game today," said George modestly. "Sometimes I slice as if I were cutting bread and can't putt to hit a haystack."

"Let me know when one of those times comes along, and I'll take you on again. I don't know when I've seen anything fruitier than the way you got out of the bunker at the fifteenth. It reminded me of a match I saw between—" Reggie became technical. At the end of his observations he climbed into the grey car.

"Can I drop you anywhere?"

"Thanks," said George. "If it's not taking you out your way."

"I'm staying at Belpher Castle."

"I live quite near there. Perhaps you'd care to come in and have a drink on your way?"

"A ripe scheme," agreed Reggie

Ten minutes in the grey car ate up the distance between the links and George's cottage. Reggie Byng passed these minutes, in the intervals of eluding carts and foiling the apparently suicidal intentions of some stray fowls, in jerky conversation on the subject of his iron-shots, with which he expressed a deep satisfaction.

"Topping little place! Absolutely!" was the verdict he pronounced on the exterior of the cottage as he followed George in. "I've often thought it would be a rather sound scheme to settle down in this sort of shanty and keep chickens and grow a honey coloured beard, and have soup and jelly brought to you by the vicar's wife and so forth. Nothing to worry you then. Do you live all alone here?"

George was busy squirting seltzer into his guest's glass.

"Yes. Mrs. Platt comes in and cooks for me. The farmer's wife next door."

An exclamation from the other caused him to look up. Reggie Byng was staring at him, wide-eyed.

"Great Scott! Mrs. Platt! Then you're the Chappie?"

George found himself unequal to the intellectual pressure of the conversation.

"The Chappie?"

"The Chappie there's all the row about. The mater was telling me only this morning that you lived here."

"Is there a row about me?"

"Is there what!" Reggie's manner became solicitous. "I say, my dear old sportsman, I don't want to be the bearer of bad tidings and what not, if you know what I mean, but didn't you know there was a certain amount of angry passion rising and so forth because of you? At the castle, I mean. I don't want to seem to be discussing your private affairs, and all that sort of thing, but what I mean is… Well, you don't expect you can come charging in the way you have without touching the family on the raw a bit. The daughter of the house falls in love with you; the son of the house languishes in chokey because he has a row with you in Piccadilly; and on top of all that you come here and camp out at the castle gates! Naturally the family are a bit peeved. Only natural, eh? I mean to say, what?"

George listened to this address in bewilderment. Maud in love with him! It sounded incredible. That he should love her after their one meeting was a different thing altogether. That was perfectly natural and in order. But that he should have had the incredible luck to win her affection. The thing struck him as grotesque and ridiculous.

"In love with me?" he cried. "What on earth do you mean?"

Reggie's bewilderment equalled his own.

"Well, dash it all, old top, it surely isn't news to you? She must have told you. Why, she told me!"

"Told you? Am I going mad?"

"Absolutely! I mean absolutely not! Look here." Reggie hesitated. The subject was delicate. But, once started, it might as well be proceeded with to some conclusion. A fellow couldn't go on talking about his iron-shots after this just as if nothing had happened. This was the time for the laying down of cards, the opening of hearts. "I say, you know," he went on, feeling his way, "you'll probably think it deuced rummy of me talking like this. Perfect stranger and what not. Don't even know each other's names."

"Mine's Bevan, if that'll be any help."

"Thanks very much, old chap. Great help! Mine's Byng. Reggie Byng. Well, as we're all pals here and the meeting's tiled and so forth, I'll start by saying that the mater is most deucedly set on my marrying Lady Maud. Been pals all our lives, you know. Children together, and all that sort of rot. Now there's nobody I think a more corking sportsman than Maud, if you know what I mean, but—this is where the catch comes in—I'm most frightfully in love with somebody else. Hopeless, and all that sort of thing, but still there it is. And all the while the mater behind me with a bradawl, sicking me on to propose to Maud who wouldn't have me if I were the only fellow on earth. You can't imagine, my dear old chap, what a relief it was to both of us when she told me the other day that she was in love with you, and wouldn't dream of looking at anybody else. I tell you, I went singing about the place."

George felt inclined to imitate his excellent example. A burst of song was the only adequate expression of the mood of heavenly happiness which this young man's revelations had brought upon him. The whole world seemed different. Wings seemed to sprout from Reggie's shapely shoulders. The air was filled with soft music. Even the wallpaper seemed moderately attractive.

He mixed himself a second whisky and soda. It was the next best thing to singing.

"I see," he said. It was difficult to say anything. Reggie was regarding him enviously.

"I wish I knew how the deuce fellows set about making a girl fall in love with them. Other chappies seem to do it, but I can't even start. She seems to sort of gaze through me, don't you know. She kind of looks at me as if I were more to be pitied than censured, but as if she thought I really ought to do something about it. Of course, she's a devilish brainy girl, and I'm a fearful chump. Makes it kind of hopeless, what?"

George, in his new-born happiness, found a pleasure in encouraging a less lucky mortal.

"Not a bit. What you ought to do is to—"

"Yes?" said Reggie eagerly.

George shook his head.

"No, I don't know," he said.

"Nor do I, dash it!" said Reggie.

George pondered.

"It seems to me it's purely a question of luck. Either you're lucky or you're not. Look at me, for instance. What is there about me to make a wonderful girl love me?"

"Nothing! I see what you mean. At least, what I mean to say is—"

"No. You were right the first time. It's all a question of luck. There's nothing anyone can do."

"I hang about a good deal and get in her way," said Reggie. "She's always tripping over me. I thought that might help a bit."

"It might, of course."

"But on the other hand, when we do meet, I can't think of anything to say."

"That's bad."

"Deuced funny thing. I'm not what you'd call a silent sort of chappie by nature. But, when I'm with her—I don't know. It's rum!" He drained his glass and rose. "Well, I suppose I may as well be staggering. Don't get up. Have another game one of these days, what?"

"Splendid. Any time you like."

"Well, so long."

"Good-bye."

George gave himself up to glowing thoughts. For the first time in his life he seemed to be vividly aware of his own existence. It was as if he were some newly-created thing. Everything around him and everything he did had taken on a strange and novel interest. He seemed to notice the ticking of the clock for the first time. When he raised his glass the action had a curious air of newness. All his senses were oddly alert. He could even—

"How would it be," enquired Reggie, appearing in the doorway like part of a conjuring trick, "if I gave her a flower or two every now and then? Just thought of it as I was starting the car. She's fond of flowers."

"Fine!" said George heartily. He had not heard a word. The alertness of sense which had come to him was accompanied by a strange inability to attend to other people's speech. This would no doubt pass, but meanwhile it made him a poor listener.

"Well, it's worth trying," said Reggie. "I'll give it a whirl. Toodleoo!"

"Good-bye."

"Pip-pip!"

Reggie withdrew, and presently came the noise of the car starting.

George returned to his thoughts.

Time, as we understand it, ceases to exist for a man in such circumstances. Whether it was a minute later or several hours, George did not know; but presently he was aware of a small boy standing beside him—a golden-haired boy with blue eyes, who wore the uniform of a page. He came out of his trance. This, he recognized, was the boy to whom he had given the note for Maud. He was different from any other intruder. He meant something in George's scheme of things.

"'Ullo!" said the youth.

"Hullo, Alphonso!" said George.

"My name's not Alphonso."

"Well, you be very careful or it soon may be."

"Got a note for yer. From Lidy Mord."

"You'll find some cake and ginger-ale in the kitchen," said the grateful George. "Give it a trial."

"Not 'arf!" said the stripling.

CHAPTER 11.

George opened the letter with trembling and reverent fingers.

"DEAR MR. BEVAN,

"Thank you ever so much for your note, which Albert gave to me. How very, very kind..."

"Hey, mister!"

George looked up testily. The boy Albert had reappeared.

"What's the matter? Can't you find the cake?"

"I've found the kike," rejoined Albert, adducing proof of the statement in the shape of a massive slice, from which he took a substantial bite to assist thought. "But I can't find the ginger ile."

George waved him away. This interruption at such a moment was annoying.

"Look for it, child, look for it! Sniff after it! Bay on its trail! It's somewhere about."

"Wri'!" mumbled Albert through the cake. He flicked a crumb off his cheek with a tongue which would have excited the friendly interest of an ant-eater. "I like ginger-ile."

"Well, go and bathe in it."

"Wri'!"

George returned to his letter.

"DEAR MR. BEVAN,

"Thank you ever so much for your note, which Albert gave to me. How very, very kind of you to come here like this and to say . . .

"Hey, mister!"

"Good Heavens!" George glared. "What's the matter now? Haven't you found that ginger-ale yet?"

"I've found the ginger-ile right enough, but I can't find the thing."

"The thing? What thing?"

"The thing. The thing wot you open ginger-ile with."

"Oh, you mean the thing? It's in the middle drawer of the dresser. Use your eyes, my boy!"

"Wri'".

George gave an overwrought sigh and began the letter again.

"DEAR MR. BEVAN,

"Thank you ever so much for your note which Albert gave to me. How very, very kind of you to come here like this and to say that you would help me. And how clever of you to find me after I was so secretive that day in the cab! You really can help me, if you are willing. It's too long to explain in a note, but I am in great trouble, and there is nobody except you to help me. I will explain everything when I see you. The difficulty will be to slip away from home. They are watching me every moment, I'm afraid. But I will try my hardest to see you very soon. Yours sincerely, "MAUD MARSH."

Just for a moment it must be confessed, the tone of the letter damped George. He could not have said just what he had expected, but certainly Reggie's revelations had prepared him for something rather warmer, something more in the style in which a girl would write to the man she loved. The next moment, however, he saw how foolish any such expectation had been. How on earth could any reasonable man expect a girl to let herself go at this stage of the proceedings? It was for him to make the first move. Naturally she wasn't going to reveal her feelings until he had revealed his.

George raised the letter to his lips and kissed it vigorously.

"Hey, mister!"

George started guiltily. The blush of shame overspread his cheeks.

The room seemed to echo with the sound of that fatuous kiss.

"Kitty, Kitty, Kitty!" he called, snapping his fingers, and repeating the incriminating noise. "I was just calling my cat," he explained with dignity. "You didn't see her in there, did you?"

Albert's blue eyes met his in a derisive stare. The lid of the left one fluttered. It was but too plain that Albert was not convinced.

"A little black cat with white shirt-front," babbled George perseveringly. "She's usually either here or there, or—or somewhere. Kitty, Kitty, Kitty!"

The cupid's bow of Albert's mouth parted. He uttered one word.

"Swank!"

There was a tense silence. What Albert was thinking one cannot say. The thoughts of Youth are long, long thoughts. What George was thinking was that the late King Herod had been unjustly blamed for a policy which had been both statesmanlike and in the interests of the public. He was blaming the mawkish sentimentality of the modern legal system which ranks the evisceration and secret burial of small boys as a crime.

"What do you mean?"

"You know what I mean."

"I've a good mind to—"

Albert waved a deprecating hand.

"It's all right, mister. I'm yer friend."

"You are, are you? Well, don't let it about. I've got a reputation to keep up."

"I'm yer friend, I tell you. I can help yer. I want to help yer!"

George's views on infanticide underwent a slight modification. After all, he felt, much must be excused to Youth. Youth thinks it funny to see a man kissing a letter. It is not funny, of course; it is beautiful; but it's no good arguing the point. Let Youth have its snigger, provided, after it has finished sniggering, it intends to buckle to and be of practical assistance. Albert, as an ally, was not to be despised. George did not know what Albert's duties as a page-boy were, but they seemed to be of a nature that gave him plenty of leisure and freedom; and a friendly resident of the castle with leisure and freedom was just what he needed.

"That's very good of you," he said, twisting his reluctant features into a fairly benevolent smile.

"I can 'elp!" persisted Albert. "Got a cigaroot?"

"Do you smoke, child?"

"When I get 'old of a cigaroot I do."

"I'm sorry I can't oblige you. I don't smoke cigarettes."

"Then I'll 'ave to 'ave one of my own," said Albert moodily.

He reached into the mysteries of his pocket and produced a piece of string, a knife, the wishbone of a fowl, two marbles, a crushed cigarette, and a match. Replacing the string, the knife, the wishbone and the marbles, he ignited the match against the tightest part of his person and lit the cigarette.

"I can help yer. I know the ropes."

"And smoke them," said George, wincing.

"Pardon?"

"Nothing."

Albert took an enjoyable whiff.

"I know all about yer."

"You do?"

"You and Lidy Mord."

"Oh, you do, do you?"

"I was listening at the key-'ole while the row was goin' on."

"There was a row, was there?"

A faint smile of retrospective enjoyment lit up Albert's face. "An orful row! Shoutin' and yellin' and cussin' all over the shop. About you and Lidy Maud."

"And you drank it in, eh?"

"Pardon?"

"I say, you listened?"

"Not 'arf I listened. Seeing I'd just drawn you in the sweepstike, of course, I listened—not 'arf!"

George did not follow him here.

"The sweepstike? What's a sweepstike?"

"Why, a thing you puts names in 'ats and draw 'em and the one that gets the winning name wins the money."

"Oh, you mean a sweepstake!"

"That's wot I said—a sweepstike."

George was still puzzled.

"But I don't understand. How do you mean you drew me in a sweepstike—I mean a sweepstake? What sweepstake?"

"Down in the servants' 'all. Keggs, the butler, started it. I 'eard 'im say he always 'ad one every place 'e was in as a butler— leastways, whenever there was any dorters of the 'ouse. There's always a chance, when there's a 'ouse-party, of one of the dorters of the 'ouse gettin' married to one of the gents in the party, so Keggs 'e puts all of the gents' names in an 'at, and you pay five shillings for a chance, and the one that draws the winning name gets the money. And if the dorter of the 'ouse don't get married that time, the money's put away and added to the pool for the next 'ouse-party."

George gasped. This revelation of life below stairs in the stately homes of England took his breath away. Then astonishment gave way to indignation.

"Do you mean to tell me that you—you worms—made Lady Maud the—the prize of a sweepstake!"

Albert was hurt.

"Who're yer calling worms?"

George perceived the need of diplomacy. After all much depended on this child's goodwill.

"I was referring to the butler—what's his name—Keggs."

"'E ain't a worm. 'E's a serpint." Albert drew at his cigarette. His brow darkened. "'E does the drawing, Keggs does, and I'd like to know 'ow it is 'e always manages to cop the fav'rit!"

Albert chuckled.

"But this time I done him proper. 'E didn't want me in the thing at all. Said I was too young. Tried to do the drawin' without me. 'Clip that boy one side of the 'ead!' 'e says, 'and turn 'im out!' 'e says. I says, 'Yus, you will!' I says. 'And wot price me goin' to 'is lordship and blowing the gaff?' I says. 'E says, 'Oh, orl right!' 'e says. 'Ave it yer own way!' 'e says.

"'Where's yer five shillings?' 'e says. ''Ere yer are!' I says. 'Oh, very well,' 'e says. 'But you'll 'ave to draw last,' 'e says, 'bein' the youngest.' Well, they started drawing the names, and of course Keggs 'as to draw Mr. Byng."

"Oh, he drew Mr. Byng, did he?"

"Yus. And everyone knew Reggie was the fav'rit. Smiled all over his fat face, the old serpint did! And when it come to my turn, 'e says to me, 'Sorry, Elbert!' 'e says, 'but there ain't no more names. They've give out!' 'Oh, they 'ave, 'ave they?' I says, 'Well, wot's the matter with giving a fellow a sporting chance?' I says. 'Ow do you mean?' 'e says. 'Why, write me out a ticket marked "Mr. X.",' I says. 'Then, if 'er lidyship marries anyone not in the 'ouse-party, I cop!' 'Orl right,' 'e says, 'but you know the conditions of this 'ere sweep. Nothin' don't count only wot tikes plice during the two weeks of the 'ouse-party,' 'e says. 'Orl right,' I says. 'Write me ticket. It's a fair sportin' venture.' So 'e writes me out me ticket, with 'Mr. X.' on it, and I says to them all, I says, 'I'd like to 'ave witnesses', I says, 'to this 'ere thing. Do all you gents agree that if anyone not in the 'ouse-party and 'oo's name ain't on one of the other tickets marries 'er lidyship, I get the pool?' I says. They all says that's right, and then I says to 'em all straight out, I says, 'I 'appen to know', I says, 'that 'er lidyship is in love with a gent that's not in the party at all. An American gent,' I says. They wouldn't believe it at first, but, when Keggs 'ad put two and two together, and thought of one or two things that 'ad 'appened, 'e turned as white as a sheet and said it was a swindle and wanted the drawin' done over again, but the others says 'No', they says, 'it's quite fair,' they says, and one of 'em offered me ten bob slap out for my ticket. But I stuck to it, I did. And that," concluded Albert throwing the cigarette into the fire-place just in time to prevent a scorched finger, "that's why I'm going to 'elp yer!"

There is probably no attitude of mind harder for the average man to maintain than that of aloof disapproval. George was an average man, and during the degrading recital just concluded he had found himself slipping. At first he had been revolted, then, in spite of himself, amused, and now, when all the facts were before him, he could induce his mind to think of nothing else than his good fortune in securing as an ally one who appeared to combine a precocious intelligence with a helpful lack of scruple. War is war, and love is love, and in each the practical man inclines to demand from his fellow-workers the punch rather than a lofty soul. A page boy replete with the finer feelings would have been useless in this crisis. Albert, who seemed, on the evidence of a short but sufficient acquaintance, to be a lad who would not recognize the finer feelings if they were handed to him on a plate with watercress round them, promised to be invaluable. Something in his manner told George that the child was bursting with schemes for his benefit.

"Have some more cake, Albert," he said ingratiatingly.

The boy shook his head.

"Do," urged George. "Just a little slice."

"There ain't no little slice," replied Albert with regret.

"I've ate it all." He sighed and resumed. "I gotta scheme!"

"Fine! What is it?"

Albert knitted his brows.

"It's like this. You want to see 'er lidyship, but you can't come to the castle, and she can't come to you—not with 'er fat brother dogging of 'er footsteps. That's it, ain't it? Or am I a liar?"

George hastened to reassure him.

"That is exactly it. What's the answer?"

"I'll tell yer wot you can do. There's the big ball tonight 'cos of its bein' 'Is Nibs' comin'-of-age tomorrow. All the county'll be 'ere."

"You think I could slip in and be taken for a guest?"

Albert snorted contempt.

"No, I don't think nothin' of the kind, not bein' a fat-head." George apologized. "But wot you could do's this. I 'eard Keggs torkin to the 'ouse-keeper about 'avin' to get in a lot of temp'y waiters to 'elp out for the night—"

George reached forward and patted Albert on the head.

"Don't mess my 'air, now," warned that youth coldly.

"Albert, you're one of the great thinkers of the age. I could get into the castle as a waiter, and you could tell Lady Maud I was there, and we could arrange a meeting. Machiavelli couldn't have thought of anything smoother."

"Mac Who?"

"One of your ancestors. Great schemer in his day. But, one moment."

"Now what?"

"How am I to get engaged? How do I get the job?"

"That's orl right. I'll tell the 'ousekeeper you're my cousin— been a waiter in America at the best restaurongs—'ome for a 'oliday, but'll come in for one night to oblige. They'll pay yer a quid."

"I'll hand it over to you."

"Just," said Albert approvingly, "wot I was goin' to suggest myself."

"Then I'll leave all the arrangements to you."

"You'd better, if you don't want to mike a mess of everything. All you've got to do is to come to the servants' entrance at eight sharp tonight and say you're my cousin."

"That's an awful thing to ask anyone to say."

"Pardon?"

"Nothing!" said George.

CHAPTER 12.

The great ball in honour of Lord Belpher's coming-of-age was at its height. The reporter of the Belpher Intelligencer and Farmers' Guide, who was present in his official capacity, and had been allowed by butler Keggs to take a peep at the scene through a side-door, justly observed in his account of the proceedings next day that the 'tout ensemble was fairylike', and described the company as 'a galaxy of fair women and brave men'. The floor was crowded with all that was best and noblest in the county; so that a half-brick, hurled at any given moment, must infallibly have spilt blue blood. Peers stepped on the toes of knights; honorables bumped into the spines of baronets. Probably the only titled person in the whole of the surrounding country who was not playing his part in the glittering scene was Lord Marshmoreton; who, on discovering that his private study had been converted into a cloakroom, had retired to bed with a pipe and a copy of Roses Red and Roses White, by Emily Ann Mackintosh (Popgood, Crooly & Co.), which he was to discover—after he was between the sheets, and it was too late to repair the error—was not, as he had supposed, a treatise on his favourite hobby, but a novel of stearine sentimentality dealing with the adventures of a pure young English girl and an artist named Claude.

George, from the shaded seclusion of a gallery, looked down upon the brilliant throng with impatience. It seemed to him that he had been doing this all his life. The novelty of the experience had long since ceased to divert him. It was all just like the second act of an old-fashioned musical comedy (Act Two: The Ballroom, Grantchester Towers: One Week Later)—a resemblance which was heightened for him by the fact that the band had more than once played dead and buried melodies of his own composition, of which he had wearied a full eighteen months back.

A complete absence of obstacles had attended his intrusion into the castle. A brief interview with a motherly old lady, whom even Albert seemed to treat with respect, and who, it appeared was Mrs. Digby, the house-keeper; followed by an even briefer encounter with Keggs (fussy and irritable with responsibility, and, even while talking to George carrying on two other conversations on topics of the moment), and he was past the censors and free for one night only to add his presence to the chosen inside the walls of Belpher. His duties were to stand in this gallery, and with the assistance of one of the maids to minister to the comfort of such of the dancers as should use it as a sitting-out place. None had so far made their appearance, the superior attractions of the main floor having exercised a great appeal; and for the past hour George had been alone with the maid and his thoughts. The maid, having asked George if he knew her cousin Frank, who had been in America nearly a year, and having received a reply in the negative, seemed to be disappointed in him, and to lose interest, and had not spoken for twenty minutes.

George scanned the approaches to the balcony for a sight of Albert as the shipwrecked mariner scans the horizon for the passing sail. It was inevitable, he supposed, this waiting. It would be difficult for Maud to slip away even for a moment on such a night.

"I say, laddie, would you mind getting me a lemonade?"

George was gazing over the balcony when the voice spoke behind him, and the muscles of his back stiffened as he recognized its genial note. This was one of the things he had prepared himself for, but, now that it had happened, he felt a wave of stage-fright such as he had only once experienced before in his life—on the occasion when he had been young enough and inexperienced enough to take a curtain-call on a first night. Reggie Byng was friendly, and would not wilfully betray him; but Reggie was also a babbler, who could not be trusted to keep things to himself. It was necessary, he perceived, to take a strong line from the start, and convince Reggie that any likeness which the latter might suppose that he detected between his companion of that afternoon and the waiter of tonight existed only in his heated imagination.

As George turned, Reggie's pleasant face, pink with healthful exercise and Lord Marshmoreton's finest Bollinger, lost most of its colour. His eyes and mouth opened wider. The fact is Reggie was shaken. All through the earlier part of the evening he had been sedulously priming himself with stimulants with a view to amassing enough nerve to propose to Alice Faraday: and, now that he had drawn her away from the throng to this secluded nook and was about to put his fortune to the test, a horrible fear swept over him that he had overdone it. He was having optical illusions.

"Good God!"

Reggie loosened his collar, and pulled himself together.

"Would you mind taking a glass of lemonade to the lady in blue sitting on the settee over there by the statue," he said carefully.

He brightened up a little.

"Pretty good that! Not absolutely a test sentence, perhaps, like

'Truly rural' or 'The intricacies of the British Constitution'.

But nevertheless no mean feat."

"I say!" he continued, after a pause.

"Sir?"

"You haven't ever seen me before by any chance, if you know what I mean, have you?"

"No, sir."

"You haven't a brother, or anything of that shape or order, have you, no?"

"No, sir. I have often wished I had. I ought to have spoken to father about it. Father could never deny me anything."

Reggie blinked. His misgiving returned. Either his ears, like his eyes, were playing him tricks, or else this waiter-chappie was talking pure drivel.

"What's that?"

"Sir?"

"What did you say?"

"I said, 'No, sir, I have no brother'."

"Didn't you say something else?"

"No, sir."

"What?"

"No, sir."

Reggie's worst suspicions were confirmed.

"Good God!" he muttered. "Then I am!"

Miss Faraday, when he joined her on the settee, wanted an explanation.

"What were you talking to that man about, Mr. Byng? You seemed to be having a very interesting conversation."

"I was asking him if he had a brother."

Miss Faraday glanced quickly at him. She had had a feeling for some time during the evening that his manner had been strange.

"A brother? What made you ask him that?"

"He—I mean—that is to say—what I mean is, he looked the sort of chap who might have a brother. Lots of those fellows have!"

Alice Faraday's face took on a motherly look. She was fonder of Reggie than that lovesick youth supposed, and by sheer accident he had stumbled on the right road to her consideration. Alice Faraday was one of those girls whose dream it is to be a ministering angel to some chosen man, to be a good influence to him and raise him to an appreciation of nobler things. Hitherto, Reggie's personality had seemed to her agreeable, but negative. A positive vice like over-indulgence in alcohol altered him completely. It gave him a significance.

"I told him to get you a lemonade," said Reggie. "He seems to be taking his time about it. Hi!"

George approached deferentially.

"Sir?"

"Where's that lemonade?"

"Lemonade, sir?"

"Didn't I ask you to bring this lady a glass of lemonade?"

"I did not understand you to do so, sir."

"But, Great Scott! What were we chatting about, then?"

"You were telling me a diverting story about an Irishman who landed in New York looking for work, sir. You would like a glass of lemonade, sir? Very good, sir."

Alice placed a hand gently on Reggie's arm.

"Don't you think you had better lie down for a little and rest, Mr. Byng? I'm sure it would do you good."

The solicitous note in her voice made Reggie quiver like a jelly. He had never known her speak like that before. For a moment he was inclined to lay bare his soul; but his nerve was broken. He did not want her to mistake the outpouring of a strong man's heart for the irresponsible ravings of a too hearty diner. It was one of Life's ironies. Here he was for the first time all keyed up to go right ahead, and he couldn't do it.

"It's the heat of the room," said Alice. "Shall we go and sit outside on the terrace? Never mind about the lemonade. I'm not really thirsty."

Reggie followed her like a lamb. The prospect of the cool night air was grateful.

"That," murmured George, as he watched them depart, "ought to hold you for a while!"

He perceived Albert hastening towards him.

CHAPTER 13.

Albert was in a hurry. He skimmed over the carpet like a water-beetle.

"Quick!" he said.

He cast a glance at the maid, George's co-worker. She was reading a novelette with her back turned.

"Tell 'er you'll be back in five minutes," said Albert, jerking a thumb.

"Unnecessary. She won't notice my absence. Ever since she discovered that I had never met her cousin Frank in America, I have meant nothing in her life."

"Then come on."

"Where?"

"I'll show you."

That it was not the nearest and most direct route which they took to the trysting-place George became aware after he had followed his young guide through doors and up stairs and down stairs and had at last come to a halt in a room to which the sound of the music penetrated but faintly. He recognized the room. He had been in it before. It was the same room where he and Billie Dore had listened to Keggs telling the story of Lord Leonard and his leap. That window there, he remembered now, opened on to the very balcony from which the historic Leonard had done his spectacular dive. That it should be the scene of this other secret meeting struck George as appropriate. The coincidence appealed to him.

Albert vanished. George took a deep breath. Now that the moment had arrived for which he had waited so long he was aware of a return of that feeling of stage-fright which had come upon him when he heard Reggie Byng's voice. This sort of thing, it must be remembered, was not in George's usual line. His had been a quiet and uneventful life, and the only exciting thing which, in his recollection, had ever happened to him previous to the dramatic entry of Lady Maud into his taxi-cab that day in Piccadilly, had occurred at college nearly ten years before, when a festive room-mate—no doubt with the best motives—had placed a Mexican horned toad in his bed on the night of the Yale football game.

A light footstep sounded outside, and the room whirled round George in a manner which, if it had happened to Reggie Byng, would have caused that injudicious drinker to abandon the habits of a lifetime. When the furniture had returned to its place and the rug had ceased to spin, Maud was standing before him.

Nothing is harder to remember than a once-seen face. It had caused George a good deal of distress and inconvenience that, try as he might, he could not conjure up anything more than a vague vision of what the only girl in the world really looked like. He had carried away with him from their meeting in the cab only a confused recollection of eyes that shone and a mouth that curved in a smile; and the brief moment in which he was able to refresh his memory, when he found her in the lane with Reggie Byng and the broken-down car, had not been enough to add definiteness. The consequence was that Maud came upon him now with the stunning effect of beauty seen for the first time. He gasped. In that dazzling ball-dress, with the flush of dancing on her cheeks and the light of dancing in her eyes, she was so much more wonderful than any picture of her which memory had been able to produce for his inspection that it was as if he had never seen her before.

Even her brother, Percy, a stern critic where his nearest and dearest were concerned, had admitted on meeting her in the drawing-room before dinner that that particular dress suited Maud. It was a shimmering dream-thing of rose-leaves and moon-beams. That, at least, was how it struck George; a dressmaker would have found a longer and less romantic description for it. But that does not matter. Whoever wishes for a cold and technical catalogue of the stuffs which went to make up the picture that deprived George of speech may consult the files of the Belpher Intelligencer and Farmers' Guide, and read the report of the editor's wife, who "does" the dresses for the Intelligencer under the pen-name of "Birdie Bright-Eye". As far as George was concerned, the thing was made of rose-leaves and moon-beams.

George, as I say, was deprived of speech. That any girl could possibly look so beautiful was enough to paralyse his faculties; but that this ethereal being straight from Fairyland could have stooped to love him—him—an earthy brute who wore sock-suspenders and drank coffee for breakfast . . . that was what robbed George of the power to articulate. He could do nothing but look at her.

From the Hills of Fairyland soft music came. Or, if we must be exact, Maud spoke.

"I couldn't get away before!" Then she stopped short and darted to the door listening. "Was that somebody coming? I had to cut a dance with Mr. Plummer to get here, and I'm so afraid he may. . ."

He had. A moment later it was only too evident that this was precisely what Mr. Plummer had done. There was a footstep on the stairs, a heavy footstep this time, and from outside the voice of the pursuer made itself heard.

"Oh, there you are, Lady Maud! I was looking for you. This is our dance."

George did not know who Mr. Plummer was. He did not want to know. His only thought regarding Mr. Plummer was a passionate realization of the superfluity of his existence. It is the presence on the globe of these Plummers that delays the coming of the Millennium.

His stunned mind leaped into sudden activity. He must not be found here, that was certain. Waiters who ramble at large about a feudal castle and are discovered in conversation with the daughter of the house excite comment. And, conversely, daughters of the house who talk in secluded rooms with waiters also find explanations necessary. He must withdraw. He must withdraw quickly. And, as a gesture from Maud indicated, the withdrawal must be effected through the french window opening on the balcony. Estimating the distance that separated him from the approaching Plummer at three stairs—the voice had come from below—and a landing, the space of time allotted to him by a hustling Fate for disappearing was some four seconds. Inside two and half, the french window had opened and closed, and George was out under the stars, with the cool winds of the night playing on his heated forehead.

He had now time for meditation. There are few situations which provide more scope for meditation than that of the man penned up on a small balcony a considerable distance from the ground, with his only avenue of retreat cut off behind him. So George meditated. First, he mused on Plummer. He thought some hard thoughts about Plummer. Then he brooded on the unkindness of a fortune which had granted him the opportunity of this meeting with Maud, only to snatch it away almost before it had begun. He wondered how long the late Lord Leonard had been permitted to talk on that occasion before he, too, had had to retire through these same windows. There was no doubt about one thing. Lovers who chose that room for their interviews seemed to have very little luck.

It had not occurred to George at first that there could be any further disadvantage attached to his position other than the obvious drawbacks which had already come to his notice. He was now to perceive that he had been mistaken. A voice was speaking in the room he had left, a plainly audible voice, deep and throaty; and within a minute George had become aware that he was to suffer the additional discomfort of being obliged to listen to a fellow man—one could call Plummer that by stretching the facts a little—proposing marriage. The gruesomeness of the situation became intensified. Of all moments when a man—and justice compelled George to admit that Plummer was technically human—of all moments when a man may by all the laws of decency demand to be alone without an audience of his own sex, the chiefest is the moment when he is asking a girl to marry him. George's was a sensitive nature, and he writhed at the thought of playing the eavesdropper at such a time.

He looked frantically about him for a means of escape. Plummer had now reached the stage of saying at great length that he was not worthy of Maud. He said it over and over, again in different ways. George was in hearty agreement with him, but he did not want to hear it. He wanted to get away. But how? Lord Leonard on a similar occasion had leaped. Some might argue therefore on the principle that what man has done, man can do, that George should have imitated him. But men differ. There was a man attached to a circus who used to dive off the roof of Madison Square Garden on to a sloping board, strike it with his chest, turn a couple of somersaults, reach the ground, bow six times and go off to lunch. That sort of thing is a gift. Some of us have it, some have not. George had not. Painful as it was to hear Plummer floundering through his proposal of marriage, instinct told him that it would be far more painful to hurl himself out into mid-air on the sporting chance of having his downward progress arrested by the branches of the big tree that had upheld Lord Leonard. No, there seemed nothing for it but to remain where he was.

Inside the room Plummer was now saying how much the marriage would please his mother.

"Psst!"

George looked about him. It seemed to him that he had heard a voice. He listened. No. Except for the barking of a distant dog, the faint wailing of a waltz, the rustle of a roosting bird, and the sound of Plummer saying that if her refusal was due to anything she might have heard about that breach-of-promise case of his a couple of years ago he would like to state that he was more sinned against than sinning and that the girl had absolutely misunderstood him, all was still.

"Psst! Hey, mister!"

It was a voice. It came from above. Was it an angel's voice? Not altogether. It was Albert's. The boy was leaning out of a window some six feet higher up the castle wall. George, his eyes by now grown used to the darkness, perceived that the stripling gesticulated as one having some message to impart. Then, glancing to one side, he saw what looked like some kind of a rope swayed against the wall. He reached for it. The thing was not a rope: it was a knotted sheet.

From above came Albert's hoarse whisper.

"Look alive!"

This was precisely what George wanted to do for at least another fifty years or so; and it seemed to him as he stood there in the starlight, gingerly fingering this flimsy linen thing, that if he were to suspend his hundred and eighty pounds of bone and sinew at the end of it over the black gulf outside the balcony he would look alive for about five seconds, and after that goodness only knew how he would look. He knew all about knotted sheets. He had read a hundred stories in which heroes, heroines, low comedy friends and even villains did all sorts of reckless things with their assistance. There was not much comfort to be derived from that. It was one thing to read about people doing silly things like that, quite another to do them yourself. He gave Albert's sheet a tentative shake. In all his experience he thought he had never come across anything so supremely unstable. (One calls it Albert's sheet for the sake of convenience. It was really Reggie Byng's sheet. And when Reggie got to his room in the small hours of the morning and found the thing a mass of knots he jumped to the conclusion— being a simple-hearted young man—that his bosom friend Jack Ferris, who had come up from London to see Lord Belpher through the trying experience of a coming-of-age party, had done it as a practical joke, and went and poured a jug of water over Jack's bed. That is Life. Just one long succession of misunderstandings and rash acts and what not. Absolutely!)

Albert was becoming impatient. He was in the position of a great general who thinks out some wonderful piece of strategy and can't get his army to carry it out. Many boys, seeing Plummer enter the room below and listening at the keyhole and realizing that George must have hidden somewhere and deducing that he must be out on the balcony, would have been baffled as to how to proceed. Not so Albert. To dash up to Reggie Byng's room and strip his sheet off the bed and tie it to the bed-post and fashion a series of knots in it and lower it out of the window took Albert about three minutes. His part in the business had been performed without a hitch. And now George, who had nothing in the world to do but the childish task of climbing up the sheet, was jeopardizing the success of the whole scheme by delay. Albert gave the sheet an irritable jerk.

It was the worst thing he could have done. George had almost made up his mind to take a chance when the sheet was snatched from his grasp as if it had been some live thing deliberately eluding his clutch. The thought of what would have happened had this occurred when he was in mid-air caused him to break out in a cold perspiration. He retired a pace and perched himself on the rail of the balcony.

"Psst!" said Albert.

"It's no good saying, 'Psst!'" rejoined George in an annoyed undertone. "I could say 'Psst!' Any fool could say 'Psst!'"

Albert, he considered, in leaning out of the window and saying

"Psst!" was merely touching the fringe of the subject.

It is probable that he would have remained seated on the balcony rail regarding the sheet with cold aversion, indefinitely, had not his hand been forced by the man Plummer. Plummer, during these last minutes, had shot his bolt. He had said everything that a man could say, much of it twice over; and now he was through. All was ended. The verdict was in. No wedding-bells for Plummer.

"I think," said Plummer gloomily, and the words smote on George's ear like a knell, "I think I'd like a little air."

George leaped from his rail like a hunted grasshopper. If Plummer was looking for air, it meant that he was going to come out on the balcony. There was only one thing to be done. It probably meant the abrupt conclusion of a promising career, but he could hesitate no longer.

George grasped the sheet—it felt like a rope of cobwebs—and swung himself out.

Maud looked out on to the balcony. Her heart, which had stood still when the rejected one opened the window and stepped forth to commune with the soothing stars, beat again. There was no one there, only emptiness and Plummer.

"This," said Plummer sombrely, gazing over the rail into the darkness, "is the place where that fellow what's-his-name jumped off in the reign of thingummy, isn't it?"

Maud understood now, and a thrill of the purest admiration for George's heroism swept over her. So rather than compromise her, he had done Leonard's leap! How splendid of him! If George, now sitting on Reggie Byng's bed taking a rueful census of the bits of skin remaining on his hands and knees after his climb, could have read her thoughts, he would have felt well rewarded for his abrasions.

"I've a jolly good mind," said Plummer, "to do it myself!" He uttered a short, mirthless laugh. "Well, anyway," he said recklessly, "I'll jolly well go downstairs and have a brandy-and-soda!"

Albert finished untying the sheet from the bedpost, and stuffed it under the pillow.

"And now," said Albert, "for a quiet smoke in the scullery."

These massive minds require their moments of relaxation.

CHAPTER 14.

George's idea was to get home. Quick. There was no possible chance of a second meeting with Maud that night. They had met and had been whirled asunder. No use to struggle with Fate. Best to give in and hope that another time Fate would be kinder. What George wanted now was to be away from all the gay glitter and the fairylike tout ensemble and the galaxy of fair women and brave men, safe in his own easy-chair, where nothing could happen to him. A nice sense of duty would no doubt have taken him back to his post in order fully to earn the sovereign which had been paid to him for his services as temporary waiter; but the voice of Duty called to him in vain. If the British aristocracy desired refreshments let them get them for themselves—and like it! He was through.

But if George had for the time being done with the British aristocracy, the British aristocracy had not done with him. Hardly had he reached the hall when he encountered the one member of the order whom he would most gladly have avoided.

Lord Belpher was not in genial mood. Late hours always made his head ache, and he was not a dancing man; so that he was by now fully as weary of the fairylike tout ensemble as was George. But, being the centre and cause of the night's proceedings, he was compelled to be present to the finish. He was in the position of captains who must be last to leave their ships, and of boys who stand on burning decks whence all but they had fled. He had spent several hours shaking hands with total strangers and receiving with a frozen smile their felicitations on the attainment of his majority, and he could not have been called upon to meet a larger horde of relations than had surged round him that night if he had been a rabbit. The Belpher connection was wide, straggling over most of England; and first cousins, second cousins and even third and fourth cousins had debouched from practically every county on the map and marched upon the home of their ancestors. The effort of having to be civil to all of these had told upon Percy. Like the heroine of his sister Maud's favourite poem he was "aweary, aweary," and he wanted a drink. He regarded George's appearance as exceedingly opportune.

"Get me a small bottle of champagne, and bring it to the library."

"Yes, sir."

The two words sound innocent enough, but, wishing as he did to efface himself and avoid publicity, they were the most unfortunate which George could have chosen. If he had merely bowed acquiescence and departed, it is probable that Lord Belpher would not have taken a second look at him. Percy was in no condition to subject everyone he met to a minute scrutiny. But, when you have been addressed for an entire lifetime as "your lordship", it startles you when a waiter calls you "Sir". Lord Belpher gave George a glance in which reproof and pain were nicely mingled emotions quickly supplanted by amazement. A gurgle escaped him.

"Stop!" he cried as George turned away.

Percy was rattled. The crisis found him in two minds. On the one hand, he would have been prepared to take oath that this man before him was the man who had knocked off his hat in Piccadilly. The likeness had struck him like a blow the moment he had taken a good look at the fellow. On the other hand, there is nothing which is more likely to lead one astray than a resemblance. He had never forgotten the horror and humiliation of the occasion, which had happened in his fourteenth year, when a motherly woman at Paddington Station had called him "dearie" and publicly embraced him, on the erroneous supposition that he was her nephew, Philip. He must proceed cautiously. A brawl with an innocent waiter, coming on the heels of that infernal episode with the policeman, would give people the impression that assailing the lower orders had become a hobby of his.

"Sir?" said George politely.

His brazen front shook Lord Belpher's confidence.

"I haven't seen you before here, have I?" was all he could find to say.

"No, sir," replied George smoothly. "I am only temporarily attached to the castle staff."

"Where do you come from?"

"America, sir."

Lord Belpher started. "America!"

"Yes, sir. I am in England on a vacation. My cousin, Albert, is page boy at the castle, and he told me there were a few vacancies for extra help tonight, so I applied and was given the job."

Lord Belpher frowned perplexedly. It all sounded entirely plausible. And, what was satisfactory, the statement could be checked by application to Keggs, the butler. And yet there was a lingering doubt. However, there seemed nothing to be gained by continuing the conversation.

"I see," he said at last. "Well, bring that champagne to the library as quick as you can."

"Very good, sir."

Lord Belpher remained where he stood, brooding. Reason told him he ought to be satisfied, but he was not satisfied. It would have been different had he not known that this fellow with whom Maud had become entangled was in the neighbourhood. And if that scoundrel had had the audacity to come and take a cottage at the castle gates, why not the audacity to invade the castle itself?

The appearance of one of the footmen, on his way through the hall with a tray, gave him the opportunity for further investigation.

"Send Keggs to me!"

"Very good, your lordship."

An interval and the butler arrived. Unlike Lord Belpher late hours were no hardship to Keggs. He was essentially a night-blooming flower. His brow was as free from wrinkles as his shirt-front. He bore himself with the conscious dignity of one who, while he would have freely admitted he did not actually own the castle, was nevertheless aware that he was one of its most conspicuous ornaments.

"You wished to see me, your lordship?"

"Yes. Keggs, there are a number of outside men helping here tonight, aren't there?"

"Indubitably, your lordship. The unprecedented scale of the entertainment necessitated the engagement of a certain number of supernumeraries," replied Keggs with an easy fluency which Reggie Byng, now cooling his head on the lower terrace, would have bitterly envied. "In the circumstances, such an arrangement was inevitable."

"You engaged all these men yourself?"

"In a manner of speaking, your lordship, and for all practical purposes, yes. Mrs. Digby, the 'ouse-keeper conducted the actual negotiations in many cases, but the arrangement was in no instance considered complete until I had passed each applicant."

"Do you know anything of an American who says he is the cousin of the page-boy?"

"The boy Albert did introduce a nominee whom he stated to be 'is cousin 'ome from New York on a visit and anxious to oblige. I trust he 'as given no dissatisfaction, your lordship? He seemed a respectable young man."

"No, no, not at all. I merely wished to know if you knew him. One can't be too careful."

"No, indeed, your lordship."

"That's all, then."

"Thank you, your lordship."

Lord Belpher was satisfied. He was also relieved. He felt that prudence and a steady head had kept him from making himself ridiculous. When George presently returned with the life-saving fluid, he thanked him and turned his thoughts to other things.

But, if the young master was satisfied, Keggs was not. Upon Keggs a bright light had shone. There were few men, he flattered himself, who could more readily put two and two together and bring the sum to a correct answer. Keggs knew of the strange American gentleman who had taken up his abode at the cottage down by Platt's farm. His looks, his habits, and his motives for coming there had formed food for discussion throughout one meal in the servant's hall; a stranger whose abstention from brush and palette showed him to be no artist being an object of interest. And while the solution put forward by a romantic lady's-maid, a great reader of novelettes, that the young man had come there to cure himself of some unhappy passion by communing with nature, had been scoffed at by the company, Keggs had not been so sure that there might not be something in it. Later events had deepened his suspicion, which now, after this interview with Lord Belpher, had become certainty.

The extreme fishiness of Albert's sudden production of a cousin from America was so manifest that only his preoccupation at the moment when he met the young man could have prevented him seeing it before. His knowledge of Albert told him that, if one so versed as that youth in the art of Swank had really possessed a cousin in America, he would long ago have been boring the servants' hall with fictions about the man's wealth and importance. For Albert not to lie about a thing, practically proved that thing non-existent. Such was the simple creed of Keggs.

He accosted a passing fellow-servitor.

"Seen young blighted Albert anywhere, Freddy?"

It was in this shameful manner that that mastermind was habitually referred to below stairs.

"Seen 'im going into the scullery not 'arf a minute ago," replied

Freddy.

"Thanks."

"So long," said Freddy.

"Be good!" returned Keggs, whose mode of speech among those of his own world differed substantially from that which he considered it became him to employ when conversing with the titled.

The fall of great men is but too often due to the failure of their miserable bodies to give the necessary support to their great brains. There are some, for example, who say that Napoleon would have won the battle of Waterloo if he had not had dyspepsia. Not otherwise was it with Albert on that present occasion. The arrival of Keggs found him at a disadvantage. He had been imprudent enough, on leaving George, to endeavour to smoke a cigar, purloined from the box which stood hospitably open on a table in the hall. But for this, who knows with what cunning counter-attacks he might have foiled the butler's onslaught? As it was, the battle was a walk-over for the enemy.

"I've been looking for you, young blighted Albert!" said Keggs coldly.

Albert turned a green but defiant face to the foe.

"Go and boil yer 'ead!" he advised.

"Never mind about my 'ead. If I was to do my duty to you, I'd give you a clip side of your 'ead, that's what I'd do."

"And then bury it in the woods," added Albert, wincing as the consequences of his rash act swept through his small form like some nauseous tidal wave. He shut his eyes. It upset him to see Keggs shimmering like that. A shimmering butler is an awful sight.

Keggs laughed a hard laugh. "You and your cousins from America!"

"What about my cousins from America?"

"Yes, what about them? That's just what Lord Belpher and me have been asking ourselves."

"I don't know wot you're talking about."

"You soon will, young blighted Albert! Who sneaked that American fellow into the 'ouse to meet Lady Maud?"

"I never!"

"Think I didn't see through your little game? Why, I knew from the first."

"Yes, you did! Then why did you let him into the place?"

Keggs snorted triumphantly. "There! You admit it! It was that feller!"

Too late Albert saw his false move—a move which in a normal state of health, he would have scorned to make. Just as Napoleon, minus a stomach-ache, would have scorned the blunder that sent his Cuirassiers plunging to destruction in the sunken road.

"I don't know what you're torkin' about," he said weakly.

"Well," said Keggs, "I haven't time to stand 'ere chatting with you. I must be going back to 'is lordship, to tell 'im of the 'orrid trick you played on him."

A second spasm shook Albert to the core of his being. The double assault was too much for him. Betrayed by the body, the spirit yielded.

"You wouldn't do that, Mr. Keggs!"

There was a white flag in every syllable.

"I would if I did my duty."

"But you don't care about that," urged Albert ingratiatingly.

"I'll have to think it over," mused Keggs. "I don't want to be 'ard on a young boy." He struggled silently with himself. "Ruinin' 'is prospecks!"

An inspiration seemed to come to him.

"All right, young blighted Albert," he said briskly. "I'll go against my better nature this once and chance it. And now, young feller me lad, you just 'and over that ticket of yours! You know what I'm alloodin' to! That ticket you 'ad at the sweep, the one with 'Mr. X' on it."

Albert's indomitable spirit triumphed for a moment over his stricken body.

"That's likely, ain't it!"

Keggs sighed—the sigh of a good man who has done his best to help a fellow-being and has been baffled by the other's perversity.

"Just as you please," he said sorrowfully. "But I did 'ope I shouldn't 'ave to go to 'is lordship and tell 'im 'ow you've deceived him."

Albert capitulated. "'Ere yer are!" A piece of paper changed hands.

"It's men like you wot lead to 'arf the crime in the country!"

"Much obliged, me lad."

"You'd walk a mile in the snow, you would," continued Albert pursuing his train of thought, "to rob a starving beggar of a ha'penny."

"Who's robbing anyone? Don't you talk so quick, young man. I'm doing the right thing by you. You can 'ave my ticket, marked 'Reggie Byng'. It's a fair exchange, and no one the worse!"

"Fat lot of good that is!"

"That's as it may be. Anyhow, there it is." Keggs prepared to withdraw. "You're too young to 'ave all that money, Albert. You wouldn't know what to do with it. It wouldn't make you 'appy. There's other things in the world besides winning sweepstakes. And, properly speaking, you ought never to have been allowed to draw at all, being so young."

Albert groaned hollowly. "When you've finished torkin', I wish you'd kindly have the goodness to leave me alone. I'm not meself."

"That," said Keggs cordially, "is a bit of luck for you, my boy.

Accept my 'eartiest felicitations!"

Defeat is the test of the great man. Your true general is not he who rides to triumph on the tide of an easy victory, but the one who, when crushed to earth, can bend himself to the task of planning methods of rising again. Such a one was Albert, the page-boy. Observe Albert in his attic bedroom scarcely more than an hour later. His body has practically ceased to trouble him, and his soaring spirit has come into its own again. With the exception of a now very occasional spasm, his physical anguish has passed, and he is thinking, thinking hard. On the chest of drawers is a grubby envelope, addressed in an ill-formed hand to:

R. Byng, Esq.

On a sheet of paper, soon to be placed in the envelope, are written in the same hand these words:

"Do not dispare! Remember! Fante hart never won

fair lady. I shall watch your futur progres with

considurable interest.

   Your Well-Wisher."

The last sentence is not original. Albert's Sunday-school teacher said it to Albert on the occasion of his taking up his duties at the castle, and it stuck in his memory. Fortunately, for it expressed exactly what Albert wished to say. From now on Reggie Byng's progress with Lady Maud Marsh was to be the thing nearest to Albert's heart.

And George meanwhile? Little knowing how Fate has changed in a flash an ally into an opponent he is standing at the edge of the shrubbery near the castle gate. The night is very beautiful; the barked spots on his hands and knees are hurting much less now; and he is full of long, sweet thoughts. He has just discovered the extraordinary resemblance, which had not struck him as he was climbing up the knotted sheet, between his own position and that of the hero of Tennyson's Maud, a poem to which he has always been particularly addicted—and never more so than during the days since he learned the name of the only possible girl. When he has not been playing golf, Tennyson's Maud has been his constant companion.

"Queen rose of the rosebud garden of girls

Come hither, the dances are done,

In glass of satin and glimmer of pearls.

Queen lily and rose in one;

Shine out, little head, sunning over with curls

To the flowers, and be their sun."

The music from the ballroom flows out to him through the motionless air. The smell of sweet earth and growing things is everywhere.

"Come into the garden, Maud,

For the black bat, night, hath flown,

Come into the garden, Maud,

I am here at the gate alone;

And the woodbine spices are wafted abroad,

And the musk of the rose is blown."

He draws a deep breath, misled young man. The night is very beautiful. It is near to the dawn now and in the bushes live things are beginning to stir and whisper.

"Maud!"

Surely she can hear him?

"Maud!"

The silver stars looked down dispassionately. This sort of thing had no novelty for them.

CHAPTER 15.

Lord Belpher's twenty-first birthday dawned brightly, heralded in by much twittering of sparrows in the ivy outside his bedroom. These Percy did not hear, for he was sound asleep and had had a late night. The first sound that was able to penetrate his heavy slumber and rouse him to a realization that his birthday had arrived was the piercing cry of Reggie Byng on his way to the bath-room across the corridor. It was Reggie's disturbing custom to urge himself on to a cold bath with encouraging yells; and the noise of this performance, followed by violent splashing and a series of sharp howls as the sponge played upon the

Byng spine, made sleep an impossibility within a radius of many yards. Percy sat up in bed, and cursed Reggie silently. He discovered that he had a headache.

Presently the door flew open, and the vocalist entered in person, clad in a pink bathrobe and very tousled and rosy from the tub.

"Many happy returns of the day, Boots, old thing!"

Reggie burst rollickingly into song.

> *"I'm twenty-one today!*
>
> *Twenty-one today!*
>
> *I've got the key of the door!*
>
> *Never been twenty-one before!*
>
> *And father says I can do what I like!*
>
> *So shout Hip-hip-hooray!*
>
> *I'm a jolly good fellow,*
>
> *Twenty-one today."*

Lord Belpher scowled morosely.

"I wish you wouldn't make that infernal noise!"

"What infernal noise?"

"That singing!"

"My God! This man has wounded me!" said Reggie.

"I've a headache."

"I thought you would have, laddie, when I saw you getting away with the liquid last night. An X-ray photograph of your liver would show something that looked like a crumpled oak-leaf studded with hob-nails. You ought to take more exercise, dear heart. Except for sloshing that policeman, you haven't done anything athletic for years."

"I wish you wouldn't harp on that affair!"

Reggie sat down on the bed.

"Between ourselves, old man," he said confidentially, "I also—I myself—Reginald Byng, in person—was perhaps a shade polluted during the evening. I give you my honest word that just after dinner I saw three versions of your uncle, the bishop, standing in a row side by side. I tell you, laddie, that for a moment I thought I had strayed into a Bishop's Beano at Exeter Hall or the Athenaeum or wherever it is those chappies collect in gangs. Then the three bishops sort of congealed into one bishop, a trifle blurred about the outlines, and I felt relieved. But what convinced me that I had emptied a flagon or so too many was a rather rummy thing that occurred later on. Have you ever happened, during one of these feasts of reason and flows of soul, when you were bubbling over with joie-de-vivre—have you ever happened to see things? What I mean to say is, I had a deuced odd experience last night. I could have sworn that one of the waiter-chappies was that fellow who knocked off your hat in Piccadilly."

Lord Belpher, who had sunk back on to the pillows at Reggie's entrance and had been listening to his talk with only intermittent attention, shot up in bed.

"What!"

"Absolutely! My mistake, of course, but there it was. The fellow might have been his double."

"But you've never seen the man."

"Oh yes, I have. I forgot to tell you. I met him on the links yesterday. I'd gone out there alone, rather expecting to have a round with the pro., but, finding this lad there, I suggested that we might go round together. We did eighteen holes, and he licked the boots off me. Very hot stuff he was. And after the game he took me off to his cottage and gave me a drink. He lives at the cottage next door to Platt's farm, so, you see, it was the identical chappie. We got extremely matey. Like brothers. Absolutely! So you can understand what a shock it gave me when I found what I took to be the same man serving bracers to the multitude the same evening. One of those nasty jars that cause a fellow's head to swim a bit, don't you know, and make him lose confidence in himself."

Lord Belpher did not reply. His brain was whirling. So he had been right after all!

"You know," pursued Reggie seriously, "I think you are making the bloomer of a lifetime over this hat-swatting chappie. You've misjudged him. He's a first-rate sort. Take it from me! Nobody could have got out of the bunker at the fifteenth hole better than he did. If you'll take my advice, you'll conciliate the feller. A really first-class golfer is what you need in the family. Besides, even leaving out of the question the fact that he can do things with a niblick that I didn't think anybody except the pro. could do, he's a corking good sort. A stout fellow in every respect. I took to the chappie. He's all right. Grab him, Boots, before he gets away. That's my tip to you. You'll never regret it! From first to last this lad didn't foozle a single drive, and his approach-putting has to be seen to be believed. Well, got to dress, I suppose. Mustn't waste life's springtime sitting here talking to you. Toodle-oo, laddie! We shall meet anon!"

Lord Belpher leaped from his bed. He was feeling worse than ever now, and a glance into the mirror told him that he looked rather worse than he felt. Late nights and insufficient sleep, added to the need of a shave, always made him look like something that should have been swept up and taken away to the ash-bin. And as for his physical condition, talking to Reggie Byng never tended to make you feel better when you had a headache. Reggie's manner was not soothing, and on this particular morning his choice of a topic had been unusually irritating. Lord Belpher told himself that he could not understand Reggie. He had never been able to make his mind quite clear as to the exact relations between the latter and his sister Maud, but he had always been under the impression that, if they were not actually engaged, they were on the verge of becoming so; and it was maddening to have to listen to Reggie advocating the claims of a rival as if he had no personal interest in the affair at all. Percy felt for his complaisant friend something of the annoyance which a householder feels for the watchdog whom he finds fraternizing with the burglar. Why, Reggie, more than anyone else, ought to be foaming with rage at the insolence of this American fellow in coming down to Belpher and planting himself at the castle gates. Instead of which, on his own showing, he appeared to have adopted an attitude towards him which would have excited remark if adopted by David towards Jonathan. He seemed to spend all his spare time frolicking with the man on the golf-links and hobnobbing with him in his house.

Lord Belpher was thoroughly upset. It was impossible to prove it or to do anything about it now, but he was convinced that the fellow had wormed his way into the castle in the guise of a waiter. He had probably met Maud and plotted further meetings with her. This thing was becoming unendurable.

One thing was certain. The family honour was in his hands. Anything that was to be done to keep Maud away from the intruder must be done by himself. Reggie was hopeless: he was capable, as far as Percy could see, of escorting Maud to the fellow's door in his own car and leaving her on the threshold with his blessing. As for Lord Marshmoreton, roses and the family history took up so much of his time that he could not be counted on for anything but moral support. He, Percy, must do the active work.

He had just come to this decision, when, approaching the window and gazing down into the grounds, he perceived his sister Maud walking rapidly—and, so it seemed to him, with a furtive air—down the east drive. And it was to the east that Platt's farm and the cottage next door to it lay.

At the moment of this discovery, Percy was in a costume ill adapted for the taking of country walks. Reggie's remarks about his liver had struck home, and it had been his intention, by way of a corrective to his headache and a general feeling of swollen ill-health, to do a little work before his bath with a pair of Indian clubs. He had arrayed himself for this purpose in an old sweater, a pair of grey flannel trousers, and patent leather evening shoes. It was not the garb he would have chosen himself for a ramble, but time was flying: even to put on a pair of boots is a matter of minutes: and in another moment or two Maud would be out of sight. Percy ran downstairs, snatched up a soft shooting-hat, which proved, too late, to belong to a person with a head two sizes smaller than his own; and raced out into the grounds. He was just in time to see Maud disappearing round the corner of the drive.

Lord Belpher had never belonged to that virile class of the community which considers running a pleasure and a pastime. At Oxford, on those occasions when the members of his college had turned out on raw afternoons to trot along the river-bank encouraging the college eight with yelling and the swinging of police-rattles, Percy had always stayed prudently in his rooms with tea and buttered toast, thereby avoiding who knows what colds and coughs. When he ran, he ran reluctantly and with a definite object in view, such as the catching of a train. He was consequently not in the best of condition, and the sharp sprint which was imperative at this juncture if he was to keep his sister in view left him spent and panting. But he had the reward of reaching the gates of the drive not many seconds after Maud, and of seeing her walking—more slowly now—down the road that led to Platt's. This confirmation of his suspicions enabled him momentarily to forget the blister which was forming on the heel of his left foot. He set out after her at a good pace.

The road, after the habit of country roads, wound and twisted. The quarry was frequently out of sight. And Percy's anxiety was such that, every time Maud vanished, he broke into a gallop. Another hundred yards, and the blister no longer consented to be ignored. It cried for attention like a little child, and was rapidly insinuating itself into a position in the scheme of things where it threatened to become the centre of the world. By the time the third bend in the road was reached, it seemed to Percy that this blister had become the one great Fact in an unreal nightmare-like universe. He hobbled painfully: and when he stopped suddenly and darted back into the shelter of the hedge his foot seemed aflame. The only reason why the blister on his left heel did not at this juncture attract his entire attention was that he had become aware that there was another of equal proportions forming on his right heel.

Percy had stopped and sought cover in the hedge because, as he rounded the bend in the road, he perceived, before he had time to check his gallop, that Maud had also stopped. She was standing in the middle of the road, looking over her shoulder, not ten yards away. Had she seen him? It was a point that time alone could solve. No! She walked on again. She had not seen him. Lord Belpher, by means of a notable triumph of mind over matter, forgot the blisters and hurried after her.

They had now reached that point in the road where three choices offer themselves to the wayfarer. By going straight on he may win through to the village of Moresby-in-the-Vale, a charming little place with a Norman church; by turning to the left he may visit the equally seductive hamlet of Little Weeting; by turning to the right off the main road and going down a leafy lane he may find himself at the door of Platt's farm. When Maud, reaching the cross-roads, suddenly swung down the one to the left, Lord Belpher was for the moment completely baffled. Reason reasserted its way the next minute, telling him that this was but a ruse. Whether or no she had caught sight of him, there was no doubt that Maud intended to shake off any possible pursuit by taking this speciously innocent turning and making a detour. She could have no possible motive in going to Little Weeting. He had never been to Little Weeting in his life, and there was no reason to suppose that Maud had either.

The sign-post informed him—a statement strenuously denied by the twin-blisters—that the distance to Little Weeting was one and a half miles. Lord Belpher's view of it was that it was nearer fifty. He dragged himself along wearily. It was simpler now to keep Maud in sight, for the road ran straight: but, there being a catch in everything in this world, the process was also messier. In order to avoid being seen, it was necessary for Percy to leave the road and tramp along in the deep ditch which ran parallel to it. There is nothing half-hearted about these ditches which accompany English country roads. They know they are intended to be ditches, not mere furrows, and they behave as such. The one that sheltered Lord Belpher was so deep that only his head and neck protruded above the level of the road, and so dirty that a bare twenty yards of travel was sufficient to coat him with mud. Rain, once fallen, is reluctant to leave the English ditch. It nestles inside it for weeks, forming a rich, oatmeal-like substance which has to be stirred to be believed. Percy stirred it. He churned it. He ploughed and sloshed through it. The mud stuck to him like a brother.

Nevertheless, being a determined young man, he did not give in. Once he lost a shoe, but a little searching recovered that. On another occasion, a passing dog, seeing things going on in the ditch which in his opinion should not have been going on—he was a high-strung dog, unused to coming upon heads moving along the road without bodies attached—accompanied Percy for over a quarter of a mile, causing him exquisite discomfort by making sudden runs at his face. A well-aimed stone settled this little misunderstanding, and Percy proceeded on his journey alone. He had Maud well in view when, to his surprise, she left the road and turned into the gate of a house which stood not far from the church.

Lord Belpher regained the road, and remained there, a puzzled man. A dreadful thought came to him that he might have had all this trouble and anguish for no reason. This house bore the unmistakable stamp of a vicarage. Maud could have no reason that was not innocent for going there. Had he gone through all this, merely to see his sister paying a visit to a clergyman? Too late it occurred to him that she might quite easily be on visiting terms with the clergy of Little Weeting. He had forgotten that he had been away at Oxford for many weeks, a period of time in which Maud, finding life in the country weigh upon her, might easily have interested herself charitably in the life of this village. He paused irresolutely. He was baffled.

Maud, meanwhile, had rung the bell. Ever since, looking over her shoulder, she had perceived her brother Percy dodging about in the background, her active young mind had been busying itself with schemes for throwing him off the trail. She must see George that morning. She could not wait another day before establishing communication between herself and Geoffrey. But it was not till she reached Little Weeting that there occurred to her any plan that promised success.

A trim maid opened the door.

"Is the vicar in?"

"No, miss. He went out half an hour back."

Maud was as baffled for the moment as her brother Percy, now leaning against the vicarage wall in a state of advanced exhaustion.

"Oh, dear!" she said.

The maid was sympathetic.

"Mr. Ferguson, the curate, miss, he's here, if he would do."

Maud brightened.

"He would do splendidly. Will you ask him if I can see him for a moment?"

"Very well, miss. What name, please?"

"He won't know my name. Will you please tell him that a lady wishes to see him?"

"Yes, miss. Won't you step in?"

The front door closed behind Maud. She followed the maid into the drawing-room. Presently a young small curate entered. He had a willing, benevolent face. He looked alert and helpful.

"You wished to see me?"

"I am so sorry to trouble you," said Maud, rocking the young man in his tracks with a smile of dazzling brilliancy—("No trouble, I assure you," said the curate dizzily)—"but there is a man following me!"

The curate clicked his tongue indignantly.

"A rough sort of a tramp kind of man. He has been following me for miles, and I'm frightened."

"Brute!"

"I think he's outside now. I can't think what he wants. Would you—would you mind being kind enough to go and send him away?"

The eyes that had settled George's fate for all eternity flashed upon the curate, who blinked. He squared his shoulders and drew himself up. He was perfectly willing to die for her.

"If you will wait here," he said, "I will go and send him about his business. It is disgraceful that the public highways should be rendered unsafe in this manner."

"Thank you ever so much," said Maud gratefully. "I can't help thinking the poor fellow may be a little crazy. It seems so odd of him to follow me all that way. Walking in the ditch too!"

"Walking in the ditch!"

"Yes. He walked most of the way in the ditch at the side of the road. He seemed to prefer it. I can't think why."

Lord Belpher, leaning against the wall and trying to decide whether his right or left foot hurt him the more excruciatingly, became aware that a curate was standing before him, regarding him through a pair of gold-rimmed pince-nez with a disapproving and hostile expression. Lord Belpher returned his gaze. Neither was favourably impressed by the other. Percy thought he had seen nicer-looking curates, and the curate thought he had seen more prepossessing tramps.

"Come, come!" said the curate. "This won't do, my man!" A few hours earlier Lord Belpher had been startled when addressed by George as "sir". To be called "my man" took his breath away completely.

The gift of seeing ourselves as others see us is, as the poet indicates, vouchsafed to few men. Lord Belpher, not being one of these fortunates, had not the slightest conception how intensely revolting his personal appearance was at that moment. The red-rimmed eyes, the growth of stubble on the cheeks, and the thick coating of mud which had resulted from his rambles in the ditch combined to render him a horrifying object.

"How dare you follow that young lady? I've a good mind to give you in charge!"

Percy was outraged.

"I'm her brother!" He was about to substantiate the statement by giving his name, but stopped himself. He had had enough of letting his name come out on occasions like the present. When the policeman had arrested him in the Haymarket, his first act had been to thunder his identity at the man: and the policeman, without saying in so many words that he disbelieved him, had hinted scepticism by replying that he himself was the king of Brixton. "I'm her brother!" he repeated thickly.

The curate's disapproval deepened. In a sense, we are all brothers; but that did not prevent him from considering that this mud-stained derelict had made an impudent and abominable mis-statement of fact. Not unnaturally he came to the conclusion that he had to do with a victim of the Demon Rum.

"You ought to be ashamed of yourself," he said severely. "Sad piece of human wreckage as you are, you speak like an educated man. Have you no self-respect? Do you never search your heart and shudder at the horrible degradation which you have brought on yourself by sheer weakness of will?"

He raised his voice. The subject of Temperance was one very near to the curate's heart. The vicar himself had complimented him only yesterday on the good his sermons against the drink evil were doing in the village, and the landlord of the Three Pigeons down the road had on several occasions spoken bitter things about blighters who came taking the living away from honest folks.

"It is easy enough to stop if you will but use a little resolution. You say to yourself, 'Just one won't hurt me!' Perhaps not. But can you be content with just one? Ah! No, my man, there is no middle way for such as you. It must be all or nothing. Stop it now—now, while you still retain some semblance of humanity. Soon it will be too late! Kill that craving! Stifle it! Strangle it! Make up your mind now—now, that not another drop of the accursed stuff shall pass your lips... ."

The curate paused. He perceived that enthusiasm was leading him away from the main issue. "A little perseverance," he concluded rapidly, "and you will soon find that cocoa gives you exactly the same pleasure. And now will you please be getting along. You have frightened the young lady, and she cannot continue her walk unless I assure her that you have gone away."

Fatigue, pain and the annoyance of having to listen to this man's well-meant but ill-judged utterances had combined to induce in Percy a condition bordering on hysteria. He stamped his foot, and uttered a howl as the blister warned him with a sharp twinge that this sort of behaviour could not be permitted.

"Stop talking!" he bellowed. "Stop talking like an idiot! I'm going to stay here till that girl comes out, if have to wait all day!"

The curate regarded Percy thoughtfully. Percy was no Hercules: but then, neither was the curate. And in any case, though no Hercules, Percy was undeniably an ugly-looking brute. Strategy, rather than force, seemed to the curate to be indicated. He paused a while, as one who weighs pros and cons, then spoke briskly, with the air of the man who has decided to yield a point with a good grace.

"Dear, dear!" he said. "That won't do! You say you are this young lady's brother?"

"Yes, I do!"

"Then perhaps you had better come with me into the house and we will speak to her."

"All right."

"Follow me."

Percy followed him. Down the trim gravel walk they passed, and up the neat stone steps. Maud, peeping through the curtains, thought herself the victim of a monstrous betrayal or equally monstrous blunder. But she did not know the Rev. Cyril Ferguson. No general, adroitly leading the enemy on by strategic retreat, ever had a situation more thoroughly in hand. Passing with his companion through the open door, he crossed the hall to another door, discreetly closed.

"Wait in here," he said. Lord Belpher moved unsuspectingly forward. A hand pressed sharply against the small of his back. Behind him a door slammed and a key clicked. He was trapped. Groping in Egyptian darkness, his hands met a coat, then a hat, then an umbrella. Then he stumbled over a golf-club and fell against a wall. It was too dark to see anything, but his sense of touch told him all he needed to know. He had been added to the vicar's collection of odds and ends in the closet reserved for that purpose.

He groped his way to the door and kicked it. He did not repeat the performance. His feet were in no shape for kicking things.

Percy's gallant soul abandoned the struggle. With a feeble oath, he sat down on a box containing croquet implements, and gave himself up to thought.

"You'll be quite safe now," the curate was saying in the adjoining room, not without a touch of complacent self-approval such as becomes the victor in a battle of wits. "I have locked him in the cupboard. He will be quite happy there." An incorrect statement this. "You may now continue your walk in perfect safety."

"Thank you ever so much," said Maud. "But I do hope he won't be violent when you let him out."

"I shall not let him out," replied the curate, who, though brave, was not rash. "I shall depute the task to a worthy fellow named Willis, in whom I shall have every confidence. He—he is, in fact, our local blacksmith!"

And so it came about that when, after a vigil that seemed to last for a lifetime, Percy heard the key turn in the lock and burst forth seeking whom he might devour, he experienced an almost instant quieting of his excited nervous system. Confronting him was a vast man whose muscles, like those of that other and more celebrated village blacksmith, were plainly as strong as iron bands.

This man eyed Percy with a chilly eye.

"Well," he said. "What's troublin' you?"

Percy gulped. The man's mere appearance was a sedative.

"Er—nothing!" he replied. "Nothing!"

"There better hadn't be!" said the man darkly. "Mr. Ferguson give me this to give to you. Take it!"

Percy took it. It was a shilling.

"And this."

The second gift was a small paper pamphlet. It was entitled "Now's the Time!" and seemed to be a story of some kind. At any rate, Percy's eyes, before they began to swim in a manner that prevented steady reading, caught the words "Job Roberts had always been a hard-drinking man, but one day, as he was coming out of the bar-parlour . . ." He was about to hurl it from him, when he met the other's eye and desisted. Rarely had Lord Belpher encountered a man with a more speaking eye.

"And now you get along," said the man. "You pop off. And I'm going to watch you do it, too. And, if I find you sneakin' off to the Three Pigeons . . ."

His pause was more eloquent than his speech and nearly as eloquent as his eye. Lord Belpher tucked the tract into his sweater, pocketed the shilling, and left the house. For nearly a mile down the well-remembered highway he was aware of a Presence in his rear, but he continued on his way without a glance behind.

"Like one that on a lonely road

Doth walk in fear and dread;

And, having once looked back, walks on

And turns no more his head!

Because he knows a frightful fiend

Doth close behind him tread!"

Maud made her way across the fields to the cottage down by Platt's. Her heart was as light as the breeze that ruffled the green hedges. Gaily she tripped towards the cottage door. Her hand was just raised to knock, when from within came the sound of a well-known voice.

She had reached her goal, but her father had anticipated her. Lord Marshmoreton had selected the same moment as herself for paying a call upon George Bevan.

Maud tiptoed away, and hurried back to the castle. Never before had she so clearly realized what a handicap an adhesive family can be to a young girl.

CHAPTER 16.

At the moment of Lord Marshmoreton's arrival, George was reading a letter from Billie Dore, which had come by that morning's post. It dealt mainly with the vicissitudes experienced by Miss Dore's friend, Miss Sinclair, in her relations with the man Spenser Gray. Spenser Gray, it seemed, had been behaving oddly. Ardent towards Miss Sinclair almost to an embarrassing point in the early stages of their acquaintance, he had suddenly cooled; at a recent lunch had behaved with a strange aloofness; and now, at this writing, had vanished altogether, leaving nothing behind him but an abrupt note to the effect that he had been compelled to go abroad and that, much as it was to be regretted, he and she would probably never meet again.

"And if," wrote Miss Dore, justifiably annoyed, "after saying all those things to the poor kid and telling her she was the only thing in sight, he thinks he can just slide off with a 'Good-bye! Good luck! and God bless you!' he's got another guess coming. And that's not all. He hasn't gone abroad! I saw him in Piccadilly this afternoon. He saw me, too, and what do you think he did? Ducked down a side-street, if you please. He must have run like a rabbit, at that, because, when I got there, he was nowhere to be seen. I tell you, George, there's something funny about all this."

Having been made once or twice before the confidant of the tempestuous romances of Billie's friends, which always seemed to go wrong somewhere in the middle and to die a natural death before arriving at any definite point, George was not particularly interested, except in so far as the letter afforded rather comforting evidence that he was not the only person in the world who was having trouble of the kind. He skimmed through the rest of it, and had just finished when there was a sharp rap at the front door.

"Come in!" called George.

There entered a sturdy little man of middle age whom at first sight George could not place. And yet he had the impression that he had seen him before. Then he recognized him as the gardener to whom he had given the note for Maud that day at the castle. The alteration in the man's costume was what had momentarily baffled George. When they had met in the rose-garden, the other had been arrayed in untidy gardening clothes. Now, presumably in his Sunday suit, it was amusing to observe how almost dapper he had become. Really, you might have passed him in the lane and taken him for some neighbouring squire.

George's heart raced. Your lover is ever optimistic, and he could conceive of no errand that could have brought this man to his cottage unless he was charged with the delivery of a note from Maud. He spared a moment from his happiness to congratulate himself on having picked such an admirable go-between. Here evidently, was one of those trusty old retainers you read about, faithful, willing, discreet, ready to do anything for "the little missy" (bless her heart!). Probably he had danced Maud on his knee in her infancy, and with a dog-like affection had watched her at her childish sports. George beamed at the honest fellow, and felt in his pocket to make sure that a suitable tip lay safely therein.

"Good morning," he said.

"Good morning," replied the man.

A purist might have said he spoke gruffly and without geniality. But that is the beauty of these old retainers. They make a point of deliberately trying to deceive strangers as to the goldenness of their hearts by adopting a forbidding manner. And "Good morning!"

Not "Good morning, sir!" Sturdy independence, you observe, as befits a free man. George closed the door carefully. He glanced into the kitchen. Mrs. Platt was not there. All was well.

"You have brought a note from Lady Maud?"

The honest fellow's rather dour expression seemed to grow a shade bleaker.

"If you are alluding to Lady Maud Marsh, my daughter," he replied frostily, "I have not!"

For the past few days George had been no stranger to shocks, and had indeed come almost to regard them as part of the normal everyday life; but this latest one had a stumbling effect.

"I beg your pardon?" he said.

"So you ought to," replied the earl.

George swallowed once or twice to relieve a curious dryness of the mouth.

"Are you Lord Marshmoreton?"

"I am."

"Good Lord!"

"You seem surprised."

"It's nothing!" muttered George. "At least, you—I mean to say . . . It's only that there's a curious resemblance between you and one of your gardeners at the castle. I—I daresay you have noticed it yourself."

"My hobby is gardening."

Light broke upon George. "Then was it really you—?"

"It was!"

George sat down. "This opens up a new line of thought!" he said.

Lord Marshmoreton remained standing. He shook his head sternly.

"It won't do, Mr. . . . I have never heard your name."

"Bevan," replied George, rather relieved at being able to remember it in the midst of his mental turmoil.

"It won't do, Mr. Bevan. It must stop. I allude to this absurd entanglement between yourself and my daughter. It must stop at once."

It seemed to George that such an entanglement could hardly be said to have begun, but he did not say so.

Lord Marshmoreton resumed his remarks. Lady Caroline had sent him to the cottage to be stern, and his firm resolve to be stern lent his style of speech something of the measured solemnity and careful phrasing of his occasional orations in the House of Lords.

"I have no wish to be unduly hard upon the indiscretions of Youth. Youth is the period of Romance, when the heart rules the head. I myself was once a young man."

"Well, you're practically that now," said George.

"Eh?" cried Lord Marshmoreton, forgetting the thread of his discourse in the shock of pleased surprise.

"You don't look a day over forty."

"Oh, come, come, my boy! . . . I mean, Mr. Bevan."

"You don't honestly."

"I'm forty-eight."

"The Prime of Life."

"And you don't think I look it?"

"You certainly don't."

"Well, well, well! By the way, have you tobacco, my boy. I came without my pouch."

"Just at your elbow. Pretty good stuff. I bought it in the village."

"The same I smoke myself."

"Quite a coincidence."

"Distinctly."

"Match?"

"Thank you, I have one."

George filled his own pipe. The thing was becoming a love-feast.

"What was I saying?" said Lord Marshmoreton, blowing a comfortable cloud. "Oh, yes." He removed his pipe from his mouth with a touch of embarrassment. "Yes, yes, to be sure!"

There was an awkward silence.

"You must see for yourself," said the earl, "how impossible it is."

George shook his head.

"I may be slow at grasping a thing, but I'm bound to say I can't see that."

Lord Marshmoreton recalled some of the things his sister had told him to say. "For one thing, what do we know of you? You are a perfect stranger."

"Well, we're all getting acquainted pretty quick, don't you think? I met your son in Piccadilly and had a long talk with him, and now you are paying me a neighbourly visit."

"This was not intended to be a social call."

"But it has become one."

"And then, that is one point I wish to make, you know. Ours is an old family, I would like to remind you that there were Marshmoretons in Belpher before the War of the Roses."

"There were Bevans in Brooklyn before the B.R.T."

"I beg your pardon?"

"I was only pointing out that I can trace my ancestry a long way. You have to trace things a long way in Brooklyn, if you want to find them."

"I have never heard of Brooklyn."

"You've heard of New York?"

"Certainly."

"New York's one of the outlying suburbs."

Lord Marshmoreton relit his pipe. He had a feeling that they were wandering from the point.

"It is quite impossible."

"I can't see it."

"Maud is so young."

"Your daughter could be nothing else."

"Too young to know her own mind," pursued Lord Marshmoreton, resolutely crushing down a flutter of pleasure. There was no doubt that this singularly agreeable man was making things very difficult for him. It was disarming to discover that he was really capital company—the best, indeed, that the earl could remember to have discovered in the more recent period of his rather lonely life. "At present, of course, she fancies that she is very much in love with you . . . It is absurd!"

"You needn't tell me that," said George. Really, it was only the fact that people seemed to go out of their way to call at his cottage and tell him that Maud loved him that kept him from feeling his cause perfectly hopeless. "It's incredible. It's a miracle."

"You are a romantic young man, and you no doubt for the moment suppose that you are in love with her."

"No!" George was not going to allow a remark like that to pass unchallenged. "You are wrong there. As far as I am concerned, there is no question of its being momentary or supposititious or anything of that kind. I am in love with your daughter. I was from the first moment I saw her. I always shall be. She is the only girl in the world!"

"Stuff and nonsense!"

"Not at all. Absolute, cold fact."

"You have known her so little time."

"Long enough."

Lord Marshmoreton sighed. "You are upsetting things terribly."

"Things are upsetting me terribly."

"You are causing a great deal of trouble and annoyance."

"So did Romeo."

"Eh?"

"I said—So did Romeo."

"I don't know anything about Romeo."

"As far as love is concerned, I begin where he left off."

"I wish I could persuade you to be sensible."

"That's just what I think I am."

"I wish I could get you to see my point of view."

"I do see your point of view. But dimly. You see, my own takes up such a lot of the foreground."

There was a pause.

"Then I am afraid," said Lord Marshmoreton, "that we must leave matters as they stand."

"Until they can be altered for the better."

"We will say no more about it now."

"Very well."

"But I must ask you to understand clearly that I shall have to do everything in my power to stop what I look on as an unfortunate entanglement."

"I understand,"

"Very well."

Lord Marshmoreton coughed. George looked at him with some surprise. He had supposed the interview to be at an end, but the other made no move to go. There seemed to be something on the earl's mind.

"There is—ah—just one other thing," said Lord Marshmoreton. He coughed again. He felt embarrassed. "Just—just one other thing," he repeated.

The reason for Lord Marshmoreton's visit to George had been twofold. In the first place, Lady Caroline had told him to go. That would have been reason enough. But what made the visit imperative was an unfortunate accident of which he had only that morning been made aware.

It will be remembered that Billie Dore had told George that the gardener with whom she had become so friendly had taken her name and address with a view later on to send her some of his roses. The scrap of paper on which this information had been written was now lost. Lord Marshmoreton had been hunting for it since breakfast without avail.

Billie Dore had made a decided impression upon Lord Marshmoreton. She belonged to a type which he had never before encountered, and it was one which he had found more than agreeable. Her knowledge of roses and the proper feeling which she manifested towards rose-growing as a life-work consolidated the earl's liking for her. Never, in his memory, had he come across so sensible and charming a girl; and he had looked forward with a singular intensity to meeting her again. And now some too zealous housemaid, tidying up after the irritating manner of her species, had destroyed the only clue to her identity.

It was not for some time after this discovery that hope dawned again for Lord Marshmoreton. Only after he had given up the search for the missing paper as fruitless did he recall that it was in George's company that Billie had first come into his life. Between her, then, and himself George was the only link.

It was primarily for the purpose of getting Billie's name and address from George that he had come to the cottage. And now that the moment had arrived for touching upon the subject, he felt a little embarrassed.

"When you visited the castle," he said, "when you visited the castle . . ."

"Last Thursday," said George helpfully.

"Exactly. When you visited the castle last Thursday, there was a young lady with you."

Not realizing that the subject had been changed, George was under the impression that the other had shifted his front and was about to attack him from another angle. He countered what seemed to him an insinuation stoutly.

"We merely happened to meet at the castle. She came there quite independently of me."

Lord Marshmoreton looked alarmed. "You didn't know her?" he said anxiously.

"Certainly I knew her. She is an old friend of mine. But if you are hinting . . ."

"Not at all," rejoined the earl, profoundly relieved. "Not at all. I ask merely because this young lady, with whom I had some conversation, was good enough to give me her name and address. She, too, happened to mistake me for a gardener."

"It's those corduroy trousers," murmured George in extenuation.

"I have unfortunately lost them."

"You can always get another pair."

"Eh?"

"I say you can always get another pair of corduroy trousers."

"I have not lost my trousers. I have lost the young lady's name and address."

"Oh!"

"I promised to send her some roses. She will be expecting them."

"That's odd. I was just reading a letter from her when you came in. That must be what she's referring to when she says, 'If you see dadda, the old dear, tell him not to forget my roses.' I read it three times and couldn't make any sense out of it. Are you Dadda?"

The earl smirked. "She did address me in the course of our conversation as dadda."

"Then the message is for you."

"A very quaint and charming girl. What is her name? And where can I find her?"

"Her name's Billie Dore."

"Billie?"

"Billie."

"Billie!" said Lord Marshmoreton softly. "I had better write it down. And her address?"

"I don't know her private address. But you could always reach her at the Regal Theatre."

"Ah! She is on the stage?"

"Yes. She's in my piece, 'Follow the Girl'."

"Indeed! Are you a playwright, Mr. Bevan?"

"Good Lord, no!" said George, shocked. "I'm a composer."

"Very interesting. And you met Miss Dore through her being in this play of yours?"

"Oh, no. I knew her before she went on the stage. She was a stenographer in a music-publisher's office when we first met."

"Good gracious! Was she really a stenographer?"

"Yes. Why?"

"Oh—ah—nothing, nothing. Something just happened to come to my mind."

What happened to come into Lord Marshmoreton's mind was a fleeting vision of Billie installed in Miss Alice Faraday's place as his secretary. With such a helper it would be a pleasure to work on that infernal Family History which was now such a bitter toil. But the day-dream passed. He knew perfectly well that he had not the courage to dismiss Alice. In the hands of that calm-eyed girl he was as putty. She exercised over him the hypnotic spell a lion-tamer exercises over his little playmates.

"We have been pals for years," said George. "Billie is one of the best fellows in the world."

"A charming girl."

"She would give her last nickel to anyone that asked for it."

"Delightful!"

"And as straight as a string. No one ever said a word against Billie."

"No?"

"She may go out to lunch and supper and all that kind of thing, but there's nothing to that."

"Nothing!" agreed the earl warmly. "Girls must eat!"

"They do. You ought to see them."

"A little harmless relaxation after the fatigue of the day!"

"Exactly. Nothing more."

Lord Marshmoreton felt more drawn than ever to this sensible young man—sensible, at least, on all points but one. It was a pity they could not see eye to eye on what was and what was not suitable in the matter of the love-affairs of the aristocracy.

"So you are a composer, Mr. Bevan?" he said affably.

"Yes."

Lord Marshmoreton gave a little sigh. "It's a long time since I went to see a musical performance. More than twenty years. When I was up at Oxford, and for some years afterwards, I was a great theatre-goer. Never used to miss a first night at the Gaiety. Those were the days of Nellie Farren and Kate Vaughan. Florence St. John, too. How excellent she was in Faust Up To Date! But we missed Nellie Farren. Meyer Lutz was the Gaiety composer then. But a good deal of water has flowed under the bridge since those days. I don't suppose you have ever heard of Meyer Lutz?"

"I don't think I have."

"Johnnie Toole was playing a piece called Partners. Not a good play. And the Yeoman of the Guard had just been produced at the Savoy. That makes it seem a long time ago, doesn't it? Well, I mustn't take up all your time. Good-bye, Mr. Bevan. I am glad to have had the opportunity of this little talk. The Regal Theatre, I think you said, is where your piece is playing? I shall probably be going to London shortly. I hope to see it." Lord Marshmoreton rose. "As regards the other matter, there is no hope of inducing you to see the matter in the right light?"

"We seem to disagree as to which is the right light."

"Then there is nothing more to be said. I will be perfectly frank with you, Mr. Bevan. I like you . . ."

"The feeling is quite mutual."

"But I don't want you as a son-in-law. And, dammit," exploded Lord Marshmoreton, "I won't have you as a son-in-law! Good God! do you think that you can harry and assault my son Percy in the heart of Piccadilly and generally make yourself a damned nuisance and then settle down here without an invitation at my very gates and expect to be welcomed into the bosom of the family? If I were a young man . . ."

"I thought we had agreed that you were a young man."

"Don't interrupt me!"

"I only said . . ."

"I heard what you said. Flattery!"

"Nothing of the kind. Truth."

Lord Marshmoreton melted. He smiled. "Young idiot!"

"We agree there all right."

Lord Marshmoreton hesitated. Then with a rush he unbosomed himself, and made his own position on the matter clear.

"I know what you'll be saying to yourself the moment my back is turned. You'll be calling me a stage heavy father and an old snob and a number of other things. Don't interrupt me, dammit! You will, I tell you! And you'll be wrong. I don't think the Marshmoretons are fenced off from the rest of the world by some sort of divinity. My sister does. Percy does. But Percy's an ass! If ever you find yourself thinking differently from my son Percy, on any subject, congratulate yourself. You'll be right."

"But . . ."

"I know what you're going to say. Let me finish. If I were the only person concerned, I wouldn't stand in Maud's way, whoever she wanted to marry, provided he was a good fellow and likely to make her happy. But I'm not. There's my sister Caroline. There's a whole crowd of silly, cackling fools—my sisters—my sons-in-law—all the whole pack of them! If I didn't oppose Maud in this damned infatuation she's got for you—if I stood by and let her marry you—what do you think would happen to me?—I'd never have a moment's peace! The whole gabbling pack of them would be at me, saying I was to blame. There would be arguments, discussions, family councils! I hate arguments! I loathe discussions! Family councils make me sick! I'm a peaceable man, and I like a quiet life! And, damme, I'm going to have it. So there's the thing for you in letters of one syllable. I don't object to you personally, but I'm not going to have you bothering me like this. I'll admit freely that, since I have made your acquaintance, I have altered the unfavourable opinion I had formed of you from—from hearsay. . ."

"Exactly the same with me," said George. "You ought never to believe what people tell you. Everyone told me your middle name was Nero, and that. . ."

"Don't interrupt me!"

"I wasn't. I was just pointing out . . ."

"Be quiet! I say I have changed my opinion of you to a great extent. I mention this unofficially, as a matter that has no bearing on the main issue; for, as regards any idea you may have of inducing me to agree to your marrying my daughter, let me tell you that I am unalterably opposed to any such thing!"

"Don't say that."

"What the devil do you mean—don't say that! I do say that! It is out of the question. Do you understand? Very well, then. Good morning."

The door closed. Lord Marshmoreton walked away feeling that he had been commendably stern. George filled his pipe and sat smoking thoughtfully. He wondered what Maud was doing at that moment.

Maud at that moment was greeting her brother with a bright smile, as he limped downstairs after a belated shave and change of costume.

"Oh, Percy, dear," she was saying, "I had quite an adventure this morning. An awful tramp followed me for miles! Such a horrible-looking brute. I was so frightened that I had to ask a curate in the next village to drive him away. I did wish I had had you there to protect me. Why don't you come out with me sometimes when I take a country walk? It really isn't safe for me to be alone!"

CHAPTER 17.

The gift of hiding private emotion and keeping up appearances before strangers is not, as many suppose, entirely a product of our modern civilization. Centuries before we were born or thought of there was a widely press-agented boy in Sparta who even went so far as to let a fox gnaw his tender young stomach without permitting the discomfort inseparable from such a proceeding to interfere with either his facial expression or his flow of small talk. Historians have handed it down that, even in the later stages of the meal, the polite lad continued to be the life and soul of the party. But, while this feat may be said to have established a record never subsequently lowered, there is no doubt that almost every day in modern times men and women are performing similar and scarcely less impressive miracles of self-restraint. Of all the qualities which belong exclusively to Man and are not shared by the lower animals, this surely is the one which marks him off most sharply from the beasts of the field. Animals care nothing about keeping up appearances. Observe Bertram the Bull when things are not going just as he could wish. He stamps. He snorts. He paws the ground. He throws back his head and bellows. He is upset, and he doesn't care who knows it. Instances could be readily multiplied. Deposit a charge of shot in some outlying section of Thomas the Tiger, and note the effect. Irritate Wilfred the Wasp, or stand behind Maud the Mule and prod her with a pin. There is not an animal on the list who has even a rudimentary sense of the social amenities; and it is this more than anything else which should make us proud that we are human beings on a loftier plane of development.

In the days which followed Lord Marshmoreton's visit to George at the cottage, not a few of the occupants of Belpher Castle had their mettle sternly tested in this respect; and it is a pleasure to be able to record that not one of them failed to come through the ordeal with success. The general public, as represented by the uncles, cousins, and aunts who had descended on the place to help Lord Belpher celebrate his coming-of-age, had not a notion that turmoil lurked behind the smooth fronts of at least half a dozen of those whom they met in the course of the daily round.

Lord Belpher, for example, though he limped rather painfully, showed nothing of the baffled fury which was reducing his weight at the rate of ounces a day. His uncle Francis, the Bishop, when he tackled him in the garden on the subject of Intemperance—for Uncle Francis, like thousands of others, had taken it for granted, on reading the report of the encounter with the policeman and Percy's subsequent arrest, that the affair had been the result of a drunken outburst—had no inkling of the volcanic emotions that seethed in his nephew's bosom. He came away from the interview, indeed, feeling that the boy had listened attentively and with a becoming regret, and that there was hope for him after all, provided that he fought the impulse. He little knew that, but for the conventions (which frown on the practice of murdering bishops), Percy would gladly have strangled him with his bare hands and jumped upon the remains.

Lord Belpher's case, inasmuch as he took himself extremely seriously and was not one of those who can extract humour even from their own misfortunes, was perhaps the hardest which comes under our notice; but his sister Maud was also experiencing mental disquietude of no mean order. Everything had gone wrong with Maud. Barely a mile separated her from George, that essential link in her chain of communication with Geoffrey Raymond; but so thickly did it bristle with obstacles and dangers that it might have been a mile of No Man's Land. Twice, since the occasion when the discovery of Lord Marshmoreton at the cottage had caused her to abandon her purpose of going in and explaining everything to George, had she attempted to make the journey; and each time some trifling, maddening accident had brought about failure. Once, just as she was starting, her aunt Augusta had insisted on joining her for what she described as "a nice long walk"; and the second time, when she was within a bare hundred yards of her objective, some sort of a cousin popped out from nowhere and forced his loathsome company on her.

Foiled in this fashion, she had fallen back in desperation on her second line of attack. She had written a note to George, explaining the whole situation in good, clear phrases and begging him as a man of proved chivalry to help her. It had taken up much of one afternoon, this note, for it was not easy to write; and it had resulted in nothing. She had given it to Albert to deliver and Albert had returned empty-handed.

"The gentleman said there was no answer, m'lady!"

"No answer! But there must be an answer!"

"No answer, m'lady. Those was his very words," stoutly maintained the black-souled boy, who had destroyed the letter within two minutes after it had been handed to him. He had not even bothered to read it. A deep, dangerous, dastardly stripling this, who fought to win and only to win. The ticket marked "R. Byng" was in his pocket, and in his ruthless heart a firm resolve that R. Byng and no other should have the benefit of his assistance.

Maud could not understand it. That is to say, she resolutely kept herself from accepting the only explanation of the episode that seemed possible. In black and white she had asked George to go to London and see Geoffrey and arrange for the passage—through himself as a sort of clearing-house—of letters between Geoffrey and herself. She had felt from the first that such a request should be made by her in person and not through the medium of writing, but surely it was incredible that a man like George, who had been through so much for her and whose only reason for being in the neighbourhood was to help her, could have coldly refused without even a word. And yet what else was she to think? Now, more than ever, she felt alone in a hostile world.

Yet, to her guests she was bright and entertaining. Not one of them had a suspicion that her life was not one of pure sunshine.

Albert, I am happy to say, was thoroughly miserable. The little brute was suffering torments. He was showering anonymous Advice to the Lovelorn on Reggie Byng—excellent stuff, culled from the pages of weekly papers, of which there was a pile in the housekeeper's room, the property of a sentimental lady's maid—and nothing seemed to come of it. Every day, sometimes twice and thrice a day, he would leave on Reggie's dressing-table significant notes similar in tone to the one which he had placed there on the night of the ball; but, for all the effect they appeared to exercise on their recipient, they might have been blank pages.

The choicest quotations from the works of such established writers as "Aunt Charlotte" of Forget-Me-Not and "Doctor Cupid", the heart-expert of Home Chat, expended themselves fruitlessly on Reggie. As far as Albert could ascertain—and he was one of those boys who ascertain practically everything within a radius of miles—Reggie positively avoided Maud's society.

And this after reading "Doctor Cupid's" invaluable tip about "Seeking her company on all occasions" and the dictum of "Aunt Charlotte" to the effect that "Many a wooer has won his lady by being persistent"—Albert spelled it "persistuent" but the effect is the same—"and rendering himself indispensable by constant little attentions". So far from rendering himself indispensable to Maud by constant little attentions, Reggie, to the disgust of his backer and supporter, seemed to spend most of his time with Alice Faraday. On three separate occasions had Albert been revolted by the sight of his protege in close association with the Faraday girl—once in a boat on the lake and twice in his grey car. It was enough to break a boy's heart; and it completely spoiled Albert's appetite—a phenomenon attributed, I am glad to say, in the Servants' Hall to reaction from recent excesses. The moment when Keggs, the butler, called him a greedy little pig and hoped it would be a lesson to him not to stuff himself at all hours with stolen cakes was a bitter moment for Albert.

It is a relief to turn from the contemplation of these tortured souls to the pleasanter picture presented by Lord Marshmoreton. Here, undeniably, we have a man without a secret sorrow, a man at peace with this best of all possible worlds. Since his visit to George a second youth seems to have come upon Lord Marshmoreton. He works in his rose-garden with a new vim, whistling or even singing to himself stray gay snatches of melodies popular in the 'eighties.

Hear him now as he toils. He has a long garden-implement in his hand, and he is sending up the death-rate in slug circles with a devastating rapidity.

"Ta-ra-ra boom-de-ay

Ta-ra-ra BOOM—"

And the boom is a death-knell. As it rings softly out on the pleasant spring air, another stout slug has made the Great Change.

It is peculiar, this gaiety. It gives one to think. Others have noticed it, his lordship's valet amongst them.

"I give you my honest word, Mr. Keggs," says the valet, awed, "this very morning I 'eard the old devil a-singing in 'is barth! Chirruping away like a blooming linnet!"

"Lor!" says Keggs, properly impressed.

"And only last night 'e gave me 'arf a box of cigars and said I was a good, faithful feller! I tell you, there's somethin' happened to the old buster—you mark my words!"

CHAPTER 18.

Over this complex situation the mind of Keggs, the butler, played like a searchlight. Keggs was a man of discernment and sagacity. He had instinct and reasoning power. Instinct told him that Maud, all unsuspecting the change that had taken place in Albert's attitude toward her romance, would have continued to use the boy as a link between herself and George: and reason, added to an intimate knowledge of Albert, enabled him to see that the latter must inevitably have betrayed her trust. He was prepared to bet a hundred pounds that Albert had been given letters to deliver and had destroyed them. So much was clear to Keggs. It only remained to settle on some plan of action which would re-establish the broken connection. Keggs did not conceal a tender heart beneath a rugged exterior: he did not mourn over the picture of two loving fellow human beings separated by a misunderstanding; but he did want to win that sweepstake.

His position, of course, was delicate. He could not go to Maud and beg her to confide in him. Maud would not understand his motives, and might leap to the not unjustifiable conclusion that he had been at the sherry. No! Men were easier to handle than women. As soon as his duties would permit—and in the present crowded condition of the house they were arduous—he set out for George's cottage.

"I trust I do not disturb or interrupt you, sir," he said, beaming in the doorway like a benevolent high priest. He had doffed his professional manner of austere disapproval, as was his custom in moments of leisure.

"Not at all," replied George, puzzled. "Was there anything . . .?"

"There was, sir."

"Come along in and sit down."

"I would not take the liberty, if it is all the same to you, sir. I would prefer to remain standing."

There was a moment of uncomfortable silence. Uncomfortable, that is to say, on the part of George, who was wondering if the butler remembered having engaged him as a waiter only a few nights back. Keggs himself was at his ease. Few things ruffled this man.

"Fine day," said George.

"Extremely, sir, but for the rain."

"Oh, is it raining?"

"Sharp downpour, sir."

"Good for the crops," said George.

"So one would be disposed to imagine, sir."

Silence fell again. The rain dripped from the eaves.

"If I might speak freely, sir . . .?" said Keggs.

"Sure. Shoot!"

"I beg your pardon, sir?"

"I mean, yes. Go ahead!"

The butler cleared his throat.

"Might I begin by remarking that your little affair of the 'eart, if I may use the expression, is no secret in the Servants' 'All? I 'ave no wish to seem to be taking a liberty or presuming, but I should like to intimate that the Servants' 'All is aware of the facts."

"You don't have to tell me that," said George coldly. "I know all about the sweepstake."

A flicker of embarrassment passed over the butler's large, smooth face—passed, and was gone.

"I did not know that you 'ad been apprised of that little matter, sir. But you will doubtless understand and appreciate our point of view. A little sporting flutter—nothing more—designed to halleviate the monotony of life in the country."

"Oh, don't apologize," said George, and was reminded of a point which had exercised him a little from time to time since his vigil on the balcony. "By the way, if it isn't giving away secrets, who drew Plummer?"

"Sir?"

"Which of you drew a man named Plummer in the sweep?"

"I rather fancy, sir," Keggs' brow wrinkled in thought, "I rather fancy it was one of the visiting gentlemen's gentlemen. I gave the point but slight attention at the time. I did not fancy Mr. Plummer's chances. It seemed to me that Mr. Plummer was a negligible quantity."

"Your knowledge of form was sound. Plummer's out!"

"Indeed, sir! An amiable young gentleman, but lacking in many of the essential qualities. Perhaps he struck you that way, sir?"

"I never met him. Nearly, but not quite!"

"It entered my mind that you might possibly have encountered Mr. Plummer on the night of the ball, sir."

"Ah, I was wondering if you remembered me!"

"I remember you perfectly, sir, and it was the fact that we had already met in what one might almost term a social way that emboldened me to come 'ere today and offer you my services as a hintermediary, should you feel disposed to avail yourself of them."

George was puzzled.

"Your services?"

"Precisely, sir. I fancy I am in a position to lend you what might be termed an 'elping 'and."

"But that's remarkably altruistic of you, isn't it?"

"Sir?"

"I say that is very generous of you. Aren't you forgetting that you drew Mr. Byng?"

The butler smiled indulgently.

"You are not quite abreast of the progress of events, sir. Since the original drawing of names, there 'as been a trifling hadjustment. The boy Albert now 'as Mr. Byng and I 'ave you, sir. A little amicable arrangement informally conducted in the scullery on the night of the ball."

"Amicable?"

"On my part, entirely so."

George began to understand certain things that had been perplexing to him.

"Then all this while. . .?"

"Precisely, sir. All this while 'er ladyship, under the impression that the boy Albert was devoted to 'er cause, has no doubt been placing a misguided confidence in 'im . . . The little blighter!" said Keggs, abandoning for a moment his company manners and permitting vehemence to take the place of polish. "I beg your pardon for the expression, sir," he added gracefully. "It escaped me inadvertently."

"You think that Lady Maud gave Albert a letter to give to me, and that he destroyed it?"

"Such, I should imagine, must undoubtedly have been the case. The boy 'as no scruples, no scruples whatsoever."

"Good Lord!"

"I appreciate your consternation, sir."

"That must be exactly what has happened."

"To my way of thinking there is no doubt of it. It was for that reason that I ventured to come 'ere. In the 'ope that I might be hinstrumental in arranging a meeting."

The strong distaste which George had had for plotting with this overfed menial began to wane. It might be undignified, he told himself but it was undeniably practical. And, after all, a man who has plotted with page-boys has little dignity to lose by plotting with butlers.

He brightened up. If it meant seeing Maud again he was prepared to waive the decencies.

"What do you suggest?" he said.

"It being a rainy evening and everyone indoors playing games and what not,"—Keggs was amiably tolerant of the recreations of the aristocracy—"you would experience little chance of a hinterruption, were you to proceed to the lane outside the heast entrance of the castle grounds and wait there. You will find in the field at the roadside a small disused barn only a short way from the gates, where you would be sheltered from the rain. In the meantime, I would hinform 'er ladyship of your movements, and no doubt it would be possible for 'er to slip off."

"It sounds all right."

"It is all right, sir. The chances of a hinterruption may be said to be reduced to a minimum. Shall we say in one hour's time?"

"Very well."

"Then I will wish you good evening, sir. Thank you, sir. I am glad to 'ave been of assistance."

He withdrew as he had come, with a large impressiveness. The room seemed very empty without him. George, with trembling fingers, began to put on a pair of thick boots.

For some minutes after he had set foot outside the door of the cottage, George was inclined to revile the weather for having played him false. On this evening of all evenings, he felt, the elements should, so to speak, have rallied round and done their bit. The air should have been soft and clear and scented: there should have been an afterglow of sunset in the sky to light him on his way. Instead, the air was full of that peculiar smell of hopeless dampness which comes at the end of a wet English day. The sky was leaden. The rain hissed down in a steady flow, whispering of mud and desolation, making a dreary morass of the lane through which he tramped. A curious sense of foreboding came upon George. It was as if some voice of the night had murmured maliciously in his ear a hint of troubles to come. He felt oddly nervous, as he entered the barn.

The barn was both dark and dismal. In one of the dark corners an intermittent dripping betrayed the presence of a gap in its ancient roof. A rat scurried across the floor. The dripping stopped and began again. George struck a match and looked at his watch. He was early. Another ten minutes must elapse before he could hope for her arrival. He sat down on a broken wagon which lay on its side against one of the walls.

Depression returned. It was impossible to fight against it in this beast of a barn. The place was like a sepulchre. No one but a fool of a butler would have suggested it as a trysting-place. He wondered irritably why places like this were allowed to get into this condition. If people wanted a barn earnestly enough to take the trouble of building one, why was it not worth while to keep the thing in proper repair? Waste and futility! That was what it was. That was what everything was, if you came down to it. Sitting here, for instance, was a futile waste of time. She wouldn't come. There were a dozen reasons why she should not come. So what was the use of his courting rheumatism by waiting in this morgue of dead agricultural ambitions? None whatever—George went on waiting.

And what an awful place to expect her to come to, if by some miracle she did come—where she would be stifled by the smell of mouldy hay, damped by raindrops and—reflected George gloomily as there was another scurry and scutter along the unseen floor—gnawed by rats. You could not expect a delicately-nurtured girl, accustomed to all the comforts of a home, to be bright and sunny with a platoon of rats crawling all over her. . . .

The grey oblong that was the doorway suddenly darkened.

"Mr. Bevan!"

George sprang up. At the sound of her voice every nerve in his body danced in mad exhilaration. He was another man. Depression fell from him like a garment. He perceived that he had misjudged all sorts of things. The evening, for instance, was a splendid evening—not one of those awful dry, baking evenings which make you feel you can't breathe, but pleasantly moist and full of a delightfully musical patter of rain. And the barn! He had been all wrong about the barn. It was a great little place, comfortable, airy, and cheerful. What could be more invigorating than that smell of hay? Even the rats, he felt, must be pretty decent rats, when you came to know them.

"I'm here!"

Maud advanced quickly. His eyes had grown accustomed to the murk, and he could see her dimly. The smell of her damp raincoat came to him like a breath of ozone. He could even see her eyes shining in the darkness, so close was she to him.

"I hope you've not been waiting long?"

George's heart was thundering against his ribs. He could scarcely speak. He contrived to emit a No.

"I didn't think at first I could get away. I had to . . ." She broke off with a cry. The rat, fond of exercise like all rats, had made another of its excitable sprints across the floor.

A hand clutched nervously at George's arm, found it and held it. And at the touch the last small fragment of George's self-control fled from him. The world became vague and unreal. There remained of it but one solid fact—the fact that Maud was in his arms and that he was saying a number of things very rapidly in a voice that seemed to belong to somebody he had never met before.

CHAPTER 19.

With a shock of dismay so abrupt and overwhelming that it was like a physical injury, George became aware that something was wrong. Even as he gripped her, Maud had stiffened with a sharp cry; and now she was struggling, trying to wrench herself free. She broke away from him. He could hear her breathing hard.

"You—you——" She gulped.

"Maud!"

"How dare you!"

There was a pause that seemed to George to stretch on and on endlessly. The rain pattered on the leaky roof. Somewhere in the distance a dog howled dismally. The darkness pressed down like a blanket, stifling thought.

"Good night, Mr. Bevan." Her voice was ice. "I didn't think you were—that kind of man."

She was moving toward the door; and, as she reached it, George's stupor left him. He came back to life with a jerk, shaking from head to foot. All his varied emotions had become one emotion—a cold fury.

"Stop!"

Maud stopped. Her chin was tilted, and she was wasting a baleful glare on the darkness.

"Well, what is it?"

Her tone increased George's wrath. The injustice of it made him dizzy. At that moment he hated her. He was the injured party. It was he, not she, that had been deceived and made a fool of.

"I want to say something before you go."

"I think we had better say no more about it!"

By the exercise of supreme self-control George kept himself from speaking until he could choose milder words than those that rushed to his lips.

"I think we will!" he said between his teeth.

Maud's anger became tinged with surprise. Now that the first shock of the wretched episode was over, the calmer half of her mind was endeavouring to soothe the infuriated half by urging that George's behaviour had been but a momentary lapse, and that a man may lose his head for one wild instant, and yet remain fundamentally a gentleman and a friend. She had begun to remind herself that this man had helped her once in trouble, and only a day or two before had actually risked his life to save her from embarrassment. When she heard him call to her to stop, she supposed that his better feelings had reasserted themselves; and she had prepared herself to receive with dignity a broken, stammered apology. But the voice that had just spoken with a crisp, biting intensity was not the voice of remorse. It was a very angry man, not a penitent one, who was commanding—not begging—her to stop and listen to him.

"Well?" she said again, more coldly this time. She was quite unable to understand this attitude of his. She was the injured party. It was she, not he who had trusted and been betrayed.

"I should like to explain."

"Please do not apologize."

George ground his teeth in the gloom.

"I haven't the slightest intention of apologizing. I said I would like to explain. When I have finished explaining, you can go."

"I shall go when I please," flared Maud.

This man was intolerable.

"There is nothing to be afraid of. There will be no repetition of the—incident."

Maud was outraged by this monstrous misinterpretation of her words.

"I am not afraid!"

"Then, perhaps, you will be kind enough to listen. I won't detain you long. My explanation is quite simple. I have been made a fool of. I seem to be in the position of the tinker in the play whom everybody conspired to delude into the belief that he was a king. First a friend of yours, Mr. Byng, came to me and told me that you had confided to him that you loved me."

Maud gasped. Either this man was mad, or Reggie Byng was. She choose the politer solution.

"Reggie Byng must have lost his senses."

"So I supposed. At least, I imagined that he must be mistaken. But a man in love is an optimistic fool, of course, and I had loved you ever since you got into my cab that morning . . ."

"What!"

"So after a while," proceeded George, ignoring the interruption, "I almost persuaded myself that miracles could still happen, and that what Byng said was true. And when your father called on me and told me the very same thing I was convinced. It seemed incredible, but I had to believe it. Now it seems that, for some inscrutable reason, both Byng and your father were making a fool of me. That's all. Good night."

Maud's reply was the last which George or any man would have expected. There was a moment's silence, and then she burst into a peal of laughter. It was the laughter of over-strained nerves, but to George's ears it had the ring of genuine amusement.

"I'm glad you find my story entertaining," he said dryly. He was convinced now that he loathed this girl, and that all he desired was to see her go out of his life for ever. "Later, no doubt, the funny side of it will hit me. Just at present my sense of humour is rather dormant."

Maud gave a little cry.

"I'm sorry! I'm so sorry, Mr. Bevan. It wasn't that. It wasn't that at all. Oh, I am so sorry. I don't know why I laughed. It certainly wasn't because I thought it funny. It's tragic. There's been a dreadful mistake!"

"I noticed that," said George bitterly. The darkness began to afflict his nerves. "I wish to God we had some light."

The glare of a pocket-torch smote upon him.

"I brought it to see my way back with," said Maud in a curious, small voice. "It's very dark across the fields. I didn't light it before, because I was afraid somebody might see."

She came towards him, holding the torch over her head. The beam showed her face, troubled and sympathetic, and at the sight all George's resentment left him. There were mysteries here beyond his unravelling, but of one thing he was certain: this girl was not to blame. She was a thoroughbred, as straight as a wand. She was pure gold.

"I came here to tell you everything," she said. She placed the torch on the wagon-wheel so that its ray fell in a pool of light on the ground between them. "I'll do it now. Only—only it isn't so easy now. Mr. Bevan, there's a man—there's a man that father and Reggie Byng mistook—they thought . . . You see, they knew it was you that I was with that day in the cab, and so they naturally thought, when you came down here, that you were the man I had gone to meet that day—the man I—I—"

"The man you love."

"Yes," said Maud in a small voice; and there was silence again.

George could feel nothing but sympathy. It mastered other emotion in him, even the grey despair that had come her words. He could feel all that she was feeling.

"Tell me all about it," he said.

"I met him in Wales last year." Maud's voice was a whisper. "The family found out, and I was hurried back here, and have been here ever since. That day when I met you I had managed to slip away from home. I had found out that he was in London, and I was going to meet him. Then I saw Percy, and got into your cab. It's all been a horrible mistake. I'm sorry."

"I see," said George thoughtfully. "I see."

His heart ached like a living wound. She had told so little, and he could guess so much. This unknown man who had triumphed seemed to sneer scornfully at him from the shadows.

"I'm sorry," said Maud again.

"You mustn't feel like that. How can I help you? That's the point. What is it you want me to do?"

"But I can't ask you now."

"Of course you can. Why not?"

"Why—oh, I couldn't!"

George managed to laugh. It was a laugh that did not sound convincing even to himself, but it served.

"That's morbid," he said. "Be sensible. You need help, and I may be able to give it. Surely a man isn't barred for ever from doing you a service just because he happens to love you? Suppose you were drowning and Mr. Plummer was the only swimmer within call, wouldn't you let him rescue you?"

"Mr. Plummer? What do you mean?"

"You've not forgotten that I was a reluctant ear-witness to his recent proposal of marriage?"

Maud uttered an exclamation.

"I never asked! How terrible of me. Were you much hurt?"

"Hurt?" George could not follow her.

"That night. When you were on the balcony, and—"

"Oh!" George understood. "Oh, no, hardly at all. A few scratches. I scraped my hands a little."

"It was a wonderful thing to do," said Maud, her admiration glowing for a man who could treat such a leap so lightly. She had always had a private theory that Lord Leonard, after performing the same feat, had bragged about it for the rest of his life.

"No, no, nothing," said George, who had since wondered why he had ever made such a to-do about climbing up a perfectly stout sheet.

"It was splendid!"

George blushed.

"We are wandering from the main theme," he said. "I want to help you. I came here at enormous expense to help you. How can I do it?"

Maud hesitated.

"I think you may be offended at my asking such a thing."

"You needn't."

"You see, the whole trouble is that I can't get in touch with Geoffrey. He's in London, and I'm here. And any chance I might have of getting to London vanished that day I met you, when Percy saw me in Piccadilly."

"How did your people find out it was you?"

"They asked me—straight out."

"And you owned up?"

"I had to. I couldn't tell them a direct lie."

George thrilled. This was the girl he had had doubts of.

"So than it was worse then ever," continued Maud. "I daren't risk writing to Geoffrey and having the letter intercepted. I was wondering—I had the idea almost as soon as I found that you had come here—"

"You want me to take a letter from you and see that it reaches him. And then he can write back to my address, and I can smuggle the letter to you?"

"That's exactly what I do want. But I almost didn't like to ask."

"Why not? I'll be delighted to do it."

"I'm so grateful."

"Why, it's nothing. I thought you were going to ask me to look in on your brother and smash another of his hats."

Maud laughed delightedly. The whole tension of the situation had been eased for her. More and more she found herself liking George. Yet, deep down in her, she realized with a pang that for him there had been no easing of the situation. She was sad for George. The Plummers of this world she had consigned to what they declared would be perpetual sorrow with scarcely a twinge of regret. But George was different.

"Poor Percy!" she said. "I don't suppose he'll ever get over it. He will have other hats, but it won't be the same." She came back to the subject nearest her heart. "Mr. Bevan, I wonder if you would do just a little more for me?"

"If it isn't criminal. Or, for that matter, if it is."

"Could you go to Geoffrey, and see him, and tell him all about me and—and come back and tell me how he looks, and what he said and—and so on?"

"Certainly. What is his name, and where do I find him?"

"I never told you. How stupid of me. His name is Geoffrey Raymond, and he lives with his uncle, Mr. Wilbur Raymond, at 11a, Belgrave Square."

"I'll go to him tomorrow."

"Thank you ever so much."

George got up. The movement seemed to put him in touch with the outer world. He noticed that the rain had stopped, and that stars had climbed into the oblong of the doorway. He had an impression that he had been in the barn a very long time; and confirmed this with a glance at his watch, though the watch, he felt, understated the facts by the length of several centuries. He was abstaining from too close an examination of his emotions from a prudent feeling that he was going to suffer soon enough without assistance from himself.

"I think you had better be going back," he said. "It's rather late. They may be missing you."

Maud laughed happily.

"I don't mind now what they do. But I suppose dinners must be dressed for, whatever happens." They moved together to the door. "What a lovely night after all! I never thought the rain would stop in this world. It's like when you're unhappy and think it's going on for ever."

"Yes," said George.

Maud held out her hand.

"Good night, Mr. Bevan."

"Good night."

He wondered if there would be any allusion to the earlier passages of their interview. There was none. Maud was of the class whose education consists mainly of a training in the delicate ignoring of delicate situations.

"Then you will go and see Geoffrey?"

"Tomorrow."

"Thank you ever so much."

"Not at all."

George admired her. The little touch of formality which she had contrived to impart to the conversation struck just the right note, created just the atmosphere which would enable them to part without weighing too heavily on the deeper aspect of that parting.

"You're a real friend, Mr. Bevan."

"Watch me prove it."

"Well, I must rush, I suppose. Good night!"

"Good night!"

She moved off quickly across the field. Darkness covered her. The dog in the distance had begun to howl again. He had his troubles, too.

CHAPTER 20.

Trouble sharpens the vision. In our moments of distress, we can see clearly that what is wrong with this world of ours is the fact that Misery loves company and seldom gets it. Toothache is an unpleasant ailment; but, if toothache were a natural condition of life, if all mankind were afflicted with toothache at birth, we should not notice it. It is the freedom from aching teeth of all those with whom we come in contact that emphasizes the agony. And, as with toothache, so with trouble. Until our private affairs go wrong, we never realize how bubbling over with happiness the bulk of mankind seems to be. Our aching heart is apparently nothing but a desert island in an ocean of joy.

George, waking next morning with a heavy heart, made this discovery before the day was an hour old. The sun was shining, and birds sang merrily, but this did not disturb him. Nature is ever callous to human woes, laughing while we weep; and we grow to take her callousness for granted. What jarred upon George was the infernal cheerfulness of his fellow men. They seemed to be doing it on purpose—triumphing over him—glorying in the fact that, however Fate might have shattered him, they were all right.

People were happy who had never been happy before. Mrs. Platt, for instance. A grey, depressed woman of middle age, she had seemed hitherto to have few pleasures beyond breaking dishes and relating the symptoms of sick neighbours who were not expected to live through the week. She now sang. George could hear her as she prepared his breakfast in the kitchen. At first he had had a hope that she was moaning with pain; but this was dispelled when he had finished his toilet and proceeded downstairs. The sounds she emitted suggested anguish, but the words, when he was able to distinguish them, told another story. Incredible as it might seem, on this particular morning Mrs. Platt had elected to be light-hearted. What she was singing sounded like a dirge, but actually it was "Stop your tickling, Jock!" And, later, when she brought George his coffee and eggs, she spent a full ten minutes prattling as he tried to read his paper, pointing out to him a number of merry murders and sprightly suicides which otherwise he might have missed. The woman went out of her way to show him that for her, if not for less fortunate people, God this morning was in His heaven and all was right in the world.

Two tramps of supernatural exuberance called at the cottage shortly after breakfast to ask George, whom they had never even consulted about their marriages, to help support their wives and children. Nothing could have been more care-free and debonnaire than the demeanour of these men.

And then Reggie Byng arrived in his grey racing car, more cheerful than any of them.

Fate could not have mocked George more subtly. A sorrow's crown of sorrow is remembering happier things, and the sight of Reggie in that room reminded him that on the last occasion when they had talked together across this same table it was he who had been in a Fool's Paradise and Reggie who had borne a weight of care. Reggie this morning was brighter than the shining sun and gayer than the carolling birds.

"Hullo-ullo-ullo-ullo-ullo-ullo-ul-lo! Topping morning, isn't it!" observed Reggie. "The sunshine! The birds! The absolute what-do-you-call-it of everything and so forth, and all that sort of thing, if you know what I mean! I feel like a two-year-old!"

George, who felt older than this by some ninety-eight years, groaned in spirit. This was more than man was meant to bear.

"I say," continued Reggie, absently reaching out for a slice of bread and smearing it with marmalade, "this business of marriage, now, and all that species of rot! What I mean to say is, what about it? Not a bad scheme, taking it by and large? Or don't you think so?"

George writhed. The knife twisted in the wound. Surely it was bad enough to see a happy man eating bread and marmalade without having to listen to him talking about marriage.

"Well, anyhow, be that as it may," said Reggie, biting jovially and speaking in a thick but joyous voice. "I'm getting married today, and chance it. This morning, this very morning, I leap off the dock!"

George was startled out of his despondency.

"What!"

"Absolutely, laddie!"

George remembered the conventions.

"I congratulate you."

"Thanks, old man. And not without reason. I'm the luckiest fellow alive. I hardly knew I was alive till now."

"Isn't this rather sudden?"

Reggie looked a trifle furtive. His manner became that of a conspirator.

"I should jolly well say it is sudden! It's got to be sudden. Dashed sudden and deuced secret! If the mater were to hear of it, there's no doubt whatever she would form a flying wedge and bust up the proceedings with no uncertain voice. You see, laddie, it's Miss Faraday I'm marrying, and the mater—dear old soul—has other ideas for Reginald. Life's a rummy thing, isn't it! What I mean to say is, it's rummy, don't you know, and all that."

"Very," agreed George.

"Who'd have thought, a week ago, that I'd be sitting in this jolly old chair asking you to be my best man? Why, a week ago I didn't know you, and, if anybody had told me Alice Faraday was going to marry me, I'd have given one of those hollow, mirthless laughs."

"Do you want me to be your best man?"

"Absolutely, if you don't mind. You see," said Reggie confidentially, "it's like this. I've got lots of pals, of course, buzzing about all over London and its outskirts, who'd be glad enough to rally round and join the execution-squad; but you know how it is. Their maters are all pals of my mater, and I don't want to get them into trouble for aiding and abetting my little show, if you understand what I mean. Now, you're different. You don't know the mater, so it doesn't matter to you if she rolls around and puts the Curse of the Byngs on you, and all that sort of thing. Besides, I don't know." Reggie mused. "Of course, this is the happiest day of my life," he proceeded, "and I'm not saying it isn't, but you know how it is—there's absolutely no doubt that a chappie does not show at his best when he's being married. What I mean to say is, he's more or less bound to look a fearful ass. And I'm perfectly certain it would put me right off my stroke if I felt that some chump like Jack Ferris or Ronnie Fitzgerald was trying not to giggle in the background. So, if you will be a sportsman and come and hold my hand till the thing's over, I shall be eternally grateful."

"Where are you going to be married?"

"In London. Alice sneaked off there last night. It was easy, as it happened, because by a bit of luck old Marshmoreton had gone to town yesterday morning—nobody knows why: he doesn't go up to London more than a couple of times a year. She's going to meet me at the Savoy, and then the scheme was to toddle round to the nearest registrar and request the lad to unleash the marriage service. I'm whizzing up in the car, and I'm hoping to be able to persuade you to come with me. Say the word, laddie!"

George reflected. He liked Reggie, and there was no particular reason in the world why he should not give him aid and comfort in this crisis. True, in his present frame of mind, it would be torture to witness a wedding ceremony; but he ought not to let that stand in the way of helping a friend.

"All right," he said.

"Stout fellow! I don't know how to thank you. It isn't putting you out or upsetting your plans, I hope, or anything on those lines?"

"Not at all. I had to go up to London today, anyway."

"Well, you can't get there quicker than in my car. She's a hummer. By the way, I forgot to ask. How is your little affair coming along? Everything going all right?"

"In a way," said George. He was not equal to confiding his troubles to Reggie.

"Of course, your trouble isn't like mine was. What I mean is, Maud loves you, and all that, and all you've got to think out is a scheme for laying the jolly old family a stymie. It's a pity—almost—that yours isn't a case of having to win the girl, like me; because by Jove, laddie," said Reggie with solemn emphasis, "I could help you there. I've got the thing down fine. I've got the infallible dope."

George smiled bleakly.

"You have? You're a useful fellow to have around. I wish you would tell me what it is."

"But you don't need it."

"No, of course not. I was forgetting."

Reggie looked at his watch.

"We ought to be shifting in a quarter of an hour or so. I don't want to be late. It appears that there's a catch of some sort in this business of getting married. As far as I can make out, if you roll in after a certain hour, the Johnnie in charge of the proceedings gives you the miss-in-baulk, and you have to turn up again next day. However, we shall be all right unless we have a breakdown, and there's not much chance of that. I've been tuning up the old car since seven this morning, and she's sound in wind and limb, absolutely. Oil—petrol—water—air—nuts—bolts—sprockets— carburetor—all present and correct. I've been looking after them like a lot of baby sisters. Well, as I was saying, I've got the dope. A week ago I was just one of the mugs—didn't know a thing about it—but now! Gaze on me, laddie! You see before you old Colonel Romeo, the Man who Knows! It all started on the night of the ball. There was the dickens of a big ball, you know, to celebrate old Boots' coming-of-age—to which, poor devil, he contributed nothing but the sunshine of his smile, never having learned to dance. On that occasion a most rummy and extraordinary thing happened. I got pickled to the eyebrows!" He laughed happily. "I don't mean that that was a unique occurrence and so forth, because, when I was a bachelor, it was rather a habit of mine to get a trifle submerged every now and again on occasions of decent mirth and festivity. But the rummy thing that night was that I showed it. Up till then, I've been told by experts, I was a chappie in whom it was absolutely impossible to detect the symptoms. You might get a bit suspicious if you found I couldn't move, but you could never be certain. On the night of the ball, however, I suppose I had been filling the radiator a trifle too enthusiastically. You see, I had deliberately tried to shove myself more or less below the surface in order to get enough nerve to propose to Alice. I don't know what your experience has been, but mine is that proposing's a thing that simply isn't within the scope of a man who isn't moderately woozled. I've often wondered how marriages ever occur in the dry States of America. Well, as I was saying, on the night of the ball a most rummy thing happened. I thought one of the waiters was you!"

He paused impressively to allow this startling statement to sink in.

"And was he?" said George.

"Absolutely not! That was the rummy part of it. He looked as like you as your twin brother."

"I haven't a twin brother."

"No, I know what you mean, but what I mean to say is he looked just like your twin brother would have looked if you had had a twin brother. Well, I had a word or two with this chappie, and after a brief conversation it was borne in upon me that I was up to the gills. Alice was with me at the time, and noticed it too. Now you'd have thought that that would have put a girl off a fellow, and all that. But no. Nobody could have been more sympathetic. And she has confided to me since that it was seeing me in my oiled condition that really turned the scale. What I mean is, she made up her mind to save me from myself. You know how some girls are. Angels absolutely! Always on the look out to pluck brands from the burning, and what not. You may take it from me that the good seed was definitely sown that night."

"Is that your recipe, then? You would advise the would-be bridegroom to buy a case of champagne and a wedding licence and get to work? After that it would be all over except sending out the invitations?"

Reggie shook his head.

"Not at all. You need a lot more than that. That's only the start. You've got to follow up the good work, you see. That's where a number of chappies would slip up, and I'm pretty certain I should have slipped up myself, but for another singularly rummy occurrence. Have you ever had a what-do-you-call it? What's the word I want? One of those things fellows get sometimes."

"Headaches?" hazarded George.

"No, no. Nothing like that. I don't mean anything you get—I mean something you get, if you know what I mean."

"Measles?"

"Anonymous letter. That's what I was trying to say. It's a most extraordinary thing, and I can't understand even now where the deuce they came from, but just about then I started to get a whole bunch of anonymous letters from some chappie unknown who didn't sign his name."

"What you mean is that the letters were anonymous," said George.

"Absolutely. I used to get two or three a day sometimes. Whenever I went up to my room, I'd find another waiting for me on the dressing-table."

"Offensive?"

"Eh?"

"Were the letters offensive? Anonymous letters usually are."

"These weren't. Not at all, and quite the reverse. They contained a series of perfectly topping tips on how a fellow should proceed who wants to get hold of a girl."

"It sounds as though somebody had been teaching you ju-jitsu by post."

"They were great! Real red-hot stuff straight from the stable. Priceless tips like 'Make yourself indispensable to her in little ways', 'Study her tastes', and so on and so forth. I tell you, laddie, I pretty soon stopped worrying about who was sending them to me, and concentrated the old bean on acting on them. They worked like magic. The last one came yesterday morning, and it was a topper! It was all about how a chappie who was nervous should proceed. Technical stuff, you know, about holding her hand and telling her you're lonely and being sincere and straightforward and letting your heart dictate the rest. Have you ever asked for one card when you wanted to fill a royal flush and happened to pick out the necessary ace? I did once, when I was up at Oxford, and, by Jove, this letter gave me just the same thrill. I didn't hesitate. I just sailed in. I was cold sober, but I didn't worry about that. Something told me I couldn't lose. It was like having to hole out a three-inch putt. And—well, there you are, don't you know." Reggie became thoughtful. "Dash it all! I'd like to know who the fellow was who sent me those letters. I'd like to send him a wedding-present or a bit of the cake or something. Though I suppose there won't be any cake, seeing the thing's taking place at a registrar's."

"You could buy a bun," suggested George.

"Well, I shall never know, I suppose. And now how about trickling forth? I say, laddie, you don't object if I sing slightly from time to time during the journey? I'm so dashed happy, you know."

"Not at all, if it's not against the traffic regulations."

Reggie wandered aimlessly about the room in an ecstasy.

"It's a rummy thing," he said meditatively, "I've just remembered that, when I was at school, I used to sing a thing called the what's-it's-name's wedding song. At house-suppers, don't you know, and what not. Jolly little thing. I daresay you know it. It starts 'Ding dong! Ding dong!' or words to that effect, 'Hurry along! For it is my wedding-morning!' I remember you had to stretch out the 'mor' a bit. Deuced awkward, if you hadn't laid in enough breath. 'The Yeoman's Wedding-Song.' That was it. I knew it was some chappie or other's. And it went on 'And the bride in something or other is doing something I can't recollect.' Well, what I mean is, now it's my wedding-morning! Rummy, when you come to think of it, what? Well, as it's getting tolerable late, what about it? Shift ho?"

"I'm ready. Would you like me to bring some rice?"

"Thank you, laddie, no. Dashed dangerous stuff, rice! Worse than shrapnel. Got your hat? All set?"

"I'm waiting."

"Then let the revels commence," said Reggie. "Ding dong! Ding

Dong! Hurry along! For it is my wedding-morning! And the bride—

Dash it, I wish I could remember what the bride was doing!"

"Probably writing you a note to say that she's changed her mind, and it's all off."

"Oh, my God!" exclaimed Reggie. "Come on!"

CHAPTER 21.

Mr. and Mrs. Reginald Byng, seated at a table in the corner of the Regent Grill-Room, gazed fondly into each other's eyes. George, seated at the same table, but feeling many miles away, watched them moodily, fighting to hold off a depression which, cured for a while by the exhilaration of the ride in Reggie's racing-car (it had beaten its previous record for the trip to London by nearly twenty minutes), now threatened to return. The gay scene, the ecstasy of Reggie, the more restrained but equally manifest happiness of his bride—these things induced melancholy in George. He had not wished to attend the wedding-lunch, but the happy pair seemed to be revolted at the idea that he should stroll off and get a bite to eat somewhere else.

"Stick by us, laddie," Reggie had said pleadingly, "for there is much to discuss, and we need the counsel of a man of the world. We are married all right—"

"Though it didn't seem legal in that little registrar's office," put in Alice.

"—But that, as the blighters say in books, is but a beginning, not an end. We have now to think out the most tactful way of letting the news seep through, as it were, to the mater."

"And Lord Marshmoreton," said Alice. "Don't forget he has lost his secretary."

"And Lord Marshmoreton," amended Reggie. "And about a million other people who'll be most frightfully peeved at my doing the Wedding Glide without consulting them. Stick by us, old top. Join our simple meal. And over the old coronas we will discuss many things."

The arrival of a waiter with dishes broke up the silent communion between husband and wife, and lowered Reggie to a more earthly plane. He refilled the glasses from the stout bottle that nestled in the ice-bucket—("Only this one, dear!" murmured the bride in a warning undertone, and "All right darling!" replied the dutiful groom)—and raised his own to his lips.

"Cheerio! Here's to us all! Maddest, merriest day of all the glad New Year and so forth. And now," he continued, becoming sternly practical, "about the good old sequel and aftermath, so to speak, of this little binge of ours. What's to be done. You're a brainy sort of feller, Bevan, old man, and we look to you for suggestions. How would you set about breaking the news to mother?"

"Write her a letter," said George.

Reggie was profoundly impressed.

"Didn't I tell you he would have some devilish shrewd scheme?" he said enthusiastically to Alice. "Write her a letter! What could be better? Poetry, by Gad!" His face clouded. "But what would you say in it? That's a pretty knotty point."

"Not at all. Be perfectly frank and straightforward. Say you are sorry to go against her wishes—"

"Wishes," murmured Reggie, scribbling industrially on the back of the marriage licence.

"—But you know that all she wants is your happiness—"

Reggie looked doubtful.

"I'm not sure about that last bit, old thing. You don't know the mater!"

"Never mind, Reggie," put in Alice. "Say it, anyhow. Mr. Bevan is perfectly right."

"Right ho, darling! All right, laddie—'happiness'. And then?"

"Point out in a few well-chosen sentences how charming Mrs. Byng is . . ."

"Mrs. Byng!" Reggie smiled fatuously. "I don't think I ever heard anything that sounded so indescribably ripping. That part'll be easy enough. Besides, the mater knows Alice."

"Lady Caroline has seen me at the castle," said his bride doubtfully, "but I shouldn't say she knows me. She has hardly spoken a dozen words to me."

"There," said Reggie, earnestly, "you're in luck, dear heart! The mater's a great speaker, especially in moments of excitement. I'm not looking forward to the time when she starts on me. Between ourselves, laddie, and meaning no disrespect to the dear soul, when the mater is moved and begins to talk, she uses up most of the language."

"Outspoken, is she?"

"I should hate to meet the person who could out-speak her," said Reggie.

George sought information on a delicate point.

"And financially? Does she exercise any authority over you in that way?"

"You mean has the mater the first call on the family doubloons?" said Reggie. "Oh, absolutely not! You see, when I call her the mater, it's using the word in a loose sense, so to speak. She's my step-mother really. She has her own little collection of pieces of eight, and I have mine. That part's simple enough."

"Then the whole thing is simple. I don't see what you've been worrying about."

"Just what I keep telling him, Mr. Bevan," said Alice.

"You're a perfectly free agent. She has no hold on you of any kind."

Reggie Byng blinked dizzily.

"Why, now you put it like that," he exclaimed, "I can see that I jolly well am! It's an amazing thing, you know, habit and all that. I've been so accustomed for years to jumping through hoops and shamming dead when the mater lifted a little finger, that it absolutely never occurred to me that I had a soul of my own. I give you my honest word I never saw it till this moment."

"And now it's too late!"

"Eh?"

George indicated Alice with a gesture. The newly-made Mrs. Byng smiled.

"Mr. Bevan means that now you've got to jump through hoops and sham dead when I lift a little finger!"

Reggie raised her hand to his lips, and nibbled at it gently.

"Blessums 'ittle finger! It shall lift it and have 'ums Reggie jumping through. . . ." He broke off and tendered George a manly apology. "Sorry, old top! Forgot myself for the moment. Shan't occur again! Have another chicken or an eclair or some soup or something!"

Over the cigars Reggie became expansive.

"Now that you've lifted the frightful weight of the mater off my mind, dear old lad," he said, puffing luxuriously, "I find myself surveying the future in a calmer spirit. It seems to me that the best thing to do, as regards the mater and everybody else, is simply to prolong the merry wedding-trip till Time the Great Healer has had a chance to cure the wound. Alice wants to put in a week or so in Paris. . . ."

"Paris!" murmured the bride ecstatically.

"Then I would like to trickle southwards to the Riviera. . ."

"If you mean Monte Carlo, dear," said his wife with gentle firmness, "no!"

"No, no, not Monte Carlo," said Reggie hastily, "though it's a great place. Air—scenery—and what not! But Nice and Bordighera and Mentone and other fairly ripe resorts. You'd enjoy them. And after that . . . I had a scheme for buying back my yacht, the jolly old Siren, and cruising about the Mediterranean for a month or so. I sold her to a local sportsman when I was in America a couple of years ago. But I saw in the paper yesterday that the poor old buffer had died suddenly, so I suppose it would be difficult to get hold of her for the time being." Reggie broke off with a sharp exclamation.

"My sainted aunt!"

"What's the matter?"

Both his companions were looking past him, wide-eyed. George occupied the chair that had its back to the door, and was unable to see what it was that had caused their consternation; but he deduced that someone known to both of them must have entered the restaurant; and his first thought, perhaps naturally, was that it must be Reggie's "mater". Reggie dived behind a menu, which he held before him like a shield, and his bride, after one quick look, had turned away so that her face was hidden. George swung around, but the newcomer, whoever he or she was, was now seated and indistinguishable from the rest of the lunchers.

"Who is it?"

Reggie laid down the menu with the air of one who after a momentary panic rallies.

"Don't know what I'm making such a fuss about," he said stoutly. "I keep forgetting that none of these blighters really matter in the scheme of things. I've a good mind to go over and pass the time of day."

"Don't!" pleaded his wife. "I feel so guilty."

"Who is it?" asked George again. "Your step-mother?"

"Great Scott, no!" said Reggie. "Nothing so bad as that. It's old

Marshmoreton."

"Lord Marshmoreton!"

"Absolutely! And looking positively festive."

"I feel so awful, Mr. Bevan," said Alice. "You know, I left the castle without a word to anyone, and he doesn't know yet that there won't be any secretary waiting for him when he gets back."

Reggie took another look over George's shoulder and chuckled.

"It's all right, darling. Don't worry. We can nip off secretly by the other door. He's not going to stop us. He's got a girl with him! The old boy has come to life—absolutely! He's gassing away sixteen to the dozen to a frightfully pretty girl with gold hair. If you slew the old bean round at an angle of about forty-five, Bevan, old top, you can see her. Take a look. He won't see you. He's got his back to us."

"Do you call her pretty?" asked Alice disparagingly.

"Now that I take a good look, precious," replied Reggie with alacrity, "no! Absolutely not! Not my style at all!"

His wife crumbled bread.

"I think she must know you, Reggie dear," she said softly. "She's waving to you."

"She's waving to me," said George, bringing back the sunshine to Reggie's life, and causing the latter's face to lose its hunted look. "I know her very well. Her name's Dore. Billie Dore."

"Old man," said Reggie, "be a good fellow and slide over to their table and cover our retreat. I know there's nothing to be afraid of really, but I simply can't face the old boy."

"And break the news to him that I've gone, Mr. Bevan," added Alice.

"Very well, I'll say good-bye, then."

"Good-bye, Mr. Bevan, and thank you ever so much."

Reggie shook George's hand warmly.

"Good-bye, Bevan old thing, you're a ripper. I can't tell you how bucked up I am at the sportsmanlike way you've rallied round. I'll do the same for you one of these days. Just hold the old boy in play for a minute or two while we leg it. And, if he wants us, tell him our address till further notice is Paris. What ho! What ho! What ho! Toodle-oo, laddie, toodle-oo!"

George threaded his way across the room. Billie Dore welcomed him with a friendly smile. The earl, who had turned to observe his progress, seemed less delighted to see him. His weather-beaten face wore an almost furtive look. He reminded George of a schoolboy who has been caught in some breach of the law.

"Fancy seeing you here, George!" said Billie. "We're always meeting, aren't we? How did you come to separate yourself from the pigs and chickens? I thought you were never going to leave them."

"I had to run up on business," explained George. "How are you, Lord Marshmoreton?"

The earl nodded briefly.

"So you're on to him, too?" said Billie. "When did you get wise?"

"Lord Marshmoreton was kind enough to call on me the other morning and drop the incognito."

"Isn't dadda the foxiest old thing!" said Billie delightedly. "Imagine him standing there that day in the garden, kidding us along like that! I tell you, when they brought me his card last night after the first act and I went down to take a slant at this Lord Marshmoreton and found dadda hanging round the stage door, you could have knocked me over with a whisk-broom."

"I have not stood at the stage-door for twenty-five years," said Lord Marshmoreton sadly.

"Now, it's no use your pulling that Henry W. Methuselah stuff," said Billie affectionately. "You can't get away with it. Anyone can see you're just a kid. Can't they, George?" She indicated the blushing earl with a wave of the hand. "Isn't dadda the youngest thing that ever happened?"

"Exactly what I told him myself."

Lord Marshmoreton giggled. There is no other verb that describes the sound that proceeded from him.

"I feel young," he admitted.

"I wish some of the juveniles in the shows I've been in," said Billie, "were as young as you. It's getting so nowadays that one's thankful if a juvenile has teeth." She glanced across the room. "Your pals are walking out on you, George. The people you were lunching with," she explained. "They're leaving."

"That's all right. I said good-bye to them." He looked at Lord

Marshmoreton. It seemed a suitable opportunity to break the news.

"I was lunching with Mr. and Mrs. Byng," he said.

Nothing appeared to stir beneath Lord Marshmoreton's tanned forehead.

"Reggie Byng and his wife, Lord Marshmoreton," added George.

This time he secured the earl's interest. Lord Marshmoreton started.

"What!"

"They are just off to Paris," said George.

"Reggie Byng is not married!"

"Married this morning. I was best man."

"Busy little creature!" interjected Billie.

"But—but—!"

"You know his wife," said George casually. "She was a Miss Faraday.

I think she was your secretary."

It would have been impossible to deny that Lord Marshmoreton showed emotion. His mouth opened, and he clutched the tablecloth. But just what the emotion was George was unable to say till, with a sigh that seemed to come from his innermost being, the other exclaimed "Thank Heaven!"

George was surprised.

"You're glad?"

"Of course I'm glad!"

"It's a pity they didn't know how you were going to feel. It would have saved them a lot of anxiety. I rather gathered they supposed that the shock was apt to darken your whole life."

"That girl," said Lord Marshmoreton vehemently, "was driving me crazy. Always bothering me to come and work on that damned family history. Never gave me a moment's peace . . ."

"I liked her," said George.

"Nice enough girl," admitted his lordship grudgingly. "But a damned nuisance about the house; always at me to go on with the family history. As if there weren't better things to do with one's time than writing all day about my infernal fools of ancestors!"

"Isn't dadda fractious today?" said Billie reprovingly, giving the Earl's hand a pat. "Quit knocking your ancestors! You're very lucky to have ancestors. I wish I had. The Dore family seems to go back about as far as the presidency of Willard Filmore, and then it kind of gets discouraged and quite cold. Gee! I'd like to feel that my great-great-great-grandmother had helped Queen Elizabeth with the rent. I'm strong for the fine old stately families of England."

"Stately old fiddlesticks!" snapped the earl.

"Did you see his eyes flash then, George? That's what they call aristocratic rage. It's the fine old spirit of the Marshmoretons boiling over."

"I noticed it," said George. "Just like lightning."

"It's no use trying to fool us, dadda," said Billie. "You know just as well as I do that it makes you feel good to think that, every time you cut yourself with your safety-razor, you bleed blue!"

"A lot of silly nonsense!" grumbled the earl.

"What is?"

"This foolery of titles and aristocracy. Silly fetish-worship! One man's as good as another. . . ."

"This is the spirit of '76!" said George approvingly.

"Regular I.W.W. stuff," agreed Billie. "Shake hands the President of the Bolsheviki!"

Lord Marshmoreton ignored the interruption. There was a strange look in his eyes. It was evident to George, watching him with close interest, that here was a revelation of the man's soul; that thoughts, locked away for years in the other's bosom were crying for utterance.

"Damned silly nonsense! When I was a boy, I wanted to be an engine-driver. When I was a young man, I was a Socialist and hadn't any idea except to work for my living and make a name for myself. I was going to the colonies. Canada. The fruit farm was actually bought. Bought and paid for!" He brooded a moment on that long-lost fruit farm. "My father was a younger son. And then my uncle must go and break his neck hunting, and the baby, poor little chap, got croup or something . . . And there I was, saddled with the title, and all my plans gone up in smoke . . . Silly nonsense! Silly nonsense!"

He bit the end of a cigar. "And you can't stand up against it," he went on ruefully. "It saps you. It's like some damned drug. I fought against it as long as I could, but it was no use. I'm as big a snob as any of them now. I'm afraid to do what I want to do. Always thinking of the family dignity. I haven't taken a free step for twenty-five years."

George and Billie exchanged glances. Each had the uncomfortable feeling that they were eavesdropping and hearing things not meant to be heard. George rose.

"I must be getting along now," he said. "I've one or two things to do. Glad to have seen you again, Billie. Is the show going all right?"

"Fine. Making money for you right along."

"Good-bye, Lord Marshmoreton."

The earl nodded without speaking. It was not often now that he rebelled even in thoughts against the lot which fate had thrust upon him, and never in his life before had he done so in words. He was still in the grip of the strange discontent which had come upon him so abruptly.

There was a silence after George had gone.

"I'm glad we met George," said Billie. "He's a good boy." She spoke soberly. She was conscious of a curious feeling of affection for the sturdy, weather-tanned little man opposite her. The glimpse she had been given of his inner self had somehow made him come alive for her.

"He wants to marry my daughter," said Lord Marshmoreton. A few moments before, Billie would undoubtedly have replied to such a statement with some jocular remark expressing disbelief that the earl could have a daughter old enough to be married. But now she felt oddly serious and unlike her usual flippant self.

"Oh?" was all she could find to say.

"She wants to marry him."

Not for years had Billie Dore felt embarrassed, but she felt so now. She judged herself unworthy to be the recipient of these very private confidences.

"Oh?" she said again.

"He's a good fellow. I like him. I liked him the moment we met. He knew it, too. And I knew he liked me."

A group of men and girls from a neighbouring table passed on their way to the door. One of the girls nodded to Billie. She returned the nod absently. The party moved on. Billie frowned down at the tablecloth and drew a pattern on it with a fork.

"Why don't you let George marry your daughter, Lord Marshmoreton?"

The earl drew at his cigar in silence.

"I know it's not my business," said Billie apologetically, interpreting the silence as a rebuff.

"Because I'm the Earl of Marshmoreton."

"I see."

"No you don't," snapped the earl. "You think I mean by that that I think your friend isn't good enough to marry my daughter. You think that I'm an incurable snob. And I've no doubt he thinks so, too, though I took the trouble to explain my attitude to him when we last met. You're wrong. It isn't that at all. When I say 'I'm the Earl of Marshmoreton', I mean that I'm a poor spineless fool who's afraid to do the right thing because he daren't go in the teeth of the family."

"I don't understand. What have your family got to do with it?"

"They'd worry the life out of me. I wish you could meet my sister Caroline! That's what they've got to do with it. Girls in my daughter's unfortunate position have got to marry position or money."

"Well, I don't know about position, but when it comes to money—why, George is the fellow that made the dollar-bill famous. He and Rockefeller have got all there is, except the little bit they have let Andy Carnegie have for car-fare."

"What do you mean? He told me he worked for a living." Billie was becoming herself again. Embarrassment had fled.

"If you call it work. He's a composer."

"I know. Writes tunes and things."

Billie regarded him compassionately.

"And I suppose, living out in the woods the way that you do that you haven't a notion that they pay him for it."

"Pay him? Yes, but how much? Composers were not rich men in my day."

"I wish you wouldn't talk of 'your day' as if you telling the boys down at the corner store about the good times they all had before the Flood. You're one of the Younger Set and don't let me have to tell you again. Say, listen! You know that show you saw last night. The one where I was supported by a few underlings. Well, George wrote the music for that."

"I know. He told me so."

"Well, did he tell you that he draws three per cent of the gross receipts? You saw the house we had last night. It was a fair average house. We are playing to over fourteen thousand dollars a week. George's little bit of that is—I can't do it in my head, but it's a round four hundred dollars. That's eighty pounds of your money. And did he tell you that this same show ran over a year in New York to big business all the time, and that there are three companies on the road now? And did he mention that this is the ninth show he's done, and that seven of the others were just as big hits as this one? And did he remark in passing that he gets royalties on every copy of his music that's sold, and that at least ten of his things have sold over half a million? No, he didn't, because he isn't the sort of fellow who stands around blowing about his income. But you know it now."

"Why, he's a rich man!"

"I don't know what you call rich, but, keeping on the safe side, I should say that George pulls down in a good year, during the season—around five thousand dollars a week."

Lord Marshmoreton was frankly staggered.

"A thousand pounds a week! I had no idea!"

"I thought you hadn't. And, while I'm boosting George, let me tell you another thing. He's one of the whitest men that ever happened. I know him. You can take it from me, if there's anything rotten in a fellow, the show-business will bring it out, and it hasn't come out in George yet, so I guess it isn't there. George is all right!"

"He has at least an excellent advocate."

"Oh, I'm strong for George. I wish there were more like him . . . Well, if you think I've butted in on your private affairs sufficiently, I suppose I ought to be moving. We've a rehearsal this afternoon."

"Let it go!" said Lord Marshmoreton boyishly.

"Yes, and how quick do you think they would let me go, if I did?

I'm an honest working-girl, and I can't afford to lose jobs."

Lord Marshmoreton fiddled with his cigar-butt.

"I could offer you an alternative position, if you cared to accept it."

Billie looked at him keenly. Other men in similar circumstances had made much the same remark to her. She was conscious of feeling a little disappointed in her new friend.

"Well?" she said dryly. "Shoot."

"You gathered, no doubt, from Mr. Bevan's conversation, that my secretary has left me and run away and got married? Would you like to take her place?"

It was not easy to disconcert Billie Dore, but she was taken aback.

She had been expecting something different.

"You're a shriek, dadda!"

"I'm perfectly serious."

"Can you see me at a castle?"

"I can see you perfectly." Lord Marshmoreton's rather formal manner left him. "Do please accept, my dear child. I've got to finish this damned family history some time or other. The family expect me to. Only yesterday my sister Caroline got me in a corner and bored me for half an hour about it. I simply can't face the prospect of getting another Alice Faraday from an agency. Charming girl, charming girl, of course, but . . . but . . . well, I'll be damned if I do it, and that's the long and short of it!"

Billie bubbled over with laughter.

"Of all the impulsive kids!" she gurgled. "I never met anyone like you, dadda! You don't even know that I can use a typewriter."

"I do. Mr. Bevan told me you were an excellent stenographer."

"So George has been boosting me, too, has he?" She mused. "I must say, I'd love to come. That old place got me when I saw it that day."

"That's settled, then," said Lord Marshmoreton masterfully. "Go to

the theatre and tell them—tell whatever is usual in these cases.

And then go home and pack, and meet me at Waterloo at six o'clock.

The train leaves at six-fifteen."

"Return of the wanderer, accompanied by dizzy blonde! You've certainly got it all fixed, haven't you! Do you think the family will stand for me?"

"Damn the family!" said Lord Marshmoreton, stoutly.

"There's one thing," said Billie complacently, eyeing her reflection in the mirror of her vanity-case, "I may glitter in the fighting-top, but it is genuine. When I was a kid, I was a regular little tow-head."

"I never supposed for a moment that it was anything but genuine."

"Then you've got a fine, unsuspicious nature, dadda, and I admire you for it."

"Six o'clock at Waterloo," said the earl. "I will be waiting for you."

Billie regarded him with affectionate admiration.

"Boys will be boys," she said. "All right. I'll be there."

CHAPTER 22.

"Young blighted Albert," said Keggs the butler, shifting his weight so that it distributed itself more comfortably over the creaking chair in which he reclined, "let this be a lesson to you, young feller me lad."

The day was a week after Lord Marshmoreton's visit to London, the hour six o'clock. The housekeeper's room, in which the upper servants took their meals, had emptied. Of the gay company which had just finished dinner only Keggs remained, placidly digesting. Albert, whose duty it was to wait on the upper servants, was moving to and fro, morosely collecting the plates and glasses. The boy was in no happy frame of mind. Throughout dinner the conversation at table had dealt almost exclusively with the now celebrated elopement of Reggie Byng and his bride, and few subjects could have made more painful listening to Albert.

"What's been the result and what I might call the upshot," said Keggs, continuing his homily, "of all your making yourself so busy and thrusting of yourself forward and meddling in the affairs of your elders and betters? The upshot and issue of it 'as been that you are out five shillings and nothing to show for it. Five shillings what you might have spent on some good book and improved your mind! And goodness knows it wants all the improving it can get, for of all the worthless, idle little messers it's ever been my misfortune to have dealings with, you are the champion. Be careful of them plates, young man, and don't breathe so hard. You 'aven't got hasthma or something, 'ave you?"

"I can't breathe now!" complained the stricken child.

"Not like a grampus you can't, and don't you forget it." Keggs wagged his head reprovingly. "Well, so your Reggie Byng's gone and eloped, has he! That ought to teach you to be more careful another time 'ow you go gambling and plunging into sweepstakes. The idea of a child of your age 'aving the audacity to thrust 'isself forward like that!"

"Don't call him my Reggie Byng! I didn't draw 'im!"

"There's no need to go into all that again, young feller. You accepted 'im freely and without prejudice when the fair exchange was suggested, so for all practical intents and purposes he is your Reggie Byng. I 'ope you're going to send him a wedding-present."

"Well, you ain't any better off than me, with all your 'ighway robbery!"

"My what!"

"You 'eard what I said."

"Well, don't let me 'ear it again. The idea! If you 'ad any objections to parting with that ticket, you should have stated them clearly at the time. And what do you mean by saying I ain't any better off than you are?"

"I 'ave my reasons."

"You think you 'ave, which is a very different thing. I suppose you imagine that you've put a stopper on a certain little affair by surreptitiously destroying letters entrusted to you."

"I never!" exclaimed Albert with a convulsive start that nearly sent eleven plates dashing to destruction.

"'Ow many times have I got to tell you to be careful of them plates?" said Keggs sternly. "Who do you think you are—a juggler on the 'Alls, 'urling them about like that? Yes, I know all about that letter. You thought you was very clever, I've no doubt. But let me tell you, young blighted Albert, that only the other evening 'er ladyship and Mr. Bevan 'ad a long and extended interview in spite of all your hefforts. I saw through your little game, and I proceeded and went and arranged the meeting."

In spite of himself Albert was awed. He was oppressed by the sense of struggling with a superior intellect.

"Yes, you did!" he managed to say with the proper note of incredulity, but in his heart he was not incredulous. Dimly, Albert had begun to perceive that years must elapse before he could become capable of matching himself in battles of wits with this master-strategist.

"Yes, I certainly did!" said Keggs. "I don't know what 'appened at the interview—not being present in person. But I've no doubt that everything proceeded satisfactorily."

"And a fat lot of good that's going to do you, when 'e ain't allowed to come inside the 'ouse!"

A bland smile irradiated the butler's moon-like face.

"If by 'e you're alloodin' to Mr. Bevan, young blighted Albert, let me tell you that it won't be long before 'e becomes a regular duly invited guest at the castle!"

"A lot of chance!"

"Would you care to 'ave another five shillings even money on it?"

Albert recoiled. He had had enough of speculation where the butler was concerned. Where that schemer was allowed to get within reach of it, hard cash melted away.

"What are you going to do?"

"Never you mind what I'm going to do. I 'ave my methods. All I 'ave to say to you is that tomorrow or the day after Mr. Bevan will be seated in our dining-'all with 'is feet under our table, replying according to his personal taste and preference, when I ask 'im if 'e'll 'ave 'ock or sherry. Brush all them crumbs carefully off the tablecloth, young blighted Albert—don't shuffle your feet—breathe softly through your nose—and close the door be'ind you when you've finished!"

"Oh, go and eat cake!" said Albert bitterly. But he said it to his immortal soul, not aloud. The lad's spirit was broken.

Keggs, the processes of digestion completed, presented himself before Lord Belpher in the billiard-room. Percy was alone. The house-party, so numerous on the night of the ball and on his birthday, had melted down now to reasonable proportions. The second and third cousins had retired, flushed and gratified, to obscure dens from which they had emerged, and the castle housed only the more prominent members of the family, always harder to dislodge than the small fry. The Bishop still remained, and the Colonel. Besides these, there were perhaps half a dozen more of the closer relations: to Lord Belpher's way of thinking, half a dozen too many. He was not fond of his family.

"Might I have a word with your lordship?"

"What is it, Keggs?"

Keggs was a self-possessed man, but he found it a little hard to begin. Then he remembered that once in the misty past he had seen Lord Belpher spanked for stealing jam, he himself having acted on that occasion as prosecuting attorney; and the memory nerved him.

"I earnestly 'ope that your lordship will not think that I am taking a liberty. I 'ave been in his lordship your father's service many years now, and the family honour is, if I may be pardoned for saying so, extremely near my 'eart. I 'ave known your lordship since you were a mere boy, and . . ."

Lord Belpher had listened with growing impatience to this preamble. His temper was seldom at its best these days, and the rolling periods annoyed him.

"Yes, yes, of course," he said. "What is it?"

Keggs was himself now. In his opening remarks he had simply been, as it were, winding up. He was now prepared to begin.

"Your lordship will recall inquiring of me on the night of the ball as to the bona fides of one of the temporary waiters? The one that stated that 'e was the cousin of young bli—of the boy Albert, the page? I have been making inquiries, your lordship, and I regret to say I find that the man was a impostor. He informed me that 'e was Albert's cousin, but Albert now informs me that 'e 'as no cousin in America. I am extremely sorry this should have occurred, your lordship, and I 'ope you will attribute it to the bustle and haste inseparable from duties as mine on such a occasion."

"I know the fellow was an impostor. He was probably after the spoons!"

Keggs coughed.

"If I might be allowed to take a further liberty, your lordship, might I suggest that I am aware of the man's identity and of his motive for visiting the castle."

He waited a little apprehensively. This was the crucial point in the interview. If Lord Belpher did not now freeze him with a glance and order him from the room, the danger would be past, and he could speak freely. His light blue eyes were expressionless as they met Percy's, but inwardly he was feeling much the same sensation as he was wont to experience when the family was in town and he had managed to slip off to Kempton Park or some other race-course and put some of his savings on a horse. As he felt when the racing steeds thundered down the straight, so did he feel now.

Astonishment showed in Lord Belpher's round face. Just as it was about to be succeeded by indignation, the butler spoke again.

"I am aware, your lordship, that it is not my place to offer suggestions as to the private and intimate affairs of the family I 'ave the honour to serve, but, if your lordship would consent to overlook the liberty, I think I could be of 'elp and assistance in a matter which is causing annoyance and unpleasantness to all."

He invigorated himself with another dip into the waters of memory. Yes. The young man before him might be Lord Belpher, son of his employer and heir to all these great estates, but once he had seen him spanked.

Perhaps Percy also remembered this. Perhaps he merely felt that Keggs was a faithful old servant and, as such, entitled to thrust himself into the family affairs. Whatever his reasons, he now definitely lowered the barrier.

"Well," he said, with a glance at the door to make sure that there were no witnesses to an act of which the aristocrat in him disapproved, "go on!"

Keggs breathed freely. The danger-point was past.

"'Aving a natural interest, your lordship," he said, "we of the Servants' 'All generally manage to become respectfully aware of whatever 'appens to be transpirin' above stairs. May I say that I became acquainted at an early stage with the trouble which your lordship is unfortunately 'aving with a certain party?"

Lord Belpher, although his whole being revolted against what practically amounted to hobnobbing with a butler, perceived that he had committed himself to the discussion. It revolted him to think that these delicate family secrets were the subject of conversation in menial circles, but it was too late to do anything now. And such was the whole-heartedness with which he had declared war upon George Bevan that, at this stage in the proceedings, his chief emotion was a hope that Keggs might have something sensible to suggest.

"I think, begging your lordship's pardon for making the remark, that you are acting injudicious. I 'ave been in service a great number of years, startin' as steward's room boy and rising to my present position, and I may say I 'ave 'ad experience during those years of several cases where the daughter or son of the 'ouse contemplated a misalliance, and all but one of the cases ended disastrously, your lordship, on account of the family trying opposition. It is my experience that opposition in matters of the 'eart is useless, feedin', as it, so to speak, does the flame. Young people, your lordship, if I may be pardoned for employing the expression in the present case, are naturally romantic and if you keep 'em away from a thing they sit and pity themselves and want it all the more. And in the end you may be sure they get it. There's no way of stoppin' them. I was not on sufficiently easy terms with the late Lord Worlingham to give 'im the benefit of my experience on the occasion when the Honourable Aubrey Pershore fell in love with the young person at the Gaiety Theatre. Otherwise I could 'ave told 'im he was not acting judicious. His lordship opposed the match in every way, and the young couple ran off and got married at a registrar's. It was the same when a young man who was tutor to 'er ladyship's brother attracted Lady Evelyn Walls, the only daughter of the Earl of Ackleton. In fact, your lordship, the only entanglement of the kind that came to a satisfactory conclusion in the whole of my personal experience was the affair of Lady Catherine Duseby, Lord Bridgefield's daughter, who injudiciously became infatuated with a roller-skating instructor."

Lord Belpher had ceased to feel distantly superior to his companion. The butler's powerful personality hypnotized him. Long ere the harangue was ended, he was as a little child drinking in the utterances of a master. He bent forward eagerly. Keggs had broken off his remarks at the most interesting point.

"What happened?" inquired Percy.

"The young man," proceeded Keggs, "was a young man of considerable personal attractions, 'aving large brown eyes and a athletic lissome figure, brought about by roller-skating. It was no wonder, in the opinion of the Servants' 'All, that 'er ladyship should have found 'erself fascinated by him, particularly as I myself 'ad 'eard her observe at a full luncheon-table that roller-skating was in her opinion the only thing except her toy Pomeranian that made life worth living. But when she announced that she had become engaged to this young man, there was the greatest consternation. I was not, of course, privileged to be a participant at the many councils and discussions that ensued and took place, but I was aware that such transpired with great frequency. Eventually 'is lordship took the shrewd step of assuming acquiescence and inviting the young man to visit us in Scotland. And within ten days of his arrival, your lordship, the match was broken off. He went back to 'is roller-skating, and 'er ladyship took up visiting the poor and eventually contracted an altogether suitable alliance by marrying Lord Ronald Spofforth, the second son of his Grace the Duke of Gorbals and Strathbungo."

"How did it happen?"

"Seein' the young man in the surroundings of 'er own 'ome, 'er ladyship soon began to see that she had taken too romantic a view of 'im previous, your lordship. 'E was one of the lower middle class, what is sometimes termed the bourjoisy, and 'is 'abits were not the 'abits of the class to which 'er ladyship belonged. 'E 'ad nothing in common with the rest of the 'ouse-party, and was injudicious in 'is choice of forks. The very first night at dinner 'e took a steel knife to the ontray, and I see 'er ladyship look at him very sharp, as much as to say that scales had fallen from 'er eyes. It didn't take 'er long after that to become convinced that 'er 'eart 'ad led 'er astray."

"Then you think—?"

"It is not for me to presume to offer anything but the most respectful advice, your lordship, but I should most certainly advocate a similar procedure in the present instance."

Lord Belpher reflected. Recent events had brought home to him the magnitude of the task he had assumed when he had appointed himself the watcher of his sister's movements. The affair of the curate and the village blacksmith had shaken him both physically and spiritually. His feet were still sore, and his confidence in himself had waned considerably. The thought of having to continue his espionage indefinitely was not a pleasant one. How much simpler and more effective it would be to adopt the suggestion which had been offered to him.

"—I'm not sure you aren't right, Keggs."

"Thank you, your lordship. I feel convinced of it."

"I will speak to my father tonight."

"Very good, your lordship. I am glad to have been of service."

"Young blighted Albert," said Keggs crisply, shortly after breakfast on the following morning, "you're to take this note to Mr. Bevan at the cottage down by Platt's farm, and you're to deliver it without playing any of your monkey-tricks, and you're to wait for an answer, and you're to bring that answer back to me, too, and to Lord Marshmoreton. And I may tell you, to save you the trouble of opening it with steam from the kitchen kettle, that I 'ave already done so. It's an invitation to dine with us tonight. So now you know. Look slippy!"

Albert capitulated. For the first time in his life he felt humble. He perceived how misguided he had been ever to suppose that he could pit his pigmy wits against this smooth-faced worker of wonders.

"Crikey!" he ejaculated.

It was all that he could say.

"And there's one more thing, young feller me lad," added Keggs earnestly, "don't you ever grow up to be such a fat'ead as our friend Percy. Don't forget I warned you."

CHAPTER 23.

Life is like some crazy machine that is always going either too slow or too fast. From the cradle to the grave, we alternate between the Sargasso Sea and the rapids—forever either becalmed or storm-tossed. It seemed to Maud, as she looked across the dinner-table in order to make sure for the twentieth time that it really was George Bevan who sat opposite her, that, after months in which nothing whatever had happened, she was now living through a period when everything was happening at once. Life, from being a broken-down machine, had suddenly begun to race.

To the orderly routine that stretched back to the time when she had been hurried home in disgrace from Wales there had succeeded a mad whirl of events, to which the miracle of tonight had come as a fitting climax. She had not begun to dress for dinner till somewhat late, and had consequently entered the drawing-room just as Keggs was announcing that the meal was ready. She had received her first shock when the love-sick Plummer, emerging from a mixed crowd of relatives and friends, had informed her that he was to take her in. She had not expected Plummer to be there, though he lived in the neighbourhood. Plummer, at their last meeting, had stated his intention of going abroad for a bit to mend his bruised heart: and it was a little disconcerting to a sensitive girl to find her victim popping up again like this. She did not know that, as far as Plummer was concerned, the whole affair was to be considered opened again. To Plummer, analysing the girl's motives in refusing him, there had come the idea that there was Another, and that this other must be Reggie Byng. From the first he had always looked upon Reggie as his worst rival. And now Reggie had bolted with the Faraday girl, leaving Maud in excellent condition, so it seemed to Plummer, to console herself with a worthier man. Plummer knew all about the Rebound and the part it plays in the affairs of the heart. His own breach-of-promise case two years earlier had been entirely due to the fact that the refusal of the youngest Devenish girl to marry him had caused him to rebound into the dangerous society of the second girl from the O.P. end of the first row in the "Summertime is Kissing-time" number in the Alhambra revue. He had come to the castle tonight gloomy, but not without hope.

Maud's second shock eclipsed the first entirely. No notification had been given to her either by her father or by Percy of the proposed extension of the hand of hospitality to George, and the sight of him standing there talking to her aunt Caroline made her momentarily dizzy. Life, which for several days had had all the properties now of a dream, now of a nightmare, became more unreal than ever. She could conceive no explanation of George's presence. He could not be there—that was all there was to it; yet there undoubtedly he was. Her manner, as she accompanied Plummer down the stairs, took on such a dazed sweetness that her escort felt that in coming there that night he had done the wisest act of a lifetime studded but sparsely with wise acts. It seemed to Plummer that this girl had softened towards him. Certainly something had changed her. He could not know that she was merely wondering if she was awake.

George, meanwhile, across the table, was also having a little difficulty in adjusting his faculties to the progress of events. He had given up trying to imagine why he had been invited to this dinner, and was now endeavouring to find some theory which would square with the fact of Billie Dore being at the castle. At precisely this hour Billie, by rights, should have been putting the finishing touches on her make-up in a second-floor dressing-room at the Regal. Yet there she sat, very much at her ease in this aristocratic company, so quietly and unobtrusively dressed in some black stuff that at first he had scarcely recognized her.

She was talking to the Bishop...

The voice of Keggs at his elbow broke in on his reverie.

"Sherry or 'ock, sir?"

George could not have explained why this reminder of the butler's presence should have made him feel better, but it did. There was something solid and tranquilizing about Keggs. He had noticed it before. For the first time the sensation of having been smitten over the head with some blunt instrument began to abate. It was as if Keggs by the mere intonation of his voice had said, "All this no doubt seems very strange and unusual to you, but feel no alarm! I am here!"

George began to sit up and take notice. A cloud seemed to have cleared from his brain. He found himself looking on his fellow-diners as individuals rather than as a confused mass. The prophet Daniel, after the initial embarrassment of finding himself in the society of the lions had passed away, must have experienced a somewhat similar sensation.

He began to sort these people out and label them. There had been introductions in the drawing-room, but they had left him with a bewildered sense of having heard somebody recite a page from Burke's peerage. Not since that day in the free library in London, when he had dived into that fascinating volume in order to discover Maud's identity, had he undergone such a rain of titles. He now took stock, to ascertain how many of these people he could identify.

The stock-taking was an absolute failure. Of all those present the only individuals he could swear to were his own personal little playmates with whom he had sported in other surroundings. There was Lord Belpher, for instance, eyeing him with a hostility that could hardly be called veiled. There was Lord Marshmoreton at the head of the table, listening glumly to the conversation of a stout woman with a pearl necklace, but who was that woman? Was it Lady Jane Allenby or Lady Edith Wade-Beverly or Lady Patricia Fowles? And who, above all, was the pie-faced fellow with the moustache talking to Maud?

He sought assistance from the girl he had taken in to dinner. She appeared, as far as he could ascertain from a short acquaintance, to be an amiable little thing. She was small and young and fluffy, and he had caught enough of her name at the moment of introduction to gather that she was plain "Miss" Something—a fact which seemed to him to draw them together.

"I wish you would tell me who some of these people are," he said, as she turned from talking to the man on her other-side. "Who is the man over there?"

"Which man?"

"The one talking to Lady Maud. The fellow whose face ought to be shuffled and dealt again."

"That's my brother."

That held George during the soup.

"I'm sorry about your brother," he said rallying with the fish.

"That's very sweet of you."

"It was the light that deceived me. Now that I look again, I see that his face has great charm."

The girl giggled. George began to feel better.

"Who are some of the others? I didn't get your name, for instance. They shot it at me so quick that it had whizzed by before I could catch it."

"My name is Plummer."

George was electrified. He looked across the table with more vivid interest. The amorous Plummer had been just a Voice to him till now. It was exciting to see him in the flesh.

"And who are the rest of them?"

"They are all members of the family. I thought you knew them."

"I know Lord Marshmoreton. And Lady Maud. And, of course, Lord Belpher." He caught Percy's eye as it surveyed him coldly from the other side of the table, and nodded cheerfully. "Great pal of mine, Lord Belpher."

The fluffy Miss Plummer twisted her pretty face into a grimace of disapproval.

"I don't like Percy."

"No!"

"I think he's conceited."

"Surely not? What could he have to be conceited about?"

"He's stiff."

"Yes, of course, that's how he strikes people at first. The first time I met him, I thought he was an awful stiff. But you should see him in his moments of relaxation. He's one of those fellows you have to get to know. He grows on you."

"Yes, but look at that affair with the policeman in London. Everybody in the county is talking about it."

"Young blood!" sighed George. "Young blood! Of course, Percy is wild."

"He must have been intoxicated."

"Oh, undoubtedly," said George.

Miss Plummer glanced across the table.

"Do look at Edwin!"

"Which is Edwin?"

"My brother, I mean. Look at the way he keeps staring at Maud. Edwin's awfully in love with Maud," she rattled on with engaging frankness. "At least, he thinks he is. He's been in love with a different girl every season since I came out. And now that Reggie Byng has gone and married Alice Faraday, he thinks he has a chance. You heard about that, I suppose?"

"Yes, I did hear something about it."

"Of course, Edwin's wasting his time, really. I happen to know"—Miss Plummer sank her voice to a whisper—"I happen to know that Maud's awfully in love with some man she met in Wales last year, but the family won't hear of it."

"Families are like that," agreed George.

"Nobody knows who he is, but everybody in the county knows all about it. Those things get about, you know. Of course, it's out of the question. Maud will have to marry somebody awfully rich or with a title. Her family's one of the oldest in England, you know."

"So I understand."

"It isn't as if she were the daughter of Lord Peebles, somebody like that."

"Why Lord Peebles?"

"Well, what I mean to say is," said Miss Plummer, with a silvery echo of Reggie Byng, "he made his money in whisky."

"That's better than spending it that way," argued George.

Miss Plummer looked puzzled. "I see what you mean," she said a little vaguely. "Lord Marshmoreton is so different."

"Haughty nobleman stuff, eh?"

"Yes."

"So you think this mysterious man in Wales hasn't a chance?"

"Not unless he and Maud elope like Reggie Byng and Alice. Wasn't that exciting? Who would ever have suspected Reggie had the dash to do a thing like that? Lord Marshmoreton's new secretary is very pretty, don't you think?"

"Which is she?"

"The girl in black with the golden hair."

"Is she Lord Marshmoreton's secretary?"

"Yes. She's an American girl. I think she's much nicer than Alice Faraday. I was talking to her before dinner. Her name is Dore. Her father was a captain in the American army, who died without leaving her a penny. He was the younger son of a very distinguished family, but his family disowned him because he married against their wishes."

"Something ought to be done to stop these families," said George.

"They're always up to something."

"So Miss Dore had to go out and earn her own living. It must have been awful for her, mustn't it, having to give up society."

"Did she give up society?"

"Oh, yes. She used to go everywhere in New York before her father died. I think American girls are wonderful. They have so much enterprise."

George at the moment was thinking that it was in imagination that they excelled.

"I wish I could go out and earn my living," said Miss Plummer.

"But the family won't dream of it."

"The family again!" said George sympathetically. "They're a perfect curse."

"I want to go on the stage. Are you fond of the theatre?"

"Fairly."

"I love it. Have you seen Hubert Broadleigh in ''Twas Once in Spring'?"

"I'm afraid I haven't."

"He's wonderful. Have you seen Cynthia Dane in 'A Woman's No'?"

"I missed that one too."

"Perhaps you prefer musical pieces? I saw an awfully good musical comedy before I left town. It's called 'Follow the Girl'. It's at the Regal Theatre. Have you seen it?"

"I wrote it."

"You—what!"

"That is to say, I wrote the music."

"But the music's lovely," gasped little Miss Plummer, as if the fact made his claim ridiculous. "I've been humming it ever since."

"I can't help that. I still stick to it that I wrote it."

"You aren't George Bevan!"

"I am!"

"But—" Miss Plummer's voice almost failed here—"But I've been dancing to your music for years! I've got about fifty of your records on the Victrola at home."

George blushed. However successful a man may be he can never get used to Fame at close range.

"Why, that tricky thing—you know, in the second act—is the darlingest thing I ever heard. I'm mad about it."

"Do you mean the one that goes lumty-lumty-tum, tumty-tumty-tum?"

"No the one that goes ta-rumty-tum-tum, ta-rumty-tum.

You know! The one about Granny dancing the shimmy."

"I'm not responsible for the words, you know," urged George hastily. "Those are wished on me by the lyrist."

"I think the words are splendid. Although poor popper thinks its improper, Granny's always doing it and nobody can stop her! I loved it." Miss Plummer leaned forward excitedly. She was an impulsive girl. "Lady Caroline."

Conversation stopped. Lady Caroline turned.

"Yes, Millie?"

"Did you know that Mr. Bevan was the Mr. Bevan?"

Everybody was listening now. George huddled pinkly in his chair. He had not foreseen this bally-hooing. Shadrach, Meschach and Abednego combined had never felt a tithe of the warmth that consumed him. He was essentially a modest young man.

"The Mr. Bevan?" echoed Lady Caroline coldly. It was painful to her to have to recognize George's existence on the same planet as herself. To admire him, as Miss Plummer apparently expected her to do, was a loathsome task. She cast one glance, fresh from the refrigerator, at the shrinking George, and elevated her aristocratic eyebrows.

Miss Plummer was not damped. She was at the hero-worshipping age, and George shared with the Messrs. Fairbanks, Francis X. Bushman, and one or two tennis champions an imposing pedestal in her Hall of Fame.

"You know! George Bevan, who wrote the music of 'Follow the Girl'."

Lady Caroline showed no signs of thawing. She had not heard of 'Follow the Girl'. Her attitude suggested that, while she admitted the possibility of George having disgraced himself in the manner indicated, it was nothing to her.

"And all those other things," pursued Miss Plummer indefatigably.

"You must have heard his music on the Victrola."

"Why, of course!"

It was not Lady Caroline who spoke, but a man further down the table. He spoke with enthusiasm.

"Of course, by Jove!" he said. "The Schenectady Shimmy, by Jove, and all that! Ripping!"

Everybody seemed pleased and interested. Everybody, that is to say, except Lady Caroline and Lord Belpher. Percy was feeling that he had been tricked. He cursed the imbecility of Keggs in suggesting that this man should be invited to dinner. Everything had gone wrong. George was an undoubted success. The majority of the company were solid for him. As far as exposing his unworthiness in the eyes of Maud was concerned, the dinner had been a ghastly failure. Much better to have left him to lurk in his infernal cottage. Lord Belpher drained his glass moodily. He was seriously upset.

But his discomfort at that moment was as nothing to the agony which rent his tortured soul a moment later. Lord Marshmoreton, who had been listening with growing excitement to the chorus of approval, rose from his seat. He cleared his throat. It was plain that Lord Marshmoreton had something on his mind.

"Er. . . ." he said.

The clatter of conversation ceased once more—stunned, as it always is at dinner parties when one of the gathering is seen to have assumed an upright position. Lord Marshmoreton cleared his throat again. His tanned face had taken on a deeper hue, and there was a look in his eyes which seemed to suggest that he was defying something or somebody. It was the look which Ajax had in his eyes when he defied the lightning, the look which nervous husbands have when they announce their intention of going round the corner to bowl a few games with the boys. One could not say definitely that Lord Marshmoreton looked pop-eyed. On the other hand, one could not assert truthfully that he did not. At any rate, he was manifestly embarrassed. He had made up his mind to a certain course of action on the spur of the moment, taking advantage, as others have done, of the trend of popular enthusiasm: and his state of mind was nervous but resolute, like that of a soldier going over the top. He cleared his throat for the third time, took one swift glance at his sister Caroline, then gazed glassily into the emptiness above her head.

"Take this opportunity," he said rapidly, clutching at the table-cloth for support, "take this opportunity of announcing the engagement of my daughter Maud to Mr. Bevan. And," he concluded with a rush, pouring back into his chair, "I should like you all to drink their health!"

There was a silence that hurt. It was broken by two sounds, occurring simultaneously in different parts of the room. One was a gasp from Lady Caroline. The other was a crash of glass.

For the first time in a long unblemished career Keggs the butler had dropped a tray.

CHAPTER 24.

Out on the terrace the night was very still. From a steel-blue sky the stars looked down as calmly as they had looked on the night of the ball, when George had waited by the shrubbery listening to the wailing of the music and thinking long thoughts. From the dark meadows by the brook came the cry of a corncrake, its harsh note softened by distance.

"What shall we do?" said Maud. She was sitting on the stone seat where Reggie Byng had sat and meditated on his love for Alice Faraday and his unfortunate habit of slicing his approach-shots. To George, as he stood beside her, she was a white blur in the darkness. He could not see her face.

"I don't know!" he said frankly.

Nor did he. Like Lady Caroline and Lord Belpher and Keggs, the butler, he had been completely overwhelmed by Lord Marshmoreton's dramatic announcement. The situation had come upon him unheralded by any warning, and had found him unequal to it.

A choking sound suddenly proceeded from the whiteness that was Maud. In the stillness it sounded like some loud noise. It jarred on George's disturbed nerves.

"Please!"

"I c-can't help it!"

"There's nothing to cry about, really! If we think long enough, we shall find some way out all right. Please don't cry."

"I'm not crying!" The choking sound became an unmistakable ripple of mirth. "It's so absurd! Poor father getting up like that in front of everyone! Did you see Aunt Caroline's face?"

"It haunts me still," said George. "I shall never forget it. Your brother didn't seem any too pleased, either."

Maud stopped laughing.

"It's an awful position," she said soberly. "The announcement will be in the Morning Post the day after tomorrow. And then the letters of congratulation will begin to pour in. And after that the presents. And I simply can't see how we can convince them all that there has been a mistake." Another aspect of the matter struck her. "It's so hard on you, too."

"Don't think about me," urged George. "Heaven knows I'd give the whole world if we could just let the thing go on, but there's no use discussing impossibilities." He lowered his voice. "There's no use, either, in my pretending that I'm not going to have a pretty bad time. But we won't discuss that. It was my own fault. I came butting in on your life of my own free will, and, whatever happens, it's been worth it to have known you and tried to be of service to you."

"You're the best friend I've ever had."

"I'm glad you think that."

"The best and kindest friend any girl ever had. I wish . . ."

She broke off. "Oh, well. . ."

There was a silence. In the castle somebody had begun to play the piano. Then a man's voice began to sing.

"That's Edwin Plummer," said Maud. "How badly he sings."

George laughed. Somehow the intrusion of Plummer had removed the tension. Plummer, whether designedly and as a sombre commentary on the situation or because he was the sort of man who does sing that particular song, was chanting Tosti's "Good-bye". He was giving to its never very cheery notes a wailing melancholy all his own. A dog in the stables began to howl in sympathy, and with the sound came a curious soothing of George's nerves. He might feel broken-hearted later, but for the moment, with this double accompaniment, it was impossible for a man with humour in his soul to dwell on the deeper emotions. Plummer and his canine duettist had brought him to earth. He felt calm and practical.

"We'd better talk the whole thing over quietly," he said. "There's certain to be some solution. At the worst you can always go to Lord Marshmoreton and tell him that he spoke without a sufficient grasp of his subject."

"I could," said Maud, "but, just at present, I feel as if I'd rather do anything else in the world. You don't realize what it must have cost father to defy Aunt Caroline openly like that. Ever since I was old enough to notice anything, I've seen how she dominated him. It was Aunt Caroline who really caused all this trouble. If it had only been father, I could have coaxed him to let me marry anyone I pleased. I wish, if you possibly can, you would think of some other solution."

"I haven't had an opportunity of telling you," said George, "that I called at Belgrave Square, as you asked me to do. I went there directly I had seen Reggie Byng safely married."

"Did you see him married?"

"I was best man."

"Dear old Reggie! I hope he will be happy."

"He will. Don't worry about that. Well, as I was saying, I called at Belgrave Square, and found the house shut up. I couldn't get any answer to the bell, though I kept my thumb on it for minutes at a time. I think they must have gone abroad again."

"No, it wasn't that. I had a letter from Geoffrey this morning. His uncle died of apoplexy, while they were in Manchester on a business trip." She paused. "He left Geoffrey all his money," she went on. "Every penny."

The silence seemed to stretch out interminably. The music from the castle had ceased. The quiet of the summer night was unbroken. To George the stillness had a touch of the sinister. It was the ghastly silence of the end of the world. With a shock he realized that even now he had been permitting himself to hope, futile as he recognized the hope to be. Maud had told him she loved another man. That should have been final. And yet somehow his indomitable sub-conscious self had refused to accept it as final. But this news ended everything. The only obstacle that had held Maud and this man apart was removed. There was nothing to prevent them marrying. George was conscious of a vast depression. The last strand of the rope had parted, and he was drifting alone out into the ocean of desolation.

"Oh!" he said, and was surprised that his voice sounded very much the same as usual. Speech was so difficult that it seemed strange that it should show no signs of effort. "That alters everything, doesn't it."

"He said in his letter that he wanted me to meet him in London and—talk things over, I suppose."

"There's nothing now to prevent your going. I mean, now that your father has made this announcement, you are free to go where you please."

"Yes, I suppose I am."

There was another silence.

"Everything's so difficult," said Maud.

"In what way?"

"Oh, I don't know."

"If you are thinking of me," said George, "please don't. I know exactly what you mean. You are hating the thought of hurting my feelings. I wish you would look on me as having no feelings. All I want is to see you happy. As I said just now, it's enough for me to know that I've helped you. Do be reasonable about it. The fact that our engagement has been officially announced makes no difference in our relations to each other. As far as we two are concerned, we are exactly where we were the last time we met. It's no worse for me now than it was then to know that I'm not the man you love, and that there's somebody else you loved before you ever knew of my existence. For goodness' sake, a girl like you must be used to having men tell her that they love her and having to tell them that she can't love them in return."

"But you're so different."

"Not a bit of it. I'm just one of the crowd."

"I've never known anybody quite like you."

"Well, you've never known anybody quite like Plummer, I should imagine. But the thought of his sufferings didn't break your heart."

"I've known a million men exactly like Edwin Plummer," said Maud emphatically. "All the men I ever have known have been like him—quite nice and pleasant and negative. It never seemed to matter refusing them. One knew that they would be just a little bit piqued for a week or two and then wander off and fall in love with somebody else. But you're different. You . . . matter."

"That is where we disagree. My argument is that, where your happiness is concerned, I don't matter."

Maud rested her chin on her hand, and stared out into the velvet darkness.

"You ought to have been my brother instead of Percy," she said at last. "What chums we should have been! And how simple that would have made everything!"

"The best thing for you to do is to regard me as an honorary brother. That will make everything simple."

"It's easy to talk like that . . . No, it isn't. It's horribly hard. I know exactly how difficult it is for you to talk as you have been doing—to try to make me feel better by pretending the whole trouble is just a trifle . . . It's strange . . . We have only met really for a few minutes at a time, and three weeks ago I didn't know there was such a person as you, but somehow I seem to know everything you're thinking. I've never felt like that before with any man . . . Even Geoffrey. . . He always puzzled me. . . ."

She broke off. The corncrake began to call again out in the distance.

"I wish I knew what to do," she said with a catch in her voice.

"I'll tell you in two words what to do. The whole thing is absurdly simple. You love this man and he loves you, and all that kept you apart before was the fact that he could not afford to marry you. Now that he is rich, there is no obstacle at all. I simply won't let you look on me and my feelings as an obstacle. Rule me out altogether. Your father's mistake has made the situation a little more complicated than it need have been, but that can easily be remedied. Imitate the excellent example of Reggie Byng. He was in a position where it would have been embarrassing to announce what he intended to do, so he very sensibly went quietly off and did it and left everybody to find out after it was done. I'm bound to say I never looked on Reggie as a master mind, but, when it came to find a way out of embarrassing situations, one has to admit he had the right idea. Do what he did!"

Maud started. She half rose from the stone seat. George could hear the quick intake of her breath.

"You mean—run away?"

"Exactly. Run away!"

An automobile swung round the corner of the castle from the direction of the garage, and drew up, purring, at the steps. There was a flood of light and the sound of voices, as the great door opened. Maud rose.

"People are leaving," she said. "I didn't know it was so late." She stood irresolutely. "I suppose I ought to go in and say good-bye. But I don't think I can."

"Stay where you are. Nobody will see you."

More automobiles arrived. The quiet of the night was shattered by the noise of their engines. Maud sat down again.

"I suppose they will think it very odd of me not being there."

"Never mind what people think. Reggie Byng didn't."

Maud's foot traced circles on the dry turf.

"What a lovely night," she said. "There's no dew at all."

The automobiles snorted, tooted, back-fired, and passed away. Their clamour died in the distance, leaving the night a thing of peace and magic once more. The door of the castle closed with a bang.

"I suppose I ought to be going in now," said Maud.

"I suppose so. And I ought to be there, too, politely making my farewells. But something seems to tell me that Lady Caroline and your brother will be quite ready to dispense with the formalities. I shall go home."

They faced each other in the darkness.

"Would you really do that?" asked Maud. "Run away, I mean, and get married in London."

"It's the only thing to do."

"But . . . can one get married as quickly as that?"

"At a registrar's? Nothing simpler. You should have seen Reggie Byng's wedding. It was over before one realized it had started. A snuffy little man in a black coat with a cold in his head asked a few questions, wrote a few words, and the thing was done."

"That sounds rather . . . dreadful."

"Reggie didn't seem to think so."

"Unromantic, I mean. . . . Prosaic."

"You would supply the romance."

"Of course, one ought to be sensible. It is just the same as a regular wedding."

"In effects, absolutely."

They moved up the terrace together. On the gravel drive by the steps they paused.

"I'll do it!" said Maud.

George had to make an effort before he could reply. For all his sane and convincing arguments, he could not check a pang at this definite acceptance of them. He had begun to appreciate now the strain under which he had been speaking.

"You must," he said. "Well . . . good-bye."

There was light on the drive. He could see her face. Her eyes were troubled.

"What will you do?" she asked.

"Do?"

"I mean, are you going to stay on in your cottage?"

"No, I hardly think I could do that. I shall go back to London tomorrow, and stay at the Carlton for a few days. Then I shall sail for America. There are a couple of pieces I've got to do for the Fall. I ought to be starting on them."

Maud looked away.

"You've got your work," she said almost inaudibly.

George understood her.

"Yes, I've got my work."

"I'm glad."

She held out her hand.

"You've been very wonderful... Right from the beginning . . . You've been . . . oh, what's the use of me saying anything?"

"I've had my reward. I've known you. We're friends, aren't we?"

"My best friend."

"Pals?"

"Pals!"

They shook hands.

CHAPTER 25.

"I was never so upset in my life!" said Lady Caroline.

She had been saying the same thing and many other things for the past five minutes. Until the departure of the last guest she had kept an icy command of herself and shown an unruffled front to the world. She had even contrived to smile. But now, with the final automobile whirring homewards, she had thrown off the mask. The very furniture of Lord Marshmoreton's study seemed to shrink, seared by the flame of her wrath. As for Lord Marshmoreton himself, he looked quite shrivelled.

It had not been an easy matter to bring her erring brother to bay. The hunt had been in progress full ten minutes before she and Lord Belpher finally cornered the poor wretch. His plea, through the keyhole of the locked door, that he was working on the family history and could not be disturbed, was ignored; and now he was face to face with the avengers.

"I cannot understand it," continued Lady Caroline. "You know that for months we have all been straining every nerve to break off this horrible entanglement, and, just as we had begun to hope that something might be done, you announce the engagement in the most public manner. I think you must be out of your mind. I can hardly believe even now that this appalling thing has happened. I am hoping that I shall wake up and find it is all a nightmare. How you can have done such a thing, I cannot understand."

"Quite!" said Lord Belpher.

If Lady Caroline was upset, there are no words in the language that will adequately describe the emotions of Percy.

From the very start of this lamentable episode in high life, Percy had been in the forefront of the battle. It was Percy who had had his best hat smitten from his head in the full view of all Piccadilly. It was Percy who had suffered arrest and imprisonment in the cause. It was Percy who had been crippled for days owing to his zeal in tracking Maud across country. And now all his sufferings were in vain. He had been betrayed by his own father.

There was, so the historians of the Middle West tell us, a man of Chicago named Young, who once, when his nerves were unstrung, put his mother (unseen) in the chopping-machine, and canned her and labelled her "Tongue". It is enough to say that the glance of disapproval which Percy cast upon his father at this juncture would have been unduly severe if cast by the Young offspring upon their parent at the moment of confession.

Lord Marshmoreton had rallied from his initial panic. The spirit of revolt began to burn again in his bosom. Once the die is cast for revolution, there can be no looking back. One must defy, not apologize. Perhaps the inherited tendencies of a line of ancestors who, whatever their shortcomings, had at least known how to treat their women folk, came to his aid. Possibly there stood by his side in this crisis ghosts of dead and buried Marshmoretons, whispering spectral encouragement in his ear—the ghosts, let us suppose, of that earl who, in the days of the seventh Henry, had stabbed his wife with a dagger to cure her tendency to lecture him at night; or of that other earl who, at a previous date in the annals of the family, had caused two aunts and a sister to be poisoned apparently from a mere whim. At any rate, Lord Marshmoreton produced from some source sufficient courage to talk back.

"Silly nonsense!" he grunted. "Don't see what you're making all this fuss about. Maud loves the fellow. I like the fellow. Perfectly decent fellow. Nothing to make a fuss about. Why shouldn't I announce the engagement?"

"You must be mad!" cried Lady Caroline. "Your only daughter and a man nobody knows anything about!"

"Quite!" said Percy.

Lord Marshmoreton seized his advantage with the skill of an adroit debater.

"That's where you're wrong. I know all about him. He's a very rich man. You heard the way all those people at dinner behaved when they heard his name. Very celebrated man! Makes thousands of pounds a year. Perfectly suitable match in every way."

"It is not a suitable match," said Lady Caroline vehemently. "I don't care whether this Mr. Bevan makes thousands of pounds a year or twopence-ha'penny. The match is not suitable. Money is not everything."

She broke off. A knock had come on the door. The door opened, and

Billie Dore came in. A kind-hearted girl, she had foreseen that

Lord Marshmoreton might be glad of a change of subject at about

this time.

"Would you like me to help you tonight?" she asked brightly. "I thought I would ask if there was anything you wanted me to do."

Lady Caroline snatched hurriedly at her aristocratic calm. She resented the interruption acutely, but her manner, when she spoke, was bland.

"Lord Marshmoreton will not require your help tonight," she said.

"He will not be working."

"Good night," said Billie.

"Good night," said Lady Caroline.

Percy scowled a valediction.

"Money," resumed Lady Caroline, "is immaterial. Maud is in no position to be obliged to marry a rich man. What makes the thing impossible is that Mr. Bevan is nobody. He comes from nowhere. He has no social standing whatsoever."

"Don't see it," said Lord Marshmoreton. "The fellow's a thoroughly decent fellow. That's all that matters."

"How can you be so pig-headed! You are talking like an imbecile. Your secretary, Miss Dore, is a nice girl. But how would you feel if Percy were to come to you and say that he was engaged to be married to her?"

"Exactly!" said Percy. "Quite!"

Lord Marshmoreton rose and moved to the door. He did it with a certain dignity, but there was a strange hunted expression in his eyes.

"That would be impossible," he said.

"Precisely," said his sister. "I am glad that you admit it."

Lord Marshmoreton had reached the door, and was standing holding the handle. He seemed to gather strength from its support.

"I've been meaning to tell you about that," he said.

"About what?"

"About Miss Dore. I married her myself last Wednesday," said Lord Marshmoreton, and disappeared like a diving duck.

CHAPTER 26.

At a quarter past four in the afternoon, two days after the memorable dinner-party at which Lord Marshmoreton had behaved with so notable a lack of judgment, Maud sat in Ye Cosy Nooke, waiting for Geoffrey Raymond. He had said in his telegram that he would meet her there at four-thirty: but eagerness had brought Maud to the tryst a quarter of an hour ahead of time: and already the sadness of her surroundings was causing her to regret this impulsiveness. Depression had settled upon her spirit. She was aware of something that resembled foreboding.

Ye Cosy Nooke, as its name will immediately suggest to those who know their London, is a tea-shop in Bond Street, conducted by distressed gentlewomen. In London, when a gentlewoman becomes distressed—which she seems to do on the slightest provocation—she collects about her two or three other distressed gentlewomen, forming a quorum, and starts a tea-shop in the West-End, which she calls Ye Oak Leaf, Ye Olde Willow-Pattern, Ye Linden-Tree, or Ye Snug Harbour, according to personal taste. There, dressed in Tyrolese, Japanese, Norwegian, or some other exotic costume, she and her associates administer refreshments of an afternoon with a proud languor calculated to knock the nonsense out of the cheeriest customer. Here you will find none of the coarse bustle and efficiency of the rival establishments of Lyons and Co., nor the glitter and gaiety of Rumpelmayer's. These places have an atmosphere of their own. They rely for their effect on an insufficiency of light, an almost total lack of ventilation, a property chocolate cake which you are not supposed to cut, and the sad aloofness of their ministering angels. It is to be doubted whether there is anything in the world more damping to the spirit than a London tea-shop of this kind, unless it be another London tea-shop of the same kind.

Maud sat and waited. Somewhere out of sight a kettle bubbled in an undertone, like a whispering pessimist. Across the room two distressed gentlewomen in fancy dress leaned against the wall. They, too, were whispering. Their expressions suggested that they looked on life as low and wished they were well out of it, like the body upstairs. One assumed that there was a body upstairs. One cannot help it at these places. One's first thought on entering is that the lady assistant will approach one and ask in a hushed voice "Tea or chocolate? And would you care to view the remains?"

Maud looked at her watch. It was twenty past four. She could scarcely believe that she had only been there five minutes, but the ticking of the watch assured her that it had not stopped. Her depression deepened. Why had Geoffrey told her to meet him in a cavern of gloom like this instead of at the Savoy? She would have enjoyed the Savoy. But here she seemed to have lost beyond recovery the first gay eagerness with which she had set out to meet the man she loved.

Suddenly she began to feel frightened. Some evil spirit, possibly the kettle, seemed to whisper to her that she had been foolish in coming here, to cast doubts on what she had hitherto regarded as the one rock-solid fact in the world, her love for Geoffrey. Could she have changed since those days in Wales? Life had been so confusing of late. In the vividness of recent happenings those days in Wales seemed a long way off, and she herself different from the girl of a year ago. She found herself thinking about George Bevan.

It was a curious fact that, the moment she began to think of George Bevan, she felt better. It was as if she had lost her way in a wilderness and had met a friend. There was something so capable, so soothing about George. And how well he had behaved at that last interview.

George seemed somehow to be part of her life. She could not imagine a life in which he had no share. And he was at this moment, probably, packing to return to America, and she would never see him again. Something stabbed at her heart. It was as if she were realizing now for the first time that he was really going.

She tried to rid herself of the ache at her heart by thinking of Wales. She closed her eyes, and found that that helped her to remember. With her eyes shut, she could bring it all back—that rainy day, the graceful, supple figure that had come to her out of the mist, those walks over the hills . . . If only Geoffrey would come! It was the sight of him that she needed.

"There you are!"

Maud opened her eyes with a start. The voice had sounded like Geoffrey's. But it was a stranger who stood by the table. And not a particularly prepossessing stranger. In the dim light of Ye Cosy Nooke, to which her opening eyes had not yet grown accustomed, all she could see of the man was that he was remarkably stout. She stiffened defensively. This was what a girl who sat about in tea-rooms alone had to expect.

"Hope I'm not late," said the stranger, sitting down and breathing heavily. "I thought a little exercise would do me good, so I walked."

Every nerve in Maud's body seemed to come to life simultaneously.

She tingled from head to foot. It was Geoffrey!

He was looking over his shoulder and endeavouring by snapping his fingers to attract the attention of the nearest distressed gentlewoman; and this gave Maud time to recover from the frightful shock she had received. Her dizziness left her; and, leaving, was succeeded by a panic dismay. This couldn't be Geoffrey! It was outrageous that it should be Geoffrey! And yet it undeniably was Geoffrey. For a year she had prayed that Geoffrey might be given back to her, and the gods had heard her prayer. They had given her back Geoffrey, and with a careless generosity they had given her twice as much of him as she had expected. She had asked for the slim Apollo whom she had loved in Wales, and this colossal changeling had arrived in his stead.

We all of us have our prejudices. Maud had a prejudice against fat men. It may have been the spectacle of her brother Percy, bulging more and more every year she had known him, that had caused this kink in her character. At any rate, it existed, and she gazed in sickened silence at Geoffrey. He had turned again now, and she was enabled to get a full and complete view of him. He was not merely stout. He was gross. The slim figure which had haunted her for a year had spread into a sea of waistcoat. The keen lines of his face had disappeared altogether. His cheeks were pink jellies.

One of the distressed gentlewomen had approached with a slow disdain, and was standing by the table, brooding on the corpse upstairs. It seemed a shame to bother her.

"Tea or chocolate?" she inquired proudly.

"Tea, please," said Maud, finding her voice.

"One tea," sighed the mourner.

"Chocolate for me," said Geoffrey briskly, with the air of one discoursing on a congenial topic. "I'd like plenty of whipped cream. And please see that it's hot."

"One chocolate."

Geoffrey pondered. This was no light matter that occupied him.

"And bring some fancy cakes—I like the ones with icing on them—and some tea-cake and buttered toast. Please see there's plenty of butter on it."

Maud shivered. This man before her was a man in whose lexicon there should have been no such word as butter, a man who should have called for the police had some enemy endeavoured to thrust butter upon him.

"Well," said Geoffrey leaning forward, as the haughty ministrant drifted away, "you haven't changed a bit. To look at, I mean."

"No?" said Maud.

"You're just the same. I think I"—he squinted down at his waistcoat—"have put on a little weight. I don't know if you notice it?"

Maud shivered again. He thought he had put on a little weight, and didn't know if she had noticed it! She was oppressed by the eternal melancholy miracle of the fat man who does not realize that he has become fat.

"It was living on the yacht that put me a little out of condition," said Geoffrey. "I was on the yacht nearly all the time since I saw you last. The old boy had a Japanese cook and lived pretty high. It was apoplexy that got him. We had a great time touring about. We were on the Mediterranean all last winter, mostly at Nice."

"I should like to go to Nice," said Maud, for something to say. She was feeling that it was not only externally that Geoffrey had changed. Or had he in reality always been like this, commonplace and prosaic, and was it merely in her imagination that he had been wonderful?

"If you ever go," said Geoffrey, earnestly, "don't fail to lunch at the Hotel Côte d'Azur. They give you the most amazing selection of hors d'oeuvres you ever saw. Crayfish as big as baby lobsters! And there's a fish—I've forgotten it's name, it'll come back to me—that's just like the Florida pompano. Be careful to have it broiled, not fried. Otherwise you lose the flavour. Tell the waiter you must have it broiled, with melted butter and a little parsley and some plain boiled potatoes. It's really astonishing. It's best to stick to fish on the Continent. People can say what they like, but I maintain that the French don't really understand steaks or any sort of red meat. The veal isn't bad, though I prefer our way of serving it. Of course, what the French are real geniuses at is the omelet. I remember, when we put in at Toulon for coal, I went ashore for a stroll, and had the most delicious omelet with chicken livers beautifully cooked, at quite a small, unpretentious place near the harbour. I shall always remember it."

The mourner returned, bearing a laden tray, from which she removed the funeral bakemeats and placed them limply on the table. Geoffrey shook his head, annoyed.

"I particularly asked for plenty of butter on my toast!" he said. "I hate buttered toast if there isn't lots of butter. It isn't worth eating. Get me a couple of pats, will you, and I'll spread it myself. Do hurry, please, before the toast gets cold. It's no good if the toast gets cold. They don't understand tea as a meal at these places," he said to Maud, as the mourner withdrew. "You have to go to the country to appreciate the real thing. I remember we lay off Lyme Regis down Devonshire way, for a few days, and I went and had tea at a farmhouse there. It was quite amazing! Thick Devonshire cream and home-made jam and cakes of every kind. This sort of thing here is just a farce. I do wish that woman would make haste with that butter. It'll be too late in a minute."

Maud sipped her tea in silence. Her heart was like lead within her. The recurrence of the butter theme as a sort of leit motif in her companion's conversation was fraying her nerves till she felt she could endure little more. She cast her mind's eye back over the horrid months and had a horrid vision of Geoffrey steadily absorbing butter, day after day, week after week—ever becoming more and more of a human keg. She shuddered.

Indignation at the injustice of Fate in causing her to give her heart to a man and then changing him into another and quite different man fought with a cold terror, which grew as she realized more and more clearly the magnitude of the mistake she had made. She felt that she must escape. And yet how could she escape? She had definitely pledged herself to this man. ("Ah!" cried Geoffrey gaily, as the pats of butter arrived. "That's more like it!" He began to smear the toast. Maud averted her eyes.) She had told him that she loved him, that he was the whole world to her, that there never would be anyone else. He had come to claim her. How could she refuse him just because he was about thirty pounds overweight?

Geoffrey finished his meal. He took out a cigarette. ("No smoking, please!" said the distressed gentlewoman.) He put the cigarette back in its case. There was a new expression in his eyes now, a tender expression. For the first time since they had met Maud seemed to catch a far-off glimpse of the man she had loved in Wales. Butter appeared to have softened Geoffrey.

"So you couldn't wait!" he said with pathos.

Maud did not understand.

"I waited over a quarter of an hour. It was you who were late."

"I don't mean that. I am referring to your engagement. I saw the announcement in the Morning Post. Well, I hope you will let me offer you my best wishes. This Mr. George Bevan, whoever he is, is lucky."

Maud had opened her mouth to explain, to say that it was all a mistake. She closed it again without speaking.

"So you couldn't wait!" proceeded Geoffrey with gentle regret. "Well, I suppose I ought not to blame you. You are at an age when it is easy to forget. I had no right to hope that you would be proof against a few months' separation. I expected too much. But it is ironical, isn't it! There was I, thinking always of those days last summer when we were everything to each other, while you had forgotten me—Forgotten me!" sighed Geoffrey. He picked a fragment of cake absently off the tablecloth and inserted it in his mouth.

The unfairness of the attack stung Maud to speech. She looked back over the months, thought of all she had suffered, and ached with self-pity.

"I hadn't," she cried.

"You hadn't? But you let this other man, this George Bevan, make love to you."

"I didn't! That was all a mistake."

"A mistake?"

"Yes. It would take too long to explain, but . . ." She stopped. It had come to her suddenly, in a flash of clear vision, that the mistake was one which she had no desire to correct. She felt like one who, lost in a jungle, comes out after long wandering into the open air. For days she had been thinking confusedly, unable to interpret her own emotions: and now everything had abruptly become clarified. It was as if the sight of Geoffrey had been the key to a cipher. She loved George Bevan, the man she had sent out of her life for ever. She knew it now, and the shock of realization made her feel faint and helpless. And, mingled with the shock of realization, there came to her the mortification of knowing that her aunt, Lady Caroline, and her brother, Percy, had been right after all. What she had mistaken for the love of a lifetime had been, as they had so often insisted, a mere infatuation, unable to survive the spectacle of a Geoffrey who had been eating too much butter and had put on flesh.

Geoffrey swallowed his piece of cake, and bent forward.

"Aren't you engaged to this man Bevan?"

Maud avoided his eye. She was aware that the crisis had arrived, and that her whole future hung on her next words.

And then Fate came to her rescue. Before she could speak, there was an interruption.

"Pardon me," said a voice. "One moment!"

So intent had Maud and her companion been on their own affairs that neither of them observed the entrance of a third party. This was a young man with mouse-coloured hair and a freckled, badly-shaven face which seemed undecided whether to be furtive or impudent. He had small eyes, and his costume was a blend of the flashy and the shabby. He wore a bowler hat, tilted a little rakishly to one side, and carried a small bag, which he rested on the table between them.

"Sorry to intrude, miss." He bowed gallantly to Maud, "but I want to have a few words with Mr. Spenser Gray here."

Maud, looking across at Geoffrey, was surprised to see that his florid face had lost much of its colour. His mouth was open, and his eyes had taken a glassy expression.

"I think you have made a mistake," she said coldly. She disliked the young man at sight. "This is Mr. Raymond."

Geoffrey found speech.

"Of course I'm Mr. Raymond!" he cried angrily. "What do you mean by coming and annoying us like this?"

The young man was not discomposed. He appeared to be used to being unpopular. He proceeded as though there had been no interruption. He produced a dingy card.

"Glance at that," he said. "Messrs. Willoughby and Son, Solicitors. I'm son. The guv'nor put this little matter into my hands. I've been looking for you for days, Mr. Gray, to hand you this paper." He opened the bag like a conjurer performing a trick, and brought out a stiff document of legal aspect. "You're a witness, miss, that I've served the papers. You know what this is, of course?" he said to Geoffrey. "Action for breach of promise of marriage. Our client, Miss Yvonne Sinclair, of the Regal Theatre, is suing you for ten thousand pounds. And, if you ask me," said the young man with genial candour, dropping the professional manner, "I don't mind telling you, I think it's a walk-over! It's the best little action for breach we've handled for years." He became professional again. "Your lawyers will no doubt communicate with us in due course. And, if you take my advice," he concluded, with another of his swift changes of manner, "you'll get 'em to settle out of court, for, between me and you and the lamp-post, you haven't an earthly!"

Geoffrey had started to his feet. He was puffing with outraged innocence.

"What the devil do you mean by this?" he demanded. "Can't you see you've made a mistake? My name is not Gray. This lady has told you that I am Geoffrey Raymond!"

"Makes it all the worse for you," said the young man imperturbably, "making advances to our client under an assumed name. We've got letters and witnesses and the whole bag of tricks. And how about this photo?" He dived into the bag again. "Do you recognize that, miss?"

Maud looked at the photograph. It was unmistakably Geoffrey. And it had evidently been taken recently, for it showed the later Geoffrey, the man of substance. It was a full-length photograph and across the stout legs was written in a flowing hand the legend, "To Babe from her little Pootles". Maud gave a shudder and handed it back to the young man, just as Geoffrey, reaching across the table, made a grab for it.

"I recognize it," she said.

Mr. Willoughby junior packed the photograph away in his bag, and turned to go.

"That's all for today, then, I think," he said, affably.

He bowed again in his courtly way, tilted the hat a little more to the left, and, having greeted one of the distressed gentlewomen who loitered limply in his path with a polite "If you please, Mabel!" which drew upon him a freezing stare of which he seemed oblivious, he passed out, leaving behind him strained silence.

Maud was the first to break it.

"I think I'll be going," she said.

The words seemed to rouse her companion from his stupor.

"Let me explain!"

"There's nothing to explain."

"It was just a . . . it was just a passing . . . It was nothing . . . nothing."

"Pootles!" murmured Maud.

Geoffrey followed her as she moved to the door.

"Be reasonable!" pleaded Geoffrey. "Men aren't saints! It was nothing! . . . Are you going to end . . . everything . . . just because I lost my head?"

Maud looked at him with a smile. She was conscious of an overwhelming relief. The dim interior of Ye Cosy Nooke no longer seemed depressing. She could have kissed this unknown "Babe" whose businesslike action had enabled her to close a regrettable chapter in her life with a clear conscience.

"But you haven't only lost your head, Geoffrey," she said. "You've lost your figure as well."

She went out quickly. With a convulsive bound Geoffrey started to follow her, but was checked before he had gone a yard.

There are formalities to be observed before a patron can leave Ye

Cosy Nooke.

"If you please!" said a distressed gentlewomanly voice.

The lady whom Mr. Willoughby had addressed as Mabel—erroneously, for her name was Ernestine—was standing beside him with a slip of paper.

"Six and twopence," said Ernestine.

For a moment this appalling statement drew the unhappy man's mind from the main issue.

"Six and twopence for a cup of chocolate and a few cakes?" he cried, aghast. "It's robbery!"

"Six and twopence, please!" said the queen of the bandits with undisturbed calm. She had been through this sort of thing before. Ye Cosy Nooke did not get many customers; but it made the most of those it did get.

"Here!" Geoffrey produced a half-sovereign. "I haven't time to argue!"

The distressed brigand showed no gratification. She had the air of one who is aloof from worldly things. All she wanted was rest and leisure—leisure to meditate upon the body upstairs. All flesh is as grass. We are here today and gone tomorrow. But there, beyond the grave, is peace.

"Your change?" she said.

"Damn the change!"

"You are forgetting your hat."

"Damn my hat!"

Geoffrey dashed from the room. He heaved his body through the door.

He lumbered down the stairs.

Out in Bond Street the traffic moved up and the traffic moved down.

Strollers strolled upon the sidewalks.

But Maud had gone.

CHAPTER 27.

In his bedroom at the Carlton Hotel George Bevan was packing. That is to say, he had begun packing; but for the last twenty minutes he had been sitting on the side of the bed, staring into a future which became bleaker and bleaker the more he examined it. In the last two days he had been no stranger to these grey moods, and they had become harder and harder to dispel. Now, with the steamer-trunk before him gaping to receive its contents, he gave himself up whole-heartedly to gloom.

Somehow the steamer-trunk, with all that it implied of partings and voyagings, seemed to emphasize the fact that he was going out alone into an empty world. Soon he would be on board the liner, every revolution of whose engines would be taking him farther away from where his heart would always be. There were moments when the torment of this realization became almost physical.

It was incredible that three short weeks ago he had been a happy man. Lonely, perhaps, but only in a vague, impersonal way. Not lonely with this aching loneliness that tortured him now. What was there left for him? As regards any triumphs which the future might bring in connection with his work, he was, as Mac the stage-door keeper had said, "blarzy". Any success he might have would be but a stale repetition of other successes which he had achieved. He would go on working, of course, but—. The ringing of the telephone bell across the room jerked him back to the present. He got up with a muttered malediction. Someone calling up again from the theatre probably. They had been doing it all the time since he had announced his intention of leaving for America by Saturday's boat.

"Hello?" he said wearily.

"Is that George?" asked a voice. It seemed familiar, but all female voices sound the same over the telephone.

"This is George," he replied. "Who are you?"

"Don't you know my voice?"

"I do not."

"You'll know it quite well before long. I'm a great talker."

"Is that Billie?"

"It is not Billie, whoever Billie may be. I am female, George."

"So is Billie."

"Well, you had better run through the list of your feminine friends till you reach me."

"I haven't any feminine friends."

"None?"

"That's odd."

"Why?"

"You told me in the garden two nights ago that you looked on me as a pal."

George sat down abruptly. He felt boneless.

"Is—is that you?" he stammered. "It can't be—Maud!"

"How clever of you to guess. George, I want to ask you one or two things. In the first place, are you fond of butter?"

George blinked. This was not a dream. He had just bumped his knee against the corner of the telephone table, and it still hurt most convincingly. He needed the evidence to assure himself that he was awake.

"Butter?" he queried. "What do you mean?"

"Oh, well, if you don't even know what butter means, I expect it's all right. What is your weight, George?"

"About a hundred and eighty pounds. But I don't understand."

"Wait a minute." There was a silence at the other end of the wire. "About thirteen stone," said Maud's voice. "I've been doing it in my head. And what was it this time last year?"

"About the same, I think. I always weigh about the same."

"How wonderful! George!"

"Yes?"

"This is very important. Have you ever been in Florida?"

"I was there one winter."

"Do you know a fish called the pompano?"

"Yes."

"Tell me about it."

"How do you mean? It's just a fish. You eat it."

"I know. Go into details."

"There aren't any details. You just eat it."

The voice at the other end of the wire purred with approval. "I never heard anything so splendid. The last man who mentioned pompano to me became absolutely lyrical about sprigs of parsley and melted butter. Well, that's that. Now, here's another very important point. How about wall-paper?"

George pressed his unoccupied hand against his forehead.

This conversation was unnerving him.

"I didn't get that," he said.

"Didn't get what?"

"I mean, I didn't quite catch what you said that time. It sounded to me like 'What about wall-paper?'"

"It was 'What about wall-paper?' Why not?"

"But," said George weakly, "it doesn't make any sense."

"Oh, but it does. I mean, what about wall-paper for your den?"

"My den?"

"Your den. You must have a den. Where do you suppose you're going to work, if you don't? Now, my idea would be some nice quiet grass-cloth. And, of course, you would have lots of pictures and books. And a photograph of me. I'll go and be taken specially. Then there would be a piano for you to work on, and two or three really comfortable chairs. And—

well, that would be about all, wouldn't it?"

George pulled himself together.

"Hello!" he said.

"Why do you say 'Hello'?"

"I forgot I was in London. I should have said 'Are you there?'"

"Yes, I'm here."

"Well, then, what does it all mean?"

"What does what mean?"

"What you've been saying—about butter and pompanos and wall-paper and my den and all that? I don't understand."

"How stupid of you! I was asking you what sort of wall-paper you would like in your den after we were married and settled down."

George dropped the receiver. It clashed against the side of the table. He groped for it blindly.

"Hello!" he said.

"Don't say 'Hello!' It sounds so abrupt!"

"What did you say then?"

"I said 'Don't say Hello!'"

"No, before that! Before that! You said something about getting married."

"Well, aren't we going to get married? Our engagement is announced in the Morning Post."

"But—But—"

"George!" Maud's voice shook. "Don't tell me you are going to jilt me!" she said tragically. "Because, if you are, let me know in time, as I shall want to bring an action for breach of promise. I've just met such a capable young man who will look after the whole thing for me. He wears a bowler hat on the side of his head and calls waitresses 'Mabel'. Answer 'yes' or 'no'. Will you marry me?"

"But—But—how about—I mean, what about—I mean how about—?"

"Make up your mind what you do mean."

"The other fellow!" gasped George.

A musical laugh was wafted to him over the wire.

"What about him?"

"Well, what about him?" said George.

"Isn't a girl allowed to change her mind?" said Maud.

George yelped excitedly. Maud gave a cry.

"Don't sing!" she said. "You nearly made me deaf."

"Have you changed your mind?"

"Certainly I have!"

"And you really think—You really want—I mean, you really want—You really think—"

"Don't be so incoherent!"

"Maud!"

"Well?"

"Will you marry me?"

"Of course, I will."

"Gosh!"

"What did you say?"

"I said Gosh! And listen to me, when I say Gosh, I mean Gosh! Where are you? I must see you. Where can we meet? I want to see you! For Heaven's sake, tell me where you are. I want to see you! Where are you? Where are you?"

"I'm downstairs."

"Where? Here at the 'Carlton'?"

"Here at the 'Carlton'!"

"Alone?"

"Quite alone."

"You won't be long!" said George.

He hung up the receiver, and bounded across the room to where his coat hung over the back of a chair. The edge of the steamer-trunk caught his shin.

"Well," said George to the steamer-trunk, "and what are you butting in for? Who wants you, I should like to know!"

My Man Jeeves

LEAVE IT TO JEEVES

Jeeves—my man, you know—is really a most extraordinary chap. So capable. Honestly, I shouldn't know what to do without him. On broader lines he's like those chappies who sit peering sadly over the marble battlements at the Pennsylvania Station in the place marked "Inquiries." You know the Johnnies I mean. You go up to them and say: "When's the next train for Melonsquashville, Tennessee?" and they reply, without stopping to think, "Two-forty-three, track ten, change at San Francisco." And they're right every time. Well, Jeeves gives you just the same impression of omniscience.

As an instance of what I mean, I remember meeting Monty Byng in Bond Street one morning, looking the last word in a grey check suit, and I felt I should never be happy till I had one like it. I dug the address of the tailors out of him, and had them working on the thing inside the hour.

"Jeeves," I said that evening. "I'm getting a check suit like that one of Mr. Byng's."

"Injudicious, sir," he said firmly. "It will not become you."

"What absolute rot! It's the soundest thing I've struck for years."

"Unsuitable for you, sir."

Well, the long and the short of it was that the confounded thing came home, and I put it on, and when I caught sight of myself in the glass I nearly swooned. Jeeves was perfectly right. I looked a cross between a music-hall comedian and a cheap bookie. Yet Monty had looked fine in absolutely the same stuff. These things are just Life's mysteries, and that's all there is to it.

But it isn't only that Jeeves's judgment about clothes is infallible, though, of course, that's really the main thing. The man knows everything. There was the matter of that tip on the "Lincolnshire." I forget now how I got it, but it had the aspect of being the real, red-hot tabasco.

"Jeeves," I said, for I'm fond of the man, and like to do him a good turn when I can, "if you want to make a bit of money have something on Wonderchild for the 'Lincolnshire.'"

He shook his head.

"I'd rather not, sir."

"But it's the straight goods. I'm going to put my shirt on him."

"I do not recommend it, sir. The animal is not intended to win. Second place is what the stable is after."

Perfect piffle, I thought, of course. How the deuce could Jeeves know anything about it? Still, you know what happened. Wonderchild led till he was breathing on the wire, and then Banana Fritter came along and nosed him out. I went straight home and rang for Jeeves.

"After this," I said, "not another step for me without your advice. From now on consider yourself the brains of the establishment."

"Very good, sir. I shall endeavour to give satisfaction."

And he has, by Jove! I'm a bit short on brain myself; the old bean would appear to have been constructed more for ornament than for use, don't you know; but give me five minutes to talk the thing over with Jeeves, and I'm game to advise any one about anything. And that's why, when Bruce Corcoran came to me with his troubles, my first act was to ring the bell and put it up to the lad with the bulging forehead.

"Leave it to Jeeves," I said.

I first got to know Corky when I came to New York. He was a pal of my cousin Gussie, who was in with a lot of people down Washington Square way. I don't know if I ever told you about it, but the reason why I left England was because I was sent over by my Aunt Agatha to try to stop young Gussie marrying a girl on the vaudeville stage, and I got the whole thing so mixed up that I decided that it would be a sound scheme for me to stop on in America for a bit instead of going back and having long cosy chats about the thing with aunt. So I sent Jeeves out to find a decent apartment, and settled down for a bit of exile. I'm bound to say that New York's a topping place to be exiled in. Everybody was awfully good to me, and there seemed to be plenty of things going on, and I'm a wealthy bird, so everything was fine. Chappies introduced me to other chappies, and so on and so forth, and it wasn't long before I knew squads of the right sort, some who rolled in dollars in houses up by the Park, and others who lived with the gas turned down mostly around Washington Square—artists and writers and so forth. Brainy coves.

Corky was one of the artists. A portrait-painter, he called himself, but he hadn't painted any portraits. He was sitting on the side-lines with a blanket over his shoulders, waiting for a chance to get into the game. You see, the catch about portrait-painting—I've looked into the thing a bit—is that you can't start painting portraits till people come along and ask you to, and they won't come and ask you to until you've painted a lot first. This makes it kind of difficult for a chappie. Corky managed to get along by drawing an occasional picture for the comic papers—he had rather a gift for funny stuff when he got a good idea—and doing bedsteads and chairs and things for the advertisements. His principal source of income, however, was derived from biting the ear of a rich uncle—one Alexander Worple, who was in the jute business. I'm a bit foggy as to what jute is, but it's apparently something the populace is pretty keen on, for Mr. Worple had made quite an indecently large stack out of it.

Now, a great many fellows think that having a rich uncle is a pretty soft snap: but, according to Corky, such is not the case. Corky's uncle was a robust sort of cove, who looked like living for ever. He was fifty-one, and it seemed as if he might go to par. It was not this, however, that distressed poor old Corky, for he was not bigoted and had no objection to the man going on living. What Corky kicked at was the way the above Worple used to harry him.

Corky's uncle, you see, didn't want him to be an artist. He didn't think he had any talent in that direction. He was always urging him to chuck Art and go into the jute business and start at the bottom and work his way up. Jute had apparently become a sort of obsession with him. He seemed to attach almost a spiritual importance to it. And what Corky said was that, while he didn't know what they did at the bottom of the jute business, instinct told him that it was something too beastly for words. Corky, moreover, believed in his future as an artist. Some day, he said, he was going to make a hit. Meanwhile, by using the utmost tact and persuasiveness, he was inducing his uncle to cough up very grudgingly a small quarterly allowance.

He wouldn't have got this if his uncle hadn't had a hobby. Mr. Worple was peculiar in this respect. As a rule, from what I've observed, the American captain of industry doesn't do anything out of business hours. When he has put the cat out and locked up the office for the night, he just relapses into a state of coma from which he emerges only to start being a captain of industry again. But Mr. Worple in his spare time was what is known as an ornithologist. He had written a book called American Birds, and was writing another, to be called More American Birds. When he had finished that, the presumption was that he would begin a third, and keep on till the supply of American birds gave out. Corky used to go to him about once every three months and let him talk about American birds. Apparently you could do what you liked with old Worple if you gave him his head first on his pet subject, so these little chats used to make Corky's allowance all right for the time being. But it was pretty rotten for the poor chap. There was the frightful suspense, you see, and, apart from that, birds, except when broiled and in the society of a cold bottle, bored him stiff.

To complete the character-study of Mr. Worple, he was a man of extremely uncertain temper, and his general tendency was to think that Corky was a poor chump and that whatever step he took in any direction on his own account, was just another proof of his innate idiocy. I should imagine Jeeves feels very much the same about me.

So when Corky trickled into my apartment one afternoon, shooing a girl in front of him, and said, "Bertie, I want you to meet my fiancée, Miss Singer," the aspect of the matter which hit me first was precisely the one which he had come to consult me about. The very first words I spoke were, "Corky, how about your uncle?"

The poor chap gave one of those mirthless laughs. He was looking anxious and worried, like a man who has done the murder all right but can't think what the deuce to do with the body.

"We're so scared, Mr. Wooster," said the girl. "We were hoping that you might suggest a way of breaking it to him."

Muriel Singer was one of those very quiet, appealing girls who have a way of looking at you with their big eyes as if they thought you were the greatest thing on earth and wondered that you hadn't got on to it yet yourself. She sat there in a sort of shrinking way, looking at me as if she were saying to herself, "Oh, I do hope this great strong man isn't going to hurt me." She gave a fellow a protective kind of feeling, made him want to stroke her hand and say, "There, there, little one!" or words to that effect. She made me feel that there was nothing I wouldn't do for her. She was rather like one of those innocent-tasting American drinks which creep imperceptibly into your system so that, before you know what you're doing, you're starting out to reform the world by force if necessary and pausing on your way to tell the large man in the corner that, if he looks at you like that, you will knock his head off. What I mean is, she made me feel alert and dashing, like a jolly old knight-errant or something of that kind. I felt that I was with her in this thing to the limit.

"I don't see why your uncle shouldn't be most awfully bucked," I said to Corky. "He will think Miss Singer the ideal wife for you."

Corky declined to cheer up.

"You don't know him. Even if he did like Muriel he wouldn't admit it. That's the sort of pig-headed guy he is. It would be a matter of principle with him to kick. All he would consider would be that I had gone and taken an important step without asking his advice, and he would raise Cain automatically. He's always done it."

I strained the old bean to meet this emergency.

"You want to work it so that he makes Miss Singer's acquaintance without knowing that you know her. Then you come along——"

"But how can I work it that way?"

I saw his point. That was the catch.

"There's only one thing to do," I said.

"What's that?"

"Leave it to Jeeves."

And I rang the bell.

"Sir?" said Jeeves, kind of manifesting himself. One of the rummy things about Jeeves is that, unless you watch like a hawk, you very seldom see him come into a room. He's like one of those weird chappies in India who dissolve themselves into thin air and nip through space in a sort of disembodied way and assemble the parts again just where they want them. I've got a cousin who's what they call a Theosophist, and he says he's often nearly worked the thing himself, but couldn't quite bring it off, probably owing to having fed in his boyhood on the flesh of animals slain in anger and pie.

The moment I saw the man standing there, registering respectful attention, a weight seemed to roll off my mind. I felt like a lost child who spots his father in the offing. There was something about him that gave me confidence.

Jeeves is a tallish man, with one of those dark, shrewd faces. His eye gleams with the light of pure intelligence.

"Jeeves, we want your advice."

"Very good, sir."

I boiled down Corky's painful case into a few well-chosen words.

"So you see what it amount to, Jeeves. We want you to suggest some way by which Mr. Worple can make Miss Singer's acquaintance without getting on to the fact that Mr. Corcoran already knows her. Understand?"

"Perfectly, sir."

"Well, try to think of something."

"I have thought of something already, sir."

"You have!"

"The scheme I would suggest cannot fail of success, but it has what may seem to you a drawback, sir, in that it requires a certain financial outlay."

"He means," I translated to Corky, "that he has got a pippin of an idea, but it's going to cost a bit."

Naturally the poor chap's face dropped, for this seemed to dish the whole thing. But I was still under the influence of the girl's melting gaze, and I saw that this was where I started in as a knight-errant.

"You can count on me for all that sort of thing, Corky," I said. "Only too glad. Carry on, Jeeves."

"I would suggest, sir, that Mr. Corcoran take advantage of Mr. Worple's attachment to ornithology."

"How on earth did you know that he was fond of birds?"

"It is the way these New York apartments are constructed, sir. Quite unlike our London houses. The partitions between the rooms are of the flimsiest nature. With no wish to overhear, I have sometimes heard Mr. Corcoran expressing himself with a generous strength on the subject I have mentioned."

"Oh! Well?"

"Why should not the young lady write a small volume, to be entitled—let us say—The Children's Book of American Birds, and dedicate it to Mr. Worple! A limited edition could be published at your expense, sir, and a great deal of the book would, of course, be given over to eulogistic remarks concerning Mr. Worple's own larger treatise on the same subject. I should recommend the dispatching of a presentation copy to Mr. Worple, immediately on publication, accompanied by a letter in which the young lady asks to be allowed to make the acquaintance of one to whom she owes so much. This would, I fancy, produce the desired result, but as I say, the expense involved would be considerable."

I felt like the proprietor of a performing dog on the vaudeville stage when the tyke has just pulled off his trick without a hitch. I had betted on Jeeves all along, and I had known that he wouldn't let me down. It beats me sometimes why a man with his genius is satisfied to hang around pressing my clothes and what-not. If I had half Jeeves's brain, I should have a stab at being Prime Minister or something.

"Jeeves," I said, "that is absolutely ripping! One of your very best efforts."

"Thank you, sir."

The girl made an objection.

"But I'm sure I couldn't write a book about anything. I can't even write good letters."

"Muriel's talents," said Corky, with a little cough "lie more in the direction of the drama, Bertie. I didn't mention it before, but one of our reasons for being a trifle nervous as to how Uncle Alexander will receive the news is that Muriel is in the chorus of that show Choose your Exit at the Manhattan. It's absurdly unreasonable, but we both feel that that fact might increase Uncle Alexander's natural tendency to kick like a steer."

I saw what he meant. Goodness knows there was fuss enough in our family when I tried to marry into musical comedy a few years ago. And the recollection of my Aunt Agatha's attitude in the matter of Gussie and the vaudeville girl was still fresh in my mind. I don't know why it is—one of these psychology sharps could explain it, I suppose—but uncles and aunts, as a class, are always dead against the drama, legitimate or otherwise. They don't seem able to stick it at any price.

But Jeeves had a solution, of course.

"I fancy it would be a simple matter, sir, to find some impecunious author who would be glad to do the actual composition of the volume for a small fee. It is only necessary that the young lady's name should appear on the title page."

"That's true," said Corky. "Sam Patterson would do it for a hundred dollars. He writes a novelette, three short stories, and ten thousand words of a serial for one of the all-fiction magazines under different names every month. A little thing like this would be nothing to him. I'll get after him right away."

"Fine!"

"Will that be all, sir?" said Jeeves. "Very good, sir. Thank you, sir."

I always used to think that publishers had to be devilish intelligent fellows, loaded down with the grey matter; but I've got their number now. All a publisher has to do is to write cheques at intervals, while a lot of deserving and industrious chappies rally round and do the real work. I know, because I've been one myself. I simply sat tight in the old apartment with a fountain-pen, and in due season a topping, shiny book came along.

I happened to be down at Corky's place when the first copies of The Children's Book of American Birds bobbed up. Muriel Singer was there, and we were talking of things in general when there was a bang at the door and the parcel was delivered.

It was certainly some book. It had a red cover with a fowl of some species on it, and underneath the girl's name in gold letters. I opened a copy at random.

"Often of a spring morning," it said at the top of page twenty-one, "as you wander through the fields, you will hear the sweet-toned, carelessly flowing warble of the purple finch linnet. When you are older you must read all about him in Mr. Alexander Worple's wonderful book—American Birds."

You see. A boost for the uncle right away. And only a few pages later there he was in the limelight again in connection with the yellow-billed cuckoo. It was great stuff. The more I read, the more I admired the chap who had written it and Jeeves's genius in putting us on to the wheeze. I didn't see how the uncle could fail to drop. You can't call a chap the world's greatest authority on the yellow-billed cuckoo without rousing a certain disposition towards chumminess in him.

"It's a cert!" I said.

"An absolute cinch!" said Corky.

And a day or two later he meandered up the Avenue to my apartment to tell me that all was well. The uncle had written Muriel a letter so dripping with the milk of human kindness that if he hadn't known Mr. Worple's handwriting Corky would have refused to believe him the author of it. Any time it suited Miss Singer to call, said the uncle, he would be delighted to make her acquaintance.

Shortly after this I had to go out of town. Divers sound sportsmen had invited me to pay visits to their country places, and it wasn't for several months that I settled down in the city again. I had been wondering a lot, of course, about Corky, whether it all turned out right, and so forth, and my first evening in New York, happening to pop into a quiet sort of little restaurant which I go to when I don't feel inclined for the bright lights, I found Muriel Singer there, sitting by herself at a table near the door. Corky, I took it, was out telephoning. I went up and passed the time of day.

"Well, well, well, what?" I said.

"Why, Mr. Wooster! How do you do?"

"Corky around?"

"I beg your pardon?"

"You're waiting for Corky, aren't you?"

"Oh, I didn't understand. No, I'm not waiting for him."

It seemed to me that there was a sort of something in her voice, a kind of thingummy, you know.

"I say, you haven't had a row with Corky, have you?"

"A row?"

"A spat, don't you know—little misunderstanding—faults on both sides—er—and all that sort of thing."

"Why, whatever makes you think that?"

"Oh, well, as it were, what? What I mean is—I thought you usually dined with him before you went to the theatre."

"I've left the stage now."

Suddenly the whole thing dawned on me. I had forgotten what a long time I had been away.

"Why, of course, I see now! You're married!"

"Yes."

"How perfectly topping! I wish you all kinds of happiness."

"Thank you, so much. Oh Alexander," she said, looking past me, "this is a friend of mine—Mr. Wooster."

I spun round. A chappie with a lot of stiff grey hair and a red sort of healthy face was standing there. Rather a formidable Johnnie, he looked, though quite peaceful at the moment.

"I want you to meet my husband, Mr. Wooster. Mr. Wooster is a friend of Bruce's, Alexander."

The old boy grasped my hand warmly, and that was all that kept me from hitting the floor in a heap. The place was rocking. Absolutely.

"So you know my nephew, Mr. Wooster," I heard him say. "I wish you would try to knock a little sense into him and make him quit this playing at painting. But I have an idea that he is steadying down. I noticed it first that night he came to dinner with us, my dear, to be introduced to you. He seemed altogether quieter and more serious. Something seemed to have sobered him. Perhaps you will give us the pleasure of your company at dinner to-night, Mr. Wooster? Or have you dined?"

I said I had. What I needed then was air, not dinner. I felt that I wanted to get into the open and think this thing out.

When I reached my apartment I heard Jeeves moving about in his lair. I called him.

"Jeeves," I said, "now is the time for all good men to come to the aid of the party. A stiff b.-and-s. first of all, and then I've a bit of news for you."

He came back with a tray and a long glass.

"Better have one yourself, Jeeves. You'll need it."

"Later on, perhaps, thank you, sir."

"All right. Please yourself. But you're going to get a shock. You remember my friend, Mr. Corcoran?"

"Yes, sir."

"And the girl who was to slide gracefully into his uncle's esteem by writing the book on birds?"

"Perfectly, sir."

"Well, she's slid. She's married the uncle."

He took it without blinking. You can't rattle Jeeves.

"That was always a development to be feared, sir."

"You don't mean to tell me that you were expecting it?"

"It crossed my mind as a possibility."

"Did it, by Jove! Well, I think, you might have warned us!"

"I hardly liked to take the liberty, sir."

Of course, as I saw after I had had a bite to eat and was in a calmer frame of mind, what had happened wasn't my fault, if you come down to it. I couldn't be expected to foresee that the scheme, in itself a cracker-jack, would skid into the ditch as it had done; but all the same I'm bound to admit that I didn't relish the idea of meeting Corky again until time, the great healer, had been able to get in a bit of soothing work. I cut Washington Square out absolutely for the next few months. I gave it the complete miss-in-baulk. And then, just when I was beginning to think I might safely pop down in that direction and gather up the dropped threads, so to speak, time, instead of working the healing wheeze, went and pulled the most awful bone and put the lid on it. Opening the paper one morning, I read that Mrs. Alexander Worple had presented her husband with a son and heir.

I was so darned sorry for poor old Corky that I hadn't the heart to touch my breakfast. I told Jeeves to drink it himself. I was bowled over. Absolutely. It was the limit.

I hardly knew what to do. I wanted, of course, to rush down to Washington Square and grip the poor blighter silently by the hand; and then, thinking it over, I hadn't the nerve. Absent treatment seemed the touch. I gave it him in waves.

But after a month or so I began to hesitate again. It struck me that it was playing it a bit low-down on the poor chap, avoiding him like this just when he probably wanted his pals to surge round him most. I pictured him sitting in his lonely studio with no company but his bitter thoughts, and the pathos of it got me to such an extent that I bounded straight into a taxi and told the driver to go all out for the studio.

I rushed in, and there was Corky, hunched up at the easel, painting away, while on the model throne sat a severe-looking female of middle age, holding a baby.

A fellow has to be ready for that sort of thing.

"Oh, ah!" I said, and started to back out.

Corky looked over his shoulder.

"Halloa, Bertie. Don't go. We're just finishing for the day. That will be all this afternoon," he said to the nurse, who got up with the baby and decanted it into a perambulator which was standing in the fairway.

"At the same hour to-morrow, Mr. Corcoran?"

"Yes, please."

"Good afternoon."

"Good afternoon."

Corky stood there, looking at the door, and then he turned to me and began to get it off his chest. Fortunately, he seemed to take it for granted that I knew all about what had happened, so it wasn't as awkward as it might have been.

"It's my uncle's idea," he said. "Muriel doesn't know about it yet. The portrait's to be a surprise for her on her birthday. The nurse takes the kid out ostensibly to get a breather, and they beat it down here. If you want an instance of the irony of fate, Bertie, get acquainted with this. Here's the first commission I have ever had to paint a portrait, and the sitter is that human poached egg that has butted in and bounced me out of my inheritance. Can you beat it! I call it rubbing the thing in to expect me to spend my afternoons gazing into the ugly face of a little brat who to all intents and purposes has hit me behind the ear with a blackjack and swiped all I possess. I can't refuse to paint the portrait because if I did my uncle would stop my allowance; yet every time I look up and catch that kid's vacant eye, I suffer agonies. I tell you, Bertie, sometimes when he gives me a patronizing glance and then turns away and is sick, as if it revolted him to look at me, I come within an ace of occupying the entire front page of the evening papers as the latest murder sensation. There are moments when I can almost see the headlines: 'Promising Young Artist Beans Baby With Axe.'"

I patted his shoulder silently. My sympathy for the poor old scout was too deep for words.

I kept away from the studio for some time after that, because it didn't seem right to me to intrude on the poor chappie's sorrow. Besides, I'm bound to say that nurse intimidated me. She reminded me so infernally of Aunt Agatha. She was the same gimlet-eyed type.

But one afternoon Corky called me on the 'phone.

"Bertie."

"Halloa?"

"Are you doing anything this afternoon?"

"Nothing special."

"You couldn't come down here, could you?"

"What's the trouble? Anything up?"

"I've finished the portrait."

"Good boy! Stout work!"

"Yes." His voice sounded rather doubtful. "The fact is, Bertie, it doesn't look quite right to me. There's something about it—My uncle's coming in half an hour to inspect it, and—I don't know why it is, but I kind of feel I'd like your moral support!"

I began to see that I was letting myself in for something. The sympathetic co-operation of Jeeves seemed to me to be indicated.

"You think he'll cut up rough?"

"He may."

I threw my mind back to the red-faced chappie I had met at the restaurant, and tried to picture him cutting up rough. It was only too easy. I spoke to Corky firmly on the telephone.

"I'll come," I said.

"Good!"

"But only if I may bring Jeeves!"

"Why Jeeves? What's Jeeves got to do with it? Who wants Jeeves? Jeeves is the fool who suggested the scheme that has led——"

"Listen, Corky, old top! If you think I am going to face that uncle of yours without Jeeves's support, you're mistaken. I'd sooner go into a den of wild beasts and bite a lion on the back of the neck."

"Oh, all right," said Corky. Not cordially, but he said it; so I rang for Jeeves, and explained the situation.

"Very good, sir," said Jeeves.

That's the sort of chap he is. You can't rattle him.

We found Corky near the door, looking at the picture, with one hand up in a defensive sort of way, as if he thought it might swing on him.

"Stand right where you are, Bertie," he said, without moving. "Now, tell me honestly, how does it strike you?"

The light from the big window fell right on the picture. I took a good look at it. Then I shifted a bit nearer and took another look. Then I went back to where I had been at first, because it hadn't seemed quite so bad from there.

"Well?" said Corky, anxiously.

I hesitated a bit.

"Of course, old man, I only saw the kid once, and then only for a moment, but—but it was an ugly sort of kid, wasn't it, if I remember rightly?"

"As ugly as that?"

I looked again, and honesty compelled me to be frank.

"I don't see how it could have been, old chap."

Poor old Corky ran his fingers through his hair in a temperamental sort of way. He groaned.

"You're right quite, Bertie. Something's gone wrong with the darned thing. My private impression is that, without knowing it, I've worked that stunt that Sargent and those fellows pull—painting the soul of the sitter. I've got through the mere outward appearance, and have put the child's soul on canvas."

"But could a child of that age have a soul like that? I don't see how he could have managed it in the time. What do you think, Jeeves?"

"I doubt it, sir."

"It—it sorts of leers at you, doesn't it?"

"You've noticed that, too?" said Corky.

"I don't see how one could help noticing."

"All I tried to do was to give the little brute a cheerful expression. But, as it worked out, he looks positively dissipated."

"Just what I was going to suggest, old man. He looks as if he were in the middle of a colossal spree, and enjoying every minute of it. Don't you think so, Jeeves?"

"He has a decidedly inebriated air, sir."

Corky was starting to say something when the door opened, and the uncle came in.

For about three seconds all was joy, jollity, and goodwill. The old boy shook hands with me, slapped Corky on the back, said that he didn't think he had ever seen such a fine day, and whacked his leg with his stick. Jeeves had projected himself into the background, and he didn't notice him.

"Well, Bruce, my boy; so the portrait is really finished, is it—really finished? Well, bring it out. Let's have a look at it. This will be a wonderful surprise for your aunt. Where is it? Let's——"

And then he got it—suddenly, when he wasn't set for the punch; and he rocked back on his heels.

"Oosh!" he exclaimed. And for perhaps a minute there was one of the scaliest silences I've ever run up against.

"Is this a practical joke?" he said at last, in a way that set about sixteen draughts cutting through the room at once.

I thought it was up to me to rally round old Corky.

"You want to stand a bit farther away from it," I said.

"You're perfectly right!" he snorted. "I do! I want to stand so far away from it that I can't see the thing with a telescope!" He turned on Corky like an untamed tiger of the jungle who has just located a chunk of meat. "And this—this—is what you have been wasting your time and my money for all these years! A painter! I wouldn't let you paint a house of mine! I gave you this commission, thinking that you were a competent worker, and this—this—this extract from a comic coloured supplement is the result!" He swung towards the door, lashing his tail and growling to himself. "This ends it! If you wish to continue this foolery of pretending to be an artist because you want an excuse for idleness, please yourself. But let me tell you this. Unless you report at my office on Monday morning, prepared to abandon all this idiocy and start in at the bottom of the business to work your way up, as you should have done half a dozen years ago, not another cent—not another cent—not another—Boosh!"

Then the door closed, and he was no longer with us. And I crawled out of the bombproof shelter.

"Corky, old top!" I whispered faintly.

Corky was standing staring at the picture. His face was set. There was a hunted look in his eye.

"Well, that finishes it!" he muttered brokenly.

"What are you going to do?"

"Do? What can I do? I can't stick on here if he cuts off supplies. You heard what he said. I shall have to go to the office on Monday."

I couldn't think of a thing to say. I knew exactly how he felt about the office. I don't know when I've been so infernally uncomfortable. It was like hanging round trying to make conversation to a pal who's just been sentenced to twenty years in quod.

And then a soothing voice broke the silence.

"If I might make a suggestion, sir!"

It was Jeeves. He had slid from the shadows and was gazing gravely at the picture. Upon my word, I can't give you a better idea of the shattering effect of Corky's uncle Alexander when in action than by saying that he had absolutely made me forget for the moment that Jeeves was there.

"I wonder if I have ever happened to mention to you, sir, a Mr. Digby Thistleton, with whom I was once in service? Perhaps you have met him? He was a financier. He is now Lord Bridgnorth. It was a favourite saying of his that there is always a way. The first time I heard him use the expression was after the failure of a patent depilatory which he promoted."

"Jeeves," I said, "what on earth are you talking about?"

"I mentioned Mr. Thistleton, sir, because his was in some respects a parallel case to the present one. His depilatory failed, but he did not despair. He put it on the market again under the name of Hair-o, guaranteed to produce a full crop of hair in a few months. It was advertised, if you remember, sir, by a humorous picture of a billiard-ball, before and after taking, and made such a substantial fortune that Mr. Thistleton was soon afterwards elevated to the peerage for services to his Party. It seems to me that, if Mr. Corcoran looks into the matter, he will find, like Mr. Thistleton, that there is always a way. Mr. Worple himself suggested the solution of the difficulty. In the heat of the moment he compared the portrait to an extract from a coloured comic supplement. I consider the suggestion a very valuable one, sir. Mr. Corcoran's portrait may not have pleased Mr. Worple as a likeness of his only child, but I have no doubt that editors would gladly consider it as a foundation for a series of humorous drawings. If Mr. Corcoran will allow me to make the suggestion, his talent has always been for the humorous. There is something about this picture—something bold and vigorous, which arrests the attention. I feel sure it would be highly popular."

Corky was glaring at the picture, and making a sort of dry, sucking noise with his mouth. He seemed completely overwrought.

And then suddenly he began to laugh in a wild way.

"Corky, old man!" I said, massaging him tenderly. I feared the poor blighter was hysterical.

He began to stagger about all over the floor.

"He's right! The man's absolutely right! Jeeves, you're a life-saver! You've hit on the greatest idea of the age! Report at the office on Monday! Start at the bottom of the business! I'll buy the business if I feel like it. I know the man who runs the comic section of the Sunday Star. He'll eat this thing. He was telling me only the other day how hard it was to get a good new series. He'll give me anything I ask for a real winner like this. I've got a gold-mine. Where's my hat? I've got an income for life! Where's that confounded hat? Lend me a fiver, Bertie. I want to take a taxi down to Park Row!"

Jeeves smiled paternally. Or, rather, he had a kind of paternal muscular spasm about the mouth, which is the nearest he ever gets to smiling.

"If I might make the suggestion, Mr. Corcoran—for a title of the series which you have in mind—'The Adventures of Baby Blobbs.'"

Corky and I looked at the picture, then at each other in an awed way. Jeeves was right. There could be no other title.

"Jeeves," I said. It was a few weeks later, and I had just finished looking at the comic section of the Sunday Star. "I'm an optimist. I always have been. The older I get, the more I agree with Shakespeare and those poet Johnnies about it always being darkest before the dawn and there's a silver lining and what you lose on the swings you make up on the roundabouts. Look at Mr. Corcoran, for instance. There was a fellow, one would have said, clear up to the eyebrows in the soup. To all appearances he had got it right in the neck. Yet look at him now. Have you seen these pictures?"

"I took the liberty of glancing at them before bringing them to you, sir. Extremely diverting."

"They have made a big hit, you know."

"I anticipated it, sir."

I leaned back against the pillows.

"You know, Jeeves, you're a genius. You ought to be drawing a commission on these things."

"I have nothing to complain of in that respect, sir. Mr. Corcoran has been most generous. I am putting out the brown suit, sir."

"No, I think I'll wear the blue with the faint red stripe."

"Not the blue with the faint red stripe, sir."

"But I rather fancy myself in it."

"Not the blue with the faint red stripe, sir."

"Oh, all right, have it your own way."

"Very good, sir. Thank you, sir."

Of course, I know it's as bad as being henpecked; but then Jeeves is always right. You've got to consider that, you know. What?

JEEVES AND THE UNBIDDEN GUEST

I'm not absolutely certain of my facts, but I rather fancy it's Shakespeare—or, if not, it's some equally brainy lad—who says that it's always just when a chappie is feeling particularly top-hole, and more than usually braced with things in general that Fate sneaks up behind him with a bit of lead piping. There's no doubt the man's right. It's absolutely that way with me. Take, for instance, the fairly rummy matter of Lady Malvern and her son Wilmot. A moment before they turned up, I was just thinking how thoroughly all right everything was.

It was one of those topping mornings, and I had just climbed out from under the cold shower, feeling like a two-year-old. As a matter of fact, I was especially bucked just then because the day before I had asserted myself with Jeeves—absolutely asserted myself, don't you know. You see, the way things had been going on I was rapidly becoming a dashed serf. The man had jolly well oppressed me. I didn't so much mind when he made me give up one of my new suits, because, Jeeves's judgment about suits is sound. But I as near as a toucher rebelled when he wouldn't let me wear a pair of cloth-topped boots which I loved like a couple of brothers. And when he tried to tread on me like a worm in the matter of a hat, I jolly well put my foot down and showed him who was who. It's a long story, and I haven't time to tell you now, but the point is that he wanted me to wear the Longacre—as worn by John Drew—when I had set my heart on the Country Gentleman—as worn by another famous actor chappie—and the end of the matter was that, after a rather painful scene, I bought the Country Gentleman. So that's how things stood on this particular morning, and I was feeling kind of manly and independent.

Well, I was in the bathroom, wondering what there was going to be for breakfast while I massaged the good old spine with a rough towel and sang slightly, when there was a tap at the door. I stopped singing and opened the door an inch.

"What ho without there!"

"Lady Malvern wishes to see you, sir," said Jeeves.

"Eh?"

"Lady Malvern, sir. She is waiting in the sitting-room."

"Pull yourself together, Jeeves, my man," I said, rather severely, for I bar practical jokes before breakfast. "You know perfectly well there's no one waiting for me in the sitting-room. How could there be when it's barely ten o'clock yet?"

"I gathered from her ladyship, sir, that she had landed from an ocean liner at an early hour this morning."

This made the thing a bit more plausible. I remembered that when I had arrived in America about a year before, the proceedings had begun at some ghastly hour like six, and that I had been shot out on to a foreign shore considerably before eight.

"Who the deuce is Lady Malvern, Jeeves?"

"Her ladyship did not confide in me, sir."

"Is she alone?"

"Her ladyship is accompanied by a Lord Pershore, sir. I fancy that his lordship would be her ladyship's son."

"Oh, well, put out rich raiment of sorts, and I'll be dressing."

"Our heather-mixture lounge is in readiness, sir."

"Then lead me to it."

While I was dressing I kept trying to think who on earth Lady Malvern could be. It wasn't till I had climbed through the top of my shirt and was reaching out for the studs that I remembered.

"I've placed her, Jeeves. She's a pal of my Aunt Agatha."

"Indeed, sir?"

"Yes. I met her at lunch one Sunday before I left London. A very vicious specimen. Writes books. She wrote a book on social conditions in India when she came back from the Durbar."

"Yes, sir? Pardon me, sir, but not that tie!"

"Eh?"

"Not that tie with the heather-mixture lounge, sir!"

It was a shock to me. I thought I had quelled the fellow. It was rather a solemn moment. What I mean is, if I weakened now, all my good work the night before would be thrown away. I braced myself.

"What's wrong with this tie? I've seen you give it a nasty look before. Speak out like a man! What's the matter with it?"

"Too ornate, sir."

"Nonsense! A cheerful pink. Nothing more."

"Unsuitable, sir."

"Jeeves, this is the tie I wear!"

"Very good, sir."

Dashed unpleasant. I could see that the man was wounded. But I was firm. I tied the tie, got into the coat and waistcoat, and went into the sitting-room.

"Halloa! Halloa! Halloa!" I said. "What?"

"Ah! How do you do, Mr. Wooster? You have never met my son, Wilmot, I think? Motty, darling, this is Mr. Wooster."

Lady Malvern was a hearty, happy, healthy, overpowering sort of dashed female, not so very tall but making up for it by measuring about six feet from the O.P. to the Prompt Side. She fitted into my biggest arm-chair as if it had been built round her by someone who knew they were wearing arm-chairs tight about the hips that season. She had bright, bulging eyes and a lot of yellow hair, and when she spoke she showed about fifty-seven front teeth. She was one of those women who kind of numb a fellow's faculties. She made me feel as if I were ten years old and had been brought into the drawing-room in my Sunday clothes to say how-d'you-do. Altogether by no means the sort of thing a chappie would wish to find in his sitting-room before breakfast.

Motty, the son, was about twenty-three, tall and thin and meek-looking. He had the same yellow hair as his mother, but he wore it plastered down and parted in the middle. His eyes bulged, too, but they weren't bright. They were a dull grey with pink rims. His chin gave up the struggle about half-way down, and he didn't appear to have any eyelashes. A mild, furtive, sheepish sort of blighter, in short.

"Awfully glad to see you," I said. "So you've popped over, eh? Making a long stay in America?"

"About a month. Your aunt gave me your address and told me to be sure and call on you."

I was glad to hear this, as it showed that Aunt Agatha was beginning to come round a bit. There had been some unpleasantness a year before, when she had sent me over to New York to disentangle my Cousin Gussie from the clutches of a girl on the music-hall stage. When I tell you that by the time I had finished my operations, Gussie had not only married the girl but had gone on the stage himself, and was doing well, you'll understand that Aunt Agatha was upset to no small extent. I simply hadn't dared go back and face her, and it was a relief to find that time had healed the wound and all that sort of thing enough to make her tell her pals to look me up. What I mean is, much as I liked America, I didn't want to have England barred to me for the rest of my natural; and, believe me, England is a jolly sight too small for anyone to live in with Aunt Agatha, if she's really on the warpath. So I braced on hearing these kind words and smiled genially on the assemblage.

"Your aunt said that you would do anything that was in your power to be of assistance to us."

"Rather? Oh, rather! Absolutely!"

"Thank you so much. I want you to put dear Motty up for a little while."

I didn't get this for a moment.

"Put him up? For my clubs?"

"No, no! Darling Motty is essentially a home bird. Aren't you, Motty darling?"

Motty, who was sucking the knob of his stick, uncorked himself.

"Yes, mother," he said, and corked himself up again.

"I should not like him to belong to clubs. I mean put him up here. Have him to live with you while I am away."

These frightful words trickled out of her like honey. The woman simply didn't seem to understand the ghastly nature of her proposal. I gave Motty the swift east-to-west. He was sitting with his mouth nuzzling the stick, blinking at the wall. The thought of having this planted on me for an indefinite period appalled me. Absolutely appalled me, don't you know. I was just starting to say that the shot wasn't on the board at any price, and that the first sign Motty gave of trying to nestle into my little home I would yell for the police, when she went on, rolling placidly over me, as it were.

There was something about this woman that sapped a chappie's will-power.

"I am leaving New York by the midday train, as I have to pay a visit to Sing-Sing prison. I am extremely interested in prison conditions in America. After that I work my way gradually across to the coast, visiting the points of interest on the journey. You see, Mr. Wooster, I am in America principally on business. No doubt you read my book, India and the Indians? My publishers are anxious for me to write a companion volume on the United States. I shall not be able to spend more than a month in the country, as I have to get back for the season, but a month should be ample. I was less than a month in India, and my dear friend Sir Roger Cremorne wrote his America from Within after a stay of only two weeks. I should love to take dear Motty with me, but the poor boy gets so sick when he travels by train. I shall have to pick him up on my return."

From where I sat I could see Jeeves in the dining-room, laying the breakfast-table. I wished I could have had a minute with him alone. I felt certain that he would have been able to think of some way of putting a stop to this woman.

"It will be such a relief to know that Motty is safe with you, Mr. Wooster. I know what the temptations of a great city are. Hitherto dear Motty has been sheltered from them. He has lived quietly with me in the country. I know that you will look after him carefully, Mr. Wooster. He will give very little trouble." She talked about the poor blighter as if he wasn't there. Not that Motty seemed to mind. He had stopped chewing his walking-stick and was sitting there with his mouth open. "He is a vegetarian and a teetotaller and is devoted to reading. Give him a nice book and he will be quite contented." She got up. "Thank you so much, Mr. Wooster! I don't know what I should have done without your help. Come, Motty! We have just time to see a few of the sights before my train goes. But I shall have to rely on you for most of my information about New York, darling. Be sure to keep your eyes open and take notes of your impressions! It will be such a help. Good-bye, Mr. Wooster. I will send Motty back early in the afternoon."

They went out, and I howled for Jeeves.

"Jeeves! What about it?"

"Sir?"

"What's to be done? You heard it all, didn't you? You were in the dining-room most of the time. That pill is coming to stay here."

"Pill, sir?"

"The excrescence."

"I beg your pardon, sir?"

I looked at Jeeves sharply. This sort of thing wasn't like him. It was as if he were deliberately trying to give me the pip. Then I understood. The man was really upset about that tie. He was trying to get his own back.

"Lord Pershore will be staying here from to-night, Jeeves," I said coldly.

"Very good, sir. Breakfast is ready, sir."

I could have sobbed into the bacon and eggs. That there wasn't any sympathy to be got out of Jeeves was what put the lid on it. For a moment I almost weakened and told him to destroy the hat and tie if he didn't like them, but I pulled myself together again. I was dashed if I was going to let Jeeves treat me like a bally one-man chain-gang!

But, what with brooding on Jeeves and brooding on Motty, I was in a pretty reduced sort of state. The more I examined the situation, the more blighted it became. There was nothing I could do. If I slung Motty out, he would report to his mother, and she would pass it on to

Aunt Agatha, and I didn't like to think what would happen then. Sooner or later, I should be wanting to go back to England, and I didn't want to get there and find Aunt Agatha waiting on the quay for me with a stuffed eelskin. There was absolutely nothing for it but to put the fellow up and make the best of it.

About midday Motty's luggage arrived, and soon afterward a large parcel of what I took to be nice books. I brightened up a little when I saw it. It was one of those massive parcels and looked as if it had enough in it to keep the chappie busy for a year. I felt a trifle more cheerful, and I got my Country Gentleman hat and stuck it on my head, and gave the pink tie a twist, and reeled out to take a bite of lunch with one or two of the lads at a neighbouring hostelry; and what with excellent browsing and sluicing and cheery conversation and what-not, the afternoon passed quite happily. By dinner-time I had almost forgotten blighted Motty's existence.

I dined at the club and looked in at a show afterward, and it wasn't till fairly late that I got back to the flat. There were no signs of Motty, and I took it that he had gone to bed.

It seemed rummy to me, though, that the parcel of nice books was still there with the string and paper on it. It looked as if Motty, after seeing mother off at the station, had decided to call it a day.

Jeeves came in with the nightly whisky-and-soda. I could tell by the chappie's manner that he was still upset.

"Lord Pershore gone to bed, Jeeves?" I asked, with reserved hauteur and what-not.

"No, sir. His lordship has not yet returned."

"Not returned? What do you mean?"

"His lordship came in shortly after six-thirty, and, having dressed, went out again."

At this moment there was a noise outside the front door, a sort of scrabbling noise, as if somebody were trying to paw his way through the woodwork. Then a sort of thud.

"Better go and see what that is, Jeeves."

"Very good, sir."

He went out and came back again.

"If you would not mind stepping this way, sir, I think we might be able to carry him in."

"Carry him in?"

"His lordship is lying on the mat, sir."

I went to the front door. The man was right. There was Motty huddled up outside on the floor. He was moaning a bit.

"He's had some sort of dashed fit," I said. I took another look. "Jeeves! Someone's been feeding him meat!"

"Sir?"

"He's a vegetarian, you know. He must have been digging into a steak or something. Call up a doctor!"

"I hardly think it will be necessary, sir. If you would take his lordship's legs, while I——"

"Great Scot, Jeeves! You don't think—he can't be——"

"I am inclined to think so, sir."

And, by Jove, he was right! Once on the right track, you couldn't mistake it. Motty was under the surface.

It was the deuce of a shock.

"You never can tell, Jeeves!"

"Very seldom, sir."

"Remove the eye of authority and where are you?"

"Precisely, sir."

"Where is my wandering boy to-night and all that sort of thing, what?"

"It would seem so, sir."

"Well, we had better bring him in, eh?"

"Yes, sir."

So we lugged him in, and Jeeves put him to bed, and I lit a cigarette and sat down to think the thing over. I had a kind of foreboding. It seemed to me that I had let myself in for something pretty rocky.

Next morning, after I had sucked down a thoughtful cup of tea, I went into Motty's room to investigate. I expected to find the fellow a wreck, but there he was, sitting up in bed, quite chirpy, reading Gingery stories.

"What ho!" I said.

"What ho!" said Motty.

"What ho! What ho!"

"What ho! What ho! What ho!"

After that it seemed rather difficult to go on with the conversation.

"How are you feeling this morning?" I asked.

"Topping!" replied Motty, blithely and with abandon. "I say, you know, that fellow of yours—Jeeves, you know—is a corker. I had a most frightful headache when I woke up, and he brought me a sort of rummy dark drink, and it put me right again at once. Said it was his own invention. I must see more of that lad. He seems to me distinctly one of the ones!"

I couldn't believe that this was the same blighter who had sat and sucked his stick the day before.

"You ate something that disagreed with you last night, didn't you?" I said, by way of giving him a chance to slide out of it if he wanted to. But he wouldn't have it, at any price.

"No!" he replied firmly. "I didn't do anything of the kind. I drank too much! Much too much. Lots and lots too much! And, what's more, I'm going to do it again! I'm going to do it every night. If ever you see me sober, old top," he said, with a kind of holy exaltation, "tap me on the shoulder and say, 'Tut! Tut!' and I'll apologize and remedy the defect."

"But I say, you know, what about me?"

"What about you?"

"Well, I'm so to speak, as it were, kind of responsible for you. What I mean to say is, if you go doing this sort of thing I'm apt to get in the soup somewhat."

"I can't help your troubles," said Motty firmly. "Listen to me, old thing: this is the first time in my life that I've had a real chance to yield to the temptations of a great city. What's the use of a great city having temptations if fellows don't yield to them? Makes it so bally discouraging for a great city. Besides, mother told me to keep my eyes open and collect impressions."

I sat on the edge of the bed. I felt dizzy.

"I know just how you feel, old dear," said Motty consolingly. "And, if my principles would permit it, I would simmer down for your sake. But duty first! This is the first time I've been let out alone, and I mean to make the most of it. We're only young once. Why interfere with life's morning? Young man, rejoice in thy youth! Tra-la! What ho!"

Put like that, it did seem reasonable.

"All my bally life, dear boy," Motty went on, "I've been cooped up in the ancestral home at Much Middlefold, in Shropshire, and till you've been cooped up in Much Middlefold you don't know what cooping is! The only time we get any excitement is when one of the choir-boys is caught sucking chocolate during the sermon. When that happens, we talk about it for days. I've got about a month of New York, and I mean to store up a few happy memories for the long winter evenings. This is my only chance to collect a past, and I'm going to do it. Now tell me, old sport, as man to man, how does one get in touch with that very decent chappie Jeeves? Does one ring a bell or shout a bit? I should like to discuss the subject of a good stiff b.-and-s. with him!"

I had had a sort of vague idea, don't you know, that if I stuck close to Motty and went about the place with him, I might act as a bit of a damper on the gaiety. What I mean is, I thought that if, when he was being the life and soul of the party, he were to catch my reproving eye he might ease up a trifle on the revelry. So the next night I took him along to supper with me. It was the last time. I'm a quiet, peaceful sort of chappie who has lived all his life in London, and I can't stand the pace these swift sportsmen from the rural districts set. What I mean to say is this, I'm all for rational enjoyment and so forth, but I think a chappie makes himself conspicuous when he throws soft-boiled eggs at the electric fan. And decent mirth and all that sort of thing are all right, but I do bar dancing on tables and having to dash all over the place dodging waiters, managers, and chuckers-out, just when you want to sit still and digest.

Directly I managed to tear myself away that night and get home, I made up my mind that this was jolly well the last time that I went about with Motty. The only time I met him late at night after that was once when I passed the door of a fairly low-down sort of restaurant and had to step aside to dodge him as he sailed through the air en route for the opposite pavement, with a muscular sort of looking chappie peering out after him with a kind of gloomy satisfaction.

In a way, I couldn't help sympathizing with the fellow. He had about four weeks to have the good time that ought to have been spread over about ten years, and I didn't wonder at his wanting to be pretty busy. I should have been just the same in his place. Still, there was no denying that it was a bit thick. If it hadn't been for the thought of Lady Malvern and Aunt Agatha in the background, I should have regarded Motty's rapid work with an indulgent smile. But I couldn't get rid of the feeling that, sooner or later, I was the lad who was scheduled to get it behind the ear. And what with brooding on this prospect, and sitting up in the old flat waiting for the familiar footstep, and putting it to bed when it got there, and stealing into the sick-chamber next morning to contemplate the wreckage, I was beginning to lose weight. Absolutely becoming the good old shadow, I give you my honest word. Starting at sudden noises and what-not.

And no sympathy from Jeeves. That was what cut me to the quick. The man was still thoroughly pipped about the hat and tie, and simply wouldn't rally round. One morning I wanted comforting so much that I sank the pride of the Woosters and appealed to the fellow direct.

"Jeeves," I said, "this is getting a bit thick!"

"Sir?" Business and cold respectfulness.

"You know what I mean. This lad seems to have chucked all the principles of a well-spent boyhood. He has got it up his nose!"

"Yes, sir."

"Well, I shall get blamed, don't you know. You know what my Aunt Agatha is!"

"Yes, sir."

"Very well, then."

I waited a moment, but he wouldn't unbend.

"Jeeves," I said, "haven't you any scheme up your sleeve for coping with this blighter?"

"No, sir."

And he shimmered off to his lair. Obstinate devil! So dashed absurd, don't you know. It wasn't as if there was anything wrong with that Country Gentleman hat. It was a remarkably priceless effort, and much admired by the lads. But, just because he preferred the Longacre, he left me flat.

It was shortly after this that young Motty got the idea of bringing pals back in the small hours to continue the gay revels in the home. This was where I began to crack under the strain. You see, the part of town where I was living wasn't the right place for that sort of thing. I knew lots of chappies down Washington Square way who started the evening at about 2 a.m.—artists and writers and what-not, who frolicked considerably till checked by the arrival of the morning milk. That was all right. They like that sort of thing down there. The neighbours can't get to sleep unless there's someone dancing Hawaiian dances over their heads. But on Fifty-seventh Street the atmosphere wasn't right, and when Motty turned up at three in the morning with a collection of hearty lads, who only stopped singing their college song when they started singing "The Old Oaken Bucket," there was a marked peevishness among the old settlers in the flats. The management was extremely terse over the telephone at breakfast-time, and took a lot of soothing.

The next night I came home early, after a lonely dinner at a place which I'd chosen because there didn't seem any chance of meeting Motty there. The sitting-room was quite dark, and I was just moving to switch on the light, when there was a sort of explosion and something collared hold of my trouser-leg. Living with Motty had reduced me to such an extent that I was simply unable to cope with this thing. I jumped backward with a loud yell of anguish, and tumbled out into the hall just as Jeeves came out of his den to see what the matter was.

"Did you call, sir?"

"Jeeves! There's something in there that grabs you by the leg!"

"That would be Rollo, sir."

"Eh?"

"I would have warned you of his presence, but I did not hear you come in. His temper is a little uncertain at present, as he has not yet settled down."

"Who the deuce is Rollo?"

"His lordship's bull-terrier, sir. His lordship won him in a raffle, and tied him to the leg of the table. If you will allow me, sir, I will go in and switch on the light."

There really is nobody like Jeeves. He walked straight into the sitting-room, the biggest feat since Daniel and the lions' den, without a quiver. What's more, his magnetism or whatever they call it was such that the dashed animal, instead of pinning him by the leg, calmed down as if he had had a bromide, and rolled over on his back with all his paws in the air. If Jeeves had been his rich uncle he couldn't have been more chummy. Yet directly he caught sight of me again, he got all worked up and seemed to have only one idea in life—to start chewing me where he had left off.

"Rollo is not used to you yet, sir," said Jeeves, regarding the bally quadruped in an admiring sort of way. "He is an excellent watchdog."

"I don't want a watchdog to keep me out of my rooms."

"No, sir."

"Well, what am I to do?"

"No doubt in time the animal will learn to discriminate, sir. He will learn to distinguish your peculiar scent."

"What do you mean—my peculiar scent? Correct the impression that I intend to hang about in the hall while life slips by, in the hope that one of these days that dashed animal will decide that I smell all right." I thought for a bit. "Jeeves!"

"Sir?"

"I'm going away—to-morrow morning by the first train. I shall go and stop with Mr. Todd in the country."

"Do you wish me to accompany you, sir?"

"No."

"Very good, sir."

"I don't know when I shall be back. Forward my letters."

"Yes, sir."

As a matter of fact, I was back within the week. Rocky Todd, the pal I went to stay with, is a rummy sort of a chap who lives all alone in the wilds of Long Island, and likes it; but a little of that sort of thing goes a long way with me. Dear old Rocky is one of the best, but after a few days in his cottage in the woods, miles away from anywhere, New York, even with Motty on the premises, began to look pretty good to me. The days down on Long Island have forty-eight hours in them; you can't get to sleep at night because of the bellowing of the crickets; and you have to walk two miles for a drink and six for an evening paper. I thanked Rocky for his kind hospitality, and caught the only train they have down in those parts. It landed me in New York about dinner-time. I went straight to the old flat. Jeeves came out of his lair. I looked round cautiously for Rollo.

"Where's that dog, Jeeves? Have you got him tied up?"

"The animal is no longer here, sir. His lordship gave him to the porter, who sold him. His lordship took a prejudice against the animal on account of being bitten by him in the calf of the leg."

I don't think I've ever been so bucked by a bit of news. I felt I had misjudged Rollo.

Evidently, when you got to know him better, he had a lot of intelligence in him.

"Ripping!" I said. "Is Lord Pershore in, Jeeves?"

"No, sir."

"Do you expect him back to dinner?"

"No, sir."

"Where is he?"

"In prison, sir."

Have you ever trodden on a rake and had the handle jump up and hit you? That's how I felt then.

"In prison!"

"Yes, sir."

"You don't mean—in prison?"

"Yes, sir."

I lowered myself into a chair.

"Why?" I said.

"He assaulted a constable, sir."

"Lord Pershore assaulted a constable!"

"Yes, sir."

I digested this.

"But, Jeeves, I say! This is frightful!"

"Sir?"

"What will Lady Malvern say when she finds out?"

"I do not fancy that her ladyship will find out, sir."

"But she'll come back and want to know where he is."

"I rather fancy, sir, that his lordship's bit of time will have run out by then."

"But supposing it hasn't?"

"In that event, sir, it may be judicious to prevaricate a little."

"How?"

"If I might make the suggestion, sir, I should inform her ladyship that his lordship has left for a short visit to Boston."

"Why Boston?"

"Very interesting and respectable centre, sir."

"Jeeves, I believe you've hit it."

"I fancy so, sir."

"Why, this is really the best thing that could have happened. If this hadn't turned up to prevent him, young Motty would have been in a sanatorium by the time Lady Malvern got back."

"Exactly, sir."

The more I looked at it in that way, the sounder this prison wheeze seemed to me. There was no doubt in the world that prison was just what the doctor ordered for Motty. It was the only thing that could have pulled him up. I was sorry for the poor blighter, but, after all, I reflected, a chappie who had lived all his life with Lady Malvern, in a small village in the interior of Shropshire, wouldn't have much to kick at in a prison. Altogether, I began to feel absolutely braced again. Life became like what the poet Johnnie says—one grand, sweet song. Things went on so comfortably and peacefully for a couple of weeks that I give you my word that I'd almost forgotten such a person as Motty existed. The only flaw in the scheme of things was that Jeeves was still pained and distant. It wasn't anything he said or did, mind you, but there was a rummy something about him all the time. Once when I was tying the pink tie I caught sight of him in the looking-glass. There was a kind of grieved look in his eye.

And then Lady Malvern came back, a good bit ahead of schedule. I hadn't been expecting her for days. I'd forgotten how time had been slipping along. She turned up one morning while I was still in bed sipping tea and thinking of this and that. Jeeves flowed in with the announcement that he had just loosed her into the sitting-room. I draped a few garments round me and went in.

There she was, sitting in the same arm-chair, looking as massive as ever. The only difference was that she didn't uncover the teeth, as she had done the first time.

"Good morning," I said. "So you've got back, what?"

"I have got back."

There was something sort of bleak about her tone, rather as if she had swallowed an east wind. This I took to be due to the fact that she probably hadn't breakfasted. It's only after a bit of breakfast that I'm able to regard the world with that sunny cheeriness which makes a fellow the universal favourite. I'm never much of a lad till I've engulfed an egg or two and a beaker of coffee.

"I suppose you haven't breakfasted?"

"I have not yet breakfasted."

"Won't you have an egg or something? Or a sausage or something? Or something?"

"No, thank you."

She spoke as if she belonged to an anti-sausage society or a league for the suppression of eggs. There was a bit of a silence.

"I called on you last night," she said, "but you were out."

"Awfully sorry! Had a pleasant trip?"

"Extremely, thank you."

"See everything? Niag'ra Falls, Yellowstone Park, and the jolly old Grand Canyon, and what-not?"

"I saw a great deal."

There was another slightly frappé silence. Jeeves floated silently into the dining-room and began to lay the breakfast-table.

"I hope Wilmot was not in your way, Mr. Wooster?"

I had been wondering when she was going to mention Motty.

"Rather not! Great pals! Hit it off splendidly."

"You were his constant companion, then?"

"Absolutely! We were always together. Saw all the sights, don't you know. We'd take in the Museum of Art in the morning, and have a bit of lunch at some good vegetarian place, and then toddle along to a sacred concert in the afternoon, and home to an early dinner. We usually played dominoes after dinner. And then the early bed and the refreshing sleep. We had a great time. I was awfully sorry when he went away to Boston."

"Oh! Wilmot is in Boston?"

"Yes. I ought to have let you know, but of course we didn't know where you were. You were dodging all over the place like a snipe—I mean, don't you know, dodging all over the place, and we couldn't get at you. Yes, Motty went off to Boston."

"You're sure he went to Boston?"

"Oh, absolutely." I called out to Jeeves, who was now messing about in the next room with forks and so forth: "Jeeves, Lord Pershore didn't change his mind about going to Boston, did he?"

"No, sir."

"I thought I was right. Yes, Motty went to Boston."

"Then how do you account, Mr. Wooster, for the fact that when I went yesterday afternoon to Blackwell's Island prison, to secure material for my book, I saw poor, dear Wilmot there, dressed in a striped suit, seated beside a pile of stones with a hammer in his hands?"

I tried to think of something to say, but nothing came. A chappie has to be a lot broader about the forehead than I am to handle a jolt like this. I strained the old bean till it creaked, but between the collar and the hair parting nothing stirred. I was dumb. Which was lucky, because I wouldn't have had a chance to get any persiflage out of my system. Lady Malvern collared the conversation. She had been bottling it up, and now it came out with a rush:

"So this is how you have looked after my poor, dear boy, Mr. Wooster! So this is how you have abused my trust! I left him in your charge, thinking that I could rely on you to shield him from evil. He came to you innocent, unversed in the ways of the world, confiding, unused to the temptations of a large city, and you led him astray!"

I hadn't any remarks to make. All I could think of was the picture of Aunt Agatha drinking all this in and reaching out to sharpen the hatchet against my return.

"You deliberately——"

Far away in the misty distance a soft voice spoke:

"If I might explain, your ladyship."

Jeeves had projected himself in from the dining-room and materialized on the rug. Lady Malvern tried to freeze him with a look, but you can't do that sort of thing to Jeeves. He is look-proof.

"I fancy, your ladyship, that you have misunderstood Mr. Wooster, and that he may have given you the impression that he was in New York when his lordship—was removed. When Mr. Wooster informed your ladyship that his lordship had gone to Boston, he was relying on the version I had given him of his lordship's movements. Mr. Wooster was away, visiting a friend in the country, at the time, and knew nothing of the matter till your ladyship informed him."

Lady Malvern gave a kind of grunt. It didn't rattle Jeeves.

"I feared Mr. Wooster might be disturbed if he knew the truth, as he is so attached to his lordship and has taken such pains to look after him, so I took the liberty of telling him that his lordship had gone away for a visit. It might have been hard for Mr. Wooster to believe that his lordship had gone to prison voluntarily and from the best motives, but your ladyship, knowing him better, will readily understand."

"What!" Lady Malvern goggled at him. "Did you say that Lord Pershore went to prison voluntarily?"

"If I might explain, your ladyship. I think that your ladyship's parting words made a deep impression on his lordship. I have frequently heard him speak to Mr. Wooster of his desire to do something to follow your ladyship's instructions and collect material for your ladyship's book on America. Mr. Wooster will bear me out when I say that his lordship was frequently extremely depressed at the thought that he was doing so little to help."

"Absolutely, by Jove! Quite pipped about it!" I said.

"The idea of making a personal examination into the prison system of the country—from within—occurred to his lordship very suddenly one night. He embraced it eagerly. There was no restraining him."

Lady Malvern looked at Jeeves, then at me, then at Jeeves again. I could see her struggling with the thing.

"Surely, your ladyship," said Jeeves, "it is more reasonable to suppose that a gentleman of his lordship's character went to prison of his own volition than that he committed some breach of the law which necessitated his arrest?"

Lady Malvern blinked. Then she got up.

"Mr. Wooster," she said, "I apologize. I have done you an injustice. I should have known Wilmot better. I should have had more faith in his pure, fine spirit."

"Absolutely!" I said.

"Your breakfast is ready, sir," said Jeeves.

I sat down and dallied in a dazed sort of way with a poached egg.

"Jeeves," I said, "you are certainly a life-saver!"

"Thank you, sir."

"Nothing would have convinced my Aunt Agatha that I hadn't lured that blighter into riotous living."

"I fancy you are right, sir."

I champed my egg for a bit. I was most awfully moved, don't you know, by the way Jeeves had rallied round. Something seemed to tell me that this was an occasion that called for rich rewards. For a moment I hesitated. Then I made up my mind.

"Jeeves!"

"Sir?"

"That pink tie!"

"Yes, sir?"

"Burn it!"

"Thank you, sir."

"And, Jeeves!"

"Yes, sir?"

"Take a taxi and get me that Longacre hat, as worn by John Drew!"

"Thank you very much, sir."

I felt most awfully braced. I felt as if the clouds had rolled away and all was as it used to be. I felt like one of those chappies in the novels who calls off the fight with his wife in the last chapter and decides to forget and forgive. I felt I wanted to do all sorts of other things to show Jeeves that I appreciated him.

"Jeeves," I said, "it isn't enough. Is there anything else you would like?"

"Yes, sir. If I may make the suggestion—fifty dollars."

"Fifty dollars?"

"It will enable me to pay a debt of honour, sir. I owe it to his lordship."

"You owe Lord Pershore fifty dollars?"

"Yes, sir. I happened to meet him in the street the night his lordship was arrested. I had been thinking a good deal about the most suitable method of inducing him to abandon his mode of living, sir. His lordship was a little over-excited at the time and I fancy that he mistook me for a friend of his. At any rate when I took the liberty of wagering him fifty dollars that he would not punch a passing policeman in the eye, he accepted the bet very cordially and won it."

I produced my pocket-book and counted out a hundred.

"Take this, Jeeves," I said; "fifty isn't enough. Do you know, Jeeves, you're—well, you absolutely stand alone!"

"I endeavour to give satisfaction, sir," said Jeeves.

JEEVES AND THE HARD-BOILED EGG

Sometimes of a morning, as I've sat in bed sucking down the early cup of tea and watched my man Jeeves flitting about the room and putting out the raiment for the day, I've wondered what the deuce I should do if the fellow ever took it into his head to leave me. It's not so bad now I'm in New York, but in London the anxiety was frightful. There used to be all sorts of attempts on the part of low blighters to sneak him away from me. Young Reggie Foljambe to my certain knowledge offered him double what I was giving him, and Alistair Bingham-Reeves, who's got a valet who had been known to press his trousers sideways, used to look at him, when he came to see me, with a kind of glittering hungry eye which disturbed me deucedly. Bally pirates!

The thing, you see, is that Jeeves is so dashed competent. You can spot it even in the way he shoves studs into a shirt.

I rely on him absolutely in every crisis, and he never lets me down. And, what's more, he can always be counted on to extend himself on behalf of any pal of mine who happens to be to all appearances knee-deep in the bouillon. Take the rather rummy case, for instance, of dear old Bicky and his uncle, the hard-boiled egg.

It happened after I had been in America for a few months. I got back to the flat latish one night, and when Jeeves brought me the final drink he said:

"Mr. Bickersteth called to see you this evening, sir, while you were out."

"Oh?" I said.

"Twice, sir. He appeared a trifle agitated."

"What, pipped?"

"He gave that impression, sir."

I sipped the whisky. I was sorry if Bicky was in trouble, but, as a matter of fact, I was rather glad to have something I could discuss freely with Jeeves just then, because things had been a bit strained between us for some time, and it had been rather difficult to hit on anything to talk about that wasn't apt to take a personal turn. You see, I had decided—rightly or wrongly—to grow a moustache and this had cut Jeeves to the quick. He couldn't stick the thing at any price, and I had been living ever since in an atmosphere of bally disapproval till I was getting jolly well fed up with it. What I mean is, while there's no doubt that in certain matters of dress Jeeves's judgment is absolutely sound and should be followed, it seemed to me that it was getting a bit too thick if he was going to edit my face as well as my costume. No one can call me an unreasonable chappie, and many's the time I've given in like a lamb when Jeeves has voted against one of my pet suits or ties; but when it comes to a valet's staking out a claim on your upper lip you've simply got to have a bit of the good old bulldog pluck and defy the blighter.

"He said that he would call again later, sir."

"Something must be up, Jeeves."

"Yes, sir."

I gave the moustache a thoughtful twirl. It seemed to hurt Jeeves a good deal, so I chucked it.

"I see by the paper, sir, that Mr. Bickersteth's uncle is arriving on the Carmantic."

"Yes?"

"His Grace the Duke of Chiswick, sir."

This was news to me, that Bicky's uncle was a duke. Rum, how little one knows about one's pals! I had met Bicky for the first time at a species of beano or jamboree down in Washington Square, not long after my arrival in New York. I suppose I was a bit homesick at the time, and I rather took to Bicky when I found that he was an Englishman and had, in fact, been up at Oxford with me. Besides, he was a frightful chump, so we naturally drifted together; and while we were taking a quiet snort in a corner that wasn't all cluttered up with artists and sculptors and what-not, he furthermore endeared himself to me by a most extraordinarily gifted imitation of a bull-terrier chasing a cat up a tree. But, though we had subsequently become extremely pally, all I really knew about him was that he was generally hard up, and had an uncle who relieved the strain a bit from time to time by sending him monthly remittances.

"If the Duke of Chiswick is his uncle," I said, "why hasn't he a title? Why isn't he Lord What-Not?"

"Mr. Bickersteth is the son of his grace's late sister, sir, who married Captain Rollo Bickersteth of the Coldstream Guards."

Jeeves knows everything.

"Is Mr. Bickersteth's father dead, too?"

"Yes, sir."

"Leave any money?"

"No, sir."

I began to understand why poor old Bicky was always more or less on the rocks. To the casual and irreflective observer, if you know what I mean, it may sound a pretty good wheeze having a duke for an uncle, but the trouble about old Chiswick was that, though an extremely wealthy old buster, owning half London and about five counties up north, he was notoriously the most prudent spender in England. He was what American chappies would call a hard-boiled egg. If Bicky's people hadn't left him anything and he depended on what he could prise out of the old duke, he was in a pretty bad way. Not that that explained why he was hunting me like this, because he was a chap who never borrowed money. He said he wanted to keep his pals, so never bit any one's ear on principle.

At this juncture the door bell rang. Jeeves floated out to answer it.

"Yes, sir. Mr. Wooster has just returned," I heard him say. And Bicky came trickling in, looking pretty sorry for himself.

"Halloa, Bicky!" I said. "Jeeves told me you had been trying to get me. Jeeves, bring another glass, and let the revels commence. What's the trouble, Bicky?"

"I'm in a hole, Bertie. I want your advice."

"Say on, old lad!"

"My uncle's turning up to-morrow, Bertie."

"So Jeeves told me."

"The Duke of Chiswick, you know."

"So Jeeves told me."

Bicky seemed a bit surprised.

"Jeeves seems to know everything."

"Rather rummily, that's exactly what I was thinking just now myself."

"Well, I wish," said Bicky gloomily, "that he knew a way to get me out of the hole I'm in."

Jeeves shimmered in with the glass, and stuck it competently on the table.

"Mr. Bickersteth is in a bit of a hole, Jeeves," I said, "and wants you to rally round."

"Very good, sir."

Bicky looked a bit doubtful.

"Well, of course, you know, Bertie, this thing is by way of being a bit private and all that."

"I shouldn't worry about that, old top. I bet Jeeves knows all about it already. Don't you, Jeeves?"

"Yes, sir."

"Eh!" said Bicky, rattled.

"I am open to correction, sir, but is not your dilemma due to the fact that you are at a loss to explain to his grace why you are in New York instead of in Colorado?"

Bicky rocked like a jelly in a high wind.

"How the deuce do you know anything about it?"

"I chanced to meet his grace's butler before we left England. He informed me that he happened to overhear his grace speaking to you on the matter, sir, as he passed the library door."

Bicky gave a hollow sort of laugh.

"Well, as everybody seems to know all about it, there's no need to try to keep it dark. The old boy turfed me out, Bertie, because he said I was a brainless nincompoop. The idea was that he would give me a remittance on condition that I dashed out to some blighted locality of the name of Colorado and learned farming or ranching, or whatever they call it, at some bally ranch or farm or whatever it's called. I didn't fancy the idea a bit. I should have had to ride horses and pursue cows, and so forth. I hate horses. They bite at you. I was all against the scheme. At the same time, don't you know, I had to have that remittance."

"I get you absolutely, dear boy."

"Well, when I got to New York it looked a decent sort of place to me, so I thought it would be a pretty sound notion to stop here. So I cabled to my uncle telling him that I had dropped into a good business wheeze in the city and wanted to chuck the ranch idea. He wrote back that it was all right, and here I've been ever since. He thinks I'm doing well at something or other over here. I never dreamed, don't you know, that he would ever come out here. What on earth am I to do?"

"Jeeves," I said, "what on earth is Mr. Bickersteth to do?"

"You see," said Bicky, "I had a wireless from him to say that he was coming to stay with me—to save hotel bills, I suppose. I've always given him the impression that I was living in pretty good style. I can't have him to stay at my boarding-house."

"Thought of anything, Jeeves?" I said.

"To what extent, sir, if the question is not a delicate one, are you prepared to assist Mr.

Bickersteth?"

"I'll do anything I can for you, of course, Bicky, old man."

"Then, if I might make the suggestion, sir, you might lend Mr. Bickersteth——"

"No, by Jove!" said Bicky firmly. "I never have touched you, Bertie, and I'm not going to start now. I may be a chump, but it's my boast that I don't owe a penny to a single soul—not counting tradesmen, of course."

"I was about to suggest, sir, that you might lend Mr. Bickersteth this flat. Mr. Bickersteth could give his grace the impression that he was the owner of it. With your permission I could convey the notion that I was in Mr. Bickersteth's employment, and not in yours. You would be residing here temporarily as Mr. Bickersteth's guest. His grace would occupy the second spare bedroom. I fancy that you would find this answer satisfactorily, sir."

Bicky had stopped rocking himself and was staring at Jeeves in an awed sort of way.

"I would advocate the dispatching of a wireless message to his grace on board the vessel, notifying him of the change of address. Mr. Bickersteth could meet his grace at the dock and proceed directly here. Will that meet the situation, sir?"

"Absolutely."

"Thank you, sir."

Bicky followed him with his eye till the door closed.

"How does he do it, Bertie?" he said. "I'll tell you what I think it is. I believe it's something to do with the shape of his head. Have you ever noticed his head, Bertie, old man? It sort of sticks out at the back!"

I hopped out of bed early next morning, so as to be among those present when the old boy should arrive. I knew from experience that these ocean liners fetch up at the dock at a deucedly ungodly hour. It wasn't much after nine by the time I'd dressed and had my morning tea and was leaning out of the window, watching the street for Bicky and his uncle. It was one of those jolly, peaceful mornings that make a chappie wish he'd got a soul or something, and I was just brooding on life in general when I became aware of the dickens of a spate in progress down below. A taxi had driven up, and an old boy in a top hat had got out and was kicking up a frightful row about the fare. As far as I could make out, he was trying to get the cab chappie to switch from New York to London prices, and the cab chappie had apparently never heard of London before, and didn't seem to think a lot of it now. The old boy said that in London the trip would have set him back eightpence; and the cabby said he should worry. I called to Jeeves.

"The duke has arrived, Jeeves."

"Yes, sir?"

"That'll be him at the door now."

Jeeves made a long arm and opened the front door, and the old boy crawled in, looking licked to a splinter.

"How do you do, sir?" I said, bustling up and being the ray of sunshine. "Your nephew went down to the dock to meet you, but you must have missed him. My name's Wooster, don't you know. Great pal of Bicky's, and all that sort of thing. I'm staying with him, you know. Would you like a cup of tea? Jeeves, bring a cup of tea."

Old Chiswick had sunk into an arm-chair and was looking about the room.

"Does this luxurious flat belong to my nephew Francis?"

"Absolutely."

"It must be terribly expensive."

"Pretty well, of course. Everything costs a lot over here, you know."

He moaned. Jeeves filtered in with the tea. Old Chiswick took a stab at it to restore his tissues, and nodded.

"A terrible country, Mr. Wooster! A terrible country! Nearly eight shillings for a short cab-drive! Iniquitous!" He took another look round the room. It seemed to fascinate him. "Have you any idea how much my nephew pays for this flat, Mr. Wooster?"

"About two hundred dollars a month, I believe."

"What! Forty pounds a month!"

I began to see that, unless I made the thing a bit more plausible, the scheme might turn out a frost. I could guess what the old boy was thinking. He was trying to square all this prosperity with what he knew of poor old Bicky. And one had to admit that it took a lot of squaring, for dear old Bicky, though a stout fellow and absolutely unrivalled as an imitator of bull-terriers and cats, was in many ways one of the most pronounced fatheads that ever pulled on a suit of gent's underwear.

"I suppose it seems rummy to you," I said, "but the fact is New York often bucks chappies up and makes them show a flash of speed that you wouldn't have imagined them capable of. It sort of develops them. Something in the air, don't you know. I imagine that Bicky in the past, when you knew him, may have been something of a chump, but it's quite different now. Devilish efficient sort of chappie, and looked on in commercial circles as quite the nib!"

"I am amazed! What is the nature of my nephew's business, Mr. Wooster?"

"Oh, just business, don't you know. The same sort of thing Carnegie and Rockefeller and all these coves do, you know." I slid for the door. "Awfully sorry to leave you, but I've got to meet some of the lads elsewhere."

Coming out of the lift I met Bicky bustling in from the street.

"Halloa, Bertie! I missed him. Has he turned up?"

"He's upstairs now, having some tea."

"What does he think of it all?"

"He's absolutely rattled."

"Ripping! I'll be toddling up, then. Toodle-oo, Bertie, old man. See you later."

"Pip-pip, Bicky, dear boy."

He trotted off, full of merriment and good cheer, and I went off to the club to sit in the window and watch the traffic coming up one way and going down the other.

It was latish in the evening when I looked in at the flat to dress for dinner.

"Where's everybody, Jeeves?" I said, finding no little feet pattering about the place. "Gone out?"

"His grace desired to see some of the sights of the city, sir. Mr. Bickersteth is acting as his escort. I fancy their immediate objective was Grant's Tomb."

"I suppose Mr. Bickersteth is a bit braced at the way things are going—what?"

"Sir?"

"I say, I take it that Mr. Bickersteth is tolerably full of beans."

"Not altogether, sir."

"What's his trouble now?"

"The scheme which I took the liberty of suggesting to Mr. Bickersteth and yourself has, unfortunately, not answered entirely satisfactorily, sir."

"Surely the duke believes that Mr. Bickersteth is doing well in business, and all that sort of thing?"

"Exactly, sir. With the result that he has decided to cancel Mr. Bickersteth's monthly allowance, on the ground that, as Mr. Bickersteth is doing so well on his own account, he no longer requires pecuniary assistance."

"Great Scot, Jeeves! This is awful."

"Somewhat disturbing, sir."

"I never expected anything like this!"

"I confess I scarcely anticipated the contingency myself, sir."

"I suppose it bowled the poor blighter over absolutely?"

"Mr. Bickersteth appeared somewhat taken aback, sir."

My heart bled for Bicky.

"We must do something, Jeeves."

"Yes, sir."

"Can you think of anything?"

"Not at the moment, sir."

"There must be something we can do."

"It was a maxim of one of my former employers, sir—as I believe I mentioned to you once before—the present Lord Bridgnorth, that there is always a way. I remember his lordship using the expression on the occasion—he was then a business gentleman and had not yet received his title—when a patent hair-restorer which he chanced to be promoting failed to attract the public. He put it on the market under another name as a depilatory, and amassed a substantial fortune. I have generally found his lordship's aphorism based on sound foundations. No doubt we shall be able to discover some solution of Mr. Bickersteth's difficulty, sir."

"Well, have a stab at it, Jeeves!"

"I will spare no pains, sir."

I went and dressed sadly. It will show you pretty well how pipped I was when I tell you that I near as a toucher put on a white tie with a dinner-jacket. I sallied out for a bit of food more to pass the time than because I wanted it. It seemed brutal to be wading into the bill of fare with poor old Bicky headed for the breadline.

When I got back old Chiswick had gone to bed, but Bicky was there, hunched up in an arm-chair, brooding pretty tensely, with a cigarette hanging out of the corner of his mouth and a more or less glassy stare in his eyes. He had the aspect of one who had been soaked with what the newspaper chappies call "some blunt instrument."

"This is a bit thick, old thing—what!" I said.

He picked up his glass and drained it feverishly, overlooking the fact that it hadn't anything in it.

"I'm done, Bertie!" he said.

He had another go at the glass. It didn't seem to do him any good.

"If only this had happened a week later, Bertie! My next month's money was due to roll in on Saturday. I could have worked a wheeze I've been reading about in the magazine advertisements. It seems that you can make a dashed amount of money if you can only collect a few dollars and start a chicken-farm. Jolly sound scheme, Bertie! Say you buy a hen—call it one hen for the sake of argument. It lays an egg every day of the week. You sell the eggs seven for twenty-five cents. Keep of hen costs nothing. Profit practically twenty-five cents on every seven eggs. Or look at it another way: Suppose you have a dozen hens. Each of the hens has a dozen chickens. The chickens grow up and have more chickens. Why, in no time you'd have the place covered knee-deep in hens, all laying eggs, at twenty-five cents for every seven. You'd make a fortune. Jolly life, too, keeping hens!" He had begun to get quite worked up at the thought of it, but he slopped back in his chair at this juncture with a good deal of gloom. "But, of course, it's no good," he said, "because I haven't the cash."

"You've only to say the word, you know, Bicky, old top."

"Thanks awfully, Bertie, but I'm not going to sponge on you."

That's always the way in this world. The chappies you'd like to lend money to won't let you, whereas the chappies you don't want to lend it to will do everything except actually stand you on your head and lift the specie out of your pockets. As a lad who has always rolled tolerably free in the right stuff, I've had lots of experience of the second class. Many's the time, back in London, I've hurried along Piccadilly and felt the hot breath of the toucher on the back of my neck and heard his sharp, excited yapping as he closed in on me. I've simply spent my life scattering largesse to blighters I didn't care a hang for; yet here was I now, dripping doubloons and pieces of eight and longing to hand them over, and Bicky, poor fish, absolutely on his uppers, not taking any at any price.

"Well, there's only one hope, then."

"What's that?"

"Jeeves."

"Sir?"

There was Jeeves, standing behind me, full of zeal. In this matter of shimmering into rooms the chappie is rummy to a degree. You're sitting in the old arm-chair, thinking of this and that, and then suddenly you look up, and there he is. He moves from point to point with as little uproar as a jelly fish. The thing startled poor old Bicky considerably. He rose from his seat like a rocketing pheasant. I'm used to Jeeves now, but often in the days when he first came to me I've bitten my tongue freely on finding him unexpectedly in my midst.

"Did you call, sir?"

"Oh, there you are, Jeeves!"

"Precisely, sir."

"Jeeves, Mr. Bickersteth is still up the pole. Any ideas?"

"Why, yes, sir. Since we had our recent conversation I fancy I have found what may prove a solution. I do not wish to appear to be taking a liberty, sir, but I think that we have overlooked his grace's potentialities as a source of revenue."

Bicky laughed, what I have sometimes seen described as a hollow, mocking laugh, a sort of bitter cackle from the back of the throat, rather like a gargle.

"I do not allude, sir," explained Jeeves, "to the possibility of inducing his grace to part with money. I am taking the liberty of regarding his grace in the light of an at present—if I may say so—useless property, which is capable of being developed."

Bicky looked at me in a helpless kind of way. I'm bound to say I didn't get it myself.

"Couldn't you make it a bit easier, Jeeves!"

"In a nutshell, sir, what I mean is this: His grace is, in a sense, a prominent personage. The inhabitants of this country, as no doubt you are aware, sir, are peculiarly addicted to shaking hands with prominent personages. It occurred to me that Mr. Bickersteth or yourself might know of persons who would be willing to pay a small fee—let us say two dollars or three—for the privilege of an introduction, including handshake, to his grace."

Bicky didn't seem to think much of it.

"Do you mean to say that anyone would be mug enough to part with solid cash just to shake hands with my uncle?"

"I have an aunt, sir, who paid five shillings to a young fellow for bringing a moving-picture actor to tea at her house one Sunday. It gave her social standing among the neighbours."

Bicky wavered.

"If you think it could be done——"

"I feel convinced of it, sir."

"What do you think, Bertie?"

"I'm for it, old boy, absolutely. A very brainy wheeze."

"Thank you, sir. Will there be anything further? Good night, sir."

And he floated out, leaving us to discuss details.

Until we started this business of floating old Chiswick as a money-making proposition I had never realized what a perfectly foul time those Stock Exchange chappies must have when the public isn't biting freely. Nowadays I read that bit they put in the financial reports about "The market opened quietly" with a sympathetic eye, for, by Jove, it certainly opened quietly for us! You'd hardly believe how difficult it was to interest the public and make them take a flutter on the old boy. By the end of the week the only name we had on our list was a delicatessen-store keeper down in Bicky's part of the town, and as he wanted us to take it out in sliced ham instead of cash that didn't help much. There was a gleam of light when the brother of Bicky's pawnbroker offered ten dollars, money down, for an introduction to old Chiswick, but the deal fell through, owing to its turning out that the chap was an anarchist and intended to kick the old boy instead of shaking hands with him. At that, it took me the deuce of a time to persuade Bicky not to grab the cash and let things take their course. He seemed to regard the pawnbroker's brother rather as a sportsman and benefactor of his species than otherwise.

The whole thing, I'm inclined to think, would have been off if it hadn't been for Jeeves.

There is no doubt that Jeeves is in a class of his own. In the matter of brain and resource I don't think I have ever met a chappie so supremely like mother made. He trickled into my room one morning with a good old cup of tea, and intimated that there was something doing.

"Might I speak to you with regard to that matter of his grace, sir?"

"It's all off. We've decided to chuck it."

"Sir?"

"It won't work. We can't get anybody to come."

"I fancy I can arrange that aspect of the matter, sir."

"Do you mean to say you've managed to get anybody?"

"Yes, sir. Eighty-seven gentlemen from Birdsburg, sir."

I sat up in bed and spilt the tea.

"Birdsburg?"

"Birdsburg, Missouri, sir."

"How did you get them?"

"I happened last night, sir, as you had intimated that you would be absent from home, to attend a theatrical performance, and entered into conversation between the acts with the occupant of the adjoining seat. I had observed that he was wearing a somewhat ornate decoration in his buttonhole, sir—a large blue button with the words 'Boost for Birdsburg' upon it in red letters, scarcely a judicious addition to a gentleman's evening costume. To my surprise I noticed that the auditorium was full of persons similarly decorated. I ventured to inquire the explanation, and was informed that these gentlemen, forming a party of eighty-seven, are a convention from a town of the name of Birdsburg, in the State of Missouri. Their visit, I gathered, was purely of a social and pleasurable nature, and my informant spoke at some length of the entertainments arranged for their stay in the city. It was when he related with a considerable amount of satisfaction and pride, that a deputation of their number had been introduced to and had shaken hands with a well-known prizefighter, that it occurred to me to broach the subject of his grace. To make a long story short, sir, I have arranged, subject to your approval, that the entire convention shall be presented to his grace to-morrow afternoon."

I was amazed. This chappie was a Napoleon.

"Eighty-seven, Jeeves. At how much a head?"

"I was obliged to agree to a reduction for quantity, sir. The terms finally arrived at were one hundred and fifty dollars for the party."

I thought a bit.

"Payable in advance?"

"No, sir. I endeavoured to obtain payment in advance, but was not successful."

"Well, any way, when we get it I'll make it up to five hundred. Bicky'll never know. Do you suspect Mr. Bickersteth would suspect anything, Jeeves, if I made it up to five hundred?"

"I fancy not, sir. Mr. Bickersteth is an agreeable gentleman, but not bright."

"All right, then. After breakfast run down to the bank and get me some money."

"Yes, sir."

"You know, you're a bit of a marvel, Jeeves."

"Thank you, sir."

"Right-o!"

"Very good, sir."

When I took dear old Bicky aside in the course of the morning and told him what had happened he nearly broke down. He tottered into the sitting-room and buttonholed old Chiswick, who was reading the comic section of the morning paper with a kind of grim resolution.

"Uncle," he said, "are you doing anything special to-morrow afternoon? I mean to say, I've asked a few of my pals in to meet you, don't you know."

The old boy cocked a speculative eye at him.

"There will be no reporters among them?"

"Reporters? Rather not! Why?"

"I refuse to be badgered by reporters. There were a number of adhesive young men who endeavoured to elicit from me my views on America while the boat was approaching the dock. I will not be subjected to this persecution again."

"That'll be absolutely all right, uncle. There won't be a newspaper-man in the place."

"In that case I shall be glad to make the acquaintance of your friends."

"You'll shake hands with them and so forth?"

"I shall naturally order my behaviour according to the accepted rules of civilized intercourse."

Bicky thanked him heartily and came off to lunch with me at the club, where he babbled freely of hens, incubators, and other rotten things.

After mature consideration we had decided to unleash the Birdsburg contingent on the old boy ten at a time. Jeeves brought his theatre pal round to see us, and we arranged the whole thing with him. A very decent chappie, but rather inclined to collar the conversation and turn it in the direction of his home-town's new water-supply system. We settled that, as an hour was about all he would be likely to stand, each gang should consider itself entitled to seven minutes of the duke's society by Jeeves's stop-watch, and that when their time was up Jeeves should slide into the room and cough meaningly. Then we parted with what I believe are called mutual expressions of goodwill, the Birdsburg chappie extending a cordial invitation to us all to pop out some day and take a look at the new water-supply system, for which we thanked him.

Next day the deputation rolled in. The first shift consisted of the cove we had met and nine others almost exactly like him in every respect. They all looked deuced keen and businesslike, as if from youth up they had been working in the office and catching the boss's eye and what-not. They shook hands with the old boy with a good deal of apparent satisfaction—all except one chappie, who seemed to be brooding about something—and then they stood off and became chatty.

"What message have you for Birdsburg, Duke?" asked our pal.

The old boy seemed a bit rattled.

"I have never been to Birdsburg."

The chappie seemed pained.

"You should pay it a visit," he said. "The most rapidly-growing city in the country. Boost for Birdsburg!"

"Boost for Birdsburg!" said the other chappies reverently.

The chappie who had been brooding suddenly gave tongue.

"Say!"

He was a stout sort of well-fed cove with one of those determined chins and a cold eye.

The assemblage looked at him.

"As a matter of business," said the chappie—"mind you, I'm not questioning anybody's good faith, but, as a matter of strict business—I think this gentleman here ought to put himself on record before witnesses as stating that he really is a duke."

"What do you mean, sir?" cried the old boy, getting purple.

"No offence, simply business. I'm not saying anything, mind you, but there's one thing that seems kind of funny to me. This gentleman here says his name's Mr. Bickersteth, as I understand it. Well, if you're the Duke of Chiswick, why isn't he Lord Percy Something? I've read English novels, and I know all about it."

"This is monstrous!"

"Now don't get hot under the collar. I'm only asking. I've a right to know. You're going to take our money, so it's only fair that we should see that we get our money's worth."

The water-supply cove chipped in:

"You're quite right, Simms. I overlooked that when making the agreement. You see, gentlemen, as business men we've a right to reasonable guarantees of good faith. We are paying Mr. Bickersteth here a hundred and fifty dollars for this reception, and we naturally want to know——"

Old Chiswick gave Bicky a searching look; then he turned to the water-supply chappie. He was frightfully calm.

"I can assure you that I know nothing of this," he said, quite politely. "I should be grateful if you would explain."

"Well, we arranged with Mr. Bickersteth that eighty-seven citizens of Birdsburg should have the privilege of meeting and shaking hands with you for a financial consideration mutually arranged, and what my friend Simms here means—and I'm with him—is that we have only Mr. Bickersteth's word for it—and he is a stranger to us—that you are the Duke of Chiswick at all."

Old Chiswick gulped.

"Allow me to assure you, sir," he said, in a rummy kind of voice, "that I am the Duke of Chiswick."

"Then that's all right," said the chappie heartily. "That was all we wanted to know. Let the thing go on."

"I am sorry to say," said old Chiswick, "that it cannot go on. I am feeling a little tired. I fear I must ask to be excused."

"But there are seventy-seven of the boys waiting round the corner at this moment, Duke, to be introduced to you."

"I fear I must disappoint them."

"But in that case the deal would have to be off."

"That is a matter for you and my nephew to discuss."

The chappie seemed troubled.

"You really won't meet the rest of them?"

"No!"

"Well, then, I guess we'll be going."

They went out, and there was a pretty solid silence. Then old Chiswick turned to Bicky:

"Well?"

Bicky didn't seem to have anything to say.

"Was it true what that man said?"

"Yes, uncle."

"What do you mean by playing this trick?"

Bicky seemed pretty well knocked out, so I put in a word.

"I think you'd better explain the whole thing, Bicky, old top."

Bicky's Adam's-apple jumped about a bit; then he started:

"You see, you had cut off my allowance, uncle, and I wanted a bit of money to start a chicken farm. I mean to say it's an absolute cert if you once get a bit of capital. You buy a hen, and it lays an egg every day of the week, and you sell the eggs, say, seven for twenty-five cents.

"Keep of hens cost nothing. Profit practically——"

"What is all this nonsense about hens? You led me to suppose you were a substantial business man."

"Old Bicky rather exaggerated, sir," I said, helping the chappie out. "The fact is, the poor old lad is absolutely dependent on that remittance of yours, and when you cut it off, don't you know, he was pretty solidly in the soup, and had to think of some way of closing in on a bit of the ready pretty quick. That's why we thought of this handshaking scheme."

Old Chiswick foamed at the mouth.

"So you have lied to me! You have deliberately deceived me as to your financial status!"

"Poor old Bicky didn't want to go to that ranch," I explained. "He doesn't like cows and horses, but he rather thinks he would be hot stuff among the hens. All he wants is a bit of capital. Don't you think it would be rather a wheeze if you were to——"

"After what has happened? After this—this deceit and foolery? Not a penny!"

"But——"

"Not a penny!"

There was a respectful cough in the background.

"If I might make a suggestion, sir?"

Jeeves was standing on the horizon, looking devilish brainy.

"Go ahead, Jeeves!" I said.

"I would merely suggest, sir, that if Mr. Bickersteth is in need of a little ready money, and is at a loss to obtain it elsewhere, he might secure the sum he requires by describing the occurrences of this afternoon for the Sunday issue of one of the more spirited and enterprising newspapers."

"By Jove!" I said.

"By George!" said Bicky.

"Great heavens!" said old Chiswick.

"Very good, sir," said Jeeves.

Bicky turned to old Chiswick with a gleaming eye.

"Jeeves is right. I'll do it! The Chronicle would jump at it. They eat that sort of stuff."

Old Chiswick gave a kind of moaning howl.

"I absolutely forbid you, Francis, to do this thing!"

"That's all very well," said Bicky, wonderfully braced, "but if I can't get the money any other way——"

"Wait! Er—wait, my boy! You are so impetuous! We might arrange something."

"I won't go to that bally ranch."

"No, no! No, no, my boy! I would not suggest it. I would not for a moment suggest it. I—I think——"

He seemed to have a bit of a struggle with himself. "I—I think that, on the whole, it would be best if you returned with me to England. I—I might—in fact, I think I see my way to doing—to—I might be able to utilize your services in some secretarial position."

"I shouldn't mind that."

"I should not be able to offer you a salary, but, as you know, in English political life the unpaid secretary is a recognized figure——"

"The only figure I'll recognize," said Bicky firmly, "is five hundred quid a year, paid quarterly."

"My dear boy!"

"Absolutely!"

"But your recompense, my dear Francis, would consist in the unrivalled opportunities you would have, as my secretary, to gain experience, to accustom yourself to the intricacies of political life, to—in fact, you would be in an exceedingly advantageous position."

"Five hundred a year!" said Bicky, rolling it round his tongue. "Why, that would be nothing to what I could make if I started a chicken farm. It stands to reason. Suppose you have a dozen hens. Each of the hens has a dozen chickens. After a bit the chickens grow up and have a dozen chickens each themselves, and then they all start laying eggs! There's a fortune in it. You can get anything you like for eggs in America. Chappies keep them on ice for years and years, and don't sell them till they fetch about a dollar a whirl. You don't think I'm going to chuck a future like this for anything under five hundred o' goblins a year—what?"

A look of anguish passed over old Chiswick's face, then he seemed to be resigned to it. "Very well, my boy," he said.

"What-o!" said Bicky. "All right, then."

"Jeeves," I said. Bicky had taken the old boy off to dinner to celebrate, and we were alone. "Jeeves, this has been one of your best efforts."

"Thank you, sir."

"It beats me how you do it."

"Yes, sir."

"The only trouble is you haven't got much out of it—what!"

"I fancy Mr. Bickersteth intends—I judge from his remarks—to signify his appreciation of anything I have been fortunate enough to do to assist him, at some later date when he is in a more favourable position to do so."

"It isn't enough, Jeeves!"

"Sir?"

It was a wrench, but I felt it was the only possible thing to be done.

"Bring my shaving things."

A gleam of hope shone in the chappie's eye, mixed with doubt.

"You mean, sir?"

"And shave off my moustache."

There was a moment's silence. I could see the fellow was deeply moved.

"Thank you very much indeed, sir," he said, in a low voice, and popped off.

ABSENT TREATMENT

I want to tell you all about dear old Bobbie Cardew. It's a most interesting story. I can't put in any literary style and all that; but I don't have to, don't you know, because it goes on its Moral Lesson. If you're a man you mustn't miss it, because it'll be a warning to you; and if you're a woman you won't want to, because it's all about how a girl made a man feel pretty well fed up with things.

If you're a recent acquaintance of Bobbie's, you'll probably be surprised to hear that there was a time when he was more remarkable for the weakness of his memory than anything else. Dozens of fellows, who have only met Bobbie since the change took place, have been surprised when I told them that. Yet it's true. Believe me.

In the days when I first knew him Bobbie Cardew was about the most pronounced young rotter inside the four-mile radius. People have called me a silly ass, but I was never in the same class with Bobbie. When it came to being a silly ass, he was a plus-four man, while my handicap was about six. Why, if I wanted him to dine with me, I used to post him a letter at the beginning of the week, and then the day before send him a telegram and a phone-call on the day itself, and—half an hour before the time we'd fixed—a messenger in a taxi, whose business it was to see that he got in and that the chauffeur had the address all correct. By doing this I generally managed to get him, unless he had left town before my messenger arrived.

The funny thing was that he wasn't altogether a fool in other ways. Deep down in him there was a kind of stratum of sense. I had known him, once or twice, show an almost human intelligence. But to reach that stratum, mind you, you needed dynamite.

At least, that's what I thought. But there was another way which hadn't occurred to me. Marriage, I mean. Marriage, the dynamite of the soul; that was what hit Bobbie. He married. Have you ever seen a bull-pup chasing a bee? The pup sees the bee. It looks good to him. But he still doesn't know what's at the end of it till he gets there. It was like that with Bobbie. He fell in love, got married—with a sort of whoop, as if it were the greatest fun in the world—and then began to find out things.

She wasn't the sort of girl you would have expected Bobbie to rave about. And yet, I don't know. What I mean is, she worked for her living; and to a fellow who has never done a hand's turn in his life there's undoubtedly a sort of fascination, a kind of romance, about a girl who works for her living.

Her name was Anthony. Mary Anthony. She was about five feet six; she had a ton and a half of red-gold hair, grey eyes, and one of those determined chins. She was a hospital nurse. When Bobbie smashed himself up at polo, she was told off by the authorities to smooth his brow and rally round with cooling unguents and all that; and the old boy hadn't been up and about again for more than a week before they popped off to the registrar's and fixed it up. Quite the romance.

Bobbie broke the news to me at the club one evening, and next day he introduced me to her. I admired her. I've never worked myself—my name's Pepper, by the way. Almost forgot to mention it. Reggie Pepper. My uncle Edward was Pepper, Wells, and Co., the Colliery people. He left me a sizable chunk of bullion—I say I've never worked myself, but I admire any one who earns a living under difficulties, especially a girl. And this girl had had a rather unusually tough time of it, being an orphan and all that, and having had to do everything off her own bat for years.

Mary and I got along together splendidly. We don't now, but we'll come to that later. I'm speaking of the past. She seemed to think Bobbie the greatest thing on earth, judging by the way she looked at him when she thought I wasn't noticing. And Bobbie seemed to think the same about her. So that I came to the conclusion that, if only dear old Bobbie didn't forget to go to the wedding, they had a sporting chance of being quite happy.

Well, let's brisk up a bit here, and jump a year. The story doesn't really start till then.

They took a flat and settled down. I was in and out of the place quite a good deal. I kept my eyes open, and everything seemed to me to be running along as smoothly as you could want. If this was marriage, I thought, I couldn't see why fellows were so frightened of it. There were a lot of worse things that could happen to a man.

But we now come to the incident of the quiet Dinner, and it's just here that love's young dream hits a snag, and things begin to occur.

I happened to meet Bobbie in Piccadilly, and he asked me to come back to dinner at the flat. And, like a fool, instead of bolting and putting myself under police protection, I went.

When we got to the flat, there was Mrs. Bobbie looking—well, I tell you, it staggered me. Her gold hair was all piled up in waves and crinkles and things, with a what-d'-you-call-it of diamonds in it. And she was wearing the most perfectly ripping dress. I couldn't begin to describe it. I can only say it was the limit. It struck me that if this was how she was in the habit of looking every night when they were dining quietly at home together, it was no wonder that Bobbie liked domesticity.

"Here's old Reggie, dear," said Bobbie. "I've brought him home to have a bit of dinner. I'll phone down to the kitchen and ask them to send it up now—what?"

She stared at him as if she had never seen him before. Then she turned scarlet. Then she turned as white as a sheet. Then she gave a little laugh. It was most interesting to watch. Made me wish I was up a tree about eight hundred miles away. Then she recovered herself.

"I am so glad you were able to come, Mr. Pepper," she said, smiling at me.

And after that she was all right. At least, you would have said so. She talked a lot at dinner, and chaffed Bobbie, and played us ragtime on the piano afterwards, as if she hadn't a care in the world. Quite a jolly little party it was—not. I'm no lynx-eyed sleuth, and all that sort of thing, but I had seen her face at the beginning, and I knew that she was working the whole time and working hard, to keep herself in hand, and that she would have given that diamond what's-its-name in her hair and everything else she possessed to have one good scream—just one. I've sat through some pretty thick evenings in my time, but that one had the rest beaten in a canter. At the very earliest moment I grabbed my hat and got away.

Having seen what I did, I wasn't particularly surprised to meet Bobbie at the club next day looking about as merry and bright as a lonely gum-drop at an Eskimo tea-party.

He started in straightway. He seemed glad to have someone to talk to about it.

"Do you know how long I've been married?" he said.

I didn't exactly.

"About a year, isn't it?"

"Not about a year," he said sadly. "Exactly a year—yesterday!"

Then I understood. I saw light—a regular flash of light.

"Yesterday was——?"

"The anniversary of the wedding. I'd arranged to take Mary to the Savoy, and on to Covent Garden. She particularly wanted to hear Caruso. I had the ticket for the box in my pocket. Do you know, all through dinner I had a kind of rummy idea that there was something I'd forgotten, but I couldn't think what?"

"Till your wife mentioned it?"

He nodded——

"She—mentioned it," he said thoughtfully.

I didn't ask for details. Women with hair and chins like Mary's may be angels most of the time, but, when they take off their wings for a bit, they aren't half-hearted about it.

"To be absolutely frank, old top," said poor old Bobbie, in a broken sort of way, "my stock's pretty low at home."

There didn't seem much to be done. I just lit a cigarette and sat there. He didn't want to talk. Presently he went out. I stood at the window of our upper smoking-room, which looks out on to Piccadilly, and watched him. He walked slowly along for a few yards, stopped, then walked on again, and finally turned into a jeweller's. Which was an instance of what I meant when I said that deep down in him there was a certain stratum of sense.

It was from now on that I began to be really interested in this problem of Bobbie's married life. Of course, one's always mildly interested in one's friends' marriages, hoping they'll turn out well and all that; but this was different. The average man isn't like Bobbie, and the average girl isn't like Mary. It was that old business of the immovable mass and the irresistible force. There was Bobbie, ambling gently through life, a dear old chap in a hundred ways, but undoubtedly a chump of the first water.

And there was Mary, determined that he shouldn't be a chump. And Nature, mind you, on Bobbie's side. When Nature makes a chump like dear old Bobbie, she's proud of him, and doesn't want her handiwork disturbed. She gives him a sort of natural armour to protect him against outside interference. And that armour is shortness of memory. Shortness of memory keeps a man a chump, when, but for it, he might cease to be one. Take my case, for instance. I'm a chump. Well, if I had remembered half the things people have tried to teach me during my life, my size in hats would be about number nine. But I didn't. I forgot them. And it was just the same with Bobbie.

For about a week, perhaps a bit more, the recollection of that quiet little domestic evening bucked him up like a tonic. Elephants, I read somewhere, are champions at the memory business, but they were fools to Bobbie during that week. But, bless you, the shock wasn't nearly big enough. It had dinted the armour, but it hadn't made a hole in it. Pretty soon he was back at the old game.

It was pathetic, don't you know. The poor girl loved him, and she was frightened. It was the thin edge of the wedge, you see, and she knew it. A man who forgets what day he was married, when he's been married one year, will forget, at about the end of the fourth, that he's married at all. If she meant to get him in hand at all, she had got to do it now, before he began to drift away.

I saw that clearly enough, and I tried to make Bobbie see it, when he was by way of pouring out his troubles to me one afternoon. I can't remember what it was that he had forgotten the day before, but it was something she had asked him to bring home for her—it may have been a book.

"It's such a little thing to make a fuss about," said Bobbie. "And she knows that it's simply because I've got such an infernal memory about everything. I can't remember anything. Never could."

He talked on for a while, and, just as he was going, he pulled out a couple of sovereigns.

"Oh, by the way," he said.

"What's this for?" I asked, though I knew.

"I owe it you."

"How's that?" I said.

"Why, that bet on Tuesday. In the billiard-room. Murray and Brown were playing a hundred up, and I gave you two to one that Brown would win, and Murray beat him by twenty odd."

"So you do remember some things?" I said.

He got quite excited. Said that if I thought he was the sort of rotter who forgot to pay when he lost a bet, it was pretty rotten of me after knowing him all these years, and a lot more like that.

"Subside, laddie," I said.

Then I spoke to him like a father.

"What you've got to do, my old college chum," I said, "is to pull yourself together, and jolly quick, too. As things are shaping, you're due for a nasty knock before you know what's hit you. You've got to make an effort. Don't say you can't. This two quid business shows that, even if your memory is rocky, you can remember some things. What you've got to do is to see that wedding anniversaries and so on are included in the list. It may be a brainstrain, but you can't get out of it."

"I suppose you're right," said Bobbie. "But it beats me why she thinks such a lot of these rotten little dates. What's it matter if I forgot what day we were married on or what day she was born on or what day the cat had the measles? She knows I love her just as much as if I were a memorizing freak at the halls."

"That's not enough for a woman," I said. "They want to be shown. Bear that in mind, and you're all right. Forget it, and there'll be trouble."

He chewed the knob of his stick.

"Women are frightfully rummy," he said gloomily.

"You should have thought of that before you married one," I said.

I don't see that I could have done any more. I had put the whole thing in a nutshell for him. You would have thought he'd have seen the point, and that it would have made him brace up and get a hold on himself. But no. Off he went again in the same old way. I gave up arguing with him. I had a good deal of time on my hands, but not enough to amount to anything when it was a question of reforming dear old Bobbie by argument. If you see a man asking for trouble, and insisting on getting it, the only thing to do is to stand by and wait till it comes to him. After that you may get a chance. But till then there's nothing to be done. But I thought a lot about him.

Bobbie didn't get into the soup all at once. Weeks went by, and months, and still nothing happened. Now and then he'd come into the club with a kind of cloud on his shining morning face, and I'd know that there had been doings in the home; but it wasn't till well on in the spring that he got the thunderbolt just where he had been asking for it—in the thorax.

I was smoking a quiet cigarette one morning in the window looking out over Piccadilly, and watching the buses and motors going up one way and down the other—most interesting it is; I often do it—when in rushed Bobbie, with his eyes bulging and his face the colour of an oyster, waving a piece of paper in his hand.

"Reggie," he said. "Reggie, old top, she's gone!"

"Gone!" I said. "Who?"

"Mary, of course! Gone! Left me! Gone!"

"Where?" I said.

Silly question? Perhaps you're right. Anyhow, dear old Bobbie nearly foamed at the mouth.

"Where? How should I know where? Here, read this."

He pushed the paper into my hand. It was a letter.

"Go on," said Bobbie. "Read it."

So I did. It certainly was quite a letter. There was not much of it, but it was all to the point. This is what it said:

"MY DEAR BOBBIE,—I am going away. When you care enough about me to remember to wish me many happy returns on my birthday, I will come back. My address will be Box 341, London Morning News."

I read it twice, then I said, "Well, why don't you?"

"Why don't I what?"

"Why don't you wish her many happy returns? It doesn't seem much to ask."

"But she says on her birthday."

"Well, when is her birthday?"

"Can't you understand?" said Bobbie. "I've forgotten."

"Forgotten!" I said.

"Yes," said Bobbie. "Forgotten."

"How do you mean, forgotten?" I said. "Forgotten whether it's the twentieth or the twenty-first, or what? How near do you get to it?"

"I know it came somewhere between the first of January and the thirty-first of December. That's how near I get to it."

"Think."

"Think? What's the use of saying 'Think'? Think I haven't thought? I've been knocking sparks out of my brain ever since I opened that letter."

"And you can't remember?"

"No."

I rang the bell and ordered restoratives.

"Well, Bobbie," I said, "it's a pretty hard case to spring on an untrained amateur like me. Suppose someone had come to Sherlock Holmes and said, 'Mr. Holmes, here's a case for you. When is my wife's birthday?' Wouldn't that have given Sherlock a jolt? However, I know enough about the game to understand that a fellow can't shoot off his deductive theories unless you start him with a clue, so rouse yourself out of that pop-eyed trance and come across with two or three. For instance, can't you remember the last time she had a birthday? What sort of weather was it? That might fix the month."

Bobbie shook his head.

"It was just ordinary weather, as near as I can recollect."

"Warm?"

"Warmish."

"Or cold?"

"Well, fairly cold, perhaps. I can't remember."

I ordered two more of the same. They seemed indicated in the Young Detective's Manual. "You're a great help, Bobbie," I said. "An invaluable assistant. One of those indispensable adjuncts without which no home is complete."

Bobbie seemed to be thinking.

"I've got it," he said suddenly. "Look here. I gave her a present on her last birthday. All we have to do is to go to the shop, hunt up the date when it was bought, and the thing's done."

"Absolutely. What did you give her?"

He sagged.

"I can't remember," he said.

Getting ideas is like golf. Some days you're right off, others it's as easy as falling off a log. I don't suppose dear old Bobbie had ever had two ideas in the same morning before in his life; but now he did it without an effort. He just loosed another dry Martini into the undergrowth, and before you could turn round it had flushed quite a brain-wave.

Do you know those little books called When were you Born? There's one for each month. They tell you your character, your talents, your strong points, and your weak points at fourpence halfpenny a go. Bobbie's idea was to buy the whole twelve, and go through them till we found out which month hit off Mary's character. That would give us the month, and narrow it down a whole lot.

A pretty hot idea for a non-thinker like dear old Bobbie. We sallied out at once. He took half and I took half, and we settled down to work. As I say, it sounded good. But when we came to go into the thing, we saw that there was a flaw. There was plenty of information all right, but there wasn't a single month that didn't have something that exactly hit off Mary. For instance, in the December book it said, "December people are apt to keep their own secrets. They are extensive travellers." Well, Mary had certainly kept her secret, and she had travelled quite extensively enough for Bobbie's needs. Then, October people were "born with original ideas" and "loved moving." You couldn't have summed up Mary's little jaunt more neatly. February people had "wonderful memories"—Mary's speciality.

We took a bit of a rest, then had another go at the thing.

Bobbie was all for May, because the book said that women born in that month were "inclined to be capricious, which is always a barrier to a happy married life"; but I plumped for February, because February women "are unusually determined to have their own way, are very earnest, and expect a full return in their companion or mates." Which he owned was about as like Mary as anything could be.

In the end he tore the books up, stamped on them, burnt them, and went home.

It was wonderful what a change the next few days made in dear old Bobbie. Have you ever seen that picture, "The Soul's Awakening"? It represents a flapper of sorts gazing in a startled sort of way into the middle distance with a look in her eyes that seems to say, "Surely that is George's step I hear on the mat! Can this be love?" Well, Bobbie had a soul's awakening too. I don't suppose he had ever troubled to think in his life before—not really think. But now he was wearing his brain to the bone. It was painful in a way, of course, to see a fellow human being so thoroughly in the soup, but I felt strongly that it was all for the best. I could see as plainly as possible that all these brainstorms were improving Bobbie out of knowledge. When it was all over he might possibly become a rotter again of a sort, but it would only be a pale reflection of the rotter he had been. It bore out the idea I had always had that what he needed was a real good jolt.

I saw a great deal of him these days. I was his best friend, and he came to me for sympathy. I gave it him, too, with both hands, but I never failed to hand him the Moral Lesson when I had him weak.

One day he came to me as I was sitting in the club, and I could see that he had had an idea. He looked happier than he had done in weeks.

"Reggie," he said, "I'm on the trail. This time I'm convinced that I shall pull it off. I've remembered something of vital importance."

"Yes?" I said.

"I remember distinctly," he said, "that on Mary's last birthday we went together to the Coliseum. How does that hit you?"

"It's a fine bit of memorizing," I said; "but how does it help?"

"Why, they change the programme every week there."

"Ah!" I said. "Now you are talking."

"And the week we went one of the turns was Professor Some One's Terpsichorean Cats. I recollect them distinctly. Now, are we narrowing it down, or aren't we? Reggie, I'm going round to the Coliseum this minute, and I'm going to dig the date of those Terpsichorean Cats out of them, if I have to use a crowbar."

So that got him within six days; for the management treated us like brothers; brought out the archives, and ran agile fingers over the pages till they treed the cats in the middle of May.

"I told you it was May," said Bobbie. "Maybe you'll listen to me another time."

"If you've any sense," I said, "there won't be another time."

And Bobbie said that there wouldn't.

Once you get your memory on the run, it parts as if it enjoyed doing it. I had just got off to sleep that night when my telephone-bell rang. It was Bobbie, of course. He didn't apologize.

"Reggie," he said, "I've got it now for certain. It's just come to me. We saw those Terpsichorean Cats at a matinee, old man."

"Yes?" I said.

"Well, don't you see that that brings it down to two days? It must have been either Wednesday the seventh or Saturday the tenth."

"Yes," I said, "if they didn't have daily matinees at the Coliseum."

I heard him give a sort of howl.

"Bobbie," I said. My feet were freezing, but I was fond of him.

"Well?"

"I've remembered something too. It's this. The day you went to the Coliseum I lunched with you both at the Ritz. You had forgotten to bring any money with you, so you wrote a cheque."

"But I'm always writing cheques."

"You are. But this was for a tenner, and made out to the hotel. Hunt up your cheque-book and see how many cheques for ten pounds payable to the Ritz Hotel you wrote out between May the fifth and May the tenth."

He gave a kind of gulp.

"Reggie," he said, "you're a genius. I've always said so. I believe you've got it. Hold the line."

Presently he came back again.

"Halloa!" he said.

"I'm here," I said.

"It was the eighth. Reggie, old man, I——"

"Topping," I said. "Good night."

It was working along into the small hours now, but I thought I might as well make a night of it and finish the thing up, so I rang up an hotel near the Strand.

"Put me through to Mrs. Cardew," I said.

"It's late," said the man at the other end.

"And getting later every minute," I said. "Buck along, laddie."

I waited patiently. I had missed my beauty-sleep, and my feet had frozen hard, but I was past regrets.

"What is the matter?" said Mary's voice.

"My feet are cold," I said. "But I didn't call you up to tell you that particularly. I've just been chatting with Bobbie, Mrs. Cardew."

"Oh! is that Mr. Pepper?"

"Yes. He's remembered it, Mrs. Cardew."

She gave a sort of scream. I've often thought how interesting it must be to be one of those Exchange girls. The things they must hear, don't you know. Bobbie's howl and gulp and Mrs. Bobbie's scream and all about my feet and all that. Most interesting it must be.

"He's remembered it!" she gasped. "Did you tell him?"

"No."

Well, I hadn't.

"Mr. Pepper."

"Yes?"

"Was he—has he been—was he very worried?"

I chuckled. This was where I was billed to be the life and soul of the party.

"Worried! He was about the most worried man between here and Edinburgh. He has been worrying as if he was paid to do it by the nation. He has started out to worry after breakfast, and——"

Oh, well, you can never tell with women. My idea was that we should pass the rest of the night slapping each other on the back across the wire, and telling each other what bally brainy conspirators we were, don't you know, and all that. But I'd got just as far as this, when she bit at me. Absolutely! I heard the snap. And then she said "Oh!" in that choked kind of way. And when a woman says "Oh!" like that, it means all the bad words she'd love to say if she only knew them.

And then she began.

"What brutes men are! What horrid brutes! How you could stand by and see poor dear Bobbie worrying himself into a fever, when a word from you would have put everything right, I can't——"

"But——"

"And you call yourself his friend! His friend!" (Metallic laugh, most unpleasant.) "It shows how one can be deceived. I used to think you a kind-hearted man."

"But, I say, when I suggested the thing, you thought it perfectly——"

"I thought it hateful, abominable."

"But you said it was absolutely top——"

"I said nothing of the kind. And if I did, I didn't mean it. I don't wish to be unjust, Mr. Pepper, but I must say that to me there seems to be something positively fiendish in a man who can go out of his way to separate a husband from his wife, simply in order to amuse himself by gloating over his agony——"

"But——!"

"When one single word would have——"

"But you made me promise not to——" I bleated.

"And if I did, do you suppose I didn't expect you to have the sense to break your promise?"

I had finished. I had no further observations to make. I hung up the receiver, and crawled into bed.

I still see Bobbie when he comes to the club, but I do not visit the old homestead. He is friendly, but he stops short of issuing invitations. I ran across Mary at the Academy last week, and her eyes went through me like a couple of bullets through a pat of butter. And as they came out the other side, and I limped off to piece myself together again, there occurred to me the simple epitaph which, when I am no more, I intend to have inscribed on my tombstone. It was this: "He was a man who acted from the best motives. There is one born every minute."

HELPING FREDDIE

I don't want to bore you, don't you know, and all that sort of rot, but I must tell you about dear old Freddie Meadowes. I'm not a flier at literary style, and all that, but I'll get some writer chappie to give the thing a wash and brush up when I've finished, so that'll be all right.

Dear old Freddie, don't you know, has been a dear old pal of mine for years and years; so when I went into the club one morning and found him sitting alone in a dark corner, staring glassily at nothing, and generally looking like the last rose of summer, you can understand I was quite disturbed about it. As a rule, the old rotter is the life and soul of our set. Quite the little lump of fun, and all that sort of thing.

Jimmy Pinkerton was with me at the time. Jimmy's a fellow who writes plays—a deuced brainy sort of fellow—and between us we set to work to question the poor pop-eyed chappie, until finally we got at what the matter was.

As we might have guessed, it was a girl. He had had a quarrel with Angela West, the girl he was engaged to, and she had broken off the engagement. What the row had been about he didn't say, but apparently she was pretty well fed up. She wouldn't let him come near her, refused to talk on the phone, and sent back his letters unopened.

I was sorry for poor old Freddie. I knew what it felt like. I was once in love myself with a girl called Elizabeth Shoolbred, and the fact that she couldn't stand me at any price will be recorded in my autobiography. I knew the thing for Freddie.

"Change of scene is what you want, old scout," I said. "Come with me to Marvis Bay. I've taken a cottage there. Jimmy's coming down on the twenty-fourth. We'll be a cosy party."

"He's absolutely right," said Jimmy. "Change of scene's the thing. I knew a man. Girl refused him. Man went abroad. Two months later girl wired him, 'Come back. Muriel.' Man started to write out a reply; suddenly found that he couldn't remember girl's surname; so never answered at all."

But Freddie wouldn't be comforted. He just went on looking as if he had swallowed his last sixpence. However, I got him to promise to come to Marvis Bay with me. He said he might as well be there as anywhere.

Do you know Marvis Bay? It's in Dorsetshire. It isn't what you'd call a fiercely exciting spot, but it has its good points. You spend the day there bathing and sitting on the sands, and in the evening you stroll out on the shore with the gnats. At nine o'clock you rub ointment on the wounds and go to bed.

It seemed to suit poor old Freddie. Once the moon was up and the breeze sighing in the trees, you couldn't drag him from that beach with a rope. He became quite a popular pet with the gnats. They'd hang round waiting for him to come out, and would give perfectly good strollers the miss-in-baulk just so as to be in good condition for him.

Yes, it was a peaceful sort of life, but by the end of the first week I began to wish that Jimmy Pinkerton had arranged to come down earlier: for as a companion Freddie, poor old chap, wasn't anything to write home to mother about. When he wasn't chewing a pipe and scowling at the carpet, he was sitting at the piano, playing "The Rosary" with one finger. He couldn't play anything except "The Rosary," and he couldn't play much of that. Somewhere round about the third bar a fuse would blow out, and he'd have to start all over again.

He was playing it as usual one morning when I came in from bathing.

"Reggie," he said, in a hollow voice, looking up, "I've seen her."

"Seen her?" I said. "What, Miss West?"

"I was down at the post office, getting the letters, and we met in the doorway. She cut me!"

He started "The Rosary" again, and side-slipped in the second bar.

"Reggie," he said, "you ought never to have brought me here. I must go away."

"Go away?" I said. "Don't talk such rot. This is the best thing that could have happened. This is where you come out strong."

"She cut me."

"Never mind. Be a sportsman. Have another dash at her."

"She looked clean through me!"

"Of course she did. But don't mind that. Put this thing in my hands. I'll see you through. Now, what you want," I said, "is to place her under some obligation to you. What you want is to get her timidly thanking you. What you want——"

"But what's she going to thank me timidly for?"

I thought for a moment.

"Look out for a chance and save her from drowning," I said.

"I can't swim," said Freddie.

That was Freddie all over, don't you know. A dear old chap in a thousand ways, but no help to a fellow, if you know what I mean.

He cranked up the piano once more and I sprinted for the open.

I strolled out on to the sands and began to think this thing over. There was no doubt that the brain-work had got to be done by me. Dear old Freddie had his strong qualities. He was top-hole at polo, and in happier days I've heard him give an imitation of cats fighting in a backyard that would have surprised you. But apart from that he wasn't a man of enterprise.

Well, don't you know, I was rounding some rocks, with my brain whirring like a dynamo, when I caught sight of a blue dress, and, by Jove, it was the girl. I had never met her, but Freddie had sixteen photographs of her sprinkled round his bedroom, and I knew I couldn't be mistaken. She was sitting on the sand, helping a small, fat child build a castle. On a chair close by was an elderly lady reading a novel. I heard the girl call her "aunt." So, doing the Sherlock Holmes business, I deduced that the fat child was her cousin. It struck me that if Freddie had been there he would probably have tried to work up some sentiment about the kid on the strength of it. Personally I couldn't manage it. I don't think I ever saw a child who made me feel less sentimental. He was one of those round, bulging kids.

After he had finished the castle he seemed to get bored with life, and began to whimper. The girl took him off to where a fellow was selling sweets at a stall. And I walked on.

Now, fellows, if you ask them, will tell you that I'm a chump. Well, I don't mind. I admit it. I am a chump. All the Peppers have been chumps. But what I do say is that every now and then, when you'd least expect it, I get a pretty hot brain-wave; and that's what happened now. I doubt if the idea that came to me then would have occurred to a single one of any dozen of the brainiest chappies you care to name.

It came to me on my return journey. I was walking back along the shore, when I saw the fat kid meditatively smacking a jelly-fish with a spade. The girl wasn't with him. In fact, there didn't seem to be any one in sight. I was just going to pass on when I got the brain-wave. I thought the whole thing out in a flash, don't you know. From what I had seen of the two, the girl was evidently fond of this kid, and, anyhow, he was her cousin, so what I said to myself was this: If I kidnap this young heavy-weight for the moment, and if, when the girl has got frightfully anxious about where he can have got to, dear old Freddie suddenly appears leading the infant by the hand and telling a story to the effect that he has found him wandering at large about the country and practically saved his life, why, the girl's gratitude is bound to make her chuck hostilities and be friends again. So I gathered in the kid and made off with him. All the way home I pictured that scene of reconciliation. I could see it so vividly, don't you know, that, by George, it gave me quite a choky feeling in my throat.

Freddie, dear old chap, was rather slow at getting on to the fine points of the idea. When I appeared, carrying the kid, and dumped him down in our sitting-room, he didn't absolutely effervesce with joy, if you know what I mean. The kid had started to bellow by this time, and poor old Freddie seemed to find it rather trying.

"Stop it!" he said. "Do you think nobody's got any troubles except you? What the deuce is all this, Reggie?"

The kid came back at him with a yell that made the window rattle. I raced to the kitchen and fetched a jar of honey. It was the right stuff. The kid stopped bellowing and began to smear his face with the stuff.

"Well?" said Freddie, when silence had set in. I explained the idea. After a while it began to strike him.

"You're not such a fool as you look, sometimes, Reggie," he said handsomely. "I'm bound to say this seems pretty good."

And he disentangled the kid from the honey-jar and took him out, to scour the beach for Angela.

I don't know when I've felt so happy. I was so fond of dear old Freddie that to know that he was soon going to be his old bright self again made me feel as if somebody had left me about a million pounds. I was leaning back in a chair on the veranda, smoking peacefully, when down the road I saw the old boy returning, and, by George, the kid was still with him. And Freddie looked as if he hadn't a friend in the world.

"Hello!" I said. "Couldn't you find her?"

"Yes, I found her," he replied, with one of those bitter, hollow laughs.

"Well, then——?"

Freddie sank into a chair and groaned.

"This isn't her cousin, you idiot!" he said.

"He's no relation at all. He's just a kid she happened to meet on the beach. She had never seen him before in her life."

"What! Who is he, then?"

"I don't know. Oh, Lord, I've had a time! Thank goodness you'll probably spend the next few years of your life in Dartmoor for kidnapping. That's my only consolation. I'll come and jeer at you through the bars."

"Tell me all, old boy," I said.

It took him a good long time to tell the story, for he broke off in the middle of nearly every sentence to call me names, but I gathered gradually what had happened. She had listened like an iceberg while he told the story he had prepared, and then—well, she didn't actually call him a liar, but she gave him to understand in a general sort of way that if he and Dr. Cook ever happened to meet, and started swapping stories, it would be about the biggest duel on record. And then he had crawled away with the kid, licked to a splinter.

"And mind, this is your affair," he concluded. "I'm not mixed up in it at all. If you want to escape your sentence, you'd better go and find the kid's parents and return him before the police come for you."

By Jove, you know, till I started to tramp the place with this infernal kid, I never had a notion it would have been so deuced difficult to restore a child to its anxious parents. It's a mystery to me how kidnappers ever get caught. I searched Marvis Bay like a bloodhound, but nobody came forward to claim the infant. You'd have thought, from the lack of interest in him, that he was stopping there all by himself in a cottage of his own. It wasn't till, by an inspiration, I thought to ask the sweet-stall man that I found out that his name was Medwin, and that his parents lived at a place called Ocean Rest, in Beach Road.

I shot off there like an arrow and knocked at the door. Nobody answered. I knocked again. I could hear movements inside, but nobody came. I was just going to get to work on that knocker in such a way that the idea would filter through into these people's heads that I wasn't standing there just for the fun of the thing, when a voice from somewhere above shouted, "Hi!"

I looked up and saw a round, pink face, with grey whiskers east and west of it, staring down from an upper window.

"Hi!" it shouted again.

"What the deuce do you mean by 'Hi'?" I said.

"You can't come in," said the face. "Hello, is that Tootles?"

"My name is not Tootles, and I don't want to come in," I said. "Are you Mr. Medwin? I've brought back your son."

"I see him. Peep-bo, Tootles! Dadda can see 'oo!"

The face disappeared with a jerk. I could hear voices. The face reappeared.

"Hi!"

I churned the gravel madly.

"Do you live here?" said the face.

"I'm staying here for a few weeks."

"What's your name?"

"Pepper. But——"

"Pepper? Any relation to Edward Pepper, the colliery owner?"

"My uncle. But——"

"I used to know him well. Dear old Edward Pepper! I wish I was with him now."

"I wish you were," I said.

He beamed down at me.

"This is most fortunate," he said. "We were wondering what we were to do with Tootles. You see, we have the mumps here. My daughter Bootles has just developed mumps. Tootles must not be exposed to the risk of infection. We could not think what we were to do with him. It was most fortunate your finding him. He strayed from his nurse. I would hesitate to trust him to the care of a stranger, but you are different. Any nephew of Edward Pepper's has my implicit confidence. You must take Tootles to your house. It will be an ideal arrangement. I have written to my brother in London to come and fetch him. He may be here in a few days."

"May!"

"He is a busy man, of course; but he should certainly be here within a week. Till then Tootles can stop with you. It is an excellent plan. Very much obliged to you. Your wife will like Tootles."

"I haven't got a wife," I yelled; but the window had closed with a bang, as if the man with the whiskers had found a germ trying to escape, don't you know, and had headed it off just in time.

I breathed a deep breath and wiped my forehead.

The window flew up again.

"Hi!"

A package weighing about a ton hit me on the head and burst like a bomb.

"Did you catch it?" said the face, reappearing. "Dear me, you missed it! Never mind. You can get it at the grocer's. Ask for Bailey's Granulated Breakfast Chips. Tootles takes them for breakfast with a little milk. Be certain to get Bailey's."

My spirit was broken, if you know what I mean. I accepted the situation. Taking Tootles by the hand, I walked slowly away. Napoleon's retreat from Moscow was a picnic by the side of it.

As we turned up the road we met Freddie's Angela.

The sight of her had a marked effect on the kid Tootles. He pointed at her and said, "Wah!"

The girl stopped and smiled. I loosed the kid, and he ran to her.

"Well, baby?" she said, bending down to him. "So father found you again, did he? Your little son and I made friends on the beach this morning," she said to me.

This was the limit. Coming on top of that interview with the whiskered lunatic it so utterly unnerved me, don't you know, that she had nodded good-bye and was half-way down the road before I caught up with my breath enough to deny the charge of being the infant's father.

I hadn't expected dear old Freddie to sing with joy when he found out what had happened, but I did think he might have shown a little more manly fortitude. He leaped up, glared at the kid, and clutched his head. He didn't speak for a long time, but, on the other hand, when he began he did not leave off for a long time. He was quite emotional, dear old boy. It beat me where he could have picked up such expressions.

"Well," he said, when he had finished, "say something! Heavens! man, why don't you say something?"

"You don't give me a chance, old top," I said soothingly.

"What are you going to do about it?"

"What can we do about it?"

"We can't spend our time acting as nurses to this—this exhibit."

He got up.

"I'm going back to London," he said.

"Freddie!" I cried. "Freddie, old man!" My voice shook. "Would you desert a pal at a time like this?"

"I would. This is your business, and you've got to manage it."

"Freddie," I said, "you've got to stand by me. You must. Do you realize that this child has to be undressed, and bathed, and dressed again? You wouldn't leave me to do all that single-handed? Freddie, old scout, we were at school together. Your mother likes me. You owe me a tenner."

He sat down again.

"Oh, well," he said resignedly.

"Besides, old top," I said, "I did it all for your sake, don't you know?"

He looked at me in a curious way.

"Reggie," he said, in a strained voice, "one moment. I'll stand a good deal, but I won't stand for being expected to be grateful."

Looking back at it, I see that what saved me from Colney Hatch in that crisis was my bright idea of buying up most of the contents of the local sweet-shop. By serving out sweets to the kid practically incessantly we managed to get through the rest of that day pretty satisfactorily. At eight o'clock he fell asleep in a chair, and, having undressed him by unbuttoning every button in sight and, where there were no buttons, pulling till something gave, we carried him up to bed.

Freddie stood looking at the pile of clothes on the floor and I knew what he was thinking. To get the kid undressed had been simple—a mere matter of muscle. But how were we to get him into his clothes again? I stirred the pile with my foot. There was a long linen arrangement which might have been anything. Also a strip of pink flannel which was like nothing on earth. We looked at each other and smiled wanly.

But in the morning I remembered that there were children at the next bungalow but one. We went there before breakfast and borrowed their nurse. Women are wonderful, by George they are! She had that kid dressed and looking fit for anything in about eight minutes. I showered wealth on her, and she promised to come in morning and evening. I sat down to breakfast almost cheerful again. It was the first bit of silver lining there had been to the cloud up to date.

"And after all," I said, "there's lots to be said for having a child about the house, if you know what I mean. Kind of cosy and domestic—what!"

Just then the kid upset the milk over Freddie's trousers, and when he had come back after changing his clothes he began to talk about what a much-maligned man King Herod was. The more he saw of Tootles, he said, the less he wondered at those impulsive views of his on infanticide.

Two days later Jimmy Pinkerton came down. Jimmy took one look at the kid, who happened to be howling at the moment, and picked up his portmanteau.

"For me," he said, "the hotel. I can't write dialogue with that sort of thing going on. Whose work is this? Which of you adopted this little treasure?"

I told him about Mr. Medwin and the mumps. Jimmy seemed interested.

"I might work this up for the stage," he said. "It wouldn't make a bad situation for act two of a farce."

"Farce!" snarled poor old Freddie.

"Rather. Curtain of act one on hero, a well-meaning, half-baked sort of idiot just like—that is to say, a well-meaning, half-baked sort of idiot, kidnapping the child. Second act, his adventures with it. I'll rough it out to-night. Come along and show me the hotel, Reggie."

As we went I told him the rest of the story—the Angela part. He laid down his portmanteau and looked at me like an owl through his glasses.

"What!" he said. "Why, hang it, this is a play, ready-made. It's the old 'Tiny Hand' business. Always safe stuff. Parted lovers. Lisping child. Reconciliation over the little cradle. It's big. Child, centre. Girl L.C.; Freddie, up stage, by the piano. Can Freddie play the piano?"

"He can play a little of 'The Rosary' with one finger."

Jimmy shook his head.

"No; we shall have to cut out the soft music. But the rest's all right. Look here." He squatted in the sand. "This stone is the girl. This bit of seaweed's the child. This nutshell is Freddie. Dialogue leading up to child's line. Child speaks like, 'Boofer lady, does i'oo love dadda?' Business of outstretched hands. Hold picture for a moment. Freddie crosses L., takes girl's hand. Business of swallowing lump in throat. Then big speech. 'Ah, Marie,' or whatever her name is—Jane—Agnes—Angela? Very well. 'Ah, Angela, has not this gone on too long? A little child rebukes us! Angela!' And so on. Freddie must work up his own part. I'm just giving you the general outline. And we must get a good line for the child. 'Boofer lady, does 'oo love dadda?' isn't definite enough. We want something more—ah! 'Kiss Freddie,' that's it. Short, crisp, and has the punch."

"But, Jimmy, old top," I said, "the only objection is, don't you know, that there's no way of getting the girl to the cottage. She cuts Freddie. She wouldn't come within a mile of him."

Jimmy frowned.

"That's awkward," he said. "Well, we shall have to make it an exterior set instead of an interior. We can easily corner her on the beach somewhere, when we're ready. Meanwhile, we must get the kid letter-perfect. First rehearsal for lines and business eleven sharp to-morrow."

Poor old Freddie was in such a gloomy state of mind that we decided not to tell him the idea till we had finished coaching the kid. He wasn't in the mood to have a thing like that hanging over him. So we concentrated on Tootles. And pretty early in the proceedings we saw that the only way to get Tootles worked up to the spirit of the thing was to introduce sweets of some sort as a sub-motive, so to speak.

"The chief difficulty," said Jimmy Pinkerton at the end of the first rehearsal, "is to establish a connection in the kid's mind between his line and the sweets. Once he has grasped the basic fact that those two words, clearly spoken, result automatically in acid-drops, we have got a success."

I've often thought, don't you know, how interesting it must be to be one of those animal-trainer Johnnies: to stimulate the dawning intelligence, and that sort of thing. Well, this was every bit as exciting. Some days success seemed to be staring us in the eye, and the kid got the line out as if he'd been an old professional. And then he'd go all to pieces again. And time was flying.

"We must hurry up, Jimmy," I said. "The kid's uncle may arrive any day now and take him away."

"And we haven't an understudy," said Jimmy. "There's something in that. We must work! My goodness, that kid's a bad study. I've known deaf-mutes who would have learned the part quicker."

I will say this for the kid, though: he was a trier. Failure didn't discourage him. Whenever there was any kind of sweet near he had a dash at his line, and kept on saying something till he got what he was after. His only fault was his uncertainty. Personally, I would have been prepared to risk it, and start the performance at the first opportunity, but Jimmy said no.

"We're not nearly ready," said Jimmy. "To-day, for instance, he said 'Kick Freddie.' That's not going to win any girl's heart. And she might do it, too. No; we must postpone production awhile yet."

But, by George, we didn't. The curtain went up the very next afternoon.

It was nobody's fault—certainly not mine. It was just Fate. Freddie had settled down at the piano, and I was leading the kid out of the house to exercise it, when, just as we'd got out to the veranda, along came the girl Angela on her way to the beach. The kid set up his usual yell at the sight of her, and she stopped at the foot of the steps.

"Hello, baby!" she said. "Good morning," she said to me. "May I come up?"

She didn't wait for an answer. She just came. She seemed to be that sort of girl. She came up on the veranda and started fussing over the kid. And six feet away, mind you, Freddie smiting the piano in the sitting-room. It was a dash disturbing situation, don't you know. At any minute Freddie might take it into his head to come out on to the veranda, and we hadn't even begun to rehearse him in his part.

I tried to break up the scene.

"We were just going down to the beach," I said.

"Yes?" said the girl. She listened for a moment. "So you're having your piano tuned?" she said. "My aunt has been trying to find a tuner for ours. Do you mind if I go in and tell this man to come on to us when he's finished here?"

"Er—not yet!" I said. "Not yet, if you don't mind. He can't bear to be disturbed when he's working. It's the artistic temperament. I'll tell him later."

"Very well," she said, getting up to go. "Ask him to call at Pine Bungalow. West is the name. Oh, he seems to have stopped. I suppose he will be out in a minute now. I'll wait."

"Don't you think—shouldn't we be going on to the beach?" I said.

She had started talking to the kid and didn't hear. She was feeling in her pocket for something.

"The beach," I babbled.

"See what I've brought for you, baby," she said. And, by George, don't you know, she held up in front of the kid's bulging eyes a chunk of toffee about the size of the Automobile Club.

That finished it. We had just been having a long rehearsal, and the kid was all worked up in his part. He got it right first time.

"Kiss Fweddie!" he shouted.

And the front door opened, and Freddie came out on to the veranda, for all the world as if he had been taking a cue.

He looked at the girl, and the girl looked at him. I looked at the ground, and the kid looked at the toffee.

"Kiss Fweddie!" he yelled. "Kiss Fweddie!"

The girl was still holding up the toffee, and the kid did what Jimmy Pinkerton would have called "business of outstretched hands" towards it.

"Kiss Fweddie!" he shrieked.

"What does this mean?" said the girl, turning to me.

"You'd better give it to him, don't you know," I said. "He'll go on till you do."

She gave the kid his toffee, and he subsided. Poor old Freddie still stood there gaping, without a word.

"What does it mean?" said the girl again. Her face was pink, and her eyes were sparkling in the sort of way, don't you know, that makes a fellow feel as if he hadn't any bones in him, if you know what I mean. Did you ever tread on your partner's dress at a dance and tear it, and see her smile at you like an angel and say: "Please don't apologize. It's nothing," and then suddenly meet her clear blue eyes and feel as if you had stepped on the teeth of a rake and had the handle jump up and hit you in the face? Well, that's how Freddie's Angela looked.

"Well?" she said, and her teeth gave a little click.

I gulped. Then I said it was nothing. Then I said it was nothing much. Then I said, "Oh, well, it was this way." And, after a few brief remarks about Jimmy Pinkerton, I told her all about it. And all the while Idiot Freddie stood there gaping, without a word.

And the girl didn't speak, either. She just stood listening.

And then she began to laugh. I never heard a girl laugh so much. She leaned against the side of the veranda and shrieked. And all the while Freddie, the World's Champion Chump, stood there, saying nothing.

Well I sidled towards the steps. I had said all I had to say, and it seemed to me that about here the stage-direction "exit" was written in my part. I gave poor old Freddie up in despair. If only he had said a word, it might have been all right. But there he stood, speechless. What can a fellow do with a fellow like that?

Just out of sight of the house I met Jimmy Pinkerton.

"Hello, Reggie!" he said. "I was just coming to you. Where's the kid? We must have a big rehearsal to-day."

"No good," I said sadly. "It's all over. The thing's finished. Poor dear old Freddie has made an ass of himself and killed the whole show."

"Tell me," said Jimmy.

I told him.

"Fluffed in his lines, did he?" said Jimmy, nodding thoughtfully. "It's always the way with these amateurs. We must go back at once. Things look bad, but it may not be too late," he said as we started. "Even now a few well-chosen words from a man of the world, and——"

"Great Scot!" I cried. "Look!"

In front of the cottage stood six children, a nurse, and the fellow from the grocer's staring. From the windows of the houses opposite projected about four hundred heads of both sexes, staring. Down the road came galloping five more children, a dog, three men, and a boy, about to stare. And on our porch, as unconscious of the spectators as if they had been alone in the Sahara, stood Freddie and Angela, clasped in each other's arms.

Dear old Freddie may have been fluffy in his lines, but, by George, his business had certainly gone with a bang!

RALLYING ROUND OLD GEORGE

I think one of the rummiest affairs I was ever mixed up with, in the course of a lifetime devoted to butting into other people's business, was that affair of George Lattaker at Monte Carlo. I wouldn't bore you, don't you know, for the world, but I think you ought to hear about it.

We had come to Monte Carlo on the yacht Circe, belonging to an old sportsman of the name of Marshall. Among those present were myself, my man Voules, a Mrs. Vanderley, her daughter Stella, Mrs. Vanderley's maid Pilbeam and George.

George was a dear old pal of mine. In fact, it was I who had worked him into the party. You see, George was due to meet his Uncle Augustus, who was scheduled, George having just reached his twenty-fifth birthday, to hand over to him a legacy left by one of George's aunts, for which he had been trustee. The aunt had died when George was quite a kid. It was a date that George had been looking forward to; for, though he had a sort of income—an income, after-all, is only an income, whereas a chunk of o' goblins is a pile. George's uncle was in Monte Carlo, and had written George that he would come to London and unbelt; but it struck me that a far better plan was for George to go to his uncle at Monte Carlo instead. Kill two birds with one stone, don't you know. Fix up his affairs and have a pleasant holiday simultaneously. So George had tagged along, and at the time when the trouble started we were anchored in Monaco Harbour, and Uncle Augustus was due next day.

Looking back, I may say that, so far as I was mixed up in it, the thing began at seven o'clock in the morning, when I was aroused from a dreamless sleep by the dickens of a scrap in progress outside my state-room door. The chief ingredients were a female voice that sobbed and said: "Oh, Harold!" and a male voice "raised in anger," as they say, which after considerable difficulty, I identified as Voules's. I hardly recognized it. In his official capacity Voules talks exactly like you'd expect a statue to talk, if it could. In private, however, he evidently relaxed to some extent, and to have that sort of thing going on in my midst at that hour was too much for me.

"Voules!" I yelled.

Spion Kop ceased with a jerk. There was silence, then sobs diminishing in the distance, and finally a tap at the door. Voules entered with that impressive, my-lord-the-carriage-waits look which is what I pay him for. You wouldn't have believed he had a drop of any sort of emotion in him.

"Voules," I said, "are you under the delusion that I'm going to be Queen of the May? You've called me early all right. It's only just seven."

"I understood you to summon me, sir."

"I summoned you to find out why you were making that infernal noise outside."

"I owe you an apology, sir. I am afraid that in the heat of the moment I raised my voice."

"It's a wonder you didn't raise the roof. Who was that with you?"

"Miss Pilbeam, sir; Mrs. Vanderley's maid."

"What was all the trouble about?"

"I was breaking our engagement, sir."

I couldn't help gaping. Somehow one didn't associate Voules with engagements. Then it struck me that I'd no right to butt in on his secret sorrows, so I switched the conversation.

"I think I'll get up," I said.

"Yes, sir."

"I can't wait to breakfast with the rest. Can you get me some right away?"

"Yes, sir."

So I had a solitary breakfast and went up on deck to smoke. It was a lovely morning. Blue sea, gleaming Casino, cloudless sky, and all the rest of the hippodrome. Presently the others began to trickle up. Stella Vanderley was one of the first. I thought she looked a bit pale and tired. She said she hadn't slept well. That accounted for it. Unless you get your eight hours, where are you?

"Seen George?" I asked.

I couldn't help thinking the name seemed to freeze her a bit. Which was queer, because all the voyage she and George had been particularly close pals. In fact, at any moment I expected George to come to me and slip his little hand in mine, and whisper: "I've done it, old scout; she loves muh!"

"I have not seen Mr. Lattaker," she said.

I didn't pursue the subject. George's stock was apparently low that a.m.

The next item in the day's programme occurred a few minutes later when the morning papers arrived.

Mrs. Vanderley opened hers and gave a scream.

"The poor, dear Prince!" she said.

"What a shocking thing!" said old Marshall.

"I knew him in Vienna," said Mrs. Vanderley. "He waltzed divinely."

Then I got at mine and saw what they were talking about. The paper was full of it. It seemed that late the night before His Serene Highness the Prince of Saxburg-Leignitz (I always wonder why they call these chaps "Serene") had been murderously assaulted in a dark street on his way back from the Casino to his yacht. Apparently he had developed the habit of going about without an escort, and some rough-neck, taking advantage of this, had laid for him and slugged him with considerable vim. The Prince had been found lying pretty well beaten up and insensible in the street by a passing pedestrian, and had been taken back to his yacht, where he still lay unconscious.

"This is going to do somebody no good," I said. "What do you get for slugging a Serene Highness? I wonder if they'll catch the fellow?"

"'Later,'" read old Marshall, "'the pedestrian who discovered His Serene Highness proves to have been Mr. Denman Sturgis, the eminent private investigator. Mr. Sturgis has offered his services to the police, and is understood to be in possession of a most important clue.' That's the fellow who had charge of that kidnapping case in Chicago. If anyone can catch the man, he can."

About five minutes later, just as the rest of them were going to move off to breakfast, a boat hailed us and came alongside. A tall, thin man came up the gangway. He looked round the group, and fixed on old Marshall as the probable owner of the yacht.

"Good morning," he said. "I believe you have a Mr. Lattaker on board—Mr. George

Lattaker?"

"Yes," said Marshall. "He's down below. Want to see him? Whom shall I say?"

"He would not know my name. I should like to see him for a moment on somewhat urgent business."

"Take a seat. He'll be up in a moment. Reggie, my boy, go and hurry him up."

I went down to George's state-room.

"George, old man!" I shouted.

No answer. I opened the door and went in. The room was empty. What's more, the bunk hadn't been slept in. I don't know when I've been more surprised. I went on deck.

"He isn't there," I said.

"Not there!" said old Marshall. "Where is he, then? Perhaps he's gone for a stroll ashore. But he'll be back soon for breakfast. You'd better wait for him. Have you breakfasted? No? Then will you join us?"

The man said he would, and just then the gong went and they trooped down, leaving me alone on deck.

I sat smoking and thinking, and then smoking a bit more, when I thought I heard somebody call my name in a sort of hoarse whisper. I looked over my shoulder, and, by Jove, there at the top of the gangway in evening dress, dusty to the eyebrows and without a hat, was dear old George.

"Great Scot!" I cried.

"'Sh!" he whispered. "Anyone about?"

"They're all down at breakfast."

He gave a sigh of relief, sank into my chair, and closed his eyes. I regarded him with pity. The poor old boy looked a wreck.

"I say!" I said, touching him on the shoulder.

He leaped out of the chair with a smothered yell.

"Did you do that? What did you do it for? What's the sense of it? How do you suppose you can ever make yourself popular if you go about touching people on the shoulder? My nerves are sticking a yard out of my body this morning, Reggie!"

"Yes, old boy?"

"I did a murder last night."

"What?"

"It's the sort of thing that might happen to anybody. Directly Stella Vanderley broke off our engagement I———"

"Broke off your engagement? How long were you engaged?"

"About two minutes. It may have been less. I hadn't a stop-watch. I proposed to her at ten last night in the saloon. She accepted me. I was just going to kiss her when we heard someone coming. I went out. Coming along the corridor was that infernal what's-her-name—Mrs. Vanderley's maid—Pilbeam. Have you ever been accepted by the girl you love, Reggie?"

"Never. I've been refused dozens———"

"Then you won't understand how I felt. I was off my head with joy. I hardly knew what I was doing. I just felt I had to kiss the nearest thing handy. I couldn't wait. It might have been the ship's cat. It wasn't. It was Pilbeam."

"You kissed her?"

"I kissed her. And just at that moment the door of the saloon opened and out came Stella."

"Great Scott!"

"Exactly what I said. It flashed across me that to Stella, dear girl, not knowing the circumstances, the thing might seem a little odd. It did. She broke off the engagement, and I got out the dinghy and rowed off. I was mad. I didn't care what became of me. I simply wanted to forget. I went ashore. I—It's just on the cards that I may have drowned my sorrows a bit. Anyhow, I don't remember a thing, except that I can recollect having the deuce of a scrap with somebody in a dark street and somebody falling, and myself falling, and myself legging it for all I was worth. I woke up this morning in the Casino gardens. I've lost my hat."

I dived for the paper.

"Read," I said. "It's all there."

He read.

"Good heavens!" he said.

"You didn't do a thing to His Serene Nibs, did you?"

"Reggie, this is awful."

"Cheer up. They say he'll recover."

"That doesn't matter."

"It does to him."

He read the paper again.

"It says they've a clue."

"They always say that."

"But—My hat!"

"Eh?"

"My hat. I must have dropped it during the scrap. This man, Denman Sturgis, must have found it. It had my name in it!"

"George," I said, "you mustn't waste time. Oh!"

He jumped a foot in the air.

"Don't do it!" he said, irritably. "Don't bark like that. What's the matter?"

"The man!"

"What man?"

"A tall, thin man with an eye like a gimlet. He arrived just before you did. He's down in the saloon now, having breakfast. He said he wanted to see you on business, and wouldn't give his name. I didn't like the look of him from the first. It's this fellow Sturgis. It must be."

"No!"

"I feel it. I'm sure of it."

"Had he a hat?"

"Of course he had a hat."

"Fool! I mean mine. Was he carrying a hat?"

"By Jove, he was carrying a parcel. George, old scout, you must get a move on. You must light out if you want to spend the rest of your life out of prison. Slugging a Serene Highness is lèse-majesté. It's worse than hitting a policeman. You haven't got a moment to waste."

"But I haven't any money. Reggie, old man, lend me a tenner or something. I must get over the frontier into Italy at once. I'll wire my uncle to meet me in——"

"Look out," I cried; "there's someone coming!"

He dived out of sight just as Voules came up the companion-way, carrying a letter on a tray.

"What's the matter!" I said. "What do you want?"

"I beg your pardon, sir. I thought I heard Mr. Lattaker's voice. A letter has arrived for him."

"He isn't here."

"No, sir. Shall I remove the letter?"

"No; give it to me. I'll give it to him when he comes."

"Very good, sir."

"Oh, Voules! Are they all still at breakfast? The gentleman who came to see Mr. Lattaker? Still hard at it?"

"He is at present occupied with a kippered herring, sir."

"Ah! That's all, Voules."

"Thank you, sir."

He retired. I called to George, and he came out.

"Who was it?"

"Only Voules. He brought a letter for you. They're all at breakfast still. The sleuth's eating kippers."

"That'll hold him for a bit. Full of bones." He began to read his letter. He gave a kind of grunt of surprise at the first paragraph.

"Well, I'm hanged!" he said, as he finished.

"Reggie, this is a queer thing."

"What's that?"

He handed me the letter, and directly I started in on it I saw why he had grunted. This is how it ran:

"My dear George—I shall be seeing you to-morrow, I hope; but I think it is better, before we meet, to prepare you for a curious situation that has arisen in connection with the legacy which your father inherited from your Aunt Emily, and which you are expecting me, as trustee, to hand over to you, now that you have reached your twenty-fifth birthday. You have doubtless heard your father speak of your twin-brother Alfred, who was lost or kidnapped—which, was never ascertained—when you were both babies. When no news was received of him for so many years, it was supposed that he was dead. Yesterday, however, I received a letter purporting that he had been living all this time in Buenos Ayres as the adopted son of a wealthy South American, and has only recently discovered his identity. He states that he is on his way to meet me, and will arrive any day now. Of course, like other claimants, he may prove to be an impostor, but meanwhile his intervention will, I fear, cause a certain delay before I can hand over your money to you. It will be necessary to go into a thorough examination of credentials, etc., and this will take some time. But I will go fully into the matter with you when we meet.—Your affectionate uncle,

"AUGUSTUS ARBUTT."

I read it through twice, and the second time I had one of those ideas I do sometimes get, though admittedly a chump of the premier class. I have seldom had such a thoroughly corking brain-wave.

"Why, old top," I said, "this lets you out."

"Lets me out of half the darned money, if that's what you mean. If this chap's not an imposter—and there's no earthly reason to suppose he is, though I've never heard my father say a word about him—we shall have to split the money. Aunt Emily's will left the money to my father, or, failing him, his 'offspring.' I thought that meant me, but apparently there are a crowd of us. I call it rotten work, springing unexpected offspring on a fellow at the eleventh hour like this."

"Why, you chump," I said, "it's going to save you. This lets you out of your spectacular dash across the frontier. All you've got to do is to stay here and be your brother Alfred. It came to me in a flash."

He looked at me in a kind of dazed way.

"You ought to be in some sort of a home, Reggie."

"Ass!" I cried. "Don't you understand? Have you ever heard of twin-brothers who weren't exactly alike? Who's to say you aren't Alfred if you swear you are? Your uncle will be there to back you up that you have a brother Alfred."

"And Alfred will be there to call me a liar."

"He won't. It's not as if you had to keep it up for the rest of your life. It's only for an hour or two, till we can get this detective off the yacht. We sail for England to-morrow morning."

At last the thing seemed to sink into him. His face brightened.

"Why, I really do believe it would work," he said.

"Of course it would work. If they want proof, show them your mole. I'll swear George hadn't one."

"And as Alfred I should get a chance of talking to Stella and making things all right for George. Reggie, old top, you're a genius."

"No, no."

"You are."

"Well, it's only sometimes. I can't keep it up."

And just then there was a gentle cough behind us. We spun round.

"What the devil are you doing here, Voules," I said.

"I beg your pardon, sir. I have heard all."

I looked at George. George looked at me.

"Voules is all right," I said. "Decent Voules! Voules wouldn't give us away, would you, Voules?"

"Yes, sir."

"You would?"

"Yes, sir."

"But, Voules, old man," I said, "be sensible. What would you gain by it?"

"Financially, sir, nothing."

"Whereas, by keeping quiet"—I tapped him on the chest—"by holding your tongue, Voules, by saying nothing about it to anybody, Voules, old fellow, you might gain a considerable sum."

"Am I to understand, sir, that, because you are rich and I am poor, you think that you can buy my self-respect?"

"Oh, come!" I said.

"How much?" said Voules.

So we switched to terms. You wouldn't believe the way the man haggled. You'd have thought a decent, faithful servant would have been delighted to oblige one in a little matter like that for a fiver. But not Voules. By no means. It was a hundred down, and the promise of another hundred when we had got safely away, before he was satisfied. But we fixed it up at last, and poor old George got down to his state-room and changed his clothes.

He'd hardly gone when the breakfast-party came on deck.

"Did you meet him?" I asked.

"Meet whom?" said old Marshall.

"George's twin-brother Alfred."

"I didn't know George had a brother."

"Nor did he till yesterday. It's a long story. He was kidnapped in infancy, and everyone thought he was dead. George had a letter from his uncle about him yesterday. I shouldn't wonder if that's where George has gone, to see his uncle and find out about it. In the meantime, Alfred has arrived. He's down in George's state-room now, having a brush-up. It'll amaze you, the likeness between them. You'll think it is George at first. Look! Here he comes."

And up came George, brushed and clean, in an ordinary yachting suit.

They were rattled. There was no doubt about that. They stood looking at him, as if they thought there was a catch somewhere, but weren't quite certain where it was. I introduced him, and still they looked doubtful.

"Mr. Pepper tells me my brother is not on board," said George.

"It's an amazing likeness," said old Marshall.

"Is my brother like me?" asked George amiably.

"No one could tell you apart," I said.

"I suppose twins always are alike," said George. "But if it ever came to a question of identification, there would be one way of distinguishing us. Do you know George well,

Mr. Pepper?"

"He's a dear old pal of mine."

"You've been swimming with him perhaps?"

"Every day last August."

"Well, then, you would have noticed it if he had had a mole like this on the back of his neck, wouldn't you?" He turned his back and stooped and showed the mole. His collar hid it at ordinary times. I had seen it often when we were bathing together.

"Has George a mole like that?" he asked.

"No," I said. "Oh, no."

"You would have noticed it if he had?"

"Yes," I said. "Oh, yes."

"I'm glad of that," said George. "It would be a nuisance not to be able to prove one's own identity."

That seemed to satisfy them all. They couldn't get away from it. It seemed to me that from now on the thing was a walk-over. And I think George felt the same, for, when old Marshall asked him if he had had breakfast, he said he had not, went below, and pitched in as if he hadn't a care in the world.

Everything went right till lunch-time. George sat in the shade on the foredeck talking to Stella most of the time. When the gong went and the rest had started to go below, he drew me back. He was beaming.

"It's all right," he said. "What did I tell you?"

"What did you tell me?"

"Why, about Stella. Didn't I say that Alfred would fix things for George? I told her she looked worried, and got her to tell me what the trouble was. And then——"

"You must have shown a flash of speed if you got her to confide in you after knowing you for about two hours."

"Perhaps I did," said George modestly, "I had no notion, till I became him, what a persuasive sort of chap my brother Alfred was. Anyway, she told me all about it, and I started in to show her that George was a pretty good sort of fellow on the whole, who oughtn't to be turned down for what was evidently merely temporary insanity. She saw my point."

"And it's all right?"

"Absolutely, if only we can produce George. How much longer does that infernal sleuth intend to stay here? He seems to have taken root."

"I fancy he thinks that you're bound to come back sooner or later, and is waiting for you."

"He's an absolute nuisance," said George.

We were moving towards the companion way, to go below for lunch, when a boat hailed us. We went to the side and looked over.

"It's my uncle," said George.

A stout man came up the gangway.

"Halloa, George!" he said. "Get my letter?"

"I think you are mistaking me for my brother," said George. "My name is Alfred Lattaker."

"What's that?"

"I am George's brother Alfred. Are you my Uncle Augustus?"

The stout man stared at him.

"You're very like George," he said.

"So everyone tells me."

"And you're really Alfred?"

"I am."

"I'd like to talk business with you for a moment."

He cocked his eye at me. I sidled off and went below.

At the foot of the companion-steps I met Voules.

"I beg your pardon, sir," said Voules. "If it would be convenient I should be glad to have the afternoon off."

I'm bound to say I rather liked his manner. Absolutely normal. Not a trace of the fellow-conspirator about it. I gave him the afternoon off.

I had lunch—George didn't show up—and as I was going out I was waylaid by the girl Pilbeam. She had been crying.

"I beg your pardon, sir, but did Mr. Voules ask you for the afternoon?"

I didn't see what business if was of hers, but she seemed all worked up about it, so I told her.

"Yes, I have given him the afternoon off."

She broke down—absolutely collapsed. Devilish unpleasant it was. I'm hopeless in a situation like this. After I'd said, "There, there!" which didn't seem to help much, I hadn't any remarks to make.

"He s-said he was going to the tables to gamble away all his savings and then shoot himself, because he had nothing left to live for."

I suddenly remembered the scrap in the small hours outside my state-room door. I hate mysteries. I meant to get to the bottom of this. I couldn't have a really first-class valet like Voules going about the place shooting himself up. Evidently the girl Pilbeam was at the bottom of the thing. I questioned her. She sobbed.

I questioned her more. I was firm. And eventually she yielded up the facts. Voules had seen George kiss her the night before; that was the trouble.

Things began to piece themselves together. I went up to interview George. There was going to be another job for persuasive Alfred. Voules's mind had got to be eased as Stella's had been. I couldn't afford to lose a fellow with his genius for preserving a trouser-crease.

I found George on the foredeck. What is it Shakespeare or somebody says about some fellow's face being sicklied o'er with the pale cast of care? George's was like that. He looked green.

"Finished with your uncle?" I said.

He grinned a ghostly grin.

"There isn't any uncle," he said. "There isn't any Alfred. And there isn't any money."

"Explain yourself, old top," I said.

"It won't take long. The old crook has spent every penny of the trust money. He's been at it for years, ever since I was a kid. When the time came to cough up, and I was due to see that he did it, he went to the tables in the hope of a run of luck, and lost the last remnant of the stuff. He had to find a way of holding me for a while and postponing the squaring of accounts while he got away, and he invented this twin-brother business. He knew I should find out sooner or later, but meanwhile he would be able to get off to South America, which he has done. He's on his way now."

"You let him go?"

"What could I do? I can't afford to make a fuss with that man Sturgis around. I can't prove there's no Alfred when my only chance of avoiding prison is to be Alfred."

"Well, you've made things right for yourself with Stella Vanderley, anyway," I said, to cheer him up.

"What's the good of that now? I've hardly any money and no prospects. How can I marry her?"

I pondered.

"It looks to me, old top," I said at last, "as if things were in a bit of a mess."

"You've guessed it," said poor old George.

I spent the afternoon musing on Life. If you come to think of it, what a queer thing Life is! So unlike anything else, don't you know, if you see what I mean. At any moment you may be strolling peacefully along, and all the time Life's waiting around the corner to fetch you one. You can't tell when you may be going to get it. It's all dashed puzzling. Here was poor old George, as well-meaning a fellow as ever stepped, getting swatted all over the ring by the hand of Fate. Why? That's what I asked myself. Just Life, don't you know. That's all there was about it.

It was close on six o'clock when our third visitor of the day arrived. We were sitting on the afterdeck in the cool of the evening—old Marshall, Denman Sturgis, Mrs. Vanderley, Stella, George, and I—when he came up. We had been talking of George, and old Marshall was suggesting the advisability of sending out search-parties. He was worried. So was Stella Vanderley. So, for that matter, were George and I, only not for the same reason.

We were just arguing the thing out when the visitor appeared. He was a well-built, stiff sort of fellow. He spoke with a German accent.

"Mr. Marshall?" he said. "I am Count Fritz von Cöslin, equerry to His Serene Highness"—he clicked his heels together and saluted—"the Prince of Saxburg-Leignitz."

Mrs. Vanderley jumped up.

"Why, Count," she said, "what ages since we met in Vienna! You remember?"

"Could I ever forget? And the charming Miss Stella, she is well, I suppose not?"

"Stella, you remember Count Fritz?"

Stella shook hands with him.

"And how is the poor, dear Prince?" asked Mrs. Vanderley. "What a terrible thing to have happened!"

"I rejoice to say that my high-born master is better. He has regained consciousness and is sitting up and taking nourishment."

"That's good," said old Marshall.

"In a spoon only," sighed the Count. "Mr. Marshall, with your permission I should like a word with Mr. Sturgis."

"Mr. Who?"

The gimlet-eyed sportsman came forward.

"I am Denman Sturgis, at your service."

"The deuce you are! What are you doing here?"

"Mr. Sturgis," explained the Count, "graciously volunteered his services——"

"I know. But what's he doing here?"

"I am waiting for Mr. George Lattaker, Mr. Marshall."

"Eh?"

"You have not found him?" asked the Count anxiously.

"Not yet, Count; but I hope to do so shortly. I know what he looks like now. This gentleman is his twin-brother. They are doubles."

"You are sure this gentleman is not Mr. George Lattaker?"

George put his foot down firmly on the suggestion.

"Don't go mixing me up with my brother," he said. "I am Alfred. You can tell me by my mole."

He exhibited the mole. He was taking no risks.

The Count clicked his tongue regretfully.

"I am sorry," he said.

George didn't offer to console him,

"Don't worry," said Sturgis. "He won't escape me. I shall find him."

"Do, Mr. Sturgis, do. And quickly. Find swiftly that noble young man."

"What?" shouted George.

"That noble young man, George Lattaker, who, at the risk of his life, saved my high-born master from the assassin."

George sat down suddenly.

"I don't understand," he said feebly.

"We were wrong, Mr. Sturgis," went on the Count. "We leaped to the conclusion—was it not so?—that the owner of the hat you found was also the assailant of my high-born master. We were wrong. I have heard the story from His Serene Highness's own lips. He was passing down a dark street when a ruffian in a mask sprang out upon him. Doubtless he had been followed from the Casino, where he had been winning heavily. My high-born master was taken by surprise. He was felled. But before he lost consciousness he perceived a young man in evening dress, wearing the hat you found, running swiftly towards him. The hero engaged the assassin in combat, and my high-born master remembers no more. His Serene Highness asks repeatedly, 'Where is my brave preserver?' His gratitude is princely.

He seeks for this young man to reward him. Ah, you should be proud of your brother, sir!"

"Thanks," said George limply.

"And you, Mr. Sturgis, you must redouble your efforts. You must search the land; you must scour the sea to find George Lattaker."

"He needn't take all that trouble," said a voice from the gangway.

It was Voules. His face was flushed, his hat was on the back of his head, and he was smoking a fat cigar.

"I'll tell you where to find George Lattaker!" he shouted.

He glared at George, who was staring at him.

"Yes, look at me," he yelled. "Look at me. You won't be the first this afternoon who's stared at the mysterious stranger who won for two hours without a break. I'll be even with you now, Mr. Blooming Lattaker. I'll learn you to break a poor man's heart. Mr. Marshall and gents, this morning I was on deck, and I over'eard 'im plotting to put up a game on you. They'd spotted that gent there as a detective, and they arranged that blooming Lattaker was to pass himself off as his own twin-brother. And if you wanted proof, blooming Pepper tells him to show them his mole and he'd swear George hadn't one. Those were his very words. That man there is George Lattaker, Hesquire, and let him deny it if he can."

George got up.

"I haven't the least desire to deny it, Voules."

"Mr. Voules, if you please."

"It's true," said George, turning to the Count. "The fact is, I had rather a foggy recollection of what happened last night. I only remembered knocking some one down, and, like you, I jumped to the conclusion that I must have assaulted His Serene Highness."

"Then you are really George Lattaker?" asked the Count.

"I am."

"'Ere, what does all this mean?" demanded Voules.

"Merely that I saved the life of His Serene Highness the Prince of Saxburg-Leignitz, Mr. Voules."

"It's a swindle!" began Voules, when there was a sudden rush and the girl Pilbeam cannoned into the crowd, sending me into old Marshall's chair, and flung herself into the arms of Voules.

"Oh, Harold!" she cried. "I thought you were dead. I thought you'd shot yourself."

He sort of braced himself together to fling her off, and then he seemed to think better of it and fell into the clinch.

It was all dashed romantic, don't you know, but there are limits.

"Voules, you're sacked," I said.

"Who cares?" he said. "Think I was going to stop on now I'm a gentleman of property? Come along, Emma, my dear. Give a month's notice and get your 'at, and I'll take you to dinner at Ciro's."

"And you, Mr. Lattaker," said the Count, "may I conduct you to the presence of my high-born master? He wishes to show his gratitude to his preserver."

"You may," said George. "May I have my hat, Mr. Sturgis?"

There's just one bit more. After dinner that night I came up for a smoke, and, strolling on to the foredeck, almost bumped into George and Stella. They seemed to be having an argument.

"I'm not sure," she was saying, "that I believe that a man can be so happy that he wants to kiss the nearest thing in sight, as you put it."

"Don't you?" said George. "Well, as it happens, I'm feeling just that way now."

I coughed and he turned round.

"Halloa, Reggie!" he said.

"Halloa, George!" I said. "Lovely night."

"Beautiful," said Stella.

"The moon," I said.

"Ripping," said George.

"Lovely," said Stella.

"And look at the reflection of the stars on the———"

George caught my eye. "Pop off," he said.

I popped.

DOING CLARENCE, A BIT OF GOOD

Have you ever thought about—and, when I say thought about, I mean really carefully considered the question of—the coolness, the cheek, or, if you prefer it, the gall with which Woman, as a sex, fairly bursts? I have, by Jove! But then I've had it thrust on my notice, by George, in a way I should imagine has happened to pretty few fellows. And the limit was reached by that business of the Yeardsley "Venus."

To make you understand the full what-d'you-call-it of the situation, I shall have to explain just how matters stood between Mrs. Yeardsley and myself.

When I first knew her she was Elizabeth Shoolbred. Old Worcestershire family; pots of money; pretty as a picture. Her brother Bill was at Oxford with me.

I loved Elizabeth Shoolbred. I loved her, don't you know. And there was a time, for about a week, when we were engaged to be married. But just as I was beginning to take a serious view of life and study furniture catalogues and feel pretty solemn when the restaurant orchestra played "The Wedding Glide," I'm hanged if she didn't break it off, and a month later she was married to a fellow of the name of Yeardsley—Clarence Yeardsley, an artist.

What with golf, and billiards, and a bit of racing, and fellows at the club rallying round and kind of taking me out of myself, as it were, I got over it, and came to look on the affair as a closed page in the book of my life, if you know what I mean. It didn't seem likely to me that we should meet again, as she and Clarence had settled down in the country somewhere and never came to London, and I'm bound to own that, by the time I got her letter, the wound had pretty well healed, and I was to a certain extent sitting up and taking nourishment. In fact, to be absolutely honest, I was jolly thankful the thing had ended as it had done.

This letter I'm telling you about arrived one morning out of a blue sky, as it were. It ran like this:

"MY DEAR OLD REGGIE,—What ages it seems since I saw anything of you. How are you? We have settled down here in the most perfect old house, with a lovely garden, in the middle of delightful country. Couldn't you run down here for a few days? Clarence and I would be so glad to see you. Bill is here, and is most anxious to meet you again. He was speaking of you only this morning. Do come. Wire your train, and I will send the car to meet you.

—Yours most sincerely,

ELIZABETH YEARDSLEY.

"P.S.—We can give you new milk and fresh eggs. Think of that!

"P.P.S.—Bill says our billiard-table is one of the best he has ever played on.

"P.P.S.S.—We are only half a mile from a golf course. Bill says it is better than St. Andrews.

"P.P.S.S.S.—You must come!"

Well, a fellow comes down to breakfast one morning, with a bit of a head on, and finds a letter like that from a girl who might quite easily have blighted his life! It rattled me rather, I must confess.

However, that bit about the golf settled me. I knew Bill knew what he was talking about, and, if he said the course was so topping, it must be something special. So I went.

Old Bill met me at the station with the car. I hadn't come across him for some months, and I was glad to see him again. And he apparently was glad to see me.

"Thank goodness you've come," he said, as we drove off. "I was just about at my last grip."

"What's the trouble, old scout?" I asked.

"If I had the artistic what's-its-name," he went on, "if the mere mention of pictures didn't give me the pip, I dare say it wouldn't be so bad. As it is, it's rotten!"

"Pictures?"

"Pictures. Nothing else is mentioned in this household. Clarence is an artist. So is his father. And you know yourself what Elizabeth is like when one gives her her head?"

I remembered then—it hadn't come back to me before—that most of my time with Elizabeth had been spent in picture-galleries. During the period when I had let her do just what she wanted to do with me, I had had to follow her like a dog through gallery after gallery, though pictures are poison to me, just as they are to old Bill. Somehow it had never struck me that she would still be going on in this way after marrying an artist. I should have thought that by this time the mere sight of a picture would have fed her up. Not so, however, according to old Bill.

"They talk pictures at every meal," he said. "I tell you, it makes a chap feel out of it. How long are you down for?"

"A few days."

"Take my tip, and let me send you a wire from London. I go there to-morrow. I promised to play against the Scottish. The idea was that I was to come back after the match. But you couldn't get me back with a lasso."

I tried to point out the silver lining.

"But, Bill, old scout, your sister says there's a most corking links near here."

He turned and stared at me, and nearly ran us into the bank.

"You don't mean honestly she said that?"

"She said you said it was better than St. Andrews."

"So I did. Was that all she said I said?"

"Well, wasn't it enough?"

"She didn't happen to mention that I added the words, 'I don't think'?"

"No, she forgot to tell me that."

"It's the worst course in Great Britain."

I felt rather stunned, don't you know. Whether it's a bad habit to have got into or not, I can't say, but I simply can't do without my daily allowance of golf when I'm not in London.

I took another whirl at the silver lining.

"We'll have to take it out in billiards," I said. "I'm glad the table's good."

"It depends what you call good. It's half-size, and there's a seven-inch cut just out of baulk where Clarence's cue slipped. Elizabeth has mended it with pink silk. Very smart and dressy it looks, but it doesn't improve the thing as a billiard-table."

"But she said you said——"

"Must have been pulling your leg."

We turned in at the drive gates of a good-sized house standing well back from the road. It looked black and sinister in the dusk, and I couldn't help feeling, you know, like one of those Johnnies you read about in stories who are lured to lonely houses for rummy purposes and hear a shriek just as they get there. Elizabeth knew me well enough to know that a specially good golf course was a safe draw to me. And she had deliberately played on her knowledge. What was the game? That was what I wanted to know. And then a sudden thought struck me which brought me out in a cold perspiration. She had some girl down here and was going to have a stab at marrying me off. I've often heard that young married women are all over that sort of thing. Certainly she had said there was nobody at the house but Clarence and herself and Bill and Clarence's father, but a woman who could take the name of St. Andrews in vain as she had done wouldn't be likely to stick at a trifle.

"Bill, old scout," I said, "there aren't any frightful girls or any rot of that sort stopping here, are there?"

"Wish there were," he said. "No such luck."

As we pulled up at the front door, it opened, and a woman's figure appeared.

"Have you got him, Bill?" she said, which in my present frame of mind struck me as a jolly creepy way of putting it. The sort of thing Lady Macbeth might have said to Macbeth, don't you know.

"Do you mean me?" I said.

She came down into the light. It was Elizabeth, looking just the same as in the old days.

"Is that you, Reggie? I'm so glad you were able to come. I was afraid you might have forgotten all about it. You know what you are. Come along in and have some tea."

Have you ever been turned down by a girl who afterwards married and then been introduced to her husband? If so you'll understand how I felt when Clarence burst on me. You know the feeling. First of all, when you hear about the marriage, you say to yourself, "I wonder what he's like." Then you meet him, and think, "There must be some mistake. She can't have preferred this to me!" That's what I thought, when I set eyes on Clarence.

He was a little thin, nervous-looking chappie of about thirty-five. His hair was getting grey at the temples and straggly on top. He wore pince-nez, and he had a drooping moustache. I'm no Bombardier Wells myself, but in front of Clarence I felt quite a nut. And Elizabeth, mind you, is one of those tall, splendid girls who look like princesses. Honestly, I believe women do it out of pure cussedness.

"How do you do, Mr. Pepper? Hark! Can you hear a mewing cat?" said Clarence. All in one breath, don't you know.

"Eh?" I said.

"A mewing cat. I feel sure I hear a mewing cat. Listen!"

While we were listening the door opened, and a white-haired old gentleman came in. He was built on the same lines as Clarence, but was an earlier model. I took him correctly, to be Mr. Yeardsley, senior. Elizabeth introduced us.

"Father," said Clarence, "did you meet a mewing cat outside? I feel positive I heard a cat mewing."

"No," said the father, shaking his head; "no mewing cat."

"I can't bear mewing cats," said Clarence. "A mewing cat gets on my nerves!"

"A mewing cat is so trying," said Elizabeth.

"I dislike mewing cats," said old Mr. Yeardsley.

That was all about mewing cats for the moment. They seemed to think they had covered the ground satisfactorily, and they went back to pictures.

We talked pictures steadily till it was time to dress for dinner. At least, they did. I just sort of sat around. Presently the subject of picture-robberies came up. Somebody mentioned the "Monna Lisa," and then I happened to remember seeing something in the evening paper, as I was coming down in the train, about some fellow somewhere having had a valuable painting pinched by burglars the night before. It was the first time I had had a chance of breaking into the conversation with any effect, and I meant to make the most of it. The paper was in the pocket of my overcoat in the hall. I went and fetched it.

"Here it is," I said. "A Romney belonging to Sir Bellamy Palmer——"

They all shouted "What!" exactly at the same time, like a chorus. Elizabeth grabbed the paper.

"Let me look! Yes. 'Late last night burglars entered the residence of Sir Bellamy Palmer, Dryden Park, Midford, Hants——'"

"Why, that's near here," I said. "I passed through Midford——"

"Dryden Park is only two miles from this house," said Elizabeth. I noticed her eyes were sparkling.

"Only two miles!" she said. "It might have been us! It might have been the 'Venus'!"

Old Mr. Yeardsley bounded in his chair.

"The 'Venus'!" he cried.

They all seemed wonderfully excited. My little contribution to the evening's chat had made quite a hit.

Why I didn't notice it before I don't know, but it was not till Elizabeth showed it to me after dinner that I had my first look at the Yeardsley "Venus." When she led me up to it, and switched on the light, it seemed impossible that I could have sat right through dinner without noticing it. But then, at meals, my attention is pretty well riveted on the foodstuffs. Anyway, it was not till Elizabeth showed it to me that I was aware of its existence.

She and I were alone in the drawing-room after dinner. Old Yeardsley was writing letters in the morning-room, while Bill and Clarence were rollicking on the half-size billiard table with the pink silk tapestry effects. All, in fact, was joy, jollity, and song, so to speak, when Elizabeth, who had been sitting wrapped in thought for a bit, bent towards me and said, "Reggie."

And the moment she said it I knew something was going to happen. You know that pre-what-d'you-call-it you get sometimes? Well, I got it then.

"What-o?" I said nervously.

"Reggie," she said, "I want to ask a great favour of you."

"Yes?"

She stooped down and put a log on the fire, and went on, with her back to me:

"Do you remember, Reggie, once saying you would do anything in the world for me?"

There! That's what I meant when I said that about the cheek of Woman as a sex. What I mean is, after what had happened, you'd have thought she would have preferred to let the dead past bury its dead, and all that sort of thing, what?

Mind you, I had said I would do anything in the world for her. I admit that. But it was a distinctly pre-Clarence remark. He hadn't appeared on the scene then, and it stands to reason that a fellow who may have been a perfect knight-errant to a girl when he was engaged to her, doesn't feel nearly so keen on spreading himself in that direction when she has given him the miss-in-baulk, and gone and married a man who reason and instinct both tell him is a decided blighter.

I couldn't think of anything to say but "Oh, yes."

"There's something you can do for me now, which will make me everlastingly grateful."

"Yes," I said.

"Do you know, Reggie," she said suddenly, "that only a few months ago Clarence was very fond of cats?"

"Eh! Well, he still seems—er—interested in them, what?"

"Now they get on his nerves. Everything gets on his nerves."

"Some fellows swear by that stuff you see advertised all over the——"

"No, that wouldn't help him. He doesn't need to take anything. He wants to get rid of something."

"I don't quite follow. Get rid of something?"

"The 'Venus,'" said Elizabeth.

She looked up and caught my bulging eye.

"You saw the 'Venus,'" she said.

"Not that I remember."

"Well, come into the dining-room."

We went into the dining-room, and she switched on the lights.

"There," she said.

On the wall close to the door—that may have been why I hadn't noticed it before; I had sat with my back to it—was a large oil-painting. It was what you'd call a classical picture, I suppose. What I mean is—well, you know what I mean. All I can say is that it's funny I hadn't noticed it.

"Is that the 'Venus'?" I said.

She nodded.

"How would you like to have to look at that every time you sat down to a meal?"

"Well, I don't know. I don't think it would affect me much. I'd worry through all right."

She jerked her head impatiently.

"But you're not an artist," she said. "Clarence is."

And then I began to see daylight. What exactly was the trouble I didn't understand, but it was evidently something to do with the good old Artistic Temperament, and I could believe anything about that. It explains everything. It's like the Unwritten Law, don't you know, which you plead in America if you've done anything they want to send you to chokey for and you don't want to go. What I mean is, if you're absolutely off your rocker, but don't find it convenient to be scooped into the luny-bin, you simply explain that, when you said you were a teapot, it was just your Artistic Temperament, and they apologize and go away. So I stood by to hear just how the A.T. had affected Clarence, the Cat's Friend, ready for anything.

And, believe me, it had hit Clarence badly.

It was this way. It seemed that old Yeardsley was an amateur artist and that this "Venus" was his masterpiece. He said so, and he ought to have known. Well, when Clarence married, he had given it to him, as a wedding present, and had hung it where it stood with his own hands. All right so far, what? But mark the sequel. Temperamental Clarence, being a professional artist and consequently some streets ahead of the dad at the game, saw flaws in the "Venus." He couldn't stand it at any price. He didn't like the drawing. He didn't like the expression of the face. He didn't like the colouring. In fact, it made him feel quite ill to look at it. Yet, being devoted to his father and wanting to do anything rather than give him pain, he had not been able to bring himself to store the thing in the cellar, and the strain of confronting the picture three times a day had begun to tell on him to such an extent that Elizabeth felt something had to be done.

"Now you see," she said.

"In a way," I said. "But don't you think it's making rather heavy weather over a trifle?"

"Oh, can't you understand? Look!" Her voice dropped as if she was in church, and she switched on another light. It shone on the picture next to old Yeardsley's. "There!" she said. "Clarence painted that!"

She looked at me expectantly, as if she were waiting for me to swoon, or yell, or something. I took a steady look at Clarence's effort. It was another Classical picture. It seemed to me very much like the other one.

Some sort of art criticism was evidently expected of me, so I made a dash at it.

"Er—'Venus'?" I said.

Mark you, Sherlock Holmes would have made the same mistake. On the evidence, I mean.

"No. 'Jocund Spring,'" she snapped. She switched off the light. "I see you don't understand even now. You never had any taste about pictures. When we used to go to the galleries together, you would far rather have been at your club."

This was so absolutely true, that I had no remark to make. She came up to me, and put her hand on my arm.

"I'm sorry, Reggie. I didn't mean to be cross. Only I do want to make you understand that Clarence is suffering. Suppose—suppose—well, let us take the case of a great musician. Suppose a great musician had to sit and listen to a cheap vulgar tune—the same tune—day after day, day after day, wouldn't you expect his nerves to break! Well, it's just like that with Clarence. Now you see?"

"Yes, but——"

"But what? Surely I've put it plainly enough?"

"Yes. But what I mean is, where do I come in? What do you want me to do?"

"I want you to steal the 'Venus.'"

I looked at her.

"You want me to——?"

"Steal it. Reggie!" Her eyes were shining with excitement. "Don't you see? It's Providence. When I asked you to come here, I had just got the idea. I knew I could rely on you. And then by a miracle this robbery of the Romney takes place at a house not two miles away. It removes the last chance of the poor old man suspecting anything and having his feelings hurt. Why, it's the most wonderful compliment to him. Think! One night thieves steal a splendid Romney; the next the same gang take his 'Venus.' It will be the proudest moment of his life. Do it to-night, Reggie. I'll give you a sharp knife. You simply cut the canvas out of the frame, and it's done."

"But one moment," I said. "I'd be delighted to be of any use to you, but in a purely family affair like this, wouldn't it be better—in fact, how about tackling old Bill on the subject?"

"I have asked Bill already. Yesterday. He refused."

"But if I'm caught?"

"You can't be. All you have to do is to take the picture, open one of the windows, leave it open, and go back to your room."

It sounded simple enough.

"And as to the picture itself—when I've got it?"

"Burn it. I'll see that you have a good fire in your room."

"But——"

She looked at me. She always did have the most wonderful eyes.

"Reggie," she said; nothing more. Just "Reggie."

She looked at me.

"Well, after all, if you see what I mean—The days that are no more, don't you know. Auld Lang Syne, and all that sort of thing. You follow me?"

"All right," I said. "I'll do it."

I don't know if you happen to be one of those Johnnies who are steeped in crime, and so forth, and think nothing of pinching diamond necklaces. If you're not, you'll understand that I felt a lot less keen on the job I'd taken on when I sat in my room, waiting to get busy, than I had done when I promised to tackle it in the dining-room. On paper it all seemed easy enough, but I couldn't help feeling there was a catch somewhere, and I've never known time pass slower. The kick-off was scheduled for one o'clock in the morning, when the household might be expected to be pretty sound asleep, but at a quarter to I couldn't stand it any longer. I lit the lantern I had taken from Bill's bicycle, took a grip of my knife, and slunk downstairs.

The first thing I did on getting to the dining-room was to open the window. I had half a mind to smash it, so as to give an extra bit of local colour to the affair, but decided not to on account of the noise. I had put my lantern on the table, and was just reaching out for it, when something happened. What it was for the moment I couldn't have said. It might have been an explosion of some sort or an earthquake. Some solid object caught me a frightful whack on the chin. Sparks and things occurred inside my head and the next thing I remember is feeling something wet and cold splash into my face, and hearing a voice that sounded like old Bill's say, "Feeling better now?"

I sat up. The lights were on, and I was on the floor, with old Bill kneeling beside me with a soda siphon.

"What happened?" I said.

"I'm awfully sorry, old man," he said. "I hadn't a notion it was you. I came in here, and saw a lantern on the table, and the window open and a chap with a knife in his hand, so I didn't stop to make inquiries. I just let go at his jaw for all I was worth. What on earth do you think you're doing? Were you walking in your sleep?"

"It was Elizabeth," I said. "Why, you know all about it. She said she had told you."

"You don't mean——"

"The picture. You refused to take it on, so she asked me."

"Reggie, old man," he said. "I'll never believe what they say about repentance again. It's a fool's trick and upsets everything. If I hadn't repented, and thought it was rather rough on Elizabeth not to do a little thing like that for her, and come down here to do it after all, you wouldn't have stopped that sleep-producer with your chin. I'm sorry."

"Me, too," I said, giving my head another shake to make certain it was still on.

"Are you feeling better now?"

"Better than I was. But that's not saying much."

"Would you like some more soda-water? No? Well, how about getting this job finished and going to bed? And let's be quick about it too. You made a noise like a ton of bricks when you went down just now, and it's on the cards some of the servants may have heard. Toss you who carves."

"Heads."

"Tails it is," he said, uncovering the coin. "Up you get. I'll hold the light. Don't spike yourself on that sword of yours."

It was as easy a job as Elizabeth had said. Just four quick cuts, and the thing came out of its frame like an oyster. I rolled it up. Old Bill had put the lantern on the floor and was at the sideboard, collecting whisky, soda, and glasses.

"We've got a long evening before us," he said. "You can't burn a picture of that size in one chunk. You'd set the chimney on fire. Let's do the thing comfortably. Clarence can't grudge us the stuff. We've done him a bit of good this trip. To-morrow'll be the maddest, merriest day of Clarence's glad New Year. On we go."

We went up to my room, and sat smoking and yarning away and sipping our drinks, and every now and then cutting a slice off the picture and shoving it in the fire till it was all gone. And what with the cosiness of it and the cheerful blaze, and the comfortable feeling of doing good by stealth, I don't know when I've had a jollier time since the days when we used to brew in my study at school.

We had just put the last slice on when Bill sat up suddenly, and gripped my arm.

"I heard something," he said.

I listened, and, by Jove, I heard something, too. My room was just over the dining-room, and the sound came up to us quite distinctly. Stealthy footsteps, by George! And then a chair falling over.

"There's somebody in the dining-room," I whispered.

There's a certain type of chap who takes a pleasure in positively chivvying trouble. Old Bill's like that. If I had been alone, it would have taken me about three seconds to persuade myself that I hadn't really heard anything after all. I'm a peaceful sort of cove, and believe in living and letting live, and so forth. To old Bill, however, a visit from burglars was pure jam. He was out of his chair in one jump.

"Come on," he said. "Bring the poker."

I brought the tongs as well. I felt like it. Old Bill collared the knife. We crept downstairs.

"We'll fling the door open and make a rush," said Bill.

"Supposing they shoot, old scout?"

"Burglars never shoot," said Bill.

Which was comforting provided the burglars knew it.

Old Bill took a grip of the handle, turned it quickly, and in he went. And then we pulled up sharp, staring.

The room was in darkness except for a feeble splash of light at the near end. Standing on a chair in front of Clarence's "Jocund Spring," holding a candle in one hand and reaching up with a knife in the other, was old Mr. Yeardsley, in bedroom slippers and a grey dressing-gown. He had made a final cut just as we rushed in. Turning at the sound, he stopped, and he and the chair and the candle and the picture came down in a heap together. The candle went out.

"What on earth?" said Bill.

I felt the same. I picked up the candle and lit it, and then a most fearful thing happened. The old man picked himself up, and suddenly collapsed into a chair and began to cry like a child. Of course, I could see it was only the Artistic Temperament, but still, believe me, it was devilish unpleasant. I looked at old Bill. Old Bill looked at me. We shut the door quick, and after that we didn't know what to do. I saw Bill look at the sideboard, and I knew what he was looking for. But we had taken the siphon upstairs, and his ideas of first-aid stopped short at squirting soda-water. We just waited, and presently old Yeardsley switched off, sat up, and began talking with a rush.

"Clarence, my boy, I was tempted. It was that burglary at Dryden Park. It tempted me. It made it all so simple. I knew you would put it down to the same gang, Clarence, my boy. I——"

It seemed to dawn upon him at this point that Clarence was not among those present.

"Clarence?" he said hesitatingly.

"He's in bed," I said.

"In bed! Then he doesn't know? Even now—Young men, I throw myself on your mercy. Don't be hard on me. Listen." He grabbed at Bill, who sidestepped. "I can explain everything—everything."

He gave a gulp.

"You are not artists, you two young men, but I will try to make you understand, make you realise what this picture means to me. I was two years painting it. It is my child. I watched it grow. I loved it. It was part of my life. Nothing would have induced me to sell it. And then Clarence married, and in a mad moment I gave my treasure to him. You cannot understand, you two young men, what agonies I suffered. The thing was done. It was irrevocable. I saw how Clarence valued the picture. I knew that I could never bring myself to ask him for it back. And yet I was lost without it. What could I do? Till this evening I could see no hope. Then came this story of the theft of the Romney from a house quite close to this, and I saw my way. Clarence would never suspect. He would put the robbery down to the same band of criminals who stole the Romney. Once the idea had come, I could not drive it out. I fought against it, but to no avail. At last I yielded, and crept down here to carry out my plan. You found me." He grabbed again, at me this time, and got me by the arm. He had a grip like a lobster. "Young man," he said, "you would not betray me? You would not tell Clarence?"

I was feeling most frightfully sorry for the poor old chap by this time, don't you know, but I thought it would be kindest to give it him straight instead of breaking it by degrees.

"I won't say a word to Clarence, Mr. Yeardsley," I said. "I quite understand your feelings. The Artistic Temperament, and all that sort of thing. I mean—what? I know. But I'm afraid—Well, look!"

I went to the door and switched on the electric light, and there, staring him in the face, were the two empty frames. He stood goggling at them in silence. Then he gave a sort of wheezy grunt.

"The gang! The burglars! They have been here, and they have taken Clarence's picture!" He paused. "It might have been mine! My Venus!" he whispered It was getting most fearfully painful, you know, but he had to know the truth.

"I'm awfully sorry, you know," I said. "But it was."

He started, poor old chap.

"Eh? What do you mean?"

"They did take your Venus."

"But I have it here."

I shook my head.

"That's Clarence's 'Jocund Spring,'" I said.

He jumped at it and straightened it out.

"What! What are you talking about? Do you think I don't know my own picture—my child—my Venus. See! My own signature in the corner. Can you read, boy? Look: 'Matthew Yeardsley.' This is my picture!"

And—well, by Jove, it was, don't you know!

Well, we got him off to bed, him and his infernal Venus, and we settled down to take a steady look at the position of affairs. Bill said it was my fault for getting hold of the wrong picture, and I said it was Bill's fault for fetching me such a crack on the jaw that I couldn't be expected to see what I was getting hold of, and then there was a pretty massive silence for a bit.

"Reggie," said Bill at last, "how exactly do you feel about facing Clarence and Elizabeth at breakfast?"

"Old scout," I said. "I was thinking much the same myself."

"Reggie," said Bill, "I happen to know there's a milk-train leaving Midford at three-fifteen. It isn't what you'd call a flier. It gets to London at about half-past nine. Well—er—in the circumstances, how about it?"

THE AUNT AND THE SLUGGARD

Now that it's all over, I may as well admit that there was a time during the rather funny affair of Rockmetteller Todd when I thought that Jeeves was going to let me down. The man had the appearance of being baffled.

Jeeves is my man, you know. Officially he pulls in his weekly wages for pressing my clothes and all that sort of thing; but actually he's more like what the poet Johnnie called some bird of his acquaintance who was apt to rally round him in times of need—a guide, don't you know; philosopher, if I remember rightly, and—I rather fancy—friend. I rely on him at every turn.

So naturally, when Rocky Todd told me about his aunt, I didn't hesitate. Jeeves was in on the thing from the start.

The affair of Rocky Todd broke loose early one morning of spring. I was in bed, restoring the good old tissues with about nine hours of the dreamless, when the door flew open and somebody prodded me in the lower ribs and began to shake the bedclothes. After blinking a bit and generally pulling myself together, I located Rocky, and my first impression was that it was some horrid dream.

Rocky, you see, lived down on Long Island somewhere, miles away from New York; and not only that, but he had told me himself more than once that he never got up before twelve, and seldom earlier than one. Constitutionally the laziest young devil in America, he had hit on a walk-in life which enabled him to go the limit in that direction. He was a poet. At least, he wrote poems when he did anything; but most of his time, as far as I could make out, he spent in a sort of trance. He told me once that he could sit on a fence, watching a worm and wondering what on earth it was up to, for hours at a stretch.

He had his scheme of life worked out to a fine point. About once a month he would take three days writing a few poems; the other three hundred and twenty-nine days of the year he rested. I didn't know there was enough money in poetry to support a chappie, even in the way in which Rocky lived; but it seems that, if you stick to exhortations to young men to lead the strenuous life and don't shove in any rhymes, American editors fight for the stuff. Rocky showed me one of his things once. It began:

Be!

Be!

   The past is dead.

   To-morrow is not born.

     Be to-day!

To-day!

   Be with every nerve,

      With every muscle,

      With every drop of your red blood!

Be!

It was printed opposite the frontispiece of a magazine with a sort of scroll round it, and a picture in the middle of a fairly-nude chappie, with bulging muscles, giving the rising sun the glad eye. Rocky said they gave him a hundred dollars for it, and he stayed in bed till four in the afternoon for over a month.

As regarded the future he was pretty solid, owing to the fact that he had a moneyed aunt tucked away somewhere in Illinois; and, as he had been named Rockmetteller after her, and was her only nephew, his position was pretty sound. He told me that when he did come into the money, he meant to do no work at all, except perhaps an occasional poem recommending the young man with life opening out before him, with all its splendid possibilities, to light a pipe and shove his feet upon the mantelpiece.

And this was the man who was prodding me in the ribs in the grey dawn!

"Read this, Bertie!" I could just see that he was waving a letter or something equally foul in my face. "Wake up and read this!"

I can't read before I've had my morning tea and a cigarette. I groped for the bell.

Jeeves came in looking as fresh as a dewy violet. It's a mystery to me how he does it.

"Tea, Jeeves."

"Very good, sir."

He flowed silently out of the room—he always gives you the impression of being some liquid substance when he moves; and I found that Rocky was surging round with his beastly letter again.

"What is it?" I said. "What on earth's the matter?"

"Read it!"

"I can't. I haven't had my tea."

"Well, listen then."

"Who's it from?"

"My aunt."

At this point I fell asleep again. I woke to hear him saying:

"So what on earth am I to do?"

Jeeves trickled in with the tray, like some silent stream meandering over its mossy bed; and I saw daylight.

"Read it again, Rocky, old top," I said. "I want Jeeves to hear it. Mr. Todd's aunt has written him a rather rummy letter, Jeeves, and we want your advice."

"Very good, sir."

He stood in the middle of the room, registering devotion to the cause, and Rocky started again:

"MY DEAR ROCKMETTELLER.—I have been thinking things over for a long while, and I have come to the conclusion that I have been very thoughtless to wait so long before doing what I have made up my mind to do now."

"What do you make of that, Jeeves?"

"It seems a little obscure at present, sir, but no doubt it becomes cleared at a later point in the communication."

"It becomes as clear as mud!" said Rocky.

"Proceed, old scout," I said, champing my bread and butter.

"You know how all my life I have longed to visit New York and see for myself the wonderful gay life of which I have read so much. I fear that now it will be impossible for me to fulfil my dream. I am old and worn out. I seem to have no strength left in me."

"Sad, Jeeves, what?"

"Extremely, sir."

"Sad nothing!" said Rocky. "It's sheer laziness. I went to see her last Christmas and she was bursting with health. Her doctor told me himself that there was nothing wrong with her whatever. But she will insist that she's a hopeless invalid, so he has to agree with her. She's got a fixed idea that the trip to New York would kill her; so, though it's been her ambition all her life to come here, she stays where she is."

"Rather like the chappie whose heart was 'in the Highlands a-chasing of the deer,' Jeeves?"

"The cases are in some respects parallel, sir."

"Carry on, Rocky, dear boy."

"So I have decided that, if I cannot enjoy all the marvels of the city myself, I can at least enjoy them through you. I suddenly thought of this yesterday after reading a beautiful poem in the Sunday paper about a young man who had longed all his life for a certain thing and won it in the end only when he was too old to enjoy it. It was very sad, and it touched me."

"A thing," interpolated Rocky bitterly, "that I've not been able to do in ten years."

"As you know, you will have my money when I am gone; but until now I have never been able to see my way to giving you an allowance. I have now decided to do so—on one condition. I have written to a firm of lawyers in New York, giving them instructions to pay you quite a substantial sum each month. My one condition is that you live in New York and enjoy yourself as I have always wished to do. I want you to be my representative, to spend this money for me as I should do myself. I want you to plunge into the gay, prismatic life of New York. I want you to be the life and soul of brilliant supper parties.

"Above all, I want you—indeed, I insist on this—to write me letters at least once a week giving me a full description of all you are doing and all that is going on in the city, so that I may enjoy at second-hand what my wretched health prevents my enjoying for myself. Remember that I shall expect full details, and that no detail is too trivial to interest.—Your affectionate Aunt,

"ISABEL ROCKMETTELLER."

"What about it?" said Rocky.

"What about it?" I said.

"Yes. What on earth am I going to do?"

It was only then that I really got on to the extremely rummy attitude of the chappie, in view of the fact that a quite unexpected mess of the right stuff had suddenly descended on him from a blue sky. To my mind it was an occasion for the beaming smile and the joyous whoop; yet here the man was, looking and talking as if Fate had swung on his solar plexus. It amazed me.

"Aren't you bucked?" I said.

"Bucked!"

"If I were in your place I should be frightfully braced. I consider this pretty soft for you."

He gave a kind of yelp, stared at me for a moment, and then began to talk of New York in a way that reminded me of Jimmy Mundy, the reformer chappie. Jimmy had just come to New York on a hit-the-trail campaign, and I had popped in at the Garden a couple of days before, for half an hour or so, to hear him. He had certainly told New York some pretty straight things about itself, having apparently taken a dislike to the place, but, by Jove, you know, dear old Rocky made him look like a publicity agent for the old metrop.!

"Pretty soft!" he cried. "To have to come and live in New York! To have to leave my little cottage and take a stuffy, smelly, over-heated hole of an apartment in this Heaven-forsaken, festering Gehenna. To have to mix night after night with a mob who think that life is a sort of St. Vitus's dance, and imagine that they're having a good time because they're making enough noise for six and drinking too much for ten. I loathe New York, Bertie. I wouldn't come near the place if I hadn't got to see editors occasionally. There's a blight on it. It's got moral delirium tremens. It's the limit. The very thought of staying more than a day in it makes me sick. And you call this thing pretty soft for me!"

I felt rather like Lot's friends must have done when they dropped in for a quiet chat and their genial host began to criticise the Cities of the Plain. I had no idea old Rocky could be so eloquent.

"It would kill me to have to live in New York," he went on. "To have to share the air with six million people! To have to wear stiff collars and decent clothes all the time! To——" He started. "Good Lord! I suppose I should have to dress for dinner in the evenings. What a ghastly notion!"

I was shocked, absolutely shocked.

"My dear chap!" I said reproachfully.

"Do you dress for dinner every night, Bertie?"

"Jeeves," I said coldly. The man was still standing like a statue by the door. "How many suits of evening clothes have I?"

"We have three suits full of evening dress, sir; two dinner jackets——"

"Three."

"For practical purposes two only, sir. If you remember we cannot wear the third. We have also seven white waistcoats."

"And shirts?"

"Four dozen, sir."

"And white ties?"

"The first two shallow shelves in the chest of drawers are completely filled with our white ties, sir."

I turned to Rocky.

"You see?"

The chappie writhed like an electric fan.

"I won't do it! I can't do it! I'll be hanged if I'll do it! How on earth can I dress up like that? Do you realize that most days I don't get out of my pyjamas till five in the afternoon, and then I just put on an old sweater?"

I saw Jeeves wince, poor chap! This sort of revelation shocked his finest feelings.

"Then, what are you going to do about it?" I said.

"That's what I want to know."

"You might write and explain to your aunt."

"I might—if I wanted her to get round to her lawyer's in two rapid leaps and cut me out of her will."

I saw his point.

"What do you suggest, Jeeves?" I said.

Jeeves cleared his throat respectfully.

"The crux of the matter would appear to be, sir, that Mr. Todd is obliged by the conditions under which the money is delivered into his possession to write Miss Rockmetteller long and detailed letters relating to his movements, and the only method by which this can be accomplished, if Mr. Todd adheres to his expressed intention of remaining in the country, is for Mr. Todd to induce some second party to gather the actual experiences which Miss Rockmetteller wishes reported to her, and to convey these to him in the shape of a careful report, on which it would be possible for him, with the aid of his imagination, to base the suggested correspondence."

Having got which off the old diaphragm, Jeeves was silent. Rocky looked at me in a helpless sort of way. He hasn't been brought up on Jeeves as I have, and he isn't on to his curves.

"Could he put it a little clearer, Bertie?" he said. "I thought at the start it was going to make sense, but it kind of flickered. What's the idea?"

"My dear old man, perfectly simple. I knew we could stand on Jeeves. All you've got to do is to get somebody to go round the town for you and take a few notes, and then you work the notes up into letters. That's it, isn't it, Jeeves?"

"Precisely, sir."

The light of hope gleamed in Rocky's eyes. He looked at Jeeves in a startled way, dazed by the man's vast intellect.

"But who would do it?" he said. "It would have to be a pretty smart sort of man, a man who would notice things."

"Jeeves!" I said. "Let Jeeves do it."

"But would he?"

"You would do it, wouldn't you, Jeeves?"

For the first time in our long connection I observed Jeeves almost smile. The corner of his mouth curved quite a quarter of an inch, and for a moment his eye ceased to look like a meditative fish's.

"I should be delighted to oblige, sir. As a matter of fact, I have already visited some of New York's places of interest on my evening out, and it would be most enjoyable to make a practice of the pursuit."

"Fine! I know exactly what your aunt wants to hear about, Rocky. She wants an earful of cabaret stuff. The place you ought to go to first, Jeeves, is Reigelheimer's. It's on Forty-second Street. Anybody will show you the way."

Jeeves shook his head.

"Pardon me, sir. People are no longer going to Reigelheimer's. The place at the moment is

Frolics on the Roof."

"You see?" I said to Rocky. "Leave it to Jeeves. He knows."

It isn't often that you find an entire group of your fellow-humans happy in this world; but our little circle was certainly an example of the fact that it can be done. We were all full of beans. Everything went absolutely right from the start.

Jeeves was happy, partly because he loves to exercise his giant brain, and partly because he was having a corking time among the bright lights. I saw him one night at the Midnight Revels. He was sitting at a table on the edge of the dancing floor, doing himself remarkably well with a fat cigar and a bottle of the best. I'd never imagined he could look so nearly human. His face wore an expression of austere benevolence, and he was making notes in a small book.

As for the rest of us, I was feeling pretty good, because I was fond of old Rocky and glad to be able to do him a good turn. Rocky was perfectly contented, because he was still able to sit on fences in his pyjamas and watch worms. And, as for the aunt, she seemed tickled to death. She was getting Broadway at pretty long range, but it seemed to be hitting her just right. I read one of her letters to Rocky, and it was full of life.

But then Rocky's letters, based on Jeeves's notes, were enough to buck anybody up. It was rummy when you came to think of it. There was I, loving the life, while the mere mention of it gave Rocky a tired feeling; yet here is a letter I wrote to a pal of mine in London:

"DEAR FREDDIE,—Well, here I am in New York. It's not a bad place. I'm not having a bad time. Everything's pretty all right. The cabarets aren't bad. Don't know when I shall be back. How's everybody? Cheer-o!—Yours,

"BERTIE.

"PS.—Seen old Ted lately?"

Not that I cared about Ted; but if I hadn't dragged him in I couldn't have got the confounded thing on to the second page.

Now here's old Rocky on exactly the same subject:

"DEAREST AUNT ISABEL,—How can I ever thank you enough for giving me the opportunity to live in this astounding city! New York seems more wonderful every day.

"Fifth Avenue is at its best, of course, just now. The dresses are magnificent!"

Wads of stuff about the dresses. I didn't know Jeeves was such an authority.

"I was out with some of the crowd at the Midnight Revels the other night. We took in a show first, after a little dinner at a new place on Forty-third Street. We were quite a gay party. Georgie Cohan looked in about midnight and got off a good one about Willie Collier. Fred Stone could only stay a minute, but Doug. Fairbanks did all sorts of stunts and made us roar. Diamond Jim Brady was there, as usual, and Laurette Taylor showed up with a party. The show at the Revels is quite good. I am enclosing a programme.

"Last night a few of us went round to Frolics on the Roof——"

And so on and so forth, yards of it. I suppose it's the artistic temperament or something. What I mean is, it's easier for a chappie who's used to writing poems and that sort of tosh to put a bit of a punch into a letter than it is for a chappie like me. Anyway, there's no doubt that Rocky's correspondence was hot stuff. I called Jeeves in and congratulated him.

"Jeeves, you're a wonder!"

"Thank you, sir."

"How you notice everything at these places beats me. I couldn't tell you a thing about them, except that I've had a good time."

"It's just a knack, sir."

"Well, Mr. Todd's letters ought to brace Miss Rockmetteller all right, what?"

"Undoubtedly, sir," agreed Jeeves.

And, by Jove, they did! They certainly did, by George! What I mean to say is, I was sitting in the apartment one afternoon, about a month after the thing had started, smoking a cigarette and resting the old bean, when the door opened and the voice of Jeeves burst the silence like a bomb.

It wasn't that he spoke loudly. He has one of those soft, soothing voices that slide through the atmosphere like the note of a far-off sheep. It was what he said made me leap like a young gazelle.

"Miss Rockmetteller!"

And in came a large, solid female.

The situation floored me. I'm not denying it. Hamlet must have felt much as I did when his father's ghost bobbed up in the fairway. I'd come to look on Rocky's aunt as such a permanency at her own home that it didn't seem possible that she could really be here in New York. I stared at her. Then I looked at Jeeves. He was standing there in an attitude of dignified detachment, the chump, when, if ever he should have been rallying round the young master, it was now.

Rocky's aunt looked less like an invalid than any one I've ever seen, except my Aunt Agatha. She had a good deal of Aunt Agatha about her, as a matter of fact. She looked as if she might be deucedly dangerous if put upon; and something seemed to tell me that she would certainly regard herself as put upon if she ever found out the game which poor old Rocky had been pulling on her.

"Good afternoon," I managed to say.

"How do you do?" she said. "Mr. Cohan?"

"Er—no."

"Mr. Fred Stone?"

"Not absolutely. As a matter of fact, my name's Wooster—Bertie Wooster."

She seemed disappointed. The fine old name of Wooster appeared to mean nothing in her life.

"Isn't Rockmetteller home?" she said. "Where is he?"

She had me with the first shot. I couldn't think of anything to say. I couldn't tell her that Rocky was down in the country, watching worms.

There was the faintest flutter of sound in the background. It was the respectful cough with which Jeeves announces that he is about to speak without having been spoken to.

"If you remember, sir, Mr. Todd went out in the automobile with a party in the afternoon."

"So he did, Jeeves; so he did," I said, looking at my watch. "Did he say when he would be back?"

"He gave me to understand, sir, that he would be somewhat late in returning."

He vanished; and the aunt took the chair which I'd forgotten to offer her. She looked at me in rather a rummy way. It was a nasty look. It made me feel as if I were something the dog had brought in and intended to bury later on, when he had time. My own Aunt Agatha, back in England, has looked at me in exactly the same way many a time, and it never fails to make my spine curl.

"You seem very much at home here, young man. Are you a great friend of Rockmetteller's?"

"Oh, yes, rather!"

She frowned as if she had expected better things of old Rocky.

"Well, you need to be," she said, "the way you treat his flat as your own!"

I give you my word, this quite unforeseen slam simply robbed me of the power of speech. I'd been looking on myself in the light of the dashing host, and suddenly to be treated as an intruder jarred me. It wasn't, mark you, as if she had spoken in a way to suggest that she considered my presence in the place as an ordinary social call. She obviously looked on me as a cross between a burglar and the plumber's man come to fix the leak in the bathroom. It hurt her—my being there.

At this juncture, with the conversation showing every sign of being about to die in awful agonies, an idea came to me. Tea—the good old stand-by.

"Would you care for a cup of tea?" I said.

"Tea?"

She spoke as if she had never heard of the stuff.

"Nothing like a cup after a journey," I said. "Bucks you up! Puts a bit of zip into you. What I mean is, restores you, and so on, don't you know. I'll go and tell Jeeves."

I tottered down the passage to Jeeves's lair. The man was reading the evening paper as if he hadn't a care in the world.

"Jeeves," I said, "we want some tea."

"Very good, sir."

"I say, Jeeves, this is a bit thick, what?"

I wanted sympathy, don't you know—sympathy and kindness. The old nerve centres had had the deuce of a shock.

"She's got the idea this place belongs to Mr. Todd. What on earth put that into her head?"

Jeeves filled the kettle with a restrained dignity.

"No doubt because of Mr. Todd's letters, sir," he said. "It was my suggestion, sir, if you remember, that they should be addressed from this apartment in order that Mr. Todd should appear to possess a good central residence in the city."

I remembered. We had thought it a brainy scheme at the time.

"Well, it's bally awkward, you know, Jeeves. She looks on me as an intruder. By Jove! I suppose she thinks I'm someone who hangs about here, touching Mr. Todd for free meals and borrowing his shirts."

"Yes, sir."

"It's pretty rotten, you know."

"Most disturbing, sir."

"And there's another thing: What are we to do about Mr. Todd? We've got to get him up here as soon as ever we can. When you have brought the tea you had better go out and send him a telegram, telling him to come up by the next train."

"I have already done so, sir. I took the liberty of writing the message and dispatching it by the lift attendant."

"By Jove, you think of everything, Jeeves!"

"Thank you, sir. A little buttered toast with the tea? Just so, sir. Thank you."

I went back to the sitting-room. She hadn't moved an inch. She was still bolt upright on the edge of her chair, gripping her umbrella like a hammer-thrower. She gave me another of those looks as I came in. There was no doubt about it; for some reason she had taken a dislike to me. I suppose because I wasn't George M. Cohan. It was a bit hard on a chap.

"This is a surprise, what?" I said, after about five minutes' restful silence, trying to crank the conversation up again.

"What is a surprise?"

"Your coming here, don't you know, and so on."

She raised her eyebrows and drank me in a bit more through her glasses.

"Why is it surprising that I should visit my only nephew?" she said.

Put like that, of course, it did seem reasonable.

"Oh, rather," I said. "Of course! Certainly. What I mean is——"

Jeeves projected himself into the room with the tea. I was jolly glad to see him. There's nothing like having a bit of business arranged for one when one isn't certain of one's lines. With the teapot to fool about with I felt happier.

"Tea, tea, tea—what? What?" I said.

It wasn't what I had meant to say. My idea had been to be a good deal more formal, and so on. Still, it covered the situation. I poured her out a cup. She sipped it and put the cup down with a shudder.

"Do you mean to say, young man," she said frostily, "that you expect me to drink this stuff?"

"Rather! Bucks you up, you know."

"What do you mean by the expression 'Bucks you up'?"

"Well, makes you full of beans, you know. Makes you fizz."

"I don't understand a word you say. You're English, aren't you?"

I admitted it. She didn't say a word. And somehow she did it in a way that made it worse than if she had spoken for hours. Somehow it was brought home to me that she didn't like Englishmen, and that if she had had to meet an Englishman, I was the one she'd have chosen last.

Conversation languished again after that.

Then I tried again. I was becoming more convinced every moment that you can't make a real lively salon with a couple of people, especially if one of them lets it go a word at a time.

"Are you comfortable at your hotel?" I said.

"At which hotel?"

"The hotel you're staying at."

"I am not staying at an hotel."

"Stopping with friends—what?"

"I am naturally stopping with my nephew."

I didn't get it for the moment; then it hit me.

"What! Here?" I gurgled.

"Certainly! Where else should I go?"

The full horror of the situation rolled over me like a wave. I couldn't see what on earth I was to do. I couldn't explain that this wasn't Rocky's flat without giving the poor old chap away hopelessly, because she would then ask me where he did live, and then he would be right in the soup. I was trying to induce the old bean to recover from the shock and produce some results when she spoke again.

"Will you kindly tell my nephew's man-servant to prepare my room? I wish to lie down."

"Your nephew's man-servant?"

"The man you call Jeeves. If Rockmetteller has gone for an automobile ride, there is no need for you to wait for him. He will naturally wish to be alone with me when he returns."

I found myself tottering out of the room. The thing was too much for me. I crept into Jeeves's den.

"Jeeves!" I whispered.

"Sir?"

"Mix me a b.-and-s., Jeeves. I feel weak."

"Very good, sir."

"This is getting thicker every minute, Jeeves."

"Sir?"

"She thinks you're Mr. Todd's man. She thinks the whole place is his, and everything in it. I don't see what you're to do, except stay on and keep it up. We can't say anything or she'll get on to the whole thing, and I don't want to let Mr. Todd down. By the way, Jeeves, she wants you to prepare her bed."

He looked wounded.

"It is hardly my place, sir——"

"I know—I know. But do it as a personal favour to me. If you come to that, it's hardly my place to be flung out of the flat like this and have to go to an hotel, what?"

"Is it your intention to go to an hotel, sir? What will you do for clothes?"

"Good Lord! I hadn't thought of that. Can you put a few things in a bag when she isn't looking, and sneak them down to me at the St. Aurea?"

"I will endeavour to do so, sir."

"Well, I don't think there's anything more, is there? Tell Mr. Todd where I am when he gets here."

"Very good, sir."

I looked round the place. The moment of parting had come. I felt sad. The whole thing reminded me of one of those melodramas where they drive chappies out of the old homestead into the snow.

"Good-bye, Jeeves," I said.

"Good-bye, sir."

And I staggered out.

You know, I rather think I agree with those poet-and-philosopher Johnnies who insist that a fellow ought to be devilish pleased if he has a bit of trouble. All that stuff about being refined by suffering, you know. Suffering does give a chap a sort of broader and more sympathetic outlook. It helps you to understand other people's misfortunes if you've been through the same thing yourself.

As I stood in my lonely bedroom at the hotel, trying to tie my white tie myself, it struck me for the first time that there must be whole squads of chappies in the world who had to get along without a man to look after them. I'd always thought of Jeeves as a kind of natural phenomenon; but, by Jove! of course, when you come to think of it, there must be quite a lot of fellows who have to press their own clothes themselves and haven't got anybody to bring them tea in the morning, and so on. It was rather a solemn thought, don't you know. I mean to say, ever since then I've been able to appreciate the frightful privations the poor have to stick.

I got dressed somehow. Jeeves hadn't forgotten a thing in his packing. Everything was there, down to the final stud. I'm not sure this didn't make me feel worse. It kind of deepened the pathos. It was like what somebody or other wrote about the touch of a vanished hand.

I had a bit of dinner somewhere and went to a show of some kind; but nothing seemed to make any difference. I simply hadn't the heart to go on to supper anywhere. I just sucked down a whisky-and-soda in the hotel smoking-room and went straight up to bed. I don't know when I've felt so rotten. Somehow I found myself moving about the room softly, as if there had been a death in the family. If I had anybody to talk to I should have talked in a whisper; in fact, when the telephone-bell rang I answered in such a sad, hushed voice that the fellow at the other end of the wire said "Halloa!" five times, thinking he hadn't got me.

It was Rocky. The poor old scout was deeply agitated.

"Bertie! Is that you, Bertie! Oh, gosh? I'm having a time!"

"Where are you speaking from?"

"The Midnight Revels. We've been here an hour, and I think we're a fixture for the night. I've told Aunt Isabel I've gone out to call up a friend to join us. She's glued to a chair, with this-is-the-life written all over her, taking it in through the pores. She loves it, and I'm nearly crazy."

"Tell me all, old top," I said.

"A little more of this," he said, "and I shall sneak quietly off to the river and end it all. Do you mean to say you go through this sort of thing every night, Bertie, and enjoy it? It's simply infernal! I was just snatching a wink of sleep behind the bill of fare just now when about a million yelling girls swooped down, with toy balloons. There are two orchestras here, each trying to see if it can't play louder than the other. I'm a mental and physical wreck. When your telegram arrived I was just lying down for a quiet pipe, with a sense of absolute peace stealing over me. I had to get dressed and sprint two miles to catch the train. It nearly gave me heart-failure; and on top of that I almost got brain fever inventing lies to tell Aunt Isabel. And then I had to cram myself into these confounded evening clothes of yours."

I gave a sharp wail of agony. It hadn't struck me till then that Rocky was depending on my wardrobe to see him through.

"You'll ruin them!"

"I hope so," said Rocky, in the most unpleasant way. His troubles seemed to have had the worst effect on his character. "I should like to get back at them somehow; they've given me a bad enough time. They're about three sizes too small, and something's apt to give at any moment. I wish to goodness it would, and give me a chance to breathe. I haven't breathed since half-past seven. Thank Heaven, Jeeves managed to get out and buy me a collar that fitted, or I should be a strangled corpse by now! It was touch and go till the stud broke. Bertie, this is pure Hades! Aunt Isabel keeps on urging me to dance. How on earth can I dance when I don't know a soul to dance with? And how the deuce could I, even if I knew every girl in the place? It's taking big chances even to move in these trousers. I had to tell her I've hurt my ankle. She keeps asking me when Cohan and Stone are going to turn up; and it's simply a question of time before she discovers that Stone is sitting two tables away. Something's got to be done, Bertie! You've got to think up some way of getting me out of this mess. It was you who got me into it."

"Me! What do you mean?"

"Well, Jeeves, then. It's all the same. It was you who suggested leaving it to Jeeves. It was those letters I wrote from his notes that did the mischief. I made them too good! My aunt's just been telling me about it. She says she had resigned herself to ending her life where she was, and then my letters began to arrive, describing the joys of New York; and they stimulated her to such an extent that she pulled herself together and made the trip. She seems to think she's had some miraculous kind of faith cure. I tell you I can't stand it, Bertie! It's got to end!"

"Can't Jeeves think of anything?"

"No. He just hangs round saying: 'Most disturbing, sir!' A fat lot of help that is!"

"Well, old lad," I said, "after all, it's far worse for me than it is for you. You've got a comfortable home and Jeeves. And you're saving a lot of money."

"Saving money? What do you mean—saving money?"

"Why, the allowance your aunt was giving you. I suppose she's paying all the expenses now, isn't she?"

"Certainly she is; but she's stopped the allowance. She wrote the lawyers to-night. She says that, now she's in New York, there is no necessity for it to go on, as we shall always be together, and it's simpler for her to look after that end of it. I tell you, Bertie, I've examined the darned cloud with a microscope, and if it's got a silver lining it's some little dissembler!"

"But, Rocky, old top, it's too bally awful! You've no notion of what I'm going through in this beastly hotel, without Jeeves. I must get back to the flat."

"Don't come near the flat."

"But it's my own flat."

"I can't help that. Aunt Isabel doesn't like you. She asked me what you did for a living. And when I told her you didn't do anything she said she thought as much, and that you were a typical specimen of a useless and decaying aristocracy. So if you think you have made a hit, forget it. Now I must be going back, or she'll be coming out here after me. Good-bye."

Next morning Jeeves came round. It was all so home-like when he floated noiselessly into the room that I nearly broke down.

"Good morning, sir," he said. "I have brought a few more of your personal belongings."

He began to unstrap the suit-case he was carrying.

"Did you have any trouble sneaking them away?"

"It was not easy, sir. I had to watch my chance. Miss Rockmetteller is a remarkably alert lady."

"You know, Jeeves, say what you like—this is a bit thick, isn't it?"

"The situation is certainly one that has never before come under my notice, sir. I have brought the heather-mixture suit, as the climatic conditions are congenial. To-morrow, if not prevented, I will endeavour to add the brown lounge with the faint green twill."

"It can't go on—this sort of thing—Jeeves."

"We must hope for the best, sir."

"Can't you think of anything to do?"

"I have been giving the matter considerable thought, sir, but so far without success. I am placing three silk shirts—the dove-coloured, the light blue, and the mauve—in the first long drawer, sir."

"You don't mean to say you can't think of anything, Jeeves?"

"For the moment, sir, no. You will find a dozen handkerchiefs and the tan socks in the upper drawer on the left." He strapped the suit-case and put it on a chair. "A curious lady, Miss Rockmetteller, sir."

"You understate it, Jeeves."

He gazed meditatively out of the window.

"In many ways, sir, Miss Rockmetteller reminds me of an aunt of mine who resides in the south-east portion of London. Their temperaments are much alike. My aunt has the same taste for the pleasures of the great city. It is a passion with her to ride in hansom cabs, sir. Whenever the family take their eyes off her she escapes from the house and spends the day riding about in cabs. On several occasions she has broken into the children's savings bank to secure the means to enable her to gratify this desire."

"I love to have these little chats with you about your female relatives, Jeeves," I said coldly, for I felt that the man had let me down, and I was fed up with him. "But I don't see what all this has got to do with my trouble."

"I beg your pardon, sir. I am leaving a small assortment of neckties on the mantelpiece, sir, for you to select according to your preference. I should recommend the blue with the red domino pattern, sir."

Then he streamed imperceptibly toward the door and flowed silently out.

I've often heard that chappies, after some great shock or loss, have a habit, after they've been on the floor for a while wondering what hit them, of picking themselves up and piecing themselves together, and sort of taking a whirl at beginning a new life. Time, the great healer, and Nature, adjusting itself, and so on and so forth. There's a lot in it. I know, because in my own case, after a day or two of what you might call prostration, I began to recover. The frightful loss of Jeeves made any thought of pleasure more or less a mockery, but at least I found that I was able to have a dash at enjoying life again. What I mean is, I was braced up to the extent of going round the cabarets once more, so as to try to forget, if only for the moment.

New York's a small place when it comes to the part of it that wakes up just as the rest is going to bed, and it wasn't long before my tracks began to cross old Rocky's. I saw him once at Peale's, and again at Frolics on the roof. There wasn't anybody with him either time except the aunt, and, though he was trying to look as if he had struck the ideal life, it wasn't difficult for me, knowing the circumstances, to see that beneath the mask the poor chap was suffering. My heart bled for the fellow. At least, what there was of it that wasn't bleeding for myself bled for him. He had the air of one who was about to crack under the strain.

It seemed to me that the aunt was looking slightly upset also. I took it that she was beginning to wonder when the celebrities were going to surge round, and what had suddenly become of all those wild, careless spirits Rocky used to mix with in his letters. I didn't blame her. I had only read a couple of his letters, but they certainly gave the impression that poor old Rocky was by way of being the hub of New York night life, and that, if by any chance he failed to show up at a cabaret, the management said: "What's the use?" and put up the shutters.

The next two nights I didn't come across them, but the night after that I was sitting by myself at the Maison Pierre when somebody tapped me on the shoulder-blade, and I found Rocky standing beside me, with a sort of mixed expression of wistfulness and apoplexy on his face. How the chappie had contrived to wear my evening clothes so many times without disaster was a mystery to me. He confided later that early in the proceedings he had slit the waistcoat up the back and that that had helped a bit.

For a moment I had the idea that he had managed to get away from his aunt for the evening; but, looking past him, I saw that she was in again. She was at a table over by the wall, looking at me as if I were something the management ought to be complained to about.

"Bertie, old scout," said Rocky, in a quiet, sort of crushed voice, "we've always been pals, haven't we? I mean, you know I'd do you a good turn if you asked me?"

"My dear old lad," I said. The man had moved me.

"Then, for Heaven's sake, come over and sit at our table for the rest of the evening."

Well, you know, there are limits to the sacred claims of friendship.

"My dear chap," I said, "you know I'd do anything in reason; but——"

"You must come, Bertie. You've got to. Something's got to be done to divert her mind. She's brooding about something. She's been like that for the last two days. I think she's beginning to suspect. She can't understand why we never seem to meet anyone I know at these joints. A few nights ago I happened to run into two newspaper men I used to know fairly well. That kept me going for a while. I introduced them to Aunt Isabel as David Belasco and Jim Corbett, and it went well. But the effect has worn off now, and she's beginning to wonder again. Something's got to be done, or she will find out everything, and if she does I'd take a nickel for my chance of getting a cent from her later on. So, for the love of Mike, come across to our table and help things along."

I went along. One has to rally round a pal in distress. Aunt Isabel was sitting bolt upright, as usual. It certainly did seem as if she had lost a bit of the zest with which she had started out to explore Broadway. She looked as if she had been thinking a good deal about rather unpleasant things.

"You've met Bertie Wooster, Aunt Isabel?" said Rocky.

"I have."

There was something in her eye that seemed to say:

"Out of a city of six million people, why did you pick on me?"

"Take a seat, Bertie. What'll you have?" said Rocky.

And so the merry party began. It was one of those jolly, happy, bread-crumbling parties where you cough twice before you speak, and then decide not to say it after all. After we had had an hour of this wild dissipation, Aunt Isabel said she wanted to go home. In the light of what Rocky had been telling me, this struck me as sinister. I had gathered that at the beginning of her visit she had had to be dragged home with ropes.

It must have hit Rocky the same way, for he gave me a pleading look.

"You'll come along, won't you, Bertie, and have a drink at the flat?"

I had a feeling that this wasn't in the contract, but there wasn't anything to be done. It seemed brutal to leave the poor chap alone with the woman, so I went along.

Right from the start, from the moment we stepped into the taxi, the feeling began to grow that something was about to break loose. A massive silence prevailed in the corner where the aunt sat, and, though Rocky, balancing himself on the little seat in front, did his best to supply dialogue, we weren't a chatty party.

I had a glimpse of Jeeves as we went into the flat, sitting in his lair, and I wished I could have called to him to rally round. Something told me that I was about to need him.

The stuff was on the table in the sitting-room. Rocky took up the decanter.

"Say when, Bertie."

"Stop!" barked the aunt, and he dropped it.

I caught Rocky's eye as he stooped to pick up the ruins. It was the eye of one who sees it coming.

"Leave it there, Rockmetteller!" said Aunt Isabel; and Rocky left it there.

"The time has come to speak," she said. "I cannot stand idly by and see a young man going to perdition!"

Poor old Rocky gave a sort of gurgle, a kind of sound rather like the whisky had made running out of the decanter on to my carpet.

"Eh?" he said, blinking.

The aunt proceeded.

"The fault," she said, "was mine. I had not then seen the light. But now my eyes are open. I see the hideous mistake I have made. I shudder at the thought of the wrong I did you, Rockmetteller, by urging you into contact with this wicked city."

I saw Rocky grope feebly for the table. His fingers touched it, and a look of relief came into the poor chappie's face. I understood his feelings.

"But when I wrote you that letter, Rockmetteller, instructing you to go to the city and live its life, I had not had the privilege of hearing Mr. Mundy speak on the subject of New York."

"Jimmy Mundy!" I cried.

You know how it is sometimes when everything seems all mixed up and you suddenly get a clue. When she mentioned Jimmy Mundy I began to understand more or less what had happened. I'd seen it happen before. I remember, back in England, the man I had before Jeeves sneaked off to a meeting on his evening out and came back and denounced me in front of a crowd of chappies I was giving a bit of supper to as a moral leper.

The aunt gave me a withering up and down.

"Yes; Jimmy Mundy!" she said. "I am surprised at a man of your stamp having heard of him. There is no music, there are no drunken, dancing men, no shameless, flaunting women at his meetings; so for you they would have no attraction. But for others, less dead in sin, he has his message. He has come to save New York from itself; to force it—in his picturesque phrase—to hit the trail. It was three days ago, Rockmetteller, that I first heard him. It was an accident that took me to his meeting. How often in this life a mere accident may shape our whole future!

"You had been called away by that telephone message from Mr. Belasco; so you could not take me to the Hippodrome, as we had arranged. I asked your man-servant, Jeeves, to take me there. The man has very little intelligence. He seems to have misunderstood me. I am thankful that he did. He took me to what I subsequently learned was Madison Square Garden, where Mr. Mundy is holding his meetings. He escorted me to a seat and then left me. And it was not till the meeting had begun that I discovered the mistake which had been made. My seat was in the middle of a row. I could not leave without inconveniencing a great many people, so I remained."

She gulped.

"Rockmetteller, I have never been so thankful for anything else. Mr. Mundy was wonderful! He was like some prophet of old, scourging the sins of the people. He leaped about in a frenzy of inspiration till I feared he would do himself an injury. Sometimes he expressed himself in a somewhat odd manner, but every word carried conviction. He showed me New York in its true colours. He showed me the vanity and wickedness of sitting in gilded haunts of vice, eating lobster when decent people should be in bed.

"He said that the tango and the fox-trot were devices of the devil to drag people down into the Bottomless Pit. He said that there was more sin in ten minutes with a negro banjo orchestra than in all the ancient revels of Nineveh and Babylon. And when he stood on one leg and pointed right at where I was sitting and shouted, 'This means you!' I could have sunk through the floor. I came away a changed woman. Surely you must have noticed the change in me, Rockmetteller? You must have seen that I was no longer the careless, thoughtless person who had urged you to dance in those places of wickedness?"

Rocky was holding on to the table as if it was his only friend.

"Y-yes," he stammered; "I—I thought something was wrong."

"Wrong? Something was right! Everything was right! Rockmetteller, it is not too late for you to be saved. You have only sipped of the evil cup. You have not drained it. It will be hard at first, but you will find that you can do it if you fight with a stout heart against the glamour and fascination of this dreadful city. Won't you, for my sake, try, Rockmetteller? Won't you go back to the country to-morrow and begin the struggle? Little by little, if you use your will——"

I can't help thinking it must have been that word "will" that roused dear old Rocky like a trumpet call. It must have brought home to him the realisation that a miracle had come off and saved him from being cut out of Aunt Isabel's. At any rate, as she said it he perked up, let go of the table, and faced her with gleaming eyes.

"Do you want me to go back to the country, Aunt Isabel?"

"Yes."

"Not to live in the country?"

"Yes, Rockmetteller."

"Stay in the country all the time, do you mean? Never come to New York?"

"Yes, Rockmetteller; I mean just that. It is the only way. Only there can you be safe from temptation. Will you do it, Rockmetteller? Will you—for my sake?"

Rocky grabbed the table again. He seemed to draw a lot of encouragement from that table.

"I will!" he said.

"Jeeves," I said. It was next day, and I was back in the old flat, lying in the old arm-chair, with my feet upon the good old table. I had just come from seeing dear old Rocky off to his country cottage, and an hour before he had seen his aunt off to whatever hamlet it was that she was the curse of; so we were alone at last. "Jeeves, there's no place like home—what?"

"Very true, sir."

"The jolly old roof-tree, and all that sort of thing—what?"

"Precisely, sir."

I lit another cigarette.

"Jeeves."

"Sir?"

"Do you know, at one point in the business I really thought you were baffled."

"Indeed, sir?"

"When did you get the idea of taking Miss Rockmetteller to the meeting? It was pure genius!"

"Thank you, sir. It came to me a little suddenly, one morning when I was thinking of my aunt, sir."

"Your aunt? The hansom cab one?"

"Yes, sir. I recollected that, whenever we observed one of her attacks coming on, we used to send for the clergyman of the parish. We always found that if he talked to her a while of higher things it diverted her mind from hansom cabs. It occurred to me that the same treatment might prove efficacious in the case of Miss Rockmetteller."

I was stunned by the man's resource.

"It's brain," I said; "pure brain! What do you do to get like that, Jeeves? I believe you must eat a lot of fish, or something. Do you eat a lot of fish, Jeeves?"

"No, sir."

"Oh, well, then, it's just a gift, I take it; and if you aren't born that way there's no use worrying."

"Precisely, sir," said Jeeves. "If I might make the suggestion, sir, I should not continue to wear your present tie. The green shade gives you a slightly bilious air. I should strongly advocate the blue with the red domino pattern instead, sir."

"All right, Jeeves." I said humbly. "You know!"

THE END

RIGHT HO, JEEVES

-1-

"Jeeves," I said, "may I speak frankly?"

"Certainly, sir."

"What I have to say may wound you."

"Not at all, sir."

"Well, then——"

No—wait. Hold the line a minute. I've gone off the rails.

I don't know if you have had the same experience, but the snag I always come up against when I'm telling a story is this dashed difficult problem of where to begin it. It's a thing you don't want to go wrong over, because one false step and you're sunk. I mean, if you fool about too long at the start, trying to establish atmosphere, as they call it, and all that sort of rot, you fail to grip and the customers walk out on you.

Get off the mark, on the other hand, like a scalded cat, and your public is at a loss. It simply raises its eyebrows, and can't make out what you're talking about.

And in opening my report of the complex case of Gussie Fink-Nottle, Madeline Bassett, my Cousin Angela, my Aunt Dahlia, my Uncle Thomas, young Tuppy Glossop and the cook, Anatole, with the above spot of dialogue, I see that I have made the second of these two floaters.

I shall have to hark back a bit. And taking it for all in all and weighing this against that, I suppose the affair may be said to have had its inception, if inception is the word I want, with that visit of mine to Cannes. If I hadn't gone to Cannes, I shouldn't have met the Bassett or bought that white mess jacket, and Angela wouldn't have met her shark, and Aunt Dahlia wouldn't have played baccarat.

Yes, most decidedly, Cannes was the point d'appui.

Right ho, then. Let me marshal my facts.

I went to Cannes—leaving Jeeves behind, he having intimated that he did not wish to miss Ascot—round about the beginning of June. With me travelled my Aunt Dahlia and her daughter Angela. Tuppy Glossop, Angela's betrothed, was to have been of the party, but at the last moment couldn't get away. Uncle Tom, Aunt Dahlia's husband, remained at home, because he can't stick the South of France at any price.

So there you have the layout—Aunt Dahlia, Cousin Angela and self off to Cannes round about the beginning of June.

All pretty clear so far, what?

We stayed at Cannes about two months, and except for the fact that Aunt Dahlia lost her shirt at baccarat and Angela nearly got inhaled by a shark while aquaplaning, a pleasant time was had by all.

On July the twenty-fifth, looking bronzed and fit, I accompanied aunt and child back to London. At seven p.m. on July the twenty-sixth we alighted at Victoria. And at seven-twenty or thereabouts we parted with mutual expressions of esteem—they to shove off in Aunt Dahlia's car to Brinkley Court, her place in Worcestershire, where they were expecting to entertain Tuppy in a day or two; I to go to the flat, drop my luggage, clean up a bit, and put on the soup and fish preparatory to pushing round to the Drones for a bite of dinner.

And it was while I was at the flat, towelling the torso after a much-needed rinse, that Jeeves, as we chatted of this and that—picking up the threads, as it were—suddenly brought the name of Gussie Fink-Nottle into the conversation.

As I recall it, the dialogue ran something as follows:

SELF: Well, Jeeves, here we are, what?

JEEVES: Yes, sir.

SELF: I mean to say, home again.

JEEVES: Precisely, sir.

SELF: Seems ages since I went away.

JEEVES: Yes, sir.

SELF: Have a good time at Ascot?

JEEVES: Most agreeable, sir.

SELF: Win anything?

JEEVES: Quite a satisfactory sum, thank you, sir.

SELF: Good. Well, Jeeves, what news on the Rialto? Anybody been phoning or calling or anything during my abs.?

JEEVES: Mr. Fink-Nottle, sir, has been a frequent caller.

I stared. Indeed, it would not be too much to say that I gaped.

"Mr. Fink-Nottle?"

"Yes, sir."

"You don't mean Mr. Fink-Nottle?"

"Yes, sir."

"But Mr. Fink-Nottle's not in London?"

"Yes, sir."

"Well, I'm blowed."

And I'll tell you why I was blowed. I found it scarcely possible to give credence to his statement. This Fink-Nottle, you see, was one of those freaks you come across from time to time during life's journey who can't stand London. He lived year in and year out, covered with moss, in a remote village down in Lincolnshire, never coming up even for the Eton and Harrow match. And when I asked him once if he didn't find the time hang a bit heavy on his hands, he said, no, because he had a pond in his garden and studied the habits of newts.

I couldn't imagine what could have brought the chap up to the great city. I would have been prepared to bet that as long as the supply of newts didn't give out, nothing could have shifted him from that village of his.

"Are you sure?"

"Yes, sir."

"You got the name correctly? Fink-Nottle?"

"Yes, sir."

"Well, it's the most extraordinary thing. It must be five years since he was in London. He makes no secret of the fact that the place gives him the pip. Until now, he has always stayed glued to the country, completely surrounded by newts."

"Sir?"

"Newts, Jeeves. Mr. Fink-Nottle has a strong newt complex. You must have heard of newts. Those little sort of lizard things that charge about in ponds."

"Oh, yes, sir. The aquatic members of the family Salamandridae which constitute the genus Molge."

"That's right. Well, Gussie has always been a slave to them. He used to keep them at school."

"I believe young gentlemen frequently do, sir."

"He kept them in his study in a kind of glass-tank arrangement, and pretty niffy the whole thing was, I recall. I suppose one ought to have been able to see what the end would be even then, but you know what boys are. Careless, heedless, busy about our own affairs, we scarcely gave this kink in Gussie's character a thought. We may have exchanged an occasional remark about it taking all sorts to make a world, but nothing more. You can guess the sequel. The trouble spread."

"Indeed, sir?"

"Absolutely, Jeeves. The craving grew upon him. The newts got him. Arrived at man's estate, he retired to the depths of the country and gave his life up to these dumb chums. I suppose he used to tell himself that he could take them or leave them alone, and then found—too late—that he couldn't."

"It is often the way, sir."

"Too true, Jeeves. At any rate, for the last five years he has been living at this place of his down in Lincolnshire, as confirmed a species-shunning hermit as ever put fresh water in the tank every second day and refused to see a soul. That's why I was so amazed when you told me he had suddenly risen to the surface like this. I still can't believe it. I am inclined to think that there must be some mistake, and that this bird who has been calling here is some different variety of Fink-Nottle. The chap I know wears horn-rimmed spectacles and has a face like a fish. How does that check up with your data?"

"The gentleman who came to the flat wore horn-rimmed spectacles, sir."

"And looked like something on a slab?"

"Possibly there was a certain suggestion of the piscine, sir."

"Then it must be Gussie, I suppose. But what on earth can have brought him up to London?"

"I am in a position to explain that, sir. Mr. Fink-Nottle confided to me his motive in visiting the metropolis. He came because the young lady is here."

"Young lady?"

"Yes, sir."

"You don't mean he's in love?"

"Yes, sir."

"Well, I'm dashed. I'm really dashed. I positively am dashed, Jeeves."

And I was too. I mean to say, a joke's a joke, but there are limits.

Then I found my mind turning to another aspect of this rummy affair. Conceding the fact that Gussie Fink-Nottle, against all the ruling of the form book, might have fallen in love, why should he have been haunting my flat like this? No doubt the occasion was one of those when a fellow needs a friend, but I couldn't see what had made him pick on me.

It wasn't as if he and I were in any way bosom. We had seen a lot of each other at one time, of course, but in the last two years I hadn't had so much as a post card from him.

I put all this to Jeeves:

"Odd, his coming to me. Still, if he did, he did. No argument about that. It must have been a nasty jar for the poor perisher when he found I wasn't here."

"No, sir. Mr. Fink-Nottle did not call to see you, sir."

"Pull yourself together, Jeeves. You've just told me that this is what he has been doing, and assiduously, at that."

"It was I with whom he was desirous of establishing communication, sir."

"You? But I didn't know you had ever met him."

"I had not had that pleasure until he called here, sir. But it appears that Mr. Sipperley, a fellow student with whom Mr. Fink-Nottle had been at the university, recommended him to place his affairs in my hands."

The mystery had conked. I saw all. As I dare say you know, Jeeves's reputation as a counsellor has long been established among the cognoscenti, and the first move of any of my little circle on discovering themselves in any form of soup is always to roll round and put the thing up to him. And when he's got A out of a bad spot, A puts B on to him. And then, when he has fixed up B, B sends C along. And so on, if you get my drift, and so forth.

That's how these big consulting practices like Jeeves's grow. Old Sippy, I knew, had been deeply impressed by the man's efforts on his behalf at the time when he was trying to get engaged to Elizabeth Moon, so it was not to be wondered at that he should have advised Gussie to apply. Pure routine, you might say.

"Oh, you're acting for him, are you?"

"Yes, sir."

"Now I follow. Now I understand. And what is Gussie's trouble?"

"Oddly enough, sir, precisely the same as that of Mr. Sipperley when I was enabled to be of assistance to him. No doubt you recall Mr. Sipperley's predicament, sir. Deeply attached to Miss Moon, he suffered from a rooted diffidence which made it impossible for him to speak."

I nodded.

"I remember. Yes, I recall the Sipperley case. He couldn't bring himself to the scratch. A marked coldness of the feet, was there not? I recollect you saying he was letting—what was it?—letting something do something. Cats entered into it, if I am not mistaken."

"Letting 'I dare not' wait upon 'I would', sir."

"That's right. But how about the cats?"

"Like the poor cat i' the adage, sir."

"Exactly. It beats me how you think up these things. And Gussie, you say, is in the same posish?"

"Yes, sir. Each time he endeavours to formulate a proposal of marriage, his courage fails him."

"And yet, if he wants this female to be his wife, he's got to say so, what? I mean, only civil to mention it."

"Precisely, sir."

I mused.

"Well, I suppose this was inevitable, Jeeves. I wouldn't have thought that this Fink-Nottle would ever have fallen a victim to the divine p, but, if he has, no wonder he finds the going sticky."

"Yes, sir."

"Look at the life he's led."

"Yes, sir."

"I don't suppose he has spoken to a girl for years. What a lesson this is to us, Jeeves, not to shut ourselves up in country houses and stare into glass tanks. You can't be the dominant male if you do that sort of thing. In this life, you can choose between two courses. You can either shut yourself up in a country house and stare into tanks, or you can be a dasher with the sex. You can't do both."

"No, sir."

I mused once more. Gussie and I, as I say, had rather lost touch, but all the same I was exercised about the poor fish, as I am about all my pals, close or distant, who find themselves treading upon Life's banana skins. It seemed to me that he was up against it.

I threw my mind back to the last time I had seen him. About two years ago, it had been. I had looked in at his place while on a motor trip, and he had put me right off my feed by bringing a couple of green things with legs to the luncheon table, crooning over them like a young mother and eventually losing one of them in the salad. That picture, rising before my eyes, didn't give me much confidence in the unfortunate goof's ability to woo and win, I must say. Especially if the girl he had earmarked was one of these tough modern thugs, all lipstick and cool, hard, sardonic eyes, as she probably was.

"Tell me, Jeeves," I said, wishing to know the worst, "what sort of a girl is this girl of Gussie's?"

"I have not met the young lady, sir. Mr. Fink-Nottle speaks highly of her attractions."

"Seemed to like her, did he?"

"Yes, sir."

"Did he mention her name? Perhaps I know her."

"She is a Miss Bassett, sir. Miss Madeline Bassett."

"What?"

"Yes, sir."

I was deeply intrigued.

"Egad, Jeeves! Fancy that. It's a small world, isn't it, what?"

"The young lady is an acquaintance of yours, sir?"

"I know her well. Your news has relieved my mind, Jeeves. It makes the whole thing begin to seem far more like a practical working proposition."

"Indeed, sir?"

"Absolutely. I confess that until you supplied this information I was feeling profoundly dubious about poor old Gussie's chances of inducing any spinster of any parish to join him in the saunter down the aisle. You will agree with me that he is not everybody's money."

"There may be something in what you say, sir."

"Cleopatra wouldn't have liked him."

"Possibly not, sir."

"And I doubt if he would go any too well with Tallulah Bankhead."

"No, sir."

"But when you tell me that the object of his affections is Miss Bassett, why, then, Jeeves, hope begins to dawn a bit. He's just the sort of chap a girl like Madeline Bassett might scoop in with relish."

This Bassett, I must explain, had been a fellow visitor of ours at Cannes; and as she and Angela had struck up one of those effervescent friendships which girls do strike up, I had seen quite a bit of her. Indeed, in my moodier moments it sometimes seemed to me that I could not move a step without stubbing my toe on the woman.

And what made it all so painful and distressing was that the more we met, the less did I seem able to find to say to her.

You know how it is with some girls. They seem to take the stuffing right out of you. I mean to say, there is something about their personality that paralyses the vocal cords and reduces the contents of the brain to cauliflower. It was like that with this Bassett and me; so much so that I have known occasions when for minutes at a stretch Bertram Wooster might have been observed fumbling with the tie, shuffling the feet, and behaving in all other respects in her presence like the complete dumb brick. When, therefore, she took her departure some two weeks before we did, you may readily imagine that, in Bertram's opinion, it was not a day too soon.

It was not her beauty, mark you, that thus numbed me. She was a pretty enough girl in a droopy, blonde, saucer-eyed way, but not the sort of breath-taker that takes the breath.

No, what caused this disintegration in a usually fairly fluent prattler with the sex was her whole mental attitude. I don't want to wrong anybody, so I won't go so far as to say that she actually wrote poetry, but her conversation, to my mind, was of a nature calculated to excite the liveliest suspicions. Well, I mean to say, when a girl suddenly asks you out of a blue sky if you don't sometimes feel that the stars are God's daisy-chain, you begin to think a bit.

As regards the fusing of her soul and mine, therefore, there was nothing doing. But with Gussie, the posish was entirely different. The thing that had stymied me—viz. that this girl was obviously all loaded down with ideals and sentiment and what not—was quite in order as far as he was concerned.

Gussie had always been one of those dreamy, soulful birds—you can't shut yourself up in the country and live only for newts, if you're not—and I could see no reason why, if he could somehow be induced to get the low, burning words off his chest, he and the Bassett shouldn't hit it off like ham and eggs.

"She's just the type for him," I said.

"I am most gratified to hear it, sir."

"And he's just the type for her. In fine, a good thing and one to be pushed along with the utmost energy. Strain every nerve, Jeeves."

"Very good, sir," replied the honest fellow. "I will attend to the matter at once."

Now up to this point, as you will doubtless agree, what you might call a perfect harmony had prevailed. Friendly gossip between employer and employed, and everything as sweet as a nut. But at this juncture, I regret to say, there was an unpleasant switch. The atmosphere suddenly changed, the storm clouds began to gather, and before we knew where we were, the jarring note had come bounding on the scene. I have known this to happen before in the Wooster home.

The first intimation I had that things were about to hot up was a pained and disapproving cough from the neighbourhood of the carpet. For, during the above exchanges, I should explain, while I, having dried the frame, had been dressing in a leisurely manner, donning here a sock, there a shoe, and gradually climbing into the vest, the shirt, the tie, and the knee-length, Jeeves had been down on the lower level, unpacking my effects.

He now rose, holding a white object. And at the sight of it, I realized that another of our domestic crises had arrived, another of those unfortunate clashes of will between two strong men, and that Bertram, unless he remembered his fighting ancestors and stood up for his rights, was about to be put upon.

I don't know if you were at Cannes this summer. If you were, you will recall that anybody with any pretensions to being the life and soul of the party was accustomed to attend binges at the Casino in the ordinary evening-wear trouserings topped to the north by a white mess-jacket with brass buttons. And ever since I had stepped aboard the Blue Train at Cannes station, I had been wondering on and off how mine would go with Jeeves.

In the matter of evening costume, you see, Jeeves is hidebound and reactionary. I had had trouble with him before about soft-bosomed shirts. And while these mess-jackets had, as I say, been all the rage—tout ce qu'il y a de chic—on the Côte d'Azur, I had never concealed it from myself, even when treading the measure at the Palm Beach Casino in the one I had hastened to buy, that there might be something of an upheaval about it on my return.

I prepared to be firm.

"Yes, Jeeves?" I said. And though my voice was suave, a close observer in a position to watch my eyes would have noticed a steely glint. Nobody has a greater respect for Jeeves's intellect than I have, but this disposition of his to dictate to the hand that fed him had got, I felt, to be checked. This mess-jacket was very near to my heart, and I jolly well intended to fight for it with all the vim of grand old Sieur de Wooster at the Battle of Agincourt.

"Yes, Jeeves?" I said. "Something on your mind, Jeeves?"

"I fear that you inadvertently left Cannes in the possession of a coat belonging to some other gentleman, sir."

I switched on the steely a bit more.

"No, Jeeves," I said, in a level tone, "the object under advisement is mine. I bought it out there."

"You wore it, sir?"

"Every night."

"But surely you are not proposing to wear it in England, sir?"

I saw that we had arrived at the nub.

"Yes, Jeeves."

"But, sir——"

"You were saying, Jeeves?"

"It is quite unsuitable, sir."

"I do not agree with you, Jeeves. I anticipate a great popular success for this jacket. It is my intention to spring it on the public tomorrow at Pongo Twistleton's birthday party, where I confidently expect it to be one long scream from start to finish. No argument, Jeeves. No discussion. Whatever fantastic objection you may have taken to it, I wear this jacket."

"Very good, sir."

He went on with his unpacking. I said no more on the subject. I had won the victory, and we Woosters do not triumph over a beaten foe. Presently, having completed my toilet, I bade the man a cheery farewell and in generous mood suggested that, as I was dining out, why didn't he take the evening off and go to some improving picture or something. Sort of olive branch, if you see what I mean.

He didn't seem to think much of it.

"Thank you, sir, I will remain in."

I surveyed him narrowly.

"Is this dudgeon, Jeeves?"

"No, sir, I am obliged to remain on the premises. Mr. Fink-Nottle informed me he would be calling to see me this evening."

"Oh, Gussie's coming, is he? Well, give him my love."

"Very good, sir."

"Yes, sir."

"And a whisky and soda, and so forth."

"Very good, sir."

"Right ho, Jeeves."

I then set off for the Drones.

At the Drones I ran into Pongo Twistleton, and he talked so much about this forthcoming merry-making of his, of which good reports had already reached me through my correspondents, that it was nearing eleven when I got home again.

And scarcely had I opened the door when I heard voices in the sitting-room, and scarcely had I entered the sitting-room when I found that these proceeded from Jeeves and what appeared at first sight to be the Devil.

A closer scrutiny informed me that it was Gussie Fink-Nottle, dressed as Mephistopheles.

"What-ho, Gussie," I said.

You couldn't have told it from my manner, but I was feeling more than a bit nonplussed. The spectacle before me was enough to nonplus anyone. I mean to say, this Fink-Nottle, as I remembered him, was the sort of shy, shrinking goop who might have been expected to shake like an aspen if invited to so much as a social Saturday afternoon at the vicarage. And yet here he was, if one could credit one's senses, about to take part in a fancy-dress ball, a form of entertainment notoriously a testing experience for the toughest.

And he was attending that fancy-dress ball, mark you—not, like every other well-bred Englishman, as a Pierrot, but as Mephistopheles—this involving, as I need scarcely stress, not only scarlet tights but a pretty frightful false beard.

Rummy, you'll admit. However, one masks one's feelings. I betrayed no vulgar astonishment, but, as I say, what-hoed with civil nonchalance.

He grinned through the fungus—rather sheepishly, I thought.

"Oh, hullo, Bertie."

"Long time since I saw you. Have a spot?"

"No, thanks. I must be off in a minute. I just came round to ask Jeeves how he thought I looked. How do you think I look, Bertie?"

Well, the answer to that, of course, was "perfectly foul". But we Woosters are men of tact and have a nice sense of the obligations of a host. We do not tell old friends beneath our roof-tree that they are an offence to the eyesight. I evaded the question.

"I hear you're in London," I said carelessly.

"Oh, yes."

"Must be years since you came up."

"Oh, yes."

"And now you're off for an evening's pleasure."

He shuddered a bit. He had, I noticed, a hunted air.

"Pleasure!"

"Aren't you looking forward to this rout or revel?"

"Oh, I suppose it'll be all right," he said, in a toneless voice. "Anyway, I ought to be off, I suppose. The thing starts round about eleven. I told my cab to wait.... Will you see if it's there, Jeeves?"

"Very good, sir."

There was something of a pause after the door had closed. A certain constraint. I mixed myself a beaker, while Gussie, a glutton for punishment, stared at himself in the mirror. Finally I decided that it would be best to let him know that I was abreast of his affairs. It might be that it would ease his mind to confide in a sympathetic man of experience. I have generally found, with those under the influence, that what they want more than anything is the listening ear.

"Well, Gussie, old leper," I said, "I've been hearing all about you."

"Eh?"

"This little trouble of yours. Jeeves has told me everything."

He didn't seem any too braced. It's always difficult to be sure, of course, when a chap has dug himself in behind a Mephistopheles beard, but I fancy he flushed a trifle.

"I wish Jeeves wouldn't go gassing all over the place. It was supposed to be confidential."

I could not permit this tone.

"Dishing up the dirt to the young master can scarcely be described as gassing all over the place," I said, with a touch of rebuke. "Anyway, there it is. I know all. And I should like to begin," I said, sinking my personal opinion that the female in question was a sloppy pest in my desire to buck and encourage, "by saying that Madeline Bassett is a charming girl. A winner, and just the sort for you."

"You don't know her?"

"Certainly I know her. What beats me is how you ever got in touch. Where did you meet?"

"She was staying at a place near mine in Lincolnshire the week before last."

"Yes, but even so. I didn't know you called on the neighbours."

"I don't. I met her out for a walk with her dog. The dog had got a thorn in its foot, and when she tried to take it out, it snapped at her. So, of course, I had to rally round."

"You extracted the thorn?"

"Yes."

"And fell in love at first sight?"

"Yes."

"Well, dash it, with a thing like that to give you a send-off, why didn't you cash in immediately?"

"I hadn't the nerve."

"What happened?"

"We talked for a bit."

"What about?"

"Oh, birds."

"Birds? What birds?"

"The birds that happened to be hanging round. And the scenery, and all that sort of thing. And she said she was going to London, and asked me to look her up if I was ever there."

"And even after that you didn't so much as press her hand?"

"Of course not."

Well, I mean, it looked as though there was no more to be said. If a chap is such a rabbit that he can't get action when he's handed the thing on a plate, his case would appear to be pretty hopeless. Nevertheless, I reminded myself that this non-starter and I had been at school together. One must make an effort for an old school friend.

"Ah, well," I said, "we must see what can be done. Things may brighten. At any rate, you will be glad to learn that I am behind you in this enterprise. You have Bertram Wooster in your corner, Gussie."

"Thanks, old man. And Jeeves, of course, which is the thing that really matters."

I don't mind admitting that I winced. He meant no harm, I suppose, but I'm bound to say that this tactless speech nettled me not a little. People are always nettling me like that. Giving me to understand, I mean to say, that in their opinion Bertram Wooster is a mere cipher and that the only member of the household with brains and resources is Jeeves.

It jars on me.

And tonight it jarred on me more than usual, because I was feeling pretty dashed fed with Jeeves. Over that matter of the mess jacket, I mean. True, I had forced him to climb down, quelling him, as described, with the quiet strength of my personality, but I was still a trifle shirty at his having brought the thing up at all. It seemed to me that what Jeeves wanted was the iron hand.

"And what is he doing about it?" I inquired stiffly.

"He's been giving the position of affairs a lot of thought."

"He has, has he?"

"It's on his advice that I'm going to this dance."

"Why?"

"She is going to be there. In fact, it was she who sent me the ticket of invitation. And Jeeves considered——"

"And why not as a Pierrot?" I said, taking up the point which had struck me before. "Why this break with a grand old tradition?"

"He particularly wanted me to go as Mephistopheles."

I started.

"He did, did he? He specifically recommended that definite costume?"

"Yes."

"Ha!"

"Eh?"

"Nothing. Just 'Ha!'"

And I'll tell you why I said "Ha!" Here was Jeeves making heavy weather about me wearing a perfectly ordinary white mess jacket, a garment not only tout ce qu'il y a de chic, but absolutely de rigueur, and in the same breath, as you might say, inciting Gussie Fink-Nottle to be a blot on the London scene in scarlet tights. Ironical, what? One looks askance at this sort of in-and-out running.

"What has he got against Pierrots?"

"I don't think he objects to Pierrots as Pierrots. But in my case he thought a Pierrot wouldn't be adequate."

"I don't follow that."

"He said that the costume of Pierrot, while pleasing to the eye, lacked the authority of the Mephistopheles costume."

"I still don't get it."

"Well, it's a matter of psychology, he said."

There was a time when a remark like that would have had me snookered. But long association with Jeeves has developed the Wooster vocabulary considerably. Jeeves has always been a whale for the psychology of the individual, and I now follow him like a bloodhound when he snaps it out of the bag.

"Oh, psychology?"

"Yes. Jeeves is a great believer in the moral effect of clothes. He thinks I might be emboldened in a striking costume like this. He said a Pirate Chief would be just as good. In fact, a Pirate Chief was his first suggestion, but I objected to the boots."

I saw his point. There is enough sadness in life without having fellows like Gussie Fink-Nottle going about in sea boots.

"And are you emboldened?"

"Well, to be absolutely accurate, Bertie, old man, no."

A gust of compassion shook me. After all, though we had lost touch a bit of recent years, this man and I had once thrown inked darts at each other.

"Gussie," I said, "take an old friend's advice, and don't go within a mile of this binge."

"But it's my last chance of seeing her. She's off tomorrow to stay with some people in the country. Besides, you don't know."

"Don't know what?"

"That this idea of Jeeves's won't work. I feel a most frightful chump now, yes, but who can say whether that will not pass off when I get into a mob of other people in fancy dress. I had the same experience as a child, one year during the Christmas festivities. They dressed me up as a rabbit, and the shame was indescribable. Yet when I got to the party and found myself surrounded by scores of other children, many in costumes even ghastlier than my own, I perked up amazingly, joined freely in the revels, and was able to eat so hearty a supper that I was sick twice in the cab coming home. What I mean is, you can't tell in cold blood."

I weighed this. It was specious, of course.

"And you can't get away from it that, fundamentally, Jeeves's idea is sound. In a striking costume like Mephistopheles, I might quite easily pull off something pretty impressive. Colour does make a difference. Look at newts. During the courting season the male newt is brilliantly coloured. It helps him a lot."

"But you aren't a male newt."

"I wish I were. Do you know how a male newt proposes, Bertie? He just stands in front of the female newt vibrating his tail and bending his body in a semi-circle. I could do that on my head. No, you wouldn't find me grousing if I were a male newt."

"But if you were a male newt, Madeline Bassett wouldn't look at you. Not with the eye of love, I mean."

"She would, if she were a female newt."

"But she isn't a female newt."

"No, but suppose she was."

"Well, if she was, you wouldn't be in love with her."

"Yes, I would, if I were a male newt."

A slight throbbing about the temples told me that this discussion had reached saturation point.

"Well, anyway," I said, "coming down to hard facts and cutting out all this visionary stuff about vibrating tails and what not, the salient point that emerges is that you are booked to appear at a fancy-dress ball. And I tell you out of my riper knowledge of fancy-dress balls, Gussie, that you won't enjoy yourself."

"It isn't a question of enjoying yourself."

"I wouldn't go."

"I must go. I keep telling you she's off to the country tomorrow."

I gave it up.

"So be it," I said. "Have it your own way.... Yes, Jeeves?"

"Mr. Fink-Nottle's cab, sir."

"Ah? The cab, eh?... Your cab, Gussie."

"Oh, the cab? Oh, right. Of course, yes, rather.... Thanks, Jeeves ... Well, so long, Bertie."

And giving me the sort of weak smile Roman gladiators used to give the Emperor before entering the arena, Gussie trickled off. And I turned to Jeeves. The moment had arrived for putting him in his place, and I was all for it.

It was a little difficult to know how to begin, of course. I mean to say, while firmly resolved to tick him off, I didn't want to gash his feelings too deeply. Even when displaying the iron hand, we Woosters like to keep the thing fairly matey.

However, on consideration, I saw that there was nothing to be gained by trying to lead up to it gently. It is never any use beating about the b.

"Jeeves," I said, "may I speak frankly?"

"Certainly, sir."

"What I have to say may wound you."

"Not at all, sir."

"Well, then, I have been having a chat with Mr. Fink-Nottle, and he has been telling me about this Mephistopheles scheme of yours."

"Yes, sir?"

"Now let me get it straight. If I follow your reasoning correctly, you think that, stimulated by being upholstered throughout in scarlet tights, Mr. Fink-Nottle, on encountering the adored object, will vibrate his tail and generally let himself go with a whoop."

"I am of opinion that he will lose much of his normal diffidence, sir."

"I don't agree with you, Jeeves."

"No, sir?"

"No. In fact, not to put too fine a point upon it, I consider that of all the dashed silly, drivelling ideas I ever heard in my puff this is the most blithering and futile. It won't work. Not a chance. All you have done is to subject Mr. Fink-Nottle to the nameless horrors of a fancy-dress ball for nothing. And this is not the first time this sort of thing has happened. To be quite candid, Jeeves, I have frequently noticed before now a tendency or disposition on your part to become—what's the word?"

"I could not say, sir."

"Eloquent? No, it's not eloquent. Elusive? No, it's not elusive. It's on the tip of my tongue. Begins with an 'e' and means being a jolly sight too clever."

"Elaborate, sir?"

"That is the exact word I was after. Too elaborate, Jeeves—that is what you are frequently prone to become. Your methods are not simple, not straightforward. You cloud the issue with a lot of fancy stuff that is not of the essence. All that Gussie needs is the elder-brotherly advice of a seasoned man of the world. So what I suggest is that from now onward you leave this case to me."

"Very good, sir."

"You lay off and devote yourself to your duties about the home."

"Very good, sir."

"I shall no doubt think of something quite simple and straightforward yet perfectly effective ere long. I will make a point of seeing Gussie tomorrow."

"Very good, sir."

"Right ho, Jeeves."

But on the morrow all those telegrams started coming in, and I confess that for twenty-four hours I didn't give the poor chap a thought, having problems of my own to contend with.

The first of the telegrams arrived shortly after noon, and Jeeves brought it in with the before-luncheon snifter. It was from my Aunt Dahlia, operating from Market Snodsbury, a small town of sorts a mile or two along the main road as you leave her country seat.

It ran as follows:

Come at once. Travers.

And when I say it puzzled me like the dickens, I am understating it; if anything. As mysterious a communication, I considered, as was ever flashed over the wires. I studied it in a profound reverie for the best part of two dry Martinis and a dividend. I read it backwards. I read it forwards. As a matter of fact, I have a sort of recollection of even smelling it. But it still baffled me.

Consider the facts, I mean. It was only a few hours since this aunt and I had parted, after being in constant association for nearly two months. And yet here she was—with my farewell kiss still lingering on her cheek, so to speak—pleading for another reunion. Bertram Wooster is not accustomed to this gluttonous appetite for his society. Ask anyone who knows me, and they will tell you that after two months of my company, what the normal person feels is that that will about do for the present. Indeed, I have known people who couldn't stick it out for more than a few days.

Before sitting down to the well-cooked, therefore, I sent this reply:

Perplexed. Explain. Bertie.

To this I received an answer during the after-luncheon sleep:

What on earth is there to be perplexed about, ass? Come at once. Travers.

Three cigarettes and a couple of turns about the room, and I had my response ready:

How do you mean come at once? Regards. Bertie.

I append the comeback:

I mean come at once, you maddening half-wit. What did you think I meant? Come at once or expect an aunt's curse first post tomorrow. Love. Travers.

I then dispatched the following message, wishing to get everything quite clear:

When you say "Come" do you mean "Come to Brinkley Court"? And when you say "At once" do you mean "At once"? Fogged. At a loss. All the best. Bertie.

I sent this one off on my way to the Drones, where I spent a restful afternoon throwing cards into a top-hat with some of the better element. Returning in the evening hush, I found the answer waiting for me:

Yes, yes, yes, yes, yes, yes, yes. It doesn't matter whether you understand or not. You just come at once, as I tell you, and for heaven's sake stop this back-chat. Do you think I am made of money that I can afford to send you telegrams every ten minutes. Stop being a fathead and come immediately. Love. Travers.

It was at this point that I felt the need of getting a second opinion. I pressed the bell.

"Jeeves," I said, "a V-shaped rumminess has manifested itself from the direction of Worcestershire. Read these," I said, handing him the papers in the case.

He scanned them.

"What do you make of it, Jeeves?"

"I think Mrs. Travers wishes you to come at once, sir."

"You gather that too, do you?"

"Yes, sir."

"I put the same construction on the thing. But why, Jeeves? Dash it all, she's just had nearly two months of me."

"Yes, sir."

"And many people consider the medium dose for an adult two days."

"Yes, sir. I appreciate the point you raise. Nevertheless, Mrs. Travers appears very insistent. I think it would be well to acquiesce in her wishes."

"Pop down, you mean?"

"Yes, sir."

"Well, I certainly can't go at once. I've an important conference on at the Drones tonight. Pongo Twistleton's birthday party, you remember."

"Yes, sir."

There was a slight pause. We were both recalling the little unpleasantness that had arisen. I felt obliged to allude to it.

"You're all wrong about that mess jacket, Jeeves."

"These things are matters of opinion, sir."

"When I wore it at the Casino at Cannes, beautiful women nudged one another and whispered: 'Who is he?'"

"The code at Continental casinos is notoriously lax, sir."

"And when I described it to Pongo last night, he was fascinated."

"Indeed, sir?"

"So were all the rest of those present. One and all admitted that I had got hold of a good thing. Not a dissentient voice."

"Indeed, sir?"

"I am convinced that you will eventually learn to love this mess-jacket, Jeeves."

"I fear not, sir."

I gave it up. It is never any use trying to reason with Jeeves on these occasions. "Pigheaded" is the word that springs to the lips. One sighs and passes on.

"Well, anyway, returning to the agenda, I can't go down to Brinkley Court or anywhere else yet awhile. That's final. I'll tell you what, Jeeves. Give me form and pencil, and I'll wire her that I'll be with her some time next week or the week after. Dash it all, she ought to be able to hold out without me for a few days. It only requires will power."

"Yes, sir."

"Right ho, then. I'll wire 'Expect me tomorrow fortnight' or words to some such effect. That ought to meet the case. Then if you will toddle round the corner and send it off, that will be that."

"Very good, sir."

And so the long day wore on till it was time for me to dress for Pongo's party.

Pongo had assured me, while chatting of the affair on the previous night, that this birthday binge of his was to be on a scale calculated to stagger humanity, and I must say I have participated in less fruity functions. It was well after four when I got home, and by that time I was about ready to turn in. I can just remember groping for the bed and crawling into it, and it seemed to me that the lemon had scarcely touched the pillow before I was aroused by the sound of the door opening.

I was barely ticking over, but I contrived to raise an eyelid.

"Is that my tea, Jeeves?"

"No, sir. It is Mrs. Travers."

And a moment later there was a sound like a mighty rushing wind, and the relative had crossed the threshold at fifty m.p.h. under her own steam.

It has been well said of Bertram Wooster that, while no one views his flesh and blood with a keener and more remorselessly critical eye, he is nevertheless a man who delights in giving credit where credit is due. And if you have followed these memoirs of mine with the proper care, you will be aware that I have frequently had occasion to emphasise the fact that Aunt Dahlia is all right.

She is the one, if you remember, who married old Tom Travers en secondes noces, as I believe the expression is, the year Bluebottle won the Cambridgeshire, and once induced me to write an article on What the Well-Dressed Man is Wearing for that paper she runs—Milady's Boudoir. She is a large, genial soul, with whom it is a pleasure to hob-nob. In her spiritual make-up there is none of that subtle gosh-awfulness which renders such an exhibit as, say, my Aunt Agatha the curse of the Home Counties and a menace to one and all. I have the highest esteem for Aunt Dahlia, and have never wavered in my cordial appreciation of her humanity, sporting qualities and general good-eggishness.

This being so, you may conceive of my astonishment at finding her at my bedside at such an hour. I mean to say, I've stayed at her place many a time and oft, and she knows my habits. She is well aware that until I have had my cup of tea in the morning, I do not receive. This crashing in at a moment when she knew that solitude and repose were of the essence was scarcely, I could not but feel, the good old form.

Besides, what business had she being in London at all? That was what I asked myself. When a conscientious housewife has returned to her home after an absence of seven weeks, one does not expect her to start racing off again the day after her arrival. One feels that she ought to be sticking round, ministering to her husband, conferring with the cook, feeding the cat, combing and brushing the Pomeranian—in a word, staying put. I was more than a little bleary-eyed, but I endeavoured, as far as the fact that my eyelids were more or less glued together would permit, to give her an austere and censorious look.

She didn't seem to get it.

"Wake up, Bertie, you old ass!" she cried, in a voice that hit me between the eyebrows and went out at the back of my head.

If Aunt Dahlia has a fault, it is that she is apt to address a vis-à-vis as if he were somebody half a mile away whom she had observed riding over hounds. A throwback, no doubt, to the time when she counted the day lost that was not spent in chivvying some unfortunate fox over the countryside.

I gave her another of the austere and censorious, and this time it registered. All the effect it had, however, was to cause her to descend to personalities.

"Don't blink at me in that obscene way," she said. "I wonder, Bertie," she proceeded, gazing at me as I should imagine Gussie would have gazed at some newt that was not up to sample, "if you have the faintest conception how perfectly loathsome you look? A cross between an orgy scene in the movies and some low form of pond life. I suppose you were out on the tiles last night?"

"I attended a social function, yes," I said coldly. "Pongo Twistleton's birthday party. I couldn't let Pongo down. Noblesse oblige."

"Well, get up and dress."

I felt I could not have heard her aright.

"Get up and dress?"

"Yes."

I turned on the pillow with a little moan, and at this juncture Jeeves entered with the vital oolong. I clutched at it like a drowning man at a straw hat. A deep sip or two, and I felt—I won't say restored, because a birthday party like Pongo Twistleton's isn't a thing you get restored after with a mere mouthful of tea, but sufficiently the old Bertram to be able to bend the mind on this awful thing which had come upon me.

And the more I bent same, the less could I grasp the trend of the scenario.

"What is this, Aunt Dahlia?" I inquired.

"It looks to me like tea," was her response. "But you know best. You're drinking it."

If I hadn't been afraid of spilling the healing brew, I have little doubt that I should have given an impatient gesture. I know I felt like it.

"Not the contents of this cup. All this. Your barging in and telling me to get up and dress, and all that rot."

"I've barged in, as you call it, because my telegrams seemed to produce no effect. And I told you to get up and dress because I want you to get up and dress. I've come to take you back with me. I like your crust, wiring that you would come next year or whenever it was. You're coming now. I've got a job for you."

"But I don't want a job."

"What you want, my lad, and what you're going to get are two very different things. There is man's work for you to do at Brinkley Court. Be ready to the last button in twenty minutes."

"But I can't possibly be ready to any buttons in twenty minutes. I'm feeling awful."

She seemed to consider.

"Yes," she said. "I suppose it's only humane to give you a day or two to recover. All right, then, I shall expect you on the thirtieth at the latest."

"But, dash it, what is all this? How do you mean, a job? Why a job? What sort of a job?"

"I'll tell you if you'll only stop talking for a minute. It's quite an easy, pleasant job. You will enjoy it. Have you ever heard of Market Snodsbury Grammar School?"

"Never."

"It's a grammar school at Market Snodsbury."

I told her a little frigidly that I had divined as much.

"Well, how was I to know that a man with a mind like yours would grasp it so quickly?" she protested. "All right, then. Market Snodsbury Grammar School is, as you have guessed, the grammar school at Market Snodsbury. I'm one of the governors."

"You mean one of the governesses."

"I don't mean one of the governesses. Listen, ass. There was a board of governors at Eton, wasn't there? Very well. So there is at Market Snodsbury Grammar School, and I'm a member of it. And they left the arrangements for the summer prize-giving to me. This prize-giving takes place on the last—or thirty-first—day of this month. Have you got that clear?"

I took another oz. of the life-saving and inclined my head. Even after a Pongo Twistleton birthday party, I was capable of grasping simple facts like these.

"I follow you, yes. I see the point you are trying to make, certainly. Market ... Snodsbury ... Grammar School ... Board of governors ... Prize-giving.... Quite. But what's it got to do with me?"

"You're going to give away the prizes."

I goggled. Her words did not appear to make sense. They seemed the mere aimless vapouring of an aunt who has been sitting out in the sun without a hat.

"Me?"

"You."

I goggled again.

"You don't mean me?"

"I mean you in person."

I goggled a third time.

"You're pulling my leg."

"I am not pulling your leg. Nothing would induce me to touch your beastly leg. The vicar was to have officiated, but when I got home I found a letter from him saying that he had strained a fetlock and must scratch his nomination. You can imagine the state I was in. I telephoned all over the place. Nobody would take it on. And then suddenly I thought of you."

I decided to check all this rot at the outset. Nobody is more eager to oblige deserving aunts than Bertram Wooster, but there are limits, and sharply defined limits, at that.

"So you think I'm going to strew prizes at this bally Dotheboys Hall of yours?"

"I do."

"And make a speech?"

"Exactly."

I laughed derisively.

"For goodness' sake, don't start gargling now. This is serious."

"I was laughing."

"Oh, were you? Well, I'm glad to see you taking it in this merry spirit."

"Derisively," I explained. "I won't do it. That's final. I simply will not do it."

"You will do it, young Bertie, or never darken my doors again. And you know what that means. No more of Anatole's dinners for you."

A strong shudder shook me. She was alluding to her chef, that superb artist. A monarch of his profession, unsurpassed—nay, unequalled—at dishing up the raw material so that it melted in the mouth of the ultimate consumer, Anatole had always been a magnet that drew me to Brinkley Court with my tongue hanging out. Many of my happiest moments had been those which I had spent champing this great man's roasts and ragouts, and the prospect of being barred from digging into them in the future was a numbing one.

"No, I say, dash it!"

"I thought that would rattle you. Greedy young pig."

"Greedy young pigs have nothing to do with it," I said with a touch of hauteur. "One is not a greedy young pig because one appreciates the cooking of a genius."

"Well, I will say I like it myself," conceded the relative. "But not another bite of it do you get, if you refuse to do this simple, easy, pleasant job. No, not so much as another sniff. So put that in your twelve-inch cigarette-holder and smoke it."

I began to feel like some wild thing caught in a snare.

"But why do you want me? I mean, what am I? Ask yourself that."

"I often have."

"I mean to say, I'm not the type. You have to have some terrific nib to give away prizes. I seem to remember, when I was at school, it was generally a prime minister or somebody."

"Ah, but that was at Eton. At Market Snodsbury we aren't nearly so choosy. Anybody in spats impresses us."

"Why don't you get Uncle Tom?"

"Uncle Tom!"

"Well, why not? He's got spats."

"Bertie," she said, "I will tell you why not Uncle Tom. You remember me losing all that money at baccarat at Cannes? Well, very shortly I shall have to sidle up to Tom and break the news to him. If, right after that, I ask him to put on lavender gloves and a topper and distribute the prizes at Market Snodsbury Grammar School, there will be a divorce in the family. He would pin a note to the pincushion and be off like a rabbit. No, my lad, you're for it, so you may as well make the best of it."

"But, Aunt Dahlia, listen to reason. I assure you, you've got hold of the wrong man. I'm hopeless at a game like that. Ask Jeeves about the time I got lugged in to address a girls' school. I made the most colossal ass of myself."

"And I confidently anticipate that you will make an equally colossal ass of yourself on the thirty-first of this month. That's why I want you. The way I look at it is that, as the thing is bound to be a frost, anyway, one may as well get a hearty laugh out of it. I shall enjoy seeing you distribute those prizes, Bertie. Well, I won't keep you, as, no doubt, you want to do your Swedish exercises. I shall expect you in a day or two."

And with these heartless words she beetled off, leaving me a prey to the gloomiest emotions. What with the natural reaction after Pongo's party and this stunning blow, it is not too much to say that the soul was seared.

And I was still writhing in the depths, when the door opened and Jeeves appeared.

"Mr. Fink-Nottle to see you, sir," he announced.

I gave him one of my looks.

"Jeeves," I said, "I had scarcely expected this of you. You are aware that I was up to an advanced hour last night. You know that I have barely had my tea. You cannot be ignorant of the effect of that hearty voice of Aunt Dahlia's on a man with a headache. And yet you come bringing me Fink-Nottles. Is this a time for Fink or any other kind of Nottle?"

"But did you not give me to understand, sir, that you wished to see Mr. Fink-Nottle to advise him on his affairs?"

This, I admit, opened up a new line of thought. In the stress of my emotions, I had clean forgotten about having taken Gussie's interests in hand. It altered things. One can't give the raspberry to a client. I mean, you didn't find Sherlock Holmes refusing to see clients just because he had been out late the night before at Doctor Watson's birthday party. I could have wished that the man had selected some more suitable hour for approaching me, but as he appeared to be a sort of human lark, leaving his watery nest at daybreak, I supposed I had better give him an audience.

"True," I said. "All right. Bung him in."

"Very good, sir."

"But before doing so, bring me one of those pick-me-ups of yours."

"Very good, sir."

And presently he returned with the vital essence.

I have had occasion, I fancy, to speak before now of these pick-me-ups of Jeeves's and their effect on a fellow who is hanging to life by a thread on the morning after. What they consist of, I couldn't tell you. He says some kind of sauce, the yolk of a raw egg and a dash of red pepper, but nothing will convince me that the thing doesn't go much deeper than that. Be that as it may, however, the results of swallowing one are amazing.

For perhaps the split part of a second nothing happens. It is as though all Nature waited breathless. Then, suddenly, it is as if the Last Trump had sounded and Judgment Day set in with unusual severity.

Bonfires burst out in all in parts of the frame. The abdomen becomes heavily charged with molten lava. A great wind seems to blow through the world, and the subject is aware of something resembling a steam hammer striking the back of the head. During this phase, the ears ring loudly, the eyeballs rotate and there is a tingling about the brow.

And then, just as you are feeling that you ought to ring up your lawyer and see that your affairs are in order before it is too late, the whole situation seems to clarify. The wind drops. The ears cease to ring. Birds twitter. Brass bands start playing. The sun comes up over the horizon with a jerk.

And a moment later all you are conscious of is a great peace.

As I drained the glass now, new life seemed to burgeon within me. I remember Jeeves, who, however much he may go off the rails at times in the matter of dress clothes and in his advice to those in love, has always had a neat turn of phrase, once speaking of someone rising on stepping-stones of his dead self to higher things. It was that way with me now. I felt that the Bertram Wooster who lay propped up against the pillows had become a better, stronger, finer Bertram.

"Thank you, Jeeves," I said.

"Not at all, sir."

"That touched the exact spot. I am now able to cope with life's problems."

"I am gratified to hear it, sir."

"What madness not to have had one of those before tackling Aunt Dahlia! However, too late to worry about that now. Tell me of Gussie. How did he make out at the fancy-dress ball?"

"He did not arrive at the fancy-dress ball, sir."

I looked at him a bit austerely.

"Jeeves," I said, "I admit that after that pick-me-up of yours I feel better, but don't try me too high. Don't stand by my sick bed talking absolute rot. We shot Gussie into a cab and he started forth, headed for wherever this fancy-dress ball was. He must have arrived."

"No, sir. As I gather from Mr. Fink-Nottle, he entered the cab convinced in his mind that the entertainment to which he had been invited was to be held at No. 17, Suffolk Square, whereas the actual rendezvous was No. 71, Norfolk Terrace. These aberrations of memory are not uncommon with those who, like Mr. Fink-Nottle, belong essentially to what one might call the dreamer-type."

"One might also call it the fatheaded type."

"Yes, sir."

"Well?"

"On reaching No. 17, Suffolk Square, Mr. Fink-Nottle endeavoured to produce money to pay the fare."

"What stopped him?"

"The fact that he had no money, sir. He discovered that he had left it, together with his ticket of invitation, on the mantelpiece of his bedchamber in the house of his uncle, where he was residing. Bidding the cabman to wait, accordingly, he rang the door-bell, and when the butler appeared, requested him to pay the cab, adding that it was all right, as he was one of the guests invited to the dance. The butler then disclaimed all knowledge of a dance on the premises."

"And declined to unbelt?"

"Yes, sir."

"Upon which——"

"Mr. Fink-Nottle directed the cabman to drive him back to his uncle's residence."

"Well, why wasn't that the happy ending? All he had to do was go in, collect cash and ticket, and there he would have been, on velvet."

"I should have mentioned, sir, that Mr. Fink-Nottle had also left his latchkey on the mantelpiece of his bedchamber."

"He could have rung the bell."

"He did ring the bell, sir, for some fifteen minutes. At the expiration of that period he recalled that he had given permission to the caretaker—the house was officially closed and all the staff on holiday—to visit his sailor son at Portsmouth."

"Golly, Jeeves!"

"Yes, sir."

"These dreamer types do live, don't they?"

"Yes, sir."

"What happened then?"

"Mr. Fink-Nottle appears to have realized at this point that his position as regards the cabman had become equivocal. The figures on the clock had already reached a substantial sum, and he was not in a position to meet his obligations."

"He could have explained."

"You cannot explain to cabmen, sir. On endeavouring to do so, he found the fellow sceptical of his bona fides."

"I should have legged it."

"That is the policy which appears to have commended itself to Mr. Fink-Nottle. He darted rapidly away, and the cabman, endeavouring to detain him, snatched at his overcoat. Mr. Fink-Nottle contrived to extricate himself from the coat, and it would seem that his appearance in the masquerade costume beneath it came as something of a shock to the cabman. Mr. Fink-Nottle informs me that he heard a species of whistling gasp, and, looking round, observed the man crouching against the railings with his hands over his face. Mr. Fink-Nottle thinks he was praying. No doubt an uneducated, superstitious fellow, sir. Possibly a drinker."

"Well, if he hadn't been one before, I'll bet he started being one shortly afterwards. I expect he could scarcely wait for the pubs to open."

"Very possibly, in the circumstances he might have found a restorative agreeable, sir."

"And so, in the circumstances, might Gussie too, I should think. What on earth did he do after that? London late at night—or even in the daytime, for that matter—is no place for a man in scarlet tights."

"No, sir."

"He invites comment."

"Yes, sir."

"I can see the poor old bird ducking down side-streets, skulking in alley-ways, diving into dust-bins."

"I gathered from Mr. Fink-Nottle's remarks, sir, that something very much on those lines was what occurred. Eventually, after a trying night, he found his way to Mr. Sipperley's residence, where he was able to secure lodging and a change of costume in the morning."

I nestled against the pillows, the brow a bit drawn. It is all very well to try to do old school friends a spot of good, but I could not but feel that in espousing the cause of a lunkhead capable of mucking things up as Gussie had done, I had taken on a contract almost too big for human consumption. It seemed to me that what Gussie needed was not so much the advice of a seasoned man of the world as a padded cell in Colney Hatch and a couple of good keepers to see that he did not set the place on fire.

Indeed, for an instant I had half a mind to withdraw from the case and hand it back to

Jeeves. But the pride of the Woosters restrained me. When we Woosters put our hands to the plough, we do not readily sheathe the sword. Besides, after that business of the mess-jacket, anything resembling weakness would have been fatal.

"I suppose you realize, Jeeves," I said, for though one dislikes to rub it in, these things have to be pointed out, "that all this was your fault?"

"Sir?"

"It's no good saying 'Sir?' You know it was. If you had not insisted on his going to that dance—a mad project, as I spotted from the first—this would not have happened."

"Yes, sir, but I confess I did not anticipate——"

"Always anticipate everything, Jeeves," I said, a little sternly. "It is the only way. Even if you had allowed him to wear a Pierrot costume, things would not have panned out as they did. A Pierrot costume has pockets. However," I went on more kindly, "we need not go into that now. If all this has shown you what comes of going about the place in scarlet tights, that is something gained. Gussie waits without, you say?"

"Yes, sir."

"Then shoot him in, and I will see what I can do for him."

-6-

Gussie, on arrival, proved to be still showing traces of his grim experience. The face was pale, the eyes gooseberry-like, the ears drooping, and the whole aspect that of a man who has passed through the furnace and been caught in the machinery. I hitched myself up a bit higher on the pillows and gazed at him narrowly. It was a moment, I could see, when first aid was required, and I prepared to get down to cases.

"Well, Gussie."

"Hullo, Bertie."

"What ho."

"What ho."

These civilities concluded, I felt that the moment had come to touch delicately on the past.

"I hear you've been through it a bit."

"Yes."

"Thanks to Jeeves."

"It wasn't Jeeves's fault."

"Entirely Jeeves's fault."

"I don't see that. I forgot my money and latchkey——"

"And now you'd better forget Jeeves. For you will be interested to hear, Gussie," I said, deeming it best to put him in touch with the position of affairs right away, "that he is no longer handling your little problem."

This seemed to slip it across him properly. The jaws fell, the ears drooped more limply. He had been looking like a dead fish. He now looked like a deader fish, one of last year's, cast up on some lonely beach and left there at the mercy of the wind and tides.

"What!"

"Yes."

"You don't mean that Jeeves isn't going to——"

"No."

"But, dash it——"

I was kind, but firm.

"You will be much better off without him. Surely your terrible experiences of that awful night have told you that Jeeves needs a rest. The keenest of thinkers strikes a bad patch occasionally. That is what has happened to Jeeves. I have seen it coming on for some time. He has lost his form. He wants his plugs decarbonized. No doubt this is a shock to you. I suppose you came here this morning to seek his advice?"

"Of course I did."

"On what point?"

"Madeline Bassett has gone to stay with these people in the country, and I want to know what he thinks I ought to do."

"Well, as I say, Jeeves is off the case."

"But, Bertie, dash it——"

"Jeeves," I said with a certain asperity, "is no longer on the case. I am now in sole charge."

"But what on earth can you do?"

I curbed my resentment. We Woosters are fair-minded. We can make allowances for men who have been parading London all night in scarlet tights.

"That," I said quietly, "we shall see. Sit down and let us confer. I am bound to say the thing seems quite simple to me. You say this girl has gone to visit friends in the country. It would appear obvious that you must go there too, and flock round her like a poultice. Elementary."

"But I can't plant myself on a lot of perfect strangers."

"Don't you know these people?"

"Of course I don't. I don't know anybody."

I pursed the lips. This did seem to complicate matters somewhat.

"All that I know is that their name is Travers, and it's a place called Brinkley Court down in Worcestershire."

I unpursed my lips.

"Gussie," I said, smiling paternally, "it was a lucky day for you when Bertram Wooster interested himself in your affairs. As I foresaw from the start, I can fix everything. This afternoon you shall go to Brinkley Court, an honoured guest."

He quivered like a mousse. I suppose it must always be rather a thrilling experience for the novice to watch me taking hold.

"But, Bertie, you don't mean you know these Traverses?"

"They are my Aunt Dahlia."

"My gosh!"

"You see now," I pointed out, "how lucky you were to get me behind you. You go to Jeeves, and what does he do? He dresses you up in scarlet tights and one of the foulest false beards of my experience, and sends you off to fancy-dress balls. Result, agony of spirit and no progress. I then take over and put you on the right lines. Could Jeeves have got you into Brinkley Court? Not a chance. Aunt Dahlia isn't his aunt. I merely mention these things."

"By Jove, Bertie, I don't know how to thank you."

"My dear chap!"

"But, I say."

"Now what?"

"What do I do when I get there?"

"If you knew Brinkley Court, you would not ask that question. In those romantic surroundings you can't miss. Great lovers through the ages have fixed up the preliminary formalities at Brinkley. The place is simply ill with atmosphere. You will stroll with the girl in the shady walks. You will sit with her on the shady lawns. You will row on the lake with her. And gradually you will find yourself working up to a point where——"

"By Jove, I believe you're right."

"Of course, I'm right. I've got engaged three times at Brinkley. No business resulted, but the fact remains. And I went there without the foggiest idea of indulging in the tender pash. I hadn't the slightest intention of proposing to anybody. Yet no sooner had I entered those romantic grounds than I found myself reaching out for the nearest girl in sight and slapping my soul down in front of her. It's something in the air."

"I see exactly what you mean. That's just what I want to be able to do—work up to it. And in London—curse the place—everything's in such a rush that you don't get a chance."

"Quite. You see a girl alone for about five minutes a day, and if you want to ask her to be your wife, you've got to charge into it as if you were trying to grab the gold ring on a merry-go-round."

"That's right. London rattles one. I shall be a different man altogether in the country. What a bit of luck this Travers woman turning out to be your aunt."

"I don't know what you mean, turning out to be my aunt. She has been my aunt all along."

"I mean, how extraordinary that it should be your aunt that Madeline's going to stay with."

"Not at all. She and my Cousin Angela are close friends. At Cannes she was with us all the time."

"Oh, you met Madeline at Cannes, did you? By Jove, Bertie," said the poor lizard devoutly, "I wish I could have seen her at Cannes. How wonderful she must have looked in beach pyjamas! Oh, Bertie——"

"Quite," I said, a little distantly. Even when restored by one of Jeeves's depth bombs, one doesn't want this sort of thing after a hard night. I touched the bell and, when Jeeves appeared, requested him to bring me telegraph form and pencil. I then wrote a well-worded communication to Aunt Dahlia, informing her that I was sending my friend, Augustus Fink-Nottle, down to Brinkley today to enjoy her hospitality, and handed it to Gussie.

"Push that in at the first post office you pass," I said. "She will find it waiting for her on her return."

Gussie popped along, flapping the telegram and looking like a close-up of Joan Crawford, and I turned to Jeeves and gave him a précis of my operations.

"Simple, you observe, Jeeves. Nothing elaborate."

"No, sir."

"Nothing far-fetched. Nothing strained or bizarre. Just Nature's remedy."

"Yes, sir."

"This is the attack as it should have been delivered. What do you call it when two people of opposite sexes are bunged together in close association in a secluded spot, meeting each other every day and seeing a lot of each other?"

"Is 'propinquity' the word you wish, sir?"

"It is. I stake everything on propinquity, Jeeves. Propinquity, in my opinion, is what will do the trick. At the moment, as you are aware, Gussie is a mere jelly when in the presence. But ask yourself how he will feel in a week or so, after he and she have been helping themselves to sausages out of the same dish day after day at the breakfast sideboard. Cutting the same ham, ladling out communal kidneys and bacon—why——"

I broke off abruptly. I had had one of my ideas.

"Golly, Jeeves!"

"Sir?"

"Here's an instance of how you have to think of everything. You heard me mention sausages, kidneys and bacon and ham."

"Yes, sir."

"Well, there must be nothing of that. Fatal. The wrong note entirely. Give me that telegraph form and pencil. I must warn Gussie without delay. What he's got to do is to create in this girl's mind the impression that he is pining away for love of her. This cannot be done by wolfing sausages."

"No, sir."

"Very well, then."

And, taking form and p., I drafted the following:

Fink-Nottle

Brinkley Court,

Market Snodsbury

Worcestershire

Lay off the sausages. Avoid the ham.

Bertie.

"Send that off, Jeeves, instanter."

"Very good, sir."

I sank back on the pillows.

"Well, Jeeves," I said, "you see how I am taking hold. You notice the grip I am getting on this case. No doubt you realize now that it would pay you to study my methods."

"No doubt, sir."

"And even now you aren't on to the full depths of the extraordinary sagacity I've shown. Do you know what brought Aunt Dahlia up here this morning? She came to tell me I'd got to distribute the prizes at some beastly seminary she's a governor of down at Market Snodsbury."

"Indeed, sir? I fear you will scarcely find that a congenial task."

"Ah, but I'm not going to do it. I'm going to shove it off on to Gussie."

"Sir?"

"I propose, Jeeves, to wire to Aunt Dahlia saying that I can't get down, and suggesting that she unleashes him on these young Borstal inmates of hers in my stead."

"But if Mr. Fink-Nottle should decline, sir?"

"Decline? Can you see him declining? Just conjure up the picture in your mind, Jeeves. Scene, the drawing-room at Brinkley; Gussie wedged into a corner, with Aunt Dahlia standing over him making hunting noises. I put it to you, Jeeves, can you see him declining?"

"Not readily, sir. I agree. Mrs. Travers is a forceful personality."

"He won't have a hope of declining. His only way out would be to slide off. And he can't slide off, because he wants to be with Miss Bassett. No, Gussie will have to toe the line, and I shall be saved from a job at which I confess the soul shuddered. Getting up on a platform and delivering a short, manly speech to a lot of foul school-kids! Golly, Jeeves. I've been through that sort of thing once, what? You remember that time at the girls' school?"

"Very vividly, sir."

"What an ass I made of myself!"

"Certainly I have seen you to better advantage, sir."

"I think you might bring me just one more of those dynamite specials of yours, Jeeves. This narrow squeak has made me come over all faint."

I suppose it must have taken Aunt Dahlia three hours or so to get back to Brinkley, because it wasn't till well after lunch that her telegram arrived. It read like a telegram that had been dispatched in a white-hot surge of emotion some two minutes after she had read mine.

As follows:

Am taking legal advice to ascertain whether strangling an idiot nephew counts as murder. If it doesn't look out for yourself. Consider your conduct frozen limit. What do you mean by planting your loathsome friends on me like this? Do you think Brinkley Court is a leper colony or what is it? Who is this Spink-Bottle? Love. Travers.

I had expected some such initial reaction. I replied in temperate vein:

Not Bottle. Nottle. Regards. Bertie.

Almost immediately after she had dispatched the above heart cry, Gussie must have arrived, for it wasn't twenty minutes later when I received the following:

Cipher telegram signed by you has reached me here. Runs "Lay off the sausages. Avoid the ham." Wire key immediately. Fink-Nottle.

I replied:

Also kidneys. Cheerio. Bertie.

I had staked all on Gussie making a favourable impression on his hostess, basing my confidence on the fact that he was one of those timid, obsequious, teacup-passing, thin-bread-and-butter-offering yes-men whom women of my Aunt Dahlia's type nearly always like at first sight. That I had not overrated my acumen was proved by her next in order, which, I was pleased to note, assayed a markedly larger percentage of the milk of human kindness.

As follows:

Well, this friend of yours has got here, and I must say that for a friend of yours he seems less sub-human than I had expected. A bit of a pop-eyed bleater, but on the whole clean and civil, and certainly most informative about newts. Am considering arranging series of lectures for him in neighbourhood. All the same I like your nerve using my house as a summer-hotel resort and shall have much to say to you on subject when you come down. Expect you thirtieth. Bring spats. Love. Travers.

To this I riposted:

On consulting engagement book find impossible come Brinkley Court. Deeply regret. Toodle-oo. Bertie.

Hers in reply stuck a sinister note:

Oh, so it's like that, is it? You and your engagement book, indeed. Deeply regret my foot. Let me tell you, my lad, that you will regret it a jolly sight more deeply if you don't come down. If you imagine for one moment that you are going to get out of distributing those prizes, you are very much mistaken. Deeply regret Brinkley Court hundred miles from London, as unable hit you with a brick. Love. Travers.

I then put my fortune to the test, to win or lose it all. It was not a moment for petty economies. I let myself go regardless of expense:

No, but dash it, listen. Honestly, you don't want me. Get Fink-Nottle distribute prizes. A born distributor, who will do you credit. Confidently anticipate Augustus Fink-Nottle as Master of Revels on thirty-first inst. would make genuine sensation. Do not miss this great chance, which may never occur again. Tinkerty-tonk. Bertie.

There was an hour of breathless suspense, and then the joyful tidings arrived:

Well, all right. Something in what you say, I suppose. Consider you treacherous worm and contemptible, spineless cowardly custard, but have booked Spink-Bottle. Stay where you are, then, and I hope you get run over by an omnibus. Love. Travers.

The relief, as you may well imagine, was stupendous. A great weight seemed to have rolled off my mind. It was as if somebody had been pouring Jeeves's pick-me-ups into me through a funnel. I sang as I dressed for dinner that night. At the Drones I was so gay and cheery that there were several complaints. And when I got home and turned into the old bed, I fell asleep like a little child within five minutes of inserting the person between the sheets. It seemed to me that the whole distressing affair might now be considered definitely closed.

Conceive my astonishment, therefore, when waking on the morrow and sitting up to dig into the morning tea-cup, I beheld on the tray another telegram.

My heart sank. Could Aunt Dahlia have slept on it and changed her mind? Could Gussie, unable to face the ordeal confronting him, have legged it during the night down a water-pipe? With these speculations racing through the bean, I tore open the envelope And as I noted contents I uttered a startled yip.

"Sir?" said Jeeves, pausing at the door.

I read the thing again. Yes, I had got the gist all right. No, I had not been deceived in the substance.

"Jeeves," I said, "do you know what?"

"No, sir."

"You know my cousin Angela?"

"Yes, sir."

"You know young Tuppy Glossop?"

"Yes, sir."

"They've broken off their engagement."

"I am sorry to hear that, sir."

"I have here a communication from Aunt Dahlia, specifically stating this. I wonder what the row was about."

"I could not say, sir."

"Of course you couldn't. Don't be an ass, Jeeves."

"No, sir."

I brooded. I was deeply moved.

"Well, this means that we shall have to go down to Brinkley today. Aunt Dahlia is obviously all of a twitter, and my place is by her side. You had better pack this morning, and catch that 12.45 train with the luggage. I have a lunch engagement, so will follow in the car."

"Very good, sir."

I brooded some more.

"I must say this has come as a great shock to me, Jeeves."

"No doubt, sir."

"A very great shock. Angela and Tuppy.... Tut, tut! Why, they seemed like the paper on the wall. Life is full of sadness, Jeeves."

"Yes, sir."

"Still, there it is."

"Undoubtedly, sir."

"Right ho, then. Switch on the bath."

"Very good, sir."

I meditated pretty freely as I drove down to Brinkley in the old two-seater that afternoon. The news of this rift or rupture of Angela's and Tuppy's had disturbed me greatly.

The projected match, you see, was one on which I had always looked with kindly approval. Too often, when a chap of your acquaintance is planning to marry a girl you know, you find yourself knitting the brow a bit and chewing the lower lip dubiously, feeling that he or she, or both, should be warned while there is yet time.

But I have never felt anything of this nature about Tuppy and Angela. Tuppy, when not making an ass of himself, is a soundish sort of egg. So is Angela a soundish sort of egg. And, as far as being in love was concerned, it had always seemed to me that you wouldn't have been far out in describing them as two hearts that beat as one.

True, they had had their little tiffs, notably on the occasion when Tuppy—with what he said was fearless honesty and I considered thorough goofiness—had told Angela that her new hat made her look like a Pekingese. But in every romance you have to budget for the occasional dust-up, and after that incident I had supposed that he had learned his lesson and that from then on life would be one grand, sweet song.

And now this wholly unforeseen severing of diplomatic relations had popped up through a trap.

I gave the thing the cream of the Wooster brain all the way down, but it continued to beat me what could have caused the outbreak of hostilities, and I bunged my foot sedulously on the accelerator in order to get to Aunt Dahlia with the greatest possible speed and learn the inside history straight from the horse's mouth. And what with all six cylinders hitting nicely, I made good time and found myself closeted with the relative shortly before the hour of the evening cocktail.

She seemed glad to see me. In fact, she actually said she was glad to see me—a statement no other aunt on the list would have committed herself to, the customary reaction of these near and dear ones to the spectacle of Bertram arriving for a visit being a sort of sick horror.

"Decent of you to rally round, Bertie," she said.

"My place was by your side, Aunt Dahlia," I responded.

I could see at a g. that the unfortunate affair had got in amongst her in no uncertain manner. Her usually cheerful map was clouded, and the genial smile conspic. by its a. I pressed her hand sympathetically, to indicate that my heart bled for her.

"Bad show this, my dear old flesh and blood," I said. "I'm afraid you've been having a sticky time. You must be worried."

She snorted emotionally. She looked like an aunt who has just bitten into a bad oyster.

"Worried is right. I haven't had a peaceful moment since I got back from Cannes. Ever since I put my foot across this blasted threshold," said Aunt Dahlia, returning for the nonce to the hearty argot of the hunting field, "everything's been at sixes and sevens. First there was that mix-up about the prize-giving."

She paused at this point and gave me a look. "I had been meaning to speak freely to you about your behaviour in that matter, Bertie," she said. "I had some good things all stored up. But, as you've rallied round like this, I suppose I shall have to let you off. And, anyway, it is probably all for the best that you evaded your obligations in that sickeningly craven way. I have an idea that this Spink-Bottle of yours is going to be good. If only he can keep off newts."

"Has he been talking about newts?"

"He has. Fixing me with a glittering eye, like the Ancient Mariner. But if that was the worst I had to bear, I wouldn't mind. What I'm worrying about is what Tom says when he starts talking."

"Uncle Tom?"

"I wish there was something else you could call him except 'Uncle Tom'," said Aunt Dahlia a little testily. "Every time you do it, I expect to see him turn black and start playing the banjo. Yes, Uncle Tom, if you must have it. I shall have to tell him soon about losing all that money at baccarat, and, when I do, he will go up like a rocket."

"Still, no doubt Time, the great healer——"

"Time, the great healer, be blowed. I've got to get a cheque for five hundred pounds out of him for Milady's Boudoir by August the third at the latest."

I was concerned. Apart from a nephew's natural interest in an aunt's refined weekly paper, I had always had a soft spot in my heart for Milady's Boudoir ever since I contributed that article to it on What the Well-Dressed Man is Wearing. Sentimental, possibly, but we old journalists do have these feelings.

"Is the Boudoir on the rocks?"

"It will be if Tom doesn't cough up. It needs help till it has turned the corner."

"But wasn't it turning the corner two years ago?"

"It was. And it's still at it. Till you've run a weekly paper for women, you don't know what corners are."

"And you think the chances of getting into uncle—into my uncle by marriage's ribs are slight?"

"I'll tell you, Bertie. Up till now, when these subsidies were required, I have always been able to come to Tom in the gay, confident spirit of an only child touching an indulgent father for chocolate cream. But he's just had a demand from the income-tax people for an additional fifty-eight pounds, one and threepence, and all he's been talking about since I got back has been ruin and the sinister trend of socialistic legislation and what will become of us all."

I could readily believe it. This Tom has a peculiarity I've noticed in other very oofy men. Nick him for the paltriest sum, and he lets out a squawk you can hear at Land's End. He has the stuff in gobs, but he hates giving up.

"If it wasn't for Anatole's cooking, I doubt if he would bother to carry on. Thank God for Anatole, I say."

I bowed my head reverently.

"Good old Anatole," I said.

"Amen," said Aunt Dahlia.

Then the look of holy ecstasy, which is always the result of letting the mind dwell, however briefly, on Anatole's cooking, died out of her face.

"But don't let me wander from the subject," she resumed. "I was telling you of the way hell's foundations have been quivering since I got home. First the prize-giving, then Tom, and now, on top of everything else, this infernal quarrel between Angela and young Glossop."

I nodded gravely. "I was frightfully sorry to hear of that. Terrible shock. What was the row about?"

"Sharks."

"Eh?"

"Sharks. Or, rather, one individual shark. The brute that went for the poor child when she was aquaplaning at Cannes. You remember Angela's shark?"

Certainly I remembered Angela's shark. A man of sensibility does not forget about a cousin nearly being chewed by monsters of the deep. The episode was still green in my memory.

In a nutshell, what had occurred was this: You know how you aquaplane. A motor-boat nips on ahead, trailing a rope. You stand on a board, holding the rope, and the boat tows you along. And every now and then you lose your grip on the rope and plunge into the sea and have to swim to your board again.

A silly process it has always seemed to me, though many find it diverting.

Well, on the occasion referred to, Angela had just regained her board after taking a toss, when a great beastly shark came along and cannoned into it, flinging her into the salty once more. It took her quite a bit of time to get on again and make the motor-boat chap realize what was up and haul her to safety, and during that interval you can readily picture her embarrassment.

According to Angela, the finny denizen kept snapping at her ankles virtually without cessation, so that by the time help arrived, she was feeling more like a salted almond at a public dinner than anything human. Very shaken the poor child had been, I recall, and had talked of nothing else for weeks.

"I remember the whole incident vividly," I said. "But how did that start the trouble?"

"She was telling him the story last night."

"Well?"

"Her eyes shining and her little hands clasped in girlish excitement."

"No doubt."

"And instead of giving her the understanding and sympathy to which she was entitled, what do you think this blasted Glossop did? He sat listening like a lump of dough, as if she had been talking about the weather, and when she had finished, he took his cigarette holder out of his mouth and said, 'I expect it was only a floating log'!"

"He didn't!"

"He did. And when Angela described how the thing had jumped and snapped at her, he took his cigarette holder out of his mouth again, and said, 'Ah! Probably a flatfish. Quite harmless. No doubt it was just trying to play.' Well, I mean! What would you have done if you had been Angela? She has pride, sensibility, all the natural feelings of a good woman. She told him he was an ass and a fool and an idiot, and didn't know what he was talking about."

I must say I saw the girl's viewpoint. It's only about once in a lifetime that anything sensational ever happens to one, and when it does, you don't want people taking all the colour out of it. I remember at school having to read that stuff where that chap, Othello, tells the girl what a hell of a time he'd been having among the cannibals and what not. Well, imagine his feelings if, after he had described some particularly sticky passage with a cannibal chief and was waiting for the awestruck "Oh-h! Not really?", she had said that the whole thing had no doubt been greatly exaggerated and that the man had probably really been a prominent local vegetarian.

Yes, I saw Angela's point of view.

"But don't tell me that when he saw how shirty she was about it, the chump didn't back down?"

"He didn't. He argued. And one thing led to another until, by easy stages, they had arrived at the point where she was saying that she didn't know if he was aware of it, but if he didn't knock off starchy foods and do exercises every morning, he would be getting as fat as a pig, and he was talking about this modern habit of girls putting make-up on their faces, of which he had always disapproved. This continued for a while, and then there was a loud pop and the air was full of mangled fragments of their engagement. I'm distracted about it. Thank goodness you've come, Bertie."

"Nothing could have kept me away," I replied, touched. "I felt you needed me."

"Yes."

"Quite."

"Or, rather," she said, "not you, of course, but Jeeves. The minute all this happened, I thought of him. The situation obviously cries out for Jeeves. If ever in the whole history of human affairs there was a moment when that lofty brain was required about the home, this is it."

I think, if I had been standing up, I would have staggered. In fact, I'm pretty sure I would. But it isn't so dashed easy to stagger when you're sitting in an arm-chair. Only my face, therefore, showed how deeply I had been stung by these words.

Until she spoke them, I had been all sweetness and light—the sympathetic nephew prepared to strain every nerve to do his bit. I now froze, and the face became hard and set.

"Jeeves!" I said, between clenched teeth.

"Oom beroofen," said Aunt Dahlia.

I saw that she had got the wrong angle.

"I was not sneezing. I was saying 'Jeeves!'"

"And well you may. What a man! I'm going to put the whole thing up to him. There's nobody like Jeeves."

My frigidity became more marked.

"I venture to take issue with you, Aunt Dahlia."

"You take what?"

"Issue."

"You do, do you?"

"I emphatically do. Jeeves is hopeless."

"What?"

"Quite hopeless. He has lost his grip completely. Only a couple of days ago I was compelled to take him off a case because his handling of it was so footling. And, anyway, I resent this assumption, if assumption is the word I want, that Jeeves is the only fellow with brain. I object to the way everybody puts things up to him without consulting me and letting me have a stab at them first."

She seemed about to speak, but I checked her with a gesture.

"It is true that in the past I have sometimes seen fit to seek Jeeves's advice. It is possible that in the future I may seek it again. But I claim the right to have a pop at these problems, as they arise, in person, without having everybody behave as if Jeeves was the only onion in the hash. I sometimes feel that Jeeves, though admittedly not unsuccessful in the past, has been lucky rather than gifted."

"Have you and Jeeves had a row?"

"Nothing of the kind."

"You seem to have it in for him."

"Not at all."

And yet I must admit that there was a modicum of truth in what she said. I had been feeling pretty austere about the man all day, and I'll tell you why.

You remember that he caught that 12.45 train with the luggage, while I remained on in order to keep a luncheon engagement. Well, just before I started out to the tryst, I was pottering about the flat, and suddenly—I don't know what put the suspicion into my head, possibly the fellow's manner had been furtive—something seemed to whisper to me to go and have a look in the wardrobe.

And it was as I had suspected. There was the mess-jacket still on its hanger. The hound hadn't packed it.

Well, as anybody at the Drones will tell you, Bertram Wooster is a pretty hard chap to outgeneral. I shoved the thing in a brown-paper parcel and put it in the back of the car, and it was on a chair in the hall now. But that didn't alter the fact that Jeeves had attempted to do the dirty on me, and I suppose a certain what-d'you-call-it had crept into my manner during the above remarks.

"There has been no breach," I said. "You might describe it as a passing coolness, but no more. We did not happen to see eye to eye with regard to my white mess-jacket with the brass buttons and I was compelled to assert my personality. But——"

"Well, it doesn't matter, anyway. The thing that matters is that you are talking piffle, you poor fish. Jeeves lost his grip? Absurd. Why, I saw him for a moment when he arrived, and his eyes were absolutely glittering with intelligence. I said to myself 'Trust Jeeves,' and I intend to."

"You would be far better advised to let me see what I can accomplish, Aunt Dahlia."

"For heaven's sake, don't you start butting in. You'll only make matters worse."

"On the contrary, it may interest you to know that while driving here I concentrated deeply on this trouble of Angela's and was successful in formulating a plan, based on the psychology of the individual, which I am proposing to put into effect at an early moment."

"Oh, my God!"

"My knowledge of human nature tells me it will work."

"Bertie," said Aunt Dahlia, and her manner struck me as febrile, "lay off, lay off! For pity's sake, lay off. I know these plans of yours. I suppose you want to shove Angela into the lake and push young Glossop in after her to save her life, or something like that."

"Nothing of the kind."

"It's the sort of thing you would do."

"My scheme is far more subtle. Let me outline it for you."

"No, thanks."

"I say to myself——"

"But not to me."

"Do listen for a second."

"I won't."

"Right ho, then. I am dumb."

"And have been from a child."

I perceived that little good could result from continuing the discussion. I waved a hand and shrugged a shoulder.

"Very well, Aunt Dahlia," I said, with dignity, "if you don't want to be in on the ground floor, that is your affair. But you are missing an intellectual treat. And, anyway, no matter how much you may behave like the deaf adder of Scripture which, as you are doubtless aware, the more one piped, the less it danced, or words to that effect, I shall carry on as planned. I am extremely fond of Angela, and I shall spare no effort to bring the sunshine back into her heart."

"Bertie, you abysmal chump, I appeal to you once more. Will you please lay off? You'll only make things ten times as bad as they are already."

I remember reading in one of those historical novels once about a chap—a buck he would have been, no doubt, or a macaroni or some such bird as that—who, when people said the wrong thing, merely laughed down from lazy eyelids and flicked a speck of dust from the irreproachable Mechlin lace at his wrists. This was practically what I did now. At least, I straightened my tie and smiled one of those inscrutable smiles of mine. I then withdrew and went out for a saunter in the garden.

And the first chap I ran into was young Tuppy. His brow was furrowed, and he was moodily bunging stones at a flowerpot.

-8-

I think I have told you before about young Tuppy Glossop. He was the fellow, if you remember, who, callously ignoring the fact that we had been friends since boyhood, betted me one night at the Drones that I could swing myself across the swimming bath by the rings—a childish feat for one of my lissomeness—and then, having seen me well on the way, looped back the last ring, thus rendering it necessary for me to drop into the deep end in formal evening costume.

To say that I had not resented this foul deed, which seemed to me deserving of the title of the crime of the century, would be paltering with the truth. I had resented it profoundly, chafing not a little at the time and continuing to chafe for some weeks.

But you know how it is with these things. The wound heals. The agony abates.

I am not saying, mind you, that had the opportunity presented itself of dropping a wet sponge on Tuppy from some high spot or of putting an eel in his bed or finding some other form of self-expression of a like nature, I would not have embraced it eagerly; but that let me out. I mean to say, grievously injured though I had been, it gave me no pleasure to feel that the fellow's bally life was being ruined by the loss of a girl whom, despite all that had passed, I was convinced he still loved like the dickens.

On the contrary, I was heart and soul in favour of healing the breach and rendering everything hotsy-totsy once more between these two young sundered blighters. You will have gleaned that from my remarks to Aunt Dahlia, and if you had been present at this moment and had seen the kindly commiserating look I gave Tuppy, you would have gleaned it still more.

It was one of those searching, melting looks, and was accompanied by the hearty clasp of the right hand and the gentle laying of the left on the collar-bone.

"Well, Tuppy, old man," I said. "How are you, old man?"

My commiseration deepened as I spoke the words, for there had been no lighting up of the eye, no answering pressure of the palm, no sign whatever, in short, of any disposition on his part to do Spring dances at the sight of an old friend. The man seemed sandbagged. Melancholy, as I remember Jeeves saying once about Pongo Twistleton when he was trying to knock off smoking, had marked him for her own. Not that I was surprised, of course. In the circs., no doubt, a certain moodiness was only natural.

I released the hand, ceased to knead the shoulder, and, producing the old case, offered him a cigarette.

He took it dully.

"Are you here, Bertie?" he asked.

"Yes, I'm here."

"Just passing through, or come to stay?"

I thought for a moment. I might have told him that I had arrived at Brinkley Court with the express intention of bringing Angela and himself together once more, of knitting up the severed threads, and so on and so forth; and for perhaps half the time required for the lighting of a gasper I had almost decided to do so. Then, I reflected, better, on the whole, perhaps not. To broadcast the fact that I proposed to take him and Angela and play on them as on a couple of stringed instruments might have been injudicious. Chaps don't always like being played on as on a stringed instrument.

"It all depends," I said. "I may remain. I may push on. My plans are uncertain."

He nodded listlessly, rather in the manner of a man who did not give a damn what I did, and stood gazing out over the sunlit garden. In build and appearance, Tuppy somewhat resembles a bulldog, and his aspect now was that of one of these fine animals who has just been refused a slice of cake. It was not difficult for a man of my discernment to read what was in his mind, and it occasioned me no surprise, therefore, when his next words had to do with the subject marked with a cross on the agenda paper.

"You've heard of this business of mine, I suppose? Me and Angela?"

"I have, indeed, Tuppy, old man."

"We've bust up."

"I know. Some little friction, I gather, in re Angela's shark."

"Yes. I said it must have been a flatfish."

"So my informant told me."

"Who did you hear it from?"

"Aunt Dahlia."

"I suppose she cursed me properly?"

"Oh, no."

"Beyond referring to you in one passage as 'this blasted Glossop', she was, I thought, singularly temperate in her language for a woman who at one time hunted regularly with the Quorn. All the same, I could see, if you don't mind me saying so, old man, that she felt you might have behaved with a little more tact."

"Tact!"

"And I must admit I rather agreed with her. Was it nice, Tuppy, was it quite kind to take the bloom off Angela's shark like that? You must remember that Angela's shark is very dear to her. Could you not see what a sock on the jaw it would be for the poor child to hear it described by the man to whom she had given her heart as a flatfish?"

I saw that he was struggling with some powerful emotion.

"And what about my side of the thing?" he demanded, in a voice choked with feeling.

"Your side?"

"You don't suppose," said Tuppy, with rising vehemence, "that I would have exposed this dashed synthetic shark for the flatfish it undoubtedly was if there had not been causes that led up to it. What induced me to speak as I did was the fact that Angela, the little squirt, had just been most offensive, and I seized the opportunity to get a bit of my own back."

"Offensive?"

"Exceedingly offensive. Purely on the strength of my having let fall some casual remark—simply by way of saying something and keeping the conversation going—to the effect that I wondered what Anatole was going to give us for dinner, she said that I was too material and ought not always to be thinking of food. Material, my elbow! As a matter of fact, I'm particularly spiritual."

"Quite."

"I don't see any harm in wondering what Anatole was going to give us for dinner. Do you?"

"Of course not. A mere ordinary tribute of respect to a great artist."

"Exactly."

"All the same——"

"Well?"

"I was only going to say that it seems a pity that the frail craft of love should come a stinker like this when a few manly words of contrition——"

He stared at me.

"You aren't suggesting that I should climb down?"

"It would be the fine, big thing, old egg."

"I wouldn't dream of climbing down."

"But, Tuppy——"

"No. I wouldn't do it."

"But you love her, don't you?"

This touched the spot. He quivered noticeably, and his mouth twisted. Quite the tortured soul.

"I'm not saying I don't love the little blighter," he said, obviously moved. "I love her passionately. But that doesn't alter the fact that I consider that what she needs most in this world is a swift kick in the pants."

A Wooster could scarcely pass this. "Tuppy, old man!"

"It's no good saying 'Tuppy, old man'."

"Well, I do say 'Tuppy, old man'. Your tone shocks me. One raises the eyebrows. Where is the fine, old, chivalrous spirit of the Glossops."

"That's all right about the fine, old, chivalrous spirit of the Glossops. Where is the sweet, gentle, womanly spirit of the Angelas? Telling a fellow he was getting a double chin!"

"Did she do that?"

"She did."

"Oh, well, girls will be girls. Forget it, Tuppy. Go to her and make it up."

He shook his head.

"No. It is too late. Remarks have been passed about my tummy which it is impossible to overlook."

"But, Tummy—Tuppy, I mean—be fair. You once told her her new hat made her look like a Pekingese."

"It did make her look like a Pekingese. That was not vulgar abuse. It was sound, constructive criticism, with no motive behind it but the kindly desire to keep her from making an exhibition of herself in public. Wantonly to accuse a man of puffing when he goes up a flight of stairs is something very different."

I began to see that the situation would require all my address and ingenuity. If the wedding bells were ever to ring out in the little church of Market Snodsbury, Bertram had plainly got to put in some shrewdish work. I had gathered, during my conversation with Aunt Dahlia, that there had been a certain amount of frank speech between the two contracting parties, but I had not realized till now that matters had gone so far.

The pathos of the thing gave me the pip. Tuppy had admitted in so many words that love still animated the Glossop bosom, and I was convinced that, even after all that occurred, Angela had not ceased to love him. At the moment, no doubt, she might be wishing that she could hit him with a bottle, but deep down in her I was prepared to bet that there still lingered all the old affection and tenderness. Only injured pride was keeping these two apart, and I felt that if Tuppy would make the first move, all would be well.

I had another whack at it.

"She's broken-hearted about this rift, Tuppy."

"How do you know? Have you seen her?"

"No, but I'll bet she is."

"She doesn't look it."

"Wearing the mask, no doubt. Jeeves does that when I assert my authority."

"She wrinkles her nose at me as if I were a drain that had got out of order."

"Merely the mask. I feel convinced she loves you still, and that a kindly word from you is all that is required."

I could see that this had moved him. He plainly wavered. He did a sort of twiddly on the turf with his foot. And, when he spoke, one spotted the tremolo in the voice:

"You really think that?"

"Absolutely."

"H'm."

"If you were to go to her——"

He shook his head.

"I can't do that. It would be fatal. Bing, instantly, would go my prestige. I know girls. Grovel, and the best of them get uppish." He mused. "The only way to work the thing would be by tipping her off in some indirect way that I am prepared to open negotiations. Should I sigh a bit when we meet, do you think?"

"She would think you were puffing."

"That's true."

I lit another cigarette and gave my mind to the matter. And first crack out of the box, as is so often the way with the Woosters, I got an idea. I remembered the counsel I had given Gussie in the matter of the sausages and ham.

"I've got it, Tuppy. There is one infallible method of indicating to a girl that you love her, and it works just as well when you've had a row and want to make it up. Don't eat any dinner tonight. You can see how impressive that would be. She knows how devoted you are to food."

He started violently.

"I am not devoted to food!"

"No, no."

"I am not devoted to food at all."

"Quite. All I meant——"

"This rot about me being devoted to food," said Tuppy warmly, "has got to stop. I am young and healthy and have a good appetite, but that's not the same as being devoted to food. I admire Anatole as a master of his craft, and am always willing to consider anything he may put before me, but when you say I am devoted to food——"

"Quite, quite. All I meant was that if she sees you push away your dinner untasted, she will realize that your heart is aching, and will probably be the first to suggest blowing the all clear."

Tuppy was frowning thoughtfully.

"Push my dinner away, eh?"

"Yes."

"Push away a dinner cooked by Anatole?"

"Yes."

"Push it away untasted?"

"Yes."

"Let us get this straight. Tonight, at dinner, when the butler offers me a ris de veau à la financiere, or whatever it may be, hot from Anatole's hands, you wish me to push it away untasted?"

"Yes."

He chewed his lip. One could sense the struggle going on within. And then suddenly a sort of glow came into his face. The old martyrs probably used to look like that.

"All right."

"You'll do it?"

"I will."

"Fine."

"Of course, it will be agony."

I pointed out the silver lining.

"Only for the moment. You could slip down tonight, after everyone is in bed, and raid the larder."

He brightened.

"That's right. I could, couldn't I?"

"I expect there would be something cold there."

"There is something cold there," said Tuppy, with growing cheerfulness. "A steak-and-kidney pie. We had it for lunch today. One of Anatole's ripest. The thing I admire about that man," said Tuppy reverently, "the thing that I admire so enormously about Anatole is that, though a Frenchman, he does not, like so many of these chefs, confine himself exclusively to French dishes, but is always willing and ready to weigh in with some good old simple English fare such as this steak-and-kidney pie to which I have alluded. A masterly pie, Bertie, and it wasn't more than half finished. It will do me nicely."

"And at dinner you will push, as arranged?"

"Absolutely as arranged."

"Fine."

"It's an excellent idea. One of Jeeves's best. You can tell him from me, when you see him, that I'm much obliged."

The cigarette fell from my fingers. It was as though somebody had slapped Bertram Wooster across the face with a wet dish-rag.

"You aren't suggesting that you think this scheme I have been sketching out is Jeeves's?"

"Of course it is. It's no good trying to kid me, Bertie. You wouldn't have thought of a wheeze like that in a million years."

There was a pause. I drew myself up to my full height; then, seeing that he wasn't looking at me, lowered myself again.

"Come, Glossop," I said coldly, "we had better be going. It is time we were dressing for dinner."

Tuppy's fatheaded words were still rankling in my bosom as I went up to my room. They continued rankling as I shed the form-fitting, and had not ceased to rankle when, clad in the old dressing-gown, I made my way along the corridor to the salle de bain.

It is not too much to say that I was piqued to the tonsils.

I mean to say, one does not court praise. The adulation of the multitude means very little to one. But, all the same, when one has taken the trouble to whack out a highly juicy scheme to benefit an in-the-soup friend in his hour of travail, it's pretty foul to find him giving the credit to one's personal attendant, particularly if that personal attendant is a man who goes about the place not packing mess-jackets.

But after I had been splashing about in the porcelain for a bit, composure began to return. I have always found that in moments of heart-bowed-downness there is nothing that calms the bruised spirit like a good go at the soap and water. I don't say I actually sang in the tub, but there were times when it was a mere spin of the coin whether I would do so or not.

The spiritual anguish induced by that tactless speech had become noticeably lessened.

The discovery of a toy duck in the soap dish, presumably the property of some former juvenile visitor, contributed not a little to this new and happier frame of mind. What with one thing and another, I hadn't played with toy ducks in my bath for years, and I found the novel experience most invigorating. For the benefit of those interested, I may mention that if you shove the thing under the surface with the sponge and then let it go, it shoots out of the water in a manner calculated to divert the most careworn. Ten minutes of this and I was enabled to return to the bedchamber much more the old merry Bertram.

Jeeves was there, laying out the dinner disguise. He greeted the young master with his customary suavity.

"Good evening, sir."

I responded in the same affable key.

"Good evening, Jeeves."

"I trust you had a pleasant drive, sir."

"Very pleasant, thank you, Jeeves. Hand me a sock or two, will you?"

He did so, and I commenced to don.

"Well, Jeeves," I said, reaching for the underlinen, "here we are again at Brinkley Court in the county of Worcestershire."

"Yes, sir."

"A nice mess things seem to have gone and got themselves into in this rustic joint."

"Yes, sir."

"The rift between Tuppy Glossop and my cousin Angela would appear to be serious."

"Yes, sir. Opinion in the servants' hall is inclined to take a grave view of the situation."

"And the thought that springs to your mind, no doubt, is that I shall have my work cut out to fix things up?"

"Yes, sir."

"You are wrong, Jeeves. I have the thing well in hand."

"You surprise me, sir."

"I thought I should. Yes, Jeeves, I pondered on the matter most of the way down here, and with the happiest results. I have just been in conference with Mr. Glossop, and everything is taped out."

"Indeed, sir? Might I inquire——"

"You know my methods, Jeeves. Apply them. Have you," I asked, slipping into the shirt and starting to adjust the cravat, "been gnawing on the thing at all?"

"Oh, yes, sir. I have always been much attached to Miss Angela, and I felt that it would afford me great pleasure were I to be able to be of service to her."

"A laudable sentiment. But I suppose you drew blank?"

"No, sir. I was rewarded with an idea."

"What was it?"

"It occurred to me that a reconciliation might be effected between Mr. Glossop and Miss Angela by appealing to that instinct which prompts gentlemen in time of peril to hasten to the rescue of——"

I had to let go of the cravat in order to raise a hand. I was shocked.

"Don't tell me you were contemplating descending to that old he-saved-her-from-drowning gag? I am surprised, Jeeves. Surprised and pained. When I was discussing the matter with Aunt Dahlia on my arrival, she said in a sniffy sort of way that she supposed I was going to shove my Cousin Angela into the lake and push Tuppy in to haul her out, and I let her see pretty clearly that I considered the suggestion an insult to my intelligence. And now, if your words have the meaning I read into them, you are mooting precisely the same drivelling scheme. Really, Jeeves!"

"No, sir. Not that. But the thought did cross my mind, as I walked in the grounds and passed the building where the fire-bell hangs, that a sudden alarm of fire in the night might result in Mr. Glossop endeavouring to assist Miss Angela to safety."

I shivered.

"Rotten, Jeeves."

"Well, sir——"

"No good. Not a bit like it."

"I fancy, sir——"

"No, Jeeves. No more. Enough has been said. Let us drop the subj."

I finished tying the tie in silence. My emotions were too deep for speech. I knew, of course, that this man had for the time being lost his grip, but I had never suspected that he had gone absolutely to pieces like this. Remembering some of the swift ones he had pulled in the past, I shrank with horror from the spectacle of his present ineptitude. Or is it ineptness? I mean this frightful disposition of his to stick straws in his hair and talk like a perfect ass. It was the old, old story, I supposed. A man's brain whizzes along for years exceeding the speed limit, and something suddenly goes wrong with the steering-gear and it skids and comes a smeller in the ditch.

"A bit elaborate," I said, trying to put the thing in as kindly a light as possible. "Your old failing. You can see that it's a bit elaborate?"

"Possibly the plan I suggested might be considered open to that criticism, sir, but faute de mieux——"

"I don't get you, Jeeves."

"A French expression, sir, signifying 'for want of anything better'."

A moment before, I had been feeling for this wreck of a once fine thinker nothing but a gentle pity. These words jarred the Wooster pride, inducing asperity.

"I understand perfectly well what faute de mieux means, Jeeves. I did not recently spend two months among our Gallic neighbours for nothing. Besides, I remember that one from school. What caused my bewilderment was that you should be employing the expression, well knowing that there is no bally faute de mieux about it at all. Where do you get that faute-de-mieux stuff? Didn't I tell you I had everything taped out?"

"Yes, sir, but——"

"What do you mean—but?"

"Well, sir——"

"Push on, Jeeves. I am ready, even anxious, to hear your views."

"Well, sir, if I may take the liberty of reminding you of it, your plans in the past have not always been uniformly successful."

There was a silence—rather a throbbing one—during which I put on my waistcoat in a marked manner. Not till I had got the buckle at the back satisfactorily adjusted did I speak.

"It is true, Jeeves," I said formally, "that once or twice in the past I may have missed the bus. This, however, I attribute purely to bad luck."

"Indeed, sir?"

"On the present occasion I shall not fail, and I'll tell you why I shall not fail. Because my scheme is rooted in human nature."

"Indeed, sir?"

"It is simple. Not elaborate. And, furthermore, based on the psychology of the individual."

"Indeed, sir?"

"Jeeves," I said, "don't keep saying 'Indeed, sir?' No doubt nothing is further from your mind than to convey such a suggestion, but you have a way of stressing the 'in' and then coming down with a thud on the 'deed' which makes it virtually tantamount to 'Oh, yeah?' Correct this, Jeeves."

"Very good, sir."

"I tell you I have everything nicely lined up. Would you care to hear what steps I have taken?"

"Very much, sir."

"Then listen. Tonight at dinner I have recommended Tuppy to lay off the food."

"Sir?"

"Tut, Jeeves, surely you can follow the idea, even though it is one that would never have occurred to yourself. Have you forgotten that telegram I sent to Gussie Fink-Nottle, steering him away from the sausages and ham? This is the same thing. Pushing the food away untasted is a universally recognized sign of love. It cannot fail to bring home the gravy. You must see that?"

"Well, sir——"

I frowned.

"I don't want to seem always to be criticizing your methods of voice production, Jeeves," I said, "but I must inform you that that 'Well, sir' of yours is in many respects fully as unpleasant as your 'Indeed, sir?' Like the latter, it seems to be tinged with a definite scepticism. It suggests a lack of faith in my vision. The impression I retain after hearing you shoot it at me a couple of times is that you consider me to be talking through the back of my neck, and that only a feudal sense of what is fitting restrains you from substituting for it the words 'Says you!'"

"Oh, no, sir."

"Well, that's what it sounds like. Why don't you think this scheme will work?"

"I fear Miss Angela will merely attribute Mr. Glossop's abstinence to indigestion, sir."

I hadn't thought of that, and I must confess it shook me for a moment. Then I recovered myself. I saw what was at the bottom of all this. Mortified by the consciousness of his own ineptness—or ineptitude—the fellow was simply trying to hamper and obstruct. I decided to knock the stuffing out of him without further preamble.

"Oh?" I said. "You do, do you? Well, be that as it may, it doesn't alter the fact that you've put out the wrong coat. Be so good, Jeeves," I said, indicating with a gesture the gent's ordinary dinner jacket or smoking, as we call it on the Côte d'Azur, which was suspended from the hanger on the knob of the wardrobe, "as to shove that bally black thing in the cupboard and bring out my white mess-jacket with the brass buttons."

He looked at me in a meaning manner. And when I say a meaning manner, I mean there was a respectful but at the same time uppish glint in his eye and a sort of muscular spasm flickered across his face which wasn't quite a quiet smile and yet wasn't quite not a quiet smile. Also the soft cough.

"I regret to say, sir, that I inadvertently omitted to pack the garment to which you refer."

The vision of that parcel in the hall seemed to rise before my eyes, and I exchanged a merry wink with it. I may even have hummed a bar or two. I'm not quite sure.

"I know you did, Jeeves," I said, laughing down from lazy eyelids and nicking a speck of dust from the irreproachable Mechlin lace at my wrists. "But I didn't. You will find it on a chair in the hall in a brown-paper parcel."

The information that his low manoeuvres had been rendered null and void and that the thing was on the strength after all, must have been the nastiest of jars, but there was no play of expression on his finely chiselled to indicate it. There very seldom is on Jeeves's f-c. In moments of discomfort, as I had told Tuppy, he wears a mask, preserving throughout the quiet stolidity of a stuffed moose.

"You might just slide down and fetch it, will you?"

"Very good, sir."

"Right ho, Jeeves."

And presently I was sauntering towards the drawing-room with me good old j. nestling snugly abaft the shoulder blades.

And Dahlia was in the drawing-room. She glanced up at my entrance.

"Hullo, eyesore," she said. "What do you think you're made up as?"

I did not get the purport.

"The jacket, you mean?" I queried, groping.

"I do. You look like one of the chorus of male guests at Abernethy Towers in Act 2 of a touring musical comedy."

"You do not admire this jacket?"

"I do not."

"You did at Cannes."

"Well, this isn't Cannes."

"But, dash it——"

"Oh, never mind. Let it go. If you want to give my butler a laugh, what does it matter? What does anything matter now?"

There was a death-where-is-thy-sting-fullness about her manner which I found distasteful. It isn't often that I score off Jeeves in the devastating fashion just described, and when I do I like to see happy, smiling faces about me.

"Tails up, Aunt Dahlia," I urged buoyantly.

"Tails up be dashed," was her sombre response. "I've just been talking to Tom."

"Telling him?"

"No, listening to him. I haven't had the nerve to tell him yet."

"Is he still upset about that income-tax money?"

"Upset is right. He says that Civilisation is in the melting-pot and that all thinking men can read the writing on the wall."

"What wall?"

"Old Testament, ass. Belshazzar's feast."

"Oh, that, yes. I've often wondered how that gag was worked. With mirrors, I expect."

"I wish I could use mirrors to break it to Tom about this baccarat business."

I had a word of comfort to offer here. I had been turning the thing over in my mind since our last meeting, and I thought I saw where she had got twisted. Where she made her error, it seemed to me, was in feeling she had got to tell Uncle Tom. To my way of thinking, the matter was one on which it would be better to continue to exercise a quiet reserve.

"I don't see why you need mention that you lost that money at baccarat."

"What do you suggest, then? Letting Milady's Boudoir join Civilisation in the melting-pot. Because that is what it will infallibly do unless I get a cheque by next week. The printers have been showing a nasty spirit for months."

"You don't follow. Listen. It's an understood thing, I take it, that Uncle Tom foots the Boudoir bills. If the bally sheet has been turning the corner for two years, he must have got used to forking out by this time. Well, simply ask him for the money to pay the printers."

"I did. Just before I went to Cannes."

"Wouldn't he give it to you?"

"Certainly he gave it to me. He brassed up like an officer and a gentleman. That was the money I lost at baccarat."

"Oh? I didn't know that."

"There isn't much you do know."

A nephew's love made me overlook the slur.

"Tut!" I said.

"What did you say?"

"I said 'Tut!'"

"Say it once again, and I'll biff you where you stand. I've enough to endure without being tutted at."

"Quite."

"Any tutting that's required, I'll attend to myself. And the same applies to clicking the tongue, if you were thinking of doing that."

"Far from it."

"Good."

I stood awhile in thought. I was concerned to the core. My heart, if you remember, had already bled once for Aunt Dahlia this evening. It now bled again. I knew how deeply attached she was to this paper of hers. Seeing it go down the drain would be for her like watching a loved child sink for the third time in some pond or mere.

And there was no question that, unless carefully prepared for the touch, Uncle Tom would see a hundred Milady's Boudoirs go phut rather than take the rap.

Then I saw how the thing could be handled. This aunt, I perceived, must fall into line with my other clients. Tuppy Glossop was knocking off dinner to melt Angela. Gussie Fink-Nottle was knocking off dinner to impress the Bassett. Aunt Dahlia must knock off dinner to soften Uncle Tom. For the beauty of this scheme of mine was that there was no limit to the number of entrants. Come one, come all, the more the merrier, and satisfaction guaranteed in every case.

"I've got it," I said. "There is only one course to pursue. Eat less meat."

She looked at me in a pleading sort of way. I wouldn't swear that her eyes were wet with unshed tears, but I rather think they were, certainly she clasped her hands in piteous appeal.

"Must you drivel, Bertie? Won't you stop it just this once? Just for tonight, to please Aunt Dahlia?"

"I'm not drivelling."

"I dare say that to a man of your high standards it doesn't come under the head of drivel, but——"

I saw what had happened. I hadn't made myself quite clear.

"It's all right," I said. "Have no misgivings. This is the real Tabasco. When I said 'Eat less meat', what I meant was that you must refuse your oats at dinner tonight. Just sit there, looking blistered, and wave away each course as it comes with a weary gesture of resignation. You see what will happen. Uncle Tom will notice your loss of appetite, and I am prepared to bet that at the conclusion of the meal he will come to you and say 'Dahlia, darling'—I take it he calls you 'Dahlia'—'Dahlia darling,' he will say, 'I noticed at dinner tonight that you were a bit off your feed. Is anything the matter, Dahlia, darling?' 'Why, yes, Tom, darling,' you will reply. 'It is kind of you to ask, darling. The fact is, darling, I am terribly worried.' 'My darling,' he will say——"

Aunt Dahlia interrupted at this point to observe that these Traverses seemed to be a pretty soppy couple of blighters, to judge by their dialogue. She also wished to know when I was going to get to the point.

I gave her a look.

"'My darling,' he will say tenderly, 'is there anything I can do?' To which your reply will be that there jolly well is—viz. reach for his cheque-book and start writing."

I was watching her closely as I spoke, and was pleased to note respect suddenly dawn in her eyes.

"But, Bertie, this is positively bright."

"I told you Jeeves wasn't the only fellow with brain."

"I believe it would work."

"It's bound to work. I've recommended it to Tuppy."

"Young Glossop?"

"In order to soften Angela."

"Splendid!"

"And to Gussie Fink-Nottle, who wants to make a hit with the Bassett."

"Well, well, well! What a busy little brain it is."

"Always working, Aunt Dahlia, always working."

"You're not the chump I took you for, Bertie."

"When did you ever take me for a chump?"

"Oh, some time last summer. I forget what gave me the idea. Yes, Bertie, this scheme is bright. I suppose, as a matter of fact, Jeeves suggested it."

"Jeeves did not suggest it. I resent these implications. Jeeves had nothing to do with it whatsoever."

"Well, all right, no need to get excited about it. Yes, I think it will work. Tom's devoted to me."

"Who wouldn't be?"

"I'll do it."

And then the rest of the party trickled in, and we toddled down to dinner.

Conditions being as they were at Brinkley Court—I mean to say, the place being loaded down above the Plimsoll mark with aching hearts and standing room only as regarded tortured souls—I hadn't expected the evening meal to be particularly effervescent. Nor was it. Silent. Sombre. The whole thing more than a bit like Christmas dinner on Devil's Island.

I was glad when it was over.

What with having, on top of her other troubles, to rein herself back from the trough, Aunt Dahlia was a total loss as far as anything in the shape of brilliant badinage was concerned. The fact that he was fifty quid in the red and expecting Civilisation to take a toss at any moment had caused Uncle Tom, who always looked a bit like a pterodactyl with a secret sorrow, to take on a deeper melancholy. The Bassett was a silent bread crumbler. Angela might have been hewn from the living rock. Tuppy had the air of a condemned murderer refusing to make the usual hearty breakfast before tooling off to the execution shed.

And as for Gussie Fink-Nottle, many an experienced undertaker would have been deceived by his appearance and started embalming him on sight.

This was the first glimpse I had had of Gussie since we parted at my flat, and I must say his demeanour disappointed me. I had been expecting something a great deal more sparkling.

At my flat, on the occasion alluded to, he had, if you recall, practically given me a signed guarantee that all he needed to touch him off was a rural setting. Yet in this aspect now I could detect no indication whatsoever that he was about to round into mid-season form. He still looked like a cat in an adage, and it did not take me long to realise that my very first act on escaping from this morgue must be to draw him aside and give him a pep talk.

If ever a chap wanted the clarion note, it looked as if it was this Fink-Nottle.

In the general exodus of mourners, however, I lost sight of him, and, owing to the fact that Aunt Dahlia roped me in for a game of backgammon, it was not immediately that I was able to institute a search. But after we had been playing for a while, the butler came in and asked her if she would speak to Anatole, so I managed to get away. And some ten minutes later, having failed to find scent in the house, I started to throw out the drag-net through the grounds, and flushed him in the rose garden.

He was smelling a rose at the moment in a limp sort of way, but removed the beak as I approached.

"Well, Gussie," I said.

I had beamed genially upon him as I spoke, such being my customary policy on meeting an old pal; but instead of beaming back genially, he gave me a most unpleasant look. His attitude perplexed me. It was as if he were not glad to see Bertram. For a moment he stood letting this unpleasant look play upon me, as it were, and then he spoke.

"You and your 'Well, Gussie'!"

He said this between clenched teeth, always an unmatey thing to do, and I found myself more fogged than ever.

"How do you mean—me and my 'Well, Gussie'?"

"I like your nerve, coming bounding about the place, saying 'Well, Gussie.' That's about all the 'Well, Gussie' I shall require from you, Wooster. And it's no good looking like that. You know what I mean. That damned prize-giving! It was a dastardly act to crawl out as you did and shove it off on to me. I will not mince my words. It was the act of a hound and a stinker."

Now, though, as I have shown, I had devoted most of the time on the journey down to meditating upon the case of Angela and Tuppy, I had not neglected to give a thought or two to what I was going to say when I encountered Gussie. I had foreseen that there might be some little temporary unpleasantness when we met, and when a difficult interview is in the offing Bertram Wooster likes to have his story ready.

So now I was able to reply with a manly, disarming frankness. The sudden introduction of the topic had given me a bit of a jolt, it is true, for in the stress of recent happenings I had rather let that prize-giving business slide to the back of my mind; but I had speedily recovered and, as I say, was able to reply with a manly d.f.

"But, my dear chap," I said, "I took it for granted that you would understand that that was all part of my schemes."

He said something about my schemes which I did not catch.

"Absolutely. 'Crawling out' is entirely the wrong way to put it. You don't suppose I didn't want to distribute those prizes, do you? Left to myself, there is nothing I would find a greater treat. But I saw that the square, generous thing to do was to step aside and let you take it on, so I did so. I felt that your need was greater than mine. You don't mean to say you aren't looking forward to it?"

He uttered a coarse expression which I wouldn't have thought he would have known. It just shows that you can bury yourself in the country and still somehow acquire a vocabulary. No doubt one picks up things from the neighbours—the vicar, the local doctor, the man who brings the milk, and so on.

"But, dash it," I said, "can't you see what this is going to do for you? It will send your stock up with a jump. There you will be, up on that platform, a romantic, impressive figure, the star of the whole proceedings, the what-d'you-call-it of all eyes. Madeline Bassett will be all over you. She will see you in a totally new light."

"She will, will she?"

"Certainly she will. Augustus Fink-Nottle, the newts' friend, she knows. She is acquainted with Augustus Fink-Nottle, the dogs' chiropodist. But Augustus Fink-Nottle, the orator—that'll knock her sideways, or I know nothing of the female heart. Girls go potty over a public man. If ever anyone did anyone else a kindness, it was I when I gave this extraordinary attractive assignment to you."

He seemed impressed by my eloquence. Couldn't have helped himself, of course. The fire faded from behind his horn-rimmed spectacles, and in its place appeared the old fish-like goggle.

"'Myes," he said meditatively. "Have you ever made a speech, Bertie?"

"Dozens of times. It's pie. Nothing to it. Why, I once addressed a girls' school."

"You weren't nervous?"

"Not a bit."

"How did you go?"

"They hung on my lips. I held them in the hollow of my hand."

"They didn't throw eggs, or anything?"

"Not a thing."

He expelled a deep breath, and for a space stood staring in silence at a passing slug.

"Well," he said, at length, "it may be all right. Possibly I am letting the thing prey on my mind too much. I may be wrong in supposing it the fate that is worse than death. But I'll tell you this much: the prospect of that prize-giving on the thirty-first of this month has been turning my existence into a nightmare. I haven't been able to sleep or think or eat ... By the way, that reminds me. You never explained that cipher telegram about the sausages and ham."

"It wasn't a cipher telegram. I wanted you to go light on the food, so that she would realize you were in love."

He laughed hollowly.

"I see. Well, I've been doing that, all right."

"Yes, I was noticing at dinner. Splendid."

"I don't see what's splendid about it. It's not going to get me anywhere. I shall never be able to ask her to marry me. I couldn't find nerve to do that if I lived on wafer biscuits for the rest of my life."

"But, dash it, Gussie. In these romantic surroundings. I should have thought the whispering trees alone——"

"I don't care what you would have thought. I can't do it."

"Oh, come!"

"I can't. She seems so aloof, so remote."

"She doesn't."

"Yes, she does. Especially when you see her sideways. Have you seen her sideways, Bertie? That cold, pure profile. It just takes all the heart out of one."

"It doesn't."

"I tell you it does. I catch sight of it, and the words freeze on my lips."

He spoke with a sort of dull despair, and so manifest was his lack of ginger and the spirit that wins to success that for an instant, I confess, I felt a bit stymied. It seemed hopeless to go on trying to steam up such a human jellyfish. Then I saw the way. With that extraordinary quickness of mine, I realized exactly what must be done if this Fink-Nottle was to be enabled to push his nose past the judges' box.

"She must be softened up," I said.

"Be what?"

"Softened up. Sweetened. Worked on. Preliminary spadework must be put in. Here, Gussie, is the procedure I propose to adopt: I shall now return to the house and lug this Bassett out for a stroll. I shall talk to her of hearts that yearn, intimating that there is one actually on the premises. I shall pitch it strong, sparing no effort. You, meanwhile, will lurk on the outskirts, and in about a quarter of an hour you will come along and carry on from there. By that time, her emotions having been stirred, you ought to be able to do the rest on your head. It will be like leaping on to a moving bus."

I remember when I was a kid at school having to learn a poem of sorts about a fellow named Pig-something—a sculptor he would have been, no doubt—who made a statue of a girl, and what should happen one morning but that the bally thing suddenly came to life. A pretty nasty shock for the chap, of course, but the point I'm working round to is that there were a couple of lines that went, if I remember correctly:

She starts. She moves. She seems to feel

The stir of life along her keel.

And what I'm driving at is that you couldn't get a better description of what happened to Gussie as I spoke these heartening words. His brow cleared, his eyes brightened, he lost that fishy look, and he gazed at the slug, which was still on the long, long trail with something approaching bonhomie. A marked improvement.

"I see what you mean. You will sort of pave the way, as it were."

"That's right. Spadework."

"It's a terrific idea, Bertie. It will make all the difference."

"Quite. But don't forget that after that it will be up to you. You will have to haul up your slacks and give her the old oil, or my efforts will have been in vain."

Something of his former Gawd-help-us-ness seemed to return to him. He gasped a bit.

"That's true. What the dickens shall I say?"

I restrained my impatience with an effort. The man had been at school with me.

"Dash it, there are hundreds of things you can say. Talk about the sunset."

"The sunset?"

"Certainly. Half the married men you meet began by talking about the sunset."

"But what can I say about the sunset?"

"Well, Jeeves got off a good one the other day. I met him airing the dog in the park one evening, and he said, 'Now fades the glimmering landscape on the sight, sir, and all the air a solemn stillness holds.' You might use that."

"What sort of landscape?"

"Glimmering. G for 'gastritis,' l for 'lizard'——"

"Oh, glimmering? Yes, that's not bad. Glimmering landscape ... solemn stillness.... Yes, I call that pretty good."

"You could then say that you have often thought that the stars are God's daisy chain."

"But I haven't."

"I dare say not. But she has. Hand her that one, and I don't see how she can help feeling that you're a twin soul."

"God's daisy chain?"

"God's daisy chain. And then you go on about how twilight always makes you sad. I know you're going to say it doesn't, but on this occasion it has jolly well got to."

"Why?"

"That's just what she will ask, and you will then have got her going. Because you will reply that it is because yours is such a lonely life. It wouldn't be a bad idea to give her a brief description of a typical home evening at your Lincolnshire residence, showing how you pace the meadows with a heavy tread."

"I generally sit indoors and listen to the wireless."

"No, you don't. You pace the meadows with a heavy tread, wishing that you had someone to love you. And then you speak of the day when she came into your life."

"Like a fairy princess."

"Absolutely," I said with approval. I hadn't expected such a hot one from such a quarter. "Like a fairy princess. Nice work, Gussie."

"And then?"

"Well, after that it's easy. You say you have something you want to say to her, and then you snap into it. I don't see how it can fail. If I were you, I should do it in this rose garden. It is well established that there is no sounder move than to steer the adored object into rose gardens in the gloaming. And you had better have a couple of quick ones first."

"Quick ones?"

"Snifters."

"Drinks, do you mean? But I don't drink."

"What?"

"I've never touched a drop in my life."

This made me a bit dubious, I must confess. On these occasions it is generally conceded that a moderate skinful is of the essence.

However, if the facts were as he had stated, I supposed there was nothing to be done about it.

"Well, you'll have to make out as best you can on ginger pop."

"I always drink orange juice."

"Orange juice, then. Tell me, Gussie, to settle a bet, do you really like that muck?"

"Very much."

"Then there is no more to be said. Now, let's just have a run through, to see that you've got the lay-out straight. Start off with the glimmering landscape."

"Stars God's daisy chain."

"Twilight makes you feel sad."

"Because mine lonely life."

"Describe life."

"Talk about the day I met her."

"Add fairy-princess gag. Say there's something you want to say to her. Heave a couple of sighs. Grab her hand. And give her the works. Right."

And confident that he had grasped the scenario and that everything might now be expected to proceed through the proper channels, I picked up the feet and hastened back to the house.

It was not until I had reached the drawing-room and was enabled to take a square look at the Bassett that I found the debonair gaiety with which I had embarked on this affair beginning to wane a trifle. Beholding her at close range like this, I suddenly became cognisant of what I was in for. The thought of strolling with this rummy specimen undeniably gave me a most unpleasant sinking feeling. I could not but remember how often, when in her company at Cannes, I had gazed dumbly at her, wishing that some kindly motorist in a racing car would ease the situation by coming along and ramming her amidships. As I have already made abundantly clear, this girl was not one of my most congenial buddies.

However, a Wooster's word is his bond. Woosters may quail, but they do not edge out. Only the keenest ear could have detected the tremor in the voice as I asked her if she would care to come out for half an hour.

"Lovely evening," I said.

"Yes, lovely, isn't it?"

"Lovely. Reminds me of Cannes."

"How lovely the evenings were there!"

"Lovely," I said.

"Lovely," said the Bassett.

"Lovely," I agreed.

That completed the weather and news bulletin for the French Riviera. Another minute, and we were out in the great open spaces, she cooing a bit about the scenery, and self replying, "Oh, rather, quite," and wondering how best to approach the matter in hand.

-10-

How different it all would have been, I could not but reflect, if this girl had been the sort of girl one chirrups cheerily to over the telephone and takes for spins in the old two-seater. In that case, I would simply have said, "Listen," and she would have said, "What?" and I would have said, "You know Gussie Fink-Nottle," and she would have said, "Yes," and I would have said, "He loves you," and she would have said either, "What, that mutt? Well, thank heaven for one good laugh today," or else, in more passionate vein, "Hot dog! Tell me more."

I mean to say, in either event the whole thing over and done with in under a minute.

But with the Bassett something less snappy and a good deal more glutinous was obviously indicated. What with all this daylight-saving stuff, we had hit the great open spaces at a moment when twilight had not yet begun to cheese it in favour of the shades of night. There was a fag-end of sunset still functioning. Stars were beginning to peep out, bats were fooling round, the garden was full of the aroma of those niffy white flowers which only start to put in their heavy work at the end of the day—in short, the glimmering landscape was fading on the sight and all the air held a solemn stillness, and it was plain that this was having the worst effect on her. Her eyes were enlarged, and her whole map a good deal too suggestive of the soul's awakening for comfort.

Her aspect was that of a girl who was expecting something fairly fruity from Bertram.

In these circs., conversation inevitably flagged a bit. I am never at my best when the situation seems to call for a certain soupiness, and I've heard other members of the Drones say the same thing about themselves. I remember Pongo Twistleton telling me that he was out in a gondola with a girl by moonlight once, and the only time he spoke was to tell her that old story about the chap who was so good at swimming that they made him a traffic cop in Venice.

Fell rather flat, he assured me, and it wasn't much later when the girl said she thought it was getting a little chilly and how about pushing back to the hotel.

So now, as I say, the talk rather hung fire. It had been all very well for me to promise Gussie that I would cut loose to this girl about aching hearts, but you want a cue for that sort of thing. And when, toddling along, we reached the edge of the lake and she finally spoke, conceive my chagrin when I discovered that what she was talking about was stars.

Not a bit of good to me.

"Oh, look," she said. She was a confirmed Oh-looker. I had noticed this at Cannes, where she had drawn my attention in this manner on various occasions to such diverse objects as a French actress, a Provençal filling station, the sunset over the Estorels, Michael Arlen, a man selling coloured spectacles, the deep velvet blue of the Mediterranean, and the late mayor of New York in a striped one-piece bathing suit. "Oh, look at that sweet little star up there all by itself."

I saw the one she meant, a little chap operating in a detached sort of way above a spinney.

"Yes," I said.

"I wonder if it feels lonely."

"Oh, I shouldn't think so."

"A fairy must have been crying."

"Eh?"

"Don't you remember? 'Every time a fairy sheds a tear, a wee bit star is born in the Milky Way.' Have you ever thought that, Mr. Wooster?"

I never had. Most improbable, I considered, and it didn't seem to me to check up with her statement that the stars were God's daisy chain. I mean, you can't have it both ways.

However, I was in no mood to dissect and criticize. I saw that I had been wrong in supposing that the stars were not germane to the issue. Quite a decent cue they had provided, and I leaped on it Promptly: "Talking of shedding tears——"

But she was now on the subject of rabbits, several of which were messing about in the park to our right.

"Oh, look. The little bunnies!"

"Talking of shedding tears——"

"Don't you love this time of the evening, Mr. Wooster, when the sun has gone to bed and all the bunnies come out to have their little suppers? When I was a child, I used to think that rabbits were gnomes, and that if I held my breath and stayed quite still, I should see the fairy queen."

Indicating with a reserved gesture that this was just the sort of loony thing I should have expected her to think as a child, I returned to the point.

"Talking of shedding tears," I said firmly, "it may interest you to know that there is an aching heart in Brinkley Court."

This held her. She cheesed the rabbit theme. Her face, which had been aglow with what I supposed was a pretty animation, clouded. She unshipped a sigh that sounded like the wind going out of a rubber duck.

"Ah, yes. Life is very sad, isn't it?"

"It is for some people. This aching heart, for instance."

"Those wistful eyes of hers! Drenched irises. And they used to dance like elves of delight. And all through a foolish misunderstanding about a shark. What a tragedy misunderstandings are. That pretty romance broken and over just because Mr. Glossop would insist that it was a flatfish."

I saw that she had got the wires crossed.

"I'm not talking about Angela."

"But her heart is aching."

"I know it's aching. But so is somebody else's."

She looked at me, perplexed.

"Somebody else? Mr. Glossop's, you mean?"

"No, I don't."

"Mrs. Travers's?"

The exquisite code of politeness of the Woosters prevented me clipping her one on the earhole, but I would have given a shilling to be able to do it. There seemed to me something deliberately fat-headed in the way she persisted in missing the gist.

"No, not Aunt Dahlia's, either."

"I'm sure she is dreadfully upset."

"Quite. But this heart I'm talking about isn't aching because of Tuppy's row with Angela. It's aching for a different reason altogether. I mean to say—dash it, you know why hearts ache!"

She seemed to shimmy a bit. Her voice, when she spoke, was whispery: "You mean—for love?"

"Absolutely. Right on the bull's-eye. For love."

"Oh, Mr. Wooster!"

"I take it you believe in love at first sight?"

"I do, indeed."

"Well, that's what happened to this aching heart. It fell in love at first sight, and ever since it's been eating itself out, as I believe the expression is."

There was a silence. She had turned away and was watching a duck out on the lake. It was tucking into weeds, a thing I've never been able to understand anyone wanting to do. Though I suppose, if you face it squarely, they're no worse than spinach. She stood drinking it in for a bit, and then it suddenly stood on its head and disappeared, and this seemed to break the spell.

"Oh, Mr. Wooster!" she said again, and from the tone of her voice, I could see that I had got her going.

"For you, I mean to say," I proceeded, starting to put in the fancy touches. I dare say you have noticed on these occasions that the difficulty is to plant the main idea, to get the general outline of the thing well fixed. The rest is mere detail work. I don't say I became glib at this juncture, but I certainly became a dashed glibber than I had been.

"It's having the dickens of a time. Can't eat, can't sleep—all for love of you. And what makes it all so particularly rotten is that it—this aching heart—can't bring itself up to the scratch and tell you the position of affairs, because your profile has gone and given it cold feet. Just as it is about to speak, it catches sight of you sideways, and words fail it. Silly, of course, but there it is."

I heard her give a gulp, and I saw that her eyes had become moistish. Drenched irises, if you care to put it that way.

"Lend you a handkerchief?"

"No, thank you. I'm quite all right."

It was more than I could say for myself. My efforts had left me weak. I don't know if you suffer in the same way, but with me the act of talking anything in the nature of real mashed potatoes always induces a sort of prickly sensation and a hideous feeling of shame, together with a marked starting of the pores.

I remember at my Aunt Agatha's place in Hertfordshire once being put on the spot and forced to enact the role of King Edward III saying goodbye to that girl of his, Fair Rosamund, at some sort of pageant in aid of the Distressed Daughters of the Clergy. It involved some rather warmish medieval dialogue, I recall, racy of the days when they called a spade a spade, and by the time the whistle blew, I'll bet no Daughter of the Clergy was half as distressed as I was. Not a dry stitch.

My reaction now was very similar. It was a highly liquid Bertram who, hearing his vis-à-vis give a couple of hiccups and start to speak bent an attentive ear.

"Please don't say any more, Mr. Wooster."

Well, I wasn't going to, of course.

"I understand."

I was glad to hear this.

"Yes, I understand. I won't be so silly as to pretend not to know what you mean. I suspected this at Cannes, when you used to stand and stare at me without speaking a word, but with whole volumes in your eyes."

If Angela's shark had bitten me in the leg, I couldn't have leaped more convulsively. So tensely had I been concentrating on Gussie's interests that it hadn't so much as crossed my mind that another and an unfortunate construction could be placed on those words of mine. The persp., already bedewing my brow, became a regular Niagara.

My whole fate hung upon a woman's word. I mean to say, I couldn't back out. If a girl thinks a man is proposing to her, and on that understanding books him up, he can't explain to her that she has got hold of entirely the wrong end of the stick and that he hadn't the smallest intention of suggesting anything of the kind. He must simply let it ride. And the thought of being engaged to a girl who talked openly about fairies being born because stars blew their noses, or whatever it was, frankly appalled me.

She was carrying on with her remarks, and as I listened I clenched my fists till I shouldn't wonder if the knuckles didn't stand out white under the strain. It seemed as if she would never get to the nub.

"Yes, all through those days at Cannes I could see what you were trying to say. A girl always knows. And then you followed me down here, and there was that same dumb, yearning look in your eyes when we met this evening. And then you were so insistent that I should come out and walk with you in the twilight. And now you stammer out those halting words. No, this does not come as a surprise. But I am sorry——"

The word was like one of Jeeves's pick-me-ups. Just as if a glassful of meat sauce, red pepper, and the yolk of an egg—though, as I say, I am convinced that these are not the sole ingredients—had been shot into me, I expanded like some lovely flower blossoming in the sunshine. It was all right, after all. My guardian angel had not been asleep at the switch.

"——but I am afraid it is impossible."

She paused.

"Impossible," she repeated.

I had been so busy feeling saved from the scaffold that I didn't get on to it for a moment that an early reply was desired.

"Oh, right ho," I said hastily.

"I'm sorry."

"Quite all right."

"Sorrier than I can say."

"Don't give it another thought."

"We can still be friends."

"Oh, rather."

"Then shall we just say no more about it; keep what has happened as a tender little secret between ourselves?"

"Absolutely."

"We will. Like something lovely and fragrant laid away in lavender."

"In lavender—right."

There was a longish pause. She was gazing at me in a divinely pitying sort of way, much as if I had been a snail she had happened accidentally to bring her short French vamp down on, and I longed to tell her that it was all right, and that Bertram, so far from being the victim of despair, had never felt fizzier in his life. But, of course, one can't do that sort of thing. I simply said nothing, and stood there looking brave.

"I wish I could," she murmured.

"Could?" I said, for my attensh had been wandering.

"Feel towards you as you would like me to feel."

"Oh, ah."

"But I can't. I'm sorry."

"Absolutely O.K. Faults on both sides, no doubt."

"Because I am fond of you, Mr.—no, I think I must call you Bertie. May I?"

"Oh, rather."

"Because we are real friends."

"Quite."

"I do like you, Bertie. And if things were different—I wonder——"

"Eh?"

"After all, we are real friends.... We have this common memory.... You have a right to know.... I don't want you to think——Life is such a muddle, isn't it?"

To many men, no doubt, these broken utterances would have appeared mere drooling and would have been dismissed as such. But the Woosters are quicker-witted than the ordinary and can read between the lines. I suddenly divined what it was that she was trying to get off the chest.

"You mean there's someone else?"

She nodded.

"You're in love with some other bloke?"

She nodded.

"Engaged, what?"

This time she shook the pumpkin.

"No, not engaged."

Well, that was something, of course. Nevertheless, from the way she spoke, it certainly looked as if poor old Gussie might as well scratch his name off the entry list, and I didn't at all like the prospect of having to break the bad news to him. I had studied the man closely, and it was my conviction that this would about be his finish.

Gussie, you see, wasn't like some of my pals—the name of Bingo Little is one that springs to the lips—who, if turned down by a girl, would simply say, "Well, bung-oh!" and toddle off quite happily to find another. He was so manifestly a bird who, having failed to score in the first chukker, would turn the thing up and spend the rest of his life brooding over his newts and growing long grey whiskers, like one of those chaps you read about in novels, who live in the great white house you can just see over there through the trees and shut themselves off from the world and have pained faces.

"I'm afraid he doesn't care for me in that way. At least, he has said nothing. You understand that I am only telling you this because——"

"Oh, rather."

"It's odd that you should have asked me if I believed in love at first sight." She half closed her eyes. "'Who ever loved that loved not at first sight?'" she said in a rummy voice that brought back to me—I don't know why—the picture of my Aunt Agatha, as Boadicea, reciting at that pageant I was speaking of. "It's a silly little story. I was staying with some friends in the country, and I had gone for a walk with my dog, and the poor wee mite got a nasty thorn in his little foot and I didn't know what to do. And then suddenly this man came along——"

Harking back once again to that pageant, in sketching out for you my emotions on that occasion, I showed you only the darker side of the picture. There was, I should now mention, a splendid aftermath when, having climbed out of my suit of chain mail and sneaked off to the local pub, I entered the saloon bar and requested mine host to start pouring. A moment later, a tankard of their special home-brewed was in my hand, and the ecstasy of that first gollup is still green in my memory. The recollection of the agony through which I had passed was just what was needed to make it perfect.

It was the same now. When I realized, listening to her words, that she must be referring to Gussie—I mean to say, there couldn't have been a whole platoon of men taking thorns out of her dog that day; the animal wasn't a pin-cushion—and became aware that Gussie, who an instant before had, to all appearances, gone so far back in the betting as not to be worth a quotation, was the big winner after all, a positive thrill permeated the frame and there escaped my lips a "Wow!" so crisp and hearty that the Bassett leaped a liberal inch and a half from terra firma.

"I beg your pardon?" she said.

I waved a jaunty hand.

"Nothing," I said. "Nothing. Just remembered there's a letter I have to write tonight without fail. If you don't mind, I think I'll be going in. Here," I said, "comes Gussie Fink-Nottle. He will look after you."

And, as I spoke, Gussie came sidling out from behind a tree.

I passed away and left them to it. As regards these two, everything was beyond a question absolutely in order. All Gussie had to do was keep his head down and not press. Already, I felt, as I legged it back to the house, the happy ending must have begun to function. I mean to say, when you leave a girl and a man, each of whom has admitted in set terms that she and he loves him and her, in close juxtaposition in the twilight, there doesn't seem much more to do but start pricing fish slices.

Something attempted, something done, seemed to me to have earned two-penn'orth of wassail in the smoking-room.

I proceeded thither.

-11-

The makings were neatly laid out on a side-table, and to pour into a glass an inch or so of the raw spirit and shoosh some soda-water on top of it was with me the work of a moment. This done, I retired to an arm-chair and put my feet up, sipping the mixture with carefree enjoyment, rather like Caesar having one in his tent the day he overcame the Nervii.

As I let the mind dwell on what must even now be taking place in that peaceful garden, I felt bucked and uplifted. Though never for an instant faltering in my opinion that Augustus Fink-Nottle was Nature's final word in cloth-headed guffins, I liked the man, wished him well, and could not have felt more deeply involved in the success of his wooing if I, and not he, had been under the ether.

The thought that by this time he might quite easily have completed the preliminary pourparlers and be deep in an informal discussion of honeymoon plans was very pleasant to me.

Of course, considering the sort of girl Madeline Bassett was—stars and rabbits and all that, I mean—you might say that a sober sadness would have been more fitting. But in these matters you have got to realize that tastes differ. The impulse of right-thinking men might be to run a mile when they saw the Bassett, but for some reason she appealed to the deeps in Gussie, so that was that.

I had reached this point in my meditations, when I was aroused by the sound of the door opening. Somebody came in and started moving like a leopard toward the side-table and, lowering the feet, I perceived that it was Tuppy Glossop.

The sight of him gave me a momentary twinge of remorse, reminding me, as it did, that in the excitement of getting Gussie fixed up I had rather forgotten about this other client. It is often that way when you're trying to run two cases at once.

However, Gussie now being off my mind, I was prepared to devote my whole attention to the Glossop problem.

I had been much pleased by the way he had carried out the task assigned him at the dinner-table. No easy one, I can assure you, for the browsing and sluicing had been of the highest quality, and there had been one dish in particular—I allude to the nonnettes de poulet Agnès Sorel—which might well have broken down the most iron resolution. But he had passed it up like a professional fasting man, and I was proud of him.

"Oh, hullo, Tuppy," I said, "I wanted to see you."

He turned, snifter in hand, and it was easy to see that his privations had tried him sorely. He was looking like a wolf on the steppes of Russia which has seen its peasant shin up a high tree.

"Yes?" he said, rather unpleasantly. "Well, here I am."

"Well?"

"How do you mean——well?"

"Make your report."

"What report?"

"Have you nothing to tell me about Angela?"

"Only that she's a blister."

I was concerned.

"Hasn't she come clustering round you yet?"

"She has not."

"Very odd."

"Why odd?"

"She must have noted your lack of appetite."

He barked raspingly, as if he were having trouble with the tonsils of the soul.

"Lack of appetite! I'm as hollow as the Grand Canyon."

"Courage, Tuppy! Think of Gandhi."

"What about Gandhi?"

"He hasn't had a square meal for years."

"Nor have I. Or I could swear I hadn't. Gandhi, my left foot."

I saw that it might be best to let the Gandhi motif slide. I went back to where we had started.

"She's probably looking for you now."

"Who is? Angela?"

"Yes. She must have noticed your supreme sacrifice."

"I don't suppose she noticed it at all, the little fathead. I'll bet it didn't register in any way whatsoever."

"Come, Tuppy," I urged, "this is morbid. Don't take this gloomy view. She must at least have spotted that you refused those nonnettes de poulet Agnès Sorel. It was a sensational renunciation and stuck out like a sore thumb. And the cèpes à la Rossini——"

A hoarse cry broke from his twisted lips:

"Will you stop it, Bertie! Do you think I am made of marble? Isn't it bad enough to have sat watching one of Anatole's supremest dinners flit by, course after course, without having you making a song about it? Don't remind me of those nonnettes. I can't stand it."

I endeavoured to hearten and console.

"Be brave, Tuppy. Fix your thoughts on that cold steak-and-kidney pie in the larder. As the Good Book says, it cometh in the morning."

"Yes, in the morning. And it's now about half-past nine at night. You would bring that pie up, wouldn't you? Just when I was trying to keep my mind off it."

I saw what he meant. Hours must pass before he could dig into that pie. I dropped the subject, and we sat for a pretty good time in silence. Then he rose and began to pace the room in an overwrought sort of way, like a zoo lion who has heard the dinner-gong go and is hoping the keeper won't forget him in the general distribution. I averted my gaze tactfully, but I could hear him kicking chairs and things. It was plain that the man's soul was in travail and his blood pressure high.

Presently he returned to his seat, and I saw that he was looking at me intently. There was that about his demeanour that led me to think that he had something to communicate.

Nor was I wrong. He tapped me significantly on the knee and spoke:

"Bertie."

"Hullo?"

"Shall I tell you something?"

"Certainly, old bird," I said cordially. "I was just beginning to feel that the scene could do with a bit more dialogue."

"This business of Angela and me."

"Yes?"

"I've been putting in a lot of solid thinking about it."

"Oh, yes?"

"I have analysed the situation pitilessly, and one thing stands out as clear as dammit. There has been dirty work afoot."

"I don't get you."

"All right. Let me review the facts. Up to the time she went to Cannes Angela loved me. She was all over me. I was the blue-eyed boy in every sense of the term. You'll admit that?"

"Indisputably."

"And directly she came back we had this bust-up."

"Quite."

"About nothing."

"Oh, dash it, old man, nothing? You were a bit tactless, what, about her shark."

"I was frank and candid about her shark. And that's my point. Do you seriously believe that a trifling disagreement about sharks would make a girl hand a man his hat, if her heart were really his?"

"Certainly."

It beats me why he couldn't see it. But then poor old Tuppy has never been very hot on the finer shades. He's one of those large, tough, football-playing blokes who lack the more delicate sensibilities, as I've heard Jeeves call them. Excellent at blocking a punt or walking across an opponent's face in cleated boots, but not so good when it comes to understanding the highly-strung female temperament. It simply wouldn't occur to him that a girl might be prepared to give up her life's happiness rather than waive her shark.

"Rot! It was just a pretext."

"What was?"

"This shark business. She wanted to get rid of me, and grabbed at the first excuse."

"No, no."

"I tell you she did."

"But what on earth would she want to get rid of you for?"

"Exactly. That's the very question I asked myself. And here's the answer: Because she has fallen in love with somebody else. It sticks out a mile. There's no other possible solution. She goes to Cannes all for me, she comes back all off me. Obviously during those two months, she must have transferred her affections to some foul blister she met out there."

"No, no."

"Don't keep saying 'No, no'. She must have done. Well, I'll tell you one thing, and you can take this as official. If ever I find this slimy, slithery snake in the grass, he had better make all the necessary arrangements at his favourite nursing-home without delay, because I am going to be very rough with him. I propose, if and when found, to take him by his beastly neck, shake him till he froths, and pull him inside out and make him swallow himself."

With which words he biffed off; and I, having given him a minute or two to get out of the way, rose and made for the drawing-room. The tendency of females to roost in drawing-rooms after dinner being well marked, I expected to find Angela there. It was my intention to have a word with Angela.

To Tuppy's theory that some insinuating bird had stolen the girl's heart from him at Cannes I had given, as I have indicated, little credence, considering it the mere unbalanced apple sauce of a bereaved man. It was, of course, the shark, and nothing but the shark, that had caused love's young dream to go temporarily off the boil, and I was convinced that a word or two with the cousin at this juncture would set everything right.

For, frankly, I thought it incredible that a girl of her natural sweetness and tender-heartedness should not have been moved to her foundations by what she had seen at dinner that night. Even Seppings, Aunt Dahlia's butler, a cold, unemotional man, had gasped and practically reeled when Tuppy waved aside those nonnettes de poulet Agnès Sorel, while the footman, standing by with the potatoes, had stared like one seeing a vision. I simply refused to consider the possibility of the significance of the thing having been lost on a nice girl like Angela. I fully expected to find her in the drawing-room with her heart bleeding freely, all ripe for an immediate reconciliation.

In the drawing-room, however, when I entered, only Aunt Dahlia met the eye. It seemed to me that she gave me rather a jaundiced look as I hove in sight, but this, having so recently beheld Tuppy in his agony, I attributed to the fact that she, like him, had been going light on the menu. You can't expect an empty aunt to beam like a full aunt.

"Oh, it's you, is it?" she said.

Well, it was, of course.

"Where's Angela?" I asked.

"Gone to bed."

"Already?"

"She said she had a headache."

"H'm."

I wasn't so sure that I liked the sound of that so much. A girl who has observed the sundered lover sensationally off his feed does not go to bed with headaches if love has been reborn in her heart. She sticks around and gives him the swift, remorseful glance from beneath the drooping eyelashes and generally endeavours to convey to him that, if he wants to get together across a round table and try to find a formula, she is all for it too. Yes, I am bound to say I found that going-to-bed stuff a bit disquieting.

"Gone to bed, eh?" I murmured musingly.

"What did you want her for?"

"I thought she might like a stroll and a chat."

"Are you going for a stroll?" said Aunt Dahlia, with a sudden show of interest. "Where?"

"Oh, hither and thither."

"Then I wonder if you would mind doing something for me."

"Give it a name."

"It won't take you long. You know that path that runs past the greenhouses into the kitchen garden. If you go along it, you come to a pond."

"That's right."

"Well, will you get a good, stout piece of rope or cord and go down that path till you come to the pond——"

"To the pond. Right."

"——and look about you till you find a nice, heavy stone. Or a fairly large brick would do."

"I see," I said, though I didn't, being still fogged. "Stone or brick. Yes. And then?"

"Then," said the relative, "I want you, like a good boy, to fasten the rope to the brick and tie it around your damned neck and jump into the pond and drown yourself. In a few days I will send and have you fished up and buried because I shall need to dance on your grave."

I was more fogged than ever. And not only fogged—wounded and resentful. I remember reading a book where a girl "suddenly fled from the room, afraid to stay for fear dreadful things would come tumbling from her lips; determined that she would not remain another day in this house to be insulted and misunderstood." I felt much about the same.

Then I reminded myself that one has got to make allowances for a woman with only about half a spoonful of soup inside her, and I checked the red-hot crack that rose to the lips.

"What," I said gently, "is this all about? You seem pipped with Bertram."

"Pipped!"

"Noticeably pipped. Why this ill-concealed animus?"

A sudden flame shot from her eyes, singeing my hair.

"Who was the ass, who was the chump, who was the dithering idiot who talked me, against my better judgment, into going without my dinner? I might have guessed——"

I saw that I had divined correctly the cause of her strange mood.

"It's all right. Aunt Dahlia. I know just how you're feeling. A bit on the hollow side, what? But the agony will pass. If I were you, I'd sneak down and raid the larder after the household have gone to bed. I am told there's a pretty good steak-and-kidney pie there which will repay inspection. Have faith, Aunt Dahlia," I urged. "Pretty soon Uncle Tom will be along, full of sympathy and anxious inquiries."

"Will he? Do you know where he is now?"

"I haven't seen him."

"He is in the study with his face buried in his hands, muttering about civilization and melting pots."

"Eh? Why?"

"Because it has just been my painful duty to inform him that Anatole has given notice."

I own that I reeled.

"What?"

"Given notice. As the result of that drivelling scheme of yours. What did you expect a sensitive, temperamental French cook to do, if you went about urging everybody to refuse all food? I hear that when the first two courses came back to the kitchen practically untouched, his feelings were so hurt that he cried like a child. And when the rest of the dinner followed, he came to the conclusion that the whole thing was a studied and calculated insult, and decided to hand in his portfolio."

"Golly!"

"You may well say 'Golly!' Anatole, God's gift to the gastric juices, gone like the dew off the petal of a rose, all through your idiocy. Perhaps you understand now why I want you to go and jump in that pond. I might have known that some hideous disaster would strike this house like a thunderbolt if once you wriggled your way into it and started trying to be clever."

Harsh words, of course, as from aunt to nephew, but I bore her no resentment. No doubt, if you looked at it from a certain angle, Bertram might be considered to have made something of a floater.

"I am sorry."

"What's the good of being sorry?"

"I acted for what I deemed the best."

"Another time try acting for the worst. Then we may possibly escape with a mere flesh wound."

"Uncle Tom's not feeling too bucked about it all, you say?"

"He's groaning like a lost soul. And any chance I ever had of getting that money out of him has gone."

I stroked the chin thoughtfully. There was, I had to admit, reason in what she said. None knew better than I how terrible a blow the passing of Anatole would be to Uncle Tom.

I have stated earlier in this chronicle that this curious object of the seashore with whom Aunt Dahlia has linked her lot is a bloke who habitually looks like a pterodactyl that has suffered, and the reason he does so is that all those years he spent in making millions in the Far East put his digestion on the blink, and the only cook that has ever been discovered capable of pushing food into him without starting something like Old Home Week in Moscow under the third waistcoat button is this uniquely gifted Anatole. Deprived of Anatole's services, all he was likely to give the wife of his b. was a dirty look. Yes, unquestionably, things seemed to have struck a somewhat rocky patch, and I must admit that I found myself, at moment of going to press, a little destitute of constructive ideas.

Confident, however, that these would come ere long, I kept the stiff upper lip.

"Bad," I conceded. "Quite bad, beyond a doubt. Certainly a nasty jar for one and all. But have no fear, Aunt Dahlia, I will fix everything."

I have alluded earlier to the difficulty of staggering when you're sitting down, showing that it is a feat of which I, personally, am not capable. Aunt Dahlia, to my amazement, now did it apparently without an effort. She was well wedged into a deep arm-chair, but, nevertheless, she staggered like billy-o. A sort of spasm of horror and apprehension contorted her face.

"If you dare to try any more of your lunatic schemes———"

I saw that it would be fruitless to try to reason with her. Quite plainly, she was not in the vein. Contenting myself, accordingly, with a gesture of loving sympathy, I left the room.

Whether she did or did not throw a handsomely bound volume of the Works of Alfred, Lord Tennyson, at me, I am not in a position to say. I had seen it lying on the table beside her, and as I closed the door I remember receiving the impression that some blunt instrument had crashed against the woodwork, but I was feeling too pre-occupied to note and observe.

I blame myself for not having taken into consideration the possible effects of a sudden abstinence on the part of virtually the whole strength of the company on one of Anatole's impulsive Provençal temperament. These Gauls, I should have remembered, can't take it. Their tendency to fly off the handle at the slightest provocation is well known. No doubt the man had put his whole soul into those nonnettes de poulet, and to see them come homing back to him must have gashed him like a knife.

However, spilt milk blows nobody any good, and it is useless to dwell upon it. The task now confronting Bertram was to put matters right, and I was pacing the lawn, pondering to this end, when I suddenly heard a groan so lost-soulish that I thought it must have proceeded from Uncle Tom, escaped from captivity and come to groan in the garden.

Looking about me, however, I could discern no uncles. Puzzled, I was about to resume my meditations, when the sound came again. And peering into the shadows I observed a dim form seated on one of the rustic benches which so liberally dotted this pleasance and another dim form standing beside same. A second and more penetrating glance and I had assembled the facts.

These dim forms were, in the order named, Gussie Fink-Nottle and Jeeves. And what Gussie was doing, groaning all over the place like this, was more than I could understand.

Because, I mean to say, there was no possibility of error. He wasn't singing. As I approached, he gave an encore, and it was beyond question a groan. Moreover, I could now see him clearly, and his whole aspect was definitely sand-bagged.

"Good evening, sir," said Jeeves. "Mr. Fink-Nottle is not feeling well."

Nor was I. Gussie had begun to make a low, bubbling noise, and I could no longer disguise it from myself that something must have gone seriously wrong with the works. I mean, I know marriage is a pretty solemn business and the realization that he is in for it frequently churns a chap up a bit, but I had never come across a case of a newly-engaged man taking it on the chin so completely as this.

Gussie looked up. His eye was dull. He clutched the thatch.

"Goodbye, Bertie," he said, rising.

I seemed to spot an error.

"You mean 'Hullo,' don't you?"

"No, I don't. I mean goodbye. I'm off."

"Off where?"

"To the kitchen garden. To drown myself."

"Don't be an ass."

"I'm not an ass.... Am I an ass, Jeeves?"

"Possibly a little injudicious, sir."

"Drowning myself, you mean?"

"Yes, sir."

"You think, on the whole, not drown myself?"

"I should not advocate it, sir."

"Very well, Jeeves. I accept your ruling. After all, it would be unpleasant for Mrs. Travers to find a swollen body floating in her pond."

"Yes, sir."

"And she has been very kind to me."

"Yes, sir."

"And you have been very kind to me, Jeeves."

"Thank you, sir."

"So have you, Bertie. Very kind. Everybody has been very kind to me. Very, very kind. Very kind indeed. I have no complaints to make. All right, I'll go for a walk instead."

I followed him with bulging eyes as he tottered off into the dark.

"Jeeves," I said, and I am free to admit that in my emotion I bleated like a lamb drawing itself to the attention of the parent sheep, "what the dickens is all this?"

"Mr. Fink-Nottle is not quite himself, sir. He has passed through a trying experience."

I endeavoured to put together a brief synopsis of previous events.

"I left him out here with Miss Bassett."

"Yes, sir."

"I had softened her up."

"Yes, sir."

"He knew exactly what he had to do. I had coached him thoroughly in lines and business."

"Yes, sir. So Mr. Fink-Nottle informed me."

"Well, then——"

"I regret to say, sir, that there was a slight hitch."

"You mean, something went wrong?"

"Yes, sir."

I could not fathom. The brain seemed to be tottering on its throne.

"But how could anything go wrong? She loves him, Jeeves."

"Indeed, sir?"

"She definitely told me so. All he had to do was propose."

"Yes sir."

"Well, didn't he?"

"No, sir."

"Then what the dickens did he talk about?"

"Newts, sir."

"Newts?"

"Yes, sir."

"Newts?"

"Yes, sir."

"But why did he want to talk about newts?"

"He did not want to talk about newts, sir. As I gather from Mr. Fink-Nottle, nothing could have been more alien to his plans."

I simply couldn't grasp the trend.

"But you can't force a man to talk about newts."

"Mr. Fink-Nottle was the victim of a sudden unfortunate spasm of nervousness, sir. Upon finding himself alone with the young lady, he admits to having lost his morale. In such circumstances, gentlemen frequently talk at random, saying the first thing that chances to enter their heads. This, in Mr. Fink-Nottle's case, would seem to have been the newt, its treatment in sickness and in health."

The scales fell from my eyes. I understood. I had had the same sort of thing happen to me in moments of crisis. I remember once detaining a dentist with the drill at one of my lower bicuspids and holding him up for nearly ten minutes with a story about a Scotchman, an Irishman, and a Jew. Purely automatic. The more he tried to jab, the more I said "Hoots, mon," "Begorrah," and "Oy, oy". When one loses one's nerve, one simply babbles.

I could put myself in Gussie's place. I could envisage the scene. There he and the Bassett were, alone together in the evening stillness. No doubt, as I had advised, he had shot the works about sunsets and fairy princesses, and so forth, and then had arrived at the point where he had to say that bit about having something to say to her. At this, I take it, she lowered her eyes and said, "Oh, yes?"

He then, I should imagine, said it was something very important; to which her response would, one assumes, have been something on the lines of "Really?" or "Indeed?" or possibly just the sharp intake of the breath. And then their eyes met, just as mine met the dentist's, and something suddenly seemed to catch him in the pit of the stomach and everything went black and he heard his voice starting to drool about newts. Yes, I could follow the psychology.

Nevertheless, I found myself blaming Gussie. On discovering that he was stressing the newt note in this manner, he ought, of course, to have tuned out, even if it had meant sitting there saying nothing. No matter how much of a twitter he was in, he should have had sense enough to see that he was throwing a spanner into the works. No girl, when she has been led to expect that a man is about to pour forth his soul in a fervour of passion, likes to find him suddenly shelving the whole topic in favour of an address on aquatic Salamandridae.

"Bad, Jeeves."

"Yes, sir."

"And how long did this nuisance continue?"

"For some not inconsiderable time, I gather, sir. According to Mr. Fink-Nottle, he supplied Miss Bassett with very full and complete information not only with respect to the common newt, but also the crested and palmated varieties. He described to her how newts, during the breeding season, live in the water, subsisting upon tadpoles, insect larvae, and crustaceans; how, later, they make their way to the land and eat slugs and worms; and how the newly born newt has three pairs of long, plumlike, external gills. And he was just observing that newts differ from salamanders in the shape of the tail, which is compressed, and that a marked sexual dimorphism prevails in most species, when the young lady rose and said that she thought she would go back to the house."

"And then——"

"She went, sir."

I stood musing. More and more, it was beginning to be borne in upon me what a particularly difficult chap Gussie was to help. He seemed to so marked an extent to lack snap and finish. With infinite toil, you manoeuvred him into a position where all he had to do was charge ahead, and he didn't charge ahead, but went off sideways, missing the objective completely.

"Difficult, Jeeves."

"Yes, sir."

In happier circs., of course, I would have canvassed his views on the matter. But after what had occurred in connection with that mess-jacket, my lips were sealed.

"Well, I must think it over."

"Yes, sir."

"Burnish the brain a bit and endeavour to find the way out."

"Yes, sir."

"Well, good night, Jeeves."

"Good night, sir."

He shimmered off, leaving a pensive Bertram Wooster standing motionless in the shadows. It seemed to me that it was hard to know what to do for the best.

-12-

I don't know if it has happened to you at all, but a thing I've noticed with myself is that, when I'm confronted by a problem which seems for the moment to stump and baffle, a good sleep will often bring the solution in the morning.

It was so on the present occasion.

The nibs who study these matters claim, I believe, that this has got something to do with the subconscious mind, and very possibly they may be right. I wouldn't have said off-hand that I had a subconscious mind, but I suppose I must without knowing it, and no doubt it was there, sweating away diligently at the old stand, all the while the corporeal Wooster was getting his eight hours.

For directly I opened my eyes on the morrow, I saw daylight. Well, I don't mean that exactly, because naturally I did. What I mean is that I found I had the thing all mapped out. The good old subconscious m. had delivered the goods, and I perceived exactly what steps must be taken in order to put Augustus Fink-Nottle among the practising Romeos.

I should like you, if you can spare me a moment of your valuable time, to throw your mind back to that conversation he and I had had in the garden on the previous evening. Not the glimmering landscape bit, I don't mean that, but the concluding passages of it. Having done so, you will recall that when he informed me that he never touched alcoholic liquor, I shook the head a bit, feeling that this must inevitably weaken him as a force where proposing to girls was concerned.

And events had shown that my fears were well founded.

Put to the test, with nothing but orange juice inside him, he had proved a complete bust. In a situation calling for words of molten passion of a nature calculated to go through Madeline Bassett like a red-hot gimlet through half a pound of butter, he had said not a syllable that could bring a blush to the cheek of modesty, merely delivering a well-phrased but, in the circumstances, quite misplaced lecture on newts.

A romantic girl is not to be won by such tactics. Obviously, before attempting to proceed further, Augustus Fink-Nottle must be induced to throw off the shackling inhibitions of the past and fuel up. It must be a primed, confident Fink-Nottle who squared up to the Bassett for Round No. 2.

Only so could the Morning Post make its ten bob, or whatever it is, for printing the announcement of the forthcoming nuptials.

Having arrived at this conclusion I found the rest easy, and by the time Jeeves brought me my tea I had evolved a plan complete in every detail. This I was about to place before him—indeed, I had got as far as the preliminary "I say, Jeeves"—when we were interrupted by the arrival of Tuppy.

He came listlessly into the room, and I was pained to observe that a night's rest had effected no improvement in the unhappy wreck's appearance. Indeed, I should have said, if anything, that he was looking rather more moth-eaten than when I had seen him last. If you can visualize a bulldog which has just been kicked in the ribs and had its dinner sneaked by the cat, you will have Hildebrand Glossop as he now stood before me.

"Stap my vitals, Tuppy, old corpse," I said, concerned, "you're looking pretty blue round the rims."

Jeeves slid from the presence in that tactful, eel-like way of his, and I motioned the remains to take a seat.

"What's the matter?" I said.

He came to anchor on the bed, and for awhile sat picking at the coverlet in silence.

"I've been through hell, Bertie."

"Through where?"

"Hell."

"Oh, hell? And what took you there?"

Once more he became silent, staring before him with sombre eyes. Following his gaze, I saw that he was looking at an enlarged photograph of my Uncle Tom in some sort of Masonic uniform which stood on the mantelpiece. I've tried to reason with Aunt Dahlia about this photograph for years, placing before her two alternative suggestions: (a) To burn the beastly thing; or (b) if she must preserve it, to shove me in another room when I come to stay. But she declines to accede. She says it's good for me. A useful discipline, she maintains, teaching me that there is a darker side to life and that we were not put into this world for pleasure only.

"Turn it to the wall, if it hurts you, Tuppy," I said gently.

"Eh?"

"That photograph of Uncle Tom as the bandmaster."

"I didn't come here to talk about photographs. I came for sympathy."

"And you shall have it. What's the trouble? Worrying about Angela, I suppose? Well, have no fear. I have another well-laid plan for encompassing that young shrimp. I'll guarantee that she will be weeping on your neck before yonder sun has set."

He barked sharply.

"A fat chance!"

"Tup, Tushy!"

"Eh?"

"I mean 'Tush, Tuppy.' I tell you I will do it. I was just going to describe this plan of mine to Jeeves when you came in. Care to hear it?"

"I don't want to hear any of your beastly plans. Plans are no good. She's gone and fallen in love with this other bloke, and now hates my gizzard."

"Rot."

"It isn't rot."

"I tell you, Tuppy, as one who can read the female heart, that this Angela loves you still."

"Well, it didn't look much like it in the larder last night."

"Oh, you went to the larder last night?"

"I did."

"And Angela was there?"

"She was. And your aunt. Also your uncle."

I saw that I should require foot-notes. All this was new stuff to me. I had stayed at Brinkley Court quite a lot in my time, but I had no idea the larder was such a social vortex. More like a snack bar on a race-course than anything else, it seemed to have become.

"Tell me the whole story in your own words," I said, "omitting no detail, however apparently slight, for one never knows how important the most trivial detail may be."

He inspected the photograph for a moment with growing gloom.

"All right," he said. "This is what happened. You know my views about that steak-and-kidney pie."

"Quite."

"Well, round about one a.m. I thought the time was ripe. I stole from my room and went downstairs. The pie seemed to beckon me."

I nodded. I knew how pies do.

"I got to the larder. I fished it out. I set it on the table. I found knife and fork. I collected salt, mustard, and pepper. There were some cold potatoes. I added those. And I was about to pitch in when I heard a sound behind me, and there was your aunt at the door. In a blue-and-yellow dressing gown."

"Embarrassing."

"Most."

"I suppose you didn't know where to look."

"I looked at Angela."

"She came in with my aunt?"

"No. With your uncle, a minute or two later. He was wearing mauve pyjamas and carried a pistol. Have you ever seen your uncle in pyjamas and a pistol?"

"Never."

"You haven't missed much."

"Tell me, Tuppy," I asked, for I was anxious to ascertain this, "about Angela. Was there any momentary softening in her gaze as she fixed it on you?"

"She didn't fix it on me. She fixed it on the pie."

"Did she say anything?"

"Not right away. Your uncle was the first to speak. He said to your aunt, 'God bless my soul, Dahlia, what are you doing here?' To which she replied, 'Well, if it comes to that, my merry somnambulist, what are you?' Your uncle then said that he thought there must be burglars in the house, as he had heard noises."

I nodded again. I could follow the trend. Ever since the scullery window was found open the year Shining Light was disqualified in the Cesarewitch for boring, Uncle Tom has had a marked complex about burglars. I can still recall my emotions when, paying my first visit after he had bars put on all the windows and attempting to thrust the head out in order to get a sniff of country air, I nearly fractured my skull on a sort of iron grille, as worn by the tougher kinds of mediaeval prison.

"'What sort of noises?' said your aunt. 'Funny noises,' said your uncle. Whereupon Angela—with a nasty, steely tinkle in her voice, the little buzzard—observed, 'I expect it was Mr. Glossop eating.' And then she did give me a look. It was the sort of wondering, revolted look a very spiritual woman would give a fat man gulping soup in a restaurant. The kind of look that makes a fellow feel he's forty-six round the waist and has great rolls of superfluous flesh pouring down over the back of his collar. And, still speaking in the same unpleasant tone, she added, 'I ought to have told you, father, that Mr. Glossop always likes to have a good meal three or four times during the night. It helps to keep him going till breakfast. He has the most amazing appetite. See, he has practically finished a large steak-and-kidney pie already'."

As he spoke these words, a feverish animation swept over Tuppy. His eyes glittered with a strange light, and he thumped the bed violently with his fist, nearly catching me a juicy one on the leg.

"That was what hurt, Bertie. That was what stung. I hadn't so much as started on that pie. But that's a woman all over."

"The eternal feminine."

"She continued her remarks. 'You've no idea,' she said, 'how Mr. Glossop loves food. He just lives for it. He always eats six or seven meals a day, and then starts in again after bedtime. I think it's rather wonderful.' Your aunt seemed interested, and said it reminded her of a boa constrictor. Angela said, didn't she mean a python? And then they argued as to which of the two it was. Your uncle, meanwhile, poking about with that damned pistol of his till human life wasn't safe in the vicinity. And the pie lying there on the table, and me unable to touch it. You begin to understand why I said I had been through hell."

"Quite. Can't have been at all pleasant."

"Presently your aunt and Angela settled their discussion, deciding that Angela was right and that it was a python that I reminded them of. And shortly after that we all pushed back to bed, Angela warning me in a motherly voice not to take the stairs too quickly. After seven or eight solid meals, she said, a man of my build ought to be very careful, because of the danger of apoplectic fits. She said it was the same with dogs. When they became very fat and overfed, you had to see that they didn't hurry upstairs, as it made them puff and pant, and that was bad for their hearts. She asked your aunt if she remembered the late spaniel, Ambrose; and your aunt said, 'Poor old Ambrose, you couldn't keep him away from the garbage pail'; and Angela said, 'Exactly, so do please be careful, Mr. Glossop.' And you tell me she loves me still!"

I did my best to encourage.

"Girlish banter, what?"

"Girlish banter be dashed. She's right off me. Once her ideal, I am now less than the dust beneath her chariot wheels. She became infatuated with this chap, whoever he was, at Cannes, and now she can't stand the sight of me."

I raised my eyebrows.

"My dear Tuppy, you are not showing your usual good sense in this Angela-chap-at-Cannes matter. If you will forgive me saying so, you have got an idée fixe."

"A what?"

"An idée fixe. You know. One of those things fellows get. Like Uncle Tom's delusion that everybody who is known even slightly to the police is lurking in the garden, waiting for a chance to break into the house. You keep talking about this chap at Cannes, and there never was a chap at Cannes, and I'll tell you why I'm so sure about this. During those two months on the Riviera, it so happens that Angela and I were practically inseparable. If there had been somebody nosing round her, I should have spotted it in a second."

He started. I could see that this had impressed him.

"Oh, she was with you all the time at Cannes, was she?"

"I don't suppose she said two words to anybody else, except, of course, idle conv. at the crowded dinner table or a chance remark in a throng at the Casino."

"I see. You mean that anything in the shape of mixed bathing and moonlight strolls she conducted solely in your company?"

"That's right. It was quite a joke in the hotel."

"You must have enjoyed that."

"Oh, rather. I've always been devoted to Angela."

"Oh, yes?"

"When we were kids, she used to call herself my little sweetheart."

"She did?"

"Absolutely."

"I see."

He sat plunged in thought, while I, glad to have set his mind at rest, proceeded with my tea. And presently there came the banging of a gong from the hall below, and he started like a war horse at the sound of the bugle.

"Breakfast!" he said, and was off to a flying start, leaving me to brood and ponder. And the more I brooded and pondered, the more did it seem to me that everything now looked pretty smooth. Tuppy, I could see, despite that painful scene in the larder, still loved Angela with all the old fervour.

This meant that I could rely on that plan to which I had referred to bring home the bacon. And as I had found the way to straighten out the Gussie-Bassett difficulty, there seemed nothing more to worry about.

It was with an uplifted heart that I addressed Jeeves as he came in to remove the tea tray.

-13-

"Jeeves," I said.

"Sir?"

"I've just been having a chat with young Tuppy, Jeeves. Did you happen to notice that he wasn't looking very roguish this morning?"

"Yes, sir. It seemed to me that Mr. Glossop's face was sicklied o'er with the pale cast of thought."

"Quite. He met my cousin Angela in the larder last night, and a rather painful interview ensued."

"I am sorry, sir."

"Not half so sorry as he was. She found him closeted with a steak-and-kidney pie, and appears to have been a bit caustic about fat men who lived for food alone."

"Most disturbing, sir."

"Very. In fact, many people would say that things had gone so far between these two nothing now could bridge the chasm. A girl who could make cracks about human pythons who ate nine or ten meals a day and ought to be careful not to hurry upstairs because of the danger of apoplectic fits is a girl, many people would say, in whose heart love is dead. Wouldn't people say that, Jeeves?"

"Undeniably, sir."

"They would be wrong."

"You think so, sir?"

"I am convinced of it. I know these females. You can't go by what they say."

"You feel that Miss Angela's strictures should not be taken too much au pied de la lettre, sir?"

"Eh?"

"In English, we should say 'literally'."

"Literally. That's exactly what I mean. You know what girls are. A tiff occurs, and they shoot their heads off. But underneath it all the old love still remains. Am I correct?"

"Quite correct, sir. The poet Scott——"

"Right ho, Jeeves."

"Very good, sir."

"And in order to bring that old love whizzing to the surface once more, all that is required is the proper treatment."

"By 'proper treatment,' sir, you mean——"

"Clever handling, Jeeves. A spot of the good old snaky work. I see what must be done to jerk my Cousin Angela back to normalcy. I'll tell you, shall I?"

"If you would be so kind, sir."

I lit a cigarette, and eyed him keenly through the smoke. He waited respectfully for me to unleash the words of wisdom. I must say for Jeeves that—till, as he is so apt to do, he starts shoving his oar in and cavilling and obstructing—he makes a very good audience. I don't know if he is actually agog, but he looks agog, and that's the great thing.

"Suppose you were strolling through the illimitable jungle, Jeeves, and happened to meet a tiger cub."

"The contingency is a remote one, sir."

"Never mind. Let us suppose it."

"Very good, sir."

"Let us now suppose that you sloshed that tiger cub, and let us suppose further that word reached its mother that it was being put upon. What would you expect the attitude of that mother to be? In what frame of mind do you consider that that tigress would approach you?"

"I should anticipate a certain show of annoyance, sir."

"And rightly. Due to what is known as the maternal instinct, what?"

"Yes, sir."

"Very good, Jeeves. We will now suppose that there has recently been some little coolness between this tiger cub and this tigress. For some days, let us say, they have not been on speaking terms. Do you think that that would make any difference to the vim with which the latter would leap to the former's aid?"

"No, sir."

"Exactly. Here, then, in brief, is my plan, Jeeves. I am going to draw my Cousin Angela aside to a secluded spot and roast Tuppy properly."

"Roast, sir?"

"Knock. Slam. Tick-off. Abuse. Denounce. I shall be very terse about Tuppy, giving it as my opinion that in all essentials he is more like a wart hog than an ex-member of a fine old English public school. What will ensue? Hearing him attacked, my Cousin Angela's womanly heart will be as sick as mud. The maternal tigress in her will awake. No matter what differences they may have had, she will remember only that he is the man she loves, and will leap to his defence. And from that to falling into his arms and burying the dead past will be but a step. How do you react to that?"

"The idea is an ingenious one, sir."

"We Woosters are ingenious, Jeeves, exceedingly ingenious."

"Yes, sir."

"As a matter of fact, I am not speaking without a knowledge of the form book. I have tested this theory."

"Indeed, sir?"

"Yes, in person. And it works. I was standing on the Eden rock at Antibes last month, idly watching the bathers disport themselves in the water, and a girl I knew slightly pointed at a male diver and asked me if I didn't think his legs were about the silliest-looking pair of props ever issued to human being. I replied that I did, indeed, and for the space of perhaps two minutes was extraordinarily witty and satirical about this bird's underpinning. At the end of that period, I suddenly felt as if I had been caught up in the tail of a cyclone.

"Beginning with a critique of my own limbs, which she said, justly enough, were nothing to write home about, this girl went on to dissect my manners, morals, intellect, general physique, and method of eating asparagus with such acerbity that by the time she had finished the best you could say of Bertram was that, so far as was known, he had never actually committed murder or set fire to an orphan asylum. Subsequent investigation proved that she was engaged to the fellow with the legs and had had a slight disagreement with him the evening before on the subject of whether she should or should not have made an original call of two spades, having seven, but without the ace. That night I saw them dining together with every indication of relish, their differences made up and the lovelight once more in their eyes. That shows you, Jeeves."

"Yes, sir."

"I expect precisely similar results from my Cousin Angela when I start roasting Tuppy. By lunchtime, I should imagine, the engagement will be on again and the diamond-and-platinum ring glittering as of yore on her third finger. Or is it the fourth?"

"Scarcely by luncheon time, sir. Miss Angela's maid informs me that Miss Angela drove off in her car early this morning with the intention of spending the day with friends in the vicinity."

"Well, within half an hour of whatever time she comes back, then. These are mere straws, Jeeves. Do not let us chop them."

"No, sir."

"The point is that, as far as Tuppy and Angela are concerned, we may say with confidence that everything will shortly be hotsy-totsy once more. And what an agreeable thought that is, Jeeves."

"Very true, sir."

"If there is one thing that gives me the pip, it is two loving hearts being estranged."

"I can readily appreciate the fact, sir."

I placed the stub of my gasper in the ash tray and lit another, to indicate that that completed Chap. I.

"Right ho, then. So much for the western front. We now turn to the eastern."

"Sir?"

"I speak in parables, Jeeves. What I mean is, we now approach the matter of Gussie and Miss Bassett."

"Yes, sir."

"Here, Jeeves, more direct methods are required. In handling the case of Augustus Fink-Nottle, we must keep always in mind the fact that we are dealing with a poop."

"A sensitive plant would, perhaps, be a kinder expression, sir."

"No, Jeeves, a poop. And with poops one has to employ the strong, forceful, straightforward policy. Psychology doesn't get you anywhere. You, if I may remind you without wounding your feelings, fell into the error of mucking about with psychology in connection with this Fink-Nottle, and the result was a wash-out. You attempted to push him over the line by rigging him out in a Mephistopheles costume and sending him off to a fancy-dress ball, your view being that scarlet tights would embolden him. Futile."

"The matter was never actually put to the test, sir."

"No. Because he didn't get to the ball. And that strengthens my argument. A man who can set out in a cab for a fancy-dress ball and not get there is manifestly a poop of no common order. I don't think I have ever known anybody else who was such a dashed silly ass that he couldn't even get to a fancy-dress ball. Have you, Jeeves?"

"No, sir."

"But don't forget this, because it is the point I wish, above all, to make: Even if Gussie had got to that ball; even if those scarlet tights, taken in conjunction with his horn-rimmed spectacles, hadn't given the girl a fit of some kind; even if she had rallied from the shock and he had been able to dance and generally hobnob with her; even then your efforts would have been fruitless, because, Mephistopheles costume or no Mephistopheles costume, Augustus Fink-Nottle would never have been able to summon up the courage to ask her to be his. All that would have resulted would have been that she would have got that lecture on newts a few days earlier. And why, Jeeves? Shall I tell you why?"

"Yes, sir."

"Because he would have been attempting the hopeless task of trying to do the thing on orange juice."

"Sir?"

"Gussie is an orange-juice addict. He drinks nothing else."

"I was not aware of that, sir."

"I have it from his own lips. Whether from some hereditary taint, or because he promised his mother he wouldn't, or simply because he doesn't like the taste of the stuff, Gussie Fink-Nottle has never in the whole course of his career pushed so much as the simplest gin and tonic over the larynx. And he expects—this poop expects, Jeeves—this wabbling, shrinking, diffident rabbit in human shape expects under these conditions to propose to the girl he loves. One hardly knows whether to smile or weep, what?"

"You consider total abstinence a handicap to a gentleman who wishes to make a proposal of marriage, sir?"

The question amazed me.

"Why, dash it," I said, astounded, "you must know it is. Use your intelligence, Jeeves. Reflect what proposing means. It means that a decent, self-respecting chap has got to listen to himself saying things which, if spoken on the silver screen, would cause him to dash to the box-office and demand his money back. Let him attempt to do it on orange juice, and what ensues? Shame seals his lips, or, if it doesn't do that, makes him lose his morale and start to babble. Gussie, for example, as we have seen, babbles of syncopated newts."

"Palmated newts, sir."

"Palmated or syncopated, it doesn't matter which. The point is that he babbles and is going to babble again, if he has another try at it. Unless—and this is where I want you to follow me very closely, Jeeves—unless steps are taken at once through the proper channels. Only active measures, promptly applied, can provide this poor, pusillanimous poop with the proper pep. And that is why, Jeeves, I intend tomorrow to secure a bottle of gin and lace his luncheon orange juice with it liberally."

"Sir?"

I clicked the tongue.

"I have already had occasion, Jeeves," I said rebukingly, "to comment on the way you say 'Well, sir' and 'Indeed, sir?' I take this opportunity of informing you that I object equally strongly to your 'Sir?' pure and simple. The word seems to suggest that in your opinion I have made a statement or mooted a scheme so bizarre that your brain reels at it. In the present instance, there is absolutely nothing to say 'Sir?' about. The plan I have put forward is entirely reasonable and icily logical, and should excite no sirring whatsoever. Or don't you think so?"

"Well, sir——"

"Jeeves!"

"I beg your pardon, sir. The expression escaped me inadvertently. What I intended to say, since you press me, was that the action which you propose does seem to me somewhat injudicious."

"Injudicious? I don't follow you, Jeeves."

"A certain amount of risk would enter into it, in my opinion, sir. It is not always a simple matter to gauge the effect of alcohol on a subject unaccustomed to such stimulant. I have known it to have distressing results in the case of parrots."

"Parrots?"

"I was thinking of an incident of my earlier life, sir, before I entered your employment. I was in the service of the late Lord Brancaster at the time, a gentleman who owned a parrot to which he was greatly devoted, and one day the bird chanced to be lethargic, and his lordship, with the kindly intention of restoring it to its customary animation, offered it a portion of seed cake steeped in the '84 port. The bird accepted the morsel gratefully and consumed it with every indication of satisfaction. Almost immediately afterwards, however, its manner became markedly feverish. Having bitten his lordship in the thumb and sung part of a sea-chanty, it fell to the bottom of the cage and remained there for a considerable period of time with its legs in the air, unable to move. I merely mention this, sir, in order to——"

I put my finger on the flaw. I had spotted it all along.

"But Gussie isn't a parrot."

"No, sir, but——"

"It is high time, in my opinion, that this question of what young Gussie really is was threshed out and cleared up. He seems to think he is a male newt, and you now appear to suggest that he is a parrot. The truth of the matter being that he is just a plain, ordinary poop and needs a snootful as badly as ever man did. So no more discussion, Jeeves. My mind is made up. There is only one way of handling this difficult case, and that is the way I have outlined."

"Very good, sir."

"Right ho, Jeeves. So much for that, then. Now here's something else: You noticed that I said I was going to put this project through tomorrow, and no doubt you wondered why I said tomorrow. Why did I, Jeeves?"

"Because you feel that if it were done when 'tis done, then 'twere well it were done quickly, sir?"

"Partly, Jeeves, but not altogether. My chief reason for fixing the date as specified is that tomorrow, though you have doubtless forgotten, is the day of the distribution of prizes at Market Snodsbury Grammar School, at which, as you know, Gussie is to be the male star and master of the revels. So you see we shall, by lacing that juice, not only embolden him to propose to Miss Bassett, but also put him so into shape that he will hold that Market Snodsbury audience spellbound."

"In fact, you will be killing two birds with one stone, sir."

"Exactly. A very neat way of putting it. And now here is a minor point. On second thoughts, I think the best plan will be for you, not me, to lace the juice."

"Sir?"

"Jeeves!"

"I beg your pardon, sir."

"And I'll tell you why that will be the best plan. Because you are in a position to obtain ready access to the stuff. It is served to Gussie daily, I have noticed, in an individual jug. This jug will presumably be lying about the kitchen or somewhere before lunch tomorrow. It will be the simplest of tasks for you to slip a few fingers of gin in it."

"No doubt, sir, but——"

"Don't say 'but,' Jeeves."

"I fear, sir——"

"'I fear, sir' is just as bad."

"What I am endeavouring to say, sir, is that I am sorry, but I am afraid I must enter an unequivocal nolle prosequi."

"Do what?"

"The expression is a legal one, sir, signifying the resolve not to proceed with a matter. In other words, eager though I am to carry out your instructions, sir, as a general rule, on this occasion I must respectfully decline to co-operate."

"You won't do it, you mean?"

"Precisely, sir."

I was stunned. I began to understand how a general must feel when he has ordered a regiment to charge and has been told that it isn't in the mood.

"Jeeves," I said, "I had not expected this of you."

"No, sir?"

"No, indeed. Naturally, I realize that lacing Gussie's orange juice is not one of those regular duties for which you receive the monthly stipend, and if you care to stand on the strict letter of the contract, I suppose there is nothing to be done about it. But you will permit me to observe that this is scarcely the feudal spirit."

"I am sorry, sir."

"It is quite all right, Jeeves, quite all right. I am not angry, only a little hurt."

"Very good, sir."

"Right ho, Jeeves."

-14-

Investigation proved that the friends Angela had gone to spend the day with were some stately-home owners of the name of Stretchley-Budd, hanging out in a joint called Kingham Manor, about eight miles distant in the direction of Pershore. I didn't know these birds, but their fascination must have been considerable, for she tore herself away from them only just in time to get back and dress for dinner. It was, accordingly, not until coffee had been consumed that I was able to get matters moving. I found her in the drawing-room and at once proceeded to put things in train.

It was with very different feelings from those which had animated the bosom when approaching the Bassett twenty-four hours before in the same manner in this same drawing-room that I headed for where she sat. As I had told Tuppy, I have always been devoted to Angela, and there is nothing I like better than a ramble in her company.

And I could see by the look of her now how sorely in need she was of my aid and comfort.

Frankly, I was shocked by the unfortunate young prune's appearance. At Cannes she had been a happy, smiling English girl of the best type, full of beans and buck. Her face now was pale and drawn, like that of a hockey centre-forward at a girls' school who, in addition to getting a fruity one on the shin, has just been penalized for "sticks". In any normal gathering, her demeanour would have excited instant remark, but the standard of gloom at Brinkley Court had become so high that it passed unnoticed. Indeed, I shouldn't wonder if Uncle Tom, crouched in his corner waiting for the end, didn't think she was looking indecently cheerful.

I got down to the agenda in my debonair way.

"What ho, Angela, old girl."

"Hullo, Bertie, darling."

"Glad you're back at last. I missed you."

"Did you, darling?"

"I did, indeed. Care to come for a saunter?"

"I'd love it."

"Fine. I have much to say to you that is not for the public ear."

I think at this moment poor old Tuppy must have got a sudden touch of cramp. He had been sitting hard by, staring at the ceiling, and he now gave a sharp leap like a gaffed salmon and upset a small table containing a vase, a bowl of potpourri, two china dogs, and a copy of Omar Khayyám bound in limp leather.

Aunt Dahlia uttered a startled hunting cry. Uncle Tom, who probably imagined from the noise that this was civilization crashing at last, helped things along by breaking a coffee-cup.

Tuppy said he was sorry. Aunt Dahlia, with a deathbed groan, said it didn't matter. And Angela, having stared haughtily for a moment like a princess of the old régime confronted by some notable example of gaucherie on the part of some particularly foul member of the underworld, accompanied me across the threshold. And presently I had deposited her and self on one of the rustic benches in the garden, and was ready to snap into the business of the evening.

I considered it best, however, before doing so, to ease things along with a little informal chitchat. You don't want to rush a delicate job like the one I had in hand. And so for a while we spoke of neutral topics. She said that what had kept her so long at the Stretchley-Budds was that Hilda Stretchley-Budd had made her stop on and help with the arrangements for their servants' ball tomorrow night, a task which she couldn't very well decline, as all the Brinkley Court domestic staff were to be present. I said that a jolly night's revelry might be just what was needed to cheer Anatole up and take his mind off things. To which she replied that Anatole wasn't going. On being urged to do so by Aunt Dahlia, she said, he had merely shaken his head sadly and gone on talking of returning to Provence, where he was appreciated.

It was after the sombre silence induced by this statement that Angela said the grass was wet and she thought she would go in.

This, of course, was entirely foreign to my policy.

"No, don't do that. I haven't had a chance to talk to you since you arrived."

"I shall ruin my shoes."

"Put your feet up on my lap."

"All right. And you can tickle my ankles."

"Quite."

Matters were accordingly arranged on these lines, and for some minutes we continued chatting in desultory fashion. Then the conversation petered out. I made a few observations in re the scenic effects, featuring the twilight hush, the peeping stars, and the soft glimmer of the waters of the lake, and she said yes. Something rustled in the bushes in front of us, and I advanced the theory that it was possibly a weasel, and she said it might be. But it was plain that the girl was distraite, and I considered it best to waste no more time.

"Well, old thing," I said, "I've heard all about your little dust-up. So those wedding bells are not going to ring out, what?"

"No."

"Definitely over, is it?"

"Yes."

"Well, if you want my opinion, I think that's a bit of goose for you, Angela, old girl. I think you're extremely well out of it. It's a mystery to me how you stood this Glossop so long. Take him for all in all, he ranks very low down among the wines and spirits. A washout, I should describe him as. A frightful oik, and a mass of side to boot. I'd pity the girl who was linked for life to a bargee like Tuppy Glossop."

And I emitted a hard laugh—one of the sneering kind.

"I always thought you were such friends," said Angela.

I let go another hard one, with a bit more top spin on it than the first time:

"Friends? Absolutely not. One was civil, of course, when one met the fellow, but it would be absurd to say one was a friend of his. A club acquaintance, and a mere one at that. And then one was at school with the man."

"At Eton?"

"Good heavens, no. We wouldn't have a fellow like that at Eton. At a kid's school before I went there. A grubby little brute he was, I recollect. Covered with ink and mire generally, washing only on alternate Thursdays. In short, a notable outsider, shunned by all."

I paused. I was more than a bit perturbed. Apart from the agony of having to talk in this fashion of one who, except when he was looping back rings and causing me to plunge into swimming baths in correct evening costume, had always been a very dear and esteemed crony, I didn't seem to be getting anywhere. Business was not resulting. Staring into the bushes without a yip, she appeared to be bearing these slurs and innuendos of mine with an easy calm.

I had another pop at it:

"'Uncouth' about sums it up. I doubt if I've ever seen an uncouther kid than this Glossop. Ask anyone who knew him in those days to describe him in a word, and the word they will use is 'uncouth'. And he's just the same today. It's the old story. The boy is the father of the man."

She appeared not to have heard.

"The boy," I repeated, not wishing her to miss that one, "is the father of the man."

"What are you talking about?"

"I'm talking about this Glossop."

"I thought you said something about somebody's father."

"I said the boy was the father of the man."

"What boy?"

"The boy Glossop."

"He hasn't got a father."

"I never said he had. I said he was the father of the boy—or, rather, of the man."

"What man?"

I saw that the conversation had reached a point where, unless care was taken, we should be muddled.

"The point I am trying to make," I said, "is that the boy Glossop is the father of the man Glossop. In other words, each loathsome fault and blemish that led the boy Glossop to be frowned upon by his fellows is present in the man Glossop, and causes him—I am speaking now of the man Glossop—to be a hissing and a byword at places like the Drones, where a certain standard of decency is demanded from the inmates. Ask anyone at the Drones, and they will tell you that it was a black day for the dear old club when this chap Glossop somehow wriggled into the list of members. Here you will find a man who dislikes his face; there one who could stand his face if it wasn't for his habits. But the universal consensus of opinion is that the fellow is a bounder and a tick, and that the moment he showed signs of wanting to get into the place he should have been met with a firm nolle prosequi and heartily blackballed."

I had to pause again here, partly in order to take in a spot of breath, and partly to wrestle with the almost physical torture of saying these frightful things about poor old Tuppy.

"There are some chaps," I resumed, forcing myself once more to the nauseous task, "who, in spite of looking as if they had slept in their clothes, can get by quite nicely because they are amiable and suave. There are others who, for all that they excite adverse comment by being fat and uncouth, find themselves on the credit side of the ledger owing to their wit and sparkling humour. But this Glossop, I regret to say, falls into neither class. In addition to looking like one of those things that come out of hollow trees, he is universally admitted to be a dumb brick of the first water. No soul. No conversation. In short, any girl who, having been rash enough to get engaged to him, has managed at the eleventh hour to slide out is justly entitled to consider herself dashed lucky."

I paused once more, and cocked an eye at Angela to see how the treatment was taking. All the while I had been speaking, she had sat gazing silently into the bushes, but it seemed to me incredible that she should not now turn on me like a tigress, according to specifications. It beat me why she hadn't done it already. It seemed to me that a mere tithe of what I had said, if said to a tigress about a tiger of which she was fond, would have made her—the tigress, I mean—hit the ceiling.

And the next moment you could have knocked me down with a toothpick.

"Yes," she said, nodding thoughtfully, "you're quite right."

"Eh?"

"That's exactly what I've been thinking myself."

"What!"

"'Dumb brick.' It just describes him. One of the six silliest asses in England, I should think he must be."

I did not speak. I was endeavouring to adjust the faculties, which were in urgent need of a bit of first-aid treatment.

I mean to say, all this had come as a complete surprise. In formulating the well-laid plan which I had just been putting into effect, the one contingency I had not budgeted for was that she might adhere to the sentiments which I expressed. I had braced myself for a gush of stormy emotion. I was expecting the tearful ticking off, the girlish recriminations and all the rest of the bag of tricks along those lines.

But this cordial agreement with my remarks I had not foreseen, and it gave me what you might call pause for thought.

She proceeded to develop her theme, speaking in ringing, enthusiastic tones, as if she loved the topic. Jeeves could tell you the word I want. I think it's "ecstatic", unless that's the sort of rash you get on your face and have to use ointment for. But if that is the right word, then that's what her manner was as she ventilated the subject of poor old Tuppy. If you had been able to go simply by the sound of her voice, she might have been a court poet cutting loose about an Oriental monarch, or Gussie Fink-Nottle describing his last consignment of newts.

"It's so nice, Bertie, talking to somebody who really takes a sensible view about this man Glossop. Mother says he's a good chap, which is simply absurd. Anybody can see that he's absolutely impossible. He's conceited and opinionative and argues all the time, even when he knows perfectly well that he's talking through his hat, and he smokes too much and eats too much and drinks too much, and I don't like the colour of his hair. Not that he'll have any hair in a year or two, because he's pretty thin on the top already, and before he knows where he is he'll be as bald as an egg, and he's the last man who can afford to go bald. And I think it's simply disgusting, the way he gorges all the time. Do you know, I found him in the larder at one o'clock this morning, absolutely wallowing in a steak-and-kidney pie? There was hardly any of it left. And you remember what an enormous dinner he had. Quite disgusting, I call it. But I can't stop out here all night, talking about men who aren't worth wasting a word on and haven't even enough sense to tell sharks from flatfish. I'm going in."

And gathering about her slim shoulders the shawl which she had put on as a protection against the evening dew, she buzzed off, leaving me alone in the silent night.

Well, as a matter of fact, not absolutely alone, because a few moments later there was a sort of upheaval in the bushes in front of me, and Tuppy emerged.

I gave him the eye. The evening had begun to draw in a bit by now and the visibility, in consequence, was not so hot, but there still remained ample light to enable me to see him clearly. And what I saw convinced me that I should be a lot easier in my mind with a stout rustic bench between us. I rose, accordingly, modelling my style on that of a rocketing pheasant, and proceeded to deposit myself on the other side of the object named.

My prompt agility was not without its effect. He seemed somewhat taken aback. He came to a halt, and, for about the space of time required to allow a bead of persp. to trickle from the top of the brow to the tip of the nose, stood gazing at me in silence.

"So!" he said at length, and it came as a complete surprise to me that fellows ever really do say "So!" I had always thought it was just a thing you read in books. Like "Quotha!" I mean to say, or "Odds bodikins!" or even "Eh, ba goom!"

Still, there it was. Quaint or not quaint, bizarre or not bizarre, he had said "So!" and it was up to me to cope with the situation on those lines.

It would have been a duller man than Bertram Wooster who had failed to note that the dear old chap was a bit steamed up. Whether his eyes were actually shooting forth flame, I couldn't tell you, but there appeared to me to be a distinct incandescence. For the rest, his fists were clenched, his ears quivering, and the muscles of his jaw rotating rhythmically, as if he were making an early supper off something.

His hair was full of twigs, and there was a beetle hanging to the side of his head which would have interested Gussie Fink-Nottle. To this, however, I paid scant attention. There is a time for studying beetles and a time for not studying beetles.

"So!" he said again.

Now, those who know Bertram Wooster best will tell you that he is always at his shrewdest and most level-headed in moments of peril. Who was it who, when gripped by the arm of the law on boat-race night not so many years ago and hauled off to Vine Street police station, assumed in a flash the identity of Eustace H. Plimsoll, of The Laburnums, Alleyn Road, West Dulwich, thus saving the grand old name of Wooster from being dragged in the mire and avoiding wide publicity of the wrong sort? Who was it ...

But I need not labour the point. My record speaks for itself. Three times pinched, but never once sentenced under the correct label. Ask anyone at the Drones about this.

So now, in a situation threatening to become every moment more scaly, I did not lose my head. I preserved the old sang-froid. Smiling a genial and affectionate smile, and hoping that it wasn't too dark for it to register, I spoke with a jolly cordiality:

"Why, hallo, Tuppy. You here?"

He said, yes, he was here.

"Been here long?"

"I have."

"Fine. I wanted to see you."

"Well, here I am. Come out from behind that bench."

"No, thanks, old man. I like leaning on it. It seems to rest the spine."

"In about two seconds," said Tuppy, "I'm going to kick your spine up through the top of your head."

I raised the eyebrows. Not much good, of course, in that light, but it seemed to help the general composition.

"Is this Hildebrand Glossop speaking?" I said.

He replied that it was, adding that if I wanted to make sure I might move a few feet over in his direction. He also called me an opprobrious name.

I raised the eyebrows again.

"Come, come, Tuppy, don't let us let this little chat become acrid. Is 'acrid' the word I want?"

"I couldn't say," he replied, beginning to sidle round the bench.

I saw that anything I might wish to say must be said quickly. Already he had sidled some six feet. And though, by dint of sidling, too, I had managed to keep the bench between us, who could predict how long this happy state of affairs would last?

I came to the point, therefore.

"I think I know what's on your mind, Tuppy," I said. "If you were in those bushes during my conversation with the recent Angela, I dare say you heard what I was saying about you."

"I did."

"I see. Well, we won't go into the ethics of the thing. Eavesdropping, some people might call it, and I can imagine stern critics drawing in the breath to some extent. Considering it—I don't want to hurt your feelings, Tuppy—but considering it un-English. A bit un-English, Tuppy, old man, you must admit."

"I'm Scotch."

"Really?" I said. "I never knew that before. Rummy how you don't suspect a man of being Scotch unless he's Mac-something and says 'Och, aye' and things like that. I wonder," I went on, feeling that an academic discussion on some neutral topic might ease the tension, "if you can tell me something that has puzzled me a good deal. What exactly is it that they put into haggis? I've often wondered about that."

From the fact that his only response to the question was to leap over the bench and make a grab at me, I gathered that his mind was not on haggis.

"However," I said, leaping over the bench in my turn, "that is a side issue. If, to come back to it, you were in those bushes and heard what I was saying about you——"

He began to move round the bench in a nor'-nor'-easterly direction. I followed his example, setting a course sou'-sou'-west.

"No doubt you were surprised at the way I was talking."

"Not a bit."

"What? Did nothing strike you as odd in the tone of my remarks?"

"It was just the sort of stuff I should have expected a treacherous, sneaking hound like you to say."

"My dear chap," I protested, "this is not your usual form. A bit slow in the uptake, surely? I should have thought you would have spotted right away that it was all part of a well-laid plan."

"I'll get you in a jiffy," said Tuppy, recovering his balance after a swift clutch at my neck. And so probable did this seem that I delayed no longer, but hastened to place all the facts before him.

Speaking rapidly and keeping moving, I related my emotions on receipt of Aunt Dahlia's telegram, my instant rush to the scene of the disaster, my meditations in the car, and the eventual framing of this well-laid plan of mine. I spoke clearly and well, and it was with considerable concern, consequently, that I heard him observe—between clenched teeth, which made it worse—that he didn't believe a damned word of it.

"But, Tuppy," I said, "why not? To me the thing rings true to the last drop. What makes you sceptical? Confide in me, Tuppy."

He halted and stood taking a breather. Tuppy, pungently though Angela might have argued to the contrary, isn't really fat. During the winter months you will find him constantly booting the football with merry shouts, and in the summer the tennis racket is seldom out of his hand.

But at the recently concluded evening meal, feeling, no doubt, that after that painful scene in the larder there was nothing to be gained by further abstinence, he had rather let himself go and, as it were, made up leeway; and after really immersing himself in one of Anatole's dinners, a man of his sturdy build tends to lose elasticity a bit. During the exposition of my plans for his happiness a certain animation had crept into this round-and-round-the mulberry-bush jamboree of ours—so much so, indeed, that for the last few minutes we might have been a rather oversized greyhound and a somewhat slimmer electric hare doing their stuff on a circular track for the entertainment of the many-headed.

This, it appeared, had taken it out of him a bit, and I was not displeased. I was feeling the strain myself, and welcomed a lull.

"It absolutely beats me why you don't believe it," I said. "You know we've been pals for years. You must be aware that, except at the moment when you caused me to do a nose dive into the Drones' swimming bath, an incident which I long since decided to put out of my mind and let the dead past bury its dead about, if you follow what I mean—except on that one occasion, as I say, I have always regarded you with the utmost esteem. Why, then, if not for the motives I have outlined, should I knock you to Angela? Answer me that. Be very careful."

"What do you mean, be very careful?"

Well, as a matter of fact, I didn't quite know myself. It was what the magistrate had said to me on the occasion when I stood in the dock as Eustace Plimsoll, of The Laburnums: and as it had impressed me a good deal at the time, I just bunged it in now by way of giving the conversation a tone.

"All right. Never mind about being careful, then. Just answer me that question. Why, if I had not your interests sincerely at heart, should I have ticked you off, as stated?"

A sharp spasm shook him from base to apex. The beetle, which, during the recent exchanges, had been clinging to his head, hoping for the best, gave it up at this and resigned office. It shot off and was swallowed in the night.

"Ah!" I said. "Your beetle," I explained. "No doubt you were unaware of it, but all this while there has been a beetle of sorts parked on the side of your head. You have now dislodged it."

He snorted.

"Beetles!"

"Not beetles. One beetle only."

"I like your crust!" cried Tuppy, vibrating like one of Gussie's newts during the courting season. "Talking of beetles, when all the time you know you're a treacherous, sneaking hound."

It was a debatable point, of course, why treacherous, sneaking hounds should be considered ineligible to talk about beetles, and I dare say a good cross-examining counsel would have made quite a lot of it.

But I let it go.

"That's the second time you've called me that. And," I said firmly, "I insist on an explanation. I have told you that I acted throughout from the best and kindliest motives in roasting you to Angela. It cut me to the quick to have to speak like that, and only the recollection of our lifelong friendship would have made me do it. And now you say you don't believe me and call me names for which I am not sure I couldn't have you up before a beak and jury and mulct you in very substantial damages. I should have to consult my solicitor, of course, but it would surprise me very much if an action did not lie. Be reasonable, Tuppy. Suggest another motive I could have had. Just one."

"I will. Do you think I don't know? You're in love with Angela yourself."

"What?"

"And you knocked me in order to poison her mind against me and finally remove me from your path."

I had never heard anything so absolutely loopy in my life. Why, dash it, I've known Angela since she was so high. You don't fall in love with close relations you've known since they were so high. Besides, isn't there something in the book of rules about a man may not marry his cousin? Or am I thinking of grandmothers?

"Tuppy, my dear old ass," I cried, "this is pure banana oil! You've come unscrewed."

"Oh, yes?"

"Me in love with Angela? Ha-ha!"

"You can't get out of it with ha-ha's. She called you 'darling'."

"I know. And I disapproved. This habit of the younger g. of scattering 'darlings' about like birdseed is one that I deprecate. Lax, is how I should describe it."

"You tickled her ankles."

"In a purely cousinly spirit. It didn't mean a thing. Why, dash it, you must know that in the deeper and truer sense I wouldn't touch Angela with a barge pole."

"Oh? And why not? Not good enough for you?"

"You misunderstand me," I hastened to reply. "When I say I wouldn't touch Angela with a barge pole, I intend merely to convey that my feelings towards her are those of distant, though cordial, esteem. In other words, you may rest assured that between this young prune and myself there never has been and never could be any sentiment warmer and stronger than that of ordinary friendship."

"I believe it was you who tipped her off that I was in the larder last night, so that she could find me there with that pie, thus damaging my prestige."

"My dear Tuppy! A Wooster?" I was shocked. "You think a Wooster would do that?"

He breathed heavily.

"Listen," he said. "It's no good your standing there arguing. You can't get away from the facts. Somebody stole her from me at Cannes. You told me yourself that she was with you all the time at Cannes and hardly saw anybody else. You gloated over the mixed bathing, and those moonlight walks you had together——"

"Not gloated. Just mentioned them."

"So now you understand why, as soon as I can get you clear of this damned bench, I am going to tear you limb from limb. Why they have these bally benches in gardens," said Tuppy discontentedly, "is more than I can see. They only get in the way."

He ceased, and, grabbing out, missed me by a hair's breadth.

It was a moment for swift thinking, and it is at such moments, as I have already indicated, that Bertram Wooster is at his best. I suddenly remembered the recent misunderstanding with the Bassett, and with a flash of clear vision saw that this was where it was going to come in handy.

"You've got it all wrong, Tuppy," I said, moving to the left. "True, I saw a lot of Angela, but my dealings with her were on a basis from start to finish of the purest and most wholesome camaraderie. I can prove it. During that sojourn in Cannes my affections were engaged elsewhere."

"What?"

"Engaged elsewhere. My affections. During that sojourn."

I had struck the right note. He stopped sidling. His clutching hand fell to his side.

"Is that true?"

"Quite official."

"Who was she?"

"My dear Tuppy, does one bandy a woman's name?"

"One does if one doesn't want one's ruddy head pulled off."

I saw that it was a special case.

"Madeline Bassett," I said.

"Who?"

"Madeline Bassett."

He seemed stunned.

"You stand there and tell me you were in love with that Bassett disaster?"

"I wouldn't call her 'that Bassett disaster', Tuppy. Not respectful."

"Dash being respectful. I want the facts. You deliberately assert that you loved that weird Gawd-help-us?"

"I don't see why you should call her a weird Gawd-help-us, either. A very charming and beautiful girl. Odd in some of her views perhaps—one does not quite see eye to eye with her in the matter of stars and rabbits—but not a weird Gawd-help-us."

"Anyway, you stick to it that you were in love with her?"

"I do."

"It sounds thin to me, Wooster, very thin."

I saw that it would be necessary to apply the finishing touch.

"I must ask you to treat this as entirely confidential, Glossop, but I may as well inform you that it is not twenty-four hours since she turned me down."

"Turned you down?"

"Like a bedspread. In this very garden."

"Twenty-four hours?"

"Call it twenty-five. So you will readily see that I can't be the chap, if any, who stole Angela from you at Cannes."

And I was on the brink of adding that I wouldn't touch Angela with a barge pole, when I remembered I had said it already and it hadn't gone frightfully well. I desisted, therefore.

My manly frankness seemed to be producing good results. The homicidal glare was dying out of Tuppy's eyes. He had the aspect of a hired assassin who had paused to think things over.

"I see," he said, at length. "All right, then. Sorry you were troubled."

"Don't mention it, old man," I responded courteously.

For the first time since the bushes had begun to pour forth Glossops, Bertram Wooster could be said to have breathed freely. I don't say I actually came out from behind the bench, but I did let go of it, and with something of the relief which those three chaps in the Old Testament must have experienced after sliding out of the burning fiery furnace, I even groped tentatively for my cigarette case.

The next moment a sudden snort made me take my fingers off it as if it had bitten me. I was distressed to note in the old friend a return of the recent frenzy.

"What the hell did you mean by telling her that I used to be covered with ink when I was a kid?"

"My dear Tuppy——"

"I was almost finickingly careful about my personal cleanliness as a boy. You could have eaten your dinner off me."

"Quite. But——"

"And all that stuff about having no soul. I'm crawling with soul. And being looked on as an outsider at the Drones——"

"But, my dear old chap, I explained that. It was all part of my ruse or scheme."

"It was, was it? Well, in future do me a favour and leave me out of your foul ruses."

"Just as you say, old boy."

"All right, then. That's understood."

He relapsed into silence, standing with folded arms, staring before him rather like a strong, silent man in a novel when he's just been given the bird by the girl and is thinking of looking in at the Rocky Mountains and bumping off a few bears. His manifest pippedness excited my compash, and I ventured a kindly word.

"I don't suppose you know what au pied de la lettre means, Tuppy, but that's how I don't think you ought to take all that stuff Angela was saying just now too much."

He seemed interested.

"What the devil," he asked, "are you talking about?"

I saw that I should have to make myself clearer.

"Don't take all that guff of hers too literally, old man. You know what girls are like."

"I do," he said, with another snort that came straight up from his insteps. "And I wish I'd never met one."

"I mean to say, it's obvious that she must have spotted you in those bushes and was simply talking to score off you. There you were, I mean, if you follow the psychology, and she saw you, and in that impulsive way girls have, she seized the opportunity of ribbing you a bit—just told you a few home truths, I mean to say."

"Home truths?"

"That's right."

He snorted once more, causing me to feel rather like royalty receiving a twenty-one gun salute from the fleet. I can't remember ever having met a better right-and-left-hand snorter.

"What do you mean, 'home truths'? I'm not fat."

"No, no."

"And what's wrong with the colour of my hair?"

"Quite in order, Tuppy, old man. The hair, I mean."

"And I'm not a bit thin on the top.... What the dickens are you grinning about?"

"Not grinning. Just smiling slightly. I was conjuring up a sort of vision, if you know what I mean, of you as seen through Angela's eyes. Fat in the middle and thin on the top. Rather funny."

"You think it funny, do you?"

"Not a bit."

"You'd better not."

"Quite."

It seemed to me that the conversation was becoming difficult again. I wished it could be terminated. And so it was. For at this moment something came shimmering through the laurels in the quiet evenfall, and I perceived that it was Angela.

She was looking sweet and saintlike, and she had a plate of sandwiches in her hand. Ham, I was to discover later.

"If you see Mr. Glossop anywhere, Bertie," she said, her eyes resting dreamily on Tuppy's facade, "I wish you would give him these. I'm so afraid he may be hungry, poor fellow. It's nearly ten o'clock, and he hasn't eaten a morsel since dinner. I'll just leave them on this bench."

She pushed off, and it seemed to me that I might as well go with her. Nothing to keep me here, I mean. We moved towards the house, and presently from behind us there sounded in the night the splintering crash of a well-kicked plate of ham sandwiches, accompanied by the muffled oaths of a strong man in his wrath.

"How still and peaceful everything is," said Angela.

-16-

Sunshine was gilding the grounds of Brinkley Court and the ear detected a marked twittering of birds in the ivy outside the window when I woke next morning to a new day. But there was no corresponding sunshine in Bertram Wooster's soul and no answering twitter in his heart as he sat up in bed, sipping his cup of strengthening tea. It could not be denied that to Bertram, reviewing the happenings of the previous night, the Tuppy-Angela situation seemed more or less to have slipped a cog. With every desire to look for the silver lining, I could not but feel that the rift between these two haughty spirits had now reached such impressive proportions that the task of bridging same would be beyond even my powers.

I am a shrewd observer, and there had been something in Tuppy's manner as he booted that plate of ham sandwiches that seemed to tell me that he would not lightly forgive.

In these circs., I deemed it best to shelve their problem for the nonce and turn the mind to the matter of Gussie, which presented a brighter picture.

With regard to Gussie, everything was in train. Jeeves's morbid scruples about lacing the chap's orange juice had put me to a good deal of trouble, but I had surmounted every obstacle in the old Wooster way. I had secured an abundance of the necessary spirit, and it was now lying in its flask in the drawer of the dressing-table. I had also ascertained that the jug, duly filled, would be standing on a shelf in the butler's pantry round about the hour of one. To remove it from that shelf, sneak it up to my room, and return it, laced, in good time for the midday meal would be a task calling, no doubt, for address, but in no sense an exacting one.

It was with something of the emotions of one preparing a treat for a deserving child that I finished my tea and rolled over for that extra spot of sleep which just makes all the difference when there is man's work to be done and the brain must be kept clear for it.

And when I came downstairs an hour or so later, I knew how right I had been to formulate this scheme for Gussie's bucking up. I ran into him on the lawn, and I could see at a glance that if ever there was a man who needed a snappy stimulant, it was he. All nature, as I have indicated, was smiling, but not Augustus Fink-Nottle. He was walking round in circles, muttering something about not proposing to detain us long, but on this auspicious occasion feeling compelled to say a few words.

"Ah, Gussie," I said, arresting him as he was about to start another lap. "A lovely morning, is it not?"

Even if I had not been aware of it already, I could have divined from the abruptness with which he damned the lovely morning that he was not in merry mood. I addressed myself to the task of bringing the roses back to his cheeks.

"I've got good news for you, Gussie."

He looked at me with a sudden sharp interest.

"Has Market Snodsbury Grammar School burned down?"

"Not that I know of."

"Have mumps broken out? Is the place closed on account of measles?"

"No, no."

"Then what do you mean you've got good news?"

I endeavoured to soothe.

"You mustn't take it so hard, Gussie. Why worry about a laughably simple job like distributing prizes at a school?"

"Laughably simple, eh? Do you realize I've been sweating for days and haven't been able to think of a thing to say yet, except that I won't detain them long. You bet I won't detain them long. I've been timing my speech, and it lasts five seconds. What the devil am I to say, Bertie? What do you say when you're distributing prizes?"

I considered. Once, at my private school, I had won a prize for Scripture knowledge, so I suppose I ought to have been full of inside stuff. But memory eluded me.

Then something emerged from the mists.

"You say the race is not always to the swift."

"Why?"

"Well, it's a good gag. It generally gets a hand."

"I mean, why isn't it? Why isn't the race to the swift?"

"Ah, there you have me. But the nibs say it isn't."

"But what does it mean?"

"I take it it's supposed to console the chaps who haven't won prizes."

"What's the good of that to me? I'm not worrying about them. It's the ones that have won prizes that I'm worrying about, the little blighters who will come up on the platform. Suppose they make faces at me."

"They won't."

"How do you know they won't? It's probably the first thing they'll think of. And even if they don't—Bertie, shall I tell you something?"

"What?"

"I've a good mind to take that tip of yours and have a drink."

I smiled. He little knew, about summed up what I was thinking.

"Oh, you'll be all right," I said.

He became fevered again.

"How do you know I'll be all right? I'm sure to blow up in my lines."

"Tush!"

"Or drop a prize."

"Tut!"

"Or something. I can feel it in my bones. As sure as I'm standing here, something is going to happen this afternoon which will make everybody laugh themselves sick at me. I can hear them now. Like hyenas.... Bertie!"

"Hullo?"

"Do you remember that kids' school we went to before Eton?"

"Quite. It was there I won my Scripture prize."

"Never mind about your Scripture prize. I'm not talking about your Scripture prize. Do you recollect the Bosher incident?"

I did, indeed. It was one of the high spots of my youth.

"Major-General Sir Wilfred Bosher came to distribute the prizes at that school," proceeded Gussie in a dull, toneless voice. "He dropped a book. He stooped to pick it up. And, as he stooped, his trousers split up the back."

"How we roared!"

Gussie's face twisted.

"We did, little swine that we were. Instead of remaining silent and exhibiting a decent sympathy for a gallant officer at a peculiarly embarrassing moment, we howled and yelled with mirth. I loudest of any. That is what will happen to me this afternoon, Bertie. It will be a judgment on me for laughing like that at Major-General Sir Wilfred Bosher."

"No, no, Gussie, old man. Your trousers won't split."

"How do you know they won't? Better men than I have split their trousers. General Bosher was a D.S.O., with a fine record of service on the north-western frontier of India, and his trousers split. I shall be a mockery and a scorn. I know it. And you, fully cognizant of what I am in for, come babbling about good news. What news could possibly be good to me at this moment except the information that bubonic plague had broken out among the scholars of Market Snodsbury Grammar School, and that they were all confined to their beds with spots?"

The moment had come for me to speak. I laid a hand gently on his shoulder. He brushed it off. I laid it on again. He brushed it off once more. I was endeavouring to lay it on for the third time, when he moved aside and desired, with a certain petulance, to be informed if I thought I was a ruddy osteopath.

I found his manner trying, but one has to make allowances. I was telling myself that I should be seeing a very different Gussie after lunch.

"When I said I had good news, old man, I meant about Madeline Bassett."

The febrile gleam died out of his eyes, to be replaced by a look of infinite sadness.

"You can't have good news about her. I've dished myself there completely."

"Not at all. I am convinced that if you take another whack at her, all will be well."

And, keeping it snappy, I related what had passed between the Bassett and myself on the previous night.

"So all you have to do is play a return date, and you cannot fail to swing the voting. You are her dream man."

He shook his head.

"No."

"What?"

"No use."

"What do you mean?"

"Not a bit of good trying."

"But I tell you she said in so many words——"

"It doesn't make any difference. She may have loved me once. Last night will have killed all that."

"Of course it won't."

"It will. She despises me now."

"Not a bit of it. She knows you simply got cold feet."

"And I should get cold feet if I tried again. It's no good, Bertie. I'm hopeless, and there's an end of it. Fate made me the sort of chap who can't say 'bo' to a goose."

"It isn't a question of saying 'bo' to a goose. The point doesn't arise at all. It is simply a matter of——"

"I know, I know. But it's no good. I can't do it. The whole thing is off. I am not going to risk a repetition of last night's fiasco. You talk in a light way of taking another whack at her, but you don't know what it means. You have not been through the experience of starting to ask the girl you love to marry you and then suddenly finding yourself talking about the plumlike external gills of the newly-born newt. It's not a thing you can do twice. No, I accept my destiny. It's all over. And now, Bertie, like a good chap, shove off. I want to compose my speech. I can't compose my speech with you mucking around. If you are going to continue to muck around, at least give me a couple of stories. The little hell hounds are sure to expect a story or two."

"Do you know the one about——"

"No good. I don't want any of your off-colour stuff from the Drones' smoking-room. I need something clean. Something that will be a help to them in their after lives. Not that I care a damn about their after lives, except that I hope they'll all choke."

"I heard a story the other day. I can't quite remember it, but it was about a chap who snored and disturbed the neighbours, and it ended, 'It was his adenoids that adenoid them.'"

He made a weary gesture.

"You expect me to work that in, do you, into a speech to be delivered to an audience of boys, every one of whom is probably riddled with adenoids? Damn it, they'd rush the platform. Leave me, Bertie. Push off. That's all I ask you to do. Push off.... Ladies and gentlemen," said Gussie, in a low, soliloquizing sort of way, "I do not propose to detain this auspicious occasion long——"

It was a thoughtful Wooster who walked away and left him at it. More than ever I was congratulating myself on having had the sterling good sense to make all my arrangements so that I could press a button and set things moving at an instant's notice.

Until now, you see, I had rather entertained a sort of hope that when I had revealed to him the Bassett's mental attitude, Nature would have done the rest, bracing him up to such an extent that artificial stimulants would not be required. Because, naturally, a chap doesn't want to have to sprint about country houses lugging jugs of orange juice, unless it is absolutely essential.

But now I saw that I must carry on as planned. The total absence of pep, ginger, and the right spirit which the man had displayed during these conversational exchanges convinced me that the strongest measures would be necessary. Immediately upon leaving him, therefore, I proceeded to the pantry, waited till the butler had removed himself elsewhere, and nipped in and secured the vital jug. A few moments later, after a wary passage of the stairs, I was in my room. And the first thing I saw there was Jeeves, fooling about with trousers.

He gave the jug a look which—wrongly, as it was to turn out—I diagnosed as censorious.

I drew myself up a bit. I intended to have no rot from the fellow.

"Yes, Jeeves?"

"Sir?"

"You have the air of one about to make a remark, Jeeves."

"Oh, no, sir. I note that you are in possession of Mr. Fink-Nottle's orange juice. I was merely about to observe that in my opinion it would be injudicious to add spirit to it."

"That is a remark, Jeeves, and it is precisely——"

"Because I have already attended to the matter, sir."

"What?"

"Yes, sir. I decided, after all, to acquiesce in your wishes."

I stared at the man, astounded. I was deeply moved. Well, I mean, wouldn't any chap who had been going about thinking that the old feudal spirit was dead and then suddenly found it wasn't have been deeply moved?

"Jeeves," I said, "I am touched."

"Thank you, sir."

"Touched and gratified."

"Thank you very much, sir."

"But what caused this change of heart?"

"I chanced to encounter Mr. Fink-Nottle in the garden, sir, while you were still in bed, and we had a brief conversation."

"And you came away feeling that he needed a bracer?"

"Very much so, sir. His attitude struck me as defeatist."

I nodded.

"I felt the same. 'Defeatist' sums it up to a nicety. Did you tell him his attitude struck you as defeatist?"

"Yes, sir."

"But it didn't do any good?"

"No, sir."

"Very well, then, Jeeves. We must act. How much gin did you put in the jug?"

"A liberal tumblerful, sir."

"Would that be a normal dose for an adult defeatist, do you think?"

"I fancy it should prove adequate, sir."

"I wonder. We must not spoil the ship for a ha'porth of tar. I think I'll add just another fluid ounce or so."

"I would not advocate it, sir. In the case of Lord Brancaster's parrot——"

"You are falling into your old error, Jeeves, of thinking that Gussie is a parrot. Fight against this. I shall add the oz."

"Very good, sir."

"And, by the way, Jeeves, Mr. Fink-Nottle is in the market for bright, clean stories to use in his speech. Do you know any?"

"I know a story about two Irishmen, sir."

"Pat and Mike?"

"Yes, sir."

"Who were walking along Broadway?"

"Yes, sir."

"Just what he wants. Any more?"

"No, sir."

"Well, every little helps. You had better go and tell it to him."

"Very good, sir."

He passed from the room, and I unscrewed the flask and tilted into the jug a generous modicum of its contents. And scarcely had I done so, when there came to my ears the sound of footsteps without. I had only just time to shove the jug behind the photograph of Uncle Tom on the mantelpiece before the door opened and in came Gussie, curveting like a circus horse.

"What-ho, Bertie," he said. "What-ho, what-ho, what-ho, and again what-ho. What a beautiful world this is, Bertie. One of the nicest I ever met."

I stared at him, speechless. We Woosters are as quick as lightning, and I saw at once that something had happened.

I mean to say, I told you about him walking round in circles. I recorded what passed between us on the lawn. And if I portrayed the scene with anything like adequate skill, the picture you will have retained of this Fink-Nottle will have been that of a nervous wreck, sagging at the knees, green about the gills, and picking feverishly at the lapels of his coat in an ecstasy of craven fear. In a word, defeatist. Gussie, during that interview, had, in fine, exhibited all the earmarks of one licked to a custard.

Vastly different was the Gussie who stood before me now. Self-confidence seemed to ooze from the fellow's every pore. His face was flushed, there was a jovial light in his eyes, the lips were parted in a swashbuckling smile. And when with a genial hand he sloshed me on the back before I could sidestep, it was as if I had been kicked by a mule.

"Well, Bertie," he proceeded, as blithely as a linnet without a thing on his mind, "you will be glad to hear that you were right. Your theory has been tested and proved correct. I feel like a fighting cock."

My brain ceased to reel. I saw all.

"Have you been having a drink?"

"I have. As you advised. Unpleasant stuff. Like medicine. Burns your throat, too, and makes one as thirsty as the dickens. How anyone can mop it up, as you do, for pleasure, beats me. Still, I would be the last to deny that it tunes up the system. I could bite a tiger."

"What did you have?"

"Whisky. At least, that was the label on the decanter, and I have no reason to suppose that a woman like your aunt—staunch, true-blue, British—would deliberately deceive the public. If she labels her decanters Whisky, then I consider that we know where we are."

"A whisky and soda, eh? You couldn't have done better."

"Soda?" said Gussie thoughtfully. "I knew there was something I had forgotten."

"Didn't you put any soda in it?"

"It never occurred to me. I just nipped into the dining-room and drank out of the decanter."

"How much?"

"Oh, about ten swallows. Twelve, maybe. Or fourteen. Say sixteen medium-sized gulps. Gosh, I'm thirsty."

He moved over to the wash-stand and drank deeply out of the water bottle. I cast a covert glance at Uncle Tom's photograph behind his back. For the first time since it had come into my life, I was glad that it was so large. It hid its secret well. If Gussie had caught sight of that jug of orange juice, he would unquestionably have been on to it like a knife.

"Well, I'm glad you're feeling braced," I said.

He moved buoyantly from the wash-hand stand, and endeavoured to slosh me on the back again. Foiled by my nimble footwork, he staggered to the bed and sat down upon it.

"Braced? Did I say I could bite a tiger?"

"You did."

"Make it two tigers. I could chew holes in a steel door. What an ass you must have thought me out there in the garden. I see now you were laughing in your sleeve."

"No, no."

"Yes," insisted Gussie. "That very sleeve," he said, pointing. "And I don't blame you. I can't imagine why I made all that fuss about a potty job like distributing prizes at a rotten little country grammar school. Can you imagine, Bertie?"

"No."

"Exactly. Nor can I imagine. There's simply nothing to it. I just shin up on the platform, drop a few gracious words, hand the little blighters their prizes, and hop down again, admired by all. Not a suggestion of split trousers from start to finish. I mean, why should anybody split his trousers? I can't imagine. Can you imagine?"

"No."

"Nor can I imagine. I shall be a riot. I know just the sort of stuff that's needed—simple, manly, optimistic stuff straight from the shoulder. This shoulder," said Gussie, tapping. "Why I was so nervous this morning I can't imagine. For anything simpler than distributing a few footling books to a bunch of grimy-faced kids I can't imagine. Still, for some reason I can't imagine, I was feeling a little nervous, but now I feel fine, Bertie—fine, fine, fine— and I say this to you as an old friend. Because that's what you are, old man, when all the smoke has cleared away—an old friend. I don't think I've ever met an older friend. How long have you been an old friend of mine, Bertie?"

"Oh, years and years."

"Imagine! Though, of course, there must have been a time when you were a new friend.... Hullo, the luncheon gong. Come on, old friend."

And, rising from the bed like a performing flea, he made for the door.

I followed rather pensively. What had occurred was, of course, so much velvet, as you might say. I mean, I had wanted a braced Fink-Nottle— indeed, all my plans had had a braced Fink-Nottle as their end and aim —but I found myself wondering a little whether the Fink-Nottle now sliding down the banister wasn't, perhaps, a shade too braced. His demeanour seemed to me that of a man who might quite easily throw bread about at lunch.

Fortunately, however, the settled gloom of those round him exercised a restraining effect upon him at the table. It would have needed a far more plastered man to have been rollicking at such a gathering. I had told the Bassett that there were aching hearts in Brinkley Court, and it now looked probable that there would shortly be aching tummies. Anatole, I learned, had retired to his bed with a fit of the vapours, and the meal now before us had been cooked by the kitchen maid—as C3 a performer as ever wielded a skillet.

This, coming on top of their other troubles, induced in the company a pretty unanimous silence—a solemn stillness, as you might say—which even Gussie did not seem prepared to break. Except, therefore, for one short snatch of song on his part, nothing untoward marked the occasion, and presently we rose, with instructions from Aunt Dahlia to put on festal raiment and be at Market Snodsbury not later than 3.30. This leaving me ample time to smoke a gasper or two in a shady bower beside the lake, I did so, repairing to my room round about the hour of three.

Jeeves was on the job, adding the final polish to the old topper, and I was about to apprise him of the latest developments in the matter of Gussie, when he forestalled me by observing that the latter had only just concluded an agreeable visit to the Wooster bedchamber.

"I found Mr. Fink-Nottle seated here when I arrived to lay out your clothes, sir."

"Indeed, Jeeves? Gussie was in here, was he?"

"Yes, sir. He left only a few moments ago. He is driving to the school with Mr. and Mrs. Travers in the large car."

"Did you give him your story of the two Irishmen?"

"Yes, sir. He laughed heartily."

"Good. Had you any other contributions for him?"

"I ventured to suggest that he might mention to the young gentlemen that education is a drawing out, not a putting in. The late Lord Brancaster was much addicted to presenting prizes at schools, and he invariably employed this dictum."

"And how did he react to that?"

"He laughed heartily, sir."

"This surprised you, no doubt? This practically incessant merriment, I mean."

"Yes, sir."

"You thought it odd in one who, when you last saw him, was well up in Group A of the defeatists."

"Yes, sir."

"There is a ready explanation, Jeeves. Since you last saw him, Gussie has been on a bender. He's as tight as an owl."

"Indeed, sir?"

"Absolutely. His nerve cracked under the strain, and he sneaked into the dining-room and started mopping the stuff up like a vacuum cleaner. Whisky would seem to be what he filled the radiator with. I gather that he used up most of the decanter. Golly, Jeeves, it's lucky he didn't get at that laced orange juice on top of that, what?"

"Extremely, sir."

I eyed the jug. Uncle Tom's photograph had fallen into the fender, and it was standing there right out in the open, where Gussie couldn't have helped seeing it. Mercifully, it was empty now.

"It was a most prudent act on your part, if I may say so, sir, to dispose of the orange juice."

I stared at the man.

"What? Didn't you?"

"No, sir."

"Jeeves, let us get this clear. Was it not you who threw away that o.j.?"

"No, sir. I assumed, when I entered the room and found the pitcher empty, that you had done so."

We looked at each other, awed. Two minds with but a single thought.

"I very much fear, sir——"

"So do I, Jeeves."

"It would seem almost certain——"

"Quite certain. Weigh the facts. Sift the evidence. The jug was standing on the mantelpiece, for all eyes to behold. Gussie had been complaining of thirst. You found him in here, laughing heartily. I think that there can be little doubt, Jeeves, that the entire contents of that jug are at this moment reposing on top of the existing cargo in that already brilliantly lit man's interior. Disturbing, Jeeves."

"Most disturbing, sir."

"Let us face the position, forcing ourselves to be calm. You inserted in that jug—shall we say a tumblerful of the right stuff?"

"Fully a tumblerful, sir."

"And I added of my plenty about the same amount."

"Yes, sir."

"And in two shakes of a duck's tail Gussie, with all that lapping about inside him, will be distributing the prizes at Market Snodsbury Grammar School before an audience of all that is fairest and most refined in the county."

"Yes, sir."

"It seems to me, Jeeves, that the ceremony may be one fraught with considerable interest."

"Yes, sir."

"What, in your opinion, will the harvest be?"

"One finds it difficult to hazard a conjecture, sir."

"You mean imagination boggles?"

"Yes, sir."

I inspected my imagination. He was right. It boggled.

-17-

"And yet, Jeeves," I said, twiddling a thoughtful steering wheel, "there is always the bright side."

Some twenty minutes had elapsed, and having picked the honest fellow up outside the front door, I was driving in the two-seater to the picturesque town of Market Snodsbury. Since we had parted—he to go to his lair and fetch his hat, I to remain in my room and complete the formal costume—I had been doing some close thinking.

The results of this I now proceeded to hand on to him.

"However dark the prospect may be, Jeeves, however murkily the storm clouds may seem to gather, a keen eye can usually discern the blue bird. It is bad, no doubt, that Gussie should be going, some ten minutes from now, to distribute prizes in a state of advanced intoxication, but we must never forget that these things cut both ways."

"You imply, sir——"

"Precisely. I am thinking of him in his capacity of wooer. All this ought to have put him in rare shape for offering his hand in marriage. I shall be vastly surprised if it won't turn him into a sort of caveman. Have you ever seen James Cagney in the movies?"

"Yes, sir."

"Something on those lines."

I heard him cough, and sniped him with a sideways glance. He was wearing that informative look of his.

"Then you have not heard, sir?"

"Eh?"

"You are not aware that a marriage has been arranged and will shortly take place between Mr. Fink-Nottle and Miss Bassett?"

"What?"

"Yes, sir."

"When did this happen?"

"Shortly after Mr. Fink-Nottle had left your room, sir."

"Ah! In the post-orange-juice era?"

"Yes, sir."

"But are you sure of your facts? How do you know?"

"My informant was Mr. Fink-Nottle himself, sir. He appeared anxious to confide in me. His story was somewhat incoherent, but I had no difficulty in apprehending its substance. Prefacing his remarks with the statement that this was a beautiful world, he laughed heartily and said that he had become formally engaged."

"No details?"

"No, sir."

"But one can picture the scene."

"Yes, sir."

"I mean, imagination doesn't boggle."

"No, sir."

And it didn't. I could see exactly what must have happened. Insert a liberal dose of mixed spirits in a normally abstemious man, and he becomes a force. He does not stand around, twiddling his fingers and stammering. He acts. I had no doubt that Gussie must have reached for the Bassett and clasped her to him like a stevedore handling a sack of coals. And one could readily envisage the effect of that sort of thing on a girl of romantic mind.

"Well, well, well, Jeeves."

"Yes, sir."

"This is splendid news."

"Yes, sir."

"You see now how right I was."

"Yes, sir."

"It must have been rather an eye-opener for you, watching me handle this case."

"Yes, sir."

"The simple, direct method never fails."

"No, sir."

"Whereas the elaborate does."

"Yes, sir."

"Right ho, Jeeves."

We had arrived at the main entrance of Market Snodsbury Grammar School. I parked the car, and went in, well content. True, the Tuppy-Angela problem still remained unsolved and Aunt Dahlia's five hundred quid seemed as far off as ever, but it was gratifying to feel that good old Gussie's troubles were over, at any rate.

The Grammar School at Market Snodsbury had, I understood, been built somewhere in the year 1416, and, as with so many of these ancient foundations, there still seemed to brood over its Great Hall, where the afternoon's festivities were to take place, not a little of the fug of the centuries. It was the hottest day of the summer, and though somebody had opened a tentative window or two, the atmosphere remained distinctive and individual.

In this hall the youth of Market Snodsbury had been eating its daily lunch for a matter of five hundred years, and the flavour lingered. The air was sort of heavy and languorous, if you know what I mean, with the scent of Young England and boiled beef and carrots.

Aunt Dahlia, who was sitting with a bevy of the local nibs in the second row, sighted me as I entered and waved to me to join her, but I was too smart for that. I wedged myself in among the standees at the back, leaning up against a chap who, from the aroma, might have been a corn chandler or something on that order. The essence of strategy on these occasions is to be as near the door as possible.

The hall was gaily decorated with flags and coloured paper, and the eye was further refreshed by the spectacle of a mixed drove of boys, parents, and what not, the former running a good deal to shiny faces and Eton collars, the latter stressing the black-satin note rather when female, and looking as if their coats were too tight, if male. And presently there was some applause—sporadic, Jeeves has since told me it was—and I saw Gussie being steered by a bearded bloke in a gown to a seat in the middle of the platform.

And I confess that as I beheld him and felt that there but for the grace of God went Bertram Wooster, a shudder ran through the frame. It all reminded me so vividly of the time I had addressed that girls' school.

Of course, looking at it dispassionately, you may say that for horror and peril there is no comparison between an almost human audience like the one before me and a mob of small girls with pigtails down their backs, and this, I concede, is true. Nevertheless, the spectacle was enough to make me feel like a fellow watching a pal going over Niagara Falls in a barrel, and the thought of what I had escaped caused everything for a moment to go black and swim before my eyes.

When I was able to see clearly once more, I perceived that Gussie was now seated. He had his hands on his knees, with his elbows out at right angles, like a nigger minstrel of the old school about to ask Mr. Bones why a chicken crosses the road, and he was staring before him with a smile so fixed and pebble-beached that I should have thought that anybody could have guessed that there sat one in whom the old familiar juice was plashing up against the back of the front teeth.

In fact, I saw Aunt Dahlia, who, having assisted at so many hunting dinners in her time, is second to none as a judge of the symptoms, give a start and gaze long and earnestly. And she was just saying something to Uncle Tom on her left when the bearded bloke stepped to the footlights and started making a speech. From the fact that he spoke as if he had a hot potato in his mouth without getting the raspberry from the lads in the ringside seats, I deduced that he must be the head master.

With his arrival in the spotlight, a sort of perspiring resignation seemed to settle on the audience. Personally, I snuggled up against the chandler and let my attention wander. The speech was on the subject of the doings of the school during the past term, and this part of a prize-giving is always apt rather to fail to grip the visiting stranger. I mean, you know how it is. You're told that J.B. Brewster has won an Exhibition for Classics at Cat's, Cambridge, and you feel that it's one of those stories where you can't see how funny it is unless you really know the fellow. And the same applies to G. Bullett being awarded the Lady Jane Wix Scholarship at the Birmingham College of Veterinary Science.

In fact, I and the corn chandler, who was looking a bit fagged I thought, as if he had had a hard morning chandling the corn, were beginning to doze lightly when things suddenly brisked up, bringing Gussie into the picture for the first time.

"Today," said the bearded bloke, "we are all happy to welcome as the guest of the afternoon Mr. Fitz-Wattle——"

At the beginning of the address, Gussie had subsided into a sort of daydream, with his mouth hanging open. About half-way through, faint signs of life had begun to show. And for the last few minutes he had been trying to cross one leg over the other and failing and having another shot and failing again. But only now did he exhibit any real animation. He sat up with a jerk.

"Fink-Nottle," he said, opening his eyes.

"Fitz-Nottle."

"Fink-Nottle."

"I should say Fink-Nottle."

"Of course you should, you silly ass," said Gussie genially. "All right, get on with it."

And closing his eyes, he began trying to cross his legs again.

I could see that this little spot of friction had rattled the bearded bloke a bit. He stood for a moment fumbling at the fungus with a hesitating hand. But they make these head masters of tough stuff. The weakness passed. He came back nicely and carried on.

"We are all happy, I say, to welcome as the guest of the afternoon Mr. Fink-Nottle, who has kindly consented to award the prizes. This task, as you know, is one that should have devolved upon that well-beloved and vigorous member of our board of governors, the Rev. William Plomer, and we are all, I am sure, very sorry that illness at the last moment should have prevented him from being here today. But, if I may borrow a familiar metaphor from the—if I may employ a homely metaphor familiar to you all—what we lose on the swings we gain on the roundabouts."

He paused, and beamed rather freely, to show that this was comedy. I could have told the man it was no use. Not a ripple. The corn chandler leaned against me and muttered "Whoddidesay?" but that was all.

It's always a nasty jar to wait for the laugh and find that the gag hasn't got across. The bearded bloke was visibly discomposed. At that, however, I think he would have got by, had he not, at this juncture, unfortunately stirred Gussie up again.

"In other words, though deprived of Mr. Plomer, we have with us this afternoon Mr. Fink-Nottle. I am sure that Mr. Fink-Nottle's name is one that needs no introduction to you. It is, I venture to assert, a name that is familiar to us all."

"Not to you," said Gussie.

And the next moment I saw what Jeeves had meant when he had described him as laughing heartily. "Heartily" was absolutely the mot juste. It sounded like a gas explosion.

"You didn't seem to know it so dashed well, what, what?" said Gussie. And, reminded apparently by the word "what" of the word "Wattle," he repeated the latter some sixteen times with a rising inflection.

"Wattle, Wattle, Wattle," he concluded. "Right-ho. Push on."

But the bearded bloke had shot his bolt. He stood there, licked at last; and, watching him closely, I could see that he was now at the crossroads. I could spot what he was thinking as clearly as if he had confided it to my personal ear. He wanted to sit down and call it a day, I mean, but the thought that gave him pause was that, if he did, he must then either uncork Gussie or take the Fink-Nottle speech as read and get straight on to the actual prize-giving.

It was a dashed tricky thing, of course, to have to decide on the spur of the moment. I was reading in the paper the other day about those birds who are trying to split the atom, the nub being that they haven't the foggiest as to what will happen if they do. It may be all right. On the other hand, it may not be all right. And pretty silly a chap would feel, no doubt, if, having split the atom, he suddenly found the house going up in smoke and himself torn limb from limb.

So with the bearded bloke. Whether he was abreast of the inside facts in Gussie's case, I don't know, but it was obvious to him by this time that he had run into something pretty hot. Trial gallops had shown that Gussie had his own way of doing things. Those interruptions had been enough to prove to the perspicacious that here, seated on the platform at the big binge of the season, was one who, if pushed forward to make a speech, might let himself go in a rather epoch-making manner.

On the other hand, chain him up and put a green-baize cloth over him, and where were you? The proceeding would be over about half an hour too soon.

It was, as I say, a difficult problem to have to solve, and, left to himself, I don't know what conclusion he would have come to. Personally, I think he would have played it safe. As it happened, however, the thing was taken out of his hands, for at this moment, Gussie, having stretched his arms and yawned a bit, switched on that pebble-beached smile again and tacked down to the edge of the platform.

"Speech," he said affably.

He then stood with his thumbs in the armholes of his waistcoat, waiting for the applause to die down.

It was some time before this happened, for he had got a very fine hand indeed. I suppose it wasn't often that the boys of Market Snodsbury Grammar School came across a man public-spirited enough to call their head master a silly ass, and they showed their appreciation in no uncertain manner. Gussie may have been one over the eight, but as far as the majority of those present were concerned he was sitting on top of the world.

"Boys," said Gussie, "I mean ladies and gentlemen and boys, I do not detain you long, but I suppose on this occasion to feel compelled to say a few auspicious words; Ladies—and boys and gentlemen—we have all listened with interest to the remarks of our friend here who forgot to shave this morning—I don't know his name, but then he didn't know mine—Fitz-Wattle, I mean, absolutely absurd—which squares things up a bit—and we are all sorry that the Reverend What-ever-he-was-called should be dying of adenoids, but after all, here today, gone tomorrow, and all flesh is as grass, and what not, but that wasn't what I wanted to say. What I wanted to say was this—and I say it confidently—without fear of contradiction—I say, in short, I am happy to be here on this auspicious occasion and I take much pleasure in kindly awarding the prizes, consisting of the handsome books you see laid out on that table. As Shakespeare says, there are sermons in books, stones in the running brooks, or, rather, the other way about, and there you have it in a nutshell."

It went well, and I wasn't surprised. I couldn't quite follow some of it, but anybody could see that it was real ripe stuff, and I was amazed that even the course of treatment he had been taking could have rendered so normally tongue-tied a dumb brick as Gussie capable of it.

It just shows, what any member of Parliament will tell you, that if you want real oratory, the preliminary noggin is essential. Unless pie-eyed, you cannot hope to grip.

"Gentlemen," said Gussie, "I mean ladies and gentlemen and, of course, boys, what a beautiful world this is. A beautiful world, full of happiness on every side. Let me tell you a little story. Two Irishmen, Pat and Mike, were walking along Broadway, and one said to the other, 'Begorrah, the race is not always to the swift,' and the other replied, 'Faith and begob, education is a drawing out, not a putting in.'"

I must say it seemed to me the rottenest story I had ever heard, and I was surprised that Jeeves should have considered it worth while shoving into a speech. However, when I taxed him with this later, he said that Gussie had altered the plot a good deal, and I dare say that accounts for it.

At any rate, that was the conte as Gussie told it, and when I say that it got a very fair laugh, you will understand what a popular favourite he had become with the multitude. There might be a bearded bloke or so on the platform and a small section in the second row who were wishing the speaker would conclude his remarks and resume his seat, but the audience as a whole was for him solidly.

There was applause, and a voice cried: "Hear, hear!"

"Yes," said Gussie, "it is a beautiful world. The sky is blue, the birds are singing, there is optimism everywhere. And why not, boys and ladies and gentlemen? I'm happy, you're happy, we're all happy, even the meanest Irishman that walks along Broadway. Though, as I say, there were two of them—Pat and Mike, one drawing out, the other putting in. I should like you boys, taking the time from me, to give three cheers for this beautiful world. All together now."

Presently the dust settled down and the plaster stopped falling from the ceiling, and he went on.

"People who say it isn't a beautiful world don't know what they are talking about. Driving here in the car today to award the kind prizes, I was reluctantly compelled to tick off my host on this very point. Old Tom Travers. You will see him sitting there in the second row next to the large lady in beige."

He pointed helpfully, and the hundred or so Market Snods-buryians who craned their necks in the direction indicated were able to observe Uncle Tom blushing prettily.

"I ticked him off properly, the poor fish. He expressed the opinion that the world was in a deplorable state. I said, 'Don't talk rot, old Tom Travers.' 'I am not accustomed to talk rot,' he said. 'Then, for a beginner,' I said, 'you do it dashed well.' And I think you will admit, boys and ladies and gentlemen, that that was telling him."

The audience seemed to agree with him. The point went big. The voice that had said, "Hear, hear" said "Hear, hear" again, and my corn chandler hammered the floor vigorously with a large-size walking stick.

"Well, boys," resumed Gussie, having shot his cuffs and smirked horribly, "this is the end of the summer term, and many of you, no doubt, are leaving the school. And I don't blame you, because there's a froust in here you could cut with a knife. You are going out into the great world. Soon many of you will be walking along Broadway. And what I want to impress upon you is that, however much you may suffer from adenoids, you must all use every effort to prevent yourselves becoming pessimists and talking rot like old Tom Travers. There in the second row. The fellow with a face rather like a walnut."

He paused to allow those wishing to do so to refresh themselves with another look at Uncle Tom, and I found myself musing in some little perplexity. Long association with the members of the Drones has put me pretty well in touch with the various ways in which an overdose of the blushful Hippocrene can take the individual, but I had never seen anyone react quite as Gussie was doing.

There was a snap about his work which I had never witnessed before, even in Barmy Fotheringay-Phipps on New Year's Eve.

Jeeves, when I discussed the matter with him later, said it was something to do with inhibitions, if I caught the word correctly, and the suppression of, I think he said, the ego. What he meant, I gathered, was that, owing to the fact that Gussie had just completed a five years' stretch of blameless seclusion among the newts, all the goofiness which ought to have been spread out thin over those five years and had been bottled up during that period came to the surface on this occasion in a lump—or, if you prefer to put it that way, like a tidal wave.

There may be something in this. Jeeves generally knows.

Anyway, be that as it may, I was dashed glad I had had the shrewdness to keep out of that second row. It might be unworthy of the prestige of a Wooster to squash in among the proletariat in the standing-room-only section, but at least, I felt, I was out of the danger zone. So thoroughly had Gussie got it up his nose by now that it seemed to me that had he sighted me he might have become personal about even an old school friend.

"If there's one thing in the world I can't stand," proceeded Gussie, "it's a pessimist. Be optimists, boys. You all know the difference between an optimist and a pessimist. An optimist is a man who—well, take the case of two Irishmen walking along Broadway. One is an optimist and one is a pessimist, just as one's name is Pat and the other's Mike.... Why, hullo, Bertie; I didn't know you were here."

Too late, I endeavoured to go to earth behind the chandler, only to discover that there was no chandler there. Some appointment, suddenly remembered—possibly a promise to his wife that he would be home to tea—had caused him to ooze away while my attention was elsewhere, leaving me right out in the open.

Between me and Gussie, who was now pointing in an offensive manner, there was nothing but a sea of interested faces looking up at me.

"Now, there," boomed Gussie, continuing to point, "is an instance of what I mean. Boys and ladies and gentlemen, take a good look at that object standing up there at the back—morning coat, trousers as worn, quiet grey tie, and carnation in buttonhole—you can't miss him. Bertie Wooster, that is, and as foul a pessimist as ever bit a tiger. I tell you I despise that man. And why do I despise him? Because, boys and ladies and gentlemen, he is a pessimist. His attitude is defeatist. When I told him I was going to address you this afternoon, he tried to dissuade me. And do you know why he tried to dissuade me? Because he said my trousers would split up the back."

The cheers that greeted this were the loudest yet. Anything about splitting trousers went straight to the simple hearts of the young scholars of Market Snodsbury Grammar School. Two in the row in front of me turned purple, and a small lad with freckles seated beside them asked me for my autograph.

"Let me tell you a story about Bertie Wooster."

A Wooster can stand a good deal, but he cannot stand having his name bandied in a public place. Picking my feet up softly, I was in the very process of executing a quiet sneak for the door, when I perceived that the bearded bloke had at last decided to apply the closure.

Why he hadn't done so before is beyond me. Spell-bound, I take it. And, of course, when a chap is going like a breeze with the public, as Gussie had been, it's not so dashed easy to chip in. However, the prospect of hearing another of Gussie's anecdotes seemed to have done the trick. Rising rather as I had risen from my bench at the beginning of that painful scene with Tuppy in the twilight, he made a leap for the table, snatched up a book and came bearing down on the speaker.

He touched Gussie on the arm, and Gussie, turning sharply and seeing a large bloke with a beard apparently about to bean him with a book, sprang back in an attitude of self-defence.

"Perhaps, as time is getting on, Mr. Fink-Nottle, we had better——"

"Oh, ah," said Gussie, getting the trend. He relaxed. "The prizes, eh? Of course, yes. Right-ho. Yes, might as well be shoving along with it. What's this one?"

"Spelling and dictation—P.K. Purvis," announced the bearded bloke.

"Spelling and dictation—P.K. Purvis," echoed Gussie, as if he were calling coals. "Forward,

P.K. Purvis."

Now that the whistle had been blown on his speech, it seemed to me that there was no longer any need for the strategic retreat which I had been planning. I had no wish to tear myself away unless I had to. I mean, I had told Jeeves that this binge would be fraught with interest, and it was fraught with interest. There was a fascination about Gussie's methods which gripped and made one reluctant to pass the thing up provided personal innuendoes were steered clear of. I decided, accordingly, to remain, and presently there was a musical squeaking and P.K. Purvis climbed the platform.

The spelling-and-dictation champ was about three foot six in his squeaking shoes, with a pink face and sandy hair. Gussie patted his hair. He seemed to have taken an immediate fancy to the lad.

"You P.K. Purvis?"

"Sir, yes, sir."

"It's a beautiful world, P.K. Purvis."

"Sir, yes, sir."

"Ah, you've noticed it, have you? Good. You married, by any chance?"

"Sir, no, sir."

"Get married, P.K. Purvis," said Gussie earnestly. "It's the only life ... Well, here's your book. Looks rather bilge to me from a glance at the title page, but, such as it is, here you are."

P.K. Purvis squeaked off amidst sporadic applause, but one could not fail to note that the sporadic was followed by a rather strained silence. It was evident that Gussie was striking something of a new note in Market Snodsbury scholastic circles. Looks were exchanged between parent and parent. The bearded bloke had the air of one who has drained the bitter cup. As for Aunt Dahlia, her demeanour now told only too clearly that her last doubts had been resolved and her verdict was in. I saw her whisper to the Bassett, who sat on her right, and the Bassett nodded sadly and looked like a fairy about to shed a tear and add another star to the Milky Way.

Gussie, after the departure of P.K. Purvis, had fallen into a sort of daydream and was standing with his mouth open and his hands in his pockets. Becoming abruptly aware that a fat kid in knickerbockers was at his elbow, he started violently.

"Hullo!" he said, visibly shaken. "Who are you?"

"This," said the bearded bloke, "is R.V. Smethurst."

"What's he doing here?" asked Gussie suspiciously.

"You are presenting him with the drawing prize, Mr. Fink-Nottle."

This apparently struck Gussie as a reasonable explanation. His face cleared.

"That's right, too," he said.... "Well, here it is, cocky. You off?" he said, as the kid prepared to withdraw.

"Sir, yes, sir."

"Wait, R.V. Smethurst. Not so fast. Before you go, there is a question I wish to ask you."

But the beard bloke's aim now seemed to be to rush the ceremonies a bit. He hustled R.V. Smethurst off stage rather like a chucker-out in a pub regretfully ejecting an old and respected customer, and starting paging G.G. Simmons. A moment later the latter was up and coming, and conceive my emotion when it was announced that the subject on which he had clicked was Scripture knowledge. One of us, I mean to say.

G.G. Simmons was an unpleasant, perky-looking stripling, mostly front teeth and spectacles, but I gave him a big hand. We Scripture-knowledge sharks stick together.

Gussie, I was sorry to see, didn't like him. There was in his manner, as he regarded G.G. Simmons, none of the chumminess which had marked it during his interview with P.K. Purvis or, in a somewhat lesser degree, with R.V. Smethurst. He was cold and distant.

"Well, G.G. Simmons."

"Sir, yes, sir."

"What do you mean—sir, yes, sir? Dashed silly thing to say. So you've won the Scripture-knowledge prize, have you?"

"Sir, yes, sir."

"Yes," said Gussie, "you look just the sort of little tick who would. And yet," he said, pausing and eyeing the child keenly, "how are we to know that this has all been open and above board? Let me test you, G.G. Simmons. What was What's-His-Name—the chap who begat Thingummy? Can you answer me that, Simmons?"

"Sir, no, sir."

Gussie turned to the bearded bloke.

"Fishy," he said. "Very fishy. This boy appears to be totally lacking in Scripture knowledge."

The bearded bloke passed a hand across his forehead.

"I can assure you, Mr. Fink-Nottle, that every care was taken to ensure a correct marking and that Simmons outdistanced his competitors by a wide margin."

"Well, if you say so," said Gussie doubtfully. "All right, G.G. Simmons, take your prize."

"Sir, thank you, sir."

"But let me tell you that there's nothing to stick on side about in winning a prize for Scripture knowledge. Bertie Wooster——"

I don't know when I've had a nastier shock. I had been going on the assumption that, now that they had stopped him making his speech, Gussie's fangs had been drawn, as you might say. To duck my head down and resume my edging toward the door was with me the work of a moment.

"Bertie Wooster won the Scripture-knowledge prize at a kids' school we were at together, and you know what he's like. But, of course, Bertie frankly cheated. He succeeded in scrounging that Scripture-knowledge trophy over the heads of better men by means of some of the rawest and most brazen swindling methods ever witnessed even at a school where such things were common. If that man's pockets, as he entered the examination-room, were not stuffed to bursting-point with lists of the kings of Judah——"

I heard no more. A moment later I was out in God's air, fumbling with a fevered foot at the self-starter of the old car.

The engine raced. The clutch slid into position. I tooted and drove off.

My ganglions were still vibrating as I ran the car into the stables of Brinkley Court, and it was a much shaken Bertram who tottered up to his room to change into something loose.

Having donned flannels, I lay down on the bed for a bit, and I suppose I must have dozed off, for the next thing I remember is finding Jeeves at my side.

I sat up. "My tea, Jeeves?"

"No, sir. It is nearly dinner-time."

The mists cleared away.

"I must have been asleep."

"Yes, sir."

"Nature taking its toll of the exhausted frame."

"Yes, sir."

"And enough to make it."

"Yes, sir."

"And now it's nearly dinner-time, you say? All right. I am in no mood for dinner, but I suppose you had better lay out the clothes."

"It will not be necessary, sir. The company will not be dressing tonight. A cold collation has been set out in the dining-room."

"Why's that?"

"It was Mrs. Travers's wish that this should be done in order to minimize the work for the staff, who are attending a dance at Sir Percival Stretchley-Budd's residence tonight."

"Of course, yes. I remember. My Cousin Angela told me. Tonight's the night, what? You going, Jeeves?"

"No, sir. I am not very fond of this form of entertainment in the rural districts, sir."

"I know what you mean. These country binges are all the same. A piano, one fiddle, and a floor like sandpaper. Is Anatole going? Angela hinted not."

"Miss Angela was correct, sir. Monsieur Anatole is in bed."

"Temperamental blighters, these Frenchmen."

"Yes, sir."

There was a pause.

"Well, Jeeves," I said, "it was certainly one of those afternoons, what?"

"Yes, sir."

"I cannot recall one more packed with incident. And I left before the finish."

"Yes, sir. I observed your departure."

"You couldn't blame me for withdrawing."

"No, sir. Mr. Fink-Nottle had undoubtedly become embarrassingly personal."

"Was there much more of it after I went?"

"No, sir. The proceedings terminated very shortly. Mr. Fink-Nottle's remarks with reference to Master G.G. Simmons brought about an early closure."

"But he had finished his remarks about G.G. Simmons."

"Only temporarily, sir. He resumed them immediately after your departure. If you recollect, sir, he had already proclaimed himself suspicious of Master Simmons's bona fides, and he now proceeded to deliver a violent verbal attack upon the young gentleman, asserting that it was impossible for him to have won the Scripture-knowledge prize without systematic cheating on an impressive scale. He went so far as to suggest that Master Simmons was well known to the police."

"Golly, Jeeves!"

"Yes, sir. The words did create a considerable sensation. The reaction of those present to this accusation I should describe as mixed. The young students appeared pleased and applauded vigorously, but Master Simmons's mother rose from her seat and addressed Mr. Fink-Nottle in terms of strong protest."

"Did Gussie seem taken aback? Did he recede from his position?"

"No, sir. He said that he could see it all now, and hinted at a guilty liaison between Master Simmons's mother and the head master, accusing the latter of having cooked the marks, as his expression was, in order to gain favour with the former."

"You don't mean that?"

"Yes, sir."

"Egad, Jeeves! And then——"

"They sang the national anthem, sir."

"Surely not?"

"Yes, sir."

"At a moment like that?"

"Yes, sir."

"Well, you were there and you know, of course, but I should have thought the last thing Gussie and this woman would have done in the circs. would have been to start singing duets."

"You misunderstand me, sir. It was the entire company who sang. The head master turned to the organist and said something to him in a low tone. Upon which the latter began to play the national anthem, and the proceedings terminated."

"I see. About time, too."

"Yes, sir. Mrs. Simmons's attitude had become unquestionably menacing."

I pondered. What I had heard was, of course, of a nature to excite pity and terror, not to mention alarm and despondency, and it would be paltering with the truth to say that I was pleased about it. On the other hand, it was all over now, and it seemed to me that the thing to do was not to mourn over the past but to fix the mind on the bright future. I mean to say, Gussie might have lowered the existing Worcestershire record for goofiness and definitely forfeited all chance of becoming Market Snodsbury's favourite son, but you couldn't get away from the fact that he had proposed to Madeline Bassett, and you had to admit that she had accepted him.

I put this to Jeeves.

"A frightful exhibition," I said, "and one which will very possibly ring down history's pages. But we must not forget, Jeeves, that Gussie, though now doubtless looked upon in the neighbourhood as the world's worst freak, is all right otherwise."

"No, sir."

I did not get quite this.

"When you say 'No, sir,' do you mean 'Yes, sir'?"

"No, sir. I mean 'No, sir.'"

"He is not all right otherwise?"

"No, sir."

"But he's betrothed."

"No longer, sir. Miss Bassett has severed the engagement."

"You don't mean that?"

"Yes, sir."

I wonder if you have noticed a rather peculiar thing about this chronicle. I allude to the fact that at one time or another practically everybody playing a part in it has had occasion to bury his or her face in his or her hands. I have participated in some pretty glutinous affairs in my time, but I think that never before or since have I been mixed up with such a solid body of brow clutchers.

Uncle Tom did it, if you remember. So did Gussie. So did Tuppy. So, probably, though I have no data, did Anatole, and I wouldn't put it past the Bassett. And Aunt Dahlia, I have no doubt, would have done it, too, but for the risk of disarranging the carefully fixed coiffure.

Well, what I am trying to say is that at this juncture I did it myself. Up went the hands and down went the head, and in another jiffy I was clutching as energetically as the best of them.

And it was while I was still massaging the coconut and wondering what the next move was that something barged up against the door like the delivery of a ton of coals.

"I think this may very possibly be Mr. Fink-Nottle himself, sir," said Jeeves.

His intuition, however, had led him astray. It was not Gussie but Tuppy. He came in and stood breathing asthmatically. It was plain that he was deeply stirred.

-18-

I eyed him narrowly. I didn't like his looks. Mark you, I don't say I ever had, much, because Nature, when planning this sterling fellow, shoved in a lot more lower jaw than was absolutely necessary and made the eyes a bit too keen and piercing for one who was neither an Empire builder nor a traffic policeman. But on the present occasion, in addition to offending the aesthetic sense, this Glossop seemed to me to be wearing a distinct air of menace, and I found myself wishing that Jeeves wasn't always so dashed tactful. I mean, it's all very well to remove yourself like an eel sliding into mud when the employer has a visitor, but there are moments—and it looked to me as if this was going to be one of them—when the truer tact is to stick round and stand ready to lend a hand in the free-for-all.

For Jeeves was no longer with us. I hadn't seen him go, and I hadn't heard him go, but he had gone. As far as the eye could reach, one noted nobody but Tuppy. And in Tuppy's demeanour, as I say, there was a certain something that tended to disquiet. He looked to me very much like a man who had come to reopen that matter of my tickling Angela's ankles.

However, his opening remark told me that I had been alarming myself unduly. It was of a pacific nature, and came as a great relief.

"Bertie," he said, "I owe you an apology. I have come to make it."

My relief on hearing these words, containing as they did no reference of any sort to tickled ankles, was, as I say, great. But I don't think it was any greater than my surprise. Months had passed since that painful episode at the Drones, and until now he hadn't given a sign of remorse and contrition. Indeed, word had reached me through private sources that he frequently told the story at dinners and other gatherings and, when doing so, laughed his silly head off.

I found it hard to understand, accordingly, what could have caused him to abase himself at this later date. Presumably he had been given the elbow by his better self, but why?

Still, there it was.

"My dear chap," I said, gentlemanly to the gills, "don't mention it."

"What's the sense of saying, 'Don't mention it'? I have mentioned it."

"I mean, don't mention it any more. Don't give the matter another thought. We all of us forget ourselves sometimes and do things which, in our calmer moments, we regret. No doubt you were a bit tight at the time."

"What the devil do you think you're talking about?"

I didn't like his tone. Brusque.

"Correct me if I am wrong," I said, with a certain stiffness, "but I assumed that you were apologizing for your foul conduct in looping back the last ring that night in the Drones, causing me to plunge into the swimming b. in the full soup and fish."

"Ass! Not that, at all."

"Then what?"

"This Bassett business."

"What Bassett business?"

"Bertie," said Tuppy, "when you told me last night that you were in love with Madeline Bassett, I gave you the impression that I believed you, but I didn't. The thing seemed too incredible. However, since then I have made inquiries, and the facts appear to square with your statement. I have now come to apologize for doubting you."

"Made inquiries?"

"I asked her if you had proposed to her, and she said, yes, you had."

"Tuppy! You didn't?"

"I did."

"Have you no delicacy, no proper feeling?"

"No."

"Oh? Well, right-ho, of course, but I think you ought to have."

"Delicacy be dashed. I wanted to be certain that it was not you who stole Angela from me. I now know it wasn't."

So long as he knew that, I didn't so much mind him having no delicacy.

"Ah," I said. "Well, that's fine. Hold that thought."

"I have found out who it was."

"What?"

He stood brooding for a moment. His eyes were smouldering with a dull fire. His jaw stuck out like the back of Jeeves's head.

"Bertie," he said, "do you remember what I swore I would do to the chap who stole Angela from me?"

"As nearly as I recall, you planned to pull him inside out——"

"——and make him swallow himself. Correct. The programme still holds good."

"But, Tuppy, I keep assuring you, as a competent eyewitness, that nobody snitched Angela from you during that Cannes trip."

"No. But they did after she got back."

"What?"

"Don't keep saying, 'What?' You heard."

"But she hasn't seen anybody since she got back."

"Oh, no? How about that newt bloke?"

"Gussie?"

"Precisely. The serpent Fink-Nottle."

This seemed to me absolute gibbering.

"But Gussie loves the Bassett."

"You can't all love this blighted Bassett. What astonishes me is that anyone can do it. He loves Angela, I tell you. And she loves him."

"But Angela handed you your hat before Gussie ever got here."

"No, she didn't. Couple of hours after."

"He couldn't have fallen in love with her in a couple of hours."

"Why not? I fell in love with her in a couple of minutes. I worshipped her immediately we met, the popeyed little excrescence."

"But, dash it——"

"Don't argue, Bertie. The facts are all docketed. She loves this newt-nuzzling blister."

"Quite absurd, laddie—quite absurd."

"Oh?" He ground a heel into the carpet—a thing I've often read about, but had never seen done before. "Then perhaps you will explain how it is that she happens to come to be engaged to him?"

You could have knocked me down with a f.

"Engaged to him?"

"She told me herself."

"She was kidding you."

"She was not kidding me. Shortly after the conclusion of this afternoon's binge at Market Snodsbury Grammar School he asked her to marry him, and she appears to have right-hoed without a murmur."

"There must be some mistake."

"There was. The snake Fink-Nottle made it, and by now I bet he realizes it. I've been chasing him since 5.30."

"Chasing him?"

"All over the place. I want to pull his head off."

"I see. Quite."

"You haven't seen him, by any chance?"

"No."

"Well, if you do, say goodbye to him quickly and put in your order for lilies.... Oh, Jeeves."

"Sir?"

I hadn't heard the door open, but the man was on the spot once more. My private belief, as I think I have mentioned before, is that Jeeves doesn't have to open doors. He's like one of those birds in India who bung their astral bodies about—the chaps, I mean, who having gone into thin air in Bombay, reassemble the parts and appear two minutes later in Calcutta. Only some such theory will account for the fact that he's not there one moment and is there the next. He just seems to float from Spot A to Spot B like some form of gas.

"Have you seen Mr. Fink-Nottle, Jeeves?"

"No, sir."

"I'm going to murder him."

"Very good, sir."

Tuppy withdrew, banging the door behind him, and I put Jeeves abreast.

"Jeeves," I said, "do you know what? Mr. Fink-Nottle is engaged to my Cousin Angela."

"Indeed, sir?"

"Well, how about it? Do you grasp the psychology? Does it make sense? Only a few hours ago he was engaged to Miss Bassett."

"Gentlemen who have been discarded by one young lady are often apt to attach themselves without delay to another, sir. It is what is known as a gesture."

I began to grasp.

"I see what you mean. Defiant stuff."

"Yes, sir."

"A sort of 'Oh, right-ho, please yourself, but if you don't want me, there are plenty who do.'"

"Precisely, sir. My Cousin George——"

"Never mind about your Cousin George, Jeeves."

"Very good, sir."

"Keep him for the long winter evenings, what?"

"Just as you wish, sir."

"And, anyway, I bet your Cousin George wasn't a shrinking, non-goose-bo-ing jellyfish like Gussie. That is what astounds me, Jeeves—that it should be Gussie who has been putting in all this heavy gesture-making stuff."

"You must remember, sir, that Mr. Fink-Nottle is in a somewhat inflamed cerebral condition."

"That's true. A bit above par at the moment, as it were?"

"Exactly, sir."

"Well, I'll tell you one thing—he'll be in a jolly sight more inflamed cerebral condition if Tuppy gets hold of him.... What's the time?"

"Just on eight o'clock, sir."

"Then Tuppy has been chasing him for two hours and a half. We must save the unfortunate blighter, Jeeves."

"Yes, sir."

"A human life is a human life, what?"

"Exceedingly true, sir."

"The first thing, then, is to find him. After that we can discuss plans and schemes. Go forth, Jeeves, and scour the neighbourhood."

"It will not be necessary, sir. If you will glance behind you, you will see Mr. Fink-Nottle coming out from beneath your bed."

And, by Jove, he was absolutely right.

There was Gussie, emerging as stated. He was covered with fluff and looked like a tortoise popping forth for a bit of a breather.

"Gussie!" I said.

"Jeeves," said Gussie.

"Sir?" said Jeeves.

"Is that door locked, Jeeves?"

"No, sir, but I will attend to the matter immediately."

Gussie sat down on the bed, and I thought for a moment that he was going to be in the mode by burying his face in his hands. However, he merely brushed a dead spider from his brow.

"Have you locked the door, Jeeves?"

"Yes, sir."

"Because you can never tell that that ghastly Glossop may not take it into his head to come——"

The word "back" froze on his lips. He hadn't got any further than a b-ish sound, when the handle of the door began to twist and rattle. He sprang from the bed, and for an instant stood looking exactly like a picture my Aunt Agatha has in her dining-room—The Stag at Bay—Landseer. Then he made a dive for the cupboard and was inside it before one really got on to it that he had started leaping. I have seen fellows late for the 9.15 move less nippily.

I shot a glance at Jeeves. He allowed his right eyebrow to flicker slightly, which is as near as he ever gets to a display of the emotions.

"Hullo?" I yipped.

"Let me in, blast you!" responded Tuppy's voice from without. "Who locked this door?"

I consulted Jeeves once more in the language of the eyebrow. He raised one of his. I raised one of mine. He raised his other. I raised my other. Then we both raised both. Finally, there seeming no other policy to pursue, I flung wide the gates and Tuppy came shooting in.

"Now what?" I said, as nonchalantly as I could manage.

"Why was the door locked?" demanded Tuppy.

I was in pretty good eyebrow-raising form by now, so I gave him a touch of it.

"Is one to have no privacy, Glossop?" I said coldly. "I instructed Jeeves to lock the door because I was about to disrobe."

"A likely story!" said Tuppy, and I'm not sure he didn't add "Forsooth!" "You needn't try to make me believe that you're afraid people are going to run excursion trains to see you in your underwear. You locked that door because you've got the snake Fink-Nottle concealed in here. I suspected it the moment I'd left, and I decided to come back and investigate. I'm going to search this room from end to end. I believe he's in that cupboard.... What's in this cupboard?"

"Just clothes," I said, having another stab at the nonchalant, though extremely dubious as to whether it would come off. "The usual wardrobe of the English gentleman paying a country-house visit."

"You're lying!"

Well, I wouldn't have been if he had only waited a minute before speaking, because the words were hardly out of his mouth before Gussie was out of the cupboard. I have commented on the speed with which he had gone in. It was as nothing to the speed with which he emerged. There was a sort of whir and blur, and he was no longer with us.

I think Tuppy was surprised. In fact, I'm sure he was. Despite the confidence with which he had stated his view that the cupboard contained Fink-Nottles, it plainly disconcerted him to have the chap fizzing out at him like this. He gargled sharply, and jumped back about five feet. The next moment, however, he had recovered his poise and was galloping down the corridor in pursuit. It only needed Aunt Dahlia after them, shouting "Yoicks!" or whatever is customary on these occasions, to complete the resemblance to a brisk run with the Quorn.

I sank into a handy chair. I am not a man whom it is easy to discourage, but it seemed to me that things had at last begun to get too complex for Bertram.

"Jeeves," I said, "all this is a bit thick."

"Yes, sir."

"The head rather swims."

"Yes, sir."

"I think you had better leave me, Jeeves. I shall need to devote the very closest thought to the situation which has arisen."

"Very good, sir."

The door closed. I lit a cigarette and began to ponder.

-19-

Most chaps in my position, I imagine, would have pondered all the rest of the evening without getting a bite, but we Woosters have an uncanny knack of going straight to the heart of things, and I don't suppose it was much more than ten minutes after I had started pondering before I saw what had to be done.

What was needed to straighten matters out, I perceived, was a heart-to-heart talk with Angela. She had caused all the trouble by her mutton-headed behaviour in saying "Yes" instead of "No" when Gussie, in the grip of mixed drinks and cerebral excitement, had suggested teaming up. She must obviously be properly ticked off and made to return him to store. A quarter of an hour later, I had tracked her down to the summer-house in which she was taking a cooler and was seating myself by her side.

"Angela," I said, and if my voice was stern, well, whose wouldn't have been, "this is all perfect drivel."

She seemed to come out of a reverie. She looked at me inquiringly.

"I'm sorry, Bertie, I didn't hear. What were you talking drivel about?"

"I was not talking drivel."

"Oh, sorry, I thought you said you were."

"Is it likely that I would come out here in order to talk drivel?"

"Very likely."

I thought it best to haul off and approach the matter from another angle.

"I've just been seeing Tuppy."

"Oh?"

"And Gussie Fink-Nottle."

"Oh, yes?"

"It appears that you have gone and got engaged to the latter."

"Quite right."

"Well, that's what I meant when I said it was all perfect drivel. You can't possibly love a chap like Gussie."

"Why not?"

"You simply can't."

Well, I mean to say, of course she couldn't. Nobody could love a freak like Gussie except a similar freak like the Bassett. The shot wasn't on the board. A splendid chap, of course, in many ways—courteous, amiable, and just the fellow to tell you what to do till the doctor came, if you had a sick newt on your hands—but quite obviously not of Mendelssohn's March timber. I have no doubt that you could have flung bricks by the hour in England's most densely populated districts without endangering the safety of a single girl capable of becoming Mrs. Augustus Fink-Nottle without an anaesthetic.

I put this to her, and she was forced to admit the justice of it.

"All right, then. Perhaps I don't."

"Then what," I said keenly, "did you want to go and get engaged to him for, you unreasonable young fathead?"

"I thought it would be fun."

"Fun!"

"And so it has been. I've had a lot of fun out of it. You should have seen Tuppy's face when I told him."

A sudden bright light shone upon me.

"Ha! A gesture!"

"What?"

"You got engaged to Gussie just to score off Tuppy?"

"I did."

"Well, then, that was what I was saying. It was a gesture."

"Yes, I suppose you could call it that."

"And I'll tell you something else I'll call it—viz. a dashed low trick. I'm surprised at you, young Angela."

"I don't see why."

I curled the lip about half an inch. "Being a female, you wouldn't. You gentler sexes are like that. You pull off the rawest stuff without a pang. You pride yourselves on it. Look at Jael, the wife of Heber."

"Where did you ever hear of Jael, the wife of Heber?"

"Possibly you are not aware that I once won a Scripture-knowledge prize at school?"

"Oh, yes. I remember Augustus mentioning it in his speech."

"Quite," I said, a little hurriedly. I had no wish to be reminded of Augustus's speech. "Well, as I say, look at Jael, the wife of Heber. Dug spikes into the guest's coconut while he was asleep, and then went swanking about the place like a Girl Guide. No wonder they say, 'Oh, woman, woman!'"

"Who?"

"The chaps who do. Coo, what a sex! But you aren't proposing to keep this up, of course?"

"Keep what up?"

"This rot of being engaged to Gussie."

"I certainly am."

"Just to make Tuppy look silly."

"Do you think he looks silly?"

"I do."

"So he ought to."

I began to get the idea that I wasn't making real headway. I remember when I won that Scripture-knowledge prize, having to go into the facts about Balaam's ass. I can't quite recall what they were, but I still retain a sort of general impression of something digging its feet in and putting its ears back and refusing to co-operate; and it seemed to me that this was what Angela was doing now. She and Balaam's ass were, so to speak, sisters under the skin. There's a word beginning with r——"re" something——"recal" something—No, it's gone. But what I am driving at is that is what this Angela was showing herself.

"Silly young geezer," I said.

She pinkened.

"I'm not a silly young geezer."

"You are a silly young geezer. And, what's more, you know it."

"I don't know anything of the kind."

"Here you are, wrecking Tuppy's life, wrecking Gussie's life, all for the sake of a cheap score."

"Well, it's no business of yours."

I sat on this promptly:

"No business of mine when I see two lives I used to go to school with wrecked? Ha! Besides, you know you're potty about Tuppy."

"I'm not!"

"Is that so? If I had a quid for every time I've seen you gaze at him with the lovelight in your eyes——"

She gazed at me, but without the lovelight.

"Oh, for goodness sake, go away and boil your head, Bertie!"

I drew myself up.

"That," I replied, with dignity, "is just what I am going to go away and boil. At least, I mean, I shall now leave you. I have said my say."

"Good."

"But permit me to add——"

"I won't."

"Very good," I said coldly. "In that case, tinkerty tonk."

And I meant it to sting.

"Moody" and "discouraged" were about the two adjectives you would have selected to describe me as I left the summer-house. It would be idle to deny that I had expected better results from this little chat.

I was surprised at Angela. Odd how you never realize that every girl is at heart a vicious specimen until something goes wrong with her love affair. This cousin and I had been meeting freely since the days when I wore sailor suits and she hadn't any front teeth, yet only now was I beginning to get on to her hidden depths. A simple, jolly, kindly young pimple she had always struck me as—the sort you could more or less rely on not to hurt a fly. But here she was now laughing heartlessly—at least, I seemed to remember hearing her laugh heartlessly—like something cold and callous out of a sophisticated talkie, and fairly spitting on her hands in her determination to bring Tuppy's grey hairs in sorrow to the grave.

I've said it before, and I'll say it again—girls are rummy. Old Pop Kipling never said a truer word than when he made that crack about the f. of the s. being more d. than the m.

It seemed to me in the circs. that there was but one thing to do—that is head for the dining-room and take a slash at the cold collation of which Jeeves had spoken. I felt in urgent need of sustenance, for the recent interview had pulled me down a bit. There is no gainsaying the fact that this naked-emotion stuff reduces a chap's vitality and puts him in the vein for a good whack at the beef and ham.

To the dining-room, accordingly, I repaired, and had barely crossed the threshold when I perceived Aunt Dahlia at the sideboard, tucking into salmon mayonnaise.

The spectacle drew from me a quick "Oh, ah," for I was somewhat embarrassed. The last time this relative and I had enjoyed a tête-à-tête, it will be remembered, she had sketched out plans for drowning me in the kitchen-garden pond, and I was not quite sure what my present standing with her was.

I was relieved to find her in genial mood. Nothing could have exceeded the cordiality with which she waved her fork.

"Hallo, Bertie, you old ass," was her very matey greeting. "I thought I shouldn't find you far away from the food. Try some of this salmon. Excellent."

"Anatole's?" I queried.

"No. He's still in bed. But the kitchen maid has struck an inspired streak. It suddenly seems to have come home to her that she isn't catering for a covey of buzzards in the Sahara Desert, and she has put out something quite fit for human consumption. There is good in the girl, after all, and I hope she enjoys herself at the dance."

I ladled out a portion of salmon, and we fell into pleasant conversation, chatting of this servants' ball at the Stretchley-Budds and speculating idly, I recall, as to what Seppings, the butler, would look like, doing the rumba.

It was not till I had cleaned up the first platter and was embarking on a second that the subject of Gussie came up. Considering what had passed at Market Snodsbury that afternoon, it was one which I had been expecting her to touch on earlier. When she did touch on it, I could see that she had not yet been informed of Angela's engagement.

"I say, Bertie," she said, meditatively chewing fruit salad. "This Spink-Bottle."

"Nottle."

"Bottle," insisted the aunt firmly. "After that exhibition of his this afternoon, Bottle, and nothing but Bottle, is how I shall always think of him. However, what I was going to say was that, if you see him, I wish you would tell him that he has made an old woman very, very happy. Except for the time when the curate tripped over a loose shoelace and fell down the pulpit steps, I don't think I have ever had a more wonderful moment than when good old Bottle suddenly started ticking Tom off from the platform. In fact, I thought his whole performance in the most perfect taste."

I could not but demur.

"Those references to myself——"

"Those were what I liked next best. I thought they were fine. Is it true that you cheated when you won that Scripture-knowledge prize?"

"Certainly not. My victory was the outcome of the most strenuous and unremitting efforts."

"And how about this pessimism we hear of? Are you a pessimist, Bertie?"

I could have told her that what was occurring in this house was rapidly making me one, but

I said no, I wasn't.

"That's right. Never be a pessimist. Everything is for the best in this best of all possible worlds. It's a long lane that has no turning. It's always darkest before the dawn. Have patience and all will come right. The sun will shine, although the day's a grey one.... Try some of this salad."

I followed her advice, but even as I plied the spoon my thoughts were elsewhere. I was perplexed. It may have been the fact that I had recently been hobnobbing with so many bowed-down hearts that made this cheeriness of hers seem so bizarre, but bizarre was certainly what I found it.

"I thought you might have been a trifle peeved," I said.

"Peeved?"

"By Gussie's manoeuvres on the platform this afternoon. I confess that I had rather expected the tapping foot and the drawn brow."

"Nonsense. What was there to be peeved about? I took the whole thing as a great compliment, proud to feel that any drink from my cellars could have produced such a majestic jag. It restores one's faith in post-war whisky. Besides, I couldn't be peeved at anything tonight. I am like a little child clapping its hands and dancing in the sunshine. For though it has been some time getting a move on, Bertie, the sun has at last broken through the clouds. Ring out those joy bells. Anatole has withdrawn his notice."

"What? Oh, very hearty congratulations."

"Thanks. Yes, I worked on him like a beaver after I got back this afternoon, and finally, vowing he would ne'er consent, he consented. He stays on, praises be, and the way I look at it now is that God's in His heaven and all's right with——"

She broke off. The door had opened, and we were plus a butler.

"Hullo, Seppings," said Aunt Dahlia. "I thought you had gone."

"Not yet, madam."

"Well, I hope you will all have a good time."

"Thank you, madam."

"Was there something you wanted to see me about?"

"Yes, madam. It is with reference to Monsieur Anatole. Is it by your wish, madam, that Mr. Fink-Nottle is making faces at Monsieur Anatole through the skylight of his bedroom?"

-20-

There was one of those long silences. Pregnant, I believe, is what they're generally called. Aunt looked at butler. Butler looked at aunt. I looked at both of them. An eerie stillness seemed to envelop the room like a linseed poultice. I happened to be biting on a slice of apple in my fruit salad at the moment, and it sounded as if Carnera had jumped off the top of the Eiffel Tower on to a cucumber frame.

Aunt Dahlia steadied herself against the sideboard, and spoke in a low, husky voice:

"Faces?"

"Yes, madam."

"Through the skylight?"

"Yes, madam."

"You mean he's sitting on the roof?"

"Yes, madam. It has upset Monsieur Anatole very much."

I suppose it was that word "upset" that touched Aunt Dahlia off. Experience had taught her what happened when Anatole got upset. I had always known her as a woman who was quite active on her pins, but I had never suspected her of being capable of the magnificent burst of speed which she now showed. Pausing merely to get a rich hunting-field expletive off her chest, she was out of the room and making for the stairs before I could swallow a sliver of—I think—banana. And feeling, as I had felt when I got that telegram of hers about Angela and Tuppy, that my place was by her side, I put down my plate and hastened after her, Seppings following at a loping gallop.

I say that my place was by her side, but it was not so dashed easy to get there, for she was setting a cracking pace. At the top of the first flight she must have led by a matter of half a dozen lengths, and was still shaking off my challenge when she rounded into the second. At the next landing, however, the gruelling going appeared to tell on her, for she slackened off a trifle and showed symptoms of roaring, and by the time we were in the straight we were running practically neck and neck. Our entry into Anatole's room was as close a finish as you could have wished to see.

Result:

1.   Aunt Dahlia.
2.   Bertram.
3.   Seppings.

Won by a short head. Half a staircase separated second and third.

The first thing that met the eye on entering was Anatole. This wizard of the cooking-stove is a tubby little man with a moustache of the outsize or soup-strainer type, and you can generally take a line through it as to the state of his emotions. When all is well, it turns up at the ends like a sergeant-major's. When the soul is bruised, it droops.

It was drooping now, striking a sinister note. And if any shadow of doubt had remained as to how he was feeling, the way he was carrying on would have dispelled it. He was standing by the bed in pink pyjamas, waving his fists at the skylight. Through the glass, Gussie was staring down. His eyes were bulging and his mouth was open, giving him so striking a resemblance to some rare fish in an aquarium that one's primary impulse was to offer him an ant's egg.

Watching this fist-waving cook and this goggling guest, I must say that my sympathies were completely with the former. I considered him thoroughly justified in waving all the fists he wanted to.

Review the facts, I mean to say. There he had been, lying in bed, thinking idly of whatever French cooks do think about when in bed, and he had suddenly become aware of that frightful face at the window. A thing to jar the most phlegmatic. I know I should hate to be lying in bed and have Gussie popping up like that. A chap's bedroom—you can't get away from it—is his castle, and he has every right to look askance if gargoyles come glaring in at him.

While I stood musing thus, Aunt Dahlia, in her practical way, was coming straight to the point:

"What's all this?"

Anatole did a sort of Swedish exercise, starting at the base of the spine, carrying on through the shoulder-blades and finishing up among the back hair.

Then he told her.

In the chats I have had with this wonder man, I have always found his English fluent, but a bit on the mixed side. If you remember, he was with Mrs. Bingo Little for a time before coming to Brinkley, and no doubt he picked up a good deal from Bingo. Before that, he had been a couple of years with an American family at Nice and had studied under their chauffeur, one of the Maloneys of Brooklyn. So, what with Bingo and what with Maloney, he is, as I say, fluent but a bit mixed.

He spoke, in part, as follows:

"Hot dog! You ask me what is it? Listen. Make some attention a little. Me, I have hit the hay, but I do not sleep so good, and presently I wake and up I look, and there is one who make faces against me through the dashed window. Is that a pretty affair? Is that convenient? If you think I like it, you jolly well mistake yourself. I am so mad as a wet hen. And why not? I am somebody, isn't it? This is a bedroom, what-what, not a house for some apes? Then for what do blighters sit on my window so cool as a few cucumbers, making some faces?"

"Quite," I said. Dashed reasonable, was my verdict.

He threw another look up at Gussie, and did Exercise 2—the one where you clutch the moustache, give it a tug and then start catching flies.

"Wait yet a little. I am not finish. I say I see this type on my window, making a few faces. But what then? Does he buzz off when I shout a cry, and leave me peaceable? Not on your life. He remain planted there, not giving any damns, and sit regarding me like a cat watching a duck. He make faces against me and again he make faces against me, and the more I command that he should get to hell out of here, the more he do not get to hell out of here. He cry something towards me, and I demand what is his desire, but he do not explain. Oh, no, that arrives never. He does but shrug his head. What damn silliness! Is this amusing for me? You think I like it? I am not content with such folly. I think the poor mutt's loony. Je me fiche de ce type infect. C'est idiot de faire comme ça l'oiseau.... Allez-vous-en, louffier.... Tell the boob to go away. He is mad as some March hatters."

I must say I thought he was making out a jolly good case, and evidently Aunt Dahlia felt the same. She laid a quivering hand on his shoulder.

"I will, Monsieur Anatole, I will," she said, and I couldn't have believed that robust voice capable of sinking to such an absolute coo. More like a turtle dove calling to its mate than anything else. "It's quite all right."

She had said the wrong thing. He did Exercise 3.

"All right? Nom d'un nom d'un nom! The hell you say it's all right! Of what use to pull stuff like that? Wait one half-moment. Not yet quite so quick, my old sport. It is by no means all right. See yet again a little. It is some very different dishes of fish. I can take a few smooths with a rough, it is true, but I do not find it agreeable when one play larks against me on my windows. That cannot do. A nice thing, no. I am a serious man. I do not wish a few larks on my windows. I enjoy larks on my windows worse as any. It is very little all right. If such rannygazoo is to arrive, I do not remain any longer in this house no more. I buzz off and do not stay planted."

Sinister words, I had to admit, and I was not surprised that Aunt Dahlia, hearing them, should have uttered a cry like the wail of a master of hounds seeing a fox shot. Anatole had begun to wave his fists again at Gussie, and she now joined him. Seppings, who was puffing respectfully in the background, didn't actually wave his fists, but he gave Gussie a pretty austere look. It was plain to the thoughtful observer that this Fink-Nottle, in getting on to that skylight, had done a mistaken thing. He couldn't have been more unpopular in the home of G.G. Simmons.

"Go away, you crazy loon!" cried Aunt Dahlia, in that ringing voice of hers which had once caused nervous members of the Quorn to lose stirrups and take tosses from the saddle.

Gussie's reply was to waggle his eyebrows. I could read the message he was trying to convey.

"I think he means," I said—reasonable old Bertram, always trying to throw oil on the troubled w's——"that if he does he will fall down the side of the house and break his neck."

"Well, why not?" said Aunt Dahlia.

I could see her point, of course, but it seemed to me that there might be a nearer solution. This skylight happened to be the only window in the house which Uncle Tom had not festooned with his bally bars. I suppose he felt that if a burglar had the nerve to climb up as far as this, he deserved what was coming to him.

"If you opened the skylight, he could jump in."

The idea got across.

"Seppings, how does this skylight open?"

"With a pole, madam."

"Then get a pole. Get two poles. Ten."

And presently Gussie was mixing with the company, Like one of those chaps you read about in the papers, the wretched man seemed deeply conscious of his position.

I must say Aunt Dahlia's bearing and demeanour did nothing to assist toward a restored composure. Of the amiability which she had exhibited when discussing this unhappy chump's activities with me over the fruit salad, no trace remained, and I was not surprised that speech more or less froze on the Fink-Nottle lips. It isn't often that Aunt Dahlia, normally as genial a bird as ever encouraged a gaggle of hounds to get their noses down to it, lets her angry passions rise, but when she does, strong men climb trees and pull them up after them.

"Well?" she said.

In answer to this, all that Gussie could produce was a sort of strangled hiccough.

"Well?"

Aunt Dahlia's face grew darker. Hunting, if indulged in regularly over a period of years, is a pastime that seldom fails to lend a fairly deepish tinge to the patient's complexion, and her best friends could not have denied that even at normal times the relative's map tended a little toward the crushed strawberry. But never had I seen it take on so pronounced a richness as now. She looked like a tomato struggling for self-expression.

"Well?"

Gussie tried hard. And for a moment it seemed as if something was going to come through.

But in the end it turned out nothing more than a sort of death-rattle.

"Oh, take him away, Bertie, and put ice on his head," said Aunt Dahlia, giving the thing up. And she turned to tackle what looked like the rather man's size job of soothing Anatole, who was now carrying on a muttered conversation with himself in a rapid sort of way.

Seeming to feel that the situation was one to which he could not do justice in Bingo-cum-Maloney Anglo-American, he had fallen back on his native tongue. Words like "marmiton de Domange," "pignouf," "hurluberlu" and "roustisseur" were fluttering from him like bats out of a barn. Lost on me, of course, because, though I sweated a bit at the Gallic language during that Cannes visit, I'm still more or less in the Esker-vous-avez stage. I regretted this, for they sounded good.

I assisted Gussie down the stairs. A cooler thinker than Aunt Dahlia, I had already guessed the hidden springs and motives which had led him to the roof. Where she had seen only a cockeyed reveller indulging himself in a drunken prank or whimsy, I had spotted the hunted fawn.

"Was Tuppy after you?" I asked sympathetically.

What I believe is called a frisson shook him.

"He nearly got me on the top landing. I shinned out through a passage window and scrambled along a sort of ledge."

"That baffled him, what?"

"Yes. But then I found I had stuck. The roof sloped down in all directions. I couldn't go back. I had to go on, crawling along this ledge. And then I found myself looking down the skylight. Who was that chap?"

"That was Anatole, Aunt Dahlia's chef."

"French?"

"To the core."

"That explains why I couldn't make him understand. What asses these Frenchmen are. They don't seem able to grasp the simplest thing. You'd have thought if a chap saw a chap on a skylight, the chap would realize the chap wanted to be let in. But no, he just stood there."

"Waving a few fists."

"Yes. Silly idiot. Still, here I am."

"Here you are, yes—for the moment."

"Eh?"

"I was thinking that Tuppy is probably lurking somewhere."

He leaped like a lamb in springtime.

"What shall I do?"

I considered this.

"Sneak back to your room and barricade the door. That is the manly policy."

"Suppose that's where he's lurking?"

"In that case, move elsewhere."

But on arrival at the room, it transpired that Tuppy, if anywhere, was infesting some other portion of the house. Gussie shot in, and I heard the key turn. And feeling that there was no more that I could do in that quarter, I returned to the dining-room for further fruit salad and a quiet think. And I had barely filled my plate when the door opened and Aunt Dahlia came in. She sank into a chair, looking a bit shopworn.

"Give me a drink, Bertie."

"What sort?"

"Any sort, so long as it's strong."

Approach Bertram Wooster along these lines, and you catch him at his best. St. Bernard dogs doing the square thing by Alpine travellers could not have bustled about more assiduously. I filled the order, and for some moments nothing was to be heard but the sloshing sound of an aunt restoring her tissues.

"Shove it down, Aunt Dahlia," I said sympathetically. "These things take it out of one, don't they? You've had a toughish time, no doubt, soothing Anatole," I proceeded, helping myself to anchovy paste on toast. "Everything pretty smooth now, I trust?"

She gazed at me in a long, lingering sort of way, her brow wrinkled as if in thought.

"Attila," she said at length. "That's the name. Attila, the Hun."

"Eh?"

"I was trying to think who you reminded me of. Somebody who went about strewing ruin and desolation and breaking up homes which, until he came along, had been happy and peaceful. Attila is the man. It's amazing." she said, drinking me in once more. "To look at you, one would think you were just an ordinary sort of amiable idiot—certifiable, perhaps, but quite harmless. Yet, in reality, you are worse a scourge than the Black Death. I tell you, Bertie, when I contemplate you I seem to come up against all the underlying sorrow and horror of life with such a thud that I feel as if I had walked into a lamp post."

Pained and surprised, I would have spoken, but the stuff I had thought was anchovy paste had turned out to be something far more gooey and adhesive. It seemed to wrap itself round the tongue and impede utterance like a gag. And while I was still endeavouring to clear the vocal cords for action, she went on:

"Do you realize what you started when you sent that Spink-Bottle man down here? As regards his getting blotto and turning the prize-giving ceremonies at Market Snodsbury Grammar School into a sort of two-reel comic film, I will say nothing, for frankly I enjoyed it. But when he comes leering at Anatole through skylights, just after I had with infinite pains and tact induced him to withdraw his notice, and makes him so temperamental that he won't hear of staying on after tomorrow——"

The paste stuff gave way. I was able to speak:

"What?"

"Yes, Anatole goes tomorrow, and I suppose poor old Tom will have indigestion for the rest of his life. And that is not all. I have just seen Angela, and she tells me she is engaged to this Bottle."

"Temporarily, yes," I had to admit.

"Temporarily be blowed. She's definitely engaged to him and talks with a sort of hideous coolness of getting married in October. So there it is. If the prophet Job were to walk into the room at this moment, I could sit swapping hard-luck stories with him till bedtime. Not that Job was in my class."

"He had boils."

"Well, what are boils?"

"Dashed painful, I understand."

"Nonsense. I'd take all the boils on the market in exchange for my troubles. Can't you realize the position? I've lost the best cook to England. My husband, poor soul, will probably die of dyspepsia. And my only daughter, for whom I had dreamed such a wonderful future, is engaged to be married to an inebriated newt fancier. And you talk about boils!"

I corrected her on a small point:

"I don't absolutely talk about boils. I merely mentioned that Job had them. Yes, I agree with you, Aunt Dahlia, that things are not looking too oojah-cum-spiff at the moment, but be of good cheer. A Wooster is seldom baffled for more than the nonce."

"You rather expect to be coming along shortly with another of your schemes?"

"At any minute."

She sighed resignedly.

"I thought as much. Well, it needed but this. I don't see how things could possibly be worse than they are, but no doubt you will succeed in making them so. Your genius and insight will find the way. Carry on, Bertie. Yes, carry on. I am past caring now. I shall even find a faint interest in seeing into what darker and profounder abysses of hell you can plunge this home. Go to it, lad.... What's that stuff you're eating?"

"I find it a little difficult to classify. Some sort of paste on toast. Rather like glue flavoured with beef extract."

"Gimme," said Aunt Dahlia listlessly.

"Be careful how you chew," I advised. "It sticketh closer than a brother.... Yes, Jeeves?"

The man had materialized on the carpet. Absolutely noiseless, as usual.

"A note for you, sir."

"A note for me, Jeeves?"

"A note for you, sir."

"From whom, Jeeves?"

"From Miss Bassett, sir."

"From whom, Jeeves?"

"From Miss Bassett, sir."

"From Miss Bassett, Jeeves?"

"From Miss Bassett, sir."

At this point, Aunt Dahlia, who had taken one nibble at her whatever-it-was-on-toast and laid it down, begged us—a little fretfully, I thought—for heaven's sake to cut out the cross-talk vaudeville stuff, as she had enough to bear already without having to listen to us doing our imitation of the Two Macs. Always willing to oblige, I dismissed Jeeves with a nod, and he flickered for a moment and was gone. Many a spectre would have been less slippy.

"But what," I mused, toying with the envelope, "can this female be writing to me about?"

"Why not open the damn thing and see?"

"A very excellent idea," I said, and did so.

"And if you are interested in my movements," proceeded Aunt Dahlia, heading for the door, "I propose to go to my room, do some Yogi deep breathing, and try to forget."

"Quite," I said absently, skimming p. l. And then, as I turned over, a sharp howl broke from my lips, causing Aunt Dahlia to shy like a startled mustang.

"Don't do it!" she exclaimed, quivering in every limb.

"Yes, but dash it——"

"What a pest you are, you miserable object," she sighed. "I remember years ago, when you were in your cradle, being left alone with you one day and you nearly swallowed your rubber comforter and started turning purple. And I, ass that I was, took it out and saved your life. Let me tell you, young Bertie, it will go very hard with you if you ever swallow a rubber comforter again when only I am by to aid."

"But, dash it!" I cried. "Do you know what's happened? Madeline Bassett says she's going to marry me!"

"I hope it keeps fine for you," said the relative, and passed from the room looking like something out of an Edgar Allan Poe story.

-21-

I don't suppose I was looking so dashed unlike something out of an Edgar Allan Poe story myself, for, as you can readily imagine, the news item which I have just recorded had got in amongst me properly. If the Bassett, in the belief that the Wooster heart had long been hers and was waiting ready to be scooped in on demand, had decided to take up her option, I should, as a man of honour and sensibility, have no choice but to come across and kick in. The matter was obviously not one that could be straightened out with a curt nolle prosequi. All the evidence, therefore, seemed to point to the fact that the doom had come upon me and, what was more, had come to stay.

And yet, though it would be idle to pretend that my grip on the situation was quite the grip I would have liked it to be, I did not despair of arriving at a solution. A lesser man, caught in this awful snare, would no doubt have thrown in the towel at once and ceased to struggle; but the whole point about the Woosters is that they are not lesser men.

By way of a start, I read the note again. Not that I had any hope that a second perusal would enable me to place a different construction on its contents, but it helped to fill in while the brain was limbering up. I then, to assist thought, had another go at the fruit salad, and in addition ate a slice of sponge cake. And it was as I passed on to the cheese that the machinery started working. I saw what had to be done.

To the question which had been exercising the mind—viz., can Bertram cope?—I was now able to reply with a confident "Absolutely."

The great wheeze on these occasions of dirty work at the crossroads is not to lose your head but to keep cool and try to find the ringleaders. Once find the ringleaders, and you know where you are.

The ringleader here was plainly the Bassett. It was she who had started the whole imbroglio by chucking Gussie, and it was clear that before anything could be done to solve and clarify, she must be induced to revise her views and take him on again. This would put Angela back into circulation, and that would cause Tuppy to simmer down a bit, and then we could begin to get somewhere.

I decided that as soon as I had had another morsel of cheese I would seek this Bassett out and be pretty eloquent.

And at this moment in she came. I might have foreseen that she would be turning up shortly. I mean to say, hearts may ache, but if they know that there is a cold collation set out in the dining-room, they are pretty sure to come popping in sooner or later.

Her eyes, as she entered the room, were fixed on the salmon mayonnaise, and she would no doubt have made a bee-line for it and started getting hers, had I not, in the emotion of seeing her, dropped a glass of the best with which I was endeavouring to bring about a calmer frame of mind. The noise caused her to turn, and for an instant embarrassment supervened. A slight flush mantled the cheek, and the eyes popped a bit.

"Oh!" she said.

I have always found that there is nothing that helps to ease you over one of these awkward moments like a spot of stage business. Find something to do with your hands, and it's half the battle. I grabbed a plate and hastened forward.

"A touch of salmon?"

"Thank you."

"With a suspicion of salad?"

"If you please."

"And to drink? Name the poison."

"I think I would like a little orange juice."

She gave a gulp. Not at the orange juice, I don't mean, because she hadn't got it yet, but at all the tender associations those two words provoked. It was as if someone had mentioned spaghetti to the relict of an Italian organ-grinder. Her face flushed a deeper shade, she registered anguish, and I saw that it was no longer within the sphere of practical politics to try to confine the conversation to neutral topics like cold boiled salmon.

So did she, I imagine, for when I, as a preliminary to getting down to brass tacks, said "Er," she said "Er," too, simultaneously, the brace of "Ers" clashing in mid-air.

"I'm sorry."

"I beg your pardon."

"You were saying——"

"You were saying——"

"No, please go on."

"Oh, right-ho."

I straightened the tie, my habit when in this girl's society, and had at it:

"With reference to yours of even date——"

She flushed again, and took a rather strained forkful of salmon.

"You got my note?"

"Yes, I got your note."

"I gave it to Jeeves to give it to you."

"Yes, he gave it to me. That's how I got it."

There was another silence. And as she was plainly shrinking from talking turkey, I was reluctantly compelled to do so. I mean, somebody had got to. Too dashed silly, a male and female in our position simply standing eating salmon and cheese at one another without a word.

"Yes, I got it all right."

"I see. You got it."

"Yes, I got it. I've just been reading it. And what I was rather wanting to ask you, if we happened to run into each other, was—well, what about it?"

"What about it?"

"That's what I say: What about it?"

"But it was quite clear."

"Oh, quite. Perfectly clear. Very well expressed and all that. But—I mean—Well, I mean, deeply sensible of the honour, and so forth—but—— Well, dash it!"

She had polished off her salmon, and now put the plate down.

"Fruit salad?"

"No, thank you."

"Spot of pie?"

"No, thanks."

"One of those glue things on toast?"

"No, thank you."

She took a cheese straw. I found a cold egg which I had overlooked. Then I said "I mean to say" just as she said "I think I know", and there was another collision.

"I beg your pardon."

"I'm sorry."

"Do go on."

"No, you go on."

I waved my cold egg courteously, to indicate that she had the floor, and she started again:

"I think I know what you are trying to say. You are surprised."

"Yes."

"You are thinking of——"

"Exactly."

"——Mr. Fink-Nottle."

"The very man."

"You find what I have done hard to understand."

"Absolutely."

"I don't wonder."

"I do."

"And yet it is quite simple."

She took another cheese straw. She seemed to like cheese straws.

"Quite simple, really. I want to make you happy."

"Dashed decent of you."

"I am going to devote the rest of my life to making you happy."

"A very matey scheme."

"I can at least do that. But—may I be quite frank with you, Bertie?"

"Oh, rather."

"Then I must tell you this. I am fond of you. I will marry you. I will do my best to make you a good wife. But my affection for you can never be the flamelike passion I felt for Augustus."

"Just the very point I was working round to. There, as you say, is the snag. Why not chuck the whole idea of hitching up with me? Wash it out altogether. I mean, if you love old Gussie——"

"No longer."

"Oh, come."

"No. What happened this afternoon has killed my love. A smear of ugliness has been drawn across a thing of beauty, and I can never feel towards him as I did."

I saw what she meant, of course. Gussie had bunged his heart at her feet; she had picked it up, and, almost immediately after doing so, had discovered that he had been stewed to the eyebrows all the time. The shock must have been severe. No girl likes to feel that a chap has got to be thoroughly plastered before he can ask her to marry him. It wounds the pride.

Nevertheless, I persevered.

"But have you considered," I said, "that you may have got a wrong line on Gussie's performance this afternoon? Admitted that all the evidence points to a more sinister theory, what price him simply having got a touch of the sun? Chaps do get touches of the sun, you know, especially when the weather's hot."

She looked at me, and I saw that she was putting in a bit of the old drenched-irises stuff.

"It was like you to say that, Bertie. I respect you for it."

"Oh, no."

"Yes. You have a splendid, chivalrous soul."

"Not a bit."

"Yes, you have. You remind me of Cyrano."

"Who?"

"Cyrano de Bergerac."

"The chap with the nose?"

"Yes."

I can't say I was any too pleased. I felt the old beak furtively. It was a bit on the prominent side, perhaps, but, dash it, not in the Cyrano class. It began to look as if the next thing this girl would do would be to compare me to Schnozzle Durante.

"He loved, but pleaded another's cause."

"Oh, I see what you mean now."

"I like you for that, Bertie. It was fine of you—fine and big. But it is no use. There are things which kill love. I can never forget Augustus, but my love for him is dead. I will be your wife."

Well, one has to be civil.

"Right ho," I said. "Thanks awfully."

Then the dialogue sort of poofed out once more, and we stood eating cheese straws and cold eggs respectively in silence. There seemed to exist some little uncertainty as to what the next move was.

Fortunately, before embarrassment could do much more supervening, Angela came in, and this broke up the meeting. Then Bassett announced our engagement, and Angela kissed her and said she hoped she would be very, very happy, and the Bassett kissed her and said she hoped she would be very, very happy with Gussie, and Angela said she was sure she would, because Augustus was such a dear, and the Bassett kissed her again, and Angela kissed her again and, in a word, the whole thing got so bally feminine that I was glad to edge away.

I would have been glad to do so, of course, in any case, for if ever there was a moment when it was up to Bertram to think, and think hard, this moment was that moment.

It was, it seemed to me, the end. Not even on the occasion, some years earlier, when I had inadvertently become betrothed to Tuppy's frightful Cousin Honoria, had I experienced a deeper sense of being waist high in the gumbo and about to sink without trace. I wandered out into the garden, smoking a tortured gasper, with the iron well embedded in the soul. And I had fallen into a sort of trance, trying to picture what it would be like having the Bassett on the premises for the rest of my life and at the same time, if you follow me, trying not to picture what it would be like, when I charged into something which might have been a tree, but was not—being, in point of fact, Jeeves.

"I beg your pardon, sir," he said. "I should have moved to one side."

I did not reply. I stood looking at him in silence. For the sight of him had opened up a new line of thought.

This Jeeves, now, I reflected. I had formed the opinion that he had lost his grip and was no longer the force he had been, but was it not possible, I asked myself, that I might be mistaken? Start him off exploring avenues and might he not discover one through which I would be enabled to sneak off to safety, leaving no hard feelings behind? I found myself answering that it was quite on the cards that he might.

After all, his head still bulged out at the back as of old. One noted in the eyes the same intelligent glitter.

Mind you, after what had passed between us in the matter of that white mess-jacket with the brass buttons, I was not prepared absolutely to hand over to the man. I would, of course, merely take him into consultation. But, recalling some of his earlier triumphs—the Sipperley Case, the Episode of My Aunt Agatha and the Dog McIntosh, and the smoothly handled Affair of Uncle George and The Barmaid's Niece were a few that sprang to my mind—I felt justified at least in offering him the opportunity of coming to the aid of the young master in his hour of peril.

But before proceeding further, there was one thing that had got to be understood between us, and understood clearly.

"Jeeves," I said, "a word with you."

"Sir?"

"I am up against it a bit, Jeeves."

"I am sorry to hear that, sir. Can I be of any assistance?"

"Quite possibly you can, if you have not lost your grip. Tell me frankly, Jeeves, are you in pretty good shape mentally?"

"Yes, sir."

"Still eating plenty of fish?"

"Yes, sir."

"Then it may be all right. But there is just one point before I begin. In the past, when you have contrived to extricate self or some pal from some little difficulty, you have frequently shown a disposition to take advantage of my gratitude to gain some private end. Those purple socks, for instance. Also the plus fours and the Old Etonian spats. Choosing your moment with subtle cunning, you came to me when I was weakened by relief and got me to get rid of them. And what I am saying now is that if you are successful on the present occasion there must be no rot of that description about that mess-jacket of mine."

"Very good, sir."

"You will not come to me when all is over and ask me to jettison the jacket?"

"Certainly not, sir."

"On that understanding then, I will carry on. Jeeves, I'm engaged."

"I hope you will be very happy, sir."

"Don't be an ass. I'm engaged to Miss Bassett."

"Indeed, sir? I was not aware——"

"Nor was I. It came as a complete surprise. However, there it is. The official intimation was in that note you brought me."

"Odd, sir."

"What is?"

"Odd, sir, that the contents of that note should have been as you describe. It seemed to me that Miss Bassett, when she handed me the communication, was far from being in a happy frame of mind."

"She is far from being in a happy frame of mind. You don't suppose she really wants to marry me, do you? Pshaw, Jeeves! Can't you see that this is simply another of those bally gestures which are rapidly rendering Brinkley Court a hell for man and beast? Dash all gestures, is my view."

"Yes, sir."

"Well, what's to be done?"

"You feel that Miss Bassett, despite what has occurred, still retains a fondness for Mr. Fink-Nottle, sir?"

"She's pining for him."

"In that case, sir, surely the best plan would be to bring about a reconciliation between them."

"How? You see. You stand silent and twiddle the fingers. You are stumped."

"No, sir. If I twiddled my fingers, it was merely to assist thought."

"Then continue twiddling."

"It will not be necessary, sir."

"You don't mean you've got a bite already?"

"Yes, sir."

"You astound me, Jeeves. Let's have it."

"The device which I have in mind is one that I have already mentioned to you, sir."

"When did you ever mention any device to me?"

"If you will throw your mind back to the evening of our arrival, sir. You were good enough to inquire of me if I had any plan to put forward with a view to bringing Miss Angela and

Mr. Glossop together, and I ventured to suggest——"

"Good Lord! Not the old fire-alarm thing?"

"Precisely, sir."

"You're still sticking to that?"

"Yes, sir."

It shows how much the ghastly blow I had received had shaken me when I say that, instead of dismissing the proposal with a curt "Tchah!" or anything like that, I found myself speculating as to whether there might not be something in it, after all.

When he had first mooted this fire-alarm scheme of his, I had sat upon it, if you remember, with the maximum of promptitude and vigour. "Rotten" was the adjective I had employed to describe it, and you may recall that I mused a bit sadly, considering the idea conclusive proof of the general breakdown of a once fine mind. But now it somehow began to look as if it might have possibilities. The fact of the matter was that I had about reached the stage where I was prepared to try anything once, however goofy.

"Just run through that wheeze again, Jeeves," I said thoughtfully. "I remember thinking it cuckoo, but it may be that I missed some of the finer shades."

"Your criticism of it at the time, sir, was that it was too elaborate, but I do not think it is so in reality. As I see it, sir, the occupants of the house, hearing the fire bell ring, will suppose that a conflagration has broken out."

I nodded. One could follow the train of thought.

"Yes, that seems reasonable."

"Whereupon Mr. Glossop will hasten to save Miss Angela, while Mr. Fink-Nottle performs the same office for Miss Bassett."

"Is that based on psychology?"

"Yes, sir. Possibly you may recollect that it was an axiom of the late Sir Arthur Conan Doyle's fictional detective, Sherlock Holmes, that the instinct of everyone, upon an alarm of fire, is to save the object dearest to them."

"It seems to me that there is a grave danger of seeing Tuppy come out carrying a steak-and-kidney pie, but resume, Jeeves, resume. You think that this would clean everything up?"

"The relations of the two young couples could scarcely continue distant after such an occurrence, sir."

"Perhaps you're right. But, dash it, if we go ringing fire bells in the night watches, shan't we scare half the domestic staff into fits? There is one of the housemaids—Jane, I believe—who already skips like the high hills if I so much as come on her unexpectedly round a corner."

"A neurotic girl, sir, I agree. I have noticed her. But by acting promptly we should avoid such a contingency. The entire staff, with the exception of Monsieur Anatole, will be at the ball at Kingham Manor tonight."

"Of course. That just shows the condition this thing has reduced me to. Forget my own name next. Well, then, let's just try to envisage. Bong goes the bell. Gussie rushes and grabs the Bassett.... Wait. Why shouldn't she simply walk downstairs?"

"You are overlooking the effect of sudden alarm on the feminine temperament, sir."

"That's true."

"Miss Bassett's impulse, I would imagine, sir, would be to leap from her window."

"Well, that's worse. We don't want her spread out in a sort of purée on the lawn. It seems to me that the flaw in this scheme of yours, Jeeves, is that it's going to litter the garden with mangled corpses."

"No, sir. You will recall that Mr. Travers's fear of burglars has caused him to have stout bars fixed to all the windows."

"Of course, yes. Well, it sounds all right," I said, though still a bit doubtfully. "Quite possibly it may come off. But I have a feeling that it will slip up somewhere. However, I am in no position to cavil at even a 100 to 1 shot. I will adopt this policy of yours, Jeeves, though, as I say, with misgivings. At what hour would you suggest bonging the bell?"

"Not before midnight, sir."

"That is to say, some time after midnight."

"Yes, sir."

"Right-ho, then. At 12.30 on the dot, I will bong."

"Very good, sir."

-22-

I don't know why it is, but there's something about the rural districts after dark that always has a rummy effect on me. In London I can stay out till all hours and come home with the milk without a tremor, but put me in the garden of a country house after the strength of the company has gone to roost and the place is shut up, and a sort of goose-fleshy feeling steals over me. The night wind stirs the tree-tops, twigs crack, bushes rustle, and before I know where I am, the morale has gone phut and I'm expecting the family ghost to come sneaking up behind me, making groaning noises. Dashed unpleasant, the whole thing, and if you think it improves matters to know that you are shortly about to ring the loudest fire bell in England and start an all-hands-to-the-pumps panic in that quiet, darkened house, you err.

I knew all about the Brinkley Court fire bell. The dickens of a row it makes. Uncle Tom, in addition to not liking burglars, is a bloke who has always objected to the idea of being cooked in his sleep, so when he bought the place he saw to it that the fire bell should be something that might give you heart failure, but which you couldn't possibly mistake for the drowsy chirping of a sparrow in the ivy.

When I was a kid and spent my holidays at Brinkley, we used to have fire drills after closing time, and many is the night I've had it jerk me out of the dreamless like the Last Trump.

I confess that the recollection of what this bell could do when it buckled down to it gave me pause as I stood that night at 12.30 p.m. prompt beside the outhouse where it was located. The sight of the rope against the whitewashed wall and the thought of the bloodsome uproar which was about to smash the peace of the night into hash served to deepen that rummy feeling to which I have alluded.

Moreover, now that I had had time to meditate upon it, I was more than ever defeatist about this scheme of Jeeves's.

Jeeves seemed to take it for granted that Gussie and Tuppy, faced with a hideous fate, would have no thought beyond saving the Bassett and Angela.

I could not bring myself to share his sunny confidence.

I mean to say, I know how moments when they're faced with a hideous fate affect chaps. I remember Freddie Widgeon, one of the most chivalrous birds in the Drones, telling me how there was an alarm of fire once at a seaside hotel where he was staying and, so far from rushing about saving women, he was down the escape within ten seconds of the kick-off, his mind concerned with but one thing—viz., the personal well-being of F. Widgeon.

As far as any idea of doing the delicately nurtured a bit of good went, he tells me, he was prepared to stand underneath and catch them in blankets, but no more.

Why, then, should this not be so with Augustus Fink-Nottle and Hildebrand Glossop?

Such were my thoughts as I stood toying with the rope, and I believe I should have turned the whole thing up, had it not been that at this juncture there floated into my mind a picture of the Bassett hearing that bell for the first time. Coming as a wholly new experience, it would probably startle her into a decline.

And so agreeable was this reflection that I waited no longer, but seized the rope, braced the feet and snapped into it.

Well, as I say, I hadn't been expecting that bell to hush things up to any great extent. Nor did it. The last time I had heard it, I had been in my room on the other side of the house, and even so it had hoiked me out of bed as if something had exploded under me. Standing close to it like this, I got the full force and meaning of the thing, and I've never heard anything like it in my puff.

I rather enjoy a bit of noise, as a general rule. I remember Cats-meat Potter-Pirbright bringing a police rattle into the Drones one night and loosing it off behind my chair, and I just lay back and closed my eyes with a pleasant smile, like someone in a box at the opera. And the same applies to the time when my Aunt Agatha's son, young Thos., put a match to the parcel of Guy Fawkes Day fireworks to see what would happen.

But the Brinkley Court fire bell was too much for me. I gave about half a dozen tugs, and then, feeling that enough was enough, sauntered round to the front lawn to ascertain what solid results had been achieved.

Brinkley Court had given of its best. A glance told me that we were playing to capacity. The eye, roving to and fro, noted here Uncle Tom in a purple dressing gown, there Aunt Dahlia in the old blue and yellow. It also fell upon Anatole, Tuppy, Gussie, Angela, the Bassett and Jeeves, in the order named. There they all were, present and correct.

But—and this was what caused me immediate concern—I could detect no sign whatever that there had been any rescue work going on.

What I had been hoping, of course, was to see Tuppy bending solicitously over Angela in one corner, while Gussie fanned the Bassett with a towel in the other. Instead of which, the Bassett was one of the group which included Aunt Dahlia and Uncle Tom and seemed to be busy trying to make Anatole see the bright side, while Angela and Gussie were, respectively, leaning against the sundial with a peeved look and sitting on the grass rubbing a barked shin. Tuppy was walking up and down the path, all by himself.

A disturbing picture, you will admit. It was with a rather imperious gesture that I summoned Jeeves to my side.

"Well, Jeeves?"

"Sir?"

I eyed him sternly. "Sir?" forsooth!

"It's no good saying 'Sir?' Jeeves. Look round you. See for yourself. Your scheme has proved a bust."

"Certainly it would appear that matters have not arranged themselves quite as we anticipated, sir."

"We?"

"As I had anticipated, sir."

"That's more like it. Didn't I tell you it would be a flop?"

"I remember that you did seem dubious, sir."

"Dubious is no word for it, Jeeves. I hadn't a scrap of faith in the idea from the start. When you first mooted it, I said it was rotten, and I was right. I'm not blaming you, Jeeves. It is not your fault that you have sprained your brain. But after this—forgive me if I hurt your feelings, Jeeves——I shall know better than to allow you to handle any but the simplest and most elementary problems. It is best to be candid about this, don't you think? Kindest to be frank and straightforward?"

"Certainly, sir."

"I mean, the surgeon's knife, what?"

"Precisely, sir."

"I consider——"

"If you will pardon me for interrupting you, sir, I fancy Mrs. Travers is endeavouring to attract your attention."

And at this moment a ringing "Hoy!" which could have proceeded only from the relative in question, assured me that his view was correct.

"Just step this way a moment, Attila, if you don't mind," boomed that well-known—and under certain conditions, well-loved—voice, and I moved over.

I was not feeling unmixedly at my ease. For the first time it was beginning to steal upon me that I had not prepared a really good story in support of my questionable behaviour in ringing fire bells at such an hour, and I have known Aunt Dahlia to express herself with a hearty freedom upon far smaller provocation.

She exhibited, however, no signs of violence. More a sort of frozen calm, if you know what I mean. You could see that she was a woman who had suffered.

"Well, Bertie, dear," she said, "here we all are."

"Quite," I replied guardedly.

"Nobody missing, is there?"

"I don't think so."

"Splendid. So much healthier for us out in the open like this than frowsting in bed. I had just dropped off when you did your bell-ringing act. For it was you, my sweet child, who rang that bell, was it not?"

"I did ring the bell, yes."

"Any particular reason, or just a whim?"

"I thought there was a fire."

"What gave you that impression, dear?"

"I thought I saw flames."

"Where, darling? Tell Aunt Dahlia."

"In one of the windows."

"I see. So we have all been dragged out of bed and scared rigid because you have been seeing things."

Here Uncle Tom made a noise like a cork coming out of a bottle, and Anatole, whose moustache had hit a new low, said something about "some apes" and, if I am not mistaken, a "rogommier"—whatever that is.

"I admit I was mistaken. I am sorry."

"Don't apologize, ducky. Can't you see how pleased we all are? What were you doing out here, anyway?"

"Just taking a stroll."

"I see. And are you proposing to continue your stroll?"

"No, I think I'll go in now."

"That's fine. Because I was thinking of going in, too, and I don't believe I could sleep knowing you were out here giving rein to that powerful imagination of yours. The next thing that would happen would be that you would think you saw a pink elephant sitting on the drawing-room window-sill and start throwing bricks at it.... Well, come on, Tom, the entertainment seems to be over.... But wait. The newt king wishes a word with us.... Yes, Mr. Fink-Nottle?"

Gussie, as he joined our little group, seemed upset about something.

"I say!"

"Say on, Augustus."

"I say, what are we going to do?"

"Speaking for myself, I intend to return to bed."

"But the door's shut."

"What door?"

"The front door. Somebody must have shut it."

"Then I shall open it."

"But it won't open."

"Then I shall try another door."

"But all the other doors are shut."

"What? Who shut them?"

"I don't know."

I advanced a theory!

"The wind?"

Aunt Dahlia's eyes met mine.

"Don't try me too high," she begged. "Not now, precious." And, indeed, even as I spoke, it did strike me that the night was pretty still.

Uncle Tom said we must get in through a window. Aunt Dahlia sighed a bit.

"How? Could Lloyd George do it, could Winston do it, could Baldwin do it? No. Not since you had those bars of yours put on."

"Well, well, well. God bless my soul, ring the bell, then."

"The fire bell?"

"The door bell."

"To what end, Thomas? There's nobody in the house. The servants are all at Kingham."

"But, confound it all, we can't stop out here all night."

"Can't we? You just watch us. There is nothing—literally nothing—which a country house party can't do with Attila here operating on the premises. Seppings presumably took the back-door key with him. We must just amuse ourselves till he comes back."

Tuppy made a suggestion:

"Why not take out one of the cars and drive over to Kingham and get the key from Seppings?"

It went well. No question about that. For the first time, a smile lit up Aunt Dahlia's drawn face. Uncle Tom grunted approvingly. Anatole said something in Provençal that sounded complimentary. And I thought I detected even on Angela's map a slight softening.

"A very excellent idea," said Aunt Dahlia. "One of the best. Nip round to the garage at once."

After Tuppy had gone, some extremely flattering things were said about his intelligence and resource, and there was a disposition to draw rather invidious comparisons between him and Bertram. Painful for me, of course, but the ordeal didn't last long, for it couldn't have been more than five minutes before he was with us again.

Tuppy seemed perturbed.

"I say, it's all off."

"Why?"

"The garage is locked."

"Unlock it."

"I haven't the key."

"Shout, then, and wake Waterbury."

"Who's Waterbury?"

"The chauffeur, ass. He sleeps over the garage."

"But he's gone to the dance at Kingham."

It was the final wallop. Until this moment, Aunt Dahlia had been able to preserve her frozen calm. The dam now burst. The years rolled away from her, and she was once more the Dahlia Wooster of the old yoicks-and-tantivy days—the emotional, free-speaking girl who had so often risen in her stirrups to yell derogatory personalities at people who were heading hounds.

"Curse all dancing chauffeurs! What on earth does a chauffeur want to dance for? I mistrusted that man from the start. Something told me he was a dancer. Well, this finishes it. We're out here till breakfast-time. If those blasted servants come back before eight o'clock, I shall be vastly surprised. You won't get Seppings away from a dance till you throw him out. I know him. The jazz'll go to his head, and he'll stand clapping and demanding encores till his hands blister. Damn all dancing butlers! What is Brinkley Court? A respectable English country house or a crimson dancing school? One might as well be living in the middle of the Russian Ballet. Well, all right. If we must stay out here, we must. We shall all be frozen stiff, except"—here she directed at me not one of her friendliest glances——"except dear old Attila, who is, I observe, well and warmly clad. We will resign ourselves to the prospect of freezing to death like the Babes in the Wood, merely expressing a dying wish that our old pal Attila will see that we are covered with leaves. No doubt he will also toll that fire bell of his as a mark of respect—And what might you want, my good man?"

She broke off, and stood glaring at Jeeves. During the latter portion of her address, he had been standing by in a respectful manner, endeavouring to catch the speaker's eye.

"If I might make a suggestion, madam."

I am not saying that in the course of our long association I have always found myself able to view Jeeves with approval. There are aspects of his character which have frequently caused coldnesses to arise between us. He is one of those fellows who, if you give them a thingummy, take a what-d'you-call-it. His work is often raw, and he has been known to allude to me as "mentally negligible". More than once, as I have shown, it has been my painful task to squelch in him a tendency to get uppish and treat the young master as a serf or peon.

These are grave defects.

But one thing I have never failed to hand the man. He is magnetic. There is about him something that seems to soothe and hypnotize. To the best of my knowledge, he has never encountered a charging rhinoceros, but should this contingency occur, I have no doubt that the animal, meeting his eye, would check itself in mid-stride, roll over and lie purring with its legs in the air.

At any rate he calmed down Aunt Dahlia, the nearest thing to a charging rhinoceros, in under five seconds. He just stood there looking respectful, and though I didn't time the thing—not having a stop-watch on me—I should say it wasn't more than three seconds and a quarter before her whole manner underwent an astounding change for the better. She melted before one's eyes.

"Jeeves! You haven't got an idea?"

"Yes, madam."

"That great brain of yours has really clicked as ever in the hour of need?"

"Yes, madam."

"Jeeves," said Aunt Dahlia in a shaking voice, "I am sorry I spoke so abruptly. I was not myself. I might have known that you would not come simply trying to make conversation. Tell us this idea of yours, Jeeves. Join our little group of thinkers and let us hear what you have to say. Make yourself at home, Jeeves, and give us the good word. Can you really get us out of this mess?"

"Yes, madam, if one of the gentlemen would be willing to ride a bicycle."

"A bicycle?"

"There is a bicycle in the gardener's shed in the kitchen garden, madam. Possibly one of the gentlemen might feel disposed to ride over to Kingham Manor and procure the back-door key from Mr. Seppings."

"Splendid, Jeeves!"

"Thank you, madam."

"Wonderful!"

"Thank you, madam."

"Attila!" said Aunt Dahlia, turning and speaking in a quiet, authoritative manner.

I had been expecting it. From the very moment those ill-judged words had passed the fellow's lips, I had had a presentiment that a determined effort would be made to elect me as the goat, and I braced myself to resist and obstruct.

And as I was about to do so, while I was in the very act of summoning up all my eloquence to protest that I didn't know how to ride a bike and couldn't possibly learn in the brief time at my disposal, I'm dashed if the man didn't go and nip me in the bud.

"Yes, madam, Mr. Wooster would perform the task admirably. He is an expert cyclist. He has often boasted to me of his triumphs on the wheel."

I hadn't. I hadn't done anything of the sort. It's simply monstrous how one's words get twisted. All I had ever done was to mention to him—casually, just as an interesting item of information, one day in New York when we were watching the six-day bicycle race—that at the age of fourteen, while spending my holidays with a vicar of sorts who had been told off to teach me Latin, I had won the Choir Boys' Handicap at the local school treat.

A different thing from boasting of one's triumphs on the wheel.

I mean, he was a man of the world and must have known that the form of school treats is never of the hottest. And, if I'm not mistaken, I had specifically told him that on the occasion referred to I had received half a lap start and that Willie Punting, the odds-on favourite to whom the race was expected to be a gift, had been forced to retire, owing to having pinched his elder brother's machine without asking the elder brother, and the elder brother coming along just as the pistol went and giving him one on the side of the head and taking it away from him, thus rendering him a scratched-at-the-post non-starter. Yet, from the way he talked, you would have thought I was one of those chaps in sweaters with medals all over them, whose photographs bob up from time to time in the illustrated press on the occasion of their having ridden from Hyde Park Corner to Glasgow in three seconds under the hour, or whatever it is.

And as if this were not bad enough, Tuppy had to shove his oar in.

"That's right," said Tuppy. "Bertie has always been a great cyclist. I remember at Oxford he used to take all his clothes off on bump-supper nights and ride around the quad, singing comic songs. Jolly fast he used to go too."

"Then he can go jolly fast now," said Aunt Dahlia with animation. "He can't go too fast for me. He may also sing comic songs, if he likes.... And if you wish to take your clothes off, Bertie, my lamb, by all means do so. But whether clothed or in the nude, whether singing comic songs or not singing comic songs, get a move on."

I found speech:

"But I haven't ridden for years."

"Then it's high time you began again."

"I've probably forgotten how to ride."

"You'll soon get the knack after you've taken a toss or two. Trial and error. The only way."

"But it's miles to Kingham."

"So the sooner you're off, the better."

"But——"

"Bertie, dear."

"But, dash it——"

"Bertie, darling."

"Yes, but dash it——"

"Bertie, my sweet."

And so it was arranged. Presently I was moving sombrely off through the darkness, Jeeves at my side, Aunt Dahlia calling after me something about trying to imagine myself the man who brought the good news from Ghent to Aix. The first I had heard of the chap.

"So, Jeeves," I said, as we reached the shed, and my voice was cold and bitter, "this is what your great scheme has accomplished! Tuppy, Angela, Gussie and the Bassett not on speaking terms, and self faced with an eight-mile ride——"

"Nine, I believe, sir."

"——a nine-mile ride, and another nine-mile ride back."

"I am sorry, sir."

"No good being sorry now. Where is this foul bone-shaker?"

"I will bring it out, sir."

He did so. I eyed it sourly.

"Where's the lamp?"

"I fear there is no lamp, sir."

"No lamp?"

"No, sir."

"But I may come a fearful stinker without a lamp. Suppose I barge into something."

I broke off and eyed him frigidly.

"You smile, Jeeves. The thought amuses you?"

"I beg your pardon, sir. I was thinking of a tale my Uncle Cyril used to tell me as a child. An absurd little story, sir, though I confess that I have always found it droll. According to my Uncle Cyril, two men named Nicholls and Jackson set out to ride to Brighton on a tandem bicycle, and were so unfortunate as to come into collision with a brewer's van. And when the rescue party arrived on the scene of the accident, it was discovered that they had been hurled together with such force that it was impossible to sort them out at all adequately. The keenest eye could not discern which portion of the fragments was Nicholls and which Jackson. So they collected as much as they could, and called it Nixon. I remember laughing very much at that story when I was a child, sir."

I had to pause a moment to master my feelings.

"You did, eh?"

"Yes, sir."

"You thought it funny?"

"Yes, sir."

"And your Uncle Cyril thought it funny?"

"Yes, sir."

"Golly, what a family! Next time you meet your Uncle Cyril, Jeeves, you can tell him from me that his sense of humour is morbid and unpleasant."

"He is dead, sir."

"Thank heaven for that.... Well, give me the blasted machine."

"Very good, sir."

"Are the tyres inflated?"

"Yes, sir."

"The nuts firm, the brakes in order, the sprockets running true with the differential gear?"

"Yes, sir."

"Right ho, Jeeves."

In Tuppy's statement that, when at the University of Oxford, I had been known to ride a bicycle in the nude about the quadrangle of our mutual college, there had been, I cannot deny, a certain amount of substance. Correct, however, though his facts were, so far as they went, he had not told all. What he had omitted to mention was that I had invariably been well oiled at the time, and when in that condition a chap is capable of feats at which in cooler moments his reason would rebel.

Stimulated by the juice, I believe, men have even been known to ride alligators.

As I started now to pedal out into the great world, I was icily sober, and the old skill, in consequence, had deserted me entirely. I found myself wobbling badly, and all the stories I had ever heard of nasty bicycle accidents came back to me with a rush, headed by Jeeves's Uncle Cyril's cheery little anecdote about Nicholls and Jackson.

Pounding wearily through the darkness, I found myself at a loss to fathom the mentality of men like Jeeves's Uncle Cyril. What on earth he could see funny in a disaster which had apparently involved the complete extinction of a human creature—or, at any rate, of half a human creature and half another human creature—was more than I could understand. To me, the thing was one of the most poignant tragedies that had ever been brought to my attention, and I have no doubt that I should have continued to brood over it for quite a time, had my thoughts not been diverted by the sudden necessity of zigzagging sharply in order to avoid a pig in the fairway.

For a moment it looked like being real Nicholls-and-Jackson stuff, but, fortunately, a quick zig on my part, coinciding with an adroit zag on the part of the pig, enabled me to win through, and I continued my ride safe, but with the heart fluttering like a captive bird.

The effect of this narrow squeak upon me was to shake the nerve to the utmost. The fact that pigs were abroad in the night seemed to bring home to me the perilous nature of my enterprise. It set me thinking of all the other things that could happen to a man out and about on a velocipede without a lamp after lighting-up time. In particular, I recalled the statement of a pal of mine that in certain sections of the rural districts goats were accustomed to stray across the road to the extent of their chains, thereby forming about as sound a booby trap as one could well wish.

He mentioned, I remember, the case of a friend of his whose machine got entangled with a goat chain and who was dragged seven miles—like skijoring in Switzerland—so that he was never the same man again. And there was one chap who ran into an elephant, left over from a travelling circus.

Indeed, taking it for all in all, it seemed to me that, with the possible exception of being bitten by sharks, there was virtually no front-page disaster that could not happen to a fellow, once he had allowed his dear ones to override his better judgment and shove him out into the great unknown on a push-bike, and I am not ashamed to confess that, taking it by and large, the amount of quailing I did from this point on was pretty considerable.

However, in respect to goats and elephants, I must say things panned out unexpectedly well.

Oddly enough, I encountered neither. But when you have said that you have said everything, for in every other way the conditions could scarcely have been fouler.

Apart from the ceaseless anxiety of having to keep an eye skinned for elephants, I found myself much depressed by barking dogs, and once I received a most unpleasant shock when, alighting to consult a signpost, I saw sitting on top of it an owl that looked exactly like my Aunt Agatha. So agitated, indeed, had my frame of mind become by this time that I thought at first it was Aunt Agatha, and only when reason and reflection told me how alien to her habits it would be to climb signposts and sit on them, could I pull myself together and overcome the weakness.

In short, what with all this mental disturbance added to the more purely physical anguish in the billowy portions and the calves and ankles, the Bertram Wooster who eventually toppled off at the door of Kingham Manor was a very different Bertram from the gay and insouciant boulevardier of Bond Street and Piccadilly.

Even to one unaware of the inside facts, it would have been evident that Kingham Manor was throwing its weight about a bit tonight. Lights shone in the windows, music was in the air, and as I drew nearer my ear detected the sibilant shuffling of the feet of butlers, footmen, chauffeurs, parlourmaids, housemaids, tweenies and, I have no doubt, cooks, who were busily treading the measure. I suppose you couldn't sum it up much better than by saying that there was a sound of revelry by night.

The orgy was taking place in one of the ground-floor rooms which had French windows opening on to the drive, and it was to these French windows that I now made my way. An orchestra was playing something with a good deal of zip to it, and under happier conditions I dare say my feet would have started twitching in time to the melody. But I had sterner work before me than to stand hoofing it by myself on gravel drives.

I wanted that back-door key, and I wanted it instanter.

Scanning the throng within, I found it difficult for a while to spot Seppings. Presently, however, he hove in view, doing fearfully lissom things in mid-floor. I "Hi-Seppings!"-ed a couple of times, but his mind was too much on his job to be diverted, and it was only when the swirl of the dance had brought him within prodding distance of my forefinger that a quick one to the lower ribs enabled me to claim his attention.

The unexpected buffet caused him to trip over his partner's feet, and it was with marked austerity that he turned. As he recognized Bertram, however, coldness melted, to be replaced by astonishment.

"Mr. Wooster!"

I was in no mood for bandying words.

"Less of the 'Mr. Wooster' and more back-door keys," I said curtly. "Give me the key of the back door, Seppings."

He did not seem to grasp the gist.

"The key of the back door, sir?"

"Precisely. The Brinkley Court back-door key."

"But it is at the Court, sir."

I clicked the tongue, annoyed.

"Don't be frivolous, my dear old butler," I said. "I haven't ridden nine miles on a push-bike to listen to you trying to be funny. You've got it in your trousers pocket."

"No, sir. I left it with Mr. Jeeves."

"You did—what?"

"Yes, sir. Before I came away. Mr. Jeeves said that he wished to walk in the garden before retiring for the night. He was to place the key on the kitchen window-sill."

I stared at the man dumbly. His eye was clear, his hand steady. He had none of the appearance of a butler who has had a couple.

"You mean that all this while the key has been in Jeeves's possession?"

"Yes, sir."

I could speak no more. Emotion had overmastered my voice. I was at a loss and not abreast; but of one thing, it seemed to me, there could be no doubt. For some reason, not to be fathomed now, but most certainly to be gone well into as soon as I had pushed this infernal sewing-machine of mine over those nine miles of lonely, country road and got within striking distance of him, Jeeves had been doing the dirty. Knowing that at any given moment he could have solved the whole situation, he had kept Aunt Dahlia and others roosting out on the front lawn en déshabille and, worse still, had stood calmly by and watched his young employer set out on a wholly unnecessary eighteen-mile bicycle ride.

I could scarcely believe such a thing of him. Of his Uncle Cyril, yes. With that distorted sense of humour of his, Uncle Cyril might quite conceivably have been capable of such conduct. But that it should be Jeeves—

I leaped into the saddle and, stifling the cry of agony which rose to the lips as the bruised person touched the hard leather, set out on the homeward journey.

-23-

I remember Jeeves saying on one occasion—I forgot how the subject had arisen—he may simply have thrown the observation out, as he does sometimes, for me to take or leave—that hell hath no fury like a woman scorned. And until tonight I had always felt that there was a lot in it. I had never scorned a woman myself, but Pongo Twistleton once scorned an aunt of his, flatly refusing to meet her son Gerald at Paddington and give him lunch and see him off to school at Waterloo, and he never heard the end of it. Letters were written, he tells me, which had to be seen to be believed. Also two very strong telegrams and a bitter picture post card with a view of the Little Chilbury War Memorial on it.

Until tonight, therefore, as I say, I had never questioned the accuracy of the statement. Scorned women first and the rest nowhere, was how it had always seemed to me.

But tonight I revised my views. If you want to know what hell can really do in the way of furies, look for the chap who has been hornswoggled into taking a long and unnecessary bicycle ride in the dark without a lamp.

Mark that word "unnecessary". That was the part of it that really jabbed the iron into the soul. I mean, if it was a case of riding to the doctor's to save the child with croup, or going off to the local pub to fetch supplies in the event of the cellar having run dry, no one would leap to the handlebars more readily than I. Young Lochinvar, absolutely. But this business of being put through it merely to gratify one's personal attendant's diseased sense of the amusing was a bit too thick, and I chafed from start to finish.

So, what I mean to say, although the providence which watches over good men saw to it that I was enabled to complete the homeward journey unscathed except in the billowy portions, removing from my path all goats, elephants, and even owls that looked like my Aunt Agatha, it was a frowning and jaundiced Bertram who finally came to anchor at the Brinkley Court front door. And when I saw a dark figure emerging from the porch to meet me, I prepared to let myself go and uncork all that was fizzing in the mind.

"Jeeves!" I said.

"It is I, Bertie."

The voice which spoke sounded like warm treacle, and even if I had not recognized it immediately as that of the Bassett, I should have known that it did not proceed from the man I was yearning to confront. For this figure before me was wearing a simple tweed dress and had employed my first name in its remarks. And Jeeves, whatever his moral defects, would never go about in skirts calling me Bertie.

The last person, of course, whom I would have wished to meet after a long evening in the saddle, but I vouchsafed a courteous "What ho!"

There was a pause, during which I massaged the calves. Mine, of course, I mean.

"You got in, then?" I said, in allusion to the change of costume.

"Oh, yes. About a quarter of an hour after you left Jeeves went searching about and found the back-door key on the kitchen window-sill."

"Ha!"

"What?"

"Nothing."

"I thought you said something."

"No, nothing."

And I continued to do so. For at this juncture, as had so often happened when this girl and I were closeted, the conversation once more went blue on us. The night breeze whispered, but not the Bassett. A bird twittered, but not so much as a chirp escaped Bertram. It was perfectly amazing, the way her mere presence seemed to wipe speech from my lips—and mine, for that matter, from hers. It began to look as if our married life together would be rather like twenty years among the Trappist monks.

"Seen Jeeves anywhere?" I asked, eventually coming through.

"Yes, in the dining-room."

"The dining-room?"

"Waiting on everybody. They are having eggs and bacon and champagne.... What did you say?"

I had said nothing—merely snorted. There was something about the thought of these people carelessly revelling at a time when, for all they knew, I was probably being dragged about the countryside by goats or chewed by elephants, that struck home at me like a poisoned dart. It was the sort of thing you read about as having happened just before the French Revolution—the haughty nobles in their castles callously digging in and quaffing while the unfortunate blighters outside were suffering frightful privations.

The voice of the Bassett cut in on these mordant reflections:

"Bertie."

"Hullo!"

Silence.

"Hullo!" I said again.

No response. Whole thing rather like one of those telephone conversations where you sit at your end of the wire saying: "Hullo! Hullo!" unaware that the party of the second part has gone off to tea.

Eventually, however, she came to the surface again:

"Bertie, I have something to say to you."

"What?"

"I have something to say to you."

"I know. I said 'What?'"

"Oh, I thought you didn't hear what I said."

"Yes, I heard what you said, all right, but not what you were going to say."

"Oh, I see."

"Right-ho."

So that was straightened out. Nevertheless, instead of proceeding she took time off once more. She stood twisting the fingers and scratching the gravel with her foot. When finally she spoke, it was to deliver an impressive boost:

"Bertie, do you read Tennyson?"

"Not if I can help."

"You remind me so much of those Knights of the Round Table in the 'Idylls of the King'."

Of course I had heard of them—Lancelot, Galahad and all that lot, but I didn't see where the resemblance came in. It seemed to me that she must be thinking of a couple of other fellows.

"How do you mean?"

"You have such a great heart, such a fine soul. You are so generous, so unselfish, so chivalrous. I have always felt that about you—that you are one of the few really chivalrous men I have ever met."

Well, dashed difficult, of course, to know what to say when someone is giving you the old oil on a scale like that. I muttered an "Oh, yes?" or something on those lines, and rubbed the billowy portions in some embarrassment. And there was another silence, broken only by a sharp howl as I rubbed a bit too hard.

"Bertie."

"Hullo?"

I heard her give a sort of gulp.

"Bertie, will you be chivalrous now?"

"Rather. Only too pleased. How do you mean?"

"I am going to try you to the utmost. I am going to test you as few men have ever been tested. I am going——"

I didn't like the sound of this.

"Well," I said doubtfully, "always glad to oblige, you know, but I've just had the dickens of a bicycle ride, and I'm a bit stiff and sore, especially in the—as I say, a bit stiff and sore. If it's anything to be fetched from upstairs——"

"No, no, you don't understand."

"I don't, quite, no."

"Oh, it's so difficult.... How can I say it?... Can't you guess?"

"No. I'm dashed if I can."

"Bertie—let me go!"

"But I haven't got hold of you."

"Release me!"

"Re——"

And then I suddenly got it. I suppose it was fatigue that had made me so slow to apprehend the nub.

"What?"

I staggered, and the left pedal came up and caught me on the shin. But such was the ecstasy in the soul that I didn't utter a cry.

"Release you?"

"Yes."

I didn't want any confusion on the point.

"You mean you want to call it all off? You're going to hitch up with Gussie, after all?"

"Only if you are fine and big enough to consent."

"Oh, I am."

"I gave you my promise."

"Dash promises."

"Then you really——"

"Absolutely."

"Oh, Bertie!"

She seemed to sway like a sapling. It is saplings that sway, I believe.

"A very parfait knight!" I heard her murmur, and there not being much to say after that, I excused myself on the ground that I had got about two pecks of dust down my back and would like to go and get my maid to put me into something loose.

"You go back to Gussie," I said, "and tell him that all is well."

She gave a sort of hiccup and, darting forward, kissed me on the forehead. Unpleasant, of course, but, as Anatole would say, I can take a few smooths with a rough. The next moment she was legging it for the dining-room, while I, having bunged the bicycle into a bush, made for the stairs.

I need not dwell upon my buckedness. It can be readily imagined. Talk about chaps with the noose round their necks and the hangman about to let her go and somebody galloping up on a foaming horse, waving the reprieve—not in it. Absolutely not in it at all. I don't know that I can give you a better idea of the state of my feelings than by saying that as I started to cross the hall I was conscious of so profound a benevolence toward all created things that I found myself thinking kindly thoughts even of Jeeves.

I was about to mount the stairs when a sudden "What ho!" from my rear caused me to turn. Tuppy was standing in the hall. He had apparently been down to the cellar for reinforcements, for there were a couple of bottles under his arm.

"Hullo, Bertie," he said. "You back?" He laughed amusedly. "You look like the Wreck of the Hesperus. Get run over by a steam-roller or something?"

At any other time I might have found his coarse badinage hard to bear. But such was my uplifted mood that I waved it aside and slipped him the good news.

"Tuppy, old man, the Bassett's going to marry Gussie Fink-Nottle."

"Tough luck on both of them, what?"

"But don't you understand? Don't you see what this means? It means that Angela is once more out of pawn, and you have only to play your cards properly——"

He bellowed rollickingly. I saw now that he was in the pink. As a matter of fact, I had noticed something of the sort directly I met him, but had attributed it to alcoholic stimulant.

"Good Lord! You're right behind the times, Bertie. Only to be expected, of course, if you will go riding bicycles half the night. Angela and I made it up hours ago."

"What?"

"Certainly. Nothing but a passing tiff. All you need in these matters is a little give and take, a bit of reasonableness on both sides. We got together and talked things over. She withdrew my double chin. I conceded her shark. Perfectly simple. All done in a couple of minutes."

"But——"

"Sorry, Bertie. Can't stop chatting with you all night. There is a rather impressive beano in progress in the dining-room, and they are waiting for supplies."

Endorsement was given to this statement by a sudden shout from the apartment named. I recognized—as who would not—Aunt Dahlia's voice:

"Glossop!"

"Hullo?"

"Hurry up with that stuff."

"Coming, coming."

"Well, come, then. Yoicks! Hard for-rard!"

"Tallyho, not to mention tantivy. Your aunt," said Tuppy, "is a bit above herself. I don't know all the facts of the case, but it appears that Anatole gave notice and has now consented to stay on, and also your uncle has given her a cheque for that paper of hers. I didn't get the details, but she is much braced. See you later. I must rush."

To say that Bertram was now definitely nonplussed would be but to state the simple truth. I could make nothing of this. I had left Brinkley Court a stricken home, with hearts bleeding wherever you looked, and I had returned to find it a sort of earthly paradise. It baffled me.

I bathed bewilderedly. The toy duck was still in the soap-dish, but I was too preoccupied to give it a thought. Still at a loss, I returned to my room, and there was Jeeves. And it is proof of my fogged condish that my first words to him were words not of reproach and stern recrimination but of inquiry:

"I say, Jeeves!"

"Good evening, sir. I was informed that you had returned. I trust you had an enjoyable ride."

At any other moment, a crack like that would have woken the fiend in Bertram Wooster. I barely noticed it. I was intent on getting to the bottom of this mystery.

"But I say, Jeeves, what?"

"Sir?"

"What does all this mean?"

"You refer, sir——"

"Of course I refer. You know what I'm talking about. What has been happening here since I left? The place is positively stiff with happy endings."

"Yes, sir. I am glad to say that my efforts have been rewarded."

"What do you mean, your efforts? You aren't going to try to make out that that rotten fire bell scheme of yours had anything to do with it?"

"Yes, sir."

"Don't be an ass, Jeeves. It flopped."

"Not altogether, sir. I fear, sir, that I was not entirely frank with regard to my suggestion of ringing the fire bell. I had not really anticipated that it would in itself produce the desired results. I had intended it merely as a preliminary to what I might describe as the real business of the evening."

"You gibber, Jeeves."

"No, sir. It was essential that the ladies and gentlemen should be brought from the house, in order that, once out of doors, I could ensure that they remained there for the necessary period of time."

"How do you mean?"

"My plan was based on psychology, sir."

"How?"

"It is a recognized fact, sir, that there is nothing that so satisfactorily unites individuals who have been so unfortunate as to quarrel amongst themselves as a strong mutual dislike for some definite person. In my own family, if I may give a homely illustration, it was a generally accepted axiom that in times of domestic disagreement it was necessary only to invite my Aunt Annie for a visit to heal all breaches between the other members of the household. In the mutual animosity excited by Aunt Annie, those who had become estranged were reconciled almost immediately. Remembering this, it occurred to me that were you, sir, to be established as the person responsible for the ladies and gentlemen being forced to spend the night in the garden, everybody would take so strong a dislike to you that in this common sympathy they would sooner or later come together."

I would have spoken, but he continued:

"And such proved to be the case. All, as you see, sir, is now well. After your departure on the bicycle, the various estranged parties agreed so heartily in their abuse of you that the ice, if I may use the expression, was broken, and it was not long before Mr. Glossop was walking beneath the trees with Miss Angela, telling her anecdotes of your career at the university in exchange for hers regarding your childhood; while Mr. Fink-Nottle, leaning against the sundial, held Miss Bassett enthralled with stories of your schooldays. Mrs. Travers, meanwhile, was telling Monsieur Anatole——"

I found speech.

"Oh?" I said. "I see. And now, I suppose, as the result of this dashed psychology of yours, Aunt Dahlia is so sore with me that it will be years before I can dare to show my face here again—years, Jeeves, during which, night after night, Anatole will be cooking those dinners of his——"

"No, sir. It was to prevent any such contingency that I suggested that you should bicycle to Kingham Manor. When I informed the ladies and gentlemen that I had found the key, and it was borne in upon them that you were having that long ride for nothing, their animosity vanished immediately, to be replaced by cordial amusement. There was much laughter."

"There was, eh?"

"Yes, sir. I fear you may possibly have to submit to a certain amount of good-natured chaff, but nothing more. All, if I may say so, is forgiven, sir."

"Oh?"

"Yes, sir."

I mused awhile.

"You certainly seem to have fixed things."

"Yes, sir."

"Tuppy and Angela are once more betrothed. Also Gussie and the Bassett; Uncle Tom appears to have coughed up that money for Milady's Boudoir. And Anatole is staying on."

"Yes, sir."

"I suppose you might say that all's well that ends well."

"Very apt, sir."

I mused again.

"All the same, your methods are a bit rough, Jeeves."

"One cannot make an omelette without breaking eggs, sir."

I started.

"Omelette! Do you think you could get me one?"

"Certainly, sir."

"Together with half a bot. of something?"

"Undoubtedly, sir."

"Do so, Jeeves, and with all speed."

I climbed into bed and sank back against the pillows. I must say that my generous wrath had ebbed a bit. I was aching the whole length of my body, particularly toward the middle, but against this you had to set the fact that I was no longer engaged to Madeline Bassett. In a good cause one is prepared to suffer. Yes, looking at the thing from every angle, I saw that Jeeves had done well, and it was with an approving beam that I welcomed him as he returned with the needful.

He did not check up with this beam. A bit grave, he seemed to me to be looking, and I probed the matter with a kindly query:

"Something on your mind, Jeeves?"

"Yes, sir. I should have mentioned it earlier, but in the evening's disturbance it escaped my memory, I fear I have been remiss, sir."

"Yes, Jeeves?" I said, champing contentedly.

"In the matter of your mess-jacket, sir."

A nameless fear shot through me, causing me to swallow a mouthful of omelette the wrong way.

"I am sorry to say, sir, that while I was ironing it this afternoon I was careless enough to leave the hot instrument upon it. I very much fear that it will be impossible for you to wear it again, sir."

One of those old pregnant silences filled the room.

"I am extremely sorry, sir."

For a moment, I confess, that generous wrath of mine came bounding back, hitching up its muscles and snorting a bit through the nose, but, as we say on the Riviera, à quoi sert-il? There was nothing to be gained by g.w. now.

We Woosters can bite the bullet. I nodded moodily and speared another slab of omelette.

"Right ho, Jeeves."

"Very good, sir."

THE INIMITABLE JEEVES

CHAPTER I
JEEVES EXERTS THE OLD CEREBELLUM

"'Morning, Jeeves," I said.

"Good morning, sir," said Jeeves. He put the good old cup of tea softly on the table by my bed, and I took a refreshing sip. Just right, as usual. Not too hot, not too sweet, not too weak, not too strong, not too much milk, and not a drop spilled in the saucer. A most amazing cove, Jeeves. So dashed competent in every respect. I've said it before, and I'll say it again. I mean to say, take just one small instance. Every other valet I've ever had used to barge into my room in the morning while I was still asleep, causing much misery: but Jeeves seems to know when I'm awake by a sort of telepathy. He always floats in with the cup exactly two minutes after I come to life. Makes a deuce of a lot of difference to a fellow's day.

"How's the weather, Jeeves?"

"Exceptionally clement, sir."

"Anything in the papers?"

"Some slight friction threatening in the Balkans, sir. Otherwise, nothing."

"I say, Jeeves, a man I met at the club last night told me to put my shirt on Privateer for the two o'clock race this afternoon. How about it?"

"I should not advocate it, sir. The stable is not sanguine."

That was enough for me. Jeeves knows. How, I couldn't say, but he knows. There was a time when I would laugh lightly, and go ahead, and lose my little all against his advice, but not now.

"Talking of shirts," I said, "have those mauve ones I ordered arrived yet?"

"Yes, sir. I sent them back."

"Sent them back?"

"Yes, sir. They would not have become you."

Well, I must say I'd thought fairly highly of those shirtings, but I bowed to superior knowledge. Weak? I don't know. Most fellows, no doubt, are all for having their valets confine their activities to creasing trousers and what not without trying to run the home; but it's different with Jeeves. Right from the first day he came to me, I have looked on him as a sort of guide, philosopher, and friend.

"Mr. Little rang up on the telephone a few moments ago, sir. I informed him that you were not yet awake."

"Did he leave a message?"

"No, sir. He mentioned that he had a matter of importance to discuss with you, but confided no details."

"Oh, well, I expect I shall be seeing him at the club."

"No doubt, sir."

I wasn't what you might call in a fever of impatience. Bingo Little is a chap I was at school with, and we see a lot of each other still. He's the nephew of old Mortimer Little, who retired from business recently with a goodish pile. (You've probably heard of Little's Liniment—It Limbers Up the Legs.) Bingo biffs about London on a pretty comfortable allowance given him by his uncle, and leads on the whole a fairly unclouded life. It wasn't likely that anything which he described as a matter of importance would turn out to be really so frightfully important. I took it that he had discovered some new brand of cigarette which he wanted me to try, or something like that, and didn't spoil my breakfast by worrying.

After breakfast I lit a cigarette and went to the open window to inspect the day. It certainly was one of the best and brightest.

"Jeeves," I said.

"Sir?" said Jeeves. He had been clearing away the breakfast things, but at the sound of the young master's voice cheesed it courteously.

"You were absolutely right about the weather. It is a juicy morning."

"Decidedly, sir."

"Spring and all that."

"Yes, sir."

"In the spring, Jeeves, a livelier iris gleams upon the burnished dove."

"So I have been informed, sir."

"Right ho! Then bring me my whangee, my yellowest shoes, and the old green Homburg. I'm going into the Park to do pastoral dances."

I don't know if you know that sort of feeling you get on these days round about the end of April and the beginning of May, when the sky's a light blue, with cotton-wool clouds, and there's a bit of a breeze blowing from the west? Kind of uplifted feeling. Romantic, if you know what I mean. I'm not much of a ladies' man, but on this particular morning it seemed to me that what I really wanted was some charming girl to buzz up and ask me to save her from assassins or something. So that it was a bit of an anti-climax when I merely ran into young Bingo Little, looking perfectly foul in a crimson satin tie decorated with horseshoes.

"Hallo, Bertie," said Bingo.

"My God, man!" I gargled. "The cravat! The gent's neckwear! Why? For what reason?"

"Oh, the tie?" He blushed. "I—er—I was given it."

He seemed embarrassed, so I dropped the subject. We toddled along a bit, and sat down on a couple of chairs by the Serpentine.

"Jeeves tells me you want to talk to me about something," I said.

"Eh?" said Bingo, with a start. "Oh yes, yes. Yes."

I waited for him to unleash the topic of the day, but he didn't seem to want to get going. Conversation languished. He stared straight ahead of him in a glassy sort of manner.

"I say, Bertie," he said, after a pause of about an hour and a quarter.

"Hallo!"

"Do you like the name Mabel?"

"No."

"No?"

"No."

"You don't think there's a kind of music in the word, like the wind rustling gently through the tree-tops?"

"No."

He seemed disappointed for a moment; then cheered up.

"Of course, you wouldn't. You always were a fat-headed worm without any soul, weren't you?"

"Just as you say. Who is she? Tell me all."

For I realised now that poor old Bingo was going through it once again. Ever since I have known him—and we were at school together—he has been perpetually falling in love with someone, generally in the spring, which seems to act on him like magic. At school he had the finest collection of actresses' photographs of anyone of his time; and at Oxford his romantic nature was a byword.

"You'd better come along and meet her at lunch," he said, looking at his watch.

"A ripe suggestion," I said. "Where are you meeting her? At the Ritz?"

"Near the Ritz."

He was geographically accurate. About fifty yards east of the Ritz there is one of those blighted tea-and-bun shops you see dotted about all over London, and into this, if you'll believe me, young Bingo dived like a homing rabbit; and before I had time to say a word we were wedged in at a table, on the brink of a silent pool of coffee left there by an early luncher.

I'm bound to say I couldn't quite follow the development of the scenario. Bingo, while not absolutely rolling in the stuff, has always had a fair amount of the ready. Apart from what he got from his uncle, I knew that he had finished up the jumping season well on the right side of the ledger. Why, then, was he lunching the girl at this Godforsaken eatery? It couldn't be because he was hard up.

Just then the waitress arrived. Rather a pretty girl.

"Aren't we going to wait——?" I started to say to Bingo, thinking it somewhat thick that, in addition to asking a girl to lunch with him in a place like this, he should fling himself on the foodstuffs before she turned up, when I caught sight of his face, and stopped.

The man was goggling. His entire map was suffused with a rich blush. He looked like the Soul's Awakening done in pink.

"Hallo, Mabel!" he said, with a sort of gulp.

"Hallo!" said the girl.

"Mabel," said Bingo, "this is Bertie Wooster, a pal of mine."

"Pleased to meet you," she said. "Nice morning."

"Fine," I said.

"You see I'm wearing the tie," said Bingo.

"It suits you beautiful," said the girl.

Personally, if anyone had told me that a tie like that suited me, I should have risen and struck them on the mazzard, regardless of their age and sex; but poor old Bingo simply got all flustered with gratification, and smirked in the most gruesome manner.

"Well, what's it going to be to-day?" asked the girl, introducing the business touch into the conversation.

Bingo studied the menu devoutly.

"I'll have a cup of cocoa, cold veal and ham pie, slice of fruit cake, and a macaroon. Same for you, Bertie?"

I gazed at the man, revolted. That he could have been a pal of mine all these years and think me capable of insulting the old tum with this sort of stuff cut me to the quick.

"Or how about a bit of hot steak-pudding, with a sparkling limado to wash it down?" said Bingo.

You know, the way love can change a fellow is really frightful to contemplate. This chappie before me, who spoke in that absolutely careless way of macaroons and limado, was the man I had seen in happier days telling the head-waiter at Claridge's exactly how he wanted the chef to prepare the sole frite au gourmet aux champignons, and saying he would jolly well sling it back if it wasn't just right. Ghastly! Ghastly!

A roll and butter and a small coffee seemed the only things on the list that hadn't been specially prepared by the nastier-minded members of the Borgia family for people they had a particular grudge against, so I chose them, and Mabel hopped it.

"Well?" said Bingo rapturously.

I took it that he wanted my opinion of the female poisoner who had just left us.

"Very nice," I said.

He seemed dissatisfied.

"You don't think she's the most wonderful girl you ever saw?" he said wistfully.

"Oh, absolutely!" I said, to appease the blighter. "Where did you meet her?"

"At a subscription dance at Camberwell."

"What on earth were you doing at a subscription dance at Camberwell?"

"Your man Jeeves asked me if I would buy a couple of tickets. It was in aid of some charity or other."

"Jeeves? I didn't know he went in for that sort of thing."

"Well, I suppose he has to relax a bit every now and then. Anyway, he was there, swinging a dashed efficient shoe. I hadn't meant to go at first, but I turned up for a lark. Oh, Bertie, think what I might have missed!"

"What might you have missed?" I asked, the old lemon being slightly clouded.

"Mabel, you chump. If I hadn't gone I shouldn't have met Mabel."

"Oh, ah!"

At this point Bingo fell into a species of trance, and only came out of it to wrap himself round the pie and macaroon.

"Bertie," he said, "I want your advice."

"Carry on."

"At least, not your advice, because that wouldn't be much good to anybody. I mean, you're a pretty consummate old ass, aren't you? Not that I want to hurt your feelings, of course."

"No, no, I see that."

"What I wish you would do is to put the whole thing to that fellow Jeeves of yours, and see what he suggests. You've often told me that he has helped other pals of yours out of messes. From what you tell me, he's by way of being the brains of the family."

"He's never let me down yet."

"Then put my case to him."

"What case?"

"My problem."

"What problem?"

"Why, you poor fish, my uncle, of course. What do you think my uncle's going to say to all this? If I sprang it on him cold, he'd tie himself in knots on the hearthrug."

"One of these emotional johnnies, eh?"

"Somehow or other his mind has got to be prepared to receive the news. But how?"

"Ah!"

"That's a lot of help, that 'ah'! You see, I'm pretty well dependent on the old boy. If he cut off my allowance, I should be very much in the soup. So you put the whole binge to Jeeves and see if he can't scare up a happy ending somehow. Tell him my future is in his hands, and that, if the wedding bells ring out, he can rely on me, even unto half my kingdom. Well, call it ten quid. Jeeves would exert himself with ten quid on the horizon, what?"

"Undoubtedly," I said.

I wasn't in the least surprised at Bingo wanting to lug Jeeves into his private affairs like this. It was the first thing I would have thought of doing myself if I had been in any hole of any description. As I have frequently had occasion to observe, he is a bird of the ripest intellect, full of bright ideas. If anybody could fix things for poor old Bingo, he could.

I stated the case to him that night after dinner.

"Jeeves."

"Sir?"

"Are you busy just now?"

"No, sir."

"I mean, not doing anything in particular?"

"No, sir. It is my practice at this hour to read some improving book; but, if you desire my services, this can easily be postponed, or, indeed, abandoned altogether."

"Well, I want your advice. It's about Mr. Little."

"Young Mr. Little, sir, or the elder Mr. Little, his uncle, who lives in Pounceby Gardens?"

Jeeves seemed to know everything. Most amazing thing. I'd been pally with Bingo practically all my life, and yet I didn't remember ever having heard that his uncle lived anywhere in particular.

"How did you know he lived in Pounceby Gardens?" I said.

"I am on terms of some intimacy with the elder Mr. Little's cook, sir. In fact, there is an understanding."

I'm bound to say that this gave me a bit of a start. Somehow I'd never thought of Jeeves going in for that sort of thing.

"Do you mean you're engaged?"

"It may be said to amount to that, sir."

"Well, well!"

"She is a remarkably excellent cook, sir," said Jeeves, as though he felt called on to give some explanation. "What was it you wished to ask me about Mr. Little?"

I sprang the details on him.

"And that's how the matter stands, Jeeves," I said. "I think we ought to rally round a trifle and help poor old Bingo put the thing through. Tell me about old Mr. Little. What sort of a chap is he?"

"A somewhat curious character, sir. Since retiring from business he has become a great recluse, and now devotes himself almost entirely to the pleasures of the table."

"Greedy hog, you mean?"

"I would not, perhaps, take the liberty of describing him in precisely those terms, sir. He is what is usually called a gourmet. Very particular about what he eats, and for that reason sets a high value on Miss Watson's services."

"The cook?"

"Yes, sir."

"Well, it looks to me as though our best plan would be to shoot young Bingo in on him after dinner one night. Melting mood, I mean to say, and all that."

"The difficulty is, sir, that at the moment Mr. Little is on a diet, owing to an attack of gout."

"Things begin to look wobbly."

"No, sir, I fancy that the elder Mr. Little's misfortune may be turned to the younger Mr. Little's advantage. I was speaking only the other day to Mr. Little's valet, and he was telling me that it has become his principal duty to read to Mr. Little in the evenings. If I were in your place, sir, I should send young Mr. Little to read to his uncle."

"Nephew's devotion, you mean? Old man touched by kindly action, what?"

"Partly that, sir. But I would rely more on young Mr. Little's choice of literature."

"That's no good. Jolly old Bingo has a kind face, but when it comes to literature he stops at the Sporting Times."

"That difficulty may be overcome. I would be happy to select books for Mr. Little to read. Perhaps I might explain my idea further?"

"I can't say I quite grasp it yet."

"The method which I advocate is what, I believe, the advertisers call Direct Suggestion, sir, consisting as it does of driving an idea home by constant repetition. You may have had experience of the system?"

"You mean they keep on telling you that some soap or other is the best, and after a bit you come under the influence and charge round the corner and buy a cake?"

"Exactly, sir. The same method was the basis of all the most valuable propaganda during the recent war. I see no reason why it should not be adopted to bring about the desired result with regard to the subject's views on class distinctions. If young Mr. Little were to read day after day to his uncle a series of narratives in which marriage with young persons of an inferior social status was held up as both feasible and admirable, I fancy it would prepare the elder Mr. Little's mind for the reception of the information that his nephew wishes to marry a waitress in a tea-shop."

"Are there any books of that sort nowadays? The only ones I ever see mentioned in the papers are about married couples who find life grey, and can't stick each other at any price."

"Yes, sir, there are a great many, neglected by the reviewers but widely read. You have never encountered 'All for Love,' by Rosie M. Banks?"

"No."

"Nor 'A Red, Red Summer Rose,' by the same author?"

"No."

"I have an aunt, sir, who owns an almost complete set of Rosie M. Banks'. I could easily borrow as many volumes as young Mr. Little might require. They make very light, attractive reading."

"Well, it's worth trying."

"I should certainly recommend the scheme, sir."

"All right, then. Toddle round to your aunt's to-morrow and grab a couple of the fruitiest. We can but have a dash at it."

"Precisely, sir."

CHAPTER II
NO WEDDING BELLS FOR BINGO

Bingo reported three days later that Rosie M. Banks was the goods and beyond a question the stuff to give the troops. Old Little had jibbed somewhat at first at the proposed change of literary diet, he not being much of a lad for fiction and having stuck hitherto exclusively to the heavier monthly reviews; but Bingo had got chapter one of "All for Love" past his guard before he knew what was happening, and after that there was nothing to it. Since then they had finished "A Red, Red Summer Rose," "Madcap Myrtle" and "Only a Factory Girl," and were half-way through "The Courtship of Lord Strathmorlick."

Bingo told me all this in a husky voice over an egg beaten up in sherry. The only blot on the thing from his point of view was that it wasn't doing a bit of good to the old vocal cords, which were beginning to show signs of cracking under the strain. He had been looking his symptoms up in a medical dictionary, and he thought he had got "clergyman's throat." But against this you had to set the fact that he was making an undoubted hit in the right quarter, and also that after the evening's reading he always stayed on to dinner; and, from what he told me, the dinners turned out by old Little's cook had to be tasted to be believed. There were tears in the old blighter's eyes as he got on the subject of the clear soup. I suppose to a fellow who for weeks had been tackling macaroons and limado it must have been like Heaven.

Old Little wasn't able to give any practical assistance at these banquets, but Bingo said that he came to the table and had his whack of arrowroot, and sniffed the dishes, and told stories of entrées he had had in the past, and sketched out scenarios of what he was going to do to the bill of fare in the future, when the doctor put him in shape; so I suppose he enjoyed himself, too, in a way. Anyhow, things seemed to be buzzing along quite satisfactorily, and Bingo said he had got an idea which, he thought, was going to clinch the thing. He wouldn't tell me what it was, but he said it was a pippin.

"We make progress, Jeeves," I said.

"That is very satisfactory, sir."

"Mr. Little tells me that when he came to the big scene in 'Only a Factory Girl,' his uncle gulped like a stricken bull-pup."

"Indeed, sir?"

"Where Lord Claude takes the girl in his arms, you know, and says——"

"I am familiar with the passage, sir. It is distinctly moving. It was a great favourite of my aunt's."

"I think we're on the right track."

"It would seem so, sir."

"In fact, this looks like being another of your successes. I've always said, and I always shall say, that for sheer brain, Jeeves, you stand alone. All the other great thinkers of the age are simply in the crowd, watching you go by."

"Thank you very much, sir. I endeavour to give satisfaction."

About a week after this, Bingo blew in with the news that his uncle's gout had ceased to trouble him, and that on the morrow he would be back at the old stand working away with knife and fork as before.

"And, by the way," said Bingo, "he wants you to lunch with him to-morrow."

"Me? Why me? He doesn't know I exist."

"Oh, yes, he does. I've told him about you."

"What have you told him?"

"Oh, various things. Anyhow, he wants to meet you. And take my tip, laddie—you go! I should think lunch to-morrow would be something special."

I don't know why it was, but even then it struck me that there was something dashed odd—almost sinister, if you know what I mean—about young Bingo's manner. The old egg had the air of one who has something up his sleeve.

"There is more in this than meets the eye," I said. "Why should your uncle ask a fellow to lunch whom he's never seen?"

"My dear old fathead, haven't I just said that I've been telling him all about you—that you're my best pal—at school together, and all that sort of thing?"

"But even then—and another thing. Why are you so dashed keen on my going?"

Bingo hesitated for a moment.

"Well, I told you I'd got an idea. This is it. I want you to spring the news on him. I haven't the nerve myself."

"What! I'm hanged if I do!"

"And you call yourself a pal of mine!"

"Yes, I know; but there are limits."

"Bertie," said Bingo reproachfully, "I saved your life once."

"When?"

"Didn't I? It must have been some other fellow, then. Well, anyway, we were boys together and all that. You can't let me down."

"Oh, all right," I said. "But, when you say you haven't nerve enough for any dashed thing in the world, you misjudge yourself. A fellow who——"

"Cheerio!" said young Bingo. "One-thirty to-morrow. Don't be late."

* * * * *

I'm bound to say that the more I contemplated the binge, the less I liked it. It was all very well for Bingo to say that I was slated for a magnificent lunch; but what good is the best possible lunch to a fellow if he is slung out into the street on his ear during the soup course? However, the word of a Wooster is his bond and all that sort of rot, so at one-thirty next day I tottered up the steps of No. 16, Pounceby Gardens, and punched the bell. And half a minute later I was up in the drawing-room, shaking hands with the fattest man I have ever seen in my life.

The motto of the Little family was evidently "variety." Young Bingo is long and thin and hasn't had a superfluous ounce on him since we first met; but the uncle restored the average and a bit over. The hand which grasped mine wrapped it round and enfolded it till I began to wonder if I'd ever get it out without excavating machinery.

"Mr. Wooster, I am gratified—I am proud—I am honoured."

It seemed to me that young Bingo must have boosted me to some purpose.

"Oh, ah!" I said.

He stepped back a bit, still hanging on to the good right hand.

"You are very young to have accomplished so much!"

I couldn't follow the train of thought. The family, especially my Aunt Agatha, who has savaged me incessantly from childhood up, have always rather made a point of the fact that mine is a wasted life, and that, since I won the prize at my first school for the best collection of wild flowers made during the summer holidays, I haven't done a dam' thing to land me on the nation's scroll of fame. I was wondering if he couldn't have got me mixed up with someone else, when the telephone-bell rang outside in the hall, and the maid came in to say that I was wanted. I buzzed down, and found it was young Bingo.

"Hallo!" said young Bingo. "So you've got there? Good man! I knew I could rely on you. I say, old crumpet, did my uncle seem pleased to see you?"

"Absolutely all over me. I can't make it out."

"Oh, that's all right. I just rang up to explain. The fact is, old man, I know you won't mind, but I told him that you were the author of those books I've been reading to him."

"What!"

"Yes, I said that 'Rosie M. Banks' was your pen-name, and you didn't want it generally known, because you were a modest, retiring sort of chap. He'll listen to you now. Absolutely hang on your words. A brightish idea, what? I doubt if Jeeves in person could have thought up a better one than that. Well, pitch it strong, old lad, and keep steadily before you the fact that I must have my allowance raised. I can't possibly marry on what I've got now. If this film is to end with the slow fade-out on the embrace, at least double is indicated. Well, that's that. Cheerio!"

And he rang off. At that moment the gong sounded, and the genial host came tumbling downstairs like the delivery of a ton of coals.

* * * * *

I always look back to that lunch with a sort of aching regret. It was the lunch of a lifetime, and I wasn't in a fit state to appreciate it. Subconsciously, if you know what I mean, I could see it was pretty special, but I had got the wind up to such a frightful extent over the ghastly situation in which young Bingo had landed me that its deeper meaning never really penetrated. Most of the time I might have been eating sawdust for all the good it did me.

Old Little struck the literary note right from the start.

"My nephew has probably told you that I have been making a close study of your books of late?" he began.

"Yes. He did mention it. How—er—how did you like the bally things?"

He gazed reverently at me.

"Mr. Wooster, I am not ashamed to say that the tears came into my eyes as I listened to them. It amazes me that a man as young as you can have been able to plumb human nature so surely to its depths; to play with so unerring a hand on the quivering heart-strings of your reader; to write novels so true, so human, so moving, so vital!"

"Oh, it's just a knack," I said.

The good old persp. was bedewing my forehead by this time in a pretty lavish manner. I don't know when I've been so rattled.

"Do you find the room a trifle warm?"

"Oh, no, no, rather not. Just right."

"Then it's the pepper. If my cook has a fault—which I am not prepared to admit—it is that she is inclined to stress the pepper a trifle in her made dishes. By the way, do you like her cooking?"

I was so relieved that we had got off the subject of my literary output that I shouted approval in a ringing baritone.

"I am delighted to hear it, Mr. Wooster. I may be prejudiced, but to my mind that woman is a genius."

"Absolutely!" I said.

"She has been with me seven years, and in all that time I have not known her guilty of a single lapse from the highest standard. Except once, in the winter of 1917, when a purist might have condemned a certain mayonnaise of hers as lacking in creaminess. But one must make allowances. There had been several air-raids about that time, and no doubt the poor woman was shaken. But nothing is perfect in this world, Mr. Wooster, and I have had my cross to bear. For seven years I have lived in constant apprehension lest some evilly-disposed person might lure her from my employment. To my certain knowledge she has received offers, lucrative offers, to accept service elsewhere. You may judge of my dismay, Mr. Wooster, when only this morning the bolt fell. She gave notice!"

"Good Lord!"

"Your consternation does credit, if I may say so, to the heart of the author of 'A Red, Red Summer Rose.' But I am thankful to say the worst has not happened. The matter has been adjusted. Jane is not leaving me."

"Good egg!"

"Good egg, indeed—though the expression is not familiar to me. I do not remember having come across it in your books. And, speaking of your books, may I say that what has impressed me about them even more than the moving poignancy of the actual narrative, is your philosophy of life. If there were more men like you, Mr. Wooster, London would be a better place."

This was dead opposite to my Aunt Agatha's philosophy of life, she having always rather given me to understand that it is the presence in it of chappies like me that makes London more or less of a plague spot; but I let it go.

"Let me tell you, Mr. Wooster, that I appreciate your splendid defiance of the outworn fetishes of a purblind social system. I appreciate it! You are big enough to see that rank is but the guinea stamp and that, in the magnificent words of Lord Bletchmore in 'Only a Factory Girl,' 'Be her origin ne'er so humble, a good woman is the equal of the finest lady on earth!'"

I sat up.

"I say! Do you think that?"

"I do, Mr. Wooster. I am ashamed to say that there was a time when I was like other men, a slave to the idiotic convention which we call Class Distinction. But, since I read your books——"

I might have known it. Jeeves had done it again.

"You think it's all right for a chappie in what you might call a certain social position to marry a girl of what you might describe as the lower classes?"

"Most assuredly I do, Mr. Wooster."

I took a deep breath, and slipped him the good news.

"Young Bingo—your nephew, you know—wants to marry a waitress," I said.

"I honour him for it," said old Little.

"You don't object?"

"On the contrary."

I took another deep breath and shifted to the sordid side of the business.

"I hope you won't think I'm butting in, don't you know," I said, "but—er—well, how about it?"

"I fear I do not quite follow you."

"Well, I mean to say, his allowance and all that. The money you're good enough to give him. He was rather hoping that you might see your way to jerking up the total a bit."

Old Little shook his head regretfully.

"I fear that can hardly be managed. You see, a man in my position is compelled to save every penny. I will gladly continue my nephew's existing allowance, but beyond that I cannot go. It would not be fair to my wife."

"What! But you're not married?"

"Not yet. But I propose to enter upon that holy state almost immediately. The lady who for years has cooked so well for me honoured me by accepting my hand this very morning." A cold gleam of triumph came into his eye. "Now let 'em try to get her away from me!" he muttered, defiantly.

* * * * *

"Young Mr. Little has been trying frequently during the afternoon to reach you on the telephone, sir," said Jeeves that night, when I got home.

"I'll bet he has," I said. I had sent poor old Bingo an outline of the situation by messenger-boy shortly after lunch.

"He seemed a trifle agitated."

"I don't wonder. Jeeves," I said, "so brace up and bite the bullet. I'm afraid I've bad news for you."

"That scheme of yours—reading those books to old Mr. Little and all that—has blown out a fuse."

"They did not soften him?"

"They did. That's the whole bally trouble. Jeeves, I'm sorry to say that fiancée of yours—Miss Watson, you know—the cook, you know—well, the long and the short of it is that she's chosen riches instead of honest worth, if you know what I mean."

"Sir?"

"She's handed you the mitten and gone and got engaged to old Mr. Little!"

"Indeed, sir?"

"You don't seem much upset."

"The fact is, sir, I had anticipated some such outcome."

I stared at him. "Then what on earth did you suggest the scheme for?"

"To tell you the truth, sir, I was not wholly averse from a severance of my relations with Miss Watson. In fact, I greatly desired it. I respect Miss Watson exceedingly, but I have seen for a long time that we were not suited. Now, the other young person with whom I have an understanding—"

"Great Scott, Jeeves! There isn't another?"

"Yes, sir."

"How long has this been going on?"

"For some weeks, sir. I was greatly attracted by her when I first met her at a subscription dance at Camberwell."

"My sainted aunt! Not——"

Jeeves inclined his head gravely.

"Yes, sir. By an odd coincidence it is the same young person that young Mr. Little—— I have placed the cigarettes on the small table. Good night, sir."

CHAPTER III
AUNT AGATHA SPEAKS HER MIND

I suppose in the case of a chappie of really fine fibre and all that sort of thing, a certain amount of gloom and anguish would have followed this dishing of young Bingo's matrimonial plans. I mean, if mine had been a noble nature, I would have been all broken up. But, what with one thing and another, I can't say I let it weigh on me very heavily. The fact that less than a week after he had had the bad news I came on young Bingo dancing like an untamed gazelle at Ciro's helped me to bear up.

A resilient bird, Bingo. He may be down, but he is never out. While these little love-affairs of his are actually on, nobody could be more earnest and blighted; but once the fuse has blown out and the girl has handed him his hat and begged him as a favour never to let her see him again, up he bobs as merry and bright as ever. If I've seen it happen once, I've seen it happen a dozen times.

So I didn't worry about Bingo. Or about anything else, as a matter of fact. What with one thing and another, I can't remember ever having been chirpier than at about this period in my career. Everything seemed to be going right. On three separate occasions horses on which I'd invested a sizeable amount won by lengths instead of sitting down to rest in the middle of the race, as horses usually do when I've got money on them.

Added to this, the weather continued topping to a degree; my new socks were admitted on all sides to be just the kind that mother makes; and, to round it all off, my Aunt Agatha had gone to France and wouldn't be on hand to snooter me for at least another six weeks. And, if you knew my Aunt Agatha, you'd agree that that alone was happiness enough for anyone.

It suddenly struck me so forcibly, one morning while I was having my bath, that I hadn't a worry on earth that I began to sing like a bally nightingale as I sploshed the sponge about. It seemed to me that everything was absolutely for the best in the best of all possible worlds.

But have you ever noticed a rummy thing about life? I mean the way something always comes along to give it you in the neck at the very moment when you're feeling most braced about things in general. No sooner had I dried the old limbs and shoved on the suiting and toddled into the sitting-room than the blow fell. There was a letter from Aunt Agatha on the mantelpiece.

"Oh gosh!" I said when I'd read it.

"Sir?" said Jeeves. He was fooling about in the background on some job or other.

"It's from my Aunt Agatha, Jeeves. Mrs. Gregson, you know."

"Yes, sir?"

"Ah, you wouldn't speak in that light, careless tone if you knew what was in it," I said with a hollow, mirthless laugh. "The curse has come upon us, Jeeves. She wants me to go and join her at—what's the name of the dashed place?—at Roville-sur-mer. Oh, hang it all!"

"I had better be packing, sir?"

"I suppose so."

To people who don't know my Aunt Agatha I find it extraordinarily difficult to explain why it is that she has always put the wind up me to such a frightful extent. I mean, I'm not dependent on her financially or anything like that. It's simply personality, I've come to the conclusion. You see, all through my childhood and when I was a kid at school she was always able to turn me inside out with a single glance, and I haven't come out from under the 'fluence yet. We run to height a bit in our family, and there's about five-foot-nine of Aunt Agatha, topped off with a beaky nose, an eagle eye, and a lot of grey hair, and the general effect is pretty formidable. Anyway, it never even occurred to me for a moment to give her the miss-in-baulk on this occasion. If she said I must go to Roville, it was all over except buying the tickets.

"What's the idea, Jeeves? I wonder why she wants me."

"I could not say, sir."

Well, it was no good talking about it. The only gleam of consolation, the only bit of blue among the clouds, was the fact that at Roville I should at last be able to wear the rather fruity cummerbund I had bought six months ago and had never had the nerve to put on. One of those silk contrivances, you know, which you tie round your waist instead of a waistcoat, something on the order of a sash only more substantial. I had never been able to muster up the courage to put it on so far, for I knew that there would be trouble with Jeeves when I did, it being a pretty brightish scarlet. Still, at a place like Roville, presumably dripping with the gaiety and joie de vivre of France, it seemed to me that something might be done.

* * * * *

Roville, which I reached early in the morning after a beastly choppy crossing and a jerky night in the train, is a fairly nifty spot where a chappie without encumbrances in the shape of aunts might spend a somewhat genial week or so. It is like all these French places, mainly sands and hotels and casinos. The hotel which had had the bad luck to draw Aunt Agatha's custom was the Splendide, and by the time I got there there wasn't a member of the staff who didn't seem to be feeling it deeply. I sympathised with them. I've had experience of Aunt Agatha at hotels before. Of course, the real rough work was all over when I arrived, but I could tell by the way every one grovelled before her that she had started by having her first room changed because it hadn't a southern exposure and her next because it had a creaking wardrobe and that she had said her say on the subject of the cooking, the waiting, the chambermaiding and everything else, with perfect freedom and candour. She had got the whole gang nicely under control by now. The manager, a whiskered cove who looked like a bandit, simply tied himself into knots whenever she looked at him.

All this triumph had produced a sort of grim geniality in her, and she was almost motherly when we met.

"I am so glad you were able to come, Bertie," she said. "The air will do you so much good. Far better for you than spending your time in stuffy London night clubs."

"Oh, ah," I said.

"You will meet some pleasant people, too. I want to introduce you to a Miss Hemmingway and her brother, who have become great friends of mine. I am sure you will like Miss Hemmingway. A nice, quiet girl, so different from so many of the bold girls one meets in London nowadays. Her brother is curate at Chipley-in-the-Glen in Dorsetshire. He tells me they are connected with the Kent Hemmingways. A very good family. She is a charming girl."

I had a grim foreboding of an awful doom. All this boosting was so unlike Aunt Agatha, who normally is one of the most celebrated right-and-left-hand knockers in London society.

I felt a clammy suspicion. And by Jove, I was right.

"Aline Hemmingway," said Aunt Agatha, "is just the girl I should like to see you marry, Bertie. You ought to be thinking of getting married. Marriage might make something of you. And I could not wish you a better wife than dear Aline. She would be such a good influence in your life."

"Here, I say!" I chipped in at this juncture, chilled to the marrow.

"Bertie!" said Aunt Agatha, dropping the motherly manner for a bit and giving me the cold eye.

"Yes, but I say...."

"It is young men like you, Bertie, who make the person with the future of the race at heart despair. Cursed with too much money, you fritter away in idle selfishness a life which might have been made useful, helpful and profitable. You do nothing but waste your time on frivolous pleasures. You are simply an anti-social animal, a drone. Bertie, it is imperative that you marry."

"But, dash it all...."

"Yes! You should be breeding children to...."

"No, really, I say, please!" I said, blushing richly. Aunt Agatha belongs to two or three of these women's clubs, and she keeps forgetting she isn't in the smoking-room.

"Bertie," she resumed, and would no doubt have hauled up her slacks at some length, had we not been interrupted. "Ah, here they are!" she said. "Aline, dear!"

And I perceived a girl and a chappie bearing down on me smiling in a pleased sort of manner.

"I want you to meet my nephew, Bertie Wooster," said Aunt Agatha. "He has just arrived. Such a surprise! I had no notion that he intended coming to Roville."

I gave the couple the wary up-and-down, feeling rather like a cat in the middle of a lot of hounds. Sort of trapped feeling, you know what I mean. An inner voice was whispering that Bertram was up against it.

The brother was a small round cove with a face rather like a sheep. He wore pince-nez, his expression was benevolent, and he had on one of those collars which button at the back.

"Welcome to Roville, Mr. Wooster," he said.

"Oh, Sidney!" said the girl. "Doesn't Mr. Wooster remind you of Canon Blenkinsop, who came to Chipley to preach last Easter?"

"My dear! The resemblance is most striking!"

They peered at me for a while as if I were something in a glass case, and I goggled back and had a good look at the girl. There's no doubt about it, she was different from what Aunt Agatha had called the bold girls one meets in London nowadays. No bobbed hair and gaspers about her! I don't know when I've met anybody who looked so—respectable is the only word. She had on a kind of plain dress, and her hair was plain, and her face was sort of mild and saint-like. I don't pretend to be a Sherlock Holmes or anything of that order, but the moment I looked at her I said to myself, "The girl plays the organ in a village church!"

Well, we gazed at one another for a bit, and there was a certain amount of chit-chat, and then I tore myself away. But before I went I had been booked up to take brother and the girl for a nice drive that afternoon. And the thought of it depressed me to such an extent that I felt there was only one thing to be done. I went straight back to my room, dug out the cummerbund, and draped it round the old tum. I turned round and Jeeves shied like a startled mustang.

"I beg your pardon, sir," he said in a sort of hushed voice. "You are surely not proposing to appear in public in that thing?"

"The cummerbund?" I said in a careless, debonair way, passing it off. "Oh, rather!"

"I should not advise it, sir, really I shouldn't."

"Why not?"

"The effect, sir, is loud in the extreme."

I tackled the blighter squarely. I mean to say, nobody knows better than I do that Jeeves is a master mind and all that, but, dash it, a fellow must call his soul his own. You can't be a serf to your valet. Besides, I was feeling pretty low and the cummerbund was the only thing which could cheer me up.

"You know, the trouble with you, Jeeves," I said, "is that you're too—what's the word I want?—too bally insular. You can't realise that you aren't in Piccadilly all the time. In a place like this a bit of colour and touch of the poetic is expected of you. Why, I've just seen a fellow downstairs in a morning suit of yellow velvet."

"Nevertheless, sir——"

"Jeeves," I said firmly, "my mind is made up. I am feeling a little low spirited and need cheering. Besides, what's wrong with it? This cummerbund seems to me to be called for. I consider that it has rather a Spanish effect. A touch of the hidalgo. Sort of Vicente y Blasco What's-his-name stuff. The jolly old hidalgo off to the bull fight."

"Very good, sir," said Jeeves coldly.

Dashed upsetting, this sort of thing. If there's one thing that gives me the pip, it's unpleasantness in the home; and I could see that relations were going to be pretty fairly strained for a while. And, coming on top of Aunt Agatha's bombshell about the Hemmingway girl, I don't mind confessing it made me feel more or less as though nobody loved me.

* * * * *

The drive that afternoon was about as mouldy as I had expected. The curate chappie prattled on of this and that; the girl admired the view; and I got a headache early in the proceedings which started at the soles of my feet and got worse all the way up. I tottered back to my room to dress for dinner, feeling like a toad under the harrow. If it hadn't been for that cummerbund business earlier in the day I could have sobbed on Jeeves's neck and poured out all my troubles to him. Even as it was, I couldn't keep the thing entirely to myself.

"I say, Jeeves," I said.

"Sir?"

"Mix me a stiffish brandy and soda."

"Yes, sir."

"Stiffish, Jeeves. Not too much soda, but splash the brandy about a bit."

"Very good, sir."

After imbibing, I felt a shade better.

"Jeeves," I said.

"Sir?"

"I rather fancy I'm in the soup, Jeeves."

"Indeed, sir?"

I eyed the man narrowly. Dashed aloof his manner was. Still brooding over the cummerbund.

"Yes. Right up to the hocks," I said, suppressing the pride of the Woosters and trying to induce him to be a bit matier. "Have you seen a girl popping about here with a parson brother?"

"Miss Hemmingway, sir? Yes, sir."

"Aunt Agatha wants me to marry her."

"Indeed, sir?"

"Well, what about it?"

"Sir?"

"I mean, have you anything to suggest?"

"No, sir."

The blighter's manner was so cold and unchummy that I bit the bullet and had a dash at being airy.

"Oh, well, tra-la-la!" I said.

"Precisely, sir," said Jeeves.

And that was, so to speak, that.

CHAPTER IV
PEARLS MEAN TEARS

I remember—it must have been when I was at school because I don't go in for that sort of thing very largely nowadays—reading a poem or something about something or other in which there was a line which went, if I've got it rightly, "Shades of the prison house begin to close upon the growing boy." Well, what I'm driving at is that during the next two weeks that's exactly how it was with me. I mean to say, I could hear the wedding bells chiming faintly in the distance and getting louder and louder every day, and how the deuce to slide out of it was more than I could think. Jeeves, no doubt, could have dug up a dozen brainy schemes in a couple of minutes, but he was still aloof and chilly and I couldn't bring myself to ask him point-blank. I mean, he could see easily enough that the young master was in a bad way and, if that wasn't enough to make him overlook the fact that I was still gleaming brightly about the waistband, well, what it amounted to was that the old feudal spirit was dead in the blighter's bosom and there was nothing to be done about it.

It really was rummy the way the Hemmingway family had taken to me. I wouldn't have said off-hand that there was anything particularly fascinating about me—in fact, most people look on me as rather an ass; but there was no getting away from the fact that I went like a breeze with this girl and her brother. They didn't seem happy if they were away from me. I couldn't move a step, dash it, without one of them popping out from somewhere and freezing on. In fact, I'd got into the habit now of retiring to my room when I wanted to take it easy for a bit. I had managed to get a rather decent suite on the third floor, looking down on to the promenade.

I had gone to earth in my suite one evening and for the first time that day was feeling that life wasn't so bad after all. Right through the day from lunch time I'd had the Hemmingway girl on my hands, Aunt Agatha having shooed us off together immediately after the midday meal. The result was, as I looked down on the lighted promenade and saw all the people popping happily about on their way to dinner and the Casino and what not, a kind of wistful feeling came over me. I couldn't help thinking how dashed happy I could have contrived to be in this place if only Aunt Agatha and the other blisters had been elsewhere.

I heaved a sigh, and at that moment there was a knock at the door.

"Someone at the door, Jeeves," I said.

"Yes, sir."

He opened the door, and in popped Aline Hemmingway and her brother. The last person I had expected. I really had thought that I could be alone for a minute in my own room.

"Oh, hallo!" I said.

"Oh, Mr. Wooster!" said the girl in a gasping sort of way. "I don't know how to begin."

Then I noticed that she appeared considerably rattled, and as for the brother, he looked like a sheep with a secret sorrow.

This made me sit up a bit and take notice. I had supposed that this was just a social call, but apparently something had happened to give them a jolt. Though I couldn't see why they should come to me about it.

"Is anything up?" I said.

"Poor Sidney—it was my fault—I ought never to have let him go there alone," said the girl. Dashed agitated.

At this point the brother, who after shedding a floppy overcoat and parking his hat on a chair had been standing by wrapped in the silence, gave a little cough, like a sheep caught in the mist on a mountain top.

"The fact is, Mr. Wooster," he said, "a sad, a most deplorable thing has occurred. This afternoon, while you were so kindly escorting my sist-ah, I found the time hang a little heavy upon my hands and I was tempted to—ah—gamble at the Casino."

I looked at the man in a kindlier spirit than I had been able to up to date. This evidence that he had sporting blood in his veins made him seem more human, I'm bound to say. If only I'd known earlier that he went in for that sort of thing, I felt that we might have had a better time together.

"Oh!" I said. "Did you click?"

He sighed heavily.

"If you mean was I successful, I must answer in the negative. I rashly persisted in the view that the colour red, having appeared no fewer than seven times in succession, must inevitably at no distant date give place to black. I was in error. I lost my little all, Mr. Wooster."

"Tough luck," I said.

"I left the Casino," proceeded the chappie, "and returned to the hotel. There I encountered one of my parishioners, a Colonel Musgrave, who chanced to be holiday-making over here. I—er—induced him to cash me a cheque for one hundred pounds on my little account in my London bank."

"Well, that was all to the good, what?" I said, hoping to induce the poor fish to look on the bright side. "I mean, bit of luck finding someone to slip it into first crack out of the box."

"On the contrary, Mr. Wooster, it did but make matters worse. I burn with shame as I make the confession, but I immediately went back to the Casino and lost the entire sum—this time under the mistaken supposition that the colour black was, as I believe the expression is, due for a run."

"I say!" I said. "You are having a night out!"

"And," concluded the chappie, "the most lamentable feature of the whole affair is that I have no funds in the bank to meet the cheque when presented."

I'm free to confess that, though I realised by this time that all this was leading up to a touch and that my ear was shortly going to be bitten in no uncertain manner, my heart warmed to the poor prune. Indeed, I gazed at him with no little interest and admiration. Never before had I encountered a curate so genuinely all to the mustard. Little as he might look like one of the lads of the village, he certainly appeared to be the real tabasco, and I wished he had shown me this side of his character before.

"Colonel Musgrave," he went on, gulping somewhat, "is not a man who would be likely to overlook the matter. He is a hard man. He will expose me to my vic-ah. My vic-ah is a hard man. In short, Mr. Wooster, if Colonel Musgrave presents that cheque I shall be ruined. And he leaves for England to-night."

The girl, who had been standing by biting her handkerchief and gurgling at intervals while the brother got the above off his chest, now started in once more.

"Mr. Wooster," she cried, "won't you, won't you help us? Oh, do say you will! We must have the money to get back the cheque from Colonel Musgrave before nine o'clock—he leaves on the nine-twenty. I was at my wits' end what to do when I remembered how kind you had always been. Mr. Wooster, will you lend Sidney the money and take these as security?" And before I knew what she was doing she had dived into her bag, produced a case, and opened it. "My pearls," she said. "I don't know what they are worth—they were a present from my poor father——"

"Now, alas, no more—" chipped in the brother.

"But I know they must be worth ever so much more than the amount we want."

Dashed embarrassing. Made me feel like a pawnbroker. More than a touch of popping the watch about the whole business.

"No, I say, really," I protested. "There's no need of any security, you know, or any rot of that kind. Only too glad to let you have the money. I've got it on me, as a matter of fact. Rather luckily drew some this morning."

And I fished it out and pushed it across. The brother shook his head.

"Mr. Wooster," he said, "we appreciate your generosity, your beautiful, heartening confidence in us, but we cannot permit this."

"What Sidney means," said the girl, "is that you really don't know anything about us when you come to think of it. You mustn't risk lending all this money without any security at all to two people who, after all, are almost strangers. If I hadn't thought that you would be quite business-like about this I would never have dared to come to you."

"The idea of—er—pledging the pearls at the local Mont de Piété? was, you will readily understand, repugnant to us," said the brother.

"If you will just give me a receipt, as a matter of form——"

"Oh, right-o!"

I wrote out the receipt and handed it over, feeling more or less of an ass.

"Here you are," I said.

The girl took the piece of paper, shoved it in her bag, grabbed the money and slipped it to brother Sidney, and then, before I knew what was happening, she had darted at me, kissed me, and legged it from the room.

I'm bound to say the thing rattled me. So dashed sudden and unexpected. I mean, a girl like that. Always been quiet and demure and what not—by no means the sort of female you'd have expected to go about the place kissing fellows. Through a sort of mist I could see that Jeeves had appeared from the background and was helping the brother on with his coat; and I remember wondering idly how the dickens a man could bring himself to wear a coat like that, it being more like a sack than anything else. Then the brother came up to me and grasped my hand.

"I cannot thank you sufficiently, Mr. Wooster!"

"Oh, not at all."

"You have saved my good name. Good name in man or woman, dear my lord," he said, massaging the fin with some fervour, "is the immediate jewel of their souls. Who steals my purse steals trash. 'Twas mine, 'tis his, and has been slave to thousands. But he that filches from me my good name robs me of that which enriches not him and makes me poor indeed.

I thank you from the bottom of my heart. Good night, Mr. Wooster."

"Good night, old thing," I said.

I blinked at Jeeves as the door shut. "Rather a sad affair, Jeeves," I said.

"Yes, sir."

"Lucky I happened to have all that money handy."

"Well—er—yes, sir."

"You speak as though you didn't think much of it."

"It is not my place to criticise your actions, sir, but I will venture to say that I think you behaved a little rashly."

"What, lending that money?"

"Yes, sir. These fashionable French watering places are notoriously infested by dishonest characters."

This was a bit too thick.

"Now look here, Jeeves," I said, "I can stand a lot but when it comes to your casting asp-whatever-the-word-is on a bird in Holy Orders——"

"Perhaps I am over-suspicious, sir. But I have seen a great deal of these resorts. When I was in the employment of Lord Frederick Ranelagh, shortly before I entered your service, his lordship was very neatly swindled by a criminal known, I believe, by the sobriquet of Soapy Sid, who scraped acquaintance with us in Monte Carlo with the assistance of a female accomplice. I have never forgotten the circumstances."

"I don't want to butt in on your reminiscences, Jeeves," I said, coldly, "but you're talking through your hat. How can there have been anything fishy about this business? They've left me the pearls, haven't they? Very well, then, think before you speak. You had better be tooling down to the desk now and having these things shoved in the hotel safe." I picked up the case and opened it. "Oh, Great Scott!"

The bally thing was empty!

"Oh, my Lord!" I said, staring. "Don't tell me there's been dirty work at the crossroads after all!"

"Precisely, sir. It was in exactly the same manner that Lord Frederick was swindled on the occasion to which I have alluded. While his female accomplice was gratefully embracing his lordship, Soapy Sid substituted a duplicate case for the one containing the pearls and went off with the jewels, the money and the receipt. On the strength of the receipt he subsequently demanded from his lordship the return of the pearls, and his lordship, not being able to produce them, was obliged to pay a heavy sum in compensation. It is a simple but effective ruse."

I felt as if the bottom had dropped out of things with a jerk.

"Soapy Sid? Sid! Sidney! Brother Sidney! Why, by Jove, Jeeves, do you think that parson was Soapy Sid?"

"Yes, sir."

"But it seems so extraordinary. Why, his collar buttoned at the back—I mean, he would have deceived a bishop. Do you really think he was Soapy Sid?"

"Yes, sir. I recognised him directly he came into the room."

I stared at the blighter.

"You recognised him?"

"Yes, sir."

"Then, dash it all," I said, deeply moved, "I think you might have told me."

"I thought it would save disturbance and unpleasantness if I merely abstracted the case from the man's pocket as I assisted him with his coat, sir. Here it is."

He laid another case on the table beside the dud one, and, by Jove, you couldn't tell them apart. I opened it and there were the good old pearls, as merry and bright as dammit, smiling up at me. I gazed feebly at the man. I was feeling a bit overwrought.

"Jeeves," I said. "You're an absolute genius!"

"Yes, sir."

Relief was surging over me in great chunks by now. Thanks to Jeeves I was not going to be called on to cough up several thousand quid.

"It looks to me as though you had saved the old home. I mean, even a chappie endowed with the immortal rind of dear old Sid is hardly likely to have the nerve to come back and retrieve these little chaps."

"I should imagine not, sir."

"Well, then—— Oh, I say, you don't think they are just paste or anything like that?"

"No, sir. These are genuine pearls and extremely valuable."

"Well, then, dash it, I'm on velvet. Absolutely reclining on the good old plush! I may be down a hundred quid but I'm up a jolly good string of pearls. Am I right or wrong?"

"Hardly that, sir. I think that you will have to restore the pearls."

"What! To Sid? Not while I have my physique!"

"No, sir. To their rightful owner."

"But who is their rightful owner?"

"Mrs. Gregson, sir."

"What! How do you know?"

"It was all over the hotel an hour ago that Mrs. Gregson's pearls had been abstracted. I was speaking to Mrs. Gregson's maid shortly before you came in and she informed me that the manager of the hotel is now in Mrs. Gregson's suite."

"And having a devil of a time, what?"

"So I should be disposed to imagine, sir."

The situation was beginning to unfold before me.

"I'll go and give them back to her, eh? It'll put me one up, what?"

"Precisely, sir. And, if I may make the suggestion, I think it might be judicious to stress the fact that they were stolen by——"

"Great Scott! By the dashed girl she was hounding me on to marry, by Jove!"

"Exactly, sir."

"Jeeves," I said, "this is going to be the biggest score off my jolly old relative that has ever occurred in the world's history."

"It is not unlikely, sir."

"Keep her quiet for a bit, what? Make her stop snootering me for a while?"

"It should have that effect, sir."

"Golly!" I said, bounding for the door.

*****

Long before I reached Aunt Agatha's lair I could tell that the hunt was up. Divers chappies in hotel uniform and not a few chambermaids of sorts were hanging about in the corridor, and through the panels I could hear a mixed assortment of voices, with Aunt Agatha's topping the lot. I knocked but no one took any notice, so I trickled in. Among those present I noticed a chambermaid in hysterics, Aunt Agatha with her hair bristling, and the whiskered cove who looked like a bandit, the hotel manager fellow.

"Oh, hallo!" I said. "Hallo-allo-allo!"

Aunt Agatha shooshed me away. No welcoming smile for Bertram.

"Don't bother me now, Bertie," she snapped, looking at me as if I were more or less the last straw.

"Something up?"

"Yes, yes, yes! I've lost my pearls."

"Pearls? Pearls? Pearls?" I said. "No, really? Dashed annoying. Where did you see them last?"

"What does it matter where I saw them last? They have been stolen."

Here Wilfred the Whisker King, who seemed to have been taking a rest between rounds, stepped into the ring again and began to talk rapidly in French. Cut to the quick he seemed. The chambermaid whooped in the corner.

"Sure you've looked everywhere?" I said.

"Of course I've looked everywhere."

"Well, you know, I've often lost a collar stud and——"

"Do try not to be so maddening, Bertie! I have enough to bear without your imbecilities. Oh, be quiet! Be quiet!" she shouted in the sort of voice used by sergeant-majors and those who call the cattle home across the Sands of Dee. And such was the magnetism of her forceful personality that Wilfred subsided as if he had run into a wall. The chambermaid continued to go strong.

"I say," I said, "I think there's something the matter with this girl. Isn't she crying or something? You may not have spotted it, but I'm rather quick at noticing things."

"She stole my pearls! I am convinced of it."

This started the whisker specialist off again, and in about a couple of minutes Aunt Agatha had reached the frozen grande-dame stage and was putting the last of the bandits through it in the voice she usually reserves for snubbing waiters in restaurants.

"I tell you, my good man, for the hundredth time——"

"I say," I said, "don't want to interrupt you and all that sort of thing, but these aren't the little chaps by any chance, are they?"

I pulled the pearls out of my pocket and held them up.

"These look like pearls, what?"

I don't know when I've had a more juicy moment. It was one of those occasions about which I shall prattle to my grandchildren—if I ever have any, which at the moment of going to press seems more or less of a hundred-to-one shot. Aunt Agatha simply deflated before my eyes. It reminded me of when I once saw some chappies letting the gas out of a balloon.

"Where—where—where——" she gurgled.

"I got them from your friend, Miss Hemmingway."

Even now she didn't get it.

"From Miss Hemmingway. Miss Hemmingway! But—but how did they come into her possession?"

"How?" I said. "Because she jolly well stole them. Pinched them! Swiped them! Because that's how she makes her living, dash it—palling up to unsuspicious people in hotels and sneaking their jewellery. I don't know what her alias is, but her bally brother, the chap whose collar buttons at the back, is known in criminal circles as Soapy Sid."

She blinked.

"Miss Hemmingway a thief! I—I——" She stopped and looked feebly at me. "But how did you manage to recover the pearls, Bertie dear?"

"Never mind," I said crisply. "I have my methods." I dug out my entire stock of manly courage, breathed a short prayer and let her have it right in the thorax.

"I must say, Aunt Agatha, dash it all," I said severely, "I think you have been infernally careless. There's a printed notice in every bedroom in this place saying that there's a safe in the manager's office where jewellery and valuables ought to be placed, and you absolutely disregarded it. And what's the result? The first thief who came along simply walked into your room and pinched your pearls. And instead of admitting that it was all your fault, you started biting this poor man here in the gizzard. You have been very, very unjust to this poor man."

"Yes, yes," moaned the poor man.

"And this unfortunate girl, what about her? Where does she get off? You've accused her of stealing the things on absolutely no evidence. I think she would be jolly well advised to bring an action for—for whatever it is and soak you for substantial damages."

"Mais oui, mais oui, c'est trop fort!" shouted the Bandit Chief, backing me up like a good 'un. And the chambermaid looked up inquiringly, as if the sun was breaking through the clouds.

"I shall recompense her," said Aunt Agatha feebly.

"If you take my tip you jolly well will, and that eftsoons or right speedily. She's got a cast-iron case, and if I were her I wouldn't take a penny under twenty quid. But what gives me the pip most is the way you've unjustly abused this poor man here and tried to give his hotel a bad name——"

"Yes, by damn! It's too bad!" cried the whiskered marvel. "You careless old woman! You give my hotel bad names, would you or wasn't it? To-morrow you leave my hotel, by great Scotland!"

And more to the same effect, all good, ripe stuff. And presently having said his say he withdrew, taking the chambermaid with him, the latter with a crisp tenner clutched in a vice-like grip. I suppose she and the bandit split it outside. A French hotel manager wouldn't be likely to let real money wander away from him without counting himself in on the division.

I turned to Aunt Agatha, whose demeanour was now rather like that of one who, picking daisies on the railway, has just caught the down express in the small of the back.

"I don't want to rub it in, Aunt Agatha," I said coldly, "but I should just like to point out before I go that the girl who stole your pearls is the girl you've been hounding me on to marry ever since I got here. Good heavens! Do you realise that if you had brought the thing off I should probably have had children who would have sneaked my watch while I was dandling them on my knee? I'm not a complaining sort of chap as a rule, but I must say that another time I do think you might be more careful how you go about egging me on to marry females."

I gave her one look, turned on my heel and left the room.

* * * * *

"Ten o'clock, a clear night, and all's well, Jeeves," I said, breezing back into the good old suite.

"I am gratified to hear it, sir."

"If twenty quid would be any use to you, Jeeves——"

"I am much obliged, sir."

There was a pause. And then—well, it was a wrench, but I did it. I unstripped the cummerbund and handed it over.

"Do you wish me to press this, sir?"

I gave the thing one last, longing look. It had been very dear to me.

"No," I said, "take it away; give it to the deserving poor—I shall never wear it again."

"Thank you very much, sir," said Jeeves.

CHAPTER V
THE PRIDE OF THE WOOSTERS IS WOUNDED

If there's one thing I like, it's a quiet life. I'm not one of those fellows who get all restless and depressed if things aren't happening to them all the time. You can't make it too placid for me. Give me regular meals, a good show with decent music every now and then, and one or two pals to totter round with, and I ask no more.

That is why the jar, when it came, was such a particularly nasty jar. I mean, I'd returned from Roville with a sort of feeling that from now on nothing could occur to upset me. Aunt Agatha, I imagined, would require at least a year to recover from the Hemmingway affair: and apart from Aunt Agatha there isn't anybody who really does much in the way of harrying me. It seemed to me that the skies were blue, so to speak, and no clouds in sight.

I little thought.... Well, look here, what happened was this, and I ask you if it wasn't enough to rattle anybody.

Once a year Jeeves takes a couple of weeks' vacation and biffs off to the sea or somewhere to restore his tissues. Pretty rotten for me, of course, while he's away. But it has to be stuck, so I stick it; and I must admit that he usually manages to get hold of a fairly decent fellow to look after me in his absence.

Well, the time had come round again, and Jeeves was in the kitchen giving the understudy a few tips about his duties. I happened to want a stamp or something, and I toddled down the passage to ask him for it. The silly ass had left the kitchen door open, and I hadn't gone two steps when his voice caught me squarely in the eardrum.

"You will find Mr. Wooster," he was saying to the substitute chappie, "an exceedingly pleasant and amiable young gentleman, but not intelligent. By no means intelligent. Mentally he is negligible—quite negligible."

Well, I mean to say, what!

I suppose, strictly speaking, I ought to have charged in and ticked the blighter off properly in no uncertain voice. But I doubt whether it's humanly possible to tick Jeeves off. Personally, I didn't even have a dash at it. I merely called for my hat and stick in a marked manner and legged it. But the memory rankled, if you know what I mean. We Woosters do not lightly forget. At least, we do—some things—appointments, and people's birthdays, and letters to post, and all that—but not an absolute bally insult like the above. I brooded like the dickens.

I was still brooding when I dropped in at the oyster-bar at Buck's for a quick bracer. I needed a bracer rather particularly at the moment, because I was on my way to lunch with Aunt Agatha. A pretty frightful ordeal, believe me or believe me not, even though I took it that after what had happened at Roville she would be in a fairly subdued and amiable mood. I had just had one quick and another rather slower, and was feeling about as cheerio as was possible under the circs, when a muffled voice hailed me from the north-east, and, turning round, I saw young Bingo Little propped up in a corner, wrapping himself round a sizable chunk of bread and cheese.

"Hallo-allo-allo!" I said. "Haven't seen you for ages. You've not been in here lately, have you?"

"No. I've been living out in the country."

"Eh?" I said, for Bingo's loathing for the country was well known. "Whereabouts?"

"Down in Hampshire, at a place called Ditteredge."

"No, really? I know some people who've got a house there. The Glossops. Have you met them?"

"Why, that's where I'm staying!" said young Bingo. "I'm tutoring the Glossop kid."

"What for?" I said. I couldn't seem to see young Bingo as a tutor. Though, of course, he did get a degree of sorts at Oxford, and I suppose you can always fool some of the people some of the time.

"What for? For money, of course! An absolute sitter came unstitched in the second race at Haydock Park," said young Bingo, with some bitterness, "and I dropped my entire month's allowance. I hadn't the nerve to touch my uncle for any more, so it was a case of buzzing round to the agents and getting a job. I've been down there three weeks."

"I haven't met the Glossop kid."

"Don't!" advised Bingo, briefly.

"The only one of the family I really know is the girl." I had hardly spoken these words when the most extraordinary change came over young Bingo's face. His eyes bulged, his cheeks flushed, and his Adam's apple hopped about like one of those india-rubber balls on the top of the fountain in a shooting-gallery.

"Oh, Bertie!" he said, in a strangled sort of voice.

I looked at the poor fish anxiously. I knew that he was always falling in love with someone, but it didn't seem possible that even he could have fallen in love with Honoria Glossop. To me the girl was simply nothing more nor less than a pot of poison. One of those dashed large, brainy, strenuous, dynamic girls you see so many of these days. She had been at Girton, where, in addition to enlarging her brain to the most frightful extent, she had gone in for every kind of sport and developed the physique of a middle-weight catch-as-catch-can wrestler. I'm not sure she didn't box for the 'Varsity while she was up. The effect she had on me whenever she appeared was to make me want to slide into a cellar and lie low till they blew the All-Clear.

Yet here was young Bingo obviously all for her. There was no mistaking it. The love-light was in the blighter's eyes.

"I worship her, Bertie! I worship the very ground she treads on!" continued the patient, in a loud, penetrating voice. Fred Thompson and one or two fellows had come in, and McGarry, the chappie behind the bar, was listening with his ears flapping. But there's no reticence about Bingo. He always reminds me of the hero of a musical comedy who takes the centre of the stage, gathers the boys round him in a circle, and tells them all about his love at the top of his voice.

"Have you told her?"

"No. I haven't had the nerve. But we walk together in the garden most evenings, and it sometimes seems to me that there is a look in her eyes."

"I know that look. Like a sergeant-major."

"Nothing of the kind! Like a tender goddess."

"Half a second, old thing," I said. "Are you sure we're talking about the same girl? The one I mean is Honoria. Perhaps there's a younger sister or something I've not heard of?"

"Her name is Honoria," bawled Bingo reverently.

"And she strikes you as a tender goddess?"

"She does."

"God bless you!" I said.

"She walks in beauty like the night of cloudless climes and starry skies; and all that's best of dark and bright meet in her aspect and her eyes. Another bit of bread and cheese," he said to the lad behind the bar.

"You're keeping your strength up," I said.

"This is my lunch. I've got to meet Oswald at Waterloo at one-fifteen, to catch the train back. I brought him up to town to see the dentist."

"Oswald? Is that the kid?"

"Yes. Pestilential to a degree."

"Pestilential! That reminds me, I'm lunching with my Aunt Agatha. I'll have to pop off now, or I'll be late."

I hadn't seen Aunt Agatha since that little affair of the pearls; and, while I didn't anticipate any great pleasure from gnawing a bone in her society, I must say that there was one topic of conversation I felt pretty confident she wouldn't touch on, and that was the subject of my matrimonial future. I mean, when a woman's made a bloomer like the one Aunt Agatha made at Roville, you'd naturally think that a decent shame would keep her off it for, at any rate, a month or two.

But women beat me. I mean to say, as regards nerve. You'll hardly credit it, but she actually started in on me with the fish. Absolutely with the fish, I give you my solemn word. We'd hardly exchanged a word about the weather, when she let me have it without a blush.

"Bertie," she said, "I've been thinking again about you and how necessary it is that you should get married. I quite admit that I was dreadfully mistaken in my opinion of that terrible, hypocritical girl at Roville, but this time there is no danger of an error. By great good luck I have found the very wife for you, a girl whom I have only recently met, but whose family is above suspicion. She has plenty of money, too, though that does not matter in your case. The great point is that she is strong, self-reliant and sensible, and will counterbalance the deficiencies and weaknesses of your character. She has met you; and, while there is naturally much in you of which she disapproves, she does not dislike you. I know this, for I have sounded her—guardedly, of course—and I am sure that you have only to make the first advances——"

"Who is it?" I would have said it long before, but the shock had made me swallow a bit of roll the wrong way, and I had only just finished turning purple and trying to get a bit of air back into the old windpipe. "Who is it?"

"Sir Roderick Glossop's daughter, Honoria."

"No, no!" I cried, paling beneath the tan.

"Don't be silly, Bertie. She is just the wife for you."

"Yes, but look here——"

"She will mould you."

"But I don't want to be moulded."

Aunt Agatha gave me the kind of look she used to give me when I was a kid and had been found in the jam cupboard.

"Bertie! I hope you are not going to be troublesome."

"Well, but I mean——"

"Lady Glossop has very kindly invited you to Ditteredge Hall for a few days. I told her you would be delighted to come down to-morrow."

"I'm sorry, but I've got a dashed important engagement to-morrow."

"What engagement?"

"Well—er——"

"You have no engagement. And, even if you had, you must put it off. I shall be very seriously annoyed, Bertie, if you do not go to Ditteredge Hall to-morrow."

"Oh, right-o!" I said.

It wasn't two minutes after I had parted from Aunt Agatha before the old fighting spirit of the Woosters reasserted itself. Ghastly as the peril was which loomed before me, I was conscious of a rummy sort of exhilaration. It was a tight corner, but the tighter the corner, I felt, the more juicily should I score off Jeeves when I got myself out of it without a bit of help from him. Ordinarily, of course, I should have consulted him and trusted to him to solve the difficulty; but after what I had heard him saying in the kitchen, I was dashed if I was going to demean myself. When I got home I addressed the man with light abandon.

"Jeeves," I said, "I'm in a bit of a difficulty."

"I'm sorry to hear that, sir."

"Yes, quite a bad hole. In fact, you might say on the brink of a precipice, and faced by an awful doom."

"If I could be of any assistance, sir——"

"Oh, no. No, no. Thanks very much, but no, no. I won't trouble you. I've no doubt I shall be able to get out of it all right by myself."

"Very good, sir."

So that was that. I'm bound to say I'd have welcomed a bit more curiosity from the fellow, but that is Jeeves all over. Cloaks his emotions, if you know what I mean.

Honoria was away when I got to Ditteredge on the following afternoon. Her mother told me that she was staying with some people named Braythwayt in the neighbourhood, and would be back next day, bringing the daughter of the house with her for a visit. She said I would find Oswald out in the grounds, and such is a mother's love that she spoke as if that were a bit of a boost for the grounds and an inducement to go there.

Rather decent, the grounds at Ditteredge. A couple of terraces, a bit of lawn with a cedar on it, a bit of shrubbery, and finally a small but goodish lake with a stone bridge running across it. Directly I'd worked my way round the shrubbery I spotted young Bingo leaning against the bridge smoking a cigarette. Sitting on the stonework, fishing, was a species of kid whom I took to be Oswald the Plague-Spot.

Bingo was both surprised and delighted to see me, and introduced me to the kid. If the latter was surprised and delighted too, he concealed it like a diplomat. He just looked at me, raised his eyebrows slightly, and went on fishing. He was one of those supercilious striplings who give you the impression that you went to the wrong school and that your clothes don't fit.

"This is Oswald," said Bingo.

"What," I replied cordially, "could be sweeter? How are you?"

"Oh, all right," said the kid.

"Nice place, this."

"Oh, all right," said the kid.

"Having a good time fishing?"

"Oh, all right," said the kid.

Young Bingo led me off to commune apart.

"Doesn't jolly old Oswald's incessant flow of prattle make your head ache sometimes?" I asked.

Bingo sighed.

"It's a hard job."

"What's a hard job?"

"Loving him."

"Do you love him?" I asked, surprised. I shouldn't have thought it could be done.

"I try to," said young Bingo, "for Her sake. She's coming back to-morrow, Bertie."

"So I heard."

"She is coming, my love, my own——"

"Absolutely," I said. "But touching on young Oswald once more. Do you have to be with him all day? How do you manage to stick it?"

"Oh, he doesn't give much trouble. When we aren't working he sits on that bridge all the time, trying to catch tiddlers."

"Why don't you shove him in?"

"Shove him in?"

"It seems to me distinctly the thing to do," I said, regarding the stripling's back with a good deal of dislike. "It would wake him up a bit, and make him take an interest in things."

Bingo shook his head a bit wistfully.

"Your proposition attracts me," he said, "but I'm afraid it can't be done. You see, She would never forgive me. She is devoted to the little brute."

"Great Scott!" I cried. "I've got it!" I don't know if you know that feeling when you get an inspiration, and tingle all down your spine from the soft collar as now worn to the very soles of the old Waukeesis? Jeeves, I suppose, feels that way more or less all the time, but it isn't often it comes to me. But now all Nature seemed to be shouting at me "You've clicked!" and I grabbed young Bingo by the arm in a way that must have made him feel as if a horse had bitten him. His finely-chiselled features were twisted with agony and what not, and he asked me what the dickens I thought I was playing at.

"Bingo," I said, "what would Jeeves have done?"

"How do you mean, what would Jeeves have done?"

"I mean what would he have advised in a case like yours? I mean you wanting to make a hit with Honoria Glossop and all that. Why, take it from me, laddie, he would have shoved you behind that clump of bushes over there; he would have got me to lure Honoria on to the bridge somehow; then, at the proper time, he would have told me to give the kid a pretty hefty jab in the small of the back, so as to shoot him into the water; and then you would have dived in and hauled him out. How about it?"

"You didn't think that out by yourself, Bertie?" said young Bingo, in a hushed sort of voice.

"Yes, I did. Jeeves isn't the only fellow with ideas."

"But it's absolutely wonderful."

"Just a suggestion."

"The only objection I can see is that it would be so dashed awkward for you. I mean to say, suppose the kid turned round and said you had shoved him in, that would make you frightfully unpopular with Her."

"I don't mind risking that."

The man was deeply moved.

"Bertie, this is noble."

"No, no."

He clasped my hand silently, then chuckled like the last drop of water going down the waste-pipe in a bath.

"Now what?" I said.

"I was only thinking," said young Bingo, "how fearfully wet Oswald will get. Oh, happy day!"

CHAPTER VI
THE HERO'S REWARD

I don't know if you've noticed it, but it's rummy how nothing in this world ever seems to be absolutely perfect. The drawback to this otherwise singularly fruity binge was, of course, the fact that Jeeves wouldn't be on the spot to watch me in action. Still, apart from that there wasn't a flaw. The beauty of the thing was, you see, that nothing could possibly go wrong. You know how it is, as a rule, when you want to get Chappie A on Spot B at exactly the same moment when Chappie C is on Spot D. There's always a chance of a hitch. Take the case of a general, I mean to say, who's planning out a big movement. He tells one regiment to capture the hill with the windmill on it at the exact moment when another regiment is taking the bridgehead or something down in the valley; and everything gets all messed up. And then, when they're chatting the thing over in camp that night, the colonel of the first regiment says, "Oh, sorry! Did you say the hill with the windmill? I thought you said the one with the flock of sheep." And there you are! But in this case, nothing like that could happen, because Oswald and Bingo would be on the spot right along, so that all I had to worry about was getting Honoria there in due season. And I managed that all right, first shot, by asking her if she would come for a stroll in the grounds with me, as I had something particular to say to her.

She had arrived shortly after lunch in the car with the Braythwayt girl. I was introduced to the latter, a tallish girl with blue eyes and fair hair. I rather took to her—she was so unlike Honoria—and, if I had been able to spare the time, I shouldn't have minded talking to her for a bit. But business was business—I had fixed it up with Bingo to be behind the bushes at three sharp, so I got hold of Honoria and steered her out through the grounds in the direction of the lake.

"You're very quiet, Mr. Wooster," she said.

Made me jump a bit. I was concentrating pretty tensely at the moment. We had just come in sight of the lake, and I was casting a keen eye over the ground to see that everything was in order. Everything appeared to be as arranged. The kid Oswald was hunched up on the bridge; and, as Bingo wasn't visible, I took it that he had got into position. My watch made it two minutes after the hour.

"Eh?" I said. "Oh, ah, yes. I was just thinking."

"You said you had something important to say to me."

"Absolutely!" I had decided to open the proceedings by sort of paving the way for young Bingo. I mean to say, without actually mentioning his name, I wanted to prepare the girl's mind for the fact that, surprising as it might seem, there was someone who had long loved her from afar and all that sort of rot. "It's like this," I said. "It may sound rummy and all that, but there's somebody who's frightfully in love with you and so forth—a friend of mine, you know."

"Oh, a friend of yours?"

"Yes."

She gave a kind of a laugh.

"Well, why doesn't he tell me so?"

"Well, you see, that's the sort of chap he is. Kind of shrinking, diffident kind of fellow. Hasn't got the nerve. Thinks you so much above him, don't you know. Looks on you as a sort of goddess. Worships the ground you tread on, but can't whack up the ginger to tell you so."

"This is very interesting."

"Yes. He's not a bad chap, you know, in his way. Rather an ass, perhaps, but well-meaning. Well, that's the posish. You might just bear it in mind, what?"

"How funny you are!"

She chucked back her head and laughed with considerable vim. She had a penetrating sort of laugh. Rather like a train going into a tunnel. It didn't sound over-musical to me, and on the kid Oswald it appeared to jar not a little. He gazed at us with a good deal of dislike.

"I wish the dickens you wouldn't make that row," he said. "Scaring all the fish away."

It broke the spell a bit. Honoria changed the subject.

"I do wish Oswald wouldn't sit on the bridge like that," she said. "I'm sure it isn't safe. He might easily fall in."

"I'll go and tell him," I said.

*   *   *   *   *

I suppose the distance between the kid and me at this juncture was about five yards, but I got the impression that it was nearer a hundred. And, as I started to toddle across the intervening space, I had a rummy feeling that I'd done this very thing before. Then I remembered. Years ago, at a country-house party, I had been roped in to play the part of a butler in some amateur theatricals in aid of some ghastly charity or other; and I had had to open the proceedings by walking across the empty stage from left upper entrance and shoving a tray on a table down right. They had impressed it on me at rehearsals that I mustn't take the course at a quick heel-and-toe, like a chappie finishing strongly in a walking-race; and the result was that I kept the brakes on to such an extent that it seemed to me as if I was never going to get to the bally table at all. The stage seemed to stretch out in front of me like a trackless desert, and there was a kind of breathless hush as if all Nature had paused to concentrate its attention on me personally. Well, I felt just like that now. I had a kind of dry gulping in my throat, and the more I walked the farther away the kid seemed to get, till suddenly I found myself standing just behind him without quite knowing how I'd got there.

"Hallo!" I said, with a sickly sort of grin—wasted on the kid, because he didn't bother to turn round and look at me. He merely wiggled his left ear in a rather peevish manner. I don't know when I've met anybody in whose life I appeared to mean so little.

"Hallo!" I said. "Fishing?"

I laid my hand in a sort of elder-brotherly way on his shoulder.

"Here, look out!" said the kid, wobbling on his foundations.

It was one of those things that want doing quickly or not at all. I shut my eyes and pushed. Something seemed to give. There was a scrambling sound, a kind of yelp, a scream in the offing, and a splash. And so the long day wore on, so to speak.

I opened my eyes. The kid was just coming to the surface.

"Help!" I shouted, cocking an eye on the bush from which young Bingo was scheduled to emerge.

Nothing happened. Young Bingo didn't emerge to the slightest extent whatever.

"I say! Help!" I shouted again.

I don't want to bore you with reminiscences of my theatrical career, but I must just touch once more on that appearance of mine as the butler. The scheme on that occasion had been that when I put the tray on the table the heroine would come on and say a few words to get me off. Well, on the night the misguided female forgot to stand by, and it was a full minute before the search-party located her and shot her on to the stage. And all that time I had to stand there, waiting. A rotten sensation, believe me, and this was just the same, only worse. I understood what these writer-chappies mean when they talk about time standing still.

Meanwhile, the kid Oswald was presumably being cut off in his prime, and it began to seem to me that some sort of steps ought to be taken about it. What I had seen of the lad hadn't particularly endeared him to me, but it was undoubtedly a bit thick to let him pass away. I don't know when I have seen anything more grubby and unpleasant than the lake as viewed from the bridge; but the thing apparently had to be done. I chucked off my coat and vaulted over.

It seems rummy that water should be so much wetter when you go into it with your clothes on than when you're just bathing, but take it from me that it is. I was only under about three seconds, I suppose, but I came up feeling like the bodies you read of in the paper which "had evidently been in the water several days." I felt clammy and bloated.

At this point the scenario struck another snag. I had assumed that directly I came to the surface I should get hold of the kid and steer him courageously to shore. But he hadn't waited to be steered. When I had finished getting the water out of my eyes and had time to take a look round, I saw him about ten yards away, going strongly and using, I think, the Australian crawl. The spectacle took all the heart out of me. I mean to say, the whole essence of a rescue, if you know what I mean, is that the party of the second part shall keep fairly still and in one spot. If he starts swimming off on his own account and can obviously give you at least forty yards in the hundred, where are you? The whole thing falls through. It didn't seem to me that there was much to be done except get ashore, so I got ashore. By the time I had landed, the kid was half-way to the house. Look at it from whatever angle you like, the thing was a wash-out.

I was interrupted in my meditations by a noise like the Scotch express going under a bridge. It was Honoria Glossop laughing. She was standing at my elbow, looking at me in a rummy manner.

"Oh, Bertie, you are funny!" she said. And even in that moment there seemed to me something sinister in the words. She had never called me anything except "Mr. Wooster" before. "How wet you are!"

"Yes, I am wet."

"You had better hurry into the house and change."

"Yes."

I wrung a gallon or two of water out of my clothes.

"You are funny!" she said again. "First proposing in that extraordinary roundabout way, and then pushing poor little Oswald into the lake so as to impress me by saving him."

I managed to get the water out of my throat sufficiently to try to correct this fearful impression.

"No, no!"

"He said you pushed him in, and I saw you do it. Oh, I'm not angry, Bertie. I think it was too sweet of you. But I'm quite sure it's time that I took you in hand. You certainly want someone to look after you. You've been seeing too many moving-pictures. I suppose the next thing you would have done would have been to set the house on fire so as to rescue me." She looked at me in a proprietary sort of way. "I think," she said, "I shall be able to make something of you, Bertie. It is true yours has been a wasted life up to the present, but you are still young, and there is a lot of good in you."

"No, really there isn't."

"Oh, yes, there is. It simply wants bringing out. Now you run straight up to the house and change your wet clothes, or you will catch cold."

And, if you know what I mean, there was a sort of motherly note in her voice which seemed to tell me, even more than her actual words, that I was for it.

* * * * *

As I was coming downstairs after changing, I ran into young Bingo, looking festive to a degree.

"Bertie!" he said. "Just the man I wanted to see. Bertie, a wonderful thing has happened."

"You blighter!" I cried. "What became of you? Do you know——?"

"Oh, you mean about being in those bushes? I hadn't time to tell you about that. It's all off."

"All off?"

"Bertie, I was actually starting to hide in those bushes when the most extraordinary thing happened. Walking across the lawn I saw the most radiant, the most beautiful girl in the world. There is none like her, none. Bertie, do you believe in love at first sight? You do believe in love at first sight, don't you, Bertie, old man? Directly I saw her, she seemed to draw me like a magnet. I seemed to forget everything. We two were alone in a world of music and sunshine. I joined her. I got into conversation. She is a Miss Braythwayt, Bertie—Daphne Braythwayt. Directly our eyes met, I realised that what I had imagined to be my love for Honoria Glossop had been a mere passing whim. Bertie, you do believe in love at first sight, don't you? She is so wonderful, so sympathetic. Like a tender goddess——"

At this point I left the blighter.

* * * * *

Two days later I got a letter from Jeeves.

" ... The weather," it ended, "continues fine. I have had one exceedingly enjoyable bathe."

I gave one of those hollow, mirthless laughs, and went downstairs to join Honoria. I had an appointment with her in the drawing-room. She was going to read Ruskin to me.

CHAPTER VII
INTRODUCING CLAUDE AND EUSTACE

The blow fell precisely at one forty-five (summer time). Spenser, Aunt Agatha's butler, was offering me the fried potatoes at the moment, and such was my emotion that I lofted six of them on to the sideboard with the spoon. Shaken to the core, if you know what I mean.

Mark you, I was in a pretty enfeebled condition already. I had been engaged to Honoria Glossop nearly two weeks, and during all that time not a day had passed without her putting in some heavy work in the direction of what Aunt Agatha had called "moulding" me. I had read solid literature till my eyes bubbled; we had legged it together through miles of picture-galleries; and I had been compelled to undergo classical concerts to an extent you would hardly believe. All in all, therefore, I was in no fit state to receive shocks, especially shocks like this. Honoria had lugged me round to lunch at Aunt Agatha's, and I had just been saying to myself, "Death, where is thy jolly old sting?" when she hove the bomb.

"Bertie," she said, suddenly, as if she had just remembered it, "what is the name of that man of yours—your valet?"

"Eh? Oh, Jeeves."

"I think he's a bad influence for you," said Honoria. "When we are married, you must get rid of Jeeves."

It was at this point that I jerked the spoon and sent six of the best and crispest sailing on to the sideboard, with Spenser gambolling after them like a dignified old retriever.

"Get rid of Jeeves!" I gasped.

"Yes. I don't like him."

"I don't like him," said Aunt Agatha.

"But I can't. I mean—why, I couldn't carry on for a day without Jeeves."

"You will have to," said Honoria. "I don't like him at all."

"I don't like him at all," said Aunt Agatha. "I never did."

Ghastly, what? I'd always had an idea that marriage was a bit of a wash-out, but I'd never dreamed that it demanded such frightful sacrifices from a fellow. I passed the rest of the meal in a sort of stupor.

The scheme had been, if I remember, that after lunch I should go off and caddy for Honoria on a shopping tour down Regent Street; but when she got up and started collecting me and the rest of her things, Aunt Agatha stopped her.

"You run along, dear," she said. "I want to say a few words to Bertie."

So Honoria legged it, and Aunt Agatha drew up her chair and started in.

"Bertie," she said, "dear Honoria does not know it, but a little difficulty has arisen about your marriage."

"By Jove! not really?" I said, hope starting to dawn.

"Oh, it's nothing at all, of course. It is only a little exasperating. The fact is, Sir Roderick is being rather troublesome."

"Thinks I'm not a good bet? Wants to scratch the fixture? Well, perhaps he's right."

"Pray do not be so absurd, Bertie. It is nothing so serious as that. But the nature of Sir Roderick's profession unfortunately makes him—over-cautious."

I didn't get it.

"Over-cautious?"

"Yes. I suppose it is inevitable. A nerve specialist with his extensive practice can hardly help taking a rather warped view of humanity."

I got what she was driving at now. Sir Roderick Glossop, Honoria's father, is always called a nerve specialist, because it sounds better, but everybody knows that he's really a sort of janitor to the looney-bin. I mean to say, when your uncle the Duke begins to feel the strain a bit and you find him in the blue drawing-room sticking straws in his hair, old Glossop is the first person you send for. He toddles round, gives the patient the once-over, talks about over-excited nervous systems, and recommends complete rest and seclusion and all that sort of thing. Practically every posh family in the country has called him in at one time or another, and I suppose that, being in that position—I mean constantly having to sit on people's heads while their nearest and dearest phone to the asylum to send round the wagon—does tend to make a chappie take what you might call a warped view of humanity.

"You mean he thinks I may be a looney, and he doesn't want a looney son-in-law?" I said.

Aunt Agatha seemed rather peeved than otherwise at my ready intelligence.

"Of course, he does not think anything so ridiculous. I told you he was simply exceedingly cautious. He wants to satisfy himself that you are perfectly normal." Here she paused, for Spenser had come in with the coffee. When he had gone, she went on: "He appears to have got hold of some extraordinary story about your having pushed his son Oswald into the lake at Ditteredge Hall. Incredible, of course. Even you would hardly do a thing like that."

"Well, I did sort of lean against him, you know, and he shot off the bridge."

"Oswald definitely accuses you of having pushed him into the water. That has disturbed Sir Roderick, and unfortunately it has caused him to make inquiries, and he has heard about your poor Uncle Henry."

She eyed me with a good deal of solemnity, and I took a grave sip of coffee. We were peeping into the family cupboard and having a look at the good old skeleton. My late Uncle Henry, you see, was by way of being the blot on the Wooster escutcheon. An extremely decent chappie personally, and one who had always endeared himself to me by tipping me with considerable lavishness when I was at school; but there's no doubt he did at times do rather rummy things, notably keeping eleven pet rabbits in his bedroom; and I suppose a purist might have considered him more or less off his onion. In fact, to be perfectly frank, he wound up his career, happy to the last and completely surrounded by rabbits, in some sort of a home.

"It is very absurd, of course," continued Aunt Agatha. "If any of the family had inherited poor Henry's eccentricity—and it was nothing more—it would have been Claude and Eustace, and there could not be two brighter boys."

Claude and Eustace were twins, and had been kids at school with me in my last summer term. Casting my mind back, it seemed to me that "bright" just about described them. The whole of that term, as I remembered it, had been spent in getting them out of a series of frightful rows.

"Look how well they are doing at Oxford. Your Aunt Emily had a letter from Claude only the other day saying that they hoped to be elected shortly to a very important college club, called The Seekers."

"Seekers?" I couldn't recall any club of the name in my time at Oxford. "What do they seek?"

"Claude did not say. Truth or knowledge, I should imagine. It is evidently a very desirable club to belong to, for Claude added that Lord Rainsby, the Earl of Datchet's son, was one of his fellow-candidates. However, we are wandering from the point, which is that Sir Roderick wants to have a quiet talk with you quite alone. Now I rely on you, Bertie, to be—I won't say intelligent, but at least sensible. Don't giggle nervously: try to keep that horrible glassy expression out of your eyes: don't yawn or fidget; and remember that Sir Roderick is the president of the West London branch of the anti-gambling league, so please do not talk about horse-racing. He will lunch with you at your flat to-morrow at one-thirty. Please remember that he drinks no wine, strongly disapproves of smoking, and can only eat the simplest food, owing to an impaired digestion. Do not offer him coffee, for he considers it the root of half the nerve-trouble in the world."

"I should think a dog-biscuit and a glass of water would about meet the case, what?"

"Bertie!"

"Oh, all right. Merely persiflage."

"Now it is precisely that sort of idiotic remark that would be calculated to arouse Sir Roderick's worst suspicions. Do please try to refrain from any misguided flippancy when you are with him. He is a very serious-minded man.... Are you going? Well, please remember all I have said. I rely on you, and, if anything goes wrong, I shall never forgive you."

"Right-o!" I said.

And so home, with a jolly day to look forward to.

* * * * *

I breakfasted pretty late next morning and went for a stroll afterwards. It seemed to me that anything I could do to clear the old lemon ought to be done, and a bit of fresh air generally relieves that rather foggy feeling that comes over a fellow early in the day. I had taken a stroll in the park, and got back as far as Hyde Park Corner, when some blighter sloshed me between the shoulder-blades. It was young Eustace, my cousin. He was arm-in-arm with two other fellows, the one on the outside being my cousin Claude and the one in the middle a pink-faced chappie with light hair and an apologetic sort of look.

"Bertie, old egg!" said young Eustace affably.

"Hallo!" I said, not frightfully chirpily.

"Fancy running into you, the one man in London who can support us in the style we are accustomed to! By the way, you've never met old Dog-Face, have you? Dog-Face, this is my cousin Bertie. Lord Rainsby—Mr. Wooster. We've just been round to your flat, Bertie. Bitterly disappointed that you were out, but were hospitably entertained by old Jeeves. That man's a corker, Bertie. Stick to him."

"What are you doing in London?" I asked.

"Oh, buzzing round. We're just up for the day. Flying visit, strictly unofficial. We oil back on the three-ten. And now, touching that lunch you very decently volunteered to stand us, which shall it be? Ritz? Savoy? Carlton? Or, if you're a member of Ciro's or the Embassy, that would do just as well."

"I can't give you lunch. I've got an engagement myself. And, by Jove," I said, taking a look at my watch, "I'm late." I hailed a taxi. "Sorry."

"As man to man, then," said Eustace, "lend us a fiver."

I hadn't time to stop and argue. I unbelted the fiver and hopped into the cab. It was twenty to two when I got to the flat. I bounded into the sitting-room, but it was empty.

Jeeves shimmied in.

"Sir Roderick has not yet arrived, sir."

"Good egg!" I said. "I thought I should find him smashing up the furniture." My experience is that the less you want a fellow, the more punctual he's bound to be, and I had had a vision of the old lad pacing the rug in my sitting-room, saying "He cometh not!" and generally hotting up. "Is everything in order?"

"I fancy you will find the arrangements quite satisfactory, sir."

"What are you giving us?"

"Cold consommé, a cutlet, and a savoury, sir. With lemon-squash, iced."

"Well, I don't see how that can hurt him. Don't go getting carried away by the excitement of the thing and start bringing in coffee."

"No, sir."

"And don't let your eyes get glassy, because, if you do, you're apt to find yourself in a padded cell before you know where you are."

"Very good, sir."

There was a ring at the bell.

"Stand by, Jeeves," I said. "We're off!"

CHAPTER VIII
SIR RODERICK COMES TO LUNCH

I had met Sir Roderick Glossop before, of course, but only when I was with Honoria; and there is something about Honoria which makes almost anybody you meet in the same room seem sort of under-sized and trivial by comparison. I had never realised till this moment what an extraordinarily formidable old bird he was. He had a pair of shaggy eyebrows which gave his eyes a piercing look which was not at all the sort of thing a fellow wanted to encounter on an empty stomach. He was fairly tall and fairly broad, and he had the most enormous head, with practically no hair on it, which made it seem bigger and much more like the dome of St. Paul's. I suppose he must have taken about a nine or something in hats. Shows what a rotten thing it is to let your brain develop too much.

"What ho! What ho! What ho!" I said, trying to strike the genial note, and then had a sudden feeling that that was just the sort of thing I had been warned not to say. Dashed difficult it is to start things going properly on an occasion like this. A fellow living in a London flat is so handicapped. I mean to say, if I had been the young squire greeting the visitor in the country, I could have said, "Welcome to Meadowsweet Hall!" or something zippy like that. It sounds silly to say "Welcome to Number 6A, Crichton Mansions, Berkeley Street, W."

"I am afraid I am a little late," he said, as we sat down. "I was detained at my club by Lord Alastair Hungerford, the Duke of Ramfurline's son. His Grace, he informed me, had exhibited a renewal of the symptoms which have been causing the family so much concern. I could not leave him immediately. Hence my unpunctuality, which I trust has not discommoded you."

"Oh, not at all. So the Duke is off his rocker, what?"

"The expression which you use is not precisely the one I should have employed myself with reference to the head of perhaps the noblest family in England, but there is no doubt that cerebral excitement does, as you suggest, exist in no small degree." He sighed as well as he could with his mouth full of cutlet. "A profession like mine is a great strain, a great strain."

"Must be."

"Sometimes I am appalled at what I see around me." He stopped suddenly and sort of stiffened. "Do you keep a cat, Mr. Wooster?"

"Eh? What? Cat? No, no cat."

"I was conscious of a distinct impression that I had heard a cat mewing either in the room or very near to where we are sitting."

"Probably a taxi or something in the street."

"I fear I do not follow you."

"I mean to say, taxis squawk, you know. Rather like cats in a sort of way."

"I had not observed the resemblance," he said, rather coldly.

"Have some lemon-squash," I said. The conversation seemed to be getting rather difficult.

"Thank you. Half a glassful, if I may." The hell-brew appeared to buck him up, for he resumed in a slightly more pally manner. "I have a particular dislike for cats. But I was saying—— Oh, yes. Sometimes I am positively appalled at what I see around me. It is not only the cases which come under my professional notice, painful as many of those are. It is what I see as I go about London. Sometimes it seems to me that the whole world is mentally unbalanced. This very morning, for example, a most singular and distressing occurrence took place as I was driving from my house to the club. The day being clement, I had instructed my chauffeur to open my landaulette, and I was leaning back, deriving no little pleasure from the sunshine, when our progress was arrested in the middle of the thoroughfare by one of those blocks in the traffic which are inevitable in so congested a system as that of London."

I suppose I had been letting my mind wander a bit, for when he stopped and took a sip of lemon-squash I had a feeling that I was listening to a lecture and was expected to say something.

"Hear, hear!" I said.

"I beg your pardon?"

"Nothing, nothing. You were saying——"

"The vehicles proceeding in the opposite direction had also been temporarily arrested, but after a moment they were permitted to proceed. I had fallen into a meditation, when suddenly the most extraordinary thing took place. My hat was snatched abruptly from my head! And as I looked back I perceived it being waved in a kind of feverish triumph from the interior of a taxicab, which, even as I looked, disappeared through a gap in the traffic and was lost to sight."

I didn't laugh, but I distinctly heard a couple of my floating ribs part from their moorings under the strain.

"Must have been meant for a practical joke," I said. "What?"

This suggestion didn't seem to please the old boy.

"I trust," he said, "I am not deficient in an appreciation of the humorous, but I confess that I am at a loss to detect anything akin to pleasantry in the outrage. The action was beyond all question that of a mentally unbalanced subject. These mental lesions may express themselves in almost any form. The Duke of Ramfurline, to whom I had occasion to allude just now, is under the impression—this is in the strictest confidence—that he is a canary; and his seizure to-day, which so perturbed Lord Alastair, was due to the fact that a careless footman had neglected to bring him his morning lump of sugar. Cases are common, again, of men waylaying women and cutting off portions of their hair. It is from a branch of this latter form of mania that I should be disposed to imagine that my assailant was suffering. I can only trust that he will be placed under proper control before he—— Mr. Wooster, there is a cat close at hand! It is not in the street! The mewing appears to come from the adjoining room."

* * * * *

This time I had to admit there was no doubt about it. There was a distinct sound of mewing coming from the next room. I punched the bell for Jeeves, who drifted in and stood waiting with an air of respectful devotion.

"Sir?"

"Oh, Jeeves," I said. "Cats! What about it? Are there any cats in the flat?"

"Only the three in your bedroom, sir."

"What!"

"Cats in his bedroom!" I heard Sir Roderick whisper in a kind of stricken way, and his eyes hit me amidships like a couple of bullets.

"What do you mean," I said, "only the three in my bedroom?"

"The black one, the tabby and the small lemon-coloured animal, sir."

"What on earth?——"

I charged round the table in the direction of the door. Unfortunately, Sir Roderick had just decided to edge in that direction himself, with the result that we collided in the doorway with a good deal of force, and staggered out into the hall together. He came smartly out of the clinch and grabbed an umbrella from the rack.

"Stand back!" he shouted, waving it overhead. "Stand back, sir! I am armed!"

It seemed to me that the moment had come to be soothing.

"Awfully sorry I barged into you," I said. "Wouldn't have had it happen for worlds. I was just dashing out to have a look into things."

He appeared a trifle reassured, and lowered the umbrella. But just then the most frightful shindy started in the bedroom. It sounded as though all the cats in London, assisted by delegates from outlying suburbs, had got together to settle their differences once for all. A sort of augmented orchestra of cats.

"This noise is unendurable," yelled Sir Roderick. "I cannot hear myself speak."

"I fancy, sir," said Jeeves respectfully, "that the animals may have become somewhat exhilarated as the result of having discovered the fish under Mr. Wooster's bed."

The old boy tottered.

"Fish! Did I hear you rightly?"

"Sir?"

"Did you say that there was a fish under Mr. Wooster's bed?"

"Yes, sir."

Sir Roderick gave a low moan, and reached for his hat and stick.

"You aren't going?" I said.

"Mr. Wooster, I am going! I prefer to spend my leisure time in less eccentric society."

"But I say. Here, I must come with you. I'm sure the whole business can be explained. Jeeves, my hat."

Jeeves rallied round. I took the hat from him and shoved it on my head.

"Good heavens!"

Beastly shock it was! The bally thing had absolutely engulfed me, if you know what I mean. Even as I was putting it on I got a sort of impression that it was a trifle roomy; and no sooner had I let go of it than it settled down over my ears like a kind of extinguisher.

"I say! This isn't my hat!"

"It is my hat!" said Sir Roderick in about the coldest, nastiest voice I'd ever heard. "The hat which was stolen from me this morning as I drove in my car."

"But——"

I suppose Napoleon or somebody like that would have been equal to the situation, but I'm bound to say it was too much for me. I just stood there goggling in a sort of coma, while the old boy lifted the hat off me and turned to Jeeves.

"I should be glad, my man," he said, "if you would accompany me a few yards down the street. I wish to ask you some questions."

"Very good, sir."

"Here, but, I say——!" I began, but he left me standing. He stalked out, followed by Jeeves. And at that moment the row in the bedroom started again, louder than ever.

I was about fed up with the whole thing. I mean, cats in your bedroom—a bit thick, what? I didn't know how the dickens they had got in, but I was jolly well resolved that they weren't going to stay picknicking there any longer. I flung open the door. I got a momentary flash of about a hundred and fifteen cats of all sizes and colours scrapping in the middle of the room, and then they all shot past me with a rush and out of the front door; and all that was left of the mob-scene was the head of a whacking big fish, lying on the carpet and staring up at me in a rather austere sort of way, as if it wanted a written explanation and apology.

There was something about the thing's expression that absolutely chilled me, and I withdrew on tiptoe and shut the door. And, as I did so, I bumped into someone.

"Oh, sorry!" he said.

I spun round. It was the pink-faced chappie, Lord Something or other, the fellow I had met with Claude and Eustace.

"I say," he said apologetically, "awfully sorry to bother you, but those weren't my cats I met just now legging it downstairs, were they? They looked like my cats."

"They came out of my bedroom."

"Then they were my cats!" he said sadly. "Oh, dash it!"

"Did you put cats in my bedroom?"

"Your man, what's-his-name, did. He rather decently said I could keep them there till my train went. I'd just come to fetch them. And now they've gone! Oh, well, it can't be helped, I suppose. I'll take the hat and the fish, anyway."

I was beginning to dislike this chappie.

"Did you put that bally fish there, too?"

"No, that was Eustace's. The hat was Claude's."

I sank limply into a chair.

"I say, you couldn't explain this, could you?" I said. The chappie gazed at me in mild surprise.

"Why, don't you know all about it? I say!" He blushed profusely. "Why, if you don't know about it, I shouldn't wonder if the whole thing didn't seem rummy to you."

"Rummy is the word."

"It was for The Seekers, you know."

"The Seekers?"

"Rather a blood club, you know, up at Oxford, which your cousins and I are rather keen on getting into. You have to pinch something, you know, to get elected. Some sort of a souvenir, you know. A policeman's helmet, you know, or a door-knocker or something, you know. The room's decorated with the things at the annual dinner, and everybody makes speeches and all that sort of thing. Rather jolly! Well, we wanted rather to make a sort of special effort and do the thing in style, if you understand, so we came up to London to see if we couldn't pick up something here that would be a bit out of the ordinary. And we had the most amazing luck right from the start. Your cousin Claude managed to collect a quite decent top-hat out of a passing car, and your cousin Eustace got away with a really goodish salmon or something from Harrods, and I snaffled three excellent cats all in the first hour. We were fearfully braced, I can tell you. And then the difficulty was to know where to park the things till our train went. You look so beastly conspicuous, you know, tooling about London with a fish and a lot of cats. And then Eustace remembered you, and we all came on here in a cab. You were out, but your man said it would be all right. When we met you, you were in such a hurry that we hadn't time to explain. Well, I think I'll be taking the hat, if you don't mind."

"It's gone."

"Gone?"

"The fellow you pinched it from happened to be the man who was lunching here. He took it away with him."

"Oh, I say! Poor old Claude will be upset. Well, how about the goodish salmon or something?"

"Would you care to view the remains?" He seemed all broken up when he saw the wreckage.

"I doubt if the committee would accept that," he said sadly. "There isn't a frightful lot of it left, what?"

"The cats ate the rest."

He sighed deeply.

"No cats, no fish, no hat. We've had all our trouble for nothing. I do call that hard! And on top of that—I say, I hate to ask you, but you couldn't lend me a tenner, could you?"

"A tenner? What for?"

"Well, the fact is, I've got to pop round and bail Claude and Eustace out. They've been arrested."

"Arrested!"

"Yes. You see, what with the excitement of collaring the hat and the salmon or something, added to the fact that we had rather a festive lunch, they got a bit above themselves, poor chaps, and tried to pinch a motor-lorry. Silly, of course, because I don't see how they could have got the thing to Oxford and shown it to the committee. Still, there wasn't any reasoning with them, and when the driver started making a fuss, there was a bit of a mix-up, and Claude and Eustace are more or less languishing in Vine Street police-station till I pop round and bail them out. So if you could manage a tenner—Oh, thanks, that's fearfully good of you. It would have been too bad to leave them there, what? I mean, they're both such frightfully good chaps, you know. Everybody likes them up at the 'Varsity. They're fearfully popular."

"I bet they are!" I said.

* * * * *

When Jeeves came back, I was waiting for him on the mat. I wanted speech with the blighter.

"Well?" I said.

"Sir Roderick asked me a number of questions, sir, respecting your habits and mode of life, to which I replied guardedly."

"I don't care about that. What I want to know is why you didn't explain the whole thing to him right at the start? A word from you would have put everything clear."

"Yes, sir."

"Now he's gone off thinking me a looney."

"I should not be surprised, from his conversation with me, sir, if some such idea had not entered his head."

I was just starting in to speak, when the telephone bell rang. Jeeves answered it.

"No, madam, Mr. Wooster is not in. No, madam, I do not know when he will return, No, madam, he left no message. Yes, madam, I will inform him." He put back the receiver. "Mrs. Gregson, sir."

Aunt Agatha! I had been expecting it. Ever since the luncheon-party had blown out a fuse, her shadow had been hanging over me, so to speak.

"Does she know? Already?"

"I gather that Sir Roderick has been speaking to her on the telephone, sir, and——"

"No wedding bells for me, what?"

Jeeves coughed.

"Mrs. Gregson did not actually confide in me, sir, but I fancy that some such thing may have occurred. She seemed decidedly agitated, sir."

It's a rummy thing, but I'd been so snootered by the old boy and the cats and the fish and the hat and the pink-faced chappie and all the rest of it that the bright side simply hadn't occurred to me till now. By Jove, it was like a bally weight rolling off my chest! I gave a yelp of pure relief.

"Jeeves!" I said, "I believe you worked the whole thing!"

"Sir?"

"I believe you had the jolly old situation in hand right from the start."

"Well, sir, Spenser, Mrs. Gregson's butler, who inadvertently chanced to overhear something of your conversation when you were lunching at the house, did mention certain of the details to me; and I confess that, though it may be a liberty to say so, I entertained hopes that something might occur to prevent the match. I doubt if the young lady was entirely suitable to you, sir."

"And she would have shot you out on your ear five minutes after the ceremony."

"Yes, sir. Spenser informed me that she had expressed some such intention. Mrs. Gregson wishes you to call upon her immediately, sir."

"She does, eh? What do you advise, Jeeves?"

"I think a trip abroad might prove enjoyable, sir."

I shook my head. "She'd come after me."

"Not if you went far enough afield, sir. There are excellent boats leaving every Wednesday and Saturday for New York."

"Jeeves," I said, "you are right, as always. Book the tickets."

CHAPTER IX
A LETTER OF INTRODUCTION

You know, the longer I live, the more clearly I see that half the trouble in this bally world is caused by the light-hearted and thoughtless way in which chappies dash off letters of introduction and hand them to other chappies to deliver to chappies of the third part. It's one of those things that make you wish you were living in the Stone Age. What I mean to say is, if a fellow in those days wanted to give anyone a letter of introduction, he had to spend a month or so carving it on a large-sized boulder, and the chances were that the other chappie got so sick of lugging the thing round in the hot sun that he dropped it after the first mile. But nowadays it's so easy to write letters of introduction that everybody does it without a second thought, with the result that some perfectly harmless cove like myself gets in the soup.

Mark you, all the above is what you might call the result of my riper experience. I don't mind admitting that in the first flush of the thing, so, to speak, when Jeeves told me—this would be about three weeks after I'd landed in America—that a blighter called Cyril Bassington-Bassington had arrived and I found that he had brought a letter of introduction to me from Aunt Agatha ... where was I? Oh, yes ... I don't mind admitting, I was saying, that just at first I was rather bucked. You see, after the painful events which had resulted in my leaving England I hadn't expected to get any sort of letter from Aunt Agatha which would pass the censor, so to speak. And it was a pleasant surprise to open this one and find it almost civil. Chilly, perhaps, in parts, but on the whole quite tolerably polite. I looked on the thing as a hopeful sign. Sort of olive-branch, you know. Or do I mean orange blossom? What I'm getting at is that the fact that Aunt Agatha was writing to me without calling me names seemed, more or less, like a step in the direction of peace.

And I was all for peace, and that right speedily. I'm not saying a word against New York, mind you. I liked the place, and was having quite a ripe time there. But the fact remains that a fellow who's been used to London all his life does get a trifle homesick on a foreign strand, and I wanted to pop back to the cosy old flat in Berkeley Street—which could only be done when Aunt Agatha had simmered down and got over the Glossop episode. I know that London is a biggish city, but, believe me, it isn't half big enough for any fellow to live in with Aunt Agatha when she's after him with the old hatchet. And so I'm bound to say I looked on this chump Bassington-Bassington, when he arrived, more or less as a Dove of Peace, and was all for him.

He would seem from contemporary accounts to have blown in one morning at seven-forty-five, that being the ghastly sort of hour they shoot you off the liner in New York. He was given the respectful raspberry by Jeeves, and told to try again about three hours later, when there would be a sporting chance of my having sprung from my bed with a glad cry to welcome another day and all that sort of thing. Which was rather decent of Jeeves, by the way, for it so happened that there was a slight estrangement, a touch of coldness, a bit of a row in other words, between us at the moment because of some rather priceless purple socks which I was wearing against his wishes: and a lesser man might easily have snatched at the chance of getting back at me a bit by loosing Cyril into my bedchamber at a moment when I couldn't have stood a two-minutes' conversation with my dearest pal. For until I have had my early cup of tea and have brooded on life for a bit absolutely undisturbed, I'm not much of a lad for the merry chit-chat.

So Jeeves very sportingly shot Cyril out into the crisp morning air, and didn't let me know of his existence till he brought his card in with the Bohea.

"And what might all this be, Jeeves?" I said, giving the thing the glassy gaze.

"The gentleman has arrived from England, I understand, sir. He called to see you earlier in the day."

"Good Lord, Jeeves! You don't mean to say the day starts earlier than this?"

"He desired me to say he would return later, sir."

"I've never heard of him. Have you ever heard of him, Jeeves?"

"I am familiar with the name Bassington-Bassington, sir. There are three branches of the Bassington-Bassington family—the Shropshire Bassington-Bassingtons, the Hampshire Bassington-Bassingtons, and the Kent Bassington-Bassingtons."

"England seems pretty well stocked up with Bassington-Bassingtons."

"Tolerably so, sir."

"No chance of a sudden shortage, I mean, what?"

"Presumably not, sir."

"And what sort of a specimen is this one?"

"I could not say, sir, on such short acquaintance."

"Will you give me a sporting two to one, Jeeves, judging from what you have seen of him, that this chappie is not a blighter or an excrescence?"

"No, sir. I should not care to venture such liberal odds."

"I knew it. Well, the only thing that remains to be discovered is what kind of a blighter he is."

"Time will tell, sir. The gentleman brought a letter for you, sir."

"Oh, he did, did he?" I said, and grasped the communication. And then I recognised the handwriting. "I say, Jeeves, this is from my Aunt Agatha!"

"Indeed, sir?"

"Don't dismiss it in that light way. Don't you see what this means? She says she wants me to look after this excrescence while he's in New York. By Jove, Jeeves, if I only fawn on him a bit, so that he sends back a favourable report to head-quarters, I may yet be able to get back to England in time for Goodwood. Now is certainly the time for all good men to come to the aid of the party, Jeeves. We must rally round and cosset this cove in no uncertain manner."

"Yes, sir."

"He isn't going to stay in New York long," I said, taking another look at the letter. "He's headed for Washington. Going to give the nibs there the once-over, apparently, before taking a whirl at the Diplomatic Service. I should say that we can win this lad's esteem and affection with a lunch and a couple of dinners, what?"

"I fancy that should be entirely adequate, sir."

"This is the jolliest thing that's happened since we left England. It looks to me as if the sun were breaking through the clouds."

"Very possibly, sir."

He started to put out my things, and there was an awkward sort of silence.

"Not those socks, Jeeves," I said, gulping a bit but having a dash at the careless, off-hand tone. "Give me the purple ones."

"I beg your pardon, sir?"

"Those jolly purple ones."

"Very good, sir."

He lugged them out of the drawer as if he were a vegetarian fishing a caterpillar out of the salad. You could see he was feeling deeply. Deuced painful and all that, this sort of thing, but a chappie has got to assert himself every now and then. Absolutely.

* * * * *

I was looking for Cyril to show up again any time after breakfast, but he didn't appear: so towards one o'clock I trickled out to the Lambs Club, where I had an appointment to feed the Wooster face with a cove of the name of Caffyn I'd got pally with since my arrival—George Caffyn, a fellow who wrote plays and what not. I'd made a lot of friends during my stay in New York, the city being crammed with bonhomous lads who one and all extended a welcoming hand to the stranger in their midst.

Caffyn was a bit late, but bobbed up finally, saying that he had been kept at a rehearsal of his new musical comedy, "Ask Dad"; and we started in. We had just reached the coffee, when the waiter came up and said that Jeeves wanted to see me.

Jeeves was in the waiting-room. He gave the socks one pained look as I came in, then averted his eyes.

"Mr. Bassington-Bassington has just telephoned, sir."

"Oh?"

"Yes, sir."

"Where is he?"

"In prison, sir."

I reeled against the wallpaper. A nice thing to happen to Aunt Agatha's nominee on his first morning under my wing, I did not think!

"In prison!"

"Yes, sir. He said on the telephone that he had been arrested and would be glad if you could step round and bail him out."

"Arrested! What for?"

"He did not favour me with his confidence in that respect, sir."

"This is a bit thick, Jeeves."

"Precisely, sir."

I collected old George, who very decently volunteered to stagger along with me, and we hopped into a taxi. We sat around at the police-station for a bit on a wooden bench in a sort of ante-room, and presently a policeman appeared, leading in Cyril.

"Halloa! Halloa! Halloa!" I said. "What?"

My experience is that a fellow never really looks his best just after he's come out of a cell. When I was up at Oxford, I used to have a regular job bailing out a pal of mine who never failed to get pinched every Boat-Race night, and he always looked like something that had been dug up by the roots. Cyril was in pretty much the same sort of shape. He had a black eye and a torn collar, and altogether was nothing to write home about—especially if one was writing to Aunt Agatha. He was a thin, tall chappie with a lot of light hair and pale-blue goggly eyes which made him look like one of the rarer kinds of fish.

"I got your message," I said.

"Oh, are you Bertie Wooster?"

"Absolutely. And this is my pal George Caffyn. Writes plays and what not, don't you know."

We all shook hands, and the policeman, having retrieved a piece of chewing-gum from the underside of a chair, where he had parked it against a rainy day, went off into a corner and began to contemplate the infinite.

"This is a rotten country," said Cyril.

"Oh, I don't know, you know, don't you know!" I said.

"We do our best," said George.

"Old George is an American," I explained. "Writes plays, don't you know, and what not."

"Of course, I didn't invent the country," said George. "That was Columbus. But I shall be delighted to consider any improvements you may suggest and lay them before the proper authorities."

"Well, why don't the policemen in New York dress properly?"

George took a look at the chewing officer across the room.

"I don't see anything missing," he said.

"I mean to say, why don't they wear helmets like they do in London? Why do they look like postmen? It isn't fair on a fellow. Makes it dashed confusing. I was simply standing on the pavement, looking at things, when a fellow who looked like a postman prodded me in the ribs with a club. I didn't see why I should have postmen prodding me. Why the dickens should a fellow come three thousand miles to be prodded by postmen?"

"The point is well taken," said George. "What did you do?"

"I gave him a shove, you know. I've got a frightfully hasty temper, you know. All the Bassington-Bassingtons have got frightfully hasty tempers, don't you know! And then he biffed me in the eye and lugged me off to this beastly place."

"I'll fix it, old son," I said. And I hauled out the bank-roll and went off to open negotiations, leaving Cyril to talk to George. I don't mind admitting that I was a bit perturbed. There were furrows in the old brow, and I had a kind of foreboding feeling. As long as this chump stayed in New York, I was responsible for him: and he didn't give me the impression of being the species of cove a reasonable chappie would care to be responsible for for more than about three minutes.

I mused with a considerable amount of tensity over Cyril that night, when I had got home and Jeeves had brought me the final whisky. I couldn't help feeling that this visit of his to America was going to be one of those times that try men's souls and what not. I hauled out Aunt Agatha's letter of introduction and re-read it, and there was no getting away from the fact that she undoubtedly appeared to be somewhat wrapped up in this blighter and to consider it my mission in life to shield him from harm while on the premises. I was deuced thankful that he had taken such a liking for George Caffyn, old George being a steady sort of cove. After I had got him out of his dungeon-cell, he and old George had gone off together, as chummy as brothers, to watch the afternoon rehearsal of "Ask Dad." There was some talk, I gathered, of their dining together. I felt pretty easy in my mind while George had his eye on him.

I had got about as far as this in my meditations, when Jeeves came in with a telegram. At least, it wasn't a telegram: it was a cable—from Aunt Agatha, and this is what it said:—

Has Cyril Bassington-Bassington called yet? On no account introduce him into theatrical circles. Vitally important. Letter follows.

I read it a couple of times.

"This is rummy, Jeeves!"

"Yes, sir?"

"Very rummy and dashed disturbing!"

"Will there be anything further to-night, sir?"

Of course, if he was going to be as bally unsympathetic as that there was nothing to be done. My idea had been to show him the cable and ask his advice. But if he was letting those purple socks rankle to that extent, the good old noblesse oblige of the Woosters couldn't lower itself to the extent of pleading with the man. Absolutely not. So I gave it a miss.

"Nothing more, thanks."

"Good night, sir."

"Good night."

He floated away, and I sat down to think the thing over. I had been directing the best efforts of the old bean to the problem for a matter of half an hour, when there was a ring at the bell. I went to the door, and there was Cyril, looking pretty festive.

"I'll come in for a bit if I may," he said. "Got something rather priceless to tell you."

He curveted past me into the sitting-room, and when I got there after shutting the front door I found him reading Aunt Agatha's cable and giggling in a rummy sort of manner. "Oughtn't to have looked at this, I suppose. Caught sight of my name and read it without thinking. I say, Wooster, old friend of my youth, this is rather funny. Do you mind if I have a drink? Thanks awfully and all that sort of rot. Yes, it's rather funny, considering what I came to tell you. Jolly old Caffyn has given me a small part in that musical comedy of his, 'Ask Dad.' Only a bit, you know, but quite tolerably ripe. I'm feeling frightfully braced, don't you know!"

He drank his drink, and went on. He didn't seem to notice that I wasn't jumping about the room, yapping with joy.

"You know, I've always wanted to go on the stage, you know," he said. "But my jolly old guv'nor wouldn't stick it at any price. Put the old Waukeesi down with a bang, and turned bright purple whenever the subject was mentioned. That's the real reason why I came over here, if you want to know. I knew there wasn't a chance of my being able to work this stage wheeze in London without somebody getting on to it and tipping off the guv'nor, so I rather brainily sprang the scheme of popping over to Washington to broaden my mind. There's nobody to interfere on this side, you see, so I can go right ahead!"

I tried to reason with the poor chump.

"But your guv'nor will have to know some time."

"That'll be all right. I shall be the jolly old star by then, and he won't have a leg to stand on."

"It seems to me he'll have one leg to stand on while he kicks me with the other."

"Why, where do you come in? What have you got to do with it?"

"I introduced you to George Caffyn."

"So you did, old top, so you did. I'd quite forgotten. I ought to have thanked you before. Well, so long. There's an early rehearsal of 'Ask Dad' to-morrow morning, and I must be toddling. Rummy the thing should be called 'Ask Dad,' when that's just what I'm not going to do. See what I mean, what, what? Well, pip-pip!"

"Toodle-oo!" I said sadly, and the blighter scudded off. I dived for the phone and called up George Caffyn.

"I say, George, what's all this about Cyril Bassington-Bassington?"

"What about him?"

"He tells me you've given him a part in your show."

"Oh, yes. Just a few lines."

"But I've just had fifty-seven cables from home telling me on no account to let him go on the stage."

"I'm sorry. But Cyril is just the type I need for that part. He's simply got to be himself."

"It's pretty tough on me, George, old man. My Aunt Agatha sent this blighter over with a letter of introduction to me, and she will hold me responsible."

"She'll cut you out of her will?"

"It isn't a question of money. But—of course, you've never met my Aunt Agatha, so it's rather hard to explain. But she's a sort of human vampire-bat, and she'll make things most fearfully unpleasant for me when I go back to England. She's the kind of woman who comes and rags you before breakfast, don't you know."

"Well, don't go back to England, then. Stick here and become President."

"But, George, old top——!"

"Good night!"

"But, I say, George, old man!"

"You didn't get my last remark. It was 'Good night!' You Idle Rich may not need any sleep, but I've got to be bright and fresh in the morning. God bless you!"

I felt as if I hadn't a friend in the world. I was so jolly well worked up that I went and banged on Jeeves's door. It wasn't a thing I'd have cared to do as a rule, but it seemed to me that now was the time for all good men to come to the aid of the party, so to speak, and that it was up to Jeeves to rally round the young master, even if it broke up his beauty-sleep.

Jeeves emerged in a brown dressing-gown.

"Sir?"

"Deuced sorry to wake you up, Jeeves, and what not, but all sorts of dashed disturbing things have been happening."

"I was not asleep. It is my practice, on retiring, to read a few pages of some instructive book."

"That's good! What I mean to say is, if you've just finished exercising the old bean, it's probably in mid-season form for tackling problems. Jeeves, Mr. Bassington-Bassington is going on the stage!"

"Indeed, sir?"

"Ah! The thing doesn't hit you! You don't get it properly! Here's the point. All his family are most fearfully dead against his going on the stage. There's going to be no end of trouble if he isn't headed off. And, what's worse, my Aunt Agatha will blame me, you see."

"I see, sir."

"Well, can't you think of some way of stopping him?"

"Not, I confess, at the moment, sir."

"Well, have a stab at it."

"I will give the matter my best consideration, sir. Will there be anything further to-night?"

"I hope not! I've had all I can stand already."

"Very good, sir."

He popped off.

CHAPTER X
STARTLING DRESSINESS OF A LIFT-ATTENDANT

The part which old George had written for the chump Cyril took up about two pages of typescript; but it might have been Hamlet, the way that poor, misguided pinhead worked himself to the bone over it. I suppose, if I heard him his lines once, I did it a dozen times in the first couple of days. He seemed to think that my only feeling about the whole affair was one of enthusiastic admiration, and that he could rely on my support and sympathy. What with trying to imagine how Aunt Agatha was going to take this thing, and being woken up out of the dreamless in the small hours every other night to give my opinion of some new bit of business which Cyril had invented, I became more or less the good old shadow. And all the time Jeeves remained still pretty cold and distant about the purple socks. It's this sort of thing that ages a chappie, don't you know, and makes his youthful joie-de-vivre go a bit groggy at the knees.

In the middle of it Aunt Agatha's letter arrived. It took her about six pages to do justice to Cyril's father's feelings in regard to his going on the stage and about six more to give me a kind of sketch of what she would say, think, and do if I didn't keep him clear of injurious influences while he was in America. The letter came by the afternoon mail, and left me with a pretty firm conviction that it wasn't a thing I ought to keep to myself. I didn't even wait to ring the bell: I whizzed for the kitchen, bleating for Jeeves, and butted into the middle of a regular tea-party of sorts. Seated at the table were a depressed-looking cove who might have been a valet or something, and a boy in a Norfolk suit. The valet-chappie was drinking a whisky and soda, and the boy was being tolerably rough with some jam and cake.

"Oh, I say, Jeeves!" I said. "Sorry to interrupt the feast of reason and flow of soul and so forth, but——"

At this juncture the small boy's eye hit me like a bullet and stopped me in my tracks. It was one of those cold, clammy, accusing sort of eyes—the kind that makes you reach up to see if your tie is straight: and he looked at me as if I were some sort of unnecessary product which Cuthbert the Cat had brought in after a ramble among the local ash-cans. He was a stoutish infant with a lot of freckles and a good deal of jam on his face.

"Hallo! Hallo! Hallo!" I said. "What?" There didn't seem much else to say.

The stripling stared at me in a nasty sort of way through the jam. He may have loved me at first sight, but the impression he gave me was that he didn't think a lot of me and wasn't betting much that I would improve a great deal on acquaintance. I had a kind of feeling that I was about as popular with him as a cold Welsh rabbit.

"What's your name?" he asked.

"My name? Oh, Wooster, don't you know, and what not."

"My pop's richer than you are!"

That seemed to be all about me. The child having said his say, started in on the jam again. I turned to Jeeves.

"I say, Jeeves, can you spare a moment? I want to show you something."

"Very good, sir." We toddled into the sitting-room.

"Who is your little friend, Sidney the Sunbeam, Jeeves?"

"The young gentleman, sir?"

"It's a loose way of describing him, but I know what you mean."

"I trust I was not taking a liberty in entertaining him, sir?"

"Not a bit. If that's your idea of a large afternoon, go ahead."

"I happened to meet the young gentleman taking a walk with his father's valet, sir, whom I used to know somewhat intimately in London, and I ventured to invite them both to join me here."

"Well, never mind about him, Jeeves. Read this letter."

He gave it the up-and-down.

"Very disturbing, sir!" was all he could find to say.

"What are we going to do about it?"

"Time may provide a solution, sir."

"On the other hand, it mayn't, what?"

"Extremely true, sir."

We'd got as far as this, when there was a ring at the door. Jeeves shimmered off, and Cyril blew in, full of good cheer and blitheringness.

"I say, Wooster, old thing," he said, "I want your advice. You know this jolly old part of mine. How ought I to dress it? What I mean is, the first act scene is laid in an hotel of sorts, at about three in the afternoon. What ought I to wear, do you think?"

I wasn't feeling fit for a discussion of gent's suitings.

"You'd better consult Jeeves," I said.

"A hot and by no means unripe idea! Where is he?"

"Gone back to the kitchen, I suppose."

"I'll smite the good old bell, shall I? Yes. No?"

"Right-o!"

Jeeves poured silently in.

"Oh, I say, Jeeves," began Cyril, "I just wanted to have a syllable or two with you. It's this way—Hallo, who's this?"

I then perceived that the stout stripling had trickled into the room after Jeeves. He was standing near the door looking at Cyril as if his worst fears had been realised. There was a bit of a silence. The child remained there, drinking Cyril in for about half a minute; then he gave his verdict:

"Fish-face!"

"Eh? What?" said Cyril.

The child, who had evidently been taught at his mother's knee to speak the truth, made his meaning a trifle clearer.

"You've a face like a fish!"

He spoke as if Cyril was more to be pitied than censured, which I am bound to say I thought rather decent and broad-minded of him. I don't mind admitting that, whenever I looked at Cyril's face, I always had a feeling that he couldn't have got that way without its being mostly his own fault. I found myself warming to this child. Absolutely, don't you know. I liked his conversation.

It seemed to take Cyril a moment or two really to grasp the thing, and then you could hear the blood of the Bassington-Bassingtons begin to sizzle.

"Well, I'm dashed!" he said. "I'm dashed if I'm not!"

"I wouldn't have a face like that," proceeded the child, with a good deal of earnestness, "not if you gave me a million dollars." He thought for a moment, then corrected himself. "Two million dollars!" he added.

Just what occurred then I couldn't exactly say, but the next few minutes were a bit exciting. I take it that Cyril must have made a dive for the infant. Anyway, the air seemed pretty well congested with arms and legs and things. Something bumped into the Wooster waistcoat just around the third button, and I collapsed on to the settee and rather lost interest in things for the moment. When I had unscrambled myself, I found that Jeeves and the child had retired and Cyril was standing in the middle of the room snorting a bit.

"Who's that frightful little brute, Wooster?"

"I don't know. I never saw him before to-day."

"I gave him a couple of tolerably juicy buffets before he legged it. I say, Wooster, that kid said a dashed odd thing. He yelled out something about Jeeves promising him a dollar if he called me—er—what he said."

It sounded pretty unlikely to me.

"What would Jeeves do that for?"

"It struck me as rummy, too."

"Where would be the sense of it?"

"That's what I can't see."

"I mean to say, it's nothing to Jeeves what sort of a face you have!"

"No!" said Cyril. He spoke a little coldly, I fancied. I don't know why. "Well, I'll be popping. Toodle-oo!"

"Pip-pip!"

It must have been about a week after this rummy little episode that George Caffyn called me up and asked me if I would care to go and see a run-through of his show. "Ask Dad," it seemed, was to open out of town in Schenectady on the following Monday, and this was to be a sort of preliminary dress-rehearsal. A preliminary dress-rehearsal, old George explained, was the same as a regular dress-rehearsal inasmuch as it was apt to look like nothing on earth and last into the small hours, but more exciting because they wouldn't be timing the piece and consequently all the blighters who on these occasions let their angry passions rise would have plenty of scope for interruptions, with the result that a pleasant time would be had by all.

The thing was billed to start at eight o'clock, so I rolled up at ten-fifteen, so as not to have too long to wait before they began. The dress-parade was still going on. George was on the stage, talking to a cove in shirt-sleeves and an absolutely round chappie with big spectacles and a practically hairless dome. I had seen George with the latter merchant once or twice at the club, and I knew that he was Blumenfield, the manager. I waved to George, and slid into a seat at the back of the house, so as to be out of the way when the fighting started. Presently George hopped down off the stage and came and joined me, and fairly soon after that the curtain went down. The chappie at the piano whacked out a well-meant bar or two, and the curtain went up again.

I can't quite recall what the plot of "Ask Dad" was about, but I do know that it seemed able to jog along all right without much help from Cyril. I was rather puzzled at first. What I mean is, through brooding on Cyril and hearing him in his part and listening to his views on what ought and what ought not to be done, I suppose I had got a sort of impression rooted in the old bean that he was pretty well the backbone of the show, and that the rest of the company didn't do much except go on and fill in when he happened to be off the stage. I sat there for nearly half an hour, waiting for him to make his entrance, until I suddenly discovered he had been on from the start. He was, in fact, the rummy-looking plug-ugly who was now leaning against a potted palm a couple of feet from the O.P. side, trying to appear intelligent while the heroine sang a song about Love being like something which for the moment has slipped my memory. After the second refrain he began to dance in company with a dozen other equally weird birds. A painful spectacle for one who could see a vision of Aunt Agatha reaching for the hatchet and old Bassington-Bassington senior putting on his strongest pair of hob-nailed boots. Absolutely!

The dance had just finished, and Cyril and his pals had shuffled off into the wings when a voice spoke from the darkness on my right.

"Pop!"

Old Blumenfield clapped his hands, and the hero, who had just been about to get the next line off his diaphragm, cheesed it. I peered into the shadows. Who should it be but Jeeves's little playmate with the freckles! He was now strolling down the aisle with his hands in his pockets as if the place belonged to him. An air of respectful attention seemed to pervade the building.

"Pop," said the stripling, "that number's no good." Old Blumenfield beamed over his shoulder.

"Don't you like it, darling?"

"It gives me a pain."

"You're dead right."

"You want something zippy there. Something with a bit of jazz to it!"

"Quite right, my boy. I'll make a note of it. All right. Go on!"

I turned to George, who was muttering to himself in rather an overwrought way.

"I say, George, old man, who the dickens is that kid?"

Old George groaned a bit hollowly, as if things were a trifle thick.

"I didn't know he had crawled in! It's Blumenfield's son. Now we're going to have a Hades of a time!"

"Does he always run things like this?"

"Always!"

"But why does old Blumenfield listen to him?"

"Nobody seems to know. It may be pure fatherly love, or he may regard him as a mascot.

My own idea is that he thinks the kid has exactly the amount of intelligence of the average member of the audience, and that what makes a hit with him will please the general public. While, conversely, what he doesn't like will be too rotten for anyone. The kid is a pest, a wart, and a pot of poison, and should be strangled!"

The rehearsal went on. The hero got off his line. There was a slight outburst of frightfulness between the stage-manager and a Voice named Bill that came from somewhere near the roof, the subject under discussion being where the devil Bill's "ambers" were at that particular juncture. Then things went on again until the moment arrived for Cyril's big scene.

I was still a trifle hazy about the plot, but I had got on to the fact that Cyril was some sort of an English peer who had come over to America doubtless for the best reasons. So far he had only had two lines to say. One was "Oh, I say!" and the other was "Yes, by Jove!"; but I seemed to recollect, from hearing him read his part, that pretty soon he was due rather to spread himself. I sat back in my chair and waited for him to bob up.

He bobbed up about five minutes later. Things had got a bit stormy by that time. The Voice and the stage-director had had another of their love-feasts—this time something to do with why Bill's "blues" weren't on the job or something. And, almost as soon as that was over, there was a bit of unpleasantness because a flower-pot fell off a window-ledge and nearly brained the hero. The atmosphere was consequently more or less hotted up when Cyril, who had been hanging about at the back of the stage, breezed down centre and toed the mark for his most substantial chunk of entertainment. The heroine had been saying something—I forget what—and all the chorus, with Cyril at their head, had begun to surge round her in the restless sort of way those chappies always do when there's a number coming along.

Cyril's first line was, "Oh, I say, you know, you mustn't say that, really!" and it seemed to me he passed it over the larynx with a goodish deal of vim and je-ne-sais-quoi. But, by Jove, before the heroine had time for the come-back, our little friend with the freckles had risen to lodge a protest.

"Pop!"

"Yes, darling?"

"That one's no good!"

"Which one, darling?"

"The one with a face like a fish."

"But they all have faces like fish, darling."

The child seemed to see the justice of this objection. He became more definite.

"The ugly one."

"Which ugly one? That one?" said old Blumenfield, pointing to Cyril.

"Yep! He's rotten!"

"I thought so myself."

"He's a pill!"

"You're dead right, my boy. I've noticed it for some time."

Cyril had been gaping a bit while these few remarks were in progress. He now shot down to the footlights. Even from where I was sitting, I could see that these harsh words had hit the old Bassington-Bassington family pride a frightful wallop. He started to get pink in the ears, and then in the nose, and then in the cheeks, till in about a quarter of a minute he looked pretty much like an explosion in a tomato cannery on a sunset evening.

"What the deuce do you mean?"

"What the deuce do you mean?" shouted old Blumenfield. "Don't yell at me across the footlights!"

"I've a dashed good mind to come down and spank that little brute!"

"What!"

"A dashed good mind!"

Old Blumenfield swelled like a pumped-up tyre. He got rounder than ever.

"See here, mister—I don't know your darn name——!"

"My name's Bassington-Bassington, and the jolly old Bassington-Bassingtons—I mean the Bassington-Bassingtons aren't accustomed——"

Old Blumenfield told him in a few brief words pretty much what he thought of the Bassington-Bassingtons and what they weren't accustomed to. The whole strength of the company rallied round to enjoy his remarks. You could see them jutting out from the wings and protruding from behind trees.

"You got to work good for my pop!" said the stout child, waggling his head reprovingly at Cyril.

"I don't want any bally cheek from you!" said Cyril, gurgling a bit.

"What's that?" barked old Blumenfield. "Do you understand that this boy is my son?"

"Yes, I do," said Cyril. "And you both have my sympathy!"

"You're fired!" bellowed old Blumenfield, swelling a good bit more. "Get out of my theatre!"

* * * * *

About half-past ten next morning, just after I had finished lubricating the good old interior with a soothing cup of Oolong, Jeeves filtered into my bedroom, and said that Cyril was waiting to see me in the sitting-room.

"How does he look, Jeeves?"

"Sir?"

"What does Mr. Bassington-Bassington look like?"

"It is hardly my place, sir, to criticise the facial peculiarities of your friends."

"I don't mean that. I mean, does he appear peeved and what not?"

"Not noticeably, sir. His manner is tranquil."

"That's rum!"

"Sir?"

"Nothing. Show him in, will you?"

I'm bound to say I had expected to see Cyril showing a few more traces of last night's battle. I was looking for a bit of the overwrought soul and the quivering ganglions, if you know what I mean. He seemed pretty ordinary and quite fairly cheerful.

"Hallo, Wooster, old thing!"

"Cheero!"

"I just looked in to say good-bye."

"Good-bye?"

"Yes. I'm off to Washington in an hour." He sat down on the bed. "You know, Wooster, old top," he went on, "I've been thinking it all over, and really it doesn't seem quite fair to the jolly old guv'nor, my going on the stage and so forth. What do you think?"

"I see what you mean."

"I mean to say, he sent me over here to broaden my jolly old mind and words to that effect, don't you know, and I can't help thinking it would be a bit of a jar for the old boy if I gave him the bird and went on the stage instead. I don't know if you understand me, but what I mean to say is, it's a sort of question of conscience."

"Can you leave the show without upsetting everything?"

"Oh, that's all right. I've explained everything to old Blumenfield, and he quite sees my position. Of course, he's sorry to lose me—said he didn't see how he could fill my place and all that sort of thing—but, after all, even if it does land him in a bit of a hole, I think I'm right in resigning my part, don't you?"

"Oh, absolutely."

"I thought you'd agree with me. Well, I ought to be shifting. Awfully glad to have seen something of you, and all that sort of rot. Pip-pip!"

"Toodle-oo!"

He sallied forth, having told all those bally lies with the clear, blue, pop-eyed gaze of a young child. I rang for Jeeves. You know, ever since last night I had been exercising the old bean to some extent, and a good deal of light had dawned upon me.

"Jeeves!"

"Sir?"

"Did you put that pie-faced infant up to bally-ragging Mr. Bassington-Bassington?"

"Sir?"

"Oh, you know what I mean. Did you tell him to get Mr. Bassington-Bassington sacked from the 'Ask Dad' company?"

"I would not take such a liberty, sir." He started to put out my clothes. "It is possible that young Master Blumenfield may have gathered from casual remarks of mine that I did not consider the stage altogether a suitable sphere for Mr. Bassington-Bassington."

"I say, Jeeves, you know, you're a bit of a marvel."

"I endeavour to give satisfaction, sir."

"And I'm frightfully obliged, if you know what I mean. Aunt Agatha would have had sixteen or seventeen fits if you hadn't headed him off."

"I fancy there might have been some little friction and unpleasantness, sir. I am laying out the blue suit with the thin red stripe, sir. I fancy the effect will be pleasing."

*   *   *   *   *

It's a rummy thing, but I had finished breakfast and gone out and got as far as the lift before

I remembered what it was that I had meant to do to reward Jeeves for his really sporting behaviour in this matter of the chump Cyril. It cut me to the heart to do it, but I had decided to give him his way and let those purple socks pass out of my life. After all, there are times when a cove must make sacrifices. I was just going to nip back and break the glad news to him, when the lift came up, so I thought I would leave it till I got home.

The coloured chappie in charge of the lift looked at me, as I hopped in, with a good deal of quiet devotion and what not.

"I wish to thank yo', suh," he said, "for yo' kindness."

"Eh? What?"

"Misto' Jeeves done give me them purple socks, as you told him. Thank yo' very much, suh!"

I looked down. The blighter was a blaze of mauve from the ankle-bone southward. I don't know when I've seen anything so dressy.

"Oh, ah! Not at all! Right-o! Glad you like them!" I said.

Well, I mean to say, what? Absolutely!

CHAPTER XI
COMRADE BINGO

The thing really started in the Park—at the Marble Arch end—where weird birds of every description collect on Sunday afternoons and stand on soap-boxes and make speeches. It isn't often you'll find me there, but it so happened that on the Sabbath after my return to the good old Metrop. I had a call to pay in Manchester Square, and, taking a stroll round in that direction so as not to arrive too early, I found myself right in the middle of it.

Now that the Empire isn't the place it was, I always think the Park on a Sunday is the centre of London, if you know what I mean. I mean to say, that's the spot that makes the returned exile really sure he's back again. After what you might call my enforced sojourn in New York I'm bound to say that I stood there fairly lapping it all up. It did me good to listen to the lads giving tongue and realise that all had ended happily and Bertram was home again.

On the edge of the mob farthest away from me a gang of top-hatted chappies were starting an open-air missionary service; nearer at hand an atheist was letting himself go with a good deal of vim, though handicapped a bit by having no roof to his mouth; while in front of me there stood a little group of serious thinkers with a banner labelled "Heralds of the Red Dawn"; and as I came up, one of the heralds, a bearded egg in a slouch hat and a tweed suit, was slipping it into the Idle Rich with such breadth and vigour that I paused for a moment to get an earful. While I was standing there somebody spoke to me.

"Mr. Wooster, surely?"

Stout chappie. Couldn't place him for a second. Then I got him. Bingo Little's uncle, the one I had lunch with at the time when young Bingo was in love with that waitress at the Piccadilly bun-shop. No wonder I hadn't recognised him at first. When I had seen him last he had been a rather sloppy old gentleman—coming down to lunch, I remember, in carpet slippers and a velvet smoking-jacket; whereas now dapper simply wasn't the word. He absolutely gleamed in the sunlight in a silk hat, morning coat, lavender spats and sponge-bag trousers, as now worn. Dressy to a degree.

"Oh, hallo!" I said. "Going strong?"

"I am in excellent health, I thank you. And you?"

"In the pink. Just been over to America."

"Ah! Collecting local colour for one of your delightful romances?"

"Eh?" I had to think a bit before I got on to what he meant. Then I remembered the Rosie M. Banks business. "Oh, no," I said. "Just felt I needed a change. Seen anything of Bingo lately?" I asked quickly, being desirous of heading the old thing off what you might call the literary side of my life.

"Bingo?"

"Your nephew."

"Oh, Richard? No, not very recently. Since my marriage a little coolness seems to have sprung up."

"Sorry to hear that. So you've married since I saw you, what? Mrs. Little all right?"

"My wife is happily robust. But—er—not Mrs. Little. Since we last met a gracious

Sovereign has been pleased to bestow on me a signal mark of his favour in the shape of—ah—a peerage. On the publication of the last Honours List I became Lord Bittlesham."

"By Jove! Really? I say, heartiest congratulations. That's the stuff to give the troops, what? Lord Bittlesham?" I said. "Why, you're the owner of Ocean Breeze."

"Yes. Marriage has enlarged my horizon in many directions. My wife is interested in horse-racing, and I now maintain a small stable. I understand that Ocean Breeze is fancied, as I am told the expression is, for a race which will take place at the end of the month at Goodwood, the Duke of Richmond's seat in Sussex."

"The Goodwood Cup. Rather! I've got my chemise on it for one."

"Indeed? Well, I trust the animal will justify your confidence. I know little of these matters myself, but my wife tells me that it is regarded in knowledgeable circles as what I believe is termed a snip."

At this moment I suddenly noticed that the audience was gazing in our direction with a good deal of interest, and I saw that the bearded chappie was pointing at us.

"Yes, look at them! Drink them in!" he was yelling, his voice rising above the perpetual-motion fellow's and beating the missionary service all to nothing. "There you see two typical members of the class which has down-trodden the poor for centuries. Idlers! Non-producers! Look at the tall thin one with the face like a motor-mascot. Has he ever done an honest day's work in his life? No! A prowler, a trifler, and a blood-sucker! And I bet he still owes his tailor for those trousers!"

He seemed to me to be verging on the personal, and I didn't think a lot of it. Old Bittlesham, on the other hand, was pleased and amused.

"A great gift of expression these fellows have," he chuckled. "Very trenchant."

"And the fat one!" proceeded the chappie. "Don't miss him. Do you know who that is? That's Lord Bittlesham! One of the worst. What has he ever done except eat four square meals a day? His god is his belly, and he sacrifices burnt-offerings to it. If you opened that man now you would find enough lunch to support ten working-class families for a week."

"You know, that's rather well put," I said, but the old boy didn't seem to see it. He had turned a brightish magenta and was bubbling like a kettle on the boil.

"Come away, Mr. Wooster," he said. "I am the last man to oppose the right of free speech, but I refuse to listen to this vulgar abuse any longer."

We legged it with quiet dignity, the chappie pursuing us with his foul innuendoes to the last. Dashed embarrassing.

*   *   *   *   *

Next day I looked in at the club, and found young Bingo in the smoking-room.

"Hallo, Bingo," I said, toddling over to his corner full of bonhomie, for I was glad to see the chump, "How's the boy?"

"Jogging along."

"I saw your uncle yesterday."

Young Bingo unleashed a grin that split his face in half.

"I know you did, you trifler. Well, sit down, old thing, and suck a bit of blood. How's the prowling these days?"

"Good Lord! You weren't there!"

"Yes, I was."

"I didn't see you."

"Yes, you did. But perhaps you didn't recognise me in the shrubbery."

"The shrubbery?"

"The beard, my boy. Worth every penny I paid for it. Defies detection. Of course, it's a nuisance having people shouting 'Beaver!' at you all the time, but one's got to put up with that."

I goggled at him.

"I don't understand."

"It's a long story. Have a martini or a small gore-and-soda, and I'll tell you all about it. Before we start, give me your honest opinion. Isn't she the most wonderful girl you ever saw in your puff?"

He had produced a photograph from somewhere, like a conjurer taking a rabbit out of a hat, and was waving it in front of me. It appeared to be a female of sorts, all eyes and teeth.

"Oh, Great Scott!" I said. "Don't tell me you're in love again."

He seemed aggrieved.

"What do you mean—again?"

"Well, to my certain knowledge you've been in love with at least half a dozen girls since the spring, and it's only July now. There was that waitress and Honoria Glossop and——"

"Oh, tush! Not to say pish! Those girls? Mere passing fancies. This is the real thing."

"Where did you meet her?"

"On top of a bus. Her name is Charlotte Corday Rowbotham."

"My God!"

"It's not her fault, poor child. Her father had her christened that because he's all for the Revolution, and it seems that the original Charlotte Corday used to go about stabbing oppressors in their baths, which entitles her to consideration and respect. You must meet old Rowbotham, Bertie. A delightful chap. Wants to massacre the bourgeoisie, sack Park Lane, and disembowel the hereditary aristocracy. Well, nothing could be fairer than that, what? But about Charlotte. We were on top of the bus, and it started to rain. I offered her my umbrella, and we chatted of this and that. I fell in love and got her address, and a couple of days later I bought the beard and toddled round and met the family."

"But why the beard?"

"Well, she had told me all about her father on the bus, and I saw that to get any footing at all in the home I should have to join these Red Dawn blighters; and naturally, if I was to make speeches in the Park, where at any moment I might run into a dozen people I knew, something in the nature of a disguise was indicated. So I bought the beard, and, by Jove, old boy, I've become dashed attached to the thing. When I take it off to come in here, for instance, I feel absolutely nude. It's done me a lot of good with old Rowbotham. He thinks I'm a Bolshevist of sorts who has to go about disguised because of the police. You really must meet old Rowbotham, Bertie. I tell you what, are you doing anything to-morrow afternoon?"

"Nothing special. Why?"

"Good! Then you can have us all to tea at your flat. I had promised to take the crowd to Lyons' Popular Café after a meeting we're holding down in Lambeth, but I can save money this way; and, believe me, laddie, nowadays, as far as I'm concerned, a penny saved is a penny earned. My uncle told you he'd got married?"

"Yes. And he said there was a coolness between you."

"Coolness? I'm down to zero. Ever since he married he's been launching out in every direction and economising on me. I suppose that peerage cost the old devil the deuce of a sum. Even baronetcies have gone up frightfully nowadays, I'm told. And he's started a racing-stable. By the way, put your last collar-stud on Ocean Breeze for the Goodwood Cup. It's a cert."

"I'm going to."

"It can't lose. I mean to win enough on it to marry Charlotte with. You're going to Goodwood, of course?"

"Rather!"

"So are we. We're holding a meeting on Cup day just outside the paddock."

"But, I say, aren't you taking frightful risks? Your uncle's sure to be at Goodwood. Suppose he spots you? He'll be fed to the gills if he finds out that you're the fellow who ragged him in the Park."

"How the deuce is he to find out? Use your intelligence, you prowling inhaler of red corpuscles. If he didn't spot me yesterday, why should he spot me at Goodwood? Well, thanks for your cordial invitation for to-morrow, old thing. We shall be delighted to accept. Do us well, laddie, and blessings shall reward you. By the way, I may have misled you by using the word 'tea.' None of your wafer slices of bread-and-butter. We're good trenchermen, we of the Revolution. What we shall require will be something on the order of scrambled eggs, muffins, jam, ham, cake and sardines. Expect us at five sharp."

"But, I say, I'm not quite sure——"

"Yes, you are. Silly ass, don't you see that this is going to do you a bit of good when the Revolution breaks loose? When you see old Rowbotham sprinting up Piccadilly with a dripping knife in each hand, you'll be jolly thankful to be able to remind him that he once ate your tea and shrimps. There will be four of us—Charlotte, self, the old man, and Comrade Butt. I suppose he will insist on coming along."

"Who the devil's Comrade Butt?"

"Did you notice a fellow standing on my left in our little troupe yesterday? Small, shrivelled chap. Looks like a haddock with lung-trouble. That's Butt. My rival, dash him. He's sort of semi-engaged to Charlotte at the moment. Till I came along he was the blue-eyed boy. He's got a voice like a fog-horn, and old Rowbotham thinks a lot of him. But, hang it, if I can't thoroughly encompass this Butt and cut him out and put him where he belongs among the discards—well, I'm not the man I was, that's all. He may have a big voice, but he hasn't my gift of expression. Thank heaven I was once cox of my college boat. Well, I must be pushing now. I say, you don't know how I could raise fifty quid somehow, do you?"

"Why don't you work?"

"Work?" said young Bingo, surprised. "What, me? No, I shall have to think of some way. I must put at least fifty on Ocean Breeze. Well, see you to-morrow. God bless you, old sort, and don't forget the muffins."

* * * * *

I don't know why, ever since I first knew him at school, I should have felt a rummy feeling of responsibility for young Bingo. I mean to say, he's not my son (thank goodness) or my brother or anything like that. He's got absolutely no claim on me at all, and yet a large-sized chunk of my existence seems to be spent in fussing over him like a bally old hen and hauling him out of the soup. I suppose it must be some rare beauty in my nature or something. At any rate, this latest affair of his worried me. He seemed to be doing his best to marry into a family of pronounced loonies, and how the deuce he thought he was going to support even a mentally afflicted wife on nothing a year beat me. Old Bittlesham was bound to knock off his allowance if he did anything of the sort; and, with a fellow like young Bingo, if you knocked off his allowance, you might just as well hit him on the head with an axe and make a clean job of it.

"Jeeves," I said, when I got home, "I'm worried."

"Sir?"

"About Mr. Little. I won't tell you about it now, because he's bringing some friends of his to tea to-morrow, and then you will be able to judge for yourself. I want you to observe closely, Jeeves, and form your decision."

"Very good, sir."

"And about the tea. Get in some muffins."

"Yes, sir."

"And some jam, ham, cake, scrambled eggs, and five or six wagonloads of sardines."

"Sardines, sir?" said Jeeves, with a shudder.

"Sardines."

There was an awkward pause.

"Don't blame me, Jeeves," I said. "It isn't my fault."

"No, sir."

"Well, that's that."

"Yes, sir."

I could see the man was brooding tensely.

* * * * *

I've found, as a general rule in life, that the things you think are going to be the scaliest nearly always turn out not so bad after all; but it wasn't that way with Bingo's tea-party. From the moment he invited himself I felt that the thing was going to be blue round the edges, and it was. And I think the most gruesome part of the whole affair was the fact that, for the first time since I'd known him, I saw Jeeves come very near to being rattled. I suppose there's a chink in everyone's armour, and young Bingo found Jeeves's right at the drop of the flag when he breezed in with six inches or so of brown beard hanging on to his chin. I had forgotten to warn Jeeves about the beard, and it came on him absolutely out of a blue sky. I saw the man's jaw drop, and he clutched at the table for support. I don't blame him, mind you. Few people have ever looked fouler than young Bingo in the fungus. Jeeves paled a little; then the weakness passed and he was himself again. But I could see that he had been shaken.

Young Bingo was too busy introducing the mob to take much notice. They were a very C3 collection. Comrade Butt looked like one of the things that come out of dead trees after the rain; moth-eaten was the word I should have used to describe old Rowbotham; and as for Charlotte, she seemed to take me straight into another and a dreadful world. It wasn't that she was exactly bad-looking. In fact, if she had knocked off starchy foods and done Swedish exercises for a bit, she might have been quite tolerable. But there was too much of her. Billowy curves. Well-nourished, perhaps, expresses it best. And, while she may have had a heart of gold, the thing you noticed about her first was that she had a tooth of gold. I knew that young Bingo, when in form, could fall in love with practically anything of the other sex; but this time I couldn't see any excuse for him at all.

"My friend, Mr. Wooster," said Bingo, completing the ceremonial.

Old Rowbotham looked at me and then he looked round the room, and I could see he wasn't particularly braced. There's nothing of absolutely Oriental luxury about the old flat, but I have managed to make myself fairly comfortable, and I suppose the surroundings jarred him a bit.

"Mr. Wooster?" said old Rowbotham. "May I say Comrade Wooster?"

"I beg your pardon?"

"Are you of the movement?"

"Well—er——"

"Do you yearn for the Revolution?"

"Well, I don't know that I exactly yearn. I mean to say, as far as I can make out, the whole hub of the scheme seems to be to massacre coves like me; and I don't mind owning I'm not frightfully keen on the idea."

"But I'm talking him round," said Bingo. "I'm wrestling with him. A few more treatments ought to do the trick."

Old Rowbotham looked at me a bit doubtfully.

"Comrade Little has great eloquence," he admitted.

"I think he talks something wonderful," said the girl, and young Bingo shot a glance of such succulent devotion at her that I reeled in my tracks. It seemed to depress Comrade Butt a good deal too. He scowled at the carpet and said something about dancing on volcanoes.

"Tea is served, sir," said Jeeves.

"Tea, pa!" said Charlotte, starting at the word like the old war-horse who hears the bugle; and we got down to it.

Funny how one changes as the years roll on. At school, I remember, I would cheerfully have sold my soul for scrambled eggs and sardines at five in the afternoon; but somehow, since reaching man's estate, I had rather dropped out of the habit; and I'm bound to admit I was appalled to a goodish extent at the way the sons and daughter of the Revolution shoved their heads down and went for the foodstuffs. Even Comrade Butt cast off his gloom for a space and immersed his whole being in scrambled eggs, only coming to the surface at intervals to grab another cup of tea. Presently the hot water gave out, and I turned to Jeeves.

"More hot water."

"Very good, sir."

"Hey! what's this? What's this?" Old Rowbotham had lowered his cup and was eyeing us sternly. He tapped Jeeves on the shoulder. "No servility, my lad; no servility!"

"I beg your pardon, sir?"

"Don't call me 'sir.' Call me Comrade. Do you know what you are, my lad? You're an obsolete relic of an exploded feudal system."

"Very good, sir."

"If there's one thing that makes the blood boil in my veins——"

"Have another sardine," chipped in young Bingo—the first sensible thing he'd done since I had known him. Old Rowbotham took three and dropped the subject, and Jeeves drifted away. I could see by the look of his back what he felt.

At last, just as I was beginning to feel that it was going on for ever, the thing finished. I woke up to find the party getting ready to leave.

Sardines and about three quarts of tea had mellowed old Rowbotham. There was quite a genial look in his eye as he shook my hand.

"I must thank you for your hospitality, Comrade Wooster," he said.

"Oh, not at all! Only too glad——"

"Hospitality?" snorted the man Butt, going off in my ear like a depth-charge. He was scowling in a morose sort of manner at young Bingo and the girl, who were giggling together by the window. "I wonder the food didn't turn to ashes in our mouths! Eggs! Muffins! Sardines! All wrung from the bleeding lips of the starving poor!"

"Oh, I say! What a beastly idea!"

"I will send you some literature on the subject of the Cause," said old Rowbotham. "And soon, I hope, we shall see you at one of our little meetings."

Jeeves came in to clear away, and found me sitting among the ruins. It was all very well for Comrade Butt to knock the food, but he had pretty well finished the ham; and if you had shoved the remainder of the jam into the bleeding lips of the starving poor it would hardly have made them sticky.

"Well, Jeeves," I said, "how about it?"

"I would prefer to express no opinion, sir."

"Jeeves, Mr. Little is in love with that female."

"So I gathered, sir. She was slapping him in the passage."

I clutched my brow.

"Slapping him?"

"Yes, sir. Roguishly."

"Great Scott! I didn't know it had got as far as that. How did Comrade Butt seem to be taking it? Or perhaps he didn't see?"

"Yes, sir, he observed the entire proceedings. He struck me as extremely jealous."

"I don't blame him. Jeeves, what are we to do?"

"I could not say, sir."

"It's a bit thick."

"Very much so, sir."

And that was all the consolation I got from Jeeves.

CHAPTER XII
BINGO HAS A BAD GOODWOOD

I had promised to meet young Bingo next day, to tell him what I thought of his infernal Charlotte, and I was mooching slowly up St. James's Street, trying to think how the dickens I could explain to him, without hurting his feelings, that I considered her one of the world's foulest, when who should come toddling out of the Devonshire Club but old Bittlesham and Bingo himself. I hurried on and overtook them.

"What-ho!" I said.

The result of this simple greeting was a bit of a shock. Old Bittlesham quivered from head to foot like a poleaxed blanc-mange. His eyes were popping and his face had gone sort of greenish.

"Mr. Wooster!" He seemed to recover somewhat, as if I wasn't the worst thing that could have happened to him. "You gave me a severe start."

"Oh, sorry!"

"My uncle," said young Bingo in a hushed, bedside sort of voice, "isn't feeling quite himself this morning. He's had a threatening letter."

"I go in fear of my life," said old Bittlesham.

"Threatening letter?"

"Written," said old Bittlesham, "in an uneducated hand and couched in terms of uncompromising menace. Mr. Wooster, do you recall a sinister, bearded man who assailed me in no measured terms in Hyde Park last Sunday?"

I jumped, and shot a look at young Bingo. The only expression on his face was one of grave, kindly concern.

"Why—ah—yes," I said. "Bearded man. Chap with a beard."

"Could you identify him, if necessary?"

"Well, I—er—how do you mean?"

"The fact is, Bertie," said Bingo, "we think this man with the beard is at the bottom of all this business. I happened to be walking late last night through Pounceby Gardens, where Uncle Mortimer lives, and as I was passing the house a fellow came hurrying down the steps in a furtive sort of way. Probably he had just been shoving the letter in at the front door. I noticed that he had a beard. I didn't think any more of it, however, until this morning, when Uncle Mortimer showed me the letter he had received and told me about the chap in the Park. I'm going to make inquiries."

"The police should be informed," said Lord Bittlesham.

"No," said young Bingo firmly, "not at this stage of the proceedings. It would hamper me. Don't you worry, uncle; I think I can track this fellow down. You leave it all to me. I'll pop you into a taxi now, and go and talk it over with Bertie."

"You're a good boy, Richard," said old Bittlesham, and we put him in a passing cab and pushed off. I turned and looked young Bingo squarely in the eyeball.

"Did you send that letter?" I said.

"Rather! You ought to have seen it, Bertie! One of the best gent's ordinary threatening letters I ever wrote."

"But where's the sense of it?"

"Bertie, my lad," said Bingo, taking me earnestly by the coat-sleeve, "I had an excellent reason. Posterity may say of me what it will, but one thing it can never say—that I have not a good solid business head. Look here!" He waved a bit of paper in front of my eyes.

"Great Scott!" It was a cheque—an absolute, dashed cheque for fifty of the best, signed Bittlesham, and made out to the order of R. Little.

"What's that for?"

"Expenses," said Bingo, pouching it. "You don't suppose an investigation like this can be carried on for nothing, do you? I now proceed to the bank and startle them into a fit with it. Later I edge round to my bookie and put the entire sum on Ocean Breeze. What you want in situations of this kind, Bertie, is tact. If I had gone to my uncle and asked him for fifty quid, would I have got it? No! But by exercising tact—— Oh! by the way, what do you think of Charlotte?"

"Well—er——"

Young Bingo massaged my sleeve affectionately.

"I know, old man, I know. Don't try to find words. She bowled you over, eh? Left you speechless, what? I know! That's the effect she has on everybody. Well, I leave you here, laddie. Oh, before we part—Butt! What of Butt? Nature's worst blunder, don't you think?"

"I must say I've seen cheerier souls."

"I think I've got him licked, Bertie. Charlotte is coming to the Zoo with me this afternoon. Alone. And later on to the pictures. That looks like the beginning of the end, what? Well, toodle-oo, friend of my youth. If you've nothing better to do this morning, you might take a stroll along Bond Street and be picking out a wedding present."

I lost sight of Bingo after that. I left messages a couple of times at the club, asking him to ring me up, but they didn't have any effect. I took it that he was too busy to respond. The Sons of the Red Dawn also passed out of my life, though Jeeves told me he had met Comrade Butt one evening and had a brief chat with him. He reported Butt as gloomier than ever. In the competition for the bulging Charlotte, Butt had apparently gone right back in the betting.

"Mr. Little would appear to have eclipsed him entirely, sir," said Jeeves.

"Bad news, Jeeves; bad news!"

"Yes, sir."

"I suppose what it amounts to, Jeeves, is that, when young Bingo really takes his coat off and starts in, there is no power of God or man that can prevent him making a chump of himself."

"It would seem so, sir," said Jeeves.

Then Goodwood came along, and I dug out the best suit and popped down.

I never know, when I'm telling a story, whether to cut the thing down to plain facts or whether to drool on and shove in a lot of atmosphere, and all that. I mean, many a cove would no doubt edge into the final spasm of this narrative with a long description of Goodwood, featuring the blue sky, the rolling prospect, the joyous crowds of pick-pockets, and the parties of the second part who were having their pockets picked, and—in a word, what not. But better give it a miss, I think. Even if I wanted to go into details about the bally meeting I don't think I'd have the heart to. The thing's too recent. The anguish hasn't had time to pass. You see, what happened was that Ocean Breeze (curse him!) finished absolutely nowhere for the Cup. Believe me, nowhere.

These are the times that try men's souls. It's never pleasant to be caught in the machinery when a favourite comes unstitched, and in the case of this particular dashed animal, one had come to look on the running of the race as a pure formality, a sort of quaint, old-world ceremony to be gone through before one sauntered up to the bookie and collected. I had wandered out of the paddock to try and forget, when I bumped into old Bittlesham: and he looked so rattled and purple, and his eyes were standing out of his head at such an angle, that I simply pushed my hand out and shook his in silence.

"Me, too," I said. "Me, too. How much did you drop?"

"Drop?"

"On Ocean Breeze."

"I did not bet on Ocean Breeze."

"What! You owned the favourite for the Cup, and didn't back it!"

"I never bet on horse-racing. It is against my principles. I am told that the animal failed to win the contest."

"Failed to win! Why, he was so far behind that he nearly came in first in the next race."

"Tut!" said old Bittlesham.

"Tut is right," I agreed. Then the rumminess of the thing struck me. "But if you haven't dropped a parcel over the race," I said, "why are you looking so rattled?"

"That fellow is here!"

"What fellow?"

"That bearded man."

It will show you to what an extent the iron had entered into my soul when I say that this was the first time I had given a thought to young Bingo. I suddenly remembered now that he had told me he would be at Goodwood.

"He is making an inflammatory speech at this very moment, specifically directed at me. Come! Where that crowd is." He lugged me along and, by using his weight scientifically, got us into the front rank. "Look! Listen!"

* * * * *

Young Bingo was certainly tearing off some ripe stuff. Inspired by the agony of having put his little all on a stumer that hadn't finished in the first six, he was fairly letting himself go on the subject of the blackness of the hearts of plutocratic owners who allowed a trusting public to imagine a horse was the real goods when it couldn't trot the length of its stable without getting its legs crossed and sitting down to rest. He then went on to draw what I'm bound to say was a most moving picture of the ruin of a working man's home, due to this dishonesty. He showed us the working man, all optimism and simple trust, believing every word he read in the papers about Ocean Breeze's form; depriving his wife and children of food in order to back the brute; going without beer so as to be able to cram an extra bob on; robbing the baby's money-box with a hatpin on the eve of the race; and finally getting let down with a thud. Dashed impressive it was. I could see old Rowbotham nodding his head gently, while poor old Butt glowered at the speaker with ill-concealed jealousy. The audience ate it.

"But what does Lord Bittlesham care," shouted Bingo, "if the poor working man loses his hard-earned savings? I tell you, friends and comrades, you may talk, and you may argue, and you may cheer, and you may pass resolutions, but what you need is Action! Action! The world won't be a fit place for honest men to live in till the blood of Lord Bittlesham and his kind flows in rivers down the gutters of Park Lane!"

Roars of approval from the populace, most of whom, I suppose, had had their little bit on blighted Ocean Breeze, and were feeling it deeply. Old Bittlesham bounded over to a large, sad policeman who was watching the proceedings, and appeared to be urging him to rally round. The policeman pulled at his moustache, and smiled gently, but that was as far as he seemed inclined to go; and old Bittlesham came back to me, puffing not a little.

"It's monstrous! The man definitely threatens my personal safety, and that policeman declines to interfere. Said it was just talk. Talk! It's monstrous!"

"Absolutely," I said, but I can't say it seemed to cheer him up much.

Comrade Butt had taken the centre of the stage now. He had a voice like the Last Trump, and you could hear every word he said, but somehow he didn't seem to be clicking. I suppose the fact was he was too impersonal, if that's the word I want. After Bingo's speech the audience was in the mood for something a good deal snappier than just general remarks about the Cause. They had started to heckle the poor blighter pretty freely when he stopped in the middle of a sentence, and I saw that he was staring at old Bittlesham.

The crowd thought he had dried up.

"Suck a lozenge," shouted some one.

Comrade Butt pulled himself together with a jerk, and even from where I stood I could see the nasty gleam in his eye.

"Ah," he yelled, "you may mock, comrades; you may jeer and sneer; and you may scoff; but let me tell you that the movement is spreading every day and every hour. Yes, even amongst the so-called upper classes it's spreading. Perhaps you'll believe me when I tell you that here, to-day, on this very spot, we have in our little band one of our most earnest workers, the nephew of that very Lord Bittlesham whose name you were hooting but a moment ago."

And before poor old Bingo had a notion of what was up, he had reached out a hand and grabbed the beard. It came off all in one piece, and, well as Bingo's speech had gone, it was simply nothing compared with the hit made by this bit of business. I heard old Bittlesham give one short, sharp snort of amazement at my side, and then any remarks he may have made were drowned in thunders of applause.

I'm bound to say that in this crisis young Bingo acted with a good deal of decision and character. To grab Comrade Butt by the neck and try to twist his head off was with him the work of a moment. But before he could get any results the sad policeman, brightening up like magic, had charged in, and the next minute he was shoving his way back through the crowd, with Bingo in his right hand and Comrade Butt in his left.

"Let me pass, sir, please," he said, civilly, as he came up against old Bittlesham, who was blocking the gangway.

"Eh?" said old Bittlesham, still dazed.

At the sound of his voice young Bingo looked up quickly from under the shadow of the policeman's right hand, and as he did so all the stuffing seemed to go out of him with a rush. For an instant he drooped like a bally lily, and then shuffled brokenly on. His air was the air of a man who has got it in the neck properly.

Sometimes when Jeeves has brought in my morning tea and shoved it on the table beside my bed, he drifts silently from the room and leaves me to go to it: at other times he sort of shimmies respectfully in the middle of the carpet, and then I know that he wants a word or two. On the day after I had got back from Goodwood I was lying on my back, staring at the ceiling, when I noticed that he was still in my midst.

"Oh, hallo," I said. "Yes?"

"Mr. Little called earlier in the morning, sir."

"Oh, by Jove, what? Did he tell you about what happened?"

"Yes, sir. It was in connection with that that he wished to see you. He proposes to retire to the country and remain there for some little while."

"Dashed sensible."

"That was my opinion, also, sir. There was, however, a slight financial difficulty to be overcome. I took the liberty of advancing him ten pounds on your behalf to meet current expenses. I trust that meets with your approval, sir?"

"Oh, of course. Take a tenner off the dressing-table."

"Very good, sir."

"Jeeves," I said.

"Sir?"

"What beats me is how the dickens the thing happened. I mean, how did the chappie Butt ever get to know who he was?"

Jeeves coughed.

"There, sir, I fear I may have been somewhat to blame."

"You? How?"

"I fear I may carelessly have disclosed Mr. Little's identity to Mr. Butt on the occasion when I had that conversation with him."

I sat up.

"What!"

"Indeed, now that I recall the incident, sir, I distinctly remember saying that Mr. Little's work for the Cause really seemed to me to deserve something in the nature of public recognition. I greatly regret having been the means of bringing about a temporary estrangement between Mr. Little and his lordship. And I am afraid there is another aspect to the matter. I am also responsible for the breaking off of relations between Mr. Little and the young lady who came to tea here."

I sat up again. It's a rummy thing, but the silver lining had absolutely escaped my notice till then.

"Do you mean to say it's off?"

"Completely, sir. I gathered from Mr. Little's remarks that his hopes in the direction may now be looked on as definitely quenched. If there were no other obstacle, the young lady's father, I am informed by Mr. Little, now regards him as a spy and a deceiver."

"Well, I'm dashed!"

"I appear inadvertently to have caused much trouble, sir."

"Jeeves!" I said.

"Sir?"

"How much money is there on the dressing-table?"

"In addition to the ten-pound note which you instructed me to take, sir, there are two five-pound notes, three one-pounds, a ten-shillings, two half-crowns, a florin, four shillings, a sixpence, and a halfpenny, sir."

"Collar it all," I said. "You've earned it."

CHAPTER XIII
THE GREAT SERMON HANDICAP

After Goodwood's over, I generally find that I get a bit restless. I'm not much of a lad for the birds and the trees and the great open spaces as a rule, but there's no doubt that London's not at its best in August, and rather tends to give me the pip and make me think of popping down into the country till things have bucked up a trifle. London, about a couple of weeks after that spectacular finish of young Bingo's which I've just been telling you about, was empty and smelled of burning asphalt. All my pals were away, most of the theatres were shut, and they were taking up Piccadilly in large spadefuls.

It was most infernally hot. As I sat in the old flat one night trying to muster up energy enough to go to bed, I felt I couldn't stand it much longer: and when Jeeves came in with the tissue-restorers on a tray I put the thing to him squarely.

"Jeeves," I said, wiping the brow and gasping like a stranded goldfish, "it's beastly hot."

"The weather is oppressive, sir."

"Not all the soda, Jeeves."

"No, sir."

"I think we've had about enough of the metrop. for the time being, and require a change. Shift-ho, I think, Jeeves, what?"

"Just as you say, sir. There is a letter on the tray, sir."

"By Jove, Jeeves, that was practically poetry. Rhymed, did you notice?" I opened the letter. "I say, this is rather extraordinary."

"Sir?"

"You know Twing Hall?"

"Yes, sir."

"Well, Mr. Little is there."

"Indeed, sir?"

"Absolutely in the flesh. He's had to take another of those tutoring jobs."

After that fearful mix-up at Goodwood, when young Bingo Little, a broken man, had touched me for a tenner and whizzed silently off into the unknown, I had been all over the place, asking mutual friends if they had heard anything of him, but nobody had. And all the time he had been at Twing Hall. Rummy. And I'll tell you why it was rummy. Twing Hall belongs to old Lord Wickhammersley, a great pal of my guv'nor's when he was alive, and I have a standing invitation to pop down there when I like. I generally put in a week or two sometime in the summer, and I was thinking of going there before I read the letter.

"And, what's more, Jeeves, my cousin Claude, and my cousin Eustace—you remember them?"

"Very vividly, sir."

"Well, they're down there, too, reading for some exam, or other with the vicar. I used to read with him myself at one time. He's known far and wide as a pretty hot coach for those of fairly feeble intellect. Well, when I tell you he got me through Smalls, you'll gather that he's a bit of a hummer. I call this most extraordinary."

I read the letter again. It was from Eustace. Claude and Eustace are twins, and more or less generally admitted to be the curse of the human race.

The Vicarage,

Twing, Glos.

Dear Bertie—Do you want to make a bit of money? I hear you had a bad Goodwood, so you probably do. Well, come down here quick and get in on the biggest sporting event of the season. I'll explain when I see you, but you can take it from me it's all right.

Claude and I are with a reading-party at old Heppenstall's. There are nine of us, not counting your pal Bingo Little, who is tutoring the kid up at the Hall.

Don't miss this golden opportunity, which may never occur again. Come and join us.

Yours,

Eustace.

I handed this to Jeeves. He studied it thoughtfully.

"What do you make of it? A rummy communication, what?"

"Very high-spirited young gentlemen, sir, Mr. Claude and Mr. Eustace. Up to some game, I should be disposed to imagine."

"Yes. But what game, do you think?"

"It is impossible to say, sir. Did you observe that the letter continues over the page?"

"Eh, what?" I grabbed the thing. This was what was on the other side of the last page:

SERMON HANDICAP

RUNNERS AND BETTING

PROBABLE STARTERS.

Rev. Joseph Tucker (Badgwick), scratch.

Rev. Leonard Starkie (Stapleton), scratch.

Rev. Alexander Jones (Upper Bingley), receives three minutes.

Rev. W. Dix (Little Clickton-in-the-Wold), receives five minutes.

Rev. Francis Heppenstall (Twing), receives eight minutes.

Rev. Cuthbert Dibble (Boustead Parva), receives nine minutes.

Rev. Orlo Hough (Boustead Magna), receives nine minutes.

Rev. J. J. Roberts (Fale-by-the-Water), receives ten minutes.

Rev. G. Hayward (Lower Bingley), receives twelve minutes.

Rev. James Bates (Gandle-by-the-Hill), receives fifteen minutes.

(The above have arrived.)

PRICES.—5-2, Tucker, Starkie; 3-1, Jones; 9-2, Dix; 6-1, Heppenstall, Dibble, Hough; 100-8 any other.

It baffled me.

"Do you understand it, Jeeves?"

"No, sir."

"Well, I think we ought to have a look into it, anyway, what?"

"Undoubtedly, sir."

"Right-o, then. Pack our spare dickey and a toothbrush in a neat brown-paper parcel, send a wire to Lord Wickhammersley to say we're coming, and buy two tickets on the five-ten at Paddington to-morrow."

* * * * *

The five-ten was late as usual, and everybody was dressing for dinner when I arrived at the Hall. It was only by getting into my evening things in record time and taking the stairs to the dining-room in a couple of bounds that I managed to dead-heat with the soup. I slid into the vacant chair, and found that I was sitting next to old Wickhammersley's youngest daughter, Cynthia.

"Oh, hallo, old thing," I said.

Great pals we've always been. In fact, there was a time when I had an idea I was in love with Cynthia. However, it blew over. A dashed pretty and lively and attractive girl, mind you, but full of ideals and all that. I may be wronging her, but I have an idea that she's the sort of girl who would want a fellow to carve out a career and what not. I know I've heard her speak favourably of Napoleon. So what with one thing and another the jolly old frenzy sort of petered out, and now we're just pals. I think she's a topper, and she thinks me next door to a looney, so everything's nice and matey.

"Well, Bertie, so you've arrived?"

"Oh, yes, I've arrived. Yes, here I am. I say, I seem to have plunged into the middle of quite a young dinner-party. Who are all these coves?"

"Oh, just people from round about. You know most of them. You remember Colonel Willis, and the Spencers——"

"Of course, yes. And there's old Heppenstall. Who's the other clergyman next to Mrs. Spencer?"

"Mr. Hayward, from Lower Bingley."

"What an amazing lot of clergymen there are round here. Why, there's another, next to Mrs. Willis."

"That's Mr. Bates, Mr. Heppenstall's nephew. He's an assistant-master at Eton. He's down here during the summer holidays, acting as locum tenens for Mr. Spettigue, the rector of Gandle-by-the-Hill."

"I thought I knew his face. He was in his fourth year at Oxford when I was a fresher. Rather a blood. Got his rowing-blue and all that." I took another look round the table, and spotted young Bingo. "Ah, there he is," I said. "There's the old egg."

"There's who?"

"Young Bingo Little. Great pal of mine. He's tutoring your brother, you know."

"Good gracious! Is he a friend of yours?"

"Rather! Known him all my life."

"Then tell me, Bertie, is he at all weak in the head?"

"Weak in the head?"

"I don't mean simply because he's a friend of yours. But he's so strange in his manner."

"How do you mean?"

"Well, he keeps looking at me so oddly."

"Oddly? How? Give an imitation."

"I can't in front of all these people."

"Yes, you can. I'll hold my napkin up."

"All right, then. Quick. There!"

Considering that she had only about a second and a half to do it in, I must say it was a jolly fine exhibition. She opened her mouth and eyes pretty wide and let her jaw drop sideways, and managed to look so like a dyspeptic calf that I recognised the symptoms immediately.

"Oh, that's all right," I said. "No need to be alarmed. He's simply in love with you."

"In love with me. Don't be absurd."

"My dear old thing, you don't know young Bingo. He can fall in love with anybody."

"Thank you!"

"Oh, I didn't mean it that way, you know. I don't wonder at his taking to you. Why, I was in love with you myself once."

"Once? Ah! And all that remains now are the cold ashes? This isn't one of your tactful evenings, Bertie."

"Well, my dear sweet thing, dash it all, considering that you gave me the bird and nearly laughed yourself into a permanent state of hiccoughs when I asked you——"

"Oh, I'm not reproaching you. No doubt there were faults on both sides. He's very good-looking, isn't he?"

"Good-looking? Bingo? Bingo good-looking? No, I say, come now, really!"

"I mean, compared with some people," said Cynthia.

Some time after this, Lady Wickhammersley gave the signal for the females of the species to leg it, and they duly stampeded. I didn't get a chance of talking to young Bingo when they'd gone, and later, in the drawing-room, he didn't show up. I found him eventually in his room, lying on the bed with his feet on the rail, smoking a toofah. There was a notebook on the counterpane beside him.

"Hallo, old scream," I said.

"Hallo, Bertie," he replied, in what seemed to me rather a moody, distrait sort of manner.

"Rummy finding you down here. I take it your uncle cut off your allowance after that Goodwood binge and you had to take this tutoring job to keep the wolf from the door?"

"Correct," said young Bingo tersely.

"Well, you might have let your pals know where you were."

He frowned darkly.

"I didn't want them to know where I was. I wanted to creep away and hide myself. I've been through a bad time, Bertie, these last weeks. The sun ceased to shine——"

"That's curious. We've had gorgeous weather in London."

"The birds ceased to sing——"

"What birds?"

"What the devil does it matter what birds?" said young Bingo, with some asperity. "Any birds. The birds round about here. You don't expect me to specify them by their pet names, do you? I tell you, Bertie, it hit me hard at first, very hard."

"What hit you?" I simply couldn't follow the blighter.

"Charlotte's calculated callousness."

"Oh, ah!" I've seen poor old Bingo through so many unsuccessful love-affairs that I'd almost forgotten there was a girl mixed up with that Goodwood business. Of course! Charlotte Corday Rowbotham. And she had given him the raspberry, I remembered, and gone off with Comrade Butt.

"I went through torments. Recently, however, I've—er—bucked up a bit. Tell me, Bertie, what are you doing down here? I didn't know you knew these people."

"Me? Why, I've known them since I was a kid."

Young Bingo put his feet down with a thud.

"Do you mean to say you've known Lady Cynthia all that time?"

"Rather! She can't have been seven when I met her first."

"Good Lord!" said young Bingo. He looked at me for the first time as though I amounted to something, and swallowed a mouthful of smoke the wrong way. "I love that girl, Bertie," he went on, when he'd finished coughing.

"Yes. Nice girl, of course."

He eyed me with pretty deep loathing.

"Don't speak of her in that horrible casual way. She's an angel. An angel! Was she talking about me at all at dinner, Bertie?"

"Oh, yes."

"What did she say?"

"I remember one thing. She said she thought you good-looking."

Young Bingo closed his eyes in a sort of ecstasy. Then he picked up the notebook.

"Pop off now, old man, there's a good chap," he said, in a hushed, far-away voice. "I've got a bit of writing to do."

"Writing?"

"Poetry, if you must know. I wish the dickens," said young Bingo, not without some bitterness, "she had been christened something except Cynthia. There isn't a dam' word in the language it rhymes with. Ye gods, how I could have spread myself if she had only been called Jane!"

*   *   *   *   *

Bright and early next morning, as I lay in bed blinking at the sunlight on the dressing-table and wondering when Jeeves was going to show up with a cup of tea, a heavy weight descended on my toes, and the voice of young Bingo polluted the air. The blighter had apparently risen with the lark.

"Leave me," I said, "I would be alone. I can't see anybody till I've had my tea."

"When Cynthia smiles," said young Bingo, "the skies are blue; the world takes on a roseate hue: birds in the garden trill and sing, and Joy is king of everything, when Cynthia smiles." He coughed, changing gears. "When Cynthia frowns——"

"What the devil are you talking about?"

"I'm reading you my poem. The one I wrote to Cynthia last night. I'll go on, shall I?"

"No!"

"No?"

"No. I haven't had my tea."

At this moment Jeeves came in with the good old beverage, and I sprang on it with a glad cry. After a couple of sips things looked a bit brighter. Even young Bingo didn't offend the eye to quite such an extent. By the time I'd finished the first cup I was a new man, so much so that I not only permitted but encouraged the poor fish to read the rest of the bally thing, and even went so far as to criticise the scansion of the fourth line of the fifth verse. We were still arguing the point when the door burst open and in blew Claude and Eustace. One of the things which discourage me about rural life is the frightful earliness with which events begin to break loose. I've stayed at places in the country where they've jerked me out of the dreamless at about six-thirty to go for a jolly swim in the lake. At Twing, thank heaven, they know me, and let me breakfast in bed.

The twins seemed pleased to see me.

"Good old Bertie!" said Claude.

"Stout fellow!" said Eustace. "The Rev. told us you had arrived. I thought that letter of mine would fetch you."

"You can always bank on Bertie," said Claude. "A sportsman to the finger-tips. Well, has Bingo told you about it?"

"Not a word. He's been——"

"We've been talking," said Bingo hastily, "of other matters."

Claude pinched the last slice of thin bread-and-butter, and Eustace poured himself out a cup of tea.

"It's like this, Bertie," said Eustace, settling down cosily. "As I told you in my letter, there are nine of us marooned in this desert spot, reading with old Heppenstall. Well, of course, nothing is jollier than sweating up the Classics when it's a hundred in the shade, but there does come a time when you begin to feel the need of a little relaxation; and, by Jove, there are absolutely no facilities for relaxation in this place whatever. And then Steggles got this idea. Steggles is one of our reading-party, and, between ourselves, rather a worm as a general thing. Still, you have to give him credit for getting this idea."

"What idea?"

"Well, you know how many parsons there are round about here. There are about a dozen hamlets within a radius of six miles, and each hamlet has a church and each church has a parson and each parson preaches a sermon every Sunday. To-morrow week—Sunday the twenty-third—we're running off the great Sermon Handicap. Steggles is making the book. Each parson is to be clocked by a reliable steward of the course, and the one that preaches the longest sermon wins. Did you study the race-card I sent you?"

"I couldn't understand what it was all about."

"Why, you chump, it gives the handicaps and the current odds on each starter. I've got another one here, in case you've lost yours. Take a careful look at it. It gives you the thing in a nutshell. Jeeves, old son, do you want a sporting flutter?"

"Sir?" said Jeeves, who had just meandered in with my breakfast.

Claude explained the scheme. Amazing the way Jeeves grasped it right off. But he merely smiled in a paternal sort of way.

"Thank you, sir, I think not."

"Well, you're with us, Bertie, aren't you?" said Claude, sneaking a roll and a slice of bacon. "Have you studied that card? Well, tell me, does anything strike you about it?"

Of course it did. It had struck me the moment I looked at it.

"Why, it's a sitter for old Heppenstall," I said. "He's got the event sewed up in a parcel. There isn't a parson in the land who could give him eight minutes. Your pal Steggles must be an ass, giving him a handicap like that. Why, in the days when I was with him, old Heppenstall never used to preach under half an hour, and there was one sermon of his on Brotherly Love which lasted forty-five minutes if it lasted a second. Has he lost his vim lately, or what is it?"

"Not a bit of it," said Eustace. "Tell him what happened, Claude."

"Why," said Claude, "the first Sunday we were here, we all went to Twing church, and old Heppenstall preached a sermon that was well under twenty minutes. This is what happened. Steggles didn't notice it, and the Rev. didn't notice it himself, but Eustace and I both spotted that he had dropped a chunk of at least half a dozen pages out of his sermon-case as he was walking up to the pulpit. He sort of flickered when he got to the gap in the manuscript, but carried on all right, and Steggles went away with the impression that twenty minutes or a bit under was his usual form. The next Sunday we heard Tucker and Starkie, and they both went well over the thirty-five minutes, so Steggles arranged the handicapping as you see on the card. You must come into this, Bertie. You see, the trouble is that I haven't a bean, and Eustace hasn't a bean, and Bingo Little hasn't a bean, so you'll have to finance the syndicate. Don't weaken! It's just putting money in all our pockets. Well, we'll have to be getting back now. Think the thing over, and phone me later in the day. And, if you let us down, Bertie, may a cousin's curse—— Come on, Claude, old thing."

The more I studied the scheme, the better it looked.

"How about it, Jeeves?" I said.

Jeeves smiled gently, and drifted out.

"Jeeves has no sporting blood," said Bingo.

"Well, I have. I'm coming into this. Claude's quite right. It's like finding money by the wayside."

"Good man!" said Bingo. "Now I can see daylight. Say I have a tenner on Heppenstall, and cop; that'll give me a bit in hand to back Pink Pill with in the two o'clock at Gatwick the week after next: cop on that, put the pile on Musk-Rat for the one-thirty at Lewes, and there I am with a nice little sum to take to Alexandra Park on September the tenth, when I've got a tip straight from the stable."

It sounded like a bit out of "Smiles's Self-Help."

"And then," said young Bingo, "I'll be in a position to go to my uncle and beard him in his lair somewhat. He's quite a bit of a snob, you know, and when he hears that I'm going to marry the daughter of an earl——"

"I say, old man," I couldn't help saying, "aren't you looking ahead rather far?"

"Oh, that's all right. It's true nothing's actually settled yet, but she practically told me the other day she was fond of me."

"What!"

"Well, she said that the sort of man she liked was the self-reliant, manly man with strength, good looks, character, ambition, and initiative."

"Leave me, laddie," I said. "Leave me to my fried egg."

* * * * *

Directly I'd got up I went to the phone, snatched Eustace away from his morning's work, and instructed him to put a tenner on the Twing flier at current odds for each of the syndicate; and after lunch Eustace rang me up to say that he had done business at a snappy seven-to-one, the odds having lengthened owing to a rumour in knowledgeable circles that the Rev. was subject to hay-fever, and was taking big chances strolling in the paddock behind the Vicarage in the early mornings. And it was dashed lucky, I thought next day, that we had managed to get the money on in time, for on the Sunday morning old Heppenstall fairly took the bit between his teeth, and gave us thirty-six solid minutes on Certain Popular Superstitions. I was sitting next to Steggles in the pew, and I saw him blench visibly. He was a little, rat-faced fellow, with shifty eyes and a suspicious nature. The first thing he did when we emerged into the open air was to announce, formally, that anyone who fancied the Rev. could now be accommodated at fifteen-to-eight on, and he added, in a rather nasty manner, that if he had his way, this sort of in-and-out running would be brought to the attention of the Jockey Club, but that he supposed that there was nothing to be done about it. This ruinous price checked the punters at once, and there was little money in sight. And so matters stood till just after lunch on Tuesday afternoon, when, as I was strolling up and down in front of the house with a cigarette, Claude and Eustace came bursting up the drive on bicycles, dripping with momentous news.

"Bertie," said Claude, deeply agitated, "unless we take immediate action and do a bit of quick thinking, we're in the cart."

"What's the matter?"

"G. Hayward's the matter," said Eustace morosely. "The Lower Bingley starter."

"We never even considered him," said Claude. "Somehow or other, he got overlooked. It's always the way. Steggles overlooked him. We all overlooked him. But Eustace and I happened by the merest fluke to be riding through Lower Bingley this morning, and there was a wedding on at the church, and it suddenly struck us that it wouldn't be a bad move to get a line on G. Hayward's form, in case he might be a dark horse."

"And it was jolly lucky we did," said Eustace. "He delivered an address of twenty-six minutes by Claude's stop-watch. At a village wedding, mark you! What'll he do when he really extends himself!"

"There's only one thing to be done, Bertie," said Claude. "You must spring some more funds, so that we can hedge on Hayward and save ourselves."

"But——"

"Well, it's the only way out."

"But I say, you know, I hate the idea of all that money we put on Heppenstall being chucked away."

"What else can you suggest? You don't suppose the Rev. can give this absolute marvel a handicap and win, do you?"

"I've got it!" I said.

"What?"

"I see a way by which we can make it safe for our nominee. I'll pop over this afternoon, and ask him as a personal favour to preach that sermon of his on Brotherly Love on Sunday."

Claude and Eustace looked at each other, like those chappies in the poem, with a wild surmise.

"It's a scheme," said Claude.

"A jolly brainy scheme," said Eustace. "I didn't think you had it in you, Bertie."

"But even so," said Claude, "fizzer as that sermon no doubt is, will it be good enough in the face of a four-minute handicap?"

"Rather!" I said. "When I told you it lasted forty-five minutes, I was probably understating it. I should call it—from my recollection of the thing—nearer fifty."

"Then carry on," said Claude.

I toddled over in the evening and fixed the thing up. Old Heppenstall was most decent about the whole affair. He seemed pleased and touched that I should have remembered the sermon all these years, and said he had once or twice had an idea of preaching it again, only it had seemed to him, on reflection, that it was perhaps a trifle long for a rustic congregation.

"And in these restless times, my dear Wooster," he said, "I fear that brevity in the pulpit is becoming more and more desiderated by even the bucolic churchgoer, who one might have supposed would be less afflicted with the spirit of hurry and impatience than his metropolitan brother. I have had many arguments on the subject with my nephew, young Bates, who is taking my old friend Spettigue's cure over at Gandle-by-the-Hill. His view is that a sermon nowadays should be a bright, brisk, straight-from-the-shoulder address, never lasting more than ten or twelve minutes."

"Long?" I said. "Why, my goodness! you don't call that Brotherly Love sermon of yours long, do you?"

"It takes fully fifty minutes to deliver."

"Surely not?"

"Your incredulity, my dear Wooster, is extremely flattering—far more flattering, of course, than I deserve. Nevertheless, the facts are as I have stated. You are sure that I would not be well advised to make certain excisions and eliminations? You do not think it would be a good thing to cut, to prune? I might, for example, delete the rather exhaustive excursus into the family life of the early Assyrians?"

"Don't touch a word of it, or you'll spoil the whole thing," I said earnestly.

"I am delighted to hear you say so, and I shall preach the sermon without fail next Sunday morning."

* * * * *

What I have always said, and what I always shall say, is, that this ante-post betting is a mistake, an error, and a mug's game. You never can tell what's going to happen. If fellows would only stick to the good old S.P. there would be fewer young men go wrong. I'd hardly finished my breakfast on the Saturday morning, when Jeeves came to my bedside to say that Eustace wanted me on the telephone.

"Good Lord, Jeeves, what's the matter, do you think?"

I'm bound to say I was beginning to get a bit jumpy by this time.

"Mr. Eustace did not confide in me, sir."

"Has he got the wind up?"

"Somewhat vertically, sir, to judge by his voice."

"Do you know what I think, Jeeves? Something's gone wrong with the favourite."

"Which is the favourite, sir?"

"Mr. Heppenstall. He's gone to odds on. He was intending to preach a sermon on Brotherly Love which would have brought him home by lengths. I wonder if anything's happened to him."

"You could ascertain, sir, by speaking to Mr. Eustace on the telephone. He is holding the wire."

"By Jove, yes!"

I shoved on a dressing-gown, and flew downstairs like a mighty, rushing wind. The moment I heard Eustace's voice I knew we were for it. It had a croak of agony in it.

"Bertie?"

"Here I am."

"Deuce of a time you've been. Bertie, we're sunk. The favourite's blown up."

"No!"

"Yes. Coughing in his stable all last night."

"What!"

"Absolutely! Hay-fever."

"Oh, my sainted aunt!"

"The doctor is with him now, and it's only a question of minutes before he's officially scratched. That means the curate will show up at the post instead, and he's no good at all. He is being offered at a hundred-to-six, but no takers. What shall we do?"

I had to grapple with the thing for a moment in silence.

"Eustace."

"Hallo?"

"What can you get on G. Hayward?"

"Only four-to-one now. I think there's been a leak, and Steggles has heard something. The odds shortened late last night in a significant manner."

"Well, four-to-one will clear us. Put another fiver all round on G. Hayward for the syndicate.

That'll bring us out on the right side of the ledger."

"If he wins."

"What do you mean? I thought you considered him a cert. bar Heppenstall."

"I'm beginning to wonder," said Eustace gloomily, "if there's such a thing as a cert. in this world. I'm told the Rev. Joseph Tucker did an extraordinarily fine trial gallop at a mothers' meeting over at Badgwick yesterday. However, it seems our only chance. So-long."

Not being one of the official stewards, I had my choice of churches next morning, and naturally I didn't hesitate. The only drawback to going to Lower Bingley was that it was ten miles away, which meant an early start, but I borrowed a bicycle from one of the grooms and tooled off. I had only Eustace's word for it that G. Hayward was such a stayer, and it might have been that he had showed too flattering form at that wedding where the twins had heard him preach; but any misgivings I may have had disappeared the moment he got into the pulpit. Eustace had been right. The man was a trier. He was a tall, rangy-looking greybeard, and he went off from the start with a nice, easy action, pausing and clearing his throat at the end of each sentence, and it wasn't five minutes before I realised that here was the winner. His habit of stopping dead and looking round the church at intervals was worth minutes to us, and in the home stretch we gained no little advantage owing to his dropping his pince-nez and having to grope for them. At the twenty-minute mark he had merely settled down. Twenty-five minutes saw him going strong. And when he finally finished with a good burst, the clock showed thirty-five minutes fourteen seconds. With the handicap which he had been given, this seemed to me to make the event easy for him, and it was with much bonhomie and goodwill to all men that I hopped on to the old bike and started back to the Hall for lunch.

Bingo was talking on the phone when I arrived.

"Fine! Splendid! Topping!" he was saying. "Eh? Oh, we needn't worry about him. Right-o, I'll tell Bertie." He hung up the receiver and caught sight of me. "Oh, hallo, Bertie; I was just talking to Eustace. It's all right, old man. The report from Lower Bingley has just got in. G. Hayward romps home."

"I knew he would. I've just come from there."

"Oh, were you there? I went to Badgwick. Tucker ran a splendid race, but the handicap was too much for him. Starkie had a sore throat and was nowhere. Roberts, of Fale-by-the-Water, ran third. Good old G. Hayward!" said Bingo affectionately, and we strolled out on to the terrace.

"Are all the returns in, then?" I asked.

"All except Gandle-by-the-Hill. But we needn't worry about Bates. He never had a chance. By the way, poor old Jeeves loses his tenner. Silly ass!"

"Jeeves? How do you mean?"

"He came to me this morning, just after you had left, and asked me to put a tenner on Bates for him. I told him he was a chump and begged him not to throw his money away, but he would do it."

"I beg your pardon, sir. This note arrived for you just after you had left the house this morning."

Jeeves had materialised from nowhere, and was standing at my elbow.

"Eh? What? Note?"

"The Reverend Mr. Heppenstall's butler brought it over from the Vicarage, sir. It came too late to be delivered to you at the moment."

Young Bingo was talking to Jeeves like a father on the subject of betting against the form-book. The yell I gave made him bite his tongue in the middle of a sentence.

"What the dickens is the matter?" he asked, not a little peeved.

"We're dished! Listen to this!"

I read him the note:

The Vicarage,

Twing, Glos.

My Dear Wooster,—As you may have heard, circumstances over which I have no control will prevent my preaching the sermon on Brotherly Love for which you made such a flattering request. I am unwilling, however, that you shall be disappointed, so, if you will attend divine service at Gandle-by-the-Hill this morning, you will hear my sermon preached by young Bates, my nephew. I have lent him the manuscript at his urgent desire, for, between ourselves, there are wheels within wheels. My nephew is one of the candidates for the headmastership of a well-known public school, and the choice has narrowed down between him and one rival.

Late yesterday evening James received private information that the head of the Board of Governors of the school proposed to sit under him this Sunday in order to judge of the merits of his preaching, a most important item in swaying the Board's choice. I acceded to his plea that I lend him my sermon on Brotherly Love, of which, like you, he apparently retains a vivid recollection. It would have been too late for him to compose a sermon of suitable length in place of the brief address which—mistakenly, in my opinion—he had designed to deliver to his rustic flock, and I wished to help the boy.

Trusting that his preaching of the sermon will supply you with as pleasant memories as you say you have of mine, I remain,

Cordially yours,

F. Heppenstall.

P.S.—The hay-fever has rendered my eyes unpleasantly weak for the time being, so I am dictating this letter to my butler, Brookfield, who will convey it to you.

I don't know when I've experienced a more massive silence than the one that followed my reading of this cheery epistle. Young Bingo gulped once or twice, and practically every known emotion came and went on his face. Jeeves coughed one soft, low, gentle cough like a sheep with a blade of grass stuck in its throat, and then stood gazing serenely at the landscape. Finally young Bingo spoke.

"Great Scott!" he whispered hoarsely. "An S.P. job!"

"I believe that is the technical term, sir," said Jeeves.

"So you had inside information, dash it!" said young Bingo.

"Why, yes, sir," said Jeeves. "Brookfield happened to mention the contents of the note to me when he brought it. We are old friends."

Bingo registered grief, anguish, rage, despair and resentment.

"Well, all I can say," he cried, "is that it's a bit thick! Preaching another man's sermon! Do you call that honest? Do you call that playing the game?"

"Well, my dear old thing," I said, "be fair. It's quite within the rules. Clergymen do it all the time. They aren't expected always to make up the sermons they preach."

Jeeves coughed again, and fixed me with an expressionless eye.

"And in the present case, sir, if I may be permitted to take the liberty of making the observation, I think we should make allowances. We should remember that the securing of this headmastership meant everything to the young couple."

"Young couple! What young couple?"

"The Reverend James Bates, sir, and Lady Cynthia. I am informed by her ladyship's maid that they have been engaged to be married for some weeks—provisionally, so to speak; and his lordship made his consent conditional on Mr. Bates securing a really important and remunerative position."

Young Bingo turned a light green.

"Engaged to be married!"

"Yes, sir."

There was a silence.

"I think I'll go for a walk," said Bingo.

"But, my dear old thing," I said, "it's just lunch-time. The gong will be going any minute now."

"I don't want any lunch!" said Bingo.

CHAPTER XIV
THE PURITY OF THE TURF

After that, life at Twing jogged along pretty peacefully for a bit. Twing is one of those places where there isn't a frightful lot to do nor any very hectic excitement to look forward to. In fact, the only event of any importance on the horizon, as far as I could ascertain, was the annual village school treat. One simply filled in the time by loafing about the grounds, playing a bit of tennis, and avoiding young Bingo as far as was humanly possible.

This last was a very necessary move if you wanted a happy life, for the Cynthia affair had jarred the unfortunate mutt to such an extent that he was always waylaying one and decanting his anguished soul. And when, one morning, he blew into my bedroom while I was toying with a bit of breakfast, I decided to take a firm line from the start. I could stand having him moaning all over me after dinner, and even after lunch; but at breakfast, no. We Woosters are amiability itself, but there is a limit.

"Now look here, old friend," I said. "I know your bally heart is broken and all that, and at some future time I shall be delighted to hear all about it, but——"

"I didn't come to talk about that."

"No? Good egg!"

"The past," said young Bingo, "is dead. Let us say no more about it."

"Right-o!"

"I have been wounded to the very depths of my soul, but don't speak about it."

"I won't."

"Ignore it. Forget it."

"Absolutely!"

I hadn't seen him so dashed reasonable for days.

"What I came to see you about this morning, Bertie," he said, fishing a sheet of paper out of his pocket, "was to ask if you would care to come in on another little flutter."

If there is one thing we Woosters are simply dripping with, it is sporting blood. I bolted the rest of my sausage, and sat up and took notice.

"Proceed," I said. "You interest me strangely, old bird."

Bingo laid the paper on the bed.

"On Monday week," he said, "you may or may not know, the annual village school treat takes place. Lord Wickhammersley lends the Hall grounds for the purpose. There will be games, and a conjurer, and cokernut shies, and tea in a tent. And also sports."

"I know. Cynthia was telling me."

Young Bingo winced.

"Would you mind not mentioning that name? I am not made of marble."

"Sorry!"

"Well, as I was saying, this jamboree is slated for Monday week. The question is, Are we on?"

"How do you mean, 'Are we on'?"

"I am referring to the sports. Steggles did so well out of the Sermon Handicap that he has decided to make a book on these sports. Punters can be accommodated at ante-post odds or starting price, according to their preference. I think we ought to look into it," said young Bingo.

I pressed the bell.

"I'll consult Jeeves. I don't touch any sporting proposition without his advice. Jeeves," I said, as he drifted in, "rally round."

"Sir?"

"Stand by. We want your advice."

"Very good, sir."

"State your case, Bingo."

Bingo stated his case.

"What about it, Jeeves?" I said. "Do we go in?"

Jeeves pondered to some extent.

"I am inclined to favour the idea, sir."

That was good enough for me. "Right," I said. "Then we will form a syndicate and bust the Ring. I supply the money, you supply the brains, and Bingo—what do you supply, Bingo?"

"If you will carry me, and let me settle up later," said young Bingo, "I think I can put you in the way of winning a parcel on the Mothers' Sack Race."

"All right. We will put you down as Inside Information. Now, what are the events?"

* * * * *

Bingo reached for his paper and consulted it.

"Girls' Under Fourteen Fifty-Yard Dash seems to open the proceedings."

"Anything to say about that, Jeeves?"

"No, sir. I have no information."

"What's the next?"

"Boys' and Girls' Mixed Animal Potato Race, All Ages."

This was a new one to me. I had never heard of it at any of the big meetings.

"What's that?"

"Rather sporting," said young Bingo. "The competitors enter in couples, each couple being assigned an animal cry and a potato. For instance, let's suppose that you and Jeeves entered. Jeeves would stand at a fixed point holding a potato. You would have your head in a sack, and you would grope about trying to find Jeeves and making a noise like a cat; Jeeves also making a noise like a cat. Other competitors would be making noises like cows and pigs and dogs, and so on, and groping about for their potato-holders, who would also be making noises like cows and pigs and dogs and so on——"

I stopped the poor fish.

"Jolly if you're fond of animals," I said, "but on the whole——"

"Precisely, sir," said Jeeves. "I wouldn't touch it."

"Too open, what?"

"Exactly, sir. Very hard to estimate form."

"Carry on, Bingo. Where do we go from there?"

"Mothers' Sack Race."

"Ah! that's better. This is where you know something."

"A gift for Mrs. Penworthy, the tobacconist's wife," said Bingo confidently. "I was in at her shop yesterday, buying cigarettes, and she told me she had won three times at fairs in Worcestershire. She only moved to these parts a short time ago, so nobody knows about her. She promised me she would keep herself dark, and I think we could get a good price."

"Risk a tenner each way, Jeeves, what?"

"I think so, sir."

"Girls' Open Egg and Spoon Race," read Bingo.

"How about that?"

"I doubt if it would be worth while to invest, sir," said Jeeves. "I am told it is a certainty for last year's winner, Sarah Mills, who will doubtless start an odds-on favourite."

"Good, is she?"

"They tell me in the village that she carries a beautiful egg, sir."

"Then there's the Obstacle Race," said Bingo. "Risky, in my opinion. Like betting on the Grand National. Fathers' Hat-Trimming Contest—another speculative event. That's all, except for the Choir Boys' Hundred Yards Handicap, for a pewter mug presented by the vicar—open to all whose voices have not broken before the second Sunday in Epiphany. Willie Chambers won last year, in a canter, receiving fifteen yards. This time he will probably be handicapped out of the race. I don't know what to advise."

"If I might make a suggestion, sir."

I eyed Jeeves with interest. I don't know that I'd ever seen him look so nearly excited.

"You've got something up your sleeve?"

"I have, sir."

"Red-hot?"

"That precisely describes it, sir. I think I may confidently assert that we have the winner of the Choir Boys' Handicap under this very roof, sir. Harold, the page-boy."

"Page-boy? Do you mean the tubby little chap in buttons one sees bobbing about here and there? Why, dash it, Jeeves, nobody has a greater respect for your knowledge of form than I have, but I'm hanged if I can see Harold catching the judge's eye. He's practically circular, and every time I've seen him he's been leaning up against something, half asleep."

"He receives thirty yards, sir, and could win from scratch. The boy is a flier."

"How do you know?"

Jeeves coughed, and there was a dreamy look in his eye.

"I was as much astonished as yourself, sir, when I first became aware of the lad's capabilities. I happened to pursue him one morning with the intention of fetching him a clip on the side of the head——"

"Great Scott, Jeeves! You!"

"Yes, sir. The boy is of an outspoken disposition, and had made an opprobrious remark respecting my personal appearance."

"What did he say about your appearance?"

"I have forgotten, sir," said Jeeves, with a touch of austerity. "But it was opprobrious. I endeavoured to correct him, but he outdistanced me by yards and made good his escape."

"But, I say, Jeeves, this is sensational. And yet—if he's such a sprinter, why hasn't anybody in the village found it out? Surely he plays with the other boys?"

"No, sir. As his lordship's page-boy, Harold does not mix with the village lads."

"Bit of a snob, what?"

"He is somewhat acutely alive to the existence of class distinctions, sir."

"You're absolutely certain he's such a wonder?" said Bingo. "I mean, it wouldn't do to plunge unless you're sure."

"If you desire to ascertain the boy's form by personal inspection, sir, it will be a simple matter to arrange a secret trial."

"I'm bound to say I should feel easier in my mind," I said.

"Then if I may take a shilling from the money on your dressing-table——"

"What for?"

"I propose to bribe the lad to speak slightingly of the second footman's squint, sir. Charles is somewhat sensitive on the point, and should undoubtedly make the lad extend himself. If you will be at the first-floor passage-window, overlooking the back-door, in half an hour's time——"

I don't know when I've dressed in such a hurry. As a rule, I'm what you might call a slow and careful dresser: I like to linger over the tie and see that the trousers are just so; but this morning I was all worked up. I just shoved on my things anyhow, and joined Bingo at the window with a quarter of an hour to spare.

The passage-window looked down on to a broad sort of paved courtyard, which ended after about twenty yards in an archway through a high wall. Beyond this archway you got on to a strip of the drive, which curved round for another thirty yards or so, till it was lost behind a thick shrubbery. I put myself in the stripling's place and thought what steps I would take with a second footman after me. There was only one thing to do—leg it for the shrubbery and take cover; which meant that at least fifty yards would have to be covered—an excellent test. If good old Harold could fight off the second footman's challenge long enough to allow him to reach the bushes, there wasn't a choirboy in England who could give him thirty yards in the hundred. I waited, all of a twitter, for what seemed hours, and then suddenly there was a confused noise without, and something round and blue and buttony shot through the back-door and buzzed for the archway like a mustang. And about two seconds later out came the second footman, going his hardest.

There was nothing to it. Absolutely nothing. The field never had a chance. Long before the footman reached the half-way mark, Harold was in the bushes, throwing stones. I came away from the window thrilled to the marrow; and when I met Jeeves on the stairs I was so moved that I nearly grasped his hand.

"Jeeves," I said, "no discussion! The Wooster shirt goes on this boy!"

"Very good, sir," said Jeeves.

* * * * *

The worst of these country meetings is that you can't plunge as heavily as you would like when you get a good thing, because it alarms the Ring. Steggles, though pimpled, was, as I have indicated, no chump, and if I had invested all I wanted to he would have put two and two together. I managed to get a good solid bet down for the syndicate, however, though it did make him look thoughtful. I heard in the next few days that he had been making searching inquiries in the village concerning Harold; but nobody could tell him anything, and eventually he came to the conclusion, I suppose, that I must be having a long shot on the strength of that thirty-yards start. Public opinion wavered between Jimmy Goode, receiving ten yards, at seven-to-two, and Alexander Bartlett, with six yards start, at eleven-to-four. Willie Chambers, scratch, was offered to the public at two-to-one, but found no takers.

We were taking no chances on the big event, and directly we had got our money on at a nice hundred-to-twelve Harold was put into strict training. It was a wearing business, and I can understand now why most of the big trainers are grim, silent men, who look as though they had suffered. The kid wanted constant watching. It was no good talking to him about honour and glory and how proud his mother would be when he wrote and told her he had won a real cup—the moment blighted Harold discovered that training meant knocking off pastry, taking exercise, and keeping away from the cigarettes, he was all against it, and it was only by unceasing vigilance that we managed to keep him in any shape at all. It was the diet that was the stumbling-block. As far as exercise went, we could generally arrange for a sharp dash every morning with the assistance of the second footman. It ran into money, of course, but that couldn't be helped. Still, when a kid has simply to wait till the butler's back is turned to have the run of the pantry, and has only to nip into the smoking-room to collect a handful of the best Turkish, training becomes a rocky job. We could only hope that on the day his natural stamina would pull him through.

And then one evening young Bingo came back from the links with a disturbing story. He had been in the habit of giving Harold mild exercise in the afternoons by taking him out as a caddie.

At first he seemed to think it humorous, the poor chump! He bubbled over with merry mirth as he began his tale.

"I say, rather funny this afternoon," he said. "You ought to have seen Steggles's face!"

"Seen Steggles's face? What for?"

"When he saw young Harold sprint, I mean."

I was filled with a grim foreboding of an awful doom.

"Good heavens! You didn't let Harold sprint in front of Steggles?"

Young Bingo's jaw dropped.

"I never thought of that," he said, gloomily. "It wasn't my fault. I was playing a round with Steggles, and after we'd finished we went into the club-house for a drink, leaving Harold with the clubs outside. In about five minutes we came out, and there was the kid on the gravel practising swings with Steggles's driver and a stone. When he saw us coming, the kid dropped the club and was over the horizon like a streak. Steggles was absolutely dumbfounded. And I must say it was a revelation even to me. The kid certainly gave of his best. Of course, it's a nuisance in a way; but I don't see, on second thoughts," said Bingo, brightening up, "what it matters. We're on at a good price. We've nothing to lose by the kid's form becoming known. I take it he will start odds-on, but that doesn't affect us."

I looked at Jeeves. Jeeves looked at me.

"It affects us all right if he doesn't start at all."

"Precisely, sir."

"What do you mean?" asked Bingo.

"If you ask me," I said, "I think Steggles will try to nobble him before the race."

"Good Lord! I never thought of that." Bingo blenched. "You don't think he would really do it?"

"I think he would have a jolly good try. Steggles is a bad man. From now on, Jeeves, we must watch Harold like hawks."

"Undoubtedly, sir."

"Ceaseless vigilance, what?"

"Precisely, sir."

"You wouldn't care to sleep in his room, Jeeves?"

"No, sir, I should not."

"No, nor would I, if it comes to that. But dash it all," I said, "we're letting ourselves get rattled! We're losing our nerve. This won't do. How can Steggles possibly get at Harold, even if he wants to?"

There was no cheering young Bingo up. He's one of those birds who simply leap at the morbid view, if you give them half a chance.

"There are all sorts of ways of nobbling favourites," he said, in a sort of death-bed voice. "You ought to read some of these racing novels. In 'Pipped on the Post,' Lord Jasper Mauleverer as near as a toucher outed Bonny Betsy by bribing the head lad to slip a cobra into her stable the night before the Derby!"

"What are the chances of a cobra biting Harold, Jeeves?"

"Slight, I should imagine, sir. And in such an event, knowing the boy as intimately as I do, my anxiety would be entirely for the snake."

"Still, unceasing vigilance, Jeeves."

"Most certainly, sir."

* * * * *

I must say I got a bit fed with young Bingo in the next few days. It's all very well for a fellow with a big winner in his stable to exercise proper care, but in my opinion Bingo overdid it. The blighter's mind appeared to be absolutely saturated with racing fiction; and in stories of that kind, as far as I could make out, no horse is ever allowed to start in a race without at least a dozen attempts to put it out of action. He stuck to Harold like a plaster. Never let the unfortunate kid out of his sight. Of course, it meant a lot to the poor old egg if he could collect on this race, because it would give him enough money to chuck his tutoring job and get back to London; but all the same, he needn't have woken me up at three in the morning twice running—once to tell me we ought to cook Harold's food ourselves to prevent doping: the other time to say that he had heard mysterious noises in the shrubbery. But he reached the limit, in my opinion, when he insisted on my going to evening service on Sunday, the day before the sports.

"Why on earth?" I said, never being much of a lad for evensong.

"Well, I can't go myself. I shan't be here. I've got to go to London to-day with young Egbert." Egbert was Lord Wickhammersley's son, the one Bingo was tutoring. "He's going for a visit down in Kent, and I've got to see him off at Charing Cross. It's an infernal nuisance. I shan't be back till Monday afternoon. In fact, I shall miss most of the sports, I expect. Everything, therefore, depends on you, Bertie."

"But why should either of us go to evening service?"

"Ass! Harold sings in the choir, doesn't he?"

"What about it? I can't stop him dislocating his neck over a high note, if that's what you're afraid of."

"Fool! Steggles sings in the choir, too. There may be dirty work after the service."

"What absolute rot!"

"Is it?" said young Bingo. "Well, let me tell you that in 'Jenny, the Girl Jockey,' the villain kidnapped the boy who was to ride the favourite the night before the big race, and he was the only one who understood and could control the horse, and if the heroine hadn't dressed up in riding things and——"

"Oh, all right, all right. But, if there's any danger, it seems to me the simplest thing would be for Harold not to turn out on Sunday evening."

"He must turn out. You seem to think the infernal kid is a monument of rectitude, beloved by all. He's got the shakiest reputation of any kid in the village. His name is as near being mud as it can jolly well stick. He's played hookey from the choir so often that the vicar told him, if one more thing happened, he would fire him out. Nice chumps we should look if he was scratched the night before the race!"

Well, of course, that being so, there was nothing for it but to toddle along.

There's something about evening service in a country church that makes a fellow feel drowsy and peaceful. Sort of end-of-a-perfect-day feeling. Old Heppenstall was up in the pulpit, and he has a kind of regular, bleating delivery that assists thought. They had left the door open, and the air was full of a mixed scent of trees and honeysuckle and mildew and villagers' Sunday clothes. As far as the eye could reach, you could see farmers propped up in restful attitudes, breathing heavily; and the children in the congregation who had fidgeted during the earlier part of the proceedings were now lying back in a surfeited sort of coma. The last rays of the setting sun shone through the stained-glass windows, birds were twittering in the trees, the women's dresses crackled gently in the stillness. Peaceful. That's what I'm driving at. I felt peaceful. Everybody felt peaceful. And that is why the explosion, when it came, sounded like the end of all things.

I call it an explosion, because that was what it seemed like when it broke loose. One moment a dreamy hush was all over the place, broken only by old Heppenstall talking about our duty to our neighbours; and then, suddenly, a sort of piercing, shrieking squeal that got you right between the eyes and ran all the way down your spine and out at the soles of the feet.

"EE-ee-ee-ee-ee! Oo-ee! Ee-ee-ee-ee!"

It sounded like about six hundred pigs having their tails twisted simultaneously, but it was simply the kid Harold, who appeared to be having some species of fit. He was jumping up and down and slapping at the back of his neck. And about every other second he would take a deep breath and give out another of the squeals.

Well, I mean, you can't do that sort of thing in the middle of the sermon during evening service without exciting remark. The congregation came out of its trance with a jerk, and climbed on the pews to get a better view. Old Heppenstall stopped in the middle of a sentence and spun round. And a couple of vergers with great presence of mind bounded up the aisle like leopards, collected Harold, still squealing, and marched him out. They disappeared into the vestry, and I grabbed my hat and legged it round to the stage-door, full of apprehension and what not. I couldn't think what the deuce could have happened, but somewhere dimly behind the proceedings there seemed to me to lurk the hand of the blighter Steggles.

* * * * *

By the time I got there and managed to get someone to open the door, which was locked, the service seemed to be over. Old Heppenstall was standing in the middle of a crowd of choir-boys and vergers and sextons and what not, putting the wretched Harold through it with no little vim. I had come in at the tail-end of what must have been a fairly fruity oration.

"Wretched boy! How dare you——"

"I got a sensitive skin!"

"This is no time to talk about your skin——"

"Somebody put a beetle down my back!"

"Absurd!"

"I felt it wriggling——"

"Nonsense!"

"Sounds pretty thin, doesn't it?" said someone at my side.

It was Steggles, dash him. Clad in a snowy surplice or cassock, or whatever they call it, and wearing an expression of grave concern, the blighter had the cold, cynical crust to look me in the eyeball without a blink.

"Did you put a beetle down his neck?" I cried.

"Me!" said Steggles. "Me!"

Old Heppenstall was putting on the black cap.

"I do not credit a word of your story, wretched boy! I have warned you before, and now the time has come to act. You cease from this moment to be a member of my choir. Go, miserable child!"

Steggles plucked at my sleeve.

"In that case," he said, "those bets, you know—I'm afraid you lose your money, dear old boy. It's a pity you didn't put it on S.P. I always think S.P.'s the only safe way."

I gave him one look. Not a bit of good, of course.

"And they talk about the Purity of the Turf!" I said. And I meant it to sting, by Jove!

* * * * *

Jeeves received the news bravely, but I think the man was a bit rattled beneath the surface.

"An ingenious young gentleman, Mr. Steggles, sir."

"A bally swindler, you mean."

"Perhaps that would be a more exact description. However, these things will happen on the Turf, and it is useless to complain."

"I wish I had your sunny disposition, Jeeves!"

Jeeves bowed.

"We now rely, then, it would seem, sir, almost entirely on Mrs. Penworthy. Should she justify Mr. Little's encomiums and show real class in the Mothers' Sack Race, our gains will just balance our losses."

"Yes; but that's not much consolation when you've been looking forward to a big win."

"It is just possible that we may still find ourselves on the right side of the ledger after all, sir. Before Mr. Little left, I persuaded him to invest a small sum for the syndicate of which you were kind enough to make me a member, sir, on the Girls' Egg and Spoon Race."

"On Sarah Mills?"

"No, sir. On a long-priced outsider. Little Prudence Baxter, sir, the child of his lordship's head gardener. Her father assures me she has a very steady hand. She is accustomed to bring him his mug of beer from the cottage each afternoon, and he informs me she has never spilled a drop."

Well, that sounded as though young Prudence's control was good. But how about speed? With seasoned performers like Sarah Mills entered, the thing practically amounted to a classic race, and in these big events you must have speed.

"I am aware that it is what is termed a long shot, sir. Still, I thought it judicious."

"You backed her for a place, too, of course?"

"Yes, sir. Each way."

"Well, I suppose it's all right. I've never known you make a bloomer yet."

"Thank you very much, sir."

* * * * *

I'm bound to say that, as a general rule, my idea of a large afternoon would be to keep as far away from a village school-treat as possible. A sticky business. But with such grave issues toward, if you know what I mean, I sank my prejudices on this occasion and rolled up. I found the proceedings about as scaly as I had expected. It was a warm day, and the hall grounds were a dense, practically liquid mass of peasantry. Kids seethed to and fro. One of them, a small girl of sorts, grabbed my hand and hung on to it as I clove my way through the jam to where the Mothers' Sack Race was to finish. We hadn't been introduced, but she seemed to think I would do as well as anyone else to talk to about the rag-doll she had won in the Lucky Dip, and she rather spread herself on the topic.

"I'm going to call it Gertrude," she said. "And I shall undress it every night and put it to bed, and wake it up in the morning and dress it, and put it to bed at night, and wake it up next morning and dress it——"

"I say, old thing," I said, "I don't want to hurry you and all that, but you couldn't condense it a bit, could you? I'm rather anxious to see the finish of this race. The Wooster fortunes are by way of hanging on it."

"I'm going to run in a race soon," she said, shelving the doll for the nonce and descending to ordinary chit-chat.

"Yes?" I said. Distrait, if you know what I mean, and trying to peer through the chinks in the crowd. "What race is that?"

"Egg 'n Spoon."

"No, really? Are you Sarah Mills?"

"Na-ow!" Registering scorn. "I'm Prudence Baxter."

Naturally this put our relations on a different footing. I gazed at her with considerable interest. One of the stable. I must say she didn't look much of a flier. She was short and round. Bit out of condition, I thought.

"I say," I said, "that being so, you mustn't dash about in the hot sun and take the edge off yourself. You must conserve your energies, old friend. Sit down here in the shade."

"Don't want to sit down."

"Well, take it easy, anyhow."

The kid flitted to another topic like a butterfly hovering from flower to flower.

"I'm a good girl," she said.

"I bet you are. I hope you're a good egg-and-spoon racer, too."

"Harold's a bad boy. Harold squealed in church and isn't allowed to come to the treat. I'm glad," continued this ornament of her sex, wrinkling her nose virtuously, "because he's a bad boy. He pulled my hair Friday. Harold isn't coming to the treat! Harold isn't coming to the treat! Harold isn't coming to the treat!" she chanted, making a regular song of it.

"Don't rub it in, my dear old gardener's daughter," I pleaded. "You don't know it, but you've hit on rather a painful subject."

"Ah, Wooster, my dear fellow! So you have made friends with this little lady?"

It was old Heppenstall, beaming pretty profusely. Life and soul of the party.

"I am delighted, my dear Wooster," he went on, "quite delighted at the way you young men are throwing yourselves into the spirit of this little festivity of ours."

"Oh, yes?" I said.

"Oh, yes! Even Rupert Steggles. I must confess that my opinion of Rupert Steggles has materially altered for the better this afternoon."

Mine hadn't. But I didn't say so.

"I have always considered Rupert Steggles, between ourselves, a rather self-centred youth, by no means the kind who would put himself out to further the enjoyment of his fellows. And yet twice within the last half-hour I have observed him escorting Mrs. Penworthy, our worthy tobacconist's wife, to the refreshment-tent."

I left him standing. I shook off the clutching hand of the Baxter kid and hared it rapidly to the spot where the Mothers' Sack Race was just finishing. I had a horrid presentiment that there had been more dirty work at the cross-roads. The first person I ran into was young Bingo. I grabbed him by the arm.

"Who won?"

"I don't know. I didn't notice." There was bitterness in the chappie's voice. "It wasn't Mrs.

Penworthy, dash her! Bertie, that hound Steggles is nothing more nor less than one of our leading snakes. I don't know how he heard about her, but he must have got on to it that she was dangerous. Do you know what he did? He lured that miserable woman into the refreshment-tent five minutes before the race, and brought her out so weighed down with cake and tea that she blew up in the first twenty yards. Just rolled over and lay there! Well, thank goodness, we still have Harold!"

I gaped at the poor chump.

"Harold? Haven't you heard?"

"Heard?" Bingo turned a delicate green. "Heard what? I haven't heard anything. I only arrived five minutes ago. Came here straight from the station. What has happened? Tell me!"

I slipped him the information. He stared at me for a moment in a ghastly sort of way, then with a hollow groan tottered away and was lost in the crowd. A nasty knock, poor chap. I didn't blame him for being upset.

They were clearing the decks now for the Egg and Spoon Race, and I thought I might as well stay where I was and watch the finish. Not that I had much hope. Young Prudence was a good conversationalist, but she didn't seem to me to be the build for a winner.

As far as I could see through the mob, they got off to a good start. A short, red-haired child was making the running with a freckled blonde second, and Sarah Mills lying up an easy third. Our nominee was straggling along with the field, well behind the leaders. It was not hard even as early as this to spot the winner. There was a grace, a practised precision, in the way Sarah Mills held her spoon that told its own story. She was cutting out a good pace, but her egg didn't even wobble. A natural egg-and-spooner, if ever there was one.

Class will tell. Thirty yards from the tape, the red-haired kid tripped over her feet and shot her egg on to the turf. The freckled blonde fought gamely, but she had run herself out half-way down the straight, and Sarah Mills came past and home on a tight rein by several lengths, a popular winner. The blonde was second. A sniffing female in blue gingham beat a pie-faced kid in pink for the place-money, and Prudence Baxter, Jeeves's long shot, was either fifth or sixth, I couldn't see which.

And then I was carried along with the crowd to where old Heppenstall was going to present the prizes. I found myself standing next to the man Steggles.

"Hallo, old chap!" he said, very bright and cheery. "You've had a bad day, I'm afraid."

I looked at him with silent scorn. Lost on the blighter, of course.

"It's not been a good meeting for any of the big punters," he went on. "Poor old Bingo Little went down badly over that Egg and Spoon Race."

I hadn't been meaning to chat with the fellow, but I was startled.

"How do you mean badly?" I said. "We—he only had a small bet on."

"I don't know what you call small. He had thirty quid each way on the Baxter kid."

The landscape reeled before me.

"What!"

"Thirty quid at ten to one. I thought he must have heard something, but apparently not. The race went by the form-book all right."

I was trying to do sums in my head. I was just in the middle of working out the syndicate's losses, when old Heppenstall's voice came sort of faintly to me out of the distance. He had been pretty fatherly and debonair when ladling out the prizes for the other events, but now he had suddenly grown all pained and grieved. He peered sorrowfully at the multitude.

* * * * *

"With regard to the Girls' Egg and Spoon Race, which has just concluded," he said, "I have a painful duty to perform. Circumstances have arisen which it is impossible to ignore. It is not too much to say that I am stunned."

He gave the populace about five seconds to wonder why he was stunned, then went on.

"Three years ago, as you are aware, I was compelled to expunge from the list of events at this annual festival the Fathers' Quarter-Mile, owing to reports coming to my ears of wagers taken and given on the result at the village inn and a strong suspicion that on at least one occasion the race had actually been sold by the speediest runner. That unfortunate occurrence shook my faith in human nature, I admit—but still there was one event at least which I confidently expected to remain untainted by the miasma of professionalism. I allude to the Girls' Egg and Spoon Race. It seems, alas, that I was too sanguine."

He stopped again, and wrestled with his feelings.

"I will not weary you with the unpleasant details. I will merely say that before the race was run a stranger in our midst, the manservant of one of the guests at the Hall—I will not specify with more particularity—approached several of the competitors and presented each of them with five shillings on condition that they—er—finished. A belated sense of remorse has led him to confess to me what he did, but it is too late. The evil is accomplished, and retribution must take its course. It is no time for half-measures. I must be firm. I rule that Sarah Mills, Jane Parker, Bessie Clay, and Rosie Jukes, the first four to pass the winning-post, have forfeited their amateur status and are disqualified, and this handsome work-bag, presented by Lord Wickhammersley, goes, in consequence, to Prudence Baxter. Prudence, step forward!"

CHAPTER XV
THE METROPOLITAN TOUCH

Nobody is more alive than I am to the fact that young Bingo Little is in many respects a sound old egg. In one way and another he has made life pretty interesting for me at intervals ever since we were at school. As a companion for a cheery hour I think I would choose him before anybody. On the other hand, I'm bound to say that there are things about him that could be improved. His habit of falling in love with every second girl he sees is one of them; and another is his way of letting the world in on the secrets of his heart. If you want shrinking reticence, don't go to Bingo, because he's got about as much of it as a soap-advertisement.

I mean to say—well, here's the telegram I got from him one evening in November, about a month after I'd got back to town from my visit to Twing Hall:

I say Bertie old man I am in love at last. She is the most wonderful girl Bertie old man. This is the real thing at last Bertie. Come here at once and bring Jeeves. Oh I say you know that tobacco shop in Bond Street on the left side as you go up. Will you get me a hundred of their special cigarettes and send them to me here. I have run out. I know when you see her you will think she is the most wonderful girl. Mind you bring Jeeves. Don't forget the cigarettes.—Bingo.

It had been handed in at Twing Post Office. In other words, he had submitted that frightful rot to the goggling eye of a village post-mistress who was probably the main spring of local gossip and would have the place ringing with the news before nightfall. He couldn't have given himself away more completely if he had hired the town-crier. When I was a kid, I used to read stories about knights and vikings and that species of chappie who would get up without a blush in the middle of a crowded banquet and loose off a song about how perfectly priceless they thought their best girl. I've often felt that those days would have suited young Bingo down to the ground.

Jeeves had brought the thing in with the evening drink, and I slung it over to him.

"It's about due, of course," I said. "Young Bingo hasn't been in love for at least a couple of months. I wonder who it is this time?"

"Miss Mary Burgess, sir," said Jeeves, "the niece of the Reverend Mr. Heppenstall. She is staying at Twing Vicarage."

"Great Scott!" I knew that Jeeves knew practically everything in the world, but this sounded like second-sight. "How do you know that?"

"When we were visiting Twing Hall in the summer, sir, I formed a somewhat close friendship with Mr. Heppenstall's butler. He is good enough to keep me abreast of the local news from time to time. From his account, sir, the young lady appears to be a very estimable young lady. Of a somewhat serious nature, I understand. Mr. Little is very épris, sir. Brookfield, my correspondent, writes that last week he observed him in the moonlight at an advanced hour gazing up at his window."

"Whose window! Brookfield's?"

"Yes, sir. Presumably under the impression that it was the young lady's."

"But what the deuce is he doing at Twing at all?"

"Mr. Little was compelled to resume his old position as tutor to Lord Wickhammersley's son at Twing Hall, sir. Owing to having been unsuccessful in some speculations at Hurst Park at the end of October."

"Good Lord, Jeeves! Is there anything you don't know?"

"I could not say, sir."

I picked up the telegram.

"I suppose he wants us to go down and help him out a bit?"

"That would appear to be his motive in dispatching the message, sir."

"Well, what shall we do? Go?"

"I would advocate it, sir. If I may say so, I think that Mr. Little should be encouraged in this particular matter."

"You think he's picked a winner this time?"

"I hear nothing but excellent reports of the young lady, sir. I think it is beyond question that she would be an admirable influence for Mr. Little, should the affair come to a happy conclusion. Such a union would also, I fancy, go far to restore Mr. Little to the good graces of his uncle, the young lady being well connected and possessing private means. In short, sir, I think that if there is anything that we can do we should do it."

"Well, with you behind him," I said, "I don't see how he can fail to click."

"You are very good, sir," said Jeeves. "The tribute is much appreciated."

Bingo met us at Twing station next day, and insisted on my sending Jeeves on in the car with the bags while he and I walked. He started in about the female the moment we had begun to hoof it.

"She is very wonderful, Bertie. She is not one of these flippant, shallow-minded modern girls. She is sweetly grave and beautifully earnest. She reminds me of—what is the name I want?"

"Marie Lloyd?"

"Saint Cecilia," said young Bingo, eyeing me with a good deal of loathing. "She reminds me of Saint Cecilia. She makes me yearn to be a better, nobler, deeper, broader man."

"What beats me," I said, following up a train of thought, "is what principle you pick them on. The girls you fall in love with, I mean. I mean to say, what's your system? As far as I can see, no two of them are alike. First it was Mabel the waitress, then Honoria Glossop, then that fearful blister Charlotte Corday Rowbotham——"

I own that Bingo had the decency to shudder. Thinking of Charlotte always made me shudder, too.

"You don't seriously mean, Bertie, that you are intending to compare the feeling I have for Mary Burgess, the holy devotion, the spiritual——"

"Oh, all right, let it go," I said. "I say, old lad, aren't we going rather a long way round?"

Considering that we were supposed to be heading for Twing Hall, it seemed to me that we were making a longish job of it. The Hall is about two miles from the station by the main road, and we had cut off down a lane, gone across country for a bit, climbed a stile or two, and were now working our way across a field that ended in another lane.

"She sometimes takes her little brother for a walk round this way," explained Bingo. "I thought we would meet her and bow, and you could see her, you know, and then we would walk on."

"Of course," I said, "that's enough excitement for anyone, and undoubtedly a corking reward for tramping three miles out of one's way over ploughed fields with tight boots, but don't we do anything else? Don't we tack on to the girl and buzz along with her?"

"Good Lord!" said Bingo, honestly amazed. "You don't suppose I've got nerve enough for that, do you? I just look at her from afar off and all that sort of thing. Quick! Here she comes! No, I'm wrong!"

It was like that song of Harry Lauder's where he's waiting for the girl and says "This is her-r-r. No, it's a rabbut." Young Bingo made me stand there in the teeth of a nor'east half-gale for ten minutes, keeping me on my toes with a series of false alarms, and I was just thinking of suggesting that we should lay off and give the rest of the proceedings a miss, when round the corner there came a fox-terrier, and Bingo quivered like an aspen. Then there hove in sight a small boy, and he shook like a jelly. Finally, like a star whose entrance has been worked up by the personnel of the ensemble, a girl appeared, and his emotion was painful to witness. His face got so red that, what with his white collar and the fact that the wind had turned his nose blue, he looked more like a French flag than anything else. He sagged from the waist upwards, as if he had been filleted.

He was just raising his fingers limply to his cap when he suddenly saw that the girl wasn't alone. A chappie in clerical costume was also among those present, and the sight of him didn't seem to do Bingo a bit of good. His face got redder and his nose bluer, and it wasn't till they had nearly passed that he managed to get hold of his cap.

The girl bowed, the curate said, "Ah, Little. Rough weather," the dog barked, and then they toddled on and the entertainment was over.

* * * * *

The curate was a new factor in the situation to me. I reported his movements to Jeeves when I got to the hall. Of course, Jeeves knew all about it already.

"That is the Reverend Mr. Wingham, Mr. Heppenstall's new curate, sir. I gather from Brookfield that he is Mr. Little's rival, and at the moment the young lady appears to favour him. Mr. Wingham has the advantage of being on the premises. He and the young lady play duets after dinner, which acts as a bond. Mr. Little on these occasions, I understand, prowls about in the road, chafing visibly."

"That seems to be all the poor fish is able to do, dash it. He can chafe all right, but there he stops. He's lost his pep. He's got no dash. Why, when we met her just now, he hadn't even the common manly courage to say 'Good evening'!"

"I gather that Mr. Little's affection is not unmingled with awe, sir."

"Well, how are we to help a man when he's such a rabbit as that? Have you anything to suggest? I shall be seeing him after dinner, and he's sure to ask first thing what you advise."

"In my opinion, sir, the most judicious course for Mr. Little to pursue would be to concentrate on the young gentleman."

"The small brother? How do you mean?"

"Make a friend of him, sir—take him for walks and so forth."

"It doesn't sound one of your red-hottest ideas. I must say I expected something fruitier than that."

"It would be a beginning, sir, and might lead to better things."

"Well, I'll tell him. I liked the look of her, Jeeves."

"A thoroughly estimable young lady, sir."

I slipped Bingo the tip from the stable that night, and was glad to observe that it seemed to cheer him up.

"Jeeves is always right," he said. "I ought to have thought of it myself. I'll start in to-morrow."

It was amazing how the chappie bucked up. Long before I left for town it had become a mere commonplace for him to speak to the girl. I mean he didn't simply look stuffed when they met. The brother was forming a bond that was a dashed sight stronger than the curate's duets. She and Bingo used to take him for walks together. I asked Bingo what they talked about on these occasions, and he said Wilfred's future. The girl hoped that Wilfred would one day become a curate, but Bingo said no, there was something about curates he didn't quite like.

The day we left, Bingo came to see us off with Wilfred frisking about him like an old college chum. The last I saw of them, Bingo was standing him chocolates out of the slot-machine. A scene of peace and cheery good-will. Dashed promising, I thought.

* * * * *

Which made it all the more of a jar, about a fortnight later, when his telegram arrived. As follows:—

Bertie old man I say Bertie could you possibly come down here at once. Everything gone wrong hang it all. Dash it Bertie you simply must come. I am in a state of absolute despair and heart-broken. Would you mind sending another hundred of those cigarettes. Bring Jeeves when you come Bertie. You simply must come Bertie. I rely on you. Don't forget to bring Jeeves. Bingo.

For a chap who's perpetually hard-up, I must say that young Bingo is the most wasteful telegraphist I ever struck. He's got no notion of condensing. The silly ass simply pours out his wounded soul at twopence a word, or whatever it is, without a thought.

"How about it, Jeeves?" I said. "I'm getting a bit fed up. I can't go chucking all my engagements every second week in order to biff down to Twing and rally round young Bingo. Send him a wire telling him to end it all in the village pond."

"If you could spare me for the night, sir, I should be glad to run down and investigate."

"Oh, dash it! Well, I suppose there's nothing else to be done. After all, you're the fellow he wants. All right, carry on."

Jeeves got back late the next day.

"Well?" I said.

Jeeves appeared perturbed. He allowed his left eyebrow to flicker upwards in a concerned sort of manner.

"I have done what I could, sir," he said, "but I fear Mr. Little's chances do not appear bright. Since our last visit, sir, there has been a decidedly sinister and disquieting development."

"Oh, what's that?"

"You may remember Mr. Steggles, sir—the young gentleman who was studying for an examination with Mr. Heppenstall at the Vicarage?"

"What's Steggles got to do with it?" I asked.

"I gather from Brookfield, sir, who chanced to overhear a conversation, that Mr. Steggles is interesting himself in the affair."

"Good Lord! What, making a book on it?"

"I understand that he is accepting wagers from those in his immediate circle, sir. Against Mr. Little, whose chances he does not seem to fancy."

"I don't like that, Jeeves."

"No, sir. It is sinister."

"From what I know of Steggles there will be dirty work."

"It has already occurred, sir."

"Already?"

"Yes, sir. It seems that, in pursuance of the policy which he had been good enough to allow me to suggest to him, Mr. Little escorted Master Burgess to the church bazaar, and there met Mr. Steggles, who was in the company of young Master Heppenstall, the Reverend Mr. Heppenstall's second son, who is home from Rugby just now, having recently recovered from an attack of mumps. The encounter took place in the refreshment-room, where Mr. Steggles was at that moment entertaining Master Heppenstall. To cut a long story short, sir, the two gentlemen became extremely interested in the hearty manner in which the lads were fortifying themselves; and Mr. Steggles offered to back his nominee in a weight-for-age eating contest against Master Burgess for a pound a side. Mr. Little admitted to me that he was conscious of a certain hesitation as to what the upshot might be, should Miss Burgess get to hear of the matter, but his sporting blood was too much for him and he agreed to the contest. This was duly carried out, both lads exhibiting the utmost willingness and enthusiasm, and eventually Master Burgess justified Mr. Little's confidence by winning, but only after a bitter struggle. Next day both contestants were in considerable pain; inquiries were made and confessions extorted, and Mr. Little—I learn from Brookfield, who happened to be near the door of the drawing-room at the moment—had an extremely unpleasant interview with the young lady, which ended in her desiring him never to speak to her again."

There's no getting away from the fact that, if ever a man required watching, it's Steggles. Machiavelli could have taken his correspondence course.

"It was a put-up job, Jeeves!" I said. "I mean, Steggles worked the whole thing on purpose. It's his old nobbling game."

"There would seem to be no doubt about that, sir."

"Well, he seems to have dished poor old Bingo all right."

"That is the prevalent opinion, sir. Brookfield tells me that down in the village at the 'Cow and Horses' seven to one is being freely offered on Mr. Wingham and finding no takers."

"Good Lord! Are they betting about it down in the village, too?"

"Yes, sir. And in adjoining hamlets also. The affair has caused widespread interest. I am told that there is a certain sporting reaction in even so distant a spot as Lower Bingley."

"Well, I don't see what there is to do. If Bingo is such a chump——"

"One is fighting a losing battle, I fear, sir, but I did venture to indicate to Mr. Little a course of action which might prove of advantage. I recommended him to busy himself with good works."

"Good works?"

"About the village, sir. Reading to the bedridden—chatting with the sick—that sort of thing, sir. We can but trust that good results will ensue."

"Yes, I suppose so," I said doubtfully. "But, by gosh, if I was a sick man I'd hate to have a looney like young Bingo coming and gibbering at my bedside."

"There is that aspect of the matter, sir," said Jeeves.

* * * * *

I didn't hear a word from Bingo for a couple of weeks, and I took it after a while that he had found the going too hard and had chucked in the towel. And then, one night not long before Christmas, I came back to the flat pretty latish, having been out dancing at the Embassy. I was fairly tired, having swung a practically non-stop shoe from shortly after dinner till two a.m., and bed seemed to be indicated. Judge of my chagrin and all that sort of thing, therefore, when, tottering to my room and switching on the light, I observed the foul features of young Bingo all over the pillow. The blighter had appeared from nowhere and was in my bed, sleeping like an infant with a sort of happy, dreamy smile on his map.

A bit thick I mean to say! We Woosters are all for the good old mediæval hosp. and all that, but when it comes to finding chappies collaring your bed, the thing becomes a trifle too mouldy. I hove a shoe, and Bingo sat up, gurgling.

"'s matter? 's matter?" said young Bingo.

"What the deuce are you doing in my bed?" I said.

"Oh, hallo, Bertie! So there you are!"

"Yes, here I am. What are you doing in my bed?"

"I came up to town for the night on business."

"Yes, but what are you doing in my bed?"

"Dash it all, Bertie," said young Bingo querulously, "don't keep harping on your beastly bed. There's another made up in the spare room. I saw Jeeves make it with my own eyes. I believe he meant it for me, but I knew what a perfect host you were, so I just turned in here. I say, Bertie, old man," said Bingo, apparently fed up with the discussion about sleeping-quarters, "I see daylight."

"Well, it's getting on for three in the morning."

"I was speaking figuratively, you ass. I meant that hope has begun to dawn. About Mary Burgess, you know. Sit down and I'll tell you all about it."

"I won't. I'm going to sleep."

"To begin with," said young Bingo, settling himself comfortably against the pillows and helping himself to a cigarette from my special private box, "I must once again pay a marked tribute to good old Jeeves. A modern Solomon. I was badly up against it when I came to him for advice, but he rolled up with a tip which has put me—I use the term advisedly and in a conservative spirit—on velvet. He may have told you that he recommended me to win back the lost ground by busying myself with good works? Bertie, old man," said young Bingo earnestly, "for the last two weeks I've been comforting the sick to such an extent that, if I had a brother and you brought him to me on a sick-bed at this moment, by Jove, old man, I'd heave a brick at him. However, though it took it out of me like the deuce, the scheme worked splendidly. She softened visibly before I'd been at it a week. Started to bow again when we met in the street, and so forth. About a couple of days ago she distinctly smiled—in a sort of faint, saint-like kind of way, you know—when I ran into her outside the Vicarage. And yesterday—I say, you remember that curate chap, Wingham? Fellow with a long nose."

"Of course I remember him. Your rival."

"Rival?" Bingo raised his eyebrows. "Oh, well, I suppose you could have called him that at one time. Though it sounds a little far-fetched."

"Does it?" I said, stung by the sickening complacency of the chump's manner. "Well, let me tell you that the last I heard was that at the 'Cow and Horses' in Twing village and all over the place as far as Lower Bingley they were offering seven to one on the curate and finding no takers."

Bingo started violently, and sprayed cigarette-ash all over my bed.

"Betting!" he gargled. "Betting! You don't mean that they're betting on this holy, sacred—— Oh, I say, dash it all! Haven't people any sense of decency and reverence? Is nothing safe from their beastly, sordid graspingness? I wonder," said young Bingo thoughtfully, "if there's a chance of my getting any of that seven-to-one money? Seven to one! What a price! Who's offering it, do you know? Oh, well, I suppose it wouldn't do. No, I suppose it wouldn't be quite the thing."

"You seem dashed confident," I said. "I'd always thought that Wingham——"

"Oh, I'm not worried about him," said Bingo. "I was just going to tell you. Wingham's got the mumps, and won't be out and about for weeks. And, jolly as that is in itself, it's not all. You see, he was producing the Village School Christmas Entertainment, and now I've taken over the job. I went to old Heppenstall last night and clinched the contract. Well, you see what that means. It means that I shall be absolutely the centre of the village life and thought for three solid weeks, with a terrific triumph to wind up with. Everybody looking up to me and fawning on me, don't you see, and all that. It's bound to have a powerful effect on Mary's mind. It will show her that I am capable of serious effort; that there is a solid foundation of worth in me; that, mere butterfly as she may once have thought me, I am in reality——"

"Oh, all right, let it go!"

"It's a big thing, you know, this Christmas Entertainment. Old Heppenstall is very much wrapped up in it. Nibs from all over the countryside rolling up. The Squire present, with family. A big chance for me, Bertie, my boy, and I mean to make the most of it. Of course, I'm handicapped a bit by not having been in on the thing from the start. Will you credit it that that uninspired doughnut of a curate wanted to give the public some rotten little fairy play out of a book for children published about fifty years ago without one good laugh or the semblance of a gag in it? It's too late to alter the thing entirely, but at least I can jazz it up. I'm going to write them in something zippy to brighten the thing up a bit."

"You can't write."

"Well, when I say write, I mean pinch. That's why I've popped up to town. I've been to see that revue, 'Cuddle Up!' at the Palladium, to-night. Full of good stuff. Of course, it's rather hard to get anything in the nature of a big spectacular effect in the Twing Village Hall, with no scenery to speak of and a chorus of practically imbecile kids of ages ranging from nine to fourteen, but I think I see my way. Have you seen 'Cuddle Up'?"

"Yes. Twice."

"Well, there's some good stuff in the first act, and I can lift practically all the numbers. Then there's that show at the Palace. I can see the matinée of that to-morrow before I leave. There's sure to be some decent bits in that. Don't you worry about my not being able to write a hit. Leave it to me, laddie, leave it to me. And now, my dear old chap," said young Bingo, snuggling down cosily, "you mustn't keep me up talking all night. It's all right for you fellows who have nothing to do, but I'm a busy man. Good night, old thing. Close the door quietly after you and switch out the light. Breakfast about ten to-morrow, I suppose, what? Right-o. Good night."

* * * * *

For the next three weeks I didn't see Bingo. He became a sort of Voice Heard Off, developing a habit of ringing me up on long-distance and consulting me on various points arising at rehearsal, until the day when he got me out of bed at eight in the morning to ask whether I thought "Merry Christmas!" was a good title. I told him then that this nuisance must now cease, and after that he cheesed it, and practically passed out of my life, till one afternoon when I got back to the flat to dress for dinner and found Jeeves inspecting a whacking big poster sort of thing which he had draped over the back of an arm-chair.

"Good Lord, Jeeves!" I said. I was feeling rather weak that day, and the thing shook me. "What on earth's that?"

"Mr. Little sent it to me, sir, and desired me to bring it to your notice."

"Well, you've certainly done it!"

I took another look at the object. There was no doubt about it, he caught the eye. It was about seven feet long, and most of the lettering in about as bright red ink as I ever struck.

This was how it ran:

TWING VILLAGE HALL,

Friday, December 23rd,

RICHARD LITTLE

presents

A New and Original Revue

Entitled

WHAT HO, TWING!!

Book by

RICHARD LITTLE

Lyrics by

RICHARD LITTLE

Music by

RICHARD LITTLE.

With the Full Twing Juvenile

Company and Chorus.

Scenic Effects by

RICHARD LITTLE

Produced by

RICHARD LITTLE.

"What do you make of it, Jeeves?" I said.

"I confess I am a little doubtful, sir. I think Mr. Little would have done better to follow my advice and confine himself to good works about the village."

"You think the things will be a frost?"

"I could not hazard a conjecture, sir. But my experience has been that what pleases the London public is not always so acceptable to the rural mind. The metropolitan touch sometimes proves a trifle too exotic for the provinces."

"I suppose I ought to go down and see the dashed thing?"

"I think Mr. Little would be wounded were you not present, sir."

* * * * *

The Village Hall at Twing is a smallish building, smelling of apples. It was full when I turned up on the evening of the twenty-third, for I had purposely timed myself to arrive not long before the kick-off. I had had experience of one or two of these binges, and didn't want to run any risk of coming early and finding myself shoved into a seat in one of the front rows where I wouldn't be able to execute a quiet sneak into the open air half-way through the proceedings, if the occasion seemed to demand it. I secured a nice strategic position near the door at the back of the hall.

From where I stood I had a good view of the audience. As always on these occasions, the first few rows were occupied by the Nibs—consisting of the Squire, a fairly mauve old sportsman with white whiskers, his family, a platoon of local parsons and perhaps a couple of dozen of prominent pew-holders. Then came a dense squash of what you might call the lower middle classes. And at the back, where I was, we came down with a jerk in the social scale, this end of the hall being given up almost entirely to a collection of frankly Tough Eggs, who had rolled up not so much for any love of the drama as because there was a free tea after the show. Take it for all in all, a representative gathering of Twing life and thought. The Nibs were whispering in a pleased manner to each other, the Lower Middles were sitting up very straight, as if they'd been bleached, and the Tough Eggs whiled away the time by cracking nuts and exchanging low rustic wheezes. The girl, Mary Burgess, was at the piano playing a waltz. Beside her stood the curate, Wingham, apparently recovered. The temperature, I should think, was about a hundred and twenty-seven.

Somebody jabbed me heartily in the lower ribs, and I perceived the man Steggles.

"Hallo!" he said. "I didn't know you were coming down."

I didn't like the chap, but we Woosters can wear the mask. I beamed a bit.

"Oh, yes," I said. "Bingo wanted me to roll up and see his show."

"I hear he's giving us something pretty ambitious," said the man Steggles. "Big effects and all that sort of thing."

"I believe so."

"Of course, it means a lot to him, doesn't it? He's told you about the girl, of course?"

"Yes. And I hear you're laying seven to one against him," I said, eyeing the blighter a trifle austerely.

He didn't even quiver.

"Just a little flutter to relieve the monotony of country life," he said. "But you've got the facts a bit wrong. It's down in the village that they're laying seven to one. I can do you better than that, if you feel in a speculative mood. How about a tenner at a hundred to eight?"

"Good Lord! Are you giving that?"

"Yes. Somehow," said Steggles meditatively, "I have a sort of feeling, a kind of premonition that something's going to go wrong to-night. You know what Little is. A bungler, if ever there was one. Something tells me that this show of his is going to be a frost. And if it is, of course, I should think it would prejudice the girl against him pretty badly. His standing always was rather shaky."

"Are you going to try and smash up the show?" I said sternly.

"Me!" said Steggles. "Why, what could I do? Half a minute, I want to go and speak to a man."

He buzzed off, leaving me distinctly disturbed. I could see from the fellow's eye that he was meditating some of his customary rough stuff, and I thought Bingo ought to be warned. But there wasn't time and I couldn't get at him. Almost immediately after Steggles had left me the curtain went up.

Except as a prompter, Bingo wasn't much in evidence in the early part of the performance. The thing at the outset was merely one of those weird dramas which you dig out of books published around Christmas time and entitled "Twelve Little Plays for the Tots," or something like that. The kids drooled on in the usual manner, the booming voice of Bingo ringing out from time to time behind the scenes when the fatheads forgot their lines; and the audience was settling down into the sort of torpor usual on these occasions, when the first of Bingo's interpolated bits occurred. It was that number which What's-her-name sings in that revue at the Palace—you would recognise the tune if I hummed it, but I can never get hold of the dashed thing. It always got three encores at the Palace, and it went well now, even with a squeaky-voiced child jumping on and off the key like a chamois of the Alps leaping from crag to crag. Even the Tough Eggs liked it. At the end of the second refrain the entire house was shouting for an encore, and the kid with the voice like a slate-pencil took a deep breath and started to let it go once more.

At this point all the lights went out.

*　　*　　*　　*　　*

I don't know when I've had anything so sudden and devastating happen to me before. They didn't flicker. They just went out. The hall was in complete darkness.

Well, of course, that sort of broke the spell, as you might put it. People started to shout directions, and the Tough Eggs stamped their feet and settled down for a pleasant time. And, of course, young Bingo had to make an ass of himself. His voice suddenly shot at us out of the darkness.

"Ladies and gentlemen, something has gone wrong with the lights——"

The Tough Eggs were tickled by this bit of information straight from the stable. They took it up as a sort of battle-cry. Then, after about five minutes, the lights went up again, and the show was resumed.

It took ten minutes after that to get the audience back into its state of coma, but eventually they began to settle down, and everything was going nicely when a small boy with a face like a turbot edged out in front of the curtain, which had been lowered after a pretty painful scene about a wishing-ring or a fairy's curse or something of that sort, and started to sing that song of George Thingummy's out of "Cuddle Up." You know the one I mean. "Always Listen to Mother, Girls!" it's called, and he gets the audience to join in and sing the refrain. Quite a ripeish ballad, and one which I myself have frequently sung in my bath with not a little vim; but by no means—as anyone but a perfect sapheaded prune like young Bingo would have known—by no means the sort of thing for a children's Christmas entertainment in the old village hall. Right from the start of the first refrain the bulk of the audience had begun to stiffen in their seats and fan themselves, and the Burgess girl at the piano was accompanying in a stunned, mechanical sort of way, while the curate at her side averted his gaze in a pained manner. The Tough Eggs, however, were all for it.

At the end of the second refrain the kid stopped and began to sidle towards the wings. Upon which the following brief duologue took place:

YOUNG BINGO (Voice heard off, ringing against the rafters): "Go on!"

THE KID (coyly): "I don't like to."

YOUNG BINGO (still louder): "Go on, you little blighter, or I'll slay you!"

I suppose the kid thought it over swiftly and realised that Bingo, being in a position to get at him, had better be conciliated, whatever the harvest might be; for he shuffled down to the front and, having shut his eyes and giggled hysterically, said: "Ladies and gentlemen, I will now call upon Squire Tressidder to oblige by singing the refrain!"

You know, with the most charitable feelings towards him, there are moments when you can't help thinking that young Bingo ought to be in some sort of a home. I suppose, poor fish, he had pictured this as the big punch of the evening. He had imagined, I take it, that the Squire would spring jovially to his feet, rip the song off his chest, and all would be gaiety and mirth. Well, what happened was simply that old Tressidder—and, mark you, I'm not blaming him—just sat where he was, swelling and turning a brighter purple every second. The lower middle classes remained in frozen silence, waiting for the roof to fall. The only section of the audience that really seemed to enjoy the idea was the Tough Eggs, who yelled with enthusiasm. It was jam for the Tough Eggs.

And then the lights went out again.

*   *   *   *   *

When they went up, some minutes later, they disclosed the Squire marching stiffly out at the head of his family, fed up to the eyebrows; the Burgess girl at the piano with a pale, set look; and the curate gazing at her with something in his expression that seemed to suggest that, although all this was no doubt deplorable, he had spotted the silver lining.

The show went on once more. There were great chunks of Plays-for-the-Tots dialogue, and then the girl at the piano struck up the prelude to that Orange-Girl number that's the big hit of the Palace revue. I took it that this was to be Bingo's smashing act one finale. The entire company was on the stage, and a clutching hand had appeared round the edge of the curtain, ready to pull at the right moment. It looked like the finale all right. It wasn't long before I realised that it was something more. It was the finish.

I take it you know that Orange number at the Palace? It goes:

Oh, won't you something something oranges,

   My something oranges,

   My something oranges;

Oh, won't you something something something I forget,

Something something something tumty tumty yet:

Oh——

or words to that effect. It's a dashed clever lyric, and the tune's good, too; but the thing that made the number was the business where the girls take oranges out of their baskets, you know, and toss them lightly to the audience. I don't know if you've ever noticed it, but it always seems to tickle an audience to bits when they get things thrown at them from the stage. Every time I've been to the Palace the customers have simply gone wild over this number.

But at the Palace, of course, the oranges are made of yellow wool, and the girls don't so much chuck them as drop them limply into the first and second rows. I began to gather that the business was going to be treated rather differently to-night when a dashed great chunk of pips and mildew sailed past my ear and burst on the wall behind me. Another landed with a squelch on the neck of one of the Nibs in the third row. And then a third took me right on the tip of the nose, and I kind of lost interest in the proceedings for awhile.

When I had scrubbed my face and got my eye to stop watering for a moment, I saw that the evening's entertainment had begun to resemble one of Belfast's livelier nights. The air was thick with shrieks and fruit. The kids on the stage, with Bingo buzzing distractedly to and fro in their midst, were having the time of their lives. I suppose they realised that this couldn't go on for ever, and were making the most of their chances. The Tough Eggs had begun to pick up all the oranges that hadn't burst and were shooting them back, so that the audience got it both coming and going. In fact, take it all round, there was a certain amount of confusion; and, just as things had begun really to hot up, out went the lights again.

It seemed to me about my time for leaving, so I slid for the door. I was hardly outside when the audience began to stream out. They surged about me in twos and threes, and I've never seen a public body so dashed unanimous on any point. To a man—and to a woman—they were cursing poor old Bingo; and there was a large and rapidly growing school of thought which held that the best thing to do would be to waylay him as he emerged and splash him about in the village pond a bit.

There were such a dickens of a lot of these enthusiasts and they looked so jolly determined that it seemed to me that the only matey thing to do was to go behind and warn young Bingo to turn his coat-collar up and breeze off snakily by some side exit. I went behind, and found him sitting on a box in the wings, perspiring pretty freely and looking more or less like the spot marked with a cross where the accident happened. His hair was standing up and his ears were hanging down, and one harsh word would undoubtedly have made him burst into tears.

"Bertie," he said hollowly, as he saw me, "it was that blighter Steggles! I caught one of the kids before he could get away and got it all out of him. Steggles substituted real oranges for the balls of wool which with infinite sweat and at a cost of nearly a quid I had specially prepared. Well, I will now proceed to tear him limb from limb. It'll be something to do."

I hated to spoil his day-dreams, but it had to be.

"Good heavens, man," I said, "you haven't time for frivolous amusements now. You've got to get out. And quick!"

"Bertie," said Bingo in a dull voice, "she was here just now. She said it was all my fault and that she would never speak to me again. She said she had always suspected me of being a heartless practical joker, and now she knew. She said—— Oh, well, she ticked me off properly."

"That's the least of your troubles," I said. It seemed impossible to rouse the poor zib to a sense of his position. "Do you realise that about two hundred of Twing's heftiest are waiting for you outside to chuck you into the pond?"

"No!"

"Absolutely!"

For a moment the poor chap seemed crushed. But only for a moment. There has always been something of the good old English bulldog breed about Bingo. A strange, sweet smile flickered for an instant over his face.

"It's all right," he said. "I can sneak out through the cellar and climb over the wall at the back. They can't intimidate me!"

* * * * *

It couldn't have been more than a week later when Jeeves, after he had brought me my tea, gently steered me away from the sporting page of the Morning Post and directed my attention to an announcement in the engagements and marriages column.

It was a brief statement that a marriage had been arranged and would shortly take place between the Hon. and Rev. Hubert Wingham, third son of the Right Hon. the Earl of Sturridge, and Mary, only daughter of the late Matthew Burgess, of Weatherly Court, Hants.

"Of course," I said, after I had given it the east-to-west, "I expected this, Jeeves."

"Yes, sir."

"She would never forgive him what happened that night."

"No, sir."

"Well," I said, as I took a sip of the fragrant and steaming, "I don't suppose it will take old Bingo long to get over it. It's about the hundred and eleventh time this sort of thing has happened to him. You're the man I'm sorry for."

"Me, sir?"

"Well, dash it all, you can't have forgotten what a deuce of a lot of trouble you took to bring the thing off for Bingo. It's too bad that all your work should have been wasted."

"Not entirely wasted, sir."

"Eh?"

"It is true that my efforts to bring about the match between Mr. Little and the young lady were not successful, but still I look back upon the matter with a certain satisfaction."

"Because you did your best, you mean?"

"Not entirely, sir, though of course that thought also gives me pleasure. I was alluding more particularly to the fact that I found the affair financially remunerative."

"Financially remunerative? What do you mean?"

"When I learned that Mr. Steggles had interested himself in the contest, sir, I went shares with my friend Brookfield and bought the book which had been made on the issue by the 'Cow and Horses.' It has proved a highly profitable investment. Your breakfast will be ready almost immediately, sir. Kidneys on toast and mushrooms. I will bring it when you ring."

CHAPTER XVI
THE DELAYED EXIT OF CLAUDE AND EUSTACE

The feeling I had when Aunt Agatha trapped me in my lair that morning and spilled the bad news was that my luck had broken at last. As a rule, you see, I'm not lugged into Family Rows. On the occasions when Aunt is calling to Aunt like mastodons bellowing across primeval swamps and Uncle James's letter about Cousin Mabel's peculiar behaviour is being shot round the family circle ("Please read this carefully and send it on to Jane"), the clan has a tendency to ignore me. It's one of the advantages I get from being a bachelor—and, according to my nearest and dearest, practically a half-witted bachelor at that. "It's no good trying to get Bertie to take the slightest interest" is more or less the slogan, and I'm bound to say I'm all for it. A quiet life is what I like. And that's why I felt that the Curse had come upon me, so to speak, when Aunt Agatha sailed into my sitting-room while I was having a placid cigarette and started to tell me about Claude and Eustace.

"Thank goodness," said Aunt Agatha, "arrangements have at last been made about Eustace and Claude."

"Arrangements?" I said, not having the foggiest.

"They sail on Friday for South Africa. Mr. Van Alstyne, a friend of poor Emily's, has given them berths in his firm at Johannesburg, and we are hoping that they will settle down there and do well."

I didn't get the thing at all.

"Friday? The day after to-morrow, do you mean?"

"Yes."

"For South Africa?"

"Yes. They leave on the Edinburgh Castle."

"But what's the idea? I mean, aren't they in the middle of their term at Oxford?"

Aunt Agatha looked at me coldly.

"Do you positively mean to tell me, Bertie, that you take so little interest in the affairs of your nearest relatives that you are not aware that Claude and Eustace were expelled from Oxford over a fortnight ago?"

"No, really?"

"You are hopeless, Bertie. I should have thought that even you——"

"Why were they sent down?"

"They poured lemonade on the Junior Dean of their college.... I see nothing amusing in the outrage, Bertie."

"No, no, rather not," I said hurriedly. "I wasn't laughing. Choking. Got something stuck in my throat, you know."

"Poor Emily," went on Aunt Agatha, "being one of those doting mothers who are the ruin of their children, wished to keep the boys in London. She suggested that they might cram for the Army. But I was firm. The Colonies are the only place for wild youths like Eustace and Claude. So they sail on Friday. They have been staying for the last two weeks with your Uncle Clive in Worcestershire. They will spend to-morrow night in London and catch the boat-train on Friday morning."

"Bit risky, isn't it? I mean, aren't they apt to cut loose a bit to-morrow night if they're left all alone in London?"

"They will not be alone. They will be in your charge."

"Mine!"

"Yes. I wish you to put them up in your flat for the night, and see that they do not miss the train in the morning."

"Oh, I say, no!"

"Bertie!"

"Well, I mean, quite jolly coves both of them, but I don't know. They're rather nuts, you know—— Always glad to see them, of course, but when it comes to putting them up for the night——"

"Bertie, if you are so sunk in callous self-indulgence that you cannot even put yourself to this trifling inconvenience for the sake of——"

"Oh, all right," I said. "All right."

It was no good arguing, of course. Aunt Agatha always makes me feel as if I had gelatine where my spine ought to be. She's one of those forceful females. I should think Queen Elizabeth must have been something like her. When she holds me with her glittering eye and says, "Jump to it, my lad," or words to that effect, I make it so without further discussion.

When she had gone, I rang for Jeeves to break the news to him.

"Oh, Jeeves," I said, "Mr. Claude and Mr. Eustace will be staying here to-morrow night."

"Very good, sir."

"I'm glad you think so. To me the outlook seems black and scaly. You know what those two lads are!"

"Very high-spirited young gentlemen, sir."

"Blisters, Jeeves. Undeniable blisters. It's a bit thick!"

"Would there be anything further, sir?"

At that, I'm bound to say, I drew myself up a trifle haughtily. We Woosters freeze like the dickens when we seek sympathy and meet with cold reserve. I knew what was up, of course. For the last day or so there had been a certain amount of coolness in the home over a pair of jazz spats which I had dug up while exploring in the Burlington Arcade. Some dashed brainy cove, probably the chap who invented those coloured cigarette-cases, had recently had the rather topping idea of putting out a line of spats on the same system. I mean to say, instead of the ordinary grey and white, you can now get them in your regimental or school colours. And, believe me, it would have taken a chappie of stronger fibre than I am to resist the pair of Old Etonian spats which had smiled up at me from inside the window. I was inside the shop, opening negotiations, before it had even occurred to me that Jeeves might not approve. And I must say he had taken the thing a bit hardly. The fact of the matter is, Jeeves, though in many ways the best valet in London, is too conservative. Hide-bound, if you know what I mean, and an enemy to Progress.

"Nothing further, Jeeves," I said, with quiet dignity.

"Very good, sir."

He gave one frosty look at the spats and biffed off. Dash him!

* * * * *

Anything merrier and brighter than the Twins, when they curveted into the old flat while I was dressing for dinner the next night, I have never struck in my whole puff. I'm only about half a dozen years older than Claude and Eustace, but in some rummy manner they always make me feel as if I were well on in the grandfather class and just waiting for the end. Almost before I realised they were in the place, they had collared the best chairs, pinched a couple of my special cigarettes, poured themselves out a whisky-and-soda apiece, and started to prattle with the gaiety and abandon of two birds who had achieved their life's ambition instead of having come a most frightful purler and being under sentence of exile.

"Hallo, Bertie, old thing," said Claude. "Jolly decent of you to put us up."

"Oh, no," I said. "Only wish you were staying a good long time."

"Hear that, Eustace? He wishes we were staying a good long time."

"I expect it will seem a good long time," said Eustace, philosophically.

"You heard about the binge, Bertie? Our little bit of trouble, I mean?"

"Oh, yes. Aunt Agatha was telling me."

"We leave our country for our country's good," said Eustace.

"And let there be no moaning at the bar," said Claude, "when I put out to sea. What did Aunt Agatha tell you?"

"She said you poured lemonade on the Junior Dean."

"I wish the deuce," said Claude, annoyed, "that people would get these things right. It wasn't the Junior Dean. It was the Senior Tutor."

"And it wasn't lemonade," said Eustace. "It was soda-water. The dear old thing happened to be standing just under our window while I was leaning out with a siphon in my hand. He looked up, and—well, it would have been chucking away the opportunity of a lifetime if I hadn't let him have it in the eyeball."

"Simply chucking it away," agreed Claude.

"Might never have occurred again," said Eustace.

"Hundred to one against it," said Claude.

"Now what," said Eustace, "do you propose to do, Bertie, in the way of entertaining the handsome guests to-night?"

"My idea was to have a bite of dinner in the flat," I said. "Jeeves is getting it ready now."

"And afterwards?"

"Well, I thought we might chat of this and that, and then it struck me that you would probably like to turn in early, as your train goes about ten or something, doesn't it?"

The twins looked at each other in a pitying sort of way.

"Bertie," said Eustace, "you've got the programme nearly right, but not quite. I envisage the evening's events thus: We will toddle along to Ciro's after dinner. It's an extension night, isn't it? Well, that will see us through till about two-thirty or three."

"After which, no doubt," said Claude, "the Lord will provide."

"But I thought you would want to get a good night's rest."

"Good night's rest!" said Eustace. "My dear old chap, you don't for a moment imagine that we are dreaming of going to bed to-night, do you?"

I suppose the fact of the matter is, I'm not the man I was. I mean, these all-night vigils don't seem to fascinate me as they used to a few years ago. I can remember the time, when I was up at Oxford, when a Covent Garden ball till six in the morning, with breakfast at the Hammams and probably a free fight with a few selected costermongers to follow, seemed to me what the doctor ordered. But nowadays two o'clock is about my limit; and by two o'clock the twins were just settling down and beginning to go nicely.

As far as I can remember, we went on from Ciro's to play chemmy with some fellows I don't recall having met before, and it must have been about nine in the morning when we fetched up again at the flat. By which time, I'm bound to admit, as far as I was concerned the first careless freshness was beginning to wear off a bit. In fact, I'd got just enough strength to say good-bye to the twins, wish them a pleasant voyage and a happy and successful career in South Africa, and stagger into bed. The last I remember was hearing the blighters chanting like larks under the cold shower, breaking off from time to time to shout to Jeeves to rush along the eggs and bacon.

It must have been about one in the afternoon when I woke. I was feeling more or less like something the Pure Food Committee had rejected, but there was one bright thought which cheered me up, and that was that about now the twins would be leaning on the rail of the liner, taking their last glimpse of the dear old homeland. Which made it all the more of a shock when the door opened and Claude walked in.

"Hallo, Bertie!" said Claude. "Had a nice refreshing sleep? Now, what about a good old bite of lunch?"

I'd been having so many distorted nightmares since I had dropped off to sleep that for half a minute I thought this was simply one more of them, and the worst of the lot. It was only when Claude sat down on my feet that I got on to the fact that this was stern reality.

"Great Scott! What on earth are you doing here?" I gurgled.

Claude looked at me reproachfully.

"Hardly the tone I like to hear in a host, Bertie," he said reprovingly. "Why, it was only last night that you were saying you wished I was stopping a good long time. Your dream has come true. I am!"

"But why aren't you on your way to South Africa?"

"Now that," said Claude, "is a point I rather thought you would want to have explained. It's like this, old man. You remember that girl you introduced me to at Ciro's last night?"

"Which girl?"

"There was only one," said Claude coldly. "Only one that counted, that is to say. Her name was Marion Wardour. I danced with her a good deal, if you remember."

I began to recollect in a hazy sort of way. Marion Wardour has been a pal of mine for some time. A very good sort. She's playing in that show at the Apollo at the moment. I remembered now that she had been at Ciro's with a party the night before, and the twins had insisted on being introduced.

"We are soul-mates, Bertie," said Claude. "I found it out quite early in the p.m., and the more thought I've given to the matter the more convinced I've become. It happens like that now and then, you know. Two hearts that beat as one, I mean, and all that sort of thing. So the long and the short of it is that I gave old Eustace the slip at Waterloo and slid back here. The idea of going to South Africa and leaving a girl like that in England doesn't appeal to me a bit. I'm all for thinking imperially and giving the Colonies a leg-up and all that sort of thing; but it can't be done. After all," said Claude reasonably, "South Africa has got along all right without me up till now, so why shouldn't it stick it?"

"But what about Van Alstyne, or whatever his name is? He'll be expecting you to turn up."

"Oh, he'll have Eustace. That'll satisfy him. Very sound fellow, Eustace. Probably end up by being a magnate of some kind. I shall watch his future progress with considerable interest. And now you must excuse me for a moment, Bertie. I want to go and hunt up Jeeves and get him to mix me one of those pick-me-ups of his. For some reason which I can't explain, I've got a slight headache this morning."

And, believe me or believe me not, the door had hardly closed behind him when in blew Eustace with a shining morning face that made me ill to look at.

"Oh, my aunt!" I said.

Eustace started to giggle pretty freely.

"Smooth work, Bertie, smooth work!" he said. "I'm sorry for poor old Claude, but there was no alternative. I eluded his vigilance at Waterloo and snaked off in a taxi. I suppose the poor old ass is wondering where the deuce I've got to. But it couldn't be helped. If you really seriously expected me to go slogging off to South Africa, you shouldn't have introduced me to Miss Wardour last night. I want to tell you all about that, Bertie. I'm not a man," said Eustace, sitting down on the bed, "who falls in love with every girl he sees. I suppose 'strong, silent,' would be the best description you could find for me. But when I do meet my affinity I don't waste time. I——"

"Oh, heaven! Are you in love with Marion Wardour, too?"

"Too? What do you mean, 'too'?"

I was going to tell him about Claude, when the blighter came in in person, looking like a giant refreshed. There's no doubt that Jeeves's pick-me-ups will produce immediate results in anything short of an Egyptian mummy. It's something he puts in them—the Worcester sauce or something. Claude had revived like a watered flower, but he nearly had a relapse when he saw his bally brother goggling at him over the bed-rail.

"What on earth are you doing here?" he said.

"What on earth are you doing here?" said Eustace.

"Have you come back to inflict your beastly society upon Miss Wardour?"

"Is that why you've come back?"

They thrashed the subject out a bit further.

"Well," said Claude at last. "I suppose it can't be helped. If you're here, you're here. May the best man win!"

"Yes, but dash it all!" I managed to put in at this point. "What's the idea? Where do you think you're going to stay if you stick on in London?"

"Why, here," said Eustace, surprised.

"Where else?" said Claude, raising his eyebrows.

"You won't object to putting us up, Bertie?" said Eustace.

"Not a sportsman like you," said Claude.

"But, you silly asses, suppose Aunt Agatha finds out that I'm hiding you when you ought to be in South Africa? Where do I get off?"

"Where does he get off?" Claude asked Eustace.

"Oh, I expect he'll manage somehow," said Eustace to Claude.

"Of course," said Claude, quite cheered up. "He'll manage."

"Rather!" said Eustace. "A resourceful chap like Bertie! Of course he will."

"And now," said Claude, shelving the subject, "what about that bite of lunch we were discussing a moment ago, Bertie? That stuff good old Jeeves slipped into me just now has given me what you might call an appetite. Something in the nature of six chops and a batter pudding would about meet the case, I think."

I suppose every chappie in the world has black periods in his life to which he can't look back without the smouldering eye and the silent shudder. Some coves, if you can judge by the novels you read nowadays, have them practically all the time; but, what with enjoying a sizable private income and a topping digestion, I'm bound to say it isn't very often I find my own existence getting a flat tyre. That's why this particular epoch is one that I don't think about more often than I can help. For the days that followed the unexpected resurrection of the blighted twins were so absolutely foul that the old nerves began to stick out of my body a foot long and curling at the ends. All of a twitter, believe me. I imagine the fact of the matter is that we Woosters are so frightfully honest and open and all that, that it gives us the pip to have to deceive.

All was quiet along the Potomac for about twenty-four hours, and then Aunt Agatha trickled in to have a chat. Twenty minutes earlier and she would have found the twins gaily shoving themselves outside a couple of rashers and an egg. She sank into a chair, and I could see that she was not in her usual sunny spirits.

"Bertie," she said, "I am uneasy."

So was I. I didn't know how long she intended to stop, or when the twins were coming back.

"I wonder," she said, "if I took too harsh a view towards Claude and Eustace."

"You couldn't."

"What do you mean?"

"I—er—mean it would be so unlike you to be harsh to anybody, Aunt Agatha." And not bad, either. I mean, quick—like that—without thinking. It pleased the old relative, and she looked at me with slightly less loathing than she usually does.

"It is nice of you to say that, Bertie, but what I was thinking was, are they safe?"

"Are they what?"

It seemed such a rummy adjective to apply to the twins, they being about as innocuous as a couple of sprightly young tarantulas.

"Do you think all is well with them?"

"How do you mean?"

Aunt Agatha eyed me almost wistfully.

"Has it ever occurred to you, Bertie," she said, "that your Uncle George may be psychic?"

She seemed to me to be changing the subject.

"Psychic?"

"Do you think it is possible that he could see things not visible to the normal eye?"

I thought it dashed possible, if not probable. I don't know if you've ever met my Uncle George. He's a festive old egg who wanders from club to club continually having a couple with other festive old eggs. When he heaves in sight, waiters brace themselves up and the wine-steward toys with his corkscrew. It was my Uncle George who discovered that alcohol was a food well in advance of modern medical thought.

"Your Uncle George was dining with me last night, and he was quite shaken. He declares that, while on his way from the Devonshire Club to Boodle's he suddenly saw the phantasm of Eustace."

"The what of Eustace?"

"The phantasm. The wraith. It was so clear that he thought for an instant that it was Eustace himself. The figure vanished round a corner, and when Uncle George got there nothing was to be seen. It is all very queer and disturbing. It had a marked effect on poor George. All through dinner he touched nothing but barley-water, and his manner was quite disturbed. You do think those poor, dear boys are safe, Bertie? They have not met with some horrible accident?"

It made my mouth water to think of it, but I said no, I didn't think they had met with any horrible accident. I thought Eustace was a horrible accident, and Claude about the same, but I didn't say so. And presently she biffed off, still worried.

When the twins came in, I put it squarely to the blighters. Jolly as it was to give Uncle George shocks, they must not wander at large about the metrop.

"But, my dear old soul," said Claude. "Be reasonable. We can't have our movements hampered."

"Out of the question," said Eustace.

"The whole essence of the thing, if you understand me," said Claude, "is that we should be at liberty to flit hither and thither."

"Exactly," said Eustace. "Now hither, now thither."

"But, damn it——"

"Bertie!" said Eustace reprovingly. "Not before the boy!"

"Of course, in a way I see his point," said Claude. "I suppose the solution of the problem would be to buy a couple of disguises."

"My dear old chap!" said Eustace, looking at him with admiration. "The brightest idea on record. Not your own, surely?"

"Well, as a matter of fact, it was Bertie who put it into my head."

"Me!"

"You were telling me the other day about old Bingo Little and the beard he bought when he didn't want his uncle to recognise him."

"If you think I'm going to have you two excrescences popping in and out of my flat in beards——"

"Something in that," agreed Eustace. "We'll make it whiskers, then."

"And false noses," said Claude.

"And, as you say, false noses. Right-o, then, Bertie, old chap, that's a load off your mind. We don't want to be any trouble to you while we're paying you this little visit."

And, when I went buzzing round to Jeeves for consolation, all he would say was something about Young Blood. No sympathy.

"Very good, Jeeves," I said. "I shall go for a walk in the Park. Kindly put me out the Old Etonian spats."

"Very good, sir."

* * * * *

It must have been a couple of days after that that Marion Wardour rolled in at about the hour of tea. She looked warily round the room before sitting down.

"Your cousins not at home, Bertie?" she said.

"No, thank goodness!"

"Then I'll tell you where they are. They're in my sitting-room, glaring at each other from opposite corners, waiting for me to come in. Bertie, this has got to stop."

"You're seeing a good deal of them, are you?"

Jeeves came in with the tea, but the poor girl was so worked up that she didn't wait for him to pop off before going on with her complaint. She had an absolutely hunted air, poor thing.

"I can't move a step without tripping over one or both of them," she said. "Generally both. They've taken to calling together, and they just settle down grimly and try to sit each other out. It's wearing me to a shadow."

"I know," I said sympathetically. "I know."

"Well, what's to be done?"

"It beats me. Couldn't you tell your maid to say you are not at home?"

She shuddered slightly.

"I tried that once. They camped on the stairs, and I couldn't get out all the afternoon. And I had a lot of particularly important engagements. I wish you would persuade them to go to South Africa, where they seem to be wanted."

"You must have made the dickens of an impression on them."

"I should say I have. They've started giving me presents now. At least, Claude has. He insisted on my accepting this cigarette-case last night. Came round to the theatre and wouldn't go away till I took it. It's not a bad one, I must say."

It wasn't. It was a distinctly fruity concern in gold with a diamond stuck in the middle. And the rummy thing was that I had a notion I'd seen something very like it before somewhere. How the deuce Claude had been able to dig up the cash to buy a thing like that was more than I could imagine.

Next day was a Wednesday, and as the object of their devotion had a matinée, the twins were, so to speak, off duty. Claude had gone with his whiskers on to Hurst Park, and Eustace and I were in the flat, talking. At least, he was talking and I was wishing he would go.

"The love of a good woman, Bertie," he was saying, "must be a wonderful thing.

Sometimes—— Good Lord! what's that?"

The front door had opened, and from out in the hall there came the sound of Aunt Agatha's voice asking if I was in. Aunt Agatha has one of those high, penetrating voices, but this was the first time I'd ever been thankful for it. There was just about two seconds to clear the way for her, but it was long enough for Eustace to dive under the sofa. His last shoe had just disappeared when she came in.

She had a worried look. It seemed to me about this time that everybody had.

"Bertie," she said, "what are your immediate plans?"

"How do you mean? I'm dining to-night with——"

"No, no, I don't mean to-night. Are you busy for the next few days? But, of course you are not," she went on, not waiting for me to answer. "You never have anything to do. Your whole life is spent in idle—but we can go into that later. What I came for this afternoon was to tell you that I wish you to go with your poor Uncle George to Harrogate for a few weeks. The sooner you can start, the better."

This appeared to me to approximate so closely to the frozen limit that I uttered a yelp of protest. Uncle George is all right, but he won't do. I was trying to say as much when she waved me down.

"If you are not entirely heartless, Bertie, you will do as I ask you. Your poor Uncle George has had a severe shock."

"What, another!"

"He feels that only complete rest and careful medical attendance can restore his nervous system to its normal poise. It seems that in the past he has derived benefit from taking the waters at Harrogate, and he wishes to go there now. We do not think he ought to be alone, so I wish you to accompany him."

"But, I say!"

"Bertie!"

There was a lull in the conversation.

"What shock has he had?" I asked.

"Between ourselves," said Aunt Agatha, lowering her voice in an impressive manner, "I incline to think that the whole affair was the outcome of an over-excited imagination. You are one of the family, Bertie, and I can speak freely to you. You know as well as I do that your poor Uncle George has for many years not been a—he has—er—developed a habit of—how shall I put it?"

"Shifting it a bit?"

"I beg your pardon?"

"Mopping up the stuff to some extent?"

"I dislike your way of putting it exceedingly, but I must confess that he has not been, perhaps, as temperate as he should. He is highly-strung, and—— Well, the fact is, that he has had a shock."

"Yes, but what?"

"That is what it is so hard to induce him to explain with any precision. With all his good points, your poor Uncle George is apt to become incoherent when strongly moved. As far as I could gather, he appears to have been the victim of a burglary."

"Burglary!"

"He says that a strange man with whiskers and a peculiar nose entered his rooms in Jermyn Street during his absence and stole some of his property. He says that he came back and found the man in his sitting-room. He immediately rushed out of the room and disappeared."

"Uncle George?"

"No, the man. And, according to your Uncle George, he had stolen a valuable cigarette-case. But, as I say, I am inclined to think that the whole thing was imagination. He has not been himself since the day when he fancied that he saw Eustace in the street. So I should like you, Bertie, to be prepared to start for Harrogate with him not later than Saturday."

She popped off, and Eustace crawled out from under the sofa. The blighter was strongly moved. So was I, for the matter of that. The idea of several weeks with Uncle George at Harrogate seemed to make everything go black.

"So that's where he got that cigarette-case, dash him!" said Eustace bitterly. "Of all the dirty tricks! Robbing his own flesh and blood! The fellow ought to be in chokey."

"He ought to be in South Africa," I said. "And so ought you."

And with an eloquence which rather surprised me, I hauled up my slacks for perhaps ten minutes on the subject of his duty to his family and what not. I appealed to his sense of decency. I boosted South Africa with vim. I said everything I could think of, much of it twice over. But all the blighter did was to babble about his dashed brother's baseness in putting one over on him in the matter of the cigarette-case. He seemed to think that Claude, by slinging in the handsome gift, had got right ahead of him; and there was a painful scene when the latter came back from Hurst Park. I could hear them talking half the night, long after I had tottered off to bed. I don't know when I've met fellows who could do with less sleep than those two.

* * * * *

After this, things became a bit strained at the flat owing to Claude and Eustace not being on speaking terms. I'm all for a certain chumminess in the home, and it was wearing to have to live with two fellows who wouldn't admit that the other one was on the map at all.

One felt the thing couldn't go on like that for long, and, by Jove, it didn't. But, if anyone had come to me the day before and told me what was going to happen, I should simply have smiled wanly. I mean, I'd got so accustomed to thinking that nothing short of a dynamite explosion could ever dislodge those two nestlers from my midst that, when Claude sidled up to me on the Friday morning and told me his bit of news, I could hardly believe I was hearing right.

"Bertie," he said, "I've been thinking it over."

"What over?" I said.

"The whole thing. This business of staying in London when I ought to be in South Africa. It isn't fair," said Claude warmly. "It isn't right. And the long and the short of it is, Bertie, old man, I'm leaving to-morrow."

I reeled in my tracks.

"You are?" I gasped.

"Yes. If," said Claude, "you won't mind sending old Jeeves out to buy a ticket for me. I'm afraid I'll have to stick you for the passage money, old man. You don't mind?"

"Mind!" I said, clutching his hand fervently.

"That's all right, then. Oh, I say, you won't say a word to Eustace about this, will you?"

"But isn't he going, too?"

Claude shuddered.

"No, thank heaven! The idea of being cooped up on board a ship with that blighter gives me the pip just to think of it. No, not a word to Eustace. I say, I suppose you can get me a berth all right at such short notice?"

"Rather!" I said. Sooner than let this opportunity slip, I would have bought the bally boat.

"Jeeves," I said, breezing into the kitchen. "Go out on first speed to the Union-Castle offices and book a berth on to-morrow's boat for Mr. Claude. He is leaving us, Jeeves."

"Yes, sir."

"Mr. Claude does not wish any mention of this to be made to Mr. Eustace."

"No, sir. Mr. Eustace made the same proviso when he desired me to obtain a berth on to-morrow's boat for himself."

I gaped at the man.

"Is he going, too?"

"Yes, sir."

"This is rummy."

"Yes, sir."

Had circumstances been other than they were, I would at this juncture have unbent considerably towards Jeeves. Frisked round him a bit and whooped to a certain extent, and what not. But those spats still formed a barrier, and I regret to say that I took the opportunity of rather rubbing it in a bit on the man. I mean, he'd been so dashed aloof and unsympathetic, though perfectly aware that the young master was in the soup and that it was up to him to rally round, that I couldn't help pointing out how the happy ending had been snaffled without any help from him.

"So that's that, Jeeves," I said. "The episode is concluded. I knew things would sort themselves out if one gave them time and didn't get rattled. Many chaps in my place would have got rattled, Jeeves."

"Yes, sir."

"Gone rushing about, I mean, asking people for help and advice and so forth."

"Very possibly, sir."

"But not me, Jeeves."

"No, sir."

I left him to brood on it.

* * * * *

Even the thought that I'd got to go to Harrogate with Uncle George couldn't depress me that Saturday when I gazed about the old flat and realised that Claude and Eustace weren't in it. They had slunk off stealthily and separately immediately after breakfast, Eustace to catch the boat-train at Waterloo, Claude to go round to the garage where I kept my car. I didn't want any chance of the two meeting at Waterloo and changing their minds, so I had suggested to Claude that he might find it pleasanter to drive down to Southampton.

I was lying back on the old settee, gazing peacefully up at the flies on the ceiling and feeling what a wonderful world this was, when Jeeves came in with a letter.

"A messenger-boy has brought this, sir."

I opened the envelope, and the first thing that fell out was a five-pound note.

"Great Scott!" I said. "What's all this?"

The letter was scribbled in pencil, and was quite brief:

Dear Bertie,—Will you give enclosed to your man, and tell him I wish I could make it more. He has saved my life. This is the first happy day I've had for a week.

Yours,

M. W.

Jeeves was standing holding out the fiver, which had fluttered to the floor.

"You'd better stick to it," I said. "It seems to be for you."

"Sir?"

"I say that fiver is for you, apparently. Miss Wardour sent it."

"That was extremely kind of her, sir."

"What the dickens is she sending you fivers for? She says you saved her life."

Jeeves smiled gently.

"She over-estimates my services, sir."

"But what were your services, dash it?"

"It was in the matter of Mr. Claude and Mr. Eustace, sir. I was hoping that she would not refer to the matter, as I did not wish you to think that I had been taking a liberty."

"What do you mean?"

"I chanced to be in the room while Miss Wardour was complaining with some warmth of the manner in which Mr. Claude and Mr. Eustace were thrusting their society upon her. I felt that in the circumstances it might be excusable if I suggested a slight ruse to enable her to dispense with their attentions."

"Good Lord! You don't mean to say you were at the bottom of their popping off, after all!"

Silly ass it made me feel. I mean, after rubbing it in to him like that about having clicked without his assistance.

"It occurred to me that, were Miss Wardour to inform Mr. Claude and Mr. Eustace independently that she proposed sailing for South Africa to take up a theatrical engagement, the desired effect might be produced. It appears that my anticipations were correct, sir. The young gentlemen ate it, if I may use the expression."

"Jeeves," I said—we Woosters may make bloomers, but we are never too proud to admit it—"you stand alone!"

"Thank you very much, sir."

"Oh, but I say!" A ghastly thought had struck me. "When they get on the boat and find she isn't there, won't they come buzzing back?"

"I anticipated that possibility, sir. At my suggestion, Miss Wardour informed the young gentlemen that she proposed to travel overland to Madeira and join the vessel there."

"And where do they touch after Madeira?"

"Nowhere, sir."

For a moment I just lay back, letting the idea of the thing soak in. There seemed to me to be only one flaw.

"The only pity is," I said, "that on a large boat like that they will be able to avoid each other. I mean, I should have liked to feel that Claude was having a good deal of Eustace's society and vice versa."

"I fancy that that will be so, sir. I secured a two-berth stateroom. Mr. Claude will occupy one berth, Mr. Eustace the other."

I sighed with pure ecstasy. It seemed a dashed shame that on this joyful occasion I should have to go off to Harrogate with my Uncle George.

"Have you started packing yet, Jeeves?" I asked.

"Packing, sir?"

"For Harrogate. I've got to go there to-day with Sir George."

"Of course, yes, sir. I forgot to mention it. Sir George rang up on the telephone this morning while you were still asleep, and said that he had changed his plans. He does not intend to go to Harrogate."

"Oh, I say, how absolutely topping!"

"I thought you might be pleased, sir."

"What made him change his plans? Did he say?"

"No, sir. But I gather from his man, Stevens, that he is feeling much better and does not now require a rest-cure. I took the liberty of giving Stevens the recipe for that pick-me-up of mine, of which you have always approved so much. Stevens tells me that Sir George informed him this morning that he is feeling a new man."

Well, there was only one thing to do, and I did it. I'm not saying it didn't hurt, but there was no alternative.

"Jeeves," I said, "those spats."

"Yes, sir?"

"You really dislike them?"

"Intensely, sir."

"You don't think time might induce you to change your views?"

"No, sir."

"All right, then. Very well. Say no more. You may burn them."

"Thank you very much, sir. I have already done so. Before breakfast this morning. A quiet grey is far more suitable, sir. Thank you, sir."

CHAPTER XVII
BINGO AND THE LITTLE WOMAN

It must have been a week or so after the departure of Claude and Eustace that I ran into young Bingo Little in the smoking-room of the Senior Liberal Club. He was lying back in an arm-chair with his mouth open and a sort of goofy expression in his eyes, while a grey-bearded cove in the middle distance watched him with so much dislike that I concluded that Bingo had pinched his favourite seat. That's the worst of being in a strange club—absolutely without intending it, you find yourself constantly trampling upon the vested interests of the Oldest Inhabitants.

"Hallo, face," I said.

"Cheerio, ugly," said young Bingo, and we settled down to have a small one before lunch.

Once a year the committee of the Drones decides that the old club could do with a wash and brush-up, so they shoo us out and dump us down for a few weeks at some other institution. This time we were roosting at the Senior Liberal, and personally I had found the strain pretty fearful. I mean, when you've got used to a club where everything's nice and cheery, and where, if you want to attract a chappie's attention, you heave a bit of bread at him, it kind of damps you to come to a place where the youngest member is about eighty-seven and it isn't considered good form to talk to anyone unless you and he were through the Peninsular War together. It was a relief to come across Bingo. We started to talk in hushed voices.

"This club," I said, "is the limit."

"It is the eel's eyebrows," agreed young Bingo. "I believe that old boy over by the window has been dead three days, but I don't like to mention it to anyone."

"Have you lunched here yet?"

"No. Why?"

"They have waitresses instead of waiters."

"Good Lord! I thought that went out with the armistice." Bingo mused a moment, straightening his tie absently. "Er—pretty girls?" he said.

"No."

He seemed disappointed, but pulled round.

"Well, I've heard that the cooking's the best in London."

"So they say. Shall we be going in?"

"All right. I expect," said young Bingo, "that at the end of the meal—or possibly at the beginning—the waitress will say, 'Both together, sir?' Reply in the affirmative. I haven't a bean."

"Hasn't your uncle forgiven you yet?"

"Not yet, confound him!"

I was sorry to hear the row was still on. I resolved to do the poor old thing well at the festive board, and I scanned the menu with some intentness when the girl rolled up with it.

"How would this do you, Bingo?" I said at length. "A few plovers' eggs to weigh in with, a cup of soup, a touch of cold salmon, some cold curry, and a splash of gooseberry tart and cream with a bite of cheese to finish?"

I don't know that I had expected the man actually to scream with delight, though I had picked the items from my knowledge of his pet dishes, but I had expected him to say something. I looked up, and found that his attention was elsewhere. He was gazing at the waitress with the look of a dog that's just remembered where its bone was buried.

She was a tallish girl with sort of soft, soulful brown eyes. Nice figure and all that. Rather decent hands, too. I didn't remember having seen her about before, and I must say she raised the standard of the place quite a bit.

"How about it, laddie?" I said, being all for getting the order booked and going on to the serious knife-and-fork work.

"Eh?" said young Bingo absently.

I recited the programme once more.

"Oh, yes, fine!" said Bingo. "Anything, anything." The girl pushed off, and he turned to me with protruding eyes. "I thought you said they weren't pretty, Bertie!" he said reproachfully.

"Oh, my heavens!" I said. "You surely haven't fallen in love again—and with a girl you've only just seen?"

"There are times, Bertie," said young Bingo, "when a look is enough—when, passing through a crowd, we meet somebody's eye and something seems to whisper...."

At this point the plovers' eggs arrived, and he suspended his remarks in order to swoop on them with some vigour.

"Jeeves," I said that night when I got home, "stand by."

"Sir?"

"Burnish the old brain and be alert and vigilant. I suspect that Mr. Little will be calling round shortly for sympathy and assistance."

"Is Mr. Little in trouble, sir?"

"Well, you might call it that. He's in love. For about the fifty-third time. I ask you, Jeeves, as man to man, did you ever see such a chap?"

"Mr. Little is certainly warm-hearted, sir."

"Warm-hearted! I should think he has to wear asbestos vests. Well, stand by, Jeeves."

"Very good, sir."

And sure enough, it wasn't ten days before in rolled the old ass, bleating for volunteers to step one pace forward and come to the aid of the party.

"Bertie," he said, "if you are a pal of mine, now is the time to show it."

"Proceed, old gargoyle," I replied. "You have our ear."

"You remember giving me lunch at the Senior Liberal some days ago. We were waited on by a——"

"I remember. Tall, lissom female."

He shuddered somewhat.

"I wish you wouldn't talk of her like that, dash it all. She's an angel."

"All right. Carry on."

"I love her."

"Right-o! Push along."

"For goodness sake don't bustle me. Let me tell the story in my own way. I love her, as I was saying, and I want you, Bertie, old boy, to pop round to my uncle and do a bit of diplomatic work. That allowance of mine must be restored, and dashed quick, too. What's more, it must be increased."

"But look here," I said, being far from keen on the bally business, "why not wait awhile?"

"Wait? What's the good of waiting?"

"Well, you know what generally happens when you fall in love. Something goes wrong with the works and you get left. Much better tackle your uncle after the whole thing's fixed and settled."

"It is fixed and settled. She accepted me this morning."

"Good Lord! That's quick work. You haven't known her two weeks."

"Not in this life, no," said young Bingo. "But she has a sort of idea that we must have met in some previous existence. She thinks I must have been a king in Babylon when she was a Christian slave. I can't say I remember it myself, but there may be something in it."

"Great Scott!" I said. "Do waitresses really talk like that?"

"How should I know how waitresses talk?"

"Well, you ought to by now. The first time I ever met your uncle was when you hounded me on to ask him if he would rally round to help you marry that girl Mabel in the Piccadilly bun-shop."

Bingo started violently. A wild gleam came into his eyes. And before I knew what he was up to he had brought down his hand with a most frightful whack on my summer trousering, causing me to leap like a young ram.

"Here!" I said.

"Sorry," said Bingo. "Excited. Carried away. You've given me an idea, Bertie." He waited till I had finished massaging the limb, and resumed his remarks. "Can you throw your mind back to that occasion, Bertie? Do you remember the frightfully subtle scheme I worked? Telling him you were what's-her-name, the woman who wrote those books, I mean?"

It wasn't likely I'd forget. The ghastly thing was absolutely seared into my memory.

"That is the line of attack," said Bingo. "That is the scheme. Rosie M. Banks forward once more."

"It can't be done, old thing. Sorry, but it's out of the question. I couldn't go through all that again."

"Not for me?"

"Not for a dozen more like you."

"I never thought," said Bingo sorrowfully, "to hear those words from Bertie Wooster!"

"Well, you've heard them now," I said. "Paste them in your hat."

"Bertie, we were at school together."

"It wasn't my fault."

"We've been pals for fifteen years."

"I know. It's going to take me the rest of my life to live it down."

"Bertie, old man," said Bingo, drawing up his chair closer and starting to knead my shoulder-blade, "listen! Be reasonable!"

And of course, dash it, at the end of ten minutes I'd allowed the blighter to talk me round. It's always the way. Anyone can talk me round. If I were in a Trappist monastery, the first thing that would happen would be that some smooth performer would lure me into some frightful idiocy against my better judgment by means of the deaf-and-dumb language.

"Well, what do you want me to do?" I said, realising that it was hopeless to struggle.

"Start off by sending the old boy an autographed copy of your latest effort with a flattering inscription. That will tickle him to death. Then you pop round and put it across."

"What is my latest?"

"'The Woman Who Braved All,'" said young Bingo. "I've seen it all over the place. The shop windows and bookstalls are full of nothing but it. It looks to me from the picture on the jacket the sort of book any chappie would be proud to have written. Of course, he will want to discuss it with you."

"Ah!" I said, cheering up. "That dishes the scheme, doesn't it? I don't know what the bally thing is about."

"You will have to read it, naturally."

"Read it! No, I say...."

"Bertie, we were at school together."

"Oh, right-o! Right-o!" I said.

"I knew I could rely on you. You have a heart of gold. Jeeves," said young Bingo, as the faithful servitor rolled in, "Mr. Wooster has a heart of gold."

"Very good, sir," said Jeeves.

Bar a weekly wrestle with the Pink 'Un and an occasional dip into the form book I'm not much of a lad for reading, and my sufferings as I tackled "The Woman" (curse her!) "Who Braved All" were pretty fearful. But I managed to get through it, and only just in time, as it happened, for I'd hardly reached the bit where their lips met in one long, slow kiss and everything was still but for the gentle sighing of the breeze in the laburnum, when a messenger boy brought a note from old Bittlesham asking me to trickle round to lunch.

I found the old boy in a mood you could only describe as melting. He had a copy of the book on the table beside him and kept turning the pages in the intervals of dealing with things in aspic and what not.

"Mr. Wooster," he said, swallowing a chunk of trout, "I wish to congratulate you. I wish to thank you. You go from strength to strength. I have read 'All For Love'; I have read 'Only a Factory Girl'; I know 'Madcap Myrtle' by heart. But this—this is your bravest and best. It tears the heartstrings."

"Yes?"

"Indeed yes! I have read it three times since you most kindly sent me the volume—I wish to thank you once more for the charming inscription—and I think I may say that I am a better, sweeter, deeper man. I am full of human charity and kindliness toward my species."

"No, really?"

"Indeed, indeed I am."

"Towards the whole species?"

"Towards the whole species."

"Even young Bingo?" I said, trying him pretty high.

"My nephew? Richard?" He looked a bit thoughtful, but stuck it like a man and refused to hedge. "Yes, even towards Richard. Well ... that is to say ... perhaps ... yes, even towards Richard."

"That's good, because I wanted to talk about him. He's pretty hard up, you know."

"In straitened circumstances?"

"Stoney. And he could use a bit of the right stuff paid every quarter, if you felt like unbelting."

He mused awhile and got through a slab of cold guinea hen before replying. He toyed with the book, and it fell open at page two hundred and fifteen. I couldn't remember what was on page two hundred and fifteen, but it must have been something tolerably zippy, for his expression changed and he gazed up at me with misty eyes, as if he'd taken a shade too much mustard with his last bite of ham.

"Very well, Mr. Wooster," he said. "Fresh from a perusal of this noble work of yours, I cannot harden my heart. Richard shall have his allowance."

"Stout fellow!" I said. Then it occurred to me that the expression might strike a chappie who weighed seventeen stone as a bit personal. "Good egg, I mean. That'll take a weight off his mind. He wants to get married, you know."

"I did not know. And I am not sure that I altogether approve. Who is the lady?"

"Well, as a matter of fact, she's a waitress."

He leaped in his seat.

"You don't say so, Mr. Wooster! This is remarkable. This is most cheering. I had not given the boy credit for such tenacity of purpose. An excellent trait in him which I had not hitherto suspected. I recollect clearly that, on the occasion when I first had the pleasure of making your acquaintance, nearly eighteen months ago, Richard was desirous of marrying this same waitress."

I had to break it to him.

"Well, not absolutely this same waitress. In fact, quite a different waitress. Still, a waitress, you know."

The light of avuncular affection died out of the old boy's eyes.

"H'm!" he said a bit dubiously. "I had supposed that Richard was displaying the quality of constancy which is so rare in the modern young man. I—I must think it over."

So we left it at that, and I came away and told Bingo the position of affairs.

"Allowance O.K.," I said. "Uncle blessing a trifle wobbly."

"Doesn't he seem to want the wedding bells to ring out?"

"I left him thinking it over. If I were a bookie, I should feel justified in offering a hundred to eight against."

"You can't have approached him properly. I might have known you would muck it up," said young Bingo. Which, considering what I had been through for his sake, struck me as a good bit sharper than a serpent's tooth.

"It's awkward," said young Bingo. "It's infernally awkward. I can't tell you all the details at the moment, but ... yes, it's awkward."

He helped himself absently to a handful of my cigars and pushed off.

I didn't see him again for three days. Early in the afternoon of the third day he blew in with a flower in his buttonhole and a look on his face as if someone had hit him behind the ear with a stuffed eel skin.

"Hallo, Bertie."

"Hallo, old turnip. Where have you been all this while?"

"Oh, here and there! Ripping weather we're having, Bertie."

"Not bad."

"I see the Bank Rate is down again."

"No, really?"

"Disturbing news from Lower Silesia, what?"

"Oh, dashed!"

He pottered about the room for a bit, babbling at intervals. The boy seemed cuckoo.

"Oh, I say, Bertie!" he said suddenly, dropping a vase which he had picked off the mantelpiece and was fiddling with. "I know what it was I wanted to tell you. I'm married."

CHAPTER XVIII
ALL'S WELL

I stared at him. That flower in his buttonhole.... That dazed look.... Yes, he had all the symptoms; and yet the thing seemed incredible. The fact is, I suppose, I'd seen so many of young Bingo's love affairs start off with a whoop and a rattle and poof themselves out halfway down the straight that I couldn't believe he had actually brought it off at last.

"Married!"

"Yes. This morning at a registrar's in Holburn. I've just come from the wedding breakfast."

I sat up in my chair. Alert. The man of affairs. It seemed to me that this thing wanted threshing out in all its aspects.

"Let's get this straight," I said. "You're really married?"

"Yes."

"The same girl you were in love with the day before yesterday?"

"What do you mean?"

"Well, you know what you're like. Tell me, what made you commit this rash act?"

"I wish the deuce you wouldn't talk like that. I married her because I love her, dash it. The best little woman," said young Bingo, "in the world."

"That's all right, and deuced creditable, I'm sure. But have you reflected what your uncle's going to say? The last I saw of him, he was by no means in a confetti-scattering mood."

"Bertie," said Bingo, "I'll be frank with you. The little woman rather put it up to me, if you know what I mean. I told her how my uncle felt about it, and she said that we must part unless I loved her enough to brave the old boy's wrath and marry her right away. So I had no alternative. I bought a buttonhole and went to it."

"And what do you propose to do now?"

"Oh, I've got it all planned out! After you've seen my uncle and broken the news...."

"What!"

"After you've...."

"You don't mean to say you think you're going to lug me into it?"

He looked at me like Lilian Gish coming out of a swoon.

"Is this Bertie Wooster talking?" he said, pained.

"Yes, it jolly well is."

"Bertie, old man," said Bingo, patting me gently here and there, "reflect! We were at school——"

"Oh, all right!"

"Good man! I knew I could rely on you. She's waiting down below in the hall. We'll pick her up and dash round to Pounceby Gardens right away."

I had only seen the bride before in her waitress kit, and I was rather expecting that on her wedding day she would have launched out into something fairly zippy in the way of upholstery. The first gleam of hope I had felt since the start of this black business came to me when I saw that, instead of being all velvet and scent and flowery hat, she was dressed in dashed good taste. Quiet. Nothing loud. So far as looks went, she might have stepped straight out of Berkeley Square.

"This is my old pal, Bertie Wooster, darling," said Bingo. "We were at school together, weren't we, Bertie?"

"We were!" I said. "How do you do? I think we—er—met at lunch the other day, didn't we?"

"Oh, yes! How do you do?"

"My uncle eats out of Bertie's hand," explained Bingo. "So he's coming round with us to start things off and kind of pave the way. Hi, taxi!"

We didn't talk much on the journey. Kind of tense feeling. I was glad when the cab stopped at old Bittlesham's wigwam and we all hopped out. I left Bingo and wife in the hall while I went upstairs to the drawing-room, and the butler toddled off to dig out the big chief.

While I was prowling about the room waiting for him to show up, I suddenly caught sight of that bally "Woman Who Braved All" lying on one of the tables. It was open at page two hundred and fifteen, and a passage heavily marked in pencil caught my eye. And directly I read it I saw that it was all to the mustard and was going to help me in my business.

This was the passage:

"What can prevail"—Millicent's eyes flashed as she faced the stern old man—"what can prevail against a pure and all-consuming love? Neither principalities nor powers, my lord, nor all the puny prohibitions of guardians and parents. I love your son, Lord Mindermere, and nothing can keep us apart. Since time first began this love of ours was fated, and who are you to pit yourself against the decrees of Fate?"

The earl looked at her keenly from beneath his bushy eyebrows.

"Humph!" he said.

Before I had time to refresh my memory as to what Millicent's come-back had been to that remark, the door opened and old Bittlesham rolled in. All over me, as usual.

"My dear Mr. Wooster, this is an unexpected pleasure. Pray take a seat. What can I do for you?"

"Well, the fact is, I'm more or less in the capacity of a jolly old ambassador at the moment. Representing young Bingo, you know."

His geniality sagged a trifle, I thought, but he didn't heave me out, so I pushed on.

"The way I always look at it," I said, "is that it's dashed difficult for anything to prevail against what you might call a pure and all-consuming love. I mean, can it be done? I doubt it."

My eyes didn't exactly flash as I faced the stern old man, but I sort of waggled my eyebrows. He puffed a bit and looked doubtful.

"We discussed this matter at our last meeting, Mr. Wooster. And on that occasion...."

"Yes. But there have been developments, as it were, since then. The fact of the matter is," I said, coming to the point, "this morning young Bingo went and jumped off the dock."

"Good heavens!" He jerked himself to his feet with his mouth open. "Why? Where? Which dock?"

I saw that he wasn't quite on.

"I was speaking metaphorically," I explained, "if that's the word I want. I mean he got married."

"Married!"

"Absolutely hitched up. I hope you aren't ratty about it, what? Young blood, you know. Two loving hearts, and all that."

He panted in a rather overwrought way.

"I am greatly disturbed by your news. I—I consider that I have been—er—defied. Yes, defied."

"But who are you to pit yourself against the decrees of Fate?" I said, taking a look at the prompt book out of the corner of my eye.

"Eh?"

"You see, this love of theirs was fated. Since time began, you know."

I'm bound to admit that if he'd said "Humph!" at this juncture, he would have had me stymied. Luckily it didn't occur to him. There was a silence, during which he appeared to brood a bit. Then his eye fell on the book and he gave a sort of start.

"Why, bless my soul, Mr. Wooster, you have been quoting!"

"More or less."

"I thought your words sounded familiar." His whole appearance changed and he gave a sort of gurgling chuckle. "Dear me, dear me, you know my weak spot!" He picked up the book and buried himself in it for quite a while. I began to think he had forgotten I was there. After a bit, however, he put it down again, and wiped his eyes. "Ah, well!" he said.

I shuffled my feet and hoped for the best.

"Ah, well," he said again. "I must not be like Lord Windermere, must I, Mr. Wooster? Tell me, did you draw that haughty old man from a living model?"

"Oh, no! Just thought of him and bunged him down, you know."

"Genius!" murmured old Bittlesham. "Genius! Well, Mr. Wooster, you have won me over. Who, as you say, am I to pit myself against the decrees of Fate? I will write to Richard to-night and inform him of my consent to his marriage."

"You can slip him the glad news in person," I said. "He's waiting downstairs, with wife complete. I'll pop down and send them up. Cheerio, and thanks very much. Bingo will be most awfully bucked."

I shot out and went downstairs. Bingo and Mrs. were sitting on a couple of chairs like patients in a dentist's waiting-room.

"Well?" said Bingo eagerly.

"All over except the hand-clasping," I replied, slapping the old crumpet on the back. "Charge up and get matey. Toodle-oo, old things. You know where to find me, if wanted. A thousand congratulations, and all that sort of rot."

And I pipped, not wishing to be fawned upon.

* * * * *

You never can tell in this world. If ever I felt that something attempted, something done had earned a night's repose, it was when I got back to the flat and shoved my feet up on the mantelpiece and started to absorb the cup of tea which Jeeves had brought in. Used as I am to seeing Life's sitters blow up in the home stretch and finish nowhere, I couldn't see any cause for alarm in this affair of young Bingo's. All he had to do when I left him in Pounceby Gardens was to walk upstairs with the little missus and collect the blessing. I was so convinced of this that when, about half an hour later, he came galloping into my sitting-room, all I thought was that he wanted to thank me in broken accents and tell me what a good chap I had been. I merely beamed benevolently on the old creature as he entered, and was just going to offer him a cigarette when I observed that he seemed to have something on his mind. In fact, he looked as if something solid had hit him in the solar plexus.

"My dear old soul," I said, "what's up?"

Bingo plunged about the room.

"I will be calm!" he said, knocking over an occasional table. "Calm, dammit!" He upset a chair.

"Surely nothing has gone wrong?"

Bingo uttered one of those hollow, mirthless yelps.

"Only every bally thing that could go wrong. What do you think happened after you left us? You know that beastly book you insisted on sending my uncle?"

It wasn't the way I should have put it myself, but I saw the poor old bean was upset for some reason or other, so I didn't correct him.

"'The Woman Who Braved All'?" I said. "It came in dashed useful. It was by quoting bits out of it that I managed to talk him round."

"Well, it didn't come in useful when we got into the room. It was lying on the table, and after we had started to chat a bit and everything was going along nicely the little woman spotted it. 'Oh, have you read this, Lord Bittlesham?' she said. 'Three times already,' said my uncle. 'I'm so glad,' said the little woman. 'Why, are you also an admirer of Rosie M. Banks?' asked the old boy, beaming. 'I am Rosie M. Banks!' said the little woman."

"Oh, my aunt! Not really?"

"Yes."

"But how could she be? I mean, dash it, she was slinging the foodstuffs at the Senior Liberal Club."

Bingo gave the settee a moody kick.

"She took the job to collect material for a book she's writing called 'Mervyn Keene, Clubman.'"

"She might have told you."

"It made such a hit with her when she found that I loved her for herself alone, despite her humble station, that she kept it under her hat. She meant to spring it on me later on, she said."

"Well, what happened then?"

"There was the dickens of a painful scene. The old boy nearly got apoplexy. Called her an impostor. They both started talking at once at the top of their voices, and the thing ended with the little woman buzzing off to her publishers to collect proofs as a preliminary to getting a written apology from the old boy. What's going to happen now, I don't know. Apart from the fact that my uncle will be as mad as a wet hen when he finds out that he has been fooled, there's going to be a lot of trouble when the little woman discovers that we worked the Rosie M. Banks wheeze with a view to trying to get me married to somebody else. You see, one of the things that first attracted her to me was the fact that I had never been in love before."

"Did you tell her that?"

"Yes."

"Great Scott!"

"Well, I hadn't been ... not really in love. There's all the difference in the world between.... Well, never mind that. What am I going to do? That's the point."

"I don't know."

"Thanks," said young Bingo. "That's a lot of help."

* * * * *

Next morning he rang me up on the phone just after I'd got the bacon and eggs into my system—the one moment of the day, in short, when a chappie wishes to muse on life absolutely undisturbed.

"Bertie!"

"Hallo?"

"Things are hotting up."

"What's happened now?"

"My uncle has given the little woman's proofs the once-over and admits her claim. I've just been having five snappy minutes with him on the telephone. He says that you and I made a fool of him, and he could hardly speak, he was so shirty. Still, he made it clear all right that my allowance has gone phut again."

"I'm sorry."

"Don't waste time being sorry for me," said young Bingo grimly. "He's coming to call on you to-day to demand a personal explanation."

"Great Scott!"

"And the little woman is coming to call on you to demand a personal explanation."

"Good Lord!"

"I shall watch your future career with some considerable interest," said young Bingo.

I bellowed for Jeeves.

"Jeeves!"

"Sir?"

"I'm in the soup."

"Indeed, sir?"

I sketched out the scenario for him.

"What would you advise?"

"I think if I were you, sir, I would accept Mr. Pitt-Waley's invitation immediately. If you remember, sir, he invited you to shoot with him in Norfolk this week."

"So he did! By Jove, Jeeves, you're always right. Meet me at the station with my things the first train after lunch. I'll go and lie low at the club for the rest of the morning."

"Would you require my company on this visit, sir?"

"Do you want to come?"

"If I might suggest it, sir, I think it would be better if I remained here and kept in touch with Mr. Little. I might possibly hit upon some method of pacifying the various parties, sir."

"Right-o! But, if you do, you're a marvel."

* * * * *

I didn't enjoy myself much in Norfolk. It rained most of the time, and when it wasn't raining I was so dashed jumpy I couldn't hit a thing. By the end of the week I couldn't stand it any longer. Too bally absurd, I mean, being marooned miles away in the country just because young Bingo's uncle and wife wanted to have a few words with me. I made up my mind that I would pop back and do the strong, manly thing by lying low in my flat and telling Jeeves to inform everybody who called that I wasn't at home.

I sent Jeeves a telegram saying I was coming, and drove straight to Bingo's place when I reached town. I wanted to find out the general posish of affairs. But apparently the man was out. I rang a couple of times but nothing happened, and I was just going to leg it when I heard the sound of footsteps inside and the door opened. It wasn't one of the cheeriest moments of my career when I found myself peering into the globular face of Lord Bittlesham.

"Oh, er, hallo!" I said. And there was a bit of a pause.

I don't quite know what I had been expecting the old boy to do if, by bad luck, we should ever meet again, but I had a sort of general idea that he would turn fairly purple and start almost immediately to let me have it in the gizzard. It struck me as somewhat rummy, therefore, when he simply smiled weakly. A sort of frozen smile it was. His eyes kind of bulged and he swallowed once or twice.

"Er...." he said.

I waited for him to continue, but apparently that was all there was.

"Bingo in?" I said, after a rather embarrassing pause.

He shook his head and smiled again. And then, suddenly, just as the flow of conversation had begun to slacken once more, I'm dashed if he didn't make a sort of lumbering leap back into the flat and bang the door.

I couldn't understand it. But, as it seemed that the interview, such as it was, was over, I thought I might as well be shifting. I had just started down the stairs when I met young Bingo, charging up three steps at a time.

"Hallo, Bertie!" he said. "Where did you spring from? I thought you were out of town."

"I've just got back. I looked in on you to see how the land lay."

"How do you mean?"

"Why, all that business, you know."

"Oh, that!" said young Bingo airily. "That was all settled days ago. The dove of peace is flapping its wings all over the place. Everything's as right as it can be. Jeeves fixed it all up. He's a marvel, that man, Bertie, I've always said so. Put the whole thing straight in half a minute with one of those brilliant ideas of his."

"This is topping!"

"I knew you'd be pleased."

"Congratulate you."

"Thanks."

"What did Jeeves do? I couldn't think of any solution of the bally thing myself."

"Oh, he took the matter in hand and smoothed it all out in a second! My uncle and the little woman are tremendous pals now. They gas away by the hour together about literature and all that. He's always dropping in for a chat."

This reminded me.

"He's in there now," I said. "I say, Bingo, how is your uncle these days?"

"Much as usual. How do you mean?"

"I mean he hasn't been feeling the strain of things a bit, has he? He seemed rather strange in his manner just now."

"Why, have you met him?"

"He opened the door when I rang. And then, after he had stood goggling at me for a bit, he suddenly banged the door in my face. Puzzled me, you know. I mean, I could have understood it if he'd ticked me off and all that, but dash it, the man seemed absolutely scared."

Young Bingo laughed a care-free laugh.

"Oh, that's all right!" he said. "I forgot to tell you about that. Meant to write, but kept putting it off. He thinks you're a looney."

"He—what!"

"Yes. That was Jeeves's idea, you know. It's solved the whole problem splendidly. He suggested that I should tell my uncle that I had acted in perfectly good faith in introducing you to him as Rosie M. Banks; that I had repeatedly had it from your own lips that you were, and that I didn't see any reason why you shouldn't be. The idea being that you were subject to hallucinations and generally potty. And then we got hold of Sir Roderick Glossop—you remember, the old boy whose kid you pushed into the lake that day down at Ditteredge Hall—and he rallied round with his story of how he had come to lunch with you and found your bedroom full up with cats and fish, and how you had pinched his hat while you were driving past his car in a taxi, and all that, you know. It just rounded the whole thing off nicely. I always say, and I always shall say, that you've only got to stand on Jeeves, and fate can't touch you."

I can stand a good deal, but there are limits.

"Well, of all the dashed bits of nerve I ever...."

Bingo looked at me astonished.

"You aren't annoyed?" he said.

"Annoyed! At having half London going about under the impression that I'm off my chump? Dash it all...."

"Bertie," said Bingo, "you amaze and wound me. If I had dreamed that you would object to doing a trifling good turn to a fellow who's been a pal of yours for fifteen years...."

"Yes, but, look here...."

"Have you forgotten," said young Bingo, "that we were at school together?"

I pushed on to the old flat, seething like the dickens. One thing I was jolly certain of, and that was that this was where Jeeves and I parted company. A topping valet, of course, none better in London, but I wasn't going to allow that to weaken me. I buzzed into the flat like an east wind ... and there was the box of cigarettes on the small table and the illustrated weekly papers on the big table and my slippers on the floor, and every dashed thing so bally right, if you know what I mean, that I started to calm down in the first two seconds. It was like one of those moments in a play where the chappie, about to steep himself in crime, suddenly hears the soft, appealing strains of the old melody he learned at his mother's knee. Softened, I mean to say. That's the word I want. I was softened.

And then through the doorway there shimmered good old Jeeves in the wake of a tray full of the necessary ingredients, and there was something about the mere look of the man....

However, I steeled the old heart and had a stab at it.

"I have just met Mr. Little, Jeeves," I said.

"Indeed, sir?"

"He—er—he told me you had been helping him."

"I did my best, sir. And I am happy to say that matters now appear to be proceeding smoothly. Whisky, sir?"

"Thanks. Er—Jeeves."

"Sir?"

"Another time...."

"Sir?"

"Oh, nothing.... Not all the soda, Jeeves."

"Very good, sir."

He started to drift out.

"Oh, Jeeves!"

"Sir?"

"I wish ... that is ... I think ... I mean.... Oh, nothing!"

"Very good, sir. The cigarettes are at your elbow, sir. Dinner will be ready at a quarter to eight precisely, unless you desire to dine out?"

"No. I'll dine in."

"Yes, sir."

"Jeeves!"

"Sir?"

"Oh, nothing!" I said.

"Very good, sir," said Jeeves.

Meet Mr Mulliner

1
THE TRUTH ABOUT GEORGE

Two men were sitting in the bar-parlour of the Anglers' Rest as I entered it; and one of them, I gathered from his low, excited voice and wide gestures, was telling the other a story. I could hear nothing but an occasional 'Biggest I ever saw in my life!' and 'Fully as large as that!' but in such a place it was not difficult to imagine the rest; and when the second man, catching my eye, winked at me with a sort of humorous misery, I smiled sympathetically back at him.

The action had the effect of establishing a bond between us; and when the story-teller finished his tale and left, he came over to my table as if answering a formal invitation.

'Dreadful liars some men are,' he said genially.

'Fishermen,' I suggested, 'are traditionally careless of the truth.'

'He wasn't a fisherman,' said my companion. 'That was our local doctor. He was telling me about his latest case of dropsy. Besides'—he tapped me earnestly on the knee—'you must not fall into the popular error about fishermen. Tradition has maligned them. I am a fisherman myself, and I have never told a lie in my life.'

I could well believe it. He was a short, stout, comfortable man of middle age, and the thing that struck me first about him was the extraordinary childlike candour of his eyes. They were large and round and honest. I would have bought oil stock from him without a tremor.

The door leading into the white dusty road opened, and a small man with rimless pince-nez and an anxious expression shot in like a rabbit and had consumed a gin and ginger-beer almost before we knew he was there. Having thus refreshed himself, he stood looking at us, seemingly ill at ease.

'N-n-n-n-n—' he said.

We looked at him inquiringly.

'N-n-n-n-n-ice d-d-d-d—'

His nerve appeared to fail him, and he vanished as abruptly as he had come.

'I think he was leading up to telling us that it was a nice day,' hazarded my companion.

'It must be very embarrassing,' I said, 'for a man with such a painful impediment in his speech to open conversation with strangers.'

'Probably trying to cure himself. Like my nephew George. Have I ever told you about my nephew George?'

I reminded him that we had only just met, and that this was the first time I had learned that he had a nephew George.

'Young George Mulliner. My name is Mulliner. I will tell you about George's case—in many ways a rather remarkable one.'

My nephew George (said Mr Mulliner) was as nice a young fellow as you would ever wish to meet, but from childhood up he had been cursed with a terrible stammer. If he had had to earn his living, he would undoubtedly have found this affliction a great handicap, but fortunately his father had left him a comfortable income; and George spent a not unhappy life, residing in the village where he had been born and passing his days in the usual country sports and his evenings in doing cross-word puzzles. By the time he was thirty he knew more about Eli, the prophet, Ra, the Sun God, and the bird Emu than anybody else in the county except Susan Blake, the vicar's daughter, who had also taken up the solving of cross-word puzzles and was the first girl in Worcestershire to find out the meaning of 'stearine' and 'crepuscular'.

It was his association with Miss Blake that first turned George's thoughts to a serious endeavour to cure himself of his stammer. Naturally, with this hobby in common, the young people saw a great deal of one another: for George was always looking in at the vicarage to ask her if she knew a word of seven letters meaning 'appertaining to the profession of plumbing', and Susan was just as constant a caller at George's cosy little cottage, being frequently stumped, as girls will be, by words of eight letters signifying 'largely used in the manufacture of poppet-valves'. The consequence was that one evening, just after she had helped him out of a tight place with the word 'disestablishmentarianism', the boy suddenly awoke to the truth and realized that she was all the world to him—or, as he put it to himself from force of habit, precious, beloved, darling, much-loved, highly esteemed or valued.

And yet, every time he tried to tell her so, he could get no further than a sibilant gurgle which was no more practical use than a hiccup.

Something obviously had to be done, and George went to London to see a specialist.

'Yes?' said the specialist.

'I-I-I-I-I-I—' said George.

'You were saying—?'

'Woo-woo-woo-woo-woo-woo—'

'Sing it,' said the specialist.

'S-s-s-s-s-s-s—?' said George, puzzled.

The specialist explained. He was a kindly man with moth-eaten whiskers and an eye like a meditative cod-fish.

'Many people,' he said, 'who are unable to articulate clearly in ordinary speech find themselves lucid and bell-like when they burst into song.'

It seemed a good idea to George. He thought for a moment; then threw his head back, shut his eyes, and let it go in a musical baritone.

'I love a lassie, a bonny, bonny lassie,' sang George. 'She's as pure as the lily in the dell.'

'No doubt,' said the specialist, wincing a little.

'She's as sweet as the heather, the bonny purple heather—Susan, my Worcestershire bluebell.'

'Ah!' said the specialist. 'Sounds a nice girl. Is this she?' he asked, adjusting his glasses and peering at the photograph which George had extracted from the interior of the left side of his under-vest.

George nodded, and drew in breath.

'Yes, sir,' he carolled, 'that's my baby. No, sir, don't mean maybe. Yes, sir, that's my baby now. And, by the way, by the way, when I meet that preacher I shall say—"Yes, sir, that's my—"'

'Quite,' said the specialist, hurriedly. He had a sensitive ear. 'Quite, quite.'

'If you knew Susie like I know Susie,' George was beginning, but the other stopped him.

'Quite. Exactly. I shouldn't wonder. And now,' said the specialist, 'what precisely is the trouble? No,' he added, hastily, as George inflated his lungs, 'don't sing it. Write the particulars on this piece of paper.'

George did so.

'H'm!' said the specialist, examining the screed. 'You wish to woo, court, and become betrothed, engaged, affianced to this girl, but you find yourself unable, incapable, incompetent, impotent, and powerless. Every time you attempt it, your vocal cords fail, fall short, are insufficient, wanting, deficient, and go blooey.'

George nodded.

'A not unusual case. I have had to deal with this sort of thing before. The effect of love on the vocal cords of even a normally eloquent subject is frequently deleterious. As regards the habitual stammerer, tests have shown that in ninety-seven point five six nine recurring of cases the divine passion reduces him to a condition where he sounds like a soda-water siphon trying to recite Gunga Din. There is only one cure.'

'W-w-w-w-w—?' asked George.

'I will tell you. Stammering,' proceeded the specialist, putting the tips of his fingers together and eyeing George benevolently, 'is mainly mental and is caused by shyness, which is caused by the inferiority complex, which in its turn is caused by suppressed desires or introverted inhibitions or something. The advice I give to all young men who come in here behaving like soda-water siphons is to go out and make a point of speaking to at least three perfect strangers every day. Engage these strangers in conversation, persevering no matter how priceless a chump you may feel, and before many weeks are out you will find that the little daily dose has had its effect. Shyness will wear off, and with it the stammer.'

And, having requested the young man—in a voice of the clearest timbre, free from all trace of impediment—to hand over a fee of five guineas, the specialist sent George out into the world.

The more George thought about the advice he had been given, the less he liked it. He shivered in the cab that took him to the station to catch the train back to East Wobsley. Like all shy young men, he had never hitherto looked upon himself as shy—preferring to attribute his distaste for the society of his fellows to some subtle rareness of soul. But now that the thing had been put squarely up to him, he was compelled to realize that in all essentials he was a perfect rabbit. The thought of accosting perfect strangers and forcing his conversation upon them sickened him.

But no Mulliner has ever shirked an unpleasant duty. As he reached the platform and strode along it to the train, his teeth were set, his eyes shone with an almost fanatical light of determination, and he intended before his journey was over to conduct three heart-to-heart chats if he had to sing every bar of them.

The compartment into which he had made his way was empty at the moment, but just before the train started a very large, fierce-looking man got in. George would have preferred somebody a little less formidable for his first subject, but he braced himself and bent forward. And, as he did so, the man spoke.

'The wur-wur-wur-wur-weather', he said, 'sus-sus-seems to be ter-ter-taking a tur-tur-turn for the ber-ber-better, der-doesn't it?'

George sank back as if he had been hit between the eyes. The train had moved out of the dimness of the station by now, and the sun was shining brightly on the speaker, illuminating his knobbly shoulders, his craggy jaw, and, above all, the shockingly choleric look in his eyes. The reply 'Y-y-y-y-y-y-yes' to such a man would obviously be madness.

But to abstain from speech did not seem to be much better as a policy. George's silence appeared to arouse this man's worst passions. His face had turned purple and he glared painfully.

'I uk-uk-asked you a sus-sus-civil quk-quk-quk,' he said, irascibly. 'Are you d-d-d-d-deaf?'

All we Mulliners have been noted for our presence of mind. To open his mouth, point to his tonsils, and utter a strangled gurgle was with George the work of a moment.

The tension relaxed. The man's annoyance abated.

'D-d-d-dumb?' he said, commiseratingly. 'I beg your p-p-p-p-pup. I t-t-trust I have not caused you p-p-p-p-pup. It m-must be tut-tut-tut-tut-tut not to be able to sus-sus-speak fuf-fuf-fuf-fuf-fluently.'

He then buried himself in his paper, and George sank back in his corner, quivering in every limb.

To get to East Wobsley, as you doubtless know, you have to change at Ippleton and take the branch-line. By the time the train reached this junction, George's composure was somewhat restored. He deposited his belongings in a compartment of the East Wobsley train, which was waiting in a glued manner on the other side of the platform, and, finding that it would not start for some ten minutes, decided to pass the time by strolling up and down in the pleasant air.

It was a lovely afternoon. The sun was gilding the platform with its rays, and a gentle breeze blew from the west. A little brook ran tinkling at the side of the road; birds were singing in the hedgerows; and through the trees could be discerned dimly the noble façade of the County Lunatic Asylum. Soothed by his surroundings, George began to feel so refreshed that he regretted that in this wayside station there was no one present whom he could engage in talk.

It was at this moment that the distinguished-looking stranger entered the platform.

The new-comer was a man of imposing physique, simply dressed in pyjamas, brown boots, and a mackintosh. In his hand he carried a top-hat, and into this he was dipping his fingers, taking them out, and then waving them in a curious manner to right and left. He nodded so affably to George that the latter, though a little surprised at the other's costume, decided to speak. After all, he reflected, clothes do not make the man, and, judging from the other's smile, a warm heart appeared to beat beneath that orange-and-mauve striped pyjama jacket.

'N-n-n-n-nice weather,' he said.

'Glad you like it,' said the stranger. 'I ordered it specially.'

George was a little puzzled by this remark, but he persevered.

'M-might I ask wur-wur-what you are dud-doing?'

'Doing?'

'With that her-her-her-her-hat?'

'Oh, with this hat? I see what you mean. Just scattering largesse to the multitude,' replied the stranger, dipping his fingers once more and waving them with a generous gesture. 'Devil of a bore, but it's expected of a man in my position. The fact is,' he said, linking his arm in George's and speaking in a confidential undertone, 'I'm the Emperor of Abyssinia. That's my palace over there,' he said, pointing through the trees. 'Don't let it go any further. It's not supposed to be generally known.'

It was with a rather sickly smile that George now endeavoured to withdraw his arm from that of his companion, but the other would have none of this aloofness. He seemed to be in complete agreement with Shakespeare's dictum that a friend, when found, should be grappled to you with hooks of steel. He held George in a vise-like grip and drew him into a recess of the platform. He looked about him, and seemed satisfied.

'We are alone at last,' he said.

This fact had already impressed itself with sickening clearness on the young man. There are few spots in the civilized world more deserted than the platform of a small country station. The sun shone on the smooth asphalt, on the gleaming rails, and on the machine which, in exchange for a penny placed in the slot marked 'Matches', would supply a package of wholesome butter-scotch—but on nothing else.

What George could have done with at the moment was a posse of police armed with stout clubs, and there was not even a dog in sight.

'I've been wanting to talk to you for a long time,' said the stranger, genially.

'Huh-huh-have you?' said George.

'Yes. I want your opinion of human sacrifices.'

George said he didn't like them.

'Why not?' asked the other, surprised.

George said it was hard to explain. He just didn't.

'Well, I think you're wrong,' said the Emperor. 'I know there's a school of thought growing up that holds your views, but I disapprove of it. I hate all this modern advanced thought. Human sacrifices have always been good enough for the Emperors of Abyssinia, and they're good enough for me. Kindly step in here, if you please.'

He indicated the lamp-and-mop room, at which they had now arrived. It was a dark and sinister apartment, smelling strongly of oil and porters, and was probably the last place on earth in which George would have wished to be closeted with a man of such peculiar views. He shrank back.

'You go in first,' he said.

'No larks,' said the other, suspiciously.

'L-l-l-l-larks?'

'Yes. No pushing a fellow in and locking the door and squirting water at him through the window. I've had that happen to me before.'

'Sus-certainly not.'

'Right!' said the Emperor. 'You're a gentleman and I'm a gentleman. Both gentlemen. Have you a knife, by the way? We shall need a knife.'

'No. No knife.'

'Ah, well,' said the Emperor, 'then we'll have to look about for something else. No doubt we shall manage somehow.'

And with the debonair manner which so became him, he scattered another handful of largesse and walked into the lamp-room.

It was not the fact that he had given his word as a gentleman that kept George from locking the door. There is probably no family on earth more nicely scrupulous as regards keeping its promises than the Mulliners, but I am compelled to admit that, had George been able to find the key, he would have locked that door without hesitation. Not being able to find the key, he had to be satisfied with banging it. This done, he leaped back and raced away down the platform. A confused noise within seemed to indicate that the Emperor had become involved with some lamps.

George made the best of the respite. Covering the ground at a high rate of speed, he flung himself into the train and took refuge under the seat.

There he remained, quaking. At one time he thought that his uncongenial acquaintance had got upon his track, for the door of the compartment opened and a cool wind blew in upon him. Then, glancing along the floor, he perceived feminine ankles. The relief was enormous, but even in his relief George, who was the soul of modesty, did not forget his manners. He closed his eyes.

A voice spoke.

'Porter!'

'Yes, ma'am?'

'What was all that disturbance as I came into the station?'

'Patient escaped from the asylum, ma'am.'

'Good gracious!'

The voice would undoubtedly have spoken further, but at this moment the train began to move. There came the sound of a body descending upon a cushioned seat, and some little time later the rustling of a paper. The train gathered speed and jolted on.

George had never before travelled under the seat of a railway carriage; and, though he belonged to the younger generation, which is supposed to be so avid of new experiences, he had no desire to do so now. He decided to emerge, and, if possible, to emerge with the minimum of ostentation. Little as he knew of women, he was aware that as a sex they are apt to be startled by the sight of men crawling out from under the seats of compartments. He began his manoeuvres by poking out his head and surveying the terrain.

All was well. The woman, in her seat across the way, was engrossed in her paper. Moving in a series of noiseless wriggles, George extricated himself from his hiding-place and, with a twist which would have been impossible to a man not in the habit of doing Swedish exercises daily before breakfast, heaved himself into the corner seat. The woman continued reading her paper.

The events of the past quarter of an hour had tended rather to drive from George's mind the mission which he had undertaken on leaving the specialist's office. But now, having leisure for reflection, he realized that, if he meant to complete his first day of the cure, he was allowing himself to run sadly behind schedule. Speak to three strangers, the specialist had told him, and up to the present he had spoken to only one. True, this one had been a pretty considerable stranger, and a less conscientious young man than George Mulliner might have considered himself justified in chalking him up on the scoreboard as one and a half or even two. But George had the dogged, honest Mulliner streak in him, and he refused to quibble.

He nerved himself for action, and cleared his throat.

'Ah-h'rm!' said George.

And, having opened the ball, he smiled a winning smile and waited for his companion to make the next move.

The move which his companion made was in an upwards direction, and measured from six to eight inches. She dropped her paper and regarded George with a pale-eyed horror. One pictures her a little in the position of Robinson Crusoe when he saw the footprint in the sand. She had been convinced that she was completely alone, and lo! out of space a voice had spoken to her. Her face worked, but she made no remark.

George, on his side, was also feeling a little ill at ease. Women always increased his natural shyness. He never knew what to say to them.

Then a happy thought struck him. He had just glanced at his watch and found the hour to be nearly four-thirty. Women, he knew, loved a drop of tea at about this time, and fortunately there was in his suit-case a full thermos-flask.

'Pardon me, but I wonder if you would care for a cup of tea?' was what he wanted to say, but, as so often happened with him when in the presence of the opposite sex, he could get no further than a sort of sizzling sound like a cockroach calling to its young.

The woman continued to stare at him. Her eyes were now about the size of regulation standard golf-balls, and her breathing suggested the last stages of asthma. And it was at this point that George, struggling for speech, had one of those inspirations which frequently come to Mulliners. There flashed into his mind what the specialist had told him about singing. Say it with music—that was the thing to do.

He delayed no longer.

'Tea for two and two for tea and me for you and you for me—'

He was shocked to observe his companion turning Nile-green. He decided to make his meaning clearer.

'I have a nice thermos. I have a full thermos. Won't you share my thermos, too? When skies are grey and you feel you are blue, tea sends the sun smiling through. I have a nice thermos. I have a full thermos. May I pour out some for you?'

You will agree with me, I think, that no invitation could have been more happily put, but his companion was not responsive. With one last agonized look at him, she closed her eyes and sank back in her seat. Her lips had now turned a curious grey-blue colour, and they were moving feebly. She reminded George, who, like myself, was a keen fisherman, of a newly-gaffed salmon.

George sat back in his corner, brooding. Rack his brain as he might, he could think of no topic which could be guaranteed to interest, elevate, and amuse. He looked out of the window with a sigh.

The train was now approaching the dear old familiar East Wobsley country. He began to recognize landmarks. A wave of sentiment poured over George as he thought of Susan, and he reached for the bag of buns which he had bought at the refreshment room at Ippleton. Sentiment always made him hungry.

He took his thermos out of the suit-case, and, unscrewing the top, poured himself out a cup of tea. Then, placing the thermos on the seat, he drank.

He looked across at his companion. Her eyes were still closed, and she uttered little sighing noises. George was half-inclined to renew his offer of tea, but the only tune he could remember was Hard-Hearted Hanna, the Vamp from Savannah, and it was difficult to fit suitable words to it. He ate his bun and gazed out at the familiar scenery.

Now, as you approach East Wobsley, the train, I must mention, has to pass over some points; and so violent is the sudden jerking that strong men have been known to spill their beer. George, forgetting this in his preoccupation, had placed the thermos only a few inches from the edge of the seat. The result was that, as the train reached the points, the flask leaped like a live thing, dived to the floor, and exploded.

Even George was distinctly upset by the sudden sharpness of the report. His bun sprang from his hand and was dashed to fragments. He blinked thrice in rapid succession. His heart tried to jump out of his mouth and loosened a front tooth.

But on the woman opposite the effect of the untoward occurrence was still more marked. With a single piercing shriek, she rose from her seat straight into the air like a rocketing pheasant; and, having clutched the communication-cord, fell back again. Impressive as her previous leap had been, she excelled it now by several inches. I do not know what the existing record for the Sitting High-Jump is, but she undoubtedly lowered it; and if George had been a member of the Olympic Games Selection Committee, he would have signed this woman up immediately.

It is a curious thing that, in spite of the railway companies' sporting willingness to let their patrons have a tug at the extremely moderate price of five pounds a go, very few people have ever either pulled a communication-cord or seen one pulled. There is, thus, a widespread ignorance as to what precisely happens on such occasions.

The procedure, George tells me, is as follows: First there comes a grinding noise, as the brakes are applied. Then the train stops. And finally, from every point of the compass, a seething mob of interested onlookers begins to appear.

It was about a mile and a half from East Wobsley that the affair had taken place, and as far as the eye could reach the country-side was totally devoid of humanity. A moment before nothing had been visible but smiling cornfields and broad pasture-lands; but now from east, west, north, and south running figures began to appear. We must remember that George at the time was in a somewhat overwrought frame of mind, and his statements should therefore be accepted with caution; but he tells me that out of the middle of a single empty meadow, entirely devoid of cover, no fewer than twenty-seven distinct rustics suddenly appeared, having undoubtedly shot up through the ground.

The rails, which had been completely unoccupied, were now thronged with so dense a crowd of navvies that it seemed to George absurd to pretend that there was any unemployment in England. Every member of the labouring classes throughout the country was so palpably present. Moreover, the train, which at Ippleton had seemed sparsely occupied, was disgorging passengers from every door. It was the sort of mob-scene which would have made David W. Griffith scream with delight; and it looked, George says, like Guest Night at the Royal Automobile Club. But, as I say, we must remember that he was overwrought.

It is difficult to say what precisely would have been the correct behaviour of your polished man of the world in such a situation. I think myself that a great deal of sang-froid and address would be required even by the most self-possessed in order to pass off such a contretemps. To George, I may say at once, the crisis revealed itself immediately as one which he was totally incapable of handling. The one clear thought that stood out from the welter of his emotions was the reflection that it was advisable to remove himself, and to do so without delay. Drawing a deep breath, he shot swiftly off the mark.

All we Mulliners have been athletes; and George, when at the University, had been noted for his speed of foot. He ran now as he had never run before. His statement, however, that as he sprinted across the first field he distinctly saw a rabbit shoot an envious glance at him as he passed and shrug its shoulders hopelessly, I am inclined to discount. George, as I have said before, was a little over-excited.

Nevertheless, it is not to be questioned that he made good going. And he had need to, for after the first instant of surprise, which had enabled him to secure a lead, the whole mob was pouring across country after him; and dimly, as he ran, he could hear voices in the throng informally discussing the advisability of lynching him. Moreover, the field through which he was running, a moment before a bare expanse of green, was now black with figures, headed by a man with a beard who carried a pitchfork. George swerved sharply to the right, casting a swift glance over his shoulder at his pursuers. He disliked them all, but especially the man with the pitchfork.

It is impossible for one who was not an eye-witness to say how long the chase continued and how much ground was covered by the interested parties. I know the East Wobsley country well, and I have checked George's statements; and, if it is true that he travelled east as far as Little Wigmarsh-in-the-Dell and as far west as Higgleford-cum-Wortlebury-beneath-the-Hill, he must undoubtedly have done a lot of running.

But a point which must not be forgotten is that, to a man not in a condition to observe closely, the village of Higgleford-cum-Wortlebury-beneath-the-Hill might easily not have been Higgleford-cum-Wortlebury-beneath-the-Hill at all, but another hamlet which in many respects closely resembles it. I need scarcely say that I allude to Lesser-Snodsbury-in-the-Vale.

Let us assume, therefore, that George, having touched Little-Wigmarsh-in-the-Dell, shot off at a tangent and reached Lesser-Snodsbury-in-the-Vale. This would be a considerable run. And, as he remembers flitting past Farmer Higgins's pigsty and the Dog and Duck at Pondlebury Parva and splashing through the brook Wipple at the point where it joins the River Wopple, we can safely assume that, wherever else he went, he got plenty of exercise.

But the pleasantest of functions must end, and, just as the setting sun was gilding the spire of the ivy-covered church of St Barnabas the Resilient, where George as a child had sat so often, enlivening the tedium of the sermon by making faces at the choir-boys, a damp and bedraggled figure might have been observed crawling painfully along the High Street of East Wobsley in the direction of the cosy little cottage known to its builder as Chatsworth and to the village tradesmen as 'Mulliner's'.

It was George, home from the hunting-field.

Slowly George Mulliner made his way to the familiar door, and, passing through it, flung himself into his favourite chair. But a moment later a more imperious need than the desire to rest forced itself upon his attention. Rising stiffly, he tottered to the kitchen and mixed himself a revivifying whisky-and-soda. Then, refilling his glass, he returned to the sitting-room, to find that it was no longer empty. A slim, fair girl, tastefully attired in tailor-made tweeds, was leaning over the desk on which he kept his Dictionary of English Synonyms.

She looked up as he entered, startled.

'Why, Mr Mulliner!' she exclaimed. 'What has been happening? Your clothes are torn, rent, ragged, tattered, and your hair is all dishevelled, untrimmed, hanging loose or negligently, at loose ends!'

George smiled a wan smile.

'You are right,' he said. 'And, what is more, I am suffering from extreme fatigue, weariness, lassitude, exhaustion, prostration, and languor.'

The girl gazed at him, a divine pity in her soft eyes.

'I'm so sorry,' she murmured. 'So very sorry, grieved, distressed, afflicted, pained, mortified, dejected, and upset.'

George took her hand. Her sweet sympathy had effected the cure for which he had been seeking so long. Coming on top of the violent emotions through which he had been passing all day, it seemed to work on him like some healing spell, charm, or incantation. Suddenly, in a flash, he realized that he was no longer a stammerer. Had he wished at that moment to say, 'Peter Piper picked a peck of pickled peppers,' he could have done it without a second thought.

But he had better things to say than that.

'Miss Blake—Susan—Susie.' He took her other hand in his. His voice rang out clear and unimpeded. It seemed to him incredible that he had ever yammered at this girl like an over-heated steam-radiator. 'It cannot have escaped your notice that I have long entertained towards you sentiments warmer and deeper than those of ordinary friendship. It is love, Susan, that has been animating my bosom. Love, first a tiny seed, has burgeoned in my heart till, blazing into flame, it has swept away on the crest of its wave my diffidence, my doubt, my fears, and my foreboding, and now, like the topmost topaz of some ancient tower, it cries to all the world in a voice of thunder: "You are mine! My mate! Predestined to me since Time first began!" As the star guides the mariner when, battered by boiling billows, he hies him home to the haven of hope and happiness, so do you gleam upon me along life's rough road and seem to say, "Have courage, George! I am here!" Susan, I am not an eloquent man—I cannot speak fluently as I could wish—but these simple words which you have just heard come from the heart, from the unspotted heart of an English gentleman. Susan, I love you. Will you be my wife, married woman, matron, spouse, helpmeet, consort, partner, or better half?'

'Oh, George!' said Susan. 'Yes, yea, ay, aye! Decidedly, unquestionably, indubitably, incontrovertibly, and past all dispute!'

He folded her in his arms. And, as he did so, there came from the street outside—faintly, as from a distance—the sound of feet and voices. George leaped to the window. Rounding the corner, just by the Cow and Wheelbarrow public-house, licensed to sell ales, wines, and spirits, was the man with the pitchfork, and behind him followed a vast crowd.

'My darling,' said George, 'for purely personal and private reasons, into which I need not enter, I must now leave you. Will you join me later?'

'I will follow you to the ends of the earth,' replied Susan, passionately.

'It will not be necessary,' said George. 'I am only going down to the coal-cellar. I shall spend the next half-hour or so there. If anybody calls and asks for me, perhaps you would not mind telling them that I am out.'

'I will, I will,' said Susan. 'And, George, by the way. What I really came here for was to ask you if you knew a hyphenated word of nine letters, ending in k and signifying an implement employed in the pursuit of agriculture.'

'Pitchfork, sweetheart,' said George. 'But you may take it from me, as one who knows, that agriculture isn't the only thing it is used in pursuit of.'

And since that day (concluded Mr Mulliner) George, believe me or believe me not, has not had the slightest trace of an impediment in his speech. He is now the chosen orator at all political rallies for miles around; and so offensively self-confident has his manner become that only last Friday he had his eye blacked by a hay-corn-and-feed merchant of the name of Stubbs. It just shows you, doesn't it?

2
A SLICE OF LIFE

The conversation in the bar-parlour of the Anglers' Rest had drifted round to the subject of the Arts: and somebody asked if that film-serial, The Vicissitudes of Vera, which they were showing down at the Bijou Dream, was worth seeing.

'It's very good,' said Miss Postlethwaite, our courteous and efficient barmaid, who is a prominent first-nighter. 'It's about this mad professor who gets this girl into his toils and tries to turn her into a lobster.'

'Tries to turn her into a lobster?' echoed we, surprised.

'Yes, sir. Into a lobster. It seems he collected thousands and thousands of lobsters and mashed them up and boiled down the juice from their glands and was just going to inject it into this Vera Dalrymple's spinal column when Jack Frobisher broke into the house and stopped him.'

'Why did he do that?'

'Because he didn't want the girl he loved to be turned into a lobster.'

'What we mean,' said we, 'is why did the professor want to turn the girl into a lobster?'

'He had a grudge against her.'

This seemed plausible, and we thought it over for a while. Then one of the company shook his head disapprovingly.

'I don't like stories like that,' he said. 'They aren't true to life.'

'Pardon me, sir,' said a voice. And we were aware of Mr Mulliner in our midst.

'Excuse me interrupting what may be a private discussion,' said Mr Mulliner, 'but I chanced to overhear the recent remarks, and you, sir, have opened up a subject on which I happen to hold strong views—to wit, the question of what is and what is not true to life. How can we, with our limited experience, answer that question? For all we know, at this very moment hundreds of young women all over the country may be in the process of being turned into lobsters. Forgive my warmth, but I have suffered a good deal from this sceptical attitude of mind which is so prevalent nowadays. I have even met people who refused to believe my story about my brother Wilfred, purely because it was a little out of the ordinary run of the average man's experience.'

Considerably moved, Mr Mulliner ordered a hot Scotch with a slice of lemon.

'What happened to your brother Wilfred? Was he turned into a lobster?'

'No,' said Mr Mulliner, fixing his honest blue eyes on the speaker, 'he was not. It would be perfectly easy for me to pretend that he was turned into a lobster; but I have always made it a practice—and I always shall make it a practice—to speak nothing but the bare truth. My brother Wilfred simply had rather a curious adventure.'

My brother Wilfred (said Mr Mulliner) is the clever one of the family. Even as a boy he was always messing about with chemicals, and at the University he devoted his time entirely to research. The result was that while still quite a young man he had won an established reputation as the inventor of what are known to the trade as Mulliner's Magic Marvels—a general term embracing the Raven Gipsy Face-Cream, the Snow of the Mountains Lotion, and many other preparations, some designed exclusively for the toilet, others of a curative nature, intended to alleviate the many ills to which the flesh is heir.

Naturally, he was a very busy man: and it is to this absorption in his work that I attribute the fact that, though—like all the Mulliners—a man of striking personal charm, he had reached his thirty-first year without ever having been involved in an affair of the heart. I remember him telling me once that he simply had no time for girls.

But we all fall sooner or later, and these strong concentrated men harder than any. While taking a brief holiday one year at Cannes, he met a Miss Angela Purdue, who was staying at his hotel, and she bowled him over completely.

She was one of these jolly, outdoor girls; and Wilfred had told me that what attracted him first about her was her wholesome sunburned complexion. In fact, he told Miss Purdue the same thing when, shortly after he had proposed and been accepted, she asked him in her girlish way what it was that had first made him begin to love her.

'It's such a pity,' said Miss Purdue, 'that the sunburn fades so soon. I do wish I knew some way of keeping it.'

Even in his moments of holiest emotion Wilfred never forgot that he was a business man.

'You should try Mulliner's Raven Gipsy Face-Cream,' he said. 'It comes in two sizes—the small (or half-crown) jar and the large jar at seven shillings and sixpence. The large jar contains three and a half times as much as the small jar. It is applied nightly with a small sponge before retiring to rest. Testimonials have been received from numerous members of the aristocracy and may be examined at the office by any bonafide inquirer.'

'Is it really good?'

'I invented it,' said Wilfred, simply.

She looked at him adoringly.

'How clever you are! Any girl ought to be proud to marry you.'

'Oh, well,' said Wilfred, with a modest wave of his hand.

'All the same, my guardian is going to be terribly angry when I tell him we're engaged.'

'Why?'

'I inherited the Purdue millions when my uncle died, you see, and my guardian has always wanted me to marry his son, Percy.'

Wilfred kissed her fondly, and laughed a defiant laugh.

'Jer mong feesh der selar,' he said lightly.

But, some days after his return to London, whither the girl had preceded him, he had occasion to recall her words. As he sat in his study, musing on a preparation to cure the pip in canaries, a card was brought to him.

'Sir Jasper ffinch-ffarrowmere, Bart.,' he read. The name was strange to him.

'Show the gentleman in,' he said. And presently there entered a very stout man with a broad, pink face. It was a face whose natural expression should, Wilfred felt, have been jovial, but at the moment it was grave.

'Sir Jasper Finch-Farrowmere?' said Wilfred.

'ffinch-ffarrowmere,' corrected the visitor, his sensitive ear detecting the capital letters.

'Ah yes. You spell it with two small f's.'

'Four small f's.'

'And to what do I owe the honour—'

'I am Angela Purdue's guardian.'

'How do you do? A whisky-and-soda?'

'I thank you, no. I am a total abstainer. I found that alcohol had a tendency to increase my weight, so I gave it up. I have also given up butter, potatoes, soups of all kinds and— However,' he broke off, the fanatic gleam which comes into the eyes of all fat men who are describing their system of diet fading away, 'this is not a social call, and I must not take up your time with idle talk. I have a message for you, Mr Mulliner. From Angela.'

'Bless her!' said Wilfred. 'Sir Jasper, I love that girl with a fervour which increases daily.'

'Is that so?' said the baronet. Well, what I came to say was, it's all off.'

'What?'

'All off. She sent me to say that she had thought it over and wanted to break the engagement.'

Wilfred's eyes narrowed. He had not forgotten what Angela had said about this man wanting her to marry his son. He gazed piercingly at his visitor, no longer deceived by the superficial geniality of his appearance. He had read too many detective stories where the fat, jolly, red-faced man turns out a fiend in human shape to be a ready victim to appearances.

'Indeed?' he said, coldly. 'I should prefer to have this information from Miss Purdue's own lips.'

'She won't see you. But, anticipating this attitude on your part, I brought a letter from her. You recognize the writing?'

Wilfred took the letter. Certainly, the hand was Angela's, and the meaning of the words he read unmistakable. Nevertheless, as he handed the missive back, there was a hard smile on his face.

'There is such a thing as writing a letter under compulsion,' he said.

The baronet's pink face turned mauve.

'What do you mean, sir?'

'What I say.'

'Are you insinuating—'

'Yes, I am.'

'Pooh, sir!'

'Pooh to you!' said Wilfred. 'And, if you want to know what I think, you poor fish, I believe your name is spelled with a capital F, like anybody else's.'

Stung to the quick, the baronet turned on his heel and left the room without another word.

Although he had given up his life to chemical research, Wilfred Mulliner was no mere dreamer. He could be the man of action when necessity demanded. Scarcely had his visitor left when he was on his way to the Senior Test-Tubes, the famous chemists' club in St James's. There, consulting Kelly's County Families, he learnt that Sir Jasper's address was ffinch Hall in Yorkshire. He had found out all he wanted to know. It was at ffinch Hall, he decided, that Angela must now be immured.

For that she was being immured somewhere he had no doubt. That letter, he was positive, has been written by her under stress of threats. The writing was Angela's, but he declined to believe that she was responsible for the phraseology and sentiment. He remembered reading a story where the heroine was forced into courses which she would not otherwise have contemplated by the fact that somebody was standing over her with a flask of vitriol. Possibly this was what that bounder of a baronet had done to Angela.

Considering this possibility, he did not blame her for what she had said about him, Wilfred, in the second paragraph of her note. Nor did he reproach her for signing herself 'Yrs truly, A. Purdue'. Naturally, when baronets are threatening to pour vitriol down her neck, a refined and sensitive young girl cannot pick her words. This sort of thing must of necessity interfere with the selection of the mot juste.

That afternoon, Wilfred was in a train on his way to Yorkshire. That evening, he was in the ffinch Arms in the village of which Sir Jasper was the squire. That night, he was in the gardens of ffinch Hall, prowling softly round the house, listening.

And presently, as he prowled, there came to his ears from an upper window a sound that made him stiffen like a statue and clench his hands till the knuckles stood out white under the strain.

It was the sound of a woman sobbing.

Wilfred spent a sleepless night, but by morning he had formed his plan of action. I will not weary you with a description of the slow and tedious steps by which he first made the acquaintance of Sir Jasper's valet, who was an habitué of the village inn, and then by careful stages won the man's confidence with friendly words and beer. Suffice it to say that, about a week later, Wilfred had induced this man with bribes to leave suddenly on the plea of an aunt's illness, supplying—so as to cause his employer no inconvenience—a cousin to take his place.

This cousin, as you will have guessed, was Wilfred himself. But a very different Wilfred from the dark-haired, clean-cut young scientist who had revolutionized the world of chemistry a few months before by proving that $H2O+b3g4z7-m9z8=g6f5p3x$. Before leaving London on what he knew would be a dark and dangerous enterprise, Wilfred had taken the precaution of calling in at a well-known costumier's and buying a red wig. He had also purchased a pair of blue spectacles: but for the role which he had now undertaken these were, of course, useless. A blue-spectacled valet could not but have aroused suspicion in the most guileless baronet. All that Wilfred did, therefore, in the way of preparation, was to don the wig, shave off his moustache, and treat his face to a light coating of the Raven Gipsy Face-Cream. This done, he set out for ffinch Hall.

Externally, ffinch Hall was one of those gloomy, sombre country-houses which seem to exist only for the purpose of having horrid crimes committed in them. Even in his brief visit to the grounds, Wilfred had noticed fully half a dozen places which seemed incomplete without a cross indicating spot where body was found by the police. It was the sort of house where ravens croak in the front garden just before the death of the heir, and shrieks ring out from behind barred windows in the night.

Nor was its interior more cheerful. And, as for the personnel of the domestic staff, that was less exhilarating than anything else about the place. It consisted of an aged cook who, as she bent over her cauldrons, looked like something out of a travelling company of Macbeth, touring the smaller towns of the North, and Murgatroyd, the butler, a huge, sinister man with a cast in one eye and an evil light in the other.

Many men, under these conditions, would have been daunted. But not Wilfred Mulliner. Apart from the fact that, like all the Mulliners, he was as brave as a lion, he had come expecting something of this nature. He settled down to his duties and kept his eyes open, and before long his vigilance was rewarded.

One day, as he lurked about the dim-lit passage-ways, he saw Sir Jasper coming up the stairs with a laden tray in his hands. It contained a toast-rack, a half bot. of white wine, pepper, salt, veg., and in a covered dish something which Wilfred, sniffing cautiously, decided was a cutlet.

Lurking in the shadows, he followed the baronet to the top of the house. Sir Jasper paused at a door on the second floor. He knocked. The door opened, a hand was stretched forth, the tray vanished, the door closed, and the baronet moved away.

So did Wilfred. He had seen what he had wanted to see, discovered what he had wanted to discover. He returned to the servants' hall, and under the gloomy eyes of Murgatroyd began to shape his plans.

'Where you been?' demanded the butler, suspiciously.

'Oh, hither and thither,' said Wilfred, with a well-assumed airiness.

Murgatroyd directed a menacing glance at him.

'You'd better stay where you belong,' he said, in his thick, growling voice. 'There's things in this house that don't want seeing.'

'Ah!' agreed the cook, dropping an onion in the cauldron.

Wilfred could not repress a shudder.

But, even as he shuddered, he was conscious of a certain relief. At least, he reflected, they were not starving his darling. That cutlet had smelt uncommonly good: and, if the bill of fare was always maintained at this level, she had nothing to complain of in the catering.

But his relief was short-lived. What, after all, he asked himself, are cutlets to a girl who is imprisoned in a locked room of a sinister country-house and is being forced to marry a man she does not love? Practically nothing. When the heart is sick, cutlets merely alleviate, they do not cure. Fiercely Wilfred told himself that, come what might, few days should pass before he found the key to that locked door and bore away his love to freedom and happiness.

The only obstacle in the way of this scheme was that it was plainly going to be a matter of the greatest difficulty to find the key. That night, when his employer dined, Wilfred searched his room thoroughly. He found nothing. The key, he was forced to conclude, was kept on the baronet's person.

Then how to secure it?

It is not too much to say that Wilfred Mulliner was nonplussed. The brain which had electrified the world of Science by discovering that if you mixed a stiffish oxygen and potassium and added a splash of trinitrotoluol and a spot of old brandy you got something that could be sold in America as champagne at a hundred and fifty dollars the case had to confess itself baffled.

To attempt to analyse the young man's emotions, as the next week dragged itself by, would be merely morbid. Life cannot, of course, be all sunshine: and in relating a story like this, which is a slice of life, one must pay as much attention to shade as to light: nevertheless,

It would be tedious were I to describe to you in detail the soul-torments which afflicted Wilfred Mulliner as day followed day and no solution to the problem presented itself. You are all intelligent men, and you can picture to yourselves how a high-spirited young fellow, deeply in love, must have felt; knowing that the girl he loved was languishing in what practically amounted to a dungeon, though situated on an upper floor, and chafing at his inability to set her free.

His eyes became sunken. His cheek-bones stood out. He lost weight. And so noticeable was this change in his physique that Sir Jasper ffinch-ffarrowmere commented on it one evening in tones of unconcealed envy.

'How the devil, Straker,' he said—for this was the pseudonym under which Wilfred was passing—'do you manage to keep so thin? Judging by the weekly books, you eat like a starving Esquimaux, and yet you don't put on weight. Now I, in addition to knocking off butter and potatoes, have started drinking hot unsweetened lemon-juice each night before retiring: and yet, damme,' he said—for, like all baronets, he was careless in his language—'I weighed myself this morning, and I was up another six ounces. What's the explanation?'

'Yes, Sir Jasper,' said Wilfred, mechanically.

'What the devil do you mean, Yes, Sir Jasper?'

'No, Sir Jasper.'

The baronet wheezed plaintively.

'I've been studying this matter closely,' he said, 'and it's one of the seven wonders of the world. Have you ever seen a fat valet? Of course not. Nor has anybody else. There is no such thing as a fat valet. And yet there is scarcely a moment during the day when a valet is not eating. He rises at six-thirty, and at seven is having coffee and buttered toast. At eight, he breakfasts off porridge, cream, eggs, bacon, jam, bread, butter, more eggs, more bacon, more jam, more tea, and more butter, finishing up with a slice of cold ham and a sardine. At eleven o'clock he has his "elevenses", consisting of coffee, cream, more bread, and more butter. At one, luncheon—a hearty meal, replete with every form of starchy food and lots of beer. If he can get at the port, he has port. At three, a snack. At four, another snack. At five, tea and buttered toast. At seven—dinner, probably with floury potatoes, and certainly with lots more beer. At nine, another snack. And at ten-thirty he retires to bed, taking with him a glass of milk and a plate of biscuits to keep himself from getting hungry in the night. And yet he remains as slender as a string-bean, while I, who have been dieting for years, tip the beam at two hundred and seventeen pounds, and am growing a third and supplementary chin. These are mysteries, Straker.'

'Yes, Sir Jasper.'

'Well, I'll tell you one thing,' said the baronet, 'I'm getting down one of those indoor Turkish Bath cabinet-affairs from London; and if that doesn't do the trick, I give up the struggle.'

The indoor Turkish Bath duly arrived and was unpacked; and it was some three nights later that Wilfred, brooding in the servants' hall, was aroused from his reverie by Murgatroyd.

'Here,' said Murgatroyd, 'wake up. Sir Jasper's calling you.'

'Calling me what?' asked Wilfred, coming to himself with a start.

'Calling you very loud,' growled the butler.

It was indeed so. From the upper regions of the house there was proceeding a series of sharp yelps, evidently those of a man in mortal stress. Wilfred was reluctant to interfere in any way if, as seemed probable, his employer was dying in agony; but he was a conscientious man, and it was his duty, while in this sinister house, to perform the work for which he was paid. He hurried up the stairs; and, entering Sir Jasper's bedroom, perceived the baronet's crimson face protruding from the top of the indoor Turkish Bath.

'So you've come at last!' cried Sir Jasper. 'Look here, when you put me into this infernal contrivance just now, what did you do to the dashed thing?'

'Nothing beyond what was indicated in the printed pamphlet accompanying the machine, Sir Jasper. Following the instructions, I slid Rod A into Groove B, fastening with Catch C—'

'Well, you must have made a mess of it, somehow. The thing's stuck. I can't get out.'

'You can't?' cried Wilfred.

'No. And the bally apparatus is getting considerably hotter than the hinges of the Inferno.' I must apologize for Sir Jasper's language, but you know what baronets are. 'I'm being cooked to a crisp.'

A sudden flash of light seemed to blaze upon Wilfred Mulliner.

'I will release you, Sir Jasper—'

'Well, hurry up, then.'

'On one condition.' Wilfred fixed him with a piercing gaze. 'First, I must have the key.'

'There isn't a key, you idiot. It doesn't lock. It just clicks when you slide Gadget D into Thingummybob E.'

'The key I require is that of the room in which you are holding Angela Purdue a prisoner.'

'What the devil do you mean? Ouch!'

'I will tell you what I mean, Sir Jasper ffinch-ffarrowmere. I am Wilfred Mulliner!'

'Don't be an ass. Wilfred Mulliner has black hair. Yours is red. You must be thinking of someone else.'

'This is a wig,' said Wilfred. 'By Clarkson.' He shook a menacing finger at the baronet. 'You little thought, Sir Jasper ffinch-ffarrowmere, when you embarked on this dastardly scheme, that Wilfred Mulliner was watching your every move. I guessed your plans from the start. And now is the moment when I checkmate them. Give me that key, you Fiend.'

'ffiend,' corrected Sir Jasper, automatically.

'I am going to release my darling, to take her away from this dreadful house, to marry her by special licence as soon as it can legally be done.'

In spite of his sufferings, a ghastly laugh escaped Sir Jasper's lips.

'You are, are you?'

'I am.'

'Yes, you are!'

'Give me the key.'

'I haven't got it, you chump. It's in the door.'

'Ha, ha!'

'It's no good saying "Ha, ha!" It is in the door. On Angela's side of the door.'

'A likely story! But I cannot stay here wasting time. If you will not give me the key, I shall go up and break in the door.'

'Do!' Once more the baronet laughed like a tortured soul. 'And see what she'll say.'

Wilfred could make nothing of this last remark. He could, he thought, imagine very clearly what Angela would say. He could picture her sobbing on his chest, murmuring that she knew he would come, that she had never doubted him for an instant. He leapt for the door.

'Here! Hi! Aren't you going to let me out?'

'Presently,' said Wilfred. 'Keep cool.' He raced up the stairs.

'Angela,' he cried, pressing his lips against the panel. 'Angela!'

'Who's that?' answered a well-remembered voice from within.

'It is I—Wilfred. I am going to burst open the door. Stand clear of the gates.'

He drew back a few paces, and hurled himself at the woodwork. There was a grinding crash, as the lock gave. And Wilfred, staggering on, found himself in a room so dark that he could see nothing.

'Angela, where are you?'

'I'm here. And I'd like to know why you are, after that letter I wrote you. Some men,' continued the strangely cold voice, 'do not seem to know how to take a hint.'

Wilfred staggered, and would have fallen had he not clutched at his forehead.

'That letter?' he stammered. 'You surely didn't mean what you wrote in that letter?'

'I meant every word and I wish I had put in more.'

'But—but—but—But don't you love me, Angela?'

A hard, mocking laugh rang through the room.

'Love you? Love the man who recommended me to try Mulliner's Raven Gipsy Face-Cream!'

'What do you mean?'

'I will tell you what I mean. Wilfred Mulliner, look on your handiwork!'

The room became suddenly flooded with light. And there, standing with her hand on the switch, stood Angela—a queenly, lovely figure, in whose radiant beauty the sternest critic would have noted but one flaw—the fact that she was piebald.

Wilfred gazed at her with adoring eyes. Her face was partly brown and partly white, and on her snowy neck were patches of sepia that looked like the thumb-prints you find on the pages of books in the Free Library: but he thought her the most beautiful creature he had ever seen. He longed to fold her in his arms: and but for the fact that her eyes told him that she would undoubtedly land an upper-cut on him if he tried it he would have done so.

'Yes,' she went on, 'this is what you have made of me, Wilfred Mulliner—you and that awful stuff you call the Raven Gipsy Face-Cream. This is the skin you loved to touch! I took your advice and bought one of the large jars at seven and six, and see the result! Barely twenty-four hours after the first application, I could have walked into any circus and named my own terms as the Spotted Princess of the Fiji Islands. I fled here to my childhood home, to hide myself. And the first thing that happened'—her voice broke—'was that my favourite hunter shied at me and tried to bite pieces out of his manger: while Ponto, my little dog, whom I have reared from a puppy, caught one sight of my face and is now in the hands of the vet. and unlikely to recover. And it was you, Wilfred Mulliner, who brought this curse upon me!'

Many men would have wilted beneath these searing words, but Wilfred Mulliner merely smiled with infinite compassion and understanding.

'It is quite all right,' he said. 'I should have warned you, sweetheart, that this occasionally happens in cases where the skin is exceptionally delicate and finely-textured. It can be speedily remedied by an application of the Mulliner Snow of the Mountains Lotion, four shillings the medium-sized bottle.'

'Wilfred! Is this true?'

'Perfectly true, dearest. And is this all that stands between us?'

'No!' shouted a voice of thunder.

Wilfred wheeled sharply. In the doorway stood Sir Jasper ffinch-ffarrowmere. He was swathed in a bath-towel, what was visible of his person being a bright crimson. Behind him, toying with a horse-whip, stood Murgatroyd, the butler.

'You didn't expect to see me, did you?'

'I certainly,' replied Wilfred, severely, 'did not expect to see you in a lady's presence in a costume like that.'

'Never mind my costume.' Sir Jasper turned.

'Murgatroyd, do your duty!'

The butler, scowling horribly, advanced into the room.

'Stop!' screamed Angela.

'I haven't begun yet, miss,' said the butler, deferentially.

'You shan't touch Wilfred. I love him.'

'What!' cried Sir Jasper. 'After all that has happened?'

'Yes. He has explained everything.'

A grim frown appeared on the baronet's vermilion face.

'I'll bet he hasn't explained why he left me to be cooked in that infernal Turkish Bath. I was beginning to throw out clouds of smoke when Murgatroyd, faithful fellow, heard my cries and came and released me.'

'Though not my work,' added the butler.

Wilfred eyed him steadily.

'If,' he said, 'you used Mulliner's Reduc-o, the recognized specific for obesity, whether in the tabloid form at three shillings the tin, or as a liquid at five and six the flask, you would have no need to stew in Turkish Baths. Mulliner's Reduc-o, which contains no injurious chemicals, but is compounded purely of health-giving herbs, is guaranteed to remove excess weight, steadily and without weakening after-effects, at the rate of two pounds a week. As used by the nobility.'

The glare of hatred faded from the baronet's eyes.

'Is that a fact?' he whispered.

'It is.'

'You guarantee it?'

'All the Mulliner preparations are fully guaranteed.'

'My boy!' cried the baronet. He shook Wilfred by the hand. 'Take her,' he said, brokenly. 'And with her my b-blessing.'

A discreet cough sounded in the background.

'You haven't anything, by any chance, sir,' asked Murgatroyd, 'that's good for lumbago?'

'Mulliner's Ease-o will cure the most stubborn case in six days.'

'Bless you, sir, bless you,' sobbed Murgatroyd. 'Where can I get it?'

'At all chemists.'

'It catches me in the small of the back principally, sir.'

'It need catch you no longer,' said Wilfred.

There is little to add. Murgatroyd is now the most lissom butler in Yorkshire. Sir Jasper's weight is down under the fifteen stone and he is thinking of taking up hunting again. Wilfred and Angela are man and wife; and never, I am informed, had the wedding-bells of the old church at ffinch village rung out a blither peal than they did on that June morning when Angela, raising to her love a face on which the brown was as evenly distributed as on an antique walnut table, replied to the clergyman's question, 'Wilt thou, Angela, take this Wilfred?' with a shy, 'I will'. They now have two bonny bairns—the small, or Percival, at a preparatory school in Sussex, and the large, or Ferdinand, at Eton.

Here Mr Mulliner, having finished his hot Scotch, bade us farewell and took his departure.

A silence followed his exit. The company seemed plunged in deep thought. Then somebody rose.

'Well, good night all,' he said.

It seemed to sum up the situation.

3
MULLINER'S BUCK-U-UPPO

The village Choral Society had been giving a performance of Gilbert and Sullivan's Sorcerer in aid of the Church Organ Fund; and, as we sat in the window of the Anglers' Rest, smoking our pipes, the audience came streaming past us down the little street. Snatches of song floated to our ears, and Mr Mulliner began to croon in unison.

"'Ah me! I was a pa-ale you-oung curate then!'" chanted Mr Mulliner in the rather snuffling voice in which the amateur singer seems to find it necessary to render the old songs.

'Remarkable,' he said, resuming his natural tones, 'how fashions change, even in clergymen. There are very few pale young curates nowadays.'

'True,' I agreed. 'Most of them are beefy young fellows who rowed for their colleges. I don't believe I have ever seen a pale young curate.'

'You never met my nephew Augustine, I think?'

'Never.'

'The description in the song would have fitted him perfectly. You will want to hear all about my nephew Augustine.'

At the time of which I am speaking (said Mr Mulliner) my nephew Augustine was a curate, and very young and extremely pale. As a boy he had completely outgrown his strength, and I rather think at his Theological College some of the wilder spirits must have bullied him; for when he went to Lower Briskett-in-the-Midden to assist the vicar, the Rev. Stanley Brandon, in his cure of souls, he was as meek and mild a young man as you could meet in a day's journey. He had flaxen hair, weak blue eyes, and the general demeanour of a saintly but timid cod-fish. Precisely, in short, the sort of young curate who seems to have been so common in the eighties, or whenever it was that Gilbert wrote The Sorcerer.

The personality of his immediate superior did little or nothing to help him to overcome his native diffidence. The Rev. Stanley Brandon was a huge and sinewy man of violent temper, whose red face and glittering eyes might well have intimidated the toughest curate. The Rev. Stanley had been a heavy-weight boxer at Cambridge, and I gather from Augustine that he seemed to be always on the point of introducing into debates on parish matters the methods which had made him so successful in the roped ring. I remember Augustine telling me that once, on the occasion when he had ventured to oppose the other's views in the matter of decorating the church for the Harvest Festival, he thought for a moment that the vicar was going to drop him with a right hook to the chin. It was some quite trivial point that had come up—a question as to whether the pumpkin would look better in the apse or the clerestory, if I recollect rightly—but for several seconds it seemed as if blood was about to be shed.

Such was the Rev. Stanley Brandon. And yet it was to the daughter of this formidable man that Augustine Mulliner had permitted himself to lose his heart. Truly, Cupid makes heroes of us all.

Jane was a very nice girl, and just as fond of Augustine as he was of her. But, as each lacked the nerve to go to the girl's father and put him abreast of the position of affairs, they were forced to meet surreptitiously. This jarred upon Augustine, who, like all the

Mulliners, loved the truth and hated any form of deception. And one evening, as they paced beside the laurels at the bottom of the vicarage garden, he rebelled.

'My dearest,' said Augustine, 'I can no longer brook this secrecy. I shall go into the house immediately and ask your father for your hand.'

Jane paled and clung to his arm. She knew so well that it was not her hand but her father's foot which he would receive if he carried out this mad scheme.

'No, no, Augustine! You must not!'

'But, darling, it is the only straightforward course.'

'But not tonight. I beg of you, not tonight.'

'Why not?'

'Because father is in a very bad temper. He has just had a letter from the bishop, rebuking him for wearing too many orphreys on his chasuble, and it has upset him terribly. You see, he and the bishop were at school together, and father can never forget it. He said at dinner that if old Boko Bickerton thought he was going to order him about he would jolly well show him.'

'And the bishop comes here tomorrow for the Confirmation services!' gasped Augustine.

'Yes. And I'm so afraid they will quarrel. It's such a pity father hasn't some other bishop over him. He always remembers that he once hit this one in the eye for pouring ink on his collar, and this lowers his respect for his spiritual authority. So you won't go in and tell him tonight, will you?'

'I will not,' Augustine assured her with a slight shiver.

'And you will be sure to put your feet in hot mustard and water when you get home? The dew has made the grass so wet.'

'I will indeed, dearest.'

'You are not strong, you know.'

'No, I am not strong.'

'You ought to take some really good tonic.'

'Perhaps I ought. Good night, Jane.'

'Good night, Augustine.'

The lovers parted. Jane slipped back into the vicarage, and Augustine made his way to his cosy rooms in the High Street. And the first thing he noticed on entering was a parcel on the table, and beside it a letter.

He opened it listlessly, his thoughts far away.

'My dear Augustine.'

He turned to the last page and glanced at the signature. The letter was from his Aunt Angela, the wife of my brother, Wilfred Mulliner. You may remember that I once told you the story of how these two came together. If so, you will recall that my brother Wilfred was the eminent chemical researcher who had invented, among other specifics, such world-famous preparations as Mulliner's Raven Gipsy Face-Cream and the Mulliner Snow of the Mountains Lotion. He and Augustine had never been particularly intimate, but between Augustine and his aunt there had always existed a warm friendship.

My dear Augustine (wrote Angela Mulliner),

I have been thinking so much about you lately, and I cannot forget that, when I saw you last, you seemed very fragile and deficient in vitamins. I do hope you take care of yourself.

I have been feeling for some time that you ought to take a tonic, and by a lucky chance Wilfred has just invented one which he tells me is the finest thing he has ever done. It is called Buck-U-Uppo, and acts directly on the red corpuscles. It is not yet on the market, but I have managed to smuggle a sample bottle from Wilfred's laboratory, and I want you to try it at once. I am sure it is just what you need.

Your affectionate aunt,

Angela Mulliner

PS.—You take a tablespoonful before going to bed, and another just before breakfast.

Augustine was not an unduly superstitious young man, but the coincidence of this tonic arriving so soon after Jane had told him that a tonic was what he needed affected him deeply. It seemed to him that this thing must have been meant. He shook the bottle, uncorked it, and, pouring out a liberal tablespoonful, shut his eyes and swallowed it.

The medicine, he was glad to find, was not unpleasant to the taste. It had a slightly pungent flavour, rather like old boot-soles beaten up in sherry. Having taken the dose, he read for a while in a book of theological essays, and then went to bed.

And as his feet slipped between the sheets, he was annoyed to find that Mrs Wardle, his housekeeper, had once more forgotten his hot-water bottle.

'Oh, dash!' said Augustine.

He was thoroughly upset. He had told the woman over and over again that he suffered from cold feet and could not get to sleep unless the dogs were properly warmed up. He sprang out of bed and went to the head of the stairs.

'Mrs Wardle!' he cried.

There was no reply.

'Mrs Wardle!' bellowed Augustine in a voice that rattled the window-panes like a strong nor'-easter. Until tonight he had always been very much afraid of his housekeeper and had both walked and talked softly in her presence. But now he was conscious of a strange new fortitude. His head was singing a little, and he felt equal to a dozen Mrs Wardles.

Shuffling footsteps made themselves heard.

'Well, what is it now?' asked a querulous voice.

Augustine snorted.

'I'll tell you what it is now,' he roared. 'How many times have I told you always to put a hot-water bottle in my bed? You've forgotten it again, you old cloth-head!'

Mrs Wardle peered up, astounded and militant.

'Mr Mulliner, I am not accustomed—'

'Shut up!' thundered Augustine. 'What I want from you is less back-chat and more hot-water bottles. Bring it up at once, or I leave tomorrow. Let me endeavour to get it into your concrete skull that you aren't the only person letting rooms in this village. Any more lip and I walk straight round the corner, where I'll be appreciated. Hot-water bottle ho! And look slippy about it.'

'Yes, Mr Mulliner. Certainly, Mr Mulliner. In one moment, Mr Mulliner.'

'Action! Action!' boomed Augustine. 'Show some speed. Put a little snap into it.'

'Yes, yes, most decidedly, Mr Mulliner,' replied the chastened voice from below.

An hour later, as he was dropping off to sleep, a thought crept into Augustine's mind. Had he not been a little brusque with Mrs Wardle? Had there not been in his manner something a shade abrupt—almost rude? Yes, he decided regretfully, there had. He lit a candle and reached for the diary which lay on the table at his bedside.

He made an entry.

The meek shall inherit the earth. Am I sufficiently meek? I wonder. This evening, when reproaching Mrs Wardle, my worthy housekeeper, for omitting to place a hot-water bottle in my bed, I spoke quite crossly. The provocation was severe, but still I was surely to blame for allowing my passions to run riot. Mem: Must guard agst this.

But when he woke next morning, different feelings prevailed. He took his ante-breakfast dose of Buck-U-Uppo: and looking at the entry in the diary, could scarcely believe that it was he who had written it. 'Quite cross?' Of course he had been quite cross. Wouldn't anybody be quite cross who was for ever being persecuted by beetle-wits who forgot hot-water bottles?

Erasing the words with one strong dash of a thick-leaded pencil, he scribbled in the margin a hasty 'Mashed potatoes! Served the old idiot right!' and went down to breakfast.

He felt most amazingly fit. Undoubtedly, in asserting that this tonic of his acted forcefully upon the red corpuscles, his Uncle Wilfred had been right. Until that moment Augustine had never supposed that he had any red corpuscles; but now, as he sat waiting for Mrs Wardle to bring him his fried egg, he could feel them dancing about all over him. They seemed to be forming rowdy parties and sliding down his spine. His eyes sparkled, and from sheer joy of living he sang a few bars from the hymn for those of riper years at sea.

He was still singing when Mrs Wardle entered with a dish.

'What's this?' demanded Augustine, eyeing it dangerously.

'A nice fried egg, sir.'

'And what, pray, do you mean by nice? It may be an amiable egg. It may be a civil, well-meaning egg. But if you think it is fit for human consumption, adjust that impression. Go back to your kitchen, woman; select another; and remember this time that you are a cook, not an incinerating machine. Between an egg that is fried and an egg that is cremated there is a wide and substantial difference. This difference, if you wish to retain me as a lodger in these far too expensive rooms, you will endeavour to appreciate.'

The glowing sense of well-being with which Augustine had begun the day did not diminish with the passage of time. It seemed, indeed, to increase. So full of effervescing energy did the young man feel that, departing from his usual custom of spending the morning crouched over the fire, he picked up his hat, stuck it at a rakish angle on his head, and sallied out for a healthy tramp across the fields.

It was while he was returning, flushed and rosy, that he observed a sight which is rare in the country districts of England—the spectacle of a bishop running. It is not often in a place like Lower Briskett-in-the-Midden that you see a bishop at all; and when you do he is either riding in a stately car or pacing at a dignified walk. This one was sprinting like a Derby winner, and Augustine paused to drink in the sight.

The bishop was a large, burly bishop, built for endurance rather than speed; but he was making excellent going. He flashed past Augustine in a whirl of flying gaiters: and then, proving himself thereby no mere specialist but a versatile all-round athlete, suddenly dived for a tree and climbed rapidly into its branches. His motive, Augustine readily divined, was to elude a rough, hairy dog which was toiling in his wake. The dog reached the tree a moment after his quarry had climbed it, and stood there, barking.

Augustine strolled up.

'Having a little trouble with the dumb friend, bish?' he asked, genially.

The bishop peered down from his eyrie.

'Young man,' he said, 'save me!'

'Right most indubitably ho!' replied Augustine. 'Leave it to me.'

Until today he had always been terrified of dogs, but now he did not hesitate. Almost quicker than words can tell, he picked up a stone, discharged it at the animal, and whooped cheerily as it got home with a thud. The dog, knowing when he had had enough, removed himself at some forty-five m.p.h.; and the bishop, descending cautiously, clasped Augustine's hand in his.

'My preserver!' said the bishop.

'Don't give it another thought,' said Augustine, cheerily. 'Always glad to do a pal a good turn. We clergymen must stick together.'

'I thought he had me for a minute.'

'Quite a nasty customer. Full of rude energy.'

The bishop nodded.

'His eye was not dim, nor his natural force abated. Deuteronomy xxxiv, 7,' he agreed. 'I wonder if you can direct me to the vicarage? I fear I have come a little out of my way.'

'I'll take you there.'

'Thank you. Perhaps it would be as well if you did not come in. I have a serious matter to discuss with old Pieface—I mean, with the Rev. Stanley Brandon.'

'I have a serious matter to discuss with his daughter. I'll just hang about the garden.'

'You are a very excellent young man,' said the bishop, as they walked along. 'You are a curate, eh?'

'At present. But,' said Augustine, tapping his companion on the chest, 'just watch my smoke. That's all I ask you to do—just watch my smoke.'

'I will. You should rise to great heights—to the very top of the tree.'

'Like you did just now, eh? Ha, ha!'

'Ha, ha!' said the bishop. 'You young rogue!'

He poked Augustine in the ribs.

'Ha, ha, ha!' said Augustine.

He slapped the bishop on the back.

'But all joking aside,' said the bishop as they entered the vicarage grounds, 'I really shall keep my eye on you and see that you receive the swift preferment which your talents and character deserve. I say to you, my dear young friend, speaking seriously and weighing my words, that the way you picked that dog off with that stone was the smoothest thing I ever saw. And I am a man who always tells the strict truth.'

'Great is truth and mighty above all things. Esdras iv, 41,' said Augustine.

He turned away and strolled towards the laurel bushes, which were his customary meeting-place with Jane. The bishop went on to the front door and rang the bell.

Although they had made no definite appointment, Augustine was surprised when the minutes passed and no Jane appeared. He did not know that she had been told off by her father to entertain the bishop's wife that morning, and show her the sights of Lower Briskett-in-the-Midden. He waited some quarter of an hour with growing impatience, and was about to leave when suddenly from the house there came to his ears the sound of voices raised angrily.

He stopped. The voices appeared to proceed from a room on the ground floor facing the garden.

Running lightly over the turf, Augustine paused outside the window and listened. The window was open at the bottom, and he could hear quite distinctly.

The vicar was speaking in a voice that vibrated through the room.

'Is that so?' said the vicar.

'Yes, it is!' said the bishop.

'Ha, ha!'

'Ha, ha! to you, and see how you like it!' rejoined the bishop with spirit.

Augustine drew a step closer. It was plain that Jane's fears had been justified and that there was serious trouble afoot between these two old schoolfellows. He peeped in. The vicar, his hands behind his coat-tails, was striding up and down the carpet, while the bishop, his back to the fireplace, glared defiance at him from the hearth-rug.

'Who ever told you you were an authority on chasubles?' demanded the vicar.

'That's all right who told me,' rejoined the bishop.

'I don't believe you know what a chasuble is.'

'Is that so?'

'Well, what is it, then?'

'It's a circular cloak hanging from the shoulders, elaborately embroidered with a pattern and with orphreys. And you can argue as much as you like, young Pieface, but you can't get away from the fact that there are too many orphreys on yours. And what I'm telling you is that you've jolly well got to switch off a few of these orphreys or you'll get it in the neck.'

The vicar's eyes glittered furiously.

'Is that so?' he said. 'Well, I just won't, so there! And it's like your cheek coming here and trying to high-hat me. You seem to have forgotten that I knew you when you were an inky-faced kid at school, and that, if I liked, I could tell the world one or two things about you which would probably amuse it.'

'My past is an open book.'

'Is it?' The vicar laughed malevolently. 'Who put the white mouse in the French master's desk?'

The bishop started.

'Who put jam in the dormitory prefect's bed?' he retorted.

'Who couldn't keep his collar clean?'

'Who used to wear a dickey?' The bishop's wonderful organ-like voice, whose softest whisper could be heard throughout a vast cathedral, rang out in tone of thunder. 'Who was sick at the house supper?'

The vicar quivered from head to foot. His rubicund face turned a deeper crimson.

'You know jolly well,' he said, in shaking accents, 'that there was something wrong with the turkey. Might have upset anyone.'

'The only thing wrong with the turkey was that you ate too much of it. If you had paid as much attention to developing your soul as you did to developing your tummy, you might by now,' said the bishop, 'have risen to my own eminence.'

'Oh, might I?'

'No, perhaps I am wrong. You never had the brain.'

The vicar uttered another discordant laugh.

'Brain is good! We know all about your eminence, as you call it, and how you rose to that eminence.'

'What do you mean?'

'You are a bishop. How you became one we will not inquire.'

'What do you mean?'

'What I say. We will not inquire.'

'Why don't you inquire?'

'Because,' said the vicar, 'it is better not!'

The bishop's self-control left him. His face contorted with fury, he took a step forward. And simultaneously Augustine sprang lightly into the room.

'Now, now, now!' said Augustine. 'Now, now, now, now, now!'

The two men stood transfixed. They stared at the intruder dumbly.

'Come, come!' said Augustine.

The vicar was the first to recover. He glowered at Augustine.

'What do you mean by jumping through my window?' he thundered. 'Are you a curate or a harlequin?'

Augustine met his gaze with an unfaltering eye.

'I am a curate,' he replied, with a dignity that well became him. 'And, as a curate, I cannot stand by and see two superiors of the cloth, who are moreover old schoolfellows, forgetting themselves. It isn't right. Absolutely not right, my old superiors of the cloth.'

The vicar bit his lip. The bishop bowed his head.

'Listen,' proceeded Augustine, placing a hand on the shoulder of each. 'I hate to see you two dear good chaps quarrelling like this.'

'He started it,' said the vicar, sullenly.

'Never mind who started it.' Augustine silenced the bishop with a curt gesture as he made to speak. 'Be sensible, my dear fellows. Respect the decencies of debate. Exercise a little good-humoured give-and-take. You say,' he went on, turning to the bishop, 'that our good friend here has too many orphreys on his chasuble?'

'I do. And I stick to it.'

'Yes, yes, yes. But what,' said Augustine, soothingly, 'are a few orphreys between friends? Reflect! You and our worthy vicar here were at school together. You are bound by the sacred ties of the old Alma Mater. With him you sported on the green. With him you shared a crib and threw inked darts in the hour supposed to be devoted to the study of French. Do these things mean nothing to you? Do these memories touch no chord?' He turned appealingly from one to the other. 'Vicar! Bish!'

The vicar had moved away and was wiping his eyes. The bishop fumbled for a pocket-handkerchief. There was a silence.

'Sorry, Pieface,' said the bishop, in a choking voice.

'Shouldn't have spoken as I did, Boko,' mumbled the vicar.

'If you want to know what I think,' said the bishop, 'you are right in attributing your indisposition at the house supper to something wrong with the turkey. I recollect saying at the time that the bird should never have been served in such a condition.'

'And when you put that white mouse in the French master's desk,' said the vicar, 'you performed one of the noblest services to humanity of which there is any record. They ought to have made you a bishop on the spot.'

'Pieface!'

'Boko!'

The two men clasped hands.

'Splendid!' said Augustine. 'Everything hotsy-totsy now?'

'Quite, quite,' said the vicar.

'As far as I am concerned, completely hotsy-totsy,' said the bishop. He turned to his old friend solicitously. 'You will continue to wear all the orphreys you want—will you not, Pieface?'

'No, no. I see now that I was wrong. From now on, Boko, I abandon orphreys altogether.'

'But, Pieface—'

'It's all right,' the vicar assured him. 'I can take them or leave them alone.'

'Splendid fellow!' The bishop coughed to hide his emotion, and there was another silence. 'I think, perhaps,' he went on, after a pause, 'I should be leaving you now, my dear chap, and going in search of my wife. She is with your daughter, I believe, somewhere in the village.'

'They are coming up the drive now.'

'Ah, yes, I see them. A charming girl, your daughter.'

Augustine clapped him on the shoulder.

'Bish,' he exclaimed, 'you said a mouthful. She is the dearest, sweetest girl in the whole world. And I should be glad, vicar, if you would give your consent to our immediate union. I love Jane with a good man's fervour, and I am happy to inform you that my sentiments are returned. Assure us, therefore, of your approval, and I will go at once and have the banns put up.'

The vicar leaped as though he had been stung. Like so many vicars, he had a poor opinion of curates, and he had always regarded Augustine as rather below than above the general norm or level of the despised class.

'What!' he cried.

'A most excellent idea,' said the bishop, beaming. 'A very happy notion, I call it.'

'My daughter!' The vicar seemed dazed. 'My daughter marry a curate!'

'You were a curate once yourself, Pieface.'

'Yes, but not a curate like that.'

'No!' said the bishop. 'You were not. Nor was I. Better for us both had we been. This young man, I would have you know, is the most outstandingly excellent young man I have ever encountered. Are you aware that scarcely an hour ago he saved me with the most consummate address from a large shaggy dog with black spots and a kink in his tail? I was sorely pressed, Pieface, when this young man came up and, with a readiness of resource and an accuracy of aim which it would be impossible to over-praise, got that dog in the short ribs with a rock and sent him flying.'

The vicar seemed to be struggling with some powerful emotion. His eyes had widened.

'A dog with black spots?'

'Very black spots. But no blacker, I fear, than the heart they hid.'

'And he really plugged him in the short ribs?'

'As far as I could see, squarely in the short ribs.'

The vicar held out his hand.

'Mulliner,' he said, 'I was not aware of this. In the light of the facts which have just been drawn to my attention, I have no hesitation in saying that my objections are removed. I have had it in for that dog since the second Sunday before Septuagesima, when he pinned me by the ankle as I paced beside the river composing a sermon on Certain Alarming Manifestations of the So-called Modern Spirit. Take Jane. I give my consent freely. And may she be as happy as any girl with such a husband ought to be.'

A few more affecting words were exchanged, and then the bishop and Augustine left the house. The bishop was silent and thoughtful.

'I owe you a great deal, Mulliner,' he said at length.

'Oh, I don't know,' said Augustine. 'Would you say that?'

'A very great deal. You saved me from a terrible disaster. Had you not leaped through that window at that precise juncture and intervened, I really believe I should have pasted my dear old friend Brandon in the eye. I was sorely exasperated.'

'Our good vicar can be trying at times,' agreed Augustine.

'My fist was already clenched, and I was just hauling off for the swing when you checked me. What the result would have been, had you not exhibited a tact and discretion beyond your years, I do not like to think. I might have been unfrocked.' He shivered at the thought, though the weather was mild. 'I could never have shown my face at the Athenaeum again. But, tut, tut!' went on the bishop, patting Augustine on the shoulder, 'let us not dwell on what might have been. Speak to me of yourself. The vicar's charming daughter—you really love her?'

'I do, indeed.'

The bishop's face had grown grave.

'Think well, Mulliner,' he said. 'Marriage is a serious affair. Do not plunge into it without due reflection. I myself am a husband, and, though singularly blessed in the possession of a devoted help-meet, cannot but feel sometimes that a man is better off as a bachelor. Women, Mulliner, are odd.'

'True,' said Augustine.

'My own dear wife is the best of women. And, as I never weary of saying, a good woman is a wondrous creature, cleaving to the right and the good under all change; lovely in youthful comeliness, lovely all her life in comeliness of heart. And yet—'

'And yet?' said Augustine.

The bishop mused for a moment. He wriggled a little with an expression of pain, and scratched himself between the shoulder-blades.

'Well, I'll tell you,' said the bishop. 'It is a warm and pleasant day today, is it not?'

'Exceptionally clement,' said Augustine.

'A fair, sunny day, made gracious by a temperate westerly breeze. And yet, Mulliner, if you will credit my statement, my wife insisted on my putting on my thick winter woollies this morning. Truly,' sighed the bishop, 'as a jewel of gold in a swine's snout, so is a fair woman which is without discretion. Proverbs xi, 21.'

'Twenty-two,' corrected Augustine.

'I should have said twenty-two. They are made of thick flannel, and I have an exceptionally sensitive skin. Oblige me, my dear fellow, by rubbing me in the small of the back with the ferrule of your stick. I think it will ease the irritation.'

'But, my poor dear old bish,' said Augustine, sympathetically, 'this must not be.'

The bishop shook his head ruefully.

'You would not speak so hardily, Mulliner, if you knew my wife. There is no appeal from her decrees.'

'Nonsense,' cried Augustine, cheerily. He looked through the trees to where the lady bishopess, escorted by Jane, was examining a lobelia through her lorgnette with just the right blend of cordiality and condescension. 'I'll fix that for you in a second.'

The bishop clutched at his arm.

'My boy! What are you going to do?'

'I'm just going to have a word with your wife and put the matter up to her as a reasonable woman. Thick winter woollies on a day like this! Absurd!' said Augustine. 'Preposterous! I never heard such rot.'

The bishop gazed after him with a laden heart. Already he had come to love this young man like a son: and to see him charging so light-heartedly into the very jaws of destruction afflicted him with a deep and poignant sadness. He knew what his wife was like when even the highest in the land attempted to thwart her; and this brave lad was but a curate. In another moment she would be looking at him through her lorgnette: and England was littered with the shrivelled remains of curates at whom the lady bishopess had looked through her lorgnette. He had seen them wilt like salted slugs at the episcopal breakfast-table.

He held his breath. Augustine had reached the lady bishopess, and the lady bishopess was even now raising her lorgnette.

The bishop shut his eyes and turned away. And then—years afterwards, it seemed to him—a cheery voice hailed him: and, turning, he perceived Augustine bounding back through the trees.

'It's all right, bish,' said Augustine.

'All—all right?' faltered the bishop.

'Yes. She says you can go and change into the thin cashmere.'

The bishop reeled.

'But—but—but what did you say to her? What arguments did you employ?'

'Oh, I just pointed out what a warm day it was and jollied her along a bit—'

'Jollied her along a bit!'

'And she agreed in the most friendly and cordial manner. She has asked me to call at the Palace one of these days.'

The bishop seized Augustine's hand.

'My boy,' he said in a broken voice, 'you shall do more than call at the Palace. You shall come and live at the Palace. Become my secretary, Mulliner, and name your own salary. If you intend to marry, you will require an increased stipend. Become my secretary, boy, and never leave my side. I have needed somebody like you for years.'

It was late in the afternoon when Augustine returned to his rooms, for he had been invited to lunch at the vicarage and had been the life and soul of the cheery little party.

'A letter for you, sir,' said Mrs Wardle, obsequiously.

Augustine took the letter.

'I am sorry to say I shall be leaving you shortly, Mrs Wardle.'

'Oh, sir! If there's anything I can do—'

'Oh, it's not that. The fact is, the bishop has made me his secretary, and I shall have to shift my toothbrush and spats to the Palace, you see.'

'Well, fancy that, sir! Why, you'll be a bishop yourself one of these days.'

'Possibly,' said Augustine. 'Possibly. And now let me read this.'

He opened the letter. A thoughtful frown appeared on his face as he read.

My dear Augustine,

I am writing in some haste to tell you that the impulsiveness of your aunt has led to a rather serious mistake.

She tells me that she dispatched to you yesterday by parcels post a sample bottle of my new Buck-U-Uppo, which she obtained without my knowledge from my laboratory. Had she mentioned what she was intending to do, I could have prevented a very unfortunate occurrence.

Mulliner's Buck-U-Uppo is of two grades or qualities—the A and the B. The A is a mild, but strengthening, tonic designed for human invalids. The B, on the other hand, is purely for circulation in the animal kingdom, and was invented to fill a long-felt want throughout our Indian possessions.

As you are doubtless aware, the favourite pastime of the Indian Maharajahs is the hunting of the tiger of the jungle from the backs of elephants; and it has happened frequently in the past that hunts have been spoiled by the failure of the elephant to see eye to eye with its owner in the matter of what constitutes sport.

Too often elephants, on sighting the tiger, have turned and galloped home: and it was to correct this tendency on their part that I invented Mulliner's Buck-U-Uppo 'B'. One teaspoonful of the Buck-U-Uppo 'B' administered in its morning bran-mash will cause the most timid elephant to trumpet loudly and charge the fiercest tiger without a qualm.

Abstain, therefore, from taking any of the contents of the bottle you now possess,

And believe me,

Your affectionate uncle,

Wilfred Mulliner

Augustine remained for some time in deep thought after perusing this communication. Then, rising, he whistled a few bars of the psalm appointed for the twenty-sixth of June and left the room.

Half an hour later a telegraphic message was speeding over the wires.

It ran as follows:

Wilfred Mulliner,

The Gables,

Lesser Lossingham,

Salop.

Letter received. Send immediately, C.O.D., three cases of the 'B'. 'Blessed shall be thy basket and thy store.' Deuteronomy xxviii, 5.

Augustine

4
THE BISHOP'S MOVE

Another Sunday was drawing to a close, and Mr Mulliner had come into the bar-parlour of the Anglers' Rest wearing on his head, in place of the seedy old wideawake which usually adorned it, a glistening top-hat. From this, combined with the sober black of his costume and the rather devout voice in which he ordered hot Scotch and lemon, I deduced that he had been attending Evensong.

'Good sermon?' I asked.

'Quite good. The new curate preached. He seems a nice young fellow.'

'Speaking of curates,' I said, 'I have often wondered what became of your nephew—the one you were telling me about the other day.'

'Augustine?'

'The fellow who took the Buck-U-Uppo.'

'That was Augustine. And I am pleased and not a little touched,' said Mr Mulliner, beaming, 'that you should have remembered the trivial anecdote which I related. In this self-centred world one does not always find such a sympathetic listener to one's stories. Let me see, where did we leave Augustine?'

'He had just become the bishop's secretary and gone to live at the Palace.'

'Ah, yes. We will take up his career, then, some six months after the date which you have indicated.'

It was the custom of the good Bishop of Stortford—for, like all the prelates of our Church, he loved his labours—to embark upon the duties of the day (said Mr Mulliner) in a cheerful and jocund spirit. Usually, as he entered his study to dispatch such business as might have arisen from the correspondence which had reached the Palace by the first post, there was a smile upon his face and possibly upon his lips a snatch of some gay psalm. But on the morning on which this story begins an observer would have noted that he wore a preoccupied, even a sombre, look. Reaching the study door, he hesitated as if reluctant to enter; then, pulling himself together with a visible effort, he turned the handle.

'Good morning, Mulliner, my boy,' he said. His manner was noticeably embarrassed.

Augustine glanced brightly up from the pile of letters which he was opening.

'Cheerio, Bish. How's the lumbago today?'

'I find the pain sensibly diminished, thank you, Mulliner—in fact, almost non-existent. This pleasant weather seems to do me good. For lo! the winter is past, the rain is over and gone; the flowers appear on the earth; the time of the singing birds is come, and the voice of the turtle is heard in the land. Song of Solomon ii, 11, 12.'

'Good work,' said Augustine. 'Well, there's nothing much of interest in these letters so far. The Vicar of St Beowulf's in the West wants to know, How about incense?'

'Tell him he mustn't.'

'Right ho.'

The bishop stroked his chin uneasily. He seemed to be nerving himself for some unpleasant task.

'Mulliner,' he said.

'Hullo?'

'Your mention of the word "vicar" provides a cue, which I must not ignore, for alluding to a matter which you and I had under advisement yesterday—the matter of the vacant living of Steeple Mummery.'

'Yes?' said Augustine eagerly. 'Do I click?'

A spasm of pain passed across the bishop's face. He shook his head sadly.

'Mulliner, my boy,' he said. 'You know that I look upon you as a son and that, left to my own initiative, I would bestow this vacant living on you without a moment's hesitation. But an unforeseen complication has arisen. Unhappy lad, my wife has instructed me to give the post to a cousin of hers. A fellow,' said the bishop bitterly, 'who bleats like a sheep and doesn't know an alb from a reredos.'

Augustine, as was only natural, was conscious of a momentary pang of disappointment. But he was a Mulliner and a sportsman.

'Don't give it another thought, Bish,' he said cordially. 'I quite understand. I don't say I hadn't hopes, but no doubt there will be another along in a minute.'

'You know how it is,' said the bishop, looking cautiously round to see that the door was closed. 'It is better to dwell in a corner of the housetop than with a brawling woman in a wide house. Proverbs xxi, 9.'

'A continual dropping in a very rainy day and a contentious woman are alike. Proverbs xxvii, 15,' agreed Augustine.

'Exactly. How well you understand me, Mulliner.'

'Meanwhile,' said Augustine, holding up a letter, 'here's something that calls for attention. It's from a bird of the name of Trevor Entwhistle.'

'Indeed? An old schoolfellow of mine. He is now Headmaster of Harchester, the foundation at which we both received our early education. What does he say?'

'He wants to know if you will run down for a few days and unveil a statue which they have just put up to Lord Hemel of Hempstead.'

'Another old schoolfellow. We called him Fatty.'

'There's a postscript over the page. He says he still has a dozen of the '87 port.'

The bishop pursed his lips.

'These earthly considerations do not weigh with me so much as old Catsmeat—as the Reverend Trevor Entwhistle seems to suppose. However, one must not neglect the call of the dear old school. We will certainly go.'

'We?'

'I shall require your company. I think you will like Harchester, Mulliner. A noble pile, founded by the seventh Henry.'

'I know it well. A young brother of mine is there.'

'Indeed? Dear me,' mused the bishop, 'it must be twenty years and more since I last visited Harchester. I shall enjoy seeing the old, familiar scenes once again. After all, Mulliner, to whatever eminence we may soar, howsoever great may be the prizes which life has bestowed upon us, we never wholly lose our sentiment for the dear old school. It is our

Alma Mater, Mulliner, the gentle mother that has set our hesitating footsteps on the—'

'Absolutely,' said Augustine.

'And, as we grow older, we see that never can we recapture the old, careless gaiety of our school days. Life was not complex then, Mulliner. Life in that halcyon period was free from problems. We were not faced with the necessity of disappointing our friends.'

'Now listen, Bish,' said Augustine cheerily, 'if you're still worrying about that living, forget it. Look at me. I'm quite chirpy, aren't I?'

The bishop sighed.

'I wish I had your sunny resilience, Mulliner. How do you manage it?'

'Oh, I keep smiling, and take the Buck-U-Uppo daily.'

'The Buck-U-Uppo?'

'It's a tonic my uncle Wilfred invented. Works like magic.'

'I must ask you to let me try it one of these days. For somehow, Mulliner, I am finding life a little grey. What on earth,' said the bishop, half to himself and speaking peevishly, 'they wanted to put up a statue to old Fatty for, I can't imagine. A fellow who used to throw inked darts at people. However,' he continued, abruptly abandoning this train of thought, 'that is neither here nor there. If the Board of Governors of Harchester College has decided that Lord Hemel of Hempstead has by his services in the public weal earned a statue, it is not for us to cavil. Write to Mr Entwhistle, Mulliner, and say that I shall be delighted.'

Although, as he had told Augustine, fully twenty years had passed since his last visit to Harchester, the bishop found, somewhat to his surprise, that little or no alteration had taken place in the grounds, buildings, and personnel of the school. It seemed to him almost precisely the same as it had been on the day, forty-three years before, when he had first come there as a new boy.

There was the tuck-shop where, a lissom stripling with bony elbows, he had shoved and pushed so often in order to get near the counter and snaffle a jam-sandwich in the eleven o'clock recess. There were the baths, the fives courts, the football fields, the library, the gymnasium, the gravel, the chestnut trees, all just as they had been when the only thing he knew about bishops was that they wore bootlaces in their hats.

The sole change that he could see was that on the triangle of turf in front of the library there had been erected a granite pedestal surmounted by a shapeless something swathed in a large sheet—the statue to Lord Hemel of Hempstead which he had come down to unveil.

And gradually, as his visit proceeded, there began to steal over him an emotion which defied analysis.

At first he supposed it to be a natural sentimentality. But, had it been that, would it not have been a more pleasurable emotion? For his feelings had begun to be far from unmixedly agreeable. Once, when rounding a corner, he came upon the captain of football in all his majesty, there had swept over him a hideous blend of fear and shame which had made his gaitered legs wobble like jellies. The captain of football doffed his cap respectfully, and the feeling passed as quickly as it had come: but not so soon that the bishop had not recognized it. It was exactly the feeling he had been wont to have forty-odd years ago when, sneaking softly away from football practice, he had encountered one in authority.

The bishop was puzzled. It was as if some fairy had touched him with her wand, sweeping away the years and making him an inky-faced boy again. Day by day this illusion grew, the constant society of the Rev. Trevor Entwhistle doing much to foster it. For young Catsmeat Entwhistle had been the bishop's particular crony at Harchester, and he seemed to have altered his appearance since those days in no way whatsoever. The bishop had had a nasty shock when, entering the headmaster's study on the third morning of his visit, he found him sitting in the headmaster's chair with the headmaster's cap and gown on. It seemed to him that young Catsmeat, in order to indulge his distorted sense of humour, was taking the most frightful risk. Suppose the Old Man were to come in and cop him!

Altogether, it was a relief to the bishop when the day of the unveiling arrived.

The actual ceremony, however, he found both tedious and irritating. Lord Hemel of Hempstead had not been a favourite of his in their school days, and there was something extremely disagreeable to him in being obliged to roll out sonorous periods in his praise.

In addition to this, he had suffered from the very start of the proceedings from a bad attack of stage fright. He could not help thinking that he must look the most awful chump standing up there in front of all those people and spouting. He half expected one of the prefects in the audience to step up and clout his head and tell him not to be a funny young swine.

However, no disaster of this nature occurred. Indeed, his speech was notably successful.

'My dear Bishop,' said old General Bloodenough, the Chairman of the College Board of Governors, shaking his hand at the conclusion of the unveiling, 'your magnificent oration put my own feeble efforts to shame, put them to shame, to shame. You were astounding!'

'Thanks awfully,' mumbled the bishop, blushing and shuffling his feet.

The weariness which had come upon the bishop as the result of the prolonged ceremony seemed to grow as the day wore on. By the time he was seated in the headmaster's study after dinner he was in the grip of a severe headache.

The Rev. Trevor Entwhistle also appeared jaded.

'These affairs are somewhat fatiguing, bishop,' he said, stifling a yawn.

'They are, indeed, Headmaster.'

'Even the '87 port seems an inefficient restorative.'

'Markedly inefficient. I wonder,' said the bishop, struck with an idea, 'if a little Buck-U-Uppo might not alleviate our exhaustion. It is a tonic of some kind which my secretary is in the habit of taking. It certainly appears to do him good. A livelier, more vigorous young fellow I have never seen. Suppose we ask your butler to go to his room and borrow the bottle? I am sure he will be delighted to give it to us.'

'By all means.'

The butler, dispatched to Augustine's room, returned with a bottle half full of a thick, dark-coloured liquid. The bishop examined it thoughtfully.

'I see there are no directions given as to the requisite dose,' he said. 'However, I do not like to keep disturbing your butler, who has now doubtless returned to his pantry and is once more settling down to the enjoyment of a well-earned rest after a day more than ordinarily fraught with toil and anxiety. Suppose we use our own judgement?'

'Certainly. Is it nasty?'

The bishop licked the cork warily.

'No. I should not call it nasty. The taste, while individual and distinctive and even striking, is by no means disagreeable.'

'Then let us take a glassful apiece.'

The bishop filled two portly wine-glasses with the fluid, and they sat sipping gravely.

'It's rather good,' said the bishop.

'Distinctly good,' said the headmaster.

'It sort of sends a kind of glow over you.'

'A noticeable glow.'

'A little more, Headmaster?'

'No, I thank you.'

'Oh, come.'

'Well, just a spot, bishop, if you insist.'

'It's rather good,' said the bishop.

'Distinctly good,' said the headmaster.

Now you, who have listened to the story of Augustine's previous adventures with the Buck-U-Uppo, are aware that my brother Wilfred invented it primarily with the object of providing Indian Rajahs with a specific which would encourage their elephants to face the tiger of the jungle with a jaunty sang-froid: and he had advocated as a medium dose for an adult elephant a teaspoonful stirred up with its morning bran-mash. It is not surprising, therefore, that after they had drunk two wine-glassfuls apiece of the mixture the outlook on life of both the bishop and the headmaster began to undergo a marked change.

Their fatigue had left them, and with it the depression which a few moments before had been weighing on them so heavily. Both were conscious of an extraordinary feeling of good cheer, and the odd illusion of extreme youth which had been upon the bishop since his arrival at Harchester was now more pronounced than ever. He felt a youngish and rather rowdy fifteen.

'Where does your butler sleep, Catsmeat?' he asked, after a thoughtful pause.

'I don't know. Why?'

'I was only thinking that it would be a lark to go and put a booby-trap on his door.'

The headmaster's eyes glistened.

'Yes, wouldn't it!' he said.

They mused for a while. Then the headmaster uttered a deep chuckle.

'What are you giggling about?' asked the bishop.

'I was only thinking what a priceless ass you looked this afternoon, talking all that rot about old Fatty.'

In spite of his cheerfulness, a frown passed over the bishop's fine forehead.

'It went very much against the grain to speak in terms of eulogy—yes, fulsome eulogy—of one whom we both know to have been a blighter of the worst description. Where does Fatty get off, having statues put up to him?'

'Oh well, he's an Empire builder, I suppose,' said the headmaster, who was a fair-minded man.

'Just the sort of thing he would be,' grumbled the bishop. 'Shoving himself forward! If ever there was a chap I barred, it was Fatty.'

'Me, too,' agreed the headmaster. 'Beastly laugh he'd got. Like glue pouring out of a jug.'

'Greedy little beast, if you remember. A fellow in his house told me he once ate three slices of brown boot-polish spread on bread after he had finished the potted meat.'

'Between you and me, I always suspected him of swiping buns at the school shop. I don't wish to make rash charges unsupported by true evidence, but it always seemed to me extremely odd that, whatever time of the term it was, and however hard up everybody else might be, you never saw Fatty without his bun.'

'Catsmeat,' said the bishop, 'I'll tell you something about Fatty that isn't generally known. In a scrum in the final House Match in the year 1888 he deliberately hoofed me on the shin.'

'You don't mean that?'

'I do.'

'Great Scott!'

'An ordinary hack on the shin,' said the bishop coldly, 'no fellow minds. It is part of the give and take of normal social life. But when a bounder deliberately hauls off and lets drive at you with the sole intention of laying you out, it—well, it's a bit thick.'

'And those chumps of Governors have put up a statue to him!'

The bishop leaned forward and lowered his voice.

'Catsmeat.'

'What?'

'Do you know what?'

'No, what?'

'What we ought to do is to wait till twelve o'clock or so, till there's no one about, and then beetle out and paint that statue blue.'

'Why not pink?'

'Pink, if you prefer it.'

'Pink's a nice colour.'

'It is. Very nice.'

'Besides, I know where I can lay my hands on some pink paint.'

'You do?'

'Gobs of it.'

'Peace be on thy walls, Catsmeat, and prosperity within thy palaces,' said the bishop. 'Proverbs cxxxi, 6.'

It seemed to the bishop, as he closed the front door noiselessly behind him two hours later, that providence, always on the side of the just, was extending itself in its efforts to make this little enterprise of his a success. All the conditions were admirable for statue-painting. The rain which had been falling during the evening had stopped: and a moon, which might have proved an embarrassment, was conveniently hidden behind a bank of clouds.

As regarded human interference, they had nothing to alarm them. No place in the world is so deserted as the ground of a school after midnight. Fatty's statue might have been in the middle of the Sahara. They climbed the pedestal, and, taking turns fairly with the brush, soon accomplished the task which their sense of duty had indicated to them. It was only when, treading warily lest their steps should be heard on the gravel drive, they again reached the front door that anything occurred to mar the harmony of the proceedings.

'What are you waiting for?' whispered the bishop, as his companion lingered on the top step.

'Half a second,' said the headmaster in a muffled voice. 'It may be in another pocket.'

'What?'

'My key.'

'Have you lost your key?'

'I believe I have.'

'Catsmeat,' said the bishop, with grave censure, 'this is the last time I come out painting statues with you.'

'I must have dropped it somewhere.'

'What shall we do?'

'There's just a chance the scullery window may be open.'

But the scullery window was not open. Careful, vigilant, and faithful to his trust, the butler, on retiring to rest, had fastened it and closed the shutters. They were locked out.

But it has been well said that it is the lessons which we learn in our boyhood days at school that prepare us for the problems of life in the larger world outside. Stealing back from the mists of the past, there came to the bishop a sudden memory.

'Catsmeat!'

'Hullo?'

'If you haven't been mucking the place up with alterations and improvements, there should be a water-pipe round at the back, leading to one of the upstairs windows.'

Memory had not played him false. There, nestling in the ivy, was the pipe up and down which he had been wont to climb when, a pie-faced lad in the summer of '86, he had broken out of this house in order to take nocturnal swims in the river.

'Up you go,' he said briefly.

The headmaster required no further urging. And presently the two were making good time up the side of the house.

It was just as they reached the window and just after the bishop had informed his old friend that, if he kicked him on the head again, he'd hear of it, that the window was suddenly flung open.

'Who's that?' said a clear young voice.

The headmaster was frankly taken aback. Dim though the light was, he could see that the man leaning out of the window was poising in readiness a very nasty-looking golf-club: and his first impulse was to reveal his identity and so clear himself of the suspicion of being the marauder for whom he gathered the other had mistaken him. Then there presented themselves to him certain objections to revealing his identity, and he hung there in silence, unable to think of a suitable next move.

The bishop was a man of readier resource.

'Tell him we're a couple of cats belonging to the cook,' he whispered.

It was painful for one of the headmaster's scrupulous rectitude and honesty to stoop to such a falsehood, but it seemed the only course to pursue.

'It's all right,' he said, forcing a note of easy geniality into his voice. 'We're a couple of cats.'

'Cat-burglars?'

'No. Just ordinary cats.'

'Belonging to the cook,' prompted the bishop from below.

'Belonging to the cook,' added the headmaster.

'I see,' said the man at the window. 'Well, in that case, right ho!'

He stood aside to allow them to enter. The bishop, an artist at heart, mewed gratefully as he passed, to add verisimilitude to the deception: and then made for his bedroom, accompanied by the headmaster. The episode was apparently closed.

Nevertheless, the headmaster was disturbed by a certain uneasiness.

'Do you suppose he thought we really were cats?' he asked anxiously.

'I am not sure,' said the bishop. 'But I think we deceived him by the nonchalance of our demeanour.'

'Yes, I think we did. Who was he?'

'My secretary. The young fellow I was speaking of, who lent us that capital tonic.'

'Oh, then that's all right. He wouldn't give you away.'

'No. And there is nothing else that can possibly lead to our being suspected. We left no clue whatsoever.'

'All the same,' said the headmaster thoughtfully, 'I'm beginning to wonder whether it was in the best sense of the word judicious to have painted that statue.'

'Somebody had to,' said the bishop stoutly.

'Yes, that's true,' said the headmaster, brightening.

The bishop slept late on the following morning, and partook of his frugal breakfast in bed. The day, which so often brings remorse, brought none to him. Something attempted, something done had earned a night's repose: and he had no regrets—except that, now that it was all over, he was not sure that blue paint would not have been more effective. However, his old friend had pleaded so strongly for the pink that it would have been difficult for himself, as a guest, to override the wishes of his host. Still, blue would undoubtedly have been very striking.

There was a knock on the door, and Augustine entered.

'Morning, Bish.'

'Good morning, Mulliner,' said the bishop affably. 'I have lain somewhat late today.'

'I say, Bish,' asked Augustine, a little anxiously. 'Did you take a very big dose of the Buck-U-Uppo last night?'

'Big? No. As I recollect, quite small. Barely two ordinary wine-glasses full.'

'Great Scott!'

'Why do you ask, my dear fellow?'

'Oh, nothing. No particular reason. I just thought your manner seemed a little strange on the water-pipe, that's all.'

The bishop was conscious of a touch of chagrin.

'Then you saw through our—er—innocent deception?'

'Yes.'

'I had been taking a little stroll with the headmaster,' explained the bishop, 'and he had mislaid his key. How beautiful is Nature at night, Mulliner! The dark, fathomless skies, the little winds that seem to whisper secrets in one's ear, the scent of growing things.'

'Yes,' said Augustine. He paused. 'Rather a row on this morning. Somebody appears to have painted Lord Hemel of Hempstead's statue last night.'

'Indeed?'

'Yes.'

'Ah, well,' said the bishop tolerantly, 'boys will be boys.'

'It's a most mysterious business.'

'No doubt, no doubt. But, after all, Mulliner, is not all Life a mystery?'

'And what makes it still more mysterious is that they found your shovel-hat on the statue's head.'

The bishop started up.

'What!'

'Absolutely.'

'Mulliner,' said the bishop, 'leave me. I have one or two matters on which I wish to meditate.'

He dressed hastily, his numbed fingers fumbling with his gaiters. It all came back to him now. Yes, he could remember putting the hat on the statue's head. It had seemed a good thing to do at the time, and he had done it. How little we guess at the moment how far-reaching our most trivial actions may be!

The headmaster was over at the school, instructing the Sixth Form in Greek Composition: and he was obliged to wait, chafing, until twelve-thirty, when the bell rang for the half-way halt in the day's work. He stood at the study window, watching with ill-controlled impatience, and presently the headmaster appeared, walking heavily like one on whose mind there is a weight.

'Well?' cried the bishop, as he entered the study.

The headmaster doffed his cap and gown, and sank limply into a chair.

'I cannot conceive,' he groaned, 'what madness had me in its grip last night.'

The bishop was shaken, but he could not countenance such an attitude as this.

'I do not understand you, Headmaster,' he said stiffly. 'It was our simple duty, as a protest against the undue exaltation of one whom we both know to have been a most unpleasant school-mate, to paint that statue.'

'And I suppose it was your duty to leave your hat on its head?'

'Now there,' said the bishop, 'I may possibly have gone a little too far.' He coughed. 'Has that perhaps somewhat ill-considered action led to the harbouring of suspicions by those in authority?'

'They don't know what to think.'

'What is the view of the Board of Governors?'

'They insist on my finding the culprit. Should I fail to do so, they hint at the gravest consequences.'

'You mean they will deprive you of your headmastership?'

'That is what they imply. I shall be asked to hand in my resignation. And, if that happens, bim goes my chance of ever being a bishop.'

'Well, it's not all jam being a bishop. You wouldn't enjoy it, Catsmeat.'

'All very well for you to talk, Boko. You got me into this, you silly ass.'

'I like that! You were just as keen on it as I was.'

'You suggested it.'

'Well, you jumped at the suggestion.'

The two men had faced each other heatedly, and for a moment it seemed as if there was to be a serious falling-out. Then the bishop recovered himself.

'Catsmeat,' he said, with that wonderful smile of his, taking the other's hand, 'this is unworthy of us. We must not quarrel. We must put our heads together and see if there is not some avenue of escape from the unfortunate position in which, however creditable our motives, we appear to have placed ourselves. How would it be—?'

'I thought of that,' said the headmaster. 'It wouldn't do a bit of good. Of course, we might—'

'No, that's no use, either,' said the bishop.

They sat for a while in meditative silence. And, as they sat, the door opened.

'General Bloodenough,' announced the butler.

'Oh, that I had wings like a dove. Psalm xlv, 6,' muttered the bishop.

His desire to be wafted from that spot with all available speed could hardly be considered unreasonable. General Sir Hector Bloodenough, V.C., K.C.I.E., M.V.O., on retiring from the army, had been for many years, until his final return to England, in charge of the Secret Service in Western Africa, where his unerring acumen had won for him from the natives the soubriquet of Wah-nah-B'gosh-B'jingo—which, freely translated, means Big Chief Who Can See Through The Hole In A Doughnut.

A man impossible to deceive. The last man the bishop would have wished to be conducting the present investigations.

The general stalked into the room. He had keen blue eyes, topped by bushy white eyebrows: and the bishop found his gaze far too piercing to be agreeable.

'Bad business, this,' he said. 'Bad business. Bad business.'

'It is, indeed,' faltered the bishop.

'Shocking bad business. Shocking. Shocking. Do you know what we found on the head of that statue, eh? that statue, that statue? Your hat, bishop. Your hat. Your hat.'

The bishop made an attempt to rally. His mind was in a whirl, for the general's habit of repeating everything three times had the effect on him of making his last night's escapade seem three times as bad. He now saw himself on the verge of standing convicted of having painted three statues with three pots of pink paint, and of having placed on the head of each one of a trio of shovel-hats. But he was a strong man, and he did his best.

'You say my hat?' he retorted with spirit. 'How do you know it was my hat? There may have been hundreds of bishops dodging about the school grounds last night.'

'Got your name in it. Your name. Your name.'

The bishop clutched at the arm of the chair in which he sat. The general's eyes were piercing him through and through, and every moment he felt more like a sheep that has had the misfortune to encounter a potted meat manufacturer. He was on the point of protesting that the writing in the hat was probably a forgery, when there was a tap at the door.

'Come in,' cried the headmaster, who had been cowering in his seat.

There entered a small boy in an Eton suit, whose face seemed to the bishop vaguely familiar. It was a face that closely resembled a ripe tomato with a nose stuck on it, but that was not what had struck the bishop. It was of something other than tomatoes that this lad reminded him.

'Sir, please, sir,' said the boy.

'Yes, yes, yes,' said General Bloodenough testily. 'Run away, my boy, run away, run away. Can't you see we're busy?'

'But, sir, please, sir, it's about the statue.'

'What about the statue? What about it? What about it?'

'Sir, please, sir, it was me.'

'What! What! What! What! What!'

The bishop, the general, and the headmaster had spoken simultaneously: and the 'Whats' had been distributed as follows:

The Bishop   1

The General   3

The Headmaster 1

making five in all. Having uttered these ejaculations, they sat staring at the boy, who turned a brighter vermilion.

'What are you saying?' cried the headmaster. 'You painted that statue?'

'Sir, yes, sir.'

'You?' said the bishop.

'Sir, yes, sir.'

'You? You? You?' said the general.

'Sir, yes, sir.'

There was a quivering pause. The bishop looked at the headmaster. The headmaster looked at the bishop. The general looked at the boy. The boy looked at the floor.

The general was the first to speak.

'Monstrous!' he exclaimed. 'Monstrous. Monstrous. Never heard of such a thing. This boy must be expelled, Headmaster. Expelled. Ex—'

'No!' said the headmaster in a ringing voice.

'Then flogged within an inch of his life. Within an inch. An inch.'

'No!' A strange, new dignity seemed to have descended upon the Rev. Trevor Entwhistle. He was breathing a little quickly through his nose, and his eyes had assumed a somewhat prawn-like aspect. 'In matters of school discipline, general, I must with all deference claim to be paramount. I will deal with this case as I think best. In my opinion this is not an occasion for severity. You agree with me, bishop?'

The bishop came to himself with a start. He had been thinking of an article which he had just completed for a leading review on the subject of Miracles, and was regretting that the tone he had taken, though in keeping with the trend of Modern Thought, had been tinged with something approaching scepticism.

'Oh, entirely,' he said.

'Then all I can say,' fumed the general, 'is that I wash my hands of the whole business, the whole business, the whole business. And if this is the way our boys are being brought up nowadays, no wonder the country is going to the dogs, the dogs, going to the dogs.'

The door slammed behind him. The headmaster turned to the boy, a kindly, winning smile upon his face.

'No doubt,' he said, 'you now regret this rash act?'

'Sir, yes, sir.'

'And you would not do it again?'

'Sir, no, sir.'

'Then I think,' said the headmaster cheerily, 'that we may deal leniently with what, after all, was but a boyish prank, eh, bishop?'

'Oh, decidedly, Headmaster.'

'Quite the sort of thing—ha, ha!—that you or I might have done—er—at his age?'

'Oh, quite.'

'Then you shall write me twenty lines of Virgil, Mulliner, and we will say no more about it.'

The bishop sprang from his chair.

'Mulliner! Did you say Mulliner?'

'Yes.'

'I have a secretary of that name. Are you, by any chance, a relation of his, my lad?'

'Sir, yes, sir. Brother.'

'Oh!' said the bishop.

The bishop found Augustine in the garden, squirting whale-oil solution on the rose-bushes, for he was an enthusiastic horticulturist. He placed an affectionate hand on his shoulder.

'Mulliner,' he said, 'do not think that I have not detected your hidden hand behind this astonishing occurrence.'

'Eh?' said Augustine. 'What astonishing occurrence?'

'As you are aware, Mulliner, last night, from motives which I can assure you were honourable and in accord with the truest spirit of sound Churchmanship, the Rev. Trevor

Entwhistle and I were compelled to go out and paint old Fatty Hemel's statue pink. Just now, in the headmaster's study, a boy confessed that he had done it. That boy, Mulliner, was your brother.'

'Oh yes?'

'It was you who, in order to save me, inspired him to that confession. Do not deny it, Mulliner.'

Augustine smiled an embarrassed smile.

'It was nothing, Bish, nothing at all.'

'I trust the matter did not involve you in any too great expense. From what I know of brothers, the lad was scarcely likely to have carried through this benevolent ruse for nothing.'

'Oh, just a couple of quid. He wanted three, but I beat him down. Preposterous, I mean to say,' said Augustine warmly. 'Three quid for a perfectly simple, easy job like that? And so I told him.'

'It shall be returned to you, Mulliner.'

'No, no, Bish.'

'Yes, Mulliner, it shall be returned to you. I have not the sum on my person, but I will forward you a cheque to your new address, The Vicarage, Steeple Mummery, Hants.'

Augustine's eyes filled with sudden tears. He grasped the other's hand.

'Bish,' he said in a choking voice, 'I don't know how to thank you. But—have you considered?'

'Considered?'

'The wife of thy bosom. Deuteronomy xiii, 6. What will she say when you tell her?'

The bishop's eyes gleamed with a resolute light.

'Mulliner,' he said, 'the point you raise had not escaped me. But I have the situation well in hand. A bird of the air shall carry the voice, and that which hath wings shall tell the matter. Ecclesiastes x, 20. I shall inform her of my decision on the long-distance telephone.'

5

CAME THE DAWN

The man in the corner took a sip of stout-and-mild, and proceeded to point the moral of the story which he had just told us.

'Yes, gentlemen,' he said, 'Shakespeare was right. There's a divinity that shapes our ends, rough-hew them how we will.'

We nodded. He had been speaking of a favourite dog of his which, entered recently by some error in a local cat show, had taken first prize in the class for short-haired tortoiseshells; and we all thought the quotation well-chosen and apposite.

'There is, indeed,' said Mr Mulliner. 'A rather similar thing happened to my nephew Lancelot.'

In the nightly reunions in the bar-parlour of the Anglers' Rest we have been trained to believe almost anything of Mr Mulliner's relatives, but this, we felt, was a little too much.

'You mean to say your nephew Lancelot took a prize at a cat show?'

'No, no,' said Mr Mulliner hastily. 'Certainly not. I have never deviated from the truth in my life, and I hope I never shall. No Mulliner has ever taken a prize at a cat show. No Mulliner, indeed, to the best of my knowledge, has even been entered for such a competition. What I meant was that the fact that we never know what the future holds in store for us was well exemplified in the case of my nephew Lancelot, just as it was in the case of this gentleman's dog which suddenly found itself transformed for all practical purposes into a short-haired tortoiseshell cat. It is rather a curious story, and provides a good illustration of the adage that you never can tell and that it is always darkest before the dawn.'

At the time at which my story opens (said Mr Mulliner) Lancelot, then twenty-four years of age and recently come down from Oxford, was spending a few days with old Jeremiah Briggs, the founder and proprietor of the famous Briggs's Breakfast Pickles, on the latter's yacht at Cowes.

This Jeremiah Briggs was Lancelot's uncle on the mother's side, and he had always interested himself in the boy. It was he who had sent him to the University; and it was the great wish of his heart that his nephew, on completing his education, should join him in the business. It was consequently a shock to the poor old gentleman when, as they sat together on deck on the first morning of the visit, Lancelot, while expressing the greatest respect for pickles as a class, firmly refused to start in and learn the business from the bottom up.

'The fact is, uncle,' he said, 'I have mapped out a career for myself on far different lines. I am a poet.'

'A poet? When did you feel this coming on?'

'Shortly after my twenty-second birthday.'

'Well,' said the old man, overcoming his first natural feeling of repulsion, 'I don't see why that should stop us getting together. I use quite a lot of poetry in my business.'

'I fear I could not bring myself to commercialize my Muse.'

'Young man,' said Mr Briggs, 'if an onion with a head like yours came into my factory, I would refuse to pickle it.'

He stumped below, thoroughly incensed. But Lancelot merely uttered a light laugh. He was young; it was summer; the sky was blue; the sun was shining; and the things in the world that really mattered were not cucumbers and vinegar but Romance and Love. Oh, he felt, for some delightful girl to come along on whom he might lavish all the pent-up fervour which had been sizzling inside him for weeks!

And at this moment he saw her.

She was leaning against the rail of a yacht that lay at its moorings some forty yards away; and, as he beheld her, Lancelot's heart leaped like a young gherkin in the boiling-vat. In her face, it seemed to him, was concentrated all the beauty of all the ages. Confronted with this girl, Cleopatra would have looked like Nellie Wallace, and Helen of Troy might have been her plain sister. He was still gazing at her in a sort of trance, when the bell sounded for luncheon and he had to go below.

All through the meal, while his uncle spoke of pickled walnuts he had known, Lancelot remained in a reverie. He was counting the minutes until he could get on deck and start goggling again. Judge, therefore, of his dismay when, on bounding up the companionway, he found that the other yacht had disappeared. He recalled now having heard a sort of harsh, grating noise towards the end of luncheon; but at the time he had merely thought it was his uncle eating celery. Too late he realized that it must have been the raising of the anchor-chain.

Although at heart a dreamer, Lancelot Mulliner was not without a certain practical streak. Thinking the matter over, he soon hit upon a rough plan of action for getting on the track of the fair unknown who had flashed in and out of his life with such tragic abruptness. A girl like that—beautiful, lissom, and—as far as he had been able to tell at such long range—gimp, was sure to be fond of dancing. The chances were, therefore, that sooner or later he would find her at some night club or other.

He started, accordingly, to make the round of the night clubs. As soon as one was raided, he went on to another. Within a month he had visited the Mauve Mouse, the Scarlet Centipede, the Vicious Cheese, the Gay Fritter, the Placid Prune, the Café de Bologna, Billy's, Milly's, Ike's, Spike's, Mike's, and the Ham and Beef. And it was at the Ham and Beef that at last he found her.

He had gone there one evening for the fifth time, principally because at that establishment there were a couple of speciality dancers to whom he had taken a dislike shared by virtually every thinking man in London. It had always seemed to him that one of these nights the male member of the team, while whirling his partner round in a circle by her outstretched arms, might let her go and break her neck; and though constant disappointment had to some extent blunted the first fine enthusiasm of his early visits, he still hoped.

On this occasion the speciality dancers came and went unscathed as usual, but Lancelot hardly noticed them. His whole attention was concentrated on the girl seated across the room immediately opposite him. It was beyond a question she.

Well, you know what poets are. When their emotions are stirred, they are not like us dull, diffident fellows. They breathe quickly through their noses and get off to a flying start. In one bound Lancelot was across the room, his heart beating till it sounded like a by-request solo from the trap-drummer.

'Shall we dance?' he said.

'Can you dance?' said the girl.

Lancelot gave a short, amused laugh. He had had a good University education, and had not failed to profit by it. He was a man who never let his left hip know what his right hip was doing.

'I am old Colonel Charleston's favourite son,' he said, simply.

A sound like the sudden descent of an iron girder on a sheet of tin, followed by a jangling of bells, a wailing of tortured cats, and the noise of a few steam-riveters at work, announced to their trained ears that the music had begun. Sweeping her to him with a violence which, attempted in any other place, would have earned him a sentence of thirty days coupled with some strong remarks from the Bench, Lancelot began to push her yielding form through the sea of humanity till they reached the centre of the whirlpool. There, unable to move in any direction, they surrendered themselves to the ecstasy of the dance, wiping their feet on the polished flooring and occasionally pushing an elbow into some stranger's encroaching rib.

'This,' murmured the girl with closed eyes, 'is divine.'

'What?' bellowed Lancelot, for the orchestra, in addition to ringing bells, had now begun to howl like wolves at dinner-time.

'Divine,' roared the girl. 'You certainly are a beautiful dancer.'

'A beautiful what?'

'Dancer.'

'Who is?'

'You are.'

'Good egg!' shrieked Lancelot, rather wishing, though he was fond of music, that the orchestra would stop beating the floor with hammers.

'What did you say?'

'I said, "Good egg."'

'Why?'

'Because the idea crossed my mind that, if you felt like that, you might care to marry me.'

There was a sudden lull in the storm. It was as if the audacity of his words had stricken the orchestra into a sort of paralysis. Dark-complexioned men who had been exploding bombs and touching off automobile hooters became abruptly immobile and sat rolling their eyeballs. One or two people left the floor, and plaster stopped falling from the ceiling.

'Marry you?' said the girl.

'I love you as no man has ever loved woman before.'

'Well, that's always something. What would the name be?'

'Mulliner. Lancelot Mulliner.'

'It might be worse.' She looked at him with pensive eyes. 'Well, why not?' she said. 'It would be a crime to let a dancer like you go out of the family. On the other hand, my father will kick like a mule. Father is an Earl.'

'What Earl?'

'The Earl of Biddlecombe.'

'Well, earls aren't everything,' said Lancelot with a touch of pique. 'The Mulliners are an old and honourable family. A Sieur de Moulinières came over with the Conqueror.'

'Ah, but did a Sieur de Moulinières ever do down the common people for a few hundred thousand and salt it away in gilt-edged securities? That's what's going to count with the aged parent. What with taxes and super-taxes and death duties and falling land-values, there has of recent years been very, very little of the right stuff in the Biddlecombe sock. Shake the family money-box and you will hear but the faintest rattle. And I ought to tell you that at the Junior Lipstick Club seven to two is being freely offered on my marrying Slingsby Purvis, of Purvis's Liquid Dinner Glue. Nothing is definitely decided yet, but you can take it as coming straight from the stable that, unless something happens to upset current form, she whom you now see before you is the future Ma Purvis.'

Lancelot stamped his foot defiantly, eliciting a howl of agony from a passing reveller.

'This shall not be,' he muttered.

'If you care to bet against it,' said the girl, producing a small notebook, 'I can accommodate you at the current odds.'

'Purvis, forsooth!'

'I'm not saying it's a pretty name. All I'm trying to point out is that at the present moment he heads the "All the above have arrived" list. He is Our Newmarket Correspondent's Five-Pound Special and Captain Coe's final selection. What makes you think you can nose him out? Are you rich?'

'At present, only in love. But tomorrow I go to my uncle, who is immensely wealthy—'

'And touch him?'

'Not quite that. Nobody has touched Uncle Jeremiah since the early winter of 1885. But I shall get him to give me a job, and then we shall see.'

'Do,' said the girl, warmly. 'And if you can stick the gaff into Purvis and work the Young Lochinvar business, I shall be the first to touch off red fire. On the other hand, it is only fair to inform you that at the Junior Lipstick all the girls look on the race as a walk-over. None of the big punters will touch it.'

Lancelot returned to his rooms that night undiscouraged. He intended to sink his former prejudices and write a poem in praise of Briggs's Breakfast Pickles which would mark a new era in commercial verse. This he would submit to his uncle; and, having stunned him with it, would agree to join the firm as chief poetry-writer. He tentatively penciled down five thousand pounds a year as the salary which he would demand. With a long-term contract for five thousand a year in his pocket, he could approach Lord Biddlecombe and jerk a father's blessing out of him in no time. It would be humiliating, of course, to lower his genius by writing poetry about pickles; but a lover must make sacrifices. He bought a quire of the best foolscap, brewed a quart of the strongest coffee, locked his door, disconnected his telephone, and sat down at his desk.

Genial old Jeremiah Briggs received him, when he called next day at his palatial house, the Villa Chutney, at Putney, with a bluff good-humour which showed that he still had a warm spot in his heart for the young rascal.

'Sit down, boy, and have a pickled onion,' said he, cheerily, slapping Lancelot on the shoulder. 'You've come to tell me you've reconsidered your idiotic decision about not joining the business, eh? No doubt we thought it a little beneath our dignity to start at the bottom and work our way up? But, consider, my dear lad. We must learn to walk before we can run, and you could hardly expect me to make you chief cucumber buyer, or head of the vinegar-bottling department, before you have acquired hard-won experience.'

'If you will allow me to explain, uncle—'

'Eh?' Mr Briggs's geniality faded somewhat. 'Am I to understand that you don't want to come into the business?'

'Yes and no,' said Lancelot. 'I still consider that slicing up cucumbers and dipping them in vinegar is a poor life-work for a man with the Promethean fire within him; but I propose to place at the disposal of the Briggs Breakfast Pickle my poetic gifts.'

'Well, that's better than nothing. I've just been correcting the proofs of the last thing our man turned in. It's really excellent. Listen:

'Soon, soon all human joys must end:

Grim Death approaches with his sickle:

Courage! There is still time, my friend,

To eat a Briggs's Breakfast Pickle.'

'If you could give us something like that—'

Lancelot raised his eyebrows. His lip curled.

'The little thing I have dashed off is not quite like that.'

'Oh, you've written something, eh?'

'A mere morceau. You would care to hear it?'

'Fire away, my boy.'

Lancelot produced his manuscript and cleared his throat. He began to read in a low, musical voice.

'DARKLING (A Threnody)

BY L. BASSINGTON MULLINER

(Copyright in all languages, including the Scandinavian)

(The dramatic, musical-comedy, and motion-picture rights of this Threnody are strictly reserved. Applications for these should be made to the author)'

'What is a Threnody?' asked Mr Briggs.

'This is,' said Lancelot.

He cleared his throat again and resumed.

'Black branches,

Like a corpse's withered hands,

Waving against the blacker sky:

Chill winds,

Bitter like the tang of half-remembered sins;

Bats wheeling mournfully through the air,

And on the ground

Worms,

Toads,

Frogs,

And nameless creeping things;

And all around

Desolation,

Doom,

Dyspepsia,

And Despair.

I am a bat that wheels through the air of Fate;

I am a worm that wriggles in a swamp of Disillusionment;

I am a despairing toad;

I have got dyspepsia.'

He paused. His uncle's eyes were protruding rather like those of a nameless creeping frog.

'What's all this?' said Mr Briggs.

It seemed almost incredible to Lancelot that his poem should present any aspect of obscurity to even the meanest intellect; but he explained.

'The thing,' he said, 'is symbolic. It essays to depict the state of mind of the man who has not yet tried Briggs's Breakfast Pickles. I shall require it to be printed in hand-set type on deep cream-coloured paper.'

'Yes?' said Mr Briggs, touching the bell.

'With bevelled edges. It must be published, of course, bound in limp leather, preferably of a violet shade, in a limited edition, confined to one hundred and five copies. Each of these copies I will sign—'

'You rang, sir?' said the butler, appearing in the doorway.

Mr Briggs nodded curtly.

'Bewstridge,' said he, 'throw Mr Lancelot out.'

'Very good, sir.'

'And see,' added Mr Briggs, superintending the subsequent proceedings from his library window, 'that he never darkens my doors again. When you have finished, Bewstridge, ring up my lawyers on the telephone. I wish to alter my will.'

Youth is a resilient period. With all his worldly prospects swept away and a large bruise on his person which made it uncomfortable for him to assume a sitting posture, you might have supposed that the return of Lancelot Mulliner from Putney would have resembled that of the late Napoleon from Moscow. Such, however, was not the case. What, Lancelot asked himself as he rode back to civilization on top of an omnibus, did money matter? Love, true love, was all. He would go to Lord Biddlecombe and tell him so in a few neatly-chosen words. And his lordship, moved by his eloquence, would doubtless drop a well-bred tear and at once see that the arrangements for his wedding to Angela—for such, he had learned, was her name—were hastened along with all possible speed. So uplifted was he by this picture that he began to sing, and would have continued for the remainder of the journey had not the conductor in a rather brusque manner ordered him to desist. He was obliged to content himself until the bus reached Hyde Park Corner by singing in dumb show.

The Earl of Biddlecombe's town residence was in Berkeley Square. Lancelot rang the bell and a massive butler appeared.

'No hawkers, street criers, or circulars,' said the butler.

'I wish to see Lord Biddlecombe.'

'Is his lordship expecting you?'

'Yes,' said Lancelot, feeling sure that the girl would have spoken to her father over the morning toast and marmalade of a possible visit from him.

A voice made itself heard through an open door on the left of the long hall.

'Fotheringay.'

'Your lordship?'

'Is that the feller?'

'Yes, your lordship.'

'Then bring him in, Fotheringay.'

'Very good, your lordship.'

Lancelot found himself in a small, comfortably-furnished room, confronting a dignified-looking old man with a patrician nose and small side-whiskers, who looked like something that long ago had come out of an egg.

'Afternoon,' said this individual.

'Good afternoon, Lord Biddlecombe,' said Lancelot.

'Now, about these trousers.'

'I beg your pardon?'

'These trousers,' said the other, extending a shapely leg. 'Do they fit? Aren't they a bit baggy round the ankles? Won't they jeopardize my social prestige if I am seen in them in the Park?'

Lancelot was charmed with his affability. It gave him the feeling of having been made one of the family straight away.

'You really want my opinion?'

'I do. I want your candid opinion as a God-fearing man and a member of a West-End tailoring firm.'

'But I'm not.'

'Not a God-fearing man?'

'Not a member of a West-End tailoring firm.'

'Come, come,' said his lordship, testily. 'You represent Gusset and Mainprice, of Cork Street.'

'No, I don't.'

'Then who the devil are you?'

'My name is Mulliner.'

Lord Biddlecombe rang the bell furiously.

'Fotheringay!'

'Your lordship?'

'You told me this man was the feller I was expecting from Gusset and Mainprice.'

'He certainly led me to suppose so, your lordship.'

'Well, he isn't. His name is Mulliner. And—this is the point, Fotheringay. This is the core and centre of the thing—what the blazes does he want?'

'I could not say, your lordship.'

'I came here, Lord Biddlecombe,' said Lancelot, 'to ask your consent to my immediate marriage with your daughter.'

'My daughter?'

'Your daughter.'

'Which daughter?'

'Angela.'

'My daughter Angela?'

'Yes.'

'You want to marry my daughter Angela?'

'I do.'

'Oh? Well, be that as it may,' said Lord Biddlecombe, 'can I interest you in an ingenious little combination mousetrap and pencil-sharpener?'

Lancelot was for a moment a little taken aback by the question. Then, remembering what Angela had said of the state of the family finances, he recovered his poise. He thought no worse of this Grecian-beaked old man for ekeing out a slender income by acting as agent for the curious little object which he was now holding out to him. Many of the aristocracy, he was aware, had been forced into similar commercial enterprises by recent legislation of a harsh and Socialistic trend.

'I should like it above all things,' he said, courteously. 'I was thinking only this morning that it was just what I needed.'

'Highly educational. Not a toy. Fotheringay, book one Mouso-Penso.'

'Very good, your lordship.'

'Are you troubled at all with headaches, Mr Mulliner?'

'Very seldom.'

'Then what you want is Clark's Cure for Corns. Shall we say one of the large bottles?'

'Certainly.'

'Then that—with a year's subscription to Our Tots—will come to precisely one pound, three shillings, and sixpence. Thank you. Will there be anything further?'

'No, thank you. Now, touching the matter of—'

'You wouldn't care for a scarf-pin? Any ties, collars, shirts? No? Then good-bye, Mr Mulliner.'

'But—'

'Fotheringay,' said Lord Biddlecombe, 'throw Mr Mulliner out.'

As Lancelot scrambled to his feet from the hard pavement of Berkeley Square, he was conscious of a rush of violent anger which deprived him momentarily of speech. He stood there, glaring at the house from which he had been ejected, his face working hideously. So absorbed was he that it was some time before he became aware that somebody was plucking at his coat-sleeve.

'Pardon me, sir.'

Lancelot looked round. A stout smooth-faced man with horn-rimmed spectacles was standing beside him.

'If you could spare me a moment—'

Lancelot shook him off impatiently. He had no desire at a time like this to chatter with strangers. The man was babbling something, but the words made no impression upon his mind. With a savage scowl, Lancelot snatched the fellow's umbrella from him and, poising it for an instant, flung it with a sure aim through Lord Biddlecombe's study window. Then, striding away, he made for Berkeley Street. Glancing over his shoulder as he turned the corner, he saw that Fotheringay, the butler, had come out of the house and was standing over the spectacled man with a certain quiet menace in his demeanour. He was rolling up his sleeves, and his fingers were twitching a little.

Lancelot dismissed the man from his thoughts. His whole mind now was concentrated on the coming interview with Angela. For he had decided that the only thing to do was to seek her out at her club, where she would doubtless be spending the afternoon, and plead with her to follow the dictates of her heart and, abandoning parents and wealthy suitors, come with her true mate to a life of honest poverty sweetened by love and vers libre.

Arriving at the Junior Lipstick, he inquired for her, and the hall-porter dispatched a boy in buttons to fetch her from the billiard-room, where she was refereeing the finals of the Débutantes' Shove-Ha'penny Tournament. And presently his heart leaped as he saw her coming towards him, looking more like a vision of Springtime than anything human and earthly. She was smoking a cigarette in a long holder, and as she approached she inserted a monocle inquiringly in her right eye.

'Hullo, laddie!' she said. 'You here? What's on the mind besides hair? Talk quick. I've only got a minute.'

'Angela,' said Lancelot, 'I have to report a slight hitch in the programme which I sketched out at our last meeting. I have just been to see my uncle and he has washed his hands of me and cut me out of his will.'

'Nothing doing in that quarter, you mean?' said the girl, chewing her lower lip thoughtfully.

'Nothing. But what of it? What matters it so long as we have each other? Money is dross. Love is everything. Yes, love indeed is light from heaven, a spark of that immortal fire with angels shared, by Allah given to lift from earth our low desire. Give me to live with Love alone, and let the world go dine and dress. If life's a flower, I choose my own. 'Tis Love in Idleness. When beauty fires the blood, how love exalts the mind! Come, Angela, let us read together in a book more moving than the Koran, more eloquent than Shakespeare, the book of books, the crown of all literature—Bradshaw's Railway Guide. We will turn up a page and you shall put your finger down, and wherever it rests there we will go, to live for ever with our happiness. Oh, Angela, let us—'

'Sorry,' said the girl. 'Purvis wins. The race goes by the form-book after all. There was a time when I thought you might be going to crowd him on the rails and get your nose first under the wire with a quick last-minute dash, but apparently it is not to be. Deepest sympathy, old crocus, but that's that.'

Lancelot staggered.

'You mean you intend to marry this Purvis?'

'Pop in about a month from now at St George's, Hanover Square, and see for yourself.'

'You would allow this man to buy you with his gold?'

'Don't overlook his diamonds.'

'Does love count for nothing? Surely you love me?'

'Of course I do, my desert king. When you do that flat-footed Black Bottom step with the sort of wiggly twiggle at the end, I feel as if I were eating plovers' eggs in a new dress to the accompaniment of heavenly music.' She sighed. 'Yes, I love you, Lancelot. And women are not like men. They do not love lightly. When a woman gives her heart, it is for ever. The years will pass, and you will turn to another. But I shall not forget. However, as you haven't a bob in the world—' She beckoned to the hall-porter. 'Margerison.'

'Your ladyship?'

'Is it raining?'

'No, your ladyship.'

'Are the front steps clean?'

'Yes, your ladyship.'

'Then throw Mr Mulliner out.'

Lancelot leaned against the railings of the Junior Lipstick, and looked out through a black mist upon a world that heaved and rocked and seemed on the point of disintegrating into ruin and chaos. And a lot he would care, he told himself bitterly, if it did. If Seamore Place from the west and Charles Street from the east had taken a running jump and landed on the back of his neck, it would have added little or nothing to the turmoil of his mind. In fact, he would rather have preferred it.

Fury, as it had done on the pavement of Berkeley Square, robbed him of speech. But his hands, his shoulders, his brows, his lips, his nose, and even his eyelashes seemed to be charged with a silent eloquence. He twitched his eyebrows in agony. He twiddled his fingers in despair. Nothing was left now, he felt, as he shifted the lobe of his left ear in a nor'-nor'-easterly direction, but suicide. Yes, he told himself, tightening and relaxing the muscles of his cheeks, all that remained now was death.

But, even as he reached this awful decision, a kindly voice spoke in his ear.

'Oh, come now, I wouldn't say that,' said the kindly voice.

And Lancelot, turning, perceived the smooth-faced man who had tried to engage him in conversation in Berkeley Square.

'Say, listen,' said the smooth-faced man, sympathy in each lens of his horn-rimmed spectacles. 'Tempests may lower and a strong man stand face to face with his soul, but hope, like a healing herb, will show the silver lining where beckons joy and life and happiness.'

Lancelot eyed him haughtily.

'I am not aware—' he began.

'Say, listen,' said the other, laying a soothing hand on his shoulder. 'I know just what has happened. Mammon has conquered Cupid, and once more youth has had to learn the old, old lesson that though the face be fair the heart may be cold and callous.'

'What—?'

The smooth-faced man raised his hand.

'That afternoon. Her apartment. "No. It can never be. I shall wed a wealthier wooer."'

Lancelot's fury began to dissolve into awe. There seemed something uncanny in the way this total stranger had diagnosed the situation. He stared at him, bewildered.

'How did you know?' he gasped.

'You told me.'

'I?'

'Your face did. I could read every word. I've been watching you for the last two minutes, and, say, boy, it was a wow!'

'Who are you?' asked Lancelot.

The smooth-faced man produced from his waistcoat pocket a fountain-pen, two cigars, a packet of chewing-gum, a small button bearing the legend, 'Boost for Hollywood', and a visiting-card—in the order named. Replacing the other articles, he handed the card to Lancelot.

'I'm Isadore Zinzinheimer, kid,' he said. 'I represent the Bigger, Better, and Brighter Motion-Picture Company of Hollywood, Cal., incorporated last July for sixteen hundred million dollars. And if you're thinking of asking me what I want, I want you. Yes, sir! Say, listen. A fellow that can register the way you can is needed in my business; and, if you think money can stop me getting him, name the biggest salary you can think of and hear me laugh. Boy, I use bank-notes for summer underclothing, and I don't care how bad you've got the gimme's if only you'll sign on the dotted line. Say, listen. A bozo that with a mere twitch of the upper lip can make it plain to one and all that he loves a haughty aristocrat and that she has given him the air because his rich uncle, who is a pickle manufacturer living in Putney, won't have anything more to do with him, is required out at Hollywood by the next boat if the movies are ever to become an educational force in the truest and deepest sense of the words.'

Lancelot stared at him.

'You want me to come to Hollywood?'

'I want you, and I'm going to get you. And if you think you're going to prevent me, you're trying to stop Niagara with a tennis racket. Boy, you're great! When you register, you register. Your face is as chatty as a board of directors. Say, listen. You know the great thing we folks in the motion-picture industry have got to contend with? The curse of the motion-picture industry is that in every audience there are from six to seven young women with adenoids who will insist on reading out the titles as they are flashed on the screen, filling the rest of the customers with harsh thoughts and dreams of murder. What we're trying to collect is stars that can register so well that titles won't be needed. And, boy, you're the king of them. I know you're feeling good and sore just now because that beazle in there spurned your honest love; but forget it. Think of your Art. Think of your Public. Come now, what shall we say to start with? Five thousand a week? Ten thousand? You call the shots, and I'll provide the blank contract and fountain-pen.'

Lancelot needed no further urging. Already love had turned to hate, and he no longer wished to marry Angela. Instead, he wanted to make her burn with anguish and vain regrets; and it seemed to him that Fate was pointing the way. Pretty silly the future Lady Angela Purvis would feel when she discovered that she had rejected the love of a man with a salary of ten thousand dollars a week. And fairly foolish her old father would feel when news reached him of the good thing he had allowed to get away. And racking would be the remorse, when he returned to London as Civilized Girlhood's Sweetheart and they saw him addressing mobs from a hotel balcony, of his Uncle Jeremiah, of Fotheringay, of Bewstridge, and of Margerison.

A light gleamed in Lancelot's eye, and he rolled the tip of his nose in a circular movement.

'You consent?' said Mr Zinzinheimer, delighted. "At-a-boy! Here's the pen and here's the contract.'

'Gimme!' said Lancelot.

A benevolent glow irradiated the other's spectacles.

'Came the Dawn!' he murmured. 'Came the Dawn!'

6
THE STORY OF WILLIAM

Miss Postlethwaite, our able and vigilant barmaid, had whispered to us that the gentleman sitting over there in the corner was an American gentleman.

'Comes from America,' added Miss Postlethwaite, making her meaning clearer.

'From America?' echoed we.

'From America,' said Miss Postlethwaite. 'He's an American.'

Mr Mulliner rose with an old-world grace. We do not often get Americans in the bar-parlour of the Anglers' Rest. When we do, we welcome them. We make them realize that Hands Across the Sea is no mere phrase.

'Good evening, sir,' said Mr Mulliner. 'I wonder if you would care to join my friend and myself in a little refreshment?'

'Very kind of you, sir.'

'Miss Postlethwaite, the usual. I understand you are from the other side, sir. Do you find our English country-side pleasant?'

'Delightful. Though, of course, if I may say so, scarcely to be compared with the scenery of my home State.'

'What State is that?'

'California,' replied the other, baring his head. 'California, the Jewel State of the Union. With its azure sea, its noble hills, its eternal sunshine, and its fragrant flowers, California stands alone. Peopled by stalwart men and womanly women....'

'California would be all right,' said Mr Mulliner, 'if it wasn't for the earthquakes.'

Our guest started as though some venomous snake had bitten him.

'Earthquakes are absolutely unknown in California,' he said, hoarsely.

'What about the one in 1906?'

'That was not an earthquake. It was a fire.'

'An earthquake, I always understood,' said Mr Mulliner. 'My Uncle William was out there during it, and many a time has he said to me, "My boy, it was the San Francisco earthquake that won me a bride".'

'Couldn't have been the earthquake. May have been the fire.'

'Well, I will tell you the story, and you shall judge for yourself.'

'I shall be glad to hear your story about the San Francisco fire,' said the Californian, courteously.

My Uncle William (said Mr Mulliner) was returning from the East at the time. The commercial interests of the Mulliners had always been far-flung: and he had been over in China looking into the workings of a tea-exporting business in which he held a number of shares. It was his intention to get off the boat at San Francisco and cross the continent by rail. He particularly wanted to see the Grand Canyon of Arizona. And when he found that Myrtle Banks had for years cherished the same desire, it seemed to him so plain a proof that they were twin souls that he decided to offer her his hand and heart without delay.

This Miss Banks had been a fellow-traveller on the boat all the way from Hong Kong; and day by day William Mulliner had fallen more and more deeply in love with her. So on the last day of the voyage, as they were steaming in at the Golden Gate, he proposed.

I have never been informed of the exact words which he employed, but no doubt they were eloquent. All the Mulliners have been able speakers, and on such an occasion, he would, of course, have extended himself. When at length he finished, it seemed to him that the girl's attitude was distinctly promising. She stood gazing over the rail into the water below in a sort of rapt way. Then she turned.

'Mr Mulliner,' she said, 'I am greatly flattered and honoured by what you have just told me.' These things happened, you will remember, in the days when girls talked like that. 'You have paid me the greatest compliment a man can bestow on a woman. And yet....'

William Mulliner's heart stood still. He did not like that 'And yet—'

'Is there another?' he muttered.

'Well, yes, there is. Mr Franklyn proposed to me this morning. I told him I would think it over.'

There was a silence. William was telling himself that he had been afraid of that bounder Franklyn all along. He might have known, he felt, that Desmond Franklyn would be a menace. The man was one of those lean, keen, hawk-faced, Empire-building sort of chaps you find out East—the kind of fellow who stands on deck chewing his moustache with a far-away look in his eyes, and then, when the girl asks him what he is thinking about, draws a short, quick breath and says he is sorry to be so absent-minded, but a sunset like that always reminds him of the day when he killed the four pirates with his bare hands and saved dear old Tuppy Smithers in the nick of time.

'There is a great glamour about Mr Franklyn,' said Myrtle Banks. 'We women admire men who do things. A girl cannot help but respect a man who once killed three sharks with a Boy Scout pocket-knife.'

'So he says,' growled William.

'He showed me the pocket-knife,' said the girl, simply. 'And on another occasion he brought down two lions with one shot.'

William Mulliner's heart was heavy, but he struggled on.

'Very possibly he may have done these things,' he said, 'but surely marriage means more than this. Personally, if I were a girl, I would go rather for a certain steadiness and stability of character. To illustrate what I mean, did you happen to see me win the Egg-and-Spoon race at the ship's sports? Now there, it seems to me, in what I might call microcosm, was an exhibition of all the qualities a married man most requires—intense coolness, iron resolution, and a quiet, unassuming courage. The man who under test conditions has carried an egg once and a half times round a deck in a small spoon is a man who can be trusted.'

She seemed to waver, but only for a moment.

'I must think,' she said. 'I must think.'

'Certainly,' said William. 'You will let me see something of you at the hotel, after we have landed?'

'Of course. And if—I mean to say, whatever happens, I shall always look on you as a dear, dear friend.'

'M'yes,' said William Mulliner.

For three days my Uncle William's stay in San Francisco was as pleasant as could reasonably be expected, considering that Desmond Franklyn was also stopping at his and Miss Banks's hotel. He contrived to get the girl to himself to quite a satisfactory extent; and they spent many happy hours together in the Golden Gate Park and at the Cliff House, watching the seals basking on the rocks. But on the evening of the third day the blow fell.

'Mr Mulliner,' said Myrtle Banks, 'I want to tell you something.'

'Anything,' breathed William tenderly, 'except that you are going to marry that perisher Franklyn.'

'But that is exactly what I was going to tell you, and I must not let you call him a perisher, for he is a very brave, intrepid man.'

'When did you decide on this rash act?' asked William dully.

'Scarcely an hour ago. We were talking in the garden, and somehow or other we got on to the subject of rhinoceroses. He then told me how he had once been chased up a tree by a rhinoceros in Africa and escaped by throwing pepper in the brute's eyes. He most fortunately chanced to be eating his lunch when the animal arrived, and he had a hard-boiled egg and the pepper-pot in his hands. When I heard this story, like Desdemona, I loved him for the dangers he had passed, and he loved me that I did pity them. The wedding is to be in June.'

William Mulliner ground his teeth in a sudden access of jealous rage.

'Personally,' he said, 'I consider that the story you have just related reveals this man Franklyn in a very dubious—I might almost say sinister—light. On his own showing, the leading trait in his character appears to be cruelty to animals. The fellow seems totally incapable of meeting a shark or a rhinoceros or any other of our dumb friends without instantly going out of his way to inflict bodily injury on it. The last thing I would wish is to be indelicate, but I cannot refrain from pointing out that, if your union is blessed, your children will probably be the sort of children who kick cats and tie tin cans to dogs' tails. If you take my advice, you will write the man a little note, saying that you are sorry but you have changed your mind.'

The girl rose in a marked manner.

'I do not require your advice, Mr Mulliner,' she said, coldly. 'And I have not changed my mind.'

Instantly William Mulliner was all contrition. There is a certain stage in the progress of a man's love when he feels like curling up in a ball and making little bleating noises if the object of his affections so much as looks squiggle-eyed at him; and this stage my Uncle William had reached. He followed her as she paced proudly away through the hotel lobby, and stammered incoherent apologies. But Myrtle Banks was adamant.

'Leave me, Mr Mulliner,' she said, pointing at the revolving door that led into the street. 'You have maligned a better man than yourself, and I wish to have nothing more to do with you. Go!'

William went, as directed. And so great was the confusion of his mind that he got stuck in the revolving door and had gone round in it no fewer than eleven times before the hall-porter came to extricate him.

'I would have removed you from the machinery earlier, sir,' said the hall-porter deferentially, having deposited him safely in the street, 'but my bet with my mate in there called for ten laps. I waited till you had completed eleven so that there should be no argument.'

William looked at him dazedly.

'Hall-porter,' he said.

'Sir?'

'Tell me, hall-porter,' said William, 'suppose the only girl you have ever loved had gone and got engaged to another, what would you do?'

The hall-porter considered.

'Let me get this right,' he said. 'The proposition is, if I have followed you correctly, what would I do supposing the Jane on whom I had always looked as a steady mamma had handed me the old skimmer and told me to take all the air I needed because she had gotten another sweetie?'

'Precisely.'

'Your question is easily answered,' said the hall-porter. 'I would go around the corner and get me a nice stiff drink at Mike's Place.'

'A drink?'

'Yes, sir. A nice stiff one.'

'At where did you say?'

'Mike's Place, sir. Just round the corner. You can't miss it.'

William thanked him and walked away. The man's words had started a new, and in many ways interesting, train of thought. A drink? And a nice stiff one? There might be something in it.

William Mulliner had never tasted alcohol in his life. He had promised his late mother that he would not do so until he was either twenty-one or forty-one—he could never remember which. He was at present twenty-nine; but wishing to be on the safe side in case he had got his figures wrong, he had remained a teetotaller. But now, as he walked listlessly along the street towards the corner, it seemed to him that his mother in the special circumstances could not reasonably object if he took a slight snort. He raised his eyes to heaven, as though to ask her if a couple of quick ones might not be permitted; and he fancied that a faint, far-off voice whispered, 'Go to it!'

And at this moment he found himself standing outside a brightly-lighted saloon.

For an instant he hesitated. Then, as a twinge of anguish in the region of his broken heart reminded him of the necessity for immediate remedies, he pushed open the swing doors and went in.

The principal feature of the cheerful, brightly-lit room in which he found himself was a long counter, at which were standing a number of the citizenry, each with an elbow on the woodwork and a foot upon the neat brass rail which ran below. Behind the counter appeared the upper section of one of the most benevolent and kindly-looking men that William had ever seen. He had a large smooth face, and he wore a white coat, and he eyed William, as he advanced, with a sort of reverent joy.

'Is this Mike's Place?' asked William.

'Yes, sir,' replied the white-coated man.

'Are you Mike?'

'No, sir. But I am his representative, and have full authority to act on his behalf. What can I have the pleasure of doing for you?'

The man's whole attitude made him seem so like a large-hearted elder brother that William felt no diffidence about confiding in him. He placed an elbow on the counter and a foot on the rail, and spoke with a sob in his voice.

'Suppose the only girl you had ever loved had gone and got engaged to another, what in your view would best meet the case?'

The gentlemanly bar-tender pondered for some moments.

'Well,' he replied at length, 'I advance it, you understand, as a purely personal opinion, and I shall not be in the least offended if you decide not to act upon it; but my suggestion—for what it is worth—is that you try a Dynamite Dew-Drop.'

One of the crowd that had gathered sympathetically round shook his head. He was a charming man with a black eye, who had shaved on the preceding Thursday.

'Much better give him a Dreamland Special.'

A second man, in a sweater and a cloth cap, had yet another theory.

'You can't beat an Undertaker's Joy.'

They were all so perfectly delightful and appeared to have his interests so unselfishly at heart that William could not bring himself to choose between them. He solved the problem in diplomatic fashion by playing no favourites and ordering all three of the beverages recommended.

The effect was instantaneous and gratifying. As he drained the first glass, it seemed to him that a torchlight procession, of whose existence he had hitherto not been aware, had begun to march down his throat and explore the recesses of his stomach. The second glass, though slightly too heavily charged with molten lava, was extremely palatable. It helped the torchlight procession along by adding to it a brass band of singular power and sweetness of tone. And with the third somebody began to touch off fireworks inside his head.

William felt better—not only spiritually but physically. He seemed to himself to be a bigger, finer man, and the loss of Myrtle Banks had somehow in a flash lost nearly all its importance. After all, as he said to the man with the black eye, Myrtle Banks wasn't everybody.

'Now what do you recommend?' he asked the man with the sweater, having turned the last glass upside down.

The other mused, one forefinger thoughtfully pressed against the side of his face.

'Well, I'll tell you,' he said. 'When my brother Elmer lost his girl, he drank straight rye. Yes, sir. That's what he drank—straight rye. "I've lost my girl," he said, "and I'm going to drink straight rye." That's what he said. Yes, sir, straight rye.'

'And was your brother Elmer,' asked William, anxiously, 'a man whose example in your opinion should be followed? Was he a man you could trust?'

'He owned the biggest duck-farm in the southern half of Illinois.'

'That settles it,' said William. 'What was good enough for a duck who owned half Illinois is good enough for me. Oblige me,' he said to the gentlemanly bar-tender, 'by asking these gentlemen what they will have, and start pouring.'

The bar-tender obeyed, and William, having tried a pint or two of the strange liquid just to see if he liked it, found that he did, and ordered some. He then began to move about among his new friends, patting one on the shoulder, slapping another affably on the back, and asking a third what his Christian name was.

'I want you all,' he said, climbing on to the counter so that his voice should carry better, 'to come and stay with me in England. Never in my life have I met men whose faces I liked so much. More like brothers than anything is the way I regard you. So just you pack up a few things and come along and put up at my little place for as long as you can manage. You particularly, my dear old chap,' he added, beaming at the man in the sweater.

'Thanks,' said the man with the sweater.

'What did you say?' said William.

'I said, "Thanks".'

William slowly removed his coat and rolled up his shirt-sleeves.

'I call you gentlemen to witness,' he said, quietly, 'that I have been grossly insulted by this gentleman who has just grossly insulted me. I am not a quarrelsome man, but if anybody wants a row they can have it. And when it comes to being cursed and sworn at by an ugly bounder in a sweater and a cloth cap, it is time to take steps.'

And with these spirited words William Mulliner sprang from the counter, grasped the other by the throat, and bit him sharply on the right ear. There was a confused interval, during which somebody attached himself to the collar of William's waistcoat and the seat of William's trousers, and then a sense of swift movement and rush of cool air.

William discovered that he was seated on the pavement outside the saloon. A hand emerged from the swing door and threw his hat out. And he was alone with the night and his meditations.

These were, as you may suppose, of a singularly bitter nature. Sorrow and disillusionment racked William Mulliner like a physical pain. That his friends inside there, in spite of the fact that he had been all sweetness and light and had not done a thing to them, should have thrown him out into the hard street was the saddest thing he had ever heard of; and for some minutes he sat there, weeping silently.

Presently he heaved himself to his feet and, placing one foot with infinite delicacy in front of the other, and then drawing the other one up and placing it with infinite delicacy in front of that, he began to walk back to his hotel.

At the corner he paused. There were some railings on his right. He clung to them and rested awhile.

The railings to which William Mulliner had attached himself belonged to a brown-stone house of the kind that seems destined from the first moment of its building to receive guests, both resident and transient, at a moderate weekly rental. It was, in fact, as he would have discovered had he been clear-sighted enough to read the card over the door, Mrs Beulah O'Brien's Theatrical Boarding-House ('A Home From Home—No Cheques Cashed—This Means You').

But William was not in the best of shape for reading cards. A sort of mist had obscured the world, and he was finding it difficult to keep his eyes open. And presently, his chin wedged into the railings, he fell into a dreamless sleep.

He was awakened by light flashing in his eyes; and, opening them, saw that a window opposite where he was standing had become brightly illuminated. His slumbers had cleared his vision; and he was able to observe that the room into which he was looking was a dining-room. The long table was set for the evening meal; and to William, as he gazed, the sight of that cosy apartment, with the gaslight falling on the knives and forks and spoons, seemed the most pathetic and poignant that he had ever beheld.

A mood of the most extreme sentimentality now had him in its grip. The thought that he would never own a little home like that racked him from stem to stern with an almost unbearable torment. What, argued William, clinging to the railings and crying weakly, could compare, when you came right down to it, with a little home? A man with a little home is all right, whereas a man without a little home is just a bit of flotsam on the ocean of life. If Myrtle Banks had only consented to marry him, he would have had a little home. But she had refused to marry him, so he would never have a little home. What Myrtle Banks wanted, felt William, was a good swift clout on the side of the head.

The thought pleased him. He was feeling physically perfect again now, and seemed to have shaken off completely the slight indisposition from which he had been suffering. His legs had lost their tendency to act independently of the rest of his body. His head felt clearer, and he had a sense of overwhelming strength. If ever, in short, there was a moment when he could administer that clout on the side of the head to Myrtle Banks as it should be administered, that moment was now.

He was on the point of moving off to find her and teach her what it meant to stop a man like himself from having a little home, when someone entered the room into which he was looking, and he paused to make further inspection.

The new arrival was a coloured maid-servant. She staggered to the head of the table beneath the weight of a large tureen containing, so William suspected, hash. A moment later a stout woman with bright golden hair came in and sat down opposite the tureen.

The instinct to watch other people eat is one of the most deeply implanted in the human bosom, and William lingered, intent. There was, he told himself, no need to hurry. He knew which was Myrtle's room in the hotel. It was just across the corridor from his own. He could pop in any time, during the night, and give her that clout. Meanwhile, he wanted to watch these people eat hash.

And then the door opened again, and there filed into the room a little procession. And William, clutching the railings, watched it with bulging eyes.

The procession was headed by an elderly man in a check suit with a carnation in his buttonhole. He was about three feet six in height, though the military jauntiness with which he carried himself made him seem fully three feet seven. He was followed by a younger man who wore spectacles and whose height was perhaps three feet four. And behind these two came, in single file, six others, scaling down by degrees until, bringing up the rear of the procession, there entered a rather stout man in tweeds and bedroom slippers who could not have measured more than two feet eight.

They took their places at the table. Hash was distributed to all. And the man in tweeds, having inspected his plate with obvious relish, removed his slippers and, picking up his knife and fork with his toes, fell to with a keen appetite.

William Mulliner uttered a soft moan, and tottered away.

It was a black moment for my Uncle William. Only an instant before he had been congratulating himself on having shaken off the effects of his first indulgence in alcohol after an abstinence of twenty-nine years; but now he perceived that he was still intoxicated.

Intoxicated? The word did not express it by a mile. He was oiled, boiled, fried, plastered, whiffled, sozzled, and blotto. Only by the exercise of the most consummate caution and address could he hope to get back to his hotel and reach his bedroom without causing an open scandal.

Of course, if his walk that night had taken him a few yards farther down the street than the door of Mike's Place, he would have seen that there was a very simple explanation of the spectacle which he had just witnessed. A walk so extended would have brought him to the San Francisco Palace of Varieties, outside which large posters proclaimed the exclusive engagement for two weeks of

MURPHY'S MIDGETS

BIGGER AND BETTER THAN EVER

But of the existence of these posters he was not aware; and it is not too much to say that the iron entered into William Mulliner's soul.

That his legs should have become temporarily unscrewed at the joints was a phenomenon which he had been able to bear with fortitude. That his head should be feeling as if a good many bees had decided to use it as a hive was unpleasant, but not unbearably so. But that his brain should have gone off its castors and be causing him to see visions was the end of all things.

William had always prided himself on the keenness of his mental powers. All through the long voyage on the ship, when Desmond Franklyn had related anecdotes illustrative of his prowess as a man of Action, William Mulliner had always consoled himself by feeling that in the matter of brain he could give Franklyn three bisques and a beating any time he chose to start. And now, it seemed, he had lost even this advantage over his rival. For Franklyn, dull-witted clod though he might be, was not such an absolute minus quantity that he would imagine he had seen a man of two feet eight cutting up hash with his toes. That hideous depth of mental decay had been reserved for William Mulliner.

Moodily he made his way back to his hotel. In a corner of the Palm Room he saw Myrtle Banks deep in conversation with Franklyn, but all desire to give her a clout on the side of the head had now left him. With his chin sunk on his breast, he entered the elevator and was carried up to his room.

Here as rapidly as his quivering fingers would permit, he undressed; and, climbing into the bed as it came round for the second time, lay for a space with wide-open eyes. He had been too shaken to switch his light off, and the rays of the lamp shone on the handsome ceiling which undulated above him. He gave himself up to thought once more.

No doubt, he felt, thinking it over now, his mother had had some very urgent reason for withholding him from alcoholic drink. She must have known of some family secret, sedulously guarded from his infant ears—some dark tale of a fatal Mulliner taint. 'William must never learn of this!' she had probably said when they told her the old legend of how every Mulliner for centuries back had died a maniac, victim at last to the fatal fluid. And tonight, despite her gentle care, he had found out for himself.

He saw now that this derangement of his eyesight was only the first step in the gradual dissolution which was the Mulliner Curse. Soon his sense of hearing would go, then his sense of touch.

He sat up in bed. It seemed to him that, as he gazed at the ceiling, a considerable section of it had parted from the parent body and fallen with a crash to the floor.

William Mulliner stared dumbly. He knew, of course, that it was an illusion. But what a perfect illusion! If he had not had the special knowledge which he possessed, he would have stated without fear of contradiction that there was a gap six feet wide above him and a mass of dust and plaster on the carpet below.

And even as his eyes deceived him, so did his ears. He seemed to be conscious of a babel of screams and shouts. The corridor, he could have sworn, was full of flying feet. The world appeared to be all bangs and crashes and thuds. A cold fear gripped at William's heart. His sense of hearing was playing tricks with him already.

His whole being recoiled from making the final experiment, but he forced himself out of bed. He reached a finger towards the nearest heap of plaster and drew it back with a groan. Yes, it was as he feared, his sense of touch had gone wrong too. That heap of plaster, though purely a figment of his disordered brain, had felt solid.

So there it was. One little moderately festive evening at Mike's Place, and the Curse of the Mulliners had got him. Within an hour of absorbing the first drink of his life, it had deprived him of his sight, his hearing, and his sense of touch. Quick service, felt William Mulliner.

As he climbed back into bed, it appeared to him that two of the walls fell out. He shut his eyes, and presently sleep, which has been well called Tired Nature's Sweet Restorer, brought oblivion. His last waking thought was that he imagined he had heard another wall go.

William Mulliner was a sound sleeper, and it was many hours before consciousness returned to him. When he awoke, he looked about him in astonishment. The haunting horror of the night had passed; and now, though conscious of a rather severe headache, he knew that he was seeing things as they were.

And yet it seemed odd to think that what he beheld was not the remains of some nightmare. Not only was the world slightly yellow and a bit blurred about the edges, but it had changed in its very essentials overnight. Where eight hours before there had been a wall, only an open space appeared, with bright sunlight streaming through it. The ceiling was on the floor, and almost the only thing remaining of what had been an expensive bedroom in a first-class hotel was the bed. Very strange, he thought, and very irregular.

A voice broke in upon his meditations.

'Why, Mr Mulliner!'

William turned, and being, like all the Mulliners, the soul of modesty, dived abruptly beneath the bed-clothes. For the voice was the voice of Myrtle Banks. And she was in his room!

'Mr Mulliner!'

William poked his head out cautiously. And then he perceived that the proprieties had not been outraged as he had imagined. Miss Banks was not in his room, but in the corridor. The intervening wall had disappeared. Shaken, but relieved, he sat up in bed, the sheet drawn round his shoulders.

'You don't mean to say you're still in bed?' gasped the girl.

'Why, is it awfully late?' said William.

'Did you actually stay up here all through it?'

'Through what?'

'The earthquake.'

'What earthquake?'

'The earthquake last night.'

'Oh, that earthquake?' said William, carelessly. 'I did notice some sort of an earthquake. I remember seeing the ceiling come down and saying to myself, "I shouldn't wonder if that wasn't an earthquake." And then the walls fell out, and I said, "Yes, I believe it is an earthquake." And then I turned over and went to sleep.'

Myrtle Banks was staring at him with eyes that reminded him partly of twin stars and partly of a snail's.

'You must be the bravest man in the world!'

William gave a curt laugh.

'Oh, well,' he said, 'I may not spend my whole life persecuting unfortunate sharks with pocket-knives, but I find I generally manage to keep my head fairly well in a crisis. We Mulliners are like that. We do not say much, but we have the right stuff in us.'

He clutched his head. A sharp spasm had reminded him how much of the right stuff he had in him at that moment.

'My hero!' breathed the girl, almost inaudibly.

'And how is your fiancé this bright, sunny morning?' asked William, nonchalantly. It was torture to refer to the man, but he must show her that a Mulliner knew how to take his medicine.

She gave a little shudder.

'I have no fiancé,' she said.

'But I thought you told me you and Franklyn....'

'I am no longer engaged to Mr Franklyn. Last night, when the earthquake started, I cried to him to help me; and he with a hasty "Some other time!" over his shoulder, disappeared into the open like something shot out of a gun. I never saw a man run so fast. This morning I broke off the engagement.' She uttered a scornful laugh.

'Sharks and pocket-knives! I don't believe he ever killed a shark in his life.'

'And even if he did,' said William, 'what of it? I mean to say, how infrequently in married life must the necessity for killing sharks with pocket-knives arise! What a husband needs is not some purely adventitious gift like that—a parlour trick, you might almost call it—but a steady character, a warm and generous disposition, and a loving heart.'

'How true!' she murmured, dreamily.

'Myrtle,' said William, 'I would be a husband like that. The steady character, the warm and generous disposition, and the loving heart to which I have alluded are at your disposal. Will you accept them?'

'I will,' said Myrtle Banks.

And that (concluded Mr Mulliner) is the story of my Uncle William's romance. And you will readily understand, having heard it, how his eldest son, my cousin, J. S. F. E. Mulliner, got his name.

'J. S. F. E.?' I said.

'John San Francisco Earthquake Mulliner,' explained my friend.

'There never was a San Francisco earthquake,' said the Californian. 'Only a fire.'

7
PORTRAIT OF A DISCIPLINARIAN

It was with something of the relief of fog-bound city-dwellers who at last behold the sun that we perceived, on entering the bar-parlour of the Anglers' Rest, that Mr Mulliner was seated once more in the familiar chair. For some days he had been away, paying a visit to an old nurse of his down in Devonshire: and there was no doubt that in his absence the tide of intellectual conversation had run very low.

'No,' said Mr Mulliner, in answer to a question as to whether he had enjoyed himself, 'I cannot pretend that it was an altogether agreeable experience. I was conscious throughout of a sense of strain. The poor old thing is almost completely deaf, and her memory is not what it was. Moreover, it is a moot point whether a man of sensibility can ever be entirely at his ease in the presence of a woman who has frequently spanked him with the flat side of a hair-brush.'

Mr Mulliner winced slightly, as if the old wound still troubled him.

'It is curious,' he went on, after a thoughtful pause, 'how little change the years bring about in the attitude of a real, genuine, crusted old family nurse towards one who in the early knickerbocker stage of his career has been a charge of hers. He may grow grey or bald and be looked up to by the rest of his world as a warm performer on the Stock Exchange or a devil of a fellow in the sphere of Politics or the Arts, but to his old Nanna he will still be the Master James or Master Percival who had to be hounded by threats to keep his face clean. Shakespeare would have cringed before his old nurse. So would Herbert Spencer, Attila the Hun, and the Emperor Nero. My nephew Frederick ... but I must not bore you with my family gossip.'

We reassured him.

'Oh well, if you wish to hear the story. There is nothing much in it as a story, but it bears out the truth of what I have just been saying.'

I will begin (said Mr Mulliner) at the moment when Frederick, having come down from London in response to an urgent summons from his brother, Dr George Mulliner, stood in the latter's consulting-room, looking out upon the Esplanade of that quiet little watering-place, Bingley-on-Sea.

George's consulting-room, facing west, had the advantage of getting the afternoon sun: and this afternoon it needed all the sun it could get, to counteract Frederick's extraordinary gloom. The young man's expression, as he confronted his brother, was that which a miasmic pool in some dismal swamp in the Bad Lands might have worn if it had had a face.

'Then the position, as I see it,' he said in a low, toneless voice, 'is this. On the pretext of wishing to discuss urgent business with me, you have dragged me down to this foul spot—seventy miles by rail in a compartment containing three distinct infants sucking sweets—merely to have tea with a nurse whom I have disliked since I was a child.'

'You have contributed to her support for many years,' George reminded him.

'Naturally, when the family were clubbing together to pension off the old blister, I chipped in with my little bit,' said Frederick. 'Noblesse oblige.'

'Well, noblesse obliges you to go and have tea with her when she invites you. Wilks must be humoured. She is not so young as she was.'

'She must be a hundred.'

'Eighty-five.'

'Good heavens! And it seems only yesterday that she shut me up in a cupboard for stealing jam.'

'She was a great disciplinarian,' agreed George. 'You may find her a little on the autocratic side still. And I want to impress upon you, as her medical man, that you must not thwart her lightest whim. She will probably offer you boiled eggs and home-made cake. Eat them.'

'I will not eat boiled eggs at five o'clock in the afternoon,' said Frederick, with a strong man's menacing calm, 'for any woman on earth.'

'You will. And with relish. Her heart is weak. If you don't humour her, I won't answer for the consequences.'

'If I eat boiled eggs at five in the afternoon, I won't answer for the consequences. And why boiled eggs, dash it? I'm not a schoolboy.'

'To her you are. She looks on all of us as children still. Last Christmas she gave me a copy of Eric, or Little by Little.'

Frederick turned to the window, and scowled down upon the noxious and depressing scene below. Sparing neither age nor sex in his detestation, he regarded the old ladies reading their library novels on the seats with precisely the same dislike and contempt which he bestowed on the boys' school clattering past on its way to the bathing-houses.

'Then, checking up your statements,' he said, 'I find that I am expected to go to tea with a woman who, in addition, apparently, to being a blend of Lucretia Borgia and a Prussian sergeant-major, is a physical wreck and practically potty. Why? That is what I ask. Why? As a child, I objected strongly to Nurse Wilks: and now, grown to riper years, the thought of meeting her again gives me the heeby-jeebies. Why should I be victimized? Why me particularly?'

'It isn't you particularly. We've all been to see her at intervals, and so have the Oliphants.'

'The Oliphants!'

The name seemed to affect Frederick oddly. He winced, as if his brother had been a dentist instead of a general practitioner and had just drawn one of his back teeth.

'She was their nurse after she left us. You can't have forgotten the Oliphants. I remember you at the age of twelve climbing that old elm at the bottom of the paddock to get Jane Oliphant a rook's egg.'

Frederick laughed bitterly.

'I must have been a perfect ass. Fancy risking my life for a girl like that! Not,' he went on, 'that life's worth much. An absolute wash-out, that's what life is. However, it will soon be over. And then the silence and peace of the grave. That,' said Frederick, 'is the thought that sustains me.'

'A pretty kid, Jane. Someone told me she had grown up quite a beauty.'

'Without a heart.'

'What do you know about it?'

'Merely this. She pretended to love me, and then a few months ago she went off to the country to stay with some people named Ponderby and wrote me a letter breaking off the engagement. She gave no reasons, and I have not seen her since. She is now engaged to a man named Dillingwater, and I hope it chokes her.'

'I never heard about this. I'm sorry.'

'I'm not. Merciful release is the way I look at it.'

'Would he be one of the Sussex Dillingwaters?'

'I don't know what county the family infests. If I did, I would avoid it.'

'Well, I'm sorry. No wonder you're depressed.'

'Depressed?' said Frederick, outraged. 'Me? You don't suppose I'm worrying myself about a girl like that, do you? I've never been so happy in my life. I'm just bubbling over with cheerfulness.'

'Oh, is that what it is?' George looked at his watch. 'Well, you'd better be pushing along. It'll take you about ten minutes to get to Marazion Road.'

'How do I find the blasted house?'

'The name's on the door.'

'What is the name?'

'Wee Holme.'

'My God!' said Frederick Mulliner. 'It only needed that!'

The view which he had had of it from his brother's window should, no doubt, have prepared Frederick for the hideous loathsomeness of Bingley-on-Sea: but, as he walked along, he found it coming on him as a complete surprise. Until now he had never imagined that a small town could possess so many soul-searing features. He passed little boys, and thought how repulsive little boys were. He met tradesmen's carts, and his gorge rose at the sight of them. He hated the houses. And, most of all, he objected to the sun. It shone down with a cheeriness which was not only offensive but, it seemed to Frederick Mulliner, deliberately offensive. What he wanted was wailing winds and driving rain: not a beastly expanse of vivid blue. It was not that the perfidy of Jane Oliphant had affected him in any way: it was simply that he disliked blue skies and sunshine. He had a temperamental antipathy for them, just as he had a temperamental fondness for tombs and sleet and hurricanes and earthquakes and famines and pestilences and....

He found that he had arrived in Marazion Road.

Marazion Road was made up of two spotless pavements stretching into the middle distance and flanked by two rows of neat little red-brick villas. It smote Frederick like a blow. He felt as he looked at those houses, with their little brass knockers and little white curtains, that they were occupied by people who knew nothing of Frederick Mulliner and were content to know nothing; people who were simply not caring a whoop that only a few short months before the girl to whom he had been engaged had sent back his letters and gone and madly got herself betrothed to a man named Dillingwater.

He found Wee Holme, and hit it a nasty slap with its knocker. Footsteps sounded in the passage, and the door opened.

'Why, Master Frederick!' said Nurse Wilks. 'I should hardly have known you.'

Frederick, in spite of the natural gloom caused by the blue sky and the warm sunshine, found his mood lightening somewhat. Something that might almost have been a spasm of tenderness passed through him. He was not a bad-hearted young man—he ranked in that respect, he supposed, somewhere mid-way between his brother George, who had a heart of gold, and people like the future Mrs Dillingwater, who had no heart at all—and there was a fragility about Nurse Wilks that first astonished and then touched him.

The images which we form in childhood are slow to fade: and Frederick had been under the impression that Nurse Wilks was fully six feet tall, with the shoulders of a weight-lifter and eyes that glittered cruelly beneath beetling brows. What he saw now was a little old woman with a wrinkled face, who looked as if a puff of wind would blow her away.

He was oddly stirred. He felt large and protective. He saw his brother's point now. Most certainly this frail old thing must be humoured. Only a brute would refuse to humour her—yes, felt Frederick Mulliner, even if it meant boiled eggs at five o'clock in the afternoon.

'Well, you are getting a big boy!' said Nurse Wilks, beaming.

'Do you think so?' said Frederick, with equal amiability.

'Quite the little man! And all dressed up. Go into the parlour, dear, and sit down. I'm getting the tea.'

'Thanks.'

'WIPE YOUR BOOTS!'

The voice, thundering from a quarter whence hitherto only soft cooings had proceeded, affected Frederick Mulliner a little like the touching off of a mine beneath his feet. Spinning round he perceived a different person altogether from the mild and kindly hostess of a moment back. It was plain that there yet lingered in Nurse Wilks not a little of the ancient fire. Her mouth was tightly compressed and her eyes gleamed dangerously.

'Theideaofyourbringingyournastydirtybootsintomynicecleanhousewithoutwipingthem!' said Nurse Wilks.

'Sorry!' said Frederick humbly.

He burnished the criticized shoes on the mat, and tottered to the parlour. He felt much smaller, much younger, and much feebler than he had felt a minute ago. His morale had been shattered into fragments.

And it was not pieced together by the sight, as he entered the parlour, of Miss Jane Oliphant sitting in an arm-chair by the window.

It is hardly to be supposed that the reader will be interested in the appearance of a girl of the stamp of Jane Oliphant—a girl capable of wantonly returning a good man's letters and going off and getting engaged to a Dillingwater: but one may as well describe her and get it over. She had golden-brown hair; golden-brown eyes; golden-brown eyebrows; a nice nose with one freckle on the tip; a mouth which, when it parted in a smile, disclosed pretty teeth; and a resolute little chin.

At the present moment, the mouth was not parted in a smile. It was closed up tight, and the chin was more than resolute. It looked like the ram of a very small battleship. She gazed at Frederick as if he were the smell of onions, and she did not say a word.

Nor did Frederick say very much. Nothing is more difficult for a young man than to find exactly the right remark with which to open conversation with a girl who has recently returned his letters. (Darned good letters, too. Reading them over after opening the package, he had been amazed at their charm and eloquence.)

Frederick, then, confined his observations to the single word 'Guk!' Having uttered this, he sank into a chair and stared at the carpet. The girl stared out of the window: and complete silence reigned in the room till from the interior of a clock which was ticking on the mantelpiece a small wooden bird suddenly emerged, said 'Cuckoo', and withdrew.

The abruptness of this bird's appearance and the oddly staccato nature of its diction could not but have their effect on a man whose nerves were not what they had been. Frederick Mulliner, rising some eighteen inches from his chair, uttered a hasty exclamation.

'I beg your pardon?' said Jane Oliphant, raising her eyebrows.

'Well, how was I to know it was going to do that?' said Frederick defensively.

Jane Oliphant shrugged her shoulders. The gesture seemed to imply supreme indifference to what the sweepings of the Underworld knew or did not know.

But Frederick, the ice being now in a manner broken, refused to return to the silence.

'What are you doing here?' he said.

'I have come to have tea with Nanna.'

'I didn't know you were going to be here.'

'Oh?'

'If I'd known that you were going to be here....'

'You've got a large smut on your nose.'

Frederick gritted his teeth and reached for his handkerchief.

'Perhaps I'd better go,' he said.

'You will do nothing of the kind,' said Miss Oliphant sharply. 'She is looking forward to seeing you. Though why....'

'Why?' prompted Frederick coldly.

'Oh, nothing.'

In the unpleasant silence which followed, broken only by the deep breathing of a man who was trying to choose the rudest out of the three retorts which had presented themselves to him, Nurse Wilks entered.

'It's just a suggestion,' said Miss Oliphant aloofly, 'but don't you think you might help Nanna with that heavy tray?'

Frederick, roused from his preoccupation, sprang to his feet, blushing the blush of shame.

'You might have strained yourself, Nanna,' the girl went on, in a voice dripping with indignant sympathy.

'I was going to help her,' mumbled Frederick.

'Yes, after she had put the tray down on the table. Poor Nanna! How very heavy it must have been.'

Not for the first time since their acquaintance had begun, Frederick felt a sort of wistful wonder at his erstwhile fiancée's uncanny ability to put him in the wrong. His emotions now were rather what they would have been if he had been detected striking his hostess with some blunt instrument.

'He always was a thoughtless boy,' said Nurse Wilks tolerantly. 'Do sit down, Master Frederick, and have your tea. I've boiled some eggs for you. I know what a boy you always are for eggs.'

Frederick, starting, directed a swift glance at the tray. Yes, his worst fears had been realized. Eggs—and large ones. A stomach which he had fallen rather into the habit of pampering of late years gave a little whimper of apprehension.

'Yes,' proceeded Nurse Wilks, pursuing the subject, 'you never could have enough eggs. Nor cake. Dear me, how sick you made yourself with cake that day at Miss Jane's birthday party.'

'Please!' said Miss Oliphant, with a slight shiver.

She looked coldly at her fermenting fellow-guest, as he sat plumbing the deepest abysses of self-loathing.

'No eggs for me, thank you,' he said.

'Master Frederick, you will eat your nice boiled eggs,' said Nurse Wilks. Her voice was still amiable, but there was a hint of dynamite behind it.

'I don't want any eggs.'

'Master Frederick!' The dynamite exploded. Once again that amazing transformation had taken place, and a frail little old woman had become an intimidating force with which only a Napoleon could have reckoned. 'I will not have this sulking.'

Frederick gulped.

'I'm sorry,' he said, meekly. 'I should enjoy an egg.'

'Two eggs,' corrected Nurse Wilks.

'Two eggs,' said Frederick.

Miss Oliphant twisted the knife in the wound.

'There seems to be plenty of cake, too. How nice for you! Still, I should be careful, if I were you. It looks rather rich. I never could understand,' she went on, addressing Nurse Wilks in a voice which Frederick, who was now about seven years old, considered insufferably grown-up and affected, 'why people should find any enjoyment in stuffing and gorging and making pigs of themselves.'

'Boys will be boys,' argued Nurse Wilks.

'I suppose so,' sighed Miss Oliphant. 'Still, it's all rather unpleasant.'

A slight but well-defined glitter appeared in Nurse Wilks's eyes. She detected a tendency to hoighty-toightiness in her young guest's manner, and hoighty-toightiness was a thing to be checked.

'Girls,' she said, 'are by no means perfect.'

'Ah!' breathed Frederick, in rapturous adhesion to the sentiment.

'Girls have their little faults. Girls are sometimes inclined to be vain. I know a little girl not a hundred miles from this room who was so proud of her new panties that she ran out in the street in them.'

'Nanna!' cried Miss Oliphant pinkly.

'Disgusting!' said Frederick.

He uttered a short laugh: and so full was this laugh, though short, of scorn, disdain, and a certain hideous masculine superiority, that Jane Oliphant's proud spirit writhed beneath the infliction. She turned on him with blazing eyes.

'What did you say?'

'I said "Disgusting!"'

'Indeed?'

'I cannot,' said Frederick judicially, 'imagine a more deplorable exhibition, and I hope you were sent to bed without any supper.'

'If you ever had to go without your supper,' said Miss Oliphant, who believed in attack as the best form of defence, 'it would kill you.'

'Is that so?' said Frederick.

'You're a beast, and I hate you,' said Miss Oliphant.

'Is that so?'

'Yes, that is so.'

'Now, now, now,' said Nurse Wilks. 'Come, come, come!'

She eyed the two with that comfortable look of power and capability which comes naturally to women who have spent half a century in dealing with the young and fractious.

'We will have no quarrelling,' she said. 'Make it up at once. Master Frederick, give Miss Jane a nice kiss.'

The room rocked before Frederick's bulging eyes.

'A what?' he gasped.

'Give her a nice big kiss and tell her you're sorry you quarrelled with her.'

'She quarrelled with me.'

'Never mind. A little gentleman must always take the blame.'

Frederick, working desperately, dragged to the surface a sketchy smile.

'I apologize,' he said.

'Don't mention it,' said Miss Oliphant.

'Kiss her,' said Nurse Wilks.

'I won't!' said Frederick.

'What!'

'I won't.'

'Master Frederick,' said Nurse Wilks, rising and pointing a menacing finger, 'you march straight into that cupboard in the passage and stay there till you are good.'

Frederick hesitated. He came of a proud family. A Mulliner had once received the thanks of his Sovereign for services rendered on the field of Crécy. But the recollection of what his brother George had said decided him. Infra dig. as it might be to allow himself to be shoved away in cupboards, it was better than being responsible for a woman's heart-failure. With bowed head he passed through the door, and a key clicked behind him.

All alone in a dark world that smelt of mice, Frederick Mulliner gave himself up to gloomy reflection. He had just put in about two minutes' intense thought of a kind which would have made the meditations of Schopenhauer on one of his bad mornings seem like the day-dreams of Pollyanna, when a voice spoke through the crack in the door.

'Freddie. I mean Mr Mulliner.'

'Well?'

'She's gone into the kitchen to get the jam,' proceeded the voice rapidly. 'Shall I let you out?'

'Pray do not trouble,' said Frederick coldly. 'I am perfectly comfortable.'

Silence followed. Frederick returned to his reverie. About now, he thought, but for his brother George's treachery in luring him down to this plague-spot by a misleading telegram, he would have been on the twelfth green at Squashy Hollow, trying out that new putter. Instead of which....

The door opened abruptly, and as abruptly closed again. And Frederick Mulliner, who had been looking forward to an unbroken solitude, discovered with a good deal of astonishment that he had started taking in lodgers.

'What are you doing here?' he demanded, with a touch of proprietorial disapproval.

The girl did not answer. But presently muffled sounds came to him through the darkness. In spite of himself, a certain tenderness crept upon Frederick.

'I say,' he said awkwardly. 'There's nothing to cry about.'

'I'm not crying. I'm laughing.'

'Oh?' The tenderness waned. 'You think it's amusing, do you, being shut up in this damned cupboard....'

'There is no need to use bad language.'

'I entirely disagree with you. There is every need to use bad language. It's ghastly enough being at Bingley-on-Sea at all, but when it comes to being shut up in Bingley cupboards....'

'... with a girl you hate?'

'We will not go into that aspect of the matter,' said Frederick with dignity. 'The important point is that here I am in a cupboard at Bingley-on-Sea when, if there were any justice or right-thinking in the world, I should be out at Squashy Hollow....'

'Oh? Do you still play golf?'

'Certainly I still play golf. Why not?'

'I don't know why not. I'm glad you are still able to amuse yourself.'

'How do you mean, still? Do you think that just because....'

'I don't think anything.'

'I suppose you imagined I would be creeping about the place, a broken-hearted wreck?'

'Oh no. I knew you would find it easy to console yourself.'

'What do you mean by that?'

'Never mind.'

'Are you insinuating that I am the sort of man who turns lightly from one woman to another—a mere butterfly who flits from flower to flower, sipping...?'

'Yes, if you want to know, I think you are a born sipper.'

Frederick started. The charge was monstrous.

'I have never sipped. And, what's more, I have never flitted.'

'That's funny.'

'What's funny?'

'What you said.'

'You appear to have a very keen sense of humour,' said Frederick weightily. 'It amuses you to be shut up in cupboards. It amuses you to hear me say....'

'Well, it's nice to be able to get some amusement out of life, isn't it? Do you want to know why she shut me up in here?'

'I haven't the slightest curiosity. Why?'

'I forgot where I was and lighted a cigarette. Oh, my goodness!'

'Now what?'

'I thought I heard a mouse. Do you think there are mice in this cupboard?'

'Certainly,' said Frederick. 'Dozens of them.'

He would have gone on to specify the kind of mice—large, fat, slithery, active mice: but at this juncture something hard and sharp took him agonizingly on the ankle.

'Ouch!' cried Frederick.

'Oh, I'm sorry. Was that you?'

'It was.'

'I was kicking about to discourage the mice.'

'I see.'

'Did it hurt much?'

'Only a trifle more than blazes, thank you for inquiring.'

'I'm sorry.'

'So am I.'

'Anyway, it would have given a mouse a nasty jar, if it had been one, wouldn't it?'

'The shock, I should imagine, of a lifetime.'

'Well, I'm sorry.'

'Don't mention it. Why should I worry about a broken ankle, when....'

'When what?'

'I forgot what I was going to say.'

'When your heart is broken?'

'My heart is not broken.' It was a point which Frederick wished to make luminously clear. 'I am gay ... happy.... Who the devil is this man Dillingwater?' he concluded abruptly.

There was a momentary pause.

'Oh, just a man.'

'Where did you meet him?'

'At the Ponderbys'.'

'Where did you get engaged to him?'

'At the Ponderbys'.'

'Did you pay another visit to the Ponderbys', then?'

'No.'

Frederick choked.

'When you went to stay with the Ponderbys, you were engaged to me. Do you mean to say you broke off your engagement to me, met this Dillingwater, and got engaged to him all in the course of a single visit lasting barely two weeks?'

'Yes.'

Frederick said nothing. It struck him later that he should have said 'Oh, Woman, Woman!' but at the moment it did not occur to him.

'I don't see what right you have to criticize me,' said Jane.

'Who criticized you?'

'You did.'

'When?'

'Just then.'

'I call Heaven to witness,' cried Frederick Mulliner, 'that not by so much as a single word have I hinted at my opinion that your conduct is the vilest and most revolting that has ever been drawn to my attention. I never so much as suggested that your revelation had shocked me to the depths of my soul.'

'Yes, you did. You sniffed.'

'If Bingley-on-Sea is not open for being sniffed in at this season,' said Frederick coldly, 'I should have been informed earlier.'

'I had a perfect right to get engaged to anyone I liked and as quick as I liked, after the abominable way you behaved.'

'Abominable way I behaved? What do you mean?'

'You know.'

'Pardon me, I do not know. If you are alluding to my refusal to wear the tie you bought for me on my last birthday, I can but repeat my statement, made to you at the time, that, apart from being the sort of tie no upright man would be seen dead in a ditch with, its colours were those of a Cycling, Angling, and Dart-Throwing club of which I am not a member.'

'I am not alluding to that. I mean the day I was going to the Ponderbys' and you promised to see me off at Paddington, and then you phoned and said you couldn't as you were detained by important business, and I thought, well, I think I'll go by the later train after all because that will give me time to lunch quietly at the Berkeley, and I went and lunched quietly at the Berkeley, and when I was there who should I see but you at a table at the other end of the room gorging yourself in the company of a beastly creature in a pink frock and henna'd hair. That's what I mean.'

Frederick clutched at his forehead.

'Repeat that,' he exclaimed.

Jane did so.

'Ye gods!' said Frederick.

'It was like a blow over the head. Something seemed to snap inside me, and....'

'I can explain all,' said Frederick.

Jane's voice in the darkness was cold.

'Explain?' she said.

'Explain,' said Frederick.

'All?'

'All.'

Jane coughed.

'Before beginning,' she said, 'do not forget that I know every one of your female relatives by sight.'

'I don't want to talk about my female relatives.'

'I thought you were going to say that she was one of them—an aunt or something.'

'Nothing of the kind. She was a revue star. You probably saw her in a piece called Toot-Toot.'

'And that is your idea of an explanation!'

Frederick raised his hand for silence. Realizing that she could not see it, he lowered it again.

'Jane,' he said in a low, throbbing voice, 'can you cast your mind back to a morning in the spring when we walked, you and I, in Kensington Gardens? The sun shone brightly, the sky was a limpid blue flecked with fleecy clouds, and from the west there blew a gentle breeze....'

'If you think you can melt me with that sort of....'

'Nothing of the kind. What I was leading up to was this. As we walked, you and I, there came snuffling up to us a small Pekinese dog. It left me, I admit, quite cold, but you went into ecstasies: and from that moment I had but one mission in life, to discover who that Peke belonged to and buy it for you. And after the most exhaustive inquiries, I tracked the animal down. It was the property of the lady in whose company you saw me lunching—lightly, not gorging—at the Berkeley that day. I managed to get an introduction to her, and immediately began to make offers to her for the dog. Money was no object to me. All I wished was to put the little beast in your arms and see your face light up. It was to be a surprise. That morning the woman phoned, and said that she had practically decided to close with my latest bid, and would I take her to lunch and discuss the matter? It was agony to have to ring you up and tell you that I could not see you off at Paddington, but it had to be done. It was anguish having to sit for two hours listening to that highly-coloured female telling me how the comedian had ruined her big number in her last show by standing up-stage and pretending to drink ink, but that had to be done too. I bit the bullet and saw it through and I got the dog that afternoon. And next morning I received your letter breaking off the engagement.'

There was a long silence.

'Is this true?' said Jane.

'Quite true.'

'It sounds too—how shall I put it?—too frightfully probable. Look me in the face!'

'What's the good of looking you in the face when I can't see an inch in front of me?'

'Well, is it true?'

'Certainly it is true.'

'Can you produce the Peke?'

'I have not got it on my person,' said Frederick stiffly. 'But it is at my flat, probably chewing up a valuable rug. I will give it you for a wedding present.'

'Oh, Freddie!'

'A wedding present,' repeated Frederick, though the words stuck in his throat like patent American health-cereal.

'But I'm not going to be married.'

'You're—what did you say?'

'I'm not going to be married.'

'But what of Dillingwater?'

'That's off.'

'Off?'

'Off,' said Jane firmly. 'I only got engaged to him out of pique. I thought I could go through with it, buoying myself up by thinking what a score it would be off you, but one morning I saw him eating a peach and I began to waver. He splashed himself to the eyebrows. And just after that I found that he had a trick of making a sort of funny noise when he drank coffee. I would sit on the other side of the breakfast table, looking at him and saying to myself "Now comes the funny noise!" and when I thought of doing that all the rest of my life I saw that the scheme was impossible. So I broke off the engagement.'

Frederick gasped.

'Jane!'

He groped out, found her, and drew her into his arms.

'Freddie!'

'Jane!'

'Freddie!'

'Jane!'

'Freddie!'

'Jane!'

On the panel of the door there sounded an authoritative rap. Through it there spoke an authoritative voice, slightly cracked by age but full, nevertheless, of the spirit that will stand no nonsense.

'Master Frederick.'

'Hullo?'

'Are you good now?'

'You bet I'm good.'

'Will you give Miss Jane a nice kiss?'

'I will do,' said Frederick Mulliner, enthusiasm ringing in every syllable, 'just that little thing!'

'Then you may come out,' said Nurse Wilks. 'I have boiled you two more eggs.'

Frederick paled, but only for an instant. What did anything matter now? His lips were set in a firm line, and his voice, when he spoke, was calm and steady.

'Lead me to them,' he said.

8

THE ROMANCE OF A BULB-SQUEEZER

Somebody had left a copy of an illustrated weekly paper in the bar-parlour of the Anglers' Rest; and, glancing through it, I came upon the ninth full-page photograph of a celebrated musical-comedy actress that I had seen since the preceding Wednesday. This one showed her looking archly over her shoulder with a rose between her teeth, and I flung the periodical from me with a stifled cry.

'Tut, tut!' said Mr Mulliner, reprovingly. 'You must not allow these things to affect you so deeply. Remember, it is not actresses' photographs that matter, but the courage which we bring to them.'

He sipped his hot Scotch.

I wonder if you have ever reflected (he said gravely) what life must be like for the men whose trade it is to make these pictures? Statistics show that the two classes of the community which least often marry are milkmen and fashionable photographers—milkmen because they see women too early in the morning, and fashionable photographers because their days are spent in an atmosphere of feminine loveliness so monotonous that they become surfeited and morose. I know of none of the world's workers whom I pity more sincerely than the fashionable photographer; and yet—by one of those strokes of irony which make the thoughtful man waver between sardonic laughter and sympathetic tears—it is the ambition of every youngster who enters the profession some day to become one.

At the outset of his career, you see, a young photographer is sorely oppressed by human gargoyles: and gradually this begins to prey upon his nerves.

'Why is it,' I remember my cousin Clarence saying, after he had been about a year in the business, 'that all these misfits want to be photographed? Why do men with faces which you would have thought they would be anxious to hush up wish to be strewn about the country on whatnots and in albums? I started out full of ardour and enthusiasm, and my eager soul is being crushed. This morning the Mayor of Tooting East came to make an appointment. He is coming tomorrow afternoon to be taken in his cocked hat and robes of office; and there is absolutely no excuse for a man with a face like that perpetuating his features. I wish to goodness I was one of those fellows who only take camera-portraits of beautiful women.'

His dream was to come true sooner than he had imagined. Within a week the great test-case of Biggs v. Mulliner had raised my cousin Clarence from an obscure studio in West Kensington to the position of London's most famous photographer.

You possibly remember the case? The events that led up to it were, briefly, as follows:

Jno. Horatio Biggs, O.B.E., the newly-elected Mayor of Tooting East, alighted from a cab at the door of Clarence Mulliner's studio at four-ten on the afternoon of June the seventeenth. At four-eleven he went in. And at four-sixteen and a half he was observed shooting out of a first-floor window, vigorously assisted by my cousin, who was prodding him in the seat of the trousers with the sharp end of a photographic tripod. Those who were in a position to see stated that Clarence's face was distorted by a fury scarcely human.

Naturally the matter could not be expected to rest there. A week later the case of Biggs v. Mulliner had begun, the plaintiff claiming damages to the extent of ten thousand pounds and a new pair of trousers. And at first things looked very black for Clarence.

It was the speech of Sir Joseph Bodger, K.C., briefed for the defence, that turned the scale.

'I do not,' said Sir Joseph, addressing the jury on the second day, 'propose to deny the charges which have been brought against my client. We freely admit that on the seventeenth inst. we did jab the defendant with our tripod in a manner calculated to cause alarm and despondency. But, gentlemen, we plead justification. The whole case turns upon one question. Is a photographer entitled to assault—either with or, as the case may be, without a tripod—a sitter who, after being warned that his face is not up to the minimum standard requirements, insists upon remaining in the chair and moistening the lips with the tip of the tongue? Gentlemen, I say Yes!

'Unless you decide in favour of my client, gentlemen of the jury, photographers—debarred by law from the privilege of rejecting sitters—will be at the mercy of anyone who comes along with the price of a dozen photographs in his pocket. You have seen the plaintiff, Biggs. You have noted his broad, slab-like face, intolerable to any man of refinement and sensibility. You have observed his walrus moustache, his double chin, his protruding eyes. Take another look at him, and then tell me if my client was not justified in chasing him with a tripod out of that sacred temple of Art and Beauty, his studio.

'Gentlemen, I have finished. I leave my client's fate in your hands with every confidence that you will return the only verdict that can conceivably issue from twelve men of your obvious intelligence, your manifest sympathy, and your superb breadth of vision.'

Of course, after that there was nothing to it. The jury decided in Clarence's favour without leaving the box; and the crowd waiting outside to hear the verdict carried him shoulder-high to his house, refusing to disperse until he had made a speech and sung Photographers never, never, never shall be slaves. And next morning every paper in England came out with a leading article commending him for having so courageously established, as it had not been established since the days of Magna Carta, the fundamental principle of the Liberty of the Subject.

The effect of this publicity on Clarence's fortunes was naturally stupendous. He had become in a flash the best-known photographer in the United Kingdom, and was now in a position to realize that vision which he had of taking the pictures of none but the beaming and the beautiful. Every day the loveliest ornaments of Society and the Stage flocked to his studio; and it was with the utmost astonishment, therefore, that, calling upon him one morning on my return to England after an absence of two years in the East, I learned that Fame and Wealth had not brought him happiness.

I found him sitting moodily in his studio, staring with dull eyes at a camera-portrait of a well-known actress in a bathing-suit. He looked up listlessly as I entered.

'Clarence!' I cried, shocked at his appearance, for there were hard lines about his mouth and wrinkles on a forehead that once had been smooth as alabaster. 'What is wrong?'

'Everything,' he replied, 'I'm fed up.'

'What with?'

'Life. Beautiful women. This beastly photography business.'

I was amazed. Even in the East rumours of his success had reached me, and on my return to London I found that they had not been exaggerated. In every photographers' club in the Metropolis, from the Negative and Solution in Pall Mall to the humble public-houses frequented by the men who do your pictures while you wait on the sands at seaside resorts, he was being freely spoken of as the logical successor to the Presidency of the Amalgamated Guild of Bulb-Squeezers.

'I can't stick it much longer,' said Clarence, tearing the camera-portrait into a dozen pieces with a dry sob and burying his face in his hands. 'Actresses nursing their dolls! Countesses simpering over kittens! Film stars among their books! In ten minutes I go to catch a train at Waterloo. I have been sent for by the Duchess of Hampshire to take some studies of Lady Monica Southbourne in the castle grounds.'

A shudder ran through him. I patted him on the shoulder. I understood now.

'She has the most brilliant smile in England,' he whispered.

'Come, come!'

'Coy yet roguish, they tell me.'

'It may not be true.'

'And I bet she will want to be taken offering a lump of sugar to her dog, and the picture will appear in the Sketch and Tatler as "Lady Monica Southbourne and Friend".'

'Clarence, this is morbid.'

He was silent for a moment.

'Ah, well,' he said, pulling himself together with a visible effort, 'I have made my sodium sulphite, and I must lie in it.'

I saw him off in a cab. The last view I had of him was of his pale, drawn profile. He looked, I thought, like an aristocrat of the French Revolution being borne off to his doom on a tumbril. How little he guessed that the only girl in the world lay waiting for him round the corner.

No, you are wrong. Lady Monica did not turn out to be the only girl in the world. If what I said caused you to expect that, I misled you. Lady Monica proved to be all his fancy had pictured her. In fact even more. Not only was her smile coy yet roguish, but she had a sort of coquettish droop of the left eyelid of which no one had warned him. And, in addition to her two dogs, which she was portrayed in the act of feeding with two lumps of sugar, she possessed a totally unforeseen pet monkey, of which he was compelled to take no fewer than eleven studies.

No, it was not Lady Monica who captured Clarence's heart, but a girl in a taxi whom he met on his way to the station.

It was in a traffic jam at the top of Whitehall that he first observed this girl. His cab had become becalmed in a sea of omnibuses, and, chancing to look to the right, he perceived within a few feet of him another taxi, which had been heading for Trafalgar Square. There was a face at its window. It turned towards him, and their eyes met.

To most men it would have seemed an unattractive face. To Clarence, surfeited with the coy, the beaming, and the delicately-chiselled, it was the most wonderful thing he had ever looked at. All his life, he felt, he had been searching for something on these lines. That snub-nose—those freckles—that breadth of cheekbone—the squareness of that chin. And not a dimple in sight. He told me afterwards that his only feeling at first was one of incredulity. He had not believed that the world contained women like this. And then the traffic jam loosened up and he was carried away.

It was as he was passing the Houses of Parliament that the realization came to him that the strange bubbly sensation that seemed to start from just above the lower left side-pocket of his waistcoat was not, as he had at first supposed, dyspepsia, but love. Yes, love had come at long last to Clarence Mulliner; and for all the good it was likely to do him, he reflected bitterly, it might just as well have been the dyspepsia for which he had mistaken it. He loved a girl whom he would probably never see again. He did not know her name or where she lived or anything about her. All he knew was that he would cherish her image in his heart for ever, and that the thought of going on with the old dreary round of photographing lovely women with coy yet roguish smiles was almost more than he could bear.

However, custom is strong; and a man who has once allowed the bulb-squeezing habit to get a grip on him cannot cast it off in a moment. Next day Clarence was back in his studio, diving into the velvet nose-bag as of yore and telling peeresses to watch the little birdie just as if nothing had happened. And if there was now a strange, haunting look of pain in his eyes, nobody objected to that. Indeed, inasmuch as the grief which gnawed at his heart had the effect of deepening and mellowing his camera-side manner to an almost sacerdotal unctuousness, his private sorrows actually helped his professional prestige. Women told one another that being photographed by Clarence Mulliner was like undergoing some wonderful spiritual experience in a noble cathedral; and his appointment-book became fuller than ever.

So great now was his reputation that to anyone who had had the privilege of being taken by him, either full face or in profile, the doors of Society opened automatically. It was whispered that his name was to appear in the next Birthday Honours List; and at the annual banquet of the Amalgamated Bulb-Squeezers, when Sir Godfrey Stooge, the retiring President, in proposing his health, concluded a glowingly eulogistic speech with the words, 'Gentlemen, I give you my destined successor, Mulliner the Liberator!' five hundred frantic photographers almost shivered the glasses on the table with their applause.

And yet he was not happy. He had lost the only girl he had ever loved, and without her what was Fame? What was Affluence? What were the Highest Honours in the Land?

These were the questions he was asking himself one night as he sat in his library, sombrely sipping a final whisky-and-soda before retiring. He had asked them once and was going to ask them again, when he was interrupted by the sound of someone ringing at the front-door bell.

He rose, surprised. It was late for callers. The domestic staff had gone to bed, so he went to the door and opened it. A shadowy figure was standing on the steps.

'Mr Mulliner?'

'I am Mr Mulliner.'

The man stepped past him into the hall. And, as he did so, Clarence saw that he was wearing over the upper half of his face a black velvet mask.

'I must apologize for hiding my face, Mr Mulliner,' the visitor said, as Clarence led him to the library.

'Not at all,' replied Clarence, courteously. 'No doubt it is all for the best.'

'Indeed?' said the other, with a touch of asperity. 'If you really want to know, I am probably as handsome a man as there is in London. But my mission is one of such extraordinary secrecy that I dare not run the risk of being recognized.' He paused, and Clarence saw his eyes glint through the holes in the mask as he directed a rapid gaze into each corner of the library, 'Mr Mulliner, have you any acquaintance with the ramifications of international secret politics?'

'I have.'

'And you are a patriot?'

'I am.'

'Then I can speak freely. No doubt you are aware, Mr Mulliner, that for some time past this country and a certain rival Power have been competing for the friendship and alliance of a certain other Power?'

'No,' said Clarence, 'they didn't tell me that.'

'Such is the case. And the President of this Power—'

'Which one?'

'The second one.'

'Call it B.'

'The President of Power B is now in London. He arrived incognito, travelling under the assumed name of J. J. Shubert: and the representatives of Power A, to the best of our knowledge, are not yet aware of his presence. This gives us just the few hours necessary to clinch this treaty with Power B before Power A can interfere. I ought to tell you, Mr Mulliner, that if Power B forms an alliance with this country, the supremacy of the Anglo-Saxon race will be secured for hundreds of years. Whereas if Power A gets hold of Power B, civilization will be thrown into the melting-pot. In the eyes of all Europe—and when I say all Europe I refer particularly to Powers C, D, and E—this nation would sink to the rank of a fourth-class Power.'

'Call it Power F,' said Clarence.

'It rests with you, Mr Mulliner, to save England.'

'Great Britain,' corrected Clarence. He was half Scotch on his mother's side. 'But how? What can I do about it?'

'The position is this. The President of Power B has an overwhelming desire to have his photograph taken by Clarence Mulliner. Consent to take it, and our difficulties will be at an end. Overcome with gratitude, he will sign the treaty, and the Anglo-Saxon race will be safe.'

Clarence did not hesitate. Apart from the natural gratification of feeling that he was doing the Anglo-Saxon race a bit of good, business was business; and if the President took a dozen of the large size finished in silver wash it would mean a nice profit.

'I shall be delighted,' he said.

'Your patriotism,' said the visitor, 'will not go unrewarded. It will be gratefully noted in the Very Highest Circles.'

Clarence reached for his appointment-book.

'Now, let me see. Wednesday?—No, I'm full up Wednesday. Thursday?—No. Suppose the President looks in at my studio between four and five on Friday?'

The visitor uttered a gasp.

'Good heavens, Mr Mulliner,' he exclaimed, 'surely you do not imagine that, with the vast issues at stake, these things can be done openly and in daylight? If the devils in the pay of Power A were to learn that the President intended to have his photograph taken by you, I would not give a straw for your chances of living an hour.'

'Then what do you suggest?'

'You must accompany me now to the President's suite at the Milan Hotel. We shall travel in a closed car, and God send that these fiends did not recognize me as I came here. If they did, we shall never reach that car alive. Have you, by any chance, while we have been talking, heard the hoot of an owl?'

'No,' said Clarence. 'No owls.'

'Then perhaps they are nowhere near. The fiends always imitate the hoot of an owl.'

'A thing,' said Clarence, 'which I tried to do when I was a small boy and never seemed able to manage. The popular idea that owls say "Tu-whit, tu-whoo" is all wrong. The actual noise they make is something far more difficult and complex, and it was beyond me.'

'Quite so.' The visitor looked at his watch. 'However, absorbing as these reminiscences of your boyhood days are, time is flying. Shall we be making a start?'

'Certainly.'

'Then follow me.'

It appeared to be holiday-time for fiends, or else the night-shift had not yet come on, for they reached the car without being molested. Clarence stepped in, and his masked visitor, after a keen look up and down the street, followed him.

'Talking of my boyhood—' began Clarence.

The sentence was never completed. A soft wet pad was pressed over his nostrils: the air became a-reek with the sickly fumes of chloroform: and Clarence knew no more.

When he came to, he was no longer in the car. He found himself lying on a bed in a room in a strange house. It was a medium-sized room with scarlet wall-paper, simply furnished with a wash-hand stand, a chest of drawers, two cane-bottomed chairs, and a 'God Bless Our Home' motto framed in oak. He was conscious of a severe headache, and was about to rise and make for the water-bottle on the wash-stand when, to his consternation, he discovered that his arms and legs were shackled with stout cord.

As a family, the Mulliners have always been noted for their reckless courage; and Clarence was no exception to the rule. But for an instant his heart undeniably beat a little faster. He saw now that his masked visitor had tricked him. Instead of being a representative of His Majesty's Diplomatic Service (a most respectable class of men), he had really been all along a fiend in the pay of Power A.

No doubt he and his vile associates were even now chuckling at the ease with which their victim had been duped. Clarence gritted his teeth and struggled vainly to loose the knots which secured his wrists. He had fallen back exhausted when he heard the sound of a key turning and the door opened. Somebody crossed the room and stood by the bed, looking down on him.

The new-comer was a stout man with a complexion that matched the wall-paper. He was puffing slightly, as if he had found the stairs trying. He had broad, slab-like features; and his face was split in the middle by a walrus moustache. Somewhere and in some place, Clarence was convinced, he had seen this man before.

And then it all came back to him. An open window with a pleasant summer breeze blowing in; a stout man in a cocked hat trying to climb through this window; and he, Clarence, doing his best to help him with the sharp end of a tripod. It was Jno. Horatio Biggs, the Mayor of Tooting East.

A shudder of loathing ran through Clarence.

'Traitor!' he cried.

'Eh?' said the Mayor.

'If anybody had told me that a son of Tooting, nursed in the keen air of freedom which blows across the Common, would sell himself for gold to the enemies of his country, I would never have believed it. Well, you may tell your employers—'

'What employers?'

'Power A.'

'Oh, that?' said the Mayor. 'I am afraid my secretary, whom I instructed to bring you to this house, was obliged to romance a little in order to ensure your accompanying him, Mr Mulliner. All that about Power A and Power B was just his little joke. If you want to know why you were brought here—'

Clarence uttered a low groan.

'I have guessed your ghastly object, you ghastly object,' he said quietly. 'You want me to photograph you.'

The Mayor shook his head.

'Not myself. I realize that that can never be. My daughter.'

'Your daughter?'

'My daughter.'

'Does she take after you?'

'People tell me there is a resemblance.'

'I refuse,' said Clarence.

'Think well, Mr Mulliner.'

'I have done all the thinking that is necessary. England—or, rather, Great Britain—looks to me to photograph only her fairest and loveliest; and though, as a man, I admit that I loathe beautiful women, as a photographer I have a duty to consider that is higher than any personal feelings. History has yet to record an instance of a photographer playing his country false, and Clarence Mulliner is not the man to supply the first one. I decline your offer.'

'I wasn't looking on it exactly as an offer,' said the Mayor, thoughtfully. 'More as a command, if you get my meaning.'

'You imagine that you can bend a lens-artist to your will and make him false to his professional reputation?'

'I was thinking of having a try.'

'Do you realize that, if my incarceration here were known, ten thousand photographers would tear this house brick from brick and you limb from limb?'

'But it isn't,' the Mayor pointed out. 'And that, if you follow me, is the whole point. You came here by night in a closed car. You could stay here for the rest of your life, and no one would be any the wiser. I really think you had better reconsider, Mr Mulliner.'

'You have had my answer.'

'Well, I'll leave you to think it over. Dinner will be served at seven-thirty. Don't bother to dress.' At half past seven precisely the door opened again and the Mayor reappeared, followed by a butler bearing on a silver salver a glass of water and a small slice of bread. Pride urged Clarence to reject the refreshment, but hunger overcame pride. He swallowed the bread which the butler offered him in small bits in a spoon, and drank the water.

'At what hour would the gentleman desire breakfast, sir?' asked the butler.

'Now,' said Clarence, for his appetite, always healthy, seemed to have been sharpened by the trials which he had undergone.

'Let us say nine o'clock,' suggested the Mayor. 'Put aside another slice of that bread, Meadows. And no doubt Mr Mulliner would enjoy a glass of this excellent water.'

For perhaps half an hour after his host had left him, Clarence's mind was obsessed to the exclusion of all other thoughts by a vision of the dinner he would have liked to be enjoying. All we Mulliners have been good trenchermen, and to put a bit of bread into it after it had been unoccupied for a whole day was to offer to Clarence's stomach an insult which it resented with an indescribable bitterness. Clarence's only emotion for some considerable time, then, was that of hunger. His thoughts centred themselves on food. And it was to this fact, oddly enough, that he owed his release.

For, as he lay there in a sort of delirium, picturing himself getting outside a medium-cooked steak smothered in onions, with grilled tomatoes and floury potatoes on the side, it was suddenly borne in upon him that this steak did not taste quite so good as other steaks which he had eaten in the past. It was tough and lacked juiciness. It tasted just like rope.

And then, his mind clearing, he saw that it actually was rope. Carried away by the anguish of hunger, he had been chewing the cord which bound his hands; and he now discovered that he had bitten into it quite deeply.

A sudden flood of hope poured over Clarence Mulliner. Carrying on at this rate, he perceived, he would be able ere long to free himself. It only needed a little imagination. After a brief interval to rest his aching jaws, he put himself deliberately into that state of relaxation which is recommended by the apostles of Suggestion.

'I am entering the dining-room of my club,' murmured Clarence. 'I am sitting down. The waiter is handing me the bill of fare. I have selected roast duck with green peas and new potatoes, lamb cutlets with brussels sprouts, fricassee of chicken, porterhouse steak, boiled beef and carrots, leg of mutton, haunch of mutton, mutton chops, curried mutton, veal, kidneys sauté, spaghetti Caruso, and eggs and bacon, fried on both sides. The waiter is now bringing my order. I have taken up my knife and fork. I am beginning to eat.'

And, murmuring a brief grace, Clarence flung himself on the rope and set to.

Twenty minutes later he was hobbling about the room, restoring the circulation to his cramped limbs.

Just as he had succeeded in getting himself nicely limbered up, he heard the key turning in the door.

Clarence crouched for the spring. The room was quite dark now, and he was glad of it, for darkness well fitted the work which lay before him. His plans, conceived on the spur of the moment, were necessarily sketchy, but they included jumping on the Mayor's shoulders and pulling his head off. After that, no doubt, other modes of self-expression would suggest themselves.

The door opened. Clarence made his leap. And he was just about to start on the programme as arranged, when he discovered with a shock of horror that this was no O.B.E. that he was being rough with, but a woman. And no photographer worthy of the name will ever lay a hand upon a woman, save to raise her chin and tilt it a little more to the left.

'I beg your pardon!' he cried.

'Don't mention it,' said his visitor, in a low voice. 'I hope I didn't disturb you.'

'Not at all,' said Clarence.

There was a pause.

'Rotten weather,' said Clarence, feeling that it was for him, as the male member of the sketch, to keep the conversation going.

'Yes, isn't it?'

'A lot of rain we've had this summer.'

'Yes. It seems to get worse every year.'

'Doesn't it?'

'So bad for tennis.'

'And cricket.'

'And polo.'

'And garden parties.'

'I hate rain.'

'So do I.'

'Of course, we may have a fine August.'

'Yes, there's always that.'

The ice was broken, and the girl seemed to become more at her ease.

'I came to let you out,' she said. 'I must apologize for my father. He loves me foolishly and has no scruples where my happiness is concerned. He has always yearned to have me photographed by you, but I cannot consent to allow a photographer to be coerced into abandoning his principles. If you will follow me, I will let you out by the front door.'

'It's awfully good of you,' said Clarence, awkwardly. As any man of nice sentiment would have been, he was embarrassed. He wished that he could have obliged this kind-hearted girl by taking her picture, but a natural delicacy restrained him from touching on this subject. They went down the stairs in silence.

On the first landing a hand was placed on his in the darkness and the girl's voice whispered in his ear.

'We are just outside father's study,' he heard her say. 'We must be as quiet as mice.'

'As what?' said Clarence.

'Mice.'

'Oh, rather,' said Clarence, and immediately bumped into what appeared to be a pedestal of some sort.

These pedestals usually have vases on top of them, and it was revealed to Clarence a moment later that this one was no exception. There was a noise like ten simultaneous dinner-services coming apart in the hands of ten simultaneous parlour-maids; and then the door was flung open, the landing became flooded with light, and the Mayor of Tooting East stood before them. He was carrying a revolver and his face was dark with menace.

'Ha!' said the Mayor.

But Clarence was paying no attention to him. He was staring open-mouthed at the girl. She had shrunk back against the wall, and the light fell full upon her.

'You!' cried Clarence.

'This—' began the Mayor.

'You! At last!'

'This is a pretty—'

'Am I dreaming?'

'This is a pretty state of af—'

'Ever since that day I saw you in the cab I have been scouring London for you. To think that I have found you at last!'

'This is a pretty state of affairs,' said the Mayor, breathing on the barrel of his revolver and polishing it on the sleeve of his coat. 'My daughter helping the foe of her family to fly—'

'Flee, father,' corrected the girl, faintly.

'Flea or fly—this is no time for arguing about insects. Let me tell you—'

Clarence interrupted him indignantly.

'What do you mean,' he cried, 'by saying that she took after you?'

'She does.'

'She does not. She is the loveliest girl in the world, while you look like Lon Chaney made up for something. See for yourself.' Clarence led them to the large mirror at the head of the stairs. 'Your face—if you can call it that—is one of those beastly blobby squashy sort of faces—'

'Here!' said the Mayor.

'—whereas hers is simply divine. Your eyes are bulbous and goofy—'

'Hey!' said the Mayor.

'—while hers are sweet and soft and intelligent. Your ears—'

'Yes, yes,' said the Mayor, petulantly. 'Some other time, some other time. Then am I to take it, Mr Mulliner—'

'Call me Clarence.'

'I refuse to call you Clarence.'

'You will have to very shortly, when I am your son-in-law.'

The girl uttered a cry. The Mayor uttered a louder cry.

'My son-in-law!'

'That,' said Clarence, firmly, 'is what I intend to be—and speedily.' He turned to the girl. 'I am a man of volcanic passions, and now that love has come to me there is no power in heaven or earth that can keep me from the object of my love. It will be my never-ceasing task—er—'

'Gladys,' prompted the girl.

'Thank you. It will be my never-ceasing task, Gladys, to strive daily to make you return that love—'

'You need not strive, Clarence,' she whispered, softly. 'It is already returned.'

Clarence reeled.

'Already?' he gasped.

'I have loved you since I saw you in that cab. When we were torn asunder, I felt quite faint.'

'So did I. I was in a daze. I tipped my cabman at Waterloo three half-crowns. I was aflame with love.'

'I can hardly believe it.'

'Nor could I, when I found out. I thought it was threepence. And ever since that day—'

The Mayor coughed.

'Then am I to take it—er—Clarence,' he said, 'that your objections to photographing my daughter are removed?'

Clarence laughed happily.

'Listen,' he said, 'and I'll show you the sort of son-in-law I am. Ruin my professional reputation though it may, I will take a photograph of you too!'

'Me!'

'Absolutely. Standing beside her with the tips of your fingers on her shoulder. And what's more, you can wear your cocked hat.'

Tears had begun to trickle down the Mayor's cheeks.

'My boy!' he sobbed, brokenly. 'My boy!'

And so happiness came to Clarence Mulliner at last. He never became President of the Bulb-Squeezers, for he retired from business the next day, declaring that the hand that had snapped the shutter when taking the photograph of his dear wife should never snap it again for sordid profit. The wedding, which took place some six weeks later, was attended by almost everybody of any note in Society or on the Stage; and was the first occasion on which a bride and bridegroom had ever walked out of church beneath an arch of crossed tripods.

9
HONEYSUCKLE COTTAGE

'Do you believe in ghosts?' asked Mr Mulliner abruptly.

I weighed the question thoughtfully. I was a little surprised, for nothing in our previous conversation had suggested the topic.

'Well,' I replied, 'I don't like them, if that's what you mean. I was once butted by one as a child.'

'Ghosts. Not goats.'

'Oh, ghosts? Do I believe in ghosts?'

'Exactly.'

'Well, yes—and no.'

'Let me put it another way,' said Mr Mulliner, patiently. 'Do you believe in haunted houses? Do you believe that it is possible for a malign influence to envelop a place and work a spell on all who come within its radius?'

I hesitated.

'Well, no—and yes.'

Mr Mulliner sighed a little. He seemed to be wondering if I was always as bright as this.

'Of course,' I went on, 'one has read stories. Henry James's Turn of The Screw....'

'I am not talking about fiction.'

'Well, in real life—Well, look here, I once, as a matter of fact, did meet a man who knew a fellow....'

'My distant cousin James Rodman spent some weeks in a haunted house,' said Mr Mulliner, who, if he has a fault, is not a very good listener. 'It cost him five thousand pounds. That is to say, he sacrificed five thousand pounds by not remaining there. Did you ever,' he asked, wandering, it seemed to me, from the subject, 'hear of Leila J. Pinckney?'

Naturally I had heard of Leila J. Pinckney. Her death some years ago has diminished her vogue, but at one time it was impossible to pass a bookshop or a railway bookstall without seeing a long row of her novels. I have never myself actually read any of them, but I knew that in her particular line of literature, the Squashily Sentimental, she had always been regarded by those entitled to judge as pre-eminent. The critics usually headed their reviews of her stories with the words:

ANOTHER PINCKNEY

or sometimes, more offensively:

ANOTHER PINCKNEY!!!

And once, dealing with, I think, The Love Which Prevails, the literary expert of the Scrutinizer had compressed his entire critique into the single phrase 'Oh, God!'

'Of course,' I said. 'But what about her?'

'She was James Rodman's aunt.'

'Yes?'

'And when she died James found that she had left him five thousand pounds and the house in the country where she had lived for the last twenty years of her life.'

'A very nice little legacy.'

'Twenty years,' repeated Mr Mulliner. 'Grasp that, for it has a vital bearing on what follows. Twenty years, mind you, and Miss Pinckney turned out two novels and twelve short stories regularly every year besides a monthly page of Advice to Young Girls in one of the magazines. That is to say, forty of her novels and no fewer than two hundred and forty of her short stories were written under the roof of Honeysuckle Cottage.'

'A pretty name.'

'A nasty, sloppy name,' said Mr Mulliner severely, 'which should have warned my distant cousin James from the start. Have you a pencil and a piece of paper?' He scribbled for a while, poring frowningly over columns of figures. 'Yes,' he said, looking up, 'if my calculations are correct, Leila J. Pinckney wrote in all a matter of nine million one hundred and forty thousand words of glutinous sentimentality at Honeysuckle Cottage, and it was a condition of her will that James should reside there for six months in every year. Failing to do this, he was to forfeit the five thousand pounds.'

'It must be great fun making a freak will,' I mused. 'I often wish I was rich enough to do it.'

'This was not a freak will. The conditions are perfectly understandable. James Rodman was a writer of sensational mystery stories, and his aunt Leila had always disapproved of his work. She was a great believer in the influence of environment, and the reason why she inserted that clause in her will was that she wished to compel James to move from London to the country. She considered that living in London hardened him and made his outlook on life sordid. She often asked him if he thought it quite nice to harp so much on sudden death and blackmailers with squints. Surely, she said, there were enough squinting blackmailers in the world without writing about them.

'The fact that Literature meant such different things to these two had, I believe, caused something of a coolness between them, and James had never dreamed that he would be remembered in his aunt's will. For he had never concealed his opinion that Leila J. Pinckney's style of writing revolted him, however dear it might be to her enormous public. He held rigid views on the art of the novel, and always maintained that an artist with a true reverence for his craft should not descend to goo-ey love stories, but should stick austerely to revolvers, cries in the night, missing papers, mysterious Chinamen, and dead bodies—with or without gash in throat. And not even the thought that his aunt had dandled him on her knee as a baby could induce him to stifle his literary conscience to the extent of pretending to enjoy her work. First, last, and all the time, James Rodman had held the opinion—and voiced it fearlessly—that Leila J. Pinckney wrote bilge.

'It was a surprise to him, therefore, to find that he had been left this legacy. A pleasant surprise, of course. James was making quite a decent income out of the three novels and eighteen short stories which he produced annually, but an author can always find a use for five thousand pounds. And, as for the cottage, he had actually been looking about for a little place in the country at the very moment when he received the lawyer's letter. In less than a week he was installed at his new residence.'

James's first impressions of Honeysuckle Cottage were, he tells me, wholly favourable. He was delighted with the place. It was a low, rambling, picturesque old house with funny little chimneys and a red roof, placed in the middle of the most charming country. With its oak beams, its trim garden, its trilling birds and its rose-hung porch, it was the ideal spot for a writer. It was just the sort of place, he reflected whimsically, which his aunt had loved to write about in her books. Even the apple-cheeked old housekeeper who attended to his needs might have stepped straight out of one of them.

It seemed to James that his lot had been cast in pleasant places. He had brought down his books, his pipes, and his golf-clubs, and was hard at work finishing the best thing he had ever done. The Secret Nine was the title of it; and on the beautiful summer afternoon on which this story opens he was in the study, hammering away at his typewriter, at peace with the world. The machine was running sweetly, the new tobacco he had bought the day before was proving admirable, and he was moving on all six cylinders to the end of a chapter.

He shoved in a fresh sheet of paper, chewed his pipe thoughtfully for a moment, then wrote rapidly:

For an instant Lester Gage thought that he must have been mistaken. Then the noise came again, faint but unmistakable—a soft scratching on the outer panel.

His mouth set in a grim line. Silently, like a panther, he made one quick step to the desk, noiselessly opened a drawer, drew out his automatic. After that affair of the poisoned needle, he was taking no chances. Still in dead silence, he tiptoed to the door; then, flinging it suddenly open, he stood there, his weapon poised.

On the mat stood the most beautiful girl he had ever beheld. A veritable child of Faërie. She eyed him for a moment with a saucy smile; then with a pretty, roguish look of reproof shook a dainty forefinger at him.

'I believe you've forgotten me, Mr Gage!' she fluted with a mock severity which her eyes belied.

James stared at the paper dumbly. He was utterly perplexed. He had not had the slightest intention of writing anything like this. To begin with, it was a rule with him, and one which he never broke, to allow no girls to appear in his stories. Sinister landladies, yes, and naturally any amount of adventuresses with foreign accents, but never under any pretext what may be broadly described as girls. A detective story, he maintained, should have no heroine. Heroines only held up the action and tried to flirt with the hero when he should have been busy looking for clues, and then went and let the villain kidnap them by some childishly simple trick. In his writing, James was positively monastic.

And yet here was this creature with her saucy smile and her dainty forefinger horning in at the most important point in the story. It was uncanny.

He looked once more at his scenario. No, the scenario was all right.

In perfectly plain words it stated that what happened when the door opened was that a dying man fell in and after gasping, 'The beetle! Tell Scotland Yard that the blue beetle is—' expired on the hearth-rug, leaving Lester Gage not unnaturally somewhat mystified. Nothing whatever about any beautiful girls.

In a curious mood of irritation, James scratched out the offending passage, wrote in the necessary corrections and put the cover on the machine. It was at this point that he heard William whining.

The only blot on this paradise which James had so far been able to discover was the infernal dog, William. Belonging nominally to the gardener, on the very first morning he had adopted James by acclamation, and he maddened and infuriated James. He had a habit of coming and whining under the window when James was at work. The latter would ignore this as long as he could; then, when the thing became insupportable, would bound out of his chair, to see the animal standing on the gravel, gazing expectantly up at him with a stone in his mouth. William had a weak-minded passion for chasing stones; and on the first day James, in a rash spirit of camaraderie, had flung one for him. Since then James had thrown no more stones; but he had thrown any number of other solids, and the garden was littered with objects ranging from match boxes to a plaster statuette of the young Joseph prophesying before Pharaoh. And still William came and whined, an optimist to the last.

The whining, coming now at a moment when he felt irritable and unsettled, acted on James much as the scratching on the door had acted on Lester Gage. Silently, like a panther, he made one quick step to the mantelpiece, removed from it a china mug bearing the legend A Present From Clacton-on-Sea, and crept to the window.

And as he did so a voice outside said, 'Go away, sir, go away!' and there followed a short, high-pitched bark which was certainly not William's. William was a mixture of airedale, setter, bull terrier, and mastiff; and when in vocal mood, favoured the mastiff side of his family.

James peered out. There on the porch stood a girl in blue. She held in her arms a small fluffy white dog, and she was endeavouring to foil the upward movement toward this of the blackguard William. William's mentality had been arrested some years before at the point where he imagined that everything in the world had been created for him to eat. A bone, a boot, a steak, the back wheel of a bicycle—it was all one to William. If it was there he tried to eat it. He had even made a plucky attempt to devour the remains of the young Joseph prophesying before Pharaoh. And it was perfectly plain now that he regarded the curious wriggling object in the girl's arms purely in the light of a snack to keep body and soul together till dinner-time.

'William!' bellowed James.

William looked courteously over his shoulder with eyes that beamed with the pure light of a life's devotion, wagged the whiplike tail which he had inherited from his bull-terrier ancestor, and resumed his intent scrutiny of the fluffy dog.

'Oh, please!' cried the girl. 'This great rough dog is frightening poor Toto.'

The man of letters and the man of action do not always go hand in hand, but practice had made James perfect in handling with a swift efficiency any situation that involved William. A moment later that canine moron, having received the present from Clacton in the short ribs, was scuttling round the corner of the house, and James had jumped through the window and was facing the girl.

She was an extraordinarily pretty girl. Very sweet and fragile she looked as she stood there under the honeysuckle with the breeze ruffling a tendril of golden hair that strayed from beneath her coquettish little hat. Her eyes were very big and very blue, her rose-tinted face becomingly flushed. All wasted on James, though. He disliked all girls, and particularly the sweet, droopy type.

'Did you want to see somebody?' he asked stiffly.

'Just the house,' said the girl, 'if it wouldn't be giving any trouble. I do so want to see the room where Miss Pinckney wrote her books. This is where Leila J. Pinckney used to live, isn't it?'

'Yes; I am her nephew. My name is James Rodman.'

'Mine is Rose Maynard.'

James led the way into the house, and she stopped with a cry of delight on the threshold of the morning-room.

'Oh, how too perfect!' she cried. 'So this was her study?'

'Yes.'

'What a wonderful place it would be for you to think in if you were a writer too.'

James held no high opinion of women's literary taste, but nevertheless he was conscious of an unpleasant shock.

'I am a writer,' he said coldly. 'I write detective stories.'

'I—I'm afraid,'—she blushed—'I'm afraid I don't often read detective stories.'

'You no doubt prefer,' said James, still more coldly, 'the sort of thing my aunt used to write.'

'Oh, I love her stories!' cried the girl, clasping her hands ecstatically. 'Don't you?'

'I cannot say that I do.'

'What?'

'They are pure apple sauce,' said James sternly; 'just nasty blobs of sentimentality, thoroughly untrue to life.'

The girl stared.

'Why, that's just what's so wonderful about them, their trueness to life! You feel they might all have happened. I don't understand what you mean.'

They were walking down the garden now. James held the gate open for her and she passed through into the road.

'Well, for one thing,' he said, 'I decline to believe that a marriage between two young people is invariably preceded by some violent and sensational experience in which they both share.'

'Are you thinking of Scent o' the Blossom, where Edgar saves Maud from drowning?'

'I am thinking of every single one of my aunt's books.' He looked at her curiously. He had just got the solution of a mystery which had been puzzling him for some time. Almost from the moment he had set eyes on her she had seemed somehow strangely familiar. It now suddenly came to him why it was that he disliked her so much. 'Do you know,' he said, 'you might be one of my aunt's heroines yourself? You're just the sort of girl she used to love to write about.'

Her face lit up.

'Oh, do you really think so?' She hesitated. 'Do you know what I have been feeling ever since I came here? I've been feeling that you are exactly like one of Miss Pinckney's heroes.'

'No, I say, really!' said James, revolted.

'Oh, but you are! When you jumped through that window it gave me quite a start. You were so exactly like Claude Masterton in Heather o' the Hills.'

'I have not read Heather o' the Hills,' said James, with a shudder.

'He was very strong and quiet, with deep, dark, sad eyes.'

James did not explain that his eyes were sad because her society gave him a pain in the neck. He merely laughed scornfully.

'So now, I suppose,' he said, 'a car will come and knock you down and I shall carry you gently into the house and lay you—Look out!' he cried.

It was too late. She was lying in a little huddled heap at his feet. Round the corner a large automobile had come bowling, keeping with an almost affected precision to the wrong side of the road. It was now receding into the distance, the occupant of the tonneau, a stout red-faced gentleman in a fur coat, leaning out over the back. He had bared his head—not, one fears, as a pretty gesture of respect and regret, but because he was using his hat to hide the number plate.

The dog Toto was unfortunately uninjured.

James carried the girl gently into the house and laid her on the sofa in the morning-room. He rang the bell and the apple-cheeked housekeeper appeared.

'Send for the doctor,' said James. 'There has been an accident.'

The housekeeper bent over the girl.

'Eh, dearie, dearie!' she said. 'Bless her sweet pretty face!'

The gardener, he who technically owned William, was routed out from among the young lettuces and told to fetch Dr Brady. He separated his bicycle from William, who was making a light meal off the left pedal, and departed on his mission. Dr Brady arrived and in due course he made his report.

'No bones broken, but a number of nasty bruises. And, of course, the shock. She will have to stay here for some time, Rodman. Can't be moved.'

'Stay here! But she can't! It isn't proper.'

'Your housekeeper will act as a chaperon.'

The doctor sighed. He was a stolid-looking man of middle age with side whiskers.

'A beautiful girl, that, Rodman,' he said.

'I suppose so,' said James.

'A sweet, beautiful girl. An elfin child.'

'A what?' cried James, starting.

This imagery was very foreign to Dr Brady as he knew him. On the only previous occasion on which they had had any extended conversation, the doctor had talked exclusively about the effect of too much protein on the gastric juices.

'An elfin child; a tender, fairy creature. When I was looking at her just now, Rodman, I nearly broke down. Her little hand lay on the coverlet like some white lily floating on the surface of a still pool, and her dear, trusting eyes gazed up at me.'

He pottered off down the garden, still babbling, and James stood staring after him blankly. And slowly, like some cloud athwart a summer sky, there crept over James's heart the chill shadow of a nameless fear.

It was about a week later that Mr Andrew McKinnon, the senior partner in the well-known firm of literary agents, McKinnon & Gooch, sat in his office in Chancery Lane, frowning thoughtfully over a telegram. He rang the bell.

'Ask Mr Gooch to step in here.' He resumed his study of the telegram. 'Oh, Gooch,' he said when his partner appeared, 'I've just had a curious wire from young Rodman. He seems to want to see me very urgently.'

Mr Gooch read the telegram.

'Written under the influence of some strong mental excitement,' he agreed. 'I wonder why he doesn't come to the office if he wants to see you so badly.'

'He's working very hard, finishing that novel for Prodder & Wiggs. Can't leave it, I suppose. Well, it's a nice day. If you will look after things here I think I'll motor down and let him give me lunch.'

As Mr McKinnon's car reached the crossroads a mile from Honeysuckle Cottage, he was aware of a gesticulating figure by the hedge. He stopped the car.

'Morning, Rodman.'

'Thank God, you've come!' said James. It seemed to Mr McKinnon that the young man looked paler and thinner. 'Would you mind walking the rest of the way? There's something I want to speak to you about.'

Mr McKinnon alighted; and James, as he glanced at him, felt cheered and encouraged by the very sight of the man. The literary agent was a grim, hard-bitten person, to whom, when he called at their offices to arrange terms, editors kept their faces turned so that they might at least retain their back collar studs. There was no sentiment in Andrew McKinnon. Editresses of society papers practised their blandishments on him in vain, and many a publisher had waked screaming in the night, dreaming that he was signing a McKinnon contract.

'Well, Rodman,' he said, 'Prodder & Wiggs have agreed to our terms. I was writing to tell you so when your wire arrived. I had a lot of trouble with them, but it's fixed at twenty per cent, rising to twenty-five, and two hundred pounds advance royalties on day of publication.'

'Good!' said James absently. 'Good! McKinnon, do you remember my aunt, Leila J. Pinckney?'

'Remember her? Why, I was her agent all her life.'

'Of course. Then you know the sort of tripe she wrote.'

'No author,' said Mr McKinnon reprovingly, 'who pulls down a steady twenty thousand pounds a year writes tripe.'

'Well anyway, you know her stuff.'

'Who better?'

'When she died she left me five thousand pounds and her house, Honeysuckle Cottage. I'm living there now. McKinnon, do you believe in haunted houses?'

'No.'

'Yet I tell you solemnly that Honeysuckle Cottage is haunted!'

'By your aunt?' said Mr McKinnon, surprised.

'By her influence. There's a malignant spell over the place; a sort of miasma of sentimentalism. Everybody who enters it succumbs.'

'Tut-tut! You mustn't have these fancies.'

'They aren't fancies.'

'You aren't seriously meaning to tell me—'

'Well, how do you account for this? That book you were speaking about, which Prodder & Wiggs are to publish—The Secret Nine. Every time I sit down to write it a girl keeps trying to sneak in.'

'Into the room?'

'Into the story.'

'You don't want a love interest in your sort of book,' said Mr McKinnon, shaking his head. 'It delays the action.'

'I know it does. And every day I have to keep shooing this infernal female out. An awful girl, McKinnon. A soppy, soupy, treacly, drooping girl with a roguish smile. This morning she tried to butt in on the scene where Lester Gage is trapped in the den of the mysterious leper.'

'No!'

'She did, I assure you. I had to rewrite three pages before I could get her out of it. And that's not the worst. Do you know, McKinnon, that at this moment I am actually living the plot of a typical Leila J. Pinckney novel in just the setting she always used! And I can see the happy ending coming nearer every day! A week ago a girl was knocked down by a car at my door and I've had to put her up, and every day I realize more clearly that sooner or later I shall ask her to marry me.'

'Don't do it,' said Mr McKinnon, a stout bachelor. 'You're too young to marry.'

'So was Methuselah,' said James, a stouter. 'But all the same I know I'm going to do it. It's the influence of this awful house weighing upon me. I feel like an eggshell in a maelstrom. I am being sucked on by a force too strong for me to resist. This morning I found myself kissing her dog!'

'No!'

'I did! And I loathe the little beast. Yesterday I got up at dawn and plucked a nosegay of flowers for her, wet with the dew.'

'Rodman!'

'It's a fact. I laid them at her door and went downstairs kicking myself all the way. And there in the hall was the apple-cheeked housekeeper regarding me archly. If she didn't murmur "Bless their sweet young hearts!" my ears deceived me.'

'Why don't you pack up and leave?'

'If I do I lose the five thousand pounds.'

'Ah!' said Mr McKinnon.

'I can understand what has happened. It's the same with all haunted houses. My aunt's subliminal ether vibrations have woven themselves into the texture of the place, creating an atmosphere which forces the ego of all who come in contact with it to attune themselves to it. It's either that or something to do with the fourth dimension.'

Mr McKinnon laughed scornfully.

'Tut-tut!' he said again. 'This is pure imagination. What has happened is that you've been working too hard. You'll see this precious atmosphere of yours will have no effect on me.'

'That's exactly why I asked you to come down. I hoped you might break the spell.'

'I will that,' said Mr McKinnon jovially.

The fact that the literary agent spoke little at lunch caused James no apprehension. Mr McKinnon was ever a silent trencherman. From time to time James caught him stealing a glance at the girl, who was well enough to come down to meals now, limping pathetically; but he could read nothing in his face. And yet the mere look of his face was a consolation. It was so solid, so matter of fact, so exactly like an unemotional coconut.

'You've done me good,' said James with a sigh of relief, as he escorted the agent down the garden to his car after lunch. 'I felt all along that I could rely on your rugged common sense. The whole atmosphere of the place seems different now.'

Mr McKinnon did not speak for a moment. He seemed to be plunged in thought.

'Rodman,' he said, as he got into his car, 'I've been thinking over that suggestion of yours of putting a love interest into The Secret Nine. I think you're wise. The story needs it. After all, what is there greater in the world than love? Love—love—aye, it's the sweetest word in the language. Put in a heroine and let her marry Lester Gage.'

'If,' said James grimly, 'she does succeed in worming her way in she'll jolly well marry the mysterious leper. But look here, I don't understand—'

'It was seeing that girl that changed me,' proceeded Mr McKinnon. And as James stared at him aghast, tears suddenly filled his hard-boiled eyes. He openly snuffled. 'Aye, seeing her sitting there under the roses, with all that smell of honeysuckle and all. And the birdies singing so sweet in the garden and the sun lighting up her bonny face. The puir wee lass!' he muttered, dabbing at his eyes. 'The puir bonny wee lass! Rodman,' he said, his voice quivering, 'I've decided that we're being hard on Prodder & Wiggs. Wiggs has had sickness in his home lately. We mustn't be hard on a man who's had sickness in his home, hey, laddie? No, no! I'm going to take back that contract and alter it to a flat twelve per cent and no advance royalties.'

'What!'

'But you shan't lose by it, Rodman. No, no, you shan't lose by it, my manny. I am going to waive my commission. The puir bonny wee lass!'

The car rolled off down the road. Mr McKinnon, seated in the back, was blowing his nose violently.

'This is the end!' said James.

It is necessary at this point to pause and examine James Rodman's position with an unbiased eye. The average man, unless he puts himself in James's place, will be unable to appreciate it. James, he will feel, was making a lot of fuss about nothing. Here he was, drawing daily closer and closer to a charming girl with big blue eyes, and surely rather to be envied than pitied.

But we must remember that James was one of Nature's bachelors. And no ordinary man, looking forward dreamily to a little home of his own with a loving wife putting out his slippers and changing the gramophone records, can realize the intensity of the instinct for self-preservation which animates Nature's bachelors in times of peril.

James Rodman had a congenital horror of matrimony. Though a young man, he had allowed himself to develop a great many habits which were as the breath of life to him; and these habits, he knew instinctively, a wife would shoot to pieces within a week of the end of the honeymoon.

James liked to breakfast in bed; and, having breakfasted, to smoke in bed and knock the ashes out on the carpet. What wife would tolerate this practice?

James liked to pass his days in a tennis shirt, grey flannel trousers, and slippers. What wife ever rests until she has inclosed her husband in a stiff collar, tight boots, and a morning suit and taken him with her to thés musicaux?

These and a thousand other thoughts of the same kind flashed through the unfortunate young man's mind as the days went by, and every day that passed seemed to draw him nearer to the brink of the chasm. Fate appeared to be taking a malicious pleasure in making things as difficult for him as possible. Now that the girl was well enough to leave her bed, she spent her time sitting in a chair on the sun-sprinkled porch, and James had to read to her—and poetry, at that; and not the jolly, wholesome sort of poetry the boys are turning out nowadays, either—good, honest stuff about sin and gas-works and decaying corpses—but the old-fashioned kind with rhymes in it, dealing almost exclusively with love. The weather, moreover, continued superb. The honeysuckle cast its sweet scent on the gentle breeze; the roses over the porch stirred and nodded; the flowers in the garden were lovelier than ever; the birds sang their little throats sore. And every evening there was a magnificent sunset. It was almost as if Nature were doing it on purpose.

At last James intercepted Dr Brady as he was leaving after one of his visits and put the thing to him squarely:

'When is that girl going?'

The doctor patted him on the arm.

'Not yet, Rodman,' he said in a low, understanding voice. 'No need to worry yourself about that. Mustn't be moved for days and days and days—I might almost say weeks and weeks and weeks.'

'Weeks and weeks!' cried James.

'And weeks,' said Dr Brady. He prodded James roguishly in the abdomen. 'Good luck to you, my boy, good luck to you,' he said.

It was some small consolation to James that the mushy physician immediately afterward tripped over William on his way down the path and broke his stethoscope. When a man is up against it like James every little helps.

He was walking dismally back to the house after this conversation when he was met by the apple-cheeked housekeeper.

'The little lady would like to speak to you, sir,' said the apple-cheeked exhibit, rubbing her hands.

'Would she?' said James hollowly.

'So sweet and pretty she looks, sir—oh, sir, you wouldn't believe! Like a blessed angel sitting there with her dear eyes all a-shining.'

'Don't do it!' cried James with extraordinary vehemence. 'Don't do it!'

He found the girl propped up on the cushions and thought once again how singularly he disliked her. And yet, even as he thought this, some force against which he had to fight madly was whispering to him, 'Go to her and take that little hand! Breathe into that little ear the burning words that will make that little face turn away crimsoned with blushes!' He wiped a bead of perspiration from his forehead and sat down.

'Mrs Stick-in-the-Mud—what's her name?—says you want to see me.'

The girl nodded.

'I've had a letter from Uncle Henry. I wrote to him as soon as I was better and told him what had happened, and he is coming here tomorrow morning.'

'Uncle Henry?'

'That's what I call him, but he's really no relation. He is my guardian. He and daddy were officers in the same regiment, and when daddy was killed, fighting on the Afghan frontier, he died in Uncle Henry's arms and with his last breath begged him to take care of me.'

James started. A sudden wild hope had waked in his heart. Years ago, he remembered, he had read a book of his aunt's entitled Rupert's Legacy, and in that book—

'I'm engaged to marry him,' said the girl quietly.

'Wow!' shouted James.

'What?' asked the girl, startled.

'Touch of cramp,' said James. He was thrilling all over. That wild hope had been realized.

'It was daddy's dying wish that we should marry,' said the girl.

'And dashed sensible of him, too; dashed sensible,' said James warmly.

'And yet,' she went on, a little wistfully, 'I sometimes wonder—'

'Don't!' said James. 'Don't! You must respect daddy's dying wish. There's nothing like daddy's dying wish; you can't beat it. So he's coming here tomorrow, is he? Capital, capital. To lunch, I suppose? Excellent! I'll run down and tell Mrs Who-Is-It to lay in another chop.'

It was with a gay and uplifted heart that James strolled the garden and smoked his pipe next morning. A great cloud seemed to have rolled itself away from him. Everything was for the best in the best of all possible worlds. He had finished The Secret Nine and shipped it off to Mr McKinnon, and now as he strolled there was shaping itself in his mind a corking plot about a man with only half a face who lived in a secret den and terrorized London with a series of shocking murders. And what made them so shocking was the fact that each of the victims, when discovered, was found to have only half a face too. The rest had been chipped off, presumably by some blunt instrument.

The thing was coming out magnificently, when suddenly his attention was diverted by a piercing scream. Out of the bushes fringing the river that ran beside the garden burst the apple-cheeked housekeeper.

'Oh, sir! Oh, sir! Oh, sir!'

'What is it?' demanded James irritably.

'Oh, sir! Oh, sir! Oh, sir!'

'Yes, and then what?'

'The little dog, sir! He's in the river!'

'Well, whistle him to come out.'

'Oh, sir, do come quick! He'll be drowned!'

James followed her through the bushes, taking off his coat as he went. He was saying to himself, 'I will not rescue this dog. I do not like the dog. It is high time he had a bath, and in any case it would be much simpler to stand on the bank and fish for him with a rake. Only an ass out of a Leila J. Pinckney book would dive into a beastly river to save—'

At this point he dived. Toto, alarmed by the splash, swam rapidly for the bank, but James was too quick for him. Grasping him firmly by the neck, he scrambled ashore and ran for the house, followed by the housekeeper.

The girl was seated on the porch. Over her there bent the tall soldierly figure of a man with keen eyes and greying hair. The housekeeper raced up.

'Oh, miss! Toto! In the river! He saved him! He plunged in and saved him!'

The girl drew a quick breath.

'Gallant, damme! By Jove! By gad! Yes, gallant, by George!' exclaimed the soldierly man.

The girl seemed to wake from a reverie.

'Uncle Henry, this is Mr Rodman. Mr Rodman, my guardian, Colonel Carteret.'

'Proud to meet you, sir,' said the colonel, his honest blue eyes glowing as he fingered his short crisp moustache. 'As fine a thing as I ever heard of, damme!'

'Yes, you are brave—brave,' the girl whispered.

'I am wet—wet,' said James, and went upstairs to change his clothes.

When he came down for lunch, he found to his relief that the girl had decided not to join them, and Colonel Carteret was silent and preoccupied. James, exerting himself in his capacity of host, tried him with the weather, golf, India, the Government, the high cost of living, first-class cricket, the modern dancing craze, and murderers he had met, but the other still preserved that strange, absent-minded silence. It was only when the meal was concluded and James had produced cigarettes that he came abruptly out of his trance.

'Rodman,' he said, 'I should like to speak to you.'

'Yes?' said James, thinking it was about time.

'Rodman,' said Colonel Carteret, 'or rather, George—I may call you George?' he added, with a sort of wistful diffidence that had a singular charm.

'Certainly,' replied James, 'if you wish it. Though my name is James.'

'James, eh? Well, well, it amounts to the same thing, eh, what, damme, by gad?' said the colonel with a momentary return of his bluff soldierly manner. 'Well, then, James, I have something that I wish to say to you. Did Miss Maynard—did Rose happen to tell you anything about myself in—er—in connexion with herself?'

'She mentioned that you and she were engaged to be married.'

The colonel's tightly drawn lips quivered.

'No longer,' he said.

'What?'

'No, John, my boy.'

'James.'

'No, James, my boy, no longer. While you were upstairs changing your clothes she told me—breaking down, poor child, as she spoke—that she wished our engagement to be at an end.'

James half rose from the table, his cheeks blanched.

'You don't mean that!' he gasped.

Colonel Carteret nodded. He was staring out of the window, his fine eyes set in a look of pain.

'But this is nonsense!' cried James. 'This is absurd! She—she mustn't be allowed to chop and change like this. I mean to say, it—it isn't fair—'

'Don't think of me, my boy.'

'I'm not—I mean, did she give any reason?'

'Her eyes did.'

'Her eyes did?'

'Her eyes, when she looked at you on the porch, as you stood there—young, heroic—having just saved the life of the dog she loves. It is you who have won that tender heart, my boy.'

'Now, listen,' protested James, 'you aren't going to sit there and tell me that a girl falls in love with a man just because he saves her dog from drowning?'

'Why, surely,' said Colonel Carteret, surprised. 'What better reason could she have?' He sighed. 'It is the old, old story, my boy. Youth to youth. I am an old man. I should have known—I should have foreseen—yes, youth to youth.'

'You aren't a bit old.'

'Yes, yes.'

'No, no.'

'Yes, yes.'

'Don't keep on saying yes, yes!' cried James, clutching at his hair. 'Besides, she wants a steady old buffer—a steady, sensible man of medium age—to look after her.'

Colonel Carteret shook his head with a gentle smile.

'This is mere quixotry, my boy. It is splendid of you to take this attitude; but no, no.'

'Yes, yes.'

'No, no.' He gripped James's hand for an instant, then rose and walked to the door. 'That is all I wished to say, Tom.'

'James.'

'James. I just thought that you ought to know how matters stood. Go to her, my boy, go to her, and don't let any thought of an old man's broken dream keep you from pouring out what is in your heart. I am an old soldier, lad, an old soldier. I have learned to take the rough with the smooth. But I think—I think I will leave you now. I—I should—should like to be alone for a while. If you need me you will find me in the raspberry bushes.'

He had scarcely gone when James also left the room. He took his hat and stick and walked blindly out of the garden, he knew not whither. His brain was numbed. Then, as his powers of reasoning returned, he told himself that he should have foreseen this ghastly thing. If there was one type of character over which Leila J. Pinckney had been wont to spread herself, it was the pathetic guardian who loves his ward but relinquishes her to the younger man. No wonder the girl had broken off the engagement. Any elderly guardian who allowed himself to come within a mile of Honeysuckle Cottage was simply asking for it. And then, as he turned to walk back, a dull defiance gripped James. Why, he asked, should he be put upon in this manner? If the girl liked to throw over this man, why should he be the goat?

He saw his way clearly now. He just wouldn't do it, that was all. And if they didn't like it they could lump it.

Full of a new fortitude, he strode in at the gate. A tall, soldierly figure emerged from the raspberry bushes and came to meet him.

'Well?' said Colonel Carteret.

'Well?' said James defiantly.

'Am I to congratulate you?'

James caught his keen blue eye and hesitated. It was not going to be so simple as he had supposed.

'Well—er—' he said.

Into the keen blue eyes there came a look that James had not seen there before. It was the stern, hard look which—probably—had caused men to bestow upon this old soldier the name of Cold-Steel Carteret.

'You have not asked Rose to marry you?'

'Er—no; not yet.'

The keen blue eyes grew keener and bluer.

'Rodman,' said Colonel Carteret in a strange, quiet voice, 'I have known that little girl since she was a tiny child. For years she has been all in all to me. Her father died in my arms and with his last breath bade me see that no harm came to his darling. I have nursed her through mumps, measles—aye, and chicken pox—and I live but for her happiness.' He paused, with a significance that made James's toes curl. 'Rodman,' he said, 'do you know what I would do to any man who trifled with that little girl's affections?' He reached in his hip pocket and an ugly-looking revolver glittered in the sunlight. 'I would shoot him like a dog.'

'Like a dog?' faltered James.

'Like a dog,' said Colonel Carteret. He took James's arm and turned him towards the house. 'She is on the porch. Go to her. And if—' He broke off. 'But tut!' he said in a kindlier tone. 'I am doing you an injustice, my boy. I know it.'

'Oh, you are,' said James fervently.

'Your heart is in the right place.'

'Oh, absolutely,' said James.

'Then go to her, my boy. Later on you may have something to tell me. You will find me in the strawberry beds.'

It was very cool and fragrant on the porch. Overhead, little breezes played and laughed among the roses. Somewhere in the distance sheep bells tinkled, and in the shrubbery a thrush was singing its evensong.

Seated in her chair behind a wicker table laden with tea things, Rose Maynard watched James as he shambled up the path.

'Tea's ready,' she called gaily. 'Where is Uncle Henry?' A look of pity and distress flitted for a moment over her flower-like face. 'Oh, I—I forgot,' she whispered.

'He is in the strawberry beds,' said James in a low voice.

She nodded unhappily.

'Of course, of course. Oh, why is life like this?' James heard her whisper.

He sat down. He looked at the girl. She was leaning back with closed eyes, and he thought he had never seen such a little squirt in his life. The idea of passing his remaining days in her society revolted him. He was stoutly opposed to the idea of marrying anyone; but if, as happens to the best of us, he ever were compelled to perform the wedding glide, he had always hoped it would be with some lady golf champion who would help him with his putting, and thus, by bringing his handicap down a notch or two, enable him to save something from the wreck, so to speak. But to link his lot with a girl who read his aunt's books and liked them; a girl who could tolerate the presence of the dog Toto; a girl who clasped her hands in pretty, childish joy when she saw a nasturtium in bloom—it was too much. Nevertheless, he took her hand and began to speak.

'Miss Maynard—Rose—'

She opened her eyes and cast them down. A flush had come into her cheeks. The dog Toto at her side sat up and begged for cake, disregarded.

'Let me tell you a story. Once upon a time there was a lonely man who lived in a cottage all by himself—'

He stopped. Was it James Rodman who was talking this bilge?

'Yes?' whispered the girl.

'—but one day there came to him out of nowhere a little fairy princess. She—'

He stopped again, but this time not because of the sheer shame of listening to his own voice. What caused him to interrupt his tale was the fact that at this moment the tea-table suddenly began to rise slowly in the air, tilting as it did so a considerable quantity of hot tea on to the knees of his trousers.

'Ouch!' cried James, leaping.

The table continued to rise, and then fell sideways, revealing the homely countenance of William, who, concealed by the cloth, had been taking a nap beneath it. He moved slowly forward, his eyes on Toto. For many a long day William had been desirous of putting to the test, once and for all, the problem of whether Toto was edible or not. Sometimes he thought yes, at other times no. Now seemed an admirable opportunity for a definite decision. He advanced on the object of his experiment, making a low whistling noise through his nostrils, not unlike a boiling kettle. And Toto, after one long look of incredulous horror, tucked his shapely tail between his legs and, turning, raced for safety. He had laid a course in a bee-line for the open garden gate, and William, shaking a dish of marmalade off his head a little petulantly, galloped ponderously after him. Rose Maynard staggered to her feet.

'Oh, save him!' she cried.

Without a word James added himself to the procession. His interest in Toto was but tepid. What he wanted was to get near enough to William to discuss with him that matter of the tea on his trousers. He reached the road and found that the order of the runners had not changed. For so small a dog, Toto was moving magnificently. A cloud of dust rose as he skidded round the corner. William followed. James followed William.

And so they passed Farmer Birkett's barn, Farmer Giles's cow shed, the place where Farmer Willetts's pigsty used to be before the big fire, and the Bunch of Grapes public-house, Jno. Biggs propr., licensed to sell tobacco, wines, and spirits. And it was as they were turning down the lane that leads past Farmer Robinson's chicken run that Toto, thinking swiftly, bolted abruptly into a small drain pipe.

'William!' roared James, coming up at a canter. He stopped to pluck a branch from the hedge and swooped darkly on.

William had been crouching before the pipe, making a noise like a bassoon into its interior; but now he rose and came beamingly to James. His eyes were aglow with chumminess and affection; and placing his forefeet on James's chest, he licked him three times on the face in rapid succession. And as he did so, something seemed to snap in James. The scales seemed to fall from James's eyes. For the first time he saw William as he really was, the authentic type of dog that saves his master from a frightful peril. A wave of emotion swept over him.

'William!' he muttered. 'William!'

William was making an early supper off a half brick he had found in the road. James stooped and patted him fondly.

'William,' he whispered, 'you knew when the time had come to change the conversation, didn't you, old boy!' He straightened himself. 'Come, William,' he said. 'Another four miles and we reach Meadowsweet Junction. Make it snappy and we shall just catch the up express, first stop London.'

William looked up into his face and it seemed to James that he gave a brief nod of comprehension and approval. James turned. Through the trees to the east he could see the red roof of Honeysuckle Cottage, lurking like some evil dragon in ambush.

Then, together, man and dog passed silently into the sunset.

That (concluded Mr Mulliner) is the story of my distant cousin James Rodman. As to whether it is true, that, of course, is an open question. I, personally, am of opinion that it is. There is no doubt that James did go to live at Honeysuckle Cottage and, while there, underwent some experience which has left an ineradicable mark upon him. His eyes today have that unmistakable look which is to be seen only in the eyes of confirmed bachelors whose feet have been dragged to the very brink of the pit and who have gazed at close range into the naked face of matrimony.

And, if further proof be needed, there is William. He is now James's inseparable companion. Would any man be habitually seen in public with a dog like William unless he had some solid cause to be grateful to him—unless they were linked together by some deep and imperishable memory? I think not. Myself, when I observe William coming along the street, I cross the road and look into a shop window till he has passed. I am not a snob, but I dare not risk my position in Society by being seen talking to that curious compound.

Nor is the precaution an unnecessary one. There is about William a shameless absence of appreciation of class distinctions which recalls the worst excesses of the French Revolution. I have seen him with these eyes chivvy a pomeranian belonging to a Baroness in her own right from near the Achilles Statue to within a few yards of the Marble Arch.

And yet James walks daily with him in Piccadilly. It is surely significant.